The Catholic School

Edoardo Albinati is a novelist and screenwriter. His novel *The Catholic School* won the 2016 Premio Strega. He lives in Rome, where he has worked as a teacher in Rebibbia prison since 1994.

THE
CATHOLIC
SCHOOL

Edoardo Albinati

TRANSLATED FROM THE ITALIAN BY
ANTONY SHUGAAR

PICADOR

First published 2019 by Farrar, Straus and Giroux, New York

First published in the UK 2019 by Picador
an imprint of Pan Macmillan
20 New Wharf Road, London N1 9RR
Associated companies throughout the world
www.panmacmillan.com

ISBN 978-1-5098-5627-5 HB
ISBN 978-1-5098-5628-2 TPB

1 3 5 7 9 8 6 4 2

A CIP catalogue record for this book is available from the British Library.

Printed and bound by CPI Group (UK) Ltd, Croydon, CR0 4YY

Visit **www.picador.com** to read more about all our books
and to buy them. You will also find features, author interviews and
news of any author events, and you can sign up for e-newsletters
so that you're always first to hear about our new releases.

And that the unclean spirit, having left a body, might find seven others even worse.

—BLAISE PASCAL, *Compendium of the Life of Jesus Christ*

Contents

Part I

Christians and Lions

I

T WAS ARBUS who opened my eyes. Not that I was keeping them shut, but I had no way of being certain of what my eyes were seeing—these might be images projected to deceive or reassure me—and I was incapable of fostering doubts about the spectacle that was presented to me every day and which we called life. On the one hand, I unquestioningly accepted every-thing that befalls a kid aged thirteen, fourteen, fifteen, and all the other years that follow in a row to bring to completion that "phase" (I've always heard it described as a "phase," a "moment," even when it lasts for quite a while, a "delicate moment," or even a "crisis," which truth be told will be followed by other moments and phases every bit as delicate or critical, com-ing one on the heels of the other in an unbroken succession until you are grown up, an adult, old, and finally dead), I partook without objection of the daily meal where the table was set with all the things that happen to any adolescent, the business he's surrounded by as he grows up, as he de-velops (there you go, "development," another keyword used by grown-ups to jimmy the padlocks of adolescence, the difficult "age of development," the "development of a personality," and then the horrible intransitive ex-pression, "he has already developed," which puts an unctuous glob of sealing wax on the secrets of the genitals), and which may not follow in any exact order, but which form the inevitable courses of any adolescent's meal: school, soccer, friends, frustrations and excitements, all of it punctu-ated by phone calls and filling up gas tanks and falling off mopeds—in other words, common experiences.

On the other hand, though, I was stung by a feeling of bafflement. Was *this* really life? That is, was this *my* life? Did I need to do something to make it mine, or was it being provided and guaranteed like this? Would I have to earn it and deserve it? Perhaps it was just a temporary life, and soon it would be replaced by the permanent one. But in that case, was it up to me to replace it, or would someone else see to that? Some external event? Life can be something extraordinary or something normal. What kind of life was mine? Until Arbus came into the story, these questions—which I am now at least capable of formulating, though I have long since given up all thought of answering them—didn't even bob to the surface, because they dissolved before even emerging into my awareness, leaving behind only the faintest of tremors.

Even the idea of calling it awareness is an overstatement.

At the very most, the sentiment of being in the world. Of being there.

Whoever projected the images that were so comfortable for me and that wrapped so snugly around me was a magician, a genius. I have to give him that. His lamp unleashed dreams that were perfect, sweet, and crystal clear, inside which I walked rapt and, indeed at certain moments, practically ravished. In other words, I was truly happy and I was truly sad. I inhaled deeply the mysterious air of the stage sets that were built around me and hastily broken down again the minute I went by. Something made me think that sooner or later a decisive event would occur that, rather than explaining one by one the previous insignificant twists and turns, would stitch them together with an irresistible thread like the kind used to bind the pages of novels so that you keep turning them until you reach the end, unable to put the book down. And so, merely resembling a piece of fiction but also possessing the implacable coherence of a piece of fiction, my life and everyone else's lives could finally be called true, and real . . .

They were moments that were precise and yet deeply troubling, I wouldn't know how to put it any better, in which I perceived with painful clarity the confusion that took possession of me. All of me. It took hold of me and left no room for anything else—say, for ideas or thoughts. I was reduced to feeling and nothing more. To be exact, what I felt was the blood that flowed, amassing in my chest, my swollen, hurting heart, I mean to say, it actually *hurt*, really really hurt, as if it were about to *leap out of my chest*, to use the language of the novels of a bygone time, but though it hurt there was also a sweetness to it, strange, a truly strange sweetness, as strange as all the rest of it.

Arbus was in the same class as me from the first year of middle school, but I only began to notice him as middle school was about to end. Just a month before final exams . . .

✛

STUDENTS ARE LEFT BEHIND by definition. All of them, with no exceptions. For that matter, teachers are also always left behind, too, they can never keep up with the study plans that they themselves drew up, and they put the blame for that on their students, which is right and wrong at the same time, since, let's just imagine that their classes were made up exclusively of little geniuses, even then they wouldn't be able to keep up, they'd still be left behind, maybe just by a page, or a line, or a millimeter. Their fate in any case is one of failure and giving up: for instance, giving up on the idea of covering all of Kant by the next-to-last year of high school. There's no explanation for it and all we can do is fall back on the enigmatic expression "the force of events." Goals are created in the first place to fall short of, it's in the exclusive nature of targets not to hit the bull's-eye. Whether it's because you run out of strength as the journey continues, or because the destination recedes imperceptibly as you go, or else because the plans were too optimistic or presumptuous or abstract in the first place, or the obstacles more daunting than expected, and the rain days or sick days or strike days or election days were just surprisingly numerous. I don't know the field of science he pursued or what he based his findings on, but a certain expert calculated that *any* project we get under way is bound to cost an average of a third more than the starting budget, and will take at least a third again as long as we estimated to complete. And this appears to be an ineluctable factor. Only the rarest of exceptions escape the dictates of this law of intrinsic delay, and one of them was Arbus.

ARBUS, ARBUS, FRIEND, you skinny old fishbone. You were so skinny that the sight of your elbows when you pretended to play volleyball to keep from flunking gym sent a shiver down my spine. A shiver of pity or revulsion. To say nothing of your upper arms or your knees, whose sharp-edged bones practically poked through the black tracksuit with green-and-yellow trim that you had special permission to wear even as late as May, or the farther reaches of June, to protect your precarious state of health. However much you might pretend to focus on the game, everyone knew that if by some chance the ball ricocheted in your direction, into the narrow slice of the volleyball court to which we'd exiled you to make sure you did as little harm to the team as possible, you wouldn't even see it hurtling downward because by then you'd be gazing in enchantment at the beams in the gymnasium roof, as if lost in calculations of the quantity of concrete required to hold it up. And if by chance, startled awake at the last instant by our shouts, you actually realized that you *had* to play (volleyball is a hysterical sport, a matter of crucial instants, in an entire game, you might or might not get your hands on the ball for a total of five seconds, and your turn comes unexpectedly), Arbus, come on! Pull it together!! Arbus, *fuuuccckkk*!! then you'd windmill your long, uncoordinated limbs, though it was unclear whether you were trying to return the ball with arms raised or loft it from below or even to catch it, which is what anyone is instinctively tempted to do when they're not paying attention and they see something coming straight at them. And in fact that's exactly what you did most of the time, you'd catch the ball in mid-flight and gather it to your chest, and then look around at your teammates as if hoping with a disoriented half smile for their approval in the very same instant that it was dawning on you that you'd screwed up for the umpteenth time, a hunch that was confirmed by the chorus of your impatient teammates, "Oh no, *noooo*, Arbus, what the *fuck* are you doing!?" And in fact, that was something that happened to you pretty regularly, that your face would have an expression sharply at variance with what you were thinking or feeling. You'd smile while people were insulting you.

The fantastic thing about Arbus was that he never got discouraged. He stayed impervious to events. Others couldn't have put up with the constant ribbing and insults, and would have just thrown the ball at their teammates or lunged into physical combat or, as the ones we called little girls would do, burst into tears at their own undeniable inadequacies: reactions that I, for instance, gave in to on numerous occasions, incapable of putting up with the pressure of other people's judgments, which always trigger a malaise or aggressivity in me even when they're flattering, leave aside when they're critical. I can't say, however, that I ever saw Arbus looking crestfallen or worried. Anyone else would have suffered through this kind of situation and found it humiliating, but not Arbus, he maintained his equanimity as if none of it mattered to him or perhaps it did matter, but his face gave no sign of it, frozen as it was in a sort of delay, unable to keep up with his much faster mind. He took forever to register what was happening and to switch one mask for another. That's it, maybe that's really how Arbus was constructed, out of modular elements that weren't synchronized each with the other, a lightning-fast mind, a cold heart, a face that was lazily incapable of shifting expression to suit the circumstance and was therefore often poised inappropriately (which is something that, as we shall see, brought him no small number of problems with his classmates, his teachers, and the authorities in general, who considered his expression to be insolent, irreverent, while his words sounded reasonable and obsequious, or the other way around).

And then of course there was his uncoordinated body. Arbus was tall and skinny, his vaguely Slavic-looking face framed by long locks of dark hair, oily as if he'd never shampooed in his life, a mouth with fleshy lips perennially arched in the half smile that proved so irritating, and then the deeply intelligent gaze behind a pair of eyeglasses that would have looked perfect on the scientist in a sci-fi or spy movie, that is, the kind of glasses that make your eyes look enormous behind lenses thick as the bottom of a glass bottle, especially if your eyes are the light blue of water as Arbus's were, or I really ought to say, as they still are, because Arbus is alive, I know that for certain, I have proof, though I have no idea where he's living or what he does.

IF HE WAS QUICK to learn (he took half the time I did, and a quarter or a tenth the time the others needed to absorb and translate theoretical lessons into practical exercises), he was every bit as good at instantly unlearning. It wasn't that he forgot, it was simply that he moved on. Once he understood them, things suddenly ceased to be worthy of attention. At year's end, he emptied out so he'd be ready to understand new things. Those who devour theories then go on to expel them. And those theories leave transparent traces of their passage through the mind, they seem to serve only to expand it, to make room for the transit of other, more complex schemes. When one's understanding is so very rapid, one has no need to store up knowledge.

Already in the first two years of high school, Arbus flabbergasted both the priests and the rest of us by going up to the blackboard and rewriting point by point the entire array of steps in a theorem that had just been set forth by the teacher only minutes ago. He would draw histograms and rotate solids in isometric projection, giving us the impression that he was *actually* observing them simultaneously from all sides—Cubism was nothing in comparison! The minute he pulled away the stick of chalk he'd sent screeching across the blackboard with nervous little strokes, without so much as an instant's hesitation, he remained there motionless, long arms dangling, clumps of hair covering his cheeks, silently staring into the void as if he were waiting to receive new instructions before venturing a movement or uttering a word. Like a robot that goes into standby mode until it receives the next command to execute. You couldn't call it boredom or impatience, if anything the opposite of that: indifference. And in fact, once the problem was solved, what more was there to add? Given that we hadn't grasped it even the first time it was set forth by our math teacher, we only realized that Arbus had replicated it exactly by the amazement painted on the priest's pointy face. He wasn't exactly pleased by how easy it was for Arbus. This facility might suggest that the teacher's job was, all things considered, superfluous. People like Arbus could simply have stayed home, curled up in bed, to leaf through the textbook and run through a month's curriculum in a comfortable half hour. There was no real difference between going to school and skipping it, after all.

Perhaps it would be better to have Arbus and the story of his well-understood genius written by someone at the bottom of the class, the behavioral problem, or the chronic underachiever, so as to bring out the full contrast. Instead the story is going to be written by me, intelligent, gifted, but not all *that* gifted, and most important of all, insufficiently endowed with the character needed to truly excel, like one of those young tennis players with enchanting backhands, for whom experts prophesy a spectacularly successful future, willing to swear up and down that they're bound to become athletic phenomena, but instead as the years go by they never actually win major tournaments because there's something they just lack. And what is it exactly that they lack? Determination? Courage? Tenacity? Balls? The killer instinct? What should we call that invisible quality without which the other, visible qualities are basically useless? Might it be no accident that we have the expression "first in the class," while no one has ever talked about the second or third, or the fifth in the class, which is what Zipoli, Zarattini, Lorco, and I were, that is, the ones who, depending on individual performance, would surge forward or fall back in the rankings, emerging into or dropping out of the top ten grinds, though never coming remotely close to threatening the number one leader of the class, Arbus, unfailingly at the top of every ranking, in spite of the few solid points that we scored with doctored classwork or oral exams in which by pure chance we were questioned on the *only* topic we had studied, or the one we'd studied *last*, and which was therefore still fresh. Hence our inevitable ups and downs. Arbus's scores, in contrast, were stunning, his results never fell below the top quartile, and so in his case the teachers were often forced to violate the great school taboo of the old days—that is, the full ten, the Italian equivalent of the A-plus. A grade that is supposed to mean: perfection. The teachers went through a moral struggle at the very idea of writing a ten in their grade books, and in fact there wasn't enough room to fit double digits into the appropriate space. But for Arbus, even the most conservative teachers understood, the ones who pointed out, "But if I give you a ten, then how should I grade Manzoni?" Well, it was unthinkable to give Arbus anything less than the highest grade, no matter how they quibbled or made planetary comparisons with ancient Chinese sages or with Descartes. Personally, I was never one to pull all-nighters, but the great thing was that neither was Arbus, much less so, in fact; I believe that at home on his own he never studied at all. And after all, homework is boring.

LATER, a great deal later, I would learn that one of the few things that Arbus did study, and systematically, were the different ways of killing people. I don't know where he got this singular passion, since he was the most mild-mannered and inoffensive young man you could ever hope to meet, especially in those years that, as we shall see in the course of the story, were marked by a very particular enthusiasm for violent abuse, an abuse that—rather than being exercised by the usual categories that are historically responsible for such abuse, that is, the rich (as a class prerogative), the poor (for survival), and criminals (by nature or profession)—was the province of just about everyone, on a scattered, individualized, personalized basis. You'd never call Arbus an aggressive or violent young man, and yet even then (though I learned of it only later, during our last years in high school) he cultivated a meticulous interest in killing, and let me be clear, killings of every kind and employing all methods or weapons—in war, of course, first and foremost, since war provides the greatest quantity and variety of killing—and then in ritual and sacrifice, in self-defense or for revenge, or else in the settling of accounts among gangsters or else to rid oneself of a boring husband or a cheating wife or out of sheer cruelty or else in the scrupulous implementation of a death sentence—in short, wherever there was a human being who for whatever reason or purpose chose to take the life of another human being, that was where Arbus turned his interest. In the pursuit of thoroughness, let me add that my classmate was also interested in the diametrically opposed situation (clearly, it was extremes that caught his attention): that is to say, not how one kills and is killed, but how one manages to survive.

As children, actually, we were immersed in a constant round of killings, for the most part imaginary but nonetheless quite appalling. Every time we went out to play, we rubbed out a vast number of enemies and almost always, at some point, our turn came to die. That was a prerequisite of the story. The scene that I believe I've played out the greatest number of times in my life is that of the gunslinger who crumples after being shot. There existed a vast array of speeds and manners of falling, bending one's legs, staggering, clutching one's chest or throwing one's arms wide, and then flinging oneself or slowly tumbling over backwards, followed by writhing and one final attempt to return fire at one's enemy before giving up the ghost. Nearly blinded as we were by blood and dust, it was hard to aim accurately and the gunshot often went wild. There is no escaping the destiny of games. Your hand would fall slack and the fingers that formed barrel and hammer would spread out empty after one last spasm, and for good. We shed rivers of blood, including our own, it was a full-fledged school of life, and now that I think back on it, it's rather strange that so few of us, after all, actually translated simulation into reality, and went out to harvest flesh-and-blood victims. It astonishes me how rarely people have recourse to violence, considering how you hear nothing but exaltations of it in books, movies, and games, and you enjoy simulations of it for decades at a time, on TV. By age twelve I'd already seen thousands of people killed or else killed them myself. I had taken part in executions by firing squad and funerals. I'd been responsible for bloodbaths. Today, you can attain the same number of kills in a few sessions with any video game, and you can send all those bastards hunkered down in the bushes straight to hell. You wipe them off the screen. The enemy has proliferated a hundredfold and the means to destroy that enemy have been perfected.

I couldn't say whether, as an adult, Arbus ever dedicated himself to these video games with their hyperrealistic graphics, which bring together the greatest imaginable verisimilitude with the sheer height of absurdity. If for no other reason than that I imagine he would like such an abstract and powerful blend, yet served up cold, by a computer. I've always thought that Arbus's life was restricted to his mind, and was therefore expansive beyond all limits. In the secret circuits of the brain—that was where things materialized. *All* things. If the phrase had already been coined back then, the world my friend inhabited might very easily have been called a virtual world. Within the sheltering shell of his intelligence, a great many more things happened than in his everyday routine as a young prodigy, that is, a day in which there was time only for school, piano lessons, and the postural gymnastics that he had to do every day, with the assistance of machinery that resembled instruments of torture, with straps and steel springs, to keep his spinal cord in alignment in spite of his growth spurt. Yet another phenomenon of development and its collateral effects. Something ungovernable and deep down, unedifying, if at the very most it took the form of a mark on the wall a few inches higher than the one carved last year. How satisfying. But in Arbus's mind there was sufficient space to contain all and every argument and adventure, and nothing was excluded from the outset because it might be too challenging or strange or dangerous or vicious. Arbus's mind was boundless, it stopped at nothing, it recognized no limits, and it overcame them practically without realizing it. It might take any hypothesis under consideration, even the most horrifying ones.

I remember that one time in class we studied the theory of a writer who had proposed, as a sort of macabre joke formulated in a solemn language (it wasn't all that clear, in other words, whether or not he meant what he said), that children be eaten as a way of alleviating the hunger of the masses. It's well known that much of what is taught in school, starting with the humanities, at first glance appears to be senseless or exaggerated or tossed out just to elicit reactions. "These people are out of their minds" is the phrase that springs to your lips every time you study a philosophical or literary doctrine, or else actual history: the emperor who had the sea whipped, the pineal gland, the theory that a cat might be simultaneously alive and dead, an excursion to the moon where the juice from the brains of men who've gone mad is kept in bottles, a chorus of mummies that sings at midnight, monads "with no doors or windows," and then the great political theorist who suggests you invite your adversaries to dinner and then have them strangled . . . Highly revered characters who hang themselves one after the other, who devour their children, have sex with their mothers, poison themselves in the belief that they can be brought back to life, the most and the least, the last who will be first, to be alive and to be dead are the same thing, and so on and so forth.

THEN WHEN THE TEACHER EXPLAINED that the author of this modest proposal was the same man who had written *Gulliver's Travels*, we understood that it was someone accustomed to retailing tall tales and felt reassured with a dose of the typical skepticism that a student employs in the face of the umpteenth loony doctrine. It goes without saying that the only one of us who found this theory sensible, although difficult to put into practice, was Arbus, who in the end was forced to admit that it was absurd, but only for considerations of hygiene.

WE WERE RATHER UNIMAGINATIVE DREAMERS. Our chief sources of stimulation were television and dirty jokes, of which I have to admit I rarely got the point, I mean to say, the whole point. I would laugh, pretending I had gotten it, while all I had gotten was that this was when I was supposed to laugh. Just as there is full nudity, there is the whole point of a joke. Let's say that I sensed it, that I did my best to guess at the point. My solitary efforts to interpret the unknown led me to original discoveries and colossal misunderstandings, some of which were never refuted and still survive today. The erotic autodidact is no better off than the scientific autodidact. At age twelve, for instance, ashamed of my ignorance but even more so of asking questions, I didn't know the meaning of the word "condom," and for an entire summer and the autumn that followed I was convinced that it was a kind of lubricant that was kept in small smoked-glass bottles, just like nose drops. It was hard for me to guess its exact use. I don't know how I deduced that piece of information. Certain of my classmates were well ahead of me in this field, but far behind me in others. The advancement of adolescents is irregular, in fact we might say that the age between twelve and fifteen doesn't really exist as an age at all, with its standard prerequisites, given that in it there coexist attitudes and events and even before that bodies, physical bodies, of every size and appearance, and of every possible sex plus other improbable sexes that exist only during adolescence and then disappear, components that have nothing to do with each other, one being diametrically opposed to the other, pure contradiction: and in fact those years are lived with a barbaric spirit, assembling the shattered suits of armor of our childhood games with the fragments of a future that is always imagined as being far more a place of science fiction than it will actually prove to be.

All games call for prizes, but especially punishments. There's usually only one prize, just as there's only one winner, and it comes at the end, while the punishments are countless, almost everyone gets them, and they are inflicted progressively over the course of the game, and every season of life has its own: depending on what is dearest to us, that is what is taken away, while what we most fear or are most ashamed of stings and drowns us, amid choruses of laughter. This is a form of "paying the penalty," doing penitence. You can be punished in your pride, in your face, watching your snack money being stolen or being obliged to study the oboe; and when the sexual games begin, of course, the sexual punishments begin with them, the most horrific of which is sexual exclusion. Rejection, however friendly the terms in which it's couched. Oh yes, even more than forced inclusion. Perhaps that's why I was trying to keep pace with the vulgarities, with the pornography, verbal even before it became visual, at the cost of having to invent explanations for everything on my own. The times and the techniques. The secret, that is, which could be found in special magazine sex supplements, shrink-wrapped inside the issue to make sure that kids couldn't peek at them on the newsstand. God, how ignorant and underdeveloped we were! The whole world conspired to keep us that way, and in the final analysis it was the priests alone, our archaic teachers, who lifted a finger to free us from that limbo. Willy nilly.

"HOLD IT RIGHT THERE, *all of you! Who gave you the condom?"*

That's exactly what he said, "condom," in the singular. I thought that it must be a kind of medicine, or anyway, who knows why, something liquid, and precious or dangerous, contained in a small bottle from which it could be doled out with an eyedropper, like a poison or, perhaps, opium. When I later discovered, without any further details, that it was a contrivance that kept girls from getting pregnant, I insisted on believing for no good reason that it was some kind of liquid, I thought that the condom needed to be sparingly applied, drop by drop, on your dick . . .

IF I WERE ASKED to begin the story of Arbus from the very beginning, I would be hard put because, as I've explained before, for a long time his presence attracted no notice in class, more or less like a rock in the desert. Immobile, off-color, he hardly even breathed. If not a rock, then let us say a reptile. His priceless way of blending in functioned almost throughout middle school, which he passed through incognito. But then when little by little he became popular (well, let's be clear on this, *relatively* popular: because in reality Arbus was never really loved at school, rather he was the object of morbid curiosity, rumor-mongering, looked upon as a phenomenon, in a certain sense, *venerated*, and therefore kept at arm's length), in other words, when Arbus became famous for his monstrous intellectual capacities, he began to be enveloped in a blizzard of legends and such hyperbolic formulations as "Arbus has no beginning nor will he ever have an end," "He is the Word," and when we began our first lessons in philosophy, all the formulations from the textbook were pinned on him, rendering them finally understandable, among other things. The tag of "unmoved mover," taken from Aristotle, for instance, fit him to a T and perfectly rendered the idea of an imperturbable power. The teachers usually didn't bother to test him, since they knew that he'd give all the right answers anyway. And the few times that they did test him, immediately after the exchange there was always someone in the back of the room who added in a solemn tone: "Ipse dixit." Moreover he was given nicknames with the most abstruse concepts, especially if expressed in Greek or foreign words, so that in correspondence with the curriculum he was called variously Apeiron, Mantissa, the Gnomon, Mummy, and Synapse.

High school students' sense of humor isn't (or wasn't) particularly inspired. In the sense that it involves relatively little imagination and almost exclusively makes use of what comes to hand, that is, in textbooks and in class. It reduces the universe to the scope of a Cliff's Notes and then continues to work on that to reduce it still smaller, miniaturizing, swept up in the same perfectionistic and caricatural delirium that led some, before classroom exercises, to copy over in characters scant microns across whole chapters on a scrap of paper that could be rolled up inside the shaft of a Bic ballpoint pen. It was a technique straight out of a spy movie, so labor-intensive that it would have been much less work simply to study those chapters. The result of this mind-set were ditties, bland parodies. "Knock, knock. / Who's there? / Euripides. / Euripides who? / Euripides trousers?" (the gags all had this dated, almost classical flavor) and "Knock, knock. / Who's there? / Eumenides. / Eumenides who? / Eumenides trousers?" The same kind of stuff that our fathers might have recited with an identical sophomoric snicker. "This is Lavinia, your future bride / feel her down under, slip your finger inside."

School in my days and Arbus's days was still in many ways as it had been in the postwar years (but how long did these blessed postwar years go on and, above all, when is it that they finally stopped stopping?), and it would change before our eyes, or perhaps I should say, under our feet—I mean to say, as children, we entered a school that seemed eternal, eternally unchanged, and when we got out, everything had changed from top to bottom, the world, the school, of course us, but even the priests who ran it were no longer the same, they were no longer the old stiff-necked bigots with the haggard faces of Spanish saints, their eyes burning with who knows what, perhaps in fact it was the priests who changed more than anything else. The only thing about them that remained the same was the tunic.

OUR SCHOOL, the SLM Institute, was a private school, religious in nature, with a monthly tuition and boarding fee, and teachers who were nearly all priests, especially in the elementary classes. In middle school and high school, the lay teachers became more and more numerous until, in the last couple of years, they were in the majority. You might deduce from this fact that the priests weren't prepared to teach anything more complicated than the lowest or most generic levels of instruction (such as: reading, writing, and arithmetic); or that, quite the contrary, they reserved for themselves the first few years in their students' education, since those are the most decisive from every point of view, including the religious sphere, which was near and dear to their own hearts and the hearts of the families (though not all of them, as we shall see). Probably both things were true. The Institute stood and still stands on Via Nomentana near the Basilica di Santa Costanza, and therefore on the eastern border of the Quartiere Trieste, a border that in fact runs along Via Nomentana, the long tree-lined boulevard, dense with traffic and romanticism, that ends at Porta Pia, where the Bersaglieri breached the walls and entered Rome. The salient events of our story will take place in the rectangle encompassed by Via Nomentana, the Tangenziale Est, or eastern bypass, Via Salaria, and Viale Regina Margherita. Nowadays the Institute, perhaps because of financial problems or for a lack of paying students, which amounts to the same thing, has been split up and reduced in size, and the buildings overlooking Via Nomentana, where the high school classes were once taught, are now occupied by a university that—before noticing the sign next to the gate, just a few yards away from the entrance to the pool where I now go to swim a couple of times a week—I had never even heard of. At the time in which this story takes place, the SLM Institute could fairly be called a very modern school.

2

THERE ARE THOSE who maintain that the cult of the Virgin Mary is an archaic holdover from the powerful and widespread matriarchal religions that came before the advent of male deities and also defied their dominion; others instead see in that cult the symbolic and highly effective reduction of a woman's role to that of mother, exclusively mother—loving mother, sorrowful, dolorous mother; yet others view it as the sole and invaluable acknowledgment—within the context of a monotheism rigidly based upon such male figures as the father, the son, and the patriarch—of the decisive importance of the female half of the species, not only in ensuring that the world exists, but also that it be both humane and inhabitable. To put it in other words, let's just be relieved that there's a woman in that gallery of bearded, highly vocal men. At least we have Her. She at least is there to rehabilitate Her sex from the beginning of things, so badly ruined by the misbegotten actions of her foremother. The religious order of the brothers of SLM was dedicated to the Virgin for all these reasons, plus the other, more obvious one, namely to ensure that there be a Mother to worry about and watch over the rearing and education of children and young men, the loveliest and most attentive and patient and indulgent of mothers, but also (as in the wonderful painting by Max Ernst, *La Vierge corrigeant l'Enfant Jésus*, or *Young Virgin Spanking the Infant Jesus in Front of Three Witnesses*) a Mother capable of administering punishment when necessary, albeit in a perfectly lighthearted manner. It really is hard to imagine (in spite of the various schools of thought about child-rearing that were progressively establishing themselves in those years, to the point that they became a sort of unquestioned common sense, maintaining exactly this view) that there could be any form of education that called for no form of punishment whatsoever. And I say this because punishments, leaving aside any consideration of whether they are just and proper retribution and whether they actually result in deterrence— it is surely reasonable to question whether they are and whether they do—in any case serve to develop in those who are subjected to them, rightly or wrongly, an anger that might prove quite useful if it can only be turned to the purposes of the education in question. Punishments, then, are useful as a way of testing and developing an individual's resistance rather than breaking it. Only those who are shattered by the punishments they receive actually transform them into pointless humiliations, which they will then proceed to resent and wallow in obsessively. For everyone else, punishments constitute merely so many ordeals to be overcome, much like the Labors of Hercules, calling upon inner resources that only in this fashion can one discover, to one's astonishment, and make use of. Strength and intelligence and even personal dignity, then, begin to run in the veins of those who resist and react to punishment, qualities that would otherwise remain in a dormant state; one would never even know that one possessed them. In other words, it's not sufficiently appreciated that morale precedes morality, but in time there is a complete confluence of the two, and that among the constituent elements of both morale and morality we should also count the resentments created by authority with its acts of repression. It's a very simple chemical reaction in the soul. Neither revolutionaries nor patriots, scientists, or even ordinary bank clerks, much less nurses and lawyers and dermatologists, would ever develop into fully formed persons unless someone along their path, much like in the game of snakes and ladders, chose to hinder their progress from time to time, by sending them back to square one, inflicting a penalty, and often for contrived reasons or at the slightest misstep. Any initiation cannot help but be painful, at least in part.

THE PRIESTS of the SLM Institute were well acquainted with the virtues of the Virgin Mary and how to make the best use of them in the course of their teaching, a pursuit that was at the basis of their calling. Just as there are military orders and mendicant orders, so there were the brothers of SLM, an order predicated upon the mission of teaching. Certainly, it was a bizarre detail that the principles of their protrectress should be applied by a community consisting exclusively of men; and that the recipients of their loving efforts should also be only and exclusively male. Teachers and students at SLM: all males, with just one great Mother and Queen, like some sort of beehive. The priests' objective—tenacious gardeners that they were, tilling a garden of pumpkins and tomatoes, was to raise young men to adulthood and eventually take them to ripe maturity as good Christians; the first of these goals was by no means an easy one, while the second, which may perhaps at the time of the order's foundation (1816) have seemed obvious and straightforward, with the passing of time had become increasingly daunting, up to and including the period in which our story unfolds, when the very expression "good Christian" had become indecipherable and everyone interpreted it as they saw fit, adding to it psychological or political shadings—the pope meant one thing by it, individual worshippers quite another, and even sinners could rightly proclaim themselves to be good Christians, indeed, perhaps the very best, seeing that they were the raw material, the ultimate evangelical resource, the latest generation of prodigal sons and potential Mary Magdalenes, an authentic seedbed worthy of tending for eventual redemption, in short, and in fact it was these last-mentioned paragons that the students of SLM wound up most closely resembling: aspiring young sinners.

According to the Eastern tradition, it is said that Mary never died but instead fell into a deep sleep, and in that state she abandoned earthly life.

I DON'T KNOW, I still don't know, I still haven't figured out what I think of priests. How I feel about them. It's a deep and lasting controversy. There are a few aspects, indeed a great many, of the priestly way that I find within myself, starting with my shoes, those shiny black lace-ups, slightly elongated, that I've always bought, never varying the style, unfailingly prompting this comment—"Once again, you've bought yourself a pair of priest shoes"—or else sandals, that's right, sandals, which are so fashionable these days, albeit in rude and daring styles, and which can be found in all kinds of stores, though I used to go buy them from a shoemaker over near the Roman Ghetto, who made them expressly for monks, with the penitential strips of black leather that crucified your foot, bruised as any martyr in a Mannerist painting, the foot of the month of May when it sticks out, pale and skinny, from beneath a pair of winter socks, courageously exposing itself to view.

Many years ago, a young woman made me blush by telling me that "you could see from my face" that I'd gone to a school run by priests, and however hard I tried to take it as a joke, wiping my forehead clean of that stain, consisting not of one scarlet letter but actually three, S, L, and M, I was actually cut to the quick. Stabbed in the heart. Indeed, for many years to come, like some young and evasive St. Peter, I concealed the truth that I had attended SLM, had been taught by priests, just as you might conceal a physical defect, avoiding the topic or outright lying, and I was lucky if the question was formulated, "What school did you graduate from?" whereupon I'd promptly reply, "Liceo Giulio Cesare!" a public high school on Corso Trieste. Neglecting to mention that I'd spent the previous twelve years at the Catholic school.

That was when I understood what it meant to be ashamed of one's own identity, to the point of hating it. To be so embarrassed that you inwardly admit the right of others to hold you in unjustified contempt. The accusers generally ask for nothing better than to be offered good reasons by those they've targeted.

In time, though, I learned that the only way to avoid shame is not so much to accept oneself (impossible to do!), but rather to boast about it, to show off the very thing you once concealed. Toss out an open challenge of defiance. Like in a gay pride parade, in other words.

From that point on, the fact that I'd been taught by priests became a jolly joker, a wild card that could be played without warning. A self-accusation, a denunciation of my own education.

✥

FOR MANY YEARS I have also imitated or worn other elements of priestly attire, more or less consciously, for instance, the black, square-cut overcoat. The rejection of color, mistrust when it comes to variety. Likewise, a vague aspiration to egalitarian garb, the forced brotherhood of the uniform that frees us from the anxious necessity of gauging ourselves, comparing each with the other, and therefore of choosing, judging, and suffering beneath the hammer of other people's opinions of us. Of course, this aspiration is defensive by nature, it's a way of protecting oneself. I confess that I am afflicted with a sort of obsession with comparison, but not on serious matters, rather on the most frivolous things, trivialities, a man who plunges endlessly into the abyss of details, and can suffer over a half-inch miscut on the hem of his trouser leg, just as he can rejoice at a brassiere that increases by a full measure the volume of its content. The only way to abolish this incessant turmoil would be not to multiply endlessly the differences, as libertarians insist, until it becomes impossible to compare individuals at all, each one unique in her or his singularity, but rather to eliminate those differences entirely and never give them another thought. One less thing to worry about. For starters, why don't we all dress alike? A world without judgments and without controls is thus implemented once and for all, in the mornings we dress without reflecting, so that no young man or young woman suffers at the thought that their T-shirt might not be quite right, or feels superior because it is. Everyone in uniform, and not another word on the matter, wouldn't that be great? A jumpsuit, a kaftan, a tunic, perhaps a hat topped with a feather. Just to make it clear who you're dealing with, whether it's a soldier a priest a fireman a factory worker a millionaire or a convict. These days, only gypsies and Carabinieri make it clear who they are . . .

Hey, this isn't some regret I'm expressing. I regret nothing at all, because even in my day uniforms no longer existed, they'd all been converted without distinction into the one obligatory uniform of T-shirt and jeans, the straitjacket of casual wear (therefore, they were by no means a marker of grim conformity, uniforms—if anything, they were proud signs of one's differences . . .), and when I did my required military service, the regulations had just been changed, which meant that off duty we could go out dressed just as we pleased. That meant that, while up until just a few months ago the city of Taranto was overrun at night by thousands of young sailors and air force men, clad in shapeless uniforms but still, somehow, dignified in their shared tawdry squalor, in the brotherhood of that ridiculous obligation, when our turn came (the draft contingent of September 1979), we were a tidal wave of oafish young men from every corner of Italy, but so very oafish . . . so grimly tumbled together and even more anonymous than if we'd all been in uniform.

A PRIEST'S TUNIC is an article of clothing that inspires respect in me, and by respect, I mean a recognition of diversity. Not a way of bridging this distance; if anything, of preserving it. Diversity is a factor of both attraction and repulsion. These days it is not generally tolerated. People say that in a faceless crowd no one pays attention to anyone else, but that's not true, a priest, for instance, or even more so, a nun, is noticed, people pay attention to their clothing, which expresses a specific choice—and this choice, since it's exclusive by nature, makes others feel uncomfortable. You're tempted to tell the priest, Hey you, why are you showing off the fact that you've dedicated your life to God, huh? Do you realize that you're offending me by making a show of how good and holy you are, or rather, claim to be? What are you trying to do, preach me a sermon? Well, listen up, you're worse than me, or maybe I should say, you're *exactly like* me, so why do you act like you're so special?

In this Western world we live in, an environment totally dominated by and devoted to sex, where sex sprays out of the wrinkles of every topic and image, in private phone calls and public billboards, clothing, politics, exercise, sports, TV programs, comedy, and so on, the prominent presence of men who don't have sex is inexplicable; or perhaps they do have sex, but only in secret, which makes hypocrites of them, or else they have no sex at all, which means they're insane. Normally, people assume the former, and in fact, in all my life I've never heard anyone denounced as damned hypocrites the way I've heard priests being condemned. But at least, if that is the case, priests would be proving that deep down they're no different from anyone else, and their alleged diversity is therefore nothing but a trick, a piece of buffoonery.

But what's really intolerable is the thought of another individual's actual chastity. First and foremost, I cannot bring myself to imagine it as anything more than a mutilation. And so, what moral authority ought I to acknowledge, for what reason on earth should I allow myself to be guided aided instructed or even just advised by a man who has so horribly mutilated himself? By giving up the only thing that makes this beastly life worth living at all, namely, love? Let's not beat around the bush here: physical love, that's right, carnal love, which includes within its domain celestial love. I don't want to waste my time listening to refined theological arguments aimed at proving that even the renunciation of love is a form of love, indeed, is an even greater form of love, as one papal encyclical claims. You can't renounce wife and children and then say: I am renouncing nothing. This is not a renunciation, *ceci n'est pas une pipe*: there are times when Catholicism appears to be a forerunner and subsequently an epigone of Surrealism. It takes any ordinary thing and then claims that that thing is the exact opposite of what it clearly and unmistakably actually is. Go to a funeral, you're feeling sad because someone you care about has died, at least this seems like a point that's beyond discussion, you just want to be left alone to mourn your loss in peace and quiet, and instead there's always a priest at the pulpit—and when I say always, I mean *always*, like a recurring curse!—assuring you that your friend or your close relative, whose loss is a burden of sadness, *isn't actually dead at all*. No, he's not dead. Or she's not dead. Enzo isn't dead. Silvana isn't dead. Cesare isn't dead. Rocco is still alive. Wait, what, aren't they *dead*?! Then what are we even doing here? No, he's not dead, he lives on, and you should all put away your sadness, you should exult with him . . . for him . . . about him . . . rejoice with him . . . Certainly, he is in paradise, where he is now happier than before, and I see what they're doing, I'm not as simple as all that: all the same, I feel that this philosophy is a mockery, a way of pulling the wool over our eyes. It triggers a boundless rage in me, I have to go outside, leave the church, I haven't been able to sit through an entire funeral service in years, I'd rather just wait around on the street for the coffin to be brought out, on the shoulders of the pallbearers, a couple of red-faced relatives and friends and the people from the funeral parlor, with bulging biceps beneath their misshapen jackets. All it seems necessary to do is take the obvious facts and turn them on their heads, and boom, you have the solution. If you're poor, then actually you're rich; diseases are gifts of God; when someone dies it's a benediction because now they're rejoicing with the angels, the first will be last, the blasphemer unbeknownst to himself praises the Lord, if you turn your back on God that means you're searching for Him, if there is no God then that surely means that He's there . . .

Could it be that in this life there's not a single thing laid down straight from the outset, that you don't absolutely feel the urge to *turn upside down*? In the midst of all the, shall we say, active virtues, that push us to be more and better than what we are, those on the other hand that are based on renunciation remain enigmatic. From the respect that we feel for those who commit acts of self-sacrifice to repugnance and ridicule is often only a short step. The typical life of a saint, of the sort frequently narrated in hagiographies, with the customary succession of mortifications and suppurating wounds, would, if replicated nowadays, be the object of universal disgust and censure. But a priest ought to bring at least a crumb of holiness with him, in a corner of his heart, or of his mind, or of his clothing, otherwise what makes him different from the rest of us? If he doesn't possess that speck of sanctity at all, then he's just bluffing, and if instead he does, then we're so unaccustomed to holiness that it frightens us or else it just bores us. The sacred is in fact a form of diversity. Those who are forty years younger than us and have yet to experience their first sexual relationship or get married are sacred, those whose skin is a different color than ours or who go barefoot are sacred, if we are male then women are sacred, if we are female then it is men who are sacred, anyone who wears a fez is sacred, or a turban or a bowler hat or a Bersagliere's plumed hat, while even a top hat rented for a wedding confers the aura of a sacred vestment for the space of an evening upon the head of whoever wears it. The unpronounceable surname of a Sinhalese housecleaner is sacred. Yesterday evening it was sacred for me to glide silently in a boat down the canals of Castello, in Venice. And it is these crumbs of the sacred, these particles of the sacred, that annoy others, unleashing tides of resentment.

SO I SUPPOSE you're someone who talks to God on a daily basis? we're tempted to say to a priest. Show me this God of yours, then, let's have a look at Him, do a miracle for me, here and now, on the spot. I realize that I often use, mentally, the same language that was used in the interrogations the earliest Christians were subjected to, to which Christ Himself was subjected, before He was nailed up on the cross. *Hic Rhodus, hic salta.* From every religious credo we demand, and not entirely without reason, that it prove itself immediately redemptive and healing: instead they all promise things far away and in the distant future, rewards that will come later, far too late, at the end of times, so that in the meantime we find ourselves settling for the lesser and propitiatory, semi-magical aspects, a smidgen of consolation from the harshness that we are forced to tolerate in the here and now, some miracle small or great, the chilly caress of the statue of a saint that protected you in some catastrophe, an airbag inflated with prayers.

One day when I happened to be in Padua, I left the hotel early in the morning and, turning the corner, realized that I was a hundred yards from the Basilica of St. Anthony (the night before, arriving half crocked in the taxi, I hadn't noticed it). I entered the church, walked toward the urn that contained the saint's remains, and I have to admit that as I got closer and closer, I could feel a powerful and inexplicable emotion growing inside me. It wasn't as if the wave of this new sentiment in any way erased my prior skepticism, since I can't even call myself a skeptic, nonbeliever, or atheist, as I'm not even any of those: I'm nothing. Personal convictions had little to do with it: perhaps it was just a kind of current, the magnetic ring formed of the vows that had been circulating around that stone structure for centuries. When I was close enough to the sepulcher that I could reach out and touch it, and did so, caressing one of its walls, I realized that the multicolored tiles that covered it were not marble inlay, as I had thought, but photographs stuck on with adhesive tape, dozens and dozens of photographs, and they were all pictures of crushed or gutted or burnt car wrecks, the kind of pictures you take after a car crash to send to the insurance company for a payout. Though, to judge from the seriousness of those wrecks, none of the cars would ever be repaired. There were cars whose entire hood had been shoved back into the passenger compartment as a result of a head-on collision, others with the roof smashed down all the way to the level of the backrests of the seats, leaving little room to the imagination of what must have become of the occupants of the vehicle. Instead, however, to my surprise, next to the photographs taken by the highway police, there were other, smaller and more recent, pictures, this time Polaroids, depicting a smiling man or woman, and a note thanking the saint for having saved them. I learned that by deciphering some of those messages, written in English or Spanish with the sort of childishly clear and rounded handwriting that, for instance, Filipinos tend to have, and in fact nearly all of the votive photographs belonged to immigrants, Asian or Hispanic, as if car crashes only befell them or else they alone, by now, in a country that is so unaccustomed to showing gratitude, felt the obligation to thank someone up there for having spared their lives. I was sorry not to have the photographs of the Honda 125 motorbike my daughter Adelaide had been riding just a few weeks earlier when she'd hit a car one morning speeding to school, and the accompanying photograph of her, smile on her face, and safe and sound. I was sorry, but I thought I might still do some good by saying a prayer, "I thank you . . . I thank you . . . for having saved her," but I didn't know exactly whom to thank, who the *you* was that I was thanking. God is far away, the saint is too busy, and in anything he's more likely to listen to those who truly believe in him. So I kept it vague, just like in one of those poems where you're certain the poet is speaking to a woman he loves, but you don't know who.

TAKING JESUS as your model doesn't help. Jesus has always been the opposite of everything. Perhaps it is in fact from Him that issues this obsessive fixation on overturning everything, always turning everything upside down, reversing appearances, overturning fixed hierarchies, overturning the money changers' tables, overturning customary ways. Overturning every instinct, beginning with the simplest of them all: if they smite you, turn the other cheek. And then Jesus overturned the final and only certainty in men's lives, that of death, by bringing Lazarus back from the dead, probably the greatest injustice ever committed. Go explain that to all the other dead who were left underground, to their families, who I doubt shed tears any less salty than those of Martha and Mary, Lazarus's sisters . . . This is a quality common to all great masters, that of overturning all at once a vision of the world after leaving it to steep for a while in the minds of their gullible disciples. They're always coming up late, the disciples, struggling in their effort to grasp and execute; when they try to apply His precepts rigidly, they come off like fools, because in the meantime the Master has chopped those precepts into bits and tossed them over His shoulders, for Him those are last week's news. He's always ten times more rigorous and a hundred times more elastic, the Master. Any priest who tried to follow Christ's example in its entirety would be paralyzed by the task.

And so each of them takes a snippet of that Christ figure and imitates it as best he can. There's the good Christ, the humble one, the teacher, the victim, the mystic, the anarchist, the consoler, the implacable one, the violent Christ, that's right, even violence can be found in that unequaled figure, or at least the violence of those who use words as swords to smite and cut, to sever. There's a mocking Christ, incurably comical, in contrast with what Nietzsche claims ("There is not one single buffoonery in the Gospels; that alone suffices to condemn a book"), and, of course, a tragic Christ. In short, He leaves His followers an entire array of characteristics and attitudes, even though each man will at most manage to take on just one of them. This was already manifest in the apostles (each of them a tile in the mosaic that, taken as a whole, depicted the Master), let alone in the priests of yesterday and today.

The brothers who taught elementary school at SLM were enthusiastic young men, driven by I have no idea what force to remain faithful to their callings. Our teacher was named Brother Germano. I remember him as a young man, open-faced, his hair trimmed short on the back of his neck, a good soccer player. He was a first-rate teacher, or at least I learned a great many things from him, indeed I would say that most of the things I learned there and still remember today were taught to me by Brother Germano. If I were to reckon up percentages of my knowledge, I'd have to guess that 90 percent dates back to my time at school. Later (at the university and in life) I didn't learn much more. Sure, a few notions of art history . . . certain political theories that called for a world ruled by very special tyrants . . . plus a bunch of other things that came in useful then and there and which I used and almost immediately forgot about. Many topics that I studied specifically to write about and then forgot. It's the only way to free oneself of an obsession.

As recently as the sixties, there were still young men in Italy who chose the harsh path of chastity and poverty (by which we mean the renunciation of individual ownership of money and property), and all this in the name of teaching, that is, in order to be able to provide young people with a Christian education. Even if eventually a chemistry teacher would have to do that, teach chemistry, which in and of itself has very little to do with matters Christian or non-Christian, and the same can be said of a French teacher or a gym teacher: what specific aspect of this is Christian I couldn't say. Is there really any reason, in order to explain to a classroom full of lunkheaded, spoiled boys how sulfuric acid is formed, or to get them to repeat the nasal French sounds of *an, en, in, on,* and *un* . . . why the teacher should take vows? The teachers, in fact, weren't even priests (I call them priests for convenience, but they were by no means priests, and they couldn't say mass), having received only minor orders, which made the meaning of their sacrifice even more mysterious. What reward awaited them in return for their efforts? To see us become good Christians, or good citizens? How many good Christians did SLM actually produce? Formed as men to go out into the world, from that confessional and nonconfessional clay. While in elementary school, our teachers were priests, enthusiastic young priests, in middle school the teaching staff was a mix, and in high school the teachers were nearly all laymen. The only priests in high school were the philosophy and chemistry teachers. The Italian teacher (who I liked very much, Giovanni Vilfredo Cosmo) was a layman, and so was the Greek and Latin teacher, likewise the math, physics, and art history teachers. I never knew if that was because of any lack of specific knowledge and preparation, that is, whether there were no priests trained to teach those subjects; perhaps it was because that order's specific choice was to devote itself to primary education, which forms individuals at an early age and in an indelible manner, while single disciplines at higher levels of education can perfectly well be imparted by qualified professionals. I've always wondered whether the lay teachers at SLM were ever asked, when they were officially hired, to make an explicit profession of faith, in other words, just how these teachers were asked to comply with the model of a Catholic school, and with its principles. When I think back to my high school teachers, none of them seemed sanctimonious to me—not even vaguely religious. Never once in class did they mention God or the Virgin Mary. Indeed, the Latin and Greek teacher, De Laurentiis, showed an unmistakable inclination toward paganism. It was the subject itself, with its erotic and heroic undertones, that sent him into a state of ecstasy, and that veil of excitement was enough to conceal the sense of ridicule and defeat that gnawed at him, and make up, at least in part, for the frustration of having to teach all those luxuriant riches to classrooms full of ignorant, spoiled boys, who simply looked on at his vehemence with pity. It is love's fate to be the target of mockery. Not one of his passions was conveyed to us, not even a line of the poets and philosophers he read out loud, emphasizing their meter, entered our heads or captured our hearts. His heavy Neapolitan accent as he declaimed Thucydides and Virgil, for that matter, left us disappointed and indifferent. Our detachment was far crueler than any mutiny could have been. Nothing could be worse than a classroom of boys who snicker at things that you personally find exciting and stirring. De Laurentiis had made up his mind to let us hear a sample of ancient Greek music, he'd obtained sheet music from some obscure source, and he'd had his son play it on an electric keyboard of some kind, I think a GEM Mini or a Bontempi organ, or else an Eko Tiger combo organ, and in class he'd played the recordings for us. They were whiny monodies, played with a single finger, and he would follow their ascending and descending notes with the hand gestures of a rapt conductor, as if painting the melody in the air, half-closing his eyes against the sunshine beaming through the branches of the pine trees outside the window, murmuring "mmm . . . mmm . . ." along with the melody as it monotonously rose and fell, rose and fell, "mmm . . . mmm . . . mmm . . . ," until the sheer joy of his exclamation, "*mmm . . . mmmusic from ancient Greece!!*" It seemed as if that thin line of notes had crossed twenty-five centuries of history just so that he could grumble along with them. Then he'd open his eyes, giddy with happiness, and discover that no one, no one except him, was even listening.

✧

BUT THESE WERE INNOCUOUS mythologies, minor ecstasies that we concede to anyone so disposed. The mania that lurks in all our hearts, if anything, is snuffed out by an excess of tolerance, and certainly Catholicism, whatever else might be said about it, is the most tolerant, elastic, and indulgent of religious professions, what with its constant habit of forgiving all and any sins, even the most infamous, and it practically gives the impression that it's justifying them, so that in its noblest and most elevated moments it skims dangerously close to amorality, its embrace is so ample that it becomes practically impossible to escape its conciliatory grip, those welcoming arms become tentacles. In a country that was still as profoundly religious as Italy in those years, where only avowed atheists were willing to step outside of and set themselves against common sentiment, evidently the fact of being a Catholic, a good Catholic, or only just someone who attends Christmas mass "because it's so charming," was considered a natural state of affairs, something along the lines of the air that you breathe. Deep down, after all, I think that our teachers were asked to do nothing more than be like everyone else. A friend of mine who had applied to teach at a private girls' boarding school a few years ago was asked a question by the headmaster, who had gathered all possible information about the candidate and checked out his extensive CV; he knew that this question would be decisive to the outcome of the interview:

"Are you married?"

"No."

"Engaged?"

"No."

"But then, tell me . . . do you like women?"

It was obviously a booby trap. My friend's instinct to lie (in reality he would drool at the sight of any even faintly desirable young woman) would have led him to reply precipitously "No!" which would have spelled his ruin. Ah, no? Liar, or pederast. But if he'd frankly replied "Yes!" that would have been even worse. At a girls' boarding school, which is more dangerous and unseemly, a teacher who likes women, or one who doesn't? What about at a boys' boarding school (this question, as we shall see, is even more interesting and would require a courageous answer . . .)? My friend, instead, improvised an answer in perfect priestly style: that is to say, a masterpiece of evasiveness.

"So, do you like women?"

"Well . . . just like any *good Christian*," he said, with a smile.

CATHOLICISM CALLS FOR a reasonable restraint of one's instincts, rather than a total repression. "For it is better to marry than to burn." There was a time, in the early eighties, when St. Augustine was fashionable, more or less like *Siddhartha*. Personally, I found that his famous yet painfully slow conversion grated on my nerves, that reluctance to be willing to become good. If one day you really understand the right thing to do, then hurry up and do it, right? I prefer, however crude and fanciful they might be, the dramatic crises, the falls from horseback, the dazzling lights and thunderous voices telling you what to do, so that you obey without hesitation—the psychology of Augustine wears me down with all its nuanced twists and turns. Our philosophy teacher was named Brother Gildo. He was a cold and meticulous man, already rather well along in years, who scrupulously prepared his lessons, though he gave the impression that the material was far away, no longer within reach, and that he'd had to study it all over again, making more than a few efforts along the way. In other words, he seemed like an aging reservist called back to active teaching in the aftermath of some emergency. Perhaps he'd studied theology as a young man, and the headmaster, encountering staffing problems, must have thought that philosophy worked more or less the same way: a succession of implacable abstractions. Strange how the science of God proceeds with roughly the same pedantry as the others, interrupted here and there by great bursts of flame. Taking the breviary out of his hand and hastily thrusting a history of philosophy (and perhaps a few volumes of Cliff's Notes) in its place, he then tossed Brother Gildo into the trenches of the classrooms. Up until Aristotle, his detached and notional lessons led us to believe that the earliest philosophers were, basically, deranged maniacs who were in the constant throes of hallucinations and saw the world as if it were made entirely of fire or water or atoms with little arms and paws to clutch at other atoms or as a slanting rain of grayish matter or other such nonsense, to say nothing of the absurd Platonic myths. Recounted, or rather coldly reported, by Brother Gildo in his nasal, incredulous voice, those daring phantasmagorias left us cold. I really found it incomprehensible that anyone could ever have taken this bullshit seriously, such as the idea of men parading back and forth like targets from a sideshow shooting gallery with statues tied to the tops of their heads, and all this just to play a game of Chinese shadow puppets in order to deceive prisoners in a cave (?), seriously, what, are we kidding? That was supposed to be philosophy? The greatest creation of human intelligence? That everything is number (which means what?) and that dogs have souls and it's forbidden to eat fava beans? And those would be the champions of world thought?

Then came Aristotle's turn. There the schematic nature that Brother Gildo wore emblazoned into his very physique, skinny and gnarled as he was, was elevated to the dignity of a system. The curly brackets on the blackboard grew thick and fast and his voice became increasingly nasal. Since he was incapable of speaking spontaneously off the cuff, he was constantly forced to refer back to his notes, which were written in such a minute script that even he struggled to decipher them, adjusting the little wire-rim spectacles that slid down his beak of a nose. In the end, he gave up the idea of explaining at all and limited himself to reading aloud variously from the textbook, now from his little sheaves of notes. Or else he'd copy his diagrams out on the blackboard, and we in our turn were expected to copy them into our notebooks. Aristotle himself is already the barest of barebones reasoning, so it is hard to imagine how he managed to render his work even more schematic than it already was. This was a charming pastime known at school as "dictating notes": a pure oxymoron. Notes that are dictated are, by very definition, *not* notes. Under dictation, the very essence of that most noble art is lost. Note-taking is the very first form of understanding and framing of a broader topic. Dictating notes is an approach that only very ignorant teachers, at the beginning of their careers, employ, or else exhausted ones, at the end. They turn on autopilot and churn along until the bell rings. The result of this further distillation of the philosopher's thoughts was an incomprehensible algebra. It seemed as if Brother Gildo, by impersonally dictating those formulations, had freed himself, and consequently us, from the duty of understanding. That is why some students are fond of this method, which has the advantage of being clear and requires no particular effort, resulting in a reasonable tacit understanding with the teacher: he is not forced to raise his voice, and peace and quiet reigns sovereign in the classroom because all the students are silent as they write.

They come out much cleaner, those pages of counterfeit notes, nice and dense, tidy, regular, and free of corrections or scratch-outs.

We had a classmate, Zipoli, who wrote the notes for all his subjects in a single notebook, in pencil. He only needed one notebook because his handwriting was so small and precise. In half a page, he could fit the entire

Renaissance. His handwriting was as fine as a hair on a newborn's head. But why in pencil? The explanation came at the end of the year. On the last day of school, Zipoli took an eraser and *deleted* everything that he had written during the year. Patiently, page by page, in a fine shower of rubber shavings. The notebook turned blank again, ready to be reused the following year. It became virgin again. In five years of high school, Zipoli only ever owned one notebook, always the same one, plus, of course, various pencils (with 3H lead?), and a set of erasers. He came from a large family, with five or six Zipoli brothers, I never knew whether they handed their notebooks down from one to the other, if they were deeded at the end of the school career. Sometimes I imagine that the entire Zipoli family used that single notebook, like the Graeae, who shared one eye among them, passing it from one to the other. (By the way, the Zipolis didn't own a TV. As far as I know, they were the only family who didn't. That fact amazed me.) Zipoli did well at school, after Arbus he was one of the best. Scrupulous, reserved, understated, he had curly blond hair so close to ash in color that it seemed white, in fact he looked old already; at age seventeen, Zipoli looked like an aged Swede. One day he asked me to lend him a helmet so he could go on a trip by Vespa, riding behind a friend, to Sweden, in fact. Two months later he brought it back to me, without a scratch on it.

Zipoli was accustomed to leaving no signs of his passage. If he did produce them, he carefully erased them.

WITH HIS PAINSTAKINGLY MINUTE WORK, Brother Gildo was successful in ruining, or perhaps we should say, in forestalling my understanding of philosophy, roughly speaking, from Thales to Kant. Something I never fully recovered. I am sorry to say that my mind grew deformed and quite modern. Those gaps in an education can't be backfilled. Subsequent readings and studies are like artificial limbs applied to a mutilated limb: however artfully made, they struggle in vain to simulate the naturalness of gestures, with their hooks at best you can reach out and clutch a glass and raise it to your lips, but you can't use them to play the piano. Certain topics or historical periods or even entire disciplines have remained out of my reach, like kingdoms that were destined to my rule, but lost before I could wear their crown. Luckily, at least Kant would be wisely reviewed by my new philosophy teacher (a *professoressa*, a woman! After a priest, *a woman!*) the following year, after I left the school run by priests for the reasons I will lay out later. She knew that there was no way ever to understand Kant sufficiently, it's not humanly possible to assimilate and remember it all after a three-month summer vacation, and I certainly couldn't have, given that I, thanks to the good offices of the elderly Marist brother, hadn't understood a single thing Kant had written, and so *she explained it all from the very start*. From first principles, which is where that body of thought itself begins, the first thought, as if it burst forth from nothingness.

My new teacher at Giulio Cesare High School felt the utmost contempt for me because I had been attending a school taught by priests. She considered me a child of wealth and privilege, spoiled and ignorant, which for that matter is the exact description I offered a few lines earlier of both myself and my classmates. The simple fact that I'd ever attended a private school at all disqualified me in her eyes. My math teacher and my Italian teacher felt the same way about me. At a public high school with a bit of a reputation, as was the Giulio Cesare of the time, anyone who came from a private Catholic school might as well have been branded with a mark of infamy. So you can just imagine if they'd transferred in senior year, in the offing for the final exams. If they didn't want him even there . . . that is what they must have thought about me. I was a piece of human detritus, in short, kicked upstairs from one grade to the next until the priests had grown heartily sick of me, so sick that they were willing to give up my tuition. I had in store for me some real ostracism and a bounty of humiliations—on one of my first days of school there, I was tossed out of class for "sitting impolitely" (that's right! In the middle of the seventies such a thing was still possible!) with the sarcastic comment, "They've spoiled him, the young master . . ." I walked out into the hallway, filled with shame and disbelief. I'd never thought of myself as "different." Apparently, however, I was.

To have studied at a school run by priests was an original sin that would have to be scrubbed out.

What does that sin consist of?

FIRST OF ALL, it's a marker of social class. Anyone who attends a private school clearly has money. And this condition of privilege, admired or envied in other ways, can have its disadvantages, its contraindications, its collateral effects. That is why even the rich are sometimes ashamed of their wealth and tread a path of purification spangled with charity, enlistment in revolutionary movements, rejection (for the interim) of the inheritances that await them, and systematic squandering of great estates. Italian society is, in fact, a class-based hierarchy, like all other societies, but it's

equipped with ingenious mechanisms of reparations, for the most part fan-
tastical in nature, just like any and all systems that dream of compensating
for injustices while leaving unaltered the harsh economic facts on which
those injustices are founded. The supposed vendetta almost always remains
on the verbal plane, where the Italians are past masters. Indeed, I would say
that the central axis of Italian culture is formed of geniuses cursed by misfortune who console and ennoble themselves, craft their vengeance, and
invent a better fate for themselves or lay waste to their enemies in a
bloodbath—all with words. The most illustrious and unattainable paragon:
Dante. But before him and in his wake there is a horde of wildcat despera-
does who tirelessly produce elegies and songs and cantos, landscapes and
dreams, virtual paradises and enchanted groves and knights and sorcerers,
and revolutions and visions and prophecies and apocalypses that were
meant to rectify (or at least help to forget for a while) the wrongs inflicted.
Only thus made whole—alas, on a strictly symbolic level—can life become
tolerable. The rigidity of social distinctions is probably less unforgiving
here in Italy than in England or France, but if wealth in any case remains
out of reach, then it is made the target of a very particular scorn. Which is
not merely the thuggish and plebeian sneer, the bow from the waist turned
on its head with an insult ("My good sir, would you care for some shit?") or
a Bronx cheer. No, what I'm talking about is the seething petit bourgeois
resentment that springs from frustrated aspirations, from dashed admiration for something to which one imagines to lay legitimate claim by proximity. Or else from a thirst for egalitarian principles that, unable to raise
one, merely degrades, incapable of elevating, hurls down, and is therefore
only too eager to exult every time a wealthy man tumbles into disgrace.
When this, all too rarely, actually happens, there is genuine jubilation. It's
time to pay for the original sin of money.

The curse of gold . . . infectious . . .

The wealthy man, this figure out of the Gospels, rendered legendary . . .

In Italian society, the rich often tend to camouflage themselves, and in
fact it is more likely that the false rich or the halfway rich show off their
Audis purchased straight out of the showroom, with zero mileage. True
wealth refracts its image deceptively, allowing others to believe what they
will, turning away gazes, fostering illusions, raising screens and mirrors.

What's more, wealth in Italy is only rarely recognized as something
that can have been acquired honestly and through merit; it is far more likely
that people will think of it as the fruit of theft or good fortune, or a blend
of the two. Rhetoric flames when it's time to stigmatize "the easily acquired

fortunes and quick profits," but only when the tax authorities are pulling up out front, rarely if ever before then. The rise and, even more eagerly, the fall of the rich are followed with all the excitement of a public lottery. And the extraordinary thing is that the catastrophe is almost never definitive, the wealthy always seem able to rise from the ashes and begin their climb again until they can reach a height from which it is worth one's trouble to fall.

(Only those who die early are permanently out of the running: this is the origin of every suicide's damned impatience . . .)

Now, the students attending SLM were for the most part the sons of a medium-to-high-level bourgeoisie, but even of the petit bourgeoisie, whose parents had decided to put on airs by sending their boy to a private school, or else hoped to protect him generically from the threats and pitfalls of the world or assure him teachers who wouldn't be replaced in the middle of the year or go on strike, a swim course and a pottery course, and maybe even procure him a few useful friendships to carry him through his life. I believe that few if any did it for any exquisitely religious preferences, that is to say, the real reason that the school existed in the first place. The tuition wasn't high enough to scare off the shopkeepers and civil servants of the Quartiere Trieste and Quartiere Africano, or even of farther-flung neigh- borhoods that back then constituted the outlying borders of the city: such as Talenti. They'd make a sacrifice, and sometimes they'd make it double or even triple, depending on how many brothers there were. If I think about those who will soon become the protagonists of this story, and who will be described in the popular press as young and pitiless nabobs—well, one was the son of a hotel desk clerk, another one's father worked in an office at the national Workers' Compensation office.

Another good reason to sneer at an alumnus of SLM was the idea (I have no way to verify this in any statistically grounded fashion) that in that school even utter dunces were passed from one year to the next just because they paid tuition. Private school considered as a professional service is a paradox, perhaps the only case in which it is the supplier of the service who judges the quality of the work, rather than the paying customer. That is the inherent contradiction of thinking of teaching as nothing more than a hired service: I do a job for you but in the end it is I who tells you that the result is unsatisfactory, and whose fault is that? Mine? No, yours . . . If a teacher is the equivalent of a dentist, and he teaches lessons the way he might drill a tooth and fill a cavity, but then the tooth splits, is it because you just didn't try hard enough as a patient? In order to avoid such a con- tradiction, I believe, rather than any full-fledged act of corruption, it was in fact rare that anyone flunked a year at SLM. And they tended to involve the edge cases, the most serious cases of misconduct. For better or worse, all the others seemed to be promoted to the next grade, this much is true.

But the genuine reason for discomfort in the presence of the new arrival was the faint scent of the sacristy. I didn't know I was emanating it. But it wasn't just the teachers, my new classmates could smell it, too.

SLM (SAN LEONE MAGNO) took its name from the great Pope Leo, who had barred the barbarian king's way by holding up the cross. Whereupon the barbarian had halted his onslaught, choosing not to invade Italy. A savior, in other words, a protector. I'm not interested to learn that this story is a legend, that the invader was actually paid off with the gold of who knows how many crucifixes melted down, and agreed to turn around and go off to devastate some other land, or some other prosaic explanation of events: the demystification of ancient stories fundamentally irritates me, having spent half my life swallowing stories like molten gold and the other half being told that not one of them was true . . . well, I'm actually much fonder of the first half. Just like the convicts I now teach, veritable sweepings of the nation's prisons, who clap their hands over their ears if I venture to tell them that the Trojan horse is a fairy tale, no, hold on a minute, I don't believe you, teacher, that can't be true! Otherwise the whole house of cards of school itself tumbles to the ground, and in fact it's been crumbling since the day they first dared to state that the heroes of antiquity were basically rogues and criminals, Gaius Mucius Scaevola a self-destructive kamikaze, Joan of Arc a schizophrenic, that it wasn't the Arabs who killed Roland at all, but the Basques, and before you know it the protagonists have vanished from the stage of history, and with them their swords and their oaths, to be replaced by an insipid socioeconomic porridge. This unmasking of history, let it be said, was sacrosanct duty, no two ways about it. Teaching is based on myths and, at the same time, like the prestidigitator who makes things appear with one hand while making them disappear with the other, the destruction of those myths. That's the intrinsic metabolism of education, the natural cycle it has to follow. But if you start straight up with disillusionment . . .

In the final analysis, what is it that a young boy should or shouldn't learn?

AND YET LEO TRULY DID DESERVE the sobriquet of Great. He spent his life refuting heretics, and in particular those who refused to acknowledge

Jesus's dual nature. Denying that dual nature was the easiest and most logical thing to do, and therefore also the stupidest, when rational thought is unwilling to give up the ghost so it fights on with its blunted weapons, A is equal to A and A is different from B. No doubt, that is the way it works here on earth, but what about in heaven? If you don't believe that Jesus was *also* a flesh-and-blood man, and that he *really and truly* died on the cross, or do you think instead that he was *only* a man, albeit a rather remarkable one . . . in that case, how can you call yourself a Christian? Why not just drop religion entirely? What's the point of mongrelizing the great mysteries with cold reason that cannot understand, will not understand, demands or pretends to understand, without even bothering to make the effort required to understand? No religion would be acceptable, no religion would make even the slightest bit of sense by the lights of the principle of noncontradiction: they would all be nothing but processions of absurdities. Why did Odin hang himself from a tree, and what does it mean that he sacrificed himself *to* himself, and how could it be that Dionysus was born from one of his father's thighs, or that Athena was born from his forehead? To common sense, practically nothing makes sense, starting with the simple fact that we're here in the world at all. Beneath its patina of reasonableness, common sense is actually the true delirium: it darkens everything with its demand of enlightenment. To these philosophers Pope SLM brought to bear the palpable chill of reason joined with the heat of action.

Yes, I admit it, I took a certain mental habit or way of thinking from the priests, made up of incessant logical reversals, sophisms, virulence banked beneath the ashes . . .

ONE OF THE DUMBEST and perhaps, for that very reason, one of the most successful pranks was this: during Brother Gildo's philosophy lessons, we would nod as he explained, let's say, Aristotle; we'd nod after each sentence he uttered. We'd gaze at him levelly and listen to every word, and with every statement he made we'd nod our heads *yes*, every last one of us, as if eager to assure him that the things he was telling us were true, that we'd understood them, and that we shared them. An entire class of students, serious and attentive, nodding their heads, heads bobbing up and down almost uninterruptedly, like the bobbing heads of those spring-loaded dogs that people used to put in the rear windows of their cars. I have nothing more to say about Brother Gildo.

Socrates tells us
And Xanthippe gives thanks
Better one fuck
Than ten thousand wanks

3

HERE IS THE IMAGE that I've always had in my mind of a class of boys in an all-male high school: crabs in a bucket, that's right, crabs heaped up in a pail.

... AND JUST *as these animals, waving claws and pincers, climb over each other's backs, hoisting themselves up the sheer walls only to fall back and start over from the beginning: the bucket teems with helpless life ...*

BUT IT IS NOT at all true that there is nothing but competition among males, quite the opposite. The profound and natural need that males feel to win love and tenderness and warmth from other males almost inevitably remains unsatisfied, and that is why it is wholly (and sometimes brutally) turned upon women; women who in turn end up, willy-nilly, invested with the unsustainability of that demand, brusquely and violently; likewise, the ritual manifestation of masculinity so often takes a menacing and disproportionate stance toward women, and is actually displayed simply to win respect from other males. Males, in other words, are the real audience other males are appealing to, especially in their teens, it is *their* judgment they depend upon, it is from *them* that they anxiously seek approval and admiration: it is from his classmates and friends that a male, only rarely able to earn love, expects at the very least recognition. And in order to obtain it, he's open to anything.

HOWEVER MUCH I may now complain about not having had girls in my classes at school, I can't really imagine what it would have been like to have them. To experience a normal adolescence at least concerning that aspect. Like the adolescence of my own children, for example.

But, come to think of it, perhaps not even my own children are experiencing one: I think of the younger one, my daughter, a student at the Righi public high school, and her girlfriends, constantly the targets of abuse and harassment, exposed to the cross fire of gossip on social media, the rankings of who is the biggest slut in the school and things like that: stuff that can knock your level of self-respect down to zero or send it skyrocketing to the stars in a giddy and hysterical oscillation . . .

At the age of fourteen they're incessantly subjected to grabbing and groping, intrusive roughhousing, offensive appraisals, and whatever terminology you may choose to apply to it, to a constant psychological and physical pressure on the part of certain of their classmates, who are however (and this is the surprising fact that perhaps deserves further discussion) not at all the early developing or fully developed "macho" males, but quite the contrary, the ones who are still half-children, and almost half-females, without a hair on their face, high-pitched voices, layers of baby fat that have not toughened into muscle or been absorbed, so that the muscle mass can break away from the bone. Their annoying persistence remains childish, but it faithfully predicts their behavior as adults. It is as if, through their bullying (which, luckily, my son, who's a little older and roughly a foot taller and attends the same high school, has promised to put an end to by delivering a pair of well-chosen punches if these students persist in bothering his sister), they fooled themselves into thinking that they thus had grown two or three years older in a single day, thus earning the status to subjugate their female classmates, especially the attractive ones.

BEING BORN a boy is an incurable disease. Arbus wasn't the only one who proved to be awkward and uncoordinated. We all constantly made ungraceful movements when we went to do any given thing, even only to throw our book satchel over our shoulders (back then there were no such things as backpacks, except for camping). If psychologists had chanced to observe our uncoordinated lunges, the way we scratched ourselves or flung our arms in the air, they would have deduced that we were mentally ill. No one realizes just how far a boy would go in order to win the approval of his classmates and pals; the quantity of abuse that he can make up his mind to tolerate, whether inflicted upon himself or inflicted upon others, in order to earn recognition. The game was wearisome and repetitive: it was necessary to prove that we were men, that is, macho males, and the minute we were done proving it, we were immediately required to prove it again, each time starting over from scratch, as if it were always possible simply to lose the masculinity that had just been measured, as if that risk always lay lurking in ambush, as if already having proven a hundred times that we were men meant nothing, because a single misstep, just one failure would erase all the results achieved, wiping out the entire stake one had accumulated. Like in card games or in those sports where the points laboriously piled up can be lost all at once on the next turn, what good does it do to prove your masculinity if just a minute later you wind up back at square one, required to prove your worth again?

And in fact, having come to this conclusion, after striving eagerly to pass these blessed tests, after posing for a lifetime so as to appear courageous, daring, virile, responsible, serious, and so on and so forth, well, once and for all, I've given up, let them take me for queer—amen.

THE GAME was very simple, it was just a matter of being fast: whoever was first to accuse someone else of being queer, wasn't. Whoever had been accused of being queer, in order to disprove the charge, had to accuse someone else, and so on. It was pointless to retort by turning the original accusation on the first one to level it: you had to pass it on to a third target. Anyone who didn't think about girls was queer; but even those who thought about them to the exclusion of all else, the whole blessed day, was equally queer. They both deserved the same amount of mockery.

Hierarchies among boys are established in a crescendo of orders, insults, alliances, and challenges.

When it came to the bullies at school, you could be:

a) Subordinate
b) Complicit
c) Persecuted/marginalized
d) Or belong to a category that was difficult to define (Nonaligned?), that the bullies left alone, considering it too much effort or basically useless to fight, sort of the way Hitler treated Switzerland. I belonged to this fourth category. The appropriate term might be "neutrality," except not enough thought is ever given to the reasons one might have for remaining neutral, and what is required in order for that status to be granted.

✦

IN ORDER TO BE FUNNY, a prank has to contain something amusing and
something hostile. A perfectly innocuous prank makes no one laugh, it
remains inexplicable: if it isn't crude, why do it? Why bother to organize
it? Even the victim, if he is in no way harmed by the prank, wonders why
he was targeted in the first place. Vulgarity, for example, remains absolutely necessary if one means to forge a bond of brotherhood: vulgarity
tends to be established on a lower level, tending toward the filthy, the trivial, the offensive, but since brotherhood per se tends to strive upward, it
is clear how one can proceed in just a few rapid steps from mongrel
wisecracks about women to the sublime love of the Dolce Stil Novo,
and from the heavy-handed spirit of the locker room to acts of altruistic
self-sacrifice and heroism, migrating from body to soul by imperceptible
degrees . . .

For instance, I've reached an age at which it is customary to consider
one's status to be an achievement gained after a lifetime of effort, and yet,
strangely enough, I care little or nothing about status now, while I cared
about it frantically when I was thirty or so and even more than that when I
was a teenager, ah, how I worried back then about how others saw me, how
I worried that I be considered the handsomest, the smartest, even the most
likable, even though I knew I was none of those things (Arbus's intelligence
knew no rivals; the laurel wreath of sheer beauty was fought over among
Zarattini—an angel—and Jervi and Sdobba, and when it came to likability,
I knew that I was struggling feebly, while both Modiano and Pilu would
have swept the vote with unanimous victories), and how I suffered at the
thought! But it wasn't only at school that this desire burned within me, but
rather during the holidays, when the landscape was adorned with girls and
the frenzy to lead the pack was focused on them. How I yearned, at the
beach, in the summer, at the ages of thirteen fourteen fifteen sixteen, how
I seethed with the desire to be held in consideration by the others my age,
boys and girls alike! I'd have done anything to please them, to win their
respect and approval! Even though I was shy and pretty much a coward,
I'd have been willing to take part in any risky or disreputable undertaking
if it would allow me to emerge from my state of anonymity, that place in
the shadows where no one ever remembers your name and they mistake
you for someone else and it always seems like they're meeting you for the
first time.

✢

WE DEVELOP those aspects of ourselves that we think others will like best. First of all for our mother, then to our young playmates, and eventually to everyone on whom we want to make a good impression, contemporaries, grown-ups, teachers, girls, we present the part of ourselves, and only that portion, that we imagine has the best chance of being approved and accepted. The rest remains in the shadows, and only someone with a very sharp eye (generally, our friends, and even more than our friends, our enemies) is able to glimpse it. The face that we present to the world, hoping that it will be accepted, the face we lay all our bets on, is called the "false self," but not because it is false—it certainly isn't, it's not a simulation or a masquerade, it belongs to us, it's authentic, it really is our face or at least an expression that comes naturally to us; it is we who falsify it by presenting it as if it were all of us, whereas it is merely a part, and not even the most significant one.

The false self can only feel alive if it is activated by a challenge to take on. It has a continuous need of outside tasks, tests to pass. Unless it acts, it might as well not even exist.

HOW DIFFICULT it is to manage one's contradictions, to hold them together! For instance, I have always had a hard time feeling alive in any sort of continuous fashion. The figure of myself that I had created to present to the attention of others was something that I was capable of sustaining for only a few hours a day, let's say, four or five, or if I had decided to tough it out, at the very most, seven or eight hours in a row, after which disaster inevitably ensued: I would collapse into abulia, complete apathy, sheer anonymity, a sort of diseased torpor that, really, wasn't such a disagreeable condition, if for no other reason than that it demanded no further efforts or displays. I didn't much like being alone, but at least solitude offered the advantage of sparing me other people's judgment, sheltering my general dereliction; and so, in the end, I grew fond of that apathy, that laziness, that exceedingly profound melancholy, and the scorn I felt toward myself for the very fact that I had spent so much time forcing myself to seem what I was not, or not really. I grew fond of that whole gloomy stew. I recognize myself more fully in those few hours of nothingness than I do in the poses put on to fortify myself.

I could feel my nerves distending until they transmitted nothing more than a weak pulsation, like guitar strings progressively slackened until they emit a dull, hollow, slightly funny sound. A useless sound. That was the ideal condition in which to read books and listen to music.

I THEREFORE CAME to the conclusion that we are nothing more than bundles of nerves and sensations to which an identity has been attributed for juridical reasons: in order to ensure that that crossroads of random and chaotic pulsations will pay the taxes, inherit his father's house, can pick up prepaid tickets in his name at the airport, and sit in his assigned seat. Nothing more. Nothing more than a convenient way of tracking you down.

And the name corresponding to this identity? Well, it's nothing more than a registration: on a magnetic card, a notarized document, the caption underneath a photograph, the bronze letters bolted to a slab of travertine, and then let's call it a day.

THE LOCKER ROOM was the place where this ritual acknowledgment of masculinity was acted out. Perhaps there can be nothing more shameful than to display one's body as a subject for comparison, even as it is still developing. When we went down to the gym and took our clothes off, there emerged from under a layer of largely equivalent clothing the bodies of boys who were more deeply dissimilar than so many stray dogs in a kennel.

With inexhaustible wisecracks designed to target alien elements, be they women or faggots, an exclusive fraternity we were celebrating, but one that, paradoxically, wound up only reinforcing the homosexual tendencies at play within the group. It is an inevitable consequence of living in a wholly male community: what with all the demeaning and dismissing, even if only in words, of women and queers and faggots, and the waving of the banner of virility, you wind up seeking only the latter. True machismo cannot be anything but intrinsically homosexual.

Very, very curious, this oscillation between the outright rejection of femininity and the almost desperate quest for it . . .

But it was all a masquerade: consisting of displays of bravado, obscene language, tremendous bullshit, either uttered or committed, risky, idiotic behavior (there's now a TV program specifically devoted to this type of behavior, steeped in a vaguely suicidal spirit: its protagonists swallow worms, strap rockets to roller skates, let themselves be flung off ceiling fans or butted by rams), in other words, any undertaking provided it is dangerous and absurd, capable of causing abrasions or making you vomit, self-destructive behavior, gratuitous violence, by which for instance I'd point to boiling a toad or filling the tank of windshield wiper spray with urine and then directing the nozzles to douse pedestrians and motorcyclists; by night, throwing cobblestones at the lions in the safari park, after luring them to the fence with the smell of raw steaks . . .

STICK A HAMSTER into a microwave oven (a traditional oven takes too long to heat up . . .), throw coins out the window at street musicians, after heating them red-hot in a pan, give an unsuspecting friend a snowball to eat, with a center of frozen piss . . .

IT WAS A TEST to which we were all subjected on a daily basis. We had to prove that we were man enough to tolerate the pressure implicit in the on-going joke in extremely poor taste that is life in an all-male boarding school. Even though I was never particularly targeted, indeed, since I belonged to the group of the luckier ones as I was exempt from any glaring physical or moral defects, and also because I've always basically minded my own business, I confess that I've given in more than once to that pressure. A palpable, tangible pressure. So how did I let off steam? By crying. If possible, without being seen. There is no better and no faster way. A couple of times by getting in fights. In the *Brief History of Punches* that one of these days I plan to write, one chapter will certainly be dedicated to fighting at school. If you leave out the fights that originate out of politics—which can be examined in a chapter all its own, a chapter that is actually very important, about fights that see the school as nothing more than a theater for a dress rehearsal of a dance that will take place on a very different stage, in the streets and in the squares—fighting in a boy's life is an integral part of his scholastic career, no less so than exams: indeed, they are just another kind of exam.

THE MOST IMPORTANT human resources are spent on gaining acknowledgment of one's role. At home, in society, at school, at work, on this earth. At certain points, it might seem that our principal pursuit was neither that of studying nor playing a sport nor watching television (which in terms of scheduling filled our days to the very brim), but rather that of playing a role. Which role? It's not that easy to say, it isn't obvious. The role of young people? The role of enterprising young males? The role of privileged young

Roman Catholic Italian males? The role of good boys or the role of vice-indulging reprobates? Probably equal measures of all of these things, simultaneously or else in alternating phases, in rotation, changing roles between winter and summer, among the family or with friends—after all, it's only normal to behave differently according to the situation, like the father and head of household who on Sunday goes out and sets fire to cars around the soccer stadium, and then Monday morning shows up right on time at his job. There's a great deal of room in a single personality—it can hold two, or three, and maybe even more. The central story of this book will confirm that you can be obedient students by day and nevertheless still go out to kidnap and rape underage girls by night.

IN KEEPING WITH a Romantic tradition with little or no foundation in reality—truly the stuff of aesthetes—a notion circulates that young people are rebellious, or at least more rebellious than adults. Nothing could be further from the truth. The vast majority of young people are superconformists. Instinct leads them to join the herd, only rarely to wander outside its bounds. If they revolt against certain rules, it's only because they are obeying the dictates of others whom they feel have greater authority. During adolescence, the herd spirit dominates life in almost every aspect: nothing lies outside its control, from the way you dress to the things you say, from how couples kiss to which and how many cigarettes should be smoked, and how to inhale without coughing. Everything, everything is learned through imitation.

PERHAPS THIS GREAT EFFORT, this continuous, endless mirroring and comparison of oneself, this interminable skirmishing with oneself even more than with others, this construction of challenges, this meeting and overcoming of them, this proving one is up to them, this hardening, as one grows wily and tests oneself, kneading one's spirit and hammering one's physique with runs around the track that leave one breathless and rounds of push-ups, this battle without quarter asked or given of crabs in a plastic bucket, well, perhaps it is nothing more and serves no other purpose than to prepare one's entry into the world of work, and that's all. Behind all these inner torments, there's just one concrete purpose: finding one's way out of the maternal Garden of Eden with the least possible amount of regret, in order to descend into the purgatory of practical, everyday life, where every conquest entails a corresponding loss, a slap in the face, a betrayal, and there are no sugar-sweet berries that simply plop into your mouth unbidden, nor do milk and honey drip from the trees. It is only so that we can tolerate this expulsion without immediately taking our own lives that we must "be men." It is with endless amounts of muscle-straining and butt-clenching and eye-squinting and cock-handling and shouting and sobbing and dreaming of oneself as the recognized leader of the World Order that one reaches a sufficient average level of insensibility that the world ceases to instill overwhelming fear . . .

I HAVE BEFORE MY EYES the last letter I received from Arbus before he exited my life. It's dated May 12, 1980, that is, six years after he left SLM, in the spectacular fashion that I'll describe in just a few pages. Let me transcribe here the passage that most struck me, hurt me, and convinced me.

"The difference between you and me, Edoardo? I understood it many years ago, but it never stopped me from being your friend. And you know what that difference is? In spite of everything, you always wanted to be accepted by our other schoolmates, and you tried to get them to like you. You'd step away, from time to time, you gave the impression of being detached from them, but only so you could make a surprise return appearance, ensuring that everyone noticed both how you went away and how you once again conceded your friendship, how you participated in the pranks and all the rest. You needed it, you couldn't live without it, just as a fish can't live out of water. You always needed the others, and there's nothing wrong with that, you need approval, admiration, even though you pretend to care nothing for it, in reality you think of nothing else and you wouldn't be capable of bidding farewell to anything or anyone. You'd only leave for a while, but you'd never make a definitive break. You're a weak and moody heart. I've seen you make trouble in class, not because you really wanted to, but because you were afraid to be the only one—aside from me and Zipoli, and let's throw in Rummo for good measure—not to be doing it . . . You were afraid, and you had fun out of a fear not to have fun. Admit it. There remain two options and they're irreconcilable: assimilate with the others, complying with all the conditions and expectations that have to do with being men; or else isolate yourself, really break away, remain pure and extraneous, noncompliant, rejecting all models. And what choice did you make?"

Yes, Arbus is right, as always, I chose the first option, or rather, it chose me: I was unable to defend my diversity, and I never really cared to defend it. I wanted to be like everybody else. Deep down, that is what I secretly aspired to, even if I was too proud to admit it. Arbus wasn't proud in the slightest. And indeed, he chose the second option, isolation.

4

WE WERE and we felt close to one another, without talking much. Better to do things together than talk about it. We were united, practically joined at the hip, and yet there was no real intimacy among us. In fact, if anything we feared intimacy.

Intimacy means feeling and being vulnerable, and also displaying that vulnerability: weakness can be exploited, trust can be betrayed, exposing yourself just opens you up to derision.

Actually, we felt no need to talk about ourselves, that is, about our hopes, our secrets, our fears, and our ambitions, no, these remained hidden and unknown, and I mean to say that, first and foremost, they were hidden from ourselves, we didn't know what they were, we didn't know who we were, how could I have confessed to my friends and classmates something that I myself didn't know? Instead, we told stories that for the most part we'd heard from others, we joked, did imitations, issued proclamations, threatened impossible things, mocked and derided one another or really (it was an asymmetrical pursuit) we'd always make fun of the same four or five classmates, always the same targets of vulgar wisecracks and pranks, a couple of whom had accepted their sacrificial role to the point that they even self-immolated, if no one else was mocking them, they'd do it themselves, insulting themselves and then proving the validity of those insults by exaggerating their awkwardness and incompetence so as to draw more slings and arrows: thus managing to appear even shyer and fatter and shorter and clumsier than they actually were. Far more powerful than degradation, in fact, is self-degradation.

INTIMACY: fear and desire. Perhaps it's just a different way of expressing similar emotions—or maybe it's a matter of awareness. You desire what you secretly fear; you fear what you unconsciously aspire to. There are those who see an absolute polar opposition between the masculine principle and the feminine one, while perhaps there are only different ways of experiencing and expressing the same forms of affection, the exact same emotions, dreams, desires fears and feelings, it's just a matter of seeing the order in which these propensities are arranged, which are visible and even exhibited, and which instead are left hidden: it's possible then that, while young women desire intimacy but subconsciously fear it, young men instead are frightened by an intimacy that, deep down, they desire, even if they're unwilling to admit it: that would smack of sentimentalism. The mutual misunderstanding springs from this hybrid, this mixed sentiment of fear and desire, which is the ambiguous cipher of sex. Fearfully. Fearfully we oscillate between fear and desire, with the paradoxical result that we flee from what we truly desire, and desire to be like those we are most afraid of . . .

Males: to hear them talk, they're vulgar, but deep in their hearts they're super-romantic, fragile, and emotional. They become dangerous when they lose their heads. A violent passion goes hand in hand with a matter-of-fact reckless kind of roughhousing. In some cases, violence against women has originated from this contradictory mixture: explicit brutality and vulgarity in practical terms, while deep in the heart there explodes a savage sentimentalism that will stop at nothing, ready even to transform the culminating apex of romanticism ("I can't live without you") into a stab wound, or thirty of them.

In existing literature on sexual differences, it's often stated that males are incapable of intimacy, that they fear it, flee it, dread it. In fact, in the context of intimacy they're at risk of being seen as weak, afraid that others might recognize this and take advantage of it. Therefore, they prefer general topics in conversation rather than more personal ones. Let's take soccer. It's a common topic of conversation among young men and even grown ones, and it seems perfectly designed to avoid personal subjects. By talking about the draft campaign being conducted by your team as it revs up for the coming championship, and doing so with an ironic or self-ironic tone, oscillating between the jokey and the tremendously serious, with expressions that range from "With the defense we've got as a team, it'll be a miracle if they don't demote us to Serie B" to "This is the year that we finally kick your ass good and hard," you start a conversation that can slither and slide for a good long time between that topic and others like it, and then eventually flicker and die, without ever having introduced anything more serious or personal.

IN ANY CASE, it's true, I've always preferred working side by side to a face-to-face interaction: not *telling each other* something, but *doing something together*. At the very most, concerning the matter of talking together, revealing oneself to another, what I find interesting is the position of those who confess their sins with respect to the confessor; there, too, the schema is an oblique one: on the one hand, there's the outline of a person whispering into a grating, on the other side is a person who lends an ear and is therefore in front yet remains invisible, protected by the door or a curtain. The separation between the two is minimal but essential. The asymmetry is a useful way to ensure that there will be some progress, to make sure that human interaction *serves* some purpose. The face-to-face interaction tends to silence, and in fact, it is ideal when you have nothing to say to each other, that is, when you love each other. In that case, it's quite enough to gaze at each other.

A CERTAIN NUMBER of us were homosexual, and the rest were homophobic. In as much as we were half-queers, we hated and laughed behind their backs at the real queers, the hundred percent, thoroughgoing ones, like Svampa, the chemistry teacher. The other part of us was turned against the first part, or to be more exact, in order to avoid acknowledging the existence of our own first part, the second part of each of us aggressively turned on the first part of the others, especially those in which the first part was even the tiniest bit more distinct, more pronounced . . . what I'm saying, in other words, is that it was fairly normal to be half-queers, queers by half, but not an iota more, no, not that, more than half an iota was too much! We'd have never admitted, for example, that there was any true love among us as classmates. That sense of transport, that quiver of pleasure at being together, even the attraction toward individual body parts of which this or that classmate might have particularly fine specimens, a pair of handsome blue eyes (that was the case with Zarattini), fine broad shoulders (in the whole class, only Sdobba and Jervi had them), nice legs (again, Sdobba, long, muscular, shimmering with blond hairs that made you want to pet them like a cat)—these feelings had to be mustered into the comradely category of friendship.

IT'S NOT AS IF we hated queers, in fact, quite the opposite, we found them fun and amusing (I'll talk later about the hilarious outbursts that followed the caresses exchanged among classmates in the classroom . . .); if anything, what we did hate was the thought that we might be taken for queers, even though we weren't (at least not all of us, or at least not entirely . . .), in other words, the possibility of a misunderstanding. What worried us was that misunderstanding.

THE FOLLOWING method had been suggested to me by a friend. He claimed it was infallible. Do you want to know if one of your classmates is a queer? Then get him to play a game of Ping-Pong. And watch him while he plays. If possible, make sure he's up against a better player. There's nothing that tests your nerves like being trounced at Ping-Pong—and the effort, the excitement, and the frustration at being unable to pull ahead in spite of all his efforts all provide the perfect setting for any individual to reveal his true nature. No one will be able to conceal their tendencies while playing a Ping-Pong match, two games out of three, or three out of five. If you're a homosexual and you mess up a decisive forehand smash—even if you've done everything you can to keep from admitting it, struggling to conceal the fact from your parents and your classmates, because you couldn't stand the mockery if they ever learned the truth—well, if your forehand smash hits the net, the queer lurking deep inside you is bound to leap out like a wounded tiger. With a little shriek, a foot-stamp of vexation, or some fretful phrase along the lines of: "I don't even like this game!" or "No fair!" or else "Jesus, what's wrong with me today?"

It's a method you can even use on yourself, if you haven't figured out whether or not you're queer. At a certain age you start to feel a lurking and generalized attraction toward others of your own sex . . . Play a game of Ping-Pong and you'll know for sure.

VIRILITY MEANS POWER. If I don't have power, it means I'm not virile. If I'm not virile, I'll never have power, the circle is unbroken.

It is, in fact, the uncertain ones who care most about seeing their half-power affirmed: the ones who have full power feel no need to prove it over and over again.

There can be no question about the fact that men as a group hold power, whereas men as single individuals rarely do. And they often react in a crazed and hysterical way to this clamorous disparity. They are going to have to invent the power they do not possess: by finding someone within reach to order around.

One of my favorite scenes from a novel comes from a book by John Fante that I read many years ago, I don't even remember which, in which the young protagonist, perhaps the famous Arturo Bandini, the author's alter ego, appoints himself King of the Crabs. (Crabs again, sure enough, they always seem to pop up . . .) His realm was the beach, his throne was the dock. From there, he shouted orders to his subjects swarming over the sand, and if they failed to obey them, he'd shoot them with a BB gun. He'd execute them one after another. He slaughtered the mutinous crabs.

Never once did they obey him.

His was a very chaotic kingdom.

BUT WHY an all-boy school, like SLM?

Perhaps it was all about that: was that the specific quality of our education? The fact that we were all students at SLM instead of some other mixed-gender school: being deprived of all contact with the world of women, with the world of mothers and sisters that had once been our family universe. The family as a feminine *couche* (class or social layer) that the boy, like a young Spartan, had to be ripped from, as young as possible. Perhaps that is the only reason our school was all male: in order to highlight that separation, make it such a customary thing that our parents and we ourselves would be convinced that it was a sage and necessary step. Who knows whether our mothers, some of whom might even feel reassured by the thought that their son was being protected from the distractions, influences, and dangers represented by young girls in flower, who can say whether they ever realized that these restrictive measures were actually directed not so much at those cunning little contrivers, but rather against them, the grand intriguers . . . and that the bosom from which we were meant to be separated was theirs, and not the unripe bosoms of the female students of the Collegio Sant'Orsola.

THE FEMALE EQUIVALENT in our quarter of SLM was, in fact, the Collegio Sant'Orsola, near Piazza Bologna.

(WHEN, YEARS LATER, several of SLM's alumni gained notoriety for their grim exploits, they became synonymous in the starkest terms with the problem of the all-male identity of the school: of its teachers, whether religious or not, and of its students. Women weren't allowed at the school, and however hard I try to remember, I can't conjure up a single female presence inside the school's walls, with the possible exception of our mothers when they came to pick us up. Maybe, yes, there might have been one woman who sold pizzas at recess . . . But when school was in session proper, the place was a veritable Mount Athos. The only woman who wasn't an intruder at SLM was the Virgin Mary. How lonely she must have been, though, there behind the altar!)

NO WOMEN among my classmates . . . oh well, it's more or less like prison. No women among the teachers . . . and this is stranger since, in Italy at least, school is predominantly feminine, an extension of the realm of the mother, a very prolonged version of nursery school. But in contrast, we, starting from elementary school, had for teachers no one but vigorous young men in tunics. Perhaps they wore tunics to remind us of the skirts from which we were torn away every morning: reminding us to reassure us, and in the meantime take it away from us, little by little, day by day.

In any case, we were unfailingly raised by individuals in skirts: first our mothers and governesses, and later, priests. We transitioned from the laps of our nannies to fluttering black tunics. How they flapped in the SLM courtyard when the wind was blowing! I personally very much like kaftans, togas, and the shalwar kameez, as well as women's dresses proper and skirts both short and long, while I have always found trousers to be crude and barbaric, acceptable only to ward off the cold.

Men in skirts are assigned the task of transforming boys into men: an all-male line.

HOMOSEXUALS, *artists, priests, and warriors all aspire to a transcendental achievement that bypasses the ordinary and mechanical process of reproduction via the feminine element. They can do without women because they create or claim to create the future in another manner, through violent acts, prayers, artworks, and teaching. They constitute self-sufficient categories of males, and they give birth to ideas or deeds instead of children. Or else they adopt other people's children to raise them themselves. While in other human groups and activities there is a continuity established over time, with the formation of dynasties, guilds, and professions handed down, as well as a family memory of shared customs, or at least a name, the celibate brother-*

hood of priests ensures that every generation dies out without leaving heirs. Priests must be replaced one by one as they die out. New priests spring up out of thin air.

THERE ARE TWO KINDS OF SCHOOLS, then: the first, in which virility emerges, is tested, and recognizes itself only in its interactions with the feminine (for the most part, that means an amorous encounter, a sexual testing of self), and the second, wherein the male finds his identity by separating himself, moving away from women, placing them between parentheses. The initiation then passes through women in the most literal sense (like the initiation of the mythical Enkidu, who becomes a man, from the half-beastly creature that he was, by means of fucking), or else it takes place by eliminating all contact with them entirely. An intermediate variant that was practiced regularly until a couple of generations before mine was to reduce the content of the initiation to its physical aspect, that is, to sexual intercourse considered as nothing more than a way of letting off steam. The place where a man was supposed to discover himself was the brothel.

THE DIFFERENCE between males and females was that both categories constituted enigmas, but the enigma of women struck me, at least, as the more interesting of the two. As did their bodies: males were flat, both physically and in their souls, it seemed to me, while females were full of curves and recesses. Given their physical and mental configuration, ideal hiding places. Where you can hide any secret, and where even males can go hide from the rest of the world (I number myself among them). Penetration itself, instead of being an act of possession, can be viewed as an act of concealment. The search for a secret place, a haven. The nonvisibility of the female genitalia has always intrigued, disconcerted, annoyed, and sometimes even frightened males, if compared with the insolent, brutal, and laughable visibility of their own sex organ, which dangles like a salami from the ceiling of a delicatessen.

WHAT IS OFTEN and crudely judged to be a flight from the essence of virility, that is, homosexuality, is, in fact, quite the contrary, and in the most concrete terms, a flight from the feminine in order to take refuge in the sphere of pure, uncontaminated masculinity, of a relationship between equals: it is a case of sexual separatism, where one swears faithfulness and love to one's own sex. You seek asylum among your own peers, your own brothers: and for that reason, I have to imagine it must be terribly tough when they treat you with contempt and expel you from their midst.

I'VE NEVER TAKEN PART—and I somewhat regret it—in conversations along the lines of "Have you ever done this? Have you ever done that?" about your first sexual experiences, about the things that girls did to you or let you do to them, how far they let you go, their mouths, their thighs, their panties, insistent focus on anatomical details, wet Kleenex, and, afterward, licorice candies in the glove compartment, to freshen her breath. I was never on close-enough terms with anyone. It was pointless to talk of such things with Arbus. Among my friends from the summer holidays, I felt too shy, since I was the least experienced of the group. I'd listen to their oratory on the subject, but I never dared to weigh in; for that matter, it was my good fortune that they left me out of it, as if I were somehow a pure spirit, and to tell the truth I really was, let's say, an already impure pure spirit, stained with nocturnal thoughts and pollutions. Continual, racking: to wake up practically every morning in a puddle of dried sperm. I can imagine the sarcastic comments of whoever had to make the bed or wash my pajama bottoms. I realized the depths of the resigned wisdom or sheer insubordination of the housekeepers from the fact that quite often at night when I went to put on my pajama bottoms I found they were quite stiff, rendered parchment-like by semen: a signal that those women were sick and tired of washing them . . . I did it all in my own room, in my twisted mind, where those perverted conversations really never stopped, where those dubious questions were asked and promptly answered.

The mind of an adolescent is a galaxy.

Sex wasn't an invention, after all, it was insistently present and manifest, inside us, planted deep in our brains even more than our bodies, a dull, thudding pulsation that made us tremble. It was a drive or a frenzy that was unquestionably natural, but where and how we were to direct it, that was much less so: this latter question was the topic of unending study, consisting in fact of fragments of phrases overheard here and there, from the orders issued to the entire team by some nameless shared sensibility, a sort of law that no one had ever set forth in clear terms, with its articles and clauses lined up one next to the other as unambiguous as commandments, which everyone or nearly everyone obeyed. What a strange thing it is when you are forced to see to your own education by peeping, perusing, winking, and yet to my mind it's the only way, at least as far as sex is concerned. And perhaps the same can be said of literature. Everything else, though, should be taught to you by someone who actually knows about it. But in those two fields, we're always self-taught and we always will be. After all, the more twisted the outcome, the better and the more authentic. You pick things up here and there, that's how it works, you can't really hope to study, you can only imitate and pilfer. Or else we're talking about an apprenticeship so panicky and hasty that it hardly deserves the name: there is none of the calm, the systematic approach, the progressive acquisition of knowledge that ought to come with true study. Lurches, violent conquests, sudden, dazzling glares of light against a background which remains that of a blessed yet ignoble ignorance.

For that matter, how much simpler and finer it would have been simply not to have it at all—a sexuality! To be cultivated, to be satisfied . . . and first and foremost, to be identified! What a relief it would have been not to feel its pressure . . . because, even if the others hadn't been there to poke and prod, to offer suggestions, to make demands, to force you to have a sexuality of some kind, there would still be your body, implacable in its re-awakenings like a dinosaur buried in the ice, and to force you sooner or later into that stupid pantomime with girls, into subterfuges with your parents and braggadocio or frustrations with your classmates, that whole rather ridiculous process that culminates in a brief venting, in four or five (and if there were a hundred, or even a thousand, what difference would that make?) thrusts of the pelvis . . . Sexuality: there exist bodies other than our own. Yes. Should we approach them or recoil from them? Which of them should we approach and from which should we recoil?

I know people who simply can't keep themselves from trying to seduce others. With smiles, a warm voice, glances. Anyone, man or woman, who is around these people must necessarily yield to their charm. While ordering an espresso in a café, or signing up for a gym membership, or paying a debt, the seducers are at work, 24/7/365: it's a pursuit you never stop engaging in, the seduction of your fellow human being. An inability to have natural interactions with others forces you to try to win them over.

For that matter, taking the sexual initiative, the thought of sex, thinking about sex, thinking about the opposite sex or one's own—all these things can hardly be anything other than *obsessive* in nature. If sex doesn't manifest itself as an obsession, then it hasn't manifested itself at all. It has no way of manifesting itself other than as a mania, a frenzy, a morbid refrain, the hammering rhythm of thought. If it doesn't pound, it doesn't exist, it's dead. There's nothing on earth whose braided fibers are so durable: it's so very difficult to cut through them, tear them asunder, just as it's almost impossible to silence the siren's voice as it echoes in your ears. Its song drives anyone who listens without taking precautions stark mad. Those fibers form an animate and palpitating continuum: it can be the one reason that keeps us alive. In an action movie, Russell Crowe asks another cop: "Are you thinking about pussy?" "No," the other cop answers. "Then you're just not concentrating," and that vulgar wisecrack possesses a certain truth. Unless sex occupies your whole mind, it hasn't really entered your mind at all. That's how the game of soccer was for my mother, or classical ballet and mountain hiking were for me. Things that concerned *other people*. Because once it gets its claws into you, sex never lets you go. If it doesn't possess you now, in this exact instant, if you don't hear the dull echo of its call, then that's something that's probably never happened at all, and which may never happen for that matter.

Back then, for us at SLM, sex was something that belonged almost entirely to the domains of chatter and dreams, in hyperbolic dirty jokes, magnified no end by the words but extremely scanty when it came to the facts and deeds, consisting by and large of the occasional masturbation onto the ceramic tiles of the bathroom with a dirty magazine propped open to the double-page spread where a smiling Junoesque dame with enormous sagging breasts displayed an incredible tawny bush between her thighs and, beneath that bush, a pink slit that the fat woman held open with her fingers, in an effort to *show it off*. Not only the slit but the entire flaccid body were an overexposed pink that verged on the hues of candied fruit, patently unreal; and the color often seeped beyond the borders that were supposed to contain it, in a delirium of imprecise details, blurred and bleeding, the enormous nipples with irregular areolas, the lips of the mouth and the lips of the slit, psychedelic gradations of pink.

WOMEN, then, were targets, and the ones in glossy magazines were easy to hit because they didn't move, and attractive because they were half-naked or entirely nude.

But that concerned my classmates, not me.

WHAT HAPPENS at night in the beds of adolescent boys is something known only to those who, the following day, while the boy is off at school, have to make his bed and change his sheets, given that in Italy it was (and I believe still is) rather rare for the moderately spoiled young man of the house to have to make his own bed, if you leave aside the dreary interval of military service, when on the first day of boot camp he is taught the extremely complicated and absurd operation of "*fare il cubo*," as the Italian would have it—"making a cube," literally—that is, transforming his pallet by folding the thin mattress over on itself and swaddling it tight with the sheets and blanket, so as to assure that it's impossible to lie down on it during the day.

As Italian mothers and housekeepers undo the bedding, they discover stains, either dry or still damp, and the same is true of the pajamas (which have long since been virtually abolished and replaced with a T-shirt and a pair of boxer shorts, as in the American series we watch on TV).

Back in the day when this story took place, male Italian adolescents still wore pajamas, and stopped wearing them—because they suddenly were perceived as something ridiculous and awkward—only with the official beginning of a true love life, with the first nights spent in bed with a girl, when it would only seem embarrassing to be seen in checkered flannel bottoms and tops, buttoned to the chin.

Whatever you wore to sleep, once the garments were stained, they went straight into the laundry hamper. I've often wondered what goes through the mind of the saintly Italian mother in those situations; whether she thinks of the word "sperm," or uses some other term, more commonplace and vulgar, or whether she simply doesn't think a thing and just goes on with her task, like any of the other routine household chores of the day, with that brisk, blind, and healthy mindlessness that preserves those who toil all day cleaning up other people's messes, their defecations, the remains of the food collectively consumed, saving them from considerations that range beyond the strictly practical: there's another load to run through the washing machine, we're almost out of fabric softener, I'm going to make stuffed zucchini for dinner, and so forth.

ITALY IS A COUNTRY where the mothers do everything, where it is said of even the most famous Son of all time that He wouldn't have achieved a thing if it hadn't been for His Mother, sainted woman that She was. Sainted women were those well-to-do matrons who found themselves, unexpectedly, dealing with problems that went well beyond the matter of grass stains on white pant legs. Sainted women are those who tolerate, conceal, and hide from the fathers the misdeeds of their sons, choking back tears.

THE SEXUAL EDUCATION that was imparted, or more often than not, *not* imparted, consisted for the most part in an assortment of prohibitions, in precepts of a negative, or else hypothetical nature: don't do this, and if you do that instead, trouble will follow . . .

Considering that it was a religious school, at SLM they were very bland and vague on this topic, aside from occasional initiatives on the part of some individual priest who was a little more rigid and old-school than the others, such as Father Saturnino, for instance, the father confessor.

5

I N ONE OF MY MOTHER'S PHOTO ALBUMS, I found a picture of my first communion.

It's taken at an angle, arranged vertically like a composition by Paolo Veronese or Tintoretto, where figures tower from on high over someone who is far below, imploring, receiving without argument; the only thing missing is fluttering banners to complete the allegory; and that tiny kneeling figure with the face turned upward is me.

My hair is neatly brushed, I'm wearing a gray jacket without lapels and a pair of gray shorts, white calf-high socks and shiny shoes, but these conventional details tell us relatively little compared with the position of the head, the neck twisted back, and the mouth open to receive the host. A position of expectant trust and concern for something that must be extraordinary.

There are three priests looming over the little boy, and I can recognize two of them. The way in which their figures are modeled, and the way they hold and intertwine their hands, and tower over the child, all seem to have been devised by a painter, starting with the elderly priest with the long white beard standing straight on the right, and if he weren't wearing a pair of eyeglasses he might just as easily have emerged from any devotional painting as the figure of a saint or a prophet. This was Father Saturnino, and he must have died many years ago. He used to come visit me at home when I was sick and missed a great many months of school, to assist me and console me, and it was with him that I said confession for the very first time.

Confession is a sacrament that may be even harder to understand than the eucharist—when you're ten years old. He would ask me what sins I'd committed and I didn't know what to answer. I would have been glad to accuse myself, in utter seriousness, of something very bad, but I searched and searched, almost desperately rummaged and struggled to feel a powerful sentiment of remorse, and nothing came to mind except for trifles and the desire to be done with it: I was, as so often happens to me, deeply moved and at the same time bored and impatient, and so I replied to Father Saturnino that I'd told lies . . . and then, that I'd disobeyed . . . disobeyed Mamma: but even that was half a lie, since I was an obedient child. Still, I was ashamed to have so little to confess and, therefore, little of which to repent; I really was embarrassed, not of my sins, but rather of their paltry number and negligible nature, and as a result I wished I could invent a few more, to make a more interesting sinner of myself, one more deserving of forgiveness, a prodigal son. I had understood that the more you sin, the greater the joy your repentance will cause. Indeed, to use the language of the religious, the greater the jubilation.

This blessed rule stupefied me then as it does now and should be classed among the things whose spiritual grandeur I am able to intuit, but it is in fact that very grandeur that upsets and irritates me, undermining my very sense of justice. This would happen to me many times in the years that followed, when I saw men of the cloth so impassioned in their devotion to sinners that they made them their pets, almost their fair-haired boys: repentant terrorists, bank robbers who have turned to painting Madonnas, murderers who, in the end, seem almost to be better people than their innocent victims, seeing that, by choosing goodness after committing so much evil, they've helped to shift the scales in which the world's good and evil are weighed, because if they stop their killing, then the dish of the scale that holds evil will in fact become that much lighter. I once thought of a way to win the Nobel Peace Prize: one sure method would be to become a terrorist, plant bombs and blow up airplanes, etc., and then at a certain point, decide to give up my wicked ways and lay down my arms and, in this exact manner, become to all intents and purposes a peacemaker, a man of peace.

Victims don't stir the same passions as a rogue redeemed, that much is obvious.

I sincerely wanted to attain redemption but I didn't know what from, so

Father Saturnino came to my aid, convinced that I was ashamed to confess my sins, while I was actually struggling with a shame of the exact opposite hue; and just as good-hearted teachers do during an oral exam, when they see that a student is having difficulty, it was he who suggested to me a few of the sins I might have committed: and even if it wasn't true or I didn't begin to understand what the specific sin might be, I hurried to answer yes, yes, to each of his questions, yes, I did that, as if I thought that in order to obtain that blessed pardon I needed to reach a certain quota, a predetermined scorecard of evil, so that I could reset that number to zero and start over, as in the card game of *sette e mezzo* or blackjack, or a loyalty program at a gas station.

And I remember very clearly just what the last sin was that Father Saturnino suggested I go and rummage around in my memory for, just in case I might have committed that one, too.

"Have you ever watched dirty movies?"

"What?"

"*Dirty* movies."

This time I hesitated to answer yes, because I really didn't know what the brother was talking about. Dirty movies? Was he possibly talking about . . . pornographic films? That couldn't be. I was ten years old. It wasn't like now, when a kid can go on the Internet and watch people having sex, or threesomes, or group sex, rapes, and orgies. Again this time, when the wise brother saw me hesitate, he decided to help me out.

"You know what I mean, don't you? Movies with *undressed* women."

Just the mere word "undressed" made me blush violently. I'd never seen undressed women, in the movies much less in real life, if you leave aside a certain episode from my childhood that I may perhaps tell you about later on. And so, deciding that enough was enough, that I'd confessed to enough sins to give an image of myself as a sufficiently wicked Candlewick, I was about to say no, when the father confessor specified: "Like, Double O Seven movies."

Secret agent 007. Bond. James Bond. And I had seen at least a couple of those movies, back then, *Goldfinger* for sure, and maybe *Thunderball*, but the women were never actually nude, when they took off their bras or when 007 unhooked them, they always had their backs to the camera, and even when they let their robes fall to the ground, the only thing you saw was their shoulders. Yes, in effect, I found those movies very unsettling, the brother had hit a bull's-eye. And in *Goldfinger* I remember that there was a girl completely naked, dead on a bed and covered from head to foot in gold, painted gold . . .

It was Father Saturnino who heard the boys' confessions, since the men I call "priests" here weren't actually fully ordained, but simply Marist brothers, and they couldn't administer the holy sacraments. Strange to live an entire lifetime as a priest but never enjoy the prerogatives of the role, that is, let's say, the powers.

The other priest I recognize in the picture is in fact a Marist, Brother Domenico, who's still just a young man in the snapshot, and who reaches up, solicitous but also serious, stern, fully taken with his role, to support the plate beneath the host. I don't know, on the other hand, who the officiant is, perhaps it's a bishop, he grips the pyx in his left hand and delicately extends the host, between the thumb and forefinger of his right hand, his gestures and faint smile suffused with calm and benevolence. A good father, in other words, or perhaps we should say, a good grandfather. The photographer showed great skill in capturing the exact moment in which the event has not yet taken place but is, in fact, still on the verge of taking place, or actually, is already in process, and though nothing has really happened it's already inevitable that it will, we now know with certainty that the host was swallowed, after that moment of imperceptible hesitation or suspension of time that can be experienced only retrospectively because reality itself flows too quickly, like in photographs of sporting events, a fleeting second that remains transfixed in an endless duration. The actors on that stage could hardly help but recognize themselves many years later, just as I am doing now, for the first time in forty years, forty years have passed since the boy in the good suit tipped back his neck and opened his mouth, and in all that time I'd never once laid eyes on that photograph, which I found rattling loose in an album where my mother keeps images of different times and places without ever making up her mind to paste them in. With the transparent adhesive corners that are still waiting to adhere. The so-called *ricordi*, or souvenirs. Children at various ages, vacations, trips, dead people, children in black and white and in full color, ceremonies, ID cards.

What emotions did I feel? Should I make a considerable effort to remember, or should I just rely on what the photograph says? Children are innocent but, at the same time, monstrously guilty, sincere and simultaneously full of make-believe, they think that the whole thing is a performance but that, if they are good actors, the performance will become reality. And they *want it to*. If a boy really concentrates on being good, then he truly will become good, and God will spring forth from the wafer that is dissolving in his mouth. After he goes back to his seat and, kneeling, rests his face in his hands in a sign of spiritual concentration, God's presence in his mouth will make itself felt, and if it doesn't, then he must once again rest his face in his hands, pumping up the level, increasing the dosage and intensity of the prayer, the pathos of that special day. It's impossible to imagine that nothing will happen. A few years later, I had the same perplexed sense of expectation while I masturbated. I was supposed to feel something, but it just kept not happening, I just kept not coming.

I know that pairing these things will sound blasphemous, but the expectation is the same and if it doesn't click, if the proper mental connection isn't there, you sit there with the communion wafer in your mouth or your dick in your hand wondering not so much *why* nothing's happening, but rather *what* is supposed to happen.

AS LITTLE CHILDREN and then as boys and young men, we were full of doubts of a legalistic nature. Do we or don't we? Are we allowed to? And under what conditions? What were the terms established, the oaths sworn? Isn't this a bizarre miracle—that something prohibited should suddenly become licit? Why? Isn't it perhaps unjust that that which is unjust should suddenly become just? Schedules, quantities, measurements, very precise calculations, boundaries not to be transgressed. As far as the gate, only up to the sign that says DANGER, no later than eight o'clock, not before meals, be back in an hour. Even games are made up of prohibitions. The observance of every commandment ends up giving more importance to the rules as such, than to the reasons those rules were established. The prohibition against going swimming after a meal is an obvious and generic precaution, but if you give it an exact duration (when I was a kid, no less than three hours! You couldn't go swimming for three hours after eating, which in our imagination meant that if you dove into the water two hours and fifty-nine minutes after polishing off a panino, you'd die the minute you hit the water . . .), when you draw an exact line, then all the forces are marshaled on one side and the other, like two armies lined up in battle, the forces of good and evil. Children are the most inflexible custodians of the given promise, of the geometry of prohibitions, and when they break their word or a prohibition, it's out of either extreme courage or desperation, never out of solid good sense, they never think, "Oh, come on, how much will it really matter . . ." the way adults do. There's no adjustment possible in the mind of a child. Home before dark, is that clear? All right, Mamma, but dark, exactly . . . when does dark *begin*?

With holy mass, the same thing happened. I had more scruples than an elderly Pharisee, and if I had been born an Orthodox Jew or a fundamentalist Muslim or any other of those many faiths brimming over with rules and prescriptions telling you that you must take care how you walk, when you breathe, what you drink, watch, and eat, which hand you use and which hat you wear and how many times you wash, painstakingly attentive to the smallest actions that are all regulated from the very outset, I think I would have been perfectly at my ease, ahhh, life would have been prescribed and guided minute by minute according to the observance of the laws, like a ticking clock, calmly, ineluctably, and once you've respected those rules you're all good, no one can say a thing to you. You're safe. You've paid in advance. The sternest law works this way, so that the very fact that you've observed it constitutes punishment enough. You punish yourself by obeying it.

The problem, though, is that little by little the moral core of the law begins to escape you, and you limit yourself to doing the basic minimum necessary to respect it, not a gram, not a lira, not a second, not a genuflection more than is strictly required. The rule is reduced to bone, worn shiny from being gnawed. Done! you can say to yourself once you've observed the precept. Done with that, now, too!

When I found out that a mass was valid once you reached the Our Father, then there was no way I was going to attend the whole service. *Never.* I split the second to make sure I got there just in time for the eucharistic liturgy after I discovered that that was all it took.

SCHOOL, for that matter, isn't exactly a place to study, or certainly not for studying alone: it's a period of your life when you explore the borders of the known world and what is permitted, when you buzz around them. And the friendships that you cultivated there were nothing more than a free zone in which to experiment and behave in ways that are otherwise forbidden, receiving support instead of scoldings. To develop our personalities, there was nothing left but to step over the borders. You achieved great progress by breaking rules, after which you either suffered cruel but fair punishments, or else you learned that there was no punishment after all. Or else, that there really was no rule, that the rule had been set up there like a scarecrow in a field, or else the rule was something completely different that we hadn't understood yet. After all, everyone knew that the rules would keep on changing, or that they would be interpreted in ever-changing ways. You grow in spurts, by making mistakes and doing reckless things, and if you don't die in the end, voilà, you're grown up now, but everything you left behind you has grown too, in its fashion, that is, becoming twisted and deformed, and it continues on its way, only in the opposite direction, growing smaller, getting older, and while you understand more and more things, an ever greater number of things, you understand them less and less clearly, until in the end you don't understand them at all.

And in the midst of all this relatively pointless anxiety there's Jesus.

Jesus, Jesus, Jesus.

Jesus remains the true and only problem. There. You can't take Him and reduce Him to nothing more than an agitator and enemy of the Romans, nor was He just a mild-mannered and permissive preacher. He claims to be the Son of God, right? As a result, He either *is* the Son of God, or else He's a liar and therefore all His other personas (prophet, revolutionary, moralist, and hippie), however charming and attractive and likable and estimable they may be to those who do *not* believe He was the son of God—and likewise everything He ever preached—all simply go out the window. There is no escaping this contradiction. You pay no attention to what a liar has said, just as you don't pick and choose among the things he said according to whether or not they're convenient for you to believe.

If Jesus was just a man, albeit a very special man, then He was a con artist, in spite of all the messages of love and brotherhood. He cannot be anything *but* God. Otherwise, if He is not God, He lied, and the Gospels aren't worth the paper they're printed on.

Nor does the commonsense interpretation apply. Is it really necessary to explain that God is unlikely to take His inspiration from plain common sense? And in His turn inspire it in us? And that faith cannot limit itself to having a mere calming effect? We have pills for that already.

If all that was needed was to put in a good word among men, then what need was there for a solution like winding up on the cross?

"WELL? How did it go?" I asked Arbus as he came back, lost in thought, from confession. "What did Saturnino tell you?"

"He told me to kill my bad thoughts."

"To kill . . . *what*?!"

"Sinful thoughts. As soon as they come out of your head, he said, take them and hurl them to the ground . . ." Arbus waved a long arm in the air. "You have to crack their skull wide open," and he suddenly lowered his arm. "On a rock."

I didn't understand. Crack the skull . . . *of your own thoughts*?

"Yes, they're just like newborn babies, tiny and adorable," Arbus explained, "and for that very reason they make you feel sorry for them . . . you'd cuddle them to your heart . . . but then they will grow and become dangerous, and by then it will be too late to stop them."

This was the first time that my classmate had been struck by a religious idea. Maybe because it was so violent.

"Have no fear, just grab them quickly," Father Saturnino had told him, "seize them by the feet, and crush them . . . kill them. It may hurt a little, true, but it's the only way to get rid of them."

"So that means we must show no mercy . . ." I murmured.

"With ourselves, with ourselves. None."

"And with the others?"

Arbus nodded. "Well, if they refuse to understand . . ."

THE NEXT DAY it would be my turn to say confession. I saw it as a sort of test I would have to take, and I wondered if I would be fully prepared for it. As long as it was a matter of repeating lessons you'd heard in class or things you'd read in a book . . . but the things you're supposed to confess aren't written down anywhere. They were going to have to come out of me, out of my soul, and what's more, they were bad things, nasty and filthy, my sins.

Whichever way it goes, you come out looking pretty bad. If you were to confess little or nothing, it might seem you were trying to conceal your wicked deeds (which in fact amounts to one more wicked deed), or else it must mean that you are such a good person—but I mean so full of sweetness and light—that you had nothing to tell the father confessor, in other words, a disgusting little angel.

To me, the intimacy required to tell someone else the harm I had done was inaccessible. You can conceal it, the harm, you can invent it, exaggerate it, or attenuate it . . . but you can never *say it*.

I've always been troubled by the doubt that what Arbus told me wasn't true. I'd never heard Father Saturnino use violent or fanatical language. His long white beard, which he let us stroke and even pull, was designed to encourage us to confide in him.

As long as I went to confession and said confession, it remained a genuine torture for me. I was sincere but, at the same time, I lied, and though I was sure I'd told the truth, at the end of confession, it seemed to me that I hadn't told the truth at all, both because the sins confessed weren't true, and because I had kept the real ones carefully hidden. I thought that I'd forgotten to mention important things, wrongs I'd committed that were far more serious than those I'd confessed, even though when I stopped to think about it, none actually came to mind. Or else I have the even more sinister sensation that I had soft-pedaled my sins, telling them in such a way that I came out looking good, so that when all was said and done I got away scot-free, I practically deserved to be congratulated, if not for having committed them, at least for having recounted them so very nicely. Too nicely, in other words, like Rousseau and his *Confessions*, which of course I hadn't read at that age but in which I'd later recognize a reflection of myself, make no mistake, not for the spiritual greatness and breadth of thought, unequaled and unattainable, but rather for the pervasive hypocrisy, about which there could be no doubt. But my greatest remorse came from the awareness that I had by no means actually repented, that is, that the repentance declared at the end of confession was in no way genuine. A convention to be respected, a formula to be recited. I only had one real regret—that I felt nothing. Nothing at all. No authentic repentance nor any impulse to make a new resolution or deep emotion or a vow to give something up. I wasn't ashamed, exactly, but neither was I proud of the wrong I had done, the way one may feel when one is truly wicked.

I FELT INSINCERE, whatever I might say or refrain from saying. My remorse was never authentic or spontaneous, my contrition was always contrived, copied from some other model, from something I'd read or heard or seen, just like so many other behaviors in my life, truth be told, that I adopted simply out of imitation, like a talented calligrapher, without ever feeling them wholeheartedly as my own for even a fleeting instant, without believing in them or, rather, believing that it was best, all things considered, to act that way, because that's just the way people act, because it's required of you, because that's what others do, because everyone else expected it of me. This is a more than adequate reason to go along: the problem is that slight feeling of being out of phase, that instant of detachment. My confession was like a song being lip-synched, with the background music playing and the lips moving as you pretend to sing, but all it takes is the slightest hitch in the timing and the fakery is revealed on the singer's face. Confession was, for me, the utmost moment of artificiality, that is, of distance not between what I was saying and what I was thinking, but rather between what I was saying and what I was *feeling*. And that, I am sorry to say, was nothing at all.

And then there was that morbid certainty of having forgotten perhaps the only real sin that was worth bothering to confess and expiate. Sincerity, courage, memory: zero. Exactly what this great buried sin might be never came to mind, no matter how hard I tried. It was there, of that I felt certain, but it remained out of my reach.

I NEVER MASTURBATED until I was old enough to be drafted and serve in the Italian army. Probably no one will believe it, but it's the truth. I mean to say, it's not as if I had never tried, I gave it a go many many times, starting when I was just a kid, I knew that my contemporaries were doing it, and I couldn't stand the idea that I was somehow different from them. But by the end of half an hour or an hour of autostimulation, with my sex erect and flame-red from the rubbing, *nothing* had happened. The application of mechanical movement hadn't produced any effect, and I was just worn out and disappointed. It all struck me as strange and I was afraid I hadn't really understood what I was supposed to do, what I could try that might be better, might be different. I continued to have wet dreams, or pollutions, as the terminology went, as I slept in the night, but if I tried to reproduce the phenomenon in a waking state, I could never bring matters to a fitting conclusion. Not once.

I must have been twenty-two or twenty-three years old, I'd already been having sex with girls for some time now, when I managed for the first time to achieve an orgasm, solitary and voluntary, and maybe you won't believe this detail either, but in the end I managed to get it done while reading a novella by Boccaccio—that's right, none other, I know it sounds like a joke or, even worse, a literary contrivance or piece of snobbery: the idea that someone, instead of using the usual pornographic pulp rag, should be aroused and actually ejaculate onto the pages of a fourteenth-century Italian classic, and yet that is exactly what happened. I was studying for an exam at the university, and I was reading the *Decameron*, and specifically, one of the dirtiest stories in the *Decameron*, the tenth tale of the third day, which has become proverbial for a very bawdy film, *Metti lo diavolo tuo ne lo mio inferno* (*Put Your Devil into My Inferno*), a box office hit and the founding example of a long-lived Italian film genre.

I had come to the part where the naïve and lusty fourteen-year-old girl, whose vagina's inferno simply would not leave her in peace, invites the hermit to fuck her for the umpteenth time, by saying to him the famous phrase, ". . . let's go put the devil back into the inferno," etc., and while reading I had had an erection, indeed, to borrow Boccaccio's phrase, a "resurrection of the flesh," whereupon my own personal devil had reawakened and was bothering me no end. With an automatic reflex I took my devil in hand.

And this time I succeeded.

6

ALREADY, toward the age of fourteen, in upper middle school, the class was divided into two parts: those who Did and those who Didn't (or at least not yet). By Didn't I mean: those who were compliant rather than arrogant, incapable of giving a soccer ball a good hard kick, uninterested in girls, beardless, as yet unfledged. Those whose mothers back home still hadn't packed all their toys away. In other words, the ones who were behind in the great race toward the conquest of masculinity: which many never entirely attain, those who will never entirely move over into the other column, the column of the Did.

It's a rough, approximate schema, but one that more or less works. There are many oblique approaches to the conquest of points of masculinity even for those who do not possess the natural endowments: power, money, perhaps even cruelty. These things do not constitute a virile identity, but they do provide satisfactory substitutes.

When it came to such sports as soccer and basketball, I wasn't particularly talented, but I was precocious. I could perform reasonably well simply because I was physically better developed than other boys my age. It's an advantage that bites back two or three years later, when the ones who are really good players actually begin to emerge, catching up with you, passing you, and finally leaving you in a cloud of dust, so you know you'll never get close to them again . . . My physical precocity, in fact, created many false impressions. At swimming and skiing, where what counts is technique and nothing else, I wasn't very good. There it doesn't help to have whiskers a year earlier than the other boys.

It is obvious that what we were looking for in sports and especially in soccer were confirmations not so much of our skills as of our masculinity. Someone who was a strong player was treated with a certain respect; the duds, on the other hand, who ran around the field leaping and prancing and waggling their asses, chasing the ball in the air as if they were bathing beauties (an expression that my mother always used to use, when I was small, as a somewhat ironic compliment: "Hey, what are you doing, where are you going, bathing beauty?" inspired by the movies with Esther Williams), could only hope to be scorned. A boy who was no good at sports, not even a little bit, was not a boy, he was just a girl. For that matter, even among the better players, scenes of utter hysteria would break out: it's a notorious fact that when a brawl erupts among soccer players it's rare to see a genuine, well-thrown punch: they're always chaotic windmills, or shoving or face-slapping, as if they're trying to scratch their opponents' eyes out. They look like screaming fights among transvestites, and the only thing missing is people hitting each over the head with handbags.

WE HAD a destructive and self-destructive attitude. Self-destruction was the science we knew best, the discipline that we practiced most assiduously. Even those who studied seriously or attended a gym on a regular basis, and thus seemed to be interested in strengthening their mind or their body, would end up distorting them both, generating maniacal thoughts or bowing themselves down under a heavy blanket of muscles. There seemed to be only two paths: either reject all exercise, or else take it to a fanatical extreme. Whichever path you took, the result was unharmonious.

We were out to conquer the world, or actually, the universe, but before doing that, we had to beat the closest adversary, even if it was just at a game of cards: there, your deskmate, that's who you had to defeat, destroy him— but at the same time, help him. That's what they taught us at SLM. The weakest must be defeated and, at the same time, helped.

It's the same contradiction we encounter so frequently these days in politicians' speeches, when in the same breath they claim to be fighting "for a meritocracy," but also to ensure that "no citizen is left behind," when it's plain as day that the first thing excludes the second.

WHAT MADE A CLASSMATE a good classmate, what made a pal a good pal? What are the qualities that make a kid a "good kid"? I'm talking about that singular, indeed unique form of coexistence that consists of being together in a classroom, a coexistence that can endure for many years through a series of coincidences, in some cases throughout one's entire scholastic career, from elementary school to high school, and might constitute for some the most long-lasting bond experienced in a lifetime, therefore providing an endless source of memories, even if those memories are increasingly distant and legendary. Well, a good classmate and pal is someone you enjoy being with, who tells funny stories or who is himself funny, who is loyal to you in the sense that when he can he helps you out and has no doubt that you in turn will help him. It's well known exactly when a person needs emergency help from a pal and a classmate: during oral quizzes and classwork, and during the study sessions leading up to these important events, sessions that fill entire boring afternoons, when the better student explains it all to the donkey from start to finish, or else when the other classmates take it out on you, and you need an ally. Plus, the bond between pals is cemented by the daily adhesive of wisecracks, smart-ass comments, jokey insults and real ones, and then gossip, tall tales, and so on . . .

You like each other, you stimulate each other, you give the other strength and you receive strength in return: if you're together with a good pal, you feel fuller, more authentic . . . protected, that's what it is, you feel protected. You could fly along with your eyes closed and you wouldn't run into anything because there's someone watching over you as you sleep. That must be what it's like in wartime when you entrust your sleep to a sentry standing guard.

At the same time, the exchange also consisted in a constant poking and prodding of your pal, continually testing him, making disgusting allusions to the sexual activity of his mother or his sisters, the small size of his dick, the fact that when he walks he swivels his hips and wiggles his ass, or else sticking a finger in his ass crack anytime he turns his back to bend over and pick something up under the desk.

We called it friendship, but it's the wrong term . . .

We were all eager to spend time together but at the same time we were terrified at the idea of opening up, revealing the truth about ourselves. Pranks and crude jokes were the best way we had to conceal our inner life, drowning it in a vulgar laugh that was always slightly awkward and embarrassed and defensive. It was in fact much simpler to show off your penis in the locker room after gym class by swinging it like a lasso than to display any other undefended part of your personality. The crudeness cauterized wounds or prevented them from being inflicted. Sports were the ideal activity for this purpose, they allowed us to spend time together without obliging anyone to open up in any real way. In fact, by playing sports with our classmates and pals, we developed a supermuscle of control. In order to protect ourselves from the risk of potential *confessions* (the kind of stuff you'd expect from young ladies), we preferred to *do* things instead of talking about them, and in sports there's next to no chitchat at all, a game is the kind of thing that after an hour and a half or two hours of insane intensity, thank heavens, comes to an end, so that you've given your all without actually giving anything specific or useful, the most burning commitment over the shortest period of time—and in fact it has many things in common with sex. That is, it allows you to emerge still virgin and uncontaminated. Risking your physical safety in sports ensures that you preserve your psychological safety. Male locker-room camaraderie, in other words, has very little in common with intimacy; instead it's something midway between vaudeville, with its rat-a-tat volley of gags and bullshit, a lineup of suspects, and a conference table surrounded by generals with maps and charts before or after a battle. The things that are said there have the muscular character of an exhibition, and the rhythm of a variety show.

Unfortunately, true intimacy doesn't exist in a partial or moderate form: it's always, by its very definition, excessive. Made up of vertical lunges. Contaminating, like saliva in French kisses. That's why we feared it, because we dimly sensed that you can never quite recover from contact with it, you can no longer veil what has once been unveiled.

Rather than opening up to your pals, then, it was necessary to conquer them, or, at least, stand up to them. Hold your own in public in such a way as to avoid being riddled with indiscreet questions. What it required were such gifts as a powerful or strident voice, the capacity to tell jokes and anecdotes (a good memory was fundamental if you wanted to keep stock of your repertory), quick repartee so that you could offer a clever or filthy riposte to any mockery, the ability to lay your audience low in helpless laughter or else make them shut their mouths with a sharp glare. What's more, sports, as practiced intensively at SLM, were a reasonably effective bulwark against the threat of girls, or at least the thought of them, seeing that there weren't any in the surrounding area. The only individual of the female gender in the entire school, as I've previously mentioned, was a woman who sold pizza at recess. Still, even a vague thought can be every bit as unsettling as a physical presence and, in some cases, even more intrusive. I, for one, can say that I've never felt females to be so incredibly close to me as the times that all I saw on all sides were other males: in my years at SLM, during my mandatory stint in the army, and in prison, I could easily swear that they were physically present, that's just how close I felt them, intensely close, upon me, inside me. It's like the old joke about the guy who goes to the doctor, claiming that he's a hermaphrodite; "What are you saying, are you sure of this?" the doctor replies. "Let me take a look . . ." Then, after an examination, the doctor reassures him: "Trust me, you're fully male, perfectly normal . . ." "No, doctor, the thing is," the guy insists, in desperation, "I have a pussy, more than one in fact, right *here!*"—and he slaps his hand against his forehead.

Nothing remained to us, in other words, but mental projections that we'd try to exorcise with chaotic basketball games, hikes, push-ups on wooden handles, kicking balls back and forth on dusty red fields, raising long trailing clouds behind us with every galloping charge, like in the cartoons with the racing ostrich. Some went so far as to try heading a seven-pound medicine ball. With actual flesh-and-blood girls, in any case, we wouldn't have begun to know what to do, what to say, it was an unknown ritual, one that most of us would learn, if anything, by testing out and rehearsing an array of phrases and acts borrowed from our older brothers like good suits, but only after we'd graduated. Once we were expelled into the real world. Only a mechanically applied ceremonial protocol would allow us to get over the shyness we'd accumulated over years of dress rehearsals.

People can't begin to imagine what a fragile fabric male shyness is, they never seem to make the effort, except perhaps to make fun of it. And they never consider, even more than the stumbling block of shyness itself, just how mortifying it is to have to make recourse to various stratagems to find one's way out of it: in pathetic little vignettes, the movies and TV have retailed the tryouts, a boy in front of a mirror rehearsing his lines, as he plans to invite a girl to dance, the declarations of love uttered to one's own image in the mirror by gawky guys who then shut their eyes and wrap their arms around their own shoulders and kiss themselves, but all this is strictly to get a laugh out of the audience, while male shyness really does have a dark, morbid side, demented and mad, which can lead variously to murder and suicide, forget about sophomoric comedies with Jack Lemmon or Adam Sandler! When you feel as if you're being strangled . . . that the air won't reach your lungs . . . and a devastating wave of desire rises to the verge of an anxiety attack, and yet it still can't breach the levee and transform itself into action. You don't lift a finger. Your voice dies in your throat. And she impatiently turns away, walks across the room, starts talking to other boys . . .

Even idiotic pranks like taking a classmate's underwear, left in the locker room during swim lessons, and drenching them thoroughly (this was a trick played frequently on Arbus, and I confess that a couple of times I myself was a member of the gang of pranksters), played a role in this process of negotiation. These were moves on the chessboard of our identities, constantly under construction. In this way, we negotiated the fear of being taken for faggots. We negotiated the desire, however small or large that desire might be, to be faggots without letting it be seen. We negotiated the rank that we were to be given in the hierarchy, where the classmate forced to wring out his sopping underwear was dropped a level or two, and if subjected sufficiently to cruel leg-pulling and ass-kicking, might sink to the very bottom of the barrel, and even remain there, a permanent pariah. To become the target of ridicule, in fact, constituted our greatest fear, a fear that we negotiated with ourselves, each of us splitting into a dual personality, at once victim and agent of the same persecution, to see which of the two personalities would be the first to collapse, the faggot within me or the real man? The serial killer or the naked girl in the shower? When you're an adolescent, it's impossible not to be both things at once. We negotiated our way through that rising tide of pointless, vulgar words and a barricade of rude and repetitive gestures pushed well beyond the bounds of the absurd (pinches, knuckle-grinders, nape-smacks, accompanied by shrill whistles and neighing, goat-nips and donkey-chomps, soldier-slaps, unannounced smacks to the testicles), struggling the whole time with our aggressivity. Put like that, I wouldn't be able to say whether we tamed those aggressive impulses or became enslaved to them like so many robots.

Since all of us were equally revolted by the thought of playing the part of the victim, we had to study, like so many would-be professional executioners, how to lop off a head, hurrying feverishly lest our own head be lopped off first. Honestly, I never really believed in even a tenth of the jerky wisecracks or extravagant boasting I spouted back then, in retaliation to those spouted by my pals and classmates, and I'm not saying that I realize that only now: I already knew it at the time. And yet, like so many others, aspiring as I did to be like everybody else and, when it came right down to it, succeeding—I said those things. I spouted them. Well, what's so bad about that? You were in trouble if you missed a chance to make a rhyme with words ending in "-ock" or "-ucker" or "-ussy" or "-unt." They just made your mouth itch at the chance. We also negotiated these succulent opportunities to show off our poetic or creative sides. To show some wit— wit, which delights in whistling through obscenities. Though none of us were born to the working classes, the low humor of our filthy nursery rhymes challenged the finest creations of an age-old tradition, in general, and Roman tradition, in particular, based on long, filthy lists and a ruthless vision of life, a cavalcade of cynicism and ass-fucking.

But foul language made us feel like good kids. Why not, a genuine community of good kids. It's often said of people with dubious reputations, even of criminals, that *deep down* they're good kids. If you scratch the surface, deep down you'll find a good kid. What is it exactly that makes a young man a "good kid"? What are we talking about? About someone who's always loyal to his buddies and ready to do what they're willing to do without hesitation, to follow them anywhere, even when we're talking about deplorable deeds, because if he tried to pull out at the last minute, then what kind of a buddy would he be, what would be so good, after all, about this good kid? A man is judged by the things he does, not by the things he says, so if someone doesn't happen to get the chance to show what he's capable of, he runs the risk of remaining a child, in the sedentary society we live in, stingy as it is with special moments. That's why sports were invented, that is, a rapid succession of acid tests that can be administered two or three times a week, even at school, without having to wait for a war to break out or an apartment building to catch on fire in order to test those who are involved, to test their courage, their emotional control, and their willingness to endure pain. With the fairly pedestrian excuse of physical exercise, improving their posture, etc.: and at SLM they'd understood all this perfectly, to the point that they outfitted the school with a very modern gymnasium, and a pool where half of the Quartiere Trieste now splashes and swims (we'll talk about that later on), as well as a sports center with basketball courts and soccer fields on Via Nomentana, where every afternoon buses full of shouting kids would pull up, and then leave several hours later full of the same kids, but now exhausted. We'd return from that sports center so sweaty and weary that often, in the winter, when night fell early and Via Nomentana was jammed with traffic, we'd fall asleep, dusty heads leaning together. Maybe males can establish relationships only in the midst of raging battle, so they re-create that condition on the playing fields.

SINCE BACK THEN the schools were very crowded, as many as thirty students in every class, or even more, in our class there were enough kids to form not one but two soccer teams, and there were even kids left over. But instead of distributing the talent pool in a uniform manner so that the two teams were more or less evenly matched, it was customary to choose the best players and put them on a Serie A team, call it major league, which would compete in the Serie A tournament, while the rest of the players formed a minor league, B team, with its own Serie B tournament.

In other words, the boys who knew how to play, the ones who might be better or worse but were, in any case, real players, and on the other hand— the jack-offs. Never in history has a discriminatory system been less called into question, even though it was questionable at best, at least around the statistical edges of the classifications, where the two categories bumped up against each other, since between a real player with serious defects and a jack-off with great energy and determination there might not be much difference when it came to actual performance on the field. All the same, the thing that astonishes is how willing the jack-offs were to be recognized as such and therefore to play on the B team. I don't remember who was in charge of the selection, as delicate and cruel as it might prove to be, I don't recall any envy or remonstrances, or demands for reclassification, quite the opposite. The jack-offs were comfortable to be grouped together and were delighted to be playing against other teams of jack-offs, soon forgetting that they'd been categorized as human garbage. Their games, however revolting they might have been in the narrowest terms of fine soccer, were still lively and hard-fought, I enjoyed watching them, and not just for their comic potential. The fascination of the struggle actually became purer amid that chaos. The ball spent nearly all the time in the air, as if the objective of the players in kicking it was to get it as high off the ground as possible, while far below, in a dense cloud of dust, the awkward bodies of the jack-offs were scrambling and flailing in jury-rigged uniforms, running and leaping without end. From the opening whistle to the game-ender, more and more chaotically and confusedly, but never slowing down in the slightest. It should in fact be said that the jack-offs proved they had almost inexhaustible stores of energy, and every bit as much determination, considering that in order to perform even the slightest acts of athleticism they squandered at least triple the effort, for instance, in delivering a corner kick or a penalty kick, for which they'd back up dozens of yards from the ball and then charge at it, head down, like excited bulls, delivering a tremendous kick with the tip of the toe but then only moving it a short distance, as if someone had secretly, at the last minute, replaced it with a cannonball. When they leaped in the air to deliver a header, they'd grind their teeth, preserving that demoniacal grimace because their tendons had trouble releasing it, and even the most elementary throw-ins from the side of the field, using the hands—something that any normally coordinated human being ought to be able to do without any particular talent or training—when done by them, seemed like extremely difficult exercises, requiring several attempts. The unsustainable level of competitive fury displayed by the jack-offs was accompanied, oddly, by a singular show of sportsmanship. In the aftermath of the frequent collisions between players caused, as often as not, by the reckless speed at which they lunged, legs extended, to take possession of the ball, in groups of three or four at a time, they would immediately leap to their feet, shaking hands with the rivals who'd been entangled in the scrimmage, though only after cleaning the dust from their hands with the tail of their shirt; afterward they'd immediately tuck the shirttails back into their shorts, as required by regulation.

ALL OF THIS TOOK PLACE in order to keep the body straight and the mind clear and to consume all our aggression in harmless skirmishing, though, mark my words, not to the point of utter exhaustion of that vein of aggressiveness, since that is what pumps life into an individual and assures he won't succumb when he comes face-to-face with the first obstacle. The correct dosage of aggression is the secret of rearing and educating males: it can't be repressed, otherwise it will build up and might erupt all at once, nor can it be denied or inverted from negative to positive, because that runs the risk of producing a litter of altar boys or (heaven forfend!) a genuine sexual inversion. Whereas if you exalt it into something healthy and vigorous, well, that's the shortest path to fascism, even if it is camouflaged in lily-white outfits. The story that this book is going to tell, alongside other stories, ought to show how, on at least one occasion, on the basis of groundwork laid long ago by numerous contributing factors, around the middle of the eighth decade of the last century—the 1970s—the priests got their formula wrong, in other words, they misjudged the dosage of various ingredients or were just plain unlucky, because what happened next was that the flammable blend caught fire and exploded.

1

EVERYONE had some problem or other with their physique. If they had a nice one, they had to cultivate it, if an unattractive one, they were required to modify it, but no matter what, they could not and must not leave it as it was, which in any case would be impossible, because in the meantime, your body would change of its own volition, and almost never according to plan, it stretched out and hunched over and twisted up. You'd never think muscles even existed in a state of nature before the invention of weights. No one would ever have developed without pumping iron. Pump, pump, pump. Otherwise your rib cage would resemble that of a little bird. Repetitive thoughts and actions lie at the basis of all training.

Swim class was a revelation, a leaden Mannerist painting: pale, misshapen bodies were exposed, jutting shoulder blades, rolls of baby fat jiggling on hips. Few of us were exempt from the urge to cross our arms to conceal our sunken chests, a gesture that people think only women perform, to cover their breasts; well, let me tell you, we did the exact same thing, out of shame but also partly because we were cold, since the priests tended to be cheap about the heating, of both the air and the water, and you'd find the big windows in the locker room thrown wide open, even in the winter.

YOUNG DENUDED VERTEBRATE, what did they do to your back? Why don't you straighten that cordillera of vertebrae, each jutting out in a different manner, like large rocks laid out hastily in the middle of a stream to cross it, why don't you tug it straight, all at once, with a pinch of pride? Your pallid back seems to stand there, just waiting for a whipping, and even if your daddy is a physician or a noted accountant, there isn't much difference between you and some slave awaiting punishment. Places like the swimming pool of an exclusive religious school, designed and built to enhance the health and development of the boys attending there, become instead theaters of the most stinging humiliations, those who aren't saddled with a bully who mocks them will just take on the job themselves—you need only to go running past a mirror, flopping along in your flip-flops, shoulders bowed, on your way to the showers, and you'll see the specter of your own adolescence go shambling past.

PROFESSOR CALIGARI, swim instructor, would line us up along the side of the pool to review us: he never said a word, he'd just stop to caress with his gaze the weak points of the various boys' constitutions, weak points that were so numerous in some of our physiques that he might stand there scrutinizing for as much as a minute, prompting us to laugh and blush. Who knows why it is that shame so often expresses itself in the form of a snicker. "There's nothing at all to laugh about here," Caligari would exclaim, "quite the opposite . . . if anything, a person ought to cry at the sight of you. You bring tears to my eyes. You're all so many charity cases. *(Titters from the class, shivering with cold.)* Though the last thing I think when I see you are charitable thoughts. *(Titters and snickers. Almost everyone is crossing their arms on their chest, rubbing themselves or covering some part of their body, alternately.)* But let's keep our hopes up. I'll take care of things. *(One or two boys slide their hands into their swimsuits. It's a childish gesture of self-protection.)* I'll turn you into living statues, you understand? You're not just going to become men, you're going to become statues," Caligari crowed. "I promise you: sta-tues!"

The exercises that our teacher assigned us to begin our sculptural transformation were only two in number, rudimentary and not especially effective: pressing our hands together in line with our sternum, or else hooking our fingers together and yanking outward, in the same position, elbows out. That's all. Ten seconds of pushing, then ten seconds of yanking, and back to the beginning. After firing a starter pistol, Caligari would count— one, two, three . . . at regular speed . . . but once he got to seven he started to go slower and slower . . . eeeighhhhttt . . . eight and a haaaalf . . . while we tried to hold that absurd position of prayer, pressing our hands together until the effort began to make them wobble, eight and three-quaaarters . . . and our elbows would tremble, and the usual involuntary snickers would explode in our sunken chests. This line of hairless boys (with the exception, of course, of Pierannunzi, about whom I'll have more to say in the next chapter), the sinews of their necks quivering, was pitiful to behold. From the corners of Busoni's mouth, straining in a grimace of effort (after ten seconds!), streamers of drool descended. Without his eyeglasses, Arbus couldn't see a thing. "Aren't we here to swim?" Zarattini, who was the skinniest and most effeminate of the kids, would ask the other boys closest to him, under his breath, but Caligari didn't miss a thing. "Excuse me, I'm not sure I heard what you said? Maybe you said that you like the water, or am I mistaken?" Whereupon he promptly ordered the others to toss him into the pool. Gladly! The skinny teenagers standing around him were suddenly transformed into musclemen, who grabbed Zarattini and hustled him over to the side of the pool, then held him right over the surface of the water, as if about to toss him over a cliff into a very deep gorge. It was an image of great festivity, and no festivity can begin without a human sacrifice. Indeed, the entire class would ally itself against Zarattini, obeying Caligari's instruction with blind and cheerful uniformity, because after he was thrown into the water, that splash served as a signal for one and all to dive in after him . . .

TRUTH BE TOLD, this happened only the first few times, we were all impatient at the thought that all the fun was to be had in the water. Instead, in the pool, you don't have much fun, and what fun you do have lasts only a few minutes: splashing, ducking others, sticking the lifesavers under your belly until they pop up out of the water: after that, you have to swim. Which is the most damnably laborious and pointless effort imaginable. The lane is packed with swimmers, it feels as if you're having to dig your way through the water, barely advancing toward the pair of feet kicking and churning froth and bubbles in front of your nose, so that if you do manage to put together a couple of more vigorous and coordinated strokes, you'll get kicked in the face for your trouble, whereas the minute you slow down the guy behind you will plow into you. If you stop in the middle of the pool you'll never get started again, and you'll sink to the bottom. Everyone gets pissed off and drinks mouthfuls of chlorinated water.

YES, among the classes of the week, the most popular and, at the same time, the most unpleasant is certainly the hour of swimming. On the one hand, nothing is as pleasurable as the prospect of being able to stop fooling around with pens and balls of crumpled paper and bothering your neighbors by plucking at the metal hooks where in theory you are supposed to hang your book bag from your desk, even though I've never seen anyone hang a book bag on one of those hooks, not once, in all the time I spent at SLM, that is, more than ten years—and then hurry out into the hallway, line up on the staircases, and then tumble down two or three stories until you reach the swimming pool and plunge into the water. Strange to imagine that in the bowels of the school it was always there, by day and by night, wobbling ever so slightly, that rectangle of green water which for only a few hours was kicked and smacked to a froth by the boys' feet and hands, while the rest of the time it rested, smooth, dark, and cold. Until the next dive. A beautiful idea, but beautiful the way only ideas can be, because in actuality the hour of swimming was the most suffocating time of the week.

We pass through pebbled-glass doors, and it's a slap in the face of hot, humid air, it seems as if we're already swimming when we descend into the locker rooms. I've always been very shy and ashamed, and stripping embarrasses me, it even embarrasses me when I'm alone and I have the door shut, if I look at my legs and belly a chill runs through me. As I enter the booth I take great care to make sure I snap the lock shut, and I keep my eye on it as I take off my shoes, my socks, I glance at it again as I remove my trousers, and then underneath, just to get done quicker, I'm already wearing my swimsuit, on Thursday mornings instead of my underwear I put on my swimsuit, and I put my clean underwear into a bag inside my gym bag.

While the air might be warm, everything else in the locker room is freezing cold, the bench, the floor, the aluminum bars speckled with chilly drops of water.

The thing that always depressed me most when I was little and I had to undress was the moment it became clear that my undershirt was tucked into my underpants. The undershirt was mandatory and mothers in the old days took care while dressing their child that it was tucked in securely under the elastic band of the underpants, and since undershirts were often bought large and loose, a size too big, "with room to grow," the extra length had to be tucked all the way down, below your buttocks. With the SLM swimsuit, which was black, pulled up over your tummy, and the white tank-top undershirt tucked into it, the image of any young boy was even more pathetic. But just as no one can say exactly what sadness is, likewise its causes are open to discussion, and you might reasonably think that it is one reason, but instead it turns out to be another, or another still, or it might even be that there are no particular reasons for being sad, you just are. Like circles under your eyes: you have them and you keep them.

✦

BEFORE VENTURING into the water, a few minutes of those calisthenics that are supposed to make us become muscular. Arbus is a laughable spectacle because he is skinny as a rail and pale as a sheet and yet he struggles to press hand against hand, wrist against wrist, and the conviction behind his effort and his scientific reliability make us think that by doing that, you really can bulk up your muscles, "Five more seconds, hold it like that . . . five, four, three . . . two . . ." and soon even Arbus will have a sculpted physique, with every single muscle defined by isometric exercise, "three . . . two . . . one and a half, one and a quarter . . . hold it like that and you'll turn into statues . . . like marble statues . . . like the statues in the Foro Italico . . . come on, now! You can release! And breathe!"

The whole swim lesson from start to finish is about holding your breath. We stick our faces in the water and pull them out only to gulp down a mouthful of air and then splash our faces back under. Everyone has the next boy's feet right in front of him, parboiled by immersion in the water. Arms windmill and the chlorine stings. Our eyes and our throats. Already after four or five laps, the water feels heavy, and our bodies, now even heavier than the water, stop bobbing and struggle to move forward beneath the surface, only the arms break through like lurching paddle wheels and the thrashing of the feet, frantic at first, begins to slow, becoming languid, reawakening periodically, when we remember that we have our feet to help us get across to the edge of the pool, and we start thrashing them hard again, just a few more yards and we'll be able to grip the edge and pretend to take a second to adjust our caps before turning and starting back across—embezzling a little more time to rest. Not even five seconds and the instructor will lean down and start smacking your head with a sandal if you don't get going. And to think how much fun it was to dive in off the starting blocks! That's what we ought to be doing, diving in, over and over again. Not struggling along, our lungs aching in the middle of a lap.

We students all wear the same black swimsuit, in a stretchy weave, with a stripe down each side, yellow and green—those are the SLM colors. And we're all pale and white, in fact, an off-green shade, or maybe that's just the light in the swimming pool, and by the end of the lesson we're even more so. Hop out, taking care not to slip, dry off. The stunned state induced by heat and chlorine and effort (not really all that much effort, truth be told, but then and there, insurmountable) merges with the hot roar of air from the wall-mounted hair dryers, which turn off after a minute so you have to start them up again with a tremendous whack on the oversized chrome-plated pommel. The head feels as if it's stuffed with heat, and you give more whacks to an ear, as you tilt your head to one side, to get the water to stream out of the other ear. Kidding around, jokes, the usual roughhousing. After the hour of swim lessons it's tough to go back to class, dragging our gym bags, they, too, black with yellow and green stripes, up the stairs. To help us get up the staircases, which suddenly seem as steep as those in a bell tower, we intone in guttural voices, "Jeee-sahel . . . Jeeee-sahel . . . ," which was a sort of biblical anthem sung by a pop group back then, with guitars and bongo drums, and a nasal voice, drawling and twangy. Only Arbus, me, and a few others in class have long hair, but not as long as the longhairs who sing the lamentatious verses of "Jesahel."

In her eyes there is light there is love . . .
In her body is the fever of pain . . .

It is always in any case an exodus, the journey of the students together in a school. They are marching toward a promised land.

She is following a light that walks
Slowly a crowd comes together . . .

8

MEN ARE INSECURE *both when they feel insufficiently masculine and when they feel too masculine: sensuality shakes an individual down to his very roots, it makes him tremble. An excess of confidence is nothing more than an inverted effect of insecurity. We were obsessed with this problem, since we had nothing but other males surrounding us—our classmates were males, our teachers were males—and we were forced to engage in a continuous struggle for placement in the hierarchies, trying to preserve or improve the ranking we'd achieved through the usual systems—foul language, sports, stealing other students' snacks, smacking, laughing, joke-telling, and our fathers' fantastic automobiles. What was missing, though, was the only reliable element to certify that a male really*

was one, namely, girls. As a result, this none-too-chivalrous tournament
was deprived of its proper audience or, rather, of its natural referee. It took
place in private, like a performance put on by inmates who are called upon
to play all the roles, including that of the widow and the seduced young
maiden, so that they dance together and kiss each other. Among other
things, it should be pointed out that in our class there weren't only awk-
ward bespectacled young men and altar boys and tubs of lard, but also
boys who, already at the ages of fourteen or fifteen, were very well devel-
oped, bursting with vitality, and yet those were the very ones who ended
badly, as if the overabundance of masculinity had led them astray or else
started to devour the organism that produced it.

IN MIDDLE SCHOOL and, later, in high school we had a very particular
classmate, who never seemed able to sit still for a minute and who looked
at least two or three years older than his actual age. He was skinny, dark-
skinned, always dressed in motorcycle garb with a pair of short boots the
rest of us could only dream of; his most salient characteristic was a pair of
long, thin eyebrows arching over a pair of wide-set eyes as inflamed as the
eyes of an Arabian stallion. His sensual gaze struck all of us, to say nothing
of the priests who taught us, who feared him a little and were intimidated
in his presence but were also indulgent toward that homegrown version of
a Middle Eastern prince, in spite of his unimpressive academic performance. His name was Stefano Maria Jervi, and he was doing poorly in a
number of subjects, starting with Italian and mathematics, which are the
load-bearing columns of the whole structure—fail them and everything
else collapses: especially if the reasons for the poor academic performance
are different and at odds between them. In fact, Jervi did poorly in Italian
because he paid no attention, when he even attended, and in mathematics
and science because he didn't understand. That meant he could neither save
himself by pointing to his unrealized potential nor by adducing the effort
he'd lavished on his studies. The truth was that school, that is, school for
adolescents, meaning the school that you had to attend because you were
legally a minor, didn't seem to suit him: he was already an adult, in mind
and body. His precocious development led him beyond the typical interests
of a high school student, prompting him to skip lessons, to evaporate outside the walls of SLM that hemmed him in. Even sports, where he ought by
rights to have excelled given his taut and fully developed physique, struck

him as nothing but a waste of time. Strictly for kids, all that running around on the grass. The only exception he made was for skiing, which he considered "totally awesome."

I have a recurring dream, in which I've flunked a year and had to repeat, and I'm being led by the hand by a headmaster who's younger than me down a row of desks to take a seat at mine, the only unoccupied desk in the classroom, ridiculously tiny, so I wind up wedged into a minuscule chair with metal legs, surrounded by snot-nosed kids who turn to look at me, amusement in their eyes, while I am consumed by the disbelief of a dreamer who knows that sooner or later he's going to awaken again, putting an end to this travesty, but also by the terror that, by the time the exams roll around, I won't be able to pass them. I'll never make it. I'm just not up to it. Those equations are too complicated for me, I won't be able to solve them, or then there's calculating mass, I don't even remember how you're supposed to find mass, or what it is, and after all, who gives a damn about equations, they don't do you a bit of good in life, I'm a grown-up now and I can confirm your suspicions, kids, take it from me, 99 percent of the stuff they teach in school won't serve any purpose later on, I'm tempted to tell them, and yet I'm deeply troubled by my unmistakable inability to perform those equations, to solve those problems, it fills me with a subtle wave of panic. There you go, inadequacy accompanied by a feeling of unjustified superiority. An adult who can't keep up with a class full of kids who, in every other aspect of life, ought to be years and years behind him. Maybe that's the way Stefano Maria Jervi felt. The drive of his hormones had already launched him far past school at a single bound, almost without realizing it. While most of us hadn't even kissed a girl, and maybe hadn't even held hands with one, it was whispered that Jervi had already had complete sexual relations.

Complete sexual relations, that was the formulation in use back then, when it was pretty well understood that girls were willing to put out, but on a sort of installment plan, in stages, or by anatomical parts, this one yes, that one no, maybe in a week from now, or maybe never. Touch, kiss, insert fingers, a Monopoly game of assorted acts, where you have to go back and start over and you lose everything just when you thought you'd reached the finish line, all because of an unlucky toss of the dice. Denuding one portion of the body, but not another, or else first one and then another but—careful—not all of them at the same time. (Truth be told, this little game is still played even when you're a grown-up, with adult and reasonably consenting women, whom you begin to strip at one end while, in the meantime, they're dressing themselves again at the other . . .) That's just how arbitrary the stages of the erotic process could be, where none of the people involved ever seemed to be fully in charge, and things would stop or move forward on what seemed to be a rather random basis. Desire, no matter how powerful, is still terribly imprecise, and female desire is even more so, creating provisional moralities instant by instant, inviolable prohibitions that are swept aside in a matter of seconds, while barriers are erected every bit as rapidly on the foundation of an ethical code that is, as it were, blinking, that exists on one day but not on the following two. To say nothing about personal will, the most ambiguous concept that's ever been coined and that, in the erotic context, practically loses all meaning or else seems eager to take on the first definition we care to give it. That we *choose* to give it. *Complete sexual relations*, in any case, remains a mocking and hypocritical expression, because there's very little about it that can be called complete, since it takes place in a very narrow anatomical area, however sought-after and sacralized or reviled it might be, depending on traditions and points of view. Was it enough to spend a few seconds there in order to be able to talk about *completeness*? The penetration of one orifice by another appendage was mistaken for the whole of the two people implicated in this welter of organs, giving rise to the most clamorous of all rhetorical figures, a synecdoche as double in nature as the helix of DNA. For that matter, was it not the greatest of all modern philosophers who described conjugal relations as nothing more than a contractual stipulation allowing each of the two parties to the agreement to make use of the genitalia of the other? But maybe it's only right that the matter should be so defined and in that definition be reduced to this, that it become simple, it's all there and there's nothing more to it, it's not always true that language delves into the depths of the topics of life, sometimes it just clarifies them with sheer brutality, and perhaps it is true that the completeness of relations between man and woman, the culmination of all that the two sexes have to communicate with each other, cannot be attained in any way other than the insertion of one organ into another. For a few minutes. And if that actually is the way it works, then Jervi was a pioneer, the explorer who in all our names put to the test the formula that allows you to enter by rights into the realm of masculinity.

THE JERVI FAMILY was wealthy in the way that only the families of high state functionaries seem able to be, that is, in a sober and mysterious manner. The Court of Audit, the Administrative Court, the State Council, the Constitutional Court, the Prefectures, the Bank of Italy—these are all state bodies that never occur to you when you think of power. You tend to identify them, instead, with the government, the parliament, or else with wealth, the public works contracts won by industrialists, financiers, bankers, oilmen, film producers, real estate developers ... And while politicians and businessmen are visible to the general public, these functionaries little by little climb the ladders of their careers inside a sort of hermetically sealed, soundproofed chamber, until they attain the chairmanship of agencies whose existence no one would even have suspected. It seems that Jervi's father had already occupied a number of these chairmanships, and was continuing his rise through the ranks, always shrouded in discretion, as if the steps he climbed were carpeted in thick felt. Some of us there at school said that he was, or had been, chairman of the Italian State Railways, others said he chaired the Olympics Committee, and there were even those who claimed that he was the supreme accountant in charge of the most mysterious Cassa Depositi e Prestiti, where, just like in Scrooge McDuck's massive money bin, he swam in a pool full of cash, from which Commendatore Jervi was able to turn on and off the faucets as he chose and pleased. Among kids, unless someone's father had a very clearly defined profession ("He's an abdominal surgeon") or else there was some other reason for special pride ("He built a dam on the Nile"), the work he did was never the subject of any specific inquiry, and that rule applied to all the other fathers as well; on the outside, at SLM, they might be classified as more or less wealthy, or not wealthy at all, according to the car they used to come and pick up our classmates in front of the school. No one dared to ask Stefano Jervi: "What does your father do?" But everyone noticed how well he dressed, his little alligator-skin ankle boots, the complete assortment, right up to the very latest model, of the leading brands of sunglasses, which most of the time he didn't even wear on the bridge of his nose, but rather perched on his forehead, to keep his raven-black bangs from tumbling over his eyes.

JERVI WAS THE FIRST one of us, and I think for a good long time, the only one, who went to the discotheque on Saturday nights and Sunday afternoons to dance, at a time when some of us classmates of his had mothers who were still hesitating as to whether they should go on buying us short pants or graduate to trousers. (I believe that I belong to the last generation of the Italian middle class that assigned this coming-of-age marker, this rite of passage: they kept boys as long as possible with their knees bare, until they finally seemed like irremediable idiots. I've thought long and hard about the possible economic motivation for this approach, which at first I believed was an attempt to prolong our childhood and therefore the pliability and obedience of male children to their parents, by forcing them to display their knees, just as it was forbidden to the daughters to display them. In reality, it was more because those shorts could be worn without having to constantly lengthen the legs or buy new ones, and they could be worn until it became impossible to fasten them at the waist.)

I COULD TELL a number of stories about Jervi at SLM, and perhaps later in this book, if you'll be good enough to listen and I haven't wandered too far afield by that point, and if they end up having anything to do with the principal story line, I'll tell them then: for now I'm going to limit myself to something that happened years later, to be exact, seven years after the end of school, which was also the last year of Jervi's life. An episode I learned about from the newspapers, identifying as my classmate—thanks to the publication of an old photograph taken from a falsified ID, in which Jervi looked absolutely identical to the way he'd looked when we were in class together at SLM, with his dazzling eyebrows, befitting a Latin American singer, and that half smile—identifying, I was saying, as Jervi a man who had been blown up while he was planting an explosive charge on the roof of the criminal insane asylum of Aversa, in the middle of the night on February 11, 1982. He'd lost his leg in the unsuccessful bombing, just like the publisher Giangiacomo Feltrinelli, and he had died in the hospital the following day without ever regaining consciousness. And so he had had no chance to reveal the objectives of his attempted attack, credit for which was not claimed by any organization. It was only after further investigation and the arrest of several of his comrades, who practically didn't have to be asked twice before spilling first and last names, Stefano Maria Jervi turned out to have been a recently enlisted member, and hardly a prominent one, of one of the numerous revolutionary groups to spring out of schisms and last-minute desperate recruitments in the final period of Italian terrorism, when it slid into its irreversible decline, producing a pyrotechnical and immensely bloody succession of shoot-outs, kidnappings, and murders, almost always committed at random or out of frustration, the last blossoming of the tree before the revolutionaries all wound up in prison or state's witnesses or fugitives abroad. His revolutionary group, if I'm remembering right, was called the UGC, Unità di Guerriglia Comunista— Communist Guerrilla Unit.

I was stunned to learn that Jervi had wound up in the UGC (how? when? and most of all, *why*?) just as the organization reached the end of its rope. A man who was about to die enlisting in the ranks of a moribund movement. What had driven him to climb onto the roof of an insane asylum on a winter night? Did he have accomplices or was he alone? Had he simply been trying to make a statement, or did he want to kill someone? And who could you be trying to kill on the roof of an insane asylum, except for pigeons or else, if you were trying to make the roof collapse, everyone in the top-floor ward with the cells of the confined inmates, which meant a bunch of criminals who were no crazier than whoever was planning to blow them up? In the newspaper article about Jervi, identified as such only two days after his death, there was some reference to the hypothesis that what was actually on the roof of the Aversa insane asylum was the arsenal or one of the arsenals of the UGC, and that my schoolmate had been killed in an accident having to do with the ordinary routine maintenance of that arsenal, in other words, while he was storing or picking up explosives.

ANOTHER CASE of overabundant but not self-destructive masculinity was Pierannunzi, the son of a toymaker on Viale Libia. He wasn't in my class, but one below me, which means that, while I was stepping over the threshold into high school, he still had another year left in middle school. At age thirteen he was as tall as he was going to be for the rest of his life, and he had a beard. Not in the sense that he could grow one, but that he actually *wore* one, and a fairly thick beard, too, like some character out of the Renaissance. It was quite something to see him with the rest of his class; he stood a head higher than them and had a full beard: Polyphemus as he's about to choose which of Ulysses's men to devour. But it was even harder to process the sight of him today, as I went past his toy shop with the exact same green neon sign that it had back then, the letters slanting to the right, in a sort of stylized script. The whole shop is the same as it was, even if now the display window is full of video games instead of dolls and six-shooters.

Pierannunzi was behind the counter, resting his weight on both elbows, with a gut, but by no means as tall as I remembered him. He wore his beard trimmed short, perhaps because it was all white, his thinning hair grown long to cover his bald spot, and now only the black bushes of his eyebrows belonged to the cyclops that he was no longer. Forty years had passed over him, not like a train but like a sandstorm that had discolored him.

I stopped to admire him, half-concealed behind the corner of the glass door as he patiently explained to an old woman, drawling his instructions with a nasal accent, exactly how to install the batteries in the back of a toy piano that she had brought back to the store, thinking it was broken.

"You see them? You see them, signora, these little marks with the plus and the minus signs?"

But the signora wasn't able to see them, even though she craned her neck over the counter.

"The batteries need to be inserted with the poles inverted, that's why it wouldn't work."

And he started tapping on the keys to test it, first at random, and then starting to play a piece of music, which he left unfinished after a couple of brief phrases. It ought to have been the first of Bach's two- and three-part inventions. Or something very similar.

Again, he went back to trying out the individual keys, pressing them the way a child with no knowledge of music might do, changing the settings so that the device produced first the sound of a trumpet, then of an organ, then of violins. Then he cut in the electronic drum set, whereupon the signora put both hands over her ears, pretending to be overwhelmed by the volume, which was actually fairly low.

"Ah, signora mine, believe me, we could raise the volume quite a bit!" Pierannunzi smiled. "You could dance to it at the disco . . ."

Then with well-rehearsed and very precise gestures, turning his eyes to the ceiling as if wishing to prove that he could do it blind, he put the keyboard back into its polystyrene cradle and pushed it back into the carton, carefully folding shut the flaps, which fit into a series of slots but had been torn by the impatient recipient in his haste to open the present. All the same, he was able to gentle them back into their proper form and the package was good as new, no different from the day it had been purchased. Maybe the gaze he turned to the ceiling was an exasperated one, or maybe I just read it that way in order to prove my thesis. The old woman thanked him and apologized for having bothered him, implicitly withdrawing her tacit accusation that the toyseller had tried to fob off a defective product on her.

"My duty, signora," the toyseller replied, "at your service. And I hope your grandson has fun with it."

I thought I had detected in this last line a note of irony. It's well known, in fact, the way things go in homes where gifts meant to produce music, say drums or other instruments, are given to children, and how as the birthday party stretches out toward its final moments and the little friends all clamor to be allowed to play, the mob of kids produces nothing but noise as nerves fray and exhaustion sets in. The most irritating examples: xylophones.

Pierannunzi had expressed his masculinity all at once in a mighty eruption between the ages of ten and sixteen, and traces of it still remained, interesting to revisit.

DEEP DOWN, adolescence is one of those rare moments in life, perhaps indeed the only one, in which you have the courage or you feel the inexorable need to venture into the labyrinth of an inner quest, something that for the rest of their lives nearly everyone avoids, either out of fear of what they've glimpsed during that search, carried out in fact when they were young, or else because all their energy is devoted to the struggle for survival, to responding to the demands and pressures placed on them by others. Only during adolescence can solitude, however much it may be feared and disliked, produce any fruit that is other than bitter, arousing authentic curiosity and holding incredible discoveries in store. Behold, this newly formed individual, newly hatched from the egg, is the very individual who is so voraciously curious to know about himself.

And how can you construct an identity for yourself, how can you even come to know yourself if not by studying, long and hard, your own image reflected in a mirror?

Who is the boy or the girl depicted behind the clothes-cupboard door, next to the stack of sweatshirts and T-shirts? Usually this dreamy posture is derided or upbraided, with the demand that it be replaced by a more adult, responsible one, open to productive interactions with other people and with the world, instead of standing there in enchanted admiration of oneself. The narcissistic lull, which is actually one of the few instants of reflection and self-awareness granted to an individual who is otherwise constantly asked to *do*, study, run, train, chat, have fun (that's right, even having fun becomes an obligation, it's constantly being devalued in the name of action and relationships). Having relationships with other people is good; having one with yourself, less so. We must immediately remind a young man who may be raptly evaluating and judging himself that only others have the right to judge him, only the evaluation that the world assigns him will be credible and valid. The young women who try on one skimpy dress after another, suffering the torments of hell over the defects that the mirror beams back to them, ought to be taken by the ear and marched away from that frustrating sight, there's plenty of other things to study instead of their own bodies, there is chemistry and computers, there's ancient Greek, art history, the buttocks of statues—those buttocks, yes, you can study them—then there's algebra, the Revolt of the Ciompi in medieval Florence, there's the piano, volunteering, the scouts, handball . . . anything, in other words, anything but an understanding of oneself, which only narcissistic self-contemplation could teach.

I, too, more vain than any of the others, in fact, vain *exactly like* the others, that is, extremely so, spent time gazing at myself in the mirror, admiring from various points of view the shape of my nose, pulling my eyebrows back toward my temples, stretching them out of shape, grimacing to bare my teeth, arranging my hair in various ways to figure out which style looked best, which was the most charming look to present to others, or to be specific, and not veer into the useless realm of the generalization, to others my age, the only beings on the planet whose existence mattered to me. Those instants of observation lasted for hours and were of a deeply upsetting profundity: I would be not just a good writer but a true philosopher if I were capable of reproducing so much as a single minute of it. The heart raced, pounding, so full of thoughts, doubts, hopes, plans, that spilled forth: spilling forth out of me, exactly, that was precisely the sensation I experienced, namely that my heart could no longer contain the wave of images and ideas churning inside it.

I misguidedly used the word "hopes": I should have referred to "fantasies." Even now I use the mirror to determine the onslaught of baldness and white hair, I live on fantasies, I nourish myself with fantasies or, rather, I slake my thirst with them like a horse at a trough, plunging my muzzle into them, I produce them and consume them on the spot, I'm obsessed with them, they possess me, I don't know what to do with these voices anymore, these images and ideas and teeming phrases. For that matter, I couldn't do without them, my life is already so bare-bones, so minimal, what would happen if the one source of daydreams were to dry up? These fantasies, moreover, serve to render astonishing the few things I do, the rare actions I actually take, which are so to speak swollen with all the aspirations, the fata morganas, the deliriums conceived in solitude, and so they give me unspeakable pleasure or scathing despair, according to whether they succeed or fail. If I fantasize about eating an ice cream and I discover that the ice cream shop is closed for a holiday, I give serious thought to the idea of killing myself. In me, sadly, the narcissistic self-contemplation of my adolescence never really came to an end: in response to the question "Who am I?" I'm afraid too many different answers have been offered to let me take any given one as correct. So, I still stand in front of the mirror, asking futile, self-regarding questions, like the queen in *Snow White*, and rejoicing or flying into a rage at the answers I receive. If I think back to Arbus and other classmates of mine, I ask myself: Which of them ever received a true, definitive answer? A single, sharp, clear, simple answer. Is there any one of them who at a certain point understood and said: Yes, I'm like *that*? I'm like that, period. Did anyone reach that point, early or late?

9

THE PRIVATE SCHOOL housed a group of young men who enjoyed the initial privilege of having been born into well-to-do families and the additional one of a solid education capable of preparing them to occupy a prominent position in the adult world. All of which was tempered by a catechism that, on paper at least, preached something like the exact opposite. It is a singular characteristic of Italian Catholicism that it carries on a millennia-old tradition of defending the least powerful while in point of fact it allies itself with the worldly interests of the most powerful. Perhaps this contradiction is the foundation of its greatness and its solidity. But it cannot escape anyone's notice, and the ones whose notice it least escaped were us, the lucky students.

✦

ANYONE who as a boy belongs to the middle class doesn't even notice the fact, in part because the privileges he enjoys or the privations he suffers aren't really all that spectacular, in the final analysis; he hardly even imagines that he can qualify as a "bourgeois young man": when he looks in the mirror he sees a young man, not a "bourgeois young man," even though that's exactly what he is and how he actually appears, even when he's in his underwear he's a bourgeois young man in his underwear, lifting weights to develop his arm muscles, in front of the mirror in the bathroom of a bourgeois home, etc. But he doesn't perceive himself that way, at age fifteen or sixteen he hardly thinks that belonging to a class is significant, and most of all he really doesn't think of himself as belonging to a social class, if anything he might consider the soccer team he roots for, the music that he likes or detests, the way he dresses, or his political beliefs, which, in the case of a middle-class young man, could vary from the extreme right wing to the extreme left without either option seeming odd.

A *borgataro* from the poorer outskirts of town or an heir to a fortune or the scion of an aristocratic family almost immediately realize who they are and where they come from and where they're heading or risk heading: the markers along the highways of their lives.

The young bourgeois man, on the other hand, will all at once perceive, on a given day that is as likely to come at age eighteen as at age thirty or forty, the class he belongs to, and in a flash it will become just as evident to his eyes that his clothing, his home, his motorcycle or his car, his very thoughts and desires and the way he has of relishing life or suffering, and even the sweetheart he has chosen or who has chosen him and who might well now be his wife, and have been for some time—all these things are the way they are precisely because he is bourgeois.

From that moment on, no matter what he might be doing, even organizing a picnic or signing an insurance policy or kissing a woman who might or might not be his wife, he'll be possessed by that awareness.

WHEN YOU ENTER SCHOOL at age six, as I did, from the warm protective safety of the family, without intermediate transitions through any form of social interaction with others, the risk is that you might acquire one of these two attitudes: either attribute to yourself a power over others, or else feel that the others have that power over you. Usually neither of the two things is real, or else it's true even if it's imaginary, like most things that a person feels and therefore does. Very few things in our lives are concrete before we ourselves make them so by materializing our fantasies, giving them a weight they didn't have in the first place. Fears, expectations, and illusions shape the world to their own image and semblance. It's rare that a concrete action takes its basis from a calculation, or else it entails a fantastic calculation which follows laws that are by no means rational, or else it might still apply an impeccable logic but to imaginary data. The person who spends the greatest amount of energy on calculation is not a mathematician, but a lunatic. Or a mad scientist, a perfect compendium between the power of reason and the delirium of the premises and the objectives. Arbus probably corresponded to that type.

BY THE SIMPLE FACT that we were enrolled in that school, by the fact that it was private, by the fact that our parents paid (thereby proving to us that we should forever be grateful to them, and to the rest of the world, which was no doubt suitably impressed that they could afford to do so) to have the teachers teach us things that all the other little kids in the country were being taught free of charge, making it clear however that what we were receiving at SLM, since it wasn't being given away for free, must necessarily be a little more valuable, more special, more exclusive, a more highly concentrated fruit juice, a more highly prized vintage of wine, an advantage, a privilege, in short, for all this and more besides we felt, to use the English word, *entitled*. I can't come up with an equivalent word in Italian: *titolati*, *aventi diritto* . . . I'll search more carefully in the Italian dictionary that I pore over every evening.

Truth be told, ours was an *entitlement* devoid of any specific title, though unmistakable, practically an emblem, a trademark, to such an extent that nearly ten years later, a young woman would notice it, that indelible brand. "Say, by any chance: did you go to a school run by priests?" "How did you know that?" "It's basically stamped on your forehead." (But I've already told you this story, haven't I?) In other words, we were young masters, *signorini*, a little rich, a little bit assholish, a little bigoted, a little bit Fascist, a little spoiled, a little bit blowhards yet at the same time shy, all these characteristics, barely hinted at or accentuated, matched the standard identikit of the former student of a private school: they made such a student easy to spot from a mile away, and apparently, I had them all in spades.

❧

FRANKLY, it doesn't seem to me that, out of that class, that year's harvest of students, many great men emerged, outstanding, noteworthy personalities. I ought to reconstruct the class rolls and delve a little deeper, but it strikes me that there's no one prominent enough to have reached my ears or come before my eyes without making specific, directed searches. Accomplished people, well advanced in their professions, a few doctors, a few accountants, one good and respected writer, Marco Lodoli, mid-ranking public officials . . . So, going on rough recollections, I know that Galeno De Matteis works in Zurich as a software developer, Alessio Giuramento took his father's place running their packaging factory, Busoni also went into his father's line of work, and is an ear, nose, and throat specialist, apparently a very good one, and in fact I was once tempted to send my son to him, he's having problems with his vocal cords, he loses his voice, but then I decided not to, I didn't feel like striking up old acquaintances just to get an office visit. And then there are certainly some honest engineers and competent lawyers . . . But really, though . . . weren't we supposed to be the new governing class, isn't that why our parents paid all that tuition? Or was it really just to keep us out of the turmoil of the strikes and the demonstrations and steer us clear of girls and drugs, to teach us the catechism, to make us good, was that why they sent us there? Or to learn to command? To help others, especially the poor and the helpless, or to gain the necessary rank to crush them underfoot, pressing down on their heads the manhole cover, like in *Metropolis*, to suppress those who march through the sewers of the underworld?

Perhaps, though, the education provided at SLM wasn't meant to hit any spectacular heights, wasn't meant to break away from the average, by preparing the students to make clamorous discoveries or achieve memorable deeds: things that no education of any sort can predict or aim at, things that are owed to an instinct which, in those cases where it is recognized ahead of time—as something already alive and in the process of development in a boy—any modern educator, especially a Catholic educator, would feel duty bound to ward off and suppress, rather than encourage. Why? Because such an instinctive impulse to achieve things out of the ordinary necessarily clashes with all and any regulations and forms of control, leads to conflict with the authorities and with the classmates. And while problems of resistance against authority might perhaps be solved in accordance with classic approaches that the priests knew and were perfectly capable of administering, and had been since time immemorial, because they'd experienced them themselves and tested them out in their own preparatory schools, seminaries, and so on, it is the conflict and detachment from their own classmates that prove unacceptable to modern educators, who look upon the idea of excelling with suspicion and consider it on a par with bullying. Education must tend toward the average, must achieve collective results, woe to those who are too far below this mediocre objective but far greater woe to him who, even without meaning to, driven by his natural gifts, surges even higher! An individual at odds with his peers, because they are not sufficiently similar to him, is eventually either domesticated or abandoned to some marginal role. Is there a way of excelling that does not entail conflict? Individuals who attain outstanding achievements are the ones who emerged victorious from the conflict, that much is obvious, but to an even greater extent, they are the ones who have emerged defeated. In fact, it is often defeat at one level that creates the occasion for triumph and redemption on some other, higher level. Now, it was that very education imparted by the priests that prevented one individual from rising above the others, that offered him Christian protection when he was at risk of sinking below them. There was no other alternative than to slog along at an average level: neither far above or far below. Whether Catholic or non-Catholic, nowadays that is how the Italian school tends to work. As soon as you emerge from its mechanisms, which at least on paper are egalitarian in nature, you plunge into the abysses of the real world.

By the way, speaking of meritocracy: if there ever were such a thing, it would be an implacable system, every bit as just as it would be illiberal, or as liberal as it would be unjust.

WEALTH . . . prosperity . . . yes.

Back then, the possessions of a young man from a well-to-do family consisted of a shelf full of records, a camera. A Vespa. And then . . . nothing else occurs to me. A stereo record player.

10

THE OBSERVATIONS that follow are taken from reading official documents from that time period, about the Catholic school in Italy and around the world, its characteristics, its vocations. The interested reader may stop to pore over them. Otherwise, she may feel free to skip a few pages.

Already in those days the great enemy was relativism, that is, the attitude that reduces all values to the setting that produces them: in other words, according to relativism, there is no such thing as an absolute value, there is nothing but an array of discourses concerning the subject of values, periods of values, values subjected to an incessant process of revision, and downgraded to mere points of view, opinions, conventions.

The Catholic school there had the mission of combating relativism with a set of absolute certainties, with perennial and nonnegotiable values.

"The Catholic school intends to shape the future Christian, allowing him to take part in the construction of the kingdom of God," and it is a precise and specific duty of all believers to "entrust their children to schools that will see to their Catholic education."

The Catholic school has an unmistakable identity and historic vocation all its own in Italy, the bearer of a vision of man as at once the fruit of reason and the gift of revelation. As a consequence, the school must be independently and authentically a school, but it must also, at the same time, achieve a synthesis between faith and culture, between faith and life. It is not easy to understand how this synthesis is attained, it's not a simple matter of addition. The Catholic school (hereinafter CS) is either identical to the public school (hereinafter PS)—but then what good is it?—or else it's different. Different how? See above. Which means that it's the same *and yet* different. But does the curriculum, do the subjects, Latin, physics, phys ed, taught in a Catholic school have anything special about them, anything specific? Is there a Catholic art class, a Catholic chemistry class? Of course not. And in that case, do the differences consist solely of the extracurricular activities, such as hearing mass or saying a rosary or going on a spiritual retreat? Which would mean, in the final analysis, that the CS is nothing more than a PS, plus prayers?

The priests knew all this perfectly well, and they had anticipated the objections, always treading the razor's edge of paradox. On the one hand they required that the CS be and remain faithful to the Gospel (and God only knows how much of a challenge that can be, both because the evangelical precepts are unnatural, starting with that "turn the other cheek," to such an extent that one can almost detect a provocative intent, a piece of sophistry, on Christ's part, by preaching them while well aware of their impracticability, and on the other hand because it is not easy to deduce from general principles what might be the specific rules to follow, to apply: are we certain, for example, that the precept "love thy neighbor as thyself" is truly positive and binding, are we in other words sure that all individuals are so in love with themselves that they will love all others to the same extent? Doesn't this equation run the risk, then, of encouraging those who hate themselves, who feel only contempt for themselves—and I'm afraid that's quite a few people—to behave toward others with the same scorn they feel toward themselves? Why should someone who has no care for his own life respect the lives of others?

For that matter, once they've established the Gospel as a prerequisite, they say that in order to be a genuine school in every way equal to the others, and therefore able to secure for those who attend it the same educational credentials offered at the PS, the CS must therefore observe "the rigor of its cultural research and a strong scientific foundation," recognizing "the legitimate autonomy of the laws and methods of research in the individual disciplines."

The CS offers its service "both to young people and to families who have made a clear choice of faith and to people who are willing to declare themselves open to the evangelical message."

So let's take the parents and forget about the child who, at age six, can hardly say how open he might or might not be to the evangelical message, let's take *my* parents: we can safely rule out the idea that they ever made "a clear choice of faith," since they never attended church in their lives except for marriages and funerals, nor did they request the comfort of religious assistance on the point of death, there is nothing we can think of them except that, in any case, given that they were reasonable people and, I believe, deeply good and kind, they fit into the category of those who do not reject out of hand the principles of the evangelical message and who show themselves through their actions to be willing to follow them: almost as if these principles already exist in the human soul, aside from any issues of faith.

It's the great unsolved issue of people who are good but not religious. Is it possible, then, to be good without faith? If it isn't, those who do not believe in God are necessarily wicked. If it is, then what difference does it make whether or not you believe?

I've never managed to find my way out of this impasse. Perhaps it's just a problem that's been posed incorrectly, but would that mean that the most important thing is *not* to be good? What more could we ask of human beings? Would we prefer a good but faithless man or a bad man who fosters an ardent faith? There may be some priests who will hasten to tell me that the latter combination is simply not possible, you can't believe ardently in God and still be evil, those two elements are simply irreconcilable. Therefore one of the two things must necessarily be false: those who claim that they believe in God and yet still commit evil acts *are lying*. I wouldn't be at all sure of that, in fact, I could produce a wide array of examples of people I've known who are deeply religious, and basically evil, some of them *very* evil.

THE CS, moreover, means to create an integrated community among its members: students, teachers, parents, and that community must have regular opportunities for meetings. The meeting is one of those myths of modern Catholicism, one of the keywords, together with "journey," "growth," "listening," and of course, "dialogue."

Already back in the day when I attended it, the CS complained about the fact that it received no public funding, "with the understandable result that it was viewed as a privileged venue, accessible only to those with the resources to secure for themselves select and costly educational resources," and in fact that's the way it was: the CS was for people with money, with a certain amount of money, not necessarily wealthy, but certainly not poor.

(Parenthesis: society was more unjust but novels were easier to write when it was possible to use terms such as "rich" and "poor" without any further commentary.)

ALL THE SAME . . . priestly education, instead of reinforcing our sense of morality, I'm not sure why, only mongrelized it, watering it down, muddling it; salting it with contradictory human case studies, and as a result the exemplary, elevated words of the Gospels seemed overblown in comparison with respect to those who served up those words to us from dawn to dusk of every day; so that it would have done no one any harm if the mouths had been stitched a little smaller while the message had been unfurled to a more substantial size.

IN THE FINAL ANALYSIS, *here there is only one lesson, repeated unchanged every single day: "How should a young man behave?" He should behave like this and like that. The teachers might even be dead and their dead lips would continue to repeat: "Like this and like that, like this and like that . . ."*

MORE THAN ANYTHING ELSE, they were worried that we might get some half-baked ideas in our heads; to prevent that, they filled our heads with an abundance of such ideas of their own, just reasonable and convincing enough, taking care not to leave any empty spaces in our consciousness where something unorthodox might sprout. A decorous absence of originality was then considered to be a distinctive feature of the respectable people the priests hoped we'd turn into, since that, after all, was their educational mission and the reason our parents had placed us in their hands. But it's no easy matter to place limits on a young boy's imagination. How I understand them, the priests! Their dialectic consisted of anticipating them, the weirdest arguments, and assimilating them preemptively, and in that way, Christianity supplied them with a formidable and versatile weapon, because it internally contemplates nearly any possible attitude and has an answer for everything: both conservation and revolution, the sweet and the bitter, the gentle and the horrifying, young people and old people, sorrow and happiness and hope and death. A doctrine unequaled in its flexibility and adaptability. Whatever the uneasiness and aspiration, whatever the context, Christ had an answer. It was as if He were incarnated continuously, in some proteiform manner, taking the appearance variously of good Son, rebel and revolutionary, alternatively capable of saving the weak, or else weak and in need of rescue Himself, on varying occasions conservative or liberal or moderate, poor as depicted in the Gospels but also ready to spring to the defense of the rich if they are threatened by the violence of the poor. The priests used Him in the manner of an encyclopedia or a superhero capable of pulling anyone out of trouble or doubt, handling Him like some immense racket capable of un-failingly smashing the ball over the net. There wasn't a corner that He couldn't reach on the double to rectify a compromised situation, righting it with a miraculous swoop. Perhaps the only subject, the only area that the priests were truly unable to cover up with their flexible interpretative and persuasive abilities, with their conciliatory method of sanding down all asperities, was sex. In that realm, there is very little that can be called reasonable, education has little if any grip, and however much times might have changed, it still remained a taboo, to be treated with incom-prehensible allegories, like the old chestnut of the "sacred mystery of life." It is no accident that it was by way of sex, that unguarded corner, that several of our schoolmates passed, going on later to become grimly noto-rious in the pulps and popular press.

IT WAS INEVITABLE: no matter how you stuff a boy's daily schedule with activities and disciplines and exercises, filling in all the boxes with various colors from eight in the morning until eight in the evening, there are still too many gaps, too many blank spaces that might be invisible to the naked eye. And then, it's a sensation strange to describe, but even though the teaching at SLM really was serious and intense, and the teachers showed up in class in rapid and punctual succession, and there was no such thing as what in the PS (and there are more and more of them all the time these days, with the school staff cut to bare bones) is called the "hour off," when the teacher is home sick and no substitute is called, but I had the feeling that we SLM students, and perhaps with us all the other students in all the schools in Italy and around the world, were destined to lengthy periods of doing nothing. Condemned to idleness, crammed in our desks, sitting on the benches in the locker room, leaning against the walls, sprawled out in our single beds, talking about nonsense or ruminating on the theorems of mathematics and the sciences or the exact formulations of religion or lists of the great French authors and the salient facts of the life of Jean-Baptiste Poquelin, *dit* Molière, which culminated in a spectacular onstage death, there was still a constant and disconcerting condition of waiting, of expectation.

Yes, of expectation . . .

✛

IN WORDS and deeds, the priests of SLM rejected the authoritarianism that had been the ruling law until just a few years ago in every school, every family, and every workplace, and therefore certainly not a prerogative unique to the priests; indeed, perhaps, among the priests the principle of authority (which in given conditions, and accepting its high costs, well, a family a factory a state an army an orchestra a team or a school has to be commanded and run with discipline, forget about these criticisms, if you're in charge you have to be in charge and if you're there to obey then you have to obey, and there's not much more to be said about it), perhaps it was precisely among the priests that this principle, so long standing and well established and tested and retested over the centuries, actually found fertile soil for revision, mitigation, softening, critiquing, or even abolition, drawing upon the abundant repertoire of maxims and concrete deeds and examples provided by the revolutionary founder of the church, Jesus: who had called into question any authority other than Our Father who art in heaven (and, in a certain sense, even that authority . . .).

THE PONDEROUS yet rigid and for that very reason creaky authoritarian control had been switched out by the priests of SLM for a bland paternalism, easier to manage, more flexible, and better suited to the times. The legitimation of those who command by means of paternalism ought in theory to derive from the fact that its subjects comply with it, relying upon it and obeying it without restrictions, indeed, almost willingly. The reasonable attitude that steers it should theoretically extend to those who are steered by it. A mild, judicious application of power is thought to be more willingly accepted by those who are subjected to it.

Well, it isn't true.

In fact, while you may either obey or rebel against authority imposed by force, since there are no other options, there are many ways to oppose a wise paternalism while pretending to accept it. And those were the methods we employed.

THEY DIDN'T GET IT. They couldn't understand. They couldn't understand that their liberal precepts turned our stomachs, since they were conceived to make us behave. Of course, we were taking advantage, we took advantage shamelessly, but we held them in contempt, manifesting our scorn as if it were an open challenge, which they saw clearly but were forced to pretend not to see. Down to the last drop, we sucked the equivocal status of permissive education. That honey squeezed out of modern doctrines and mixed with traditional goodness. We reviled anyone who tried or expected to "understand us." Those of us who committed full-blown crimes, I believe they ended up committing them for the fun of seeing how far they could push it, by continuing to be "understood."

The knife cuts into understanding as if it were butter.

SINCE WE OURSELVES WERE PRODUCTS of those progressive fairy tales about upbringing and education, we knew perfectly well how to disprove them, or perhaps we should say that we were the living, breathing disproof: proof that it worked the other way around. The first generation to have enjoyed almost limitless liberty made the worst possible use of it, which is after all the only use possible, the most significant use, because of how exceptional and extreme it is. Pure liberty consists of nothing more than this. And it is its very purity that kindles fear.

INTO THE VOID. The danger of the end of school. A great, great danger, a cliff. After you graduate, at the moment your daily commitments suddenly come to an end, the mandatory alarm clock at seven, etc., every day, year-round . . . something that's been going on since you were small and then, suddenly, breaks off. A structure collapses, the scholastic regime, a regime guiding your life. Whose sheer repetitiveness helps, in a boy, to stitch the various parts of you and hold them together, and even the bad mood caused by all the activities you're pursuing against your will serves as an adhesive, it integrates you, it gives form to your persona. Your frustration or resentment against the teachers, the discipline against whose bars you bang your head and rub your back, all help you to gain awareness of your own head, your own back. The various pieces that make up a boy search for a limit within which they are contained, and they are grateful to that barrier, even as they never stop complaining about it for even a minute, as it prevents them from collapsing and being scattered, like the pages of a manuscript flying off in a gust of wind. The ineluctable duty of school wins over even those who hate it, indeed, it is only reinforced by that hatred. An unbroken chain of tyrannical inanities keeps those who are subjected to them awake.

BUT BEFORE THE END, every summer, the long, very long, practically endless summer vacation! So long that we'd forget everything. Whoever had been sent back for a new set of final exams in September would show up after the summer holidays even more ignorant than they had been in June.

It wasn't recovery, though that was the term used for it! It was a regression.

There were those who claimed that such a long break was harmful to the boys, there were others who were convinced we absolutely needed it, to "recharge our batteries." All I know is that it was a time of great joy. Unquestionably the greatest pleasure of our lives: the only wish that was granted, 100 percent, the summer would come, necessarily, all we had to do was wait and the vacation would come, school ended, locked its doors, you could count on it, you could bet money that that long-awaited event would actually occur. When? June sixth, eighth, maybe ninth. At the very latest, the twelfth. You just had to be able to wait.

IT WASN'T JUST THE THINGS we had studied during the school year that were forgotten, but rather the very existence of school itself. Three, nearly four months of time off erased it. June, July, August, September: each of these months had its own special color and sound, yes, it resonated in an unmistakable manner.

June: Yellow Astonishment City Expanding Ultramarine Ardor.

July: Fullness Red Buzzing Discovery.

August: Burnt White Dust and Emptiness.

September: Melancholy Thought Unknown City Heart Pounding in Your Throat.

UPON OUR RETURN, the city was new, our home was new, the furniture had never been glimpsed before. Reentering our bedroom, retaking possession of it, jumping onto the bed, it all starts over from scratch . . .

Two opposite sensations, the first prompted by the return home with the frantic excitement at seeing friends and classmates and starting a new life over again, the second caused by the impending end of vacation as we already mourned our summer adventures, those experienced and those missed out on—these two sensations electrified the last days before school:

excitement and sadness, which usually present themselves at different times, swelled and grew until they reached high points of an overwhelming intensity and mingled in a single sentiment, like certain vegetables that can be found at the market only when they are in season, lasting no more than a few weeks and then vanishing for the rest of the year. There is no other month quite like September, no other set of feelings quite so special: you might feel happy or disgruntled or angry or fearful or envious at any given moment, and then on for the rest of your life, albeit with differing gradations and nuances, but the distinct sensation that seizes a boy by the throat in the month of September really has no equal.

WHEN I WAS LITTLE, though, how I loved to go to school! Inconsolable if I was forced to stay home sick. And intolerable the idea of going home when lessons were over. What happened to me was the exact opposite of what happened to young Törless as a student: just like when he was away from home, when I was away from school, that is, from SLM, there descended over eyes and heart a damp veil of melancholy; and I sometimes struggled to choke back my sobs. When as the sun set I found myself alone, eating a snack, standing at the kitchen counter, dipping slices of zwieback into my milk, and watching the way the wet half would break off and drop into the mug, I felt like the last man on earth and, seriously, I had to make an effort to choke back the tears. In reality, I was by no means alone, my brother was at home, likable and glad to socialize, and so was my little sister, and the maid, and at the far end of the apartment, in her bedroom, on the bed reading or making a phone call or drinking a cup of tea, my mother. In my bedroom I had plenty of toys and books and comic books and records to pass the few hours left till dinner. Nonetheless, I felt every bit as lifeless and aimless. Because what I missed was my classmates. And the gym, the courtyard, the chapel, the priests.

II

THE HEADMASTER of SLM wore dark glasses, but only partially dark, like the ones I've seen only certain prelates, local notables, and ophthalmic patients wear. Behind those lenses, you can glimpse the eyes, but the lenses make the expression inscrutable. Those who peer at you through those eyeglasses don't conceal themselves entirely, in fact, they don't conceal themselves at all, but instead reveal only as much of themselves as they feel it's worth the bother of unveiling, which is to say, their power: which alludes without ever displaying itself, without being transformed into a clear, concrete image, a specific act. The most indisputable and sovereign gesture would only limit the scope of that power. And however magnetic a look may be, you end up being yoked far more effectively to its dominion by the absence of certainty as to where it's directed and what it expresses: whether it's monitoring us or ignoring us, whether it approves of us or holds us in contempt.

Our headmaster never exercised his prerogatives: he never punished, never suspended anyone, he literally did little or nothing; but he cared very much about giving the impression of always being on the verge of doing so, always ready, always on the brink of taking very grievous initiatives that would surely impact us with incalculable consequences. If there had been precedents of punitive measures of any description, or for any specific variety of infractions, we might have had a way of imagining what might ensue if and when we committed them, rendering them commensurate with those of the past. But as far as I am able to recall, nothing had ever happened deserving of anything more serious than his ironic and cutting scoldings, and come to think of it, not even those seemed to spring from the individual shortcomings of any particular classmate, but were rather directed at all of us students as an amorphous, indistinct mass.

Or perhaps not, perhaps something terrible had already happened which had been buried or suppressed without ever coming into the light of day. But we didn't know what that might be.

That was what constituted the halo at once menacing and faintly laughable, the aura that surrounded the headmaster. We were afraid of him, I have to admit it, in part because we were all basically cowards and if by chance anyone really rebelled, he did it out of pure idiocy and was almost never capable of sustaining for any length of time the consequences of his decisions, which were therefore reduced to sheer buffoonery, and fell into the ranks of parsonage pranks, oratory out of a sports locker room, where the boys lose all shame and then, in the end, are deeply ashamed of themselves. They're outbursts that don't manage to vent a single real thing.

We would prick the skin of the beast and then turn to run as fast as our legs would carry us.

So we were afraid of the headmaster, we were very afraid of him, but it wasn't a serious fear and so, really, it wasn't real fear at all. We knew that in any case he couldn't lay a finger on us. He did not really stir the obscure depths of our fear.

And do you know why? Because, whatever happened, *it was we who paid his salary.*

The truth is that we can never really fully fear someone whose survival we guarantee, *out of our own pockets.* That is an economic law even before it's an emotional one, or maybe it's just a law of emotional economics. The fear that the headmaster struck into us was a conventional, theatrical effect, due to the roles that we played at school, surely more powerful than the fear emanating from the individual teachers but still not enough to hold back our lack of respect, which sprayed out of our attitudes the minute the panic caused by his unannounced appearances began to subside. In fact, if we didn't mistreat our headmaster it was only because we had already exhausted our imagination and energy in mocking the teachers, objectively less powerful: the religion teacher, poor Mr. Golgotha, the art history teacher, the French teacher, and the music teacher, people who walked into the classroom already well aware they didn't count for shit. No two ways about it, sovereign power cannot derive from the subjects over which it is exercised, which means that in democracies, too, the true power, the real power, is either not democratic or else it is not power. There is no point in wasting any more chitchat on it, anyone who wishes to understand will already have grasped the point. And then if it is based on a dependency of economic nature . . . specific and binding . . . the kind that only money can generate . . . then that's that. Neither love, nor violence, nor culture: it is money that can subjugate one man to another, independent of his beliefs and his actions. Maybe it's just a few stray spores of Marxism that have wafted onto me from the recent past that make me say it and reiterate it, today: who can really know? The bonds of money may be patent or they may remain invisible, like the leash woven to capture the monstrous wolf, son of Loki, but these bonds cannot be torn or severed.

And so: would a captain whose salary was paid by his own crew ever dream of ordering a swabbie keelhauled for insubordination or malingering? And you, rank-and-file musicians of a symphony orchestra, would you suck up without blinking an eye the tantrums of a conductor whose salary your own families paid, depositing a monthly sum in his account? And what else was the tuition fee that our parents paid, if not a demand for certain services, and at the same time, a guarantee of impunity?

I think back nowadays with a greater understanding that, yes, certainly, we were afraid of the headmaster, we hid from his sight . . . but it was he who had a leash around his neck, not us.

WHATEVER THE CASE, his unruffled, ironic manner of speech made him especially odious to us, given that it reduced our rare acts of insubordination to a level so insignificant and ridiculous as to destroy any pleasure we might take in having committed them. He never took us seriously, in other words. He never spoke directly to us, because we didn't deserve it. Protected behind his lenses, his eyes seemed to look a foot or so above our heads, as if to communicate to us his disappointment, his impatience, and something like his disgust at seeing that we had not grown up sufficiently. Moral and intellectual midgets is what we were, if not midgets in actual, physical fact. What conflict can there be with someone who refuses to consider you as an individual? To the headmaster we were merely a motley crew, a mass, a mass of idiots, idiots and nothing more, but so lacking in the basic prerequisites that constitute a person that it wasn't worth wasting on us even a drop of genuine anger. Let alone respect. We were mildly harmful microbes, numbered slots on the class ledger, nicknames, ghosts. In his presence, I, who thought of myself as fairly independent and proud, felt like a piece of shit devoid of personality. All it took was his dark glasses and the occasional wry phrase tossed off in the midst of his generic statements, in which he never had it in for anyone in particular, perhaps to make it clear to us that we were always and in any case *all* guilty, even when we hadn't done a thing, because just doing nothing was itself a wrong, a fault. But a petty one, inane. At a certain point in his sermon he would stop, fall silent, slowly turn his head toward a corner of the classroom from which a tiny buzz had arisen, point to a student who wasn't doing anything in particular, and warn him: "Hey, you . . . that's right, you . . . *a little less cocky.*"

The classmate would be seized by doubt, since the headmaster had employed nothing more specific than his invisible gaze to single him out, his hands had remained crossed over his large belly in that all-too-priestly position that telegraphs tranquillity and amiability at all costs, or else hooked by the thumbs to the sash that held the tunic around his waist, and frequently because of this intentional equivocation about the actual identity of the accused, two or three other students would grimace in disbelief, as if to say, "Me? Are you speaking to me? What do I have to do with any of this?"

But it was perfectly clear who he was speaking to.

"Yes, that's right, you, I'm talking to you . . . *a little less cocky.*"

Sometimes, after a stretch of silence, he would add: ". . . So are we clear, *sweetheart*? Fine."

THE HEADMASTER, in fact, ended every sentence with a "fine," just as Shylock in *The Merchant of Venice* said "well" at the end of each sentence. Any proposal brought to him or objection raised or request submitted, his answer, whether it was positive or negative, always ended with a "fine."

CLASS REPRESENTATIVE: "Mr. Headmaster, sir, could school let out an hour early, today? Mr. Golg . . . that is, the religion teacher is absent . . . his mother has been admitted to the hospital."

HEADMASTER: "I know all about it. No, I'm sorry, you can't leave early, I'll make sure and send you a substitute. Fine."

IMPERO BAJ (*custodian*): "The third-floor bathroom is flooded, what should we do?"

HEADMASTER: "Tell the kids in the scientific high school to use the bathroom on the second floor, and the ones from the classical high school to go to the fourth floor. Is that all clear, Baj? Fine."

IMPERO BAJ: "Maybe someone ought to call a plumber, I don't know . . ."

HEADMASTER: "I'm already picking up the receiver, you see that? I've already dialed the number. All right, fine."

HEADMASTER: "Well?"

SCOLDED STUDENT: "I won't do it again."

HEADMASTER: "Is it a promise?"

SCOLDED STUDENT: "It's a promise."

HEADMASTER: "Fine."

It wasn't a simple verbal tic, but instead something quite serious. It was fine, the inevitable conclusion of any issue had to be good, well, fine, positive, even matters that at first glance seemed thorny or painful.

It may be more useful for me to explain with an example, and perhaps the readers will understand—if, indeed, they are benevolent—my difficulties in explaining myself otherwise, especially because the example I intend to bring up does not constitute a digression, but rather a direct and immediate continuation of the story.

So, one day the headmaster found himself face-to-face with an extra problem and he took it on as was his wont. Three or four of the older boys had cornered one of my classmates, Marco Lodoli, during recess. With at least a hundred boys running around, milling, and shrieking all at once, no one had noticed that Marco had been targeted. What was the reason for that ill-intentioned interest? The fact that Marco, slight and skinny, tall, bespectacled, was also long-haired: an ash-blond halo of frizzy hair around an intelligent and invariably slightly mocking face. That's why the upperclassmen had long since sized him up as a target, and that day they started shoving and jerking him around, grabbing him by his shirt front, giving him little slaps that at first seem friendly but then increase in intensity, and finally grabbed his glasses and half-broke them, yep, that's right: one of them, without a word of explanation for what he was doing, pulled off Marco's eyeglasses and snapped, with the strength of his fingers, in a single sharp move, the bridge that held together the two lenses. Then he handed them back to him. As I said, nobody had noticed a thing, but when we returned to class, everyone noticed that our classmate was forced to hold his eyeglasses up, pressing them onto his nose with his fingers.

Cosmo, our Italian teacher, jumped in.

And he asked Marco what had happened to him.

It was clear that he didn't really want to say what had happened, and he muddled along, trying to come up with an excuse ("They fell off while I was running . . ." "I banged my face in the bathroom . . ."), piling up contradictory versions, until his voice cracked and he finally fell silent. He just stood there, holding his thick eyeglasses by the temples, hands trembling with nervousness.

The suspicion began to circulate that the guilty party might be one of our classmates, even if there weren't any bullies or even any boys especially given to horseplay, aside from Chiodi, and possibly Jervi, who had never shown signs of any cruel or treacherous behavior, but then, without warning, it was the other Marco in our class, Marco d'Avenia, a chubby young boy with rosy skin and a blank look in his eyes, who got to his feet and told Cosmo and all the rest of us exactly what had happened. D'Avenia, in fact, tended to go off on his own during recess for fear that one of the older boys might steal his snacks or knock them to the ground with a rough shove, and so he hid behind the boxwood hedges that ran along the outside wall of SLM, and in the safety of that refuge he was able to devour his pizza in peace and quiet. From that vantage point, his mouth crammed full of tomato sauce, he'd been able to watch the bullying unfold. No one had noticed him hiding behind the hedge, and no one but him, in that corner of the courtyard, had noticed the older boys roughing up Lodoli. The boys had in fact surrounded him in such a way that no one could see what was happening inside the knot of bodies. D'Avenia, however, saw it all and told what he knew.

IT WAS A RARE THING to see Cosmo angry, or even irritated. Maybe he was neither this time. But when he strode out of the classroom after assigning Rummo to maintain a minimum level of order until his return, I'm quite certain I heard him utter, under his breath, the following words: "It's high time someone taught a lesson to these gallows birds."

THE TERM "gallows bird" had already long since fallen from common use in the time when this story unfolds: in fact, I place it primarily in the context of reading, the deliciously outmoded written language, books in other words, the yellowed and unequaled adventure novels I read, many of them in translation from the English, the French, and the Russian. And in particular I am reminded of a beautiful old large-format volume, perhaps twelve inches by sixteen, with magnificent illustrations, that I owned as a boy and which I must have read through, from cover to cover, dozens of times, until I had practically memorized the whole thing. It was titled *Pirati, Corsari e Filibustieri—Pirates, Corsairs, and Filibusters.* Cosmo liked to express himself in precise, ironic, literary turns of phrase, which were vividly realistic nonetheless. Since then I have been unable to forgo using the term myself. Gallows birds, that's right, they were nothing but gallows birds, and for the crime they would commit not long after this episode, they would once have surely been hanged.

FOUR STUDENTS were summoned to the headmaster's office after being reported by Cosmo, and for now at least I'm not going to reveal their names. A couple of those names will become significant in the second half of this book. As I said, they were a year older than us. In any case, I have no way of knowing what the headmaster said to them, how he confronted them, and in what terms he asked them to account for what they had done. I might try to re-create here—using the technique impudently picked up from the pages of Thucydides or Tacitus, when they imagine the speeches of generals before engaging in battle or diplomats determined to restore peace—a certain type of scolding lecture, in the style at once dismissive and elusive that was so typical of the headmaster, but that would simply be a waste of time because the only thing I know for certain is that no measures were actually taken against the four students, and that fact appears much more significant than any number of words, which after all, given the benefit of hindsight, we now know to have been spoken into the wind. Not even a disciplinary note on the school ledger, or a day of suspension, or a letter to the parents. I imagine that the matter of Marco Lodoli's eyeglasses was simply filed away as a case of excessive physical boisterousness, incidental vectorial by-products of the kinetic energy that drove the bodies of those adolescents to clash in narrow spaces, like the swirling atoms in the visions of the ancient philosophers. That the incident had turned out for the best, at least from the point of view of our headmaster, was proven by the fact that a few days later, Ottetti (as we had nicknamed our custodian Impero Baj, on account of the *otto etti*, Italian for 800 grams, nearly two pounds, of pasta that he claimed to eat every day at lunch) came to Lodoli's class to bring him a brand-new pair of frames, Lozza brand, or maybe Persol, to be fitted with his thick lenses. No one ever knew whether it had been the bullies themselves out of their own pockets, or the school, who had paid for them: the important thing is that Lodoli regained his sight, and SLM regained its equilibrium, for a while.

WE HAVE a deeper and more extensive knowledge of another significant day, that is, the day that Arbus went to the headmaster's office to lodge a complaint because he wasn't learning anything. The lessons were too dull and repetitive, the teachers were too lazy and predictable. Really, we classmates were the least responsible for that trend. It was the school itself that worked badly. An incredible number of hours and days, precious, irretrievable, spent amid those four walls—to learn so little!

With a cunning tactical move, the headmaster immediately summoned to the office Rummo, who was our class representative, so that he could either confirm or deny Arbus's claim: actually, though, because he wanted the presence of another student as a witness, and he was convinced that to have one would restrain Arbus from expressing excessively radical judgments. Evidently, he didn't know Arbus well enough (Who can claim to have ever really known him, that young man? Not even I can boast that I understood him, and perhaps I won't succeed, right up to the last page of this book), and in fact Arbus spoke as if Rummo wasn't even present in the headmaster's office, in fact, truth be told, as if the headmaster himself weren't there. It was, in fact, Rummo himself who told us about it later, filled with admiration. That was characteristic of guys like Arbus, if there has ever been anyone else like him: to pay no attention to their interlocutor, neither his rank nor his mood, to feel no need to come to terms with him, to worry about how he might react, and therefore adapt the things he might say to fit the circumstances, the way we do out of courtesy or fear or self-interest or mere hypocrisy. None of all that: Arbus wanted to say what he believed to be the truth, but without any demands or self-regard in teaching a lesson or laying down a challenge. He wanted to say, in short, what was right to say, even though it might be disagreeable or scandalous: almost without a care for what effect he might have, in fact, without even noticing that there might be any. Pure, ingenuous, innocent, pitiless, automatic: that's what my friend Arbus was like. The presence of the unfortunate Rummo, in the final analysis, served only one purpose: to let us know, subsequently, how that meeting had gone. In contrast with what he did before the assembled class, which he treated with scorn, this time the headmaster reserved a treatment of utmost respect for Arbus. My classmate deserved it.

"SCHOOL? It's just one more way of locking us up in a safe place and making sure we don't cause any trouble. The teachers are nothing more than our prison guards. If they teach us anything at all, it's by accident, or purely random, a collateral effect. Do you have any idea, Headmaster, how we could put the time we spend in here to better use?"

"That'll do, Arbus, I understand your point. If I simply said that you were wrong, on the specific point, or else if I said that, no two ways about it, you're not in charge of deciding how your scholastic career is to unfold, and that that's up to your parents, I'd be insulting your intelligence, and at your age, that's not a good thing to do. Fine. So how old are you?"

"Fifteen. Almost sixteen."

"Almost. Fine. It is in that *almost* that we can find the answer to your complaints; which, in any case, I have no intention of overlooking. I've recorded them word for word, and I'll take advantage of your input to improve the quality of the service that we, with all our limitations, are called upon to provide to you, to give you students . . . This is our *vocation*, and you know what that term means, don't you? 'Vocation.' It means that ours is not a choice, but rather a simple answer: the answer to a calling. Fine. Don't worry. I'll make sure that this vocation is tested, teacher by teacher, and that is a promise: without making any distinction between the religious brothers, like me, and the laymen. They, too, answer to the same appeal, and if it does not come directly from God, it will surely come from their professional conscience. But I feel sure that you know these things already. And that, deep down, you appreciate them. Fine. I believe, for that reason, that it is unnecessary to summon your parents to let them know about your dissatisfaction. Perhaps you've already informed them on your own initiative, back at home, is that right? Have you talked to them? Did you? Oh, you didn't? That's exactly what I thought: you didn't. Fine. Very good. The first piece of advice, in fact, that I want to give you, is always to try to solve problems *within* the context where those problems have arisen, never outside, never, never . . . never expanding them, never extending the problem to a broader circle, never allowing them to migrate elsewhere, contaminating others with the leprosy of these problems . . . Discretion and determination, that's what it takes. Is there something not working here at school? Fine. We'll resolve it here at school. Among ourselves. Among those who are close to that problem, who know it, who are capable of intervening, changing things, taking action. Fine. It's like the interior of our souls: if difficulties arise, the struggle must be an inner struggle, us against ourselves. The true target of any revolution lies in whoever undertakes it, not outside him. Pointless to involve the others, to upset them, to make them worry, just as your father and your mother would be worried if they were informed of the criticisms that you're leveling against the school. I don't criticize you in the slightest, and for that matter, with someone like you, so wide-awake and mature, what good would that do, right? All right, then, let's put it in these terms: we aren't perfect, either as men or as religious, much less as teachers. Fine. Could anyone but Our Lord Jesus Christ claim to be? Claim, that is, to be the finest man or the finest teacher possible? No, certainly not. Fine. The fact is that, my dear Arbus, my very dear boy, neither are you. Neither are you the perfect student. Or are you convinced that you are?"

"No, of course not."

"Fine. You see it yourself. You're an *almost* ideal student. Chronologically speaking, you're *almost* a man. In strictly theoretical terms, given your intelligence, you'd be capable of studying all by yourself what remains to be studied from here to the end of high school. Is that what you want? Do you think that it would amount to the same thing, if you stayed at home with your books, instead of coming to school each day? What do you still lack to attain your objective? I'll tell you what: you lack something *that you'll never have*. And it's the same thing that we priests lack, we teachers, we adults, and in fact all men and women lack, even your father and mother, if it comes to that. Becoming adults, we've never become perfect, you know? The margins of improvement were great . . . but even if they had been small, and we improved a little more, every day a little more, day after day, and we still do our best to do so, well, we'd still fall an inch, half an inch, a quarter inch short . . . and we'd never bridge that gap. If you learn, from this day forward, to accept this constitutional shortcoming, this lack in you, maybe you'll be able to better understand the same shortcoming in others. And after all, it's not a matter just of making better use of your own time: it's a simple matter of letting it pass, of overlooking it, do you understand me, Arbus? Because it's the time that passes that makes us grow, even if we don't realize it, even when we have the sensation of standing still, we aren't, time still sweeps us away, it transports us over great distances, like the current of a river, as long as we oppose no resistance. Fine. At the end of this journey, you'll be a changed person, a greatly changed person, my boy, much more than you could ever imagine, and independently of any lesson in Italian or geometry, while you will have received other lessons without ever realizing that they were imparted to you. And it strikes me that this is a good, a fine thing.

"We'll be behind you, I assure you of that, Arbus, we'll help in every way imaginable to keep you from feeling like an outsider, so you don't feel special: we'll teach you to be normal, that is, to accept what all the others accept. *Everyone*. This is a lesson, too, the most important lesson you can learn. Fine, fine.

"As for your outlandish belief that you can't learn anything here, you're as wrong as can be about that. Of course you can learn here, Arbus. Absolutely. You can, if you want to. Fine. Do you want to know something? Do you want to know where you can begin? First of all, you should learn to know those who are around you. Your schoolmates. They are the first subject you should be studying, you know that? The human subjects are the most interesting ones, they come before history and geography and science, and they're worth making an effort, at least an attempt to get to know them, don't you think, Arbus? Fine, fine, that's fine. Let's take your teachers, just as an example. Are you convinced that you really know them? Or have you judged them without really understanding them? And I'm not talking about the subjects they teach, I'm talking about the people. Don't you think you might have been a little too hasty in your judgments, perhaps, in your condemnations? Why, fine, that's fine, I understand you. We understand you. You're impatient because you're intelligent, the two things often go hand in hand, and instead you ought to remain calm. Much calmer. *Nice and calm*, Arbus, understood? That's fine."

ARBUS'S COMMENT once he was back in the classroom was terse and concise. After being informed of all that had happened by Rummo, we asked Arbus how it had gone with the headmaster.

"Simple: he conned me."

As if he couldn't care less about it now. He had better things to think about.

12

I'S ALWAYS DIFFICULT to relate to school, either critically or with narrative intent—virtually impossible during your time there as a student, almost invariably in a resigned or resentful tone if you teach there, inevitably sentimental if you limit yourself to remembering it years later, as an integral part of your youth.

The "well, it's something we all went through" approach renders memories of school in general largely one-note, sentimental, anecdotal, and foggy. Paradoxically, for such a fundamental and universal and enduring institution, it is safe to say, with almost mathematical certainty, that the only true moment of joy that it offers is when its doors shut behind you for the very last time. And if it's not joy, it's relief.

Going to school is not something open to discussion; something that's so clearly not open to discussion that it becomes natural, and therefore no longer conceivable as anything different from what it is, the most prolonged and cerebral artificial experience of our lives, considered by one and all to be an obligation that it would be uncivil to avoid: little boys and girls, teenagers of both sexes forced to spend many hours a day in virtual immobility, for a variable number of years, in closed rooms, to do what, basically? To bend their spinal cords over desks and clog their brains with classical or scientific or technical tirades spouted by out-of-breath tutors, hoarse from shouting, whose actual, unstated function, tacit yet obvious and primary in nature—as Arbus had so rightly understood (I only realize it now, he'd figured it out at age sixteen: that's the enormous difference)—is to keep the students occupied to ensure they do no harm to themselves or others, serving as little more than custodians or guards, really, a job assigned to them by a society that must fill the void of surveillance created at the moment that exhausted families push their children out of the house, at least for a certain portion of the day, at an age when the world of labor is not yet ready to accommodate them inasmuch as they don't yet know how to do anything (truth be told, they'll know even less by the time they're done with their academic careers, but "that's another matter"). This period of latency, by the way, has become so extraordinarily prolonged in the contemporary world that it lasts, when all is said and done, as long as fifteen years. Fifteen years to become adults ready to be ground up in the machinery. Fifteen years of an experiment that can yield (according to statistical probability more than any real method) some good fruit, there's no way to deny it, but if considered dispassionately for what it truly is, it's more appalling than vivisection itself.

AND THEN there are the academic subjects themselves, or perhaps we should say, the subjects that have been *rendered* academic—that is to say, boring, remote, and incomprehensible . . .

Not that the curricula themselves were mistaken, quite the contrary. They were full of interesting topics, the curricula. It's so strange that at the political and bureaucratic level, people always seem to have a bone to pick with the curricula, which are blamed for being so damned antiquated, narrow, moldy, the curricula, junk from the last century—and maybe that's because it's easy to change the curricula, far less easy to change the people. It takes only a busy afternoon to rewrite all the curricula with ink on paper, maybe even inventing new subjects that have never been taught before or giving new names to the old subjects (one can only applaud the rhetorical variations that turn good old calisthenics into physical education, while what remains of history, the old subject featuring Hannibal's elephants and the emperor's red beard, has been rebaptized, alliteratively, historical and social studies . . .).

And the teachers, whether priests or non-priests, could hardly be blamed for any of this. Generally speaking, they were unfortunate wretches,

obsessed and at the same time repulsed by their subjects after years of having to repeat the rote formulations that, over time, had turned into nursery
rhymes, which they might as well learn by heart and recite in a singsong,
like Tibetan prayers, and in fact over the years some of their voices had
taken on the same nasal and guttural tonality that can be heard from the
priests of all religions when they recite their psalms, a droning lullaby that
emphasizes certain syllables in a single exhalation of breath, and which we
in our oral examinations tended to replicate word for word, with all the
very same pauses.

So whose fault was it?

I DON'T KNOW if I'm alone in remembering school in these terms; probably
there are those who were enthusiastic schoolgoers or who now imagine or
remember the experience, finding themselves pining for the good old days,
since it's impossible to surgically remove the bloc of "school" without destroying the larger bloc of "youth," so that people wind up believing that
the two were the same thing; there are some who can say in all sincerity
that they "had fun" at school, that they loved their classmates or teachers,
and if I were to maintain, with contempt, that "nothing of the sort ever happened to me," I'd no doubt come off as a miserable person, well, all right,
then, I too had fun, but it was always fun with clenched fists, and I made
friends, but it wasn't the school that created those friendships, indeed, if
anything, the school ostracized them, shoving us all together like thirty
mice in a shoebox. More than friends, we were fellow prisoners, and I can
safely say that I learned at my own expense just how illusory, albeit briefly
intoxicating, this kind of solidarity can be—the camaraderie engendered
by constraint, how morbid and rotten the "us against the world" kind of
companionship can be, the involuntary brotherhood celebrated by the
poets of wartime.

SCHOOL, then, was conceived as a patient period of waiting, a gestation
lasting many years, over the course of which formidable and explosive
things took place, first and foremost in our bodies and our minds, which
seemed to be under the effect of extremely powerful narcotics, so great were
the psychedelic transformations (the product of our minds and bodies
themselves, certainly not the effect of any of the lessons . . .), and even more
so in the outside world, which was bursting with new developments to the

point of becoming unrecognizable, another world, just a completely different chapter of history, between 1962 and 1975, that is, from when I entered that school dressed in a student's smock until I left wearing elephant bell bottoms. You need only compare photos and TV footage from the period.

A period as changeable and dangerous as a serpent slithering through the forest.

And what were we doing, in the meantime, at school? We were waiting. We were waiting, ruminating over formulas, poetry, theorems, lists, transcribing, erasing everything with the white eraser or the blue one, chalking up blackboards, tossing medicine balls, carving into the grooves on our school desks with our penknives, looking at the trees outside the window . . .

If it were possible to pile up all in one place the rubber shavings produced by our furious erasures, if we could fill up a swimming pool with all of the ink spilled, I'm not even saying in all our translations from ancient Greek and from Latin, from start to finish, but just the ink used in making mistakes, in writing the words that were destined to be marked wrong by the teacher in red pencil, and if it were possible to line up, end to end, all the red segments of the corrections . . .

PERHAPS as late as age fourteen or fifteen, it was still possible to coexist with school, doing no more than to mock and parrot the teachers the second they had their backs turned, aping their physical defects and the way they spoke, and, in the breaks between these exercises in boorishness, absorbing here and there scraps of lessons, the more elementary passages or, now and then, the more difficult ones, for no purpose other than to recite them later, during the oral exams, mindlessly verbatim, without having actually understood a thing. Deep down, it was an easy, cowardly recipe that anyone—unless they were just talentless or truly rebellious, by which I mean rebellious to the depths of their soul—could put into practice and scrape by one year after another. We needed only to behave and keep a low profile to avoid trouble and this, really, was the only condition that the priests insisted on our respecting, to hell with matters like scholastic achievement, broadening our horizons, knowledge, and all that, what was actually required was a modicum of hypocrisy and contrition, just like in the confessional, and we were sure to be promoted to the next year, or, in other words, absolved of our sins. And allowed to run free like little lambs frolicking on a hillside. There are religions that ask their faithful nothing more than this: pray, bow, turn the other way when I tell you to, murmur and whisper instead of shouting, and as for the rest, do more or less as you please. Pay a small, small bail fee and you're free! Our priests were actually not very demanding, even a Nazi could have met their requirements, and it's no surprise that more than one actually did. They accepted, accepted, and accepted—in accordance with the mystical precept of "accept everything." That is, the totality of a man, with all his deplorable aspects. That was the credo handed down by the founder. They forgave and forgave, or else they simply overlooked. We, on the other hand, refused, hindered, rejected, and we'd have rejected school as a whole if it hadn't been so simple, in the final analysis, to just put up with it, its burden distributed throughout the span of the year, and in exchange, as part of the pact, while we agreed to be good (*buoni*, or better, increasingly Roman in inflection, *boni, boni*, "*state bboni* . . ."), we accepted a handful of vignettes of surreal humor, the occasional furtive snicker, and passing grades in the class ledger—passing grades, just eked out, conceded graciously, squeaking past, amended, rounded upward, but perfectly valid.

But after that a singular phenomenon unfolded: even though we all remained so many ignorant and incomplete amoebas, suddenly we felt superior to our teachers, as if by some automatic promotion due to seniority, a sudden promotion on the field of battle, we had, that is, the impression that we had caught up with them and overtaken them and that therefore none of them (except for Cosmo) was any longer capable of striking fear in our hearts. Respect was something they had never been able to inculcate. In certain of our classmates who were particularly self-confident and arrogant, this meant treating them like doormats. This was all about money, in the final analysis and as usual, as I've said before. They had discovered, that is, that the all-powerful teachers actually had very little money of their own.

Others instead felt (rather unjustified) intellectual haughtiness; convinced that they now knew and understood far more than their teachers in the very subjects they taught. Giovanni Lorco, for instance, had convinced himself that the priests must necessarily be a herd of ignorant bumpkins drafted straight out of divinity school and sent into the classrooms after being given a hasty scrub: whereas the others, the lay teachers, had no certificates or degrees, and were losers from the outset who had figured out a work-around to avoid civil service exams, turning up at a private institute of education the same way they might show up at a soup kitchen. And so

Lorco was always checking his books to make sure the things they said in class were accurate. He was just waiting for a chance to catch them making a mistake.

Others still were seized by a singular enthusiasm that made them feel ready to experience extraordinary adventures; these classmates thought of school as nothing but useless ballast and the teachers as heavy objects, like so many carved marble animals to be used as bookends. These students already had an eye on afterward, the years after school, and couldn't wait to be emancipated from the flock of children and their grim custodians.

Part II

Flesh for Fantasies

I

THOSE WERE HAPPY TIMES, when in order to live the way you're supposed to all you had to do was follow a script! Faithfully, adding only a few personal variations. For instance, the roles of men and women. Well written, extensively tested, invariably recognizable to those around you who witnessed your performance and judged it. From which you could, at the very most, escape by committing an act of conscious revolt, violating its rules. By rebelling. But if there are no rules at all, how are you supposed to break them or change them? And here you are, then, a prisoner of the absence of rules, or else wandering, blinded by their nebulous vagueness. How bitterly ironic, to be a slave to rules that don't exist. The problem with vows never uttered is that they cannot be broken. Study, work, mate, have children, age . . . die . . . but also laugh, quarrel, fight, and kill . . . these were all things for which the individual, according to sex and age and social condition, found models ready to use, only asking to be applied, boilerplate to be slotted in, with a little patience and care, like the patterns you could find in knitting magazines for making a pullover or a cardigan: we only needed to follow instructions step-by-step. Everything seemed boring and oppressive and, really, it was, but at the same time, how very reassuring! Reassuring even for those who chose *not* to follow the script. The risk, so to speak, possessed a solid certainty all its own: like the opposition in a dictatorship, you knew perfectly what faced you, the penalties meted out to those who rebel. Not the way things are these days when, even if you take all your clothes off and have sex with a sheep in front of the Italian Senate, either no one pays the slightest attention to you, or else your act will be interpreted as a laudable provocation or a statement of protest toward which we should all express our solidarity inasmuch as it is an expression of a widespread malaise or even as a piece of performance art. The muscle of interest is riddled in vain by the tickle of the most violent and foolish provocation: it won't start, it won't react. Today, we troop out into life in scattered order, so many stragglers, with no signal (with the possible exception of money, perhaps, which is at least *something*) to tell us from the outset what we ought to do and what we ought to refrain from doing, what we should aspire to and what we should avoid. Everyone goes their way, stitching together as they go a random patchwork of attitudes and half-conventions scavenged here and there, to avoid being left naked and incomprehensible to other people, even though you can see from a mile away that it's all made up, improvised or borrowed, cadged off TV series or talk shows, advice columns, and tidal waves of online recommendations. There is no substance, there's no deep foundation, and there isn't even a nice, fully rounded form of hypocrisy to be adopted, a well-enameled surface, a vacuous yet impeccable model, compact in its social array, like what we had, for example, until not that long ago, in the bourgeois model. In this harlequinade, in the assemblage of incongruous patchworks of identity and social models, there is a hierarchy of males, distinguished by their levels of resentment and frustration and ridicule, perhaps because their traditional mold has been shattered to smithereens, not for dramatic and progressive reasons, as was the case for women with feminism, but in a derisory and regressive fashion. Feminist radicalism had, at least, an obtusely heroic aspect, an epic thrust the way that all protest movements do at the moment they first arise, when they spontaneously gather and wave the banner. Male fumbling in search of a new role resembles nothing so much as the jerky movement of a lizard's severed tail, the nervous laughter that greets a witticism or a wisecrack that has simply baffled instead of amused. So the man becomes hysterical, the woman becomes combative, strange, isn't it? So at variance with the old clichés . . . all of these new and contradictory images began to rain down on us right around the time when this story unfolds. While we were just boys. There were those who weren't at all in search of a new role for men, and who took up stances in favor of the old ways, of their crumbling walls.

YOUNG MEN back then found themselves ping-ponging between two diametrically opposed conditions, each equally unsettling: one, the most commonplace and quotidian, was the frustration of not fucking, the other, the anxiety of performing adequately when they did in fact fuck. Sex, both desired and practiced, caused a general uproar in one's entire being. To say that we were agitated and uncertain about how our genitalia would react when put to the test, even though we could hardly wait to have the chance, would be a gross understatement. It was a suffocating blend of anguish and morbid curiosity. This adolescent fear would accompany every male for the rest of his life, unless he were to decide to take a vow of chastity and managed to stick to it. The authentic will to power, in fact, is expressed not in coitus, but in the renunciation of coitus. That is why the rare individuals who are actually chaste are often intolerable to be around: because they make a muscular display of their choice. By repressing themselves, they've liberated themselves, and now their intact, undispersed energy becomes a brash, overbearing social tool, a sort of cat-o'-nine-tails with which they can lash the world. The frightful farsighted power of the celibate man! No objective is out of his reach. Baudelaire used to say that we have two ways to elude the tedium of death: one is work, the other is pleasure. The sole difference between the two is that work increases your strength, pleasure consumes it. Actually, though, it is my modest opinion that both work and pleasure consume your strength.

SEX was a subject to be studied at the drawing board, a difficult theorem to explicate and to apply. There was nothing natural about it, except that muffled, imprecise drive, the pulsation that verged on queasy sickness, impossible to translate into concrete acts unless they smacked of banality: banality pervaded the things you had to say to get there, banality infused the ways in which we groped and stroked, truly grotesque when it came to the act of removing your underwear, and ridiculous the way they tended to twist and tangle around your ankles ... And stranger still is the way we had of trying to resolve it, once we managed to get on top of a female body, by delivering great and awkward thrusts, frantic back-and-forth of the pelvis, with a soundtrack of grunting. Is that really how it was supposed to go? As if those enthusiastic and clumsy efforts could solve the brainteaser. Some clearly thought that it might be a way of leaping to conclusions—the harder you pushed, the closer you got. No different from a test of strength at an amusement park.

NOW THE DESTINIES have become star-crossed, the customs have been overturned, and the exact point of the crossover were the years of my youth:

in a more puritan society, in the early years of psychoanalysis, people learned for the first time that many nonsexual acts had a hidden sexual source; now, in contrast, we realize that many sexual behaviors have a nonsexual motivation. In the old days we used to hasten to strip the body bare and reveal its nudity; today, in order to understand something, we have to dress it again. The symbolism has been overturned: a girl with a popsicle in her mouth was, deep down, sucking a cock, nowadays she might be sucking a cock but maybe she's really thinking about a popsicle.

2

UNTIL PUBERTY, it's not even a matter for discussion, it doesn't even come up. Then, over the course of a single season, the girls are transformed in such an explosive and spectacular fashion that their diversity becomes unbearable: too powerful to look at, too powerful to think about. It's no longer possible to pretend nothing's happened. The countless series of American films with porkies and pom-pom girls and lunatics and nerds and Elvis wannabes and taking girls' dormitories by siege and showers with holes in the walls so you can peek inside—none of these give even the slightest idea of the whiplash that young men undergo while witnessing the uncontrollable flowering of secondary female sexual traits: any comparison with the tortuous and strained development of their virility, which unfolds in parallel, seems unfair, manifesting itself laughably in the form of goatees and acne and breaking falsetto voices and the tendency to hunch over due to the weight of muscles that, truth be told, they don't yet possess. That diversity changes from virtual, statistical, to tangible, corporeal: and whether because it's attractive or because it's repugnant, sometimes because of both things at once, it's unlikely to leave you indifferent.

Yes, of course, there are adolescents who care nothing about the phenomenon of young girls in flower: out of every five young men, there is one who is so sure of himself and his charm that he'll inevitably lay waste to a bevy of female hearts precisely because he's cold and imperturbable; one who feigns indifference strictly because he is paralyzed by a shyness so great that it prevents him from even thinking of talking to girls, much less actually talking to them; a third is seriously uninterested, and what comes first in his hierarchy of personal interests is: the soccer team he roots for, his mother, his collections, chemistry, cars, or even (yes, there are kids who are already thinking about it at age fourteen . . .) money; a fourth young man, perhaps the most common type, is simply slow to catch up, he's a few time zones behind on the meridian of sexuality, capable of remaining firmly attached to that childish point of view until he turns sixteen or even twenty, or even maintaining that virginal trait, stuck to him for the rest of his life; the fifth young man is queer and still doesn't know it because he doesn't feel anything yet, or else does feel something, but strictly for other boys.

THERE WAS ONE CLASSMATE in particular who seemed simply incapable of making sense of the metamorphosis—Iannello. His discomfort was unmistakable. The discovery had caught him off guard, wrong-footed him. But perhaps it was he who had changed, his gaze, from the end of one school year to the beginning of the next, had so to speak grown heavy, seeing that women had existed previously, but he had simply never noticed. I mean to say that the libido splashed and sprayed out of his own eyes, rather than out of the bodies that those gleaming eyes, alight with curiosity, pursued with such feverish interest.

"Those bodies, fuck! Those bodies!" Iannello murmured. I spent a tormented school year sitting next to him.

"All you need to do is go away for the vacation and when you come back . . . they're practically scary! And my sister, the same thing, how she changed this summer, her eyes, her hair . . . you won't believe it, but even her hair has *changed*, for fuck's sake! I don't know how to explain it. Now her hair looks like my mother's hair, and I'm sure of it, she didn't do anything at all, she didn't go to the beauty parlor . . . but her hair doesn't look the way it used to."

It was obvious that Iannello was taking care not to refer to the most evident aspect of the changes in his sister Annetta: the incredible pair of breasts that had erupted from her chest, round and proud like the breasts on the goddesses carved on the façades of Indian temples. In any case, Annetta strongly resembled a slave girl out of the *Arabian Nights* or an Indian princess: all the Iannellos, father, mother, and children, were dark-skinned, with glittering eyes, red lips, and white teeth, as in the descriptions of Eastern poets, and very much like a fabulous actress from those years, Claudia Cardinale. And Annetta was just fourteen years old, in fact she might not yet have turned fourteen! How can a boy her age who, in the meantime, has only grown bigger, pimplier, and clumsier handle the bruising impact of *all that*? And what do you suppose *all that* even is, if not the normal progress of life?

Which means that life itself is unbearable for a boy, then for an adult, and then for an old man or an old woman, the protagonists or perhaps the victims of this incessant metamorphosis.

"It's not as if a guy doesn't have a dick . . ." Iannello went on, in astonishment, under his breath, turning to look at me during our science lesson, "and then from one day to the next he finds he has one dangling between his legs!"

I clearly understood my classmate's point of view and his disappointment. He was referring to the fact that breasts, which previously had simply not existed, something that girls didn't used to have, when they were just as flat as us boys, had suddenly begun to swell, protrude, outthrust . . . and unexpectedly become the central focus of attraction and comment, something to dress up and undress, support, fondle, blame . . . Something that just a few months ago hadn't existed was now planted firmly at the center of our collective attention and concern.

"They're ruining my life . . ." Iannello hissed, before being forced to turn back around to face the front of the room, summoned sharply by Svampa. We've encountered Svampa before, he's the chemistry teacher.

"Hey, dark-haired boy, there, in the front row . . . what's got into you today to make you so . . ." and he struck him on the hand with the long pointer he used to indicate the position of the elements on the periodic table that hung on the wall, "make you so *distracted*, eh?" Iannello shut his eyes, waiting for a second, harder whack of the pointer. In the meantime, his mind's eye continued, indifferent to all the calls to attention, to wander off in pursuit of a pair of twin shapes, protruding from a slender torso, apparently with the sole objective of creating mental upset in someone like him, and in many others. (No, if you please, don't let's start arguing about whether those breasts serve or will someday serve another purpose, a noble purpose, a maternal purpose . . . in reality, the way they're made and where they're located, they can't serve any purpose at all, that is, no purpose other than to become the object of female concerns and male obsessions and fantasies. Pointless, in other words, to try to remind us that these are mammary glands, and that they're there to feed our little ones, exactly like so many other mammals have them. Have you ever taken a look at them, the tits of other animals, of dogs, monkeys, I don't know, *dolphins*, and where they're located? It's written in plenty of books that the day we stood upright, we for all time inverted the order of our functions, putting the objective of sexual attraction in first place. And these days, breasts are popping out earlier and earlier, practically while they're still little girls, whereas women have children later and later, and in ever smaller numbers, and they breast-feed them for shorter and shorter periods: which means that, if all goes according to schedule, it might be a good fifteen or even twenty years before those uselessly precocious boobs will feel the hungry mouth of a newborn baby, and then another or at the very most two more little rugrats, meaning a total of just a few months over the arc of an entire human lifetime . . . while, over that same period of time, dozens of male adolescents or adults or old men will dream of doing the same thing, touching, squeezing, biting, sucking those breasts, and a few will succeed.

Before winding up in the mouth of a newborn child, at least in Western countries, those nipples are going to be sucked on by a great number of grown men; and once the suckling child has been forcefully removed from the source of nourishment that in theory was created expressly for it, and successfully guided toward powdered milk and disgusting baby foods, then sure enough its daddy, and maybe other grown men to whom the mommy is willingly and well disposed, will latch back onto those nipples. Taking turns. Hungrily. Greedily.

So now I have to ask myself: When all is said and done, who has sucked a woman's breast *less* than her own children?)

It is inevitable that in the presence of a pair of naked breasts, a male will regress. Proof of the fact is the enduring popularity of the famously big-breasted woman, that is to say, women famous for being big-breasted—it would be as pointless as simple to draw up a list of them here, seeing that any one of us can easily get hold of that list instantly, accompanied by an eloquent array of images. And in those images, these ladies do nothing other than to thrust forward or pretend to hide and shield their gifts of nature, hefting them, pressing down on them with both hands or compressing them into skimpy outfits or tops or bras . . . and by pretending to hide them they show them off, because it really is impossible to keep them at bay, make them sit in a corner, as if in punishment, no, because they're simply too much, they're just too damned . . . *eruptive*. Perhaps that's the adjective I'm looking for.

(I CONFESS that what has always attracted me most in the female body is the bosom, the breasts, the source of the greatest pleasure and frustration that a man can experience through physical contact, or when that contact is denied him, in simple line of sight: a lovely pair of breasts exalts, unnerves, caresses, and disturbs the male eye much the same way that phosphenes do, those mysterious sparks that swim across our field of vision. One cannot hope for anything better than to see those breasts laid naked, freed from the miserable constraints of corsets, girdles, bustiers, bra cups, underwires, spaghetti straps, elastic undergarments . . . The apparition of a fine bosom freed of all that paraphernalia has something superb and, at the same time, utterly pure about it, a form without compromise that astounds: it's "like a stag stepping out of the forest." The dazzling beauty of a pair of breasts is assisted by the fact that it need express nothing at all, unlike the human face, that field of battle devastated by sentiments and thoughts, which everyone looks at to interpret, everyone scrutinizes to know what you're feeling, what you're thinking. There's nothing more to be learned from a fine pair of breasts.)

FROM THE MOMENT that girls began to exist for me, the thorniest problems were always shyness and awkwardness.

What were the right things to say, the right things to do? Uneasiness, uneasiness, uneasiness . . . it took years before we could find a passable way of communicating with the opposite sex, the same manner that I still use today. When I looked at a girl back then, I almost immediately blushed and turned away, at the thought that she might have similar fantasies and intentions to those that had come into my mind. That's what embarrassed me most, to imagine that girls could read my mind or that I might read theirs and find that it was the same as mine, or even much filthier.

IF I THINK BACK to the girls I had crushes on, during the vacations, in a confused but venomous way, to the point that I was incapable of thinking about anything other than them, of their eyes, which seemed like deep wells of wonder, their artfully pouty lips, their hair, their thighs, and that invisible thing they clamped tightly between those thighs, well, I can't help but agree with those who believe that behind that figure of an ordinary girl, more or less unexceptional (just as my own figure was unexceptional, the persona of an infatuated kid), there lurked a luminous image, not entirely of this world, a radiant form capable of enchanting and subjugating, a form with which I was entering into contact for the first time through those very same pallid fourteen-year-old girls, just as they were doing through me, and through mine. Ephebic adolescents, slender, almost haggard, on the boundary of the insignificant: it was unthinkable in a way that they all on their own might be able to give rise to such heat, such splendor, that they— if someone loves them and desires them, or even just if they feel themselves being observed, if someone watches them with a furtive glance—can unleash an energy with all the scorching power of a hydrogen bomb, sucking the air out of the atmosphere for miles in all directions around their mighty sphere of flame. How can all this be explained? Since I've watched the same thing happen to my children, I'm convinced that it functions precisely as described. Yes, it's a mystical experience, what else could it be? An experience of which we pallid figures are the substrate, the vehicle.

IT THEREFORE HAPPENS that the crucial years of scholastic learning coincide with the years of maximum emotional turbulence, when one's sexuality emerges from oblivion, frightening and seducing and confusing and scorching the brain of those who cross the vast expanse of adolescence, the baking sands.

BUT NOT ARBUS. Arbus was different. He always had been, and in every way. While we were kicking soccer balls around on the crunchy ash of the playing field, he was secretly constructing his mind. He never revealed—as far as I know, or at least not as long as I was still in contact with him—his weakness, his frenzy toward images of women; he never fell into rapt enchantment, as Iannello did, at the thought of those shapes, those faces. Or else he was capable of masking it successfully, as he did so many other thoughts.

Then, when I lost track of him, he must have discovered it, after his fashion, or invented it, seeing that he actually got married.

That's right, Arbus found a woman, I came to hear of his singular marriage much further on, and in a few pages, if you have the patience to bear with me, I'll tell you how.

3

S VAMPA, our chemistry teacher, the elderly priest with the thin, nasal voice, used his pointer with all the agility of a fencer pointing his foil.

In spite of the fact that it was so very long, he whirled it and nailed the target spot-on for the most part.

And in fact, he never clubbed us, it was more like striking a billiard ball, as if trying to run the boys through, which wasn't all that different really from what he would have liked to do in another context, in compliance with his repressed erotic desire.

But was it, after all, so very repressed?

We wondered that quite often.

That he was head-over-heels a homosexual, there could be no doubt: but no boy at SLM that I ever met or spoke to told me that he'd been molested by him if, as I trust and hope, we don't consider molestation the loving phrases he lavished on his pets, the most attractive and effeminate young boys, or those, on the contrary, who were precociously virile, the young men like Iannello, in other words.

That "I could just eat you alive with kisses, Riccardino mine!" aimed at Modiano, who at the time had an angelic head of hair, fine and fluffy and blond, sadly, the kind of hair that falls out early, was actually just a form of scholastic encouragement, when Svampa gave him back his classroom assignment with a passing grade.

THE SCIENCE CLASS might just as fairly have been called the alchemy class.

Although they taught modern sciences there, it was like a piece of the Middle Ages set in the rationalist building of SLM, the cabinet of Doctor Faustus, upholstered with symbols, skeletons, creatures pickled in formaldehyde, carnivorous plants that masticated and swallowed insects, nourishing a fleshy, purple flower, which blossomed for a single night, surviving only the following day, and ultimately causing the death of the plant, drained of its life force by having engendered it.

Gas was Svampa's assistant.

A filthy, bowed little old man with long white hair and enormous snowy eyebrows, who must have worked every type of job and disgusting endeavor known to man before donning the rough, stained gray lab coat, spotted with sprays of chemical substances; without ever uttering a word, he helped Svampa to clean up the lab when the experiments were over. The flasks, the bottles, the alembics, the electrical generators, the mirrors for optical experiments.

Svampa, in fact, was very messy, terribly disorderly, and as he explained things his excitement mounted to the verge of euphoria, as he shrieked in a falsetto, and if it hadn't been for Gas's assistance, he would surely have blown the whole school sky-high, especially when he amused himself by boiling his potions over the Bunsen burner—and as often as not, he'd forget to extinguish the flame.

Gas never opened his mouth, and looked at us, over Svampa's shoulders, with true hatred, especially when Svampa abandoned himself to his amorous tirades aimed at the more attractive of my classmates, the usual ones: Jervi, Modiano, or Zarattini.

He'd review us one by one with that hate-filled glare, amplified by his enormous scruffy white eyebrows.

Gas hated every last one of us pampered brats, without exception.

IN FACT, it could just as easily have been Merlin or Paracelsus in Gas&Svampa's stead.

While the two old men stood bowed and busy over the workbench where they did their experiments, they looked like a couple of corpse thieves, the notorious Burke and Hare. For that matter, among the many rumors concerning Gas, there was one going around that, before being hired at SLM, already in his late fifties, he'd been a morgue attendant, perhaps working in the office of the medical examiner, responsible for washing the corpses and reassembling them after autopsies. It was also said that he had been an alcoholic, and some insinuated that he still was. In any case, whether truth or legend, there's nothing to be done about it. Scientists are just one notch above, or below, shamans and sorcerers.

AS IF THAT WEREN'T ENOUGH, Svampa was convinced that a young man's talents and character were inscribed in his features: as a result, it was not only because he was a homosexual that he would scrutinize each of us with a gaze that seemed to physically palpate the face and grope the body. If he decided that one of us wasn't suited to the study of chemistry because, let's say, of the shape of his nose or his forehead or hands, then he'd abandon any effort to teach him, he'd never test him, he wouldn't answer his question or requests for further explanations and—this was the topper—he'd just put a D on his report card so that he wouldn't have to waste any more of his time or breath on him.

ONE TIME, Jervi and Chiodi played a tremendous prank on him. An unforgettable one. Even now, the alumni of SLM talk about it. Svampa had in fact raised this very rare agave plant, which he tended with loving care while awaiting the day it would finally bloom. It was supposed to flower just once in its lifetime, and Svampa waited months for it to blossom, the way an expectant mother awaits a child. You could say, without rhetorical overreach, that he watered that agave plant with his tears, the tears of an old repressed queer priest, and there must have been plenty of those tears, shed both over the sins he'd committed and those merely imagined, let alone for his continual sacrifices and frustrations. By now the solitary agave bud was swollen and juicy as a young artichoke, and you had the impression you could feel the petals within pushing their way out, eager to open up and display their garish colors, which would instantly redeem the little shrub's unassuming appearance: a grayish trunk that, if it hadn't been for that monstrous sucker ready to open out, you would have thought was withered and dead. During the last class held before the prank—if that's what we want to call it—was played, Svampa had seemed distracted more than once, and had turned his gaze toward the vase, set just below the window to accelerate its vegetal processes, as if he wanted to witness the exact moment of the blossoming. But the miracle seemed to be slightly delayed. When Gas, leaving the laboratory unguarded, the keys left carelessly in the keyhole, went down into the cellar to get some cleaning soap (though some claimed he went down there to drink), my two classmates Jervi and Chiodi scampered in and poured half a bottle of bleach into the agave's vase. To hear the two of them tell it (though it might well have been an invented horror-film detail), they'd actually given the plant "an injection," directly into the stalk. The effect, in any case, was already unmistakable the next day. It was a Tuesday, a day on which we had no science lesson, but word spread in a flash down the hallways: Svampa was sitting in the laboratory, head cradled in his hands, and before him was the agave in its vase. He was unable to restrain his sobs. His shoulders heaved uncontrollably. The boys who had gone in at the sound of his laments had found him in that position. We arrived too, on the run, the minute the bell rang for recess, crowding around the laboratory door, and Svampa was still there, rapt in his wake for the flower that had died unborn. The plant, in fact, was as gray as ever, but its succulent bud—through the partially opened corolla in which you had been able to glimpse the red thread of its petals until just the day before—had fallen off the stalk, tumbling to the floor. Now Svampa was turning it over and over between his fingers, dead, dry, and colorless; he seemed to be trying to figure out what had happened, but if you ask me, he knew perfectly well. And he bowed his head in tears.

Standing next to him was Gas, red in the face, his white hair standing on end and his eyebrows even more tousled. He kept a solicitous hand placed on Svampa's shoulder, where the priest's black tunic was worn and almost shiny. But consoling the broken teacher was not the first of his concerns. He knew that before long the headmaster would begin an investigation into his failure to adequately safeguard the laboratory. And he looked at us students with a hatred that I doubt has ever been felt in any human soul toward his fellow men. A pure, absolute, justified hatred.

And all for a flower.

4

ERE HE IS, the pimply young male, anxious, excessive, bipolar by nature, busy running to and fro, zigzagging like in some video game between crevasses and gorges that open suddenly on either side and the narrowly averted obstacles of latent homosexuality, social ridicule, failure, or pure and simple capitulation in the face of women. All of these are minefields, territories where, if you once set foot, you can be blown straight into the air. His battles are not against the opposite sex, but rather against the fears engendered by his membership in his own sex. As a male, he has been set certain standards to attain and honor, and nothing can frighten him more than the doubt that his masculinity has turned out poorly, incomplete, wounded, whiny: as in point of fact it almost always is.

As a result, all the trouble he gets into, big and small, is precisely in order to make up for these terrors, to patch the holes with which his virility is riddled.

COMRADELY ATTRACTION, fear, competition, and especially sensitivity, that's right, sensitivity, an insanely delicate sensitivity that no one would ever imagine in young men but that, instead, is in fact present, a highly acute and childish sensitivity toward the judgments and gazes of the other boys. An obsession bound together the classmates and at the same time offended them and drove them apart. They spent all their time measuring themselves against one another to see where they stood in the ranking of masculinity, and what score they would assign to the others. Females formed part of this competition only because they allowed males to gain higher rankings in the hierarchy of masculinity, and so males used them to judge one another, to settle their reckonings. They served as markers, indicators, like athletic achievements or musical tastes or the way they dressed. Anyone who thinks that it's only girls who compare their clothing with other girls' clothing is making a terrible mistake: males scrutinize one another with perhaps even greater attention to detail, and with an even more curious and relentless eye: nothing can drop your ranking like the wrong T-shirt, pair of shoes, or trousers.

When, from one day to the next, in your early adolescence, you convince yourself that you have discovered the difference between being male and being female, a competition begins, with the objective of distinguishing oneself, standing out. In order to prove that they have understood the role, like so many insecure actors, the boys overdo their performance, they load up on attitudes. Adolescents pose as men and women with an awkward and watchful seriousness, proportional to their fear of not being taken seriously, to the point of producing parodistic imitations of masculinity and femininity, caricatures, in other words, *Guys and Dolls*, a sort of *Grease*-style musical: boys cursing and girls squealing. For the males, the simplest way of proving that they are, in fact, male is to hold femininity in contempt: it is a clear negative precept, whose simplified formula tells us that in order to be men, it is sufficient not to be women. Even the fathers of bygone times (and maybe, to some small extent, those of today) worked in terms of a process of exclusion: rather than encouraging their sons to behave in a manly manner, they did everything they could to prevent them from behaving in a girlish one. A boy emerged from childhood with only one clear idea in mind, that is, to make sure he didn't get dragged into sex.

Any interest in anything that was even vaguely sexual was already considered in and of itself feminine. Any attention paid to one's own body was taboo: looking at yourself in the mirror, combing your hair, paying attention to the way you dress. Any healthy young male ought to turn up his nose at all this, dress sloppily, wash infrequently, let his hair grow wherever it will, twisted and curly. The object that best sums up this foul-smelling slovenliness is the *scarpa da ginnastica* (that's what gym shoes were called back then, now they have no name in Italian). This no-nonsense and slightly filthy model of masculinity has nothing new about it, indeed it dates back to many schools of philosophy of the ancient world; it finds its most extreme and polemical exposition in the writings of Julian the Apostate: this anachronistic emperor who, in the name of a thrifty and soldierly ideal, rejected the idea of shaving body hair, found baths enervating, and rejected the culture of massages and beauty care, in short, all the oriental faggotry that had softened Rome, muddling the roles of the sexes and making the imperial city no better than any of its client satrapies.

AT THAT AGE, the doubt of "not feeling like the others" becomes a certainty: no one can be or feel "like the others," such a thing is impossible, everyone feels and actually is different, whether they think of themselves as very special or are afraid that they might be a scoundrel or a rogue or a monster.

And so there were two ways of expressing one's anger against other males: either by subduing them with crude words and violent acts, proving in other words that you were more masculine than them, bigger and stronger than them, or else with a hysterical tantrum borrowed from the feminine repertory, that is, with an unnaturally piercing falsetto voice, scratching faces, shedding tears. Often the two styles, which share a common array of dirty words, are mixed . . . and there is no need to be effeminate for that to happen. The inexhaustible search for company, approval, similarity, and solidarity that males seek from other males, when it is frustrated, unleashes a resentment that may even be stronger than what can be felt toward the opposite sex: being rejected by one's fellow male leads to a dramatic uncertainty concerning one's own identity, even worse than the not entirely unexpected rejections that one receives from the opposite sex, which, however disagreeable, may even serve to strengthen that identity. A young man who rejects your friendship can hurt you more deeply than a young woman who rejects your love.

OFFICIALLY, if there is one thing that men seem to take pleasure in boasting about, it's the fact that they are not women; but deep down, there is a widely circulating curiosity, an envy, and even a desire—or a frenzied lust—to be a woman, or at least to take the opposite gender for a test drive, so to speak, and to think with a woman's head, to feel curving hips and bouncing breasts, your heart beating in a different way, and then to feel pleasure like a woman, to cry the way women cry, and if the experiment were to last over a longer period of time, then, yes, miraculously become pregnant, and give birth like a woman . . . all things that are off-limits to men, things that appeal to men every bit as much as they frighten them.

SO WHAT DOES IT MEAN to be male? How, and by virtue of what, are men recognized as males? Since most men by and large fail to match the commonly accepted image of a male, and don't possess at all the presumed identity of the real man, a male amounts to being other than the way one actually *is*—it means being the way one *ought* to be. A male isn't someone who *is* male, but someone who *has to be* male, and it is in this absolute requirement that we find its essence. A male, then, is a non-being or rather a being-for, a potential being, a volition, an edge concept, a guiding principle.

Effort, demonstration, proof of self. You aren't born a man, you become a man. There is no such expression as "Be a woman!" equivalent to the well-known "Be a man!" (See, for example, the terrifying Kipling poem "If," the worst and most banal thing that great narrator ever wrote, and there are even people who hang it on the wall and force you to learn it by heart . . .)

THE COST OF LIVING up to expectations, to fit the role that you imagined a boy, a man, a male was supposed to play. Just what was that role? What price did we pay?

I personally paid that price. In this book I have told and will go on to tell about various episodes, of how and where and how much I paid, in short, the payments of my debt of maleness. Of how I never managed to pay off that debt. Of how unfair and yet inevitable it was that that repayment would be demanded, from me and from all my schoolmates and all the males who have looked, or are now looking, and may someday look over the threshold (should I say over the brink of the cliff?) of adolescence. I'm not talking about women here: they have their own substantial debts to pay, and each of them owes a share. There is surely a female deity to whom these tributes are donated, perhaps something like the Artemis of Ephesus, or some big-bosomed pre-Columbian, or Kali, or else a cherub.

NOW LET'S NOT OVERSTATE THIS solidarity among males. A man is certainly different from a woman, but truth be told, he's also different from all other men. And in fact he might prove to be much more different from most men than he is from certain individual women. While the difference from women is taken for granted from the very first day, from the pink or blue ribbons hanging outside the door of the hospital room in the maternity ward (a horrible custom, which I hope is falling into disuse, that marks from the very beginning the unbridgeable sexual gap: even before the name, or the skin, or the family, or the social rank, before anything else, it is in that catalogue that you come into the world, "a fine bouncing baby boy has been born . . ."), the differences among men become clear along the path, and for the most part they come as a disagreeable surprise, and in some cases might prove to be far more acute and strident. When you realize that those who ought to be *like you* aren't at all . . . then it comes naturally to say, I'm not a bit like them . . . I'm not at all like them, even though I, too, have a thingy dangling between my thighs. This apparent similarity does nothing other than widen the disparity. So there are two types of diversity, which are too often mixed up: one is interspecific, the other intraspecific. It's like the differences among peoples: there can be no doubt that the Italians are different from the Germans, but there is less average diversity between an Italian and a German than there might be between certain Italians at the farthest extremes from one another. Groups, genders, social categories, and peoples have abyssal internal differences.

WE USE as yardsticks the ability to keep uncertainty under control, to eliminate it or suffocate it, or at least not to allow oneself to be overwhelmed by it. Uncertainty is in its turn engendered by one's personal inability to respond adequately to situations of danger, novelty, or mere contact with other people. For some (and I am one), it is an immense challenge to be in the same room as ten other people: I get the impression that they're all looking at me, judging me, want to threaten me or seduce me or be seduced by me, or else that they're intentionally ignoring me; while the truth is that none of them gives a damn about me, about who I am or what I do. The uncertainty comes from the feeling of being threatened, and at the same time, the desire for emotional intimacy.

ANY YOUNG MALE wishes to be further masculinized. The masculinity that he possesses, nine times out of time, is inadequate, hesitant, uncertain, and so it needs to be remodeled and buttressed. If it tends toward the feminine, then it needs to be straightened and redirected. If, on the other hand, it is too accentuated, then brakes need to be put on it. Strength is not the only indicator of masculinity, in fact an even greater indicator is the ability to get that strength under control (more or less the same thing that the ads for a well-known brand of tires say, or what soccer coaches preach when they recruit a talented but reckless young player).

THE CHALLENGES that masculinity had to overcome when I was born, at the time of my boyhood and youth, were no longer considered universally valid, and they were already subject to disapproval and ridicule by the time I became a man, that is, when it was my turn to overcome them. From John Wayne and Steve McQueen we'd passed on to Dustin Hoffman and Al Pacino: instead of manly men and men's men, the model had shifted to short, neurotic men.

THE TRUE OPPOSITE of masculinity wasn't femininity but homosexuality: a perilous border. The masculine ideal could be defined as a negation: the exact opposite of a man wasn't a woman, it was a queer.

The most intolerable fear for us males was that someone might laugh at us . . .

Do you know what it means to fight all the time, all the time, against fear and shame? I'm talking about the fear of being made fun of, of being considered a faggot.

If by chance you were considered a faggot, to fight back, you had to immediately find another kid who might act a little effeminate, or weak, or shy and fearful. Carry out a police operation along the border between the sexes. A sort of night watch.

✤

FROM WHEN I WAS EVEN SMALLER . . . at the park . . . I remember dramatic and deeply stirring games that were dubbed with such familiar nicknames as "hide and seek" and "tag," names that tell you nothing about the immense frustration, indeed, the despair of those who were found or taken prisoner, because they weren't fast enough or clever enough, the true victims of those cruel games, who had to count on the speed and spirit of sacrifice of some other friend willing to liberate them.

I remember that little girls were a source of contamination, they always wanted to kiss you, they'd chase after you with their lips pursed and pouty. I remember the hatred I felt toward fat girls and girls with glasses, and the instantaneous love toward the pretty ones.

But even the pretty ones were destined to suffer abuse. They were invited to play, for instance to jump rope, and for a while the game proceeded normally, the boys would turn the rope at the right rhythm for the girls to jump . . . then the boys who were turning the rope would speed up the pace or reverse direction and the girl would wind up tripping and falling, and everyone would run away, variously laughing or shrieking. The girls were so used to being interrupted or tricked in the course of their play, or having their toys stolen or destroyed, that they'd developed rituals to make up for the mistreatment the males had inflicted upon them: if the guilty parties hadn't already run away of their own volition, they'd dismiss them, waving them away with a sigh of resignation that was already fully adult, resuming their game, consoling the girls who were crying. They'd pretend that nothing at all had happened. "Ah, those dopes . . ." was the comment, and if they were sometimes angry at the treatment, at the same time they might also be amused at the stupid pranks that were played on them.

> *to penetrate the space of others*
> *the space of girls*
> *to violate their space, their conversations*
> *to violate their body*

LITTLE BOYS might not know what sex is, but they know perfectly well what domination is, and therefore they tend to interpret sex as domination and defeat ("Papà is hurting Mamma, and in fact, listen to her scream . . ."). Some boys maintain this identification, even when they're adults.

PLAYING AT SOMETHING is the first step on the path that leads to seriously doing something, a sort of dress rehearsal. The performance of aggression toward young girls was innocuous only because and only as long as it remained a performance, but its content remained valid once the game was over, as something that could always be put into practice when the time was right. Doing things as a joke is the most effective way to learn how to do them for real. Playful terrorism.

THEY CONTAMINATED MALES *with their touch, their kisses, their saliva, their feelings . . . or just with their presence!*

TO HAVE THE FEELING *one needs to overcome a wall of resistance. Even when there isn't one. To have to win out at all costs, after some lighthearted skirmishing, then turned serious, determined, angry, or desperate.*

AND THEN, once you've grown up, also the sensation that you need to *get the better* of a woman to fuck her. It would seem to be a reasonably well-founded idea, psychologically speaking, but at the same time, in factual terms, it's not true in the slightest, at least for me and, I believe, for all the men of my generation. If I think back to the women I've gone to bed with in my life, well, let's say a third of them did, in fact, make me work for it, at least a little. Some of them a lot, some just according to standard ritual, I wouldn't know. The ones who made me work too hard, I just gave up on, but I have no evidence of whether or not I did the right thing. Maybe if I'd insisted, who can say . . . Of the other women, a good half of them (meaning a further third of the total number) had the same thing in mind as I did, and we found ourselves in each other's arms with admirable promptitude.

The other third simply lunged right at me.

PUSH AWAY, push away, push away. In our destiny as young male animals, this too was written: that males separate, and females unite. Starting right from the matter of how his or her body is built, or ought to be built, the male defines, distinguishes, identifies; the female accommodates, shares, mingles. She aspires to union, we aspired to separation . . .

IN MY DAY and in my social class the typical young woman was: fragile, vague, docile. Fair-haired but not actually blond. Silent but not really sad, other people could make her laugh, now and then. You can make her laugh, even if you're not the most charismatic guy around, still, you seem to be enough for her. The first great explorer of the human mind maintained that apathetic young women are particularly desirable on the matrimonial market. A man can take her as she is, empty, and fill her with the contents that best suit him, whether real or imagined. That was true in his day, but also in my day.

> Fragile, docile, apathetic, vague:
> toward this lovely woman it's almost
> a chivalrous obligation to appear as protective
> as indulgent . . .

OUR PARENTS, whether enlightened conservatives or cautious liberals, wound up bending to the new aspects of the period, unwillingly but still they gave in—sexual freedom, foul language, sloppy dress, political extremism, provided there was no action to suit the fiery words, informality of all kinds—with that form of annoyed or worried indulgence that sociologists call "grinding acceptance," which to my Italian ear sounds like acceptance with clenched teeth. The new ways filtered into our family like a fine dust, while in other families they had already pervaded every aspect of life, and in others still, they simply hadn't penetrated, at least theoretically, because of the staunch, die-hard resistance put up by the parents of our classmates to change of any kind. We were the eldest children, the firstborn, already sapped and weakened by the new effeminate culture, based on desire instead of personal sacrifice and hard work. There were those who chose to react with spectacularly symbolic and violent actions, in the belief that bombs and rapes were essential to the restoration of a society ordered according to manly principles, a society that could once again be called masculine. Paradoxically, it turns out that many of these were the most spoiled children of all, anything but spartan!

5

'M TAKING THIS PATH for the first time, with all of you. Follow me if you can, if you have the willingness, the time, the patience . . .

ALREADY IN THOSE DAYS, masculinity was considered to be in crisis, threatened, since it seemed necessary to rescue it, vindicate it in the face of the danger constituted by women homosexuals and hippies.

It was urgent to react. We couldn't stand by, twiddling our thumbs. We couldn't bear witness to the collapse indifferently. React, react, react against the degeneration of civilization that had made men look more and more like women, suffice it to think of the fashion of long hair, equally detested by the Fascists, by Pier Paolo Pasolini, and by old factory workers. The Fascists wanted a crop of healthy, vigorous young Italian men, ready to fight, Pasolini wanted them with the napes of their necks shaved clean and bangs hanging over their foreheads, and the factory workers were old-school, they wanted things the way they used to be. The permissive culture, in contrast, measured its advancement by the degree to which it had succeeded in feminizing males. I remember the sheer disgust with which the average adult watched longhairs on TV (singers, etc.). I myself wore my hair long, and I would have let it grow longer, but the fact is that it tended to grow upward instead of hanging down, puffing out at the sides, like the hairstyle of a female host on some show on RAI TV, especially if I tried to brush it. As a result, it never hung down over my shoulders, the way it did for those blessed with smooth, silky hair.

The obsession was always with masculine identity: to confuse it and bring it closer to the identity of the opposite sex (hair, earrings, etc.) or, on the contrary, to believe that you could safeguard it with a pair of scissors.

There were back then (and still exist today) the custodians of the virile myth. In their eyes, femininity softens a male, inducing flaccidity. They see femininity as an infection, they fear being contaminated with it, they guard virility as a closed, compact system, impermeable to the softness that contact with the feminine evokes and provokes. The fear, in other words, of being taken back to the nursing baby's condition of dependency. The cock is hard until, after sexual intercourse, it softens. In truth, it was soft before intercourse as well, but what is most striking is always what comes *after*, just as the question of what there will be after death is always more frightening than what there was before life. However you choose to put it, sex is enervating. It is considered not as proof of potency, but quite to the contrary, as the main cause of potency's loss. It is therefore undervalued or feared. All this has a plastic obviousness: with love, from stiff and strong, the body turns languid, tender, relaxed, and soft, just like a woman's body, come to think of it . . .

Sex, then, would be nothing more than a trap laid for the man by the woman to debase and thereby subjugate him. To make him her slave by using a magic capable of causing weakness, of draining the energies or rerouting them into a bestial life, like that of the men transformed into wild animals by Circe (it's interesting that Ulysses should use sex in a preemptive manner to prevent that from happening to him: he subjugates the sorceress by forcing her to engage in intercourse, which, curiously, weakens her, not him! This is a very rare case of a reversal of the rule, which instead applies inflexibly even among the gods, for example Ares and Hephaestus, one the lover, the other the husband, are both knocked out of combat by Aphrodite's amatory arts). Sex is the means but at the same time the end of the project of seduction: it is what the man obtains as playful reparation for having accepted female domination, a gratification that actually enslaves those whom it renders happy, at least to the untrained eye. They believe that they have won, but what they receive is a consolation prize. Feminine allure is therefore a particular and, so to speak, very flexible variation of strength. It manifests itself not as a banal form of hardness but rather according to subtlety and invisibility.

Along with attraction, males always feel a vague terror of or repugnance toward intimacy, they fear intimacy with females and, to an almost equal degree, they fear it with other males, a scandalous impulse that must be repressed. The fact of desiring and inhibiting one's desire can recur in each instance, or it may have happened once and for all during adolescence, when, in a more or less conscious manner, one makes one's own sexual choice. During their first sexual experience, arms wrapped around a woman, young men are unable to breathe, they feel as if they're suffocating, trapped. A very different matter from possessing, conquering, dominating! A man feels he's enveloped in coils, wrapped tight in tentacles, buried in the yielding softness of the shape of a female body, and when he enters

her, it is as if he had just entered his own grave. To his immense pleasure
and upset, the disconcerting novelty of softness.

IT'S NOT EASY TODAY to distinguish what makes sex different from sports,
from the purchase of luxury goods, and from violence. What boundaries
separate it from these other practices, seeing that the way it is depicted is
no different from athletic or commercial performance, or a rape. Sports,
consumerism, and violence form a single category these days, and the only
things that conventionally divide them are the thematic channels on satel-
lite TV. Sports, consumer purchases, and pornography, the great contemporary surrogates for experience, the substitutes for war: strain and effort,
limitless physical appropriation of goods and bodies. The objective of an
athletic competition is simple and unequivocal: to win. The rest is just talk.
Either the ball goes in the net or it doesn't, there's no point in arguing about
it, even if the frustrated sports fans will go on doing so for weeks or even
years, relitigating the disallowed goal, the ball that missed the net by a fraction of an inch . . . the result remains the same. It remains the law of the
strongest and the best, and that means the team or the athlete who wins.
Something very similar to this brutal, categorical spirit, as unfair as you
please, but at least crystal clear, can be applied to courtship: So when it's all
said and done, did you fuck her? Did you fuck her or didn't you? The rest is
so much empty chatter.

   Once you have grasped this erotic-athletic nexus, it isn't hard to see the
link between the twin worlds that, revolving with all their numerous satel-
lites, occupy so much space in the male imagination, until their orbits coincide, now that sports, once an almost ascetic practice with overtones of
elitism and puritanism, is the most highly eroticized and popular domain
in the world. That said, I remember without the slightest twinge of regret at
least a couple of non-fucks, in fact, probably more, at least three or four episodes among the many in which my soccer ball hit the upright, the penalty
shot was misjudged or not even kicked, out of laziness or awkwardness or
lack of perspicacity or a curious lack of interest that surfaced at the last minute: the culmination of a singular desire to play, yes, but only a little, to play
a friendly exhibition game, so to speak, without anything at stake, without
anyone winning anything. Without necessarily getting kinged, without dipping your biscuit, to use the explicit rhetorical figures of tradition (Roman,
thuggish). There was a time when I believed that this spirit was exclusively
feminine. A little provocative, slightly capricious, naturally inclined to make

sure that nothing happened, just interested in seeing what might shake out, what might turn up. Women often like to sprinkle a little magic dust around the place, flap their wings, raise the temperature, without really looking for anything in particular . . . and then stop at a certain point for no particular reason, without explanation, pushing the game all the way along and then calling a halt all at once, and good night, Irene . . . the kind of thing that drives lots of men crazy and in certain cases has made me come close to losing my grip. Wait, what? You were willing to come over to my house, and now you're already half-naked, and blah blah blah.

And yet I can say that I've done more or less the same with certain women, and that certain other women have done the same with me: shift from pedal to the metal to slamming on the brakes, or perhaps on the clutch, so that the engine races frantically: you can still hear the roar but the car slows down and comes to a halt . . . the excitement is at its peak, is it really necessary to go any farther? There is a wonderful and carefree moment, a senseless instant, in that suspension . . . Or perhaps it's a profound fear, who can say . . . But fear of what?

And so, if I've experienced the same thing myself, does that mean that men and women are more similar than we suppose? That the whole rhetoric of getting to home base whatever the cost is false? Or that it's not exclusive to males? Or that once you've hurled yourself headfirst into the enterprise of seduction, the actual fucking is actually only relatively important?

TO COUNTERBALANCE THESE, there have been other episodes when I wound up determined to fuck at all costs, practically in spite of myself, as if with my eyes closed, just to honor the principle of not doing without. Fleeting, senseless instances of intercourse in which, if I raped anyone, I raped myself, and like an athlete clenching his teeth on the last lap, thinking only of the finish line, managed to break the ribbon only to collapse immediately afterward into a heap of utter indifference.

PERHAPS WE DON'T EVEN realize to what extent much (these days, almost the totality) of our sexual experience is indirect and vicarious. However long and however many times we might have kissed, touched, and made love, we've seen, read, peeped at, spied on, eavesdropped on someone else who was doing it or talking about doing it a millions times more. In a single screenshot on any old site on the Internet there flashes more sex than we've had or will have in our entire lifetimes. I'm not just talking about pornography, though these days pornography is the world's most important medium of communication, and at the same time, the most widespread message; I'm talking about the thousand channels via which sex reaches us. Our direct experience of coitus, the experiences of it that we've personally consumed, is nothing compared with the indirect experience, and we can therefore say that the latter is far more substantial and important than the former. Even if we're just talking about kisses, however many of them I may have given (something that I found repugnant when I was kid but now like it better than all the rest), it's still just an infinitesimal percentage of the kisses I've seen given: by other people in flesh and blood, on TV, at the movies, on the street, at parties, between men and women, and men and men, and women and women, in museums, in snapshots, many of them anonymous and many of them memorable, as memorable if not more so than the ones I've given and received with my own lips . . .

Even if we grant that a guy has only ever known the woman he married, well, from the very outset that's not true: there have been at least a thousand or ten thousand different women, that is, as many as have filled his eyes, naked, since he was a boy. And many of them he will have shared with vast numbers of other men. Along with that crowd, he will have formed an image of sexuality that is far more vast than that experienced in his conjugal observatory. The disproportion between your real and imaginary activity, that is, made up of images, but no less concrete than the former, is almost enough to make your head spin. The same thing could be said of the relationship between the life you are obliged to live and the alternative existences lived by proxy when reading novels or watching movies.

Back in the days of elementary and middle school, the stars were Ursula Andress and Raquel Welch, in their skimpy bikinis or skintight jumpsuits or animal pelts. In the period when this story unfolds, less explosive female stars were triumphing, ones that were more complicated, morbid, and ambiguous, such as Charlotte Rampling or Sylvia Kristel.

FOR THAT MATTER, pornography and the novel were born together and they spread in parallel. They are two tools that are basically similar in the way that they amplify the individual experience in a fantastic manner, by collecting a series of adventures, which could only rarely be lived in person, through fictional characters. A difference that may amount to mirror images of each other, complementary roles: while the audience for novels par excellence was feminine, pornography targeted almost exclusively men.

The most common image—and the most commonly visited image—on the web is of a woman without clothing. What can explain the fact that yesterday I spent at least an hour online searching for photos of a skinny Belgian model with big tits? Why does sexual freedom so closely resemble slavery? This story unfolds at the apex of the curve of a great change, exactly a quarter of a century before the end of the millennium, long before sexual liberation—which a number of people before us had fought for—came to resemble a form of sexual oppression, with its unprecedented prescriptions and persecutions, and the pillorying and shaming and banishments . . . How can it be that the good thing which others before us battled for should transform itself so rapidly into the evil against which we now have to battle? The more my freedom grows, the more I become a slave. Sexualization of domination. A sexualization that affects every corner and aspect of life, especially those of a commercial nature: from food and work and how little girls and brides dress to the way they sell a package vacation . . . Power is sexualized, soccer is sexualized, infancy and old age are sexualized, war is hypersexualized . . . Politics is pure pornography. And then journalism, or what remains of it, is an unbroken erotic message, a thoroughgoing eroticization with here and there, scattered throughout, the occasional fact or even a flood, a revolution, an earthquake . . . crashing airplanes . . .

And yet true sexual freedom ought to include freedom *from* sex as well. More than pedagogy, it's a full-blown dictatorship: even back then, at the time when this story unfolds, the main source and authority in the sexual education of young males was pornography. Aside from personal confidences from some older friend with more practical knowledge and fewer illusions, and specialized magazines full of specious descriptions that you had to read and reread, like assembly instructions, the basic laws of sex were crudely imparted by porn films but, especially, pulpy porn magazines. A rudimentary but effective pedagogy, useful at least in scraping away the worst forms of ignorance. It was pornography that showed us, albeit after its own fashion, that is, in a hyperbolic, inimitable manner, the things that happen between men and women, the positions in which they couple, what's underneath the clothing, how the various parts of the body are to be employed.

FOR INSTANCE, let's take the sealed supplements that came with the magazine *Due+*. I remember, from those exhausting readings, a brief chapter on a special technique of oral sex known as the "butterfly kiss" or maybe "butterfly wings": you put your face between the girl's open thighs, and then you shake your head from side to side, slowly at first and then faster and faster, and faster still, as if you were saying no a thousand times over, running the tip of your tongue as stiff as an arrow over the girl's clitoris, just barely grazing it, the way the wing of a crazed butterfly might do. There, I put it in my own words, and I'm a little ashamed to have done so, but in the magazine it was all more technical, and long-winded: they seemed like instructions for operating an electric appliance of some sort, or performing a rehabilitation exercise for deaf-mutes. If correctly performed, with the right degree of delicacy and rapidity, it was supposed to take the girl to the heights of ecstasy.

(Auxiliary sexual metaphor: like a pick on the strings of a guitar . . .)

AFTER SEX, nowadays the vast revenue and allied industries of the world of crime are far more extensive than the criminal activity itself; the exploitation extends to countless TV series and networks dedicated to the investigation of techniques of killing, a vast branch of the publishing industry, with dictionaries of crime, the biographies and confessions of murderers, and more or less novelized versions of true crime stories. There are judges who, after undertaking judicial investigations on the activities of criminal gangs, have written screenplays and articles about them for TV and the press, making their protagonists incredibly popular; murderers who tell the story of their killings in written form, in search of human understanding or fame; the incessant creation of inspectors and detectives, speaking dialect or proper Italian, with a side gig as gourmets or philosophers or lotharios, who—between fine lunches and dinners—solve the mysteries of some murder or other; the flourishing of a brand-new school of noir or detective fiction whose authors gained their knowledge about the underworld firsthand, working with it in careers previous to their rebirth as writers, and whose suspense novels, someone commented, aren't worth reading because you always know in advance who the killer is: the author. This book of mine also belongs to the genre of true crime exploitation, though at arm's length, as we'll see later on. Now more than ever, crime *pays*.

THE ABUSE AND TORTURE inflicted upon a woman can always be retailed as entertainment. The Rorschach blots of violence give reliable, unvarying answers. If you see a naked man being tortured, what comes to mind is either political persecution or a criminal vendetta. If you see a naked woman being tortured, what comes to mind is sex. If the most unspeakable taboos are violated within the context of some pornographic intent, instead of triggering indignation they will stir feelings of excitement, or else both indignation and excitement, the excitement barely concealed beneath the overlaid veil of indignation. In the prose employed by the popular press, a diction and tone are deliberately trotted out for descriptions of sex crimes that are designed to titillate the reader. That's to say nothing of TV, which has, if possible, an even more morbid relationship with its viewers, supplying them from dawn to dusk, in its various formats, ranging from news broadcasts to TV series—adjacent in style and content but often mingling and even overlapping one with another—an ongoing celebration of eroticized crime, the most powerful stimulant on earth, since it's an intertwined embodiment of the most fundamental impulses. There is nowadays only one degree of separation between a flesh-and-blood criminal and an imaginary one on TV, and often not even a single degree, since it has been clearly established that real criminals provide excellent raw material for creating fictional ones, or can even take their place entirely. The most prosperous and ubiquitous industry on earth, the flesh trade, continues to expand limitlessly until it constitutes an unbroken pornographic continuum that takes in the territories of crime reporting, given that these territories are where excitement runs most unbridled, expertly camouflaged behind the moral condemnation that we customarily reserve for true stories and events that actually occurred. In tune with the universe of sexualized fiction, a sensation of continuity propagates busily through space and time. The oil that glistens on the ass cheeks of porn actresses has been smeared over the world at large, enveloping it like a translucent patina, its tremulous reflection illuminating the still watches of the night and the daylit boredom of millions of viewers at their computers. It takes no special effort to translate real events into pornographic fantasies, and vice versa: the most objective, barebones exposition of the facts concerning sex crimes can be transformed into an erotic short story, where the same morbid features that trigger indignation and horror also serve to stir up excitement. It is by communicating in this way that imagery which is sadistic and disgusting becomes pornographic, that is, every bit as sadistic and disgusting, and yet exciting as well. Pornography in fact consists of the arousal and excitement that an object manages to deliberately trigger in a given individual, whether consciously or passively: an excitement that can be calculated in advance and calibrated according to fine-grained standards capable of predicting the effect of a certain word, or an image, and even a fragment of that image, a half-inch of flesh photographed a half-inch higher or lower than usual . . . We find it in newspaper headlines, product advertising, scenes of violence, objects arranged in a shop window, in the incessant stream of double entendres that constitutes 90 percent of all TV comedy, in locker-room humor.

And indeed on screens, which are mirrors to real life, the mirror of the desires and fears that make up our lives, all we see people doing is fucking or murdering, murdering or fucking. In detective movies, crime flicks, horror, romance, police, psychological, erotic, war, and adventure films, characters kill or have sex as if these were the two fundamental activities of human existence, the only ones worthy of being depicted. Lovers and murderers; bare-naked ladies and bullet-riddled corpses. Nothing could be more obvious than to connect the two themes and reduce them to a single act, an unbroken succession of fucking and killing, all in perfect continuity.

RAPE IS CONTIGUOUS or intertwined with other acts of violence, war, robbery, vendetta, of which it can represent the culmination, the initial purpose or else a secondary objective, after the fact, a garnish or side dish, a transfer, a variant, or even an improvised invention. If an armed robber comes up empty-handed, he can always rape the lady of the house. If he rapes her, he can always kill her. If he had planned to rape her, he can always change his mind and simply beat her senseless. Or else he can do all these things combined. Rape and plunder always go hand in hand. When there isn't much to plunder, you can just rape instead: the principle of appropriation can be applied more or less indifferently to inanimate objects and living beings. These various eventualities are like adjacent keys on a piano. The scales may already be written in the musical score or else improvised on the spur of the moment, depending on the occasion and the mood: and in any given harmonic chord, you may choose to let resonate the dominant note of rape, or mute it, keeping it as a minor chord, or even choose to leave that key unplayed entirely. As in wartime, the line of conduct will vary according to the minute-by-minute changes in the situation, with the tactics best suited to the terrain and the adversary; or else, contrarywise, the mission might be pursued in single-minded fashion: a man goes out in search of a woman to rape, and in the end, a woman will be raped. Roughly two-thirds of all rapes are planned in advance, like the one I am going to tell you about farther on in this book, a crime that developed out of the setting that I'm describing here. Far from being a crime committed under the urgent impulse of uncontrollable instincts, rape is often worked out at the drawing board, especially when it's not an individual but rather a group doing the planning, choosing a target and taking all necessary steps to ensure that one is in an advantageous position with respect to that target, thus assuring that the victim can neither fight back nor oppose resistance without risking her life. Though she may still be risking her life even when she puts up no resistance.

THE EVENT THAT GAVE rise to this book is the so-called Circeo Rape/ Murder, September 29, 1975: hereinafter the CR/M.

What can be rightly asked about the case of the CR/M is whether the murder was a continuation of the sexual violence, one further step, more or less planned out on a continuum with the abuse and torture and rape, or whether instead the rape was nothing more or less than a prelude to the murder, a preparatory phase. Before killing the girls, they wanted to have some fun with them. Or else: having raped them, they therefore decided to kill them.

THE PURPOSE OF WAR is the utter domination and defeat of the enemy, right? Which can take place in one of two ways, either through killing or appropriation. War, in other words, basically consists of a series of violent acts designed to kill the men who have been declared enemies and to possess their women, thereafter either to kill them, too, or else to let them live as slaves. Depending on your point of view, these killings and these rapes can equally justifiably be considered as means or objectives, or as incidental casualties of war itself. And even if no war is under way, the rapist still behaves just like the soldier of an invading army. He has the same mind-set, guided by thoughts of vengeance and plunder. The man whose women (wives, mothers, daughters, sisters) are raped is thus forced to admit his helplessness, his impotence, and therefore his substantial lack of manliness. Instead, that term can rightly be applied to he who can show that he is both capable of protecting his own women and ravish with impunity other men's women. If you carefully follow the twists and turns of this line of thought, you can see how many acts of violence against women are actually not directed against them at all, or not only against them, but should instead be taken as acts of outrage or defiance or contempt toward their men. It is other men that rapists want to hurt, by ricochet. The bodies of raped women are nothing more than the physical medium used to send a message to their men: a clear, brutal, mocking message. That is the reason that so often the woman's husband or father or boyfriend is immobilized and forced to witness the woman's rape: that's not an extra dose of sadistic violence, an afterthought. It is, rather, the true objective of the rape. A quintessential affirmation of supremacy. By inflicting violence on one person, you lash out at two. Virility, then, is measured by the ability both to protect women and to assault them.

THE AFFIRMATION OF MASCULINITY would seem to imply the submission of the female counterpart. So, one sex affirms itself by subjugating the other? That's a simplification of the schema whereby every living being, in order to affirm itself, must subjugate other living beings. One expresses one's own vital will only by bending the will of others. If we imagine, then, a specific essence of masculinity, it manifests itself in the dominion of femininity, but the reverse might equally be the case, that is, in its turn, the feminine element might manifest itself in all its power and its authentic nature when it is able to dominate the male principle: only, instead of availing itself of physical force, which it possesses to a lesser extent, it makes recourse to cunning, seduction, the sapping and undermining of the opposing force, by weakening it, feigning submissiveness and compliance only to gain the upper hand through duplicity. It's the typical strategy, the last-ditch resource available to those who are subordinate, the age-old school of the oppressed that teaches how to reverse the power relations, not by some spectacular act, destined to failure, but instead with a slow, invisible, and silent conquest . . .

That is why, as a counterstroke, the sword of force slices through the cloud of seduction. Like Alexander the Great, who slices the Gordian knot in half—no more dilemmas, no more complicated issues and subtleties and feints and courtships and skirmishes. Instead, an overt act. That is the ethic of virility that Fascist activism took as its emblem: a club to be wielded against the ambiguities and sophistries, a mace to be brought down on the head of those who would stall for time, raise objections, slow-walk, fend off, recoil or nitpick or play. This is how a man justifies his competitiveness: he overwhelms the woman, he is duty-bound to overwhelm her, lest he be sub-jugated by her instead. It's a preemptive move: unless the feminine element is fought to a standstill, it will ultimately enslave its male counterpart—either with sexual love or else the mechanisms of family life. The man in either case will end up in chains. In any case, to defy and master feminin-ity requires not just any ordinary individual—it takes a hero. Capable of dominating the woman and defanging her, rendering her helpless. But even a hero can sometimes lay down his arms, bowing to the unmistakable fact that the woman possesses and exercises a power greater than his, greater than all other powers, unequaled, the power of conception. Impossible to subdue that enigmatic might, that earthshaking force. The hero can com-bat femininity like any of the monsters that block his path—giants, drag-ons, dragonesses—we forget how often those superhuman creatures are female, Medusa, the Sphinx, the Hydra, Giambattista Basile's enchanted doe, Grendel's mother in *Beowulf*, the pythoness that Apollo killed, to say nothing of the Sirens and the Harpies, filthy and seductive. The hero strug-gles to master this subject, in the name of (male) spirituality in defiance of the (female) corporeal, and for that reason he must either kill or succumb, if he is to eradicate all and every material residue.

The truth is that a male is generally unwilling to tolerate feminine sex-uality in whatever form it expresses itself: every attitude displayed by a woman can cause resentment or contempt or fear in a man: whether she is rejecting the offered relationship, or giving in too easily. Chastity and erotic licentiousness are both seen as equally disagreeable and fearsome, two de-viant forms of behavior. He can't tolerate a woman being hostile to sex or being a sex maniac. But even so-called normality has a disquieting side to it. A man deplores and at the same time envies feminine sexuality in that which is supposed to be its most obvious faculty, namely maternity, even when it's regimented and legitimized within the context of matrimony: he's frightened by it, intimidated, he obscurely fears the development of some-thing that is entirely outside his control. Certainly, as a father he'll be able to enjoy his children and feel pride in them: but he will still in a certain sense have to adopt them, even if they really are his own offspring, he'll somehow have to *make* them his.

Thus, whatever form feminine sexuality may take is bound to hurt a man, attracting him at the same time that it irritates him, frightening him and subjugating him, or driving him mad. He is either abjectly dismayed or driven into a furious rage by any woman who denies her own femininity by declining to have relations with him, and has the same reaction to the woman who, at the opposite extreme, gives in promiscuously to anyone who asks, and last of all, to the woman who behaves in a perfectly ordinary fashion, in the innocuous context of monogamy, who by the simple contingency of becoming pregnant chains the man to his fatherly responsibilities and duties. This places a ball and chain around his ankle for good. In this sense, marriage can be even more deadly than chastity, promiscuity, and prostitution. Needless to say, men traditionally perceive the family as a feminine invention and demand. An enterprise that immediately proves to be exhausting and expensive to run. Whether she is a church lady, a young woman of loose morals, or the mother of a family, a man is invariably troubled by the sexual faculties of any given woman, which constitute a challenge to him, a provocation: the woman must be defeated, or protected, saved, or held at arm's length, but in any case she cannot be trusted, her lures and wiles must be outwitted, he must not be taken prisoner by her maneuvers, and he must gird himself against her menace. But what can there be about a woman that is so terribly threatening? The overabundance of life implicit in her nature. Life, a dangerous matter. If the poet writes that April is the cruelest month, he means that this vital overexuberance is a threat and a source of suffering. It never leaves the man in peace, it is bound to torment him. Against this uncontrollable exuberance of the feminine element, a man wages an ascetic battle.

Even if they will never confess to it, males experience an atavistic fear of sex, of contact with the opposite sex; the original terror that they have of sex is at least equal to their curiosity and desire. The fear and trembling and recoil of the virgin in the presence of the erect phallus is, after all, much easier to explain than the male hesitation and reluctance to venture into a woman, literally, to go inside her. What awaits a man at the end of this journey of initiation? Is it really advisable to undertake it? Perhaps what they fear most of all is their own pliability, that is, the possibility that they might abandon themselves to the influence of the feminine element, which has come to unsettle their already intrinsically precarious equilibrium. And so they must behave in a far more hostile fashion toward women than they actually feel like doing: this performance of hostility is meant for other males lest they feel betrayed by any male who might devote too much attention to women and too little toward his pal. That is why any male who gets engaged and breaks away from a group of friends and isolates himself in the dreamscape of love is so often looked down upon and considered lost, someone who—poor fellow—has really gone around the bend. He instantly becomes the target of wisecracks inspired by pity and envy.

It is unlikely that, in one form or another, in reality or on the symbolic plane, a man, even an independent and vigorous man, will fail to bow down before the inexplicable power that a woman exercises over him. However much he may manifest his strength and claim his independence, a slender but strong chain will bind him at last, and what is even more unpredictable, almost always with his tacit consent, producing in him a curious sobbing happiness. He luxuriates in the dominion established over him: which suggests that happiness in its purest state consists of this, an abandonment, giving oneself up to something mysterious, portentous, and yet which can be perceived at the same time as natural. No longer recalcitrant, therefore . . . Abandoning oneself, surrendering. It is thought that women do this, by their nature or in the face of persistent courtship, the pressure of a man's advances, the pulsation of male desire, capable of sweeping away any and all obstacles in the blind stampede toward fulfillment. I believe, in contrast, that there is nothing that can be compared with the almost infantile relief of feeling that one has been defeated, expropriated of a strength that it costs nothing to lose because, in reality, one never really possessed it in the first place, nothing could ever be as authentic and sweet as a man's abandonment of himself onto the bosom of what he feels existed before, after, and in spite of him: the feminine element. "That blessed sensation verging practically on stupidity," Turgenev calls it; he was one of its most intimate and precise narrators. Something like a cause of which we are merely the effect. To which we can look back with gratitude, like all the times in which we experience the feeling of truly being in the presence of a *principle*, an absolute principle, past which we cannot track back, an originating matrix: in the presence of ancient monuments, hearing a forgotten language being spoken, yielding to sleep, floating in the ocean, acknowledging the death of a beloved person or an animal that we have lived with and held dear.

Yes, something desirable. To feel oneself to be in the throes, dispossessed, pure instruments of someone else's will and pleasure is at once the most sinister of sensations yet also a fundamental element of the amorous experience, without which there can be no opening, no relation, no knowledge. Every passion arises from a kidnapping, it is itself a kidnapping, that is, the loss of actual mastery over oneself, one's body, one's identity, which will be turned inside out like a glove, subjected to exalting and mortifying ordeals, and then abandoned like some useless burden. Passion consists of abolishing all rights, all guarantees, all the laboriously conquered insignia of individuality, once considered inalienable: ideas, sentiments, convictions, property, physical and moral integrity, even one's name, the last surviving residue of personal definition, will be set aside in that rush of passion, to be replaced by embarrassing and generic pet names, childish or grotesque, and obscene. Anyone who proudly cares about his own name must steer clear of these passions and their undermining infection.

And yet our envy of the feminine remains very powerful, and there is no way to remedy it. The only thing you can do is avail yourself of a brutal piece of compensation. It's a law we've glimpsed before: when the angel of God takes the soul, then the devil will declare himself master of the body. Since it is always a woman who is at the source, a man out of spite will usurp the right to put an end, thus placing himself at the far extremity of life, where the ancients nonetheless imagined that female deities stood watch. The reasoning is simple: if I can't go down in history for having built the Colosseum, then I'll go down in history for having destroyed it. If I can't give someone life, then my only option is to take it from someone else.

IN REALITY, the universe is asymmetrical; everything is asymmetrical, un-balanced; the most deceptive symbol, the Taoist symbol of the perfect equi-librium between yin and yang, between light and dark . . . give me a break! Everything in life, life the way it really is, is asymmetry and unbalance, crushing forces that are never, let me repeat, never equal to one another. Equilibrium, suspension—they last for an instant . . . then an implacable gravitational force makes it all teeter and fall in one direction. When people nowadays talk about armed conflict and use the term "asymmetric war-fare," I have to choke back my laughter: Why? Are you saying that there was ever such a thing as balanced, symmetrical warfare? When it's always been three against one, ten against one, David against Goliath! Always! In all the great and legendary battles I've ever read accounts of, one side of the forces in the field was always outnumbered. Now, that doesn't necessarily mean that the side with the most troops always won, of course, but it means then that the asymmetry was attained in other domains, in armaments, in the perspicacity or the cowardice of the generals, in the way the soldiers were nourished . . . or how many days it had been since they'd eaten on the day of the battle. Not even Chip 'n' Dale are symmetrical, not even Castor and Pollux, or twins in general: there's always one who leads, one who commands.

THE THING THAT THE MALE WORLD most fears, at first glance, is dependency. That is because pure masculinity ought to consist in that quality's diametric opposite, that is, autonomy, fierce independence: to have and preserve jealously within oneself one's beginning and one's end. In contrast, a woman seeks those things elsewhere, in the Other: in her encounter with a man, but even more, with her children, which are a significant shift of the center of gravity of one's life outside oneself. This schema corresponds to the idea that the ascetic impulse is typically male while sexuality, understood as the regime of desire and dependency and procreation, is a feminine characteristic. This line of reasoning, then, concludes with an inference: if a man so frequently abandons his ascetic path, the only path that could keep his masculinity safe from the mortal threat of dependency, it happens because he has been drawn into the maelstrom of sexuality, feminine in nature. He therefore plummets into amorous and family-oriented sexual dependency, thus abdicating the very principle of masculinity. By abandoning himself to the arms of a woman, he will be lost . . . happy, satisfied, contented, but lost.

(There is no other explanation of the celibacy of Catholic priests.)

And so the man seeks retribution for this loss, a certain compensation: if I'm going to have to fall, and lose my dignity and even my male identity in this fall, then she who's dragging me down with her will have to pay dearly for that of which she might boast, namely, the fact that she has stolen my independence, left me chained, bound to the stake, sucked me dry of all strength. Once enslaved, I can no longer regain my liberty and control over my own life, but I will at least do my best to destroy the one I consider guilty for what happened to me. If Samson must die, etc., but the ones dying with him won't be the Philistines, rather it will be that woman who was capable of making me as weak as a woman. A part of the hostility that the man brings with him into intercourse, in some cases exasperated to the point of cruelty, is due to this complex of the fall. A complex that does not seem to expect to reinforce a domination; quite the contrary, it takes on the connotations of revenge exacted by someone who feels that *he* has been dominated. (But this vision of feminine domination exercised through passivity remains very mysterious . . .)

Not long ago, I finished writing this tirade and then went to the beach for a dip in the water. It's late September and the weather is uncertain, but between one cloud and another the sun shines warm. The beach was deserted, except for five young Germans, who had camped behind the dune. Farther down the beach, I laid out my own towel. The young men were hulking and unsightly, relaxed, wearing multicolored swim shorts that hung down below their knees. Just a couple of yards from the water's edge they had built an enormous sandcastle, which was still wet. If you looked closely, it wasn't as much a castle as it was a fortress, a bunker, squared off, massive, with turrets at the corners and high enclosure walls. For no special reason, except that it, too, had been built by Germans, I was reminded of Spandau Prison. Spandau, in Berlin, where Rudolf Hess had been held prisoner, the Nazi with the small eyes and the massive jaws. The biggest of the group of young men, a true lardball, strolled with a bored step down toward the water, loitered lazily around the walls of the sand prison, extended a foot toward the tip of one of the turrets, and let it hover just above its conical roof, fanning all five toes. He seemed to be meditating on an important decision. Then he lowered his foot and the rest of his substantial bulk onto the sand tower, crushing it. Again, he grew meditative. He began performing a series of strange pirouettes, spinning around in place. Then he moved on to the next turret, and I expected him to do the same work of careful demolition with that one, but this time he threw all caution to the winds and jumped into the fortress with both feet, excavating a large hole where he landed. Once inside the walls, he looked back at his friends, laughed, and began a sort of frantic dance. He jumped and kicked, and his pale fat rings bounced above his waistline, while the walls of sand collapsed one after another. But the fortress was so large and solid that it would take some time for him to raze the whole structure: they'd built it painstakingly, using hundreds of pounds of wet sand. And so his friends came running to his aid, and in short order there were five German teenagers leaping like lunatics, without a word, on their own project of beach engineering, leveling it to the ground. They were expressing every sign of happiness. I watched them for a while and then, lost in thought, I went to dive into the water. I swam out far from shore. From where I was, I could see them still hard at work on the ruins of their sandcastle . . .

Then when I got back home, I started writing again. What did I write? The following chapter.

6

T HE PROMISCUOUS WOMAN seduces the man because she is promiscuous, the shy and modest woman because she is shy and modest. Whichever angle you want to look at it from, the outcome remains the same, so that one begins to suspect that the man is attracted quite independent of whatever a woman may or may not do, may or may not be, much like the moth with the lantern. All that is required is for the lantern to be lit, for the woman to be alive. Philosophers who tend to explain all behavior in an antiphrastic manner, glimpsing in it some hidden wisdom of nature, an instance of cunning or some biological trick, maintain that feminine modesty is by no means designed to drive men away, but rather to excite them. Woman's show of reserve, then, has little if anything to do with purity and chastity, seeing that it only serves to kindle the flames of masculine desire, to select among her suitors those who are better equipped with the energy necessary to overcome the obstacle of that reserve. Which is thus not a shield but a magnet. It seems to protect and repel, while it actually seduces. Once explained in these terms, the feminine unwillingness to engage in coitus can be read in reverse, that is, as an invitation, however cunningly masked, camouflaged as its opposite, as a way of seeing how the man will react, whether he will be discouraged in the face of that no, which has actually been set out there only to test his capacity to vault over it. The hypothesis that the no actually does mean quite simply and definitively that "no" can be taken into consideration only in hindsight, or else ignored entirely. Erased. A woman who says no without at least some tiny part of her twisting and writhing in the desire to say yes is quite inconceivable. With women, you only need to *insist*. It is the level of persistence, the kind of pressure, and the spiritual or physical surface upon which that persistence is applied that makes every case different from another, in successive gradations, or nuances, which range from obstinate courtship to molestation and onto rape, all of them unified by the idea that the reluctance is strictly ritual and need only be won over, or at least that one ought to give it a try, and see if you can win it over. Otherwise, you'll never know how it might have turned out. I don't have the certainty that this point of view is entirely false. Indeed, you can't say it's untrue in any other walk of life where you *truly* desire to obtain something—satisfaction, recognition, money, justice, success, even love, yes, even for love this is the way it works: insistence is capable of knocking down any barrier, reversing any initial position and declaration. The path that leads from a no to a yes can be crooked and uneven but that doesn't mean that that path doesn't exist or that it is, in and of itself, immoral to try to travel it. I see no reason why, out of all the various human pursuits, sex and sex alone ought to prove an exception to the logic of negotiation. How did a man win a woman's favors (such a delightful vintage expression, which I intentionally choose to use here)? By the use of seduction, persuasion, gifts, payment (a noneuphemistic variant of the gift), by means of marriage, by means of coercion. Even after the revolution in sexual customs, those same methods remain valid, perhaps in a less overt form or under some different name. People struggle to keep the path of abuse wide open: if the coercion exercised through arranged marriages is abolished, then the same impulse will take the form of rape.

IN EFFECT, passivity and inactivity do have their advantages. Those who remain immobile, those who can afford to maintain their immobility, are sovereign; while those who instead are forced to bestir themselves to work are subjugated. While they may give the impression of great vigor because they take the initiative and guide activities, in truth they are slaves to those activities, that is, servants of the purpose that they've set themselves. Male erotic entrepreneurship resembles the duties of a mere workman, executing the plans of others, obliged to struggle to hit the target, neurotic and as stressed out as any salesman who has to bring home that contract, make that sale, at all costs. It is therefore fair to say that the well-known proverb that, in love, he wins who flees is largely inaccurate: in love, in reality, he wins *who does nothing*. Or who does as little as possible. The desired one, not the desiring one, who is entirely taken up in the vortex of his initiatives. He's no different, in the end, than a delivery boy who takes on a vast number of packages. The only ones to benefit, in the end, are his lazy female customers. He hurries from place to place, he exhausts himself, he scurries in and out of imperially immobile pussies, which in the end—according to the notorious verdict of Tiresias, the only one capable of judging from both points of view—take nine-tenths of the pleasure to be harvested from all that effort and energy.

The struggle between the rich and the poor, between old and young, men and women: these battles have been waged for millennia, and the last named is perhaps the least spectacular, but it's also perhaps the oldest one. While other wars experience moments of truce or stagnation, this war does not, unless we are to consider love as a sort of armistice or interlude of peace, which is quite absurd if you remember that what is causing the conflict is precisely the reciprocal attraction and need, and in the twists and turns of love that conflict can attain high points of the maximum virulence. (Let's say that, in love, the war between the sexes experiences its greatest epic splendor and, however it may turn out, creates episodes of heartbreaking beauty.) If men and women could live and ignore each other, then not the slightest violence would be unleashed between them, and it is highly unlikely that men would ever have decided to subject women to slavery exclusively for their own convenience, something that happens only in the aftermath of sex, as a secondary, albeit stubborn, effect of the fatal attraction that binds men to women.

Most important of all, while the poor and the rich run into each other much more rarely, almost only by accident, and lead separate lives, since wealth is, by definition, nothing other than the very possibility of enforcing that distinction, that separation, which keeps the poor out of the enclosures surrounding the guarded mansions, armor-plated cars, residential gated communities, deserted beaches, "exclusive" lounges and clubs and restaurants (the term itself designates a regime of segregation), and while old men and young men generally don't want to have anything to do with each other, men and women in contrast meet and clash and mingle and couple constantly and ubiquitously. The way they incessantly rub up against each other produces an imperceptible music like that of the celestial spheres, which spin one within the other. If only we could hear the sound of this constant friction, it would be a roar loud enough to shake the earth! Naïve to think that it is copulation that will put an end to all conflict, which instead takes on different forms, it is so to speak fixed and sublimated, regulated and rendered endemic, whereas it is within that copulation that the clashes take place, the harshest battles. Copulation can actually render the conflict permanent, perpetuating it at a level of low intensity. In those cases the dose of torment to be inflicted reciprocally is maintained just a millimeter beneath flash point, the level of explosion, where it would be lethal, and it serves to cement together the members of the couple with the adhesive of a bland but durable sadomasochism.

In some cases, rare but not exceedingly so, and very significant, sexual intercourse takes on the pure form of the clash, brief and violent: and this is rape. But there is no bright line distinguishing between the various forms of contact between the sexes: each one has much in common with all the others, each leads in a few moves to its opposite, from the gentlest to the most brutal.

"AND RAPE FOR HER is like a gift."

IN TRUTH, only love, when it doesn't exacerbate it, can obviate the primordial hostility between the sexes. Love offers at the same time the best opportunity for clash and identification, conflict and attraction. People often wind up getting married in order to stop fighting, or in order to go on doing so under the auspices of an institution that regulates conflicts and fixes them in conventional forms, which wind up going straight into the repertory of jokes about married life.

(One of the most implacable forms of these jokes is the one about the monk and the nun who, for reasons there is no need to go into, and which form the basis of any joke, find themselves obliged to spend the night in the same bed. Good night, good night, they say to each other, and they turn their backs on each other. But the nun gets cold, and so the monk gets up to fetch her a blanket, he drapes it over her. After another little while, the nun complains again: "Brother, I'm freezing . . ." and he gets up to bring her another blanket. But she still can't get warm, "I'm cold, I'm still so cold," and he very kindly brings her yet another blanket. The nun won't give up, and this time she offers another suggestion, "Brother, I'm still so terribly cold in this bed . . . what do you say, why don't we act like husband and wife?" Whereupon he replies: "Ah, you want to act like husband and wife? In that case, go get your own damn blankets!")

AT SCHOOL, studying ancient Greek was challenging and dull, and I never learned it well, but luckily there was always the mythology. I'd developed a passionate love for it ever since I was a child. That is why I cite it so frequently, and its teachings are the only ones I believe. Among the Greek gods, the most virile personage is unquestionably Athena, followed closely by Artemis. At a considerable remove comes Ares, who nonetheless represents only the death-dealing aspect of the male character, then Zeus, who may appear very macho with all his amorous adventures and lovers, whereas in truth he is very much compromised by the feminine side of things, going so far as to reproduce it, to include it in himself: for that matter, if his power must be free to deploy itself in all directions, then it stands to reason that it cannot be limited and constrained by the boundaries of a sexual identity, which is why Zeus actually gets pregnant. And he gives birth to Athena, who issues from his brain, and Dionysus, born of his thigh, just to show that he is capable even of that: bringing a pregnancy to term. His energy is so overabundant that it can reproduce or incorporate within him feminine virtues. A male who is far more typical in his fashion is Hephaestus, whose virility is constantly being excited and frustrated: by his unhappy sham marriage with Aphrodite, the farcical struggle to possess the armed virgin Athena, which ends with a spurt of sperm in the dust. A cuckold and an onanist, Hephaestus is the emblem not of how males ought to be, that is, valiant warriors, irresistible seducers, unquestioned family authority, etc., but rather how they actually are. Desperately in need of a crumb of sensual tenderness, not only a cripple in his legs but also in his ability to love and be loved, the poor man takes it all out in his work, forging with mighty mallet blows thunderbolts not his, those symbols of power, too, having been expropriated from him, rejected by his mother, mocked by his father, abandoned on a nightly basis by his wife, and with a monster brat for a son, born with a serpent's tail out of his father's grotesque, inept act of pollution . . .

On the feminine side, immediately after Aphrodite comes Dionysus, dancing, with hair and rounded hips like a young girl. Here, too, we are dealing with a power that can't be confined sexually, in contrast with Apollo, the god of clear separation, who in fact suffers and inflicts suffering with the cutting, painful clarity of his initiatives. Dionysus is liquid like a beverage, he slithers like a snake, he steeps the virtuous adherents of the authoritarian, that is, male principle, with himself and his folly. When the pirates who had kidnapped him as a boy decide to fuck him, everything aboard their ship suddenly turns twisted, serpentine, soft and swaying, the shrouds become liana vines and field bindweed, and the oars turn to snakes . . .

Then there's Demeter, perfectly symmetrical to Ares in giving shape to one and only one of the aspects that characterize their sex. Both of them accentuate the difference between masculine and feminine to the point of exasperation: every bit as much as Ares is obtusely violent, so does Demeter play the mother in an exclusive and possessive manner, the Great Mother, the uterus ready to welcome to swell to germinate, the generous and

disconsolate mother, the fecund and afflicted matrix . . . By no means interested in any other games, she has nothing in mind but her destiny of becoming pregnant, only to be deprived of her fruit. If young Ares plays with
his weapons, in ferocious and solitary manner, Demeter from when she was
a young girl rocks a cradle. They both have an autistic tendency and are
possessed by a fixation: the one with procreation, the other with destruction.

Hey, are you still listening to me?
Do you still want me to continue?
Then I'll go on for a little longer.

THIS STORY TAKES PLACE during a time when women, nearly all women,
became in a very short time, a matter of a few years, far more available to
men, ten times more available, and as a result, ten times more threatening.
The new erotic freedom, coming hand in hand with other forms of emancipation and therefore amplifying them, seemed at first to enhance their
influence. In every historical period, from the Greece of Socrates to the
chivalrous Middle Ages to the court of Louis XV, sex has had this effect—of
sending a chill down the back, sharpening awareness to the verge of the
painful, throwing open new fronts upon which, in good time, science, ethics, philosophy, and politics would eventually battle. You might say that
sex has to do with individuals' private lives, their bedrooms alone, but in fact
it shakes society as a whole from top to bottom, reshaping it into new entities, repositioning all values, reformulating all relationships. Erotic relations
between man and woman, man and man, woman and woman, are what
cause movement in both individual and collective lives, the reason wars are
fought and peace is established, the foundation of intelligence, the cause and
at the same time the objective of every enterprise, the key to unlock mysteries
and the hidden significance of any clue . . . Sexual relations occupy the young
man's mind and, obsessively, the old man's mind, too, if not as desire, then
as dream, memory, regret, and they permeate the thoughts of the chaste
every bit as much as the licentious. Sexual passion is the very origin of the
personality and the way that that personality can draw upon itself.

Men back then felt that they still had to pay for this easier access to intercourse, pay for it not with cash, but with the coin of an anxiety never
hitherto experienced. An anxiety caused when they found themselves
face-to-face with an unknown feminine power, unleashed by new sexual

customs and by the pill, a contraceptive that made them virtually unstoppable. For men, in other words, fucking continued to have a cost, though an undeclared one, less easily identified than in a former time, and therefore not as easy to pay, or perhaps we should say, to pay off. How? How much? To whom? Feminine availability, at first celebrated as a form of liberation or, more cynically, as a feast of plenty for the males, who dove in headfirst, in time began to reveal its more unsettling aspects, once the early pioneering stage was a thing of the past. Everything that has no clear limitations, no obvious stopping point, is disquieting. As it had done a century earlier, a specter was haunting the West, festively menacing. It lent itself famously to frightening the bigots and church ladies, it was ideal for mocking them, but this irreverent use was a trifle when compared with the genuine subversion that it brought in its wake: this was something that shook the branches of the Tree of the Knowledge of Good and Evil, making all the fruit tumble to the ground.

1

THE DESIRES, incompatible with reality, that drive a young boy or an adolescent are destined to wane, and it's a tormented decline. Sex life at that age can be considered intensely pure, immaculate, practically crystalline, or to the contrary, exceedingly impure, since it consists solely of dreams and desires, and almost never of actual experience. Now, which is more perverse: a dream or reality?

Like many other boys, but I believe with an acuity that was out of the ordinary, that sunset in me was accompanied by an immense, inexplicable suffering. And this suffering, this monstrous uneasiness, never ceased, continuously changed shape and intensity, and from the moment that it became possible to satisfy at least a part of those boundless if vague fantasies that shot through me like meteors day and night, instead of improving the situation it only worsened it, the frustration at not being able to satisfy all the other fantasies swelled disproportionately, becoming a thorn in my side, an obsession, a genuine well of unhappiness. Unhappiness about what? Because of what? I could say that up until now I had enjoyed a full and fortunate life, and in fact I do say so, comparatively speaking, at least.

So what am I wasting your time complaining about? Nothing. What's the problem? There is none. I'm not complaining, I *am* a complaint. I suffer every single instant that I'm not being touched, that I can't hug, clutch, caress, that I can't penetrate: therefore, a very considerable part of the time I'm alive. My hunger is never placated. Forget about good breast and bad breast! All breasts are mean to me, the ones that are denied me but also those that are conceded to me, that I clutch, caress, and suck, because they are never conceded to me sufficiently, I'd like to squeeze them and suck them *uninterruptedly*. The good breast isn't good, because, as I already know, as I know in advance (and this is why I hate it), it will soon turn bad, it will be denied to me.

It is happiness, it is fulfillment itself, touched ever so briefly, that engenders unhappiness. It gives us some sense of the yawning gap that separates the possibilities of life from ordinary life as we know it. It seems clear to me that someone who had never experienced any satisfaction of their desires would be far less unhappy as a rule, someone who had always been denied access to breasts; his unhappiness would be clear, unsullied, crystalline, not stained here and there by patches of pleasure that make it not only unbearable, but also obscene, filthy, indecorous, and even ridiculous, that's right, ridiculous, because if someone stands there constantly whining for them to give back his toy, the toy that they took from him, his yo-yo, the soft, swelling bosom, the illusory and boundless sweetness until just an instant before the stimulus, the frenzy begins again. I'm such a frenzied individual that when I was a child I was forced to learn the harsh law of the postponement of pleasure, by dint of necessity, at school, at home, I understood and digested that cruel lesson, but then I forgot it, I'm afraid so, it may sound incredible but as I grew older, I forgot it, and at age eighteen there I was again, whining and stamping my feet, at age twenty-five, let's not even mention it, and at forty and fifty even worse, things continue to deteriorate with the passing of the years. The further into the past my childhood recedes and the more I'm choked with rage and self-pity, if they don't immediately give me back my yo-yo, then I turn red in the face and I suffocate with rage and sorrow, if they don't find the breasts and bring them back to me. I lived on these rewards and these offers, which I believe to be undeserved, and which always come unexpectedly, but unless they arrive promptly, every time that I feel the need for them (which is to say, *always*), every day and every minute of my life, I am filled with fury and tears. Mine is not a narcissistic wound, as books describe these things: it's a veritable sinkhole. A cleavage that splits me in two from head to foot, like those characters in Dante, or Italo Calvino's famous cloven viscount, though with a significant difference: that in the book by Calvino, the cleavage split Medardo of Terralba into two distinct and opposite parts, one good and the other wicked, while the two halves into which I am split both love, lust after, want, suffer, and contend for the same things: food, beauty, respect, sex, oblivion, thrills, intelligence, abandonment, and rest, but it's only one of the halves that manages to gather a few scraps, while the other half goes hungry. So there's always a part of me that suffers, abandoned to itself, while the other half has a high old time: the part that suffers is the part that foresees the instant in which the enjoyment will come to an end, and it despairs at the thought. The blade of narcissism splits me into two equal parts that look at each other in the mirror and admire themselves, pity themselves, detest themselves, and feel contempt for their helplessness.

In spite of the fact that I spent countless hours studying and striving to practice the highest forms of human wisdom, and although it was well within reach of my spiritual means, the frenzy by no means diminished over time, all that subsided eventually was the energy with which that frenzy expresses itself, in fainter but for that very reason more piercing forms: in other words, I'm now an older, but no means a wiser man. And what with the insistent determination of their stubborn persistence, these frenzied and limitless desires, uncensorable, which eventually dwindled to one and one alone, the desire to be loved, yes, to be loved whatever that expression may mean, and whatever nuance or shape that desire may assume and in whatever gesture it may present itself, the infinite extension of the same state and still of the same reaction to that state (as I was saying, a mixture of anger, self-pity, languor, passivity, pride, and even brutality, something in the depths of which I was able to glimpse how the feminine traits and the virile aspects of the human character, more than intertwining, *coincided*, became one, possessing in reality a single identity, which showed me once and for all that men and women possess the same identical nature—that they want and desire and fear the same things, or else different things but in the same exact way, that they are constituted, that is, by a single desiring element . . . and that there cannot exist a desire more hysterical and irritable than the lust for arms instead of for clothing and jewelry, which seriously means that Achilles is in no way different from Deidamia, he lunges at the swords and axes with the same frenzy that the princess and her sisters experience as they grab and snatch at pearls and silks—what changes if the object is different but the excitement is the same?), and what with the repeating and repeating the same illusion and disappointment, like a moth continually bumping against a lantern whose light attracts it, banging into the glass, finding the strength to beat its wings only to slam up against the glass again, each time feeling the same disappointment and yet unable to register that stubborn fact, or else inventing the monstrous formula whereby that foolish slamming against glass actually becomes pleasurable in and of itself, that's right, pleasurable, and in the end that is the objective, after all, the object of the desire has simply changed, and it has become the pursuit of pain and hurt, as painful as possible, by slamming against that hard barrier. It hardly even matters anymore that there is a light behind the glass, the moth can't even see that light now, all that matters is the pane of glass against which it bangs its head, the pain growing ever greater, the noise growing louder, scattering the colorful dust from the wings as they frantically beat. I've grown fond of this repetition, as one grows fond of anything that has accompanied a person for a long time, even if it's negative, so in the end I've developed a bond, since by now I've become that thing, that crazed moth. And here I am, then, happily unhappy, satisfied in my dissatisfaction. As long as I haven't thrown myself out a window, it means that things have been going smoothly, life goes on, where I couldn't say, and yet it's gone on until, in fact, it reaches that sill and that wide-open window. Only the window is a guarantee. In terms of comprehension, the real problem is that, by repeating and repeating, I still haven't understood a jot more than I'd already understood at age eighteen. The endless recapitulation of the same schema protected me, I curled up inside it. And even now, I don't want to know about anything else. I know that I suffer and that no one can understand me, including those who understand me, no one loves me, including those who love me, in fact, I hate them all the more, I'm furious at them, since, considering that they love me, well, in that case, they ought to love me *more*, much much more than they do, they shouldn't stop loving me for so much as an instant, thinking about me and dedicating themselves wholeheartedly to me. But instead what do they do? At a certain point, they just *stop*. They turn elsewhere. They think of other things, they love other people. And the cloud of suffering envelops me. Nothing exists but that dark, clammy fog that pricks me, that pierces me.

My words are nothing but an ongoing lament, I know that, but it's what I feel, what I think, even in this exact moment as I write I'm feeling and thinking this and nothing other than this, you might not believe it but I have a heart swollen with bitterness and self-pity, for no good reason. It's a beautiful day out, full of sunshine and wind, I acknowledge the wonderful things that have happened to me, the unforgettable places I have visited, the extraordinary people I have met and come to know, whose works I have read and listened to and admired, the fantastic individuals I have had beside me or whom I've even helped to engender with my semen, and yet even to this book I only want to confide the desire to climb up and over that windowsill. All fine things conspire against my mood, by showing me, pointing out to me, that which, if I ever had it, I have nonetheless lost. I have lost it precisely because I have had it. Fulfillment, contentment, are unbearable terms of comparison, their blinding radiance kills. I feel perennially exiled from that fulfillment, that complete happiness, in the instants in which I have enjoyed it (not few in number, truth be told, but fleeting, as frequent as they have been ephemeral) it was not possible for me to enjoy it in full. When one ought to enjoy, one cannot, one enjoys only *afterward*, in a subsequent moment, which might even arrive quite soon, but only after the fullness of the enjoyment has ended, one then enjoys thinking and remembering just how much one has enjoyed and regretting that one can no longer enjoy in that manner. Those who take pleasure, in the instant of that pleasure, feel nothing, since pleasure is only retrospective, and it is precisely that, the sign that you are taking pleasure: the fact that you feel nothing. Pleasure will lie in the interpretation, the regret, the abandonment, it is there that it establishes and finds its measure, and therefore it inevitably contains within itself displeasure, without which it would not know how to value itself, appreciate itself.

That's what every novel always is: the narration of an unhappiness. Even when the author joyfully lays claim to the fullness, the exuberance of life, or proclaims its aridity, invariably and in every case he is narrating his unhappiness about something that went away after being there, or else something that he awaited in vain, or that passed close by, very close, even too close, such as love, for Uncle Vanya, or glory, for Bolkonsky, but they didn't move fast enough to seize it. I, for example—I partly remember the time in which this story unfolds, I partly studied it or heard other people talk about it, I dream of it a great deal, to an even greater extent I invent it depending on what the story requires: it's a snake in the grass that you glimpse for a fleeting instant, and there is more of a sensation of having seen it, relived it in a shiver that runs down my spine, than a clear sighting of it before my eyes.

ARBUS HAD TAUGHT ME not to trust: it's not much, as lessons go, but at least it's clear. Certainly, it's not especially inspiring: you'd prefer to receive a lesson that runs along the lines of "This is," rather than "This might not be," or "It's not the way you think it is."

And the first people you'd better not trust, according to Arbus, are precisely the masters, the authority figures, the grown-ups, the teachers, the ones who are supposed to know. The ones who are supposed to know, don't: they think they know things they don't, they don't know that they don't know, so they presume. Their authority is based on nothing. On this point, Arbus was categorical: I never once saw him take a statement at face value, whether it was written in a book, or spoken by a teacher, much less the stories that circulated among us students in such legendary forms that they should certainly be taken with a large grain of salt just on principle alone. The funny thing is that Arbus had nothing to hold up against the truths propounded by our teachers, in fact, even more than mistrusting them, he said, we'd be well advised not to trust ourselves. Let's take the unhappiness I was talking about earlier: well, Arbus didn't seem to be touched by it even in the slightest. I never saw him, even once, sad and concerned, I never heard him complain: and yet he'd have had good reason, certainly more than I ever did. He'd never had a father; his mother seemed to be much happier to have, say, his friends at their home (for instance, me) than her own son, taking every opportunity to mock him, practically humiliate him, for his awkward physical appearance, because he dressed badly, because he was shy, because he didn't understand any part of what was important or pleasurable in life: and in effect, Arbus, even leaving aside the acne that tormented him, was homely, poorly dressed, seldom washed (especially his hair), and didn't seem to be liked by anyone, or almost anyone, nor did he make any effort to be liked. I often wondered whether the friendship that I endowed upon him was a product of the confidence it gave me to know that I was handsomer and luckier than him, even if I wasn't as smart. Arbus was more intelligent than me and all the others, no doubt about it, and not by a small margin, but by leaps and bounds; in every other aspect, however, I was a genuine Prince Charming in comparison with him, and it may be that I bonded with him as a gracious princely concession. Or else that extraordinary intelligence of his really did exert a power over me, it was the magnet that drew toward him all other emotions, interests, predilections, even a singular physical attraction. That's right, Arbus, so gangly, oily, and bony, attracted me physically. Not enough to want to hug him (something I doubt I did even once in my whole life) but enough to leave me in a rapt state of enchantment, gazing at him, especially at school, admiring his profile, and the gleaming black shocks of hair that dangled from his temples down to the corners of his mouth. This was his study posture, while he read or wrote. He wrote slowly, never lifting the tip of his pen from the sheet of paper, because he used a special unbroken style of handwriting, which he had invented himself.

At school, when in-class exercises were assigned, at the end of several minutes of concentration, during which his eyes remained half-shut behind the thick, dirty lenses of his glasses, he would suddenly start writing and he wouldn't raise his head or his pen from the sheet of legal paper until he had completed the translation or the series of problems in mathematics or physics. He never seemed pleased or dissatisfied, much less worried, as if those exercises that mattered so much to everyone else meant nothing to him. And in fact, his grades weren't always excellent.

CONSIDERING HOW INTELLIGENT HE WAS, it's strange that he never got a higher grade than a six—what Americans would call a D—in Italian literature. Barely a passing grade, and sometimes not even that. Class essays irritated him. "What you wrote is accurate but devoid of thought," Signor Cosmo would tell him, handing him back his classroom assignment, untouched since it had been turned in. Not a mark, not a correction. What Arbus lacked was the reason and the incentive to write.

ONE OF THE VERY FEW TIMES he ever vented to me, he did so using more or less the following words:

"I don't like Italian class. What kind of subject is that supposed to be, Italian? To speak and write in your own language, and then what? Essays. Actually, what is it I'm supposed to say? And who am I saying it to? And does Cosmo seriously care what I think? What twenty-eight adolescent kids think about Paolo and Francesca in the *Inferno*? I have no desire to talk about love with Cosmo. At least in mathematics or physics, there are rules, whether or not you understand them, whether or not you apply them, and the result of an equation or a problem, in the end, will be right or it will be wrong. There's no middle ground. Here, instead . . . What does it mean to say that an essay is *nice*? Why do people say that one poem is beautiful and another isn't? There's no one on earth who can prove it, I mean to say, actually prove it, and it's pointless to grasp at straws, the way Cosmo does when he's run short on chatter, it's useless to latch on to that whole rigama-role of meter, accents, and rhyme . . . I could sit down and write a hundred poems, with meter and everything. A hundred poems, one worse than the last. And then this idea that you're supposed to express yourself, your opin-ions, your emotions . . . talk about things *in your own way* . . . give a *personal* interpretation . . . How can I help it if I don't have any personal interpre-tation of anything? If Catullus or Petrarch feel lonely, well, I'm sorry for them . . . best of luck . . . it's not as if I don't understand them, I get it, they feel solitary and sad, but what am I supposed to add to it all? I might even like literature, if they'd just stop asking me my opinion about everything. My comment. Certain pieces, well, I can see that they're written well, but when it all comes down to it?"

ARBUS NEVER COMPLAINED. He accepted it all with a faint smile that might just as easily have been calm and serene or scornful or even conceal-ing who knows what devilry. Maybe all he meant to convey is that he didn't care at all about grades, school, priests, or us, his classmates. In that case, what *did* he care about? Well, I believe that he was curious about things themselves, about their shapes, the way they worked, how they differed each from the other, what might be the best way to distinguish among them and catalogue them. That mattered to him, that was something he liked: he liked to observe, without judging and without being judged, without turn-ing ideas into performance, speculation into academic achievement, dis-coveries into grades on a report card. The exact opposite, in other words, of the rest of us, who only wanted to exploit to the maximum what little we knew and especially what we didn't know, falling back on any trick imag-inable to trade off our wily ignorance.

THERE WERE SOME WHOSE SKILL at deceiving the teachers during class-room essays and exams approached a level of genius, or maniacal obsession, something that always has a certain link to genius. And instead of study-ing, rather than studying, with an investment of time and effort that was certainly equal to and in some cases required far greater dedication and work than what would have been sufficient to prepare adequately for quiz-zes or classroom assignments, Giuramento, Chiodi, Crasta, a.k.a. Three-

Toed Sloth, and even Lorco, who was actually a good student, would spend afternoons at a time miniaturizing on little strips of paper, narrow and long, dozens of names and the works of philosophers, theorems, tables with verb conjugations, and then they'd devote endless painstaking efforts to slipping those tiny scrolls into the transparent bodies of their ballpoint pens, twisting them in cunning spirals around the cartridge tube, which held the ink, only to unroll them in secret during the classroom assignment, in an equally delicate process, which was by and large pointless, since you had to know how to make use of those formulas, not just transcribe them onto the exam paper. Those reasonings would need to be recapitulated from start to finish, dates and names included in a narrative or argument with a shred of sense to it, and for those purposes these strips of paper or the inked tattoos on the forearm or the sheets of flimsy paper slipped into dictionaries weren't often especially helpful. It would have been much, much easier and more productive, in the final analysis, to study. But for some of us that was unthinkable, a shameful alternative. Lowering ourselves to studying . . . never in life! If there was at least a chance of deceiving, of taking a shortcut, which, as I've pointed out, in many cases proved longer and twistier than the main road, if it looked at least remotely thinkable that you could get by without effort or achievement, well, then that constituted the achievement, that is, the fact of being capable of sleight of hand, prestidigitation, of being fortune-tellers, pickpockets, cat burglars, in other words, anything other than diligent students.

THE OTHER SOLUTION was to copy. Copying from your neighbor or deskmate is the oldest ploy in the book, it dates back to the caveman, it corresponds to an atavistic impulse, suggesting that the weak should copy the strong, believe them and obey them, entrust themselves to their generosity, or else to their reliability. Whatever the grind sitting at the desk on either side of you is writing on his sheet is certainly right, the correct answer, the proper translation. And if your deskmate is a hopeless donkey, then you do your best to sit elsewhere, move closer to the reliable source, the way a scrupulous historian or an investigator might do; or at least link together a chain winding from the knowledgable to the ignorant in need of help through a series of intermediaries, just as in ancient times signals were sent from one tower to another, so that a message could hopscotch across hundreds of miles. There were two main problems, though: that there are only one or two truly knowledgable students in a given class, or at the most three or four in each subject, and not all of those few are willing to hand over their classroom assignment; for example, Gedeone, Gedeone Barnetta, who was good at Latin and Greek, made sure to build barriers of books on one side and used his left arm on the other, so as to cover what he was writing, while Zipoli, strong at math, wrote with a fine-point, very-hard-lead pencil, in a handwriting so minuscule that you couldn't have deciphered it even with a magnifying glass. That meant that the reliable sources in some cases dwindled to a single student in the whole class.

In that case, what ensued was a bizarre phenomenon of anarchy. Everyone copied from everyone else, from the good students and even from the bad ones, in a maelstrom of total mistrust of themselves, and there were even those who erased the equations they'd solved for themselves, and copied them number for number from the most ignorant student in the class, say Giuramento or Crasta. Who knows why it is that when you copy from your neighbor, you always have the sensation that you're thus doing better than you would have done on your own. And by a strange law of statistics, similar to Murphy's Law, between two classmates handing around a translation or comparing a math problem, it was almost certain that they would settle on the solution that was furthest from being right. You might derive a philosophical or scientific or psychological rule from this fact, delineating some very grave consequences for any kind of community or society that might emerge: namely that error is transmitted more *easily* and *rapidly* than truth. If one person copies from someone else, more often than not they replicate the errors and miscues of whoever they've taken as a model, or misinterpret him. Error, in other words, is more convincing, more attractive. I'm able to test out that rule, this morning, in the class I teach in prison: two of my Romanian students are conferring in low voices over a sheet of paper with a grammar exercise, and then they seem to come to an agreement and one of them corrects what he had written, correcting it to match what the other one had written. Walking around the desks, and brushing close past the doorway of the bathroom, which has no door, I come up behind them, and I look down at the first line of their official worksheet, and all I need to do is read the first few words: *mio fratelo a comprato na moto*. My brother bought a motorcycle. In correct Italian, it would have read: "*mio fratello ha comprato una moto.*"

All right, aside from the double consonant, so alien to the Romanian ear, I can see at least that Nicusor had written the verb correctly, "*ha comprato*," but then, peeking over at Ionut's paper, he had erased the *h*, in fact, he had not merely erased it, he'd actually buried it under a layer of ballpoint ink. I told him: "You see that? You're only capable of handing each other mistakes . . . but the good things, each of you keep those for yourselves. So everyone might as well do their own work, don't you agree?"

Sometimes I emphasize the point with a crude image: "Everyone might as well take their own *shits* with their own *assholes*." It's vulgar, but it packs a punch. No one here would want their own asshole used to expel someone else's shit, and the same thing ought to apply to their thoughts. Let everyone produce their own, right or wrong though they might be, and then we'll see. (In that "and then we'll see," my provisional approach to pedagogy is aptly summarized.) But I'm speaking as a teacher, while back then I spoke and I thought as a student. Taking it for granted that the best students were few in number, well out of reach, and unlikely to share their work (that was, for example, true of Sanson) or else terrorized by the teachers' monitoring, which was in truth very mild and indulgent, strictly pro forma in most cases, the strongest temptation was to ask just about anyone who had a passing grade, however low, or even undeserved, and then copy, copy everything, without posing any useless scruples or double-checking their work, without asking permission or begging their kindness or promising repayment just to get your hands on a single phrase or formula. That was where someone like me came into play; I had been a good student in middle school, but now that I was in high school, except when it came to Italian, my performance had started to slip in subjects I used to be good at; whereas on the new subjects such as ancient Greek or physics, I'd never gotten a feel for them, and gradually, as time went on and I neglected my studies and tended to other things and missed classes, in other words, what with my failure to take seriously both the teachers and the lessons, constantly assuming I was a good student without however bothering to study, constantly skipping especially challenging school days with a "Mamma, today I just don't feel like it" (which was enough to allow me to stay in bed, with a caress from my sweet and overindulgent mother), the lazy young man that I was began to develop shortfalls that no amount of brilliant improvisation or sparkling patter or self-confident demeanor—the kind of thing that can persuade teachers to consider the students sitting across from them to be better and more thoroughly prepared than they actually are, and thanks to that brash display of confidence alone, looking the teacher who's testing you right in the eye and speaking in a strong, loud voice, using such clever formulations as "certainly, it goes without saying that . . ." after which you add nothing, or else "one might also say a great deal about . . . ," in short, empty clauses that nonetheless invariably make a certain impression, and I was a bit of a master at flourishing these circumlocutions—I finally got to a point where all these contrivances and expedients were no longer enough to bridge my shortcomings.

My translations from Greek and from Latin, therefore, became increasingly half-baked, improbable, the result of guesswork, with interpretations tossed out at random because, since I hadn't studied the grammatical rules that govern those languages with implacable rigor, I had no alternative but to rely on my ear or on random chance.

... I HAD NO ALTERNATIVE but to rely on my ear, on random chance, or on instinct.

The decline of my mathematical abilities, which at ages ten or twelve had been remarkable, was quite pronounced, and I was the first to notice. While at first I understood everything at first glance, with an intuitive leap, on the first round of explanations, I suddenly stopped following so closely, began understanding less and less, which in a certain sense is worse than understanding absolutely nothing; the same thing happens with languages, because if you just don't understand them at all, their alien melody can prove to be enjoyable, it costs you no effort to sit and listen to it: but if, instead, you can pick up one word out of ten, then it turns into sheer torture, and before giving up, you make a tremendous effort to grasp the meaning of the nine other words, which are incomprehensible. Understanding mathematics only halfway, in dribs and drabs, in fragments, was a decisive factor in my decision to stop studying it. I don't think I opened the textbook even once in my time at high school.

In Latin and ancient Greek I continued to scrape by: in spite of the fact that my linguistic ignorance only continued to grow, at least there I was dealing with books, with poetry, with poems, with writers, and I found myself in a familiar world, even if De Laurentiis, the classics teacher, did all he could to disabuse us of the idea that those writers were saying anything interesting and beautiful. Even though I remained a mediocre translator, during the classroom assignments there were still classmates who wanted me to pass them my version. Matteoli, Scarnicchi a.k.a. the Dormouse, even Chiodi, who as classroom assignments approached, shifted from a state of catatonia to one of uncontrollable frenzy, thereafter relapsing into the utmost indifference the second after handing in the embossed sheet of official test paper, scribbled over beginning from the wrong side, the inside of the fold, indifferent even to the grade he'd struggled so hard for during the classroom assignment, all this academic fibrillation focused its intensity on me, as well, eyes hungering for help, meaningful dancing of the eyebrows, lips curled, whispers practically shouted across the room, lightning bolts of hissing trained in my direction, but I had two limitations, two scruples: I was afraid of being caught by De Laurentiis, and that foolish fear was in any case sufficiently powerful to embarrass me. Second of all, honestly, I knew perfectly well that, along with my translation of, let us say, Livy, I'd also be letting him copy plenty of mistakes I'd made, I'd be giving him a *contaminated* assignment. Who knows why, since I had already shown on many different and far more important occasions that I was a reasonably courageous young man, or at least reasonably coolheaded in confronting risks and emergencies, I should still have been frightened by threats of such a small, minuscule proportion: such as being stopped by the highway police, who might discover that my registration had expired, or that a teacher might catch me passing a note. Such prospects practically terrorized me, and it is perhaps interesting to notice how I always feel these dangers looming up at me from the world of the law, the public institutions, the vested authorities—while I was never scared of armed bandits. Strange, I felt absolutely no fear at the sight of pickup trucks packed with Taliban militants with submachine guns slung around their necks; but during my early years as a teacher I literally trembled if I was summoned to the headmaster's office. What could I have done wrong? What can they have uncovered concerning some shortcoming or misdeed that I most *assuredly* have committed, but I'm so careless that it's simply slipped my mind entirely? There you go, carelessness. Maybe it's on account of carelessness that I've gotten into trouble and it's always due to carelessness that I've deleted that trouble from my conscience, stowing it away someplace where someone else may stumble upon it: which is exactly what I expect from one moment to the next. Practically every night I dream of being in prison, locked up for armed robberies I pulled right after I became an adult . . . Could that be, could I really have been an armed robber when I was a young man? Evidently so, evidently at that age I must have figured I could make money that way, it must have seemed easy . . . Then someone must have talked . . . and I wound up behind bars. In the dream I clearly knew that this wasn't a case of mistaken identity, no miscarriage of justice, no, I *really had* done those armed robberies. And the law had pursued me, tracked me down, and was now punishing me. Yes, the only thing I seriously fear is the law. With all the capriciousness that it emanates, for example, the fact that it can come for you so many years after and at such physical distance from the commission of the crime. That is what so scares me, the fact that your misdeed might *resurface*, that it was never buried deep enough, and after years, and covering miles and miles, as if it had miraculously traveled underground, the corpse bobs to the surface . . .

> *The girl is buried already*
> *and it all happened a long time ago . . .*

I DIDN'T IMMEDIATELY COMPLY with the furtive requests of my classmates. But it was Scarnicchi's big staring eyes, or the thumb Chiodi ran menacingly over his throat, that convinced me to hand over the sheet of paper with my rendition. They copied it in less time than it takes a champion 400-meter runner to do a lap around the track, I don't know how they did it, they seemed to have a panoramic view, a photographic impression, but evidently not faithful enough, so that they added new errors to the ones I'd already committed, due either to haste or lack of understanding or that bizarre law of literature whereby any scribe, unfailingly, will introduce creative variations in the text that he is given to copy. I remember one in particular: it was none other than Chiodi who transmuted, while copying, the siege that the Romans had laid on *"una certa città,"* a certain city, into the siege of "Macerata." When he handed back the assignments with his corrections, De Laurentiis, who had developed a falcon eye for plagiarism and copying between one version and another, was almost speechless. His freckles turned beet red as he spoke, and a crust of dried saliva formed an off-white ring around his lips. More than anger, you could describe the sentiment that clearly gripped him as one of astonishment, mystification, and horror, clearly pushing him to the edge of collapse. His life was teetering on the brink of an absurd and unfathomable abyss: and all this merely because Chiodi had written "Macerata." What? Why? But why? Wait, seriously, what?

All blood had drained from his face, aside from the freckles that flamed on that muzzle of a tame tapir, and De Laurentiis was clearly having difficulty breathing, his respiration caught in his throat, he was stammering, waving Chiodi's classroom assignment in the air.

"But I . . . Chiodi . . . Macerata! Where did you get that? Where, *Dio mio* . . . where is it . . . ? I . . . I . . . I just can't . . . ! It isn't . . . it's not . . . I must be dreaming! Chiodi! Well, then . . . Chiodi . . . Macerata. But I ask myself . . .

I truly wonder . . . Macerata . . . *queshto* . . . *queshto* . . . Good Lord above! Good Lord Almighty! Blood of a ram, it's your . . . eh! *reshta* . . . *reshta l'unica* **sh***piegazzione* . . . *'na possessione diabbolica* . . ." The mushy esses were pure Neapolitan.

As he grew progressively angrier, his Neapolitan accent swelled, like rising yeast, because that's the way De Laurentiis was, or perhaps it's the way all Neapolitans are, that when they're swept away on an emotional or intellectual wave, a gust of sorrow or anger or amusement or focused reason, they immediately start talking with a strong accent and an inflection of the mother dialect, and in fact, when he was in a good mood, De Laurentiis, smiling and jovial, turned into something like the local *maschera*, a character out of commedia dell'arte, a strolling serenader or a Pulcinella clown, and the same thing happened to him in those outbursts which weren't, as I said, anger pure and simple, but rather sorrowful astonishment.

"*Agge ritto che solo 'o demonio . . . Chiodi . . . solo 'o riavulillo pote fa' chiove 'rinto 'o competo tuje 'sta parola: Macerata!*" "I said that only the devil . . . Chiodi . . . only Satan himself could have wedged that word into your paper: *Macerata*!"

But the strangest thing is that, in the end, Chiodi had been given a passing grade because his version (that is, 99 percent mine, aside from Macerata) had only six mistakes, two of which were serious (two points off), and four were minor, half a point off each, which meant four points off, hence, six. The Macerata error had so shocked De Laurentiis that he hadn't counted it.

In fact, I got a six myself, that time.

I WANT TO MAKE one thing clear about my friend Arbus, lest he seem like a pompous ass, a know-it-all. He really wasn't. Even when they were noteworthy or brilliant, Arbus always undercut his statements by framing them with "in my opinion," peppering them with "maybes" and "perhapses," and thus presenting them as ideas that wanted nothing better than to be contradicted and proven wrong, while to me they immediately rang clear as irrefutable. I don't know if he did this out of insecurity, or in mockery, or because he'd already attained the type of wisdom that intentionally avoids formulating categorical ideas, considering them intrinsically to be the epitome of stupidity.

8

CERTAINLY, Arbus's acne-inflamed face was no treat for the eyes.

It looked as though his skin had been raised at certain points and dug out at others, like land carved by the plow, so red and flushed that it was repulsive just to think of him washing it, putting his hands on it every morning, that pockmarked face.

It wasn't until ten or fifteen years later, when I met a man in London who'd been disfigured by erysipelas, or St. Anthony's fire, as it is also known—only then did I see anything more horrifying than Arbus's face at the peak of its inflammation.

Arbus, my poor friend!

It was clear to the eye that he was embarrassed, pained, resentful.

Many of us had zits scattered over our cheeks, our chins, our shoulders, and in the middle of our backs.

Iannello and Chiodi had them, for instance, and I, too, around age fourteen, that is, when I started to shave, felt those painful bumps start to erupt on my chin or in the folds of flesh behind my nostrils on either side of my nose; sometimes they broke the surface, other times instead they remained pulsating just under the reddened skin, unable to find an outlet. My mother would prepare plasters of boiling-hot salty water, after which she'd give me a grayish liniment with a repugnant odor to apply to my face: "Put it on, it helps the pimple to *ripen* . . ." and I still can't say which of these things was more disgusting, the slimy liniment itself, with its nauseating odor, or the very idea that you had to *ripen*, as if it were some kind of fruit, that lump swelling beneath my face, upon my lovely adolescent face; in short, all us kids, or nearly all of us, suffered from skin problems, some had skin that was too shiny, for others it was too greasy, too scaly, too oily, too dry, too *something*, as if the organism itself were incapable of regulating its hormone and sebum pumps.

But nothing came close to Arbus's face.

What about his mother? Didn't she do anything for him?

Couldn't she be troubled to lift a finger?

9

EVER SINCE I was a small boy, but also in the heart of my adolescence and then on into my years as a young man, in spite of my total naïveté and, so to speak, growing up in the shelter of this overextended and, therefore, guilty innocence, and feeding on it all the while, like a termite concealed in the heart of a plank of tender wood, there lived in me a ravaging and overwhelming sensuality—all the more overwhelming because it was veiled behind a very powerful strain of modesty. While other kids my age let loose with rowdy and bumptious manifestations, speaking in vulgar terms of genitalia, slutty women, condoms, men's semen and women's saliva spattered and dripping in all directions, I—who grew troubled and scandalized and fell uneasy prey to this explicit language of theirs—was trembling deep inside at the power of that sensuality they were expressing so recklessly, I could feel it pumping through my veins a thousand times more powerful, impetuous, dangerous, and invincible than that of all the young males I knew put together. That sensuality made my head spin, it filled me with nausea, it made me dizzy until I felt I was suffocating and falling.

I'd like to cite two episodes, both linked to an object, the mere mention of which, now, as I write, stirs in me an inexplicable agitation so enduring that I know, even now, that once I'm done writing I'm going to get up from my desk and I'll start wandering aimlessly through the rooms, I'll climb downstairs and up, at first touching myself furtively between the legs, and then in an increasingly determined manner, until I end up masturbating—in fact, I'm afraid that I'm going to have to start doing it immediately, now, before I even manage to begin narrating these episodes, and all this because they both have to do with a subject, indeed, because in both of them the same object plays a role, and that object is a swimsuit, and the mere expression, "swimsuit," written or visualized, unleashes in me such a tempest that it shakes me from head to foot, I can feel a riptide, a hot whirlpool draining life force from my legs, I can feel this vital fluid pulsating and turning and concentrating at the height of my hips, torn away from other parts of my body, weakening them, so that my hands tremble and my sight blurs, all merely because I'm sitting here writing about a *swimsuit*, a soft, colorful object, drenched with water, I have to run off to masturbate, that's right, just because of that, because of the simple verbal wrapping of the word "swim-suit," two sounds, all it takes is two syllables, and because my love is not here, otherwise I'd go from room to room in search of her, wandering in a random and nervous fashion, ravening, I'd find her, I'd wrap my arms around her from behind, I'd put my hands beneath her breasts, lifting them, I'd tell her how beautiful she is today as I rub up against her, overcoming her objections because I interrupted her while she was busy doing something else, like reading, writing letters, cooking, talking on the phone, brushing her hair, putting things away, still I'd try to get her clothes off and lay her down to make love, or not even strip her entirely, because all I'd need would be to get her naked just enough to slip inside her quickly, right then and there where I found her, still standing.

This demon is always with me, it's been living inside me for a lifetime, it never abandons me for an instant, so much so that if one day I no longer felt it churning my blood and thickening it, well, I'd assume I was dead, that I'd died without noticing it. A powerful surge in my heartbeat is the way it has of knocking from within. I felt it once when I was little more than a child, in a changing booth at the seaside resort of San Felice Circeo—shame, excitement, curiosity, a throbbing in my temples and a heat in my thighs and on my back—and on the beach at Terracina—the sea murky with sand, bathers laughing as they were slapped by the waves, and my cousin, whose disgusted face I can still see before me if I meet her on the stairs, and my own face, morbidly enchanted.

Even though I had not the faintest idea of what sexual desire might be, I could still sense its presence every time that even the simplest events, the most ordinary gestures and glances started to seem strange to me, directed specifically at me, and to torment me precisely because I had no explanation for what was happening. I couldn't yet describe that state as arousal . . .

I HAD BEEN INVITED to the Circeo by Zarattini, my best-looking classmate in middle school. And after going swimming over and over again in the sea off the resort club where his family kept their chairs and beach umbrella, we went to the changing booth to get out of our suits. Back then, the heavy fabric of the suit would get drenched and stay wet for hours. "You go get out of that wet suit right away" was a typical thing for a mother to say, with the equally typical anticipation of the pronoun at the beginning of the sentence. Zarattini and I changed with our backs to each other, out of modesty. I tried to change very quickly and I got snagged, coming close to tripping in my haste to pull the suit up. Rather than paradise or the starry sky, the specific dim light and cool air of the changing booths represent for me, in the most literal terms, the ineffable: what human words are incapable of describing, at least, the ones that I know how to use. For instance: the almost-shiver of cold that catches you in there, while the sun beats down furiously outside, the sandy floor, the smell of salty mold. What made me start and almost lifted my heart into my throat, as if I had suddenly gone mad with shame, was the dull thud behind me of Zarattini's swimsuit, drenched with water, as it fell onto the rough concrete surface immediately after he'd taken it off, and the thought that he at that moment was nude unsettled me to a far greater extent than, an instant earlier, I had been filled with embarrassment by the fact that *I* was.

AT TERRACINA, on the other hand, an event occurred that was, if possible, even more insignificant, and yet which still echoes and resonates inside me. The seawater was cloudy, because of the waves that were kicking up sand from the seabed. But the kids were going swimming anyway, wearing scuba masks. Not that there was anything to see, beyond the yellowish wall of sand in suspension, but that way you could stick your head underwater without burning your eyes, dive in, guess at the shadows of the friend standing closest to you in the water, and grab him as a prank. Instead, there was someone who saw something. It was my cousin, a couple of years older than me, and she was swimming a little farther out than where the rest of us were splashing and wallowing. We saw that she was heading in with great and powerful strokes, struggling through the waves, windmilling her arms, her hands paddling flat. She was indignant. She pulled off her mask and swept back the locks of wet hair. She was shaking with outrage. "Just disgusting!" she said, once she was close to us. "Why, what happened?" She turned around, pointing to a couple in the distance who appeared and disappeared beyond the foam of the breakers. The two of them had their arms around each other and were kissing, or at least their heads were close, as they bobbed on the passing waves. I remember, she had a yellow swim cap: I can still see that as a fundamental detail, I'd be willing to swear to it in a court of law. My cousin's voice was cracking with the emotion. "I was swimming over there, around them, and I almost ran straight into them . . ." While she was talking and we were listening to her, a wave caught us by surprise, slapping right into our faces. My cousin emerged from the water, her face grimacing in disgust. "But I could see that she . . . that he was taking her swimsuit off . . . the *bottom part!*"

The bottom part of her swimsuit . . . the "bottom part" . . . the "bottom" . . . of the "swimsuit" . . . I felt myself flushing red at that information. I was swept by an immediate fever, a fever that has never since subsided.

ALL OF THIS SENSUALITY, like several other morbid inclinations of mine, comes I believe from my mother and her side of the family, consisting of a small undivided army of neurasthenics. Among themselves, like in some novel from the olden days, they talked about their nerves as if they were an autonomous entity, independent of the person they inhabit, like so many tenants incorrigibly behind on their rent, sleepless and insolent, who just won't stop bothering the landlord with their inopportune misbehavior: loud shouting, violent crises, nighttime commotion, arguing, screams. These nerves, my nerves, calm my nerves, I don't know what's up with my nerves today, she gets on my nerves, oh, my poor nerves! I haven't really heard that expression for some time now, but in those days it was the terminology of the day. People spoke of "nervous breakdowns" as if they were always lurking around the corner, on the steep edge of which everyone was blithely strolling, possibly without a clue of the danger. My mother and everyone else in her family, all they ever seemed to do was tip over that brink and be heroically wrestled back up over it. Today the expression "nervous breakdown" has been replaced in everyday Italian by "stress," but that's hardly the same thing at all . . .

EVEN THOUGH I've often felt abandoned and alone, and being well aware that I was fighting battles that were lost before they were begun, or worse, that most people wouldn't even understand in the name of what I stubbornly insisted on fighting them, at various moments of my life I've experienced the subtle pleasure of continuing to act that way, a pride that verges on the cheerful, the mocking, the enjoyment of doing something exotic, of serving a deity whose identity was unknown to me. A characteristic that I think has been with me since I was a child, in fact, *that I had especially* as a child, was that my mind wasn't occupied by a single thought, but rather by a great number of different discordant thoughts at the same instant. Which caused me a strange happiness, the singular sensation of always having company, along with a constant sense of apprehension, to say nothing of confusion and uncertainty. Uncertainty, that is, about *what* I actually thought, and what I believed about any given topic, since I was well accustomed to thinking one thing and its exact opposite at the same time, along with a series of intermediate thought processes; and the same thing applied to my convictions and even my desires. I liked everything and every person and, at the same time, I disliked them, and I wanted to do everything and at the same time I feared doing it or I thought it was wrong. I wasn't really the master of my own thoughts, rather it was the thoughts that entered or exited me or remained there as they pleased, it was they that inhabited and possessed and governed me, to such a degree that, in fact, it seemed wrong to me to refer to those thoughts as *mine,* any more than a meadow might venture to describe as *its sheep* the sheep that graze upon it. In that case, who was I? To which of those thoughts and desires could I attach my own name? It was when I was out walking that I was especially able to notice just how dense was the crowd of thoughts and different voices that swarmed inside me. Even for very short walks, like the one I took every morning to school, to the SLM Institute, which measured by my present-day pace and stride is roughly one hundred fifty steps, while with my legs back then it might have been two hundred. Well, those two hundred steps were sufficient to produce in me a trancelike state, so raptly did follow the various threads intertwining in my head, twining around the slightest notion or idea, or image or word, to the point that I lost all contact with the reality that surrounded me, namely the street, whether I was walking along it or crossing it, Via Bolzano, Via Tolmino, the square of Santa Costanza. And more than once, while walking to school, I realized that I had gone past the bronze-colored gates with SLM written above them (a few years ago, those gates were repainted a harsh yellow color) and I was already proceeding along Via Nomentana, beneath the trees that run along that thoroughfare, in the direction of Sant'Agnese, dazedly listening to the string of thoughts that were my guests without daring to interrupt them, the way you let someone talk whom you're afraid to contradict. My mind did nothing, the same as it does today: it just let me talk.

I STILL LULL MYSELF in the childish hope that it might all at once become possible to reconcile all incompatibilities; the ones that I feel within myself, overwhelmingly powerful, and between myself and the others, for now irremediable . . . And because this dream tends to vanish as quickly as it appears, I feel as if I'm the unhappiest person in the world, and naturally I exaggerate when I feel this way, and display that state of mind to those who are close to me, I exaggerate my affliction, and it is here that I find my chief and abiding vanity: because I know that human points of view are far too disparate for there ever to be any hope of reconciling their divergences, and yet I feel them within me, as vivid and immediate as thorns.

AT AGE TWELVE I was already stunned and excited to the verge of agony by my readings of myths and chivalric exploits, I knew by heart all the adventures of Siegfried, the Valkyries, Jason, Mordred, Arthur, Hagen (or Högni), and Sir Kay, all the misdeeds of Loki and the wily cunning of Hermes as a child, the murderous folly of both Apollo and Hercules, the mocking cruelty of Dionysus . . . and I had taken in hand the various swords, Excalibur, Durandal, and Balmung, windmilled them mercilessly against the frost giants, Mjölnir, the hammer of Thor. I read so greedily that I almost didn't have time to grasp or understand.

I COULDN'T SAY whether I have a tireless mind housed in a lazy body, or a lazy mind curled up inside a tireless body. There's one thing I feel and know for certain, however: that since the day I was born, and all the more now that I have reached and passed middle age, my mind and my body don't get along, so to speak, they don't keep the same hours, when one is awake the other is catnapping, and when the other boils over with vigor the one languishes, weakened. My metabolism is staggered into two series that never meet and never coincide. That's why I'm never entirely alert and never fully placated. I know neither the fully waking state nor complete repose. At night, for example, my physical exhaustion becomes the ideal setting for insistent, tormented, hallucinatory thoughts, extremely lucid in their obstinate determination to create a perfect delirium. While at other moments a simple and obtuse force applies and squanders itself in actions amid which I feel stupid, blind, inanimate as an automaton. In full agreement, at peace with myself? Never.

ASIDE FROM ARBUS, the unrivaled champion, the fact that I might have been the most intelligent, or at least considered such, wasn't actually such a huge source of satisfaction, nor is it even now when, far less frequently, truth be told, this refrain emerges once again, the idea that I'm supposedly the most intelligent in any given category, which may vary in type and dimension: of my school, of my contemporaries, of the contestants for a literary prize (where I usually place or show, coming in second or third, and in those instances it's said in the spirit of consolation), the entire array of living Italian writers ... Aside from the fact that it's false, I take no pride from this primacy in relation to any of these categories; because what good are a man and his ideas, if he doesn't know what to do with them?

I cannot use even the one thing I possess in abundance.

I recopy this phrase taken from a novel: "And looking up at the celestial vault above me, immovable, dumb, I felt like a tiny speck of life under that vast, transparent corpse."

AND MY CULTURE? My endless and inquisitive knowledgeability in such subjects as film titles Norse sagas nicknames of soccer players etymologies and word origins made me a sterile little champion out of some TV quiz, but one who stays at home, that is, the guy who answers the question from his easy chair, beating the contestant on screen by a tenth of a second ("Come on, Papà, why don't you enter as a contestant yourself? You'd win for sure!"), in other words, the kind of know-it-all that everybody vies to get on their team when it's time to play Trivial Pursuit.

I MUST CONFESS that as a boy and later, as a teenager, I was inclined to tell stories invented out of whole cloth, or willfully false, in the hopes of arousing the interest of other people. If I'd had as many stories available that were just as interesting but true, I'd surely have told those instead of lying, but that was not the case. I was obliged to invent things because the reality that I knew was devoid of attractions, and my experience of extraordinary things was quite limited. The life of a boy from a respectable family in the city is rather empty and must necessarily be filled and supplemented with imaginary or borrowed adventures: I think that applies to a great many others, not just to me. Love and fantasies on the theme of amorous endeavors, for example, how could those two topics enter the life of an adolescent born in the middle of the twentieth century, unless it was in the form of half-lies and feeble boasts? When you still haven't kissed a girl (and zero, the original, absolute zero, as we all know, isn't even a number but a metaphysical entity), how can you help but lie, stating, with studied nonchalance, that you're already on number ten? This could be called a lie, or perhaps it's actually an advance on later luck, as if you were just helping yourself out a little in your reckoning by including the future kisses, which are sure to be given and received eventually, to the ones that for now exist only in dreams. Could this be a sort of loan, or a down payment?

IT IS BY NO MEANS true that young men are superficial and inclined to distractions and amusements: in reality everything that seemed more solemn and serious than usual fascinated us. Only those things appeared very rarely.

10

EVEN THOUGH THEY ARE SECOND-RANK PLAYERS in the development of the story, a book like this can hardly fail to include a chapter on my gym teachers. Namely: Brother Curzio and Tarascio at SLM, and the Painter of Nudes, also known as Courbet, at the Giulio Cesare classical high school, where I took my battery of final exams in 1975. I call them gym teachers using the old terminology, even if the official description is "physical education," and in some classes of school it's even been modified into the still more generic and abstract "motor skills education." That increasingly distilled and denatured language no longer dares to mention the subject or the concrete actions or the instruments employed in work: this is part of the process, gradual yet unstoppable, of the dematerialization of existence, which seeps from words to life and back again (the beginning of this mutation took place with "trashman" or "street sweeper," replaced by "environmental engineer," a classic, textbook example).

A phys ed teacher in an Italian school is an alien body, or rather, he is a *body*, surrounded by so many other brains minds and souls, conversations, trains of thought, and calculations, and theories, and he's just been placed there to remind them all, for a couple of hours a week, that students have legs and arms and lungs to breathe with and that, in short, there's also another part of their individuality that is in need of training, needs to be rendered lithe and elastic, helped to grow, examined and, in the end, judged. Just like one's intellectual resources, one's physical resources need to be used and measured, even if that's at a 1:10 or 1:20 ratio with the mental resources. The ability to leap over a horizontal bar or do a certain number of push-ups or shove a volleyball straight down into the face of the girl who was jumping up to the net with her eyes closed will be infinitely less appreciated than the skills that help you to find your way through the graph of Kant's transcendental categories or let you solve for a square root. And yet they offer the subject, they have a teacher dedicated full-time to that subject, it's not just fun and letting off steam and the exuberance of teenagers set free after hours of deformation of the spinal cord, nailed to the desk like so many geese being stuffed with vague notions. The most restless period in a lifetime—while in the body galaxies of unknown energies collide and a squall is blowing that would be capable of uprooting all and every thought—is spent in a state of physical immobility, like in some Byzantine mosaic. And then people complain about how kids are *restless . . . !*

To meet their tapping feet partway, we have a period of phys ed.

BROTHER CURZIO wasn't all that young, but he had a trim physique. Always in a tracksuit, with the zipper half-open in the front, and underneath, over his chest, a simple white T-shirt (I'm talking about the skintight tracksuits of the time, in a semisynthetic fabric, with zippers on even the ankles). He was short, dark-complected and dark-haired, hair that he always wore neatly combed, parted to one side, with a five o'clock shadow even after he shaved. To just see him like that in the street, you'd never have guessed that he was a priest, compared with other priests with their emaciated look, or else the fat and jovial ones, like monks from the Middle Ages. But the right question to ask wasn't whether he seemed like a priest, but rather *why* he was one, why he had ever become a priest. Was it out of a vow of some sort, or was it a form of self-mortification, in the aftermath of a long-ago crime, in search of forgiveness, like Manzoni's Fra Cristoforo, or the knight played by Robert De Niro in the movie *Mission*? In fact, he was always serious, almost moody, very reserved indeed. None of us students had ever seen him in his tunic, nor had we ever heard him speak about God or the Madonna, and during his physical education classes he never referred—the way his brother priests did, even when they were talking about subjects that had nothing to do with them—to sins we were to avoid, temptations we were to reject, the importance of maintaining intact and chaste our bodies which were, literally, the raw material upon which

Brother Curzio was paid to work (even though I never did understand how things worked with the stipends or salaries paid to priests in general and those at SLM in particular: whether their vow of poverty was absolute, whether they were given a per diem at least for their petty expenses, I don't know . . . let's say, in that case, that he was "called" to work, that that was his pedagogical and religious vocation). But more than once we had wondered whether among the priests, the ones who were assigned to teach physical education might not actually be the ones incapable of doing anything else, the most ignorant ones, in other words, the ones who hadn't studied; or whether instead Brother Curzio had scrupulously studied as an athletic coach, with special courses in anatomy, physiology, and nutrition, or whether it had been Brother Curzio's physique itself—compact, virile, lithe, shoulders straight, torso deep, tense, taut legs, not an ounce of fat, a belly tucked inward, but it wasn't a pose, it was constitutional—that had persuaded the elder brothers to assign him to teach sports, something they might never have practiced. It's a strange thing, but in all the sports I've taken classes in, whether on an ongoing basis or a one-time, occasional thing, the instructor has always been as good at teaching as he was ungifted in the practice of the sport itself: my soccer coach was a terrible player, only capable of passing the ball flat-footed, hitting it with his foot open like a golf club, my swim instructor never let himself be seen in the water because he would have struggled to stay afloat, the elderly and very gay basketball coach would show us gracefully how, at the height of the jump, floating in midair, you could whipcrack your wrist to make sure the ball, spinning opposite to its direction of travel, would arc through the air, but his demonstration shots always hit the ring, so that he stubbornly tried four or five times until he'd turned red in shame and out of breath. Which only goes to show you that the better you are at teaching something, the worse you are at actually doing it.

Good teachers transmit the best of themselves, instead of doing it in the first person; they arouse in others that same passion that in them often led to failure.

End of the parenthesis, just to say that while Brother Curzio might very well have had an "incredible physique," at age forty, ten times more powerful and tireless than us teenagers, he still seemed completely useless in its application to actual sports, such as, say, volleyball, which is probably the most widely pursued group physical activity in Italian schools, both private and public, all you need to do is take the kids and split them into two teams, on either side of the net, throw a ball into the air, and something is bound to happen. The Marist brother had only to give the signal, with a blast or two on the whistle around his neck, and the dances were on, and he could retreat behind the screen of his reserved personality. We loved him, actually, when all was said and done, if only for his distance from the standard priestly model: he might just as easily have been a factory worker, or a cameraman, or the proprietor of a hardware store, or probably even a soldier, that's right, a soldier. The Madonna wasn't foremost in his thoughts, nor was She the last thing on his mind. In rewards and punishments, hope and charity, he showed no interest at all. So why should someone like him have ever become a priest at all? Was he really a priest, then, Brother Curzio, or was there someone else hidden under that tracksuit, an escaped convict, or a deserter, a former mercenary who had murdered who could say how many negroes in his previous life, and who was paying the price of those crimes by presiding over those volleyball tournaments between no-talent weaklings?

AN ANSWER THAT FAILS to provide a true explanation, but rather adds only a further tile of mystery to the mosaic, came late one night as we were tooling along on a moped down the long, dark Viale di Tor di Quinto, between Via Flaminia and Via Olimpica. I was on my way back from a soccer match played on one of the countless five-a-side fields that line the banks of the Tiber, shrouded in the mist rising from the river, forming a sort of luminous cube of humidity. I was with Rummo, and I was perched on the scanty little tail end of the saddle of his Morini 50 cc, a Corsarino, which in those days represented the dream conveyance of any and every adolescent.

We had just pulled up in front of the shooting range when, by the light of a bonfire, we saw a man leaning out of a compact car to haggle over prices with the prostitutes who were warming themselves by the flames. There were two of them, both middle-aged, one in front, the other lingering farther back, almost entirely out of the circle of dancing light flickering tremulously around the steel drum with the fire burning inside it. The first one was blond, the second brunette, both with their hair teased out and short skirts revealing solid legs planted in ankle boots; and the man who was arguing about prices with them, his elbow protruding from the window of the Fiat 850, one of the classic Fiats of those years, a car that is inconceivable today for the barren simplicity of its features, well, that man was none other than Brother Curzio, identifiable from a good distance by the swept-back bangs and the serious grimace on his face. For that matter, the Fiat 850 was very familiar, since it served as the official runabout of both the headmaster and the school, and we knew like the back of our hands its squared-off silhouette, which we'd seen parked so many times outside the front gate of SLM or inside the courtyard of the school, which faced Via Nomentana. The chrome trim designed, as a child with a crayon might have done, its simple outline, its blocky back, with the grillwork on the hatch to give air to the engine: perhaps the most straightforward and familiar vehicle of those years.

I doubt that Brother Curzio recognized us as we putted past, slowing down to take in the spectacle, on the service road. Viale di Tor di Quinto, in fact, is a broad thoroughfare with tree-lined service roads running alongside it, next to which are further turnaround areas. In later years, alongside the banks of the Tiber, a large tent theater would be set up, specializing in musicals, the cause of lengthy traffic jams due to the throngs of spectators arriving and leaving, but back then the dense shadows harbored only the bonfires and folding chairs of the prostitutes; while on the far side of the thoroughfare the Carabinieri barracks had not yet been built, and there were only meadows, and the soccer field where S.S. Lazio practiced.

So was it him, Brother Curzio, the man who was frequenting these meretricious women? In spite of the fact that my eyes had certainly seen what they'd seen, a doubt still lingered as we shot to the right around the traffic jam of cars backed up along Via Olimpica. But Rummo rid me of my misgivings, swiveling his head to one side and twisting his mouth to make sure I heard him in the rush of wind.

"Of course that was him. And what do you find strange about that? Did you think priests didn't go with women? They go, oh, they go . . ."

I was amazed that Rummo—who was a traditionalist, I'd even have said a bit of a conformist, if the term really has any meaning when applied to an adolescent, Rummo who served communion at every blessed holy mass—should prove to be such a realist, so cynical. But he was right. From that day forward, I saw priests in a different light. As if all of a sudden a glow or an aura had been revealed around them that had previously been invisible, a frothy wake made up of all the actions, the instincts, ideas, and desires, all of the missing parts of their lives, I mean to say, the parts that were missing to us students in order to complete their image as *men*, and not priests. Isn't it only natural that this full-blooded man, full of repressed energy, should go out in search of a woman? And since he couldn't fall in love with that woman, since he couldn't actually declare his feelings for her and set up housekeeping together, since he couldn't marry her and have children with her, what else was he supposed to do, if not pay her and fuck her, pay her to fuck her? I started to wonder whether *all*, I mean every last one of the priests, did it. No, impossible. There were some whom you truly couldn't even imagine embracing, touching a woman's breasts, others still who perhaps had the strength to resist, and yet others who clearly didn't really like women so for them it wasn't that much of a sacrifice to renounce their company. Just as men are different one from another, priests likewise differ, indeed, within their ranks they may be more widely diversified than the human race taken as a broad whole, and the uniformity imposed by the credo and the tunic is strictly one of appearance, indeed if anything it highlights the difference. There are all sorts of things, there are all sorts of people under that collar!

In any case, the next year, after the summer, we went back to school and Brother Curzio wasn't there anymore.

HE HAD BEEN REPLACED by a lay teacher, Tarascio, muscular and wrinkled and twisted, perhaps from lifting too much weight over the course of a lifetime. Tarascio spoke with a strong southern twang, so that he never completed his words, striking the accent on the next-to-last syllable and simply cutting off the last one: at first, he'd give us orders with a moan, but he'd complete them in something approaching a shout. Those orders would always end with a word like "exercise" (esercita*zione*), "solution" (solu*zione*), or "justification" (giustifica*zione,*) with a double "z" and the last syllable cut off.

"*Fate at-ten-ZZIO'* . . . *che ora faccia-mo la pre-pa-RA-ZZIO'* . . . *pe' la corretta ESECUZZIO'* . . ." Pay close at-ten-TTIO' . . . now we're go-ing to do some pre-pa-ra-TTIO' . . . for the correct EXECUTTIO' . . .

We had no idea what had become of Brother Curzio. Some said that he had gone to South America. Others maintained that he had been defrocked for unspecified reasons, reasons that appeared all too clear to me. I still had the doubt that what we had seen in the dim light off Viale di Tor di Quinto, in the dancing glow of the flames and the passing headlights, might not be common knowledge, that is to say, that it hadn't been an isolated episode at all, but rather a routine outing: what priests call a vice, in fact, *the* vice, the vice by very definition, and that the other brothers had caught him. In those cases, what happens? How does the system of investigation and repression proceed, who judges, who decides? What is the punishment? Are you expelled, and that's that, or what else? Is a pardon even a possibility? And if so, then was Brother Curzio doing penitence who knew where, and who could say how much and indeed whether he still thought of women, which is to say, *all* women, not just the women in the street, the working girls, but also the mothers waiting for their children outside the school, actresses, images on newsreels, naked statues and women swimming at the beach and swimmers in pools . . . maybe even nuns.

(A parenthesis about the last-mentioned category. Misogyny and resentment and perverse morbid fascination find an easy target in nuns. Far more than against priests, widespread anti-Catholic sentiment tends to be vented against these regimented creatures, who are easier to classify and place as a group or subgroup, as a caricature and through stereotypes and jokes, than as independent individuals.

When talking about a girl who plays hard to get or is shy or dresses in a depressing style, or too prudishly, or doesn't wear makeup, or goes to church, it is said with some annoyance that she is a nun, while it would never occur to anybody to say of her male equivalent that he is a priest.

Which means that a nun has to be short and homely, with a mustache, or else, if she's pretty, then it's obvious that she must be a sort of latter-day Nun of Monza, that is to say, a slut in a habit, her lustful body barely concealed by her ample tunic, ready at any moment to explode, as is regularly described in a specialized sector of the pornographic film industry.

Males and females, priests and nuns.)

WITH TARASCIO, it was quite another matter. He manifested his maleness proudly, wearing a tank top even when the gym was freezing, and showing off his freckly old flesh, sagging slightly above the taut firm muscles of his shoulders, his visible deltoids, his pectorals covered with twisted white hairs. He seemed delighted to be able to show us the results of thousands of push-ups, performed over the course of various decades, the wrinkly gun shows of his biceps, and in fact, we were very impressed with the show. Despite all this, Tarascio struck us as an exceedingly ancient man, a mummy, a plaster cast of some athlete or boxer found under the ashes of Herculaneum: among other things, because Tarascio, all told, stood five feet tall, like the men of antiquity, to judge from their armor and the height of the doorways they passed through, short, muscular, virile.

Tarascio was fixated with virility. It was his obsession, the purpose of his life, that we, his students, should be *masculine*, and if we weren't already, that we should become sufficiently virile, what with weight lifting and Swedish stall bars.

✦

FROM THE FRUSTRATION of these fitful starts, these lunges at virility, there arose a singular form of narcissism. Precisely because we were losers, we had failed, and we continued to fail in the face of any challenge, even the slightest ones, we might be summoned to withstand when it came to virility, we were all the more inclined to fantasize our perfect virile identity, and we leaned over it to gaze at our images in it, as if in the image dreamed of we could see the reflection of our virility, and that reflection could shimmer onto our flesh-and-blood self, finally rendering it worthy, complete, fully achieved. How we admired ourselves! How we studied our reflections! But not because we loved ourselves, quite the contrary! The core of narcissism isn't self-love, it's anger.

Among the various ways of getting to know yourself: gaze at length into the mirror, get sick, write letters, play soccer or Ping-Pong, fall in love, read, struggle. Or even returning insults, that is, the instinctive way we do it, hysterically, or menacingly and calmly, can tell us a great deal about who we are. If in fact we don't subject ourselves to challenges that prove who we are and if fate doesn't hold any in store for us, because the period doesn't consider them important or the class we're born into or the place we're born exclude them from the outset, then virility has no option but to express itself through one's outward appearance and attitude. Then our shoulders, the muscles in our arms, our pectorals replace courage, determination, decisiveness, and initiative. What we *don't* do is underpinned by a great many other things that we do, a vast amount of agitation, bending, pumping, lifting, or thrusting: in the absence of a single action that can seriously be considered noteworthy and significant, we perform a myriad of other actions, in series of ten, twenty, or thirty at a time. The body in training repeats the same act countless times, it's hungering for action but it's forced to break that action down into minimum sequences, replicating them ad infinitum. In a gymnasium, an action *is never complete*. With Tarascio, we exhausted ourselves with push-ups, even though we knew the whole time that we had done *nothing at all*. But still, we'd feel that we were bigger and more confident, as we touched our chests through our T-shirts.

BUT WHY AM I TALKING about gym teachers from my old school days? What is so interesting or particular about them? Can the sticky material that covered the gym floor become an object of regret? I don't know, I doubt it. Perhaps it's because they were the only ones to come a little closer to what truly touched us, to what troubled us and disturbed us, and turned us into the men we are now, the disordered bodies we are now, deployed between a urology clinic and the little apartment with the loft bed where a lover lives we see so infrequently that the affair might go on for ten or twenty years. (This last phrase is vulgar and intentionally striking, perfectly suited therefore to a book by a contemporary writer, which is what I am, but in part it also corresponds to the reasons a phys ed teacher and his students, males all—even if they never say anything meaningful to one another, and even though the teacher limits himself to bellowing orders and scolding the students, who swarm wholesale through a gymnasium where the squeegeeing footsteps of their rubber soles on the linoleum echo through the air—*always* share a profound secret.)

LIKE ANY OTHER HUMAN RESOURCE, the body is made to be modified. That is, shaped, engraved, sculpted, with various intents, but in accordance with typically artistic procedures: make the clearly defined forms emerge from the indistinct, which is what adolescent bodies almost always are, emaciated, twisted, or still clothed in baby fat, which the kids make jiggle as they run or jump in their awkward ways. The body thus becomes a virgin expanse, ideal for experimentation. On that parade ground, all sorts of exercises and maneuvers are undertaken. To Tarascio, the idea of leaving his signature on the bodies of the fifteen-year-olds he sculpted was a source of delight. Why, of course, Gian Lorenzo Tarascio, like a Renaissance maestro. And in fact, when he wasn't shouting, he was accustomed to murmuring under his breath, as if rapt in meditation: "The Discus Thrower . . . yes . . . the Gladiator . . . the Bronze Boxer . . . Michelangelo's David," as he supervised the completion of the series of exercises that were meant to push us closer, day by day, to those sculptural models.

For a certain period, Matteoli and I, and a few other schoolmates, determined once and for all to build up our physiques, attended his private gymnasium, which was located in the area around Ponte Mammolo. We would go in formations of two or four, on our scooters with gym bags slung over our shoulders. For the most part I rode on the back of Matteoli's scooter. He had a small gray Vespa. Matteoli was without a doubt the most faithful adherent of Tarascio's, and the one who had most wholeheartedly signed on to the project to build up our strength, the same process that in those years was being applied, in fact, to the Vespa 50 cc scooters. Indeed, with a few simple modifications—so simple that even I, who knew next to nothing about engines, managed to complete them—a Vespa 50 cc became capable of going twice as fast as the legal, unmodified version. It's a known fact that a 50 cc has the potential of becoming a veritable rocket ship, and that only the special devices and calibrations of the manufacturers limit their performance in order to comply with the rules of the road. Well, all you have to do is remove the manufacturer's restrictions: pull out the diaphragms, widen the caliber of the carburetor, empty the muffler, and use a hacksaw to shorten the exhaust pipe . . . Modifications roughly equivalent to the ones being done to motor scooters behind closed garage doors were being carried out by Tarascio on the bodies of the boys who came to his gym near Ponte Mammolo, which, for that matter, must once have been a garage. Back then we had none of the complicated fitness equipment that nowadays even the most down-at-the-heels gyms possess, and the gym was equipped with nothing more than a couple of sets of stall bars, weight benches, a few barbells, kettlebells, chest expanders, back extenders, and other junk nineteenth-century bodybuilders might have used.

OF THE FIGURE of Brother Curzio nothing remains to me now but a few fleeting images, including, as I've described, the unforgettable snapshot of Tor di Quinto, and the memory of a phrase that he once let slip while watching Arbus. "This isn't calisthenics, Santa Madonna! This is St. Vitus's dance!" he said, almost frightened at my classmate's lack of coordination, along with the vigorous frenzy of his movements, his way of making up for his awkwardness.

I can't be 100 percent sure, but I think that I saw him again a couple of years ago, in the center of town, along the river, at the point where they were planning to excavate an underpass but then had to give up the project for fear that the million tons of Castel Sant'Angelo might collapse in upon it. He was old, unshaven, and on his head he wore a wig, thick and raven black, shiny as an animal's pelt. How was I able to recognize him? You'll never believe it, but he was wearing a tracksuit, that's right, the old tracksuit from SLM, black with yellow and green trim, faded from repeated washings but not yet entirely in tatters. It must have been made of some really durable fabric! Curzio (perhaps it's wrong to think of using the salutation "brother" now) was wandering around in circles, lost in his thoughts, then a shrill voice called to him, and a homely woman, who up until then had been rummaging around one of the last specimens of a pay phone in the city of

Rome, caught up with him and grabbed him brutally by the hand, forcing him to stroll with her along the parapet overlooking the river, swinging their arms back and forth, like some parody of a couple of young lovers. Then he said to her: "You whore," and in that single word I recognized the voice of my old phys ed teacher. He couldn't manage to twist loose from that woman's grip.

Witnessing that scene, I assumed they were husband and wife.

I'LL CALL the third phys ed teacher the Painter of Nudes, also known as Courbet.

Courbet might have been thirty-five years old or so, but he always spoke of himself in the past tense, like a man in his sunset years, to whom all the good or bad things that are going to happen have already happened. We were astonished, amused, and worried by this tic. Could the arc of a male's life be so brief? Feel oneself to be done for before middle age—could that happen to a vigorous man who, like our teacher, loves art and sports and women? Perhaps someone like Courbet felt it more than others, in a more intense fashion. What did he feel? His decline. Which for an athlete or an aesthete comes just after age thirty, and the exceptions certainly don't contradict the rule, and even they, at a certain point, obey it. Courbet in a T-shirt and trousers, and I think of it every time I see him these days, crossing the piazza downstairs from my apartment, brushing close to the wall of LUISS University, or on Via Bellinzona, as he wanders hunched over through the Quartiere Trieste, or QT, dragging his feet as if he were shod in boots of lead, his gray hair hanging over his shoulders and his nose hooked like the beak of a bird of prey, resembling an elderly Apache, the faded leather of his face and a pair of stark, staring eyes, *panting*, if you can use an adjective like that one for a person's gaze.

But in those days, he struck us as a perfect specimen of the sensuous Italian male, gleaming hair, gypsy gaze, shiny white teeth, and the rest of him a bundle of clearly defined muscles and nerves so taut and responsive that you could bet money that he'd always be the first to strike the blow, pitiless. His skinniness made him look almost menacing, men without fat on their bodies and jutting cheekbones often are menacing or at least look it, which amounts to the same thing, since menace is a pure phantom quality.

Now Courbet is nothing but a ghost . . .

II

OURBET'S NICKNAME came from the fact that he was not only a gym teacher, but also a painter. In fact, he was first and foremost a painter.

He immediately established good relations with the few male students of class 5M, the last section of Giulio Cesare High School, the class of reprobates, decimated by their systemic flunking, to which I had been assigned the day I enrolled, with stamped on my forehead, like the mark of Cain, the emblem of the private school that I had left of my own initiative and free will, while at Giulio Cesare they just assumed I'd been expelled. It didn't take long, a couple of months from the beginning of the school year, before one afternoon Courbet invited us to his studio, ten minutes away from the school. No more tossing the balls and sprinting from one side of the gym to the other. Far more serious and intense things awaited us here. His atelier was a barren cellar space that gained what little light it had from a pair of transom windows just above street level. A few large electric lamps illuminated a full-size bed, hastily remade, a long table made of construction planks and sawhorses, with paintbrushes and jars of paint, and then stretched canvases stacked along the walls. The whole place was white but dotted with stains, rumpled, grayish. Even the bedsheets, with the consistency of cardboard, seemed to have been painted white, rather than washed: and painted upon that white field were the shadings of the rumpled sheets. Seated or half-lying on those sheets, on Courbet's bed, with cigarettes in our mouths, we watched the exhibition of his paintings, which our gym teacher turned toward us one at a time, without comments.

He was good, Courbet was. And obsessive. He drew and painted only in black and white. He reproduced bodies of naked women nude in obscene poses or others sprawled so languidly they looked like they were dead. He did it with noteworthy, I'd say almost excessive, skill.

It was then that I guessed at the link between artistic technique and masturbation, in every field of art where the virtuoso, the great virtuoso, capable of performing with the utmost mastery, is always, basically, masturbating: and that was, in fact, what Courbet did when he was painting, and what he wanted the audience of his paintings to do, canvases in which he reproduced with great minutiae the pubic hairs and the folds of the feminine bellies and the wrinkles in the models' erect nipples, women who were for the most part dark, mature, in fact, slightly decrepit, who gave every indication of having been his lovers. Technique is a sophisticated way of producing excitement, and that is what the great virtuosos (Salvador Dalí, Carlo Emilio Gadda, Glenn Gould, Alvin Lee) are doing with the vortex of their feverish, skillful fingers: a whirlpool of autoeroticism.

THEY WERE STRANGE and instructive afternoons, the ones we spent in Courbet's studio. He'd pour himself glasses of whiskey and offer us orangeade, with a faint smile of scorn and superiority, but also of brotherhood, in the manner that an elder brother has, or ought to have, when he teaches his younger brethren about life: he enchants them, he weans them, and he pushes them away, out into open waters. Once we'd drunk our orangeade, we'd start looking at the nude women, thighs splayed, that Courbet had painted. Those open thighs ought to have united us, but the element that united us was, at the same time, a thousand miles away, out of our reach.

FROM THE THINGS he said and the canvases he painted, you'd say that our teacher thought about nothing but women, only then he would surprise us with paradoxical lines of thought, which both amused us and filled us with doubts.

"Sure, you talk, you all talk and talk . . ." while in fact we were saying nothing, ". . . but deep down, there's not all that big of a difference in fucking someone in the ass and getting fucked in the ass . . . sticking it in a hole or having your hole stuck, what's the big deal, after all?"

At the sight of our baffled faces he would drive on. "The idea that a man should get all worked up over something like this strikes me as ridiculous. Do you feel like taking it up the ass? Then go ahead!"

And then other prophecies we didn't understand, concerning age and the passage of time, which was of course the exact reason we didn't understand them.

"You have no idea what it means for a man to get out of bed in the morning, bend over, and touch the tips of his toes . . . and what an immense miserable satisfaction there is in being able to do it."

He painted a lot and, from what he told us, sold his work briskly, at least a painting a week. When he ran out of canvases to show us, he limited himself to teaching.

"SO YOU THINK that the fact that you like nude women means you're safe, right? If women excite you, you figure that you're wired correctly . . . well, not necessarily. It's just another way, a different way, of being effeminate. In reality, all men are queers, that's right, all of them. The ones who don't like women and who like to take it up the ass, they're queers, obviously. But what about the ones, instead, who spend all day every blessed day thinking about women, like me . . . ? Or like you? What kind of men are they, or I should say, what kind of men are we, what sort of males are those who have nothing but pussy in their heads? Who think about nothing but legs, skirts, high-heeled shoes . . . are these virile thoughts, in your opinion?

"As a result, men can be divided into two categories: queers, who love other men, and half-queers, who love women. A real man ought to hang around with men only, but if he does that, then he's queer. And in fact, in the old days, all those bands and gangs were queer . . . monks, sailors, pirates . . . even Robin Hood and his merry men!"

And he'd throw back another glass of whiskey, at four in the afternoon. "So what's left? The only thing left is to possess women brutally. To hold them in contempt. That's the only way a male can feel safe from the risk of effeminacy. By scorning what you desire. But it's such a depressing thing . . . so vulgar . . ." And at that point a great wave of melancholy swept over him.

IT'S INEVITABLE that men who really like women sooner or later desire, not only to have women, but also to *be* women, that they should be curious, that is, to experience the same sensations that women experience, wear their clothing, turn men's minds inside out, go all languid . . . fondle a breast that doesn't jut out from or hang off someone else's body, but their own. The attraction for the female sex organ can't help but push you into the fantasy of having one of your own. The act of hiking up a skirt is every bit as stirring if you perform it on yourself. The feminine potential of so-called lady killers is very highly developed, and it doesn't matter whether or not it becomes explicit. A man who is seriously virile can't be fully attracted to the opposite sex: he has to take substantial part in the nature of the thing that he desires, the theory of gender complementarity, if it's not a flat-out piece of stupidity, is in any case an oversimplification, scholastic in nature, like the distinction made between Classicists and Romantics, Guelphs and Ghibellines, just to be clear. Desire is not fostered only by difference but above all by similarity, by semblance, and a womanizer's narcissism is so acute that he dies of curiosity to know what a woman feels when she is wrapped in his arms . . . since when he is embracing a woman, he's embracing himself.

A man of that kind might desire women as an ornament or a consolation, he might win them over, if only to paint them, he might molest them, humiliate them, emulate them, allow himself to be subjugated by them, or avoid them entirely. Or else it might be they who avoid him.

> *There was a time when taking it up the ass relaxed you, now*
> *it pisses you off. Strange but true how the arc*
> *of a long love story can be summarized that way.*
> (poem by Courbet)

A COUPLE OF YEARS after school ended I convinced Arbus to come back to the gym, just to "stay in shape." At first he was reluctant, but then he accepted. His gaunt physique was growing increasingly bent with the passing of the years and, incredible but true, at age twenty, skinny as he was, Arbus was already showing something of a gut. He had completely given up the postural gymnastics that had been prescribed to straighten him. The initiative of buying memberships in the gym was perhaps the last thing we ever did together; the last thing I did with my friend before losing sight of him forever. We chose the gym across the street from my house, it was convenient. The proprietor, Gabriele Ontani, instructor for male customers, was a fanatic who reduced everything to two fundamental truths: "man is a beast" and "woman is a work of art." As a result, he did everything he could to ensure that we became even more beastly. In the end, that wild animal and that work of art were destined to meet and couple, but we had to be worthy of them, and adequately prepared. It's obvious that if you spend a whole lifetime redesigning bodies, reshaping backs, arms, chests, and legs, you can never overlook the sexual use to which those bodies will be put. And so Ontani spurred us on, stimulated us with insults of every kind (focused on the fact that we were beasts, since "man is a beast"), strictly to prepare us for the woman or women who awaited us, in order that we might be worthy when the moment finally came; and every effort we made, all the push-ups and the sweat and the constant repetition of the same movements (accompanied by Ontani's imprecations and his typical method of setting the rhythm: "*Go-go-go—come on now—come on—go-go . . . and Go-go-go-go-go-go . . . man is a beast!*") served chiefly to train us for intercourse.

That means that Ontani is the fourth gym teacher to appear in this book.

WE HELD OUT in there for a couple of months. I obeyed Ontani as best I could, executing his commands right up to the threshold of pain. As I said, few gyms back then had sophisticated equipment, and Ontani's had none to speak of, sophisticated or otherwise. His was the old system of free body calisthenics, which have nothing at all to do with freedom, that is to say, push-ups, toe touches, sit-ups, bench press, the wheelbarrow, hand weights, bench weights, all very homemade and obsessive, and then exercises in pairs where you were supposed to lift your partner and haul on his arms until you'd practically yanked them out of their sockets. As an exercise partner, Arbus was implacable. He really pushed and yanked with all his strength, and sometimes, under my breath so that Ontani couldn't hear me, I had to beg him, "Hey, cut that out!" especially in one exercise that involved sitting face-to-face, legs spread, feet arched toward the partner's feet, and then, grabbing each other's wrists, one had to pull the other forward into a bow until, if possible, his forehead grazed the floor, which is something you can do only if you are limber from plenty of training. Otherwise, stabbing pains and stitches beneath the thighs. If it had been up to Arbus, who I discovered to my great amazement possessed a grip of steel, he would have hauled until he broke my back. And yet it was because of Arbus that we quit Ontani's gym, and it was precisely because of his notorious slogan. While we were executing the third or fourth set of ten push-ups, Ontani came to stand over me and Arbus as we were slaving away. My arms were trembling with every push-up, Arbus on the other hand was pumping up and down quickly and had almost finished the set, when Ontani leaned down until his face was level with our heads as if he was afraid we might not hear him clearly and, stopping his counting, he burst out with his usual catchphrase:

"Man is a beast!"

ARBUS STOPPED EXERCISING and sat on the floor. Without his eyeglasses, he looked at Ontani, who was still bending over, his hands braced on his knees, and was therefore close enough for Arbus to focus on his falsely threatening face, which was actually playful and mocking. Arbus said to him in a low voice: "Listen, sir, let's get one thing straight: I *am not a beast.*" Ontani's face maintained its smiling smirk but now it stiffened. "So you can stop once and for all shouting in my ears," added Arbus, as he got to his feet. Ontani stood up too. He continued smiling, certain that my classmate was joking: it must never once have happened to him in his years of honorable career as a gym instructor that anyone had rejected his anthropological theory, and especially not the way Arbus had done, that is, taking it literally. For perhaps the first time, Ontani lost his proverbial arrogance. He was stumped, he held both hands on his hips as Arbus gazed at him with his mole-like stare, opaque but level, firm, and calm. At that point Ontani gave him a slap in the face. "Show respect for your elders!" was all that he managed to blurt out to justify an act that had disqualified him, revealing him to be an arrogant and easily provoked person, an act that everyone in the gymnasium, I am quite certain, deplored.

However stubborn and devoid of wit, Arbus in contrast came off famously.

I REMEMBER WHEN, at the end of lengthy construction projects that had torn up the pavement of the courtyard of the middle school, the SLM swimming pool was finally inaugurated. It was a grand event. From that day forth, the hours of physical education were split up between the gymnasium (with a very high ceiling and lots and lots of light) and the shadowy, dank pool, its walls covered with artistic majolica tiles. As far as athletic activities were concerned, there was quite a difference between swimming in a pool built especially for your school and kicking a ball made of crumpled paper down the hallway, as I would find myself doing later on, at Giulio Cesare High School.

SWIM CLASS WAS PUNCTUATED BY LINES LIKE: "You've got tits like a woman!" "And you have a tiny dick!"

There was this obsession with being somehow defective. You mocked others and were in turn mocked for the same old story. The mockery was crude, monotonous, and stupid: for example, if a pal or classmate was bending over, you'd run your finger upward between his buttocks, and in the meantime murmur into his ear: "The *ssshaarkkk* is here!"

Your classmate would jerk upright after being grazed by the "shark."

Sometimes it was more than just a grazing.

And you never, never bent over to tie your shoes or pick up a folder off the floor. They'd knock your pen off the desk to make you bend over to get it . . . and while you were bent over . . . here it comes up behind you . . . the *sss-shaaarkkkk*!

AT SLM like so many deranged zoo animals we wound up wooing any female surrogate—any image or substitute object—attractive classmates, elementary school kids, even priests and their tunics that billowed in the wind like skirts, long and languid evening gowns, and then figures we cut out to glue into our theme essays, a statuette of the Madonna, milk white and sky blue, and our classmates' mothers, who were women in flesh and blood, certainly, albeit unreal and untouchable. Once we were older, we'd reserve our unexpressed chivalry for the stark-naked girls of *ABC* magazine and, at home, in the corners of our little bedrooms, directing our eyes there, in that metaphysical void, in search of a point of reference, an apparition, like little shepherd boys ready to be blinded. There were those who fell in love with their classmate, their deskmate, others who fell in love with their own book bag and the books it held, some who fell in love with money (I believe that many great fortunes were built specifically to make up for this lack of a woman), while others still vented with soccer or sheer insanity. Crasta, a.k.a. Kraus, the stupidest one of us all, fell head over heels in love with the matron who sold pizza during recess, a woman well along in years whose enormous shapeless bosom kept her from moving freely.

12

ANOTHER REMARKABLE MARIST BROTHER, Brother Barnaba, is in charge of the SLM swimming pool. He is known as the intelligent priest. His intelligence is unquestioned, there's no need to give any proof of it, everyone knows he's smart, it's like a hidden tattoo everyone talks about even though no one's seen it. Tall and gangly, he walks silently, putting one foot in front of the other, along a sort of pre-drawn line down the hallways, with sharp right-angled turns at the corners. When he talks he's subtle, cautious, laconic, and cool. He, too, like the headmaster—and in fact, he's the headmaster's right-hand man—wears smoked-glass spectacles with steel frames on the tip of his nose. Barnaba probably owes his fame as an intelligent priest to the fact that he has been put in charge, with great skill and success, it should be said, of the school's extracurricular activities: in particular, of course, the management of the swimming pool, the playing fields, and the film forum. Activities that put us in relation with the outside world and normal life, the life led by men and women. And he is the one who establishes this contact. Barnaba is in fact the priest whom we can most easily imagine, the easiest to guess what he would have been like if he hadn't been a priest. The fact that he is one seems like the result of crossed wires: as if one fine morning, while hastily getting out of bed, he had dressed in the dark without realizing that there, on the chair, was a tunic instead of his usual clothing, and once he was out on the street it was already too late, by now he could no longer take off that clothing, he had become one with his priestly habit. In the old days, ships would shanghai sailors by getting them drunk, then hitting them over the head, and the next morning the new sailor would wake up, aboard ship, land already out of sight. As a result, Barnaba is the one we admire the most, but also the one who makes us angriest, he remains a mystery, it's not clear what he's doing at SLM and why he doesn't just discard his tunic and go out into the world, open an engineering office or a law firm like our fathers, get married and start a family and go the beach for his summer vacation instead of continuing to say mass and mumble prayers and sleep in the narrow single cot in his tiny room.

The rooms where the Marist brothers live and sleep on the upper floors of the school resemble college dorm rooms: they're small and unadorned, devoid of the mystical allure of a monastic cell. The grown men who live in them lie down alone every night, reading a few pages always from the same books before dropping off to sleep. Aside from the breviary, the Holy Scriptures, and the textbooks for the subjects they teach—which each of them goes over scrupulously before their lessons because nothing could be worse than to be caught flat-footed by a smarty-pants student—I've never known a priest to read a book just for the pleasure of it. Reading must be useful, it must serve a purpose, and that purpose is growth. To grow as a human being, to grow spiritually, to grow as individuals, and to grow as a community with others—growth is the true obsession of all priests, and even as adults they never cease to grow and to expand their knowledge, their awareness, their faith, their hope, and their love. Their personal condition, as men or as Christians. In religious discourses the verb, in a succession of hammering anaphoras, is repeated with the addition of all the prepositions imaginable— we grow with love, we grow for love, we grow in the midst of love, thanks to love, we must grow with others, among others, amid others, for others, in others . . . All the things that happen in life, and especially the bad things, the misfortunes and the sorrows, are opportunities for growth. Our readings must contribute to this growth, otherwise they are only a waste of time. And yet, at every age, the little rooms where the priests live remain dorm rooms, typical of a boarding school or a university, but much neater. Perhaps it is celibacy that extends youth beyond all reasonable limits . . .

The priests I have known maintained for many years, even into their forties, a boyish appearance. Not only in their faces but also in their way of behaving. Their annoyance and their astonishment and their happiness were all expressed in infantile grimaces. And then their anger, which suddenly cast a shadow over their faces, as if they'd never learned how to contain it.

ONE TIME, in Seoul, in South Korea, I had a long conversation with a Buddhist monk, young and handsome, who had a round face, smooth pudgy hands, and eyes and mouth that glistened like a newborn's. I talked to him for a long time, in part because his English, as is the case with nearly all Koreans, was fragmentary and incomprehensible, but it didn't matter, since every sentence he uttered was followed by a radiant smile and his little eyes winked, that's right, they winked, communicating a sort of happy disinterest toward the concepts that our mouths were trying, in the meantime, to transmit, with some considerable effort. Perhaps—in fact, certainly—he understood me, I didn't understand the words he was saying at all, but the rest, his calm, the way he almost made fun of me, his lips twisted in disenchanted laughter, was very clear to me. To be able to talk to people like that more frequently! People who don't argue, don't harangue, don't refute. Although we were taking part in an important ceremony with the official attendance of the highest religious and civil authorities, he wore his white tunic, with dirty sleeves, but truly filthy, and such indifference to appearance on the one hand astonished me, on the other, reassured me. It was as if he feared nothing, he wasn't even afraid of appearing or being impure, and he suggested that I do the same. (I had already noticed during that trip various oddities, like the fact that the Buddhist monks were always clutching their cell phones, of which they sometimes had several, the very latest models, which they allowed to ring during ceremonies and religious services, absolutely indifferent to the noise, and they'd loudly answer calls with great bursts of laughter . . .)

After roughly an hour of nonconversation, interrupted only by the mouthfuls of food we'd fish off the dishes scattered around the table, an operation in the course of which the holy man had cheerfully further bespattered and begrimed himself, he insisted that I guess his age and tell him mine (when it comes to the way we managed to communicate these details between us, I'll refer only to the fact that he took my right hand, turned it palm upward and laid it in his hand, and then, with his thumbnail, which he probably hadn't cut in months, he traced grooves on it the way prisoners do to count, lots of parallel lines, crossed by a diagonal every so often. The number of years, the passing of time. With his fingernail he crossed and recrossed my Life Line).

I looked at him carefully as he lifted a fish ball to his lips and slurped it into his mouth with his gleaming tongue. He looked like a very young man but he couldn't be all that young, his race and his way of life had preserved him, so I added five or six years to my initial evaluation and took a stab: "Thirty-two?" He burst out laughing. "Thirty-five?" He shook his head. Perhaps the meditation he practiced all day long really had spared him the passage of time. Just like in a basketball game, the chronometer was simply stopped while he was intently praying. In the void, his metabolism went at half my rate. In that case, I thought, if he looked twenty, he must be forty. "Forty . . . but I can't believe it . . . you're forty years old . . . !" Not so. The monk continued smiling and ran his hand over his shaven head. I noticed that there were numerous scars on his flesh as if someone had whipped him with a belt when he was a child. At those points, the scars kept his hair from growing back. His lips pursed into the shape of a heart, he carefully enunciated: "Fif-ty . . . se-ven . . . !"

THEN FROM ONE DAY to another they get old. From young boys they suddenly are covered with wrinkles and their hair turns white all at once. Barnaba was perhaps the only one who looked his exact age, in short, he was a man and not an aged child. For some the desire of perfection can take no other form than a separation from the world. That was not the case for Brother Barnaba. He, too, had a thorn planted in his body.

IT'S A PROD, a thorn in the flesh, which produces an infection, and the infection eventually reaches the heart.

The thought is an autonomous entity. The thought speaks, suggests, insinuates, makes figures dance before your eyes.

The thought must be subjected to punishment.

A woman's body is fire, a young boy's body is fire.

But even without making contact with another body you can sin. You sin with your mind, which can be even more impure than your body.

If that thorn has spared you so far, it's no merit of yours. It means that the devil just didn't consider you worthy of fighting with him.

13

UPON MR. GOLGOTHA'S ENTRANCE, Eleuteri started singing vaguely in his faint contralto voice: in spite of the fact that he had a small dark mustache, the voice itself hadn't changed since he had wandered whimpering and whining down the hallways of middle school because someone had stolen a piece of pizza from him, tearing it roughly out of his hands. And in fact, that's what high school kids did: incursions among the younger students, not so much *stealing* their lunches and snacks as *destroying* them. One piece remained in the interloper's hands, the rest flew onto the floor, tomato sauce down, smeared on the linoleum. (Linoleum, what a material: in twenty years, no one will know what it is, we'll have to footnote it.) Since then, Eleuteri had grown, taller and stouter, but his voice had remained high-pitched and nasal and made us all, actually, not just teachers but us students, too, want to straight-armed slap him to make him shut up: you know, the kind of disagreeable sound, like fingernails scratching on metal. Hiding behind rows of drooping shoulders that no Brother Curzio would ever be able to straighten with his barked commands, his one-two, one-two, up-down, come-on-get-going, making us bend down and squat ten or twenty times over the little wooden cubes, and yet revealed unmistakably by that nasal tone of voice, Eleuteri struck up his blasphemous nursery rhyme to welcome Mr. Golgotha, our religion teacher:

> *Take a little nail . . .*
> *And a little hammer . . .*
> *Come and join us, drive a nail or two . . .*

To the tune of "Bibbidi-Bobbidi-Boo," the novelty song from Disney's *Cinderella*, it was a blasphemous little ditty about the Crucifixion. Something so stupid and embarrassing that Mr. Golgotha didn't even manage to understand it, indeed, didn't even perceive it, taking it for background noise from the classroom and the hallways, from the school as a whole. A school, in fact, is nothing other than an enormous echo chamber for bothersome noises, or a concert hall where all the instruments are being tuned. Along with the orchestra, there's a choir vocalizing in voices high and low, light and dark, a thousand singers, all rehearsing their parts. How could Golgotha have noticed that little ditty, how can you single out one individual piece of idiocy when you're soaking all day every day in a sea of idiocy? Every student is well aware of the fact, and if it ever happens that the student in question one day becomes a teacher, and he chances to find himself, so to speak, in the somewhat hyperbolic phrase, "on the other side of the barricades," he'll certainly bring that awareness with him: the fact that teachers notice practically nothing of what their students say, think, and scheme behind their backs, and not even the things that they do openly before them; they cannot control the reactions and the laughter and the passed notes and the smirks and the whispers and the obscene gestures; they manage to grasp one out of ten of the wisecracks that target them.

STRANGE TO SAY IN A SCHOOL run by priests, but our religion teacher wasn't a priest. Who knows why. The most crucial subject at a religious school was taught by someone who wasn't a religious, by a dilettante, so to speak, even if he was animated by a great and abiding passion. Perhaps too much passion. In fact, the students called him Golgotha, or Mr. Golgotha. Golgotha was the refrain in nearly all the things he had to say, which revolved around Mount Golgotha, in fact: the image of Golgotha, the prophecy of Golgotha, the Golgotha that can be found inside each of us, and if it's not inside us it's right before us, before our eyes, in our destiny, on the

horizon, even if we can't see it, and if we don't see it, that's because we don't
want to see it, but the Golgotha is there, right there, awaiting us.

Why don't you come hammer with us . . .
Hammer the nails of Baby Jesus
Put an end to all this fuss!

Without any need to respond to Eleuteri's provocative ditty, Mr. Golgotha already had tears in his eyes, they'd been there even before he set foot
in the classroom. It had been a difficult year for him, more than difficult,
insurmountable. The idea of hiring a layman to teach religion in a school
run by priests had been a risky one. Perhaps it had been done in order to
demonstrate the openness and modernity of a school that nonchalantly
chose to entrust the teaching of the subject that constituted its very reason
for existence to an outsider. Good job, smart choice, compliments on your
democratic pluralism. The problem was that, as a result, it wasn't clear, and
especially not to us students, just what authority Mr. Golgotha enjoyed,
whence it derived, since he was not a priest, in other words, why on earth
we ought to sit and listen to someone like him talking to us about Jesus,
after the priests themselves had already talked about Him quite a bit, more
than enough I'd say, at catechism and at mass. We'd have been willing to undergo the umpteenth tirade about the Christ who illumines, the Christ who
magnifies, the Christ who redeems, the Christ who forgives, the Christ
who loves, if it was being delivered by a young brother filled with the spirit,
newly graduated from the seminary, or else a hidebound old priest, who
would harshly throw his appeals to goodness into our faces like so many
roundhouse punches: but how could we believe and obey that hypersensi-
tive, ill-shaven young man, whose vocation for that matter was so weak and
uncertain that it hadn't even led him to wear the black skirt?
    Since Mr. Golgotha was anything but stupid, he had understood imme-
diately, from the very first day, the atmosphere he was going to be working
in, and that the year he was going to spend with us was going to be sheer
torture if he tried to follow the path of catechism and doctrine like any
other priest: he absolutely had to emphasize the difference. He had therefore chosen to play the extremely risky card of the innovator: someone who
wants to change, be more modern and up to date, bring a breath of fresh
air. Now, this type of teacher tends to arouse among his students very little
enthusiasm and a great deal of suspicion, and among them there are

immediately those who plan to take advantage of him. What's the trick? wonders the majority. While a disciplined minority, naïve or idealistic, follows the teacher in his revolutionary programs, the more cynical students scheme to make a fool of him. That's the price progressivism always has to pay. And if the subject matter is religion, it's not clear how you can lay it down in a new way. And yet Mr. Golgotha had given it a try.

HE HAD PROMISED from the very first lesson that he wouldn't talk about God (a subject about which we already knew all there was to know, that is, truth be told, *nothing*), but instead about ourselves. What is that supposed to mean, "ourselves"? Well, about our problems. About our psychological problems. About our problems "as young people today" (in every historical period, obviously, there are "young people today" and they always have their own specific set of problems). "We want to talk about our problems" meant nothing more than an aspiration to say something, anything, to vent. At least, that's what Golgotha seemed to think. Who knows why he imagined that young people's problems are always psychological in nature, and therefore inevitably stem from the family, when instead it's pretty evident that what's really making them suffer is first and foremost their physique, their body, their skin, their hair, their stomach, their genitals, their muscles, their legs—maybe too short or too skinny or too hairy—and then their gums and oily flesh and armpits and hair follicles and acid reflux and body odors and dry skin and dandruff . . . all being traced back to their psyches, as if these were mere projections, fantasies, ghosts.

(Might it not be appropriate to talk about zits with a religion teacher, would it be too basic to put zits first in your thoughts, in your "problems" . . . ?)

Adolescents are stuffed into their bodies like so many sausages, often with hormone levels raging out of control, and in spite of that, they are still peered at through the lens of the soul, by people trying to figure out what it is that's not working right in their heads. For that matter, in the years during which this story unfolds, psychoanalysis entered—in some cases on tiny cat feet, in others with impetuous recklessness, touted as an explanation, a solution, a discovery, or a revolution—into a vast and diverse array of settings, the companion piece to any conversation or topic. A psychoanalytical interpretation came hurrying to the rescue of a rather feeble theory, in the midst of a controversial debate, and it was used as a crowbar to force open unsolvable problems, revealing the mechanisms that lay behind all decisions. Everything could now be reviewed and explained through the lens of psychoanalysis, which magnified to a dizzying extent details, revealing things that had never been seen before: politics, literature, art, society, the family, war, fascism, cinema, as well as history and even the hard sciences could be colored with meaning from the spectrum of psychoanalysis now being beamed onto them. So why not religion, too? What difference does it make if, instead of the soul, we talk about the psyche? That's changing just one word, a word that, for that matter, means the same thing. And in place of the usual brandishing of menacing passages from Holy Scripture, offer current, personal experiences, taken from our everyday lives. Instead of Jacob and Elijah, the stories of your friends—and your own stories, too. Setting aside the old books, numbered line by line, let's talk about ourselves instead, freely, let's talk about "our problems" (some these days might talk about "problematics").

Like any progressive teacher, Golgotha thought he could get away with it, with this reduction of God to ego, of metaphysics to history and of history to current events, of religious doctrine to run-of-the-mill advice about how to live, in the belief that that's what we needed, what we were thirsting for. If I toss the Bible overboard and instead start talking about Oedipus complexes and obscure drives, or about sexuality, this longtime taboo, the boys will stir out of their apathetic boredom, they'll pay attention to what I have to say or at the very least they'll stop shooting spitballs at me when I have my back turned, busily writing the names of the prophets on the chalkboard: that's what Mr. Golgotha must have had in mind. But he'd miscounted his aces. Just imagine. With his idea of letting us open our hearts and bare our thoughts, he had no idea what he was up to. In fact, here is a good phrase from the Gospels that would have suited him to a tee: Forgive him, Lord, for he knows not what he does. He did not know, in other words, that we had no thoughts in our heads whatsoever, and the thoughts that we did have were unspeakable, unconfessable, that we would never have dreamed of revealing them to anyone, and certainly not to a teacher in front of the rest of the class, or else that we might even have done it, and this actually happened, I think, only a couple of times in all, and was greeted with a hail of laughter and shrill whistles as the other boys mocked whatever our classmate was confessing. Deep down, this is what Golgotha wanted from us: he wanted to hear our confessions, he wanted us to reveal our sins, and to feel relieved in so doing, with no expectation of the shame that would envelop them, these revelations, or the gusts of noisy heckling that would sweep them away.

Therefore, poor, mortified Golgotha often found himself standing there spouting soliloquies, preaching in the wilderness of our indifference and mistrust, reading practically incomprehensible passages taken from the classic texts of psychoanalysis, passages that left no marks on our consciousness, our slumbers interrupted only by the clanging bell marking the end of the hour. This, of course, is the common fate of all those who teach a subject considered to be of lesser importance, with only a few hours spread out among a great many classes and a vast number of students who, after months and months, barely know who the teacher is, so rarely have they laid eyes upon him, and who can scarcely remember his name, much less Mr. Golgotha, who fooled himself into believing that he could draw an individual psychological profile of each of us. Who actually believed that he could use *The Interpretation of Dreams* or *The Psychopathology of Everyday Life* to bring out our obsessions and heal them.

And who had even dared, to the absolute astonishment of us students, to venture into the seething-hot territory of sex, questioning us about our desires, sampling and testing our knowledge and expectations, a truly courageous undertaking, all things considered, or else completely mad or reckless, a pioneer of a new subject, a religious studies teacher in a school run by priests venturing within a footstep, just a hairbreadth from sex education! That subject, about which a debate was raging at that time, in the wake of the larger reforms in society's morals and customs, as to whether it ought to be taught at school, introduced as a full-fledged topic of instruction as, for example, it was said they were doing in Sweden—sure, of course, Sweden, the eternal touchstone, the emblem of an advanced nation behind which ours lagged, underdeveloped as always. Sex education was just added to the list of great innovations discussed and called for in those years, when people advocated "reading the newspaper in class" (which newspaper? Our unfailing response was *Il Corriere dello Sport*, basically the sports pages, in other words, while among the magazines most often suggested, we offered *Le Ore* and *Caballero*, rough Italian equivalents of *Hustler* or *Playboy*) or suggested that instead of going on field trips to the Reggia di Caserta or to Bomarzo, we should be carted off to farms or factories to get a closer look at manual labor, executed by those callused hands which, when displayed, according to a parable still touted in our elementary school primers, one would promptly gain admission through the pearly gates.

Until someone came along who decided to pay Golgotha back in the same coin. It was, in fact, the same day that Eleuteri had greeted our

religion teacher with his mocking and irreverent little ditty. But it was Arbus, unexpectedly, who took the pantomime to the next level.

That morning, in fact, Golgotha had got it into his head to take on the
topic, without warning, of the "drug problem," that is, one of the main
"problems" of "young people today," the biggest new development with respect to the same old problems as ever. It would have been a safe bet that he
would get there eventually, there wasn't a single adult in the world, and for
that matter there isn't one now, who didn't glimpse the sinister shadow of
drugs looming over any given aspect of young people's lives; much less
would any of these adults give up the chance to refer—perhaps in strictly
ritual terms, as a verbal duty that must be performed, whatever the situation—to the "dangers of drugs." There were two possibilities: that drugs
were the cause of the problems, or else their consequence; either you have a
problem because you're on drugs or else you're on drugs because you have
a problem. From the words he used that day, it was clear however that
Mr. Golgotha set out from the assumption that he was introducing us to a
totally unfamiliar topic, one we were familiar with only because we'd heard
about it from others. He wanted, in other words, to protect us, to put us on
our guard: it never would have occurred to him that the chosen topic could
be anything more than a useful moral exercise, a simulation undertaken as
a sort of preemptive war game, if we ever actually happened, someday in
the distant future, to come face-to-face with those problems.

"It is the weakness of the spirit," he said, "that drugs take advantage of."

Golgotha talked about drugs as if they were a single person, endowed
with will and awareness, and it was always therefore treated in the third
person singular. Drugs were a treacherous individual, a dangerous companion who offers to lend a hand, then takes everything for himself.

"But you can't let drugs offer to help you."

"Then who?"

It was Arbus who had posed the question. He asked it with curiosity, not
insolence, though the two things tend to resemble each other to an uncomfortable extent in any adolescent, let alone Arbus, our own Nobel laureate.
If someone asks questions, it means they're not satisfied with what's been
said, or they don't entirely buy into it, and therefore every question, even
the most guileless and innocent, is bound to be seen as a criticism, or a
challenge.

"You don't know, Arbus? Of course you know."

"No, teacher, I don't know. Why don't you tell me?"

"Do you have friends you can count on?"

"Real friends, teacher?" and Arbus ran his eyes around the class and in the end sat gazing at me, though not for long, just long enough that everyone understood that his gaze was a clear indication, an answer to Golgotha. I didn't enjoy being dragged into the challenges, intellectual and nonintellectual, that Arbus stubbornly insisted on hurling at teachers, at priests, and at authority in general. I didn't like mental arm wrestling back then, and I'm sure I never will enjoy it. If I fight back, I do so instinctively, but I'm never the first to wave a red flag, I'd rather stay out of squabbles, neither create them nor wade into them, it bores me to watch them and I feel anxious when I have to take part in them. Having been tapped by Arbus to participate, it meant I had to take sides, or rather that, like it or not, I had already taken sides with him in what promised to be a diatribe, a stupid diatribe, and with whom? With that wretch Golgotha! Fun times! Start something up with a teacher like him! Why couldn't he just have let him spout off on his own? Golgotha would eventually have run out of steam, and with him, like the flickering flame of a wax taper burning down to the candleholder, the religion class. But at the same time, under the annoyance at being called into combat in that manner by Arbus, I felt a warm surge, a physical pleasure not unlike the touch of an unexpected caress. That glance of his was a fine declaration of friendship, which embarrassed me and filled me with pride at the same time. Nonetheless, I didn't return the gesture, and I did so deliberately, I turned my eyes away from my friend's eyes and looked at the floor instead.

"Well, teacher? Is it enough to have a friend to defeat the scourge of *ddh*rugs?" That's how he pronounced that last word, in an imitation of the drawling cadence that Golgotha practiced in his sermons, a cadence that surfaced especially when he grew heated. Some in the class, among the few who were actually paying attention to the exchange of views between student and teacher, laughed, but it was clear that Arbus wasn't putting on a show for them, he hadn't parodied the teacher for their benefit, or had he, though? After a fashion, Arbus enjoyed a curious popularity, in other words, he was a character.

Mr. Golgotha went on, placidly inspired. It was clear that he was falling back on his last remaining resources, he'd consumed all the rest during that year spent preaching to the four winds, winds so powerful that the seeds he'd scattered didn't even touch the ground but simply went spinning into the whirlwind and then blew back into his face. Residual energies seem to have a special quality, it's firewood that burns bright, and so what he said next was truly inspired and yet, at the same time, incomprehensible, both because of the elevated concepts contained in his words, and because those words sank into an even darker gulf of dialect, verging on some other language, you might call it a dead tongue, like Ancient Greek or Aramaic. Blessed were those who did understand him, because that very day he entered into heaven. I certainly didn't understand him, so profound were the things he said, I couldn't follow them in the slightest, they made an impression on me, sure, but I didn't really grasp them, and that is why I can't reproduce them here. Only Arbus seemed to follow the thread. Then, when he descended from the realms of the empyrean back to the sphere my intellect could reach, and once again began speaking in Italian, a dazzling archaic Italian full of laments, not unlike what I imagine was spoken by Giordano Bruno—*Il Nolano*—or Tommaso Campanella, or Bernardino Telesio, he said more or less the things that I render here in a somewhere simplified language.

"CALL THEM by the names that you prefer . . . the opportunities to err are numerous. We have countless numbers of different ways to get things wrong and a frequency that is daunting just to consider. Once a minute. Therefore it is a true miracle if at the end of a day, we've made only four or five mistakes, rather than a thousand, and if we're lucky, none of those mistakes are grave ones, we haven't killed anyone, our carelessness and our lies haven't caused any apartment buildings to collapse, and the small change stolen from a dresser drawer, tomorrow, if we so choose, we can always put back, with no one the wiser. In fact, this is what almost always happens: we make mistakes without witnesses. We can make up for our mistakes, and we can pray that they go unnoticed, or that they're almost immediately pardoned or forgotten. If there were no forgiveness, the defects of memory would ensure the same outcome: which is to say, that we never pay the price of our errors. The police fail to catch us, or if they do, they don't have the time or interest to go after small fry like us, there are more serious problems to solve. The world doesn't consider us the way we deserve for the good things that we do, much less for the bad things. The world is otherwise occupied, too distracted by the larger wounds, by the craters, the atomic blasts, to worry about tiny scratches. And that is how we start out, this is why we go on, but the conclusion will be different. We start out with a tickle, but we wind up burned alive. The scanty interest aroused by our misdeeds tempts us, first of all, to repeat them without fear, and then to make them intentionally much worse. Two-bit criminals that we are, we ought to be punished immediately, not because our infractions are so significant, but because the only way we have of emerging from the nameless crowd is to commit more spectacular ones. For that matter, you might reasonably say that it does no good to punish them, after all, the level would rise all the same, either because of the punishment or because of its absence. There are individuals for whom forgiveness, punishment, indulgence, or indifference all amount to the same thing, and obtain the same effect. They are an equation that, in whatever order you put the factors, and however you add them up or subtract them, multiply them or divide them, the result is always the same, namely zero."

WAS HE TALKING ABOUT US? Was he talking *to* us? Golgotha had set off on a tangent. No one could stop him now, no one could stop his sermon, which wasn't really a sermon at all, since he didn't seem bound to convince or convert anyone. It was, rather, a soliloquy, that's right, a way of letting off steam. When Golgotha grew animated, instead of growing more vivid and colorful, he just became dull and gray, his dark little goatee seemed to get damp, his eyes, already sunken in their sockets, turned tiny and blazed with a desperate, diabolical flame. It was, in fact, as if he were possessed. Flecks of slobber formed at the corners of his mouth, stirring in us a sense of disgust and of the ridiculous, but in the end, almost, of fear. Fear of what? Of him? Of his punishing us? Inasmuch as an agent of goodness, an angel of truth, while we were all sinners? Or was it fear of the fact that he had gone mad, and that he was actually the devil, concealed beneath the garb of a miserable, mild-mannered, unfortunate soul, in his face and in body and attire and certainly in the pittance that the priests paid him, this little religious studies teacher? What figure could be better suited to that role than this grim and emaciated Molise-born man of the cloth as an emissary of the Evil One? I didn't know whether to sneer at him or admire him. So, most of the time, I did both, alternately, or joined in a single grimace, the face that you see in someone admiring a canvas in which a martyrdom is depicted, let's say, the scene of a saint sliced to bits or burned at the stake or gimleted by his executioners, his tormentors, where the disgust, the absurdity, and the ridicule of certain sadistic details and sheer heroism are fused into a single figure, inextricably—*that*, in the end, is the sentiment that the painting inspires.

"... THE REAL TRAGEDY is when everyone is right, when everyone has a valid reason for doing what they do, which is to say, for doing evil. Or at least a smidgen of a reason, a crumb of a reason, the kind that drives us to take vengeance, for example, in the belief that we're doing justice, righting a wrong, acting within the right. For that matter, if you don't have justice, then you do justice, and you do it quickly, you make it at home, like you distill aquavit or you can chopped tomatoes, justice, too, can be taken into one's own hands. You can't live without justice, it's something we need, without it we feel we can't breathe, and that's the reason for the eternal conflict among men, who are fundamentally unsuited to life and so they try to make up for their inadequacy by falling back on all means, legitimate or illicit, right out to the bounds of the absurd and the grotesque, and all this to procure the surrogate, whatever it is that can stand in for their missing arm, their diminutive stature, their poor pronunciation, or their shortage of money or intelligence. To put an end to those injustices, they create new ones. We are like broken dolls, from the very outset, it's not as if someone twisted off that arm and broke it, it's not like the dog ate it, we simply never had it at all! And it's only normal that we object and we fasten on to the faintest hope, a lottery ticket. Here, we talk all the time about faith, don't we? They talk to you about it, right? As something evident, normal, and concrete, true? Well, it's not at all clear where the boundary falls between a true faith and just any old superstition, that is the great problem, knowing how to tell the difference, because once again truth and reason seem to be all over the place, even the devil has reason on his side, sometimes, and he makes his fine arguments that are not entirely devoid of their logic, quite the opposite, his arguments hold up, in fact, they hold up beautifully! He's not all wrong, the devil.

"My lads, get used to thinking that the devil will show up punctually every time that you're right, when you have right on your side, and when you're pleased to be on the side of the angels, behold, that is when he shows up, as if he were bound and determined to cash in a part that we owe him, a commission for having kept his tools bright and shiny. The devil arrives at the very instant you feel inebriated, then, I mean to say, by your own honesty, your own correctness. Forgive me if I speak to you about Jesus and the Gospel, I'd promised not to do it ... but that is exactly what Jesus criticized the Pharisees for: you are servants of the devil when you're in the right, that is, when you cannot be criticized for anything, because that is exactly when, in such an abundance and culmination of honesty, you are actually full of the devil, of his impeccable logic, so typical of those who *always* and only perform their duty, and do it scrupulously, with precision . . . with style!"

"Teacher, sir, you're delirious!" spoke up a voice from the desks, interrupting Golgotha before he could get started again.

It was Rummo.

"Stop for a moment and catch your breath . . ."

"You're right, Rummo, you're correct when you say that I should stop. But I'm not delirious at all, you know that? What I'm saying to you I say in full cognizance . . ."

"Yes, but in practical terms, unless I've misunderstood, sir, you're telling us that when we behave as we ought to, we're actually complying with the devil's suggestions. And that," Rummo said, shaking his head, "is impossible. Or else it's impossible for me to understand."

Golgotha massaged his temples. He stepped down from his dais and went on in an even hoarser voice, which turned shrill as he uttered the key words. "It's the age-old question of the *law*," and in fact when he pronounced the word "law," it came out on a very high note. "The law, you understand, something that offers no margin. Something you can never get free of. Either you are crushed by it, or else you obey it just to avoid punishment, and therefore, in either case, you flee from it, or else you break it and you pay the consequences. Which means that the law will have its way, in any case. You can't escape it, whether you respect it or you transgress it. Think about it, think about it: this dates back to the prohibition against eating from the Tree of the Knowledge of Good and Evil, in the Garden of Eden. With that prohibition, sin became inevitable in its way, because it would have been a sin *not* to eat it, that apple, just to have left it there on the tree, what do you think? By respecting that prohibition, man would never have had access to the human condition, he would never have attained his fullness which, you may not believe this because it will seem absurd, but that fullness consists exactly, *ex-act-ly*, in its absence, that is, in sin! In other words, he would not have been a man while obeying, and he became a man only by falling, tumbling . . . becoming lost. There was no alternative. And there is none even now . . . perhaps."

"What do you mean, perhaps?" Rummo had gotten a little heated. "You need to give us clear indications, teacher, sir! Otherwise, we can't follow you. You're saying, in other words, that we can become men only by doing evil, right or wrong?"

"When we commit evil and when we suffer evil. But in order to suffer evil, there necessarily has to be someone who inflicts it, no? Jesus couldn't exactly clamber up onto the cross all by Himself, now, could He!"

Such a clamorous phrase had never before been heard at SLM. Perhaps not even outside its walls. But it had a logic all its own.

AT THAT POINT it became clear that Golgotha was gone now, out of his head. It was clear that the thoughts he was expressing were improvised, and yet they grew out of a long-pursued process of reasoning, a solitude that was macerated, decomposed, and anxious. How can it be, I thought to myself, that they always send us these bizarre individuals, on the verge of despair, to teach us? What's behind that, what are they trying to tell us, what plan lies behind the idea of abandoning a defrocked man without a calling like Mr. Golgotha to the tossing waves of a class made up of misfit rich kids? Maybe they want to know what we learn from human failure. Maybe they're starting us out from there, to help us avoid it ourselves? But at this point, I start to wonder, is it really avoidable at all? Or is it not more like a universal destiny that drags us all downward, toward misery? Or maybe they just want to let us sink our talons into an animate object, the way cats do. And Golgotha is our ball of yarn, they tossed him to us so that we could bat him back and forth between our paws. Thinking back upon it with hindsight, I find it only normal that these human cases should be found on a school faculty, where they serve as targets, as lightning rods, upon which the cruelty of the student body can be vented, thus sparing the other teachers: it's a statistical law. Still, though, the religious studies teacher, of all the subjects, such a fundamental one, in a school run by priests! How could they ever have thought of hiring a maniac to teach us to believe? Could it be because they themselves don't believe . . . ? Or else, this could be the truth, they think that only a raving lunatic would be able to kindle a flame in our hearts . . .

"It is necessary, in other words, that this should happen," Golgotha went on, recovering clarity and calm for a moment. "So we shouldn't be surprised. The division of labor between good and evil takes place *inside* us, most of the time . . ."

And here I started to sense that I understood, or at least that I was starting to understand, more clearly. The division is inside us, yes, I thought so myself. And I'd experienced it, it was true, that was an experience I'd had many times: feeling divided myself. "One part does the evil, the other part suffers it . . ."

It was a part of being alive, this schism.

"Listen, couldn't you explain this concept to us again?" asked Rummo.

"Shhh!" I silenced him. "Let him talk."

"Don't worry if you don't understand, boys, don't worry about it," said Golgotha. "Just try to get used to the idea that the threat doesn't come from other people . . ."

That's right, I thought to myself, other people aren't the threat . . .

"It doesn't come from other people, the threat, it comes from ourselves. The left hand conspires against the right. We already have drugs in our blood, there's no need to inject it, is that clear, do you understand it, yes or no?"

"No," said Rummo.

"Maybe," said Arbus. "Maybe," he repeated.

I was unsure whether Mr. Golgotha really was a holy man, a sage we didn't deserve, or simply nothing more than a miserable wretch, a charlatan, like those who sold miracle potions capable of curing any and all diseases. But in that case, why didn't he cure himself first and foremost? If he had come so close to the truth, then why had he allowed himself to be worn down into that state, with sweat on his forehead and temples, his suit wrinkled and rumpled and shiny at the elbows? Could it be that the truth manhandles those who discover it, leaving them in such dire straits? In the things he said, there was something that made me admire him, but it was the same thing that made me scorn him.

"If that's the case, then it is the blood of the weak and innocent inside us that is shed, and shedding that blood is the strong, the bullying, the violent one that is in us. Cain and Abel, you see? In the beginning, they were a single person. They were an only son . . ."

No, in that case he's crazy, I thought to myself.

"Teacher, just a minute . . ."

". . . then, in order to avoid confusing the simple souls, those who composed the Bible, skillful dramatists that they were, divided this son in two, doubled him into two, and there you have the two brothers, the shepherd and the farmer, the fair-haired and the dark . . ."

". . . hold on, just a minute!" Rummo objected.

"The good and the bad," Arbus added ironically.

"It would be more appropriate then to speak of suicide, for the first man born on earth, from the belly of his mother, and born already split . . ."

"No, that's enough!"

IT'S A SINGULAR THING to see how two or three people having a spirited discussion can seem, as soon as they raise their voices a bit, as if they're quarreling. Perhaps attracted by these sonic peaks and valleys, without anyone noticing that the door had been opened, the headmaster had materialized in the doorway, motionless, arms crossed. We leaped to our feet, a few who had been slumbering in the back rows were late in rising, imitating the others without understanding. From the position of his head, it seemed as if the headmaster were looking at us students, but I was almost certain that behind his dark glasses, his eyes were turned to look fixedly at Golgotha. Who was standing in front of the first row of desks, hands extended backward toward his desk, gripping it. The headmaster was sniffing the air, his head turning jerkily. Then he unfolded his arms, and in the process of that movement, he caressed the crucifix, repositioning it in the exact center of his chest, along the buttons.

"I thought I heard . . . how to put this . . . some uproar, in here. Fine. What sort of problem do we seem to have here, teacher?"

14

JESUS, Jesus, Jesus.

ONLY A PARADOXICAL FORM OF INJUSTICE, that gives up the idea of punishing the evil done, can reestablish peace. By restoring history to the point of departure, at a hypothetical year zero. The debt will be forgiven, the wrong erased.

THE HOLY SCRIPTURES ARE DISCOMFITING: a series of stories about treachery and great falls. Eve deceived by the serpent, then Adam by Eve, Abel murdered by his brother, Esau cheated again by his brother, Joseph in Egypt (beware of your brothers, rings the chief warning of the Bible), and then the universal flood, Sodom and Gomorrah, the Tower of Babel, there isn't one story that doesn't end with punishment of some misdeed, variously grandiose or petty, and the heroes, too, like Samson, are regularly betrayed and perish, or else others who seemed to be perfectly respectable wind up behaving far worse than the villains that they had defeated. Take David, for instance, the giant-killer, who in order to enjoy Bathsheba all to himself sent her husband off to die in the wars. The scandal lies in the fact that the murderer is allowed to live in the same world where the victim is cursed to die. And I can't swallow this thing, it sticks in my craw, it won't go down: I'm talking about David, the dancing youth . . . so you can just imagine when it comes to the other kings of Israel or any other realm. It seems as if all or almost all the kings in history were hysterical bloodthirsty lunatics, parasitically exploiting their kingdoms, tireless fornicators or anemic phantoms, as they appear in the portrait galleries of the museums of Europe, where our pilgrimages come to a respectful halt before long lines of debauched lethargic dolts with goatees, with large vacuous eyes, or else small vicious ones, or else lovely dreamy eyes, for which credit is due only to the painter's bravura or shameless flattery, by which I mean, the painter was the one who interpolated that splendor in the eyes, between the heavy lids and puffy bags eloquent of nights of heavy celebrating or unanswered prayers. The kings of Israel are no exception, indeed they offer a full array of case studies ranging from the degenerate to the murderous despot, the ambitious conniver, the coward, and the terrorist; the Good, the Brave, the Wise, the Judicious, the Magnificent, but who do we think we're talking about? Who ever called them that but their official historians?

WHAT WE FOUND most thrilling and novelistic about the stories in the Bible was at the same time exactly what made us angriest. What struck us in the end as most absurd and unjust. It wasn't clear how you could consider a bunch of real bastards as teachers, masters, leaders of the people, spiritual guides, with all the crimes that had sullied their hands.

With the benefit of hindsight, looking back from my current vantage point, the Bible appears very realistic and almost Machiavellian, adventuresome and far more profound than any modern psychological novel: but back then, when I was a boy, it seemed crazy that it should serve as the foundation to a religion that was also said to be a religion of goodness, charity, and love, etc. Elements that were practically missing from the scene. You might as well read the Greek myths, in that case.

In the Bible, the obsession with guilt suggested that human beings had been assigned no other destiny than this, to sin, sin, and sin some more, to fall, no, better yet, to plunge, deviate, betray, degenerate, be corrupted, rot, give the lie to every slightest illusion that could be entertained about them. If I had believed these negative prophecies to the letter and if I had known enough about him, something that was highly unlikely in a Catholic school at the time, perhaps I would have become a follower of Luther. The idea that man by his very nature is made to fall can be a simple observation or something to fight against or even a morbid indulgence that voluptuously embraces evil while at the same time denouncing it: when it comes right down to it, there is no real difference.

EVEN JESUS'S DEATH struck me as pointless. A sacrifice for its own sake, admirable and yet utterly in vain, seeing that since then mankind hadn't improved in the slightest. If even killing the Son of God wasn't enough to make mankind better, or at least a little less evil, then that means it's just not possible, or else that the right approach hadn't been used, it's pointless to shed blood, cut lambs' throats, immolate the innocent, the procedure of sacrifice washes away no sin, it doesn't cancel the crime, if anything it just becomes one more. Why should one murder absolve you of other murders? Instead of making me milder, the death of Jesus, when I was a boy, just increased my thirst for revenge. Forgiveness be damned! What I wanted was a savage reprisal. Perhaps people fail to take into account the fact that, once you've reached a certain level of emotion and pathos, once you've heard enough stories of martyrdom and persecution (whether the protagonists are saints or refugees, or detainees in German concentration camps, or poor Jesus, spat upon, beaten, whipped, and crucified), beyond that teary point what snaps into action is a reaction that is hardly unpredictable: either you feel like burning those Christians alive yourself, or else you're tempted to lead the uprising against their persecutors.

In teaching lessons about how goodness is the tolerance of evil, people always forget that you can hardly expect such sage wisdom from a boy, that the real goodness in our nature would be the one that refuses to tolerate injustice, that rises up against it, to put an end to it, to remediate it, and that therefore the monstrous iniquities suffered by the martyrs can only teach us to revolt against them, and certainly not to submit to them with an ecstatic smile—that is a prerogative of saints. The edifying stories aim to accentuate the sentimental aspect of injustice and cruelty (for example, the cruelty that was inflicted upon Jesus), pushing us to be stirred to emotion, remaining passive, like so many spectators in tears in a movie theater, whereas if they have any effect at all on those who listen to them, it is to bring to the surface their instinctive sadism, reawakening through imitation the latent violence lurking in the individual, until you realize that you too want to stone the adulteress, of course, after all, deep down that slut deserves to die and I wouldn't mind smashing in her skull with a rock, or else, to the contrary, it stirs a chivalrous sense that aspires to return blow for blow, picking the rock up off the ground and hurling it into the face of the one who first threw it. Observing the succession of persecutions suffered by innocent people at the hands of wicked people only stirs you to join forces with the latter and to have a good time doing so, taking it out on that sniveling mass of Christians, Jews, women, and defenseless old people, or else to spring to their defense, but for real, with a club, with a sword, in the tradition of the Seven Samurai—with rifles, in other words, not with prayers.

That's the effect the story of the cross has always prompted in me: it makes my fists itch. I think about Jesus every day. Jesus! Of all the religion there is, You're the most curious, necessary, and disconcerting figure. I'd be able to accept You more easily if You were only God or merely a prophet. But both things taken together! You're just insatiable!

No objections to be made concerning the individual figures, if taken separately. Rather conventional, actually. Indeed, compared with the pagan religions, on the one hand, and folklore and practical wisdom on the other, pretty drab, no special flair if you think of a Zeus or an Indra or a Shiva; as a paradoxical philosopher, as a street preacher, Christ possesses a spectacular simplicity and fluidity, fair enough, but the concepts He expresses don't have a great deal extra compared with the ones you might find scattered here and there in Socrates, Zhuang Zhou, or even Marcus Aurelius. If He had only been a man, Jesus's teachings might be the subject of a chapter in the *Lives of Eminent Philosophers* by Diogenes Laërtius, with the famous anecdotes, the parables, the magnificent Sermon on the Mount, and then, in a few brief lines, or even in a long and heartbreaking episode, the trial, the torture, and the death.

. . . It's something I seem capable of taking seriously only on paper, when reading, reading the Gospel, or Holy Scripture, or the powerful tirades of the Church Fathers, or looking at the apocalypses painted by artists, the resurrections of the dead bodies, with skeletons emerging from the ground, the sweet Marys, their cheeks tinged with modesty . . . but which ceases to make sense as soon as I return to reality and find myself at a mass and all the emotion I'd experienced in my reading vanishes as I watch the sad line that forms at the center of the church, ladies in raincoats heading up to receive the wafer. It's a lightning cut for me, a break with any form of adherence, credulity, faith. It's already difficult for me to *believe*, to believe anything, even to believe in myself, believe that I even exist . . . so you just imagine how hard *this* is.

Only in the formal or figurative perfection or in the elevation of thought, perhaps, or in the abyss of last acts, do I glimpse even a scrap of possibility, but in that case, rather than *believing*, I am *dominated*, I feel that I'm at the mercy of some greater force that brusquely demands that I put away my skepticism. In other words, I surrender. Let's just say that, without believing, I obey.

Normally, instead, I'm just there *observing*, I observe and nothing more, perhaps tickled by a slight irritation, let me be clear, not toward the faithful, but toward myself . . . and taking on the point of view of the entomologist or the satirist or the person who "just wants to understand" does nothing whatsoever to make up for the chilly initial sensation of detachment, it doesn't transform it, it fails to redeem it.

I've said that I obey. And yes, that's correct. I obey beauty, for instance, and its extremely powerful redemption. I even obey when I would have strong objections to the objects upon which that beauty draws my attention in order to oblige me to venerate them, the figures before which it demands that I prostrate myself, the values that it conveys or propagandizes. I'm almost never in agreement with the authors or artists I admire. But it's the power or the beauty of the way they work, in other words, the form or technique they create and then apply, after having created it . . . it's almost never the arguments themselves that persuade me, or should I say, bend me, instead, it's the argumentation. In the Gospel, for example, the terse economy of the discourse; the inexorable unpredictability of the logical transitions; the hammering, simple style with which the examples are produced, why of course, the parables, with their hooks, impossible not to dangle impaled upon them, snagged. Yes, this is the sensation that Jesus's words—paradoxical at first blush—provoke: the desire to obey them.

But the reason this happens isn't because I devalue the reality of things in favor of ideas, theory, or fantasy. Quite the contrary, I'm attracted by the concentrated, amplified, intensified reality of the molding and shaping, the implementation of the form. I am by no means interested in abolishing or escaping reality, rather what I want is to confront reality, take it on its most powerful expressions, when sadly I usually find it under my nose in a diluted, watered-down form. What can I do if people and their actions are almost always disappointing with respect to ideas? Is it the ideas' fault, or the fault of the people who put them into practice? And for that matter, if ideas aren't applied by people, then who on earth are they intended for? The sagas, the myths, and the legends that so captivated me as a boy still make my heart race today (I'm nothing other than a failed mythographer, or rather a failed-almost-everything, a failed musician, a failed mathematician, engineer, photographer, psychoanalyst, maybe even priest, yes, that's it, a failed priest), don't those myths and legends and sagas spring out of human beings, and aren't they aimed at human beings? Power and precision and authenticity and profundity exist solely in written or sculpted or painted form: then the word tarnishes in a split second, and everything conspires to prove the opposite, to give the lie, corrupt, and water down. If that's what religion is, then I'm not interested. It will *never* kindle me, *never* light my fire. Christ is something else. Yes, but where *is* Christ? Who truly follows Him?

But after all, I wonder, why always that central Italian accent, from the Marche, Abruzzo, Molise, straight out of a dialect play, as if they were from the home town of Padre Pio, exchanging "g" for "c," "d" for "t," *lo Sbirito Sando gi assisde, Gristo gi vete e gi sende* ... the Holy Sbirit assisds us, Ghrist sees us and hears us, who knows why all these preachers always have a raucous voice, a piercing, hoarse timbre, which whispers into the microphone as if through the grate of a confessional, and why they're always full of amazement as if they'd just opened their eyes onto the world only now, for the first time, as if they were witnessing a miracle, why of course, the miracle ... the miracle of grace, the miracle of forgiveness, the miracle of human contact, the miracle of gratitude, the miracle of goodness and repentance, of the sun that rises every morning, the miracle of life, the miracle of this, that, and the other thing ... Yes, when I'm in the car, I listen to two kinds of radio broadcasts—the kind for and by AS Roma fans, and the kind done by priests: the former amuse me, the latter are the subject of my study. Both categories are absolutely incorrigible, which is what I like about them.

> *I don't care if it rains or freezes*
> *As long as I have my plastic Jesus*

But if I put it like that, then you might be led to believe that my sole contact with faith comes through reading St. Thomas Aquinas or Dante. Not at all the case. The closest I've ever come to a religious experience dates back, as is perhaps true for everyone, to my childhood. And it was at my grandmother's house that this minuscule miracle took place. There, too, entrusted to my grandmother by my parents so they could go off on their wonderful and romantic trips, the biggest problem for me was sleep. In the still hours of the night, thoughts and feelings became terrifyingly prehensile. I believe that I managed to grasp, in the sense of understanding, most of the important things in my life at night, before age twelve. Everything that's happened since has been a matter of applications and consequences.

Yes, specifically by night, guided like a divining rod by that form of mad, overemphatic lucidity. But those conquests came at a cost, from when I was very small, the cost of hours and hours of hallucinatory wakefulness spent crushing and forming my pillow into every imaginable shape. At my grandmother's house, though, there was a figure that stood awake beside me. I could see it glow from the night table, not far from my head. I'd blink my eyes and rub them to see it better, but its cerulean blue remained vague and ill defined. So I'd reach out my hand to touch it. It was a phosphorescent Madonna about four inches tall. Clutching Her in my hand, I'd remember what She was and why She was there: to protect me. And, in fact, She protected me. From what?

From my own thoughts, from the looming shadows, from the illusions generated in darkness, from the dangers created by my own mind. The frightful dimensions of my nocturnal obsessions, clutching the luminous Virgin Mary in my hand, were slowly restored to the scope of normality, and they ceased to threaten me—especially the most insidious, the most radical, the most implacable of all the thoughts that burdened me, namely, the thought of death. By night, in fact, I became aware, acutely aware, to the brink of the intolerable, of death. Not so much of the fact that I would someday die and that there was always a risk of dying, from one cause or another, but rather the fact that *everything* dies, that everyone dies, and in the end, there is nothing left . . . And did the Madonna do anything to overturn or counteract that conclusion? Not at all. Very simply, though, she rendered it innocuous, she emptied it of all anguish. Death therefore became a conquest and no longer a stabbing wound. One problem, however, arose: if I held the statuette in my fist and clutched it tight, it disappeared. I could no longer see its glow in the darkness. My touch extinguished it, like when you catch a firefly in a glass and in its alarm, it stops glowing.

And so I had found a system for remaining in contact with Her, without dimming Her light: I limited myself to clutching the pedestal between thumb and forefinger, so that the rest of the little figure would continue to glow. And so, I believe that with my arm extended toward the night table, fingers touching the base of the phosphorescent Madonnina, I must have spent many hours of my childhood, reassured by Her, protected by Her faint light. And in that position, having thought everything thinkable, and imagined everything imaginable and unimaginable, and after feeling the tide of dismay subside within me, I would finally manage to fall asleep.

A FEW YEARS AGO a weekly newsmagazine asked me to reply to a list of questions, which was called, for some reason that eludes me still, "The Proust Questionnaire." Flat questions, answers of half a line or a single word, about the things you like best or hate most, such as: your favorite book, your favorite film, what impresses you most about a woman, or a man, the saddest day of your life, the happiest, and so on. I can no longer find that copy of the magazine. I'm certain that 90 percent of the answers I gave then would be different today, in fact, they would already have been different one week after the interview. Not because I might *change my mind*, no. But because I have many different thoughts and ideas in my mind, it's not as if I change it or repudiate it, no, let's just say that I alternate my mind and the ideas in it, in rotation, like 45s in a jukebox. My tastes, memories, passions, books . . . there are so many of them, and variety is such a wonderful thing! What a stupid thing a fixation is, or perhaps I should say, how foolish to have just one! For instance, I remember that I didn't include Karl Malden among my favorite actors, and now I would, and the same goes for Aroldo Tieri. There's only one answer that I remember giving that I would probably give today, exactly the same.

Question: Who is your favorite historical figure?
Answer: Jesus.

I WAS BEING ASKED, basically, to believe in something I couldn't understand, and—in spite of the fact that it's clear to me now that this and this alone is the true meaning of the word "believe," that is, to place faith in something that you can't understand or verify, because something that you *can* understand need only be acknowledged, you only need to recognize its existence, which means, therefore, that there is no need to believe in it—at the time such a demand struck me as unacceptable.

If there is something that by its very nature is unintelligible, fine, let's leave it right there, where it is, in its splendid world beyond our comprehension: what need is there to attain it or ingratiate ourselves with it or make an alliance or jolly it along, get it on our side, to resist it or surrender to it, since no matter what we do, you can neither predict what it will do in advance nor understand what it does afterward, nor, in the final analysis, does it have any obligation to justify its actions, so that if it sends you an earthquake or a cancer or it lets you win the lottery, it really all adds up to the same thing, the meaning behind that choice remains mysterious, look what it did to Job or allowed to be done to its own chosen people, does any of this strike anyone as logical? Exalted sinners and innocents burned at the stake or crucified.

ARBUS WAS THE ONLY ONE of us who had no hesitation in declaring and demonstrating his absolute lack of any religious sentiment whatsoever. Among our classmates, even the most foulmouthed and profane, if really questioned closely, would have admitted that, deep down, well, yes, they believed in God, at least a little, and that they perceived something supernatural in the world, or they could sense it, they were afraid of something! Maybe of hell. In short, they believed in Jesus, or in the Resurrection, or in the angels. Scattered scraps of faith or residues of catechism or snatches of prayers accompanied by the powerful and obscure sensation "there has to be something out there." Not Arbus. It's as if his exceedingly pure, automatic mind had been liberated—and God only knows to what extent that actually constituted a liberation—from the desperate and naïve need to believe.

"Man fears God the way that monkeys fear snakes." Arbus feared nothing, that's all there was to it.

For that matter, my friend didn't particularly like to argue. "Arguments are rarely useful and they are mostly a waste of time and the cause of unpleasantness." For that reason, too, we were forced to guess at many of the notions and beliefs that Arbus certainly possessed, because he took care not to make them known to us, first of all to spare himself the effort of having to explain them, and then having to defend them from our muddled and misguided confutations. The few times that he actually bothered, he had a ready response to our objections: unlike what most people do, namely to pile up the greatest possible number of arguments in favor of the position they hold, he was accustomed to considering and evaluating all the opposing reasons, like the true scientist that he was (if it strikes you as absurd that I use the term "scientist" to describe a fifteen-year-old boy, well it suits nobody I've ever met as well as it does Arbus, yes, he was a scientist just as Tartaglia, Newton, or von Neumann might have been, Harvey or Volta, even if, in the end, as far as I know, he never discovered or invented anything of any importance, or hasn't yet, who can say . . .), so that he had already tried to find the answers to those objections by posing them to himself.

ONE TIME HE TOLD ME: "You have to understand that it was simple for Jesus Christ. What He did and what He said went together. And if He had wanted, He could have straightened everything out. My problem is that I can't: that's the difference between me and Him. My willingness, my intention would not be sufficient in any case. I just can't do it, and that's that. Jesus isn't even an example for me. He's nothing, nothing more than the usual fucking hero."

(DO YOU KNOW who really was a hero within Arbus's reach? None other than Tartaglia, Niccolò Tartaglia. And just who would that be? A great mathematician. A short while ago I was deeply stirred as I read his brief online biography. Niccolò Tartaglia, of Brescia, got his name—Tartaglia ["stammerer"]—because a French soldier disfigured his face and mouth, out of sheer cruelty, when he was just twelve years old. With his ravaged, restitched mouth, he was unable to speak normally. His father was murdered on that same occasion: and Niccolò, who had until then been illiterate, grew up an orphan and self-taught.)

15

E VERY RELIGION TAKES AS ITS SUBJECT AND, *at the same time, as its driving force that feeling typical of any adolescent crisis, namely: dissat-isfaction, the searching need for meaning, feelings of inadequacy and incompleteness, the demand for answers. But what was our initiation? Confirmation, a sacrament whose meaning has long since been lost, and even when we received confirmation, they had a hard time explaining to us what it was and what purpose it served. They told us during our catechism: "You'll become a soldier of Jesus!" What's that supposed to mean? Once we'd been confirmed, what war were we supposed to fight?*

JUST ABOVE THE NAPE OF MY NECK, there's a pointy bump on the back of my head. I can feel it particularly when I rest my head against a wall. Since it's a popular saying that having a bump on your head means you possess a propensity or fixation for a certain discipline, and that you are inclined toward that discipline from birth, I asked an expert in phrenology what a bump like mine was supposed to mean. After touching it and examining it, and asking me to get my hair cut with a high fade, so that he could examine and photograph it, and forward the picture in turn to other experts and discuss the matter with them, he told me that he had identified it as such a well-developed bump for religion that it would have sufficed for ten priests.

It's an odd thing, then, that I should always have nurtured a strong intellectual interest in religion but also, shall we say, a natural skepticism, instinctive and emotional; how little I've ever felt the sensation or the conviction that we call "faith" or "belief." It's not illogical or absurd to believe in something we cannot understand; but I've never actually felt it inside me. I've never felt, in other words, a sentiment of trust growing inside me, an ardor, a sense of transport toward the Creator, the original author of those stories that, in any case, certainly captivated and stirred me, starting with the Bible stories, like the destruction of Sodom and Gomorrah, with the angels warning Lot to flee, and then what happens to his wife, transformed into a pillar of salt, and his daughters, who get their father drunk and have sex with him. All the same, I never could hear those stories with a different shiver of horror than the one I felt as I read about Palinurus's death or the terrifying night Thor and Loki spent in the giant's glove. I never managed to rise to Him who is in the heavens, I never ventured so high, and that's why I liked myths and heroes instead, things that we can find, shall we say, midway between earth and sky: people a thousand times better than me, more powerful and more courageous, no doubt, but at the same time, actually, similar, even close to me, comprehensible, full of shortcomings and desires, sometimes even ridiculous ones, the way the gods so often are, in contrast with the Almighty.

THE RELIGIOUS SENTIMENT does not depend on any particular process of reasoning; it is not a conviction, like those that can be attained through reason; it's something different, impossible to define, which will always remain so, something the atheists' objections will never manage to undermine, because they're always talking *about something else*. It's not as if the atheists are *wrong* to say what they say, it's just that they remain on the outside, they aren't really talking about faith, they can't talk about something if they don't know what it is. I may know what it is, but I still don't have it.

WE WERE ACCUSTOMED to defending ourselves from their sermons by paying no attention: this is true of priests and of grown-ups in general, but of priests in particular, because the style of their reasoning and the way they blandly admonished or implored or offered benediction was always the same, monotonous, querulous, and always seemed to fall back on the same basic arguments, indeed, it seemed like one single speech recorded on a disc that spun slowly at first and then at normal speaking speed and, as soon as it was over, started again from the beginning. It consisted of four basic ingredients: scolding, hope, humility, and forgiveness. Scolding was the general key the sermon was tuned to, its bitter undercurrent, the way it unfolded, heartbroken at the certainty that whoever was listening to it was inevitably at fault, was obliged to acknowledge his or her faults and begin to mend them. Everyone, no one excluded. Even if Jesus and the Madonna had been sitting in a pew listening to the sermon, They too would have been treated to the usual upbraiding, exhorted not to be lazy, to devote Themselves more to others, more and more and more, to acknowledge Their own sins, even the smallest ones—this is important, especially the little ones!—to cherish hope, and to show Themselves to be humble and forgive others. Hope and humility and forgiveness were in fact the most important contents rolled up in and, so to speak, protected by the verbal shell of the scolding. To infuse hope, send positive messages, turn ugly things toward beauty, detect benign signals amid great difficulties, engage in a constant effort to translate evil into goodness. And most of all, to learn to wait, learn to wait without impatience, learn to wait patiently for whatever the future held for us. But not the simple future, the ulterior future, the one that lies beyond the future, because it lies beyond life, after death. At the age of fifteen it's already quite something to try to imagine what will become of us at ages twenty or thirty, much less trying to think of what it will be like when we're no longer around. And indeed, this exercise of hope was the hardest one to kindle inside us, the most artificially induced, and the priests made great rhetorical efforts to guide us onto the path of hope.

With humility, it was already a simpler matter. It's a clear concept, verging on the crude, and the concept of humility itself is humble, modest, rough as the sackcloth that represents it, but understandable, even if not necessarily something you subscribe to, or share; and after all, the Gospel is full of examples to explain it. It's not very hard to understand what it means to be humble: it's a much greater challenge to actually achieve humility, actually become humble, in real life, everyday life. In effect, though, I can safely say that among my classmates there were at least three or four boys who were truly humble, Gedeone Barnetta, for example, and then De Matteis, Vandelli, and Scarnicchi, a.k.a. the Dormouse, even though in the case of the last-named paragon of humility it was perhaps more a matter of laziness and passivity, rather than genuine humility: attitudes and states of mind often border each other or even overlap, depending on where a person's true center lies, they can be fundamental attributes or strictly tangential, lying along the peripheral orbits, where they interfere as they encounter other feelings, yielding in force or gaining in meaning. I wouldn't know whether these classmates were humble in that way by inborn character, or because they had been gently encouraged in that direction by the upbringing and education they received at home and at SLM. I was certainly never humble, and I'm not humble now, and to tell the truth, I've never been sorry in the slightest not to be, but that is due precisely to the fact that I'm not. So I'd venture to think that it's a quality you can't easily acquire along the way, you're either born with it or you aren't, but it remains true that, if you have it, it's a good idea for your teachers to reassure you that it's a quality, a virtue, not a defect.

Last of all, forgiveness.

Here the matter begins to twist and turn. The priests no longer seemed quite as confident of what they were saying. The problem of forgiveness lies, in fact, in its conflict with the natural sense of justice: why should someone who has done wrong be forgiven, instead of punished?

Forgiveness is, de facto, an imbalance to the advantage of the malefactor. Rather than following the maxim of *suum cuique*, "may all get their due," it ensures that those who have already taken from others are also given a gift of indulgence. Now God, in His limitless sovereignty, may be able to afford the luxury of issuing pardons and amnesties, that is, to go beyond the scope of the law and, in a sense, abolish it, deleting the punishment called for by due process, and remitting unpaid debts. But human beings? Don't those who issue amnesties and pardons commit a sin of pride, setting themselves up as comparable to God in their sovereign decision not to carry out the punishment? If in God punishment is a right, in human beings it ought to be an obligation, on pain of loss of their very humanity, their sense of justice. Is it possible to be so magnanimous without verging on presumption or the ridiculous or, in the final analysis, the abject state of those who would rather wash their hands of the whole matter, because they're simply unwilling to take on the highly disagreeable role of castigator? In their games, why do children always want to be robbers and not policemen? And not just in Scampia, outside Naples, but in the QT as well. Because the guardians of the law are always considered pains in the ass, except when you're frantically calling them because you're in danger yourself. Yes, indeed, that's the way it works, no point in arguing with the facts: from the very outset, the lay of the land favors the bandit: the elevated novel and the romantic potboiler, the movies, the Catholic religion, our collective imagination—they're all clamorously rooting for the bandit, and it's pointless for a priest to turn up the volume from time to time on his righteous indignation against Camorristi and Mafiosi because, after all, by definition, they too are lost sheep, sadly led astray, and the father awaits their return with open arms to throw the fatted calf on the grill in celebration. Hate the sin and forgive the sinner . . . But are they really two such different things? How can you distinguish between them? How do you tell the dancer from the dance?

IT SEEMS, in other words, that evil adds a new element to life, tingeing life with new possibilities, a sort of bet, a challenge to see how the individual involved will come out of it: the culprits, the victims or their nearest and dearest, society as a whole—it's as if they were all subjected to a new ordeal, a salutary exercise. Granted, no one can ever restore the condition existing prior to a given crime or sin, either in the material state of things or in the people affected, least of all in their feelings and ideas, which evil and damage have already irreversibly changed, and it is therefore necessary to create new solutions, come up with new approaches. Evil, then, becomes the chief agent of this transformation, and a stimulus to the invention of ways to repair it, overcome it, even take advantage of it, in order to ensure that things become better than before. Evil, then, brings great new things and it is not only God who uses it to attain His mysterious and concealed objectives; good people can also make use of it to achieve progress. It may sound like an inappropriate and cynical comment to add that the first to benefit are, in any case, the wicked.

Therefore, only a very particular form of injustice, a wholesale amnesty of the evil done, can restore peace: the chain of reprisals and punishments would stretch out endlessly, and therefore the decision is made, at a certain point, to break the chain, leaving unpunished the latest of the evildoers and his misdeeds, putting an end to it there, with forgiveness, renouncing any efforts to prosecute the wrongs done, forgoing reparations, canceling them from the record, in brief drawing a clear line beyond which all debts are remitted, and we start over again from scratch. We not only find this moral approach in Christianity; it is also expressed in the classic Neapolitan song "Simmo 'e Napule, Paisà!" which says: "*Chi ha dato ha dato ha dato, chi ha avuto ha avuto ha avuto . . .*" (The ones who gave, have given, and they gave, and the ones who got, have got, and they got) with the further invitation "*scurdammoce 'o ppassato*" (Let's forget the past) addressed to those who, fair to say, if they really were to keep a running tab of the wrongs done by each to all and all to each, would still be waging war against each other until the last day of recorded time. Still, there is a difference; and that difference is there, in the past, a past that for Christianity can never be erased or forgotten, but which can also never lay a claim on the present, because it would continue to demean, in an intransigent manner, the reparation of the damage done: the inexhaustible theme of the novella *Michael Kohlhaas* by Heinrich von Kleist.

The substance of peace and its first active measure is amnesty. Or, in more cynical terms, amnesia.

It is true that coexistence among human beings demands that wrongs be righted: if evil is never sanctioned, if reparations are never made, a community falls apart. And so, forgiveness at once contradicts and satisfies this need.

Discretionality undermines any law. And forgiveness cannot help but be discretional, unilateral, and gratuitous, otherwise it's not forgiveness, but a simple logical deduction, while forgiveness is the opposite of logic and utility, it's sheer overabundance. I've always found it bizarre that in Italy the dicastero del Guardasigilli, that is, the Ministry of the Keeper of the Seals, which would be the Lord Chancellor's office in Britain and the Department of Justice in the United States, should have been described as the Ministry of Grace and Justice. Why combine two such contradictory principles? Wasn't the latter of the two sufficient on its own?

NOW I WONDER, asking perhaps ahead of time, in terms of the telling of the tale: can we offer forgiveness to the protagonists of this crime which, page by page, I'm coming ever closer to exploring and treating (too slow, too rambling, this journey of mine, you might well say? He certainly is taking his time about it? You're right: but it was the very nature of the crime that demanded that its background and preliminaries be recounted; or should I say, the concentric circles that wrap around it, the rings that on the one hand lead to it, and on the other lead away from it, like in certain animated neon signs. The school, the priests, males, the quarter, families, and politics. It might turn out that the bull's-eye on that target isn't the crime in question at all, but something else entirely . . . and if you have the patience to follow me through this, we'll find out together), can the guilty parties be pardoned, leaving aside the fact of whether they have or haven't served the sentence imposed upon them by the state? And if not full Christian forgiveness, at the very least, indulgence, or simple forgetfulness? (Forty years have gone by, and it appears fairly certain that the most dangerous of them all, the fugitive from justice, is already dead and buried. Another one has been released from prison. The third is serving time for new crimes.)

Can we get their personas out from underfoot once and for all? Will I, at least, *I* who was their classmate, at the same school as hundreds of other kids just like me, ever be able to stop thinking of their faces, their smiles?

What is the rate sheet, not exclusively penal in focus, that makes it possible to determine whether the price for that crime has been fully paid, or expiated? The law cares very little about the emotional consequences of evil upon those subjected to it, but if religion, too, winds up overlooking those consequences and prefers instead to focus on the redemption of the evildoer, then who will devote themselves to the suffering of the victim, who will lend the victim an ear, once the wave of momentary scandal and indignation has subsided? It's not true that the testimony of evil, if ignored at sufficient length, simply disappears: to the contrary, that witness never dies out, that testimony is never consumed, indeed, it is fixed, it coagulates, it becomes autonomous, isolating itself from the rest of time and from the other events that are ground up and overrun by time's headlong course, ultimately becoming a perfect example of what has been called "a past that shall not pass." A clot, an embolism. What must be done, then, to ensure that that crime passes once and for all, that both its culprits and its victims finally move on? Is it enough to wait for them all to die, and for us, too, who lived at the time of those rapes and that murder, to all be dead, in twenty years or so, or to be optimistic, thirty? And what role does this book play, does it extinguish or preserve?

THE INSTRUMENT OF MERCY (*grazia*, or "grace," in the highly Catholic-centric Italian legal system; the Italian Ministry of Justice, until the end of the twentieth century, was called the Ministry of Grace and Justice) can only be brought to bear on the guilty parties, never the victims. If the culprits are sentenced to the death penalty, then they are brought back to life when they were already virtually dead, while victims can never be resuscitated, they are beyond the reach of any human action and even, strictly speaking, any divine measures. It would therefore have been very interesting if one of the miracles narrated in the Gospels concerned not a sick man, but rather someone who had been murdered, in other words, a Lazarus who had been executed or killed in a brawl, or say, by brigands or bandits, because in that case life would have been restored not only to the one it had been taken from, but also to the one who took it. And the murder would instantly come under full amnesty. A twofold miracle, then, an intervention the likes of which we have no record of in Holy Scripture and whose interpretation might have entailed even greater problems than the already tangled issues attendant upon other marvels and prodigies performed by Christ. Resurrection, then, seems to affect the two categories in different manners: for the evil, it's available in this life, through the agency of forgiveness, for their victims, strictly in the afterlife, in the beyond.

THEY SAY THAT EVIL is our burden to bear if destiny assigns it to us. It's an objective form of suffering, a fact of nature, crudely realistic. But if, instead, it is *we* who engender evil and we're even pleased to see it in action, then it's only right that there should be no indulgence shown us, no remission of our sins. Or does a fissure open, even in this morbid case, through which clemency can pass? Would it be, after all, its very morbidity, then, the very pleasure taken in committing evil, that becomes its justification, or at least a mitigating circumstance, a natural factor, inevitable because intrinsic to our character, something that makes this evil, too, a thing to be tolerated, a burden to be borne, something we accept with a shrug, without demanding in exchange at least some punishment of the culprit? In the Middle Ages, people punished horses that had unseated and killed their knight, hanging or drawing and quartering them, after a trial held in accordance with legal procedure. But we are no longer in the Middle Ages, nor are these the times of Xerxes, who ordered the waves of the Hellespont whipped when they refused to subside. If someone enjoys torturing and raping and killing "because it's in his nature," what can ever make him change that nature?

IN SPITE OF THAT FACT, people say that all that's needed to put things back the way they ought to be is remorse, confession. "Feeling horrible" is supposed to guarantee forgiveness to those who experience it. What matters are feelings, true or false though they may be, rather than facts or deeds. In Italy, especially, feelings have always gotten the better of facts, which are considered accidental elements, erasable at will, or subject to interpretation so subtle and casuistic as to bring about a complete inversion of polarity. It is always possible to get rid of inconvenient facts. The paradoxical lesson of Christianity trains the mind to perform this stunt, to turn the information provided by commonsense experience on its head, so that however things may go, the sinner redeemed will always be in the front row, offering lessons on the path followed to that point, displaying the misdeeds committed as a testament to his profound humanity. No one will ever have the nerve at that point, no one will call him a bastard after the path he has walked. If a lamb fails to get lost so that she can be searched for, found, and saved; unless a pilgrim wanders off the straight path, well, he'll never get a speck of attention, in fact, he can just go fuck himself, him with all his rectitude.

WHEN I WAS TALKING about sermons, above, I wasn't just referring to ones delivered in church, after the reading of Holy Scripture. It's obvious that the preaching done in those situations had the tone of a sermon, otherwise, why bother? I'm talking, instead, about the things the priests would tell us, or the discussions we'd have with them, perhaps to talk about snacks or the formation of the soccer teams taking the field for a tournament, or Christmas vacations, or any other topic you care to name: in all those instances, it was inevitable that they'd eventually take on that distinctive cadence and, along with the cadence, the objective. I mean to say that their pedagogical vocation would get the better of any other communicative or expressive intent, in the end, the voice you'd hear was inevitably that of the wise teacher with life lessons or else the watchful guardian with your best interests at heart, or else perhaps we were merely reading an undertone into perfectly neutral statements, but they sure sounded to us like a string of admonishments. Even the cries of Brother Curzio when he wanted us to pick up the pace of our languid warm-up trots around the gymnasium, "Come on, get going, a little faster! Faster! Put your heart into it, come on!!" and even his sharp shrills on the whistle contained an unmistakable allusion to the troubles that afflict a young man who gives in to laziness. If Brother Franco winked an eye at Barnetta during recess and told him: "Pizza with tomato sauce is good, isn't it?" Barnetta, who was about to chomp down, to prevent the tomato sauce from sliding off the side of the pizza that had folded precipitously downward (in fact, it was always that thin, greasy, gooey pizza, heavily laden with tomato sauce and therefore extra delicious, especially at 11:30 in the morning, an item sold throughout the schools of Rome, in every order and grade, now and stretching back into the past), Barnetta immediately halted, pulled his hand back, extracting the slice that was already halfway into his gaping maw, convinced that the priest was alluding to the sin of gluttony.

MORE THAN THE CONTENTS, much of it understandable and, in the final analysis, easy to subscribe to, and some of it even exciting because it was so similar to stories of magic or adventure tales, what made us lose all and any religious impulse and annihilate what lingering enthusiasm might have survived was, in fact, the *tone*. Yes, the tone, the tone, I've said it before but I'll never tire of repeating it, the unmistakable Catholic tone: the tone in which that content and those stories were foisted off on us, that psalmodizing preachy tone, slightly high-pitched, nasal, raucous, exasperating, a sort of inspired and prophetic falsetto, as if the speaker had shut his eyes to better savor the vision conjured up by his words, and as he speaks, he smiles, that's right, he smiles complacently. The complacency of priests derives, I believe, from the fact that they're constantly mingling sin and goodness, and pointing out how the latter is sure to triumph in the end. Goodness absolutely *had* to triumph. Sin lay in ambush everywhere, it lurked, slithering along the edges of our words, images, actions, with the same treacherous undulation as the serpent in the Garden of Eden: but after giving the impression that it would always prevail, it ultimately got the worst of it. When the head of the serpent that poisons the world with its treacherous breath was finally crushed underfoot, the already querulous tone would begin to pitch upward, taking on a coloratura of indignation, turning almost vengeful, really, and then it would placate itself, turning magnanimous, relaxed, pastoral, drinking in the peace and quiet that reigned in the pastures once the wolf had been chased into the woods. The curve of the graph according to which the priests treated any subject was invariably the same, first rising then falling, with the peak situated around three-quarters of the way through the discourse: exposition/admonishment against the risks of sin/development of arc from sinfulness/indignation/redemption/pacification.

We knew the shape of the curve so intimately that, at mass, we could trace it in the air with our hands, waving an imaginary conductor's wand, miming the tempestuous *fortissimo* and then the inevitable closure of reconciliation.

I can't say if that was faith or something else, whether it was faith or stupidity, if it was faith or a conscious lie, if it was a false certainty or a thought so insistent that it came true, at least for those who had repeated it in their heads so many times that in the end they no longer even needed to think about it, one assurance of life and another of death, a contract signed and set aside, under a stack of other assorted papers, I don't know if that faith was truly faith, or a gift, or a grace, the true faith, the true simple faith of someone who believes that God exists, that He created us out of nothingness, and awaits us in the afterlife, with a reward or a punishment ready to hand, depending on what we do now, here, today, me, you, us, everyone, judged one by one, and if you have this faith, then maybe you'll get by, and if you don't, then you'll just muddle through and hope for the best, maybe there'll be a final act of clemency, for which, strictly speaking, you can't even hope, since you don't believe in it. What kind of hope, faith, or charity can skeptics practice, and if they practice these virtues anyway, then what difference is there between them and believers? Just the fact that God isn't brought into it? And the very word "credo"—literally, "I believe"—in the final analysis, what does it mean, what does it prove, what does it matter, truth be told, whether or not you believe? In the final analysis, I can even believe in what's not there, what isn't true, and in fact there are plenty of people who believe with all their heart in some genuinely crackpot things, flying saucers, vampires, that Hitler loved mankind and wanted to save it, that Hitler isn't dead and Paul McCartney is, but does their vibrant faith by chance make their convictions any more true? And if instead they don't believe, they refuse to believe, and they say that the death camps never existed, does that disbelief somehow make the smoke go back down the chimneys and reassemble the incinerated bodies of the children, does it bring them back to life? The fact that they don't believe in the crematoriums, in the ovens, does that by any chance cancel their existence, does it make it any less solid, does it transform the bricks into mist? All of this emphasis on believing or not believing struck me, since I was a boy, as overstated, a false problem, an overvalued factor, a totem. Faith, sure, faith, all faith is nothing more than a way of hiding the truth or an attempt to get to it by taking a shortcut, almost, so to speak, by deceit, by trickery. To understand, certainly, to explore, yes, to try out and to seek, but *to believe*? Is it really that important?

FROM THESE TWELVE YEARS at a school run by priests, from the incessant preaching, sometimes explicit, at other times tacit, to which I was exposed, I have developed two different attitudes, mutually contradictory: the first is utter hatred for emphasis, whatever the text or discourse in which I find it; the second is the involuntary tendency to take on the tone and the pacing of a sermon the minute I start talking about a subject that is dear to my heart. In social occasions, for instance, I often say nothing, for as long as possible, but once I start talking, if for any reason I feel that I ought to provide a clearer explanation of what I think, before long I've slipped into the posture of a preacher, hammering and obsessive, eventually overwhelming or boring those I'm talking to, and that is also the reason I prefer to remain silent.

AND WHAT HAPPENED, after all, when I prayed? Nothing. I'd pray with my mind drifting to other things, then, ashamed of my distraction, I'd try to steer my wandering thoughts back onto the subject of my prayer, but I'd draw a blank: what had been the subject, what had been the intention? God was in my mouth and I did nothing other than to chew on His name. Peering around, I decided that if the others, kneeling like me, with their hands cupped in front of their faces or their fingers intertwined beneath their chins, were doing the same thing, then it meant it was possible, it was possible to pray, it meant something, and therefore it was simply a matter of being patient, of doing the same as them and waiting for a different sentiment to spring from those formulations, an emotion unlike anything I'd experienced so far. Or else, and this was another opportunity to assign meaning to that ceremony, even if I didn't feel anything special as I was doing that praying, it would still prove effective in satisfying the requests I had made: another case in which it was a matter of waiting and seeing how it turned out. Patience remained the main structure upon which the entire matter hinged. I found this second hypothesis to be much less attractive than the first one: I didn't like the idea of begging for charity in order to obtain this or that, and since I was a rather fortunate young boy, I had no special graces to implore or wishes so great that they couldn't possibly be satisfied by my father and my mother, who were so very generous and affectionate with me and my brothers. In that case, better to turn to them directly for my requests. And so I limited myself—as the priests had suggested I do, drawing upon the equivalent of a preprinted form to be filled out—to praying for the continued health of my family members . . . for their happiness . . . to help me to be a good boy . . . right, and then . . . and then . . . as a generic and all-inclusive appeal, well, certainly, I prayed for peace among men . . . indeed, according to the standard formula, for "peace on earth." To judge from subsequent developments, you'd hardly say that my requests had been heard. Peace on earth? Not even the shadow of it (though as far as that request goes, I have to admit that I wasn't expecting great results), and as for my family, it's been decimated by disease or other misfortunes (five died young of cancer, one suicide, and one who was killed while tearing along at high speed on his motorcycle). Still skeptical about the efficacy of my prayers as well as anyone else's for "peace on earth," what I do hope for is the protection so vainly invoked for my family back then, possibly shifted forward with more effective power to the family that I've created myself now; and so I suspend all judgment and I wait and wait . . .

NEARLY ALL BELIEVERS, for that matter, cut and stitch themselves a religion to fit, holding on to the things that suit them best and deleting the more restrictive or disagreeable chapters, behaving more or less like that pirate who took the Tablets of the Law to sea with him, and scratched off a certain number of Commandments.

Part III

Victory Is Making You Suffer

I

ARBUS WAS TOO FAR AHEAD of all the other students, so in the second year of *liceo*—eleventh grade—he withdrew to study two years in one and present himself for the final high school exams. In order for this to be permitted, the candidate had to have a an average of nine—roughly, an American A, a 4.0 GPA—but that was no problem for Arbus because he excelled in all the subjects, except for Italian, even better than Zipoli or anyone else, and the teachers were willing to help him, raising his average by a few points if that should prove needful. Arbus was ready to make the great leap forward and we prepared ourselves to bid him farewell. It was a shame to see him leave, but it was also the right thing. Our class was losing the most advanced and diabolical brain, if by this adjective you are referring to logical and connective capacity, taken to extreme consequences without fear of anything.

Some time ago I studied the character of Satan and I discovered that his image oscillates between the two extremes of an absolute glittering intelligence and the most absolute, abysmal, black stupidity. According to tradition, the devil is either very astute or else foolish or even demented, given that he seems to be ready to fall into any trap set for him by a barely functional peasant. In general, in any case, his way of thinking, even when it appears to be dizzyingly subtle or wily, remains deep down mechanical, a matter of applied intelligence: he is a deducer, a calculator, but he seems incapable of making quantum leaps or significant advances from the plane upon which he conceived his initial thought. The devil, in short, is a logical fellow, indeed, he is absolute logic incarnate in a being of immense power, and this may perhaps help to explain the contradiction between intelligence and stupidity, given that even the latter quality is the product of a mental process that is, in its way, irrefutable. Idiocies are usually perfectly logical. And the fool who allows himself to be deceived in the medieval tales isn't incapable of reasoning, indeed, if anything, he does *too much* reasoning: in the most literal sense, he has reason on his side, and he remains convinced that he has it on his side even after the prank being played at his expense has been fully consummated. What makes us laugh behind his back is in fact precisely this: not his error, but the way in which he is right—the eternal and useless rightness of Shylock, the law that succumbs to the exception, reason and rightness (deep down, blind and obtuse) defeated by a small twist, a loophole that in the end proves victorious. The absence of the law proves superior to any law. Freedom is superior to logic—freedom, which the devil does not rule.

Which is why he is the implacable accuser of God and of His defects. It is precisely the devil's frenzy to bring his reasonings to completion, reaching for the most absurd or dolorous implications (that is, in fact, why he is, in the final analysis, a servant: the servant of his own mind), making him so exquisitely sensitive to the endless injustices of Creation. It is enough for him to turn his gaze around him, and lo the devil twists aghast in suffering: everywhere, he sees contradiction dominating, which is a knife to the heart for a logical fellow like him. Divine action—by the light of the diabolical mentality, which is rectilinear—is unjustifiable. The Grand Inquisitor's question is unquestionably diabolical in nature: why do children suffer, why are the innocent left to die? As he asks it, the devil, who spouts it through the mouth of Ivan Karamazov, no doubt has reason on his side. And he is a thousand times right to be infuriated at the tiny little tear shed on a deathbed, allowing the soul of a perfect bastard (Buonconte da Montefeltro) to fly away to heaven in the arms of an angel. How can this be? Doesn't no one deserve hell, not even a scoundrel like him? In that case, what point is there, what difference does it make whether we are good or bad? In that case, the devil might as well become good. "Hate must make a person productive; otherwise one might as well love." Like those revolutionaries who aspired to justice and who, once they had witnessed the defeat of their ideals, decided that it had become pointless to continue their opposition, and instead chose to accept, indeed embraced and practiced with the most cynical realism, the injustices they had once fought against, similarly the devil— who had once been blinded by his thirst for justice, only to become resigned to the inconsistent law of general injustice that governs the world as it was created by the Lord God—limits himself to torturing the occasional just man, like Job, in his spare time. Evil has become his weary work, his routine, as horrifying as it is taken for granted, and now it is only rarely that we espy the old glint of rebellion in his eye.

NOW ARBUS WAS A SORT of latter-day Ivan Karamazov. In fact, he did seem like a young Russian of the particularly bloodless sort, austere, his flesh lustrous, his lips swollen, his raven hair silky and long, eyeglasses with heavy black frames, just as we might imagine the prototype of a sorcerer's apprentice or a young scientist or, even better, a science fiction author. And in fact, Arbus was the perfect incarnation of the nerd who patents infernal machines in his garage, or the young musician who practices obsessively, repeating scales on the piano, over and over.

> They hate you if you're clever and they despise a fool
> Till you're so fucking crazy you can't follow their rules

NERD. Back then, the term was unknown in Italy. The so-called nerd is a student who exclusively pursues intellectual interests, and remains segregated from the social aspects of student life, such as parties, fashion, relationships, and sports. He is therefore synonymous with shyness, awkwardness, isolation, and anachronism. He is antiquated and futuristic at the same time. His intellectual superiority—almost always manifested in scientific and technical subjects, which sometimes leads the nerd to merge into the stereotype of the mad scientist, of which he is the youthful prefiguration—is counterbalanced by his ineptitude when it comes to human relations. The nerd is by definition unpopular: he is mistreated by his more athletic classmates, mocked and humiliated by the more desirable females. He wears eyeglasses with thick lenses and celluloid or Bakelite frames and, in the version handed down to us, his shirt pocket is decorated with countless pens and pencils. He wears his hair short and neatly groomed, or else long and greasy and unkempt. His unimpressive appearance might serve as a mask or a provisional identity beneath which may lie concealed a superhero like Clark Kent or Peter Parker: but not even the special powers and the admiration aroused by his heroic alter ego are sufficient to cancel out the introversion and the ineptitude at human relations of the original character, who is awkward, shy, and incompetent. Which inspires a blend of irritation, compassion, and fear toward the nerd. In the reverse situation, in fact, it might happen that the nerd, embittered by his failures in love and the humiliations he has suffered, decides to take revenge, transforming himself into a diabolical character such as, in fact, a mad scientist capable of causing catastrophes. His intelligence, just like the sciences and technologies in whose service he has enlisted, giving up any and all other forms of satisfaction, since it presents itself as a neutral element that could as easily be directed toward good as toward evil, is nonetheless and in any case fearsome. There is nothing more fearsome than a nerd's revenge, precisely because it's guided by a superior intelligence. When a nerd emerges from the phase of deep reflection and finally goes into action, his technical abilities and his inventive resources prove to be utterly implacable (suffice it to think of the movie *Straw Dogs*, 1971), and his apparent emotional coldness, which once constituted an obstacle in terms of human relations, becomes the ideal instrument for shrewdly aiming his strategic moves.

In psychological terms, nerds are introverted and intuitive. They are interested in and stimulated by ideas and objects, more than by people. They can spend many hours alone, absorbed in their pursuits, whether that means studying, computers, comic books, television, collecting, various compilations, model-building, trading cards, model trains, chess, extinct animals, or classical music but also punk rock and heavy metal, and books with a distinct inclination toward fantasy. They are more at ease with abstract concepts than direct experience. They prefer reasoning to emotions and they almost always prove that they are every bit as incapable of conveying their own emotions as they are of understanding those of others. The social alienation of young nerds can be so profound and intense that some create imaginary friends to keep them company. Often, they are pedantic, using coded or exaggeratedly formal language, on occasion displaying a lightning-quick sense of humor, usually based on wordplay. While they ought by rights to be model students, they often feel deeply uncomfortable when it comes to doing homework, or taking tests or facing other learning challenges in which they may paradoxically achieve mediocre results, despite their generally superior qualities. Instead of being proud of them and coddling them, some teachers find them annoying and turn mistrustful or even hostile toward the nerds who pop up in their classes, ultimately stigmatizing them as bad students, apathetic and unable to complete tasks, or else, on the other hand, as potential competition in terms of mastery of the subject. Targeted for classroom bullying on account of their inability to react in accordance with established social standards, nerds obey those norms only within the limits whereby they are able to perceive them, or only until, having taken the time to analyze them, they fully realize the irrational nature of those artificial constructs. Their misfit status also derives from their inability to acknowledge hierarchies and authority, toward which they largely, and by and large unconsciously, take a defiant stance. If provoked, their moral or political neutrality may then easily be transformed into open rebellion.

TOGETHER WITH ARBUS, and for one season with Gedeone Barnetta (what a coincidence, the first three names in the roll of attendance . . .), who however decided the next year not to renew his season subscription— from the last year of *ginnasio*, to middle school, to the second year of *liceo*, or high school, that is, eleventh grade—I attended the concert season at the SLM auditorium. Even though the performers were rarely first class, the program was varied and interesting, in Arbus's opinion, and I believe I missed very few of those Tuesday evening performances. For us students, the subscription was quite affordable, and we were also allowed to move from the cheap seats at the back of the room down to the front rows, where there were a few empty seats, in the last few minutes before the concert began.

Arbus generally said little while we waited for the musicians to come on stage and begin to play, but his carefully measured words meant more to me than any program notes that might be handed out. Aside from the usual Vivaldi, Mozart, Chopin, and Bach, pieces were performed by composers I'd never heard before, or even ever heard of: and in those cases, Arbus provided me with succinct introductions to their body of work. Those were the loveliest and most interesting lessons that I've ever sat through. In five minutes, my classmate was capable of preparing me for what we were about to hear, without delving too deeply into the technical details; neither, however, did he settle for a few superficial impressions or spur-of-the-moment judgments or generic comments along the line of "He is a very passionate composer" or "He delves into the depths of the human soul." He was never willing to translate music into petty sensations. Afterward, moreover, he was capable of explaining to me whether the execution had actually been a fine one, something that I usually barely even noticed, or where the performer had shown weaknesses, and whether they were minor or grave. There were times when chamber groups or small orchestras would perform, but most of the time they were either soloists or, more frequently, pianists. In those cases, Arbus's expertise—expressed without any arrogance or pedantry, but in the simplest of terms, direct, light-years away from the affectations that blight the conversation of connoisseurs of classical music and, in general, the maniacal aficionados of any other discipline—was to me a source of endless pleasure. When all was said and done, along with the lessons of Professor Cosmo, Arbus's lessons on the basics of music, delivered in the few minutes before the concerts in the SLM auditorium, were the most valuable learning experiences I ever enjoyed, and they introduced me to an understanding of and appreciation for things, facts, forms, and personalities, the vastest array of sentiments, the broadest expanse of ideas, and all of this thanks to a high school classmate who had invited me along. A young weirdo, no doubt about it, but an invaluable one!

Barnetta was wrong to stop coming with us: but he got bored at the concerts, and very few adversaries manage to get the better of boredom.

DEEP DOWN I, too, was a nerd, even though I didn't need to wear glasses and I was rather good-looking, but still, I possessed a fair quotient of nerd in my personality, and perhaps I still do, and perhaps I would have written my books in a different way if I hadn't remained a nerd at heart; perhaps we should just say that I was, as in so many other episodes in my life, a *part-time* nerd. There is no affiliation or identity or conviction to which I have adhered in any lasting way. Frequently, in fact, I have juxtaposed three or four, until nothing made sense anymore, and I could no longer say who I was or what I wanted. More than the body, I had the brain of a nerd. What boy at age fifteen, after all, could take serious interest in . . . what was the name of the composer, atonal and yet structurally classical in approach? Honegger? Hindemith . . . ? Yes, who would have chosen to spend their evenings listening to Hindemith or talking about Hindemith (or was it Honegger?) with Arbus, instead of taking a girl on a date?

THE FIRST TIME that I went over to Arbus's house one afternoon, his mother called his sister out of the room where she had been studying and invited her children to perform a four-handed piece on the piano for me. I watched them from behind, brother and sister, as they raised and lowered their hands over the keyboard, the backs of their bowed heads, and I almost didn't listen to the music at all, so taken was I, it struck me as a scene from bygone times, even though the rapidity with which Arbus's sister fled back to her room and shut the door once they had finished the piece, and the suddenly glassy look in my classmate's eyes, made it clear to me just how unwillingly that performance had been executed.

An obligation, one of the many obligations that dot the day of an adolescent. Heads bowed over the piano keyboard, as if in punishment. Education is a forced journey. Its results are attained by forcing nature but it's only by forcing nature that you comply with it . . .

Even without seeming to put any passion into it, his mind traveled with great agility through every kind of schema or diagram or musical score. At a certain point, school must have weighed down upon him, an uninteresting burden, to be off-loaded or sidestepped as soon as possible. Or perhaps it was his family pushing him to step up the pace so that he could attend university at the earliest opportunity.

There was a time when having a child who was "a year ahead" at school was a considerable source of pride. My folks tried to enroll me a year early, but I was not accepted. In any case, it is true that in Italy school lasts too long, at age eighteen what you really need is to be out in the world, to get plenty of fresh air, fill your lungs full of it! Away from the lunchroom mini-pizzas and teachers calling roll and bells marking the end of class, our whole educations should be shortened, intensified, and abbreviated, while nowadays instead we tend to drag it out, we luxuriate in it, taking our time, and what with postgraduate degrees and various specializations, there are those who find themselves going bald but still walking around with a stack of books under their arm, indeed it would seem that the pedagogues are advocating the idea of a "permanent education," perhaps because that would even allow them to test out their theories on little old men and little old ladies. Each and every discipline seeks to expand its dominion, to take possession of different fields and age groups. After decades of swings from the progressive to the conservative, I have come to the conclusion that the ideal educational model is the one described by Descartes in the autobiographical portion of his *Discourse on the Method*: until age twenty, he studied very hard, then from ages twenty to thirty, he turned away from books and delved into "the great book of the world," which is to say, traveling, trading, fighting, accumulating experiences, and then, at age thirty, he began his adult efforts, harvesting the fruit of everything he had learned, in books and afterward. At that point, there are no longer any excuses you can turn to or stories you can make up: whatever you're going to be capable of doing is what you do then.

WHAT DID ARBUS do the last day before leaving school? What was his farewell to the Catholic school?

No one saw him, no one noticed as he worked away, nor was it possible afterward to figure out how he had done it or what technique he had employed, but when he stood up to go, the desktop was inked, from top to bottom and from one side to the other, in banner letters that formed the two words of the most common profanity.

The first letter was a "g" and the last was an "n": seven letters in black-ink block print, fifteen inches high.

It was supposed to be his last day of school. He turned around for a second on his way out the classroom door and said to us, quite simply: "Ciao."

THE NEXT DAY, however, he was back, accompanied by the headmaster, who slid into the classroom like a shadow right behind him and announced that our classmate, before leaving to study for his final exams on his own, had one last thing to say to us. Then Arbus spoke.

His head remained bowed, with locks of hair hanging down on either side of his face and the glint of his eyeglasses preventing us from seeing his eyes; his voice, too, was low and it quavered slightly, yet I had the impression that the corners of his mouth were tilted upward in a sort of smile. Just the faintest ironical twist. He said, without beating around the bush, that he was very sorry he had written that profanity on the desktop and had thus offended not only God, but all those who believe in Him. Then a bottle of denatured alcohol and a rag appeared in his hands, objects that no one had noticed, and Arbus set about cleaning the desktop, in utter silence. He had been forced to abjure and to erase his profanity, and in fact, after twenty minutes of alcohol and elbow grease it had, sure enough, disappeared, and no one could say it had ever been there. The case was closed just twenty-four hours after it had first exploded. It was a masterpiece of diplomacy.

Once I got over my astonishment and my sense of distaste at that retreat, which resounded like such an act of cowardice to me, and above all, a ridiculous one, I felt an admiration growing inside me, in a way that hasn't wavered since, for that double, twofold hypocrisy: the hypocrisy of the one willing to abjure (Galileo), and the hypocrisy of those willing to accept the abjuration (the Church) even though they knew it was insincere. Two formally impeccable positions that made it possible to move past the impasse caused by that profanity. Because it was obvious that Arbus, after that painstaking project of blasphemous scribbling, could forget about his A minus GPA, which was what he needed to gain admission to the final high school exam: that must have been the argument the priests had inserted their crowbars under and exerted their leverage.

If he wanted to make the quantum leap and go straight to the final examination, Arbus would have to apologize. And there was nothing on earth that Arbus desired so ardently as to get out of our school, and as quickly as possible. Nowadays, it is very common for people to be asked to make public apologies: both institutions and individuals who have been guilty of both horrendous crimes and negligible instances of bad manners are asked to beg publicly for forgiveness, either a few hours after the offense, or else decades and even centuries after the crime in question. "If they'd only at least say they're sorry," is the demand. It's not enough that they are thrown in prison or treated to universal reprobation: they have to *apologize*. Politicians, soccer referees and misbehaving players, TV sorceresses, popes and former monarchs, tycoons of high finance lurching into bankruptcy, hit-and-run drivers, kids who've thrown rocks off bridges over highways, distant heirs to long-extinct ideologies, soccer hooligans, surgeons and chief physicians, all now say they're sorry. The religious custom of asking forgiveness has migrated into the layman's conscience, along with the profound sense that it is a ritual to be commemorated, if possible, with open declarations on TV or over the Internet; and yet this by rights ought to be the farthest thing from the layman's mind-set, the idea of a verbal or emotional reparation for the harm done, with a resulting pardon. That's right, because once the offenders have felt remorse and asked for forgiveness, then the pardon *must* follow, it's practically obligatory. When the parents of a young woman murdered for trivial reasons, and with grave cruelty, appear in public, the first thing that the journalists hasten to ask is this: "Have you forgiven, eh? Have you forgiven the murderer?"

Arbus apologized.

He apologized, which is something that requires no particular effort, as proven by the glint that I'm certain I saw in his eyes the minute he looked up at the end of his act of contrition, in fact, it's simple as can be, a mere formal statement, which can actually be done in a manner that's more offensive than the original offense, as is so clear in those children who, when forced by their mother to make amends with a friend or a younger sibling, shout a loud "Sorry!" into their face, causing more hurt than the punch given previously.

Arbus apologized and that became his last day of school.

A FEW YEARS LATER while I was leafing through some pulp newsweekly, such as *Oggi* or *Gente*, while waiting my turn at the barber shop, I noticed a photograph in which two policemen in riot gear, billy clubs raised high, were dragging a half-unconscious student by the armpits, his knees dragging across the asphalt. The caption said that the officers were "assisting a demonstrator." I thought I recognized in that emaciated, long-haired young man Arbus, and of course his eyeglasses, which dangled from one ear, with the lenses shattered.

The demonstration where he had been beaten, inside the University of Rome campus, would in time become quite famous, because a twofold battle had been waged during it, between the union demonstrators and the revolutionary students, and then between the revolutionaries and the police.

The security forces of the various political groups certainly didn't use a soft touch: the last demonstration I attended, a few months after the one at the university, also grimly famous because a young woman was killed at it, was my last one, because of handguns tucked in belts and under the tails of jackets and raincoats.

And I'm talking about handguns stuck in the belts of demonstrators, not just those of the policemen.

And so, on the Garibaldi Bridge, while the sounds of the first shots reached our ears, I turned on my heels and, from that day forth, I was done with politics, understood in that sense.

I was done, period.

And I'm glad I was, it meant I'd have done one thing right in my life.

I HAD HEARD that Arbus was involved with a group of Nazi-Maoists.

That is, the people who chose the worst—or in their opinion, the best— of right-wing and left-wing extremism.

I don't know how reliable this rumor is and I know very little about the Nazi-Maoists, nor for that matter am I very interested in knowing much more.

In a certain sense, it's a fairly obvious point of arrival for anyone battling against capitalism.

It's a political model that remains relevant today, indeed, if anything, perhaps more so than forty years ago.

But in that period, the names and acronyms of groups of lunatics and fanatics flourished and proliferated and the only reason you'd even be aware of them was if you yourself were a member of one of those splinter groups or else, to your misfortune, happened to be targeted by one of them. In that case, you did start to pay attention to their combative proclamations. There were vast numbers of combatants in the field, militants and militiamen, squads, flying units, enforcers making their rounds, and platoons. Like cells on a microscope slide, they pullulated, they split and divided and hastily rushed to outflank one another, to the right or to the left, formulating planks and platforms that were increasingly delirious or vague. Movements, fronts, cells, brigades, battle committees, counterforce committees. It didn't take much to throw together a few scattered shreds of ideology and shape them around the need for action because that, action, was what everyone lusted after and hailed. For someone like Arbus, becoming a Nazi-Maoist wasn't really all that strange. In effect, nothing was strange for someone like him: after all, he was the outsider, the alien. When you're light-years away from everything, even the most absurd things can ring familiar to you. Persons, things, ideas—Arbus seized at them all with his telescopic pincers and brought them close for observation beneath the thick lenses of his eyeglasses, and in them he saw things that he alone could see. He did experiments to provoke reactions. He was a chemist who regularly scorched his fingertips. I believe that what he was seeking in that curious political position was precisely the irreconcilable: if it hadn't already existed, then he would have invented Nazi-Maoism himself expressly for that purpose, in order to disgust not only the fearful, the right-thinking, and the respectable, but above all his hypothetical extremist allies. You wound up borrowing from every last one of them. An isolated, radical, and ambiguous position, that was the ideal place for Arbus.

I heard reports about him at long intervals, decades at a time: that he had become an expert on wolves, and that he'd camp out in the mountains for months on end to catch sight of one, then that he had become a specialist in artificial intelligence and spent his time building robots.

Concerning the reliability of this information, I certainly wouldn't swear an oath.

But then, I wouldn't swear to anything, for that matter.

2

I ONCE ENTERED A CHAPTER OFFICE of the neo-Fascist Italian Social Movement (MSI). Salvatore, a classmate of mine, took me. I was at his house on Via Tolmino, maybe to study or to play or else for one of those visits that have no real purpose, at thirteen you go out just for the sake of going out, the afternoons drag out endlessly, empty, a quick phone call and a brisk walk can take you over to see the most accessible classmates, the easiest to reach, with a mamma who makes snacks or the stereo or a courtyard in the rear and neighbors who don't complain if you play soccer: and that gets you to dinnertime.

"Can I come by your house?" means that a kid is running away from his own house.

In those houses, you're always welcome.

AFTER WE'D RUN OUT of things to do, Salvatore asked me if I wanted to go down to the MSI office, downstairs just a short walk away. I agreed. We found the chapter in a basement room, a short flight of stairs beneath street level. I feel comfortable in those kinds of places, they're familiar to me. In Rome it's in those basement-level offices that all the extracurricular activities took place, it was there that all a boy's free time unfolded: in a basement I played the saxophone, in various basements I played pool, took part in Ping-Pong tournaments, listened to records, exercised, wrote and rehearsed school plays. Small windows with security grates, concrete-framed glass panels, the smell of mold. The blithely unaware feet and legs of people walking by on the street, while down here life teems and thrives.

The MSI office was shadowy, and not only because of the grim tone of the posters hanging on the walls: as if penetrating into its inner recesses was part of a process of initiation. The slogans invited you to dare. Everywhere were trophies, symbols, and dangling pennants, slightly dusty-looking: everything was stagnant and old.

The only luminous objects, like so many phosphorescent globes in the dim light, were busts of the Duce's head, white or in ivory.

Each of them one and a half times or twice normal size.

Mussolini's head has been described countless times, far too many for me to care to try again.

Features far too distinct to be able to avoid the temptation of caricature.

The Duce's body, about which books have been written, was little more than an appendage to that famous head.

The most voluminous and spectral bust was perched atop a cabinet, and from its lofty vantage point, it looked down on anyone who entered the room, which was also the farthermost, the innermost, the darkest room in the chapter.

THE PROBLEM IS THAT THIS VISIT, which may or may not have lasted all of five minutes, had consequences, or perhaps I should say, it didn't, because of my father's prompt intervention. I was naïve enough to tell him that very same evening, at dinner, where my classmate had taken me, in response to the ritual question, "What did you do today?" posed to one child after another.

His face darkened.

"Why did you go?"

"Why? No reason, just to have something to do . . ."

He insisted on finding out exactly what had happened in that place.

"Nothing."

"What do you mean, nothing?"

"Nothing, nothing at all happened . . . We took a look around and then we left."

"And there was no one there?"

There had been someone, actually. Beneath the last of the busts of the Duce, at the foot of the cabinet, there was a young man sitting at a desk. He'd turned out to be very nice. He'd asked who I was and Salvatore had spoken up for me, he'd introduced me, he'd given the young man my first and last name. And the young man had written them down.

"Where?" my father asked in a brusque tone of voice that wasn't customary with him. "Where did he write them down?"

In a ledger book. The MSI clerk had taken note of my name, and then he had asked me my home address. It didn't seem to me that a person's address was much of a secret, you can find it in the phone book. In part because I lived not a hundred yards from Via Tolmino. But from the way my father's face changed when I told him that I'd given the MSI clerk my address, that is, *our* address, I realized that I had made a huge mistake, and suddenly I felt as if I were a traitor, or a fool, a foolish child who had played the spy.

"I'm sorry, Papà, but I didn't think that . . . I just went there to keep my friend company . . ."

He clearly manifested the depth of his rage by saying nothing. He no longer uttered a single word about it. Silence at my house was always the way in which a broad array of feelings and states of mind were expressed, ranging from simple disapproval to full-blown rage. The subtraction of words made you inscrutable and in any case unsettling, even when the clouds cast only passing shadows. My father's concern transmitted itself to me and proliferated into my own concern, and for a while I thought about nothing but the extremely stupid mistake I had made. And yet I didn't understand what could be so serious about it. I'd set foot in the place, and that was all. I'd seen posters with the Fascist lictor's staff, the black shirts, and a bust of Mussolini's bald head. To me, it meant nothing much more than the curly-headed bust of the philosopher, a copy of a sculpture by Vincenzo Gemito, which stood in the entrance to our apartment with a cigarette stuck between the lips as a joke.

Well, we could have put the same sort of thing in the Duce's mouth. Maybe a cigar.

Clearly, though, something serious must have happened, because the next morning my father went down to the chapter office and succeeded in getting my name taken off the list. I have no idea what system he used, jovial, friendly, or threatening. For all I know, starting a file on a thirteen-year-old boy is illegal.

I heard about it later from my mother. Had my father acted out of ideological conviction? To keep me out of trouble? Did he hate Fascists? Did he fear them? Was he defending his good name?

This book is unable to answer a great many questions.

STRANGE THAT HE HAD TAKEN it so seriously. He had always taken a mocking approach to this sort of thing, like when he told us how, one day, during a visit by the Duce (the real one, in flesh and blood) to his school, Giulio Cesare, the middle schoolers like him had been lined up along the staircases to greet him, and the dictator, out of breath after the first flight of stairs, had stopped on the landing where my young teenaged papà was standing and had patted him on the cheek, putting on a gruff and paternal tone, whereas he actually just wanted to catch his breath. "Bravo, good boy," Mussolini had said. As he told this story, my father would turn his cheek to his mother-in-law, my grandmother, telling her: "Go on and touch my cheek, signora, touch right here . . ." and when my grandmother reached out her hand, "Touch right here . . . it's still there, nice and warm, the Duce's handprint." And his eyes would glitter, ironically. "Since that day, you know, I haven't washed my face once."

And my grandmother became indignant because she'd taken him seriously, and she yanked her hand back as if the sense of ridicule had scalded it.

"EVERY TIME that politics surfaces in literature, it does so in the form of impotent hatred." This is a phrase of Stendhal's that I never tire of reflecting upon, and in the meantime I go in search of examples that contradict it, valid exceptions to the rule. I rarely find them.

SALVATORE WAS A CLASSMATE with red hair, shy and polite. He had a slightly awkward way of moving. He was a very good boy, which made him generally well liked but not particularly interesting. By which I mean that no one was interested in busting his chops, but no one cared much about him at all. It was his good luck that the reckless and bullying classmates had an array of targets to take it out on (Marco d'Avenia and Picchiatello, better known as Pik), otherwise someone like Salvatore could very easily have become the next chosen target. There are those who claim the opposite, that is, that it's only a way of stimulating dangerous levels of competition among males, but I personally believe that the presence of females in a class mitigates the aggressivity, forces them to moderate their impulses, exert some self-control, come to an overall judgment concerning their behavior. At a mixed school, the girls serve as mirrors in which the boys can see their reflections, every time they open their mouths or do something. Like in a gymnasium, where you use mirrors to check whether you are exercising correctly. It is true, of course, that females can be even crueler and more implacable in rejecting and marginalizing someone. They do it with a perfect dosage of contempt and indifference, an invisible cordon sanitaire drawn around the unfortunate victim.

In an all-male school, on the other hand, the threat can be sensed in a physical way, as it is among dogs. I say this, having had twelve years' experience of it as a student and another twenty as a teacher with all-male classes. To say nothing of the time I spent living in barracks during my mandatory military service. Teaching in prison, in the past few years I've had a few transsexuals in my classes, and all it takes is one to change the atmosphere, they enter the classroom and it's as if a gust of wind had suddenly thrown open the windows, in part because someone of that gender and in that setting has the impact of three or five. Insinuating his, or her, physical charms, which are usually explosive to say the least, into the grim and gray compactness of the manly group, she re-creates for an instant the natural mixing of life on the outside, of normal life, the life prior to being segregated from the world. Males are monotonous, and monotony tends to evolve into frustration, and frustration in its turn splits into melancholy or aggression. Spending time among males is like talking to yourself. Only a woman can interrupt the basso continuo of foul language, the verbal and mental automatism. Without the needle-sharp disturbance of a feminine presence, all language turns into slang: the jargon of fishermen, truck drivers, soldiers, where the absent woman is evoked in dribs and drabs, bits and pieces, broken down into her orifices and protuberances, but the same thing happens in learned language, like that used by philosophers. As with any prolonged privation, it can even lead to elevated and spiritual results. To a sort of dizzying or horrifying purity.

SLM WAS AN ALL-MALE educational institution until 1979, five years after I left. It would seem that the admission of girls was a decision due to nothing more complicated than a lack of enrollees.

The opposite sex wasn't banished in absolute terms, merely kept away during classtime. This meant that gender segregation was specific to an idea about teaching, about the transmission of knowledge. Women, mothers, sisters younger and older crowded the school's courtyards every day, when they came to pick up the students at the front entrance or spent time with them during their afternoon activity or attended mass on Sunday—mass was celebrated in the big modernist church. Dozens of women leaned over, elbows braced on the balcony railing as they watched their sons churn up the water in the pool, waiting for the end of the swimming lesson to take their boys home. There were a thousand and one occasions of mixing and mingling. I understand the point of Mount Athos, but once you've admitted those female creatures into the enclosure, why not just enroll them in classes, let them attend the school? Is it just to avoid the problem of differentiated latrines? What harm could they actually have done? I've always wondered what the mothers thought, when they came to get their sons outside a school where they, as little girls, wouldn't have been admitted. Could it be that they approved of this discrimination or found it to be salutary? To offer a variation on Groucho Marx's famous line: I do want to belong to any club that doesn't care to have me as a member. Why would these priests, devotees of the cult of a woman, according to whom it was a woman who crushed the serpent's head and saved all our souls, these priests who exhorted us to pray to her with the words "our life, our sweetness and our hope, hail!" those priests whose very order bore her name—why would they exclude women?

More than a religious interdiction it was a social legacy. Perhaps females really were considered to be too great a distraction, an element of persistent disorder or sexual alarm (at eight years of age?). Maybe the families were happy to know that their daughters and sons were separated at least during their hours of study, reciprocally safe from each other. Maybe for that dozen or so years it would be better to have each gender off on its own, bent over their books, separated by a partition that was in any case easy enough to sidestep or climb over, after all we were going to spend the rest of our lives together in a campaign of mutual destruction, in love or in hate. The war of the sexes, some claim, is something you want to get started at the earliest possible opportunity, and in fact these voices propose returning to a separation by gender beginning in elementary school, to protect little girls from the harassment of violent males, since there is no longer any way or even any intent of restraining or repressing these violent boys and young men. Maybe so. All it ever did to me was harm, and I've spent thirty years licking the real and imaginary wounds produced by that segregation. The tree of love came up crooked, the code of relations with the opposite sex had too many chapters censored or overblown, so that I was forced first to indulge in endless conjectures and then to leap straight to conclusions. Something excessive, maniacal, in both the shyness and the brutality, something hasty and furtive, but devoid of the sweetness that furtiveness would still possess at an innocent age, something like reparations repeatedly demanded but never obtained, no matter how many women you might go on to have or even collect in your life, afflicts those who spent their school days the way we did at SLM. In elementary school, deep down, it's easy, even natural, you advance across the chessboard like so many pawns, all equal, all the same, and in fact it's almost an advantage not to have those whining, detestable little girls underfoot; in middle school it already starts to sound odd, it's become increasingly clear that half the world is missing in there, but the unhappiness of developing male bodies is still thus protected from all embarrassing comparisons and can be vented almost entirely in sports and fisticuffs; in high school, the realization is tinged with bitterness, becomes derisory, you decide that a mocking, contemptuous god locked you up in there for no good reason, you're a clueless idiotic Sabine male whose women were all stolen away from you, and if you want to get your own back you're going to have to go fishing for them with a long pole, outside the safety of the port, in the open waters plied by experienced and hostile ships. Relations with the opposite sex have become a desperate parody. Forced to become more enterprising and predatory than other boys, you turn shy. Your moves are tosses of the dice and applications of abstract rules. No everyday experience, no familiarity, no natural interactions, ever, with the opposite sex: it's like trying to learn Arabic with a collection of cassette tapes. You can do it, that much is clear, but it requires efforts that will only embitter your results. And there can be nothing more dispiriting than the lack of spontaneity.

There is one extreme consequence of this predatory attitude toward women, caused by an absence of familiarity: and that is rape.

THE OTHER POSSIBLE VARIANT, men being with men: homosexuality.

PEOPLE FREQUENTLY ASK SOMEONE like me who works in a prison whether convicts in there practice homosexuality or become homosexuals just because they're always among men, and can see women only during visits, when they can only lust after them in vain. Like a sum of cash uninvested, then, their sexual desire would be assigned to the only gender available. To say nothing of those cases, so often depicted in movies about prison, in which homosexual relations are imposed by force, usually upon a new arrival, who finds himself tossed into a cell with rough and powerful men, horny and implacable; or else upon someone too weak to defend himself.

PAS DE CHANCE was tattooed on the bodies of the convicts described by Cocteau, with arrows pointing to the anus.

If I turn the same question around and ask the convicts, they give me only evasive answers. The only confessions, the only stories that I hear waver somewhere between the sarcastic and lascivious, concerning some "goodfella," who might very well have a wife and children back home, but who in prison got a crush or actually fell head-over-heels in love with a transsexual in the G8 wing who was making goo-goo eyes at him. Sure, you know the way things go . . . love is love . . . but if you stop to think about it, this, too, is a desperate quest for the lost feminine component, rediscovered between the hard, upright tits of some male Brazilian nearly six feet tall. Strictly speaking, there's very little about prison that can be called homosexual, indeed, often these love stories are brimming over with the classic saccharine boy-meets-girl formula. And there's another curious detail worth adding: the ones who really fall hard for the trannies are often the guards.

ONE TIME, this is how it went.

There was a tranny in tenth grade.

The cells that serve as classrooms are arranged in pairs, one across from the other, at the far end of a short corridor, twenty or twenty-five feet long, which in turn feeds into the wide hallway that leads to the G11 wing.

The school occupies four of these side corridors, for a total of eight cells, five of them used as classrooms, where lessons can be taught, two others as workshops with computers, and one as a teacher's room, with lockers, a Xerox machine, stationery, and all the rest.

Between one period and the next, the students leave class to stretch their legs and smoke a cigarette as they wait for the teacher for their next class, who is often, however, arriving from a different wing of the prison: for example, he might be coming down out of the maximum security wing, which is two stories higher up and requires you to pass through a number of gates.

Some of those gates are opened remotely, others by hand so you have to wait for the guard to show up with the keys: this manual opening may be done with haste, indifference, insolence, deliberate slowness; kindly or brusquely.

The normal shifting of teachers at the end of the period can draw out into a full-fledged recess.

But the convict students don't take advantage only of the time between periods to loiter in the side corridor: often, during the lessons, they will ask permission to step out and smoke a cigarette or else, on their return from medical examinations or meetings with their lawyers, instead of going immediately back into class to face up to the formulas with which the teacher is filling the blackboard, they'll hang out there to savor those few minutes of paradoxical liberty that consists of being locked up in neither a cell nor a classroom, but instead in that sort of no-man's-land which is, in fact, the little side corridor, seven or eight paces, no more.

There is a relative margin of tolerance toward this custom: the teachers turn a blind eye, and the guards who are in charge of keeping an eye on the school are satisfied that the convicts don't go out into the main corridor, but remain confined in the side corridors.

To prevent too many comings and goings, every once in a while the guards will shout down from their lookout points, in weary voices, "Everyone inside . . ." or else, "You knooooow iiit, don't you? . . . that you're not allowed to haaaang oooout in the haaaallways . . ." after which they walk the side corridors to shut all the gates with the pebbled glass inserts, so that the loitering prisoners sneaking a smoke won't be noticed by any superior officers who may be walking down the main corridor, thus avoiding unnecessary dressings down, remonstrances, and reports that might ensue—to the detriment of both prisoners and guards.

Anyway, there was a tranny in tenth grade who spent more time outside the classroom than in it.

She had a hard time paying attention to the lessons, she had to get up and stretch that body which, since the last time it had been immobilized behind a desk in school, had unquestionably became more shapely. *Too* shapely.

She had fairly discreet manners, certainly not as shameless as the pair of explosive beach balls that swung from her chest.

She was standing with her back against the wall, at the far end of the side corridor, frequently with one long leg stretched forward and the other one bent with the heel against the wall, smoking and chatting, with a tremulous, nasal voice, along with the eleventh-grade students, who had also come out of the classroom out of boredom or tobacco addiction.

We had all noticed, as we walked down the main corridor between periods, or on our way to the laboratory, that nearly every time the tranny was out of the classroom, on the other side, leaning with both elbows on a radiator in the central corridor, there was a prison guard, a handsome, relaxed young man.

They would talk to each other from that safe distance, in a faint voice just loud enough for each to appreciate the other's wisecracks: every so often the guard would flash smiles while the tranny laughed, flattered, with those squawks and gurgles and high-pitched squeaks typical of those who have hormonal imbalances and mucous linings permanently inflamed by cocaine.

When the rest of us walked between them, we were never able to make out a single word of what they were saying to each other, whereas they understood perfectly.

It was like a secret code they were speaking.

And yet the current of interest between those two was quite visible, it became almost instinctive to apologize as you passed through the middle of it.

IT SHOULD COME as a surprise to no one.

The guards are ordinary young men and the transsexuals are more womanly than real women.

Not all of them, but certainly some, possess a communicative charge that is not merely erotic in nature; what's more, they give the impression of successfully having escaped from the grim reality of prison.

As they sashay along the corridors and hallways with their awkward or regal gait, depending on the length of their thighs, they joke, they constantly joke, they poke and prod one another, they pretend to quarrel and to take offense, it's never clear whether or not they're serious, they preen and promenade, they flirt for the most part with one another, they conduct their conversations with extremely rapid exchanges in falsetto like in an opera buffa, transforming the prison into a theater where even vulgarity becomes poetic and the custodians leaning on the handles of their mops are the audience.

This amateur production can irritate or seduce, or it can be the target of sarcasm (I, for example, feel all three reactions at the same time): but when the phantasmagoria fails to culminate and the colorful dust evaporates off the butterfly's wings after too much flapping, it veers toward the darkest tragedy.

And the hysterical butterfly dies.

AFTER A FEW WEEKS, we noticed that the prison guard had narrowed the distances, now he was standing at the threshold of the pebbled-glass gate that leads into the side corridor, that is, the gate that he was duty-bound to close to keep the smokers from getting out.

With his legs in the main corridor and his torso leaning toward the interior of the side corridor, he would sway on the threshold of the gate, while the tranny was still down at the far end, giggling and shaking her hair.

Gradually, as their friendship became explicit, almost flaunted, well beyond the bounds of prison protocol, their conversation grew increasingly intimate, an uninterrupted swap meet of jests and tender words, tinged with the airy irony that only those who truly understand can achieve, those who express themselves in a language that is allusive, but perfectly clear to them.

Their, shall we say, professional relationship, of prison guard to convict, had evaporated into a human, personal flow.

A miraculous naturalness that aroused concern in some of us, annoyance in others; still others, and I was among them, were filled with admiration at the way the life force finds a way, stubbornly burrowing along like the grass that flourishes in the cracks in the pavement and sidewalks.

I know, I know, that a prison guard should never have such close relations with a convict.

Especially not a convict with great big silicone-filled tits.

There can be vicious twists, sexual extortion and all sort of dirty dealings, and in fact it is normally in the wings where trannies are imprisoned that this sort of business flourishes, at night.

Let's be clear on this point.

But there, at school, in broad daylight, right before the eyes of one and all, the story took on another aspect.

If it had happened in any ordinary high school instead of behind prison bars, you could have imagined it as a platonic love story between a custodian and a female student.

Something that runs against commonsense rules but not against the deeper nature of desire.

In a school in the outside world, it all would have been settled with muffled laughter at the expense of the two lovers and at the very most a dressing down from the headmaster.

But this is prison, all adults, and there is no headmaster, and the guards are cops.

IT CONTINUED like that until the last days of school. The beauty let her locks hang over the balcony, and the prison guard resumed his serenade, on the threshold of the side corridor, and occasionally from the interior, as if with all that swaying on his arms, his impetus had catapulted him inside.

Closer to his fair interlocutor, her smile.

Until one fine day, when the lessons are over and the classrooms have emptied out and the students have all gone back to their wing, a female teacher who has stayed late in the laboratory straightening up the equipment is walking silently down the main corridor on her way to the exit. She still has to go through six gates before she can leave the building, but in her mind she's already in the outside world, she's thinking about other things by now, about preparing lunch and her son who will be getting out of his school soon, and as she passes down the corridor she darts a glance into the secondary side corridors, out of an inbred prison instinct that drives you to always look around corners, to check every intersection.

The gate is open, there's no one there, at the far end the doors are thrown open, the classrooms are deserted.

She walks past the first side corridor, the second, and then when she comes to the third she has a moment's hesitation and a double take that pushes her to retrace her steps . . .

It's strange, through the gap in the half-closed gate she glimpses someone down at the end of the side corridor: could it be that the custodians are cleaning up now, when it's time to start making dinner? she wonders, and stopping in her tracks and almost leaning backward, she goes back to peering through the gap in the gate that's standing ajar.

Only from there can she see clearly.

At the end of the side corridor with his back to the wall is the guard, his eyes closed and his hands resting on the shoulders of a person who's kneeling before, shaking her long hair and moving her head up and down, to the right and to the left, pulling away suddenly and then plunging back down into the man's pelvis.

Despite the unmistakable meaning of this scene, the teacher cannot seem to connect this image right away with its significance, and she was ashamed afterward of that fact.

Otherwise, she would immediately have turned her gaze away and taken to her heels.

Instead she stood there for a few seconds, in any case, for too long, staring at the scene, openmouthed, until the guard opened his eyes wide and saw the teacher, in the gap between the sheets of pebbled glass, their eyes meeting.

He didn't say a word, he was flushed with pleasure.

There's a short story by Chekhov in which a peasant overeats, splurging on caviar, gets indigestion, but can't stop eating, until he finally dies, but the caviar was just too good, he couldn't stop.

The head continued to bob up and down, yessir, with those side shakes that instead suggest a negation, a refusal.

The female teacher slipped away, trying not to make any noise with her heels on the cement floor.

A LOVELY SCENE, canonical, after its fashion.

Deeply moving.

It was the only way the two of them could enter into contact, in the briefest and most intense manner possible, like a move out of the martial arts, which concentrates in a single gesture, applied to a single point, the power of the entire body.

They had concentrated their desire.

Love manages to express itself even in a narrow range of actions, and after so many words, all that was left for the two of them was to burn it up in a physical act, and little did it matter that it was the exact same act that the convict regularly performed, in the outside world, for pay.

The maximum amount of spontaneity in there couldn't express itself in any way but a typical meretricious performance.

A blow job.

I'm willing to swear that in the outside world, that would have been a kiss.

3

I HAVE OFTEN THOUGHT THAT GOD EXISTS, that it's right that He should exist, and that if there is no God it's because there are a great many gods and they inhabit the things of the world and are inside us, they speak through our voices. But between this elementary thought and a true faith there stretches an abyss, and I don't have the necessary courage, but not even the basic impulse, to cross it. I am moved when I listen to "My Sweet Lord," but I don't experience any of the feelings described in the song.

In other words, even if God exists, I don't love Him.

He loves me but I don't burn with desire to meet Him (*I really want to see you . . .*), I imagine that He'd scorch me to a crisp, like a dry leaf.

But I necessarily have to place a subject in all these sentences I write: God. It is just like in the exercises of grammatical analysis that I invent for my students, they're interchangeable grammatical schemes such as "The peasant harvests the wheat" or "Gianni's dog bit a policeman," as I write them on the blackboard I'm certainly not thinking about who this peasant or the dog-bit policeman might be, instead of a policeman as far as I'm concerned he might as well be a thief, a direct object he remains, I like the fact that the language manages to function on its own, but instead my students immediately start asking me who this Gianni is, and they laugh with satisfaction at the fact that that bastard of a policeman should have been bitten by the dog, good work, Gianni, you trained your dog right! In other words, they're able to believe the words, so they're willing to believe in God, who cannot be anything more than a concept for them. If you name something, you've already brought it into existence.

My students are ontological by nature.

I'm not.

I'm not ready.

I don't even match the evangelical cliché of the "man of little faith."

I remain outside the temple, even after I've entered it.

But because I've always liked words, if for no reason other than their sound, I would read Holy Scripture at mass.

I'D ALWAYS REFUSED to serve the mass.

But I still needed to pile up points for the end-of-year prizes, and you could earn points not only by serving mass, but also by doing the readings.

Why not? I liked the idea.

Readings were more dignified, there was no need to dress up like an altar boy or to obey anyone's orders: your moment arrived, you went to the lectern, and you read aloud.

Once you had finished the assignment, you went back to your seat.

The first times I read, I just took care to enunciate each word clearly.

Then there was what we might call an actorial period: once I started to feel a little more sure of myself, I started to interpret and dramatize the text, with pauses and changes of the tone and register of my voice, when the characters in the Gospel speak in the first person.

"What would ye that I should do for you?"

"Lord, that our eyes may be opened!"

I would make my childish voice ring out as impressively as possible . . .

"O faithless and perverse generation, how long shall I be with you, and suffer you?"

And I intoned such emotions as indignation and compassion; I let ring tones of prophesying.

"And if thy right hand offend thee . . . cut it off, and cast it from thee! And if thy right eye offend thee . . . pluck it out, and cast it from thee!"

One day it dawned on me just how ridiculous I was.

Since then, I have always felt a certain mistrust toward actors, who are good at performing but almost never good at reading, because they're never satisfied to just read.

As soon as I stopped insisting on being inspired and moved, I realized that the inspiration and the emotion were there, yes, but they were in the text, in the words before my eyes, they were already inspired and it did no good to add emphasis or drama, it wasn't necessary to push them or hurl them like stones, it was enough to let them slide one after the other, give them back, *give them back*, that's right, you need to give them back the way you would do with something borrowed that has only been entrusted to us for a while.

And the time comes to give it back.

Every time that book was opened and read, its words went back to where they had come from.

To give them a further interpretation would mean hindering them, trying in vain to stop them on their course.

Instead, you have to make the voice vanish, be gone, light or heavy or terrible or consoling, these words must go away as if they were vanishing from the page as you read them.

Once I understood this, I began to experience a genuine pleasure.

Which has never since left me.

I paid only intermittent attention to the rest of the mass, immersed as I was in other thoughts and looking around me or above me, toward the ceiling of the church; when I was little, mass was said in Latin, but then when they changed it to Italian, it became even more incomprehensible, at least beforehand there had been something mysterious, like those songs in English that you learn without understanding.

At a certain point they introduced guitars and bongo drums, to accompany the singing, which became noisy and rhythmic, that new type of mass known as a beatnik mass, which I found even harder to take seriously.

So similar to the junk you could hear on the radio, only much much worse.

In this, you have to admit that the priests at SLM were true innovators. They wanted to keep up with the times, open up to the outside world.

On Sunday an intelligent and learned priest came to say mass. His name was Don Salari, he delivered sermons in which he invited everyone to engage in dialogue. The priests at SLM rubbed their hands in delight because it brought in a lot of people, some from outside the Quartiere Trieste, and everyone was astonished and filled with admiration at how progressive the school had turned out to be.

I STOPPED going to mass once and for all when the custom was introduced of turning to your neighbor, after the Our Father, and shaking hands. It turned into a sort of mandatory thing. The priest would order, "Exchange a sign of peace," and you had to turn to your right and your left, and toward the pew behind you, and say hello and smile at everyone who was around you, extending your hand or even exchanging hugs. To do it was embarrassing, not to do it was offensive, if you didn't shake hands it seemed as if you had it in for whoever was there, or as if you had a black soul, curled up like a porcupine. At school during mass, we SLM students found ourselves exchanging gestures of peace between classmates or even deskmates and the first few times we'd shake hands firmly with a deep bow like oriental ambassadors, all of it accompanied by smiles and mocking glances. Or else the extended hand could suddenly snap into an almost face-slap. Barracks humor triumphed over all. I won't conceal the fact that the moment, if spared the arrows of sarcasm, could be touching, literally speaking, that is, the touch might have a strange effect, like an electric shock. It's not necessarily a bad thing to be forced into something we'd be ashamed to do in a spontaneous manner. In any case, if among ourselves, we classmates exchanged the sign of peace in a buffoonish or threatening way—so that it wound up resembling its diametric opposite, a promise to exchange punches—with strangers it was more of a source of uneasiness and it left a bitter sense of hypocrisy. Pretending to love or be reconciled with someone you never actually had a fight with makes you veer automatically toward vile thoughts such as, "Actually, I don't give a flying fuck about you," thoughts that would never have crossed your mind if it hadn't been for that paradoxical invocation: "Exchange a sign of peace." The fact is that for me, the sign of peace was the end of my practice of religion.

WHEN I ATTENDED mass this morning at SLM, after all these many years, on a warm, excessively warm February morning, I noticed that all the trees are dwarf trees. You practically have to bow down to avoid poking yourself in the eye with a branch. And then there's no one in sight. Not a living soul—and it's not like it's sunrise, it's eleven a.m. Via Tolmino, the asphalt repaved, echoes only to the sound of my heels, which are those good English ones, purchased on Corso Trieste where my father used to buy his. Sunday shoes, according to a concept of Sunday that has been obsolete for a long time now. Made in Northamptonshire, where Church's and Grey's shoes are manufactured, to come all this way to tread the dark and odorous asphalt, under the dwarf trees of Via Tolmino, sticky and black in spite of the illusory arrival of springtime.

TO MY ENORMOUS SURPRISE, Don Salari is still there, saying mass. Old, very old, but still perfectly lucid. Practically a soothsayer, a seer. And what I have tried to transcribe in the following chapter was his sermon. Or at least the part of it that struck me.

4

WHY DID JESUS go into the desert to fast? Forty days . . . immersed in His most profound thoughts. Does God need to reflect in order to decide what to do? Isn't everything already clear and luminous in the divine mind, isn't everything already written? It's in that exact moment that Jesus is about to undertake the path that will lead Him to become the Christ. The fact that He feels the need to withdraw and to meditate shows us that this line of action is not the only one possible, it would not be inevitable, and that the decision still entails a doubt, many doubts, as well as sacrifices that will have to be accepted as the price of excluding all other possibilities.

"Just as the Jews had to wander for forty years in the desert before reaching Israel, and just as during their stay in the desert they fall into temptation and on many occasions are on the verge of retracing their footsteps, it is likewise right that Jesus should face up to and overcome the same obstacles that stand in the way of Him attaining His destiny. Careful, however: if for the Jews at the end of their long wandering lies the Promised Land, for Jesus there is death. And while what was tempted by the devil was a people's human weakness, with Jesus what was tested was His boundless divine power. He must fast and suffer, then, not in order to save Himself, but to degrade Himself.

"Let this be clear: it isn't the human part of Christ that is being tempted, or it isn't only the human part; it is in fact the divine part. It is God, not man, who is uncertain. In order for God to accept His own diminution, for Him to accomplish fully the plan that He Himself conceived, the necessary amount of time must pass in order to make the scope of its daring fully understandable. It takes courage, in other words, a quality that is by no means as instinctive as is commonly thought, but which instead requires reflection and ripens with time: a product of patience and doubt. A quality that springs not from the fullness of strength, but rather from its lack—which indeed courage fills in for. God does not possess it: being courageous is not part of his endowment, that would be an admission of inferiority, a man can be courageous, God cannot. Courage is required to achieve things that loom far above us, that are greater than us. Jesus instead has to find that courage in order to face up to a fate too puny and squalid for His divine nature: suffering and death.

"Hence the fasting, which is the mortification of his energy.

"Hence the temptations of the devil, who is actually subordinate to Him, as Holy Scripture tells: and he promises Him realms that the devil has received from God to manage. Ridiculous, offensive: it's as if a servant offered hospitality to the master of the house.

"Jesus goes into the desert to find His own humanity, whole and complete, to perfect its imperfection, and in fact, at the end of His fast, He is hungry. Real hunger, a hole in His stomach. He has fully become a man and now He is ready, capable of dying. From unconscious divine sovereignty, He has passed into conscious human precariousness. Clearing up His mind with His meditation in the desert, His ideas have become smaller, so that they can transform themselves into words and actions. We humans, too, when we are able to define our objectives, it's because we've reduced them. To choose means setting limits, eliminating alternatives, destroying possible worlds. An undecided man is infinitely richer, and that is why he hesitates, because he does not want to give up his riches. Human life feels the insult of partialness. Life is short, we receive little, we know even less, we under-stand almost none of it. And then it all ends. In the desert, Jesus comes to know and experiences this nightmare of partialness. The relativity of exis-tence becomes palpable, physical in the desert, there is nothing but sand in all directions, rough rocks, the monotony of the landscape and the sky, never changing, dominated by the blazing sun. The desert is the place where the solitary voice of every prophet is born, as he attempts to inhabit, to animate the nothingness. Even a shout is enough to populate that void, and it is likely that even the hermit's profound meditations are nothing more than a muttering, a stammering, a little ditty sung in the silence, maybe even a snatch of doggerel. The sole consolation of a sentry aban-doned in a solitary place is the singsong that keeps him company. In the desert, Jesus experiences the relativity of human life, first with suffering, then as a precious glint of the entirety of the divine life. He no longer suf-fers over it, He enjoys it. It's a revelation. A valid announcement for all humans. To be destined for death and not to possess the truth in its en-tirety, instead of being cruel privations, qualify as signals of eternal life and fundamental truth. That breath of life need no longer feel guilty for the fact that it is merely a breath.

"Certainly, human existence is only a clue, but it's a very precious one. In its paltriness, in fact, it serves to indicate, to announce, and for that rea-son it must be exemplary, and an example means nothing unless it refers back to a significance that transcends the mind, and therefore can never be comprehensible as a whole, but rather only in fragments, through allusions, parables, enigmas. Our way of thought, enslaved by partialness, yearns to redeem it, aspiring to the absolute dominion of matter, through an exercise that we call reason. It does not know how to yield to an obstacle. Quite to the contrary, it ought to treasure partialness. It illuminates us in an elo-quent fashion about the nature of things, starting with our own nature. And for that matter, a point of view is certainly not mistaken just because it is partial.

"Let me offer you the example brought by an ancient thinker.

"We are in the Christian East. Imagine a Byzantine church. Observing from a distance the golden cupola that rises atop its bell tower, I receive a particular image of it according to my location, which will be different for another observer looking at the bell tower from the opposite side as me. If I myself change my position, if I move closer to the bell tower or farther away, or if I circle around it, my new view will change from the previous view, and in some sense I will find myself different, uncertain, I will find myself in conflict with myself, uncertain as to which image is more significant or real among the various images I have seen. In other words, I and some other observer will have different and partial views. This difference is certainly irreconcilable, there is no discussion or openness to dialogue that can remedy it. The distance remains intact, even among willing interlocutors. A person might even make a special effort and in his enthusiasm renounce his own point of view in order to embrace and take as his own the other person's point of view: however admirable in and of itself, the sacrifice wouldn't change the difference, and in fact, this renunciation might even strike some as cowardly.

"In other words, I will always have a different view from another observer. That doesn't change the fact that we are looking at the same bell tower, the same cupola that glitters in the distance. Its gold is no less splendid for the fact that I see only a sliver of it. The partialness, the relativity of the experiences that we can have does nothing at all to undermine their overall significance. The gold doesn't lose its value, it isn't divided up into sections, if you multiply the points from which it is seen, indeed, everyone can glimpse a reflection of it, the gleam that would otherwise be lost if it weren't seen and enjoyed from there, from that exact spot, and only from there, from that particular angle . . .

"Often we mistake this relativity for relativism, the conviction, that is, that one idea is as good as any other, and that there is no foundation for stating that anything has universal validity. Contradicting its own underlying concept, relativism confidently states that no absolute bond exists between the truth and statements that concern the truth. One statement, in the final analysis, is equivalent to another. Relativity is quite another thing. Full awareness of the constitutional weakness of our being and the need to revise and update our point of view on things oblige us to a never-ending quest. During this migration, no answer given at any specific moment can ever be all encompassing in its validity because, in the meantime, the question itself has already radically changed. Or perhaps we should say, the point from which that question is asked. Question oneself, verify, reformulate the questions.

"That is why even Jesus, God on earth, needs forty days in the desert to update His point of view, multiply it, revealing its relativity. And that is why He allows himself to be subjected to the temptations/hallucinations, like any human who stays too long with nothing to eat or drink. His power could easily sweep away all misunderstandings in an instant, but it would be a shortcut that would contradict the meaning of the incarnation. This is His supreme sacrifice: He immolates the truth itself, its divine entirety, and from this point forward He will only express it in an allusive form, through enigmas, as is inevitable when you pass through the locks and channels and the clauses of human language, and as the prophets did before Him. However deadly its precision, the language of the Gospels does not represent the mastery over being, but instead its emergence in so violent a manner as to leave one stunned, breathless. The phrases of Jesus loom up with dazzling precision, at the limit of comprehensibility or well beyond it. The parables explain nothing, they don't even explain themselves . . ."

USUALLY IT IS OLD PEOPLE who attend holy mass, a greater number of women than men, let's say in a ratio of four to one, I imagine because the men (that is, their husbands) have already been dead for several years, or else because although they're still alive, they don't go to mass, because they consider religion to be a somehow feminine business, or else because they're convinced that only one member of the family need practice it. In the large modern church where, among other things, my mother's funeral was held, the ladies who attend mass have hairdos dyed an indefinable color, abstract, somewhere between ocher yellow and titian, a shade not found in nature, a hue that sparkles with a faint phosphorescence when they turn their heads or bow them as they kneel upon their return from the Eucharist. Their hairdos are swollen with hairspray and by the light that passes through it. While in everything else they constitute a model of resigned bourgeois normality, the color of their hair offers a delirious touch to their appearance, as if they were fairies or witches.

IT'S ASTONISHING just how faint collective singing can be. There's nothing vital or joyous about it. A community gathered in church shows itself to be shy, chilled, deeply Western. Laboring under the illusion that the courage to proclaim their faith will only grow among his parishioners along with the volume of their voices, the priest tries to bolster their enthusiasm, he dogs them, thundering into his microphone, from one verse to the next, but in so doing all he manages to do is to cover up the few voices that actually rise from the pews. Once they've exhausted the scant impetus of the refrain, the chorus goes back to murmuring in an almost inaudible fashion. It's not as if people simply don't sing, quite the contrary: it's that when they do sing they do it sotto voce, barely moving their lips, as if lip-synching. They are ashamed of letting their voices be heard, as if that were somehow unseemly or fanatical. The same thing happens during the prayers, when the priest urges the faithful to repeat a ritual phrase, such as: "We, Your faithful, full of weeping, humbly ask You, Oh Lord, to dry our tears" or else "The gates that protect Your kingdom are not locked, but only ajar" or even "We have knocked at Your door in the night and the cold and in the end, we were admitted." Whether complicated or easy to memorize, these phrases are mumbled or even substituted by a generic grumbling in which all that can be heard is the first and last words. "The lamb which . . . mmnyuhmmnyuh nguhnguhnnnnnn awanyuhmanyuhngnuh wanyawanya . . . nyahnyamugnognuh . . . purification!"

Sometimes one voice stands out above all the others, shameless, rising above the subdued chorus. This is usually one solitary fanatical woman, or possibly someone who's hard of hearing and has no idea that they're practically shouting.

I HAVE NOTICED that when people pray these days, they no longer put their hands together but instead hold them out, palms raised flat, at chest height, in imitation of the paintings on the walls where the saints receive a divine vision or else martyrdom. This posture is in fact a very lovely and ecstatic one: the worshipper does not hunch over in isolation after receiving holy communion, as if trying to protect his soul from prying eyes, but instead exposes himself to a sort of wind or light emanating from the altar.

TODAY, Easter Sunday, I have braved the pouring rain to go back to mass at SLM. I left my little spring-loaded collapsible umbrella, which wasn't working anyway, outside the church's bronze portal, dangling from the foot of the little boy to whom the founder of the Marist order benevolently imparts a lesson, or a benediction, but the bronze foot was wet, too smooth or slanted just that little bit too far, and the umbrella slid to the ground. I left it there and went in. There weren't many people, and it was cold inside the church. They'd brightened the floors with carpets, and at the center of the nave they'd placed a large table lined with flowers. Around that table there was room for at least twenty people to sit for the Easter luncheon. You could hear the raindrops tapping on the roof while inside water dripped from the raincoats of the faithful, scattered among the pews, nearly all of them elderly people, stiff with the dank chill of this Easter, so grim and early. Similarly grim was the priest, his loquacious rambling had no idea what path to take, and, looking at him more closely now, I saw that he was old, a fragile little old man with white hair, who was chiefly trying to warm up his homily in order to warm himself up. But he couldn't do it, and after a few minutes and more than one false argumentative start, he finally gave up. I expected him to justify his failure by informing his listeners that he was indisposed, but instead he moved on without delay to the subsequent phases of the ceremony. A mass, after all, is basically just a mass, period. It needn't necessarily be *aesthetically pleasing*, it's not as if we're at the theater, or at the stadium for a soccer match. The order of the prayers really did strike me as distant and muddled, and I wound up growing completely distracted.

A few yards away from me sat a mother with a small boy in a stroller, sitting quietly, big blue eyes, fair exceedingly fine hair, emitting little noises of contentment, turning his head to look at his mother and trying to grab the various objects that she held out to him in an order so natural and precise that it seemed preordained. The child had small, white, very prehensile hands.

5

ANOTHER TIME I WENT TO SALVATORE'S HOUSE was much more interesting and unsettling than our visit to the MSI chapter.

This time, my friend asked me: Do you want to see something?

What are you supposed to say to a question like that?

He went into his brother's bedroom—his brother wasn't home—rummaged around anxiously in a drawer as if he were afraid that his brother might be about to come in at any moment, and pulled out a stack of Polaroids.

We hurried back to Salvatore's room and sat down on the bed to examine them.

From the very first I was swept by a violent emotion that took my breath away.

They were pictures of nude girls.

I'd seen naked girls before, in various porn magazines, in *Caballero*, which was a tabloid newspaper, and in *Le Ore*.

It wasn't uncommon to find pages torn out of these magazines, or their covers, blowing along the street, or abandoned beside garbage cans, or in public bathrooms: as if whoever had managed to get their hands on them hadn't been able to resist ripping them to pieces.

And so the magazine was divided and multiplied.

It was common for packing paper or food wrappings to consist of pages from erotic magazines.

But I had never before seen pictures of nude girls taken in private, girls who were, so to speak, real girls.

Their very reality somehow made them repugnant.

The flash lit up their bodies in dazzlingly white close-ups, or not so much white as gray, as if they were dead, and the rest of the room remained partially in shadow.

It wasn't entirely clear whether some of these bodies were female or male.

They were glabrous and boneless, the bellies and backs dotted with moles, the thighs and the nipples purplish.

Nearly all of them lacked heads, that is, the photographs were framed from the necks down to the knees.

Salvatore would pull one Polaroid off the top of the stack, hand it to me, wait for me to examine it thoroughly while he observed my reactions with a somewhat stupid-looking smile, then he'd give me another.

He gave the impression that he knew them all by heart and was interested to know what I thought of them.

I gulped down my saliva in silence and put the photo I'd just viewed at the bottom of my stack, the way you might do with a hand of cards.

The stack in Salvatore's hands was dwindling while the one in mine was thickening.

I was tempted to ask Salvatore some questions, but I was throttled by my heart as it pounded in my throat.

The girls were different, yes, I'd have to guess that they were all different, lying down with their long hair draped along their backs or else bent over, both hands pulling their buttocks wide open.

The one characteristic they all had in common was that none of them was very well developed and by no means attractive.

One in particular made a very strong impression on me. The only girl to have been photographed more than once, in various positions. She was bronzed and had white bikini marks on her skin, a nonexistent bosom, and very skinny hips. Completely naked. From behind, you might have taken her for a little boy if it weren't for the pale line left by the elastic strap of her brassiere, which ran horizontally beneath her protruding shoulder blades. She was posed in a standing position, squatting on the floor, curled up on the bed, lying belly down and spread-eagled. Only in one shot could her face be glimpsed, and that might have been an accident. Her face looked scared.

I DON'T THINK Salvatore really liked girls.

At that age it was hard to say which of us students at SLM liked girls and which didn't, we had no way of making it evident, either to ourselves or to others.

Puberty is a crystal inferno.

Salvatore had a short, stout deskmate named Marco d'Avenia, childish to the verge of retardation, the kind of young boy who remains beardless and asexual until he becomes an adult.

In class, the two of them sat at the first desk on the right, next to the hallway door, clearly visible both from the teacher's desk and podium and from all the rest of our desks. They were also therefore most vulnerable to the unannounced arrivals of the headmaster, who was fond of making visits as sudden as they were contrived, on flimsy pretexts, not so much for the purpose of checking on the student as on the teachers, who in fact feared these intrusions much more than we did and were very visibly ashamed and mortified if there was uproar or disorder.

The door would open without anyone knocking first and we'd all freeze, paralyzed in our various and grotesque poses: one might have a hand raised as he prepared to throw a crumpled ball of paper, another might be pretending to push his desk as if it were a bobsled about to take off, and then leap onto it to mimic the swerving and jolting of the track, others might be strangling each other, their hands around each other's throat, and the teacher would be standing there, both arms high in the air like the conductor of a demented orchestra.

The silence that followed was broken only by his embarrassed small coughs and by the last metallic twangs of the hooks for our book bags being played as a sort of jew's harp.

THE LESSONS seemed endless.

I would spend them almost entirely immobile, my hands perched on either side of my face, my elbows braced on my desktop.

I would do my very best to pay attention because I've always hated studying at home in the afternoon, but it was hard to maintain concentration for anything more than ten or fifteen minutes, after which I no longer changed position, but instead of looking toward the teacher's desk or the podium or the blackboard, my eyes would lift a few degrees, toward the classroom ceiling, and after that I slipped into a trance.

I would be filled with an irresistible lassitude.

It happens to me still, and in the least advisable situations, I still drop off to sleep . . . not long ago it happened to me during a conference in Padua, seated at a table next to several important speakers.

Luckily, I happened to be wearing sunglasses and I hope and trust that nobody saw my little catnap.

Instead my classmates were in a constant frenzy, agitated as they tirelessly invented new ways of interrupting the lesson, some of them, I have to admit, decidedly brilliant.

There was one method in particular, and I occasionally took part in it myself, as it didn't require you to move a muscle to participate, and most important of all, it was impossible to identify the culprit.

In Rome, every day at noon, aside from the famous cannon shot fired from the top of the Janiculum Hill, which was however too far away from SLM for us to be able to hear it, a siren sounded. It signaled lunchtime in the factories, which back then were still operative and working.

Yes, back then there were factories in Rome, though we've long since forgotten them, not just in Milan and Turin.

It came from over near Tiburtina Station, from the Pietralata quarter.

It lasted a minute.

Theoretically.

Because nearly everyone in the class would hum along to the note of the siren, mouths closed, an almost imperceptible moan, which went on after the sound of the siren had ceased.

Mmmmmmmmm . . . Mmmmmmmm . . .

We'd continue a while longer and eventually the teacher necessarily realized that the sound was going on too long, he'd stop teaching and shake his head in amazement.

Stupefied by such idiocy.

He would look at us disconsolately and probably mused sorrowfully on the failure of his calling as a teacher, one he'd embraced so many years, in a terrible error.

So these were the results?

These were the creations, these the men?

Inside our mouths, lips compressed, and in our noses, the siren would continue to resonate like a Buddhist om, and then, little by little it would start to dwindle, dying out bit by bit as each of my classmates stopped their moaning, first one, then another, then a third, and then all the others would fall silent with one last exhalation, except for one solitary voice holding out until the end of that last breath, tremulous, and silence would return to the classroom.

By then, it was three minutes after noon, or perhaps five minutes after noon.

A small, unpunishable collective crime.

Idiocy gives you a giddy dizziness of pleasure.

We were practically of legal age, almost men, and yet we still howled at high noon, like a pack of stray dogs, rendered giddy by the joy of staring our teacher right in the eye with a glint of defiance, leaving him powerless against us.

The most frustrated teacher was always De Laurentiis, who taught ancient literature and so dearly cherished Greek music, and who would let himself go into ritual, endless soliloquies, the targets of countless imitations.

All you needed to do was put on something of a Neapolitan accent, and imitate the grim, false curve of his bulbous blue eyes, his hands clasped in a prayer to San Gennaro to put an end to all the "con-few-shun."

"Alas! Alack! And to think that the lot of you are zitting here warming your zeats inshtead of out shoveling coal . . . and all because your mishguided parents can afford to pay a little money . . ."

The cold hard truth that he couldn't avoid—so that after a little while he'd fall silent and start back up with the *Aeneid*—was that the very same money paid his salary.

It was our well-to-do parents who paid that miserable wretch.

He made a living off our ignorance, and I almost felt as if he owed us a debt of gratitude.

Even those of us who were blithely unaware of this relationship still loved to exercise with great cruelty this social prerogative, whereby a teacher is nothing more than a salaryman at the service of his students, less respectable in that way than a housecleaner whom you pay by the hour— because she at least cleaned your house and you could see the results, while the lessons of ancient Greek had virtually no perceptible results at all.

The teacher-as-office-clerk, the teacher-as-supplier, the teacher-as-butler, the teacher-as-nanny.

The phantom of his authority created on the basis of grades, threats of flunking, notes on the classroom ledger—it was all merely a scarecrow, a boogeyman.

Eliminate that, and what you have left is a day worker.

Although it was once found exclusively in private schools, that attitude can now be found in schools everywhere.

BUT THE TWO BOYS in the front row didn't care about being so visible, they just didn't notice or else they simply didn't care about all the eyes focused on them.

And often they *touched each other*.

Actually, it was Marco who touched Salvatore.

He'd do it at moments when his classmate was closely attending to the lesson: he'd stealthily extend a hand under the desk and lay it flat on the crotch of his pants.

Almost before Salvatore even had a chance to notice it, Marco would already have withdrawn his hand and was once again sitting with both arms crossed in front of him on the desk, in the impeccable position of the good student, obedient to the injunction to "sit up properly."

Ten or fifteen minutes would pass.

He'd reach out his hand again.

As if he were indifferent or insensitive to it, Salvatore would say nothing.

Only a couple of times could you notice him lurching slightly, perhaps because his classmate had lowered his paw a little too vigorously into his lap and had hurt him.

When the class began to notice this peculiar behavior, it became the subject of interest and study.

We'd all sit there, raptly watching, waiting for the moment that Marco would reach out his hand.

It was strange that he should have acted so hastily but, at the same time, so explicitly, as if he cared nothing whether he was seen by one and all as he rummaged around between his neighbor's thighs.

He seemed to be too caught up in the game.

And the very rapidity of his gesture, the way he touched and then withdrew, palpating his classmate and then sitting up straight and proper at his desk, had something of the compulsive and unconscious about it, as if, by doing it, not only Salvatore but even he himself would not have enough time to realize what had just happened.

And, in fact, nothing at all had happened.

Crossing his arms again, it was as if he were saying: "What did I do? Nothing. I have my hands on the desk, as you can see. I'm listening to the teacher . . ."

Soon, though, he'd be seized by the desire to try it again.

We'd see him practically shaking in his good-boy posture.

It was obvious that the hand was about to go back there.

In the meantime, Salvatore continued placidly to listen to the lesson, like a large grazing ruminant.

He had the same clueless slowness that he had displayed when he'd shown me the Polaroids that his brother had taken.

NEVER ONCE must Marco have sensed the fervor behind him with which his filthy move was awaited by his classmates, to their great and mocking amusement.

In fact, what he did didn't scandalize a soul, it just left us flat on the floor with laughter.

In school, what with all the repressing of laughter, it is eventually transformed into a sort of asthmatic death rattle.

6

LET ME MAKE ONE THING CLEAR: *before anything else, before being Caucasian, Italian, baptized as a Roman Catholic, middle-class, left-wing, and a Lazio fan, I am a male. This is my most evident identity, my salient feature, my most distinctive characteristic, something I was called to account for the minute I emerged from my mother's belly. I therefore have much more in common with a poor black Muslim born in Sudan than I do with a female lawyer born in the Parioli neighborhood, or with the female Ukrainian caregiver who makes broth for that lawyer's mother. Though great gulfs may well separate me from the sub-Saharan Muslim, I still bear the same physiological stigmata as he does, fraternally because involuntarily, the same faults and perhaps a comparable and equally unjustified sense of pride, I cherish similar desires, I cultivate twin frustrations. My body functions the same way his does, and to a roughly 90 percent correspondence, so does my mind, that enormous submerged part of the mind that the environments in which he and I grew up can't even begin to touch.*

I FEEL an authentic veneration for Sigmund Freud: and yet I couldn't say whether his work is more misbegotten for the fact that he stitched together a demented theory about femininity based on the discovery of not having a penis, or for the fact that he roundly ignored the fact that, if we think that not having a penis is tragic, having one can often be far worse. The misunderstanding comes from a worldview that was still quite common in his day, dating back to the Bible, of the man as the original figure, and of the woman as somehow derived from the man, or a poor imitation of him, as a mutilated, incomplete, and therefore uncomfortable male: a woman, then, is a sort of Fisher King, who sadly contemplates the wound between her legs.

As a result, Freud formulated the doctrine of "penis envy," but not the corresponding theory of "penis embarrassment" or "penis inconvenience," which would have had a much more solid foundation: in part because in the development of any scientific theory, you'd expect to obtain better results by studying the consequences of something *that exists* rather than those, purely hypothetical, of something *that doesn't*. The theory of penis envy may well be intermittently valid, but the other one is incontrovertibly evident, as engraved in the experience of any male alive. While women's problems may be ascribed, with a breathtakingly daring form of reasoning, on something women *lack*, men's problems can be clearly and easily attributed to something that men very evidently *have*. The problematic and mysterious fact of being male is taken for granted, as if it were an obvious point of departure, something there a priori, Adam, the subject, the little figure inscribed by Leonardo da Vinci in that circle as a measure of all things.

At a rough guess, however, you'd have to say that it's more harmful to have a penis than not to have one.

It is in fact male sexual identity that is awkwardly overabundant, rather than its female counterpart being in any way deficient. The penis is not something of which women have been mutilated, but rather something extra that men have found themselves possessing, something that will accompany them for the rest of their lives, like a saprophyte, a sharer who is by no means secret, and who behaves extravagantly, living a parasitic existence parallel to that of its host. Even more than it is threatening to others, or to other women in particular, the erect penis is threatening to those who see it poke out from beneath their bellies, at once haughty, quizzical, and ridiculous. It does not answer to any command, neither mental nor even, often, manual. Its sheer independence is the source of pride, depression, and horror. Its power is felt as an alien, almost enemy presence, so capable of dragging the rest of the person after it that it can make you think and say and commit any atrocity, and to an equal degree, its laziness and weakness can be deeply demoralizing: and the entire delicate mechanism of self-esteem dangles absurdly from this oscillation. I believe that it was St. Augustine who said that God had intentionally endowed man with such a fickle sex, so independent of his will, precisely in order to limit his pride, to deprive him of any illusion that he was capable of becoming the master of the earth, seeing that he cannot even master an anatomical appendage. God created sexual impotence, not only chronic impotence but more evocatively, episodic impotence, which strikes precisely when you least expect it, in order to strip man of all confidence, to diminish him, and to keep him from nurturing dreams of corporeal perfection. Thus, only spiritual perfection should be his goal.

As a result, the virile male member is in fact the least virile part of the man. The very symbol of uncertainty.

THE AUTHORS who tried to illustrate the idea of "penis inconvenience" in their books have failed to do so (it was inevitable), instead merely generating lunatic duets. Classical sculptors, on the other hand, were fully aware of it as they girded themselves to complete a project, finding themselves obliged to give form and dimension to an incongruous organ extraneous from the rest of the body that they had shaped in perfect harmony, and so they decided to diminish its size, certainly not out of any modesty, because they recognized in the sex attribute, in fact, an unbalancing, a pleonasm, the unharmonious element capable of rendering ridiculous the entire form, first and foremost due to its morbid ability to attract the observer's gaze to it. Suffice it to think of the immediately unnerving and comical effect of depictions of a classical body with an erect penis. Nonetheless, the models for those athletes, soldiers, chariot drivers, and discus throwers must necessarily have had erections! The very improbable metamorphosis of the organ induces embarrassment in cataloguing it. Pornography aside, what would be the correct way of looking at it? How should a scientific portraitist depict it, one of those illustrators capable of rendering plants, leaves, fish, and snakes down to the millimeter, or great artists such as Pisanello or Dürer? When can it be said to be more specifically itself, in repose or in erection? Which of the two states (to say nothing of the other intermediate states, which can only be catalogued in filthy conversations) would be more amply representative?

(It is possible that a flaccid dick expresses a man's emotions far more precisely than a hard one can. Or his authentic corporeal essence, which is fragile far more than it's potent.)

To consider women to be incomplete and envious cloned copies then leads to negative attitudes in men, who find themselves living next to mutilated creatures, to be contemplated with horror and contempt, or else with compassion. A *castrato*. Who herself is ashamed of her wound, and therefore hides it. The masochistic desires of a woman over the course of her life, according to respected female psychologists: to be devoured, to be whipped, pierced, or perforated. Coitus, basically, is reduced to receiving blows. Hence the resemblance of the sex act, if viewed by someone who, hypothetically, had no idea of what was going on, to a punishment of some sort (I no longer remember whether it was Baudelaire or Laforgue who spoke of a "surgical procedure" . . .).

(THE FIRST ONES to be undermined by the suspicion that the myths about their inferiority may actually represent the truth, rather than mere propaganda, are women themselves. That is the risk that every subjugated or bullied group runs: that of giving credit to those who bully them, acknowledging the foundation of the legends that tell how and why this relationship of subjugation has always existed and must continue to remain in place. The power of myths in fact lies in their permanence: beyond all the other variants, the substance of what the myth tells us remains identical. In classical times, we find an agreement between the victor and the vanquished, the dominator and the dominated, that their relationship, thus established, has no other alternatives, that it is just, or even necessary. The victor and the vanquished see that dominion in the same manner: that it must be viewed as a natural event, which means that it is immutable. The way things stand has no reason to be called into question, and for that matter, who would even dare to try such a thing? As if, placed under hypnosis, dominator and dominated were to repeat the same identical formula, which is no longer imposed by the victor, in fact, which even he finds himself repeating without clearly understanding who actually suggested it to him. They limit themselves to handing down that which they have received, and it finds its legitimation precisely in the fact that it is being handed down: if it were not legitimate, it would long ago have vanished. If it endures, that means that it's well founded. When everyone says the same thing, then it happens in fact that no one can even remember who said it first, or when. It is in this way that commonplace truths are formed.)

All of this, however, stopped all at once when women began to show themselves off proudly, shamelessly, with an exhibitionism nowadays turbocharged by the technology that makes it possible to display your body, or the juiciest parts of it, live, to a vast, unlimited audience, and with relative ease compared with males whose nudity (setting aside the peculiar sense of modesty that, in my opinion, is actually stronger among men than women) obliges them to that oscillating dangle, half comical and half pornographic, and the inevitable comparisons that ensue.

MALE SELF-RESPECT in erotic terms is often expressed in numbers. If they are not displayed, they are secretly reckoned. The number of women one has had, the number of sex acts performed in a single night, the endurance of the coitus, the length of the dick, and so on and so forth. Numbers, in short, numbers, numbers, no different than in a stock exchange or in the world of sports. The test to be passed these days in order for a man's sexual performance to be considered satisfactory is not to have an orgasm himself but to make sure that his female lover has one: this is the metric by which his sexual competence will be judged (by her, by himself, by those of both sexes to whom the details will be confided). Which of course can be the source variously of a surge of pride or just as easily of fearsome lurches of anxiety and mortification.

How many girls have you taken to bed; how many times did you fuck; how often do you get a hard-on, how many times did you come, and how many times did you make the girl you were fucking come, etc. Data, mere data. Calculations. There was a time when you could measure a man's prowess by the number of children he had brought into the world with his seed. The record is said to belong to Genghis Khan, who raped so many women during his incursions and raids that nowadays in Asia, nearly eight centuries after his death, it is estimated that one person in twenty has some chromosomes from the great military leader.

THE FEMALE BODY then becomes an interchangeable, accumulable object, which circulates in men's conversations like a coin, allowing them to get to know one another, understand one another, compare themselves with one another, establishing certain hierarchies among themselves in accordance with who is wealthiest. Women constitute one of the methods, for some men the principal one, by means of which a man can affirm his own identity in the eyes of other men. Like money, women serve this purpose, allowing men to establish a certain credit. "He's a guy who knows how to handle women . . ." If women didn't exist, then men would be obliged to square off in open and direct competition, they'd have to vanquish one another: instead they conquer women and show them off as trophies. The men deserve admiration because they have been skilled and ruthless, because the women they have conquered are pretty, or else because they're numerous, or else the women hang eagerly on their lips, admiring their speech. If women didn't exist, there would be a constant state of war among men. But, of course, there would also be more love. Instead, a great deal of both the fascination and the brutality is unloaded upon the women as intermediate bodies.

The desire to fuck many women or a single woman many times may be viewed as an inexhaustible quest of the male identity. Every time I enter a woman I can tell myself: yes, I am a man.

ACCORDING TO A HALF-BAKED theory that was circulating when I was a boy, a man is capable of producing a limited quantity of sperm in a lifetime, corresponding to a certain number of orgasms. Have you ever heard this idea? I swear that I witnessed and was tempted to take part in a number of discussions of this topic, despite the fact that I was entirely ignorant about the subject. They unfolded roughly along these lines.

They're like bullets.

What do you mean?

You shoot them out.

And so . . .

When you're out of ammunition, you're out of ammunition.

And just how many of these "bullets" are we supposed to have, tell me.

Three thousand.

Three thousand? That's quite a few.

Not as many as you might think, if you count the times you jack off.

You have to count them?

Of course you do.

What difference does it make? It's an ejaculation like any other.

True enough . . .

"Ejaculation" is the most ridiculous word I've ever heard in my life.

I couldn't agree more.

It's only a technical term.

But I must have jacked off a thousand times, by now . . .

. . . if not more! Ha ha ha!

(On this specific point, I would be as evasive as possible, hoping not to be pinned down for the reason I've mentioned previously.)

But then, when you get to three thousand, what happens then?

You can't get it up?

You can't come anymore?

Do you die?

I've read that there are orgasms where you don't come.

What's that supposed to mean?

You come inward instead of outward.

Inward?

That seems impossible.

Wait, you still haven't answered my question. When you get to three thousand . . . ?

Well, I don't really know what happens: but for sure, you're going to have trouble.

Or else, utter peace.

So what if it was more? Like four thousand, or even five thousand?

But what if it was less . . . ?

Maybe it's just different for every man.

A porn actor must have a bigger reservoir.

Right. Otherwise by the time he turns thirty, he's out of a job.

Then it would probably be a good idea to start as late as possible.

I know that there are people capable of fucking for hours without ever coming.

How do they do it?

Even all day long.

Fantastic!

Sounds boring!

Sure, but how do they do it?

They exert mental control over themselves. Over their bodies. They're like . . .

Like fakirs?

Sure, like fakirs.

Some pretty fucked-up fakirs.

So why do they do it?

To preserve their energies.

And do they attain nirvana?

What does nirvana have to do with any of this?

If you ask me, plenty.

FOR ME, these discussions were the source of considerable embarrassment. Still, I couldn't help but listen eagerly.

"It only counts if you get it inside her" (the words of a student at a summer Spanish course in Salamanca, 1979). "Listen, you have to get it up her ass. With a woman, it only counts if you can fuck her in the ass. Otherwise, it's like you never even fucked her at all" (assertion of an Italian literary critic, 1989).

Masculinity, as we are taught by Don Juan, is not something you have, it's something you always have to *still* have, it's something you are constantly required to test, you must *make* your masculinity, and each time you *create* it with a woman. Like Sir Gawain, who every night of his life as a knight-errant, in order to win hospitality in a castle, was required to refresh his reputation as a great lover by bedding the latest chatelaine who, invariably, teases his honor, while in fact all he is looking for is a pallet and to be allowed to rest undisturbed, similarly Don Juan lives uncomfortably exposed in an interminable demonstration of his amatory endowments, and even though his reputation as a cocksman might accompany him, indeed, precisely because it does, his virility is continuously being subjected to testing, subjected to judgment, referred from bed to bed, postponed to the next conquest, the next amorous adventure. It is in fact the sum of his conquests that has elevated him to such erotic heights that he is now in danger, like an athlete constantly forced to outdo himself. However self-confident he may appear, he is instead consigned to everlasting uneasiness about his own endowment, his own virility, sooner or later bound to leave him in the lurch, and therefore fatally destined, like any hedonist, to disappointment: since these qualities, once they have reached their peak, by the relentless laws of statistics, cannot do anything but decline, wane, the hair turning gray beneath the powdered wig, just as the pubic hair must do, the cock that either slouches helpless or else remains stiff for hours, incapable however of emitting semen, neither giving nor receiving pleasure, like a dried-out club, a ridiculous umbrella.

Those who feel obliged to reaffirm their strength and confidence every minute of the day prove the exact opposite, demonstrating that they are actually fragile. A certificate of masculinity is never going to be issued once and for all to an individual: he might always fail the next test that awaits him, and suddenly reveal to the world the weakness of his nature. All it takes is a minus sign to reverse into a negative number the entire sum of virility acquired at such a high price.

These are scientific data: males are nursed longer and weaned later, they need to be carried even when they're pretty big, they have a harder time learning, they're lazy when it comes to being toilet trained, and they are unable to control their bladders at night until embarrassingly late ages. All these things, in brief, point to their fragility, their greater attachment to their mothers. They behave in ways that are inexplicable, endangering themselves and others, and they present all sorts of unsettling symptoms. They get themselves into all kinds of trouble. They don't know how to handle the losses and wounds that are inflicted on their perennially developing masculinity, and above all, they don't want to talk about it, and they won't tolerate having others talk about it. They remain humiliated forever by the compromises that growing up costs them. They mistake gratuitous risk-taking with bravery.

ADOLESCENCE, then: adolescence was the optimal moment. Before it polarizes and is channeled into forms of sexual expression, and then, eventually, into one's work, virility is in its pure, liquid state. It's like a deposit of flammable material: precious, unquestionably, and perhaps useful as well, but finding a use for it is no easy task. There are disparate and sometimes interchangeable modes, one may abandon one of them to embrace another: friendship, which is fickle as it spins the wheel of its preferences, the occasional artistic inclination, tending toward solitary fixations, such as the guitar or the drums, collecting things, fighting, athletic mysticism, self-destructive impulses and pursuits. Today we have personal computers, which we didn't have back then, along with all the interests and obsessions that go with them. But in short, there are a great many options and they might all be adopted together, in select groups, or alternately. There is no force comparable to that of a desire that has no exact object. The original desire, the most scalding one, consists in fact of the quest for an object of one's own desire. The more powerful its impact, the vaguer the objective toward which it is directed. There is a willingness for *anything*. Hesitant and at the same time reckless, virility that has not yet found its name takes on forms as fleeting and virulent as any exanthematic outbreak, it manifests itself in the manner of a skin rash, which can come close to disfiguring anyone who comes down with it, but then it almost always passes, replaced by some other, further symptom. From case to case, veering with unpredictable randomness, it may result in a dramatic catastrophe or deflate into a trivial nothing, often in the context of a drama that grows out of some trifle. Lies and illusions help to produce very high levels of reality. Entire lives can be shaped by misunderstandings. Disproportionate, out of bounds, and at the same time petty and tawdry, adolescent virility still hasn't experienced sex, or perhaps it has and yet it already recoils from it or else it fosters it and fondles it and dreams of it in some morbid fashion, and when it finally encounters it, they are like chemical products that mix all at once—perhaps nothing will happen, or any of an array of reactions may take place, heat, freezing, dissolution, evaporation, or else the volatile blend may detonate, blowing everything to smithereens . . .

JUST LIKE GIRLS with the abstract ideal of femininity, as we tried to live up to the abstract masculine ideal we were forced to sacrifice much of ourselves, while amplifying qualities that we possessed only to a very small degree. We'd blow them up the way you might a rubber dinghy, inflating them by mouth, exhausting our lungs. If we didn't possess those qualities at all, then we'd borrow them, we'd imitate them. I, who am taken for an independent person, verging on fierceness or even foolishly punctilious, have actually spent my whole life imitating the behavior of others, their gazes, their postures, the way they hold their shoulders, their ways of greeting upon arrival or departure, and a great many phrases and a vast number of expressions I use I have simply copied from others; perhaps I had no reason for constructing a personal culture on the basis of books and films, except as a way of upholstering my identity, layering it with references in order to make it appear more solid and durable than it actually is; even the way I have of curving my mouth after a smile isn't actually original with me. And if in the end I've resigned myself to being what I am, it's only been out of exhaustion.

The abstract ideal of virility, well, it's almost impossible to nail it, the vast majority of men fail to come even close over the course of a lifetime, remaining on the distant margins of the model—leaving aside those who don't individually meet the required standards, there are also entire categories excluded a priori, teenagers, old men, skinny weaklings, homosexuals, even the poor, if the idea of a fully attained masculinity is associated with professional success and financial self-sufficiency. If you're queer and you're unemployed, from that point of view, it amounts to the same thing. Like the painted figures in an allegory, the archetypal evolution of the male through the ages of life ought to experience these phases: as a boy, a loyal friend; as an adult, a responsible father; as an old man, an unflappable sage. Well, I've never met anybody who answers to this ideal figure.

Male desire is viewed as a voracious force, a tireless potency, a need that must at all costs be satiated. Pornography presents vigorous and insatiable males, while the actual experience of real men is, quite to the contrary, for the most part, precarious, contradictory, and insecure. I believe that this happens to men every bit as much as it does to women, indeed, perhaps, even more so: feeling not quite up to the challenge, unsatisfactory in terms of one's sexual performance, and not just now, in the aftermath of the various revolutions in the way we live our lives, but always, it's always been like that, that is to say, one's virility has always dangled by a thread, precarious, fragile, subject to the evaluation of a judgment that is not only that of women, but first and foremost the judgment that the man issues of himself . . .

Fragility, sense of inadequacy, anxiety, fear of judgment, of being unable to satisfy the expectations of others, fear of failure. The braggadocio and aggressive stances were nothing but poses. We put on a front of confidence that 90 percent of the time we never possessed in the slightest. The things one really does possess in a lasting way, one feels absolutely no need to show off. That confidence was just a form of camouflage, and in fact it was often unmasked, causing shame and ridicule. If the phallus is a symbol of power, as is carved into stone walls in half the known world and as we can read in every corner of every page in anthropology textbooks, well, then it is a very fallacious symbol, we might say, a very poorly chosen one, seeing that it all too often fails to live up to its reputation, proving to be seldom or not at all the master of the situation or of itself, a weapon that often jams and fails to fire and, even if it doesn't, always still might . . . from one moment to the next. Thus it is the very same powerful and predatory image of men in general that so decisively puts individual men in the permanent

condition of risking failure. The possibility of failure is the deep and intimate root of being men, and God planted its symbol right in the middle of
the body, clearly visible, in order to ensure that each man is well aware, not
of his own power, but rather of his own fallibility: as in fact that long-ago
Church Father stated in such a convincing and reasonable manner, God
made sure that the erection should be a capricious thing to keep at bay
our sense of omnipotence, crushing it, undermining it at its very roots.
If we must harbor doubts about our ability to perform even the simplest
act, the very act that ensures the existence of our species on the face of the
earth, then how are we likely to feel about everything else?

WHEN WE WANT to change something about ourselves, we almost inevitably begin with our physical being. Muscles are vital and significant. People
say that men's self-respect is proportional to the development of the upper
part of their body. I once asked a friend, who spent a lot of time in gyms,
why the biceps were so often developed to the exclusion of all else. "Because
you can see them," he replied with disarming simplicity. And with that, he
meant to say that, sure other people can see them, especially if you're wearing a T-shirt, but you—first and foremost—can see the gun show you have
on your own arms, you can feel them, you can palpate them, there they are.
For that matter, what drives these young men to pump iron is a sense of
insecurity: the greater the insecurity and the more iron they will pump.
They are engaged in a strenuous struggle to conceal their vulnerability.
Stutterers, dyslexics, fat boys, short guys, four-eyes—in the end, they're the
ones who pump iron more than anyone else. It is an original weakness that
swells our biceps, thus transforming itself into strength. In this alchemy lies
the secret of the male personality. For that matter, our body is *always* wrong,
and I'm not just talking about the bodies of midgets, of homely dogs, of
those who want to change their sex . . .
    Let's delete entirely from the puzzle the word that doesn't belong: "plea-
sure." When we're young, we have sexual experiences for any reason but
that of experiencing pleasure. Perhaps only mature men and women, very
experienced, can devote themselves to pleasure with conscious attention;
seeking it, earning it, comparing the nuances, the specialties . . . It's like
with food. When we're kids, we eat because we're hungry, not to savor who
knows what delicacy. From a lengthy observation of myself and my contemporaries, it strikes me that when someone begins to take an interest in
fine cuisine, exquisite wines, carefully prepared delicacies, and to enjoy

them, for real, it means that they're getting old. But then, if not for pleasure, why did we quest after sex, why do we seek it now even more than before, and you can find it on any street corner without even having to look
for it? Respected scholars and experts claim that we boys cared so much
about taking girls to bed only to prove to one another that we weren't faggots. And the girls? Why did they come to bed with us, then? What were
they trying to prove?

WHEN, after many repeated efforts to obtain a valid exemption, and after
various deferrals for my university studies, I was finally drafted, and enough
time had passed that I was the oldest one in my barracks in Taranto, there
were those who tried to comfort me by hauling out a stupid proverb: "Whoever isn't good enough for the king, isn't good enough for the queen." Its
meaning, just in case my readers fail to get the metaphor (and at first I certainly failed to get it) is as follows: if when you go in for your physical, they
don't find you to be man enough to serve the king, then you also won't be
man enough to satisfy his wife, the queen, and by extension, any other
woman. Cold comfort for anyone conscripted to serve in the military, to
imagine that they had received a certificate of virility, while those who remained home with a nice fat exemption were merely impotent cripples: a
formula that hadn't worked in wartime, much less in peacetime. If anything, I find more interesting a reverse formulation of the same saying: if
you're not good enough for the queen, then you're not good enough for
the king. If you're not a man in bed, then it's pointless to try to be one
elsewhere. The minimum measure of virility is sexual. In this form, the
proverb would still be false, since the impetus that drives many men to
fight and to prove themselves in battle, availing themselves of all the aggressivity they possess, is in fact to redeem themselves for their own lack of
erotic capacity.

There's probably a connection between this insecurity and the number
of women raped: as the insecurity increases, the number of rapes rises cor-
respondingly. And the rape isn't caused by testosterone, if anything, it's a
surrogate for it. Violent behavior stands in for a libido that is frequently
lacking, it serves as a sort of supplement. Experts say that if anything, it
may be aggressive behavior that produces testosterone—not the other way
around.

It is therefore with rape that one is able to free oneself at a single stroke
from this constraint, the forced sex act has entirely different ends, different

meanings, physical enjoyment is no longer at stake, neither one's own nor that of others, which is relegated to second place. It is hard to define exactly what pleasure one enjoys in coitus at all: certainly the pleasure that one procures when raping a woman is completely separate from the sexual realm, and it may have some tiny overlap with a consensual sex act, but the rest must be different, specific, connected rather with the exercise of force per se, with the subjugation of someone else's will to your own, the humiliation of whoever you subjugate, in other words, the specific pleasure that derives from power, that is, when we are capable of obligating others to do, not what they want to do, but what we want them to do. Which can actually happen in a consensual sex act, too: that is, we can allow the other person to do what they want to us, in order to allow them to taste an intoxicating power.

MASCULINITY MANIFESTS itself through two contradictory impulses: on the one hand, the rejection or avoidance of the feminine (family and maternal affection, childish or effeminate attitudes), on the other hand, the pursuit of the feminine (courtship, coupling). In order to become a male, you ought to repudiate the beloved feminine part of you, inherited from, literally sucked out of your mother, and at the same time go and get, and touch, and suck other women's breasts.

Break away from women—erase your mother—delete the feminine traits within yourself—devalue anyone who incarnates them, which means all women—and despite that devaluation, desire them. (Line in a cop movie: "Are you thinking about pussy?" "No, not really . . ." "Then you're just not concentrating." Yes, I know, I already used it once, but it's just such a great line.) Turning your back on women—rejecting your mother—rape *as a way to keep from seeing her*—rape as a form of sexual relations "with the back turned."

A man ought to be judged by what he does, not what he says: but it's not as if there are all that many occasions to do, to do anything significant and concrete, in the modern world we live in: a person limits himself to performing a certain number of routine actions, and then you're done.

But a real male is not so much someone who does certain things, it's first and foremost someone *who doesn't do* certain other things. Like what? Like crying, for example. Like betraying a friend. Putting on effeminate poses. Constantly changing your mind. More than any other form of behavior, so-called manly behavior is transmitted through imitation. Instructions are of little or no value, there is no need for explicit orders or a code of behavior learned by heart. A man has to deduce the commandments from examples offered by flesh-and-blood people or, more often, glimpsed in movies or read in novels: various heroes, warriors, as well as gangsters, bandits, or great seducers—but already these latter figures, the great cocksmen, appeared less all of one piece, more compromised with the feminine, designed to please women rather than us men: the handsome actor with the languid eyes, the living daydream of all girls everywhere, but whom the boys considered insipid or obnoxious . . . in the years when my own uncertain masculinity was being formed, the classical model (which would only last for a few more years) was that of the American western, cowboys, in other words, who shortly thereafter would be extinct as moral and physical figures, in the wake of the onslaught of the anticonformist cinema of the little big men, of the soldiers blue, of the midnight cowboys, figures that all heaved onto the scene at the end of the sixties to chase the all-of-a-piece pistoleros off the sound stage.

7

FOR A MALE, to have a sister is a sort of miracle. Inexplicable, in and of itself, and yet it helps to explain a great many things, nearly *everything*. I would venture to state that men without sisters grow up to have a prejudicial and narrow experience of the world. Their views are limited, and so are the ways they feel and communicate to others what they feel and see. The angle is restricted to the repetition of a landscape that never changes. In that case, better to be an only child, a condition that at least forces you to invent relationships in all directions because no one is handed to you as a natural sibling. A male with one or more brothers is a prisoner in a hall of mirrors, he just sees himself reflected in figures that compete with one another, imitating or avoiding one another, struggling and fighting, making alliances and helping one another and sliding into jealousies and envies, killing each other precisely because they're similar, all too similar.

Brotherhood conceals, deep down, a treacherous twist that springs from an excess of affinity that, when it is not limited to the merely physical, can dramatically affect the role and the fate of each. There is always the risk of muddling those roles and fates, stealing them, as Jacob did with Esau. Identity engenders rivalry. Dozens of origin stories tell of the danger of an overabundance of males, which forces you either to eliminate your rival or else hand yourself over to him, bound hand and foot—the Bible alone so overflows with these stories that it might reasonably be described as the tragic book of the absence of sisters, or else the book of murderous brotherhood, of the plethora of virility. Not that brothers necessarily have to deceive and slaughter each other, and yet you always have the impression that there's one too many, one who turned out badly, one who bosses the other one around, or the other ones, and it is his or their lot to obey. Or else they refuse to do so. The same matrix can produce a series of different individuals (sometimes very different indeed, even polar opposites, the kind of thing that can only happen between brothers) who are subjected to a pitiless comparison, something they cannot flee even if they run away from home or disavow their family, since their very flight will become one of the pieces of evidence that goes into the judgment hanging over them. Murderous brothers fooled themselves into believing that they could avoid that judgment when they killed. In their violent act was the desire to put an end to the natural but unhealthy competition among peers who are supposed to have come into this world in order to love each other and cooperate (ah, brotherhood, so frequently and mistakenly invoked, how many misunderstandings about the actual scope of its appeal! with no realization that it's a matter of reawakening an original lust for destruction!) but who instead find themselves in conflict on account of their fundamental equality. Rather than subjugating their own double, they wanted to merge with him, eliminating the repetitions that are so often the source of disorder and dismay.

All brothers are necessarily Karamazov.

A sister, instead, is a gift beyond compare. If she's older, you can love her and take her as your shield, if younger, then you dote on her adoringly. If she is a replica of us, or if we are a replica of her, the simple fact of belonging to the opposite sex makes her a unique, extraordinary creature, because at once utterly familiar and entirely alien.

An enigmatic precept, applicable to a broad array of fields; if a person is searching for something worthwhile, it prescribes: always look for what's closest in what's far away, and farthest away in what's close.

In a sister, though, you've found it. A sister matches the definition in full, she occupies that place, that point. With her you can experience the otherness of which a mother cannot be the owner, even if she comes first. For instance, I could never conceive of the idea that my mother was a woman, a female, that she belonged to the sex opposite to my own, so closely was I fused with her, so greatly did she represent the entirety. A sister, on the other hand, is the very rhetorical figure of contiguity, in some cases a synecdoche, in all cases a metonymy; through a sister, men are able to free themselves of the disheartening constrictions of sexual identity, yet still remain in *their own*, within the limits of their own flesh and blood. They feel that they can grow, expand, until they can include the figure that they glimpse behind the mirror.

If I were to draw up a list of my classmates' interesting sisters, I wouldn't know where to begin. My own sister was too young and hardly counted. At age nine or ten, you're necessarily the child of the house, and that's what you'll remain until you're fifty and there no longer is a house. She was a miniature blonde with freckly skin so thin, so fine, that if you brushed against it, the freckles seemed to swim on its surface. Would she become a pretty girl, an attractive woman? We didn't care. For us elder brothers, she could remain unchanged for all time and I'd continue to admire and ignore her, like a fragile, unusable toy that is therefore always left on the shelf, but my brother instead took delight in torturing her, after all, she never complained and that only drove him to torture her more. He would lure her onto my parents' bed with some cunning excuse, and there he promised they'd play a wonderful game, come on, it'll be fun, and instead he'd nail her to the mattress, crucifying her there and subjecting her to all and every form of harassment and abuse, though she'd never protest or cry. She'd never go running to tattle to Mamma. I would walk past my parents' bedroom and there they would be, frozen in their customary position: him on top, immobilizing her with his weight, she underneath, arms spread, wrists clamped, and face turned aside in a grimace of disgust that contained quivers of terror and amusement, because at that instant my brother was busy letting a streamer of drool drip down toward her from his mouth, so that it dangled almost onto her, without ever breaking from his lips, only to suck it back up and start over, up and down, up and down, the streamer of spit rose and descended from my brother's mouth like the string of a yo-yo.

And this was my sister.

Jervi instead had a sister just one year younger who was stunning. Beautiful. Skinny with a dark complexion, tall with long black hair and a face that wasn't just pretty, something more, mysterious, beaming, mischievous, intense, secret, promising. It was clear that that girl had been put on earth expressly to arouse a swell of attraction and then ride it like a surfer on the ocean. That was the image of her that remained stamped in my mind from that very first meeting. No one, seeing her bundled up for warmth on a rainy winter day with her mother, when they would come to stand outside the school together to pick up Jervi, no one could fail to fantasize about how she would look in summer, that is, lithe and slender, her long black hair dangling down her back, tips touching the elastic waist of her skimpy bikini as she ran down to where the sand met the waves, the very embodiment of a television commercial for ice cream, that is to say, in slow motion. Back then the cloth bikinis could be scanty scraps of material, rumpled, basically rags, and we were confidently sure—even though we'd never even glimpsed it under the unflattering bulky winter overcoats—that she had a small, firm, perfect ass, indeed we were mathematically certain, thanks to those media-proffered visions. Her body was a subject for soothsayers and seers. Most important of all, she was by no means shy, and she would joke and call us by name, we her brother's classmates, as if to provoke and test our reactions, which were invariably mistaken, overblown, in our feigned nonchalance as well as in our shyness.

(I was the latter.)

Let's admit that Jervi was proud to have a sister who was so *sorca* (such a piece of pussy, I use this word because I'm sure that I heard him describe his sister with it, at least a couple of times, with full awareness, preceding the vulgar term with the usual formula, "*un pezzo di sorca . . .*"), but he was proud of her more or less the way you might be proud to own a nice motorcycle, no more, no less: his *sorca* sister, that is, placed him a step above those who didn't have one.

Yes, indeed, I was always captivated, transported by an ideal love for the sisters of my classmates at school: the two older, beautiful blond sisters of Marco Lodoli, much older than him, whom I have the impression of remembering as already married, and with children, Jervi's stupendous sister, Iannello's miraculously well-developed sister, and then Barnetta's sister, known as the *muzhika* because of her stout, powerful legs and the red apples on her cheeks, and last of all Leda, Arbus's silent sister.

It was common at SLM to have pairs or even trios of brothers. With their range of ages, they covered entire eras of that school's history, often inheriting the same teachers, for instance Cosmo, or Svampa or Brother Curzio. There were the Ducoli brothers, the Abbadessa brothers, the Di Marziantonio brothers, the Sferra brothers, the Bellussi brothers, the Pongelli brothers, the brothers Giannuzzi, two Cerullos, the Dall'Oglio brothers, the Rummos, and even the Albinati brothers . . .

Back in the day when this story unfolds, families were large, with lots of children and cousins, which allowed them to express and contain a high if capricious erotic potential, in the sense that you could peruse and review the entire family, pondering and fantasizing, lingering enjoyably over the examination and the many doubts that surfaced as you did so, striving to determine which of the brothers or the sisters would be most exciting to fall in love with, which would be the smartest to marry, just who was the prettiest or most handsome in the family, a judgment that might well take in parents, as well, as there were frequently mothers who far outstripped their daughters in terms of personal attractiveness. A mythology of those years, fomented by the movie *The Graduate*, stirred dizzyingly obscene fantasies and projections around the subject of alluring women in their forties.

Now I have to wonder, concerning these abusers and torturers of women who will take on the role of protagonists in this book, or at least in a section of it, serving as leading characters; well, I have to wonder, as I was saying, just what kind of relationship did they have with their mothers, with their sisters (if they had any), that is, with the women closest to them? Contempt, morbid love, jealousy, long-simmering rage? Or was there something pure, who can say? Who was it they were actually yearning to deflower, sodomize, and strangle? Who was it they wanted to punish, and who had, perhaps, humiliated and punished them in the first place?

The classic formulation would be: absentee father + morbid mother = psycho. But I've never found that to be especially persuasive. There's something second-rate about it, the work of an unimaginative screenwriter.

IN THE CHAPTERS THAT FOLLOW, I'll have some stories to tell about one of these women, one of these mothers, the mamma of my dear classmate and friend, perhaps the most interesting of all the mothers I've ever met, the strangest, and as far as I can remember, the most beautiful or, in any case, the one who made the strongest impression on me. Beautiful just like my mother, though very different, physically the diametric opposite: a redhead, freckle-faced, with small green eyes. When I speak of Ilaria Arbus, I'll speak of the mothers of the period, all the mothers I've known, the mothers of my classmates, the Signoras of the QT. Together, let's turn this page.

8

LOVELY, she was lovely. Pretty, she was pretty. And I'd say unhappy, as well. Unhappy with that sort of lurking unhappiness that tormented mothers with a family, between the ages of thirty and forty, who have brought children into the world, fed them, dressed them and cared for them, and now that they were no longer children, found themselves with an almost empty life. These days it doesn't happen so much because everything starts later, but back then it was normal that a woman at age thirty-five or so should have already substantially completed her maternal duties, at least those that consisted in care and feeding, strictly speaking. She no longer had anything to take care of with fanatical intensity. She still had her daily round of household chores, but the heroic phase was over. And now. What remains to be done, to do? What is to be done with one's life, beyond grocery shopping and planning the weekly menu and the management of the bills and the mending of worn-out cuffs and collars? At the age of thirty and change, one might say that three emotional cycles of a woman's young life were now concluded, the one in her original family, the one with her husband, unlikely to fully resume after the shock of conjugal life, and the one with her child or children, perhaps the most exclusive and demanding love story of them all, which is transformed from a visceral dependency into a problematic relationship, no longer exclusive, marked instead by the fracture of the mythical union between mother and child. So now what?

For a certain period of time, the same years in which the main part of this story took place, Italian mothers oscillated between radically different options, although they sprang from the same sense of uncertainty. Some of them embraced wholeheartedly and for time without end, as if taking confirmatory vows, the role of vestals of the family, and they managed to carry on with that role as long as possible, even with a husband largely indifferent and children now grown and married in their turn, organizing and staging with disarming punctuality the domestic rites of times now past: meals, holidays, birthdays, presents, vacations (if bourgeois) or outings (if working class), even the quarrels and the insults and the misfortunes and

the periods of mourning seemed to have been planned out in detail by these
women who wanted to remain mothers and abbesses and queens and governesses of nothing, but a nothing kept in perfect order, overseen, dominated,
regulated, administrated, managed, an enclosure, in short, from which
escape would be sheer sacrilege; others, in contrast, the more emancipated
Italian mothers, with the demeanor of one who wishes to prove who she really
is, having left behind the reproductive phase, threw themselves headlong
back into their studies, either never undertaken in the first place or else interrupted or pointlessly completed, into the careers that they'd set aside for
such a lengthy period of time that they basically had to start over again
from scratch, or else come up with a brand-new one; among the women of
my mother and Arbus's mother's generation, for instance, one who already
had a degree in law was finally able to practice her profession; another
opened a toy store specializing in Swedish natural wood toys, and another
still founded a music school where children were taught the notes as physical gestures in sequence: raising an arm or a leg, taking a step forward,
a step sideways, jumping in the air; with surprising moves these women
founded associations, started newspapers and magazines, research centers,
corporations, joined political movements, in short, they did all they could to
explain with deeds, and not in words, that a new life had begun for them,
indeed, in some cases, that *that* was their real life, as opposed to the preceding conjugal-maternal version; others, suddenly realizing that they were still
desirable to anyone who wasn't their spouse, frequently the only man they'd
ever been to bed with, and starving for love or something different, after decades of rigorous fidelity, decided to take the path of sentimental and sexual
adventures, in the vast majority of cases, experienced without stepping outside the network of old acquaintances and the circle of the lives they'd always lived, therefore taking as lovers classmates from school or university,
encountered by chance after all these years, or else the husbands of their
longtime girlfriends, emitting signals in a code so allusive as to allow them
to be interpreted as innocent, manifesting an interest in them not limited
to the conventional niceties, making it clear that there could exist between
them an affinity extending to planes beyond that of the collective choice
of a movie theater or a restaurant; and then their sons' classmates and even
their daughters' boyfriends who, excited but at first reluctant, wound up
giving into the morbid fascination of the idea—in which they could luxuriate, looking back, of having had both mother and daughter, that is, the
high point of the male erotic imagination, especially that of the Italians,
which reserves a place of honor in its anything but limitless repertoire

for the maternal figure (nowadays, celebrated and scorned by the deplorable acronym of MILF). Most of them, and I believe that Arbus's mother was among them, didn't choose to take on any of these clear-cut positions, but instead limited themselves to floating in the void of the everyday passing of time: the children at school, her husband, Professor Lodovico Arbus, absorbed by academic life (or at least so everyone believed), the home silent, neat and tidy, and in no need of attention any more paranoid and obsessive than, say, sitting down to polish the pewter ware, the world outside buzzing, face and body reflected in the mirror . . . under examination . . .

The mothers of my classmates and the matrons and housewives of the QT in that period expressed their will to power in the form of a maternal instinct. To them, the whole world, or nearly the whole world, was formed of objects to tend to and mouths to feed: children first and foremost, of course, but also friends their age and classmates from school and friends from sports activities, in a radius stretching ever outward, and then, unfortunate or sick relatives, pets, elderly parents, poor people who attended the same parish church, all those people whose lives needed to be straightened out, brought under control. If by any chance there was a momentary shortfall of charity cases, the mothers weren't about to stand around twiddling their thumbs, they went out looking for them. It would be a terrible thing if all of a sudden no one had any need of their tender loving care anymore.

There were other mothers less decisive and less interventionist, who, having suffered the invasive treatment of their own mothers, took great care not to replicate it with their children. My mother, for example.

Ah, Arbus's mamma, with what transports of delight she laid into her son! I realized that I yearned to be given the same treatment, but she made it clear that she had no wish to make me the target of her harassment, so that when it came right down to it, by treating me kindly, she mocked me, and was well aware of the fact. I wasn't worthy of her, in other words, I was unworthy even of being treated as an unworthy creature, as a slave, a parasite, a speck of mold, a storm-tossed hulk. Arbus was her target, the target of her love. I had been found to be, at the same time, too young and too full grown: too young as a male to bother subjugating, too unripe to procure any satisfaction, and yet too full grown to be cradled in her arms, cradled and knocked to and fro, cradled and tormented. In other words, I wasn't sufficiently defenseless but then I also lacked sufficiently formidable defenses . . .

She'd make me an afternoon snack, carefully spreading butter and jam out to every corner of the slices of bread, but instead, when she made one for Arbus she'd knock it to the floor, after slapping on a spoonful of jam to make sure that it would overturn, tipping off the edge of the plate. "And this is all for our Edo," she'd say, handing me the bread and then, as she watched me eat, she'd ask: "Happy?" How could I remain indifferent to her mocking intent?

When it came to the zwieback, things were even worse: she'd give me the intact pieces, while Arbus would always get the cracked ones, which crumbled in his hands the minute he picked them up. Pointless to specify that the broken pieces fell to the floor butter-side down.

"What a clumsy son I have . . . what on earth do you have in that big head of yours? What are you thinking about? *Who* are you thinking about, heh?"

And saying over and over again "Who? Who?" she would knock on the top of her son's head with her knuckles. Arbus pretended it didn't bother him, as the sharp raps increased in intensity and frequency, and he went on meticulously recopying his notes, then he'd dodge his head to one side, without a word.

"There's no secret in here," his mother would say, pretending she was out of sorts.

Then she'd turn to me with a smile and ask, "But you have secrets, don't you? And just what are you hiding, come on, let's hear."

"Me?"

"Yes. The things you won't tell your mother. Come on!"

"Well . . . I hardly tell her anything at all . . ."

And so the afternoons at Arbus's house were always exciting and unpredictable. I mean, they were actually deadly boring, but the boredom of studying was continuously interrupted by the incursions of Signora Arbus. Interruption was the cutlass she brandished. Whatever we might be doing, she sank the blade of her proposed alternatives into the heart of it. If we were watching TV, she demanded that we turn off the set then and there, and that my friend get up and play some Scarlatti. As soon as he had started playing a piece, she ordered him to play a different, more challenging one, and then she'd bring a snack to ensure that his fingertips would be sticky with jam or mayonnaise. One time, we were studying chemistry. Prostrate at the death of his flower, Svampa had sworn that from now on he'd make us put everything in writing, no more explanations, no more oral examinations, he no longer wanted to talk himself hoarse, waste his squawking voice, or hear us spouting singsong renditions of the acid chains, he'd only give extremely challenging written homework that would leave us with no alternative but to study the subject on our own, poring over our textbooks— get busy, then, he had told us, his eyes puffy with angry weeping mixed with genuine sorrow: get busy if you're so smart. And so Ilaria Arbus had entered her son's bedroom in her bathrobe, with her hair wrapped in a towel, perched on her head like a turban, interrupting our litanies.

"What are you doing? I'll bet that you're wasting time as usual, aren't you, Edo?"

"Why no, signora, we're just doing our chemistry homework," I had begun eagerly to explain, "and . . ."

"Not one is turning out right," she promptly ended my sentence for me.

Ilaria Arbus was only partially right. Despite the fogged-up eyeglasses and the ostentatious disinterest in such a crude subject ("People who like to fool around with test tubes," he dismissively called chemists, even if they were Lavoisier or Madame Curie), her son still successfully solved at least two-thirds of the questions, while I would always get at least one step wrong, sending my answers sadly askew.

"Let me take a look," she said, and yanked the sheet of paper out of my hand, on which were written the exercises that Svampa had dictated to us.

"All right . . . let's see," and she ran down the list, ". . . a sulfuric acid molecule (H_2SO_4) has a molecular weight of 98 AMU . . . Hey, what does AMU mean?"

Arbus snorted. "Atomic mass unit."

"Of course it does, that's obvious," his mother continued, "atomic mass unit . . . a-m-u . . . all right then, yes . . . it has a weight of 98 AMU. Calculate the percentage of oxygen present in the molecule."

She glanced up from the sheet of paper and looked at us, with a smile. "You know how to do it, don't you? The percentage of oxygen. It's not that hard."

"No, it's not that hard . . . but I just don't know how to calculate it," I confessed. "I can't remember."

"What about you, Mamma, do you know?" Arbus asked in a mocking tone.

"*Caro*, if you'll just let me think for a minute, I'll come to it. I studied this stuff twenty years ago!"

Well, while it was unmistakable that she didn't understand a thing about chemistry, I still expected her to get the right answer from one minute to the next, as if it had been suggested to her by an angel. Both of us watched her, Arbus with annoyance, me with anxiety. Seeing her furrow her brow, I made the effort that she was only pretending to exert. I struggled to remember the last lesson that Svampa had taught us, before going on strike over the death of his flower.

AND I FOUND the solution.

While Arbus continued to stare at his mother with a look of defiance, I wrote the answer in the margin of the book, hoping I had done my calculations right: 65.2 percent.

The signora spotted what I had done without her son noticing. She peeked at the number. Then she heaved a deep sigh and tucked back a lock of hair that had tumbled out from under her turban while she was studying the problem.

"Well, actually you two ought to be telling me . . . but let's not waste our breath, it's sixty-two percent, the oxygen, or actually, to be exact, it's sixty-five point two percent, am I right?" and she shot her son a look of defiance that matched his, in a way that I found irresistible.

"WELL THEN, seeing that we already know our chemistry, what do you say to a little game?" proposed Signora Arbus, causing every zit on her son's face to blush beet-red.

"A game of what?" I asked in surprise.

"A game of cards, what a question. Poker, if you feel like it."

"Mamma, really! The idea of playing cards!"

"You don't want to because you're no good at cards. And you're afraid you'll lose your allowance . . . Aren't you?"

"Mamma! I'm not afraid of anything."

"Of course you are," said Signora Arbus, sitting down on the desk as if to cover the chemistry textbooks, as if she wanted to use her body (in fact, a noteworthy body it was) to prevent us from studying, and thereby letting a leg slip out of her bathrobe, and that leg hung there, dangling and swinging, before my eyes.

"You're afraid of having fun. That's all. Did you know, Edo, that your little friend is *terrified* of having fun?"

I was so embarrassed that my embarrassment actually became pleasurable, to feel myself dazed, filled with admiration for the sheer shamelessness of Arbus's mother and, let's admit, her extraordinary beauty, to which it was agreeable as it was surely fatal to submit wholeheartedly for someone like me who has never found more cogent arguments than a smooth white leg to put an end to all reasoning. In order for my mind to draw a whole and complete blank, a vision like that was more than sufficient: Arbus's mamma, in a bathrobe looming above us, towering over us, two students crammed into our little folding chairs, pencils in our mouths so we could underline. Anyway, that day we gave up studying chemistry and played poker, I lost what little money I had with me in just a few hands (Signora Arbus soon grew bored and, clutching the bathrobe to her chest as if with that gesture she wished to allude to the sheer insolence of the way my eyes had strayed there, she left the room), and the next day I was forced to pretend I was sick with a fever in order to avoid a classroom assignment in chemistry that I would certainly have flunked. And yet I can safely say that that day, at Arbus's house, unlike my classmate, I had enjoyed myself.

I'll never forget my visits there, the afternoons with Arbus and his mamma, who treated him like a teddy bear, to be hugged and mistreated with the same vehemence. She always seemed to be on the verge of yanking his eyes out and then sewing them back on, weeping, the way slightly sadistic little girls will do with their dollies.

Speaking of eyes: whenever Arbus's mother was around, provoking him, tormenting him, tickling him, his eyes, behind those thick, smudged lenses, narrowed until they became a pair of horizontal slits . . .

She would torture him, convinced that this was the right way to treat him, then she'd offer reparations in the form of a wave of love. But those reparations never reached him.

9

HER MOOD WAS INFINITELY CHANGEABLE. If she wasn't playful, if she wasn't kidding around, then she was pensive. One time I went over to their house, without calling ahead. I rang the doorbell.

"Is Arbus home?"

I always called him that. And I had discovered that at home his family called him by his surname as well.

"No. But I think he'll be home soon. Come in."

I followed her into the hallway. When I came even with my friend's bedroom, the door was open, the desk was neat and tidy, the bed was made, and I turned to go on in, but Ilaria Arbus swiveled quickly and grabbed me by the arm.

"No, not here. Come with me. There's something I want to show you." And she continued to walk down the shadowy hallway. I followed behind her.

She ushered me into her bedroom. "Come in, come in." I was embarrassed. The room was fairly small and almost entirely occupied by the bed, which appeared to me, perhaps for that reason, larger than a normal bed, a walnut dresser, and an armoire, from the knobs of which hung necklaces. I studied them, in the dim light that the curtains filtered into the room: they were costume jewelry.

"Sit down, Edoardo." There was no place else to sit but on the bed. I looked up at her in consternation. She had turned away, had opened one of the bottom dresser drawers, and was looking for something in the drawer. She said it again, "Sit down," still leaning over with her back turned to me, or really, with her derriere turned to me, swathed in the cotton dress beneath which I could make out the stripes of the elastic bands of her panties. I would have chosen to sit at the foot of the bed, but it was occupied by a massive wrought-iron structure, painted black, with a large ball perched atop each corner. For that reason, I had no alternative but to sit at the center of the bed, right behind Signora Arbus, who was still bent over, rummaging through the drawers, on the side of the bed where she slept, since I had noticed bottles of medicine and a pack of wax earplugs on the night table, along with a couple of a detective novels, while the other night table was empty, and the reading lamp was unplugged from the wall socket.

"Look here, look at this," and she straightened up with a manila folder in one hand, then sat down next to me on the edge of the bed, which sank swaybacked beneath our weight. She pulled out of the folder a stack of paper, different-size sheets of varying weight, and started handing them to me, one by one.

The first few sheets must have been torn from a medium-size spiral notebook, and were lightweight and unlined. On each page, drawn with heavy blue marker, was a cityscape, but a depiction of an imaginary city, never glimpsed by human eyes, or seen only in dreams, with tall buildings, churches, towers, skyscrapers with daring shapes very similar to those with which, in the past thirty years or so, the most highly paid architects on earth have amused themselves by dotting the skylines of the world's great cities, rendering them even more spectacular . . . and then there were parks, elevated highways, lakes, bunkers, fortifications . . . They were beautiful architectural projects, and each city—even though the line with which it was drawn remained the same in each case—was very different from the last, as if each one constituted an exact and very distinct model. Arbus's mother would hand me one and at the same time take back the one I had just studied, putting it back at the bottom of the stack; then she'd look at me and smile in a way that I couldn't quite categorize, unsure whether she was being ironic, or simply amused at my astonishment. "Wow, these are really nice . . ." were the only words I could manage to get out in return for that smile. She was so close to me that I actually couldn't see her whole face, only the mouth but not the rest, or else the eyes and not the rest.

But it was not until she had handed me the last of these urban landscapes that I noticed a surprising detail, which had been hidden from my eyes precisely by the densely elaborate nature of their execution. That was when I realized that the drawings had been done without once lifting the marker from the paper. They consisted, in other words, of a single unbroken line that started at one point and, by way of scrollwork, zigzags, verticals and diagonals, returned to the starting point after having given shape to that astonishing mass of buildings. That, by the way, was what gave proof of the incredible conceptual consistency, the sheer compactness of the thing: because each of them was the result of a single thought, or perhaps I should say a single action, an uninterrupted movement of the hand, which had lifted the pen from the paper only once the whole drawing was complete.

"He did these when he was five years old."

"They really are incredible . . ." I murmured, and I was tempted to ask Arbus's mother to give me back the ones she'd already showed me, to see whether they were all drawn with that same extraordinary single line, but she'd already taken the last sheet out of my hand and was now giving me another.

"Five years old . . ."

The new series consisted of genuine drawing paper, thick, rough sheets. On it, drawn in pencil, were depictions of domestic interiors. The style was completely different from the one glimpsed in the cityscapes: every bit as much as the cityscapes were airy, abstract, stylized, and, so to speak, graphic, these were minutely detailed, hyperrealistic, and extraordinarily painstaking in their faithful depiction of every object present in the room that the artist had before his eyes as he began to fill up the sheet of paper. That's right, "filling up" is the right phrase: because, in spite of the fact that the pencil line was in any case a faint dark track across the white of the paper, the whole space appeared to have been transformed into background, adorned, from top to bottom, from left to right, creating a singular effect of a photographic survey, or better, a digital scan: as if the eye of the observer had slowly rotated from one edge of the field of view to the opposite side, and then had transferred an identical reproduction to the paper. The only perceptible difference lay in a slight, barely detectable deformation, or fluctuation of the space, which here and there tightened or tilted as if the point of view had shifted by a degree or two or as if the object portrayed had been twisted ever so slightly on its axis.

Let me give an example that will help you to grasp what I'm talking about, taken from the first drawing that Arbus's mother handed to me. It depicted a living room, or perhaps I should say, what was called a parlor in the apartments and houses of the bourgeoisie. I wouldn't be capable of replicating with anything like the same minute attention to detail everything that appeared in the drawing, because what really astonished were certain very vivid and realistic details that gave it the casual quality of a snapshot. There were two sofas arranged in L shapes and two armchairs with high backrests, padded on the sides, whose flowered fabric was here reproduced with the exactitude of certain canvases by Vuillard, and there, draped over the backrest, another layer of fabric meant to protect the upholstery, and then carpets on the floor and paintings on the walls, which looked familiar to me. From the frame of one of those pictures, a man looked out into the parlor, arms crossed over his chest, a proud air about him, in an elegant smoking jacket, and the draftsman had also remembered to reproduce the embroidery just over the breast pocket, the mouthpiece of a pipe sticking out of the pocket, and a monogram just under the embroidery, L.A., as if this were evidently a significant detail. Atop an oval table with four Viennese canework chairs turned, not inward toward the center of the table but, irregularly, facing away, as if whoever had been sitting in them had suddenly stood up and left the room without bothering to put them back where they belonged, there was a deck of cards, and cards had been dealt out, three per hand, to at least a couple of the players before that round of the game had been interrupted. Beside and below the armrest of one of the two sofas stood a trelliswork metal magazine holder, and through the holes in the metal it was possible to read some of the letters of the mastheads of at least three newsweeklies that had been rolled up and jammed in there by some cleaning woman or housewife, impatient but determined to restore some order, and beside or beneath those letters forming the name of the magazine, the illustrator had even gone so far as to reproduce the visible portions of the rolled-up covers: a woman's leg, a hand loaded down with large rings, a lock of light-colored hair. The only title that could be reconstructed on the basis of the letters that could be read was *L'Espresso*.

A specially built piece of furniture that consisted of two stacked cubes housed the turntable and the amplifier of a stereo and a not particularly extensive collection of albums; because it was shown at an angle, it was possible to make out the cover of the first one, the famous *Abbey Road*, but only the two figures on the right could be seen, Lennon with a beard and long hair hanging over his shoulders, all in white, and Ringo in an elegant black suit, as they crossed the zebra stripes.

Now I could go on with my enumeration (against one wall, an upright piano with sheet music set askew, and a few loose sheets that had actually slipped down onto the keyboard . . . the back half of a black cat emerging from a door standing ajar on the right . . . the crystal drop chandelier hanging over the scene . . . and so on) but I stop instead to point out that these objects, the sofas, the piece of furniture with the stereo, the photographs, the paintings, were all as precisely depicted as they were faintly deformed, or else placed in space from an array of different vantage points, varying ever so slightly, so that for instance the table appeared to be inclined toward the observer so that all the cards threatened to slide toward him, whereas the arrangement of the paintings on the walls gave the impression that the angle where the walls met at the far end of the room was acute, suggesting that the entire parlor had been built in the prow of a ship.

"That's the part of him that we lost. Forever."

The smile on Ilaria Arbus's lips had died, and her green eyes were full of inexplicable tears.

I couldn't begin to imagine that roughly eight years later, I would be lying with her daughter Leda on that very same bed.

10

A H, IF I THINK of the enormous amount of energy that I've wasted over the years trying to justify myself... to give meaning in hindsight to my actions, so that what I did might be, or at least seem, or sound *right*, even if it wasn't, especially if it wasn't, or wasn't entirely, and that what I *didn't* do might seem right not to have done, right to have avoided, in short, that my refusal (ah, how often I refused, so often, too often) came not out of fear or laziness or snobbery, but rather out of some noble, albeit obscure, principle of consistency.

The daisy chain of my "I would prefer not to"s is so very long!

The truth, though, is that it would be better not to stoop to dig up reasons, and to illustrate the reasons for your reasons: if you avoid doing that, you just feel stronger. It sounds arrogant, but it's actually honest, and it spares you a great deal of hypocrisy, and it spares your fellow man a great deal of illusions. If other people like what you do and who you are, fine, otherwise, why worry about it, and what good does it do you to justify it? If you're in the right, then why waste time explaining it, and if you aren't, it's certainly not going to be your words or your poses that will put you there.

And if, in the end, everything you do is completely wrong, then you will be the one who pays the consequences, or reaps the benefits, so at least with yourself, there's no point cooking the books, now, is there?

OH, OH, talking about yourself...

It isn't easy. It is by no means easy to talk about your own misdeeds, your infamy, and, even worse, your own normality: it's like having a knife and using it to kill someone, but it won't cut, it's dull, the blade lacks an edge and won't slice into the flesh, try as you might, press down on it with all your strength... And the deeper you carve, the farther away this stranger moves.

Who are you? Halt. Let me get my hands on you.

Hee, hee. Let who get whose hands on who?

Let *me*!

But you can't, you know. I *am* you.

You're me?!

That's right.

But I can't see you . . .

And you never will!

THERE ARE NO SINCERE PHRASES, none of them are ever sincere *enough*, and there are no revealing accounts in all this talking of yourself, shuffling, shuffling, and reshuffling until you have gotten the deck completely drunk and, with it, the figures printed on each card . . .

One of those figures, as far as I was concerned, was Arbus.

Another was a woman, or actually a girl, but at first I didn't recognize her. Will I know who she is, at the end of this book? How many important girls have there been in your life, how many decisive women? The ones that you love, the ones that you dream of, the ones that you marry . . . will the ones that make you suffer be more or less important in the end than the ones you made suffer?

Shall we draw up a list? Who has never made a list of all the lovers they've had? And how many they never had, either because the other person didn't want to, or because the list maker didn't, or else because something went sideways, the taxi never came, the room was taken, the look wasn't caught or it was but misunderstood—of course, I had a fever of 104 and a plane to catch early the next morning.

How haphazard, how random it all is! No literature will ever be able to recapture this chance series of events. And even if it could, it wouldn't want to! It won't! A novel is the exact opposite of chaos, it is the natural enemy of disorder. That is why talking about yourself or about others is nothing but a waste of time.

All right, then, shut the book.

Put the cap on your pen.

Turn off your computer or your iPad.

Turn off the light, too.

Throw the windows open wide and let in the evening air. It's dense, heavy with the perfume of flowers and exhaust. The evening is out there, and it's immense and wide open.

II

A GOOD TEN YEARS HAVE GONE BY, perhaps even more, since the episode I'm going to tell you about here. My calculations of the date are pretty certain, a fixed point, what in historical research is called (I believe) a terminus ante quem, being 2005, the year I played my last soccer match, or really, just a friendly little game at home in my yard with some kids: when, in order to gain control of a ball that was descending in a high arc, and to prevent a twelve-year-old from taking possession, I leapt vigorously, lifting and stretching my right leg, and just as it made contact with the ball I heard a noise behind my thigh, *inside* my thigh, a sort of snapping sound, and I fell to the ground, my leg still stretched out, the way male Russian dancers do at the conclusion of their acrobatic performances.

That tear in my biceps femoris marked the end of my soccer career, which, for that matter, I had been dragging along behind me only in five-a-side games, and even then, not as often as I ought to have.

And so it was certainly before 2005 that I met—at a sports club where the fields are wedged between the hillside made up of fluvial detritus and the Tiber, over which hovers a mist that makes the synthetic grass sparkle with humidity beneath the floodlights—my old classmate Rummo.

I can't imagine how he managed to recognize me in the locker rooms, thirty years later.

"Excuse me, but aren't you Albinati?"

We were both in our underwear and both in a hurry, the hour we had reserved began in just three or four minutes, and in fact the other players had already left the locker room, reminding the last of us who took the field to remember to lock the door.

"Yes . . . and you. I'm sorry . . . ?"

"Rummo. Don't you remember? We both went to . . ."

"Rummo . . . ? To SLM! Of course. You've—"

"I've changed a lot, eh?"

And with a smile he ran his hand over his bald head where, back in the time when the most important chapter of our history was unfolding, a mane of beautiful wheat-blond hair had once grown, fine and abundant.

I reassured him that all of us had changed considerably.

"Are you a psychiatrist, too?" Rummo asked me.

That question might strike the reader as odd, but those Tuesday evening soccer games were in fact organized by a psychiatrist, and the other players were generally his colleagues and a few male nurses from the mental health centers: all of them rather particular individuals, not full-fledged lunatics, let me be clear, like in Edgar Allan Poe's famous short story "The System of Doctor Tarr and Professor Fether," but still, some genuine oddballs, and in fact more than one of the games had been broken off because of the eccentricities of the players. There were those who were ready for a brawl, others got their feelings hurt, others still, for no apparent reason, would simply stop playing. I was one of the few players who didn't work in the mental health sector, and I went every Tuesday evening for two or three years, since psychiatrists are pretty poor soccer players, sufficiently unskilled and untrained that I could keep up, and disorganized enough that someone like me could venture to dictate the geometries of the plays on the field.

It is inevitable that, in soccer, the level of play and of the players allows you to change position: as a boy, when I was playing with stronger companions, the best I could hope for was to play the rough-and-ready stopper, with these miserable middle-aged players, I could be a deep-lying playmaker, and thanks to the limited size of the field, I could even dare to kick with my left foot, since I only had to move the ball five yards away, no more.

"A psychiatrist? No."

"Then you're a psychoanalyst, aren't you?"

Truth be told, I wished I could tell Rummo that I was. Perhaps that profession is the only one I would have liked to undertake.

"Lacanian, I'd bet money on it."

I shook my head. "And why Lacanian?"

"I don't know, I just would have sworn . . ."

"No, I teach. Literature."

Rummo asked at which university. "No university. Just at school."

"Ah. So you're one of those guys who never really left school at all. You went out the door and climbed back in through the window."

"More or less."

"That shows a singular attachment."

"Very singular, true." I rummaged deep in my gym bag. "Listen, Rummo, you wouldn't happen to have an extra pair of gym socks, would you? Otherwise, I'm going to have to play with these," and I pointed down at the lisle knee-high socks I wore. "I always forget something."

"Of course. Here," and he tossed me a rolled-up pair of terry-cloth socks. "Three pair, five euros. But we'd better get going."

I laced up my old track shoes with the cracked toes.

"Actually, I teach in prison."

Rummo looked up. "Really? In prison!"

"Funny, isn't it?"

"Not so funny."

"Actually, if you're a psychiatrist . . . which of us deals with the weirder people on our jobs, you or me?"

"Do you ever see anyone from our old class?"

"No, no one."

After thirty years, go out for a pizza on Via Alessandria and talk about what? About whom? About De Laurentiis and ancient Greek music? About Mr. Golgotha? About Gas&Svampa?

(For that matter, what else am I doing right here? I talk and rant about those people: Who will ever be interested?)

IT'S UNBELIEVABLE how many misfits we had in that class. Out of twenty-four of us, at least five belonged in an insane asylum, and I'm not just saying that—in fact, several of them wound up in one. A wing nut every six boys: but if you were to consider the big and medium-size eccentricities, then you'd have five nuts out of every six students, or even all of them, except for one. Except for me. I think that I'm the one who saves himself temporarily because it's his job to recount the follies of the others and therefore can't completely give in to his own madness: once he's accomplished his mission, in all likelihood, even the last one will go mad, and perhaps that's why he's postponing the completion of his work.

THE MISFITS in our class:
  PIK: autistic (?)
  CHIODI: sadist, with suicidal tendencies
  CRASTA (better known as Kraus or Three-Toed Sloth): mental defective
  D'AVENIA: masochist
  ARBUS: the jury is still out

✦

"HOW ABOUT YOU, for instance, have you ever seen d'Avenia again? Do you know what became of him?"

Rummo shook his head.

"I've heard lots of different things. That he became an incredibly wealthy and slightly shady businessman, and that he lives out of the country . . . they say he's been married two or three times, to beautiful South American women. On account of how rich he is."

"And Three-Toed Sloth?"

"I think he's the same as ever."

"Okay, let's get moving," and I left the locker room.

Rummo broke into a little run, his heels clacking on the cement. A bit of a gut wobbled over the elastic of his shorts.

Outside it was starting to turn dark and they had turned on the flood-lights along the succession of five-a-side soccer fields, enclosed in high nets to make sure the ball didn't end up in the next field or in the river. It was a long, smeary stain of light. I took a deep breath of the air, which reeked of rot.

"And Chiodi?" I asked Rummo as we galloped toward the field that we'd been assigned, for the match to be played by psychiatrists, male nurses, a few nut jobs, and me.

"Oh . . ." Rummo sighed. "Chiodi. Chiodi."

"Why?"

"He was one of my patients for a while. Let's not talk about it."

This exclamation, however, just made me want to talk about it more. But by now we had reached the field. The others were waiting for us with their hands on their hips; one of them was letting off steam by taking penalty kicks into the empty goal.

"Where the *fuck were* the two of you?"

"How the *fuck* long did you take getting dressed?"

We were welcomed with these phrases and play began immediately. During the game, when people called to each other to pass the ball or to warn them that they were about to pass to them, I noticed that I didn't re-member Rummo's given name. At school, he was just called by his sur-name: Rummo, period. It was only toward the end of the game, after much mulling and casting my mind back, that I remembered: Gioacchino. Gio-acchino Rummo.

"Listen, Rummo, I have to confess . . . I'm writing a book . . ."

"Really? That's great. What about?"

"Oh, I couldn't say . . . sort of about that school, that period of time . . . our classmates."

"What is it, nonfiction . . . ?"

"No, it's a sort of . . . ehm . . . a novel, even if a lot of things I talk about really happened. That is, they're based on things that really happened. So . . . this thing with Chiodi. Interesting."

"You think? Not really all that interesting, if you ask me."

"Well, for my book it would be. I'd like to include it. You wouldn't have held on to anything about his case . . . a file, some notes?"

"Sure, of course, I still have the notes. Just like for all my patients."

"And his therapy . . . ?"

"For the time I had him as a patient, yes. But why?"

"It would come in handy for me to have that material and use it."

"Use it?"

"For my book."

"You couldn't. Patient privacy."

"Ohhh," I snorted, in exasperation, "come on now, with this patient privacy . . . If we let the privacy rules guide everything, we wouldn't know a thing, about anything or anybody. No history, no literature. No jurisprudence. And no psychiatry, for that matter. It's all always private, but all the most interesting things are *private*!"

"It's a matter of someone's illness. Professional ethics, you know that better than I do."

"What about if I change his name in the book, would that be enough?"

"No, it wouldn't be enough. He'd still be recognizable."

"But how?"

"If you write that he was a member of your class at school, then you automatically identify him by age. Roman, born in 1956 or thereabouts, he attended SLM, with that pathology . . . and what happened to him. It wouldn't take a great lawyer to find a number of good reasons to sue you. And then to sue me, since I was treating him."

"All right, I'll change something else . . . I promise you. And I'll just use your notes as a rough basis, I'll rewrite it all so no one will be able to identify the source. That's what I always do."

"But wait, what about me, am I in your book?"

He looked up at me. It was a question that quivered with a note of emotion. It sounded like "Am I worthy of existing, too?"

"What kind of a question is that . . . of course you are, Rummo."

This page is proof of the fact. And when I talked about Brother Curzio frequenting whores, it was with Rummo that I happened to be passing by Tor di Quinto, that night, on a scooter, remember? Many pages back. Certainly, he isn't a prominent character in the book . . . I'd have to give him more space, if I wanted to lay my hands on Chiodi's clinical file.

"Everyone's in the book." A half-truth. "I try to be faithful to what happened, you know?" Complete lie.

"And what about Arbus, do you talk about him?"

"Yes, about him, too."

"Have you seen or talked to him lately?"

"No." I was determined not to add a word.

"Now I'd like to get a better understanding of this interest of yours for Chiodi. When we were at school together, you didn't give a damn about him . . ."

You had a point, Rummo: but when you're dealing with someone who is right, the only thing to do is to insist stubbornly.

"So, are you going to give me this file?"

"Listen, I don't do that kind of thing." As he said it, it was clear that he was tempted. Rummo had a trusting nature. "But you'll let me read it when it's done, right?"

CERTAINLY, if then your patient kills himself . . . the way Chiodi did . . .

TWO DAYS LATER, I had eight closely printed pages, though fairly faint, probably produced by an old-fashioned dot matrix printer on an "economy" setting, the kind that used continuous-feed sheets with the sprocket holes on the side, that come away in one longer perforated strip. I felt a deep surge of embarrassment, but I soon overcame it. Let me try to summarize part of what was in it.

AS A CHILD, *he seemed to feel no emotions, either toward relatives and family, or toward others his age. With his parents he was cold and detached. At school he behaved in an inexplicable manner, concerned only with himself, as if his classmates and teachers didn't exist. Intellectually gifted, he didn't know how to make use of those gifts. As a young man, he wavered between mystical impulses and fundamentalist materialism. Now he would pore over books of theology, at other times, textbooks of the natural sciences. When he enrolled at the university, his fellow students considered him to be insane. He would read all day, for instance, for a solid month, nothing but Leopardi, without understanding a word of it. Total lack of interest in the opposite sex. Once he happened to have a sexual relation, by chance, practically by accident, and certainly against his will, with a female student at the university who was at least as crazy as he was but, unlike him, very obsessive about matters erotic. He realized that he had felt absolutely nothing, no desire beforehand, no pleasure during, no satisfaction afterward. He found coitus to be absurd and he had no desire to repeat the experience. For no particular reason, he was often visited by thoughts of suicide, though he didn't feel driven toward it by any particular despair or anguish. He made suicide the subject of a pseudophilosophical dissertation, in which he maintained that, much like masturbation, it was an act both justifiable and comprehensible. After repeated experiments with various poisons, he attempted suicide by swallowing fifty-seven tranquilizer tablets, but it was an unsuccessful attempt, he was saved and sent to a psychiatric clinic. He had no moral instinct, no sense of decency, no social spirit. In his writings, to all appearances serious and profound, he displayed only coldness and an attention to trifles. He possessed chaotic bodies of knowledge and the logic that would have allowed him to organize them and make use of them was somehow distorted in him. He treated everything and everyone, even the most sublime subjects or the most praiseworthy individuals, with a blend of cynicism and irony. He argued the cause of suicide with lines of reasoning that were patently nonsensical and self-serving, departing from premises that he first and foremost showed no sign of believing, as if he were trying to persuade idiots and therefore chose to make use of equally idiotic argumentation. As if it were a subject that had little if anything to do with him, indeed, as if the matter left him entirely indifferent, he proclaimed nonetheless that as a result of this and such incontrovertible considerations, he intended to take his own life. And indeed, he did in fact make numerous suicide attempts. He complained that his pocketknife had been taken away from him, otherwise he would have used it to cut his wrists in the manner of Seneca, in the bathtub. One time a friend had given him, instead of poison, a powerful laxative. Instead of being transported into the afterlife, he'd spent a whole day on the toilet. Only the Grim Reaper himself, with a swoop of his scythe, would be able to free him of his fatal obsession. From time to time he was seized with an obsessive thought that forced him to occupy his mind with the most pointless and unreason-*

able problems, employing and exhausting all his energies on interminable and laborious internal disputes, at the end of which, enervated, and unable to settle any single matter to his satisfaction, he was simply incapable of coming to any decision. He had busied himself with problems of a theological nature with the goal of founding a new church, since in his opinion Christ had spread false hopes, fooling people, and had with his miracles deceived the whole world, which was now in desperate need of a truth cure that could be put off no longer. The treatments to which he was subjected conflicted and overlapped in a contradictory manner, and he lost all faith in those who had prescribed them. In spite of that fact, his latest therapies, finally well suited to his difficult-to-diagnose case, had obtained some good results. He had given signs of wanting to start talking about his malaise again, explaining the reasons for it to those who would listen. He took his life at the age of thirty-eight, jumping off a fifth-floor balcony.

FAREWELL, Chiodi.

Thank you, Rummo.

Look, I'm not just throwing you a bone here, by giving you a little more space in the book, the way you have to do with certain actors or actresses who complain that their part is too short and so you pad it, writing them a few more lines; it's really that I was reminded of an episode that really might be worth telling the readers about, something I'll do in a few chapters from now. I don't know whether, in the end, Rummo will be satisfied with it.

Just to make it clear, though, I can say here and now that I consider him a wonderful person.

THE ONLY ONE OF THE MISFITS I hadn't asked about, there, on the soccer field, was Picchiatello, that is, Pik. My memories of him from when we were at school together are more than enough. And, what's more, I confess, I was afraid that Rummo might tell me he was dead. He, too, dead, like Chiodi and like Jervi. In fact, I felt sure of it. Young men with that kind of pathology aren't destined to live long.

I avoided telling him that for years I had cultivated a fantasy about poor Picchiatello's mother, Coralla Martirolo. I fantasized that my hair was wet either because I had just stepped out of the bathtub or else because I'd been caught out in the rain, and she was drying it with a hair dryer. She was drying my hair and combing it, tugging at the still-wet locks. I could see myself, seated, and her, tall, standing behind me, dressed in black, both of us reflected in the bathroom mirror. I laid the nape of my neck back against her belly.

"What nice hair you have . . ." Coralla was saying, "what nice hair . . ." and my hair was as long as hers.

12

PICCHIATELLO, that is, the one who in his delirium tells the most obvious truths that none of the others are allowed to utter.

His cranium was oversized, bigger than normal. And the idea of shearing his hair very short and close, reducing it to a sort of blondish fuzz no longer than a tenth of an inch, didn't make his head look any smaller, in fact if anything it only emphasized how disproportionate it really was. It *magnified* it . . .

THERE WERE TIMES that we tried to involve Pik in our nights out with the classmates. There's no point in specifying whether our invitation was extended to Pik out of pity or so we could laugh at him behind his back. It was probably for both reasons, since there is no one on earth—certainly no adolescent, much less a male adolescent, who is good through and through, who is *only* good, and there is no goodness that isn't mixed with its exact opposite, otherwise goodness would be an intolerable, asphyxiating sentiment.

In any case, we invited him to go out with us two or three times, just to eat a pizza . . . but it was clear immediately that it hadn't been a very good idea. You couldn't have a normal evening out if he was there. One time, at the pizzeria, he just got up from the table and vanished. Up till that point, he'd been very tense: playing with the utensils, tossing his glass in the air, exasperating everyone else at the table. When he stood up and left, we were all relieved. "If you call him one more time, I swear that I'll stop coming," Matteoli threatened, forcing us into a corner, as if his presence were indispensable. "Oh, come on, really, what did he do wrong?" I asked, defending Pik mildly, not because I was any less irritated than Matteoli by Picchiatello's annoying tics: it annoyed me the way he played with his forks, wedging them together to create a sort of catapult, but that was just part of Pik, it was

Pik in all of those balancing acts, Picchiatello, our classmate, crazy as the woodpecker that was his namesake, and if you can't get over your irritation with a classmate, an unfortunate classmate like him, then you have to explain to me where the difference lies between a friend and someone who isn't one. Between a friend and an enemy? So that meant we had to take Pik the way he was and like it. Period. My sense of justice only activates like this, in reaction, in this case against Matteoli's irritated impatience.

If I had been alone with Picchiatello I'd have choked the life out of him, but with the others I defended him as a foregone conclusion.

Then, unexpectedly, Pik reappeared. He was wearing a waiter's jacket, and he had a cloth napkin dangling from his left forearm, possibly imitating some sketch or funny cartoon he'd seen, because in reality no one had ever seen a waiter who looked anything like that. His torso was leaning forward, his chin was raised, ready and at attention to take an order. In fact, he approached us, zigzagging his way through the other tables.

"Have the gentlemen already placed their orders?" he asked, raising his eyebrows and flaring his nostrils.

HE WAS FUNNY, but unnerving, Picchiatello. In class or at recess, everyone else would play and joke around with him, in part because he was likable and everyone liked him, or put up with him, in short, how can you really dislike someone like Picchiatello: but after school, in the afternoons or on Sundays or during the holidays, no one wanted anything more to do with him. Everyone had their friends, from school or otherwise, their soccer or basketball team or their tennis or swimming lessons, and then they had people they played guitar with and their cousins, male and female, and the movies, plus homework, getting help where possible on classics translations and math problems from some classmate who was better at them. Jervi went dancing every afternoon as soon as the discos opened. And in all this churn of activity, Picchiatello had simply not found a place for himself.

A number of times, Mr. Golgotha had put forth the idea of "doing something together" to "involve him" (yes, the verb "involve" was often trotted out in those years, to indicate a collective initiative, that might make everyone feel united and engaged . . .), but nothing had ever come of it. Picchiatello's life outside of school therefore remained a mystery. People said of him and his family that they were rich, seriously rich: a gleaming black Mercedes came to pick him up at school, so long that the driver took ages to walk around it and open the back door for our classmate, who would wave back to us before getting in. He was laughing but it wasn't hard to imagine him later, back home, lonely and sad.

Poor Pik, we'd think to ourselves or say to one another, shaking our heads. It was less work to pity him briefly than to spend any amount of time with him.

Perhaps it was because he saw that I was well disposed toward him, perhaps because I was among the few, or perhaps the only one, who never made fun of him with the usual wisecracks, wisecracks whose wicked cruelty surfaced almost unwittingly, in something approaching innocence, during the games among classmates, whom I can hardly blame for it, let me say it again, theirs was an all-too-natural cruelty, an automatism that went part and parcel with the very game we were playing, and if I never unleashed my cruelty upon Picchiatello, it was only because those amusing cruelties never came to mind, and therefore *not* because I was a better person than the others, but only because I wasn't as quick-witted, I wasn't as funny. And in fact I laughed at those wisecracks of theirs, I laughed as much as anyone . . . Perhaps that was why Pik started to ask me, at first sporadically, and then more insistently, five or ten times in a row, to come over to his house to do our homework together. "Will you come over, eh, will you come over?" "Well, actually . . ." "Tell me you'll come over . . . Will you come over? Today? Eh? Today? This afternoon?" "Look, I really need to . . ." "So, we're in agreement? At three o'clock? Three thirty? Three fifteen?"

I couldn't seem to stem the rush of his requests. As he peppered me with them, interlarding them with his incessant refrain of "eh? eh?" he kept looking up at me with those bulbous eyes of his, a chilling blue, and at every "eh?" he'd squeeze me with his rigid fingers at the socket of my shoulder, which got to be pretty annoying.

YES, HE WAS FUN, and he was unnerving. Pik represented what you can't really tell how to take, that which you don't know what to do with. At school, in his family, with us classmates. He would often be targeted and surrounded by some small cluster of kids, molested, you might say, practically tortured, but then released because he wasn't worth the trouble, at the very worst they might force him to swallow a few crumpled paper balls.

"HEY, PICCHIATELLO, why don't you tell us what you think about things?"

"Picchiatello, who dressed you like that?"

"Who bought you those blue jeans that are too long?"

"You need to cuff them, but with two-inch cuffs, so they look funny. Just ridiculous!"

"Pik, hcy, Pik, listen up: you're never going to grow up, you'll never have a woman, you'll never have a fiancée or a wife."

"Everyone smiles at you, everyone acts as if they're happy to see you, they hug you and they're nice to you because they have to be, because that's the right thing to do. It would be disgusting to treat someone like you badly and people really want to show what good folks they are . . ."

"Hey, you have a butterfly on the tip of your nose. Did you notice that, Picchiate'?"

"Butterflies land on people who smell bad."

"It's the stink that attracts them, did you know that?"

"Hey, Picchiatello, you sweat like a horse, you're a lake of sweat, your hands are all clammy."

"You know, people say that you don't have any feelings. That you're like an animal, like a plant."

"You don't understand, you don't suffer, you don't have fun, in other words, you aren't *alive*."

"You're useless and slobbery."

"Hey, Picchiatello!"

"You don't talk, you just drool."

"String one streamer of drool after another and that would be a conversation with you."

"All the same, Picchiatello, when you look in those big blue eyes of yours, sometimes it really seems like you've understood everything we say . . ."

"Hey, Pik? Does it hurt you if someone sticks a needle under your fingernail?"

"Come here, Pik. Kneel down. Right here, in front of me. No! Don't look at me. Look at the ground. No, I said on your *knees*, you get it? Now start crying. That's right, cry. Let me see if you know how to cry. If you can't do it, think of something sad. Think about your parents not wanting you. That they didn't want you before you were born, and afterward they wanted you even less, seeing what you're like. There, now cry. And you still aren't crying? Just think, Pik, how happy they'd be if they'd had a different son instead of you. I told you not to look at me. Cry, Pik. It would be better for you. Oh, at last, there you are. Good job. Bravo. Now dry your face. That's enough. Dry your face. You're getting my shoes wet. Stop it. Stop it, Pik. You're pretending, aren't you, Picchiatello? I'm sick of this. I know that you're just making believe. Your sorrow is fake. I'll give you something to cry about, if you don't stop. You've cried enough and it's time to stop."

PERHAPS I WAS THE ONLY ONE who understood him. Or rather, I might not have understood him, but I accepted him. And even that's not true. I didn't accept Picchiatello, that was impossible, impossible for anyone to accept him: let's just say then that I was *studying* him. I was studying his diversity. The nervous exhaustion that he provoked in anyone who spent more than fifteen minutes around him wasn't enough to crowd out the interest I felt for him. I'm sorry I didn't write down his better sayings, in detail, because now, collected along with his doings, no less surprising and unpredictable, they would constitute an opus comparable in genre to those of certain Chinese sages, or the whimsical Mittel-European aphorists of the early twentieth century. The Sayings of Pik.

FOR A LONG TIME, I resisted his invitations. Then, in view of an upcoming classroom assignment in Latin that promised to be decisive for the final, year-end grade (even though everyone knew that the priests were going to pass Picchiatello, *no matter what*), I gave in, and I went over to his house "to study together."

PIK'S HOUSE WASN'T A HOUSE, it was a wonderful villa concealed by a high perimeter wall overflowing with plants and flowers. The garden, shaded by palms and strange trees, with stout twisted trunks and violet leaves, looked like it belonged to a colonial residence: the architect who must have designed it in the 1920s, or thereabouts, had stuffed into it nearly all the styles available to him, playing with turrets, round-arched and Gothic-arched windows, bow windows, pediments and aedicules, super-steep pitched roofs, majolica wall coverings crowded with young women dancing in skimpy skirts, and then there were swans, swans, and more swans.

Parked under an awning that was made more modestly of corrugated sheet metal, although it was covered with a dense carpet of Virginia creeper, there were two antiquated automobiles impeccably buffed to a high gleam, the black Mercedes that used to take him to and from school, and a bottle-green Fiat 500 "Topolino," a model of car that flickers among my earliest memories, when we'd cram into its narrow interior and my grandfather would hunker over the steering wheel, Borsalino on his head. But I'm not going to linger on these details which, later in the book, I'll explore at greater length in order to give a little color and shape to this blessed QT. By so doing, I hope I'll help you understand the mentality of its inhabitants, which has been so shaped as to fit with great exactitude into those spaces, like those panels on which small children work industriously to find the right hole into which they can insert stars, triangles, hexagons, squares, and thus receive the praise of their parents. Because the most alluring element of Pik's home was without a doubt the figure of his mother, of whom until that day I had only seen half, the upper half, when she would roll down the window of the Mercedes in front of the school and wave to Pik to climb in. Dark glasses, dark dress, black hair, it wasn't as if much of her could be seen in that hasty glance, but still I saw enough to notice that she was gorgeous. At school, in the conversations that sprang up around the both unfortunate and comical personality of our classmate, it was said of her that she was an actress, or rather that she had been one, in the fifties, until Picchiatello was born. I had actually never seen any of her movies, not even on TV, and so that mythology remained intact, and I had no desire to subject it to any further investigation, for fear that might spoil it. It was, however, a common occurrence in those days that a woman's film-acting career would be suspended or terminated entirely upon her first pregnancy, which in fact producers and press offices did their best to keep secret as long as possible; nevertheless, the arrival of Pik must have been something quite different from the usual family incident. A meteorite, rather, hurtling to earth from an intricate stellar nebula: the beautiful young starlet, with such a startling resemblance to Lucia Bosè, till then considered her rival, giving birth to a mentally handicapped son.

IT WAS SHE WHO ANSWERED the door and let me in. There are people who know how to reconstruct every single item of apparel worn by the people they met in certain situations, whereas I never pay the slightest attention, even if they're decisive meetings, meetings that change your life. And yet I remember with extreme precision, with a clarity and resolution befitting the grain of a photograph, exactly how Coralla Martirolo, Pik's mamma, was dressed: a black knee-length skirt that fit her very snugly and a white blouse with the cuffs bias-cut, fastened at the throat with a ruby brooch, and high heels. I'd never seen anyone, no mother, no girl, no woman dressed like that at home in the afternoon.

I WOULD HAVE LIKED to hear her voice, but as if she had taken a vow of silence, she led me without a word through the villa's maze of hallways, to my classmate's bedroom. Before opening the door, she turned to give me what on the face of another person would have been called a perfunctory polite smile: but which Coralla gave such a melancholy interpretation that you might think she was on the verge of tears. Her eyes studied me with an intensity and sadness so profound that it shook me to my foundations, and I was tempted to lay my hand on hers as it already gripped the doorknob, and help her to complete, together, that rotary movement, which seemed to be costing her an unheard-of effort, and by so doing, inform her: "Signora, I understand you. I'm with you, I'm at your side. I'd gladly change places with your son. I'd like to do something, something more, and believe me I'd do it for you, and not for that nutty woodpecker of a son that fate bestowed upon you. What injustice! No doubt, he's a young man deserving of our pity, but the person who really deserves our sympathy is you, signora, you are the victim here. Please allow me to help you to turn this door handle in order to enter the room. Let's do it together. Then I promise I'll look after your boy Pik for the rest of the afternoon and you can occupy yourself with other, more enjoyable things. Put your mind at peace. You can't? It's impossible to do? You can't seem to rid your mind of this affliction, this cross that is yours to bear? I can just imagine. I know so very many things about you, signora, things that I learned from your son. If I promise to be kind to him from now on, if I promise to help him, to protect him from the bullshit of his other classmates, will you take that into consideration? Will you repay me? And how could you repay me? Why, it's simple. By embracing me. By throwing your arms around me and holding me tight."

She opened the door and I found myself doing Latin homework next to Pik, who kept giving me annoying little taps on the shoulder.

I CAME BACK ANOTHER TIME. Coralla Martirolo wasn't at home. A maid answered the door. My frustration rocketed to the stars. I hated Picchiatello.

BUT THE NEXT TIME, she was there. As soon as I saw her I abandoned myself once again to my fantasies. My heart was brimming over with joy. I don't know why. I had immediately gone back to nurturing a feeling toward Pik that was a mix of fondness and pity, and he amused me with his various tics and his eccentricities. Staring me right in the eye, he dared to ask: "My mamma's pretty, isn't she?" and I nodded, unable to lie, with downcast gaze. The boy had read my mind. I said it before, Pik was magic. "Mamma!" he called. "Mamma, come here, come here now!" he shouted even louder, and I was afraid that he was about to spill the beans, telling Signora Martirolo something about me, something along the lines of "Did you know, Mamma, that he likes you?" pointing at me, "Did you know that he's fallen in love with you?" with a singsong chant, "Edo loves my mamma . . . Edo loves my mamma . . ." Instead, luckily he just wanted a snack.

AROUND SEVEN, when Coralla Martirolo walked me back to the door (Pik had been forced by the maid to take a bath, and at that moment, he was already naked in the tub, loudly protesting, while she inundated him with water), she finally opened her mouth, and she not only spoke, she actually caressed my head.

"You have nice hair," she told me.

13

WHEN PICCHIATELLO PRETENDED to be a waiter, there, in the pizzeria, he surprised the rest of us, his classmates, but not a bit the other waiters, the real ones: in fact, they just played along, treating him as if he really were the youngster who had just started working there and was a little lost, in dire need of gruff advice. When he had finished jotting down our orders on his notepad (we'd each gone for a margherita pizza and a fountain Coke: the cheapest items on the menu), an older mustachioed waiter came up behind him and pulled the order pad out of his hand, dressing him down the way you do with a new hire, a green beginner. "How the devil did you write these orders? The *pizzaiolo* isn't going to be able to make heads or tails of this!" and with a rapid shorthand he transcribed the orders onto a scrap of paper that he then impaled on the long spike that stood on the counter next to the wood-fired pizza oven.

This seemed to demonstrate only one thing, but in a very clear, precise manner: that the only way to deal with Pik was to take his buffoonery seriously. Not to unmask it. One had to be neither indulgent nor consolatory (after all, poor thing, you see the way he is?), instead one had to act on the plane of reality. Sure, fair enough, that's the only plane there is: everything is real, even our dreams, even monsters.

TIME WENT BY and he remained unchanged. I want to tell the story of the time that we went out together, Pik, two girls, and me. Maybe it was the year before I left SLM. It was the riskiest and most decisive experiment, and once it had been run it would become possible to issue a definitive judgment on the case of Pik, a question that had so interested psychologists, professors, and therapists, namely, whether he could be salvaged. I realized that deep down I was almost wishing for a full-blown disaster, a catastrophe, with the girls scandalized offended disgusted etc., after which I could just be done with Pik entirely, like so many others before me.

I HAD MET ONE OF THE GIRLS Pik and I were supposed to squire out and about that evening at the beach, the previous summer. Her name was Monica. Back then, many, many girls, in numbers that defied belief, at least in Rome, were named Monica, and I couldn't guess the reason: toward the end of the fifties and at the start of the following decade, the name of St. Augustine's mother had influenced pregnant women, both in the bourgeoisie and the working classes. Now, this Monica had become very fond of me over the course of the summer, she'd call me, talk to me, laugh at my efforts to get her to like me, so much so that I was tempted (and at the same time concerned, of two minds) to try to see whether her interest in me was strictly in the vein of friendship, or whether, instead, she *liked* me, that is, if she'd go so far as to consider me a potential boyfriend. It wasn't easy and it still isn't, even though the signals they send have become more explicit, to read women's minds, and it is true that they can wind up taking offense either at having their openness misinterpreted as emotional and sexual availability, or at it *not* being taken that way: I believe that the reason is first and foremost because what reigns in their heads is confusion, that is, about whether being desired represents an ambition or a burden to them. With a view to clarifying this doubt, and making it clear to myself whether, in the final analysis, I really liked Monica after all, that is, whether I liked her, aside from any question of her potential availability, I had phoned her after finding her phone number on a sheet of graph paper that had survived being washed in the back pocket of a pair of jeans where I had tucked it away two months earlier, outside a gelato shop at Monte Circeo, with the promise that I'd call her. I hadn't given her my number because of a stupid shamefacedness, inexplicable, unless you adduce the factor of my shyness back then.

I had thought, that is, that if I'd given her my number, she would have been able to call me whenever she wanted, and she certainly would have done it, one fine day, and her call would have caught me off guard, which was exactly what I wanted to avoid, I didn't want to find myself standing there with the receiver in hand, paralyzed by my emotion. That your shyness must at all costs be masked, concealed, is the obsession of the shy. But since I had her number, I could comfortably pick and choose, both the time and the suitable mood, the appropriate day, I could ready the things I was going to say, the opening line to start the phone call, acting detached, as if I didn't care all that much about her in the first place, which experts in matters amorous had told me was the right attitude to display with girls, because too heated an interest in them, instead of attracting them, would chase them away, it almost annoyed them, whereas they were captivated by insolent manners, that approach summarized in the advertising slogan of an aftershave of the time, intended for the type of man "who doesn't have to try too hard," the man who is his own boss, who doesn't lift a finger and just waits for women to fall into his arms.

I told Pik to make the phone call. That's right, I had Picchiatello call Monica. He improvised very well indeed, smoothly passing himself off as my secretary, saying that he wanted to set up an appointment with her. He made her laugh: then he passed me the receiver.

"Wait, who was that?"

"A friend of mine. Nice guy, right?"

"Sure . . . nice guy. A little strange."

"I'm strange, too."

"Of course you are. If you decide to invent a personal secretary . . ."

"Still, it worked."

"By which you mean what?"

I took a deep breath.

"Now you and I have a date."

"Silly. I would have gone on a date with you, even if you'd just called yourself. What, were you ashamed to call me?"

I was about to deny it, instinct told me to deny it, what are you talking about, me ashamed? Why would I be ashamed? But for once I managed to resist the impulse to defend myself, to justify myself, an impulse that hasn't given me peace since the day I was born and to which, perhaps, I owe the fact that I became an intellectual: essentially to defend myself, to justify myself, by finding the best examples and reasons in books. After all, what in the final analysis have Italian writers been doing for the past five or six hundred years? Nothing other than defending themselves, justifying themselves.

Better to be straight with Monica, so the truth came out of my mouth like a fish leaping out of the water, instinctively.

"Yes, I was ashamed."

"Don't tell me that you're shy. I don't believe it."

"I'm shy."

"If you say so, then it means that you aren't."

The usual little game, I thought to myself. The game of catching you in a contradiction.

"Ehm . . . you wouldn't happen to have a girlfriend, would you? A girlfriend who could come, too?"

"Wait, I'm not enough for you?"

"Not for me, for my friend. The one you talked to on the phone."

"What's his name?"

"Pik."

"Is that a name?"

"Yes. Actually, his name is Pico." Pico della Mirandola had popped into my mind. Better not to explain the real reason for his nickname. "He's from an aristocratic family."

"Ah . . . and is he cute, your friend Pik?"

"Well, no. But he's really likable . . ." and here I wasn't lying. "Anyway, it's just for one date, it's not like your girlfriend has to marry him or anything . . ."

"But I have to marry you?"

I fell silent. And this silence of mine turned out to be important for the future twists of the story.

14

WE WOUND UP at Monica's house; her parents were away.

The other girl, Erika, got it into her head to be affectionate with Pik.

She had taken it as a mission.

And that way, she thought she was giving me and Monica a hand, to do who knows what.

Pik was in seventh heaven.

He couldn't thank me enough for having brought him along with me.

And he couldn't stop asking me which of the two girls I wanted to fuck, and which one he could fuck himself.

"Pik, cut it out. Get those things out of your head."

"No fucking?"

"No way."

"Fucking?"

"Don't start any trouble, Pik, or else I'll . . ."

"Oh, come on, I was just kidding. I was just kidding! Can you really not understand when I'm just kidding around?"

"Exactly, Pik, take it from me: no kidding around. Be a good boy. Otherwise, we're going home."

"Certainly, my lord, certainly," Pik said, with a deep bow.

The real mistake was letting him drink.

Alcohol has unpredictable effects on anybody's head and body.

Normally, I open up and become more likable.

That evening, Monica stopped posing as a heartbreaker and turned out to be much more fragile than I could have imagined.

Erika transfigured herself until she seemed almost pretty, or at least so she appeared to our eyes, though only after we had downed a bottle of one of those liqueurs with an unlikely name that you can find in the liquor cabinet in any home.

Her eyes, which were small and blue, had grown, and so had her nostrils, and even her legs were longer.

Pik . . . well, with Pik it was as if his highly carbonated mind had been shaken up and down and then the cork had been popped.

He couldn't stop talking and laughing, and making us laugh.

Luckily, he had set aside his sexual plans, which I so greatly feared.

Or at least, he had set them aside for the moment.

Erika, sitting on a sofa, had allowed him to lie down next to her, and had taken his big head in her lap and was stroking his hair.

Picchiatello could barely contain his moans of pleasure.

"Erika, you're the most fantastic girl I've ever met in my life. For real!"

"Thanks. And you, too . . . you're really a special kind of guy."

And Erika looked at Monica and me, with a smile that had nothing ironic about it.

I thought to myself: these great girls, who are spending the evening with us.

Who are going along with this rather strange date.

Then both of them stood up and disappeared.

They must have gone to the bathroom, I thought, together, the way girls do, who knows why they do that.

Picchiatello got up off the sofa and came over.

He kneeled down in front of me.

"Listen . . . I've never been with a girl."

"Don't worry. You're not going to tonight, either."

"But Erika . . ."

"Erika just likes you, that's all. Because you, as you know, my friend, tend to win girls over."

"You think? You really think so? For real? And what else?"

"And nothing else. That's already plenty and enough."

"No, it's not enough. Don't try to make a fool of me. I know there's more to it."

"There's nothing more to it."

"Oh, yes there is."

"No there isn't."

"But Erika . . ."

"Oh, come on, Pik! She's a good girl. And she's cute. She's being nice to you."

"Exactly! So what am I supposed to do next?"

"Listen. You *don't* need to do anything, Pik. You don't need to *do* anything. *Nothing at all*, got it? Have fun. Let's have fun, and nothing more. It's a nice night out. We're having a good time together, right?"

"The two of us together?"

"The two of us and our girlfriends."

Pik laughed and clapped his hands.

"Fantastic!" he exclaimed. "They're fantastic!"

"Right. And we are two gentlemen. Their gentlemen."

"You can say that again!" and he clapped his hands again loudly.

"We're lucky boys, aren't we?"

"I'll say!"

"Very lucky."

"So which one of them do you want to fuck?"

"No, listen, Pik . . . please . . ."

"Do you think that I can fuck Monica instead of Erika? Huh? Monica instead of Erika? Can I leave Erika for you?"

"Oh, so you haven't listened to a thing I've said . . ."

"What can I do about it? I like her better. I like Monica better than Erika."

"Do I have to explain it all over to you, from the beginning?"

"There's no need, I understand, I get it. It's just that I like Monica better. That's all."

"Well, so what, Pik, I like Monica better, too, but that doesn't really matter now . . ."

"Ah, so you see? We both feel the same way about it. So, what do you say, can I take her to bed? Do you mind? Can I make her get undressed? Can I tell her to take off her clothes? Do you think that Monica will let me suck on her ass?"

"Her . . . *what* . . . ?!"

"Can I take her to bed, Monica? On top of the bed?"

"What *bed* are you taking about, Pik, for fuck's sake!!"

"What did I say that was wrong? There, now you've gotten mad."

"I'm not mad."

"You just made a face . . ."

"But I assure you, I'm not mad."

"Then why are you cursing?"

"Look . . . I didn't mean to . . . oh, listen, Pik, let's just not start causing trouble now of all times . . ."

"What trouble? I'm not causing trouble. Never have, not once in my life."

"Then listen to me, listen to me for once."

"Haven't caused a bit of trouble, not ever in my life. I don't cause trouble."

"I believe you, I believe you. It's all been great up till now, right, Pik? It's been great, hasn't it? Say so."

"Very. Very, very nice. I'd even say it's been wonderful."

"Oh, there you go! So why ruin everything now?"

"Right. Because you think it would ruin everything?"

"That's exactly right."

"Then what are you trying to tell me? What is it you're saying to me?"

"You know exactly what I'm saying, Pik."

"So are you, maybe, telling me that . . . that I shouldn't . . . fuck things up?"

"Exactly."

"I shouldn't fuck things up?"

"No, you shouldn't."

"So don't fuck things up?"

I shook my head no, back and forth, repeatedly.

"Don't fuck things up."

"So I won't fuck things up, I promise."

"You promise?"

"I promise, I promise. Don't you trust me?"

"No, I don't trust you . . . !"

"And you're right not to trust me!" Pik burst out laughing, crossing both fingers over his mouth and kissing them. "I didn't swear, you know! I didn't swear!"

"But you promised."

"That's not the same thing."

"Oh, for God's sake, fuck it to hell, Pik . . . !" I blurted out, impatiently, and my irritation caused me to throw back another half a glass of aquavit.

"I was just kidding, hey, I was just kidding, don't get mad, I was just kidding. I was kidding! I swear it, I was kidding, this time, I swear, okay? 'Cause I was kidding . . ." Picchiatello begged me, putting his hands together.

At that point, the girls came back into the living room.

They must have talked things over between them, they must have washed their faces and redone their makeup, their eyes were sparkling, their lips were red.

I reflected on the fact that Monica really was pretty, not just a cute young woman, and that if I had gone to all that trouble just to allow my classmate Picchiatello to spend an evening out, away from home, then I really was an idiot.

And was I doing it all for *him*, really?

Just for him?

Let's tell the truth: I was doing it because I was head over heels with his beautiful mother.

What the hell, Picchiatello could go fuck himself, fuck his nervous tics and his watery, bulging eyes: it was Coralla Martirolo, in her chaste outfits, with her heaving breasts, who was stirring my compassion.

Her red heart, stabbed with daggers ever since the birth of that mental defective.

Coralla Martirolo moved my spirit, and she stirred all the rest: thinking about her made me tremble with pity, which is the most sensual sentiment of them all, the most physical, you feel it like a shiver, a thorn in your flesh that gives you a pain that's sharp and then sweet, so to speak, celestial.

Mercy, mercy.

Have mercy on us, oh Lord.

Have mercy on Coralla Martirolo.

Have mercy on this poor nut job.

Have mercy on Erika with the *k* that they stuck in her poor name.

Have mercy, oh Lord, on those who seek You and on those who don't seek You and on those who have given up trying.

Mercy, mercy, mercy.

Have mercy on me and I will show you the same mercy.

I will seek among the Christians for someone like me, and if I don't find him, I'll seek him among the non-Christians, and I will find him.

Ecce homo. Behold the Man.

Pik's face appeared to me even more deformed than it actually was.

"What shall we do now?" the girls asked cheerfully, wobbling on their heels.

They couldn't handle the alcohol any better than we could.

Oh, yes, yes, decisiveness and indecisiveness: the two poles between which my life has always swerved.

Very frequently, in fact, nearly always, I've acted in a clumsy, brusque, and excessive manner, only because otherwise I run the risk of not acting at all, it's all or nothing, either I jump out the window or else I'll be stuck here, lost in thought in a chair, either I say nothing or I scream, there are no alternatives, it's either inertia or head-on crash.

And so I staggered to my feet, shoved Pik aside—he was just getting in my way with his oversized, extraterrestrial head—and I reached the girls, blurry because of the alcohol, and I roughly grabbed Monica by the hand, pulled her after me, and groped and stumbled my way down the dark hallway.

Turning around for a moment, I saw Pik with a confused, alarmed look on his face, his eyes round as balls, begging me for help, but I wasn't going to give it to him.

It was hopeless.

Monica protested in monosyllables.

"Come on," I answered her brusquely, "come on."

We entered a room at random, and there was a bed in it.

I pushed her onto the bed.

"Wait," she said.

"No, I'm not going to wait," and I jumped on top of her, crushing her into the mattress.

"Wait, not like that," she said again, and I who could feel a roaring of water in my head ignored her because, I'm sure of it, if I had waited, it all would have ended at once, the girl and the room would have vanished, but luckily it was my own physical weight, the weight of my head and the weight of my body, that dragged me like lead on top of her.

For the third time, Monica asked me to wait.

But wait for *what*?

I wanted to give her a kiss, but in order to give her that kiss I would have to scale a mountain and plunge down a bottomless cliff . . .

All right then, kiss her, kiss her immediately, a french kiss, press my own bruised, dry mouth down upon that mouth aflame, right now.

I did it.

And afterward all I said was: "Oh, Monica . . . ," and the words fled from my mouth like a lament.

And I flipped over next to her, I relaxed, in a state of abandonment, as if I were exhausted, but from what, after all? Looking up at the ceiling as it swayed, slid back and forth, a white rectangle that was sliding away, going back where it belonged, and then sliding off to one side again.

My spirit had run aground in that soft and passionate kiss.

Monica's face appeared above me, and she looked down at me, astonished.

"You're completely crazy," she said and laughed.

She stroked my face and she tried to give me a more delicate, deeper kiss than the last one.

Just at that moment, Picchiatello entered the room.

He seemed terribly far off, and tiny, there, two yards away.

"It's time to go," he said.

Behind him, Erika entered the room.

An Expressionist painting.

"I'm sorry," she murmured, "I'm so sorry . . . I . . ."

Monica in the meantime had sat up on the bed and was smoothing her skirt over her legs.

Pik was blinking his eyes and looking first in one direction and then in the other.

In a metallic voice, he repeated that he had to get back home.

"Right-a-way."

He spoke like a tape-recorded message.

At that point, Erika burst into tears.

Between sobs, she was stammering: "I don't know . . . I don't know what . . . it was just . . . just . . ." then she ran across the room to grab the handle of a small door on the far side of the room, as if she were about to fall down, then she opened it and disappeared through it.

The next instant, she could be heard vomiting.

"Shall we go? I'm ready," Picchiatello said, calm and indifferent.

His enormous eyes were glassy, there was dried slobber at the corners of his mouth, and he was smoothing his shirt with his hands to tuck it in under the belt of his too large, too loose trousers.

"Certainly, certainly," I replied, "I'm ready, too," and I let my legs dangle over the side of the bed.

From the bathroom came the last sounds of retching, dry heaves, when nothing more will come up.

Really, a special evening.

I'm sort of sorry for Monica.

15

RUMMO IS A COMPOSED PERSON. He was even when he was young. He treated everyone respectfully and gave them his full attention. I saw further confirmation of this trait in how he approached five-a-side soccer: a sport, or rather, a game that is quite eloquent, capable of bringing out all the players' frustrations and hysteria after just a few passes and exchanges, especially in those who are getting along in years and yet stubbornly insist on continuing to play, even as they grow less agile and more likely to commit fouls and complain about it. In five-a-side soccer, you can't camouflage or disguise your nature. And so, Rummo is a good, clean player, he passes the ball when he ought to, his elbows are no sharper than they need to be, he doesn't shout or whine or kick the ball angrily off the field when he gets kicked. He acknowledges without arguing his own fouls and those committed by his teammates. He is a psychiatrist by profession, and yet you'd think that he rejects the more dramatic hues of life in advance, abjuring them.

Tragedies are just vast misreadings: if we were only capable of seeing them from the right angle, we'd understand that they're ideal occasions, opportunities . . .

RUMMO CAME FROM a large and happy family. His parents were devout Catholics who had married very young and had given all their children names of characters out of Holy Scripture, some famous, others less so. The first born was Ezechiele, or Ezekiel, then came Lea (Leah), the third was Gioacchino (or Joachim, and he was in fact my classmate), followed by Elisabetta (Elizabeth), Rachele (Rachel), Tobia (Tobias), and last of all Giaele (Yael)—in Italian, it was only when you saw her that you realized Giaele was a girl's name. Therefore, enrolling Rummo at SLM (as they had enrolled, a few years earlier, Ezechiele, better known as Ezi, or Lele, and after him, Tobia, who had just begun middle school) made good sense: his family believed strongly in Catholic teaching, in the Catholic school as offering the best kind of education in absolute terms, and not merely because it conferred a certain distinction to attend the school. The Rummos really weren't that kind of people. Before they moved to Rome, they'd lived in Naples, and the beauty of their large Neapolitan house with its view of the sea was often summoned up with great yearning and regret by Gioacchino (it doesn't come natural to me to call him by his given name instead of the appellation usually assigned him in roll call at school); to Rummo, the city of Rome constituted a place of exile, and the QT, so deeply loved and appreciated by most of its residents, appeared cramped and suffocating to him.

The Rummo brothers and sisters when all assembled in one place constituted quite a spectacle. On weekends, they would go for long hikes in the mountains, the two adults and seven children, ranging from the eighteen years of age of the eldest down to Giaele, age four, all dressed in what we might nowadays call technical gear, but scavenged, down-at-the-heels: oversized shapeless heavy sweaters, tattered and riddled with holes, felt trousers worn out at the knees in which a great many pairs of legs had hiked before the legs of the current occupant, athletic socks of some indefinable color that sagged around the ankles.

I watched them set out once, at the beginning of a long holiday weekend, in their van equipped to sleep nine, though God only knows how. I was especially struck by an aspect of the family to which I have always been morbidly sensitive, and which was dizzying in the Rummos: the color of their hair. Long or short, the hair of all nine members of the family displayed all the possible gradations of blond, with coppery or tawny highlights, or hues of wheat, honey, gold, and ash, ranging all the way down to the almost colorless and extremely fine hair of the littlest girl, Giaele. On Tobia's head, practically shorn bald, the blond bristles changed color every time he would nod or turn his head.

THERE ARE TWO TRAILS that run around the Lago dell'Angelo, or Angel Lake: one off to the right, the other to the left. The one to the right cuts through dense woods whose trees run down to the lakeshore, while the opposite shore is high, bare, and rocky; at certain points the drop to the dark lake water must be fifty or even a hundred feet. In order to determine which path is shorter, the Rummos decide to split up into two groups, each of which will try out one of the two trails. Whichever group reaches the opposite side of the lake first will be the one that took the quicker route. Once the two groups have met at the far side, they'll each come back taking the opposite trail, splitting up into the same two groups, each of which will return on the trail that the other group took on the way out, so that at the end of the hike both will have hiked the entire perimeter of the lake, one clockwise, the other counterclockwise.

"Listen, though, no running, understood?" the architect Rummo tells his youngsters with a smile; he likes to imagine these geometric circuits, plot and calculate the routes of their hikes, as if he could see them sketched out in a luminous streak before his eyes, on a life-size map. "We hike at our usual pace. Otherwise it's no fair!" He reckons it will take a couple of hours to complete the circuit: a good long walk. But the boys and girls eye each other as they ready themselves for what they see as a game, and games are something you either win or you lose.

The two teams were chosen by lot as follows: Davide Rummo, the father, with Ezechiele, Elisabetta, and Rachele would go to the left along the rocky ridge; Eleonora Rummo, the mother, with Lea, Gioacchino, Tobia, Giaele, to the right, through the woods. "But what if Giaele gets tired, and doesn't want to walk?" asked Lea, who was always something of a critic: a young woman with reddish hair, glasses, and freckles. "Then you'll just have to carry her piggyback, you and Gioacchino," their mother laughed, and the group set out. The other group, with Davide, Ezechiele, and the middle girls got moving, too. "Don't forget, along the way, collect, collect!" called Eleonora Rummo, before plunging into the trees.

ELEONORA RUMMO, an architect like her husband, liked to spend her free time assembling compositions of tiny found natural elements, such as acorns, berries, pebbles, dried flowers, insect larvae, seashells, eggshells, shells of all sorts, feathers, pieces of quartz, and twigs, gathered on their mountain hikes or on the beach during the winter; she would then glue them to a background of gray or ocher cardboard and frame them as abstract artworks. Her children had developed the habit of filling their pockets and then offering their finds to their mother. This, too, turned into a sort of competition, to see who could find the loveliest and most curious objects. A dead lizard an inch long, desiccated and mummified. A piece of mother-of-pearl. A shard of glass burnished by the weather. The cap of an acorn. A fragment of blue or yellow majolica. So when they hiked they always had their eyes on the ground. Sometimes their pockets were packed so full that the memorabilia would crumble into dust, especially the more delicate objects such as snail shells or the exoskeletons of sea urchins, dotted with holes; so when they put in their hands to pull out their finds, they retrieved only a fistful of shards and dust. What a disappointment!

THE GROUP WITH MY CLASSMATE moves off through the trees. The trail is just a faint track marked by the recent passage of other hikers who have trodden down the underbrush: there are no other blazes or markings. It's a little chilly. The single file tends to straggle and break up. Tobia hurries ahead, keenly aware of the importance of arriving first. "There's no point in running!" his mother yells after him, "wait for us," and Lea echoes her mother's admonition; today Lea is lost in thought, walking slowly and bringing up the rear. Gioacchino is holding Giaele's hand and telling her a story. My classmate has no imagination, he doesn't know how to invent anything original, so he falls back on the stories he's heard and studied at SLM starting in elementary school. This time he chooses Pharaoh's dreams and the one who was able to interpret them, young Joseph. Rummo has often wondered why his parents didn't give him that name, so simple and lovely—Giuseppe in Italian—rather than Gioacchino, so uncommon. He can't imagine that before just twenty or thirty years have passed, many of these extremely common Italian boy's names, such as Giuseppe, in fact, or Giovanni, or Mario, will be practically extinct. "What is a Pharaoh?" Giaele asks, and Rummo (forgive me if I go back to calling him Rummo, I can't help it) patiently sets aside his story to lay out a brief history lesson, and while he's at it, a little art history as well. "A great king, very mighty, so powerful that in order to bury him they built the biggest tomb of all time, just think, all just for him! A pyramid!"

THERE THEY ARE, my classmate Rummo's parents, walking in opposite directions, though in the end their paths will bring them all back together, which is the destiny of their lives. Davide is a very positive, energetic man, still young, who has a simple and convincing solution for every problem and a word of comfort for anyone assailed by doubts or difficulties. He's brilliant and generous, honest and reasonable, and he has only one defect, though it's a grave one, which derives, paradoxically, from those very same fine qualities he possesses in such abundance, the good fortune and the happiness he enjoys: he is, so to speak, overwhelmed with self-satisfaction, contentment with his work, which is thriving, with his beautiful family, and with those hikes they all set out on together, so enthusiastically, even though his children have such a wide range of ages. Davide is puffed up, you might say turgid with satisfaction for his children and his wife, Eleonora, still lovely after so many pregnancies, whom he loves just as much as the first day, indeed, even more, much more, since the experiences they have lived together in almost twenty years have just made their love deeper and richer and more nuanced. It is, in fact, on account of these very same experiences, so intense and exhausting, that Eleonora, though she, too, loves her husband as much as ever, no longer wishes to have relations with him, for fear she might become pregnant again. Already with her last child, Giaele, who fell from heaven a full six years after Rachele's birth, when Eleonora Rummo was convinced she'd finished her childbearing years, it was an event accepted as yet another of God's many graces, but an ordeal nonetheless. Though Davide was beside himself with delight when he heard the news, dazzled with the pleasure of that blessed surprise, for the first time she sensed that she *did not want* another child, that she did not desire *that* new baby about to arrive, which had been thrust upon her in the capricious way that God disposed of human lives, and about which Davide instead seemed to be so enthusiastic, as if this were the very proof of His existence. She would gladly have done without, foregone that last gift, but she could not turn it down—she could only make sure it was the last one. And so, when she chose the name with which that child would be baptized, a name that she had chosen all by herself, and not in common accord with her husband—and of course when this baby girl came into the world, she was loved by her mother every bit as much as, if not more than the six others—it may just be that there was an unconscious or mischievous reference to the episode that characterizes the biblical heroine Yael (again, the English version of Giaele), making her figure famous among those who are serious scholars of the Bible, and not like her husband, a childish and superficial reader of Holy Scripture.

In an episode recounted almost hastily, the young Yael kills a fearsome enemy of the Israelites, first by getting him drunk, and then by driving a large nail into his temple. And so Yael is always depicted, the hammer lifted high in the air by her muscular arm.

That nail, Eleonora had felt it inside her, at the beginning of her pregnancy, the way it scratched her, pierced her, right in the spot where Giaele's developing fetus lay, and then, as she grew accustomed to the idea of giving birth and nursing and, all things considered, starting over yet again with all the chores and tasks that have to do with caring for a little one (they'd had to buy a new Snugli and a stroller because they'd given away the ones they'd used for all their other children to younger mothers), from one day to the next she had no longer felt that nail. In a remote area of her consciousness, another image had appeared: the nail that little Giaele would one day drive into the head of her father.

The shared beliefs and faith and the lengthy marriage and the blond hair might make you think that Davide and his wife resemble each other, but they don't. Eleonora has an artistic temperament, gentle only in appearance but, in reality, stubborn and tenacious, and in spite of the web of relationships, of blood and of friendship that goes with such a large family, or perhaps precisely because of this unbroken expenditure of self upon others, she has always maintained with considerable reserve a zone of thoughts and feelings that excludes the others. And it is a zone that is far more vast and profound and mysterious than that happy-hearted Davide can even begin to imagine.

ELISABETTA AND RACHELE hopped nonchalantly along the steep brink of the cliff over the lake. Their father didn't think he needed to keep too tight a rein on them. It was clear that they were accustomed to taking care of themselves, having been raised to be self-reliant as early as nursery school, where the sinks were set fifteen inches off the floor, and they each had a locker all their own with a set of personal effects, and every child from the age of three up dressed themselves, washed up on their own, kept their things neat and tidy, hoed their own little vegetable garden, learned to knead and bake bread, as well as learning reading and writing and arithmetic. The singular destiny of the Rummo girls is that, since their parents couldn't enroll them at SLM, since they were female, from Lea to Giaele they had all attended very advanced elementary and middle school, coed, boys and girls together, and they had therefore become independent much sooner than their brothers. The idea that they might attend schools run by nuns the same way that their brothers attended schools run by priests had been ruled out from the start. The Rummos had at first discussed this disparity in education according to sex, and the same subject had surfaced over the years, every time they had to choose a new nursery school for one of their daughters, but Davide had managed, if not to convince Eleonora completely on the matter, at least to persuade her to set aside her doubts, presenting that compromise as the best available, given the situation. They needed to be realists, without undermining their own principles. Provisional decisions can sometimes prove to be as appropriate as if they had been the outcome of carefully pondered choices. Davide was convinced that he was doing the right thing when he allowed himself to be guided by solid common sense, and he liked to repeat the motto that he had learned from his spiritual master, an old Egyptian Jew who had lived as a layman until the age of forty, when he had converted and taken the vows: "Perfection is the enemy of the good." This was the chief legacy, the essence of the many teachings, far more complex and articulated, imparted by old Maimone, and Davide Rummo had accepted it with such fervor because he had glimpsed in it a summation of the best of both worlds, of the life experiences of that man who struck him as a saint: the secular world and the religious one. Tolerance, openness to the world, and above all, a quest for what, then and there, without prejudice, may prove to be the best path available: Maimone had grown old and had died without once giving the lie to this proverbial, affable doctrine. Davide had often repeated it to his children when he saw them growing rigid in the face of any necessary compromise, when they chose to give up an opportunity if they felt unable to pursue it without doing some form of wrong. "You know that perfection is the worst enemy of the good."

He was certain that he and Eleonora shared this moral outlook without even having to discuss it, and in that belief Davide was a little naïve, or perhaps he preferred to be thought of as such.

"POP, do you think I could take the van next Friday?"

"The van? Why not? I think so."

"It's to go out with a few friends," Ezechiele specified, with entering into details.

"Why not?" Davide Rummo says again. "But we may need it. Your mother and I were thinking of taking a trip to Gubbio, all of us together."

"To Gubbio?"

"Yes. It's a beautiful little city." His eyes lit up. "None of you have ever been there. Maybe your mother, but when she was a girl, with the scouts, and she's not sure. And all around it, there are magnificent woods . . . So, now, you were saying? Sure, of course, certainly. If you need the van and you don't feel like coming with us, one way or another we'll figure it out. Too bad, though, because Gubbio is really worth the trip, believe me, it's worth it . . ."

"It doesn't matter, Pop, I'd be glad to come with you. I'd be glad of a chance to see Gubbio, ag—" said Ezechiele, hastily, eager to skip over the matter, and avoiding any further reference to the fact that he had already been to Gubbio once before, four years earlier, and had spent a week there, for a basketball workshop, when he was so tall for his age that they thought he might be an excellent player. The super-gay basketball coach at SLM had shown great interest in him, in every sense of the word. Then he stopped growing, six foot two, tall, handsome, well proportioned, but not tall enough to be one of the real giant players, nor was he quick and technically proficient enough to become one of the "little" players of that sport. Davide Rummo no longer remembers the fact, but with seven children that's more than understandable. Already it's a tremendous achievement and a sign of goodwill that he only rarely mixes up names, places, and activities.

ELISABETTA WAS MORE OR LESS complaining for the fun of it, more than anything else to keep the line connecting her with her younger sister taut and active. When two young girls are so close in age (they were only a year and ten months apart), the elder of the two tends to give the line the occasional jerk and then reel the lure back in, like a fisherman. Even though it's not necessarily the case that it's the elder sister who always has the fishing pole in hand.

"I've made up my mind: this is the last time that I'm going to carry the water."

"Then why don't you drink it? That way the canteen will weigh less."

Elisabetta was at once struck both positively and negatively by Rachele's observation, at once intelligent and cynical.

"If I do that, then Papà and Ezi will think that I'm just selfish . . ."

"So, what are you saying, that you're not?" asked Rachele, grimacing in a way that was funny for her age, making the face of an adult saying something that's taken for certain: eyebrows arched, corners of the mouth twisted downward in disdain.

"No. No . . . ! Well, sure, I'm selfish, I'll admit it."

"And so?"

"I don't want them to know," she said, pointing to their father and Ezechiele, who were walking a little way ahead and talking as they walked. The architect Rummo was leaning on a stout branch, stripped of bark, that he had picked up during a previous hike, not because he needed any support, but because that improvised walking stick really was beautiful, and it was nice to spin it, twisting his wrist, before digging it into the ground and, afterward, slinging it forward for the next step. It helped him to set a rhythm as he hiked.

"But you think I am?" Rachele resumed; she knew Elisabetta's weakness for their father and how important it was to her sister not to have him think any the less of her.

"What do I care about you? You're selfish too. We're even."

"It's not true that I'm selfish," Rachele murmurs, and her voice cracks. "It's not true one little bit," and tears start to well up in her eyes.

They walk along in single file for a stretch.

Choking back her tears, Rachele suddenly says, "Lis, I'm thirsty," and leaps, both feet planted, over next to her sister. "Let me have some water."

"No."

"Give me the canteen."

"I'm not giving it to you."

"Elisabetta! Give it to me."

"Rather than give it to you, I'll pour all the water onto the dirt," and Lis unscrewed the cap and made the gesture, but only the gesture, of tipping the canteen.

"But then what if Papà tells you he's thirsty?"

"He can just ask Ezechiele, he has a canteen too. Plus, it's not hot out. Not one little bit."

"No one would ever think you're two years older than me. You're acting like a little girl. And even though I am still a little girl, I wouldn't act like that."

"You're not a little girl anymore, you're *already* ten years old!" Elisabetta retorted, in utter conviction. "Whereas, in a certain sense, I'm still a little girl, I *still* haven't turned twelve!"

They heard their father's voice.

"Hey, you two! You're not fighting, are you?"

"No, Papà, not at all. We were just talking," his daughters explained.

"Good girls. But while you're talking, look out for where you put your feet. And put your hats back on."

Both Elisabetta and Rachele had their hats hanging down their backs by the chin strap.

The rocky ridge, bare of vegetation, along which they were walking, now that they were halfway to their destination, was at the highest point over the lake, and the stone was riddled with fissures and cracks.

"Have you had some water? Because it's nice and hot out today."

Elisabetta unslung the canteen from around her neck, the same canteen that she had previously threatened to pour out onto the ground. She handed it to her sister. Rachele gathered her long wheat-blond hair and tied it in a crude braid, while Elisabetta waited, arm extended. Then, unhurried, she took the canteen, drank off two long swigs, dried her mouth, and handed it back to her sister, who also took a careful, measured drink of water. Then she put the canteen back over her shoulder, "Oh, right," said Elisabetta, and she put her floppy hat back on her head, covering her short hair, much darker than Rachele's, with reddish shocks here and there. Rachele did the same.

"YOU HAVEN'T COLLECTED anything for Mamma."

"Neither have you."

"You want to bet that I can find more nice things than you can?"

"Look, I'll just let you win that bet, I don't much feel like it today, and Mamma has more than enough of that junk already. She doesn't know where to put it anymore. The other day I saw her tossing a bag of it in the trash when she thought no one was looking!"

TO SEE THEM WALKING through the woods, Lea and her mother, Eleonora, look like two girls rambling aimlessly, even though one of them is forty-two years old and the other is surrounded by the bubble of parenthood carefully crafted by her mother, a bubble capable of withstanding any pressure, both from without and from within; nothing could shatter it. Both of them sense this bubble as an incomparable source of support and an impediment. Both are happy and unhappy in equal measure. Or perhaps we should say, in each of them, their sensations upend and reverse, first in one direction and then in the other, overturning their moods, like an hourglass being turned, from wretched to dreamy and enchanted . . .

THE ARCHITECT RUMMO is a woman who is just now beginning to consider the immense effort made to arrive where she is now. She hadn't sensed it while she was accomplishing it, but she senses it now that the burden is decidedly lighter. Only a few years ago, she had her professional obligations plus six children who looked to her for everything, her and her eager and willing, loving and enterprising spouse, who however could perhaps be categorized in certain ways as the seventh of the children she cared for, if it hadn't been for the fact that an actual seventh child was on the way, the unplanned-for Giaele. And yet it is this very same exhaustion that lets her slide forward now, without friction against things and people, without the spasmodic attachment that had once held sway. She's afraid that she might have to attribute to early aging this serenity, so similar to indifference, and the serenity barely savored is immediately converted into anguish and fear. Another few years, and she will be done with it all, with all *this*, and she'll have to find new reasons for living that are planted on this earth and not in the realms of hope or faith—and the good things about those are that they help you to get through difficulties, projected as they are into the future, a limitless and glorious future, but they're not enough to fill the present, they aren't designed to fill the present, if the present is empty, but only to tolerate it, if it's a present made up of hard work or sorrow. For Eleonora, and perhaps for everyone, religion has always been a bet placed on the future. Now that she is midway through her life, gluing together artworks with bark and clusters of juniper berries collected on vigorous hikes gives her a sense of time, frees her of her anxieties; when it becomes an occupation, and she needs to fill the time instead of emptying it, then she'll have to confer weight and substance to it instead of lightening it, then those cheery and picturesque collages promise to strike anguish into her heart.

GIOACCHINO HAD LONG since run through the story of Joseph and Pharaoh, enriching it with the further adventures in Egypt of Moses and Aaron, the plagues, and the parting of the Red Sea, as well as Baby Jesus taking refuge there while King Herod slaughtered all the newborns in Israel. Giaele didn't seem particularly horrified by his account of the massacre, and in fact she had just continued to ask for more specific details.

"But did the soldiers cut the children's heads off?"

"Well, yes, I think so, that, too . . ."

"And did they poke holes in their tummies with their swords?"

"Yes, yes . . ."

"And did their mommies cry?"

"All the tears they had in their eyes."

My classmate Rummo is starting to get worried about the little girl's morbid and unquenchable curiosity. "Poor little children, but what had they done wrong? And did they hang them by the neck? The little girls too?"

"Now, enough is enough, Giaele. Anyway, no, not the little girls. There was no need."

He wished that Lea might intervene now, and help to break the taut span of Giaele's attention with a wisecrack, or by pretending to trip her and make her fall, or by picking her up with both hands under her arms and swooping her through the air. "Fly, fly, fly . . ."

"YES," Lea thinks, "he's a very good-looking boy, but he is the way he is. I doubt it will last." It just so happens that the boy she's developed a crush on for the past couple of weeks is Stefano Jervi, I don't know if anyone remembers him, a classmate of both Gioacchino and your author, a charming character, in effect, capable of making a big impression on anyone, boys and girls and adult women. Luckily, Lea's is nothing but a passing infatuation, though right now it fills every last fiber of her mind and her skinny, elongated body, devoid of any feminine curves. Sooner or later, it will wane. Stefano has managed to take her to bed twice, but that's not actually an accurate description of what happened with Lea, because the girl was an active participant, in fact, more active than him, and certainly not unaware that those encounters were fleeting and unlikely to lead to anything more.

In the Catholic religion as it was shaped and practiced so fervidly by Lea, sexual relations are sparks cast off by the great bonfire of universal love. "My own private Jesus," she would describe her Savior with candid irony. With the very same casual offhandedness she handled religious images, the way they do in India, shuffling them carelessly. She drew pictures of Christ completely naked, she hung dozens of little images of Mexican Madonnas, dressed to the nines and made up and crowned, on the back of the door of the armoire in her bedroom, in place of a mirror, and she would dress in front of them every day, gazing at herself in their reflection. As she walks listlessly through the woods, she keeps both hands in the pockets of her shorts, which belonged to Ezechiele when he was thirteen, and which now fit her because she has no hips, clutching tight in her right fist a tiny crucifix fastened with a fine chain to a serpent biting its tail. She often fantasizes about seeing small animals crucified, such as fox cubs or dormice, or little girls, or old men with long white beards, and as she imagines these things she feels impetuous transports of love toward those tortured figures.

"Do you remember, Mamma?"

"Yes? Remember what, Lea?" Eleonora Rummo replies, torn from her vague thoughts.

"That time when I was a little girl and I dreamed I had stabbed Jesus with a pitchfork and hoisted Him on high."

"What on earth are you talking about, Lea?!"

"Sure, come on, I woke up in a cold sweat . . . and He was twisting and writhing, like a lizard . . ."

"No, I don't remember any such thing."

She shakes her head. She decides that Lea has just made up that traumatic memory, perhaps in perfectly good faith, the way you might remember a dream, taking it for something that had actually happened. Lea had dreamed that she had dreamed. When she was born, her parents had been about to add an "h" to the end of her very short name, like in English, but then they had decided not to gild the lily.

IT MUST BE THE WOODS with its shadows that is generating this refraction effect among the members of the team that Gioacchino is walking with, giving the impression that each of them is walking on their own. Only Giaele keeps moving around from one sibling to the other.

Unlike the biblical heroine from whom she takes her unwieldy name—a name about which she has never complained or felt ashamed, the way children with odd names so often do—Giaele doesn't use nails, but instead a tiny pin that she plants in the brains of her brothers and sisters: and that pin is her insatiable and intrusive curiosity.

"What is this?"

"And what is this other thing?"

"And who does this belong to?"

"Listen, Giaele, why don't you gather a few berries or some little rocks for our artworks?"

TOBIA SHOUTS AND WAVES his arms: "Hurry up, Mamma!"

"We're not in any hurry at all," she replies, pensively. Oh, gosh, what children I have. Each one different from the last. All of them special. "Tobia, did you see how nice these woods are? Did you notice all the lovely trees?"

"Sure, they're beautiful, but they all look the same to me . . . Mamma, come on!"

"No, it's not true, look closely. Look at them from up close."

Asking Tobia to do such a thing is nonsensical. To him, they are all just so many wooden cylinders with leaves. Stakes driven into the ground, to swerve around in a slalom. His desire to compete sweeps away all details. He'd burn that whole forest to the ground just to light a torch to carry up to a mountaintop.

WHEN THE TWO GROUPS spotted each other, they were both about the same distance from the agreed-upon meeting point, on the opposite shore of the Lago dell'Angelo, a little restaurant built entirely out of wood that had been closed for months. That meant that whether you went around the lake on the western side or the eastern side, it took the same amount of time: roughly an hour and a half. On the restaurant's deserted terrace, the two teams of the Rummo family greeted each other as if it had been who knows how long since the last time, they crossed themselves, they hastily gobbled down the snacks that Davide had carried for them all on his own shoulders, and then they split up again to head back. "I wanted to go with her . . ." Rachele complained under her breath, pointing to her mother. Ezi pointed out to her that there was no changing the teams that had been drawn by lots at the beginning. "But why not?" Ezechiele hesitated, he didn't know what answer to give. "Will you come with me, then?" Giaele asked, taking her hand, but Rachele replied, "No, I can't," and brusquely shook her hand free from her little sister's grasp, turned on her heels, and went running toward the woods, to ensure that no one else could witness her disappointment and her stifled tears, choked back for the second time in the back of her throat. Her father laughed when he saw how eager she was to resume the hike. "Those girls just never get tired," he said to his wife, as he slung his rucksack onto his shoulders. The tie between the two teams in their circuit around the lake had embittered Tobia, who now had no desire to run, or even really to walk. He got back to his feet and began trudging along, all hunched over, kicking to the side with each step.

THEY HADN'T BEEN WALKING ten minutes before Giaele asked Gioacchino to pick her up and carry her. "All right, but only for a little way, then you'll have to walk." He let her climb up onto his back and wrap her little legs around the back of his neck. But from that moment on he had to take great care not to trip and fall: the rock he was walking on was crumbly and riven with sudden cracks and fissures. After he had walked a hundred yards or so, Giaele began kicking her heels against Gioacchino's chest, rocking from side to side like a cowboy breaking a wild horse in a rodeo. "Cut it out, or I'll put you down," he threatened her, but she wouldn't stop and instead started singing aimlessly. "Stop it, Giaele, that's bothering me," and he clenched both ankles tight to hold her little feet still. "Ouch! No, you're the one who's hurting *me*!" the little girl complained.

"All right, that's enough, now get down."

Giaele showed no sign of climbing down from up there.

"Get down!"

Their mother hurried up and pulled the little girl down off her brother's shoulders, lowered her to the ground, and gave her a little smack on the bottom to encourage her to walk. Lea finally realized it might be time to weigh in and suggested to Giaele that they sing together the nonsense song that the little girl had been singing while riding on Gioacchino's shoulders.

"No, because you don't know the words."

"Oh, yes I do."

"Then sing it."

> Cecco Rivolta
> Hurt himself when he bolted
> Slid all the way downstairs
> Laughing like he had no cares
> Like a human slinky
> Only to break his pinky.

Almost offended, Giaele ran on ahead.

NOW SHE'S CLIMBING and hopping on the rocks, like a goat . . .

She leans out over the lake. She runs back because the height makes her head spin, then she ventures close to the rocky edge again. She looks down and sees herself in the lake. Then she poses with her arms at right angles, like an ancient Egyptian, so that the others will notice her.

Freed of the burden, Gioacchino whistles the chorus of "Aqualung" by Jethro Tull under his breath. He can't wait to get home so he can listen to it again. Our classmate Arbus let him borrow the record. Rummo has to make a tape of it and then give it back. Duration of the loan: three days. It's already been two days.

THE LITTLE GIRL rummaged in her pocket. She pulled out a small red berry that she had picked on the way out. She ran to her older sister to show it to her, hand raised.

"Look, Lea."

"What is it?"

"It's for Mamma, but don't tell her." She lowered her voice. "It's a surprise." She opened her hand.

Eleonora had lagged behind, on the far side of a rocky outcropping. As always, running late, but she would catch up.

"Did you find it?" Gioacchino asked, also bending over to take a look.

"Yes," the little one replied proudly.

Lea wanted to get a closer look at it and tried to take it, but Giaele withdrew her arm and shut her fist tight.

"It's very pretty, but . . ."

At that very moment, they heard their mother let out a yell. Lea and my old classmate ran back.

Eleonora Rummo had set her foot wrong and had caught her hiking boot in a crack in the rock. With a delicate operation, her children helped her to get free, but once she was able to move the foot, their mother burst out in a genuine scream of pain. Her eyes welled over with tears of rage. And she began to curse.

"Fuuuuck! Fucking damn it to hell!"

"Come on, Mamma . . ."

Lea's fright was due to the fact that she had never heard her mother curse before. She had used a different voice, this sounded more like a roar.

"Ahhhrrr!"

"Please, Mamma . . ."

"Nooo! Not this, not now!! Goddamn it all!! Goddamn it all to hell!!"

"Enough! That's enough!!" Gioacchino yells at her, trying to shut her up.

Lea covers her ears with her hands in utter horror.

WHEN THEY GO BACK to Giaele, to reassure her, the little girl seems to have a small rock in her mouth.

"What do you have there?" Gioacchino asks her.

"Open your mouth!" Lea orders her.

Giaele opens her mouth and atop the frighteningly swollen tongue, there it is, poised on the redness: the berry, likewise red, that she had shown off earlier with such pride.

"Spit it out!"

"Spit that thing out now, Giaele!"

"Spit it out!"

And Giaele, drooling, spits out the little piece of fruit into Gioacchino's hand.

"What happened? What's happening?" shouts the mother. Then she screams again at the pain in her ankle and her last scream is muffled into a moan.

THEY TRY TO CALL across the lake, to pass word of the emergency, but it's too far and the group being led by their father is deep in the thick of the woods. When their trail emerges and runs along by the lakeshore again, only Ezechiele, who is the last in line, thinks that he can see someone waving their arms on the far shore, at the edge of the rocky ridge, but he just assumes they want to wave hello and he waves back, then calmly goes on walking, light-footed, unhurried, the way his father has always told him to do. And in the meantime, he looks around carefully, an eye out for acorns or bird feathers or little twigs with interesting shapes to collect for his mother.

ELISABETTA AND RACHELE have made peace. Too much peace. They walk through the woods, arms around each other, which makes it difficult to sidestep obstacles: where one could get through easily, the other has to stoop in order to avoid taking a branch in the face, or else trips over a root hidden beneath the leaves, but it doesn't matter. Marching along close beside her, Lis plants frequent kisses on her sister's cheek and, sniffing at her, pays her exaggerated compliments, which ring false but are utterly sincere. "What nice hair you have . . . how shiny and sleek. It looks like, I don't know, a fur coat . . . a cat's fur coat. It almost tickles. And it smells so nice . . ."

"I used some of Mamma's shampoo," Rachele confesses.

"And didn't she notice that you'd used it?"

"Not at all!" Rachele explains that she added a little water to the bottle, leaving it at the same level. They laugh and hug each other closer.

"Your hair looks good like that," and with a little smack she knocks Lis's hat behind her back, after all, there's no need for it in the woods, it's cool in the shade of the trees, and she caresses the short tousled locks.

WHEN THEY GET BACK to the point of departure, from which the lake trails split in two directions, they find no one but Eleonora Rummo, overwhelmed with pain and sobbing, sitting on a rock, with her ankle ligaments torn. The rest of the group to which my classmate Gioacchino belonged had headed on down the trail to the valley at top speed, in search of a possible rescue.

"Stay here with your mother!" Davide orders Ezechiele, who can do nothing other than to obey and remain there, as his father lopes back down the slope. Taking giant steps, despairing lunges, he gathers up his children, first encountering Lea, who instead of walking is lurching, on the verge of a nervous breakdown, and then Tobia, who's striding along briskly, head bowed, wiping his tears with the sleeves of his denim shirt. Gioacchino Rummo, at the head of the line, is almost running with his little sister in his arms, down toward the bottom of the valley, where they left the van. By now, Giaele's face is so swollen that her eyes can no longer be seen, and from her puffy, bluish lips comes a rattling breath, in increasingly quick, short puffs.

"Come on, Gia', keep breathing . . ." Rummo tells her in a faint voice, ravaged by exhaustion. His arms hold his sister, who at first was light as a feather: but now those arms are heavy as lead, and his knees are on fire. "Keep breathing, girl, keep breathing, it's not far now . . ." and "Look at me, Giaele, look at me! We'll be there soon and then you'll be fine . . ." At last Davide Rummo catches up with him and tears his daughter out of his son's arms. Rushing away down the hill as fast as his legs will carry him, he yells at Gioacchino, by now out of strength and out of breath: "Run! Run!"

IT TURNED OUT to be the unfortunate intersection of a very slight quantity of toxic content in the berry and the little girl's elevated allergic sensitivity, of which there had been no prior indication. This sort of episode usually manifests only in the very young, tending to lessen with age or disappear entirely. By the time they got Giaele to the hospital she'd been dead for ten minutes. All efforts to revive her in the car had been fruitless: the architect Rummo, the father that is, had been driving with the horn blaring while my classmate tried to blow air into his sister's clamped mouth. Spasm of the glottis is what this phenomenon is called. *Solanum dulcamara*, or bittersweet nightshade, is the name of the poisonous plant. Gioacchino had dutifully kept in his pocket the berry that Giaele had sucked on, now withered and pruned, and he showed it to the doctors. It was useful only in that it gave them something specific to put down on the death certificate.

I HEARD THIS STORY from Ezechiele Rummo, the firstborn, many years later. Gioacchino would never have told me about it. For Ezechiele that had been the great torment, the true regret of his life, not to have been able to do anything to help his little sister; and indeed, to have wasted time along the way gathering twigs and stupid acorns: acorns, at age eighteen!

My classmate, on the other hand, somehow succeeded, I could never guess how, in transforming it into an "opportunity" to become a grown-up, a man. And I say that with nothing but the greatest admiration.

DEAR GIOACCHINO, this was the story that came spontaneously to me to tell, not some other. Yes, I know that it's more about your lovely family, and your sister, and the misfortune that befell you all, than it is about you. I hope that you aren't too upset. Likewise, I hope that this doesn't infuriate any of the others I talk about, faithfully or unfaithfully, at length or only briefly, in this book.

16

HAD MET EZECHIELE RUMMO at his house, around the year 2000. He was throwing a party for the tenth anniversary of the founding of his publishing house, not particularly big but quite active, which I consider to be a worthwhile and courageous undertaking, more than a great many others would be capable of. The sign of a very distinctive obstinacy and faith. It is work, it is only work that opens paths where no roads exist. Connecting his surname to that of my classmate, I recognized in him the unmistakable family trait: he was a tall, corpulent man, with a shy smile, and little patches of blond still popping up here and there among his largely gray hair. I was struck with curiosity about the collages made of items from nature that dotted the entire wall behind the desk in his office, and I asked him who had made them, and when. They really were quite lovely, and I would say, if the expression itself weren't the exact opposite of what it's meant to signify, "in fine taste." It was odd that someone with a personality as reserved as his should have willingly set out to tell me the whole story, with its tragic conclusion. The thing that made him most uncomfortable while also stirring a sort of bitter amusement, so that he smiled as he shook his head, was the account of his mother's stream of profanities. "She was cursing without the slightest idea that it wasn't that, that it wasn't a broken ankle that offered a good reason to curse God!"

Referring to Gioacchino, he too admitted that he was amazed at the way that young man had managed to find a state of equilibrium.

He called Gioacchino a young man, though he was now my age, that is, over forty, because of the natural habit of considering younger brothers youngsters for the rest of your life.

"That which is a source of suffering must become the source of the most profound joy. Yes, that's it, that must be how it is . . ." Ezechiele murmured. "But it's a miracle that I have no idea of how to explain, and one that, unfortunately, was not afforded to me: bad things remain bad, and the same is true of the good things, fortunately. I don't know if the same has been true for you, Edoardo . . ." I nodded my head in a way that might have conveyed assent, and yet it was true, and how. "Those things might possibly fade or become more vivid, kindle with light, but they never shift from plus to minus or vice versa, they are never transmuted into something new . . . No, what never happens is that grief takes on a positive significance, that it becomes a reason to live, and to live better . . . to live more fully."

Ezechiele Rummo sighed and looked down at me, clearly moved, from the height of his massive frame. I felt like throwing my arms around him. There is no good reason for cursing God. But just then the leading author of Rummo Books had arrived: practically all on her own, with her popular series of novels all set in Sardinia, she was keeping the publishing house running, bringing in 80 percent of recent revenue, and Ezechiele turned away to give her a hug.

17

OF THE MANY SPIRITUAL RETREATS that I went on in all my years at SLM, I remember only two things.

The first was the bread meat loaf.

AS IS WELL KNOWN, when you're mixing up a meat loaf, you have to knead in along with the meat and everything else some breadcrumbs, stale slices of bread crumbled up or else grated: it's to bind the other ingredients together and bulk them up. It's all in the quantity, just like in any dish. But in the case of the meat loaf that they served in the lunchroom at SLM and at the religious shelters where we went for our spiritual retreats in preparation for Easter, the recipe was taken to an extreme, and the concept of percentage started to lose meaning, because among the various ingredients, bread had expanded to take up 90 or 95 percent of the volume, and in fact, unless I'm misremembering, they actually called it "bread meat loaf."

THE SECOND THING is a story that I'll tell at some greater length.

During one of those spiritual retreats we discovered (where exactly? In the bunkroom, I think, or else down some hallway, or perhaps in the bedroom of the spiritual director, where we snuck in while he was in church at prayer . . . I tend to lean toward this third possibility because now, as I write, I seem to have it before my mind's eye, hanging over an iron bedstead, practically bigger and heavier than the bed itself . . .) a painting of the flagellation of a saint.

It wasn't clear which saint this was, since the image was dark, grim, except for the glittering halo around the head turned up to heaven, imploring divine aid.

Behind the saint's back, strapping powerful men reared up, taking turns delivering the blows: one had the whip raised high, the other was lashing the saint on the lower back, which gleamed white and was discolored with bruises in the shadows.

After we went back to the bunk room, we persuaded Marco d'Avenia to strip down, that is, to take off his sweater and shirt so he could play the martyr ("What are you whining about? It's the leading role!"), and then we started in on him, at first at a gentle rhythm, as if in slow motion, and then beating him a little faster. We pounded his naked, pudgy shoulders with a pair of cords we had knotted at various points along their length. We delivered the blows with symbolic majesty, with a sweeping, theatrical gesture accompanied by oaths and words of derision, like the executioners in one of those films they still show on TV during Holy Week, in Technicolor: blue and yellow cloaks, pink faces, streaks of bright blood on Jesus's back . . .

IT WAS A HOLY SPECTACLE. We had stamped evil grins onto our faces. On his knees, with both hands tied behind his bare back in the middle of the bunk room, Marco d'Avenia was begging for mercy, at first as part of the game, just as we had promised him a flagellation as part of the game, and then for real. He lurched each time the whip came down, even though it was little more than a love tap. Tears welled up in his eyes and then streaked down his cheeks. At last he burst into tears. "Stop, I'm begging you!" he shouted, and the authentic fear he was displaying made a few of the torturers want to stop, while others wanted to go on, intensifying the blows, until d'Avenia's fear was transformed into real pain.

Now you could hear the whistle and snap of the cords on our classmate's flesh. "Listen to me, that's enough! Let me go," and on his fat, freckled shoulders you could start to see the welts raised by the lashes he had received. Marco had bowed his head, pulling it in between his shoulders to hide his terror. He'd stopped breathing. He awaited each lash and received it with a moan, and during the intervals, which were actually growing shorter and shorter, we too held our breath. After one blow that was harder than the others, d'Avenia raised his head, shouting: "Have mercy! What did I ever do to you? *Why?*" and his sniveling broke into outright sobbing.

At that point, to give a crumb of meaning to that punishment, and to steer it back onto the tracks of the sacred passion play or, actually, a parody of one, that it had started out being, one of the torturers stopped whipping him, lowered his arm, and demanded of d'Avenia: "If you wish to be spared, then will you disavow your faith?" D'Avenia was so racked with sobs that he failed to understand the question and Chiodi had to repeat it to him, remaining firmly within the phrasing he had taken from some Sunday reading, the Acts of the Apostles, the Acts of the Martyrs, etc.

"Let me repeat it to you one more time. It's up to you to save your own life. Abjure your God!" "Which God?" d'Avenia stammered, and bubbles of tears mixed with saliva formed on his lips. It was painful to see, but also ridiculous. At this point one or two of our classmates muttered in a low voice: "Maybe we should stop. What if someone comes along?" and I, too, as if coming to from my torpor, added my own protest to those feeble objections, "Yeah, now that's enough . . ." and yet my voice was lost in the air crackling with tension, so much so that I began to wonder whether I had really spoken at all, and I cleared my throat to speak again. But the executioner was indifferent to us, determined to complete his inquisition of the martyr. "You know *perfectly well* which God! The God in which you have had the insolence to claim you believe. That's the God you need to abjure, you filthy pig. Now deny Him!" And as further proof of the fact that his victim had no other way of saving himself than to disavow his faith, he lashed his shoulders with another blow of the belt, this time really hard, so hard that it tore a genuine scream of pain from our classmate's lips.

"Nooo!"

SPRAYING SPIT FROM HIS MOUTH, like a dog, d'Avenia tried in vain to free himself from the twine bindings we'd used to fasten his wrists behind his back, the thin kind of string you use to truss a roast for the oven, with no result other than to dig the bindings deeper into his flesh, and he tried to get back on his feet, staggering from one side to the other, awkwardly flaccid, incapable of getting up unless someone helped him. Having called out to them to stop, but seeing that they defiantly continued, that they persisted, I was tempted to turn and leave so that at least I was no longer responsible for what was happening, which I had at first found amusing, but then it had turned absurd. Absurd precisely because increasingly true-to-life, real. I personally like performances, but I care less for reality. Often, that's how I've gotten by, by avoiding reality. All you need to do is get out of it, leave the room, turn your attention elsewhere, if possible, toward another performance. This attitude of mine was very similar to that of Pontius Pilate, seeing that I did not approve of what was happening, but I did little or nothing to prevent it, except to murmur a series of barely audible urgings to stop. Those appeals to reason, the kind you know in advance aren't going to do any good unless they are accompanied by a forcefulness at least as great as whatever they are meant to halt. No less cowardly, then, were my classmates, or maybe they really were just carried away by the ceremony. I could sense their excitement. Not merely reason, but mildness and pity are swept away once the action has built up inertia, on its downhill course. Another lash of the whip.

A HORRIFIED SCREAM, feminine this time, followed by a prolonged cry of anguish that broke into a piercing high note.

"Nooooo . . . ! Stop whipping me! That's enough!" and d'Avenia turned his eyes up to the ceiling of the bunk room. Exactly as the saint in the painting was doing, toward the dark sky where his Savior lurked in hiding, every bit as much a coward. Then he tried to turn his head as far as he could, craning around to see his torturers standing behind him.

"I . . . I . . ."

His lips were swollen and there was a chaotic glint in his eyes.

"I don't believe in *anything*!"

At this point the flails, the whips, fell to the sides of the torturers.

AT LAST I TOOK A BREATH. We all took a breath. We came back to earth, or perhaps it had been on the earth, the bare, dirty earth, that we had been standing for the ten minutes that Marco d'Avenia's auto-da-fé had lasted. He, too, was breathing heavily, drenched in sweat, looking over his shoulder to see if any other lashes of the whip were on the way, even after his abjuration. It was then, as I gazed at his face, that I fully grasped the situation, from a detail that had escaped me until then. Something obvious, that is to say, belonging to the category of truths to which my otherwise renowned intelligence (which was vivid and gleaming, especially at that age, during my adolescence, at school) *always* arrives later, regularly the last to pull up, revealing itself to be, therefore, a form of reverse obtuseness, a sort of presbyopia that can glimpse that which is far away but not what is right before your eyes, grasping that which is abstruse, not things that are glaringly evident.

In Marco's face, chaos wandered freely. The things that form in the soul of someone who has undergone an injustice without even understanding whether it was truly unjust: astonishment horror mortification and hope for the cessation of the punishment . . .

But there was also something else. A tautening of his features, his face seemingly split into two bands at odds with each other, at the top, suffering still, while below that . . .

His brow furrowed, his eyebrows raised high, very high, his eyes red and bulging as if about to burst out of their sockets with the effort of bracing for each blow. But on his unnaturally swollen goatish red lips there fluttered a mindless little smile that one might have thought was due to his relief at the cessation of the torture. Well, actually, that's not what it was at all.

IF I HADN'T LIKED this game of making a martyr of d'Avenia with the excuse of staging a passion play, and if I had done cowardly little to put an end to the game once it had stopped being one, he instead, who had been tied up, forced to kneel, and whipped, had actually liked it.

Yes, he had liked it. A lot, really a lot . . .

SUDDENLY I REALIZED that those eyes gleaming with tears were actually swollen with pleasure, and perhaps the only sincere glint of pain that I could see in them was a shadow of disappointment that the punishment had been suspended. More, those eyes were saying, *more!* Then why had his lips called out stay, enough? Had fear won out over pleasure? I mean to say, the fear of experiencing an even more intense pleasure, and to show it in that obscene fashion before the whole class? Or had he faithfully recited the oathbreaker?

"YOU'RE A COWARD, and this will suffice," said Executioner Number One, Stefano Maria Jervi. "No God would demand to win back the faith of a coward." And he gestured at Executioner Number Two, which is to say, Chiodi, who pulled a penknife out of his pocket that he normally used to carve words and pictures into his desk at school. Jervi instructed Chiodi to cut the bonds on the prisoner's wrists. A number of classmates immediately swarmed around Marco d'Avenia and helped him to his feet. I hung back, watching him. His smile of pleasure was angelically transformed into one of gratitude. As he was straightening his shirt and tucking it in, he came toward me, still escorted by his more solicitous classmates, the one who had suffered most as they watched him being mistreated, among them Rummo, and I realized that the marks of the lashes on the white and sweat-drenched flesh of his back were nothing more than thin, pinkish stripes, not unlike the marks you might get almost without noticing if you walk barelegged through high grass. The streaks of blood like those seen in the painting of the praying martyr were just a trick of the imagination! Was I the only one who had had it, or was the whole class laboring under the same hallucination? Marco smiled at me, still in that same stupidly ecstatic manner, and then turned suddenly serious, as if he recognized me as one of those who, with their objections, had put an early end to the ceremony. "Listen, believe me, I didn't do a thing!" I felt like telling him, laying eager claim to what I had most regretted just a moment before, my hesitation to make my voice heard.

At that moment, there rang out a clap that echoed through the bunk room as if we were in an underground cavern. It was the spiritual director, standing erect in the doorway. From his panoramic glance around the room, it was clear that he had realized clearly that in that place, until just a moment earlier, something impassioning, deeply impassioning, had taken place, and that the excitement had subsided all at once, emptying the gestures of meaning and, at the same time, fixing them in place, like those games where you're supposed to freeze on the spot, all at once: but he was a man with too much experience of the world to think for a minute that he could delve into an event through a series of retrospective questions.

Without a word, nor did he repeat the initial signal he had sent by clapping his hands, he turned and left the bunk room, without ever having actually entered it, and all of us, including d'Avenia, who was still buttoning his shirt and staining it with sweat the minute the fabric touched his flesh, silently straggled out of the room after the director, from the big room that was almost too bright to the shadowy hallway. Out in the hallway I found myself walking behind Jervi; I caught up with him and took him by the arm, slowing his pace. He seemed satisfied but still grim-faced, as if he hadn't yet abandoned the character he'd been playing a short while before.

"DID YOU DO IT on purpose?" I asked.

"Of course, what else did you think?"

"Me? Nothing. Just like he said."

"What do you mean by that?"

"I mean, I don't think, I don't believe anything. Still, though, maybe you could have spared him . . ."

And I made it clear to him with a grimace that there had been no need to excite the other members of the class, to arouse their instincts.

"After this lovely first example, anyone is going to feel authorized to inflict punishment on anyone they please . . . perhaps to start them down the path of redemption."

"Don't say that, even in jest," he said, again fully striking the grim pose of the inquisitor.

"You're the ones who are joking around, and then you punish anyone who has agreed to go along with your game."

"What game are you talking about? It's not a game, I told you that. And after all, if we want everything to function properly, it's enough to ensure that the punishments fall on those who deserve them . . . and who in fact already expect them. In fact, they can't wait to be punished."

He shot me a wink and then he looked me right in the eyes to see which side I was on, to see, that is, whether for once I would make up my mind to be on one side rather than another, and cut it out with all this fluttering high above everything and everyone, looking like someone who just happened past by pure chance.

"You know what I mean?"

I nodded without another word and lowered my eyes. Jervi pulled his arm out of my grip and walked on quickly, taking three or four long strides, but then coming to a stop and turning his head, he whispered close to my ear: "You know yourself that he deserved it. He deserved it, didn't he? That half-queer. If at least he was a whole queer!"

IN THE MEANTIME, Marco walked on ahead, at the front of the group, smiling, no, actually laughing, forgetful of it all. We turned down the large staircase and the whole class started descending the steps, leaping down them, taking them two or three at a time, with headfuls of brown and blond hair dancing in front of me, and the silence broke into the usual silly little screams, wisecracks, beginnings of jokes. It's over, it's over, it's over . . .

Why half-queer, I thought, too late. D'Avenia is 100 percent queer. Being half-queer, then, would be far more deplorable.

I WAS SO STRUCK with pity and filled with horror and curiosity by the scene of the flagellation that I imagined it being me, in my turn, who was stripped and thrust to my knees, to be whipped by my classmates. They took turns doing it, handing the rope around. For that matter, it was true that Marco had experienced pleasure in being whipped, but I had also glimpsed a gleam of pleasure in the eyes of those who were punishing him, and now I saw it glitter in the eye of the one taking the knotted cord to beat me with it. Yes, they enjoyed it, too, there was no doubt about it, whether camouflaging their excitement or manifesting it openly, and they seemed to relish punishing me in particular. What could the reason be? Was it because my martyrdom made sense, or because it was more enjoyable to take revenge on me, or because I had a greater number of sins to expiate, or quite the contrary, because I was innocent and the blood I shed was pure, and therefore precious? But what blood, what punishment? What am I talking about? In my fantasy it was all just a joke, in the end it was hugs all around . . .

Or at least, that's what I believe happened, though maybe instead I was dying and my classmates were embracing me, bidding me a final farewell, as befits a martyr.

In any case, if this is the law, if everyone takes equal pleasure in the sacrifice, then there was no getting out of it: you were either the executioner or the victim or else one of the onlookers, but in any case, with full satisfaction and awareness.

SCHOOL WAS ONCE A LONG and complicated game of prizes and punishments. When you could claim that you'd learned its rules, that you'd finally learned how to play the game, then you left.

SO ANYWAY, Marco d'Avenia. With the episode of the flagellation, he came out into the open. At the end of my classmates' violent games, whoever had lost was expected to get down on all fours and carry the winner on his back, and it required no order or threat to make him kneel down, because the defeated one was already down, in fact, it was that humiliating position that proclaimed his defeat.

When is it in a battle that you proclaim victory or defeat? Who decides?

Well, while all the rest of us were humiliated by it, and we laughed hysterically and in a rage at having been put under, he liked it. He lost without a word, and if he hadn't already been the weakest member of the class, except for Pik, I feel certain that he would have lost on purpose just to make sure he'd be put under and punished, used as a beast of burden by the victors, who were already kicking their heels into his ribs to spur him on, the way you do when you're riding a donkey, and he, as the heels pounded against his sides with a pitiful sound, a sound I wished I'd never heard, *he was smiling.*

18

BUT ISN'T THE PRECEPT "Turn the other cheek," deep down, masochistic, rather than generous and affectionate? Give your neighbor a kiss, now that, yes, would be a loving commandment, rather than: let your neighbor beat you silly without saying a word.

A punishment for a masochist is the proof of his guilt; the factors are inverted: you aren't being punished because you're guilty, you're guilty because you're being punished; and all the more pleasurable is the punishment, all the more grave must have been the guilt, until these two series, the pleasure of the punishment and the displeasure of the guilt, move away from each other respectively, they diverge to such an extent that the individual is lacerated, torn in two, as if he had been drawn by horses in opposite directions.

While it is perhaps possible and certainly our duty to try to resist our sadistic impulses, leaving them safely anchored to the plane of fantasy, why should we fight against masochistic ones? The moral brake is less effective here: after all, the masochist may think, I do no harm to others, and I must surely be free to harm myself. Countering masochistic tendencies is therefore more difficult, in part because it is more difficult to understand the scope of such things or to stigmatize them. A person must surely be free to suffer, as long as they don't *make other people* suffer, right? Isn't that what morality demands? And in fact, don't morality, any morality, and education, any education (a Christian education in particular), always have a masochistic foundation? Don't they teach, after all, that the highest value is that of self-sacrifice, to let the other person have the better portion of food, sit in the most comfortable chair, become our master? To put oneself at the service of the other, acting out a relationship of subordination, that is what courtesy demands: at your orders, your wish is my command, at your service, consider me your servant, I kiss your hands, and even the short word of greeting we use when we're in a hurry, the most famous Italian word in the world, "*ciao*," doesn't that come from the word "slave," I am your slave, do as you will with me, dispose of me as you think best, isn't that what we say to each other in a ritual manner, dozens of times a day: enslave me, subjugate me, and I will be happy with it? Ethics consists of the purest masochism: the renunciation of power, the renunciation of pleasure, sacrifice yourself so that someone else can enjoy in your place, be as mild as any lamb, let yourself be nailed to the cross, give up your bed, your cloak, your portion of food, your money, your body, allow yourself to be flagellated, let yourself be martyred. There must be a form of pleasure in the renunciation of pleasure. There is no martyr who doesn't revel in his martyrdom, and not only out of pride, as Thomas Becket had so clearly understood, and that is why he tormented himself, that is, he tormented himself with tormenting himself, but precisely for the physical pleasure of undergoing torture. A violent feral pleasure in a reversal of poles, swiveled around 180 degrees, just like the suicide's pistol in Hitchcock's *Spellbound*; to see blood flow and take joy in it, but not the blood of victims, not the giddy ecstasy of the wolf, but rather your *own* blood, intoxicated on your own blood instead of the blood of your prey—isn't there, deep down, an extraordinary resemblance between these two spectacles, between these two phenomena?

And yet we always allow the masochist a certain margin of clemency, and of empathy, given that in his spirit we see mirrored entire cultures and roles and categories of humanity. Women are sweetly masochistic, all of them, apparently, inasmuch as they are women. Their approach to sex could be called masochism in the purest state. Priests—if it weren't that some of them are sadists, as if this were the exception that proves the rule—perfectly personify the figure of the masochist, as do ascetics, eremites, gurus, and fakirs. In any married couple, at least one is a masochist and often they both are, in alternating phases, or else in different and complementary forms. Heroes are by and large masochists, if in nothing other than the epilogue of their story. Leonidas was a masochist and Pisacane was a masochist and so was Che Guevara; likewise, Saints Francis and Clare were of course masochists. Kissing a leper might belong in Krafft-Ebing rather than in the *Little Flowers of St. Francis.* That visceral love for the flesh—rotting, raped, wounded, crushed underfoot—for one's own tortured flesh that is preferable, all of a sudden, overturning a thousand-year tradition, to the handsome and healthy and sound and athletic ethos of ancient statuary, rags and pus-oozing wounds, sackcloth and hair shirt and stigmata instead of taut quivering muscles and rounded buttocks—aren't these perhaps symptoms of a raging masochism? I believe that it was *this*, in the final analysis, that the priests were trying to teach us, however unsuccessfully: to be masochists, in full serenity, to take joy in our suffering, to redeem our pain and sorrow by discovering in the end that they are pleasurable, to love the wounds of Jesus as if they had been inflicted on our own bodies, and thus prepare ourselves for when this was bound to happen sooner or later: suffering. Suffering: the great and the only theme. The theme of all the novels and tragedies and works of history and poetry and textbooks of philosophy and compendiums of wisdom of all time. A daunting task, the one facing the priests! Extremely difficult, recklessly so. Because in fact their teachings and the examples they set and the words spoken all, constantly, grazed the bounds of the morbid, of a perverted love for disease, verging on the territory of sins far graver than those from which they were meant to safeguard us. To say nothing of the, so to speak, *biological* resistance to such a principle. A young body pushes back against the notion that its purpose is to allow itself to be mistreated, that its salvation lies in its mortification, that is, literally, *to become dead*. Every single indicator of vitality rebels against the very idea.

To compensate for and integrate this penitential and masochistic out-look, SLM administered the antidote of athletic activities, a safety valve to let off overabundant energy. The young, immature body: since they couldn't crush it beneath the crushing press of martyrdom (this is no longer the his-torical period, and what's more, the rest of us were attending the school not in hopes of earning sainthood but, at the very most, a diploma), it was necessary to douse those energies in some taxing endeavor, chasing back and forth on dusty fields or climbing poles or thrashing the water in a swimming pool with our hands and feet. This feature of SLM really was unrivaled, especially in the Quartiere Trieste, which in spite of its reputa-tion did not offer (and still does not) anything at all to its athletically minded youth, except for a few tennis courts wedged between the condo-minium apartments around Piazza Verbano, or terraced into the lovely slope beneath the hill of Santa Costanza, now defaced by the horrible metro station, and if you otherwise wanted to do any swimming, you had no al-ternative but to be friends with a resident of the apartment house at Via Appennini no. 34, on the majolica-decorated façade of which, for several hours a day, there glitter the reflections of a sky-blue pool.

NOW, however, the parents who were gratified at having enrolled their young son at a religious educational institution so amply supplied with reg-ular recreational and athletic activities (soccer, swimming, basketball, vol-leyball, gymnastics, judo, Ping-Pong) would have a chance to ponder a little more thoroughly the reason for this contradiction—perhaps only a matter of appearance, but still, visible to the eye at least—between the care for the students' spirits and the care for their bodies, the emphasis that was placed on the latter, for example, in the advertisements for this private school ("It has wonderful playing fields in the green meadows along Via Nomentana! And then there's the swimming pool!"), the modern facilities, and so on and so forth.

TROTTING, jumping, kicking, calling for a ball to be passed to you, fearing the violence of its arrival . . . balls thudding into your face, your stomach . . . and shouting . . . shouting until you were out of breath . . . but still they knocked you out of the game. I don't think I've ever been so tired in my life as on certain dark afternoons, on our way back from the renowned playing fields on Via Nomentana. At age fourteen, at six in the evening, lying on my bed instead of sitting at my desk and finishing my homework, with one arm covering my face, listening to the savage pounding of my heart, I felt as if I were seventy years old, and when they called me for dinner, I'd just ignore them. I was voiceless.

With the excuse of strengthening the body, you actually extinguish it like a candle, with two saliva-dampened fingers crushing the wick.

LIKEWISE, the art lover, the opera fanatic, the ballet fiend, the connoisseur of all things, the aficionado of any artistic specialty or discipline and especially those in which what predominates is corporeal virtuosity (opera singers, gymnasts, dancers, and so on)—all of these are pure masochists. Their pleasure consists of being dragged and subjugated and strangled, to the verge of suffocating in their pleasure, by great pianists, brilliant conductors of symphony orchestras, sopranos who cruelly eviscerate those who listen to them, and phantasmagorical ballet dancers. Those who frequent the theaters where these human phenomena perform take joy in being overwhelmed and crushed by the genius of maestros and étoiles. Even when directing a pianissimo, the maestro's wand whistles through the air like a riding crop . . .

AND SO, yes, behold, the whole world appears to be, the whole world unexpectedly reveals itself to be masochistic: the whip lashed by the carriage driver, the pinch on the chin that the teacher gives the pupil, the sight of imposing women, with large breasts and swaying hips, who crowd the streets teetering on platform stacks; yes, women, though on average they may be smaller than men, can nonetheless appear immense, towering, and can instill an enjoyable yet morbid sense of inferiority, not so much because of their overall bulk and heft as much as certain elements that go to make up that figure, and which the male gaze is accustomed to disincorporating and examining separately, such as, for example, the ass. Perhaps it is only for this reason that the sight of women's large breasts and large bottoms awakens admiration mixed with something approaching terror, and the need to react, that's right, to react one way or another, by letting yourself go, with vulgar or hyperbolic or ecstatic comments, or else by turning your gaze elsewhere, as if trying to avoid a dangerous sight, or else by taking hastier and even brutal initiatives; the bigger they are, the more convulsive the reaction of enthusiasm, terror, hilarity, and excitement will be, not because they're beautiful, in fact, those breasts and those bottoms, not because they're especially pretty (and if they're really big, only rarely are they pretty), it has nothing to do with beauty, because what attracts and arouses male excitement is merely the *size*, in the face of which males, displaying an illusory confidence that they will easily be able to possess them, dominate them, actually experience a masochistic sense of submission and inadequacy. That is what their vulgar comments actually signify: impotence, a hysterical signal of impotence masquerading as virility, which may proudly talk a good game, promising who knows what sexual exploits, but in reality takes pleasure in being utterly disqualified in an outmatched encounter with those phenomena. There is no male on earth who can genuinely take them on, certain large sets of tits on women, contain them in his own hands, heft them, gauge them: they are measureless and in fact, ideally, they just keep on growing in scope and volume. That is why (brilliant intuition, this one), young Federico in *Amarcord*, instead of sucking on the enormous boobies that the female tobacconist pushes toward him, or rather, we should say, covers him with, submerges him in, instead of sucking on them, *he blows*. He blows to push them away from him, to resist that feminine immensity that is lowered upon him, descending out of a male fantasy but taking it to extremes, as in a nightmare. He blows to make them get even bigger. What with all the huffing and puffing and inflating of breasts in erotic fantasies, it becomes clear that those masculine projections pushed well beyond the bounds of caricature, those outsized shapes, really do exist, and they return from the realm of wishes, in a sense, to take their revenge on those who first imagined them, like the monsters in *Forbidden Planet*, and that they were invented by nature (which already has its own intrinsic tendency to veer toward the monstrous) long before they were invented by any manga illustrators. As with the different silhouettes and sizes of the various breeds of dogs, and with the decisive contribution of human design, which is bound and determined to bring its sketches to life, no matter how demented, there exists an incredible variety of female anatomical shapes, vast enough to form categories independent of the bodies that, so to speak, host them, and of whose profile they are a distinctive trait. The male eye, aside from any matters of erotic interest or disinterest, remains astonished by the feminine body. "Astonished," yes, perhaps that is the right word. By what the feminine body *lacks*, certainly, as psychoanalysis textbooks now a century old tell us (and this is perhaps why in recent years so many regular patrons of prostitutes have begun to become affectionate frequenters of transsexuals, and find themselves so comfortable with them, because they certainly *don't lack* a thing . . .), but especially what they have extra, those phenomenal forms, better if they're big, really big, enormous (when I read in certain classified ads that a young lady promises "pneumatic bliss" with a 42-inch bra, my head starts to spin . . .), because they are proof of a genuine monstrosity. More than an object of desire, hyperdeveloped breasts are a smoking gun, evidence for the prosecution. For those who are attracted to women while detesting them, that is, who are attracted to them precisely because they detest them and find detestable the extortion of the attraction they feel, and who therefore wish to punish those who cause it, and whatever the shape of their breasts, that shape becomes a provocation, triggering rage or mockery; if they are small, you can only laugh at them, if they are normal, you would like them larger, if they're beautiful they intimidate and one is tempted to deform them, in order to make them stop their insolent, dazzling beauty, if they are large and heavy then they seem ideal to mistreat and crush, thus mortifying the woman who has to carry around with her those two soccer balls of flesh . . . It is the breast per se that signals the abnormality of the female body, its excess. A diversity that can attract, intimidate, annoy, make one wish to steer clear or latch on tight, to merge with it, take out your anger on it, delete it, destroy it . . .

(A SHORT WHILE AGO, on the beach, I watch a short middle-aged woman walk by, bowed over by the weight of her shapeless breasts, which the straps of her bra sagging from her shoulders struggle to hold up, and the cups as large as serving plates can barely contain, and suddenly I smile at the thought of how much happiness that pair of tits brought to how many, not all that many years ago. That the breasts she now carries around with her like an inconvenient suitcase, making young boys wink and snicker, were long ogled and yearned after and served as the content of fantasies and the object of strenuous negotiations with a view to squeezing and fondling them, and I imagine how various men had spurted their semen onto the bathroom tiles or into their wives' vaginas as they merely dreamed of those breasts naked and bouncing. That thought could so easily depress me, instead I find it amusing and a consolation.)

(AS I HAVE SAID BEFORE, I have never understood the classical theory, that is, the idea of women somehow being mutilated and the envy that they are supposed to feel for what they do not possess: a feeling that I, myself, have never, let me repeat, never encountered in any of them, while I personally have experienced and have shared with many men the sensation of being brought face-to-face with a feminine overabundance, a volume, a power expressed first and foremost in their physical form . . . the ample architecture of the pelvis, the generosity of the bosom, the hair . . .)

So let's face it: the coitus that women were once obliged to say they were obliged to take part in, that they insisted they didn't do for their own pleasure, etc. (and many of them really thought that, so profoundly rooted was the commandment), is also a duty for many males, more often than not. A task to be performed. Instead of doing it to please God, as the old litany ran, men do it because they fear the cruel judgment of their own woman, of women in general, and, writ large, of their entire society.

An impotent male or, perhaps almost worse, one who is uninterested in sex, what kind of a man is he?

"Don't let anything come between you" is the slogan of a TV commercial that depicts erectile dysfunction as a barrier separating a couple in love at dinner in a chic restaurant, who aren't even able to look at each other because there is an enormous basket of flowers on the table, while in another commercial two matches are in bed together, they rub against each other a little bit but before you know it, one of them has burst into flame, burns up in a flash, and then, completely charred, bows its little head, saddened by its premature ejaculation. The shame of being unable to satisfy a woman ("Three million Italians suffer from problems," etc. . . .) is thought to be second only to the shame of not even wanting to.

At the time in which this story takes place, a young man who wasn't interested in women received only the scantiest of consideration from either sex, from men and women, boys and girls: everyone felt sorry for him, or even held him in contempt. Even those who were most reluctant to venture out into the open in that arena, even if they felt within themselves no stimulus more lively than that of trying to go along with the behavior of their contemporaries, still had to hurl themselves into it, in what might perhaps be an awkward and ill-advised manner, like someone who is shoved from backstage out onto the boards, even though they knew only a couple of lines for their role by heart. I could see this behavior in operation at parties,

I've been watching it and studying it ever since then and, to some extent, I impersonated it myself: and that is how I learned the rudiments of a science of sexual behavior, from the way, that is, that I could see the bodies standing up from settees and sofas to go out and dance in the middle of a room, from the phrases that I heard in the misty atmosphere overheated by cigarettes and music. Records that you had to get up and change every three minutes . . .

PEOPLE IMAGINE THAT WOMEN, being the weaker sex, faint more frequently than men. That is not true. Likewise, people have theorized that the feminine gender is masochistic by nature. Again, completely false. Masochism is spread equitably among the sexes and it is not hard to convince women to play the dominant role in cases where they might not be inclined to do so by their personal character. It is a typical request that men make of them in private, even when they're keen to make it thought in public that they, as men, maintain control. Women are used to this. They're so used to it that their bullying and abuse becomes subtle and invisible. To see this in action, just carefully observe any couple chosen at random: in couples that have been together for many years, the dynamic can be glimpsed in transparency behind the codified roles of male and female, even after those codified roles had been shattered precisely in the period in which our story unfolds. Perhaps some men, by allowing themselves to be subjugated individually, were unconsciously convinced or attempted to make up for centuries of general male domination of women. Male masochism, far more widespread than is often thought, might then be seen as a form of reparation in psychic terms for all that has been taken from women in economic and social terms. But I believe that there is something far deeper at play here, and that it is bound up with human relations per se. All human relations, independent of gender.

Masochism, in fact, is one of the great load-bearing structures of the world, and perhaps of the entire universe, but certainly of human society, which is thoroughly based upon masochistic acts. Beat, prick, scold, or caress: actions that differ by degree and are based upon one another. Whether literally or metaphorically, an incalculable number of people enjoy being oppressed, violated, subjugated, and tortured, with the proviso that this treatment is alternated or mixed, from time to time, with the occasional caress. The concluding caress inverts the governing sign of the beatings from negative to positive, transforming them into gestures of care and attention. Thus, people willingly get themselves into pitiable situations, coupling, marrying, joining political parties, and becoming part of groups where the members are ruled with tears and blood by charismatic leaders, who sometimes claim the title of teachers or masters; others happen to wind up in these situations through no intentional doing of their own, in spite of themselves, by sheer chance, because life is like that, but they soon adjust to it, and by adjusting to it they end up enjoying the mistreatments they suffer, and in the end, find that they love them and desire them. If you took those mistreatments away all at once, they would suffer. The burden of bullying and abuse, if lifted away all at once, might be perceived as an intolerable vacuum. And so there are those who seek out for themselves masters, teachers, doctors, guides, persecutors, prophets, trainers, and dominatrixes, and when they chance to lose one, they replace them with another. But the sweetest pressure to tolerate, the most pleasurable pain to feel applied to one's body and one's spirit, is the one that everyone inflicts upon us and that everyone stands ready to inflict upon us. Nothing could be as delicious to a masochist as an all against one.

. . . DANTE AND PETRARCH WERE MASOCHISTS, but even more so Guido Cavalcanti and the whole school of poets kneeling before their cruel, beautiful lady, their belle dame sans merci, moaning at the punishment that she inflicts upon them, even as she maintains at times a sweet and gentle demeanor. Dominatrix. Stern. Dispenser of murderous glares. She crushes her lovers beneath a sovereign wrath and an indifference remote by light-years. The entire Middle Ages, and we're not just talking about ascetics and hermits, should be reexamined by the light of masochism, here, and right away. How lovely it is to let your heart bleed, have it ripped from your chest, allow yourself to be flayed alive! And we are by no means dealing with metaphors here. The highest aspiration is to become a beast of burden, a servant of the glebe, a doormat to be wiped underfoot: which will give us, along with the pain, *"gran piacimento"*—great pleasure. Pleasurable pain, delighting in torture, high above, on the cross. Consider, if you will, the extremely pure masochism of nearly all love poetry (I'd say, with the exception of Ovid: frosty Ovid), where the poet is unfailingly mistreated, only to delight in it, how he enjoys himself! The entire armamentarium of S&M torture is already complete in the very language of love, abounding as it is with enslavement, bonds, chains, our cross and our delight, suffering, sores, wounds, fire, burns, and imprisonment . . . Among the openly avowed masochists were Rousseau and Baudelaire and Pascoli, and even T. S. Eliot was a masochist, after his fashion, which is to say, both active in nature and passive and submissive. Who among the great men of history didn't relish his own suffering? Doesn't being crucified constitute the highest form of greatness? Isn't being swollen with love a condition in which you experience the irreversible dissolution of the boundary between pleasure and pain? Equally so, the renunciation of it, the disavowal of one's passion? What else could abnegation be, but this? Always and inevitably, the dependence of one individual on another is masochistic. This submission leads those who find themselves under its yoke to perform dolorous acts that go *against* their own interest and health, and often drive against all morality and every law. Obscene, degrading, destructive and self-destructive acts. Once again, it's a question of intensity: we all feel an identical sentiment of dependency, the feeling that you cannot go on living unless a certain person exercises upon you a certain influence that might be benevolent but also severe, brutal, authoritarian, and to keep this influence from being taken away, we'd be willing to do anything, nay, actually, *almost* anything.

The next step is to abolish that *almost*.

ONE NEED ONLY TAKE a single step to lose one's balance and plunge into absolute, pathological submission. Slaves of love of whatever gender become literal expressions. Anyone who finds themselves in this state experiences it in a masochistic manner. For that matter, it would also be a form of masochism to reject love. The love that accepts the tyranny of the beloved becomes a love of tyranny itself, the emotion that you feel toward the person who dominates is transferred entirely to the exercise of domination per se, and a linked pleasure derives from being dominated: it no longer matters who or what that person is, but only what they *do*, or perhaps we should say, what they do to *us*. If the person hits and humiliates us, then we love the blows and the humiliations. Thus, the original masochism is little by little and day by day *cultivated*. Any noble tradition, be it self-sacrifice, martyrdom, or chivalry, can transform itself, intensifying into perversion, transmuting physical suffering into emotional enjoyment.

TO COMMAND IS EXCITING, but never as much as it is to obey.

VIEWED FROM THE OTHER SIDE, the impulse to make an impression upon the object of one's desire, or curiosity, in the most profound and enduring way—that is, to change them, to stimulate them, to overwhelm them—so typical of all sexual impetus, can then degenerate into the temptation and, eventually, into the frenzy to inflict pain upon them: pain, which of all the stimuli is the most violent but, more important, it is the one that can be provoked with the least effort and the paltriest degree of inventiveness. I can't be certain that my witticism will make a girl laugh, or that my gaze will fascinate her, but for sure, a slap or a punch will make her cry. Pain is a guaranteed effect of certain actions, while pleasure cannot be generated with anything like the same mechanical likelihood, because it comes only as the culminating product of an elaborate procedure that offers no assurances it will succeed. It takes no special effort to hurt someone, on the other hand: a razor blade, a cigarette stubbed out on their arm, and the reaction will be immediate. It may be that people opt for pain for this reason alone: it's a shortcut, it's a simple, tried-and-true way of interacting, to draw a response from one's interlocutor's nervous system, or even a surrogate. If I am incapable and I'm too impatient or in any case for whatever reason I'm unsuccessful or uninterested in getting another individual to feel pleasure (after all, why all this solicitous concern, why all this altruism?), then I can just make them suffer, and there's no need to be a Chinese torturer to succeed. While you must gain mastery of some technique in order to engender pleasure, whether it is the skill of a great violinist or that of an expert lover, causing your victim to shriek in agony and terror is child's play. Within reach of anyone. Once again, the positive things prove to be more articulated and complex than the negative ones. I'll hurt you, then, because it doesn't cost me anything to do so. Here, see how you like this—and I haul off with a smack to the face. Rip out your hair, twist your nipples: easy to do, now or later. It's plausible that in the context of the cruel crime I am soon going to talk about in this book, as in all situations in which someone has full dominion over someone else, it was the extreme ease and simplicity with which harm could be done to helpless young women that induced their captors to inflict that harm. It's like with a stereo amplifier: even if the music is never going to be listened to at the speakers' maximum volume, because it would simply be deafening noise and nothing more, there is always the temptation to turn that knob all the way, as far as it will go. It's an experiment. Let's see how far we can take it. We can certainly take it a long way. But you never know how far until you try. No one can say, until you put it to the test, just what level your own brutality can reach, and how intense someone else's suffering can become, how loud a young woman can scream. And how loud can she scream before she stops screaming for good?

The normal occasions for meeting girls (which weren't normal at all, but rather extraordinary), such as dances, parties, the movies, didn't interest him. He had never chatted with girls or tried to smoke a cigarette with them, leaning on a windowsill, or asked them if they cared to dance. Until that time, at private parties for adolescents, birthdays, etc., there ruled a strict code of conduct almost typical of a dance hall, but deep down not all that different from the behavior of the aristocrats at balls described in novels like *War and Peace*, except that the girls didn't have a little notebook in which to mark down their future *beaux chévaliers*, and it all took place in a far more disorderly fashion, even if the basic concept remained the same: girls sitting on sofas and settees waiting for someone to approach them with an explicit invitation, "Would you care to dance?" or the more succinct and generic: "Wanna dance?" (which might be greeted with any of several answers, "No," "Yes," "Sure, but not with you," "No, but with you, maybe"), right up to the version that could be read, depending on the tone of voice, as either desperate or else, quite the contrary, almost proof of brash arrogance: "Dance with me?"

Which, of course, applied to slow dances, which demanded direct contact, but also for the faster kind.

Marco d'Avenia recoiled from all this.

DURING PHYS ED, he was visibly excited, albeit inept and awkward in his movements, especially when he wrapped his arms and legs around the climbing pole and hung there, motionless, five feet off the floor, like a lemur clinging to a tree trunk: instead of pulling himself up with the strength of his arms, he just rubbed up against it, clamping the pole between his thighs as his gaze took on a defenseless light, mortified but at the same time brimming over with beatitude.

Even though he feared it as a disaster, in the final analysis he preferred solitude, in the abiding fear that the other boys might discover his tendencies or mock him or attack him. In reality, he felt no desire or erotic impulse, and for the sole reason that this absence of sexual interest of his might be viewed badly or misunderstood by the others, he allowed it to torment him, only the judgment of others made his condition disagreeable, and made him experience it as a fault, a shortcoming. Because, truth be told, if it hadn't been for this overriding fear, he often felt a curious sweetness, a strange warmth like what you feel when you wet the bed, which is a disgraceful thing that brings with it scoldings and threats, but long, long after it's happened, whereas then and there, in the immediate aftermath, it's a wonderful sensation, to feel your body warming itself from interior to exterior, miraculously, as if it wished to wrap itself in a hot, damp, reassuring film. Marco often felt this sensation, on various occasions, almost immediately, though, exactly the way it feels when you pee yourself, accompanied by the worry of being caught and mocked and punished, not so much for having done something you shouldn't, as for having taken pleasure in it. He feared that in the long run this would ruin his life. As a result, although it was punctuated by so many episodes of forbidden pleasure, happily consigned to oblivion, in which he forgot everything, and first and foremost, himself, regressing toward a sort of cradle of beatitude, the present for Marco d'Avenia was pure misery and his entire future life shaped up in his mind as a burden to be borne.

Since he had a yielding, submissive nature, he had intentionally constructed an attitude designed to conceal his true character. He tended to reject all human interactions, or else he would suspend them the minute they became even slightly more personal, because he knew in advance that he was bound to show himself to be compliant, which he actually was: his shyness was only a mask concealing a languid soul and a flaccid body.

I DON'T THINK that we were particularly cruel, but cruelty fascinated us all. Certainly, the cruelty that is expressed in words and images. We were crazy about Nero and the way he burned Christians or fed them to the lions. What was supposed to inspire pity in *Quo Vadis?* just met with our enthusiasm. When the gates were flung open and the lions burst into the arena from their underground cages in the Colosseum, we were on the lions' side. Burn the heretics, crucify the mutinous slaves. *No pity for Ulzana.* I remember being disturbed and fascinated by a movie where they find the body of a man who had been tied up by Indians at the base of a tree, seated, with a fire burning between his legs, which have been spread open and staked in place. As the men are untying the unfortunate corpse, burned alive and charred from his genitals to his face, one of them comments along these lines: "The Indians are sure good at making sure their prisoners die slowly, suffering as long as possible . . ." Yes, it might have been in *Ulzana's Raid*, an atypical and nihilistic Western. The movies in those years launched a genre that still hasn't died out: movies about cruelty being inflicted on the helpless. What was it that was so irresistible about cruelty? The fact that it was gratuitous, unpredictable, and at the same time, curiously realistic.

And therefore necessary. If we compared it to all the sickly sweet things the priests had to say about the need to love one another, hug one another, extend the hand of friendship, sing songs together of jubilation and brotherhood, well, those ferocious Indians who took such brutal revenge seemed to us far more real, and therefore more human in that sense, at least as much as the soldiers in blue who had been sent to massacre them. And the same went for the barbarians with horns on their helmets, or else the Greeks with the Trojans. If this was the way that things had always gone, everywhere and throughout history, wasn't it simply hypocritical to preach all those sermons to us about relations between people of goodwill and full of optimism, looked down upon from the clouds on high by a God of "infinite goodness," a God who nonetheless from the beginning of time had never done anything but strike the earth with lightning bolts, flood it, allowing its cities to be consumed by flames and the inhabitants to be put to the sword, without lifting a finger to save them, indeed, expressly ordering them to be exterminated? So where was all this much-ballyhooed mercy, what was the nature of justice anyway if not in a flaming sword unsheathed to punish, or a hail of thunderbolts, or a plague of locusts, or blood, or a rain of frogs . . . (all of them, of course, things that we loved, those incredibly cruel punishments that struck so many innocent people, since we'd sat through at least ten showings of *The Ten Commandments* with Charlton Heston playing Moses, with a beard that grew longer and whiter scene by scene, but after all, was it right for us to love bloodbaths the way we did, even if they took the form of divine justice? And what should we say, in fact, about the infinite goodness of that God who killed all the firstborn sons including the newborns and infants, just to get Pharaoh to finally straighten up and fly right?), and after all, in this cruel world, wasn't He, the Lord God, the cruelest being of them all? Wasn't the purpose of prayers merely to jolly Him along a little, to calm His bottomless wrath? Instead of going in search of Him, pursuing Him in every corner of Creation, in the deserts and in the depths of our own hearts, wasn't He actually someone to look out for, whose talons you could only hope to elude, even though you'd done nothing wrong, seeing that in those (nonetheless riveting) Bible stories it was always the guiltless who died, consumed by fire or drowned in the sea?

If you just barely scratched the surface of the teachings that we were given, a very different version emerged, another religion, a reversal of the moral.

You only had to go a few lines down or a few pages further on, among the episodes less frequently recounted, concealed among the parentheses and the summaries, such as when Achilles slits the throats of a few Trojan prisoners, to celebrate Patroclus's funeral. There you go! He cuts their throats while they have their hands bound behind their backs. This is stuff they teach you at school (or they used to teach, not anymore, but in my day they taught it—and how) to little kids, age thirteen or fourteen, and they taught it as examples of heroism, models to be imitated, I mean to say, yes, the great Achilles, a legend, a hero! Not a Nazi criminal. And just what was this hero like? Cruel. Indeed, cruel, and that was what was especially superlative about his heroism. Perhaps even crueler than him, because slyer, craftier, was the other hero, for whom we rooted feverishly: Ulysses. The king of Ithaca. Who on an expedition into Troy cut the throats of his enemies as they lay deep in sleep. And Hector's young son? Ulysses had him hurled off the walls of the city in flames. Once he returned home, he disarmed the suitors so he could massacre them at his ease, and then hanged from the rafters of his palace all the unfaithful serving women. A glourious basterd: but that's why we liked him. When he drives the stake into the cyclops's eye, blinds him, and then mocks him . . .

Then there were Tiberius, Caligula, Claudius, Nero (who ordered his mother executed) . . . our forefathers.

Nothing can be as arbitrary as cruelty.

By rights, you could describe anything as cruel that might just as easily have been spared the person who is subjected to it. Mistreatment of a prisoner, for example: if the only purpose of his imprisonment is to render him harmless, then why throw in the beating? If all I want to do is immobilize him, then why do I bother cutting him up with a razor blade? Cruelty therefore is the overabundant, anything that goes beyond the strict purpose (and which thereby reveals that strict purpose not to be the real purpose). Whatever contains no practical objective, save for pure enjoyment, on the one hand, and on the other hand a reputation to which, by acting with cruelty, a soldier or a bandit aspires, in order to become more fearsome. They want it known just how pitiless they really are.

Anything that might just as easily have *not* been done is cruel, when he who has already won could decide to make do without, if only he chose, without his victory being therefore called into question. Cruel is that which is inflicted on those who are incapable of defending themselves, if that cruelty is practiced solely for the reason that they cannot defend themselves. Cruelty is that which offers no right of reply, and therefore it has as its condition and its very reason for being the weakness of those who are subjected to it. Weakness is cruelty's favorite target. If cruelty is unleashed on the weak, that is not only because he who practices that cruelty *can* do it without encountering resistance, but because he *loves* to. It is not merely an obvious ratio of force. Weakness arouses a cruelty that otherwise wouldn't exist. A person becomes cruel when catching a whiff of someone else's weakness. And so the ideal object of cruelty is the hostage, the kidnap victim. You can only inflict pain on them pointlessly, because the cruelty does nothing to increase the dominion exercised, which is already total.

Let's take a frog caught by a gang of kids. It's certainly not to keep it from escaping that they cut its legs off with a jackknife, or pour a pan of boiling water over it, or stick a lit cigar in its mouth. And so: frogs, lizards, children, sick people, girls, old men and old women, the mentally handicapped, kidnap victims, hostages, prisoners. Cruelty is the way we have of highlighting their subalternate status. It's a tautology: that which is defenseless doesn't deserve to be defended. That is why those who act cruelly can convince themselves that they are merely applying in an exemplary fashion a law that cannot be evaded by either those who suffer its rigors or those who inflict them. What can I do about it if you're incapable of defending yourself from my mistreatment? That is why I inflict that mistreatment upon you. Cruelty is engendered by the inequality among its actors, it has no purpose or objective other than to reiterate itself, whether on a transitory or permanent basis, and whether it responds to an unmodifiable law of nature or a contingent social situation, or merely a fortuitous circumstance whereby you, now, have fallen into my hands, and are therefore *at my mercy.*

AFTER HAVING HEARD a great deal about it in the past, for the first time I saw on the Internet the series of grainy black-and-white photographs of a Chinese man sentenced to death, who is tied to a pole and, little by little, cut to pieces, that is, literally sliced apart, so that he remains alive and alert while one piece of flesh after another is cut off him, his muscles are resected with great precision, vertically, first his pectoral, then his buttocks, then his thighs, until all that remains of him is a sort of long stump, almost entirely stripped of flesh, with the ribs and other bones glinting white, clearly visible. Only his face is spared the razor, as if they wished to allow the crowd to savor the spectacle of the sensations that he is experiencing minute by minute as he is flayed alive. The procedure is called lingchi. A philosopher who was a scholar and fan of the excessive, Georges Bataille, thought he detected on the lips of the condemned man a smirk that resembles a faint, ineffable smile, probably due only to a nervous contraction, and went so far as to claim that the man was actually enjoying the experience, in a virtually superhuman manner, and that he was in a state of ecstasy. Supreme pain resembles or is even identical to pleasure in one aspect: the out-of-body nature of the experience. While pleasure and pain, joy and terror, are and remain distinctly different things, they do share the quality of being *extraordinary*, that is, they shatter the normal course of the everyday.

SINCE WICKEDNESS CAN PARTLY BE HEALED, and is partly irremediable, sticks can beat out that which can be modified, that which can be corrected, while axes can lop off that which is incorrigible, says an ancient author. The problem is that corporal punishment is an inadequate form of education, because then there will always be those who receive too much of it, those who (like me, for instance) have been given too little, or none at all. It is difficult to apply just the right amount to make it effective: too much deforms, too little tickles, none at all causes regret.

YOU COULD SPIT IN SOMEONE like Marco d'Avenia's face ten times a day, if you wanted to.

Part IV

Struggle of Interests in a
Contest of Inequality

I

NO, YOU CAN'T. No, you don't. No, you mustn't. And, no, that's not something you can say.

You don't point your finger at people, you don't whisper in people's ears, you don't yawn without putting your hand in front of your mouth, you don't show familiarity with strangers, you don't keep people waiting if you have an appointment, you don't betray promises you've made. You don't bother people. I grew up with only one oath in my heart: I shall not disturb. Ever. Anyone. Not even if you're dying of blood loss with an arrow piercing your throat, even then you don't bother other people by pestering them with requests for help. Not disturbing means not disturbing the peace, not interrupting the brief postprandial nap (sacred), the serenity of the after-dinner interlude (likewise, sacred), and therefore, no phone calls to a home after eight o'clock in the evening. In a certain sense, you shouldn't even disturb yourself. I have to confess that this minor and apparently secondary precept, just as it was first taught to me, remains one of the few valid ones among my ever-vacillating convictions: I try to practice it as best I can, and I am endlessly grateful to those who observe it when it comes to me, and thus spare me any given disturbance. That's right, they spare me. From the dubious education and upbringing that I received, what I have preserved is the counterintuitive principle that warmth, love, and affection can also be shown to us by *not* doing something, by avoiding, by letting slide, remaining silent, and steering clear, in fact, by sparing us bitternesses, annoyances, useless punctilios, interruptions, intrusions. How often, instead, the manifestation of one's ideas and sentiments, even the positive ones, takes the form of afflicting one's neighbor! Therefore, to emotions displayed I prefer emotion contained, a sentiment that clearly shows some effort has been made to control it.

In a previous book of mine, in order to characterize his personality, I wrote that my father did not love music. Now I've reached the conclusion that he considered it deserving of classification with any other garden variety of *disturbance*. In other words, an incomprehensible and deliberate violation of silence, however refined and even sublime it might be, which if anything only makes things worse, inasmuch as it is thus the work of people not bereft of civility, who therefore ought to have known better. Those orchestral eruptions, such as Beethoven's Ninth—how they must have rung conceited and unasked-for to his ears! What need was there to splash in the face of other people such a tidal wave of the tragic, and at top volume? Or the noisy dancing cheerfulness of the *Pastorale*? And the horns, the brass section? Why can't you go blare it somewhere else, and not under my window, he seemed to be saying, as if there were no real difference between the Berlin Philharmonic and a chorus of car horns in a traffic jam. To say nothing of pop music or rock or jazz or easy listening . . .

(I won't even begin to say what it was like to sit next to my father on the sofa, watching a broadcast of videos of Devo doing their covers of "Satisfaction" or "R U Experienced?")

THE UPBRINGING I RECEIVED was necessarily contradictory, as was the upbringing I handed down, in turn, to my own children. Made up of a grab bag of disparate elements—hygiene language ethics culture and so on— that are in part consciously inherited in part adopted by default and in part fabricated on one's own—it may seem advanced in some areas and quite backwards in others. Here and there I have applied to my own children norms dating back perhaps to my grandparents or great-grandparents or even farther—nineteenth-century relics, in short. In many ways, my parents were more open than I am and they certainly were if you consider the years in which they played their roles: for instance, I don't recall them ever sticking their noses into my personal business, monitoring my phone calls, and so on. Since every family lies at the intersection of multiple generations, and therefore constitutes an overlay of different customs, every family winds up being at once traditional and modern, both archaic and reckless to a fault. The boundary between old and new ways is a jagged one, a patchwork of behaviors convictions and punctilios: as they jostle and take each other's place, the generations first reject and then wind up adopting at least in part the rules handed down from their parents, remodeling them on their own children and their own times. Certain pat phrases, mindless gestures, automatisms. Systems concerning which I said to myself: "The day I have children of my own, that's something I will never do," well, in the end, that was exactly what I did end up doing. All the same fateful words, "This house is not a hotel, you know," no, I never once uttered them. If ever a family could be in everything and entirely traditional or modern, in a clear, unequivocal way, then all internal debates would die aborning, or else they'd break out into open conflict. Instead they go on endlessly nurturing and feeding on incongruities.

So fragmented is the transmission, the way things are handed down, that the institute of the family must be refounded each time from scratch, but not from zero, because it will inevitably make use of the legacy of the previous generations, inheriting from them not the best traditions but only the best-preserved ones, or those that are least difficult to adapt to the changed circumstances of the present day. If you're moving into a smaller house, you move in the more modest pieces of furniture. You don't choose your inheritance, but you can pick and choose among the things that you inherit.

... *THEY HAD HALF PRESERVED and half forgotten the old way of life, and what they had preserved they hadn't necessarily understood. It is easier, in fact, to understand what you abandon and you betray than it is to understand what you remain faithful to: faithfulness is always blind, you perform acts and rituals whose meaning you've long since lost track of, whose source has run dry, or the rope to the bucket has been lost down the well, but you certainly can't call everything into question and start over from scratch. You receive the rule and you don't argue about it, you understand it only once you've broken it. When you obey, you never understand exactly what it is you're obeying, much less why. The whys are assigned in hindsight, as a consolation prize, a pat on the cheek of the child who gave the correct answer.*

THE FAMILY IS BY DEFINITION the place of compromises, since it is, first and foremost, a territory of exchange and interaction among different sexes and ages.

For some time now, an absolutely strict upbringing has been unthinkable, but the thought is almost never abandoned entirely. In order to be able to conceive of the thing, you have to be able to think of it as inconceivable. Parents are sometimes tempted by the idea of a counterreformation, they threaten to go back in time, decades if not centuries, restoring chastisements, very stern reprimands, etc.

Screen and filter of disturbing experiences, point of encounter with the real, place where the benefits received are reciprocated, a compensation chamber to transition from one age to another, crossroads between sexes and generations, the family is also a warehouse for all the family models from the past: each one recapitulates all the families of all time, both in handing down and roundly reviling their customs. The models of bygone eras supply the contemporary family with limbs and organs: a bourgeois head, a romantic heart, a medieval stomach all animate a body that walks on the legs of archaic respect for one's parents. Those legs often wobble.

The ethico-practical collage includes an array of rules, from how to sit at the table, to how you appear in public, to the acceptable or most effective ways of advancing your career, to how many times a day you should wash your hands or brush your teeth, to exactly how you should tear off and fold the toilet paper before using it to wipe your ass, to the political party you should vote for, what god to pray to and which to make fun of. Some of them are rules dictated by frequency, others by a moral imperative that may be applied a couple of times in your whole life or else, in concrete terms, never. It turns out that the former are more important than the latter, because they're put into practice on a daily basis—the precept "Thou shalt not kill," for instance, is rarely needed, while "Thou shalt chew thoroughly before swallowing" often is.

Equally obligatory are those things that are usually done and those that entail a punishment if they are not done. Which is followed by the chapter of chastisements. Of punishments. It's already hard to establish which ones are fair, much less implement them.

THE DECLINE OF FAMILY AUTHORITY, which had certainly begun well before the time in which this story is set, but which had just then begun to become obvious, did not by any means produce more autonomous and independent people. If before, minors were subjected to the laws laid down by their parents, afterward they found themselves forced to obey the certainly no-less-ironbound laws of the market, of fashion, the suffocating obligations of belonging to their generation and social sharing. Capillary laws that penetrate every aspect of life and even dictate the way you breathe, the way you lick an ice cream cone or take a picture, the things you must and the things you absolutely, at all costs, must *not* do. Young people are anything but free, they move through an air that is solid, so dense is it with prescriptions. By eluding parental control, at least in part, they've handed themselves over entirely to community control. Before they had one master and now they have many, as deviously authoritarian as the one master was openly authoritarian. Especially in Italy: where the idealization of the institution of the family was so pervasive and detached from reality as to produce the paradoxical effect whereby the family, considered invincible, could be abandoned in all tranquillity to its fate ... The decline in fact is all the more catastrophic when it occurs to the detriment of something that had been deemed all-powerful and is still considered as such: for a certain period its ghost hovers on the stage, and that is the moment of the gravest misunderstandings, when the supporters deny its unmistakable deterioration and the protesters become increasingly vociferous even as the target of their outrage dwindles and wanes.

What runs along this ridgeline is the battle between tradition and innovation in the field of ethics; a field in which the arguments themselves count less than who proffers them: if I absolutely have to say that someone is right, if I am going to pay heed to the voice of an authority in the realm of morality, what do you think, am I better off agreeing with the pope or Sabrina Ferilli?

Who will wander farthest from the truth? Who offers the most persuasive testimonial?

Who is most authoritative? Who could I trust?

When I was a boy, who were the modern parents and what it did mean to be one? A good question.

AND NOW WE COME to the bourgeois family that this book is about: challenged ideologically or devastated practically speaking, loosened, expanded, decimated demographically, deprived of its canonical appendages (servants, summer holidays, socializing with visiting extended family, initiation ceremonies).

Certainly this seems at first glance to be a venue of conservation rather than one of renewal. Suffice it to think of the implacable monotony upon which the routines of Sunday hinge and pivot.

Something that becomes a law by the simple fact that it is replicated, invariably unchanging. The doubt arises that rules, and I mean all of them, literally all rules, even the wisest and most sacrosanct rules, consist of nothing more than those things that we lack the strength or the imagination to change. Encrusted sediments of habits, such as drinking our espresso without sugar, or leaving the sheet folded over the top of the blankets in a single width, exactly a hand's width, on a precise line with the pillow. There isn't a single family on earth that doesn't complain, for example, about the unchanging sameness of the meals, "No, but really, we always eat the same stuff!" (that complaint itself is a ritual that can be counted on to repeat, unvarying . . . just the same as the way we once used to cross ourselves before each meal), and frequently the first to complain about it are the very same women who established that menu over time with their own grocery shopping and a well-tested but not limitless ability to cook it. In other words, the "house specialties." Let's say, meat loaf. Stuffed zucchini. Baked tomato with rice. Spaghetti with butter and parmesan cheese. Vegetable casseroles soaked in béchamel sauce. Steak *pizzaiola*. Potato timbale. Baked pasta. Consummate skill, sheer boredom, lack of time, relying on a sure thing, "I don't want to have to think about it," depression—it all dissolves into a profound indifference that might itself be the solution. The frenzy for change can ruin lives every bit as much as the rat race of routine, the humdrum existence, the dull snore, the tra-la-la. Even if magazines and TV shows overflow with glorious recipes in which every ingredient is photographed in the most sexual manner imaginable, thighs and breasts, musky grottoes damp with liqueur, glistening mucus and quivering cones, glazes and custards—at home you almost always wind up eating pasta with meat sauce, a can of peeled tomatoes, an onion, and you're done.

FOR INSTANCE, I clearly remember dinners that consisted of a Galbanino cheese. It loomed on a platter in the middle of the table. Solitary. It stood, in fact, alone. Its oblong shape, like that of a large yellow salami, and the wax crust that encased the Galbanino, were for many years, until the attainment of the age of reason, and beyond, the only physical context with which I associate the noun "cheese." Unmistakable flavor and shape. The modest alternative that the Galbanino offered was the choice of whether to peel off the wax casing for a certain distance, or else slice it whole for the fun of then peeling off the wax rings one by one. The first approach might be the more civilized one, but certainly less gratifying. In any case, at the end you had the heel of the Galbanino, which you could pop whole into your mouth.

Round slices of Galbanino, fresh from the refrigerator, were the communion wafers of my childhood and adolescence.

The groceries were ordered over the phone by the maid, in a particular language. It was already a miracle that she and the deli man could understand each other at all. She used words that had only the faintest resemblance to the words usually used in Italian.

"*Cripiera*" meant "*groviera*," or Gruyère.

"*Salamelle de iusti*" were "*wurstel*," or frankfurters.

"*Chittà*" stood for Kitekat for cats; but it also meant Tic Tac mints.

Maybe that was why Galbanino was always present, there was no debate or misunderstanding about its name, at least. There was no possible error and so, bring on the Galbanino, for years and years.

And when she had to pick up the phone and order sunflower seeds for the hamster, in Italian, *criceto*, she referred to it as the "*griscile*."

". . . *Da magna' pel griscile.*"

THE FAMILY SETTING has the character of a container, a warehouse in which objects and experiences are stored, memorable phrases and photographs, all those things that pop up when you move house, stirring deep emotions, annoyance, regret, and astonishment at the unbelievable and largely useless baggage that we haul along behind us over time. The motto, "Never throw anything away": carved marble fruit covered by a glass bell. And life observed in transparency.

What we preserve in particular is inequality, and where inequality is lost, once parity has been attained, the family ends and dissolves like a successful game of solitaire, where each and every card goes back to its place and the king at that point counts every bit as much as the jack or the two. The most conservative of us all, in any case, are children, opposed on general principle to any changes. It's extraordinary how attached they can be to the family home, or the vacation house, or certain objects that, when they become adults, they'll be all too eager to get rid of.

IT IS THE FAMILY that secretes the adhesive capable of joining together the discontinuities of life; it provides identity and succor; it merges past and future with the generations; it transcends the individual. Its metabolism is the transformation of the unfamiliar into the familiar. That which is experienced outside of the home is relived, processed, and allowed to decant. Just as you prepare food, cleaning dicing and cooking it and then serving it on a plate, the same happens for everything else. When you make fun of a friend because at age forty he still "goes to his mother's for lunch," you aren't considering how profound and grateful a thing it is to entrust yourself to someone who is willing to take on the task of feeding us. There seems to be no appreciation of the gratitude that we should always and invariably feel toward anyone who makes us a meal, and shops transports peels dices slices fries sauces and garnishes. To say nothing of the catabolic phase, the clearing up, the destruction of the leftovers, washing up . . .

DOMESTIC MORALITY is the very essence of the family, there is no way to describe family life other than through the rules that punctuate it. Stereotypes, rituals, formulas, locutions, interjections, detailed lists of things that ought to be done or ought not to be done, do's and don'ts, threats, sermons, sanctions. Even the proper place to put things, pliers, passports, knee pads, talcum powder, "In the usual place . . . ," "In the third drawer from the top . . . ," ". . . Certainly, unless someone's taken it and left it somewhere it doesn't belong . . . !" The mystical principle upon which a family is founded is nothing more than a certain *custom*, a way of doing things, people venerate the way people do things (all things considered, negligible details) as if they dated back thousands of years, and the fundamental offset is the fact that *they really don't*. These family customs are balanced precariously on nothing, they are formed and then they are forgotten, but for the brief instant in which they apply, they appear to be extremely rigorous, inappellable, for those who dictate them and those who respect them. To put on makeup and brush your hair before going out, always, no matter what (the way my grandmother did). A kiss under the mistletoe, the little mouse that brings a coin in exchange for the baby tooth in the box under the pillow. Thou shalt not bear false witness. Thou shalt not covet thy neighbor's wife, much less, and far more important, their property. Always give your guests clean towels. Morality as a domestic art is, in fact, an invention—a bourgeois contrivance, something that came in handy—the defenseless mollusk of the conscience that finally found a hard shell it could scoot its flaccid body into. The bourgeois family, entirely deboned, invertebrate, is able to hold itself erect thanks to this exoskeleton, and secrete an ever-flowing

gluey stream of rules to strengthen it, endowing it with a rigid, solid configuration, at least in appearance, and a renewed justification. To expect
moral reasonings and demeanors from the aristocracy or from the plebs is
a sheer waste of time. That is why they have practically gone extinct, and
meanwhile the shelled mollusk has become universal. It has spread over the
face of the earth and it now rules unopposed.

A WOMAN I WORK WITH, laughing in embarrassment, told me something
that she'd been meaning to confess for some time, namely that at her house
the cash was hidden between the pages of one of my books. My book about
prison. Like in a safe, the cash is concealed in those pages: and when she
needs money, to give some to her children, for example, she'll go to the
bookshelf, open the book, and get the cash. I keep my money in an anthology of German Romantic poets, but as soon as this book is published, I'll
change my hiding place. In my parents' home, instead, the cash was hidden in Trevelyan's *History of England*, so in response to the question:
"Mamma, can I have two thousand lire?" the answer was: "Get it yourself."
    "Where?"
    "In England."
    For brevity's sake, England was our family's bank.

*THE ONLY THING A FAMILY can't protect itself against is itself. When within
it the unfamiliar manifests itself.*

2

T HE FAMILY WAS BORN in the groove of abandonment. "Therefore shall
    a man leave his father and his mother" (Genesis 2:24). In order to form
    a new family, members must be subtracted from two already existing
families (which are thinned out, dismantled . . .). More than originating
under the sign of a new union, therefore, the new nuclear family is developed under the sign of subtraction, the symbolic space, and often the actual

concrete space as well, is obtained by cutting it out of older nuclear families that are, as often as not, better formed.

THE UNDERLYING PARADOX of the family is that it originates from sexuality but is destined to become an institution. It springs from a seething desire that brings together but, at the same time, destroys, burns, consumes, erodes, so that in the end the marriage is charred, or the bride and groom are, or just one of them. Perhaps out of these ashes, from the gray and now-sterile panorama of the morning after the blaze, a further cycle of cohabitation can emerge, or the preceding one can be extended in the burnt cradle of love. What gives origin to cohesion can also undermine that pact and make it crumble, either with its dissolution or else with its excessive and scandalous duration. A husband who still loves his wife twenty years later is almost a suspicious figure, like the Japanese soldier who wanders through the jungles of a desert island, twenty years after the war is over.

The one who first fails to understand him is his wife . . .

And so love is at the same time the promoter and the saboteur of modern marriage. Incompatible with each other are the visions that call love necessary to marriage and claim durability as its principal objective.

Like in an opera, the theme of sentiment is emphasized. That which by its very nature is intolerant of all bonds has been turned into a single and unique bond. "Do you love him? Do you really love him? Then marry him!"

Procreation would be the one sure way of disarming and defusing sexuality by giving it an objective, an end. A sexuality that is not procreative by principle allows the destructive components of eros to dominate. The full deployment of sexuality leads to limits beyond which there is nothing but its own nullification. The erotic potential has a vast array of implementations, which can by equal rights claim to form part of a single horizon that ranges from mere promiscuity to platonic love, from rape to bringing children into the world, from incest to masturbation to becoming mothers or grandmothers with grandchildren on your knee and bedtime fairy tales—all of them phenomena belonging to the same universe. Forget about S&M games: the most perverse game of them all, but at the same time the only one that conducts its practitioners to a subsequent stage, is procreation. Fertilization-conception-pregnancy-birth, that is the chain of events that radically transforms individuals, and shelters us from one form of uneasiness (engendering another . . .) that lovers perceive even in the throes of their intercourse, as if they are somehow aware of the destructive element that lies in the depths of the amorous impulse, and were hoping to find a remedy for it.

IN REALITY, in the male, uneasiness is caused by procreation, more than solved; indeed, it induces a genuine state of panic. Conception is always intentional, even if that intention remains buried in the subconscious. One wants something powerfully without knowing that one wants it. That is why we once contrasted conjugal eroticism, as a profoundly bound form, with homosexual eroticism, rather than the eroticism of the single or the libertine. Because it would be pure eros, happily (or unhappily) unproductive. Though even that seems now to be a thing of the past . . .

There was a time, long ago, when love was banished from the family, and considered its most dangerous enemy, its natural adversary (the most classic love story of them all: Lancelot and Guinevere). Then everything was turned upside down and love was chosen as the necessary condition and foundation of family ties.

While love originates in sentiments and sex, the family rests upon a singular intertwining of blood and duties. Two fickle elements against two permanent ones. You can get a new wife but you can't get new children. That is why there are those who insist that once the marriage is over, the family must go on, indeed, it goes on in any case. Extended families are the confirmation of the institution's elasticity, capable of adapting and rebuilding themselves from their own ashes, grinding up marriages and kneading the old materials into new shapes . . .

And (extraordinary fact!) someone has calculated that the percentage of dissolved marriages isn't as high nowadays as it was a couple of centuries ago. Nowadays divorce takes care of it, back then it was the premature death of the spouse. Divorce, in other words, has reestablished by legal means what once took place naturally, and the figure of the divorced man has taken the place of the widower.

(How often have I mused, though I have always regretted the thought—whether or not it is true—that my ex-wife would have been less upset if, instead of leaving her, I had simply died.)

MARRIAGE HAS BEEN put at grave risk by love. After Romanticism it became inevitable to unite in holy matrimony out of love, and to dissolve that matrimony once the love was no longer there. When there had never been any love in the first place, then matrimony lost nothing along the way, if anything it acquired something by way of familiarity and habit. Love is a necessary but destabilizing force, capricious and uncontrollable, and the conviction that we have a right to happiness, if not to possess it, at least to yearn for it and lay claim to it (therefore a hypothetical right, the right to obtain something that you almost never actually have, rather than to hold on to what you actually do have), only leads to frustration. Marriage is the grave wherein love is laid only in the case that something is there to be killed: otherwise what prevails is a functional, practical, social, protective, procreative aspect. That is exactly why it is so exemplary of the bourgeois model of life: the aspiration to recognition is very hard at work in it. And so we might fairly reverse the saying: love is the grave wherein marriage is laid.

THE PAGANS HAD A GOD FOR LOVE, the Christian God is for matrimony; the former has a transgressive character, the latter a legalistic one. Both gods command imperiously and are quick to wrath if their dictates are not obeyed. They are both equally violent in their demands that you either make love or not make love. One obliges his worshippers to that which the other forbids, and therefore, no matter what you do, the same action will constitute both obedience and disobedience. Consequently, punishment guaranteed. There exists, in fact, as it were, a twofold hell, just as the great writers about love have described it, with an abundance of details: one is where those who have given into the temptations of lust wind up, the other is where those who refused those temptations are sent. So nobody gets away with it in the end. Much like love, matrimony is a potent but primitive magic, an elementary formula, and in order to function it has to be believed by those who practice it, right down to the bitter end, and this happens from the beginning of both the amorous frenzy and the desire to take a wife (or husband), blindly and with a variable duration. Frighteningly demanding at the moment that vows are taken, as soon as they are deprived of devotion, the conjugal rites wane so far into languidity as to lose track of even the memory of why they were entered into in the first place. The weapons that the two deities use to fight each other are sexual pleasure and children: opposing phenomena that are nevertheless descended from the same vitality, one the cause of the other. In the obscure depths of each and every act of intercourse lurks conception. And this is why, however contradictory and symmetrical they may be to each other, the Christian God enjoys a fundamental advantage over His pagan counterpart, because He includes that Other within Himself or at least tends to do so, just as Christianity has always swallowed up preceding religions, taking possession of their temples, rites, customs, symbols, feasts, and superstitions, stealing their priestly crosiers and tiaras. Thus, matrimony claims to absorb love, indeed, it is actually founded on it. Sexual pleasure is not denied, if anything it is exalted and celebrated, while being ushered toward its family outcome, which, even as it denies it, nonetheless, paradoxically, embodies it, incarnates it. And behold, children, duration . . .

WHAT ARE AT WORK in marriage are forces, conveniences, and intentions that are unequal for the spouses, and which can only be made approximately equitable with a considerable effort at conversion. They must be summed up and then translated one into the other, assigning arbitrary values to ensure that the numbers add up, at least at first, whereupon the couple should take hasty advantage of that provisional point of equilibrium (hurry, hurry!) to get married. When they both seem, for reasons that are often quite different, to ardently desire the same thing. The desire for children, protection, love, friendship, continuity, and new things, for a different life, quiet or adventurous, to get away from home or to start a new one, fear of loneliness, hunger for social advancement, self-destruction, resignation, imitation of one's own mother or father or of some girlfriend. Intelligence, wisdom, or recklessness. Enchantment, seduction, fraud. Faith in the future. One is running away from something, the other is running toward it. Not only do the requirements have different weights, but they speak different languages, they don't even use the same alphabet. Like any other form of encounter between the sexes (starting with coitus), but in an infinitely more complex manner, since it includes them all, marriage is a form of asymmetrical warfare.

OR PERHAPS IT WAS, and in part still is, an exchange. Reciprocity is assured even if the object being exchanged is not the same, the important thing is that it should have equal value for those who receive it. Normally the husband offered stability, first and foremost economic stability, while the wife offered the gratifications available within the family circle: love, care, and sex, the sex that lies at the origin of progeny, and that comes after it as well. The first, the husband, operates from without, the second, the bride, from within.

Put in the simplest possible terms: a man secures the right to fuck at the end of the day, and in exchange, he provides food and lodging.

Protection in exchange for sex: when reduced to its bare-bones essence, the matrimonial barter consisted of these primary and irreplaceable services. Let's grant that it's not necessarily the man who provides the former and the woman the latter, but in any case the outcome remains the same: at the moment that one spouse ceases to provide the other spouse with the expected service (or provides it in an inadequate or discontinuous manner), the other spouse might well consider themselves freed of the bond. The courts say it's so. Matrimony: to always have a man (or a woman) beside you to fuck. If however they don't want to fuck, if they no longer feel like fucking, then the basic foundation of the marriage threatens to collapse. There's no two ways about it, it's in the basic code of the bond, which precisely with its clause of exclusivity becomes hypersexualized, seeing that it demands that sexuality be exercised only within the confines of marriage. How then can it oblige you to something that it cannot itself ensure? Inasmuch as it is the exclusive venue of the exercise of eroticism, which by its very nature would be the exact opposite of exclusivity, it becomes a trap with no exit. This incurable contradiction ensures that, in real life, at least from a certain point onward, the extraconjugal exercise of sex can be deliberately tolerated by both spouses—or by one of them if it's only the other spouse that practices it—if not actually approved and encouraged. How long does it take for this to happen? How many months or years or decades after the wedding does this become normal?

It would appear that only in recent centuries have conjugal eroticism and maternal love appeared. Both are now considered unrenounceable elements for a happy marriage. While the family sees its functions decline, many of them delegated to the state or the community (such as education, health, or the search for a job), the expectations on the part of its members increase to a dizzying extent, as do the reciprocal obligations and commitments, whereby a husband now not only expects his wife to give him children and look after the house, but also that she be attractive and active, that she advise him and show solidarity in his work-related decisions, that she develop her own personal interests, and that she perhaps be capable of earning a salary of her own. He expects, then, love, friendship, sex, child care, domestic virtues, personal initiative, and finally money. You'd have to be a perfect individual to satisfy all these demands, in order to play all these roles.

The fathers of my time certainly loved their children, but they couldn't openly express that feeling, the manifestation of which was instead the prerogative of the mothers. It would have undermined their authority, it would have been seen as a sign of weakness. It was up to the mothers to be understanding and indulgent, to forgive, caress, be stirred to pity, clutch their children to their breast.

NOTHING COULD BE MORE MISTAKEN than the Marxist affirmation that the bourgeoisie had stripped family relations of their deeply moving sentimental veil by reducing them to a "pure monetary relationship." Actually, emotions and the accumulation of money are by no means mutually exclusive, in fact, a morbid and sticky characteristic of the bourgeois family is that love and money are constantly being mixed together, as are bonds of affection and economic ties, strengthening each other reciprocally. If only it were possible to distinguish between them! The bourgeois family would run like a clock if nothing but naked self-interest were at play within it, pure calculation, "open, shameless, direct, arid" exploitation. The most savage resentments have their dark origins in the matter of money, just as demands of an economic nature are almost always compensation for some emotional harm, and people labor under the illusion that that money can heal wounds of the heart. Two kinds of balance sheet face off, as in a double-entry accounting ledger: on one page are the records of family love, given and received, and on the other page are the records of money, income and outlay. The income and outlay entries cannot be deleted. The debts are unpayable. At the very most, a transaction might be accepted, money in exchange for love. Mama always loved you best, she couldn't stand me, that's why she left you the apartment and left me the garage. The reading of a will is an Oresteia, a board meeting, or both things.

What exactly is patrimony?
And what is matrimony?
A bourgeois life exists between these two poles.

(PLEASE BEAR WITH ME as I continue for the next few pages to talk about family. If I didn't write a few more words about the subject, if I didn't take the time to reason about it in some depth, the young men in this book would just be pasted like trading cards to large blank sheets. The house, the parents, the routines, the rules, the silences, love, money: I need to fill in those blank spaces. It's the family, a certain type of family, a type of family that's by no means special, in fact, quite common, the place that gave origin to what I'm going to describe altogether in the tenth chapter, that is, in fifty pages or so. As if vomiting it all out.)

THE FAMILY IS THE VENUE of embarrassment. Everyone knows or thinks they know, and they wonder how much others know about them, and whether they know the right things. Over the years, we can hide a great many things from our families, but still less than we manage to hide from others. We are eyewitnesses, in a family, of a myriad of indicative events, we have heard countless statements, witnessed and taken part in a significant number of revelatory scenes. Quarrels, lies, secrets that are not secret at all. We know our family members like the back of our hands and they know that, but they know us, too, they have proof in hand, a memory of things that if they wrote them down would fill thousands of pages, like the documentation in a trial, and especially among siblings, it's hard to escape each other's judgment, the years and years spent together constitute an unbroken period of observation. And once you are adults, this can create a veil of embarrassment, skepticism, sarcastic incredulity, because when an adult claims this or that, we can see behind her words and actions the child that did and said the exact opposite, or we think that we know the real reason for this or that behavior. "That's a hell of a thing to hear from you of all people . . ."

In the same way that we can pick out inconsistencies in other people, we can also call attention to the continuity of certain annoying attitudes. "That's you all over!" "You never change!" "There you go, you're always the same. You just want to be the center of attention, you want it all for yourself, like when you grabbed the baby bottle . . ."

It's not necessary for the objections to be put into explicit form, indeed, most of the time this doesn't happen. They float in midair, like something implicit and unstated, they serve as subtitles to official speeches, during family reunions, the major holidays, the assemblies during which it's necessary to argue, when it's finally time to face up to "a problem that's been festering for far too long," when we "all have to make a decision together," when those unspoken considerations hover overhead like fat clouds, swollen and black.

And yet these testimonies are, in the end, tainted, falsified by their own overabundance. Familiarity distorts the meaning of each individual act, when it is repeated on a daily basis for years and years. A perfectly normal amount of attention can become persecutory or, contrariwise, a morbid attitude mistaken for love. Every word threatens to transform itself into an accusation and we put our hands over our ears to make sure we can't hear it, discretion and silence taken for indifference. Parents cannot be anything other than spectators of the malaise of their children, something they can do nothing about, just as the children are helpless to slow the physical decline of the parents and the chill or the crisis afflicting them, between them, the kind of thing that, when it happens, is unmistakable to everyone in the house. Many young people (I myself was one) in the presence of any family problem withdraw to their space, which might just as easily be their bedroom or their mind.

It's up to you, take your pick.

EMBARRASSMENT AS AN ATTRIBUTE and reflection of sexuality, both the parents' sexuality—the deployment of which is authorized yet limited—and the more or less secret, pioneering, and so to speak amateurish sexuality of the children. The blessed conjugal sex (almost always reduced to a pale flicker) and the barbaric explosions of youthful sex (which in my day we used to describe, hypocritically, as "premarital," defining it by the one quality it lacked—like saying prehistoric, extraparliamentary, subnormal). Shame and embarrassment of the children because the parents fornicate, embarrassment of the parents because the children do the same, and that fact either annoys them or worries them or makes them proud or scandalizes them—but in any case, it's highly unlikely that they aren't going to take at least some position on the matter. The children generally limit themselves to pretending not to know about their parents' erotic activity, and yet they're curious or disgusted or else, at the very least, consider it amusing, in part because young people always find their parents to be elderly if not ancient, far older than they actually are, and the image of the two of them engaging in carnal union, their half-naked bodies writhing in copulation, the idea of the two little old people going at it with Mamma shrilling and Papà snorting, and the puffing and panting and sweating and the hair in disarray and the rush to the bathroom to get washed after they're done, they find all this fairly ridiculous. The distaste takes the form of grimaces and hysterical laughter. A father's hard cock or a mother's wet pussy . . . well, these are unlikely images, even just in verbal terms. Parents are always far too old to have sex and when, by chance, a baby brother is born, the joy and the jealousy are accompanied by the realization that those two are still making love, they still like each other, they still touch each other.

EVEN THE MOST FERVENT IDEALIST must acknowledge the fact that there is no marriage in which, at least subconsciously, there is not a certain aspiration to prosperity, to an improvement in one's living conditions, necessary prerequisites to satisfactions of a higher order: emotional, erotic, moral. The latter, which are unquestionably more serious, more profound, ultimately overshadow the former, which may be instrumental but remain, so to speak, even more fundamental—as is almost always the case with the unconfessable as compared with the openly declared. Marriage, then, has an open, manifest objective and another, subterranean one, and it is fairly rare that anyone attains the former independently of the latter. There is no *happiness* without *money*, in other words. Personal assets, in fact, are the unspoken aspect of every respectable couple who have placed far different values at the official foundation of their pact of cohabitation, first and foremost love (the true fetish of contemporary ideology, at once worshipped and reviled, and paradoxically the last barricade of the Catholic conception of matrimony . . . a conception that thus finds itself clutching for its edifying purposes at the most unpredictable and volatile of all human sentiments, clinging to that which for centuries was its most implacable adversary— love!!), but this certainly doesn't mean that it disappears from the horizon, and we're not merely talking about the bourgeois family, quite the contrary, it's always ready to reemerge, especially at the most difficult moments, in the decisions to be made without delay, in the bottlenecks, when things are tight, there it is, the subject of money. The longer it is buried, the more pungent the stench of rot released upon its sudden emergence in thoughts and conversations, indeed, it's like a corpse being exhumed, a cadaver, which every patrimony resembles, in effect, even physically, lying there in the dark, in its safe-deposit box, in the depths of land registries, like in so many deep-dug graves. It's not a Marxist sin, these aren't the last spores wafting out of the untilled, abandoned fields of the Communist mind-set sowing their seeds in me, when I state that the family serves the purpose of "fixing" patrimonial structures, reproducing the social relationships that made it possible to pursue those structures as if they were untouchable schemes—now whether or not that effort is successful is a horse of a different color, the family aspires to achieve this exact thing, and perhaps it's unsuccessful, it can no longer achieve it, it's a retrograde and incompetent agent, which is however not to say that it has changed its nature. What has done a great deal to undermine its solidity is no doubt love: that very same sentiment whose disappearance from the cynical world of today is so frequently lamented, has actually contributed more than anything else to triggering this crisis.

With the affirmation of the idea that every individual has the right to choose their own path to happiness (or unhappiness . . .), we increasingly demand that the conjugal bond be based on love, thus believing that we make it stronger, more lasting, and more authentic, while instead it has actually knocked that bond into a permanent state of emergency. How can a long-lasting relationship be based upon the most capricious sentiment of them all, by very definition?

Matrimony as the grave wherein love is laid, were we saying? In that case, better to have the grave be empty, that there be nothing at all to bury, as back in the day of arranged marriages, because that which was never born cannot die; while there can be nothing sadder than the funeral of a passion.

Erotic individualism is only one aspect of the individualism beneath whose powerful drive the family has no choice but to succumb, and, succumbing, to unleash one last halo of community spirit, emitting glimmers of solidarity, mutual aid, donation, reciprocity, becoming in other words the ideal object of nostalgia and regret that alone, as it wanes and vanishes, manages to push its faults into the background. No one remembers what is hidden behind the little statues of the Christmas crèche once they've been shattered in an outburst of rage and the pieces have been swept away. The immense bazaar of consumer choice and sexual options can hardly help but sweep aside the fair-trade flea market where gifts are repurposed, along with used shoes, the hairy kisses of the aunts, the *maybe when you're older*'s, the *learn to stay in your place*'s, the *I refuse to allow you to use that tone of voice with me*'s, the *what's on TV tonight*'s?, the *we'll work it out, sweetheart*'s, the *leave me be*'s, the *I'm sick of repeating myself a thousand times*'s, the *what do you say to a soft-boiled egg*'s?; and if there seems to be no getting rid of it all entirely, it's only because of its dull, stubborn capacity for resistance, which can hardly help but batten off the residual scraps of an ethics that is retrograde, merely biological, and therefore unassailable in the terms that apply to discourses about mere utility. To hell with matters of practicality and modernity. The family listens to no one: it would rather die than give in to flattery and insults. Like a boxer in the corner, it can only huddle in a defensive crouch, trying to offer as little exposure as possible to the hail of punches, offering only the least sensitive parts, at least until it becomes clear that the punches come from within, from beneath his guard, and how can you defend against the blows that you unleash against yourself? The intimism steeped in impotence into which families curl up like hedgehogs (a diehard legacy of the bourgeois model of family that as it spreads, declines, and as it declines, spreads: privacy) offers only a semblance of protection, the principles with which we bandage ourselves, the values that we deploy to screen ourselves really do become a burden, they crush those whose foundations are too fragile to lay claim to them, but at the same time they offer very little protection against the attack from without.

Like a suit of armor that can be easily pierced.

THEREFORE THE ONLY PATH REMAINING is compromise. The tacit strategy of "everything can be worked out." Everyone's demands and the promise to everyone of a space of their own, a destiny of their own . . .

The Italy with a Mamma complex, Catholic Italy, bourgeois Italy, and even the Italy that was Communist, all blend together, creating a hue in which one shade or another might prevail, but familism remains the same, and demands its mediation.

And finally the apotheosis in which everyone reconciles, weeping on TV, thanks to a small army of fake mailmen delivering letters oozing remorse.

The family has, or perhaps once had, multiple reasons to exist and countless benefits; in less developed societies, where the individual was by no means independent of the group, if you were outside the nuclear family, you simply died—proof of this is the hardy survival of the model in risky situations, where the individual alone would never survive. But if, instead, these protective functions are performed by other institutions; if the advantage of starting a family becomes hypothetical and its duties are neglected (education, upbringing, protection) or secondary (procreation) or performed by others (care and assistance in case of disease); if the family, in other words, instead of *facilitating* and *protecting*, actually *hinders* the individual, then it is natural that it should wane. If an individual can live perfectly well as a single, or even better than others because freed of responsibilities and free to invest his own earnings only for himself, if the costs of starting a family outweigh the benefits, then why would anyone think of embarking on such a challenging and laborious undertaking?

The family in purely theoretical terms ought to ensure unconditionally human treatment. With our blood relations we ought to be more sincere, more devoted, and more disinterested than with other people. If we need help, who will give it to us? Relations between the generations, bonds of authority, the setting of examples, ties of ideological dependency, all of which were once powerful, are now practically null, while the bonds of economic dependency have increased: they think for themselves, but they don't have a penny to their name, that is the condition of the new generations. As a result, their parents are obliged to disburse more and more money in exchange for being increasingly ignored.

RELATIONS THAT ARE CONTINUOUS, immediate, and free of charge: to put it with brutal matter-of-factness, you don't have to pay your wife for sex, nor do you have to hire your son to bring you the newspaper (or, in the old days, to dig up potatoes). And in theory, that's 365 days a year, talk about affordability. Certainly, your wife and your son may get sick and tired, and in fact, nearly all of the wives and almost all of the children did get sick and tired, and they no longer obey, in bed or at home, and, if you stop to think about it, they no longer receive orders because the head of household no longer dares to issue them, in part because there simply *is no such thing anymore* as a head of household.

THE NEED FOR ORDER, guidance, and protection. The need for communion, the need for law. Family as a "framework" that holds life together. It's not just the weak woman, the weak children who need this protection, the shield that was once wielded, in the election posters of a bygone time, to ward off the serpents of moral dissolution.

We are all so exposed, so fragile, all at the mercy of fate (a thin sheet of ice), at the mercy of our nerves, of the ill will of others and our own stupidity, we're exposed to the even more ruinous winds of our desires, our dreams, the cutting wind of frustrations, riddled with wounds, skinned alive . . .

THAT WHICH IS BORN in secret sooner or later aspires to make itself manifest. The invisible has ambitions to become visible: even though it is superior to the visible, without visibility it feels incomplete. Until He descends to earth, not even God can fully call Himself God. When one discovers the intimate connection that can link two beings, it becomes urgent to tell the whole world about this wonderful discovery, and to all appearances, the world has not yet gotten tired of hearing the announcements of these obvious discoveries, that is to say, that the seeds of another possible life exist in us. Deprived of social visibility, in time even the greatest love turns arid, is mortified; if it remains hidden, secret, people will say that it's not true love, if it lacks courage, if it is ashamed of itself—"What, are you afraid to let others know that you're with me? Why don't you introduce me to your friends, your parents?" It was and still is women in particular who demand this recognition, who desire a step up toward visibility, even though this public aspect might represent the decay of a very pure sentiment into trite, banal, conventional forms.

The traditional expression of all that is matrimony. The decisive step: when sexual attraction becomes a public matter.

THE FAMILY MYSTIQUE demands a totem.

You worship it from childhood.

It's often physical, sensual in nature—it may be your father's authority or charisma, your mother's beauty, all the more celebrated as it drifts toward its sunset ("She was the prettiest girl in all of Parioli . . . ," "He went head over heels, but for real, he went down on his knees . . . ," "All the boys were in love with her . . .")—the financial legacy, or the genetic one, resemblance in facial or bodily features. I've known families-qua-tribes that stood principally on the extraordinary physical resemblance between parents and children, and then of the children (frequently numerous) to one another, with the testimonial of checkerboards of photographs dotting the walls or else framed on sideboards or shelves or bulking up in stacks of photo albums, with robust bindings in the finest English style, and as you leaf through their pages you could also note to your astonishment that the parents, incredibly, resembled each other, in fact, they were actually identical, like brother and sister, whether that was because they met and chose each other on the basis of this fatal familiarity that already pumped through their bloodstreams, or else because long years of cohabitation wound up influencing their physiognomies, until they overlapped and merged . . . It happened especially to the fair-haired families, such as the Rummos, in fact.

Unity can also be based on money: around the family fortune, the domestic prosperity that must be handed down at all costs. Which emits gleams of light even in the darkness, even when shut up in a coffer, like the treasure in a fairy tale. Nothing could be more sacred; no one can dare, for whatever reason, to endanger it; there can be no argument, taste, idiosyncrasy, predilection opinion whim or personal critique that isn't relegated to a secondary status with respect to the preservation of that prosperity. The game of differences and personalities ceases immediately when money comes into play, that's no laughing matter, in any family.

AS PREVIOUSLY NOTED, love toward children, too, seems to have been a rather recent invention, more or less a couple of centuries old. Before then, people paid less attention to them, little or none at all, they gave them to wet nurses to suckle, they'd send them as far away as possible. Those who had money seemed to want to get rid of their children quickly and those who had none tried to do the same, selling them as servants or soldiers. When the children were small, they swaddled them tight like tiny mummies, and they left them alone for hours and hours to wail and sob, until they finally tired themselves out. Given that the husband, by definition, didn't love his wife, and vice versa, for what reason would this couple, so hand in glove, have ever thought to love their children? You popped them out, one after the other, and at least half of them died on you, so better not to get too fond of them. If your veal calf died on you, that was certainly a catastrophe, but no one was paying too much mind to the death of a son or daughter! And then they'd head down to the village, buying on the same shopping trip the syrup for the child on his deathbed and the nails to hammer down the lid, "no point in making two separate trips."

Do you remember Dino Risi's *Opiate '67*, originally titled *I Mostri* (*Monsters*), and one of those monsters spends his last thousand lire, not in the pharmacy to buy medicine for his sick little boy, but instead at the stadium, to see a match with his favorite team, *'a Rooomaaa!!!*

Well, there was a time when everyone was a monster like that, it was normal.

Was it the fathers alone who were authoritarian, rigid, and intransigent? Not on your life, it was the mammas, too, the blessed mammas who kept an eye on the children with methods worthy of the secret police (in fact, we can safely say that the principal methods used in espionage were copied from homemade investigative systems—and at home we defended ourselves against this intrusive spying by counterespionage measures of the same kind—invisible inks, secret letters, ciphers and codes, hiding places, disguised

voices, misinformation, fake phone calls from cooperative friends to throw
the investigators off the trail—methods that have been brought up to date
these days with passwords, etc.). For that matter, weren't spies the reigning
heroes of the movies of those years? The people you need to keep the closest
eye on are the ones who live right next to you; if not for purposes of repression, those measures will be taken to satisfy the invincible demands of curiosity. The inquisitorial gaze of mothers knew no moral stumbling blocks
inasmuch as they themselves were a moral instrument (here, too, the beneficent objective wins out over any and all scruples), and in fact nearly all my
friends and, in particular, the girls we grew up with knew their mail was being monitored, their evening stops outside the downstairs entrance to the
apartment buildings were under observation from on high, their phone calls
were eavesdropped on or even monitored from the other line in the next
room, the unmistakable background noise of the receiver of the second phone
delicately lifted and every bit as delicately set back down after the shouted
protest, "Mamma, would you please hang up the phone?!" since you certainly
couldn't fight back against the right of others to stick their noses into your
business in terms of principles, but only on the more concrete grounds of
shouting, that is, on a passionate, visceral level, which only wound up binding
those spied upon to those spying in an even tighter fashion.

WE HAVE LIBERATED OURSELVES from family ties and community controls, we have started to see marriage as the result of free choice, of a physical and loving attraction between future spouses, and the disparity between
husband and wife has gradually been reduced. Which is a good thing. Every
member of the family, even the smallest ones, has demanded recognition
as a person, and the freedom of an exclusive sphere of action, in search of
individual fulfillment. And that's a good thing. A wave of individualism,
free market, and emotions has swept over the family as an institution, shaking it to its foundations. And that's a good thing. Likewise, love toward
one's children, until not long ago something that was practiced only rarely
or with extreme embarrassment, has now become fervent, exclusive, passionate; which has engendered freer relations between parents and children,
more balanced, without a doubt, stickier, weaker relations in terms of authority but still, more intimate and richer in emotional content, perhaps
even too rich, so much so that the generational rings arranged neatly one
after the other have started to overlap and entangle among themselves, giving rise to issues of identification that delay the reciprocal detachment,

almost eliminating the differences that still, in so many ways, have never been as great as they are today, in the sense that the present-day world as it is experienced by kids and the way they inhabit it has almost nothing in common with the world of, let's say, thirty years ago, and yet here we see parents who dress and talk like kids, mothers with their underwear hanging out of their pants just like their daughters, daughters who are practically glued to their mammas, the so-called *bamboccioni*, children who haven't grown up . . . The gooey and intrusive love in these overblown communities . . . And that's a good thing.

When we lament the decline of genuine community feeling, the egalitarian spirit, the values of solidarity and sharing, the capacity to sacrifice oneself in order to meet the needs of the collective, we hardly ever notice the way in which the experience of fraternity, brotherhood in its literal and original meaning, has been so drastically reduced or entirely eliminated with the disappearance of large families. Before, we proceeded to found a political and social realm of the imagination, that's what brotherhood was: how can we expect such a thing to have any meaning for only children? And so we see parents obliged to become older siblings to those who have no natural siblings of their own.

DON'T SQUANDER YOUR PATRIMONY, don't allow your assets to fall into the hands of others, and for that reason, make sure, by means of faithfulness (an institute or value that is entirely pragmatic, as we shall see), that the children you raise are actually of your own blood, which nowadays, with DNA testing, is child's play to determine, in other words, don't let it happen that you slave away for a lifetime to leave part of your nest egg to a bastard. Doubts, for that matter, legitimized by the incredible percentage in the results of those exams: one child out of every five has been found to have another father.

And then, this is the principal engine driving people to work, to earn more, to venture beyond the mere, bare necessities: even the most selfish individual needs to be able to envision the handing down of the fruit of his labors in the form of an inheritance, thus fully satisfying his original selfishness and egotism, making him immortal and beneficent, deserving of gratitude. Why would we even be doing it, if we were only working for ourselves? We are almost never the objective of our own actions. We feel the need to transcend ourselves: and if that does not take the form of writing a memorable symphony, or standing up to the enemy on the walls of your city, then we might always try pushing a heap of money beyond the horizon of our life, like a croupier's rake moving toward the winner of a hand of cards. This is demonstrated by the state of abulia into which people without any prospects or responsibilities toward others so often slip—be they confirmed bachelors, irreducible singles, those who chiefly cultivate their own individual welfare. To think only of oneself, take one's own pulse, do push-ups and drink centrifuged carrot and pomegranate juice, is cloying and, over the long run, fails to produce gratitude in anyone else, and ultimately ends up depressing even the very narcissistic impulses that generated the egotistical thoughts in the first place. We make those so-called sacrifices first and foremost in order to get into the game, to throw ourselves into the action, for the thrill of risk, otherwise we might just as well stay at home and do nothing. I've never understood, for example, how certain people manage to cook just for themselves. Dishes like risotto, *peperonata*. They could just throw together a sandwich and be done with it. After all, nobody is going to compliment them on the risotto, no one's going to sit in rapt admiration of the dome of their soufflé before deflating it with the tines of a fork. Almost all the things we do, we do to others or for others, but it's not altruism by any stretch of the imagination, rather it's the need to express ourselves, to make ourselves seen and heard, we have a desperate need for an audience, clients, recipients, guinea pigs, beneficiaries, and victims of our actions . . . whip, chop, mince, sauté, flambé, lard, stuff . . . *and all for yourself?* Just the names of these various culinary techniques lose their meaning. Any gesture that rises above the level of the most elementary is inevitably performed *toward* someone.

Parents are the audience for whom the children tread the stage every evening. Siblings are the audience for their siblings. And then the performance is put on with roles reversed, and the actors go to take their orchestra seats.

3

THE RULES IN A FAMILY are dictated by financial resources. If they are abundant, then they tend to lay out what you *can* do. If they are restricted, they prescribe that which you *must* do. The family's patrimony is the beginning of everything; the individual always comes on stage after the show has begun. The patrimony is the very purpose of the family, to be protected and increased, or else, in some cases, to be torn to shreds, squandered, destroying it: in the chronicles of lines of inheritance, stories are handed down of legendary spendthrifts, poker-playing uncles, or others who spent freely on women, grandfathers with crazy entrepreneurial impulses, who bet it all on engines that ran on water or on a business selling boiling ice, champions of carelessness or full-fledged embezzlers, who ran through the whole sum in a single night, or in a decade or so, carving hemorrhages into the destinies of their descendants. In other words, people who influenced our lives long before we even came into the world. A bankrupt forebear swings from the ceiling in the gallery of every family. Next to him there are, instead, illustrious paranoids who spent an entire lifetime obsessed with the defense of their patrimony. Let us honor their neuroses, thanks to which we can nowadays purchase our salmon presliced.

The scope of the economic damage that we can tolerate gives the exact measurement of our wealth. True luxury would be to blithely ignore any such harm, or to leave unpunished whoever inflicts that loss upon us through carelessness or incompetence, especially if we are talking about ourselves: we really would like to be able to pardon ourselves with some noble gesture. But in order to be able to afford the nonchalant elegance of epic squandering, those who scraped together the fortune in the first place must have come before us. Much of the cohesiveness of the bourgeois family springs up (or until some time ago sprang up) around the multiplication and handing down of assets. I had a classmate named Busoni, number four in the class ledger after your author, Arbus, and Barnetta, who was obliged to hurry home to drink a toast with his father every time the old man landed a deal. It happened a number of times: after a phone call he'd turn serious, apologize to his friends, and then hurry away home to pop the cork on the champagne. With his father, his mother, and his siblings, I'd imagine, gathered in the living room, or perhaps in the kitchen, close to the fridge. The ceremony might seem grotesque but, after all, if you think about it, why not? It wasn't really all that strange: that something should have been shown off and celebrated in order to cement the bond among the family members, allowing them to join in as participants in their father's success, was in contrast carefully concealed in my family, censored, unspeakable, and barely even visible through the indirect forms it took such as paintings or porcelain: earnings, profits. What was vulgar was not, of course, the fact of getting money—but to display it, *that* unquestionably smacked of great vulgarity. It is typical of bourgeois families both to show off money and the prosperity that comes with it, and to conceal it or, rather, to make it implicit, refer to it only discreetly: we have it, thank heavens, but we are not to speak of it. *Ever.*

IN THOSE DAYS, bourgeois families *were* the bourgeoisie, they represented their class in its entirety. You cannot imagine or illustrate bourgeois life as anything other than family life, nor can you feature the bourgeois home except as a residence designed to house a family. The alleged individualism of the middle class in its original form presents itself as an attribute of the nuclear family. The family is the true bourgeois subject, much more than the individual people who make up that family, it is the organism struggling to attain its ultimate affirmation, the purveyor of a supremely selfish and combative vision of the world. And it cannot be identified in the single leadership figure of the father, old-school style, or be reckoned up in terms of the mere addition of individuals that compose it: in other words, the bourgeois family possesses a very specific personality and strength. To say nothing of its vices and diseases.

I REMEMBER HOW I once tried out the scornful Marxist vernacular while arguing with my father. The subject was political engagement. He didn't consider it to be necessary nor of any superior moral worth in comparison with the activity of honestly pursuing one's own personal interests. In response to his somewhat peeved question: "What if someone thinks of nothing in life but his own family, his children?" "Then he's a filthy pig," I replied.

THE CONSTITUENT ELEMENTS of a family are: a) the people and b) the things, plus a third category that bonds the first two together, and that is c) the relations, which in their turn fall into one of three types: 1) relations between people and other people, 2) between people and things, and last of all, 3) again between people and other people but this time as a function of, or through, the property owned. This last relationship, then, can be described as between "proprietors." That is, between people who own things. This relationship is usually a competitive one, and therefore to prevent conflicts within the traditional family no one, except for the head of the family, possessed anything of their own, nor could they claim any financial independence (in a quick aside we might note that those who have no economic independence have no independence at all). It is the head of the family who, at his own discretion, distributes money to the other family members ("loosens the purse strings" is the apt expression—coughs up, antes up, or the equivalents in Italian: *sganciare*, or unhook, *scucire*, or unstitch). Things don't change much if the distributions are generous or miserly, if they take place in wealthy or poverty-stricken settings. A vow of poverty, so to speak, on the monastic model, can regulate a wealthy family, if that which passes through your hands can never accurately be called yours, truly your own. Property means just that, an exclusive possession, proper to one person. At my house, nothing could be said to belong to anyone and everything belonged to everyone. The sense of property was abolished. Selfishness and egotism were unthinkable. If a Vespa was purchased for, let's say, me, then that Vespa, even if I drove it, implicitly belonged to my brothers, who would have the right to use it whenever they wanted. Gifts, too, were often collective in nature. In our minds and, actually, in cold hard fact, *everything* belonged to my father: it originated with him and was endowed by him to the rest of us only in usufruct, if at all. That fact led my brothers and me to encounter some serious issues of both a practical and a symbolic nature with our management of the family estate after the death of the head of the family, whereupon the estate was split up and entrusted to each of us. It wasn't a matter of conflict among us, as is so often the case, but quite the opposite, a matter of confusion, of blurring, as if that patrimony were still held in common and had remained intact. Who is supposed to pay for what, who is in charge of what, who is responsible for . . . ? Even the documentation, twenty years after my father's death and the divvying up of the property, all of the documentation pertaining to the estate is held together in one place, and not out of any bitterness or regret. When I got married and I had to file a declaration making all my property jointly owned with my wife, I literally owned *nothing.* Maybe a motor scooter. Even now I have a hard time referring to the property that my father left me in his will as "mine." I continue to think of it all as belonging to him and therefore, inasmuch as his, indirectly *ours.* But certainly not *mine.* A truly singular kind of communism. The one exception to that regime are the gifts my father gave my mother: dresses, shoes, jewelry, all those were, obviously, jealously and morbidly personal. But there we're not talking about family, we're talking about love.

SO, ARE WE TO ASSUME that succession, the hereditary transmission of property, is the principal factor holding the bourgeois family together? It might be the motive driving the hard work of the head of the family, but in point of fact, it can actually constitute an element of division and enmity, quite the opposite of cohesion, since every family is destined to split up into new families that the children will form with perfect strangers, who might be viewed as saboteurs of the family's original, underlying integrity.

By the essentially egalitarian nature of the right of inheritance, the patrimony of a bourgeois family is something that, it is well known, will eventually be split up, shared out: it exists as an intact structure only formally, and for no more than a generation, whereupon it is dismembered. Dismemberment is inscribed in its makeup from day one: that is the fate assigned to it.

THE TRANSCENDENTAL IMPULSE in the accumulation of a patrimony also manifests itself in the exquisitely religious nature of its transmission, the way it's handed down. The last will and testament in which that transmission is formalized and sealed is a gift that a dying person bestows upon the living to secure for themselves a serene and untroubled journey into the afterlife. Let's call it a form of restitution, an offering . . . The dying man performs that act not out of any particular generosity or as a celebration of self, or even out of attachment to his own flesh and blood, but rather as a preliminary step of separation, the unclothing of the earthly aspects of oneself. While a powerful man once took all his most precious goods with him so that his soul presented itself to the gods of the underworld decked out and richly adorned, he now has to show up naked. At the very instant in which he relinquishes his possessions, he is given one last opportunity to make a great show of equanimity: the drafting of his will. I remember as if it were yesterday the meticulousness with which my father calculated and recalculated the portioning out of his belongings, applying countless different parameters, and on the basis of these reckonings he created a testamentary disposition that ensured that each of his heirs was given the right amount. The right amount? The problem is that the right amount never remains right over the course of time: it oscillates, it varies, in order to update it would require an endless array of reparations and compensations. In the last few months of his life, it had become an obsession, the sole occupation of his aggravated soul, the one paradoxical form of faith in an afterlife, since, riddled with metastases as he was, he might just as easily have ignored entirely the problem of whether the parking space in the basement on Via Parenzo was to go to me or my brother.

He would sit in his dressing gown at the table where he usually played hands of solitaire, but instead of a deck of cards he would have a calculator and graph paper notepads, which he'd fill with dense, crabbed calculations. In pencil. He'd work the numbers over and over again, a thousand times. He'd tirelessly update his estimations, some of which could be attained by simple and reasonably objective calculations, valid for the immediate present, while others were more evanescent, fluctuating, the fruit of predictions that necessarily extended out many years after his impending death, and there the margins of subjective guesswork were proportional to the level of anguish unleashed at the thought of his own passing, his own nonexistence. In the throes of a scrupulousness that verged on the hysterical, he strove to exert a mastery over time that was well out of his reach. It's very much like someone tied to a chair trying to seize an object that is several yards away. The right amount is never the product of a mathematical calculation, otherwise all you would have to do is divide it all by four and your job would be done.

And instead: predispose correctives and amortizations, hypothesize devaluations, adjust the shares in accordance with the personal profile of each heir; whose needs were never the same, according to age, sex, aspiration . . .

How can you determine if a son or daughter will or won't be successful? Will he make his fortune, will he earn money by the bucket, will she marry a rich man, will he marry a rich woman, and then maybe be divorced, will he end up living on the street, will he commit suicide, will he lead a sober and dignified life with just a hint of squalor, will he fail miserably at everything he sets out to do, will he set himself goals beyond his scope or beneath his abilities, attaining them with too little effort and even less satisfaction, will he squander the money left him by his daddy, eating away at the estate, in small mouthfuls, until nothing is left but the crumbs . . . will he become a rock star, a surgeon with gifted hands and bank accounts in Luxembourg, a highly respected university professor . . .

My father spent the last hours of his life tapping numbers into a virtual calculator that, after his death, proved to be fallacious, through no fault of his own, but because reality never stands around waiting, and more important, the numbers that you use to measure an estate, an inheritance, never really stand still for a second, they zip up and down like rubber balls.

Some values dropped and others remained there, motionless, or else skyrocketed.

OF THE RICHES that belong to us unjustly, we are the usurpers and thieves; of those to which we instead have fair and just title, we are only the temporary managers. There exists a scrupulous and exacting ethical standard according to which all the things we own are nothing but loans, which we are called upon to return the day we die, the way you return your room key when you check out of a hotel. We inhabited it, and nothing more. Even though we think the exact opposite of him, in other words, that he is attached to his possessions, I believe that the bourgeois has to a very large extent actually adopted the morality in question. He is bound and obliged, on point of death, to return his patrimony, *amplified and enhanced*, or at the very least, identical, certainly undiminished with respect to what was consigned to him; that would be worse than humiliating, it would be nefarious. If that happens, then what was the point of his life? It we accept that nothing actually belongs to us, it certainly doesn't mean that we're not expected to scrupulously preserve and increase the gifts that fate assigned to us. What renders imperative the duty of accumulation, and what defends the bourgeois against any and all negative considerations concerning the vanity of attachment to material things, is in fact the powerful awareness that the restitution of that patrimony at the end of his life will not benefit some blurry and indistinct whole, say, the world or society at large, but his *own children*. Even his own body, his corpse, will be assigned to his children. A bourgeois without money and without children is by definition no longer a bourgeois, he has no title to the name, and if a bourgeois isn't a bourgeois then he isn't really even a human being.

MY FATHER'S ANCIENT, sublime, simple gesture of reaching for his wallet. I can't remember, I think, a single time when he said no. At the very most, a faint skeptical smile, a hint of sarcasm accompanied by the pride of always, and in every case, being able to *fork over*. To be ready with cash in pocket, rolls of bills fresh from the bank, to satisfy any and every need, whether for my mother or anyone else in the house who might need cash. Ready to lay down "cash on the barrelhead." It seemed endless, to us children, the wads of money folded in the back pockets of his trousers, bound together in bundles with yellow rubber bands, or else tucked away inside the ample covers of Trevelyan's *History of England* (who knows why that book out of all others), as I wrote a few pages back, which, moreover, was a book of mine,

I had received it as a gift for my fourteenth birthday. Who would dare give Trevelyan to a fourteen-year-old boy nowadays, instead of, say, a PlayStation, even if that boy was a shy and bookish grind, without expecting to have it flung at their head the minute the gift was unwrapped . . . ? Who can imagine what my parents supposed, what they expected from me, when they gave me that demanding, burdensome gift. I read Trevelyan's history from the first line to the last without the slightest idea of why I was doing it: perhaps the best way to read it. The War of the Roses pierced my chest and settled down into my kidneys, and the countless Henrys stood watch around the perimeter of my bedroom, menacing and bloody. Once merely a book, it later became the household coffers, our family treasure chest. The cash was stuffed into the middle of that book, somewhere around the Gunpowder Plot. Whenever you took out a banknote or two, you couldn't help but read details about how Guy Fawkes was hanged and quartered. "Remember remember / the Fifth of November . . ." The money available to us was in fact far from endless, as it had once seemed, and I have the sensation it must have dwindled in the last years of my father's life, from a certain point onward the cycle reversed—more money went out than came in. A tendency that only accelerated after his death.

In the old denominations, lira pound peseta, you could sense the physical weight of money, a bag full of coins that was untied and reknotted. "Disburse," related to "purse," now there's a word with heft.

THE BOURGEOIS FAMILY is destined by its very essence to crumble and collapse. Both its mission and its pride consist in withstanding time and the impulses of disintegration, in proving solid and protective, internally as well as to the eyes of strangers, while at the same time its nature is to fall apart: an organism that battles against the very disease that is inscribed in its genetic code. Little by little, it loses elasticity, it turns rigid, and while to the untutored eye it appears more stubborn and refractory, in reality it has become fragile, delicate: it has begun to disintegrate. The death agony may feature accents and episodes that are variously heroic or ridiculous, heartbreaking or grotesque, and the course of the illness may be so slow that it is not perceived at all and is taken for complete health and silently handed down to the following generation, so that the children of a highly respected family, when it comes their time to set up housekeeping, engender ramshackle, disastrous relationships. The children who were brought up wearing white kneesocks and pageboy haircuts, with a wise mother who regulated the flow of dirty clothing with a sorcerer's touch, well, those very same children are the ones who so often turn out to be misfits, who reject wholesale the model of happiness offered them by their parents, or else ape that model in a pathetic fashion.

4

TODAY, July 3, 2008, someone called me up to ask if I wished to be the subject of a literary quiz on the radio: my name was supposed to be the "right answer," the listeners would be given hints concerning my books, over the course of the broadcast, at first vague but increasingly revealing. I declined the offer. The official reason is that I dislike culture quizzes, and that's true, I'm not fond of them.

The real reason, though, is that I was afraid I might not be recognized. Maybe no one would guess.

I'd like it if my reputation as a writer were sufficiently great that I could hope to have a street named after me in my city, just a little, out-of-the-way street, as long as it's not one of those streets newly built on the outskirts, no, I'd like it if my name on the corner replaced another name, for example, that a street should be renamed Via Edoardo Albinati that is currently Via Nino Oxilia, a small cross street of Viale Parioli in Rome, where my grandmother bought socks on the market stands and would give them to me after repackaging them in wrappers from Schostal, the well-known linen and underwear shop on Via del Corso. In fact, she had the drawers of her credenza full of bags and packages from Schostal and other shops such as Frette or Caccetta, neatly folded and stacked away, the hallmark of a generation that, in a gift, cared at least as much about the container as the content. I discovered the fact one Christmas, when the socks that she had given me turned out to be far too big, and I told my grandmother, "It doesn't matter," that I'd just go by Schostal and exchange them, but she insisted on taking back the gift package, "Let me go, I'll be glad to go . . . ," "Don't worry about it, Grandma, all the way over to Via del Corso . . . give them to me, come on, I'll take care of it," but she wouldn't relinquish the package, "What's got into you, I told you that I'd go myself!" she was losing her temper until she was finally forced to confess.

"It's just that, well, you see . . . they're not from Schostal."

"What do you mean?"

"They're just not."

She let go of the bag. And then she told the truth, which for someone like my grandmother really must have been quite a comedown. Good manners require that the truth should *always* be concealed. Inside I was laughing, proud of her contrivance. Devilish old woman. Certainly, the notion of a certain Turin-based/Parioli-inflicted respectability that she had chosen to defend with the trick of the bag from Schostal had been spoiled by the revelation (just think: the market stands on Via Oxilia! The ones that these days are run by the Sinhalese, indeed, they're long gone, the market has closed down, all that survives are the remainders shops selling DVDs), but in and of itself it was perfect, indeed, that scheme delighted her. Since she was hardly made of money, to save money on the purchase, and then trick it out so decorously, adding nothing more than a glittering shell, the lovely gold-appliquéd bags from the shops in the center of town, and all just to obtain . . . that hint of distinction.

Something formally impeccable.

Moreover, the socks weren't badly made at all. I still have them in my drawer, immense, beige, like size 11s.

NINO OXILIA DIED at the Battle of Caporetto, before he even turned thirty. He'd written plays and made movies when the film industry was just getting started. In his soldier's rucksack he had some poetry, later published in a book that came out posthumously, *Gli orti*. He was considered a genius. Well, I could have a marker with my name there, for a hundred years or so, roughly as long as Oxilia, and then I could be replaced by another notable.

EVEN THOUGH WE TEND to think of the wealthy residents of Parioli and the QT as rich moneybags, for the most part they were simply dignified specimens of the middle class.

It is true that they had an affection that verged on a morbid obsession for good labels and trademarks, but an equally strong fondness for counterfeits, which allow you to save 50 percent on the price.

IN ANY FAMILY, trouble is caused to an equal extent by that which is said and that which is left unstated. It is said that it takes three generations to "make" a psychosis. At my house, the second of the two errors was committed: thanks to a stubborn and actually admirable practice of discretion, understatement, and shame taken to a sovereign and almost mystical measure of indifference toward all dramas, one's own and those of others, a vocation for self-control that could be broken only by some unexpected accident, like a condom breaking during sex, very powerful cases of maladjustment developed . . . But all family novels are necessarily neurotic, and equally neurotic is anyone who assembles one making use of an album compiled of lists of the good and the bad and the mediocre, the dramatic, "money shot" scenes, and the need for meaning so typical of those who believe it is right there, within reach.

THE BOURGEOIS FAMILY was once composed not only of blood relatives but also messenger boys, chauffeurs, clothing pressers, and housekeepers. Perhaps the household serving women represented the family even more essentially than did their employers—the essence of its continuity.

My mother used to go out to the small towns and villages to find her housekeepers. Once she went all the way to Sardinia and returned home with not one but two young Sardinian women, diminutive and dark-complected, practically identical, Saveria and Filomena, known as Mena—I think they were probably sisters—who beat me silly when they discovered I had ogled them secretly through the keyhole while they were taking their bath together, in one of those small tubs with a step/bench so you could wash yourself while seated, and yet they were so tiny that they both fit in together, one of them sitting on the step. I don't know what mistake I committed, how I was found out, maybe I coughed. How I wished that keyhole were bigger! I couldn't see much, but I did see enough to learn how women were made, their bushes of hair, and they had three each, therefore three black tufts dripping water while Saveria and Mena took turns swiveling to allow themselves to be sprayed down, in front and back, one of them gripping the hand-held showerhead, and the other soaping up her bushes, moving her shower sponge from one tuft to the next, scrubbing hard as if she were determined to tear them out, uproot them. I still don't know how they were able to hear me breathing with all that splashing water.

AT HOME, fully entitled members of my family lived ate slept and worked until that title was revoked by dismissal. Aside from performing household tasks, the presence of the domestic staff also helped to establish an image of decorum and prestige: for example, a cook, a presser, a chauffeur.

For that same reason, we had a married couple in our service for only a couple of months. It became clear almost immediately that the man of the couple was superfluous, he had nothing to do in the house, much less outside, since my father had no need of a driver and the school was right around the corner, so there was no need to pick us up or take us there. The few times I saw this handsome gentleman with his head of white hair waiting for me outside the gate at SLM, with a deferential demeanor, I was so ashamed that I asked my parents please not to send him again.

(THE REASON A PRIORI for household service staff: the low cost of labor. The reason a posteriori: the multiplicity of family jobs performed.)

I REMEMBER that in the conversations of well-to-do women, their favorite topic was their household staff. For those who can still afford to have them today, that hasn't changed. Certain matrons, chatting with their girlfriends, amuse themselves by depicting their servants with all there is about them of the curious or the ridiculous, or they even speak of them as if they were their worst enemies, living under the same roof by some sort of tragic mishap. Others, instead, are exaggeratedly fond of their maid, whom they love to describe as a "pearl," their "salvation," a "blessed hand," seriously "irreplaceable," and they are so possessive of them that no one had better dream of trying to "poach them" or "steal them away"—as if they were a necklace or a pair of earrings.

When I was a child and I listened to them chatter, I imagined that the most terrible job in the world had to be the "changing of the armoires," which was what they called the seasonal rotation of the wardrobes. It was an operation run like a military campaign. And I wondered: Why is the queen in chess the most powerful piece? And if so, then why do you win the game by checkmating that good-for-nothing, that half-handicapped king? Why is the queen the very emblem of sovereignty, and yet she does not rule?

Italy was a distinctly singular form of matriarchy where the women counted for little or nothing outside the home.

The other favorite topic of conversation, and the purpose for which so much chitchat, often malicious, intertwined, was the painstaking and detailed social classification of neighbors and acquaintances, carried out by reviewing such indicators as language, attire, education, children, homes. This patient work of description and cataloguing, befitting an eighteenth-century botanist at work on the vegetation of a newly discovered tropical island, proved however aleatory, provisional, because unlike biological species, social roles underwent continual and sometimes very rapid modifications, and the point of the diagram where single individuals were placed, along with families and groups, had to be updated, drawing on an ever-changing harvest of data, the collection of which could never be considered complete: news, gossip, secrets that were no longer secrets at all, insinuations, indiscretions, revelations.

ONE'S GOOD NAME, anonymity, gossip, and distinction: it was between these four corners that the generations-long game played out within good families. The adults did everything they could to maintain a low profile, to drown their own personalities, often quite strong, in the professions they practiced, their family role, the specific decorum of the class they belonged to—a decorum, in fact, that consisted of an obstinate discretion around the sources of their own prosperity, their income and their assets, which manifested itself in the form of cars and houses and villas and travel, but never ostentatious, never shown off, in fact, quite the opposite, almost concealing them, so to speak, hiding them in the shadows or dim light. Hence came the popularity of certain vacation spots where the lovely residences were almost invisible, built as they were in the thick of the forests and pine groves, allowing the wealth of those who lived there to be guessed at while in fact hiding it; contrariwise, in the young people, the passionate desire to distinguish themselves would be capable of coming up with the most improbable exploits.

THE CULMINATING MOMENT of family life is the evening meal. It remains the principal and often the only occasion on which the members of the family see one another. In situations where the custom of eating together disappears, due to differences in needs or disinterest or reciprocal annoyance, when adducing schedules that fail to meet by twenty minutes or half an hour family members hasten to wolf down their food, perhaps not even sitting down, eating with their hands, in the kitchen, on the living room side table, barricaded in their bedrooms and curled up on their beds, anything in order to avoid embarrassing community sittings, then the family only really exists at a formal level, strictly on paper, they all live together like students in a group house. The duration of the meal is inversely proportional to the solidity of the ties between those who eat that meal together. Haste is the worst indicator. Everything else, everything else can perfectly well be done all along, in a separate setting, you wash and bathe alone, you make phone calls, study, smoke, and watch TV alone, people even talk to themselves when they're alone—but eating is something you should do together. Why? Because that's the way it is, and that's that. It's the fundamental ritual of cohesion: you exchange information, you comment on the events of the day, you talk about plans and projects and decisions that must be made, you announce news of greater and lesser importance, you crack jokes and make the others laugh, or you arouse their curiosity or make them angry, you discuss the fate of the baby bird that fell out of its nest and how if it doesn't eat by nightfall it's bound to die, there, in the Stan Smith shoebox lined with cotton padding—all this while you all sate your hunger. This is the place and the time (for the most part, residual time) where parents can perform some minimum educational task. The proof of the pedagogic function that the family meal serves is this: in my day, since my frustrated parents (that is, my mother) were unable to focus that function on important topics, they sidetracked it onto the formal aspects of eating at the table, hands washed, elbows pressed to your sides, not drinking in the midst of chewing, and please, no belching. A secondary but tangible objective—that of etiquette. The scolding about our awkwardness at the table, in fact, struck us as somehow less subjective, though every bit as boring for us—the targets—than the usual abstract tirades about values such as honesty, sincerity, and personal hygiene (each of which were, as I have mentioned, always, for my mother, "the first thing"). As a further confirmation of this function of the shared meal, we have the embarrassing comportment of kids nowadays who slurp and chomp and slouch, indications that their parents have abdicated so much as a dusting of education and upbringing concerning formalities, a crucial surrogate of education concerning matters more substantial.

But why? Was it because, aware that they had received an upbringing consisting of hypocritical formalities, they chose not to replicate that approach with their own children, out of either a love of sincerity or mere laziness? In other words: if I can't straightforwardly teach my son or my daughter what is right and good (in part because at age forty, I still have no idea, or I'm not as certain of it as I might once have been . . .), what's the point of telling them that you never raise your glass to your lips before wiping your mouth with your napkin?

In any case, when we were little (but not even all that little), my brother and I never ate at the same table with our parents, but at a low side table, sitting on two small plastic chairs.

THE MURDERERS WHOSE CRIME I'm now preparing to write about also went home to dinner with their parents. To keep them from worrying. In the pauses between inflicting torture on their victims, they ate lunch while watching TV. At least, one of them did. I could no longer say in which Russian novel (perhaps *The Golovlyov Family*?) the household rules include having the samovar "always on the boil," and the members of the family "putting their knees under the table five times a day"—or perhaps even more, seeing the sheer number of snacks, early dinners, tidbits, and dishes they consumed, a never-ending munching of cucumbers and spreading of butter. It goes without saying that a family so deeply united and unshakable in their customs with respect to meals would fall apart—a fate that seems inevitable for any and all families in novels. The group that appears on stage in the first act will have broken apart by the time the curtain falls on the third act, that's the narrative law. Let me say it again: every family novel is the story of a neurosis. The desperate yearning for meaning, so typical of novels, triumphs in the conclusions that we draw about our past, providing a fantastic alibi for anything that has happened but also for the things that have yet to happen; after all, literature is a life insurance policy that allows us to give up the effort to build a different kind of life, to build another me, another self that is better or more courageous, what good would it do if I had literature to serve as a substitute, novels, ah, novels, daydreams, "fantasy" worlds (how much ink has been spilled in celebration of "fantasy," a virtue more or less nonexistent in any person of real worth), and this or that character can do a perfectly fine job of taking my place from now on, why certainly, I'll send him on in my place, he'll do fine, and I can simply step out of view. And so we shape and we fix the fleeting and foolish mask of character, "my" character, an accumulation of banalities held together in a chronology. It is said that literature magnifies life, enlarges it, multiplying the number of paths you can follow in your fantasies, in your imagination, as if it were possible to add to our own lives the lives of all the characters read about in books, until they form a sort of tribe of ghosts capable of anything, of standing in for everything . . .

Fantasy worlds are trotted out in lectures, at conferences, in hopes we can get students to read a book or two.

BUT PERHAPS the main interest that novels offer, their fundamental or perhaps only reason for existence, is that in them, worlds that have long since been swept away live on. Or worlds that will soon be swept away. For that sole reason, realistic novelists have an advantage over purely fanciful ones— if such a thing still exists, that is—since the world of the latter, never having actually existed, cannot disappear, and is therefore indestructible, which, while it may seem like a good thing in terms of durability, nevertheless deprives that text of the heartbreaking splendor that emanates from an endangered, vanishing universe.

What is truly *marvelous* is that which no longer exists.

Every great novel becomes incomprehensible.

And it is this very state of incomprehensibility that sucks us in.

5

WHAT ELSE CAN WE DO *with them now?*
Nothing.
We've already done everything we could think of to them.
You don't waste a speck of the hog, from snout to tail.
They're turning cold.
I can't think of a single thing.
They're no good to us anymore.
They just disgust me.
They were disgusting before.
Well, that's not true. They're kind of cute.
Not anymore.
And they really weren't at first, either.
We didn't take them because they were cute.

There are thousands more just like these two. Rome is full of girls just like them.

That's why they're perfect, because there are plenty more just like them. We're not done with them. We can start over again tomorrow.

From scratch.

From scratch?!

Don't you feel like it?

I don't think I really like them all that much.

Who don't you like, these two?

Women. Women in general.

Oh well, why don't you just go ahead and like the fact that you don't like them?

If we liked them, then we wouldn't treat them like this.

We treat them like this because we like to.

If we didn't like them, we wouldn't be going out looking for them . . .

We aren't looking for them: we're hunting them.

How is that different?

When I see them like this, I'd like to choke the life out of them.

Today that's what you did.

Why choke them?

To make them shut up.

But even if they shut up, it's as if they were still talking.

They whine. Or else they're arrogant. Arrogant and whiny.

And stupid!

So stupid.

All of them?

All of them. Do you think you know any who aren't?

Mmm . . . your mother?

My mother? My mother isn't stupid, my mother is deranged.

If she could hear you say that!

Trust me, she hears me. I say it to her, what do you think? I say it to her face.

What a bastard!

Like, what do you say, sorry? What do you say to her?

"You're just a pathetic mess. A slut. A deranged lunatic."

You tell your mother she's a slut? I don't believe you.

Neither do I.

All right, okay, I don't say it to her face, outright. But I make sure she knows it, I let her know what I think.

What do you think?
Oh, lord.
What's wrong?
I feel full . . . And when I feel full, I have to explode.

6

PRACTICALLY ALL FAMILIES have become bourgeois families, the model has spread like an infection. With no reference to their actual income, nowadays every family is bourgeois in the broadest sense, or rather, perhaps, we ought to say that the very effort involved in creating a family, running it and protecting it, is bourgeois, just as the methods used to dissolve a family are also bourgeois.

In any case, the pure and simple duration of the conjugal bond remains synonymous with its success. If it lasts, then it was meant to be; if it doesn't, then it wasn't. In order to complete the tasks that pertain to marriage, whatever they may be, years are required; and confirmations, the lapse of time, the repeating of things, latencies, growing accustomed, seasons that come and go, the slow construction of a past, endless variations on a beloved theme, obstacles, sicknesses, recoveries—in other words, diachrony. Faithfulness, if we choose to use the word not in the sense of exclusivity but of persistence. If someone by any chance wishes for happiness, they will have to wait, they must be patient, not that they're necessarily unhappy in the meantime, that's not what I'm saying, but they may eventually understand their happiness, that is, how happy they really were, only some time later. Unhappiness, on the other hand, can be detected immediately, there's no need to let it decant: it's there, today, right in front of you. Time gives a retrospective gleam and glow, the instant burns with absolute pain. But today we wish, in fact, we demand happiness, we have a right to it *now*, not on some random day in the future, when, looking back . . .

THERE IS NO TOPIC like the family capable of inspiring and unleashing the virulence of writers, thinkers, ideologues: it's as if there was a reckoning awaiting. It seems as if they are taking vengeance on their own families by writing against families in general. A more-or-less veiled autobiographism veins and drives the more ideological attacks. There is no theme better suited to poisoning the language: against fathers, mothers, spouses, siblings, and even one's children, that's right, one's children, we talk very seldom about the hatred that parents feel toward their children and prefer to give voice to the less surprising revolt of the children against their parents; even though the myth of Chronos is far older than the myth of Oedipus.

Modernity consists of this overflow of resentment, and its legitimation, when the right to murder the adjoining generation is overturned: there was a time when fathers held the unquestioned right of life and death over their children ("you clothed these wretched meats, / and you undressed them . . ."), but from the revolutionary era on, it is the opposite that rings sacrosanct, that the children have the right to rid themselves of their fathers. More than anything else, though, it is precisely the family as a structure that prompts scorn and irony among writers. Novelists, philosophers, psychoanalysts have all enjoyed good sport in mocking the abstract principles and concrete sins upon which the family rests, and in the course of just a couple of centuries, they have succeeded with the force of their arguments, but to an even greater extent, with the sweep of their style (normally tinged with cruelty, a satirical spirit, subtlety, but above all, resentment), in overturning millennia's worth of celebrations of the virtues and serenity of that notorious institution. The nest of vipers, in other words, needed to have its lid torn off, and there may be not a single worthwhile book or short story from Romanticism on that hasn't echoed as a specific *j'accuse*. The absolute masterpiece of the genre is Kafka's *The Metamorphosis*, the story of a young man transformed into a cockroach, even though we are inclined to think that he already was a cockroach before the transformation because of the simple fact that he lived in the narrow tunnel of a bourgeois family. The story begins after the metamorphosis has already taken place, but it must have followed a lengthy incubation. A stroke of genius to have written no prologue, and just begin like that, because it's already all clear . . .

WE BELONG TO OUR OWN TIME from head to foot: by rejecting it, we belong to it. We are distinctive products, exclusive property of a given time, which guards us jealously.

At the time when this story took place, the bourgeois family was still standing, even though the campaign to liquidate it was well advanced. The death of the family was being prophesied as something inevitable and preached as something just. The best way of demolishing an institution is to ascertain its advanced state of crisis, with instruments thought to be neutral. A body that has already decomposed cannot be preserved—unless you wish to hold on to the rot, the stench. Under the form of sociological and statistical observation, one is able to accelerate the very processes you are studying. If the term "death" might have seemed melodramatic, suggesting a hint of regret and remorse at the loss, because no one likes to see corpses lying around, especially when you consider that there were millions of those corpses of families still lying around—in that case the euphemistic "outmoded" was used instead of "dead." To a historical-clinical glance, the family was *outmoded*. There was very little likelihood of being able to fight against obsolescence, pointless to kick back: when your black-and-white TV, your nonflat screen, your cell phone that doesn't take pictures or really do anything, your PC with little if any memory are all "outmoded," then there is nothing to do but replace them. For that matter, the old models will be promptly taken off the market, and even if someone wished to wallow in retrograde attitudes, they would no longer be able to find them. After all, let's admit, there is nothing that could be snootier and more snobbish than this digging-in of feet. If something new comes along with a very clear identity and specific creators, then you can resist it and fight against it; but if it is presented as an impersonal force that acts according to fate, then you feel as if you are already possessed, in short, we have already made the choice without realizing it, or rather, it is we who have been selected, called, commanded. We have been living like sleepwalkers in a condition for some time now, and like sleepwalkers someone finally opens our eyes to our state. It is irresistible to comply with something that washes over all our heads like a wave. If we leaf through it like the page of a newspaper, the last century is dotted with death announcements. "It is with great bereavement . . ." or with a sigh of ill-concealed relief that we proclaim: the death of literature, the death of the novel, the sunset of movies, the fact that we're running out of petroleum, the collapse of values, the disappearance of communism, the end of history . . . Why shouldn't the family die, too?

The first exam I took at the university, just a few months after the CR/M, had to do with exactly these topics: the critique of the family. If I remember correctly, the course was in the Department of Moral Philosophy: under that umbrella, various seminars were held on all manner of topics, ranging from flower power to the language of schizophrenics. Schizophrenics were very widely studied, at the time, beloved of one and all, practically revered: in their feverish minds a revolutionary formula lay hidden. As I drew up my plan of studies, I'd opted out of philosophy courses that focused on such figures as Plato or Leibniz, whom I had already trudged through unhappily under the tutelage of Brother Gildo. They struck me as largely out-of-date and irrelevant compared with the ones we'd be studying in the Moral Philosophy course; all of them belonged to the so-called school of antipsychiatry, nearly all of them in agreement in their determination to liquidate that inconvenient, vicious, discriminatory, pathogenic, and unproductive institution: the family. The founder of the movement was the famous R. D. Laing, author of *The Divided Self* and *Knots*, books that I would go and read every morning on Piazza di Siena. I carefully underlined as I read. A great deal of my youthful interest was devoted to topics that were fashionable at the time: South American literature, progressive rock, conceptual art . . . It is these days, sadly, that I can no longer easily identify fields of interest to pursue, perhaps a sign of my own declining interest in life. I can remember the delightful vintage sound of those books as if they were so many songs by Pink Floyd: for example, Cooper, the legendary David Cooper, who apologized for being obliged to use in his writings such archaic and reactionary terms as "father" and "mother." The idea that these figures were agents of a treacherous and powerful repressive apparatus. Our parents: useful idiots or enthusiastic executioners. The maternal instinct, rhetorical and deceitful; the paternal impulse, intrinsically authoritarian. Or the notion that the insane were simply misfits that the bourgeoisie (there you go again! the usual suspect!) had hustled out of the way, creating insane asylums and locking them up, so that they could go about their business in blessed peace. Anyone who opposes the accumulation of capital will be interned. Anyone who stands in the way will be shoved aside. Anyone who disturbs the family peace will be sent away and confined: that is the nature of "the cure." In fact, back then it was a commonly held belief that peace was desired only by profiteers and oppressors, and that in any case peace constituted in and of itself a hypocritical concept, a conciliatory mask worn in order to better look after one's own interests. I rejected peace on general principle and I despised peacemakers, or rather, I considered them to be sly dogs, like the ones at Giulio Cesare High School who weighed in, trying to separate the warring sides during the brawls that broke out, uttering words full of good sense (fuck them and their moderation, one of them became a cabinet minister, and here I am, still teaching the object complement and the agent complement to convicts in prison . . . strange, isn't? *Agent* complement, the grammatical form expressed in: "the thief was caught *by the police*" . . .).

Families were death-dealing organisms, as soon as a child was born its family would saddle it with the name of a dead person. A ballast to lug after oneself in life. Upon baptism, a dead person was tied to a living one, the way the Nazis did before tossing Jews into the Danube, and the metal wire was the family tradition . . . to hell with that, too, if in order to respect that tradition I would have had to be named GERVASO! It's a good thing my parents showed me that clemency, it's just a good thing that in my ancestry, the Albinati clan, descended from Alba Longa, they were sufficiently uncertain of their karma that they changed their own names: there was a cousin of my grandfather's who was named Mario in the legal registry (a perfectly normal name, right?), but instead he chose to be called Luigi—why on earth?!

You're born hand in hand with a corpse. So during the course of your upbringing and education your parents will a thousand times prefer a docile zombie to a rambunctious child: a little boy who is basically already dead will be heaped with praise, while the one with a spark of life will be given regular punishments. "There are no bad children . . . there are only constipated children!" ran the ad for a laxative pill "with the sweet flavor of prunes." Wickedness, as a moral concept, was the target of humor, and even more roundly mocked was its opposite number, goodness. The wicked were celebrated. Rehabilitated. Publicly acclaimed. When I was a boy, lots of things happened, to me and to the others. Things worth trying, or believing in, or fighting against.

As in any revolutionary era, the praise of infamy was dutifully sung.

AT MY FIRST EXAM, I met a young man who had gotten the highest possible grade, an A-plus-plus. Our conversation began with a perfectly ordinary question from me: "Are you studying philosophy?" and it ended a short while later.

"Yes, but philosophy only interests me somewhat. I want to be a psychiatrist, even though I'm not sure how much I like the term."

"What term?"

"'Psychiatry.'"

"Why, what would you call it instead?"

"I wouldn't call it anything. To give things or people names is to do them violence."

"Do them . . . *violence*?!"

✤

THE LASTING SUCCESS of the family is due primarily to an absence of work-able alternatives. Like the *Settimana Enigmistica*, Italy's popular weekly puzzler, it boasts countless attempts at imitation, and in defiance of them all, it continues to sell better than the competition, that is, all the surrogates, parodies, or applications of the same principles with accompanying vices and virtues, on a different scale. Once you'd abolished the family, its problems were bound to resurface intact, often without even being able to enjoy the advantages of the old model, much less the new ones created by its demolition. The imagination of philosophers and politicians, of radical reformers and abolitionists, gave rise in the best of cases to a collectivization, at first perhaps joyous in spirit but, in time, inevitably forced and unnatural, of the canonical functions performed by the couple—love, sex, responsibility for and education of children, transmission of expertise, and so on.

THE BOURGEOIS WORLD is always a microcosm, and therefore it represents the entire cosmos to perfection. And this is how my quarter is introduced, the Quartiere Trieste, QT, a miniature universe all its own: homogeneous, smooth, devoid of handholds, of any nooks or crannies to hide in, since the quarter is itself a refuge: and how can you hide there *if you're already in a hiding place*? How can you hide from the others if they're curled up hiding in there with you? In the shadows where things are neither invisible nor truly visible . . .

It's the syndrome of those who feel they're being held prisoner by their own bodyguards: they're supposed to be protecting me but, actually, look at this, they're laying siege to me instead. How many times have I heard matrons complain about the presence in their home of their own housekeeper! "I'd far prefer to do it all myself than to have to find her constantly underfoot!" even though in point of fact they'd last two and a half days, no longer, without a maid, and so, it's true, they heave a sigh of relief the minute she leaves for her weekly day off, but they heave the same sigh of relief that evening when the key turns in the door and she's back.

They feel suddenly abandoned and suddenly invaded.

THE OBSESSION, even in the QT, was with security. Everyone had done all they could to ensure a quiet, untroubled life, even at the cost of renouncing any new and exciting opportunities. Existence had been sanded to a smooth finish, stripping it of any irregularity that might constitute either a worry or a joy—be done with it, plane it smooth. Their prayers had been answered. When I was born, the war had been over for eleven years. No one would ever have wanted to slip back for so much as an instant into the privations and discouragement of the old days of danger and poverty. The quarter had stabilized its image, and it had been sprinkled with prosperity, in the little apartment houses around the Parco Nemorense, in the detached villas of Via Arno and Via Reno, in the large intensive farming tracts along Viale Eritrea there was no mistaking the flow of fresh money, pumping into that dignified shell the one element truly necessary to achieve respectability. Yes, because honesty, decorum, courtesy, and hard work count up to a certain point, but after that, what you need is money. And at last, there was no shortage of money, there was plenty of ham on the table and crystal-drop chandeliers and a TV in front of the Naugahyde armchairs, impatiently champing at the bit to be replaced by a color set, in fact, there were a few people who already owned one, and they delighted in the incomparable *"prove tecniche di trasmissione,"* morning and afternoon—color test patterns and random snippets of film. I would go over especially to see them at the home of a friend, Riccardo Modiano, now my CPA, and Lodoli, Barnetta, Pilu, Puca, and Rummo would come, too; we'd all gather at three o'clock in front of the big black Philco set . . .

IN 1975, *RAI television started its regular technical test broadcasts in color, with a special programming broadcast twice a day, in the time slots from 10 to 11 a.m. and 3 to 4 p.m. It went on for years. Almost without meaning to, the "prove tecniche di trasmissione" became a part of the history of our television network; in fact, it seems unbelievable that such a program, conceived for purely experimental purposes, and with that disquieting woman's voice-over, repeating at regular intervals, "Prove tecniche di trasmissione"— "Technical test broadcasts"—could ever have become so popular, especially among those who were kids at the time. This is how these test broadcasts were organized: after a few minutes of video of colored stripes and audio with a shrill, constant frequency, the first part would begin, consisting of a sequence of motionless images. To the warm notes of the Sonata for Strings in C major by Gioacchino Rossini, the following images would appear:*

- *elegantly dressed young woman in a sixties-style kitchen;*
- *child surrounded by toys, wearing an Indian headdress;*

- *anthurium flowers, one red, the other green;*
- *a matron with dark hair, intently applying makeup, with lipstick and perfume atomizer in plain view;*
- *young woman with tennis racket and ball, glimpsed through the net on a tennis court.*

Having completed the first part of the broadcast, there followed several minutes of the new color monoscope, then began the second part, consisting of a sequence of film clips:

- *matron who comes home from doing her grocery shopping and starts making dinner, in a pleasant household atmosphere accompanied by refined and relaxing music;*
- *studio of painters working in various mediums: watercolor, oil, collage, charcoal. The musical commentary is the Adagio from the Concerto for Oboe and String Orchestra in D minor, op. 9, no. 2, by Albinoni;*
- *fabric salesmen who shows a rich sampling of satin scraps to two very beautiful young women, one with long blond hair, the other with Asian features and a pageboy hairstyle. Here, too, a musical commentary of great beauty: the Nocturne in E-flat major, op. 9, no. 2, by Fryderyk Chopin;*
- *the same young Asian woman strolling in a garden in Rome, admiring the colorful flowers. Soundtrack, the stirring dialogue between English horn and transverse flute, taken from the* William Tell *Overture by Gioacchino Rossini;*
- *scene at the Rome Zoo, to the tune of the Overture to* La Gazza Ladra, *by Gioacchino Rossini.*

After another brief intermission with the Philips monoscope, the third part brought to an end the technical test, repeating the same images as the first, but with a background of music from the Baroque period. There were a considerable number of people at the time who watched the technical test broadcasts every day, going so far in certain cases as to watch them twice a day and even record the soundtrack. The increasingly powerful desire for color, the sense of an imminent future of high technology, the beauty of the music, the delicacy of the scenes aired, the details with the most powerful chromatic effect, cunningly highlighted by the way they were photographed or filmed, the continuous exercise of the imagination on the part of the many viewers who still owned a black-and-white television set, can all explain why these tests met with such approval.

✣

IT WOULD BE A LOW BLOW, the kind of thing a manipulative screenwriter might come up with, running two scenes in parallel, to say that we were sitting there filling our eyes with brightly colored flowers, while a few hundred yards away rapes were committed and murders planned by people we'd seen that very morning at school, pushing past one another in line to buy a slice of pizza.

THE OBSESSION WITH SAFETY. Just now that we'd finally emerged from the hardships and the horrors (because it's the feeling of narrowly averted economic danger that dominates the QT in those years, leave aside the notion of wealthy and pitiless, for the most part the place was inhabited by people who just a few years ago had started to let their belts out a few notches, set aside a nest egg, finally feel as if they might have reached safety), here we were, tumbling right back into the abyss, or actually, not back into it, because this kind of threat had never existed before.

7

WHAT GIVES AN EXCLUSIVE VALUE to the bourgeois universe is nothing but a piece of verbal magic, whose effects can vanish, in a flash, like a potion whose antidote you drink, whereupon the gaze becomes lucid, pitiless. Let us take, for instance, Via Archimede, or Vigna Clara, or Vigna Stelluti: an enfilade of "fine" apartments that have nothing fine about them, save for the quality that is conferred upon them by the classification into zones by the real estate agencies; buildings defined as "prestigious" that actually emanate no prestige whatsoever, luxury residences that have nothing luxurious about them, except for the amplification of the spaces . . . And so, all of a sudden, once the veil of verbal decorum is rent asunder, the universe of the middle class may appear thus to the disconsolate eyes of those who want nothing so much as to flee; and the bourgeois even goes so far as to dream of making a trade with those who envy him, to take a few steps down, provided he . . . provided he . . . but he lacks the strength, has neither the courage nor any authentic desire to do so.

No! Not even in jest can we play at being poor.

Back then, nothing could drive a father and head of household into a rage quite as much as the ostentatious sight of a son dressed like a bum, the masquerade of fake poverty is in ab-so-lute-ly the worst sort of taste, and it even tempts fate, jinxes the present by alluding to the possibility of a potential ruinous expulsion from the Garden of Eden, which is hardly something that can ever be ruled out confidently, since the family business could face a downturn at any moment. Even Eve, the nude sinner, forced to abandon the Earthly Paradise, weeps in disappointment like a matron forced to say farewell forever to her lovely apartment, caress the leaves of her plants and flowers for the last time, look out from the spacious terraces with fine views, the penthouse apartment sold off to pay a mountain of debts.

In the context of social ascent, we find clear confirmation of just how easy it is to get used to wealth and comfort, and how intolerable it is, to the verge of the monstrous, to be forced to give it up. Invincible forces act on our senses, modifying them by force of habit: all you need is a few months sleeping on a memory foam mattress or driving a Mercedes to make it seem as if any other surface you lay your back on is bare rock. While the increase of prosperity is perceived as natural, and people almost stop noticing it as it occurs, the diminishment of prosperity is experienced as a punitive event, literally degrading.

Those who have been indigent, and fortunately no longer are, spend the rest of their lives in the sheer terror of becoming indigent once again. It's a sort of recurring nightmare, and even when we're not talking about full-blown terror, it still takes on the nature of a dull implicit threat wielded by a variety of different agents: the state, the government, the stock market, the banks, thieves, con artists, the Chinese, relatives who squander and children who are layabouts . . .

Although in the period during which this story unfolds, poverty had been eradicated in the QT, like smallpox or polio, there still persisted a sort of genetic legacy, latent but ready to spring back to life and sow the fear that it might return, more horrible and frightening than ever. To have to turn suit jackets inside out, to live in an unheated apartment, or to be entirely homeless . . .

It happened only rarely in the QT that you would cross paths with people who had fallen so low, but if you wanted to find examples aplenty, you needed only to take a walk, for instance, down to Via di Pietralata (less than a kilometer from my house), which was then lined with hovels and shacks. If not in the time span of the individual, in the collective space, at least, poverty was still disagreeably close at hand. The inhabitants of the QT had three ways of dealing with it: by pitying and assisting the poor, holding them in contempt, or ignoring them entirely. Which means charity (for the most part, through Catholic institutions), arrogance, or else indifference. I'll let you guess which was the option most widely adopted.

THE REAL, overpowering danger, then, wasn't dishonor, but poverty, which is in and of itself dishonorable; not the loss of decorum, but the loss of one's status of affluence. The true horror: to be poor, to go back to being poor for those who once had been poor, to become poor for the first time for those who never had. But during the years in which this story unfolds, in spite of the oil crisis and the state of the world economy and the political struggle in Italy, which was growing bloodier, that was a fairly remote eventuality, and indeed it rarely happened that a bourgeois family was sent back to "Go" in the social game of Monopoly, a fate that instead, today, looms over the European middle class taken as a whole. The image of the hellish descent below the threshold of prosperity, or even that of subsistence, was a nightmare from which one awoke in the middle of the night, a bizarre phantom— while it is instead taking shape day by day for the present generation. A quarter century before the end of the millennium, Italy and Europe and the West, though ravaged by cyclical crises of a scale that would later prove to be relatively modest, was still buoyed up on the wave of expansion that had been triggered in the postwar years, the "social escalator," or consumer price index, was still conveying the average family upward, and there would still be a good twenty years of prosperity and lavish spending, of reckless wealth, sure, with speculative bubbles that burst every now and then, making loud noises . . . but not the general decline we're experiencing now.

THE MIDDLE CLASS, eager to be admired for its reasonableness and the maturity of the way it understands life, placid, modest, a stranger to excess, actually preserves a childish or possibly adolescent trait, brusque, irritable, and naïve—a tendency to defy the rules that it is forced to observe by none other than itself. It is by no means true that it always and invariably obeys. On the one hand, certainly, it feels a spasmodic need for security. On the other hand, it does all it can to escape from the order that reassures it. The unconditional adherence to the model requires, like some sort of test of the validity of the schema adhered to, that it be repeatedly stressed, the way you rap your knuckles on an object to test its soundness before buying it. If the object withstands our experimental violence, we find that reassuring; the same way that adolescents sometimes feel reassured if adults react firmly in the face of their provocations. Whatever the case, the order called into question must be abolished and then rebuilt in a different manner, in order to affirm one's personality and prove one is capable of independence. Often, at the end of that process, this reconstruction will prove to be almost identical to the order that was found to be so objectionable, but the important thing is to have transformed it for at least a certain period into a state of disarray. To conform and to disobey, to conform and to distinguish oneself, to join and to protest, to obey and to rebel, the movement is as incessant as a pumping heart, until the blood stops and the contradiction ceases. "A violent order is a disorder," says the poet, and, "A great disorder is an order," in any case. An incessant reforming is reminiscent of artistic processes, much the same as with style, an original intertwining of tradition and departure from tradition. It can't be one thing or the other, it must necessarily be both.

It's a well-known fact, for that matter, that any man reputed to be civil and inoffensive can prove to be capable of actions that are nothing more nor less than replicas of the deeds of his ancestors, full of ill will and cruelty.

TO ABANDON THE LAZY RITUALITY and the lengthy time periods of study and work and domestic life, to seek shortcuts in order to grasp "at a single stroke" the results of those normally slow procedures: in order to possess, that is, money, sex, a pleasant life, and recognition. Whatever respectable citizens may say about it, however much they may turn up their noses, crime is a very powerful promoter of social recognition, and it is in fact practiced to that end: in order to win respect. Power and wealth generate respect, force generates respect, violence, whether it is acted out or merely threatened, imposes respect, which is a feeling in the end not that different from reverential fear, and which in any case marks a distance imposed upon the gaze. *To strike*: thrust in, impress, shake, batter, hammer, drive in forcefully . . .

THE MOST FEROCIOUS ENEMIES of the family are: first and foremost, plaque (a threat looming like the barbarians pressing in upon the borders of the empire), and after that, tooth decay and halitosis, body odor, smelly feet and teenagers' gym shoes, dandruff, excessive body hair—in other words, the by-products, the wood shavings of our intimate parts, the wastage from the incessant processing of the body, details concerning whose repugnance advertisers hammer relentlessly to alarm all the members of the family the minute they stick their noses out their front door.

Woe betide them if they aren't immediately halted by the correctives offered by the market.

8

D O YOU FEEL *like an ice cream?*
An ice cream?
Yes, an ice cream cone.
No, I don't feel like one.
How about a cup?
Come on, you want one.
Even if I don't much want one, okay, let's get some ice cream. Whatever you guys want.
It's all the same to me.
But where?
The usual place.
And where would that be?
The usual. The usual place. The one where we get ice cream.
Okay, I get that, but which one?
The one on the piazza.
On the piazza, no?
Ah, that place.
But do you still feel like ice cream?
Me? I didn't want any in the first place. I told you that, didn't I?
Oh, in that case . . .
Let's go anyway.
I feel full . . . And when I feel full, I have to explode.

9

*F*AMILIES, *I hate you. Yes, I know, dear readers, if you're sick of this topic, just skip to the next, decisive chapter. I'd understand you, I'd forgive you, and I only hope that you'll forgive me. It's just too bad because a couple of lines of reasoning (which aren't flour from my bag, as we say in Italian, not original with me: in this book of mine, I've only contributed the yeast to make the dough rise) might perhaps be worth the time it takes to read them. But you can always just set these pages aside and come back to them at some later date, if you choose, after you've finished the book, retrace your steps, or else go forward, continue reading, if you find them dull, if you don't enjoy, at least a little, letting yourselves be tortured.*

IT'S A PROBLEM that has no voice. That has no shape, no visage. There is something unspeakable at the heart of family life, a secret that doesn't necessarily conceal unseemly or repugnant details (child abuse, mistreatment of the mother, dubious paternity, pilfered inheritances, terrible lies . . .), since it is everyday domestic life itself, even when that life is wonderfully peaceful and unruffled, that constitutes the enigma. Peace and quiet is no less indecipherable than horror, perhaps even more so. Horror can burst to the surface and explode, leading to a confession or an accusation, a vendetta, but peace and quiet is itself the unruffled surface, with barely a ripple . . . How could it erupt out of itself?

You can't escape peace.

The victims of peace and quiet manifest very distinctive symptoms. Lassitude, apathy, lack of lust for life, a frenzy devoid of any object, moods of dreariness that are unlikely to rise to the level of a full-fledged breakdown, but then again, beatific happiness, unalloyed satisfaction, and sheer serenity, what is it that you expect them to have to say, and to whom? Who would even be interested in listening to such an elusive story, who'd understand anything about it, and who, even if they do grasp something, wouldn't feel an envy so deep that it would rapidly transmute into hatred or contempt (as if those who are contented feel that way just because they're willing to settle, because they were willing to take peace at a discount)? Or else, on the other hand, if the people listening happen to be experiencing that same joy and delight in their own lives, why would they bother to pay attention to something they already possess?

It's by no means true that the happiness in every happy family is alike, as the opening words of the famous novel declare: perhaps the sensation of uniformity is due to the disinterest that such situations, in truth each very different from the other, eventually cause, boring observers until they all begin to look alike.

AMONG MY CONTEMPORARIES, I know hardly anyone whose memories aren't inhabited by a depressed mother, in the throes of inexplicable migraines, subjected to sleep cures or other therapies, mothers unwilling to get out of bed or leave the bedroom during the long, shadowy winter afternoons. A mother with perfect posture who heaves deep sighs, each respiration as if she were inhaling opium, as coils of steam rise from the cups of tea sipped in the parlor with her mother-in-law or the girlfriends who drop in for a visit. As they leaf through their photo albums, these elegantly dressed young housewives, often very beautiful, exude an unconstrained sadness, their mascaraed eyes staring down at the gray sea, the silhouette of the Alps, the happy moments that appear static, however, too heartrending, almost painful in the end, even if we're just talking about a vacation, it wasn't wartime, after all. Their hairstyles look alike.

WHO IS THE AUDIENCE before whom the gleaming silver is displayed, who will bother to notice the absence of dust on the credenzas and shelving? Once upon a time, it was the ranks of kith and kin, aunts, grandmothers, cousins, whose numbers have dwindled in recent years, as has the frequency of their visits, as their judgments have gradually become less and less crucial, while many guests deep down would be delighted to abolish even these last remaining processional displays. Christmases, birthdays, communion and confirmation parties. Do people even still go through confirmation, these days? And if so, what's the result? That the silver remains buried in old suitcases tucked away in closets, like stolen property (and in a certain sense, maybe it is . . .), the furniture with the fingerprints, the poorly ironed shirts, the plastic utensils, the children just so many little savages, and everyone even more frustrated than before, women most of all, since that residual list of chores to be added to work already won as a right instead of rejected as a sentence, a burden, will just be added to the responsibilities they already face.

In the families where the mother did nothing other than to look after the children, when the children grew up and became adults and moved out, the mother would slide into a crisis, starved for both affection and a reason to live. To what could she devote herself? In any case, the best way to continue to keep her busy is to cause all sorts of dismay, keep her up nights, break her heart. Like troublesome children, the criminals who committed the rape and murder in a villa on the coast kept their families very busy, causing trouble at the age when children normally *stop* causing it. The mother who goes to clean up the house after the torture, as if it were some sort of New Year's party, the father of another one of the criminals who bribes correctional officers. Seriously, those parents were forced to work overtime and went on looking after the scions of the family for the rest of their lives, handing out tips and paying lawyers' fees, opening special accounts, bribing functionaries, hiring expert witnesses, fabricating documents, phoning apprehensively overseas, just like the families that send their children to study English in Oxford over the summer.

HOW TO MAKE ONE'S WAY in the world? The best way was to listen to your parents' instructions, because they knew all the right recipes. All you had to do was apply them. Then the world started speeding up, faster and faster, and then too fast. Little by little their expertise began to be called into question, their experiences and their tastes began to fall behind. A son, however obedient, felt torn whether to accept notions (technical, and also moral) that were now useless and out of date, imparted by his parents, or else to accept more recent notions that were in clear and open conflict with the former. For their part, the more self-aware parents began to realize uneasily that their body of knowledge was being drained of its significance: even though some of their axioms still sounded right and just, at least in abstract terms, how could they honestly hand them down to their children? It would be like asking them to study geography with an atlas bearing the borders of 1989, 1939, or 1914. Every parent suddenly became nineteenth-century in their beliefs and knowledge. They were backdated with a sudden shove that knocked them into the arms of their grandparents. And they found themselves (as they still do) in the condition of the immigrant whose children know much better than he or she does the language and the customs of the country they live in. Parents became chronic misfits, deserving of faint smiles of commiseration. Therefore, in a way that was at once tragic, ridiculous, and steeped in heartbreaking pathos, a good parent must refrain from handing down ideals and rules of behavior (codes that they have followed all their lives) lest they cause their children to become maladjusted. Those ideas remain valid, but only for them, and they will cherish them as long as they live, but those good parents will not be able to profess them openly nor teach them. What is required of a parent, if they wish to be a good parent, is that they simply cease to act like a parent. Let it be, it's what common sense and my own fatherly or motherly love demand, I'll stop teaching them about a subject I don't actually know as well as I once thought I did: life. That's what a good parent says to himself, and by this point he has shrunk so tiny that he vanishes from the horizon. Careful, though, weak parents are by no means the same as unimportant parents, because other people's weaknesses, like our own, are decisive in our lives. If previously children were subjugated by force, now they depend upon weakness. A silken leash is every bit as hard to break as a steel one. Starting in the years in which this story unfolds, an implacable law was taking shape, which marked the new relations between parents and children: less prestige = more affection. Less authority = more love. Countless fathers and mothers therefore came to this conclusion: well, then, seeing that I can no longer be believed or feared or respected, I might as well see about being loved. I won't do anything that might endanger the love that my children feel for me. Let me take myself as an example. Many, I'd even say all of the mistakes that I've made in my children's upbringing have been due to this spasmodic, slightly cowardly need for affection, my failure to meet the less agreeable duties of a parent in order to ensure myself gratitude, benevolence, and fondness from my children. "Deep down, I'm a good father . . . proof of the fact is that they love me." A father, in other words, as a sort of indulgent grandfather, or an understanding—because in the final analysis irresponsible—elder brother.

Relations between generations, then, instead of a system of reciprocal duties and bonds, became an extortionate sentimental game.

My generation found itself teetering between the influence of a declining parental authority that remained, however, still powerful, utterly unwilling to give up its prerogatives—and the growing domination of fashion, the sway of the markets of taste and behavior, consumerism as the only way to enter into contact with the world. Perhaps during this interregnum we were freer, since the new gods had not securely seated themselves on the thrones just abandoned by those that had fled—or perhaps we were the servants of two masters and not just of one, as had been the case for the previous generation, which had been entirely subordinated to the command of the family, and as it would be for the subsequent generation, wholly enslaved by the market. Without recognized masters or else serving under a double yoke. The topic of this book is entirely wrapped up here, in this question: How free were we? Free *of what*? Free *to do what*? Many of us experienced scraps of old-style family oppression, hybridized or alternating with a permissiveness that was still the product of our parents' specific beliefs, not due to their exhaustion, the waning of their mental energies, or poor habits. In order to be modern and open-minded, nowadays, with your children, you need only ignore them and the game is done. I mean to say that this was a period when freedom still had a price and was not merely a by-product, a collateral effect. It was conquered in brusque, sharp episodes, or else conceded in pioneering open-minded awakenings, by a reformer proud to have undertaken real change. In other words, both in order to be stubbornly old-fashioned and in order to establish freer relations in the family, parents had to make a conscious investment, and that took a great deal of conviction. There existed no clear trend to go along with. The arrows of morality pointed in all directions—a veritable compass rose. While nowadays freedom is like one of those immense Atlantic beaches from which the tide has withdrawn, leaving the sand covered with litter, and you find that expanse at your disposal without having had to do a thing, and nothing is exactly what you will be able to do when the ocean decides to reclaim it.

AUTHORITY, unless it wishes to become arbitrary and repressive, must be based on reasonableness and affection, but by so doing, it liquidates the very principle of authority.

The idea, reasonable at first glance, that reasonableness provokes automatic consensus and compromise from one and all is very naïve.

My generation scorned the word and the concept of obedience.

To obey was tantamount to making oneself ridiculous, pitiable, pathetic.

What had been considered for centuries to be a precious value, and was still touted as such, was to us a humiliating practice.

We were disgusted by the prospect of having to be inducted, sooner or later, into military service.

There, in the barracks, we were going to be obliged to *obey*.

Orders and commands devoid of sense, such as moving bags from one side of the courtyard to the other, gave a good measure of the concept.

There was nothing more unjust than an order.

Every word of imposition had to be contradicted.

We worshipped and revered anyone who refused to truckle under, who rejected obedience: rebels, revolutionaries, anarchists, conscientious objectors, banditti, *cangaceiros*, the ones who never keel and never bow their heads.

But we bowed ours.

We obeyed.

We obeyed, at school, at home, on Saturdays with our friends, we obeyed unwritten laws, but we did nothing to undercut their binding force.

I think of myself as an independent kind of guy, and I'm foolishly proud of the fact, but in reality I've never done anything else in my life but to obey the rules that are woven around me in an invisible but very stout spider-web, indeed, at certain points I have clutched them tight, the way you might cling to a safety net, or perhaps I myself was the spider that spun those webs of rules, produced them and walked on them, those webs protected me, if I observed them, and if I chanced to tear them, I would have plunged into the void below.

And in the meantime, how we scorned the obedient ones! Soldiers, monks, functionaries, lackeys, servants (who in reality almost always disobey).

IF YOU UNDERTAKE a brief bibliographic research project nowadays, you will find that the term "obedience" can be found exclusively in religious publications. You obey, or rather you ought to obey, God, and the authorities who represent Him on earth. The Church is the last earthly institution that seriously demands obedience.

A BOURGEOIS EDUCATION CONSISTS of obeying not others but oneself, obeying laws that you impose upon yourself. They teach them to you in your family, that is true, but then you go on respecting them and in the end you wind up preaching them yourself because you have become convinced that there could be nothing better, difficult not to be in agreement with them, not to see that there is no higher form of civilization than that which teaches you to reduce disagreeable occasions to the bare minimum attainable, to spare yourself and other people those occasions. Curse words, yawns, references to feces and urine, arrogance, rudeness, sources of annoyance. On this plane, minor annoyances can be even more deadly than outright evil because, as etiquette tells us, one may be exposed to them repeatedly and on a daily basis, causing us each time a small displeasure that, however, building up little by little over time, in countless instances, can become immense, just as the minor virtues end up being more beneficial than the great ones, given that the former are performed far more often than the latter. The unbroken sting of mosquitoes is, from a statistical point of view, more annoying than the unlikely bite from a lion, and therefore, you should reach for a bottle of insecticide, not a rifle. Numbers trump weight. It is on this sage axiom that the bourgeois education and upbringing is based, so we can hardly complain if it focuses for the most part on minutiae, because its universe is in fact that of mosquitoes and horseflies, not tigers and lions, which, let's face it, you'll never once run into in a lifetime. Everyday annoying people, not murderers, call us on the phone. How often in modern bourgeois life does one have an opportunity to display courage? Courage is a virtue that has application in rare and exceptional circumstances. Of nearly all the people I know (and the same goes for myself), I would be unable to say whether they are courageous or cowardly, since I have never once seen them actually put to the test, and I can proceed only by suppositions, with imaginary projections into dramatic scenarios, where they would be required to prove once and for all just who they are, and what they would be capable of, and I'd be basing myself on the attitudes they have displayed in far less significant circumstances, the kind offered by everyday life. You'd have to hypothesize events that normal existence rules out or renders unlikely. There was a time, no doubt, when a man would require some guts to go from Rome to Tivoli, or to cross a river or walk through a forest, nowadays only a victim of truly unfortunate circumstances can actually learn what lies at the bottom of his heart, and there are people who live an entire lifetime without getting that chance. Ignorant of themselves. Therefore the term and the very concept of courage recede toward a milieu out of something like novelistic fancy, turning into a papier-mâché creation like the ship in *The Black Corsair*, or else they're trivialized in metaphorical phrases of this sort: "It takes some courage to wear that dress to the party!" or else restricted to a very specific context, albeit terribly common, specifically the way certain sick people face up to their disease, depicted as an enemy to be combatted, even more treacherous in that it is internal, whereas perhaps other words might be better suited, such as firmness or patience. When life seems to offer no opportunities to put one-self to the test, then we reproduce them "in vitro," in a laboratory, or we go out intentionally in search of them: by jumping off a bridge into a gorge hanging from a giant rubber band, etc.

THEREFORE, even if someone is courageous, they have no way of knowing it, and a person himself is the first to be surprised if he finds himself react-ing in a resolute manner in the face of an emergency. After surviving it, they look around full of amazement. Was that really me who dove into the water like that . . . ? Who responded defiantly to that huge powerful guy and his friends . . . ? Well, how about that, I did all right . . . You unexpect-edly find that you're an intrepid, audacious soul, and you might even be impatient to find another opportunity to put these virtues to the test and feel the thrill, the instinctive charge, but the thing is, you don't know ex-actly how to make that happen, where and how, so you're forced to create the conditions intentionally, by taking risks or even putting someone else in danger. It's hard to tell courage from recklessness, self-destructiveness, or even sheer imbecility, the boundaries aren't entirely clear. A subtle vein of idiocy wends its way through every undertaking that would otherwise be difficult to accomplish; it's different from cases in which idiocy is the only discernible motive for one's actions. That also explains why sometimes it is people who are absolutely stupid that carry out particularly risky deeds, and why in certain groups that commit violent acts, the leader might be a full-blown psychopath, who lacks important elements of executive function and self-control and therefore dares to do things at the thought of which others would quail. I have often wondered whether those who lack inhibi-tory brakes are mental defectives or superior beings, in short whether they have something more or something less than other people. There is a sin-gular grandeur and an equally profound poverty in a willingness to stop at nothing, no act, no intention. To dare incessantly may sharpen our minds and sling them farther and farther until they plunge into the indistinct mist; once you've outstripped conventional limitations, it's difficult to set others that cannot, in their turn, be surpassed, you move in other words through a boundless field of *feasibility*, any new initiative becomes obsolete on the spot, and therefore you are obliged to intensify all your mental and physical excesses, you have to strive to do or say titanic, outrageous, mon-strous, glorious, infamous challenges, never sufficient, never sufficiently monstrous and glorious. This is exactly what a hero is. This is a hero's delirium. His ability to produce salvation and violence is bottomless, until eventually the two things come to equal each other: like the tip of Achilles's spear, which wounds and then heals.

BOURGEOIS MORALITY IS NOT REQUIRED to deal with extraordinary events, and therefore neither does it countenance the qualities required to confront them. The proverb says: you go to the market with coins, not with gold ingots. Courage, therefore, is not contemplated in this book of etiquette. Courtesy, on the other hand, is indeed a virtue no doubt less glorious, along with good manners, discretion, qualities that we employ countless times a day. They affect a far greater number of people around us, with frequency such that they can profoundly alter their lives and ours. Without these traits life descends into pure barbarity. A rude or obnoxious person has a thousand opportunities to embitter us, while a truly evil, vicious person, who might certainly have far more serious and weighty effects upon us, nonetheless has objectively fewer chances to do so. They can do us great harm, this is true, but we need only steer clear of those few occasions and we will be safe. It seemed that there were never any lions lurking around the corner, ready to rend someone limb from limb in the QT, and indeed there couldn't have been. So what we worried about was how to keep down the mosquitoes. Our education was based on euphemism, attenuation, and accommodation. In conversation, what had to be avoided were vulgarities, of course, but also subjects that tended to overheat the temper, or topics that were too profound and touching. (The purpose of conversation, in fact, is not to clash and argue, but to reassure ourselves that we belong to the same group.) You must never point at the people you're talking with and never, never mock those with physical defects. At the dinner table, you were not to stretch or yawn or whistle or sing or scratch yourself. When the serving platter arrived, and you must never call for it, you were to serve yourself with moderation and then pass it on. Good manners were exercised in both the things you did and the things you did not do, in speaking but especially in remaining silent. The list of inappropriate words and phrases varied from family to family. At my house, it was considered bad manners to say "*Che schifo*" ("How disgusting"), and it was an enormous relief, on a trip once with our parents, to discover that there exists a Renaissance villa called Schifanoia, in Ferrara, and we toured it. From that day on, it made no sense for them to forbid us to use such a lofty and cultivated word.

This rather strict upbringing gave rise to its reversal, point by point, that is, a counteretiquette that consisted entirely of belching and farting, foul language trotted out with stubborn determination and a complete doggedness, and then rude gestures, filthy and blasphemous nursery rhymes, obscenities and profanities—these latter relatively rare, but blasted out with particular delight in that school run by priests.

I remember one guy in middle school, Puca, who would curse after taking communion. He'd stand in line to take the wine and the wafer, then he'd retrace his steps slowly and mournfully, kneel at the pew, the wafer still in his mouth, and I'd hear him murmur a profanity, head bowed, hands clasped, and who knows why, what pleasure he took from it . . .

At school, a new and blasphemous nursery rhyme was sent around every day.

THE GOLGOTHA GRAN PRIX *was held today: winner, Jesus, riding Barabbam, showing in second place, Judas Iscariot, riding Matra Dito, and coming in third, Pontius Pilot.* (Brabham: a famous Formula One racing team founded by the ace driver Jack Brabham; Matra: an auto manufacturing group that also made race cars and won the Formula One championship in 1969.)

IN OTHER WORDS, there was a delight in defiling and disfiguring anything that we had been taught was good or just or sacred or decorous: all good manners, starting with polite language. At school we vented that tendency with pervasive vulgarity.

> *Say, what is the law of Gay-Lussac?*
> *My dick up your ass goes clickety-clack.*
> *And what, pray tell, is the rule of Tartini?*
> *My dick up your ass won't make bambini.*

> *The goddess Kali*
> *Ate bowls of rice*
> *and shat out arancini*

> *Took a boat to North Korea*
> *and Sandokan had diarrhea*

10

AROUND ELEVEN AT NIGHT on September 30, 1975, from the window of his apartment, a resident of Viale Pola 5 (two hundred yards from where I live), notices two young men parking a Fiat 127 in the apartment building driveway, then they get out of the car, discuss something animatedly, and then leave.

Later, in the middle of the night, he is awakened by his mother, who tells him that she heard noises downstairs; he goes again to the window, and looks down into the street. He notices that the trunk of that Fiat 127 is shaking, as if being pounded by someone locked inside. First he calls the Carabinieri, then he goes down into the street and walks over to the vehicle.

He calls out, asking who could be in there.

A young woman's voice replies: "The guys who pulled off the Bulgari kidnapping locked me in here . . . I'm wounded and I'm wrapped around a dead woman's body." And then: "Open the trunk, I can't take it anymore . . ."

In the meantime, another tenant has emerged from the same apartment building.

"Don't leave, they haven't gone far!"

Before long, the Carabinieri arrive. They force open the trunk, from which moaning and cries for help can be heard.

INSIDE WAS A BULKY OBJECT WRAPPED in a blanket and behind it, wedged against the back of the rear seat, the wounded girl was groaning. The Carabinieri had a hard time understanding what she was saying, and getting her out of the car as well: she was half-naked and smeared with blood. It was only after she'd almost completely emerged from the trunk that they understood that there was another girl in there; that the bulky object concealed in the blanket was the body of another young woman, naked and lifeless. They pulled out the corpse and laid it on the asphalt, after extracting it from the sheets of plastic wrap that the murderers had used to transport it.

✧

TWO OF THEM WERE ARRESTED immediately. They were wandering around the quarter and couldn't provide any explanation of their presence in the street at that hour. With respect to Viale Pola, they lived so to speak right around the corner, one on Via Capodistria—the street that ran parallel to Viale Pola, likewise a cross street of Via Nomentana—and the other on Via Tolmino. By sheer coincidence, one of them was arrested downstairs from the apartment of the other, where the Carabinieri had gone in search of the father, who was named on the documents as the owner of the Fiat 127. They asked him where his son might be, were duly informed, of course, that he wasn't home, and then, on their way out, right in the courtyard of the palazzo on Via Capodistria, they picked up that son's accomplice.

The other one was spotted, also in the vicinity, by a security guard on night patrol. When asked to explain his presence on the streets late at night, the suspect took to his heels, while the security guard fired shots in the air in order to attract the attention of the police, who were carpeting the QT by this point, in the aftermath of the discovery of the two girls locked in the car trunk. The chase was a long one and the security guard was running out of breath so, panting, he shouted at the fugitive: "Stop, or I'll shoot you!" The other man stopped and leaned against the wall, every bit as exhausted as his pursuer. While the security guard caught up to him, his weapon leveled, he said: "I didn't kill the girls!"

THE THIRD CULPRIT in the crime will never be apprehended.

WHAT HAPPENED is in its way fairly elementary and yet tangled, not such a simple story to tell, in part because, aside from the two victims and the three culprits, it also involves a considerable number of costarring walk-ons who, one after another, or in pairs, come on stage and leave it rather randomly, with no clear explanation why they did so, what their role was, and especially where they went and came from; if their movements were traced on a map with the QT at the center, it would eventually be blackened with lines. Just the comings and goings of that one night, between September 30 and October 1, 1975, on Viale Pola (a lovely tree-shaded little street that resembles anything but the boulevard of its name, "viale," since it is a one-way street with a single lane of traffic, and till then it was known only for the presence of the most respected private university in Rome, whose frontage lined a good long section of the street), reveal an astonishing frequency, like the fibrillation of a seismograph. It is on that same narrow street that two of the main players live, who were at first swept up in the investigation, questioned, and so on. It is also hard to say, quite honestly, when talking about this story, exactly where it begins and ends, its onset and its conclusion. And so I'll make use of abbreviations, omissions, and simplifications.

NOW, let's take a short step back in time, to five days earlier, Thursday, September 25, when two young women are given a ride from in front of the Empire cinema (Viale Regina Margherita, southern boundary of the QT) by a young man who tells them his name is Carlo, even though it's not true, since his real name is Gian Pietro. Courteous, solicitous, he drives them to the Termini train station, where they'll be able to catch the metro to E.U.R. Of the two girls, only one, D.C., the one with the curly hair, will wind up half-dead in the trunk of the Fiat 127; and the self-proclaimed Carlo (that is, the same student who had smashed my classmate Marco Lodoli's eyeglasses), though arrested immediately after the rapes and murder, will be found to have had nothing to do with it. In short, of the three people who begin the episode, only one will wind up in the torture villa made so notorious by the press accounts.

Two days later, on Saturday, September 27, the young man who claimed his name was Carlo calls D.C. and suggests they meet for a date in a place so characteristic and typical of those years that it has been immortalized in films and TV series, while I couldn't say that it's as popular and busy these days. It's at the southern end of E.U.R., which means it's at the outskirts, indeed in many ways already outside the city, where the scent of the sea is in the air and the light is different, clean, windy; it's known as "Il Fungo," that is, the Mushroom, because it's a tower and at the top it spreads out into a large ring that in fact resembles a mushroom cap, and inside that ring is housed a restaurant with a panoramic view. A smaller-scale but nonetheless spectacular precursor, sensational in its time, of the famous Landmark Hotel and Casino in Las Vegas, the one that the aliens blow up in *Mars Attacks!* A longtime meeting spot for genuine Fascists and two-bit *fascistelli*, identifiable as Fascists only by their speech and their attitudes, or else ordinary people stopping off there to meet friends and then continue on their way to the beach at Ostia. D.C. went to the appointment accompanied not by her girlfriend of two days earlier, Nadia, who had other plans (she was at the Lunapark amusement park with two other girlfriends), but another young woman, let's say, a substitute, the unfortunate R.L., who will end up a corpse on the asphalt of Viale Pola; while "Carlo" (let me remind the reader once again, if the reader has any need, that I am not changing his name here out of any authorial prudence, but rather that it was he who from the very outset declined to give his real name, and later had a hard time explaining to the police the reason for his masquerade: "I just did it, for no special reason . . .") showed up together with a young man I'll call Subdued and with Angelo, who had joined the crew, apparently, by pure chance, happening to meet the so-called Carlo at Piazzale delle Muse. A half hour of conversation at Il Fungo and then a new date for the following Monday, out front of the Ambassade cinema, which is also near E.U.R.; now that there are three boys, there is talk of reaching out to Nadia, the girlfriend from the Empire.

On Monday, however, "Carlo" has some studying to do, with a university classmate, after which he has to attend a mathematical analysis class, which means he'll miss the date, leaving Angelo and Subdued to go alone; there, they will find that there are also only two girls, the same ones who came to Il Fungo for that aperitif, since once again Nadia couldn't come, as she was feeling unwell. So Nadia twice narrowly misses a bitter fate, the first time going off to shriek on the roller coasters of Lunapark at E.U.R. with her girlfriends, the second time because of painful menstrual cramps. "Carlo" remains on the sidelines of the story, though he continually brushes against it, intersecting it, given that that same evening of Monday, September 29 (a date that a few years earlier the pop group Equipe 84 had made memorable, with the first major hit written by Lucio Battisti), while the two girls were already being held prisoner in the villa at Monte Circeo (though "Carlo" doesn't know this . . .), he joins one of the murderers, Subdued, who had returned to Rome, on the street downstairs from his apartment, and together they go to pay a call on the third, the Legionnaire, who has not yet entered directly into the mechanics of the crime—he tells them that he is tired and doesn't feel like going out. The next day, the usual routine for "Carlo": that is, studying, class, more studying (with what remains a less-than-ironclad alibi, still sufficient to convince the investigators), but, once night falls, who does he go to meet, outside the Rocci bar at the corner of Via Nomentana and Via di Santa Costanza, around midnight? Angelo. That's right, none other. On foot. "Carlo" tells him to get in the car and together they drive around aimlessly for a couple of hours, and in that time, his friend and classmate never once makes any reference to the fact that he has just returned from Monte Circeo with two young women, swathed in plastic wrap, in the trunk of the car. First of all, the two young men are starving, so they go to the café at the metro station on Piazza Euclide, to eat a couple of sandwiches, then they go to ogle the prostitutes on Via Veneto, and from there to Viale Pola, where Angelo wants to ring his friend's buzzer, outside whose building they parked the Fiat 127 a few hours earlier, but "Carlo" dissuades him from it. And so the person who first turned the handle that set the engine of kidnapping and murder running, and who through the various phases of the crime managed to meet in person all three of the kidnappers and murderers, gets off scot-free.

OCTOBER 1, 1975. As soon as day dawns, the investigators go in search of the mysterious location where the two girls were tortured and beaten. The fragmentary information provided by D.C. ("We were already close to Via Pontina . . . on the left was a hotel with a red sign . . . we turned down a road that was only partially paved . . .") was enough to send the Carabinieri outside Rome, beyond Latina, to Monte Circeo, and after searching the most sparsely inhabited areas for hours and hours, they were able to iden-tify a villa in Punta Rossa at four in the afternoon, a place that they de-cided might well match the description provided by the surviving victim. A French window overlooking the garden stood wide open, but there were no signs of breaking and entering. At last, they decide to go in. The house is a mess, and the Carabinieri find traces of blood in the parlor, along with clumsy attempts to clean it up; most important of all, there are spattered bloodstains on the wall next to the phone. Only a few minutes have passed since the investigators first set foot inside the villa at Monte Circeo, and the officers are already starting to gather evidence of the crimes that were committed there (according to the verdict: murder and attempted murder, with the aggravating factors of manifest intention of concealment of the crime, abject motives, the tortures and cruelty brought to bear, the relative defenselessness of the victims, the abuse of the obligations of hospitality; and after that, abduction and rape; last of all, illegal possession and carry-ing of a firearm), when the owner and her son rush into the villa, namely and respectively, the Legionnaire's mother and brother. They both declare to the officers that they had read about the murder committed at Monte Circeo in that morning's edition of *Il Messaggero*, but that that was not the reason they urgently left Rome to come to the villa. "I had some things to take care of in the house," the woman claims: the villa had been left in a mess after a weekend spent there the week before.

Even though, and again it is the Legionnaire's mother who makes the statement, along the way to Monte Circeo, she had begun to feel a twinge of apprehension when she stopped to purchase another newspaper, *Momento-Sera*, and saw a photo of Angelo published there, next to an article about "serious violent crimes" at Monte Circeo; this reawakened the suspicion that her son might have lent his house keys to Angelo, despite the fact that he had absolutely been forbidden to have any interactions with that individual.

Her other son, too, who had precipitously accompanied his mother there, had also felt a "faint doubt," along with the need to make sure that "everything was shipshape" at the house.

WHETHER THEY THOUGHT the family villa was perfectly shipshape or a complete mess, it's impossible that either the Legionnaire's mother or his brother that morning could possibly have read *any* news about the crime. It had been discovered too late at night, when *Il Messaggero* was already printed and ready to ship to the newsstands. Eh, these are the contradictions, the frayed nerves, the stuttering argumentation of those who hardly expected to stumble into a police questioning session and therefore hadn't had the time to stitch together the facts on the ground with a basic logical thread. They both stubbornly denied having spoken on the phone with the wanted young man or having any idea of his whereabouts, a young man who since that day never ceased to be a person wanted by the police and the subject of relentless pursuit.

BUT LET US NOW TRACK BACK to a few days earlier, that is, to that notorious Monday, September 29, 1975, outside the Ambassade cinema. It was supposed to be a normal date, boys and girls going out together. But since that's not at all what was going on, let's skip right over the so-what-should-we-do, the where-should-we-go, the to-the-movies? the deceitful suggestion, "Let's go to Lavinio, to Carlo's house, and he'll catch up with us later." Instead let's leap straight to the villa at Monte Circeo. It's an isolated place and the road to reach it is so inaccessible that to get there the young people in the car were forced to stop more than once to ask directions.

✛

IT WAS ABOUT SIX IN THE EVENING, and the girls had promised they'd be home early. Angelo opened the door with a key he pretended to have found near the front gate. The young men couldn't find their way around the house very successfully, though they'd been there before, and couldn't even find the light switches. There were a few preliminary come-ons but the girls refused to take their clothes off. They claimed they were still virgins, and that they wanted to go home now. So one of the two young men pulled out a gun and threatened them: "We're in the Marseille gang! We've got all the police on our tail, they're hunting for us high and low!" and added that soon their boss would be joining them—Jacques, a terrifying guy. The girls, frightened, insisted that they wanted to be taken back to Rome. Whereupon the two boys grabbed them and shoved them into a bathroom, shutting the door and locking it.

A little while later, the one I'm calling Subdued went back to his home in Rome, to have dinner with his parents, after which he drove around town with his friends, between the QT and Piazzale delle Muse, as I described at the beginning of the book, before heading back to Monte Circeo. Angelo had told the girls that his friend had gone to get some sleep. He let R.L. out of the bathroom, then brought her back completely naked, asked D.C. to come out of the bathroom, and locked R.L. back inside. He dragged the girl to a bedroom and threatened her, "*Se strilli, ti addobbo*"—literally, "If you yell, I'll deck you out." "*Addobbare*," or "deck" as in "deck the halls," or decorate, is a neo-Romanesco term, a late addition to Rome's dialect and already largely obsolete, almost invariably used as a threat: "*Guarda che t'addobbo*"—"Look out or I'll deck you out," often with a further specification, "*come 'n arbero de Natale*," literally, "like a Christmas tree," meaning "I'll beat you black and blue." After which, Angelo made her strip naked and forced her to take his penis in her mouth. It was in that context that, either to frighten her or else, according to him, to establish an atmosphere of reciprocal trust, he invented the lie that he had helped to pull off the Bulgari kidnapping, which had taken place a few months earlier.

IN HER STATEMENTS TO INVESTIGATORS, the surviving girl said that the tenor of the rest of the night remained unchanged. It was one in the morning, or possibly later, and in the meantime Subdued had returned from Rome.

"Angelo came back into the bathroom. He assured us that he'd let us go, but then he said that if Jacques wanted him to, he'd have to kill us. With Angelo was his friend. They forced me to take his penis in my mouth. He got mad and told me that I didn't know how to do a single thing right. A short while later they told me to call my friend. 'We need to take one of these girls' virginity.' We begged them to let us go and they laughed, they were making fun of us."

Then Subdued placed his member in R.L.'s mouth and pledged to Angelo that he would take her virginity. In the meantime, Angelo was fondling D.C. but said he wouldn't be up to deflowering her.

They locked them back in the bathroom, naked, until the morning. After a nap, around dawn, they moved the car out of the villa's courtyard, worried that the gardener might show up and see it. R.L. continued screaming and moaning, and Subdued threatened the girls with his belt, unfastening it from his trousers, cursing and shouting, "Shut up, the two of you, or I'll kill you," while Angelo kept a pistol trained on them. They moved the girls from one bathroom to another, still naked, and then put them back in the first bathroom. Until the afternoon of Tuesday, September 30, that's the way things went in the villa at Monte Circeo, or that's the point at which they remained fixed, as if rerunning repeatedly the same brief clips: the boys threatened the kidnapped girls, made them come out of the bathroom, first one then the other, then one of the boys would force one of the girls to take his member in her mouth, the girls would beg, the phone would ring. Subdued thought that the most serious thing they'd done hadn't been to beat the girls up or force them to perform fellatio, but to lock them in the bathroom. It turned it into a case of kidnapping. But they absolutely had to wait until Jacques got there. In the meantime, the girls, locked in the bathroom, had caused a minor disaster . . .

AND THE MINOR DISASTER WAS THAT, it's unclear exactly how, the faucet on the bathroom sink broke. In these vacation homes, the plumbing doesn't get much use, the pipes oxidize and corrode, the washers crumble. The water sprays out of the broken faucet and floods the bathroom. The young men fly into a rage and start slapping their prisoners around. Then, again under the threat of the pistol, for the umpteenth time, they transfer the two young women to the other bathroom, this one also windowless.

UNTIL AROUND FOUR IN THE AFTERNOON, the stalemate is broken by the arrival of Jacques, the Marseillais, from Rome. The future Legionnaire. Jacques immediately takes control of the situation. He talks with the girls (without any French accent, of course), reassures them, and explains to them that no more harm will be done to them, as long as they swear they won't breathe a word about what's happened so far. "If you don't want to go to bed with me, I won't insist." Then, though, he tells them that they have to make love with each other, in front of him. He forces them to embrace and touch each other. Then he chooses R.L. and leads her into a bedroom. Angelo keeps the other girl with him and once again tries to penetrate her. He lunges on top of her, crams a pillow over her face, while Subdued starts kicking her. D.C. shrieks in pain and fear, and no matter how hard Angelo might try, rubbing his sex against the girl's pudendum and manipulating it to obtain an erection, he can't manage to penetrate her. Angrily, he tells his accomplice to take care of it, but Subdued refuses. "I don't like this one."

From behind the closed door of the room where Jacques has taken the other girl, her screams can be heard. Subdued assumes that Jacques is deflowering her, opens the door, and sees R.L. on the bed and Jacques on top of her. They're both naked. The girl is shrieking with pain. Subdued shuts the door again.

WHEN SHE EMERGED FROM THE ROOM, R.L. had blood between her thighs. She was bewildered, her legs wobbly. "Can I go get washed up?" she asked in a toneless voice. Jacques, completely naked, ordered the other girl to come with him, and told the other men to take the girl he had just raped to the top floor. He was gentle with D.C., he kissed her and told her not to worry, they would take the two of them home after putting them to sleep. In the meantime, outside, it was getting dark. The occupants of the villa didn't notice because the shutters had been closed the whole time, since the previous afternoon.

THE LEGIONNAIRE PULLED OUT some vials. He also had a length of surgical tubing, for use as a tourniquet, and a syringe. He went back down to the ground floor, taking D.C. with him, opened the box of vials, broke four of them into an ashtray, filling it with a red liquid, drew it into the syringe, and injected it into the girl's arm. Then he went upstairs to do the same with the other prisoner, who was confined on the top floor. After that, he went back downstairs and gave D.C. a second injection because the first one hadn't had any effect. What effect was it supposed to have? Put her to sleep? Kill her? Then he went back up to the top floor. In the meantime, Angelo was playing with the tourniquet, and saying: "You can't guess how many people I've strangled with these things."

THE TWO MEN ON THE GROUND FLOOR started to get dressed again. They let D.C. put on her pants. After being subjected to further maltreatment, more of the same, D.C. passed out. They took advantage of the opportunity to go clean up a little and mop up the water from the leak in the bathroom. But when they go back to the living room, they realize that the girl is awake and has dialed the phone and is holding the receiver in her hand. She's called 113, the Italian 911. "Hello, they're murdering me . . ." Subdued rushed over to her, grabbed the phone out of her hand, hung up, and then kicked her in the face. The girl's blood sprayed onto the wall behind the phone, staining it. She got up and tried to rush toward the outside door, which was unlocked, but Subdued beat her to it and, using a tool he'd found in the yard, hit her on the head and at various places all over her body. The tool was a steel-reinforced club. The Legionnaire, who had come back down to the ground floor, ordered them to hurry and dial other phone numbers so that it wouldn't be possible to trace the last call from the villa. The others hastened to do as he said. Then Angelo took the belt from his pants and wrapped it around D.C.'s neck. He dragged her around the house. She screamed. "If you scream again, I'll throttle you." Evidently, she continued to scream and Angelo choked her, tighter and tighter, until the belt broke. Then he hit her with the pistol butt, while Subdued went on beating her with the steel-tipped club.

ON THE TOP FLOOR of the villa at Monte Circeo, R.L. was drowned in the bathtub. Aside from the other evidence found, during the autopsy, in the re-spiratory passageways (a thick mucus, foam, and froth plug, massive emphysema caused by pulmonary hyperexpansion, subpleural hemor-rhagic petechiae—all phenomena typical of drowning rather than a slower

asphyxiation), the ecchymosis and swelling on her face could also be attributed to the violent and repeated immersion of R.L.'s head in the bathtub.

SO ONE OF THE GIRLS was dead before the group began its trip back to
Rome. The second girl showed no signs of life. They had beaten her so hard
and so long that they were exhausted. Subdued kicked her one last time to
see whether she was alive or dead. During his depositions, he would claim
that he'd seen her move, though just barely. She was bleeding badly. To keep
from getting blood on themselves, Angelo and Subdued wrapped the body
in plastic sheeting, but it kept slipping out of their hands, sliding around,
so they put the body back down and wrapped it in a blanket. Then they took
it to the trunk of the Fiat 127, which had been driven back to the villa's
courtyard, and shut the trunk, leaving the keys in the lock. As proof that
they thought she was still alive, Subdued tells the investigators that in the
past he had even locked his dog in the trunk, when he went hunting with
his father in Manziana, and that enough air got in for it to breathe. Then
they went back into the house to do a quick cleanup, mopping the blood off
the floor and wiping it off the walls. The Legionnaire alone would take care
of transporting R.L.'s corpse downstairs and placing it in the trunk. They
started off in two cars, Subdued's Fiat 127, with the two young women in
the trunk, and the yellow Mini Minor belonging to the Legionnaire, alias
Jacques the Marseillais. On the way back to Rome, Angelo rode with him.
They stopped to buy a couple of cans of Coca-Cola. Then, when they had
almost reached Viale Pola, Angelo moved over to the Fiat 127.

DURING THE TRIP BACK, the girl who was still alive tried shaking the other
girl with her elbow, but she remained inert. Pressed against her, in the darkness of the car trunk, D.C. couldn't even figure out where R.L.'s head and
feet were. But she understood that she was dead. In any case, she refrained
from calling her name and speaking to her for fear that the two men might
hear her. She heard one of them saying: "Shhh, what good little sleepers
these two are . . ." and "Silence! We have two dead women here."

THE VERSION OF THE CR/M provided by Angelo is dreamlike, somnambulis-
tic, and yet still full of details, annotations, and interpretations and descriptions of states of mind, real or fictitious. Aside from telling, in all likelihood,

a considerable array of lies to the investigators, Angelo candidly confesses all the lies that were told to the young women. But he may be lying even when he confesses to the lies. They are, so to speak, lies squared. Not only the lies that were necessary to lure them into the trap; during the long phase of the kidnapping, while the young women were being held captive, he invents a bunch of stories, embellishments, he likes to exaggerate, invert, or romanticize human interactions, introducing moments of intimacy and something approaching naïveté that give a certain color to his personality. His shifts in mood and attitude are sudden and wild. When the actual kidnapping begins, Angelo narrates that moment as if there were uncontrollable forces at work inside him that overwhelmed his very conscience. "I didn't realize that by locking the girls in the bathroom our friendship would be damaged and that that would mean the end of any dialogue with them." Dialogue? Dialogue?! (Ah, that word so beloved of the priests and the school run by priests that he and I had both attended until the previous year . . .) The dialogue had come to an end in spite of him, and to his chagrin. The realization that he was committing a crime had passed through Subdued's mind, but not Angelo's; and so he doesn't give his friend time to hesitate and think it over, he pushes the girls into the bathroom and locks the door.

From that moment on, all sorts of anxiety and concern spangle the night. "I thought my mother might be crying. Every time that I came home late, I found the family worried, all of them just a wreck." "I had left word for my father that I was staying with a friend of mine, at his villa at Monte Circeo, and that the next day I'd be going to the American market [flea market] in Latina," where you could buy used shirts and jeans like new for a handful of lire, but you had to go very early. When, at dawn, he unlocks the bathroom door and finds the two girls inside, naked and terrified, on their knees begging to be allowed to leave, he justifies himself by telling them he can't do as they ask because in the meantime other men who are wanted by the law have arrived, and are upstairs in the villa, so he can't reveal the presence of the two hostages to them, otherwise things would just be so much the worse for them. "At this point I started to get the impression that the girls no longer believed the stories I was telling them."

BUT THE SEQUENCE OF LIES *and fantasies traced back to the very outset. Aside from the story of the Marseille gang and the Bulgari kidnapping, when the girls ask for the first time to be taken back home, otherwise they won't know what to tell their parents if they get back late, how they'll be able to explain,*

Angelo suggests that they just tell them a lie, that is, that they had been forced into a car by a bunch of thugs who had taken them to a pine grove. That is, he recommends that they gin up a fairy tale that just happens to be a chilling copy of the truth: as if they weren't him and Subdued, he invents a bunch of thugs and kidnappers to help the young women find a way out of their unpleasant quandary. To stir them to pity, he tells them that his mother died of heartbreak when he was in prison in Marseille. He gets irritated when the home phone keeps ringing and it might be the Legionnaire's parents calling, or the Legionnaire himself calling to let them know that his parents are arriving. So it's probably best not to answer. He asks the two girls "as a joke, in a humorous tone" to have sex with each other: and that's because, according to him, R.L. had confessed to him that she had a weakness for girls, and for D.C. in particular. Even though he feels riddled with anguish and dark thoughts, among them emerges the awareness that he's going to spend the night away from home, which will make his parents worry: "But, now that I was here, I might as well enjoy the night."

IF HE DOESN'T BEHAVE in an entirely rational manner, it's because he's sleep-deprived. He continually steps away for a brief nap. He says that he didn't have the pistol, his accomplice had it, then he doubts his own statement: "I don't know where he got the pistol and whether he really had told me that or whether I'd imagined it. Sometimes I imagine things that I believe are true, things that refer to higher levels, meaning emotions." Angelo in fact confesses that he is very sentimental and emotional: he never quite recovered from the way a troubled relationship ended, a romance with a girl he loved, nor from the "collapse of his political ideals." He's afraid of this and that, he's alarmed, tense. Then, however, he promises D.C., "Now I'm going to take your virginity," and his friend piles on, but just to scare her a little, "No, I'll deflower you, but with a broom handle." After Jacques arrives, his tension seems to subside somewhat and a strange disinterest takes over concerning the ending of an affair that has been dragging on for too long already. He is struck only by certain details: the phone that flies out of D.C.'s hands when Subdued hits her, the dog that Subdued took "to Manziana," locked in the trunk, his revulsion at the blood on D.C.'s face, after she has been kicked repeatedly. He's almost chivalrous when he asks the young woman if she'd rather be put to sleep with an injection, "or if you like with a blow to the head." On Via Pontina, when the Legionnaire's Mini Minor stops "right in front of a police station" and Angelo gets out to buy the cans of Coca-Cola, *he forgets to collect the change from the barista. "I'm sure that the people in the bar noticed my condition, I was a wreck, and they were looking at me." He always feels eyes on the back of his neck.*

Once he'd returned to Rome, his wanderings in the few hours between September 30 and October 1 are too random and intricate to be described without inducing confusion. Angelo wanders like a robot, starving and exhausted, he passes and repasses through Viale Pola, the last time without even noticing that where they had left the Fiat 127, the Carabinieri are now gathering, he's just looking for a water fountain where he can wash his face, "because my head was exploding."

||

AH, YES, GOOD MANNERS. They guaranteed a net savings of time and mental energy: by observing them you eliminated all doubts and pointless hesitations. Nothing creates greater anxiety than uncertainty about the right thing to say or do, exposing yourself on positions that few others will support or share.

(The same thing happens with *bad* manners.)

Going along, in any case, entails a lower cost than standing out for going your own way. And even if everyone likes the idea of being considered a nonconformist, a dispassionate reckoning would show us that most of the times that we wandered away from the majority consensus, we've turned out to be wrong. The effort to distinguish ourselves led us astray from the path of justice; rather than imitating the others when they spoke the truth, we chose to swear to the false.

THE THREE PILLARS OF ANY EDUCATION, any upbringing, were these: persuasion, threat, punishment. But more than pillars, they were phases. If the first one worked, then there was no need to apply the successive phases. If the first two phases were sufficient, then the last one remained unutilized. But if after the explanations—reasonable—and the threats—disproportionate—the subject remained adamant, unmoved, then it was necessary to *punish him*. The chapter of punishments had not yet been drawn up because in that period there were no longer any valid, well-tested ones, none that could be applied without a second thought, such as a whipping or bed without dinner, and the punishments of modern pedagogy were still in an experimental phase. We were raised during the interval when everything was allowed and where, for the same infraction (a bad grade in math or a lie or a theft), among families that were otherwise quite similar to one another, in one family you might be punished by being sent to your room, in another by having your allowance cut or being grounded for the week, and in a third by the suspension of expensive gifts or your favorite foods, or else with straight-armed smacks to the face, verbal sarcasm ("You're a pathetic moron, a mental defective"), or else with the exaction of the simple promise "I won't do it again," and the matter was closed. Alongside these common approaches, which parents made use of on a fairly random basis, there were a few others, custom-tailored, personalized.

The most singular case might have been the writer who, having made the ideological decision never to punish his daughter, punished himself instead. He would stand in the doorway of his daughter's bedroom, look her right in the eye, and list her misdeeds in a brokenhearted yet chilly voice ("You smoke hash, I know you do, even though I begged you not to . . ."), and then he'd start banging his forehead against the doorjamb. Bam, bam, bam, gently at first, then bam-bam-BAM! harder and faster.

And as he did, he murmured: "There's nothing I can do about it. But I just want you to know that you're causing me a great deal of pain through your actions . . ."

And the head-banging continues.

I read once that in England up until the eighteenth century it was customary to pair a scion of the nobility with a son of peasants the same age, to serve as a sort of double, a proxy. A relationship of equivalency between the two boys: since the aristocrat could not be given corporal punishment, whenever he committed some misdeed, the peasant boy was whipped in his stead. And he was dubbed, in fact, the whipping boy. Had the rich boy stolen jam from the kitchen? Then the poor boy got the whipping, and what was the result? That the rich boy, even if he hadn't tasted the blows of the switch, was thought to suffer from pangs of guilt and sorrow for the blows his poor companion had received. In the case that I described above, it was the parent who chose to take the role of whipping boy for his daughter: he maltreated himself instead of punishing her. The spectacle was a pathetic one, but the self-punishment did achieve the goal of afflicting the guilty party, that is the girl, who in fact became increasingly eccentric over time and finally went completely mad.

In middle school, I had a classmate named Venanzio, one of the very few students at SLM who managed to flunk entirely, and so he transferred to a different school. At his house, his parents went old-school, pounding away, beating him for the slightest shortcoming, until this habit of theirs caused a very singular incident.

He must have been about twelve years old when his mother, infuriated because he had been outside playing, instead of inside studying, gave him a good hard smack, only the latest in a long succession of them, and not a particularly violent one, but it was well aimed. Where? At the seat of his pants. The seat of the pants where, for centuries, the corrective frenzy of schoolteachers and kin had found its target. And Venanzio's mother had such an extra-fine, well-honed technique that she could have taken on the task of serial-spanking all the kids of the quarter. But the fact is that Venanzio, on that afternoon out and about with the rest of us, had stocked up on firecrackers (left over from the New Year's celebrations), and at the very moment his mother let fly, the back pocket of his trousers was stuffed full of them.

Miccette is what we call in Rome those little firecrackers an inch and a half or two inches in length, their fuses braided into strings of twenty or so: light that fuse and they go off in rapid succession, making a tremendous racket. Venanzio must have had a hundred or so *miccette* in his pocket, but his mother didn't happen to notice the bulge, and she had no time to notice because the minute my friend walked into his home, after the door opened at his knock, his mother, without a word, simply stepped aside and let him walk past her, and then spun around and hit him, with her hand opened wide, like a spatula, right on his ass.

It was the most powerful spanking ever given in all of human history. Upon impact, the *miccette* all went off at the same time with a roar and Venanzio was propelled forward, rocketing across the room with a spectacular burst of flame that burned his mother's hand but that especially burned him. It took three weeks in the hospital and then months of ointments and bandages before the burn was entirely healed; it seemed to be incurable, as if the absurd manner in which it had been procured somehow had a negative effect on the normal process of scar formation, and even now Venanzio has an unfortunate reminder between buttock and hip, a sort of round stamp the diameter of a tea saucer, he sometimes tugs down the elastic band of his trunks to show it off at the beach. The flesh there is white and fibrous.

And about that scar he says, ironically but almost with regret, that justice would have been better served if it had been shaped like his mother's hand.

His mother was so shocked by what happened that she never raised a hand to him again, never employed any other means of correction, and indeed no one in his home ever again dared to so much as scold the boy, who thus grew up wounded but happy, and utterly savage. His manners provoked at the very most a little grumbling, but never any actual sanctions.

When he was older, and the memory of the dramatic event had faded, his father regained the nerve to scold him, or perhaps it was just his personality that, as he aged, had become increasingly choleric. The thing in particular that drove his father crazy was Venanzio's way of sitting down to meals, which was in fact particularly slovenly, and since he had also grown a sparse beard, whenever he ate, this beard was always spattered with tomato sauce. His father gazed at him, turgid with scorn.

Until he finally couldn't take it, and blurted out a succession of insults in front of his siblings and mother.

"Venanzio, you're *a filthy pig*!" and he'd get up from the table in disgust, tossing aside his napkin.

"Nothing but a fil-thy pig," he'd carefully enunciate. Then he'd be seized by a realization, and he'd correct himself.

"No . . . you're not a pig, pigs are *useful* animals . . . you're just plain useless, harmful, in fact!"

IT'S A TRUISM THAT, without violating the dictates of fine manners, you can wind up gutting each other in a knife fight. Etiquette frowns upon cleaning your fingernails at the dinner table or spitting on the floor, it cautions against disturbing your neighbor's afternoon nap, but it makes no mention whatsoever, doesn't even criticize, the act of stabbing someone. So, take it from me, you'd better not annoy him with loud music, but you can certainly murder him. As I've had ample opportunity to learn from my contacts behind bars, it's possible to be an extremely courteous murderer, a chivalrous strangler, a paid killer and yet positively ceremonious. It's true that in these cases what's at stake isn't etiquette, but rather the divine commandments. But perhaps it's no accident that when people focus on surface aspects, on the formal boundaries of behavior, a void remains at the center. We naïvely take it for granted that this void will automatically be filled in by the most obvious moral principles, such as thou shalt not kill, thou shalt not steal. While I have frequently scolded my children for sitting down to a meal with filthy hands, sending them straight off to wash them, I've never felt it was necessary to explain to them that you mustn't murder a person. It struck me as unnecessary, almost offensive to explain to a young mind, in part because children have always seemed to me to be very clear-minded when it comes to morality, indeed, far more rigid than adults. Rarely will a child accept compromises on what is true and what is false, the kind of compromises so often adopted by adults. They want no shadows, no middle ground, no shades of gray. The stubborn child, I believe, is the creature that inspired the evangelical precept "But let your communication be, Yea, yea; Nay, nay: for whatsoever is more than these cometh of evil" (Matthew 5:37), and for that matter, there is a childish punctiliousness about all of Christ's preachings, they are characterized by a deeply infantile intransigence. The fanaticism of innocence, the pure eye, the mouth of truth. The mouths of babes. The Pharisees, in contrast, they are certainly wise, they are adult. Pontius Pilate is too, with his half-measures, such as fustigation, after all, that was an acceptable compromise, wasn't it?

No, it wasn't.

That is why it is thought useless to spend time explaining the fundamentals, and why we concentrate instead on details, we specialize. The same thing happens in schools today, where general curricula are no longer studied, but extremely detailed local research projects are carried out instead, on a theme, creating explicative panels, elaborating creative texts, and by the end of elementary school, although the pupils have no idea of where Brescia or the Danube might be, they do know everything about a certain farm that produces organic foods, where they went on a field trip.

SOMETHING TELLS ME that at least one of the murderers sat at the table with perfect posture, elbows tight at his sides . . .

A CRIME like the one I've just narrated so concisely was an exceptional event in the QT and, as such, it ought to have stood out in the conscience of the quarter's inhabitants, so alien was it to their mind-set and their shared experience. Ponderation, caution, hard work, prudence, decorum, what did all these things have to do with that monstrosity? Among good people, certain things just don't happen. The graver and rarer an infraction, the more it ought to encourage the citizens to feel upright, encircling them in an isolating barrier, cordoning them off. The alliance among honest citizens is the sole positive fallout of a crime. The moral reaction that makes it possible to restore the values offended, to recognize them as fundamental and defend them collectively. Instead, that's not what happened at all. That crime did nothing to bring the inhabitants of the QT into a common point of view, it simply terrorized them and made them suspicious of one another. It actually drove them to doubt themselves, which is the most worrisome schism of them all. Reading the newspapers, as you might gaze down a well where, in the depths, your own image flickers, quivering, dim and shapeless, they thought they could recognize a hidden flaw, a demon stirring at the foundations of that way of life. Instead of being sterilized by a solid, united moral front, the wound grew infected and spread total uncertainty about *who* had done *what*, and *why*, and about who had been, in any case, capable of doing it, willing and ready to do it; in every home, on every street, in every classroom in all the schools, in every group of friends or family, the crime proliferated with a refraction effect that made it infinitely possible, because the elements that went to make it up were in point of fact common and available everywhere you looked— boys and girls, a car and a vacation home, phones ringing, plastic bags, university textbooks to underline, jeans, ice cream. There was no need for any special scenario, no need for urgent motivations nor any particular succession of events, in other words, it wasn't even particularly necessary to be criminals to commit that kind of crime. The crime was gratuitous, the crime was for sheer dilettantes, which meant it was within reach of *anyone*. Easy, convenient, no one was ruled out as either a perpetrator or a victim. The indignation of the first few days gave way to a new realization that sent shivers down the spine: the discovery, that is, that the margins of prevention and protection against what had happened were much more slender than anyone had ever dreamed, indeed, those margins *simply didn't exist*. They never had. It was pointless to go on expressing pointless astonishment and indignation: it was the very same practical bourgeois spirit that unveiled the fault, just like when a solid professional accountant goes over the ledgers with a fine-tooth comb, recalculates the accounts, and discovers the trick. All it took was a pinch of reasonable understanding to see that an entire life built entirely on reasonable understanding didn't guarantee a damned thing, in fact, it had thrown open the gates to the very thing it should have warded off: the unreasonable, the demented. Pure horror. An ordinary mistake, starting from which all the subsequent calculations had turned out to be mistaken. Believing that they were immunizing themselves against evil by simply never exposing themselves to it, never even acknowledging the remote possibility of it, they had developed an extremely weak organism, atrophied, incapable of reacting to that which was no longer familiar. Which meant there were no longer (or more accurately, there never had been) any safe places or settings, and the ones that had been deemed safe now revealed themselves to be potentially the most dangerous of all.

An unspeakable consternation began to settle over all those families that had sent their children to the same school as the murderers, a place that they had considered until then as a further special reservation of safety, inside an already well-protected world, as was the QT. And instead of steering them clear of trouble, they had plunged them right into the midst of it. To protect them from contagion, they'd locked them up with a bunch of sick people. The type of panic caused by this revelation manifests itself in the form of the so-called cold sweats. The internal agitation, unable to vent itself, expresses itself as a stiffening and a stale sheen of perspiration that bathes the temples and drips down your back. Everything you've done or said or believed until then suddenly appears false. No action can be undertaken, you can neither attack nor defend yourself, all meaning has vanished into thin air. It is no longer a rhetorical expression to say that time stands still.

IT IS SAID THAT AFRICAN VILLAGES, once night has fallen, are besieged, right up to the doors of the houses, by the spirit of the wild. It is as if with darkness the savanna reclaims possession of everything that man has taken away from it by the light of day, in the pitiful illusion that he has conquered that wilderness for good. Human space shrinks, people barricade themselves indoors, leaving everything else to the mercy of dark and menacing forces. The same thing happened in the QT. We only felt safe shut up in our homes, our apartments, in the dining rooms where the rules of family life reigned, a way of life that unfolded at its constant lazy pace, lulled by the humming of the refrigerator and the chirping of the radio, as if nothing could ever alter it; the preparation of meals, sleep, study, the washing of clothes, the ritual, harmless arguments between the generations over the dinner table. Let's be clear, it's not as if private life was exempt from drama and tragedy, but those cases were never sufficient to call into question, to throw into crisis the entire system. The death of a father or a daughter who's been shooting up alone isn't enough to bring down an entire civilization: a civilization that in the QT, just like in so many other places around the world, continues undisturbed to evolve or decay, but at rhythms that are so slow and with changes that are so subtle that it requires several generations to even register them and metabolize their meaning. Indoors, in other words, things turn slowly, "the silent calm of an aquarium reigns over all." But between one apartment house and the next, the space proved to be riddled with booby traps. A gust of wind was enough to erase all the rules that had guided our lives, indeed, the very idea that there ever had been such a thing as a law. Immediately outside the private setting of the home, the tree-lined streets, the piazzas, and the wide stretches of road in the QT, which in terms of their decorum and anonymity perfectly matched the domestic interiors, could easily turn every bit as savage as any canyon. A cold wind, perhaps simply a shiver down your back, a strange shadow might materialize without warning within a panorama that remained utterly familiar in every way, in its everday image exempt from the slightest shadow of danger: Bar Tortuga, the photo booth, the scooters parked in front of Giulio Cesare High School, the 38 bus roaring past, heading for Piazza Istria.

WHILE IN A TRENCH DURING WARTIME, you expect to die from one moment to the next, you're there for that very reason, that's the right place and the right time to catch a bullet between the eyes, the murder victims of the QT had not even the slightest idea that this day might be their last, as they were hurrying to catch the bus, walking their dog, opening their apartment house door, leaning against a car smoking a cigarette: and many of them didn't even realize that anyone was about to kill them. There was no reason to expect it, no warning signs, it was an ordinary day.

ON PAPER, the QT is bounded to the west by Via Salaria, to the south by Viale Regina Margherita, on the east by Via Nomentana, and to the north by the Aniene River. But the true boundaries of the QT were marked like those of the city of Sparta, as stated by one of its generals: Sparta stretches as far as my spear will reach.

SO PAY CLOSE ATTENTION TO THIS POINT: patience, tolerance, restraint, and prudence are constantly on the verge of being turned upside down and transformed into their opposites, indeed they're often nothing more than paradoxical manifestations of their exact contrary: calm is merely fury in disguise, tolerance is a "coded" performance of aggression, the domination we impose upon ourselves is no less relentless than the domination we'd gladly impose upon others, if only we could, decorum is a mask we apply to a face devastated by obscene desires, and if you examined it with sufficiently close attention, you'd notice how diabolically the features emerge. So much furor beneath the surface, all that magma boiling under that peaceful crust! Violence announces itself in its most threatening way precisely as repressed violence. The virtues bear subtle traces of the delirium out of which they originated, and which might at any instant snatch them back, taking renewed possession of them. If modesty is born of sin, it resembles it as a son resembles the father. Sovereign mastery over one's feelings, detachment, and self-control, which constitute the principal bourgeois contribution to morality, only increase the inner gap by means of which people can observe and judge themselves as if they were safe on the far shore, on the opposite cliff face, across the yawning gorge, but if you are forced to cross back over, clinging to a dangling rope, at that point the oscillation truly begins to swing wide, the velocity becomes dizzying, and you find yourself catapulted into the void if you release your grip for so much as an instant.

AND SO, in perfect unison, everyone thought the same thing but did not say it, they didn't dare to openly utter their thoughts, instead they barricaded themselves in their doubt. They preferred to battle alone against nothingness, which in the end drives you to embrace it. There can be no more ferocious form of conformism than the kind that expresses itself in segregated, incubated forms, where everyone thinks the same thing but in private, refraining from communicating those thoughts. When everyone curses the same god in their thoughts. I believe that there was never a time around here in which people did so little talking as in the aftermath of the CR/M; among fathers and mothers and sons and daughters, between husbands and wives, between the sexes, a strange laconicism descended; everyone might have encountered grounds for criticism in everyone else, the right to upbraid one another for faults more or less blindly, but knowing by now that no matter what direction you hurled that stone of blame, even at random, you were bound to hit something (insofar as young, insofar as old, insofar as male or female, insofar as bourgeois, you were certainly implicated and you had a sin to expiate), it was better for everyone to remain silent and when all was said and done it would have been difficult even to establish *what* exactly was up for discussion, the topic defied analysis. The fear of letting a detail slip out, something that might later be used as evidence against you, meant it was probably best to keep your lips zipped even with the people you trusted: because they in particular might easily become the most fearsome accusers. Truth be told, any aspect of life was already weighty evidence of guilt, sufficient to bring a conviction. Aspects that might at first glance seem positive, for instance, could prove to be red-handed proof. If you were an honest, hardworking father, then you were guilty of absentee distraction. If you'd married well and lived a quiet life, so much the worse. And let's even talk about your bank account, or cheerful family vacations, all images of respectable conformity that could be turned inside out as so many crushing exhibits of evidence, proof of guilt. A dignified appearance—you could swear that it concealed nasty surprises. And so, in short order, out of convenience, the respectable mask of indignation and wholesale rejection was put back on. The problem was put away and forgotten because of its monstrosity, the declarations of horror became ritual and detached, as if we were talking about a catastrophe fallen from the sky or a disease, an earthquake. "How could it be that such good boys . . ." It sank out of sight, and the surface closed over it.

THE OTHERS COME BEFORE US: in families the imperative reigns of doing things "for others" and not "for yourself."

It is necessary to respect, to honor others, not to offend, listen to them when they speak, be courteous, if possible satisfy their demands. In reality, what is requested is often strictly an exterior tribute: a minimum of etiquette to facilitate the normal flow of everyday actions. Perhaps the least foolish aspect of bourgeois morality is in fact its pronounced formalism, which never demands the complete adherence to what one says and does, and indeed always safeguards a certain quota of inner freedom, even though in the final analysis this margin is reduced to being able to say one thing while thinking another. To being, in short, the first not to believe in your own words. Liberty, therefore, coincides with the shadow beneath which hypocrisy protects true feeling, it is specifically that dimly lit space, devoid of faith, ambiguous. The cool shade of disbelief. The virtual identity of bourgeois morality and Christian morality breaks at this point. Bourgeois morality seemed to be nothing more than a double for Christian morality, but it proves to be autonomous where it defends in a punctilious manner superficial choices, latter-day Phariseeism, as opposed to the total adhesion of the soul that Christ demands. Its underlying principle is based on a practical order: let's say that I am well behaved, or pretend to be, in the end what matters is whether my behavior is or is not good, independent of whether or not it is heartfelt, if it's the fruit of conviction or deceit. You may even feel proud of yourself when you go along with standard opinion even though you don't share it a bit. If any correct behavior is artificial, the bourgeois can rightly expect it from anyone: if you're not good, you still have to behave *as if* you were. And that's the point, *as if*. The child who yawns while having dinner with his grandparents, though no one can demand that he not be bored (impossible!), one may rightly demand that he "politely" place his hand over his mouth when he yawns. That is the only reasonable demand that can be made . . . Act *as if* . . .

How much hatred the truth produces! While secrecy renders light and free not only those who conceal it, but especially those who overlook it, who do not know. "No, please, I don't want to know anything about it" is the formula of those who wish to remain free.

THE REAL PROBLEM with the truth is whether or not to speak it.

12

ICERO: "Is there anything more sacred, anything more surrounded by all kinds of inviolability than the individual citizen's home?" "His haven is inviolable." I think it was Ernst Jünger, in less lofty terms, who reminded us that the inviolability of the domicile isn't some abstract right elaborated in the archives of generations of jurists, but rather that this principle springs from a concrete and archaic image: that of the father of the family who, accompanied by his sons, appears with the ax on the threshold of his dwelling. Just try and get into that home. That is *real* inviolability: if you cross that threshold without their permission, they'll cut you into pieces. The Vikings don't quibble over fine points. Well, the present-day bourgeois may not stand guard at night at the front door to his apartment, but when he locks that door behind him, armor-plated or not, he can sit around in his boxer shorts watching TV and not even the king or the pope have the right to enter.

That is how the concept of privacy was born.

The cult of separation: from the succession of rooms, the enfilade of the aristocratic palazzo, devoid of any and all privacy since you must walk through one room after another to get from one place in the building to another, and where everything unfolds, from morning awakening to donning one's clothes, to meals and business and conversations, beneath the eyes of a crowd of people, for the most part household staff (which is the reason for the invention of the so-called cabinets, where one can be alone or keep secret company), to the bourgeois hallways along which side rooms open up.

The myth of the *locked door*.

The only thing that could penetrate the barrier of the locked door was noise.

Records, hair dryers, laughter.

Musical instruments.

And then the sounds of sex: sex between parents; sex among children, solitary or in couples.

A young woman I met at Giulio Cesare High School gave me a memorable account of her first sexual experiences, around the age of sixteen. Back then, it was normal to have a couple of boyfriends you'd let feel you up and kiss you in a more or less adventuresome fashion, and then the right boy would come along and you'd take him to bed. And if he wasn't the right *boy* then it was the right *time* to do it, in fact, around that age, sixteen or seventeen, a little earlier or a little later, depending on lots of different factors. The girls of my generation were the first female Italians to have *all* lost their virginity before marriage. They did it because they felt like it, out of desire, at the insistence of their boyfriends or in emulation of their girlfriends. The distinction had vanished between easy girls and respectable girls, as the males of the preceding generations had designated them, the males who, like Alberto Sordi, had to travel to Sweden to meet available young women (back then the adjective used was "uninhibited"), or else pay for sex. Boys my age only had to show some patience or have some luck in finding a girlfriend who was already emancipated or ready to become emancipated. There was a line dividing the high school girls between those who "had already done it" and those who "hadn't done it yet," but that was just a matter of time. We already knew everything about some girls, about others we could only guess. In any case, I didn't know about the subject as long as I stayed at SLM.

The first time that Linda had sex with her boyfriend was in her own bed; her father was at work and her older sister was in her bedroom with the door shut. After they'd had sex, confident that no one was spying on them, Linda smoked a cigarette, stretched out naked with her legs propped up against the wall, in a pose that was very cinematic, perfect for the poster of a movie about the sexual revolution, maybe to let her boyfriend get a better look at her, or else just because space was limited for the two of them in her single bed. Without knocking or in any other way alerting her, her father, who had just come home from work, strode into the bedroom and was greeted by that scene: on his face was the struggle to contain his poorly disguised astonishment.

The two kids in the bed, paralyzed, didn't even think of trying to cover themselves.

Then her father, in a high-pitched, angry voice: "What is this, Linda . . . since when do you *smoke*?"

And he slammed the door behind him.

In my family, when presented with a closed door, the rule was clear: you never enter a room without knocking. You *always* knock *first*. And not only the door to the parents' bedroom: the children had the same right to that respect. Even among brothers and sisters, the same discretion was expected. You weren't allowed to lock your door, that was true, because privacy couldn't stand as an obstacle to first aid if, say, someone fell ill in the bathroom, for example. Over the bathtub in the old days there hung a bell pull you could yank on if you felt unwell. That same sense of alarm was transmitted to me. The bathtub becomes a place of drowning or electrocution. The ceramic tiles, damp with steam, glisten insidiously. In the overheated bath water, it's as if the veins on my wrists had already been slashed.

THE PRESTIGE OF THE BOURGEOIS RESIDENCE was associated with the diversification of the various rooms: front hall, antechamber, living room, parlor, dining room, study, library, "office" (the English word, or was it French?), laundry room . . . the partition walls distinguished among the various functions and multiplied the privacy of each act of domestic life, reading, eating, talking on the phone, receiving visitors, resting, making food and storing it, preparing clothing and putting it away—and in fact these days when people renovate old apartments, it seems like all they do is knock down partition walls.

Concealing and displaying are the two poles between which bourgeois domestic life oscillates, tucking away the unpleasant aspects and illustrating the prestigious ones. Then there are precious things that are hidden, only to trot them out on special occasions—jewelry, for instance. Though they were conceived to be shown off, they spend most of their time enclosed in cases, inside safes or hiding places, where burglars can't find them, only to burst into the light on grand occasions.

IN ITS MOST TYPICAL EXPRESSION, by now virtually extinct, bourgeois life emitted more light than heat. It was supposed to be buffed to a high gleam in every single detail. That is the reason for the obsession with keeping the marble, the enamel, and the metal clean; the constant polishing of fine silver that was almost never used in everyday life, and only enjoying its sparkle when you opened that drawer by accident; the full-blown cult of parquet floors, brushed and polished until it assumed that dark glow.

The service sets of silverware and porcelain for important occasions were stored in cubbyholes, hidey-holes, cabinets large and small, cupboards, and sideboards under lock and key. In the homes of respectable folk, you couldn't count the rooms that were off-limits, the corners protected by latches you needed a key to open . . .

(I've never understood what people meant by the non-Italian term "office" . . . why that term is used . . .)

THE BOURGEOISIE, unfailingly unsure whether to conceal or exhibit its prosperity, often does both things at the same time.

No one in Italy is eager to reveal their income, they conceal it from other people and, if possible, from the state, while scattering in all directions unmistakable markers of wealth.

Only property prevents the bourgeoisie from aspiring to communism, which would be the natural outcome of social envy. Bourgeois joy consists of the sentiment of contrast: possessing what others do not and what they therefore envy. Apartments, suits, automobiles, and women, wives or lovers selected like pieces of fine silver or paintings or tapestries or rare furniture.

THE EFFECT OF DISTINCTION is obtained through elements of decoration: furniture, drapery, carpets, memorabilia from travel, precious or extravagant objects. A handsome credenza placed in just the right place can redeem an otherwise dreary living room. Entire homes rotate around the totem of an antique hutch. There's a kind of home whose walls are dotted with African masks or in whose corners, as deep and shadowy as jungles, there are lush stands of ferns and ficus with cloying scents. The owners are often attractive matrons filled with yearning for the exotic landscapes from which those objects were taken, in homage to the aesthetic law of dislocation. Life seems too cramped for them, and their eyes are almost always blue or green, glittering luminous against their suntans even in the depths of winter, they look out, beyond Italy, soaring above mountain ranges and broad oceans. Real life would appear to be elsewhere, and those lovely homes, luxuriant with begonias, are to some extent compensation for having given it up. There is not a more ascetic creature in existence than the well-to-do housewife. The alternate hypotheses to the lives that they actually do lead, luxurious but so very dull, radiate around their faces like an aura, sometimes conferring upon them a magical splendor. If the men of the same class routinely compare the relative degrees of success they've obtained, their wives instead live their lives in a constant comparison of their respective sacrifices. There are those who sacrificed a professional career to help their husband's career, or to make sure he wasn't jealous, others who gave up having children or sacrificed having more or fewer than they actually did have, there are women who gave up the true love of their lives, and this effort to bury alive the emotion that still stirs deep in their hearts gives them a sad loveliness.

Pleasure and wealth cannot coexist, since pleasure in fact consists of the transition from a state of malaise to a state of well-being.

AND THEN THERE'S COLLECTING: paintings, books, pipes, antique weapons, porcelain, or those who collect their own past, a wake of vases, bottles, musical instruments, hats, photographs . . . each one dating back to a specific episode or period . . . or a trip, hanging there on the wall like an icon.

The home is the place where you lay down the traces of a permanent way of life, the signs of the continuity of existence. The habitation—both as place and activity—gives the sense of having something and continuing to have it over time. Yesterday, today, tomorrow, I was, I am, and I will be *here*. In the precipitation of dramatic events, just as in the slow accumulation of everyday acts, there is nothing like a house to confer a glimmer of significance and hold together one's identity. Especially nowadays when the elements of recognizability have grown muddled, there's almost nothing left but your house to tell others (and yourself) who you are, in some cases, who you once were, what you want, what you like or don't like. And how much money you earn. That's the way it is, the class war never ends: and unless it's in the form of a clash between opposing social giants, like in a Mayakovsky poster—the factory worker in overalls against the capitalist fat cat in a tailcoat—it shatters into a myriad of intermediate and local conflicts, at low intensity, often between social groups that are close to each other, neighboring each other, in income or in physical proximity—so close that they seem identical. It's the logic of the dogfight. Which in forms less sadistic or spectacular than attacks on Roma camps also take place within the variegated bourgeois social structure. The class struggle becomes a struggle for classification. On the ever-shifting horizon of social relations where the positions attained are continuously undermined, the home stands there, firm, solidly rooted, as evidence of *stability*, continuity, certainty—things that in reality last no more than a couple of generations. Already, children who grew up in spacious bourgeois apartments, once they're grown up and married, have had to migrate to smaller homes, or to less prestigious quarters.

From Parioli to Talenti, from Prati to Torpignattara.

It is a mathematical law governed by the division sign.

For some people, the veins of gold ore began to run out as early as the seventies and the eighties. The children of prominent professionals who lived lives cushioned by cotton wool, shielded from sharp edges by their wealth, fooled themselves into thinking that that golden mean constituted an unchanging horizon, but one fine day they reawakened to the sound of retrenchment under way.

EVEN THE BOURGEOIS VISION of the home is magical. Its symbols are no less sacred for the fact that they belong to an everyday universe. Certain objects or spaces are charged with power. Others are forbidden, like the Tree of the Knowledge of Good and Evil. Certain thresholds must never be crossed, on pain of perdition, certain keys must never be turned in certain locks except by the shaman who is entitled to do so. In the film *Il marito* Alberto Sordi takes his newlywed wife to a new apartment, on the outskirts of town, in fact, practically in the countryside, true, but a very nice place, and proudly shows her a little terrace, which will be their private nest, the setting for their carefree days, but before you know it the mother-in-law draws with a piece of chalk the floor plan of the room she wants built there, for her to live in. On the floor, she writes, "Mamma's bedroom." And what does Sordi do, when he learns of this project? He takes the hose used to water the flowers and he sprays it away. *"Anvedi 'sta mandrucona . . . ! Ush! e che t'eri messa in testa, eh? Mo' te sistemo io . . ."* In his inimitable Roman accent, he derides her, as he washes off the chalk.

There are two forms of magic, one involving chalk, the other involving water, the first one evocative, the second a genuine, full-fledged exorcism.

To build a house, to buy it or even just rent it, is a foundational act. Nowadays, when renting your home is less common, as is building a new home, and buying one is a titanic enterprise, the activity in which the average bourgeois homeowner invests money and spare time, her expectations and his taste is, rather, the renovation of a home: the renovation of stables, barns, farmhouses—the *masseria*, the *trullo*, the *dammuso*, ruins outside the city to be used as vacation homes.

THERE ARE BARDS OF THE QT: often they grew up there as children or young people and then were obliged to move away, and they dream of coming back one day, in spite of the fact that in the meantime real estate prices have skyrocketed to prohibitive levels. Just as the Latin poets inveighed against the chaotic and corrupt way of life in Rome, celebrating in contrast the tranquillity of a small plot of land in the countryside, likewise the bards of the QT exalt it in contrast with the city's historic center— which is no doubt a very pretty place, stupendous, unrivaled on earth, etc., but also noisy, filthy, overrun by traffic and sidewalk tables of bars and restaurants and tourists and the various night owls who fill the piazzas with broken-bottle brawls or pillow fights that the aficionados of the QT, who so love the narrow streets already deserted at nine in the evening, detest.

AND YET, even here in the QT, there is the usual widespread deterioration and decay of Rome. Dumpsters overflowing, never emptied. Cars nonchalantly double- and even triple-parked. People walking dogs that, thighs a-tremble, defecate in front of apartment house doors, testers of mini-motorcycles built in garages or other remote-controlled devices (NB: these aren't kids, these are men in their fifties), and then graffiti artists, "writers" or "taggers" are the terms used in Italian, in other words those jerk-offs who defile walls with their monotonous scrawls, the kind of work that some alumnus of the DAMS school or former member of parliament from the Communist Refoundation Party (but why? why? *why did I vote for you?*) stubbornly insists on defending as an artistic manifestation or symptom of "the malaise of the young."

It isn't clear why graffiti on the walls of the city should have been identified as an expression of a youthful malaise any more than letting dogs shit on sidewalks should be seen as an expression of a malaise of the elderly.

NOWADAYS, at first glance, neither your clothing nor the car you drive nor the language you speak reveal your social affiliation. It's all fluid, blurred, indistinct. From time to time, because of my slovenly attire, I'm taken for a homeless person. I see it from the way people look at me, how they address me . . . then I need only don a jacket and shave properly, and the way they feel about me is reversed. These are fleeting, provisional impressions.

One's home had remained perhaps the last unmistakable marker to define a style, a bourgeois aesthetic, a bourgeoisie that in its behavior, its manner of dressing and speaking and even in its political orientation (with the invention of the so-called left-wing bourgeoisie) had almost entirely abandoned the cult of distinction, which it had been carefully observing for at least a couple of centuries now. The new bourgeois generation of those years (my generation) was born under the sign of white socks and dark blue sandals with eyelets and real leather soles, and within just a few years, had grown up ragtag, informal, promiscuous, free, potty-mouthed, and filthy.

THE ONLY CURIOSITY MY FATHER ever expressed when I returned home after studying at a classmate's home, or from a birthday party, was: "What was the house like?" or "What was the apartment like?" and I never knew how to answer.

"What's their apartment like?"

"I don't know! It's an apartment . . . sure, it's nice . . . I guess!" since at the age of twelve you weren't exactly blown away by the fact that a home had three full bathrooms, and you're not tempted to poke around in the apartment's hallway in search of the laundry room. I had no way of knowing that to my father that question was tantamount to asking the profession or the income of my friend's parents, replacing the old snobbish query: "Who are their people?"

These are all things that I understood only much later . . . Only when I was in my early thirties, in the aftermath of a home renovation, did I begin to grasp the meaning of such evocative terms as "winter garden," which to me carried echoes of a Russian novel, a piece of stage direction in Chekhov, a lyrical expression like the roses that bloom out of season, "late roses filled with early snow," or the beach in winter, "a concept that the mind doesn't consider."

PERHAPS THE ONLY ACCESSORY a residence could possess that made any difference to us was a swimming pool. Ah, the pool. Whoever had a pool, private or open to all the tenants of the apartment building, also had a great many not entirely disinterested friends. Toward May that friendship tends to stir and quicken, in June it begins to glow, and in July and August it explodes, a renewed fondness toward those with access to and use of a swimming pool.

It was in fact at the side of the swimming pool at Via Appennini 34 (I'd managed to get in there thanks to I no longer remember which personal contact), newly filled with water for the summer season, that one fine day in June I happened to notice a slender blond girl: she was on her own, reading a book, stretched out on her tummy, legs bent at the knee, lolling in the sun. At first glance I didn't recognize her, not even when I took a second and then a third glance, but someone told me that she was Leda Arbus, my classmate's sister. For real? Leda Arbus? Oh, of course. The faded bikini almost blended into the pallor of the flesh. With one hand she was pressing her hair against the back of her neck, to keep it from spilling over her shoulders, with the other she was bracing up her chin, elbow pressed against the cement. It looked like a very uncomfortable position. When I'd seen her at the Arbus home she was, of course, fully dressed. Now she was almost naked. The comparison troubled me. So I steered clear of her, intentionally ignoring her.

THE BOURGEOISIE ALWAYS WANTS to interact with life using the formal form of address, in Italian the "lei," keeping interactions on a stiff, remote basis, never reducing the distance by so much as a fraction of an inch, interacting with a world populated by functions and ghosts, professional figures and silhouettes, beings with a title but never a name. They'd rather address blood and betrayal and disease in the formal, address death and ask it: "Pardon me, sir, I'm sure you'll understand, in your line of work, but would you be so good as to come back again at a later date, let's say, in a couple of years, or ideally, in ten or so?" At all costs, preserve a certain detachment, which may sound, variously, serious or ironic, shy or arrogant, and in any case springs from the need to maintain control over the darker forces, avoiding contamination, sterilizing, refrigerating. And if the given name, the first name, ever surfaces in regular use, it's only to mark a social distance, in addressing a social inferior (the fruit vendor, Luigi, Bartolo, Natale, the housecleaner whose surname you've never uttered, and who will always remain Amalia, Amalia and nothing more, Aurora, Rosi, Bice, Corazón, Tania, Svetlana . . .). My father was known only as "l'Ingegnere"—the Engineer. "Ingegnere" had become his real name, the appellation used to distinguish him from other people, and when he died most of the people attending his funeral at the Church of Sant'Agnese thought, "L'Ingegnere is dead," l'Ing. Carlo, or rather, Carlo Ingegnere, like Chauncey Gardiner, Chance the Gardner in the film, and they kept saying to me, while choking back tears: "What a good, kind person l'Ingegnere was . . ." When I dictated the death announcement over the phone, I naïvely told them Carlo Albinati, leaving off the professional prefix, L'Ing.—L'Ing. Carlo Albinati—and oh, how pissed off my grandmother was! She said that we had dishonored my father's memory. Without the cloak of that L'Ing., he must have flown up to heaven naked as a worm, blushing in shame.

ASPIRING TO "DISTINCTION" as a fundamental value, the bourgeoisie wishes to be recognized by society and therefore break away from it, marking an unbridgeable boundary. In colloquial language this took the form of the negative locution "not to dare." Don't you dare stick your nose into my business. How dare you. Don't you dare use such manners—such a tone of voice, such language . . .

In order to cross that thin line and enter into the territory, the home, the business of others (a line for which we nowadays use the pallid English term "privacy"), it is in fact necessary to obtain permission, which the good bourgeois issues only with the greatest parsimony and mistrust. Normally he will hunker down defensively behind that line. The spirit of the façade, the so-called decorum, far more than a hypocritical fiction, actually means that beyond that impeccable appearance, no one has the right to venture. Even the subject feels unauthorized to enter his own inviolable thoughts, to be, so to speak, indiscreet with himself. More than concealing, the mask *protects*. It does not serve to deceive, that is, to pretend to be someone else, but rather to keep others from knowing who you really are. The only statement made toward the outside world will be your economic standing, and it is well known that money has no personality, money doesn't lie but then again, it doesn't tell the truth either, money says nothing and that is why members of the middle class often appear interchangeable, anonymous, just as the inhabitants of the QT were, and remain today.

DISCRETION CONSISTS OF KEEPING ourselves distant from knowledge. Choosing not to delve deep, not to ask questions, not to know anything more than our interlocutor has deliberately decided to tell us, indeed, in certain cases, not even wanting to hear that much. Nothing, I don't want to know anything. Sweetheart, please, don't say another word. Words serve no purpose . . . The delicacy with which one holds oneself aloof from the intimate sphere of one's neighbor can sometimes verge on indifference, which for that matter is the feeling one often comes to after facing difficulties and privations. If I fully sacrifice my curiosity about others, if I become accustomed to mortifying that curiosity as a rule, it is likely that, little by little, others will cease to interest me. The life of another person, enclosed in his most secret thoughts, will slip out of my reach. If one insists on asking nothing, one winds up having nothing more to say. Those who are accustomed not to ask, also soon stop replying. If, moreover, such discretion seems motivated by the determination not to wound others, not to trouble them, if you look more closely you will find that that discretion actually serves to avoid being hurt oneself. Protecting oneself from potentially disagreeable truths. Those who are discreet do in fact avoid a bunch of problems and disappointments, whereas the indiscreet are always at risk of being caught up and dragged into trouble. You can be indiscreet and show a lack of respect even toward yourself, revealing too openly, out of recklessness or a love of sincerity, things that it might well be best for others not to know about you. That is an even more foolish and serious sin: the intrusiveness of those who are determined at all costs to tell you things that are their business, not yours.

ON THE WHOLE, we tend to overestimate the weight of the gaze that rests upon us. Out of insecurity or vanity, we believe that other people have nothing better to do with their time than to study and judge us, while most of the time we actually go, by and large, unnoticed. The sheer mass of expectations, concerns, and self-referential thoughts that make a man or a woman tremble when they make their entrance into a crowded room and feel every eye in the place focused upon them is normally out of proportion to the interest they actually stir.

13

THERE IS A CURIOUS FACT about the bourgeoisie.
If you study history, the bourgeoisie always seems to be in the process of being born.
In fact, every new age seems to inaugurate the rise of the bourgeoisie.
During the reign of Octavian Augustus, it seems that the bourgeoisie was beginning its rise. In the Middle Ages, historians claim, the bourgeoisie came into existence, in the Renaissance it enjoyed a rebirth, the eighteenth century was the century of the bourgeoisie, and so was the nineteenth century, in other words this darn bourgeoisie was always there, developing, elbowing its way, pushing ahead with its values and its interests . . .
(In prison, a student of mine, who had been in the Red Brigades, claimed that even during the Stone Age, the bourgeoisie was already exploiting the proletariat—right there, in the caves.)
The bourgeoisie holds the record for hatred and scorn aroused in those belonging to other classes, and that is understandable, but what is truly sensational is the depth of the hatred prompted within its own class: the most livid tirades against the bourgeois spirit have been conceived, written, and psalmodied during rallies, in hails of invective, and at demonstrations, by members of the bourgeoisie. Perhaps that is because it is the bourgeois themselves who are the first to be disappointed or disgusted by the prosperity that

they themselves attain. It is an aspect, a particular but not contradictory declension of the very insatiability and intense desire for social promotion. When people get rich, they ought to become happier, and yet they seem to experience a singular whiplash that drives them to scorn what they once yearned for. Since there are limits to one's capacity for self-deception, once you have obtained what you lusted after with all your heart, and once you have convinced yourself that it was this, the very thing you most desired, there arises a profound disappointment that might have psychological or metaphysical causes, or else simply chronological ones, since one almost invariably achieves one's desires a long time after first setting them, that is, far too late: you can finally afford to acquire something you've dreamed of only when the fact of owning it is no longer so important or prestigious, and others have already ensured that that ownership is no longer exclusive. If the fetish of the seventies, the fur coat, is something that all women possess, then the matron who doesn't own one will feel like a cripple, an amputee, for not having one, while the matron who owns one will take no pleasure in the fact.

We often would like objects but can't afford them. We'll be able to afford them when they are no longer so desirable.

With the rise in the level of education, the level of discontentment rises as well. With the increase in prosperity, dissatisfaction rises in your throat.

In other words, those who accumulate material goods may subsequently be disappointed by them, ultimately finding that they detest them or hold them in contempt. If it is not the bourgeois who feels repugnance toward them, it may perhaps be his children. One oscillates between the obsessive yearning for possession and the more or less sincere condemnation of the perverse effects that enrichment itself has caused: in us, in the environment, in the nation, on earth. Everyone wants to be more comfortable and yet everyone complains about being more comfortable, since greater comfort has brought these things with it: exasperated levels of individualism, amorality, inner emptiness, consumerism, abandonment of values, the death of the spirit of community, a leveling of tastes, pollution, a flavorless life, an even greater dissatisfaction. The possessions first sought after and subsequently obtained, at the cost of great effort and even greater compromises, suddenly look foolish, repulsive, detestable. In American movies, the rich executive who's living high on the hog suddenly realizes that his life is deeply inauthentic. It is always from the heart of Hollywood that the attack is launched against Hollywood. Because, and this is an important point, it is culture itself that produces both the frenzy for possession and its harshest critique, and occasionally it is the very people who are drowning in money who proclaim for all to hear that they are disgusted by money: and that stance is not, or it is not merely, hypocrisy. Attraction and repugnance may perhaps represent two aspects of the same vital impulse, which is made up of spasmodic tensions. The sensation that prosperity is a will-o'-the-wisp that fails to warm life up is more profound than we can concede to what definitively appears to be classic false consciousness: to think one thing and in the meantime do the opposite. This schism forms the bourgeois consciousness from the very outset, a conscience whose values are easy to mock, as writers, artists, singers and songwriters, prophets and religious leaders, moralists, and satirical authors have done for centuries, and with them many left-wing orators and politicians, but even more often their right-wing counterparts, who need only utter three phrases of invective against the vices and contradictions and softness of the bourgeois in order to inflame the street . . . the morality of shopkeepers . . . their cowardice, the way they live off the flesh of others . . . the devout hypocrisy . . . the famous formulation "warriors against merchants" . . .

vecchia piccola borghesia *little old bourgeoisie*
per piccina che tu sia *small though you may be*
non so dire se fai più rabbia *I can't say if you prompt more anger*
pena schifo o malinconia *pity disgust or melancholy*

THE BOURGEOISIE HAS ALWAYS BEEN the polemical idol of itself. Even the entry in the Encyclopaedia (a cultural institution whose origin and conception is due to the bourgeois spirit), which you might expect to be supremely neutral, positively quivers with a certain irony, if not ill-concealed contempt, in the definition that it gives.

Here it is.

Mental and emotional characteristics: reluctance, repulsion, jealousy, hostility, aridity, spiritual distress. A skeptical, dubious, diffident, grimy, greedy, cowardly man.

His sole and exclusive interest: to do business deals, buy land and houses, sell them, found profitable companies, be a leader in his profession, advance in a career in public administration, so as to emancipate himself once and for all from the sense of social inferiority toward the nobility and the rich, emphasizing his distance from the lower classes. Merchants, bankers, jurists, notaries, businessmen, and lawyers.

Abandonment of chivalrous ideals and feelings.

Underlying secularism blended with religious conservatism. Religious fervor, when present, lukewarm: what you might call Sunday religion.

Deep down, the bourgeois has always been averse to religion, even when he formally submitted to it. From a certain moment on, he found himself allied with it only because he considered it the last bulwark of the threatened vestiges of traditional life. Accustomed to reason and quibble about every aspect of the world that concerns him (business, law, rights, education), the bourgeois winds up demanding a reckoning from the faith he once professed without further discussion. "I'm starting litigation with God," so to speak, he's suing Him, he's demanding an explanation for His way of operating, he moves his way of thought toward God like a chess piece on the board. He tends to build himself his own doctrine and shape it according to his own needs. He doesn't submit to the precepts of humility; accustomed as he is to the well-pondered calculation of his best interests, he is repelled by the idea of an Almighty Providence that dominates him. And so the last chance of maintaining a certain religious spirit is to lay claim to a Christianity without death, without Providence, without sin, without religion.

Theoretically averse to money, practically speaking, devoted to it. No one talks about money, they just make it. Eager to obtain riches, but also ease and comfort. Interested in public office, he despises politics as an arena of intrigue.

The bourgeois is never sufficiently unaware to be truly happy. As he ages, his strength gradually subsiding with the years and the horizon of his expectations progressively shrinking, his disappointment swells exponentially. Life dwindles away and very few can claim to have truly lived it. Inasmuch as he is the guardian of a contradictory idea of stability and continuity (which in fact conflicts with the canonical model, the model of social advancement), he would like to put an end to the uncertainty that dominates his life. If that happens, however—if, that is, he does indeed secure a margin of economic security, then behold the arrival of boredom and monotony, seeing that pleasure and joy spring from discontinuity, from the unexpected. It is the arch and mocking mechanism governing the law of desire. People curl up on prosperity as if seated in a chair but immediately thereafter, their derrieres begin to tingle and grow numb from restricted circulation. To say nothing of the fact that economic tranquillity, which we suppose is acquired in a permanent fashion, does little if anything to keep you safe from the other misfortunes perennially lurking in ambush, disease, the death of one's loved ones, or one's own death—events that can sneak up on the most prosperous merchant or the most renowned lawyer. Indeed, if you listen to the words of certain holy parables, it is precisely upon these people that destiny strikes down with particular savagery, it is prosperity that the hand of God smites with exemplary fury, in order to ensure that each and every one of us should gain a better understanding of the actual worth of the things of this world. Money, success, beauty, the pleasures of the flesh, the vanities of the spirit—all crushed to dust. Rich landowners stripped of all their wealth in the course of a night, merchants afflicted with disgusting cases of scabies or blinded by bird shit, opulent hoteliers swallowed up by earthquakes, cabinet ministers who lose their posts and wind up with their heads on the executioner's block before the sun sets.

This is something the bourgeois can smell well in advance. His anxiety can never be placated, those forces might be unleashed against him at any point.

And so, beneath a conventional patina of optimism donned with a view to decorum, like a clean shirt and a pair of neatly pressed pants, one must be prepared for the worst ("The worst will come, it's at the gates, it's only a matter of time . . ."). In the bourgeois mentality, that which is transitory is intolerable. And since *everything* is transitory, in the end *everything* turns out to be intolerable. At that point, there is nothing left but dreams, illusions. If you persist in believing in nothing you will ultimately end up believing in the most ludicrous of fairy tales. The myth of permanence, ruminated and chewed over by the aristocracy down through the centuries, is injected into the veins of the bourgeois like a drug. All that's required is a few generations and a renovated ruin in order to fool yourself into believing you've founded a dynasty. That you've sunk deep roots, assuring yourself of an ongoing return of memories and deeds upon which time will progressively place its seal. Though he never opens his mouth without singing the praises of pragmatism and reasonableness, no one believes in symbols more implicitly than the bourgeois, and he clings to them in times of crisis: in comparison with him, the aristocrats and the plebeians are brutally realistic.

Actually, the bourgeois has taken a vow of unhappiness by definition: his morality may encourage the accumulation of wealth and prestige, but it cannot bring joy to those who adhere to it. The congruence of means and ends rarely arouses enthusiasm. The Arnolfini couple, man and wife, hardly seem to be bursting with happiness. And aside from the occasional sated or arrogant gaze here and there, the images handed down by the paintings of these well-to-do gentlemen and couples always seem to betray traces of an irrepressible anguish of living. The age of anxiety, in short, had begun long, long ago, a very long time back.

> *vecchia piccola borghesia . . .*   *little old bourgeoisie . . .*
> *per piccina che tu sia . . .*   *small though you may be . . .*

AFFLICTED BY ITS VERY WISDOM, it would be tempted to get rid of it with impulsive bolts from the blue or authoritarian coups, and sometimes it allows itself to be seduced by extraneous forces in which it believes it recognizes instinct, vigor, spontaneous joy, since it is incapable of such things, incapable of understanding what it actually wants, what it really and truly *desires*. Postponed till the end of the world the idea of liberation, and the dream of attaining an authentic liberty, it is obliged in the meantime to be scrupulous at every instant, to take seriously an infinite array of minutiae and weigh them carefully to see if there is any profit to be had from them. The principle of personal advantage multiplies human contacts but ruins them from the outset. The quantity of things that must be measured exceeds all measure. If the noble was for the most part a layabout and yet happily *active* in his passions, the bourgeois is *reactive*—nothing that he does is autonomous, gratuitous, spontaneous, original—not even his amusements—everything in him originates as a reaction to something else, as a response, as a resentment or a retort, a recovery, a counteroffer, a negotiation. He can consider virtuous only that which puts him in a condition to be as productive as possible; everything else doesn't count or, even worse, is a luxury, it becomes a shameful waste to be a person with impulses and faults; all inefficiency must be discredited, all waste. Even health is useful, a certain food is good for you, knowledge is money, cornering the market on beauty can be profitable, luxury confers prestige, the mountains help you relax, they soothe your nerves.

> *sei contenta se un ladro muore*   *you're happy if a thief dies*
> *se arrestano una puttana*   *if they arrest a whore*
> *se la parrocchia del Sacro Cuore*   *if the parish of the Sacred Heart*
> *acquista una nuova campana*   *purchases a new church bell*

Those were the lyrics that Claudio Lolli sang in 1972 and that we psalmodized along to, as we listened to the record of this grim antibourgeois nursery rhyme. With the dreamy conviction of those who are captivated by the music: an emotional vector capable of transporting any content whatsoever.

The song perfectly nails the rhyme of *puttana/campana* (whore and church bell) which points to the sharpest point of contrast between the respective moralities, the libertarian and transgressive morality of the prostitute, and the shuttered, bigoted, resentful morality of some hypocritical Catholic church lady. It's obvious that, romantically, our preference veers toward the former, in songs and poetry the whore wins hands down over the respectable matron, just as the bandit and the rebel gobble up the office worker in a single bite. Difficult to conceive of the ballad of a bank clerk, if not as a parody. Those tightfisted church ladies, conformist and decorous, who were responsible for keeping Italy running, at least according to reactionary thought, are always good for a caricature, it matters little whether ferocious or good-natured, once it's made clear that we're talking about figures unworthy of being taken seriously. Decorum, in literature, is in fact the very apex of the indecorous. At the very most, it can be accorded contempt. From the day that the bourgeoisie made its entrance into literature, literature has done nothing but insult and mock it, and rightly so I might add, since the bourgeoisie shoved aside the fine characters of the old days, heroes and heroines, musketeers and princesses, replacing those fine people with greedy social climbers, governesses, pharmacists, and depressed functionaries. Two-bit extras, in other words. It's a singular thing how the very authors who first offered free access in the world of art to these characters devoid of attractive qualities should hate them or look down upon them from the bottoms of their hearts, even when they identify with them: it's as if they hated themselves and the novel was their pressure valve, a desperate "coming out," to use the English term. Yes, I'm grimy-fisted, envious, devoid of titles, and yet I want to be princely and beloved as such. I deserve it, if for no other reason than my own frankness in admitting that I don't deserve it. Since nearly all writers were parvenus, who dragged themselves up out of the swamps of their social origins with acts of sheer will, aestheticizing and invariably verging on desperation, a form of self-legitimizing bootstrapping, like Munchausen pulling himself up out of the water by his ponytail, like Tartuffe, who builds a solid position on the fascinating nothingness of words, they know perfectly well that they're lying but they're so fond of and stirred by their lie that they seriously believe in it, to the point of becoming genuinely heartbreaking for the faith with which they recount it. The original sin is washed clean by art. It's an exorcism. Those who have risen through the social ranks blow the dust of their origins off their shoes, those who are well-to-do redeem that fault by joining movements that preach their own destruction.

The bourgeois creates and administers his own investiture with his own two hands. He is condemned to extrapolate rules from the absolute absence of rules, and without hands up or connections from on high. That is what makes secular morality such an uncertain thing. And he conceals his inherent weakness with his aggressiveness. Those who are forced to be self-made men need to be sarcastic and cutting. If, instead, the bourgeois, for the most part because of a lack of time to devote to the ideal elaboration of morality, for example in the propulsive era of great profits and the accumulation of personal fortunes, when there is no time to do anything but pile up cash, if, as we were saying, the bourgeois in that case is willing to accept an inherited, traditional morality, though only accepting it as transitory and provisional (for example, a Catholic morality), he inevitably falsifies it. His skeptical breath freezes it. From a tumultuous and mystical religion, Christianity becomes terse and pragmatic. The intense and nauseating odor of rot that wafts off martyred flesh is swept away by the brisk breeze of good hard work . . . where by sacrifice at the very most we're talking about devotion to one's job and domestic frugality. Hygienicized and internalized, to avoid scandalizing with excessively ardent testifying, amputated of all awkward and overenthusiastic impetus, its quotient of superstition reduced but not quite to zero, in a bid to keep the lower social orders at least clamoring to drink from the trough watered by the spring of mysteries, apparitions, and bleedings, Christianity proved eminently suited to its new function. All you needed to do was switch a plus sign to a minus or vice versa on certain symbolic equations: for example, the anathema against money, which had thundered out from day one on the very lips of the Master, in unequivocal terms. So it had remained for many centuries, and it had worked to perfection: the Christian soul and the bourgeois spirit were fellow travelers, each playing along with the other's game, and perhaps the Church thought that it was riding the tiger, employing that distinctive brand of Realpolitik that has brought it up to the present day, a blend of shrewd and ruthless alliances with its bitterest adversaries, making use of them to render them harmless, in view of the triumph that awaited them in the bright tomorrow: instead, once it had been sucked well and thoroughly dry, and when all that remained of it was a burdensome, inconvenient shell, religion was tossed aside, first by the bourgeoisie—the bourgeoisie, of all categories!—and then by everyone else, all the others. It no longer worked, its "propulsive force" had run out. In any case, too old-fashioned, too restrictive, bristling with obstacles and dense with precepts, however much they might have been softened and rounded and hollowed out.

Nowadays, in Europe, Christianity is an eccentric belief system practiced only by a minority, and where that is not the case, if it does not accept being bracketed in that manner, it simply no longer exists, it has been expunged from the horizon of everyday life. Even where it ardently wishes it could bring a little warm, young blood back into circulation, it can no longer afford the luxury of outright fanaticism, seeing the unfair competition it is facing on this plane from other radical religious persuasions, so it is constantly obliged to retrench, tread carefully, remain tolerant through clenched teeth, hypocritically conciliatory, though everyone realizes that a faith cannot survive on the basis of such weak and generic feelings. (This is Islam's unforgivable crime in the world of the present: it has and it cultivates a faith that no longer exists in the West and is no longer cultivated there. *This* and nothing else is the cause of the fear and disgust, but also a hint of envy, experienced by Westerners.) There really is no need of a God to persuade people to respect stoplights, pay their tithes, and recycle conscientiously (oh Lord, maybe so in Italy, only hellfire is enough to make us toe the line: but in Sweden, in Switzerland?). Everything seems to conspire to abolish religion as an antiquated luxury or replace it with a less demanding kind of mortgage. Faith is madness, a flame that is flickering out and dying if fed only with the arid communion wafers of reasonableness. That which can be proven has very little value.

And then there is a clause in the contract with which Christianity signed itself over to the bourgeois spirit, appointing it as its proxy or sole and exclusive agent, which has proven disadvantageous over the long run: by which I mean the negotiation whereby, in order to conquer the rest of the world in the wake of the imperialist fleets, the Church lost Europe. That was the collateral, this the trade-off. Well, the contract has been honored, Europe was lost, I believe once and for all, proof of which can be seen in the fact that its legislatures are ashamed to name Christianity as one of their underlying principles: ancient Greece, certainly, the Romans as well, the tradition of the Enlightenment as well, but Christ, the first one to say that all men are equal, no. There you go, if Europe has turned its back on Jesus, Jesus remains bound hand and foot to Europe, like a hostage who must necessarily go wherever his kidnappers take him.

If Christianity could not possibly be, for the bourgeoisie, anything more than a morality provisionally taken on for instrumental purposes, and which has yet managed to cling stubbornly to the bourgeoisie for so many, many years, this is because the bourgeoisie, in the meantime, has proven incapable of developing any other morality to replace it. In spite of the efforts of some first-rate minds, the bourgeoisie has failed ever to go beyond generic affirmations and abstract enunciations. With the collapse of Christian ethics, quite simply we have remained without ethics, and we have been obliged to jury-rig and stitch together bits and pieces of other religious or moral codes, tatters of liberalism or socialism, with which feudally partitioned shares we see represented on the political commissions assigned to lead the discussion of such matters as euthanasia, artificial insemination, birth control, the family. Perhaps the patchwork can serve as a model for a modern society, but certainly not the general body of ethics that governs it.

In the same exact way, as if it had never believed it before, and hadn't placed it at the center of an entire system of values, the middle class abandoned the patriotic rhetoric it had battened off for a hundred years and through a pair of world wars, wars it had marched off to with resounding hurrahs and tossing of hats in the air, replacing that rhetoric with a pacifism based on the same selfish set of values that propped up the ideology it had just tossed overboard. Many rainbow flags flutter nowadays for the same reason national flags waved just a few decades ago: the unashamed defense of one's own interests, or at least the interests that people believe, rightly or wrongly, to be theirs. War "no longer interests us," whereas it used to "be in our interest," and therefore it had to be waged, right or wrong, it hardly matters. In point of fact, there are no right wars or wrong wars, there are only wars you win and wars you lose. In any case, we don't want to know anything about it. Keep us out of it, please. It used to be that we believed our interests had to be defended with our blood, nowadays it seems that blood, especially innocent blood, when all is said and done, only hurts them. Peace. Peace. Leave us in peace. Then what has become of that word, which once scalded our mouths and our hearts, the Fatherland, the Homeland—what filled the void left by that concept? Or weren't those words themselves a void, mere names, verbal idols to hold our lives together? If God and Country no longer warm up the vocabulary of the middle class, it is bound to freeze over, crumpling like the poet's withered leaf. If you don't possess or aren't possessed by a rhetoric, then you fall silent. I'm not saying you're left without ideas, but genuinely silent, speechless. The other infatuations, such as culture and communism, were too fleeting, and after all they remain fundamentally extraneous to the spirit with which the bourgeoisie undertook its long struggle, while money alone does not provide a sufficient legitimation, not even a self-legitimation. Even when it really is the one purpose for which you live, well, you never have the courage to declare that fact aloud, "All I care about is money" is a phrase you might utter when you're stinking drunk or defiantly or to show off your cynicism or while beating your chest and scattering ashes on your head at the culmination of an act of self-denunciation, but it would be unbearable if spoken seriously, in a levelheaded manner, it can't stand up for itself, money isn't a value, or maybe it is, but it can only be tendered for anything but as a value, so if money cannot be spent, then it ceases to be what it is, it contradicts its own nature, it dissolves into thin air, money, in other words, exists but it can't be spoken of, it's a means not a subject, and in fact the richer you are, the less you talk about it, you have money, and you shut up about it, only those who have very little money ever talk about it.

In Italy, there existed a sole exception to this rule, and it was a person who never spoke about anything but his own money, obsessively, and in spite of the fact that he was and remains the wealthiest man in the country, he talked about it as if he needed to convince himself first and foremost that he possessed it, that he needed to touch his cash with the tip of his tongue, the same way that, in the old days, to reassure oneself that it was still where it belonged, you would plunge your hands under the mattress to make sure your wad of cash was still there, well, instead he would stick his tongue into his money, every time that he needed to make it clear who he was, he'd open his mouth and speak of his money. And there's something heartbreaking about the ritual, like the one practiced by Fagin in *Oliver Twist*, when he pulled his treasure out of the hidey-hole and ran it through his fingers.

Nearly all his statements in every field or sector, even in matters that had nothing to do with money, were always completed and sealed by the same turn of phrase: "And you can all trust someone like me, who's made a bundle of cash!" There are those who claim that his continual harping on money is due to his incurable fear of death. Others think it's the parvenu's revenge, the need to lord it over those he's overtaken and outstripped in terms of wealth. Others think that he mentions it constantly in order to arouse admiration and the desire to identify with him, because, in their view, the Italians now have money as their sole and exclusive value. Others still believe that it's simply an imitation of the manners of American businessmen, who show no false modesty in declaring the size of their fortunes, "Last year wasn't a particularly good one, I *only* made thirty-five million dollars . . ." even though I doubt that they do it with such ostentation, just as I doubt that a retiree trying to make his pension last until the end of the month can be induced to identify with a man who's delighted to boast so shamelessly of his wealth, and admire him rather than hating him. I, personally, would be heartily sick and tired of hearing someone constantly say, "Look at me, take me for a model . . . !" the way this man does. What the hell kind of model, a model *of what*? Enjoy your millions and shut up about it, mutters the grouchy old man deep inside my heart, into whom I'll be transformed physically, as well, in the fullness of time, waving a cane. Other people's outrageous good fortune generally doesn't arouse our finest feelings, our empathy or our benevolence. Quite the opposite.

Others still have built a theory about this incredibly successful entrepreneur and politician, namely that he actually represents the average Italian raised to a power, as it were, an ordinary Italian cubed, the sum and amplification of both fine qualities and defects, but especially of the common traits, neither good nor bad, that make up the Italian character: a sort of turbo-Italian, in other words, to use the phrasing employed during the war in the former Yugoslavia to describe the most vociferous nationalists of the various ethnic groups, turbo-Serbs and turbo-Croats. He, then, would be in fact a turbo-Italian, a faithful scale projection of the image that the Italians like to present of themselves, endowed with repulsive and undeniable vices and shortcomings, in some cases with impressive virtues. This opinion is expressed with the faintly disgusted tone, a note of commiseration, generally used to talk about Italy. What else can you expect, ladies and gentlemen, this is what an Italian is like . . . there's nothing to be done about it. Lazy and hardworking, wise and utterly brainless, skeptical and fanatical, afflicted at the same time with an inferiority complex and a superiority complex, it seems that his amphibious character lends itself perfectly to the experiments of politicians and the fiery declamations of moralists, to both of whom he remains, deep down, completely indifferent. Let them write what they please. The scandal of his mobility and versatility cannot be solved by opinion pieces brandishing indignant prose or broadsheets of civic poetry. For that matter, when a national conscience is based almost entirely on rhetorical proclamations and crystallizations of legendary figures as saints and bandits, all it takes is a well-thrown rock to shatter it, and once the stained-glass windows that tell of their exploits have been smashed to smithereens, you plunge straight into the darkness of a lack of identity. Indistinctness remains the sole alternative to lies. Either the Italian is a half-true myth or else he doesn't exist at all. From exaltation we go straight to a lynching. Even our bourgeoisie must be begged on bended knee to behave like a bourgeoisie, at least a little, what the devil, at least like others do in the rest of the civilized world, toward whom we have always nourished a profound envy mixed with scorn—the emotion that a sly servant feels toward a foolish master. Impossible to put ourselves on the same level as the others, we always have a special destiny, we Italians, a supremacy to boast of or a shame to conceal. The philanthropist turns out to be a pedophile, the hero that everyone adored actually broke into the offerings box, confirming the sensation that it was all just a trick, a well-devised deception that lay at the origin of their positive image. Theater, in other words, all on stage, and so we see the reason for our unyielding love of grand opera, not as an artistic genre, but rather as a social posture.

Periodically, and often at the hands of their illustrious compatriots, the Italians are scolded for not being French, or English, or Scandinavian, but rather, what they are, namely Italians. Already a century before the character in question, the great corruptor, entered onto the scene, there were already those who accused the Italians of worshipping the Golden Calf. Of having sold their souls. Which soul? With how many souls do we come equipped? We hadn't yet even acquired a shred of identity and already we were complaining about having lost it.

NOW WE'VE COME TO THE POINT. Perhaps he, whose obvious name I will refrain from stating, is the only bourgeois who has ever had the impudence to manifest his own resentment, to vent it without restraint or inhibitions. Along with that resentment, his otherwise inconfessable ambitions: boundless aspirations. I am capable of; I am sufficiently wealthy to; I possess; I can do—*everything*. My purchasing power is *limitless*. I'm a friend and a father. As a well-known comedian likes to say about him, at a wedding he wants to be the groom, at a funeral he wants to be the corpse. The hundreds of jokes that circulate about him, making fun of his megalomania and his frenzy to be Napoleon, Jesus Christ, or, worst case, pope (with the name of Pio Tutto, an Italian pun on the name Pius and a phrase in Roman dialect that translates to "I take it all"), don't fall far from the truth. What we can see in him is the extreme immoderation typical of an era that has overflowed its banks, where everyone is acknowledged the sacrosanct right to aspire to *anything*. In the bourgeoisie, grand ambitions are either lacking entirely or else they manifest themselves to a catastrophic extent. In a world divided into castes, the lives of individuals were assigned rigid tasks and horizons, from which it was impossible to escape, and greatness was measured precisely in the acceptance of those impositions of status and role, whatever they might be. In the world of the present day, the constraints have been loosened to such an extent that one can imagine, either with a dollop of anguish or boundless delight, that one has no destiny, no limitation marked in advance. You can never settle for what you've achieved and attained, and the boundary between mediocrity and glory becomes so blurred that people are constantly taking one for the other and vice versa, so that it becomes necessary to raise the ante for fear one might have set one's sights too low. Hence the torment of having chosen the wrong path, both in the sense of having chosen the wrong objective and of having taken the wrong path to get to it, or else of lacking the pace needed to beat the others to the destination, getting there too late to keep them from taking the prize in your place. If the first error, choosing the wrong path, reveals an existential uncertainty, the second and third, following the wrong path or being too slow, are perhaps even more humiliating, because they mean you'll find yourself outstripped in your lane by other competitors with greater skills or gifts, or who are perhaps simply more ruthless. Since no one is precluded from the outset from any objective (at least in theory), any goal that is attained proves frustrating because it might promptly be rendered vain by some other daring exploit.

There remained, in fact, on this same line, sex. Sex is the new frontier upon which commodification and merchandising and global saturation proceed: and it was in fact sex, a virtually uninterrupted bacchanal, it was that euphoric orgy of the thoroughgoing possession of *everything*, from the intimate body parts of young women dressed as candy stripers to the titillated minds of the fellow diners witnessing the group sex, it is no accident that sex was the triumphal apex as well as the beginning of the decline of the bourgeois champion I was talking about earlier. It is a physiological curve: the ultimate utilization, the extreme conversion of cash cannot be anything other than to buy the body, or multiple bodies, to reacquire the corporeal dimension from which it originates, its first provenance, to reincarnate. From the primitive force of the hand that hammers or scythes, to the rounded curve of two ass cheeks spreading to reveal a pussy and an asshole. It all returns to there. And after making that choice—to begin necessarily to grow old and die. It's no longer economics or politics, it's physiology.

But will the bourgeoisie ever manage to become entirely pornographic?

14

T HE STAGES THEN WENT AS FOLLOWS: *from an absolute ethic of sacrifice to be attained whatever the cost, to a morality of sacrifice for a cause considered rationally just, to the rejection of sacrifice for a cause considered rationally unjust, to the rejection in any case, whatever the considerations, of any sacrifice whatsoever. I don't mean to imply that each of these ideas doesn't have its own degree of truth and justification, nor that it's impossible to survive with the ethics of the preceding phase in the following one.*

ARE YOU STILL LISTENING TO ME? You are? Or are you getting tired? Do you want to put down the book and go to sleep, return it to whoever gave it to you as a gift, go to the bookstore and demand your money back? Well, I'm certainly sorry. It's too late for me, but not for you. I could recommend skipping a few chapters and go directly to Part V, which is titled "Collective M." That's right, M, like the monster of Düsseldorf. In the meantime, I'll go on for a while longer, observing the middle class under a magnifying glass. Who knows if I'll manage to winkle out the little insects I'm looking for. Their sting can cause surprising effects. I myself was stung by them, and infected, and driven to this obsessive inquest.

IF SOMEONE TELLS ME, *"Stop!" I go on.*

THE GRAVEST THREAT to the middle class comes not from below, as it always believed, but from its own innovative spirit. It is for this very reason that there exists a fraction of the middle class that remains conservative to the verge of sheer obtuseness, that struggles to hold tight, with tooth and nail, to the old ways in order to avoid being swept away by the velocity at which the world is spinning, after the shove it was given by the other fraction. The world spins, whirls, and as it whirls it flicks out of their orbits all those who failed to sink strong roots, or at least that's the anguished sensation from which they flee headlong, hastily erecting anchorages that create at least the semblance of a continuity, of a tradition. The patrimony—in appearance the one thing for which the bourgeois are willing to fight, even if that means fighting against members of their own family—is the symbol or the equivalent of what must be defended from erosion, namely, life itself, with its values, its meaning, which appears every bit as ephemeral and at risk. The danger that capital runs on a daily basis shows just how precarious all the rest is: and the success or failure of a business proposition goes well beyond the simple economic outcome—that is why these operations must either be celebrated in a triumphal manner or alternatively cause abysmal dismay, given that they are the only indicators that can establish whether or not progress has been made in the correct direction. It's not that the bourgeois are so grimy-hearted that they can think of nothing other than money: but what other parameter ought they to measure themselves against? Their hearts, like everyone's, are swollen with desires, confused dreams, delicate ideals or violently romantic ones. The unit of measurement, however, remains cash. The admirable and pathetic efforts with which they often seek to emancipate themselves from the dictatorship of the economic principle (for example, by treading the paths of cultural reparations, attending exhibitions and concerts, becoming collectors, patrons of the arts, connoisseurs of taste of style) do nothing but confirm the supremacy of that principle and its almost irresistible magnetism, and I say "almost" because there can be no doubt that it's possible to break away from it, with an act of pure will, or else as a result of a distinctive psychological inclination—let's go ahead and call it a perversion. I confess that I feel a sense of solidarity by and large with those old-school professionals, be they functionaries or industrialists, who trembled at the thought of seeing their sons manifest artistic ambitions: it's inevitable to consider such aspirations a form of degeneration, a self-deceit, a betrayal, or even worse, the high-toned claim to be spiritually superior to their fathers. You want to be the conductor of a symphony orchestra instead of running the woolen mill? Good boy, that way you'll feel that you're better than me . . . There is always something healthy about anti-intellectualism, something almost naïve, creatural, a sort of intuitive realism that knows how to identify the levers that move the world and seize them unhesitatingly. With the same nonchalance displayed in handling money. It's only logical then that the well-to-do should be worried if a son of theirs displays a vocation that might lead him astray from the principle of utility, even if in this new role he were to be kissed by fame and success. However illustrious, he would remain forever subalternate, strictly decorative.

Intellectuals: the dominated portion of the dominant class.

That's the real point. Allowing yourself to be swept away by the sublime execution of a piano piece does not, unfortunately, redeem the soul from original sin; rather it indicates that the flame of suffering for that sin will never die out. A love of the beautiful often springs from an inability to produce it. Or even understand it. There is no school of thought more mercilessly bourgeois than Marxist thought, in the version that reduces and consigns all phenomena to the economic sphere. Determinism only produces more determinism, just as money produces more money. That which is denounced or unmasked, by that very fact triumphs. Like fate in a Greek tragedy, the more you hurl yourself against it, the more ineluctable it becomes, the more gigantic it looms. Marx's thought is a form of bourgeois thought, stripped of all hypocritical decorum, and from this brutal stripping bare comes the clear-eyed, humorous nature of certain of his pages, and the reason that they now lie abandoned—leaving aside the fact that they failed in political terms. Too cynical, too brilliantly simplistic to appear credible. Denuded of its ideological and aesthetic ornaments, the dominion of the economic factor becomes truly grotesque or slides toward the Jewish joke, like the one about Isaac the shopkeeper, who on his deathbed, by now almost blind, wanted all his children gathered around him: "David, are you here?" "Yes, Father, I'm here." "And you, Rebecca, are you here, too? And Sarah and Myriam? And Daniel?" "Yes, Father, we're all here." "And Benjamin? Where is my little Benjamin?" "I'm here, too, we're all at your side." "Oh, really, you're all here? Then *who the hell is looking after the store*?!?"

The key term is "sharp-eyed," which is to say, having a keen eye on everything: eyes to monitor, calculate, weigh, measure, and compare *everything*.

Like the eye of God, watching over every material and spiritual activity, is the economic spirit, which scrutinizes and gauges from on high, or perhaps we ought to say, from down below, since it underlies every initiative or thought. Even the incommensurable and the sublime can be quantified, by calculating the worth of a canvas, its present-day quotation with a view to its future value. The art collector perfectly represents this almost mystical abandonment to the apparition of the aesthetic event, yoked without inhibition to the calculation of self-interest. Will it be a good investment? While one eye grows languidly moist at the beauty in which it is being bathed, the other eye studies the price list. And the impressive thing is that this does nothing to induce cross-eyedness, no, the aesthetic eye and the economic eye *are actually both looking in the same direction*. It is along this parallel that the bourgeois identity travels, always teetering and in tension lest its paths diverge. It holds itself together thanks to *diligence* and *application*. It has none of the natural arrogance of the aristocrat, none of the wild spontaneity of the working class, but it is capable of affecting both the former and the latter, and when necessary making use in an instrumental fashion of things that do not inherently belong to it, be they style or ignorance. It is, in short, a *modular* identity, which can be assembled as desired, and as such demands incessant updating and feedback. How far can I go with the means at my disposal? How can I field more effective tools in order to obtain more resources than the means I currently lack? If the objective were clear and established once and for all, you could simply accept the challenge or decide to throw in the towel from the outset: the problem is that the middle class never explicitly declares its objectives, such as for instance personal enrichment, because if it were to do so, it would lose all decorum, in its own eyes first and foremost, but it also can't agree to declare itself satisfied with its current status, which would amount to admitting that it sets itself no objectives, and therefore lives a pointless existence. Between a looming sense of uselessness and the concealment of its own unconfessable objectives, the gamut of existential solutions opens out. Certainly, the minimum objective remains that of defending a certain status, of preserving a tradition: even if it's difficult to claim that a little holiday villa at Ansedonia constitutes in and of itself a solid tradition, there is no question that being forced to sell it due to emerging financial difficulties can constitute a harsh blow from which more than a few have never recovered. The way it was for my aged grandmother, when she was forced to move from Parioli to the outskirts of Vigna Clara, to an apartment half the size of the previous one, and as a renter, not an owner.

In short, in order to understand this conservative mentality, you need to imagine a permanent state of siege . . .

AMONG THE ARTISTIC PASSIONS brandished as marks of distinction, pride of place is owned by the visual arts and music, rather than literature—and why is that? If I were the set designer assigned to reproduce an interior of the high bourgeoisie in the seventies, I'd know exactly what artworks to deck the walls with. Certainly, the visual arts lend themselves as a way to yoke together the aesthetic function with its economic counterpart; while on the opposite slope, music is the ideal art because through it one can attain the ambition of placing the greatest distance between oneself and material obligations. The tension toward the pure artistic form and the disinterested enjoyment of it, then, would be nothing more than a reflection of a social inclination: to put at the farthest possible reach the world of need, redeem oneself from the principle of utility, opposing it with form, soul, and beauty. Obtaining the maximum profit from the uselessness of Beethoven. Which just goes to show that pure disinterest doesn't exist, and never can.

REASONINGS, reasonings, reasonings . . . what good are they?

Having worked our way through all the various reasonings, nothing remains but the prophecy, much as, having eliminated out of pride or idealism or laziness the various paths of the professions and businesses, a well-to-do young man is left with no options but to become an artist—actor, writer, or musician. Since he does not know how to produce, he'll just have to create; with no talent for measurable quantities, he finds himself obliged to pursue the infinite and the boundless. I know of some young men who had all the paths to wealth and honor spread before them, if only they'd been willing, with a crumb of humility, to learn how to handle basic arithmetic, like honest greengrocers who tot up the prices with a pencil on graph-paper notebooks; but no, instead they turned up their noses at this straightforward option, they passed up the prospect of working with the tangible, the material, with all the prose of those petty numerical concerns—and in their arrogant purity they went on to write film reviews for newspapers where they could have and should have risen to become treasurers or trustees, on whose boards they might easily have been sitting by now if they hadn't been possessed by a foolish intellectual frenzy. Too full of themselves to command, they chose instead to submit and, from below, criticize.

REALISM WAS THE BITTER MEDICINE that the bourgeois spirit had the courage and the impertinence to administer to the world in order to cure it. The world wasn't cured by that vaccination, but the problem is that even the bourgeoisie was unable to swallow that bitter dose without making faces. The acid taste of reasoning in the maxims of everyone from Machiavelli to Karl Kraus thrills those who wade through them, it's a slashing razor, an ice-cold spray in the pestilential air of fairy tales, but over the long run it too can become depressing, suffocating. Radical realism certainly has many merits but relatively little appeal, and it can be hard to take, it entails a certain existential monotony, an implacable fixity of thought, so that even the most disenchanted spirit at a certain point would like to fill his head with clouds and dreams, just for a change, abandoning for a moment the fine-honed gaze that the falcon trains on this world, flying off elsewhere freely in his thoughts. Anywhere else, as long as it's *outside* of reality. What's more, the pitiless knowledge of one's limitations can be a prod to excel as much as a source of frustration, it can encourage wise and manly behavior as much as it can drive one to abandon himself to despair. Someone who fires a bullet into his head is, in a way, a realist; in many aspects, suicide is the most realistic act that a person can commit—it is, in contrast, staying alive that is an illusion, a deception. And so, if we were all realists . . .

WE WIND UP being afraid not only of the future, but even of the past. If fear is born of uncertainty, at some point in life it is legitimate to nurture doubts about what has already happened, about the meaning we should assign to what we have already done, perhaps even more than to what has yet to take place. We fear the past as if it could sneak up behind us, shoot us in the back, defraud us. As if within the purple cavities of a dream, concealed truths lie in the past, truths capable of shaking us and devastating us. In any case, in the course of these meditations pregnant with feelings that agitate the heart and disturb the surface of the river that ought by rights to flow quietly between its well-established banks, the present is never taken into consideration, the present, that is, the only time that we are in fact living and which is therefore, curiously, overlooked. There is nothing more mysterious than the present, and there is no graver blindness than that which comes over us in the presence of the things that lie right before our eyes. We turn our gaze away from the wound of the present.

The middle class thrives on regrets and fears: it sees missed opportunities and shattered traditions behind it, and dark clouds gathering on the horizon ahead of it. Even in times of peace and calm, when nothing dramatic troubles the order of events, it keens its ritual lament, its neurotic complaint, in the twofold form of a declamation of the objective decadence of the current way of life (the world has grown vulgar, the honesty of times gone by lost forever, the children poorly brought up and ignorant, the housekeepers and maids incompetent) twinned with the heralding of impending disasters (recession, squandering of savings, unsatisfactory marriages of one's heirs, physical and mental degeneration). While fooling itself that it controls life in every slightest aspect and that it can direct to its own profit all inclinations imaginable, whether good or bad, like a sailing ship that can set its sails to gain headway from contrary winds every bit as much as favoring winds to keep its course, the middle class is racked with the shiver of perennial insecurity: when that insecurity isn't real, then mental, and if not psychological, then actual and effective insecurity, as it is now, in these times of crisis. Insecurity is the pond in which its neurotic vitality pullulates, insecurity is the prod, the painful stimulus, the thorn that forces you to feel alive even when all the primary objectives would seem to have been attained, as well as the secondary ones, and so on down the hierarchy. Without the tremor of fear, there would be no civilizing progress, and perhaps there would be no progress of any kind. The frantic oscillations of the stock market clearly represent this fickle condition: something to trust in, but something one always wishes to protect oneself against. The ritual demand that investors, especially small and medium investors, make of their stockbrokers and advisers assumes a curiously oxymoronic form: please, let me speculate but don't scare me, bet my savings but don't cut into them, gamble without gambling, what I'm trying to say is, I want to run risks without running risks, is that clear? It's like the Holy Church of Christ without Christ in the novel *Wise Blood*. Ah, a church like that would truly be perfect, without that bothersome man crucified on the wall! The ability to perform the calculations required precisely to prevent disaster derives strictly from some previous disaster, from an initial terror, similar to the original sin of religion. Indeed, you might say that the star of reasonableness under whose enlightening protection the bourgeois has chosen to let his footsteps be guided is nothing more than a residual form of fear, fear sharpened, rarified, and systematized, set to monitor and rein in the dangers and unforeseen twists that threaten his existence. Reason is nothing more than structured panic. Essentially a mechanism of self-defense, it preserves an aggressiveness equal to that of the other feelings, the love or the anger or the thirst for revenge, that inhabit and animate man. He learns to chill the hot burst of terror, transmuting it into the crystalline form of law, but even this cooling is itself an instinct, no different from that of insects that feign death in order to elude predators. It is to forestall all objections concerning its behavior that reason simulates a mechanical, necessary, impersonal, objective state. The common sense that structures its discourses, although at first glance it would seem to be nothing more than a neutral and dispassionate instrument of logical control, actually originates with the inner panic it works so hard to set aside. Reason, in other words, comes before reason, it too comes from the heart or the belly, from the chest, from the guts, and its thirst for domination overall is nothing other than a residue and clear proof of its physiological character. If reason really were abstract and superior and pure and disinterested, what need would it have to establish itself with such virulence? It develops itself in order to defend itself and, in time, subdue all others. During headlong flight, the ability to calculate the width of a crevasse is no less necessary than the muscular strength required to make the leap. The exactitude of that reckoning may well be a matter of life and death.

And so, common sense itself is a complete myth, which has cultivated the claim that it can present itself as an anti-myth, capable of unmasking the lies behind all other myths, religions, hallucinations, fairy tales, customs, and phantoms of certainties that have coagulated into systems of thought and law. Originating out of insecurity, exactly like the bodies of belief that it claims to suppress, it grows weak and starts to fail just when people start to feel most confident, when it seems as if the certainties are sufficient, in the periods when the danger seems to have retreated, when in fact the middle class luxuriates in ease and comfort and becomes a dissident from itself, abandoning its obedience to the precepts of caution that had long protected it.

The threat of a danger over the long term may prove less harmful than the superficial euphoria caused by its apparent cessation. If the middle class lives in fear, in other words, it lives better, or perhaps it may even live worse but it more closely resembles itself, and even in its state of anguish, whether for good cause or for nothing at all, it will suffer less from issues of identity. When subjected to stress, its qualities of endurance and stamina prove truly outstanding. I could cite numerous examples from my grandmother's life: she was a bourgeois woman who lived through fascism, pregnancies, war, semipoverty and semiwealth, a husband who went insane and a son who killed himself in a motorcycle crash, never turning a hair through it all, impeccable, never wavering for an instant from her personal style, whose creation and the oath she swore to remain faithful to it forever came at elevated costs, superhuman efforts, floors gleaming like mirrors, face powder, fur coat, black hat, Paglieri perfume, espresso at Il Parnaso and dinner at Il Caminetto. That is where the backbone of the middle class is rooted, its unyielding formalism, its hypocrisy that never falters or subsides, becoming wonderfully unreasonable at the darkest moments: always setting the table with double sets of utensils and two glasses, even when there's nothing to eat. Hunger, but not proletarian hunger, so melodramatic and

heartfelt, no, bourgeois hunger is an admirable spectacle, sterile and strident. Never despair, even when you die. Pretend, obstinately pretend, always pretend.

On the other hand, when it suddenly stops making sacrifices, saving,
toiling, keeping its lip zipped, wearing the polka-dot tie, buying trays of
finger pastries on Sunday, dangling from one finger the hangman's noose
of curly pink ribbon, then its moan of complaint truly becomes intolerable,
and the middle class, paradoxically, discovers its seditious and anarchistic
vocation. The tranquillity it had always aspired to but never attained is suddenly too tight for comfort. It turns apathetic, lazy, surly, and threatening.
It believes itself to be omnipotent and, in the meantime, raves frantically
over its own impotence. It demands compensation for wrongs supposedly
suffered. It feels ill-used and demands vengeance. It's sick and tired of
self-control and pious dissimulation, which have for so long been the pillars
of its way of being, sick and tired of shrewdly administering its household,
and of cutting sharp deals, and of filling the freezer with dishes and sauces
to be consumed at regular intervals, more or less as if it had freeze-dried its
whole life. The middle class rebels against the religion of monotony it invented itself. It feels the urge to go plant bombs on trains, and then it really
does go and plant them. In the end, it's even capable of killing the very same
policemen who were once the revered guardians of its vaunted tranquillity.
It self-destructs with drugs, skepticism, and unbridled financial exposure. It
introduces shapeless baggy workout pants as part of its wardrobe. It is
tempted to vote differently from how it has always voted in the past, or even
to stop voting entirely. It no longer obeys. No longer obeys whom? Itself.
Decorum, the cult of hard work, reputation, restraint—it throws all of it
into the briar patch, but then regrets having done so the minute it does,
since it cannot replace the suit of clothes it has stripped off with anything
that it actually finds persuasive, above and beyond its first burst of superficial curiosity, neither yoga, nor Buddhism, nor volunteering, nor the permissive upbringing of its children, who turn on it, throwing tantrums of
episodic severity, belated and ineffective, nor does smoking joints work any
better than giving up those same joints, not even Pilates or evening belly-
dancing classes. In short, it's as if they never know *why* they behave like
this. What with this furious process of hearing the hypocrisy of its values
denounced and unmasked, along with family and social conventions,
empty formalities and insincere attitudes, it finds itself unable to take up
new ones that aren't every bit as fake as the ones it abandoned, if not more
so. Because deciding to become an underwater photographer instead of a

commercial notary like Papà wanted is by no means a step forward if this decision, exactly like all the ones before it, is made solely as a way to stand out, a way of getting attention. In other words, for the same reasons as ever. If before they believed very little in the things they were doing but clung to them in ritualistic fashion, since repetition of the same acts renders them sacred by the simple fact of performing them regularly, every day, without any need or further addition of faith, now they are forced to believe, to *really* believe in what they do, something they are sincerely not cut out to do. Faith, a true faith, could be embraced only by giving in to madness, by falling apart, smashed to smithereens like a house abandoned and invaded by the wilderness. The self-control and dissimulation of one's feelings were undoubtedly a form of hypocrisy, but at least they drove in a specific direction, they had an objective that could be shared above and beyond the personality of a given individual, like a trademark, a class affiliation: remaining consistent with oneself, sheltering behind a frosty shield of reserve, a façade behind which no one was allowed to venture, but so obstinately that in the end the façade eventually comes to coincide with the innermost essence of one's being; or perhaps one might simply forget entirely that anything exists behind that façade, no longer requiring that any means be hidden behind the attitudes, the poses, the habits, the rules, the barriers. Fully adherent to appearance, sacrifice to it—and thereby saved. Saved from themselves. "Protect me from what I want."

Desires, like the horns of snails, recoil upon contact with reality; and once retracted, or ten times, or a hundred times, they no longer extend. An order must surface amid the most chaotic of visions, out of the most frightening and tangled phenomena. And yet the little compass of vigilance and reasonableness finds its needle spinning crazily in the opposite direction when it chances to pass by magnetic fields, buried or forgotten deposits of lodestone, and it becomes clear just how easy it is to find deep in one's soul all the hidden violence, nurtured and lovingly fostered precisely because it has been repressed for so long. The blind nest, the warm litter of unconfessable feelings are all preserved much better than those vulnerable to the daily wear of exposure and display. At this point, once the field shift has been completed, the polarity inverted, the discipline instilled and learned can be applied and implemented unchanged in the opposing field, the values function even if they are marked by a negative instead of a positive sign: bankers and bank robbers both obey, they perform their duties, they're faithful to a pact. Evil, too, possesses a strict logic all its own and a persuasive code of ethics. Crime is as plausible as an honest life. Its organization, once you choose to apply it, is every bit as perfect. There, too, you can be industrious, laborious, diligent, and dispassionate . . .

Speaking in more general terms, when a dam has been built and the dam suddenly collapses, the damage caused by the rushing waters is much more grievous than if they had been allowed to flow off gradually. An identity made up of rules is guaranteed as long as possible, and if one is incapable of imposing order upon one's soul, one seeks it elsewhere, one manifests it beginning with the outer appearance, this was the exchange, the sublime convention of the middle class: if we are to recognize that the soul is none too decorous, at least let the (pressed) trousers and (buffed and polished) shoes be. The rest you can fake—but not the shoes. It was in fact one's shoes that once presented the chief obsession and concern; as a decisive thought, an element in which one's fate was eminently focused, how to find a job, get married, be recognized by a community; and "Am I presentable?" was perhaps the most crucial and heartfelt question that one could ask oneself, in all honesty. My grandmother, for example, would ask herself that question in a tone accentuated with pride and a hint of desperation, in her lovely eyes, made up to perfection, especially once she was old and her stroll before the implacable gaze of the ladies of the quarter had become a risky ritual, a bet that was being run increasingly close to the breaking point, veering nearer and nearer to the point of no return, each time might well be the last one, since her reputation as a lovely and elegant woman was day by day endangered by the indecorous threat of looming old age. Horrible, horrible. Until one fine day she decided not to go out again, and she never did, seriously, she never again set foot outside her house. No afternoon coffee in her black hat and fur.

My hands, she would say, are already too ugly, and she'd display and touch her protruding veins.

15

THE STAGES OF THIS DECLINE were likewise logical. At first, there was only the struggle, a harsh battle for domination. With this end in mind, there is a modification of the Christian precept of renouncing things on one's own behalf in order to give them instead to others, transforming that

precept into renunciation of oneself in favor of oneself: it is the puritan mo-
rality that places nonlife as the highest model of life. Thereafter, what is left is
only the sacrifice of others. The haters of men begin by detesting their own
person, and then go on to detesting others; deep down it is nothing more than
a generalization of the same scorn. That is why you must always beware of
anyone who says: "I am hard on myself, therefore I have every right to be hard
on others." People who have been severe with themselves ought actually to
have learned to be indulgent with others.

BY SHOWING OFF the morality of sacrifice, the middle class at least succeeded in rebutting all accusations of selfishness, of egotism, since the
accumulation of wealth took place in exchange for a total depersonaliza-
tion. The bourgeois spirit showed a capacity for a melancholy acuity in its
self-diminution, its belittling of itself, behind the screen of such mediocre
qualities as modesty and parsimony. By donning the suit of armor of a sober and anonymous ethics, it meant to protect itself from both the blame
of moralists and its inner unrequited restlessness. And yet this latter quality seemed to be impossible to get rid of, a constituent element of the bourgeois spirit which, once it had won its age-old battle, found itself fighting
nothing other than itself. During the course of a war that was far more violent than is normally depicted within the gilded picture frame of the Rights
of Man, the bourgeoisie eliminated the nobility, staggering on its last legs,
and a couple of centuries later finally rid itself as well of the proletariat,
armed with an embarrassing ideology that ultimately misfired, leaving it
dwindling and defenseless, at least in the West. In the countries where up
until just a few years ago the proletariat wielded its magniloquent dictatorship, nowadays not a single voice is raised in defense of the oppressed and
the government has passed directly into the hands of profiteers. It was a
doctrine whose very aggressiveness made it, in the end, incapable of defending itself. A revolutionary machine is extremely delicate; it has an engine that must always be kept running, warmed up because, once it has
stalled, there is no one capable of getting it started again. The ancien régime and communism both collapsed under the weight of their inadequacy. The law of large numbers and the pervasive and proteiform spirit of
adaptation acknowledged the middle class's victory.

And yet the phantom of uncertainty continues to obsess it, to sink its
talons into it. The middle class has no real right to complain, seeing that
such insecurity was created or at the very least accelerated by the dynamism

that the middle class itself introduced into the social fabric, something that the other classes tended to consider unalterable. What can you do if you find yourself at the same time the most conservative *and* the most frantic component of society?

TASTE CONSISTS OF PUTTING the greatest possible distance between you and your material needs, displaying a detachment from the primary necessities of existence and from those who, by their social position, are conditioned by them. Only that which is free of charge, in fact, is beautiful, decorous, or elegant, where the sole interest is in fact appearing to be disinterested. The only thing, in theory, that can be satisfying is that which satisfies no needs: all the rest is "vulgar." It is vulgar to want it is vulgar to ask for help it is vulgar to show agitation it is vulgar to summon the waiter it is vulgar to add up the check it is vulgar to eat in haste, every bit as vulgar as it is to chew with your mouth open . . . it is vulgar to say "pleasure to meet you" and it is vulgar to say "*buon appetito.*" A distinguished person instinctively hates a vulgar person. He will find him repulsive. What happens though is that, in order to ward off all and any suspicions that one might labor under some need, one ends up becoming a slave to another need, and that is to say, the need for distinction: the eternal condemnation to show off one's superiority. There is no describing the repugnance that the bourgeoisie at every level manifests toward the style expressed by the level immediately inferior to its own. The best way of marking one's identity is through disgust and phobias. Hairstyles, clothing, furnishings, tastes and predilections when it comes to films, music, food, pronunciations of words, are all systematically caricatured mocked and held in revulsion; we contrast ourselves with that which we fear we might be confused with, taken for, within the context of the bourgeoisie itself, amid the component factions of the same, in a perennial rivalry with one another, far more than with any more distant social strata. The haute bourgeoisie, especially if it has cultural traditions or ambitions, scorns with all its soul the petit bourgeois style but not necessarily the plebeian style, toward which it may show a certain sympathy or even admiration (consider the parodistically "thuggish" manners of certain individuals of elevated social extraction . . .). Although the bourgeois may feel physically threatened by them, like an industrialist in his Jaguar facing off with the workers picketing the factory (sure, sure, I realize, that's an obsolete image, at least thirty years out of date . . .), he certainly runs no risk of being contaminated by their style. Distinction must not falter even in a state of emergency: a proper lady after a car crash must emerge from the twisted wreckage bloodied but with her clothing perfectly composed, like those suicides who, before leaping off the top floor of their aristocratic palazzi, made sure to fasten the hem of their dress with a safety pin lest they be found, once they smashed down onto the asphalt, in unseemly poses.

For that matter, they don't teach you at school how to dress and how to furnish your home. Elements of a domestic style that probably no longer exists, whose typical atmosphere was redolent of winter afternoons, formed of musical phrases played on a piano, repeated and interrupted, and then repeated again, the scent of jasmine tea, the buzz of a hair dryer after a succession of baths with loud objections from those left with the cold water at the end . . . records playing behind closed doors, adjoining yet separate worlds, the secrecy of the children's rooms, of murmuring telephone conversations in the father's study, the kitchen where a maid, either grim or cheerfully singing, makes a sauce for the boiled beef: all of them extremely close but light-years away from one another. Parsley olive oil garlic bread crumbs capers anchovies . . . mince, squeeze, sift.

Yes, but without domestic help and without a certain number of children engaged in endless quarreling over who gets to use the phone, that atmosphere vanishes, evaporated from the hermetically sealed container of the family apartment.

Taste is sacred, ideas are profane.

IN THE CONCEPT OF DISTINCTION, primacy belongs to the eye. To the "you can see at a glance that . . ." You can see at a glance that . . . she's a respectable young woman, he's a young man from a good family. You can see at a glance that . . . business is booming for her husband. You can see at a glance that . . . she studied at one of the better high schools. The signs of prestige are first and foremost visual: it's from tiny details that you can perceive someone's status. This need to display and be seen, however, contrasts with another bridgehead of bourgeois style, namely restraint, discretion, where an idea of inviolable intimacy is expressed at its highest degree. But what can you do to ensure that others will have sufficient access to this inaccessibility to recognize it? How can you immodestly show off your modesty? Is there such a thing as brazen discretion? The more accentuated the individualism, the more it demands recognition from others. Unfortunately, the so-called marks of distinction can prove to be dreary marks of an utter lack of distinction. You need only show them off. If done ostentatiously, they lose their value, like a demagnetized compass.

LET ME CITE AN EXAMPLE. My mother's best friend, Vicki, was an extremely elegant woman and her refinement could be seen everywhere, on her person and in her surroundings, scattered like the finest gold dust. She was a set and costume designer for the theater, her home was a splendid cornucopia of objects, fabrics, lamps, and a rainbow of color. According to my mother, no one had a wardrobe like hers, the most refined and at the same time simple, perfect, and rigorous that could be obtained from the couturiers of the time. Vicki affirmed her tastes in an imperious manner.

Then they found cysts in her brain.

She underwent three operations, in Italy and abroad, and they saved her life. But afterward, she was different. That is, her mental and physical facilities remained intact—she spoke and thought clearly, she could move and walk like before. But she had become *vulgar*. Yes, incredible but true, she had lost every ounce of taste. She bought bric-a-brac and embroidered doilies. She dressed like a shopgirl twenty years her junior. She grew sloppy or garish. Lots of times men would follow her when she left home wearing a tattered T-shirt and a pair of jeans stuck into the high tops of a pair of pointy-toed boots. Over her hair, which she used to have done in a permanent three times a month, she'd jam a woolen cap with a pompom that got filthy over time, a head covering that became famous throughout the quarter, but she refused to stop wearing it. She'd smear a heavy layer of cherry-red lipstick on her mouth and don heavy pendant earrings. She gave away her family furniture and replaced it with pompous designer objects that struck her as more chic, and in particular, the old dining room table was traded in for an enormous slab of glass supported by a crosspiece of chrome-plated tubing. It wasn't that the things she was doing now were wrong, no, it's worse, she had merely lost her sense of aesthetics, which had once been the light on the headland of her life.

For that reason, and for that reason alone, in spite of the fact that she was perfectly capable of making decisions about anything else, and she still appeared to be mentally lucid, her children were able to have her declared of unsound mind. She was fifty-six years old. The loss of her personal style, her sloppy way of living and dressing, were sufficient proof that "she was no longer herself." And the court that issued the decisions was right. By that point, Vicki was another person, a stranger.

Taste is sacred
ideas are profane.
The body is sacred
the mind is profane.
Woman is sacred
man is profane.
Man is a beast
woman is a work of art!

SELF-RESTRAINT, IN FACT, consists of the ability to resist, to master, to tame, to keep from giving in to vulgar or dangerous inclinations. Which can mean that once the levee breaks, there is no bottom, there are no more limits to the actions that take joy in the savage delight of being liberated . . . and by the sheer force of inertia continue their course without hindrance. Into the void. From rigid conformity to outright perversion, the distance is not only short, it can be a single step. You should further consider that pitiless and bullying acts, while they may sorely restrict the freedom of those upon whom they are inflicted, unleash the freedom of the person inflicting them. And they therefore constitute at the same time the maximum level of oppression and the maximum level of liberty, both coercion and unbridled freedom. There is no point in trying to resist the argument: rape and murder are liberatory, if viewed with the eyes of those who commit them. Perfect circularity between these two extremes is attained when those who have been oppressed by violence utilize it in their turn to achieve liberation: the joy of those who suddenly stop obeying, submitting, restraining themselves, being patient—and simply explode. Suffice it to think of the celebration of this turnaround that can be seen in countless revenge films, of which the founding father remains *Straw Dogs*, where the professor, the civilized man who has been the victim of mistreatment, suddenly reverses the situation by making use of the same violence that was used against him, but amplified tenfold by his frustration and brilliant mind. Malevolent energy concealed behind the screen of good manners.

SO LET IT BE SAID as an introduction to the central theme of this book: why shouldn't our bourgeoisie, with its frenzy, its thirst for recognition, why shouldn't it produce criminals? Perhaps it does so in a somewhat more controversial manner, or with a slightly higher dose of remorse, while the lower classes simply produce them without thinking twice. More self-aware = guiltier.

There is no country like Italy, nowhere that criminals are so envied, coddled, pitied, or mythologized . . . taken as paragons, imitated . . . both when *they redeem themselves* and when *they do not redeem themselves*. In the first case, they are admired for having been able to complete a courageous internal journey, in the second case for having shown themselves to be tough and pure. Seeing the error of their ways or showing resoluteness . . . both of these attitudes are capable of fabricating compassion or allure, and no doubt, life stories that are more interesting than those of some honest husband or admirable housewife. How many times have I heard absolutely respectable individuals boast of having made friends with a murderer, or several, and in them I could detect a genuine sense of transport, an indubitable enthusiasm, the same you will find in the die-hard sports fan who gets the autograph of a soccer champion, or the young girl with a TV star. Venturing to express doubts about the sense, or at least the advisability of such friendships, only seems to have the opposite effect of reinforcing them.

That's right, there's no country like Italy when it comes to taking pity on, mobilizing in favor of, or justifying the actions of some criminal, even if it means climbing towering and intricate conceptual castles of cards. There is not a criminal in Italy, common street criminal or political criminal, armed robber or terrorist, prominent or secondary (provided that the second-rank criminal has spent some time with his first-rank counterparts and can drop their names knowingly), who hasn't dictated his autobiography, like Silvio Pellico. His version of events, truer than true. Or else he's written a crime novel, or a noir novel, making good use of his knowledge of technical details in the realm of murder, such as cartridges and slides and bolts and how and when they jam. We may all shudder at the horror of America with its maniacal cult of weapons, where a boy in middle school who forgot to do his homework can just walk into a school and mow down his classmates with an Uzi; but here in Italy, among the many who are violent in their words and yet mild-mannered inoffensive individuals, the very few who actually know how to handle a Browning sidearm create an aura of respect around them, if not an actual halo of legend. Just a few years may go by after some bloody incident, and before you know it a movie, a TV drama, a tell-all book sets out to celebrate the exploits in question, after the TV newscasters have already done their part, churning out specials, panel discussions, in-depth documentaries, live prime-time confessions, chomping hungrily on the flesh and blood of the crime.

16

It's not the pussy that's tight, it's the head!
It's women's heads that need to be
stretched . . . It takes character
not compassion, so they understand.
When they've finally gone too far
you can get any and every thing from them.
When one of them dies, you just replace her.

I fought, I won, I tore out
all and any feeling from my heart
that might stand in the way of my will.
But if your will is no longer guided
by sentiment, if it is no longer bound by
or fond of anything, what can it want?
It can only be guided by itself
it will be pure will, a wanting to want
that takes things over
only to discard them an instant after
getting them, only to destroy them
and thus keep the will
purified of all individual feelings,
intact, active, and perennially unsatisfied.

True happiness, the great, indescribable happiness
of feeling, and being, above all others,
breaking the laws that others
have bound themselves to respect . . .
having known this supreme happiness gives you the right
not to be like them, not to think the way they do
not to respect them, and to be able to abuse them whenever you
  please.

You can have a greater pleasure
from someone who hates you
than someone who loves you.

17

THE ARDOR WITH WHICH WE PURSUE prosperity is equaled only by our terror at having missed the opportunity to achieve it. Damn it, I didn't buy a house or an apartment when they were dirt cheap, I was reluctant to invest when the stock market was booming, and I only made my mind up to do so a week before the meltdown of Argentine bonds, or Parmalat, of American mortgage-based securities, etc. The bourgeoisie is constantly tempted to speculate, tormented by doubt, unsure whether it's worth the trouble to take and plant elsewhere, in some safer place, in some more fertile terrain, the seeds of its shifting ambitions. With his impersonal adherence to the role and the status assigned him by destiny and his clan, his ancestry, in ancient times a man could at least forget himself, in part, while it only rarely happens in the mobile bourgeois world that anyone can create such stability and continuity that they can subsume themselves into it entirely, nullifying themselves in it: the individual with his whims and his ambitions always pops his head up eventually. Even first names, once handed down in a family, are now assigned in an arbitrary and fleeting fashion, because there is so little of the past that is now deemed worthy to hand down to our children, and if from time to time that sort of need endures in the form of a singular attachment to some relic or piece of furniture or family custom like spending Christmas or the summer holidays in a given place (which sadly, in Italy at least, you can almost swear has been disfigured and ruined in the meantime by wildcat development and mass tourism, making your stay there unpleasant and comparisons with the past depressing), there is always something weak and ridiculous about such resistance, as if it were a mania, a tic, a reference, which an ounce of realistic wisdom would recommend abandoning, so that you could then at some later date regret it, and yearn for it nostalgically.

The bourgeois is assailed by doubts. Constantly. The purchase of a car, or phone, or a computer, becomes a brain twister, more than it would be for someone who has very little money or a great deal. An instant after the purchase, even as he's leaving the dealership or the shop, he's already thinking: I bought the wrong thing, or else, I paid way too much, or even, I bought it now instead of waiting for the new model, I bought it but actually no one else is going to like it, or it's me who isn't going to like it, or the truth is I don't need it, so why did I buy it in the first place? But he can't retrace his steps. You can't go back, because that would mean confirming a mistake, reiterating it. In the fields of taste and culture, this happens even more frequently. Let's take shows. Once you've bought the ticket, you feel obliged to use it, even if you don't much want to. You can't stand the idea of having wasted your money, and you'd rather inflict two hours of utter tedium upon yourself. And so you'll wind up suffering twice as much. The curve of human benefits never matches the curve of economic costs. If, at the insistence of his wife or friends, he goes to a concert, for example, to hear classical music, paying top dollar for the seats because it's a famous conductor or a great orchestra or a fantastic virtuoso, and the tickets are practically impossible to get hold of, or else if he subscribes to an entire cycle of concerts, or a theater season, for the simple reason that by going to the opera or the theater he can prove to others and, first and foremost, to himself that he's doing something of cultural relevance, something that qualifies him as person, even if he actually understands little or nothing when it comes to music and theater, and they bore him to death, well, this man will suffer twice, the first time as he lays out the price of the ticket or the subscription, the second time as he sits through shows he doesn't like but for which he's already paid a head-spinning price. From these two torments added together, paradoxically, a certain pleasure may spring, a pained, contradictory, ecstatic pleasure, because the bourgeois is forced to leave his body, transcend himself, twice in order to conquer his greed and his inner grumblings. If he were seriously to apply the economic principle that his class is said to have been guided by since the Middle Ages, and which is highlighted in textbooks as the first rule of his way of life, then he ought by rights to avoid spending to suffer instead of to enjoy himself, and if he truly isn't able to enjoy himself, at least let him be bored for free, the way you do when you go to a terrible show but with tickets you didn't have to pay for, so at least you can tell yourself: "Just think if I'd had to pay for that!" The idea that he might have wasted his money is enough to drive him crazy, and that is why he prefers to lie to himself, proclaiming himself well pleased. The funny thing is that sometimes he's truly convinced that he is delighted, because he has mistaken the uproar in his heart over his authentic discontent for an aesthetic afflatus. The transfiguration will take on enduring features, and he will be able to be deeply stirred by the memory of a trip through artistic cities and castles during which he was truly bored, feeling nostalgia for places and events that at the time had only disappointed him.

Therefore, the idea of some shabby bourgeois utilitarianism is, in its turn, a legend: the idea that the bourgeois acts in accordance with a clear-eyed calculation of convenience and self-interest is one of the fables of the theory. Equally off-target is the idea that competition pushes people toward progress and that it rewards only the best: maybe so, if they don't have many competitors, if individuals can manage social comparisons and are motivated to make a rational choice, but if there are too many social actors at play, if the competition tends to fall into uniformity, then the choice becomes bewildering. Those who are forced to evaluate themselves in relation to a great number of competitors, in terms of personal resources, ability, and success, over the long term will tend to perform less and less well, in both professional and human terms. Instinctively, we tend to compare ourselves not with those who are in our same social position, but instead with those who are *at least one step above us.* This is a natural inclination, often a mortifying one, offset from time to time with the consolatory corollary of measuring ourselves against those who are *one step down.* But the frustration engendered by the first tendency will never be wholly compensated by the relief prompted by the second.

(*DO YOU REMEMBER? When the lights were turned out and the children were lined up by age, starting with the youngest little cousins all the way up to the adults and bringing up the rear of the procession was the grandmother, and each one carried one of those little candles that spray sparks and spread fear and astonishment because they don't burn your hand but only tickle it, prickling it enjoyably, and you can wave them around, creating luminous streaks that linger in your eyes, with the one shortcoming being that by the time you light the last in line, already the candles of the littlest children are already starting to burn down, they're just about to flicker out, hurry, we have to get moving into the dark room full of gifts, singing, hurry! before the sparks die out entirely . . .*)

18

SUBMIT, subjugate. The bourgeoisie is capable of fostering both instincts, simultaneously and with the same force, which by and large are distinctive features of, respectively, the lower and upper classes. The dichotomy is caused by that law of society, valid for one and all but almost pathologically vivid in the middle class (as if it had been created especially for that specific class), which obliges us to submit to conventions and, at the same time, stand out against them, distinguish ourselves, lest we become anonymous, nondescript. To obey, to fit in, to conform—to be independent, to differentiate ourselves, to distinguish ourselves. The bourgeois institution par excellence, the institution in which the middle class had found its most classic expression, with all that is solemn, ridiculous, cruel, and piteous that can be concentrated in a human relationship, that is to say, matrimony, lends itself ideally to perform this twofold function, whereby with the foundation of a new nuclear family unit, one separates oneself, one emancipates oneself—and at the same time, one goes along, one settles, and in certain cases, *one actually resigns oneself* to the greatest possible degree of conventionality. We have all experienced this sentimental-economic short circuit, this paradoxical point of fusion between two urges that, in any case, remain irreducible, generated by eroticism with the end result of killing that same eroticism, the culminating point of identification of self and other (only you, you alone exist for me, and only by your side do I exist), which inexorably plunges into the most obvious and banal of liturgies, the wedding registry, the in-laws, the mantra of evening soups, the nauseating byplay of faithfulness/betrayal, the skyrocketing utility bills, the children's orthodontist and their braces, the mismatched silverware, the measurement and purchase of matrimonial linen, deciding where to spend the vacation, wherever you like, it makes no difference to me—in other words, the sublime and monotonous muddling through of life. You save your skin and you commit suicide in one single act. The acid test that proves the physiological necessity of settling is the fact that even homosexuals, previously excluded, or should we say, exempted, now demand the right to "be like everyone."

BOURGEOIS MATRIMONY, then, is a tightrope stretched between two mountains, to be walked without ever looking down: on the one hand there is the social utilitarianism of the classical conception, on the other, the aspiration to the erotic fusion of the romantic, modern world. Matrimony ought to contain at once self-interest and passion. If you stop to think about it, it may be the only institution that, in the transition from the ancient world, which considered it a necessary but purely pragmatic ritual, and the modern world, which exalts lovers' free will to choose, rather than being desacralized over time and directed toward the pure principle of utility, as has been the case with all other forms of human expression, art, politics, and work, has instead been spiritualized, idealized . . . It was the introduction of the sacrosanct "right to happiness" that first sabotaged marriage. The expectation of happiness has rendered intolerable the fact of not being happy, or of not being happy anymore. By basing marriage on emotion, which is as exciting as it is capricious, it has been undermined and made unnecessary. If I no longer love my husband, the honesty of my desire authorizes me to get a new one. Now, instead of taming a shrew, you just dump her.

THE DECISION TO LIVE a bourgeois life often comes before its concrete achievement (alongside who to live that life, where, exercising what profession, etc.), presenting itself as an overarching plan, a sketch full of blank spots still to be filled in, whereas in other cases it is precisely the details, the preconditions, or the underlying context (a girlfriend eager to become a wife, an apartment that was supposed to come on sale and finally does, your father's office that is in need of young blood . . .) that dictate the transition from a bohemian lifestyle as a student to a very different one, of rigidly observant bourgeois ways: children—office—German sedan—business dinners—carefully planned vacations—cancer of the uterus or the prostate. You suddenly find yourself at age thirty, then forty, then fifty, with no idea of how it happened.

The change came about little by little—and then, all at once, from one day to the next, an avalanche.

> *And you may find yourself*
> *in a beautiful house, with a beautiful wife . . .*

And you may ask yourself
well . . . how did I get here?

CERTAINLY, NOTHING COULD BE more bourgeois than to reject bourgeois conventions, so that from a certain point onward, acceptance or rejection end up becoming the same thing, morally speaking. To oppose resistance, rebellion, is not always a sign of firm resolution; on the other hand, there can be something truly courageous, almost heroic, in the acceptance of a state of fact. It is clear that those who are always forced to distinguish themselves and in any case fear that they may not be particularly recognizable, often choose to avail themselves of controversial poses, the display of eccentricities and idiosyncrasies. On the other hand, sensitive people may choose to don the mask of conformist behavior, adhering to it without argument, so as to preserve intact a margin of inner freedom.

Although it usually displays a very rigid table of commandments, along with an ample array of values to be observed, in reality the middle class is incapable of identifying once and for all with a single model that establishes a clear social contract. Not even the "morality of elderly aunts" can offer a permanent moral code, and in fact, if the bourgeoisie had ever seriously respected the code that it displays as its social ethics (parsimony, shrewdness, etc.), it never would have taken a single step forward, it would still be right where it was at the start, in the Middle Ages. It is therefore a class that progresses by contradicting itself, that defines itself by its opposite. Perhaps that is why, as perhaps its most illustrious bard, Thomas Mann, maintains, it is the class with the greatest number of points of contact and things in common with the human race as a whole.

If we wanted to send a paragon of humanity into space to meet the aliens, then we ought to send an accountant, or maybe make it two humans, and throw in a school principal.

19

WHAT FOLLOWS WAS WRITTEN while thinking of the QT.

The following coexist in the middle class:

• a gray zone of people who are indifferent to almost every-thing, pleasures, ideas, dangers, impulses, tragedies, even money, in a word, to life itself; closed up like snails in a translucent shell, they seem to withstand the pressure of the outside world, holding their breath the whole time; the slightest change would cause them pain and embarrassment, even if it were a change for the better; they're afraid of being found out and judged for their detachment; in real-ity, it is they who judge the world, given that the indifference they display toward that world is perhaps far more ferocious than an openly leveled *j'accuse*; they love no one and no one loves them;

• the hedonists who chase after luxury and the superfluous, and who live for no reason other than to dazzle others with their suits and their watches and their jewelry and a style that calls attention to itself from afar;

• the good fathers and mothers who administer their patrimony as if it were a gift, without showing off, something to be preserved and not squandered, ensuring the members of their family a pros-perity so solid and discreet that in the long run it becomes practically imperceptible, something that can cause substantial confusion, such as the sensation of being poor, since they never acquire the luxury goods that others instead possess and flash freely;

• those, increasingly numerous these days, who live just a couple of steps above the poverty line, obsessed by the limits of their bud-gets, and therefore forced to second-guess their everyday behavior and expenses, taking note of each day's outlay on a monthly grid, so that a movie ticket, an espresso at the café, and the daily sports pa-per all become entries in a balance sheet.

No matter which of these categories they belong to, any member of the middle class feels that he is represented by no one, neither by the institutions, nor by the political parties, nor by the trade unions or the newspapers, and least of all, here, in the city of the pope, by the Catholic Church. Any direct involvement in political activity is viewed with skepticism, if not outright disapproval, in part because it is thought (not entirely mistakenly) that politics is the territory in which any individual's worst inclinations tend to be freed.

Disenchantment has often prevented the inhabitants of the city from taking on positions that were either too fanatical or intransigent.

THE TRADITIONAL ITALIAN CHRISTMAS DINNER with eel, a cold serpent garnished with slices of hard-boiled egg—the farewell kisses on the hairy cheeks of the old women—confessing your own childhood sins, which were for that matter practically nonexistent, to a strange man hiding behind a wooden grate: the power of conventions is so powerful and binding that it makes us accept things that are annoying or incomprehensible, the enchantment of our subjugation. The more arbitrary a rule, the greater the obligation to honor and obey it. Being constantly subjected to the will of others was, once upon a time, the core of one's upbringing, a sort of forced march into absurdity. If this explains, among other things, the unbelievable docility with which generations of men allowed themselves to be marched off into military bloodbaths, in wars fought over the possession of a few miles of weed-ridden land, on its flip side it clearly demonstrates that there can be nothing so absurd that it defies belief, and therefore that human beings are infinitely malleable, and that we are therefore willing to make incredible leaps of faith while remaining within our basic nature. That means that it is legitimate to mistrust *any* nature because it might contain the seeds of a character that is antithetical to the apparent one, and that therefore *any* convention, even one derived from the most innocuous proverb recited by a grandmother, is always on the verge of being reversed into its own opposite.

STANDING OUT isn't that hard after all, except that those very signs of distinction, on the one hand, while they do separate you from the general code of taste, also tend to lump you with a smaller, more elite circle inside of which everyone is far too alike. Possessing as they do the same prerequisites and cultivating the same idiosyncrasies, the members of the club wind up becoming practically interchangeable. It's the fate of restricted groups, of select bodies, that the very process of selection makes them as different from the outside world as they are homogeneous on the interior. A regiment of mounted cavalrymen engaged in the changing of the guard will certainly impress passersby with their extraordinary height and their plumed helmets, but it will then be very difficult for those same passersby to distinguish the new sentinels from the ones they just replaced: they all look the same. It is really rather frustrating to fight for the privilege to socialize exclusively with people of your same rank and, in the end, for that very reason, find them boring.

WE'RE TALKING ABOUT A CLASS THAT, in actual reality, aspires to possess what only a very narrow portion of its membership in effect owns. Thus, social affiliation is measured not so much in terms of the property or titles held as of aspiration to do so. The more scalding that desire, the more marked the hallmarks of membership. To be dying of envy for something is far more typically bourgeois than to own it. This characteristic, emotional rather than economic in nature, has assured that, in the opinions of some, the proletariat strictly speaking has ceased to exist in Italy, not because it has been emancipated from the bonds of poverty—instead, it vanished at the point at which it began to share in the aspirations and frustrations of the bourgeoisie. Since nine times out of ten the outcome of any given desire is frustration, it might make better sense to redesign the profiles of sociological investigations to fit the curve of a (shall we say) "index of impotence." What that would entail is taking into account not the actual consumption that single individuals or families can afford, but rather the one that it might lay claim to, even though it might be beyond their economic reach. Everything, in other words, that they feel, rightly or wrongly, they've been *cheated out of.* According to this new calculation, then, we *are* chiefly that which *we lack* in order to be able to be what we are. We consist, then, of our deficits, of the things that we lack. There is practically no family on earth in which everyone doesn't feel they've been made the victims of cruel injustices and depredations on the part of their blood kin. Or else family members believe that they've done a great deal but that it will be others who enjoy the fruit of their labors. You have to work hard to conquer the right to leisure, but since the phases of that process cannot be synchronous, they are spread over numerous generations, so that it was the father who broke his back in order to allow his children to awaken at noon.

We work today in order to be able to laze about tomorrow. Saving up money means saving up time. The generations follow each other in successive waves of hardening and softening.

But the sense of impotence is not only a reference to frustrated ambitions, to the frenzy of possession. It can also have a broader, deeper scope, and ultimately include every aspect of life, extending beyond life itself. It is as if the disappointment caused by one's awareness that one is no longer influencing things in any substantial way were vented in an obsessive effort to exert control over the external appearance of those same things. Hence the cult of the façade, the propensity to consider the aesthetic exterior, the need to "keep up appearances," whatever the cost. If a parent can do nothing to control his children's savage hearts, if he is unable to pilfer their secret thoughts, then that parent will unleash his efforts on the clothes they wear, ensuring those children at least go out into the world clean and tidy, uttering no foul language. This was true thirty years ago, nowadays the children of those children and, to an even greater degree, the daughters of those daughters swear like truck drivers, and are only sporadically reprimanded for being potty mouths. The frustration of indulgent parents is due to the fact that they never wanted or managed to exert power that in the form of educational necessity—directed therefore toward the children's upbringing, meant for their own good—might in any case afford them a pleasant sensation. Not so much of authority in the traditional sense, but rather of the ability to shepherd the chaos of things into an established form, to master them, at least in their external aspect.

If you can't get into their heads, you can at least force them to go to the barber.

IF YOUR ULTIMATE GOALS fall short, then retrench to the intermediate ones. Often the values that you have assigned as your objective are so elevated and out of reach that you are forced to fall back on the instrumental aspects that served to attain them: thus, since you are never going to be able to satisfy entirely your aspirations to social prestige or happiness, you'll settle, normally, on *money*. A spiderweb of intermediate objectives, of partial successes, of special interests winds up veiling and concealing that which you once thought was the only thing worth living for. You move to the middle, if you can't reach your ultimate destination, you lull yourself in movement, in transit.

THIS SOCIAL MODEL has a very precise equivalent in aesthetic terms, according to which one's natural inclinations, idiosyncrasies, and passions must be sacrificed and shaped in order to ensure that they comply with a higher-order schema: in bourgeois life, in fact, that would mean work and the family—in creative pursuits, works of art. Individual drives must be "placed at the service" of an objective that fulfills them but at the same time transcends them. In this sense, marriage, too, after its fashion, is a work of art—a portentous psychological and social artifact. The melancholy bourgeois aestheticism, on the one hand, aspires to and yearns for vitality, pure and simple, while in contrast it also recoils from it or aspires to tame it with the teaching of good manners, with the asceticism of renunciation, precisely as an artist does when, immersed in the array of options and seductions, in order to achieve his work of art, he must stylize with brutality, discarding pages and pages, rough drafts, and in some cases truly outstanding materials. Though they are viewed in common parlance as diametrically opposed and antithetical, the bourgeois and the artist actually turn out to be similar and close, at least in terms of the ruthless and cynical use that they make of life. Neither an artist nor a spouse, if self-aware, expects to claim any right to personal happiness, since that is not the goal to which they aspire: they are at the service of their creation far more than that creation can be said to be in service to them. The effort of the bourgeois, moreover, is twofold, since for various and curious reasons, every story, every adventure that concerns him (sentimental, conjugal, and even commercial) is already at the outset a story of degradation. It's inevitably a *Death in Venice*. When the bourgeois protagonist achieves success and becomes wealthy, his advance constitutes nothing more than the prelude to a subsequent ruin, either partial or total. The state of equilibrium so laboriously attained is invariably lost the minute it is achieved. His peace of mind—threatened and disfigured. While he seems to be committed to the struggle to improve his condition in life, the bourgeois is every bit as determined to make an attempt to restore the harmony that he had achieved up to that moment. As he advances inexorably toward the future, his eyes are fixed on a past that he no longer knows where to situate. What is the past for a member of the bourgeoisie, exactly where is it to be found? Life must be redeemed, transformed, if necessary overturned, its polarity reversed: by definition, the existential art is that of transforming the banal into the sublime, the sublime into the familiar. The order that derives from this series of painful acts of censorship will, in the end, prove broader, more complex, and more generous than the possibilities, immense though they might be, that have been excluded.

Similar even in their contradictions, the bourgeois and the artist unite prudence and audacity, method and recklessness, they scrape together their winnings, patiently, day by day, and then, like thieves, they suddenly lay their hands on great riches. But if there hadn't been a hard and daily routine of preparatory labor, they would have been unable to pull off their capers, their business deals, their brilliant hunches. They achieve dexterity through practice. Both bring to fruition not only their virtues, as is right and self-evident, but also their vices. Their invaluable bad inclinations. It is from their malevolent impulses, appropriately channeled, that they draw the force for renovation. Precisely like a resentful member of the bourgeoisie, or a cunning merchant, an artist finds the strength to outdo himself and his competitors in the shape of the resources that can be drawn from his ignoble side, aspects that stimulate his inventiveness. Dark deposits and veins of ore, glittering with inspiration. The raw material, awaiting refinement. Out of anguish, out of envy, out of desperation, out of remorse, out of perversion, and even out of infamy, he will draw the contents of his works and, most important, the sheer energy needed to shape it. He could not do without vice, which allows him to learn to know and administer himself. Likewise, the artist, every bit as much as, and even more so than the bourgeois, yearns to distinguish himself. To the point that this aspiration to recognition can turn into a delirium. He nourishes himself bitterly on his irony toward the results thus far attained. If he has sold fifty copies of his book, he wishes he'd sold fifty-one. If he has sold five hundred thousand, he still wishes he had sold one more. Otherwise, it is suffering, and suffering is infinite. But we're not talking about money here. This is not merely a financial frenzy, and numbers are just the most accessible form in which it manifests itself. So simple that it might engender a misunderstanding: "All he ever thinks about is money." Exactly the same thing that befalls the middle-class man. A comparable disquiet troubles the bourgeois and the artist. They each possess a vulpine spirit that affords them not an instant of true peace. They must prance, delve, roam, stick their nose where it doesn't belong, sniff at life and then sink their fangs into it or else flee. When he hoists a statuette in one fist, displaying it to an audience of his peers who failed to receive one this time, the gesture is at once an act of acknowledgment and of vendetta. Take this, you stinking assholes, thank you, thank you so much, I owe you everything, I love you. The thirst for money that strikes certain artists in such a morbid fashion can only be explained as a boundless, disconsolate impulse to get even.

An incessant speculator, the artist is normally depicted as a spendthrift with his head in the clouds, incapable of making himself a cup of coffee or doing basic arithmetic, and this may even be true in certain exterior aspects, but within his domain the artist is an entrepreneur who plays his cards with utter ruthlessness. The game of chance cannot spare the most intimate, delicate, and dolorous aspects, the mysteries concealed at the bottom of the heart. Any artist worthy of the name speculates on everything: on the skin of others, on his own flesh, on his innermost pains and sorrows, on his secret loves. He must take misery and make it pay, he must transform it into a work of art, this is his mandate. His wager, his investment. He cannot leave in blessed peace his brother who committed suicide, the young servant girl who died of consumption, his infant child in a Negro land, his father who was driving a buggy when he was murdered. As he celebrates their eternal rest in the grave, with hot, copious, scalding tears, he reawakens those dead. He brings them back to life, only to kill them again, as in a curse for ghosts. His need to give shape is greater than any self-restraint, exactly as is the accumulation of wealth for the bourgeois. There can be no other form of redemption for them, otherwise life would have no meaning. An artist's patrimony is his works, his purpose is to increase their number and worth. Like the members of the bourgeoisie once they finally managed to get their hands on the large landholdings of the nobility, the artist endows value by fixing it in some formal plane to what lay uncultivated in the depths of the soul of the collective. He reclaims disease-ridden swamps, and with his work he makes them fertile and practicable. Thanks to the artists of the twentieth century, we can journey through the twists and turns of the psyche, and thanks to the bourgeoisie, we can travel the highways of the earth.

IN ORDER TO WRITE OR BRING to completion works of art, the impulse of resentment is not in and of itself sufficient, but it can always come in handy. It acts as a vehicle, as a fuel enabling propulsion, as an energy source from which you can draw renewed vigor when the forces of rational planning begin to fall short. While it may seem rather tawdry to depict the motivation or the very content of the artwork (as is the case for many moralistic and satirical writers, especially when they are working in the format required by newspapers and magazines, creating targets on a daily basis upon which to vent their frustration), it is, in contrast, the act of limiting themselves to providing the necessary energy that proves so very fertile. One of the bare essentials: like the provisions and the medicines that one packs before setting off on a journey. In and of itself quite repugnant, resentment over the long run can become a moral resource. Especially when it's a matter of toughing it out and completing the artwork or volume, lavishing painful efforts that cannot be deemed justifiable in any other manner, not even to the eyes of those doing the work, much less anybody else's. A man shut up in a room talking to himself (which in the final analysis is what writing really is), another man who spends months daubing at a picture, neither of them is likely to be met with much understanding by those who are instead motivated by a more evident or less self-centered utility. Since an artwork has no foundation other than itself, those who create it are driven by an impulse that is not only creative but also destructive. Otherwise, it would not be sufficient. The violence of the impulse neither offers nor asks for reasons. There's a desire to get in a fight, make a clean sweep, make them pay dearly. But make whom pay dearly, and for what? Often, that's unclear, and this in fact is one of the defining characteristics of resentment: that it rages and aspires and fights *against who knows who*. You put the worst and most detestable part of yourself into your work. As long as you can make it work, make it flow in the direction of the artwork. Hatred must be productive, otherwise, you might as well love. The secret desire for revenge on the world, or at least for redemption in the eyes of those who looked down on you with contempt, or didn't bother to look at you at all, is kindled in even the noblest souls, it is the element of resentment that gives the bourgeois writer the urge to write. A true aristocrat would never go to the trouble and effort of finishing a novel.

AH, TASTE. Taste is more distinctive than opinions. It marks an individual in an indelible fashion, without any need to probe his principles. A print hanging on a wall or the choice of restaurant are far more powerful than any profession of creed or faith. Our egos are more deeply offended by disapproval of our tastes than of our ideas, since the former are intrinsic to our person and characterize it in a far more intimate and precise fashion than do the latter. It is easy to change your mind, while it is rare to acquire or lose style. In the years when this story is set, a respectable citizen would suffer far less grievously at the thought that his daughter might be a Communist than the sight of her going out in public dressed like a gypsy, wearing wooden clogs and long, loose flower-print skirts. In the life of any self-respecting family, what remains memorable are the furious lectures about clothing. Certain prohibitions concerning the merely exterior ("You can forget the idea of going out dressed like that, young lady!") are every bit as neurotically imperative as the chief moral precepts, thou shalt not steal, thou shalt not lie, get that makeup off your face, *there*, that's where you see true authoritarianism snapping into action, when it comes to matters of taste. At my house, there were no problems of the sort, but I do remember clearly when my eleven-year-old sister, the most morally rigid little girl in the world, asked permission to go with her classmates to the hotel of an actor who was at the time playing the character of Sandokan on TV. Sandokan, the Malaysian pirate. It was nothing more than a matter of waiting outside the hotel to get an autograph. That's all, an autograph. What are you *talking* about?! That's completely out of the question. No way on earth. Have you lost your mind? Are you seriously asking me that? My mother refused to give her permission with, more than indignation, genuine astonishment. At that point, my sister, who never asked for a thing, never a thing at all, dug in her heels and insisted on being given that permission, which all things considered would have cost them nothing; she begged, she teetered on the brink of despair, she burst into tears, incredulous in her turn that she should be denied something that her girlfriends from school were allowed to do without any particular fuss—so why am I the only one who can't go? *Why can't I but the other girls can?* The crisis went on for a whole day, as she lay on her tear-soaked bed. The prohibition remained in place, the time for the stakeout at the hotel where the Tiger of Mompracem was staying came and went, with the tragic solemnity of all those opportunities that will never return in your lifetime, and the entire affair was erased as if it were a sort of family shame, buried deep, even though we, her brothers, went on for years afterward, alluding to it mischievously, every now and then, without warning. My sister would walk into a room, and we'd burst out in chorus: *Sandokaaan . . . Sandokaaan . . .*

I DON'T REMEMBER if she was ever told the reason. Aside from the generic explanations, such as "Just forget about it," "That's not the way," "We just don't, and that's that," "It's simply a stupid thing to do," parents weren't obligated to explain the reasons for a refusal of that kind, and for that matter, they wouldn't have known how. I believe that the argument against it was implicit and meant to remain that way: someday my sister would understand on her own, and then she would agree with my mother's stern attitude; I felt certain that this hurt my mother as much as it hurt my sister, but she could not simply abandon her principles. Both of them, my mother and my sister, Alessandra, suffered a great deal over nothing, but that nothing was as solid as a rock. Insurmountable, impassable. A matter of taste.

So I'll tell you the reason.

Because waiting for hours in the street for a television star to give you an autograph is not only stupid, it is, far worse . . . *something only housekeepers would do.*

Fine, nobody has housekeepers anymore, or if they do, they certainly don't call them housekeepers, and they no longer read magazines like *Grand Hotel* and the kind of pulp novels housekeepers read, which in the meantime have become the core of modern fiction and literary imprints, with an avalanche of titles in the second person, often in the imperative mood, *Let Me Look at You, Take Me, Forget Me, Don't Move, Carry Me Off, Grab Me, Lay Me Down, Hold Me Tight, Listen to Me,* etc.

THE BOURGEOIS VIRTUES ARE ECONOMIC in nature, they administer quantity more than they exalt quality. They are economic virtues: shrewdness, farsightedness, frugality . . . and then there's punctuality, prudence, circumspection, thrift, honesty. I call honesty a strictly economic virtue when it requires no other quality in order to be observed. It's by no means a despicable quality, let's not misunderstand, but it ought to go without saying, like giving a customer correct change.

When other human qualities are required, for example, it accompanies courage, in the willingness not to conceal an inconvenient truth, or to reject compromises that violate one's convictions, or else admitting one's mistakes, and only then does honesty rise to the rank of the qualities that stand beside it.

RESENTMENT, on the one hand, can lead you to reinforce your honesty, as you proclaim your indignation toward those who, by failing to practice the same virtue, have obtained advantages greater than yours (at my house we referred to such people by the old-fashioned term of "scoundrels"), or on the other hand, it can push you to imitate them. If you can't fight them, join them. This whispers a sense of impotence into the ear of those who see people less meritorious than themselves nevertheless advancing across the social chessboard. It is difficult to remain calm in the face of scandal. We wish to punish the protagonists and yet, at the same time, we envy them, tempted to do the same thing, even though our conscience depicts it as deeply repugnant, or even better, we'd like to enjoy the advantages without having to pass through the necessary and degrading act. We'd like to become rich without having to steal, in other words, have beautiful women without having to corrupt them or buy them. Which would mean remaining innocent. Without punishment, in the long term, the sense of guilt disappears as well. Just think what Pleasure Island would be without the donkey ears. The cult of legalism among the bourgeoisie is always poised on the verge of being overturned into its opposite, so powerful is the pressure of the resentment that drives it. The ideal equality to which envy aspires produces violent lurches far greater than the gaps it meant to bridge in the first place. Isolation from everyone and homogeneity with everyone. It is in fact leveling that causes the attitude of comparison in the first place and, as a result, an envy honed to razor sharpness on the most trivial of details: when there aren't immense fortunes, castles, and horse-drawn carriages to eat your heart out over, then envy (and the desire for self-affirmation) focuses on, say, a pair of boots. Perhaps that was truer when I was a kid—nowadays the sheer overabundance of consumer goods has made our appearances roughly indecipherable, and the indicator of the things we buy is no longer a reliable marker of our social affiliation. Consumption has become deceptive. The indicators of wealth, now slippery. The objects that assign status, affordable and interchangeable. A 500-euro cell phone seems to be within reach of anyone who wants it, and even a Lamborghini doesn't necessarily imply a wealthy heir behind the wheel. It may sound strange, but the objects of our envious resentment are not the incalculable fortunes, the estates of the great financiers. The imagination falters when it tries to grasp what it actually means to be Bill Gates, it can't scale those heights. Instead, we tend to envy that which is *almost* within reach. We envy that which we believe we have every right to possess. We envy our neighbors, not people who are radically different from us. Those who are like us in quality, age, social category, similarity of fate.

I've never envied Gianni Agnelli or his grandchildren.

All right, then, whom have I *really* envied?

❖

IF WHAT I'VE SAID so far is true, then the literary world is the most bour-geois of them all! The situation, from the outset, is here, too, one of sup-posed equality and an apparent homogeneity of means and ends. A particle physicist, a financial analyst, the conductor of a symphony orchestra are all unrivaled, unattainable in their specific fields of knowledge, it would take twenty years of study to be able even to have an intelligent conversa-tion with them: but what does it take to write a book? Since we're all capa-ble of stringing a few words together (there may be those who are better at it, or worse, but that's a secondary matter), theoretically anyway, we'd all be able to write a bestseller, which may not be true but it's certainly con-ceivable, open to infinite conjecture. Another characteristic of resentment: the fact that it hammers relentlessly, obsessively: a "malevolent rumina-tion" that will never give you peace, and while at first it may be directed toward a specific person, in time it spreads and extends to the world at large. Twenty years ago, when Susanna Tamaro published an enormously successful book (and about time: the first bestseller of my g-g-generation!), I remember just how aghast the writers her age were, especially the women. They thought of Susanna as being closer, more similar to them, no differ-ent in other words, and so? What are you saying, that I have no sensibility? Don't I have a grandmother of my own? I must be able to squeeze a few tears out of my readers! That's what they all seemed to be thinking, be-tween one faint dismissive smile and the next. We were all good enough to write *Follow Your Heart*, in other words, and a few thought they were bet-ter than good enough.

A society of our peers creates spasmodic and boundless desires. And lots and lots of Schadenfreude, malevolent joy.

You could say that prosperity creates discontentment, instead of placat-ing it. As it was for the French at the time of the Revolution, according to de Tocqueville, the position of the bourgeois becomes all the more intoler-able the more it improves. One's dissatisfaction with the goods acquired only grows in direct proportion to their number. Along the path of social promotion, the awareness that there is an infinite number of goods still to be acquired becomes intensely painful. Logic might tell you that every search, every quest begins from a state of total privation. Instead, that is not the case: it actually starts from a state of incomplete possession. And every possession, in fact, is incomplete. Thus, the greater the possession, the greater the lack that accompanies it, like a shadow to a body. Who possesses much, lacks much. The little virtues, the sweet ironies of life, the measured and tranquil pleasures, the myth of the family nest, the morality of thrift, of the saying "*parva sed apta mihi*," which has been translated as "Small is my humble roof, but well designed"—all these things are nothing more than a modest covering, or perhaps the antidote that the bourgeois Dr. Jekyll frantically produces to sedate the Mr. Hyde who rages frantically in his laboratory. It is this retentive morality that compresses even the most savage resentment beneath its chaste surface.

What appears to be an unresolvable contradiction is in reality a movement of systole and diastole, absolutely consistent and something that ought to be perceived in a unified manner as it manifests itself through opposing phenomena: on the one hand, an aspiration to anonymity, on the other, the excessive yearning for self-affirmation.

The fact that prosperity amplifies your sense of malaise is something that can be viewed in the form of a negative in certain archaic societies, where once you've satisfied your primary needs, food and shelter, say, there is nothing else you can think of. No particular needs drive competition among individuals or families. People live without any special expectations. Society remains unchanged, if you set aside the resentment that would normally drive the spirit of initiative. Resentment is the worst enemy of laziness. Resentment is almost always what drives men of action: businessmen, travelers, merchants, politicians. Only when introduced from without (by TV, by foreigners, etc.) are reasons felt for dissatisfaction, only then do they desire anything more than a meal and a cot. I remember what people said to me as I went through certain far-flung villages to the south of Kandahar, in Afghanistan: "Here, my friend, if you can manage to survive, life is very relaxing."

RESENTMENT IS AN EMOTION but also a form of thought, reactive in nature, and therefore social and political: it develops only in response to the surrounding environment, in contact with one's neighbor, and it obliges the person who falls victim to it to relive a negative experience or one that, most of the time, actually isn't negative at all, only experienced as such, as a form of injustice. The closer a person or a situation that causes resentment is to us, the more it is pushed right before our eyes, so to speak (a next-door neighbor, an indignity suffered at your workplace, or a glaring privilege given to a teacher's pet or a favorite sibling, thereby upsetting the theoretical equality among all children), the more intense the resentment becomes. The families and the offices where people live cheek by jowl, in accordance with hierarchies subtly called into question, are the ideal terrain for this proliferation of ill feeling, which, by the way, let us recall, may originate out of an authentic thirst for justice. After all, the brothers of the prodigal son, just like the laborers in the Gospel who had been toiling in the vineyard since dawn, have every reason to be pissed off when someone comes along, fresh and rested, to sweep up their full reward at the very last minute. The very particular aspect of resentment, however, is that it is not manifested openly. It is repressed or masked or buried deep in one's soul, where it lurks in silence, becoming rancor. If it manifested itself, it would promptly dissolve into thin air. But it will not or cannot reveal itself. Shyness or decorum prevent that. One is tempted to answer the insult or the outrage with a retort, but that answer is put off, deferred, out of either fear or self-control (and frequently the former is palmed off as the latter), and so you sit there, silent and well behaved, biding your time until the ideal moment comes along, the blade is sharpened and honed ten thousand times, what with your constant mulling over and refining, your plans for revenge are brought to a high sheen, until so much time has passed that a retort is now out of the question, or the recipient would simply not even understand it anymore. In that case, the rancor that has been sitting there, incubating, now breaks away from the individual with whom it originated and spreads out like a patch of oil, a veil of grease, overlaid on people and things. You no longer hate the individual doctor who got the diagnosis wrong, now you hate the entire professional class of doctors: incompetent thieving murderers, self-centered gasbags, full of hot air. You no longer envy the brownnoser who managed to get a promotion at your office, but everyone who manages to climb the ladder in life, by whatever means, so that even legitimate methods start to look dishonest and hypocritical to you. You no longer nurture rancor toward the individual neighbor who has failed to pay his share of the condo heating fees for the building, but now toward all the tenants in the building, or even in the quarter: in fact, toward the whole human race, made up as it is of evildoers who, if there were such a thing as justice, or at least one worthy of the name, would be hauled out and horsewhipped on the public square, subjected to painful and ridiculous punishments. In my mind, I have a fanciful sampling of tortures with which to subject a list of people, whose names I keep to myself, along the lines of those inflicted at the Caudine Forks; otherwise I might emulate the Michael Douglas character in *Falling Down*, the stressed-out everyman who one day gets out his

Uzi and starts settling scores, giving everyone exactly what they deserve; but let's be clear, here too, the character played by Douglas isn't just paying back those who did him wrong, he's taking it out on entire human categories that he runs into during his demented trek across Los Angeles: wealthy golfers, neo-Nazis, policemen, Hispanic gang members, price-gouging shopkeepers, etc.

His frustration has risen to levels high enough that he's ready to lash out at anyone: if no one is without sin, then we all still deserve punishment. The executioner's whip strikes all of society and spares not even the flogger, who may hate himself every bit as much as he hates all others. Indeed, the fact that he considers himself a miserable wretch may help him to cultivate his feelings as honest and straightforward and, in the final analysis, even noble. Perhaps some may have noticed how professional haters (among writers, for example, Thomas Bernhard) obtain consensus and even admiration or a sort of ethical license to exercise their malevolence, given that they turn it first and foremost against themselves: that is to say, by proclaiming themselves to be, from the very outset, vile creatures, vicious, miserable, squalid—but still honest enough to admit it.

The only good and effective thing about a vendetta, at least in theory, is the way it allows you to vent your negative instincts. At the moment of action, those instincts would ideally be vaporized, burned to a crisp. If instead you are forced by your own weakness or by social conventions to put a good face on things and smile as you gulp down the healthy portions of crow your envy serves you, then the impossibility of revenge is transformed into a form of genuine inner torment. A resentful man no longer lives within himself, he no longer lives his own life, but exists only as a function of other people's lives. He listens through a stethoscope, he scrutinizes, spies, and registers every slightest variation in the status of others, as sensitive as the needle of a Geiger counter. And then he compares. He compares the results, the successes, the failures, the engine size of the cars parked on the street where he lives. There exists no investigative spirit, no aptitude for espionage, no introspective brooding more attentive than that of the envious bourgeois, who—and it is no accident—first invented the psyche and the relative instruments for penetrating that psyche. Incapable of the aristocrat's sovereign indifference, the bourgeois is always wide awake and keenly attentive, and he keeps track, he keeps track of everything. He interrogates himself, in an ongoing inquisition. I've never understood why the best-known novel about the Italian bourgeoisie, Alberto Moravia's *The*

Indifferent Ones, should have been given that title. Perhaps to stigmatize, with the moralistic approach that is so typical of every young author, a sin that is considered abominable—that of no longer feeling authentic sentiments and affections? But if only the sin of the bourgeoisie was indifference; if only! If only the bourgeois really did let life slide off his back, as holy men and wild animals are able to do . . . Quite to the contrary, there is no creature on earth more highly alert than he. His existence unfolds under the banner of an incessant comparison and measurement between himself and others. Just the slightest detail is enough to make a difference, for better or for worse. Set inside a Leonardesque circle, arms and legs spread, but in a suit and tie. The comparison with one's competitors can be glimpsed in a thousand different objects and details, so that if you are or if you feel inferior in one aspect, you can always regain ground in another. In the case that one has, for example, a homely or unfaithful or shrewish wife, or all three things together, you can make up for it, perhaps, with prestigious residences and vacations, successfully landed contracts, children at good universities, sailboats that handle better than others. Furnishings, automobiles, athletic activities, checking accounts, severance agreements and fringe benefits, the thickness and color of the hair on your head, the frequency of sexual relations, highly placed friends, and invitations to dinner, square footage and cubic inches: there are countless types of status symbols. Happiness at this price is impossible; its modest stand-in, satisfaction; while frustration is the almost perennial, virtually universal state of mind of bourgeois life. In many historic periods (including this one), at every turn of the economy, it is the middle class that feels disappointed and punished more than any other: either because it is unable to improve its own conditions or else because it sees them increasingly undermined and threatened. When the chilly bourgeois heart heats up, it is because it feels that it has been cut out of the distribution of wealth in a time of fatted calves, or else because it is in danger of descending or even plunging toward the bottom in a period of lean and haggard cows. The loss of an acquired benefit or else the inability to take full advantage of new opportunities that appear on the horizon terrorizes the bourgeois, tormenting him and humiliating him ("How the fuck can it be that I'm the only one who's never made a penny on the stock market?" is the scolding that who knows how many people have given themselves after a speculative bubble has popped, to say nothing of those who plunged in too late, for whom the purchase of tech stocks or bonds in developing nations, which instead of skyrocketing have decided to plunge suddenly into a state of anarchy, has turned into a grotesque nightmare that has burned through the savings of twenty years in just a few short weeks . . .). The problem of bourgeois identity is by definition unsolvable. The bourgeois need for differentiation goes beyond the mere biological need for subsistence. In its grimmest moments, it must defend itself tooth and nail, but it will never lower itself to considering survival as its sole objective, it would be demoralizing and indecorous to have to struggle, as the poor must, for a meal and a roof over one's head.

Politically the bourgeois will vote for anyone who'll promise him that the gap between him and inferior social classes will remain unchanged, at the very least; as long as he can ward off the risk of being downgraded on the social chessboard, he's ready to give his wholehearted and enthusiastic support to adventurism that is anything but peaceful, thereby giving the lie to his own spirit of moderation, thereby unleashing a fanaticism as understated as it is deadly, in comparison with which the populist frenzy of the sansculottes merely pales, feebly; whereas the revolutionary fury of the sansculottes flares up in violent gusts, gusts that are frequently short-lived, the treacherous embers of bourgeois resentment seethe quietly, burning for years, fired by the fuel of deep-seated frustrations; and in the absence of any solid guarantees defending their own status, the bourgeois are willing to settle for a bare minimum of symbolic gratifications. Certainly, a novel can never limit itself to providing a portrait of a social class, even though it may proclaim that to be its intent and narrative horizon, as in the case of *Madame Bovary* or *Anna Karenina*, and it is surely no accident that both of these novels have women as their protagonists, women who, even more than men, seem to belong body and soul—without reservation, in an almost sacrificial manner, as if they had taken some ironclad vow—to their respective classes: it is in their destiny as victims that they reveal their radical essence. While the men climb, plummet, accumulate fortunes, only to lose them over the course of a night, attempting to forge their destiny with a knife blow, soaring across the social panorama like rockets glaring in the night, illuminating the trenchworks excavated across those landscapes by convention: and those men are all to some extent Barry Lyndons and Bel Amis and Lucien de Rubemprés and Counts of Monte Cristo, come back to take their vengeance, I was saying, at the same time the women remain *figées* to the torture wheel of a surname and, after marrying the provincial doctor, their escapist fantasies can never be anything more than dreams. It might seem romantic to dream and to wallow in illusions, but there can be nothing more predictable and obvious than dreams. In order to fill the void, people transfer themselves body and soul into another person's life, or other people's lives, or into their earlier life, when they're afraid they might be incapable of living wholeheartedly what remains of that life. Too late, too late . . . In certain cases, the agonizing comparison is with youth, idealized and envied in its dazzling glow, or else spangled with regrets for the missed opportunities, often for the lack of boldness in taking advantage of them when they presented themselves. In other words, regrets for one's upbringing. The education one received. You slap yourself for having cleaved to a moral code to which, as often as not, you were clinging out of weakness, that is, a lack of the courage required to commit the acts that such morality abhors. I was too reserved, too honest, in a world of profiteers—that is the unfailing regret of the properly brought up individual. I never let my own self-interest come first, and here is the result: the others got ahead and I didn't. Who will ever recognize this sacrifice of mine? There can be no more intense and lasting sentiment than the bitterness of the bourgeois who was, remains, and always will be unable to vent his frustrations. His wife and children rarely understand this effort of his, indeed, to tell the truth, they never even notice it. Which only adds insult to injury. How could they be grateful for or admiring of something that by its very definition remains invisible or inexplicable? The secret of a man who does nothing but inhibits and restrains himself really does run the risk of leaving no traces. If only we were capable of turning the other cheek without letting the insult thus swallowed stagnate and putrefy somewhere deep inside us! This sublime and controversial moral precept almost unfailingly turns into: I'll put up with it now, but one day I'll make you pay. In fact, I'll make *all of you* pay. A postponement, in other words; and the expansion of one's plans for vengeance until they encompass an entire community of individuals by whom one was done wrong, wrongs that are variously real and imaginary.

THAT'S WHY THE TITLE, *The Indifferent Ones*, formidable though it is, strikes me as somehow disjointed from the book, if its aim was to depict the middle class. Perhaps it should have been called *The Dissatisfied Ones*.

20

A s I've mentioned before, my grandmother was furious (in muffled silence, only to explode and throw it in my face many years later . . .) that in my father's obituary he had been called "Carlo Albinati" and not "Ing. Carlo Albinati"—"Carlo Albinati, Engineer." That Ing. before the name made all the difference, in her opinion; it was in that Ing. that the meaning of a lifetime could be found (and really, looking back, I can't disagree with her), and not having added it to the dead man's name was tantamount to desecrating the corpse.

I wrote that death notice myself. I chose not to name either of my sons Carlo precisely because, when saying the name, I would have been hard put to avoid adding the unfailing prefix "Ing."

IN A SINGLE SPIRIT there can coexist inventive flair—which must necessarily shatter inherited traditions in order to blaze new and profitable trails that frequently verge on the illegal—and caution, honesty, attachment to old habits, the fear of innovation. Often the two souls are phases or generations of a process of development, one following on the heels of the other—first come the adventurers, and then come the accountants, those who found the empires and those who administer and consolidate them. After them come the wastrels, who squander those fortunes.

In Italy, it requires only three generations for the cycle to be complete; in this country the anthropological malleability is stunning. Even in the physical features, you can see a metamorphosis that recapitulates the economic transformation, or even precedes it.

ASIDE FROM SUCCEEDING each other chronologically, the two opposing spirits belong in principle to two distinct types of middle class: on the one hand, the entrepreneurs (industrialists, builders, etc.), devoted to risk by definition, and on the other hand, functionaries, to the same extent by definition alien to risk.

THE AFFIRMATION of a quantitative conception of the world, followed by its technical translation into a virtually infinite production of consumer goods, likewise valued in economic terms, thereby conferring little by little an indisputable dignity to the bourgeois way of thought, convincing the middle class—and along with that class, the members of the upper and lower classes, who were obliged to fall into line with it—of the universal goodness and the practical and moral superiority of the bourgeois model of life. The underlying formula being: everything must be calculated on the basis of functions and objectives. Everything must be placed under control, safely secured, regulated and measured according to economic principles. The earth, the sky, heaven, love, the air, our gestures, the relics of the past, the days of our lives, even our amusements and our leisure time must be profitable, otherwise they make no sense. Land left untilled makes no sense, an apartment left unrented, vacant, makes no sense, an asset poorly allocated, even less. A vacation from which you return untanned, without a portfolio of sexual satisfactions or monuments toured, is scandalous. All of life resembles a membership in a gym or a swimming pool, which must be earned out, made to pay. The costs and benefits of every undertaking must be closely evaluated. You eat one kind of food because "it's good for you," you perform a physical activity because it "keeps you fit" or it "relaxes you." You replace the joy of running or jumping with the maniacal care of the body as if it were a piece of machinery that needs its regular tune-up. Even unrequited love, which in the classical world was a standard figure of eros, a quintessential form of passion, and the fatal consequence of the capricious act of some god or other, becomes a tragic and ridiculous mishap only in the bourgeois world (to which Romanticism, of course, is the winged repercussion), where it is simply intolerable to think that some given investment yields no return. It doesn't pay off, in other words, or the yield is less than might have been expected. Whether they are short-term returns, with a one-night stand, or long-term returns, with a marriage, the amorous investment must in either case be profitable, it must be successful, otherwise it was a mistake or a folly. Unhappy love will cause dismay, no different than a bad business deal. The sense of loss is accompanied by a bitter realization of one's own recklessness or ineptitude, the same as when you buy a basket of strawberries only to realize that the ones at the bottom are spoiled, or when you buy stock and it drops in value, or defective merchandise, or a house that turns out to have a lien on it. In other words, you could have gotten a better deal, even in love, by turning a sharper eye, by evaluating more carefully, making a better choice, stopping in time, or to the contrary, by being more daring, throwing yourself into the erotic fray more wholeheartedly, taking greater risks (because if there's a shortcoming of which the bourgeois loves to accuse himself in a ritual and self-gratified fashion, it's coldness, or actually, even worse, tepidness, being lukewarm about things; emotional distraction, a heart that beats too slow; disenchantment, in other words, the resigned impotence of those who fail to live life to the utmost, like a hero, or not even to the zero degree, like an ascetic or a hermit, but rather, with the tachometer running right in the middle).

However he operates, with cold opportunism or overemphatic enthusiasm, the bourgeois often suspects that he's done something wrong, that he's failed to consider the alternatives thoroughly enough, that he's run a needless risk or clipped his own wings foolishly, misplaying his cards, let his finest qualities become his worst shortcomings. "What was I thinking?" "How did I ever get myself into this mess?" are perhaps the most typical phrases in his repertory of discontentment. Incapable of identifying with a specific destiny, he is convinced that he'll be able to revise it endlessly, correcting it, fine-tuning it, recalibrating it thanks to updated calculations, retouching existence as if it were a hairdo, a financial regulation, the optionals on an automobile, a construction project that flies just under the building code, one of those gifts that "if you don't like it, you can always return it to the store." Life as it actually is is always a little too tight for comfort, in any case. Let it be spangled with success or lived under a gray cloud cover of monotonous squalor, it never matches up with what he had planned or expected, in part because the planning, endlessly revised and expanded, has become completely illegible. For example: the plan to get rich. Nothing wrong there, it's a perfectly clear and legitimate desire. But since there is no limit to wealth, when is it that I can say: *There*, I've achieved my objective? Is this enough, am I satisfied now? Practically never. When you have one million or one billion, you can always get another. No different from a gambler or an armed robber, who tells himself each time: "Just this last caper, and then I retire," the objectives that the bourgeois sets for himself are perforce partial. In vain does he proclaim that once he's achieved these, he'll be contented. He need only take a quick look around: others just like him might have achieved better results or in less time. The spirit of comparison is implacable. Did you buy yourself a nice house? It's mathematically certain: there will always be some friend or acquaintance who bought a nicer one or paid less.

Like homosexuals on a public beach or penguins standing erect on Antarctic shoals, the bourgeois look around, constantly, to their right and left, checking out what the others are doing. You never know. There are succulent opportunities you don't want to miss, there are dangers to flee. Even the office worker with the safe job and the monthly paycheck calculated down to the last penny, with deductions and incentives, might feel he has fallen prey to the slings and arrows of chance, or has become the victim of injustices as gross as they are treacherous, colossal in their apparent insignificance, ranging from a dimly lit desk to not having been invited to the company five-on-five soccer tournament. Likewise, he can exult in victories that are practically imperceptible and relish subliminal mockeries. When a case of alleged workplace mobbing winds up in court, the judge is frequently stunned: he finds himself examining exhibits of evidence that seem to promise to point to cases of extreme cruelty, only to pop like so many soap bubbles that only the tormented mind-set of jealous comparison was able to conjure up.

The perpetual suffering of believing himself to be the victim of some injustice (or perhaps, the torment of actually being a victim of it), the perpetrators of which are, variously, the government, one's superiors or colleagues at work, one's family members, one's wife, the competition, the criminal element, is replaced, or mixed up with the pleasure of imagining one's vendetta. A delicious desire, a fantasy in which you picture yourself paying back twofold the wrongs inflicted upon you, pleasurably warms the life of the bourgeoisie every bit as much as a fire crackling merrily away in the fireplace of the little country house on the weekend, gradually warming them. It can even go so far as to scorch the soul. The bourgeois heart is as deep as a black abyss, and that is why its feelings never rise to the surface. Passions lie concealed in its shadows whose existence you could never begin to imagine, like the sea monsters that live in the depths of the ocean trenches.

Just because something has never been seen, doesn't necessarily mean that it doesn't exist.

For a long time, he has become accustomed to the idea of putting up with the insolent abuse, the minor mistreatments, the laughable injustices, because that is how he was brought up, and that is how he, in his turn, will bring up his offspring; but deep in his heart, he mulls and plots, he savors and anticipates his *vendetta*. There need be absolutely no valid justification for the day he finally unleashes it, quite the contrary; bourgeois vengeance almost never bursts into action after some grave wrong is done him, as it

would be in the blood feuds that erupt in the lower classes. In fact, by taking revenge, he wants to pay back, at a single blow, all the people and all
the things, and not a specific episode against a specific person. The all-
encompassing and widespread nature of the bourgeois dream of vengeance
has to do with life as a whole and is designed to lay waste to an entire army
of adversaries, of whom those who are actually struck by this vendetta are
only a minor sampling. The ones he wants to make pay are "them." The
bourgeois vendetta is a demented response to a myriad of provocations that
have piled up over time: it might snap on the tenth, or the hundredth, or
the thousandth time, or never go off at all, remaining for all time concealed
beneath the jacket and tie, never entirely laid to rest. That third person plural, "they, them," covers any number of sworn enemies: the poor, the rich,
the greedy relatives, the city cops, the bureaucracy . . .

What's more, it's not at all true that the bourgeois is a liar. A hypocrite,
okay. He's more likely to conceal the truth than invent a falsehood, and this
capacity may, when necessary, be reversed into its positive side, that is, as
an instance of good manners, as the construction of a more livable world,
tidier, more comfortable, where the unpleasant truths have been pushed
into the background, hidden from view. (The objective correlative of this
psychological aptitude are the broom closets, nooks, and clothes closets of
bourgeois apartments that even now elicit little cries of admiration from
the ladies during a tour of the house—convenient spaces in which to stow
away, out of sight, all the objects devoid of a permanent and dignified domestic collocation.) Nothing could be more disconcerting than a shame
that cannot be placed within a pattern. The unplaceable is the true secret
tenant of every house and every life in the middle class. It could be a suit, a
rowing machine, a demented cousin, a sloppily sentimental book, the photograph of a dead lover, a piece of jewelry never returned to whoever lent it
to you. A bourgeois falls back on a lie only in case of emergency, if obliged to
make up a fib then and there, he feels it goes against his nature. He may or
may not succeed, but the fact that he might be able to do it doesn't make
him a liar in the conventional sense of the term. The art of fabricating an
existential alibi is, rather, a slow process of weaving, something that takes
years, rendering increasingly opaque over time certain aspects of his original personality, and at the same time adding glitter and luster to others.

Though we may feel certain we're very perspicacious, and capable of
unmasking the lies of others, in reality we allow ourselves to be deceived
easily and often, since at the base of this deception can be found, more than
stupidity, self-interest. We want to *persuade*, but perhaps even more strongly,

we want to *be persuaded.* Persuaded of that which is good and right, but also of that which is neither: persuaded of an error seems better to us than to be uncertain or convinced of nothing.

If it is true that a society is based on the presupposition that its members tell one another the truth, but if it's also true that every other time they open their mouths, they lie—truth, lie, truth, lie—then this means that we prefer in any case, and on general principle, *to believe*, to believe things that if we had even a smidgen of good judgment we would immediately recognize as *false*. In other words, it is more painful to unmask those lies than it is to maintain intact a naïve trust in our fellow man.

As a result, those who persist in denouncing falsehood ultimately win not the gratitude but the irritation of the collective, a general response of dismay. People prefer to assign the features of truth to that which has been determined to be false, as long as it helps to hold a social structure together. That which is false by logic can be true by conscience.

ANYONE WHO HAS BEEN BROUGHT UP in a rigid manner to take it for granted that everyone tells the truth, that is, not only that everyone *ought* to tell the truth but that everyone actually *does tell the truth*, in short, anyone who has been accustomed to trusting other people *on principle*, in a state of total credulity, the day that they discover that it isn't true, that it isn't *always* true, that in fact it's *almost never* true, runs the risk of becoming all at once the most suspicious and skeptical person in the world. Having never before experienced anything of the sort, all of a sudden they have the giddy, dizzying sensation that *everyone* is lying, and that they actually do nothing but tell lies—do nothing but tell *them* lies. The revelation can be so pitiless, and at the same time, so mocking (in fact, you feel like an utter fool), that it drives you to the opposite excess. While before this person believed everything and everyone, indiscriminately conceding his trust (which constitutes a fine savings of mental energy: mistrusting others so that you can unmask them is, in fact, an exhausting exercise, a continuous mulling of hypotheses, an effort of interpretation that never leads to any certain outcome), he now believes nothing and no one. EVER. The world has become a carnival of lies.

In the utter collapse of credulity, the first one to pay the price, the first one I stop trusting is me. I tell myself: okay, you're not fooling me again. You won't take me in again with your deceits. You can't enchant me with your palpitations. Normally people assume that it's impossible to falsify your feelings, that is, they suppose that feelings are by definition sincere, authentic, how could someone pretend to *feel* something? Oh, I don't know what: say, love, regret, gratitude . . .

On the contrary, I am convinced that there is nothing that can be so easily falsified as feelings, nothing about which people are more likely to fool themselves. In truth, we never know exactly *what* we're feeling, certainly, we're feeling *something*, it feels as if we're crossing through a tempest, but not even that, deep down, is all that certain.

LET US NECESSARILY GO BACK to the subject of money. In response to the question "how much," the only legitimate answer is "lots." (The answer "not much" is inconceivable, it would be obscene.) Even when we have stopped wanting to purchase the objects we needed money to buy, money still remains desirable in and of itself.

Money has the unsettling characteristic of being a pure and infinite *possibility*, an equivalent through which everything in the world intersects and becomes one with all the others. In that abstract place, a multiplicity of heterogeneous and unattainable objects and stimuli converge. At the same time, money enhances the possibility of contact with different persons and things (travel, hotels, automobiles, art, technological accessories, clothing, wine, styles . . .) but spares you the need to explore that contact in depth. While it seems to bring the immediacy of life and the world within reach, it also erects itself as a protection against it. Money serves as a trailer hitch but also as a shock absorber, as a hook but also a buffer with respect to reality. At a certain point, you can always break loose. Those who have a great deal of money know both more and less than those who have very little. They may have been to the Laccadive Islands, but they have no idea where Tor Tre Teste or Casalotti are, on the outskirts of Rome. They may know how to fly a jet plane, but they wouldn't know how to find their way through a bus station.

(TRUTH BE TOLD, though, the wealthy people I've met knew more than I did about everything, from fine food to economics, from antiques to horseback riding, from painting to fine tailors to mountain climbing to sex. Perhaps only in literature could I have held my own: but it's not by talking about Kierkegaard that you impress someone else and intimidate them . . . And I have to confess that, at least lately, they had read more novels and seen far more movies than I had, they were better informed even about those things! They knew more people, they had more friends, and they cultivated a vast and detailed array of interests and hobbies, they owned collections, they had traveled everywhere, they knew about wines and vineyards, horses and dogs, automobiles, fabrics, helicopters, silk ties, fine cheeses, magazines, cocktails, restaurants in New York, boats, and women, they knew a hundred times as much as I did, and in comparison with them I felt like a provincial, a pathetic little booger. They knew how to cook, ski, play squash, backgammon, Yahtzee, and mahjong.)

IN MINIATURE, I understood all that, I understood life, work, contacts, I understood Milan, I understood myself and others when, one evening many years ago, I was invited to a dinner party with a number of journalists or editors and publishing executives, or perhaps they belonged to other equivalent professional categories: thirty years later, I can hardly remember, but I do remember that they were capable people, enterprising, reasonably likable. A girlfriend of mine had invited me along with a fairly sociable intention, "I want you to get to know them," and maybe it would prove useful to be introduced to them. Useful? Why? For my career. What career? My literary career, which was still just beginning.

Unfortunately, with me, that sort of intention rarely works out, and nothing interesting has ever resulted from arranged meetings, or hardly ever: whereas chance encounters, random fleeting involuntary interactions have brought me the benediction of my life.

I still remember just one thing about that evening out in a fashionable restaurant in Milan, and it's not who the people were that I had just met and dined with, as they neither entered nor remained part of my life any more than I entered theirs, and who probably now occupy positions even more prestigious than the ones that they, still young, already occupied back then, but I do clearly recall a detail that fell toward the end of the dinner when, not having thus far taken a particularly active role in the conversation and having heard one of my tablemates mention that he had a passion for sailing, and owned a boat, and took it to sea regularly, I tried to dive into the flow of chatter for a few exchanges, at least to offer a tidbit of satisfaction to my friend and the way she had "been so keen to get me to know them," etc., because by now she was losing hope that I would jibe with her friends, so I tossed out something along the lines of, "Oh, oh, I like to sail myself . . . I competed in regattas aboard a Flying Dutchman, when I was a boy . . .

and once I was even shipwrecked . . . ," and I told a couple of anecdotes from the time. Anyone who's ever gone to sea, maybe even just in the summer, without necessarily being this great navigator, has it as part of their personal baggage: magnificent inlets, that one time they lost the anchor, tremendous southwesterly gales, blows to the head by a swinging boom, a man overboard, the radio out of commission, some beautiful girl in the boat moored alongside, and so on. I displayed a disproportionate enthusiasm for sailing, well out of scale to my actual experience, I overstated it a bit, but unless I overstate things, if I don't exaggerate, if I fail to attribute importance with excited words to any given subject, I have the impression that nothing has any importance.

By so doing, in any case, I earned myself an invitation to go out on their boat.

"Well then, if you'd care to, why don't you come out with us sometime for a sail?"

"Certainly! That would be wonderful," I replied with slightly ginned-up enthusiasm that was, nevertheless, heartfelt, because the idea of leaving Milan—where I was then spending the better part of my time—and going down to Liguria to face the challenge of the winter sea, the icy spray, the black waves, in the company of experienced people with a genuine, serious passion for it, excited me, it really excited me, here was a fine opportunity, one I didn't want to miss, and my friend flashed a satisfied smile as if her plan of introducing me to those acquaintances of hers had finally worked out, even though it didn't seem to point to any assignments, no sign of a job on the horizon or even any articles to write for newspapers or magazines, just a promise of a sail on the open sea, but you know what they say, one thing leads to another, socializing can lead to opportunities, there are people in this country who've risen to the rank of president or chairman of something and it all started out over a Ping-Pong table. And so my enthusiastic acceptance of the invitation to go out for a sail on a certain date met with benediction in the form of broad smiles; except that, when the guy who had invited me out on his sailboat, or to be perfectly frank, on whose sailboat I had actually *invited myself*, pulled out his datebook to see when might be a good time, the first slot he had open (as far as I was concerned, *anytime* was fine, the next day, or that coming Saturday, or the one after that . . .), was a little later on, his weekends were pretty busy for a while . . .

"So listen, how would March thirteenth work for you? Do you have anything planned that day?" he asked, with the typical Milanese drawl, the protracted, teeth-clenched *e* in the word "*bene*," turning it into "*beeene*." "Is that fiiiine for you? Are you freeee that daaaay?"

He'd invited me for a sail in mid-March.

This was in November.

That means he had every weekend already spoken for, for the coming four months.

Anyway, I told him yes.

THE PROBLEM WITH HAVING THE WORLD within your grasp, without limits and without repercussions, is that you can develop a sense of omnipotence, whereby every act, even destructive ones, can be taken to its ultimate conclusion and then withdrawn, leaving the person who committed the act untouched. Weaned but still a virgin. Ready to give it another shot. Like an amazing rubber band, a little bit of money can catapult you into the middle of the most vivid experiences but then yank you back before the consequences begin to make themselves felt. In other words, a person can labor under the illusion that they are free to do almost anything, or even, in fact, anything at all. Money is supposed to protect you, even if you leap off the diving board into an empty swimming pool, like a cushion of air.

It's fun to be rich and out of control.

This explains at least in part the character of the youthful protagonists of this story in the era in which it takes place. On the one hand, they had grown up, as people once said, coddled in excelsior: spoiled by their families, attending private school, with young foreign ladies as their nannies. Protected from any impact, swaddled in precautions designed to insure them against any wound as they encountered the tiny hindrances of life. And thanks to this miraculous immunity, they could push into the opposite extreme, into the realm of danger and violence, convinced that they'd always get away with it. Every new provocation expanded the horizon of their liberty, marking a new, distant point. So distant that, once they'd returned to home base, to the trusted hideouts of the little villas of the QT, they were convinced they were well out of reach, untouchable by the consequences of their actions. Indeed, that these actions could not possibly have, by their very nature, any consequences whatever.

They grew up with the deep-seated certainty that they had the right to do anything.

Part V

Collective M

I

A STROLL. WHY, YES! Let's go take a *nice* stroll! Why, is there such a thing as a horrible one?

There, the evening stroll before dinner. The thing that I found most incomprehensible when I was a boy, when it was my parents going out for that stroll, during the period of rehabilitation that followed my father's heart attack; and around five, later in the evening during the summertime, the couple (and they were hardly elderly, they were much younger than I am now! My mother was still ravishing . . . no dogs to take out for a walk . . .) would go out for a hike through the quarter—three quarters of an hour, an hour or so. What's the purpose of it, I'd wonder, this wander through the narrow streets of the QT, always turning at the same intersections, skirting around apartment houses, measured from the ground floor to the wash-houses on top with the engineer's professional eye a thousand times over, the ivy, the imposing front gates, the little balconies with their iron railings, the majestic entrances that give a building such prestige . . . and at a certain point along the way, as if the two of them had suddenly realized they had ventured too far, it was time to begin their anabasis, their trek home, making turns at right angles a couple of times and taking parallel streets in order to avoid retracing their exact paths on the way back, and finally finding themselves back at the base, in front of the last doorway on the little uphill section of Via Tarvisio—with a slight heaving in my father's respiration, and the well-earned approach of the evening meal. Why do they do it? What on earth can they have discovered during their walk? Aside from the aspect of improved health for the heart-attack survivor, which gave a melancholy tinge to the whole exercise, I couldn't see the point. Perhaps it helped to strengthen my parents' relationship, maybe they talked as they walked along arm in arm, in fact, I know they did; it was a custom in the neighborhood, a sign of affection in the QT.

SINCE YESTERDAY, January 17, 2007, I've moved my meager belongings, two suitcases and my computer, and now I sleep in a ground-floor apartment on Via Tolmino, facing the apartment house where a former student at SLM, Angelo, once lived. Three days ago, he was found guilty in criminal court of murdering two women, a mother and a daughter. I was in the same class as his younger brother, Salvatore. This date marks my return, after more than twenty years, to live in the QT. The TV broadcast closeups of Angelo's face, now horribly obese, upon which there floated, as always, a faint smile, while his bulbous eyes rolled and darted incessantly, without ever coming to a stop on any person present in the hall of justice; in the newspapers appeared statements by him that were every bit as mocking and sarcastic, about how the two victims hadn't been able to understand just how much of a "sentimental guy" he really was, and that the two poor women "just hadn't known how to handle him," otherwise "things might have ended differently," in other words, not in a double homicide. If my teenage memories don't mislead me, this was the exact same building, the one I'm looking at now, whose two symmetrical wings must have been repainted recently in two different hues of yellow, one slightly pinkish, the other more of an acid hue. From the windows, I can see cars driving up and down Via Tolmino, or turning up the hill onto Via Gradisca, and occasionally a motorcyclist who takes advantage of the empty, straight street to race through the gears. Truly peaceful, Via Tolmino. It always has been.

My soul, too, after months of raging tempests, is more serene. Or perhaps we should say, not serene, but suspended. I am therefore in the right condition to try to understand what it is that's so special about this quarter, to the casual eye so nondescript, so anonymous. What is it that my parents saw here, at the end of their late-afternoon promenades? And why was it here, of all places, in the QT, in those years, that the greatest and most concentrated number of gratuitous murders, political attacks and ambushes, premeditated killings and accidental killings, manhunts, and reprisals took place? It was on this borderland that bellicose young men converged from every other quarter in Rome, from all walks of life, of every political ideology. You might say that a place like this, precisely because of its neutrality, was a perfect place to fight. And to kill.

OVER SOME OF THE TREE-LINED STREETS of this urban checkerboard, such as Via Volsinio or Via Benaco, for example, lours the perennial shadow of foliage that has never been cut back, from trees that have grown until their branches meet and intertwine on high, forming a roof of greenery, beneath which it is lovely to zip along on a scooter at the height of summer—something for that matter that is not uncommon in Rome, where the trees of the city's streets are abandoned to their own devices, as if in some magical forest, until they attain monstrous sizes and shapes, sending chills down your back, until the clock strikes the x hour and, as if to punish them for their luxuriant growth, they are pruned down to mere stumps, perhaps because that means doing the job "once and for all," or else, with some weak botanical justification, sawed off just above the base, while instead it is obvious that the job has the unmistakable flavor of a reprisal. The Parks Department takes action in an intimidatory and exemplary fashion, like the police under some oppressive regime, and one fine day the green tunnel is simply gone, and the streets find themselves barren, stripped naked under the glare of a sun they haven't seen in years and, just like that—surprise!—you can see the pale façades of the buildings again, and even the windows on those façades with railings and art nouveau decorations whose very existence had been kept a secret, and whose inhabitants no longer even dared to look out them, thrust back into their apartments by the branches' menacing proliferation. The sheer power of nature . . . until the chain saws of the city's botanical dogcatchers come riding to the rescue.

After they've come through, two rows of sawn-off stumps protrude from the sidewalks. Institutionalized neglect in Rome, in fact, manifests itself in one of these two extreme forms: either nothing is done, or else it's a massacre.

A further surreal effect burst loose yesterday evening on Via Benaco, as I was walking along, hands clasped behind my back, pondering who I ought to put in the next scene and how to give that person shape, and as I thought, I slowly entered the gallery of greenery, whereupon, raising my eyes, I realized that I had stepped into that famous painting by Magritte: under the vault of foliage it was already dark night, the bright yellow streetlamps casting shadows, a gloomy silence like some provincial city—while overhead, above the branches, you could still glimpse clear and luminous the sky of Rome, crisscrossed by darting swallows.

High above, there was still daylight.

On the ground, darkest night.

Sort of like in this story. Divided by a line where opposites meet, even though the canvas is the same, and so is the instant. Even the protagonists are the same, whether they act in the darkness or in the light of day. There, it is as if the light itself produces the darkness, as if its splendor engenders the darkness, and I'm certain that this contradiction in terms has some meaning of its own, that's right, that it is prosperity itself that engenders malaise. I can't find this meaning, I can't find it on my own, I have to reach out to my memory and my imagination for help. You might say to me, what help are you looking for, whose help are you asking for, in that case? Whose help, if you are still the one, who remembers and invents. But the memory and the imagination aren't mine, I'm not really *me*, the forces that come to my aid as often as not also abandon me. If they really were mine, they'd do as I say, wouldn't they? Like a hand that reaches out to grasp a glass. Hand, grab that glass, and my hand grabs it. Lift it to my mouth. Tip it . . .

A thirst-slaking gulp of water.

I have no choice, though, but to hope that memory and imagination come to visit me, and I cannot expect anything certain, maneuverable, from them. I have begun to suspect that these are not two separate, distinct forces, recollection and fantasy, but rather a single force, and that the words come from the same spring, they are neither true nor are they false, neither authentic nor invented, there is just one voice that recounts and reasons, and I have no option but to listen to it. Trustingly.

TRAGEDY IS NOTHING other than this, then: to show the other side of things, places, and people, revealing a reality considered impossible, which is instead the possibility of a different reality. The same scene suddenly turns into a dark and unsettling world, even though it mirrors the world we already knew and which seemed, if not festive, at least innocuous. Remaining identical to its former self, that world is turned inside out. In just the same way that, after the first crime, the CR/M, from one day to the next my quarter became an antiquarter, a sinister shadow of the quarter it had once been. No one had ever noticed that they were living on the edge of a swamp: neat rows of tidy apartment houses, small balconies bursting with flowers, palm trees extending high over the enclosure walls, sheathed in Virginia creeper, pedestrians who greet each other as they cross paths . . .

all suddenly become dark and trembling, uneasy profiles, pale silhouettes on the black surface of the stagnant water. The images of the QT remained the same, only now they were tinged with a leaden hue and caressed by the quavering of the reflections on the water, unreal even though they replicate reality with maniacal exactitude, perhaps with excessive exactitude, just the way in fact a maniac would do, a lunatic, the way madmen act out their pantomimes, betrayed only by the faint, chilling tremor that stirs beneath the surface of their otherwise letter-perfect imitations. Something like a solar eclipse, a reality that has been drained of color and stripped naked, a treacherous world: that is what the QT became in the days following the rape/murder.

ALL ALONG CORSO TRIESTE, instead of the doormen from the Marche region that used to populate the neighborhood, Sinhalese doormen now poke their heads out to toss bucketfuls of mop water into the street, broad and docile faces topped with locks of gleaming hair, yellowish eyes, and skin pockmarked by acne. In the buckets, the water is tinged with the grime from the travertine staircases.

Many of the small villas behind Giulio Cesare High School, along the small streets reduced to jungle habitat by the uncontrolled growth of trees and plants, seem partially abandoned. Shutters fastened, front yards piled high with detritus . . .

PALAZZINE. Apartment houses.

They are normally five stories tall, built very close to one another. Someone once described them as "boxes with a lid": their lids are the elevated penthouse structures that have transformed washhouses and common areas into inhabitable apartments. The old shared terraces over which cement awnings once stood have since been filled in with walls and windows, erected in violation of the building code, but long since consecrated as official dwellings by successive waves of regulatory amnesties. If you look up, you can still make out the shapes of the compartments that once held water tanks and washhouses, now visible in the structure of the penthouse apartments that incorporated them.

Their exterior appearance is dignified. An understated style, intelligent use of materials, and not much more. If you rule out daring structural approaches, the so-called décor almost always takes the form of ornamental inserts, or else it incorporates effects designed to add scale: the monumental ambition of certain apartment houses and small villas, for example, was expressed by their ground-floor street presence with entrances so grand that they jutted out beyond the second-story façade. These are cases of grandeur typical of the QT, touching, after their fashion. As I walk past them, on Corso Trieste, and I admire these colonnades, these spacious, shadowy atriums that lead into buildings that, all things considered, are really quite modest, I think of the effort, yes, the sheer effort to attain distinction: the interplay of recessed and jutting sections of the façade, the obsessive motif of pocket balconies and terraces, which forced the architects to pursue an exhausting succession of variations on such a narrow theme, as well as the use of materials that were more or less precious and appropriate. On the façades, the brick curtain wall alternates playfully with travertine and plaster.

All this because, in spite of how widespread it is, the apartment house, specifically, the small, three-story apartment house, the *palazzina*, is a structural model so amorphous that it doesn't even seem to merit a clear and specific definition. In the architecture textbooks that I've consulted, there is no mention of it. Very commonly used, on the other hand, is the term derived from it, "*palazzinaro*," the "building speculator," the developer, without whom the Roman social landscape would be left incomplete and, in many ways, inexplicable. But I don't want to delve into the topic. I myself am the son of a "*palazzinaro*."

I walk and I walk, and I look, and I walk, and I think.

It's true, the work of inventing things all concerns the surface, not the form. These are purely graphic expedients, they are to architecture as illustration is to painting . . .

Via Sabazio, Via Topino, Via Sebino, Via Taro . . . so lovely, with the stringcourses marking each floor designed in a pseudosculptural fashion, decorated with cornices of foliage and flowers . . . the little balconies shaped like upside-down bells, so tiny that you can barely open the window and step out, one person at a time . . . and then there are little loggias, arches, Latin inscriptions, and mosaics. Around Piazza Verbano, the décor is smeared onto buildings that would otherwise be strictly working class in character . . . and peering in, the courtyards of the apartment buildings, well tended, deserted . . . because inflexible building regulations prohibit children from chasing one another around the palm trees, bicycles and motor scooters from parking, and playing soccer is forbidden.

Decent housing for white-collar workers, that's the source of all of Rome's modernization.

While for the working classes, a home is a shelter from the elements, the middle class sees it as a mark of distinction and a sign of social recognition: the QT is the middle class's reward. In one case it's the alternative to living in a hovel, a favela, in the other it's a way of assuring that someone (the doorman, your barber, the mailman, a city courier, the grocer's delivery boy) will say, "Accountant Filacchioni/Construction Surveyor Pedetta/Professor Sacripante . . . lives there," in that apartment house with the fine moldings around the windows and the Jugendstil dripstone.

I look at those little balconies filled with flowers: they're meant to liven up the façade, give it a rhythm. I'm thinking in formal terms. In existential terms, they're good for going out and smoking a cigarette, now that you can no longer do it indoors.

There was a time when in the stately apartment houses, the *palazzi signorili*, the balcony was not used to bask in the sun or enjoy a cool breeze: no one seemed to feel any need for the outdoors. The outdoors was vulgar, opening to the exterior was a weakness, a crack through which strangers and enemies could penetrate to the heart of the building. The balcony was a place where a gentleman or a lord could look out or, more likely, show himself to the populace. Something of this closure toward the exterior, and of a perch where the master could display himself on official occasions, can still be found in certain small villas or *palazzine*, whose windows are curiously smaller than one might expect or the dimensions might allow, as if the occupants weren't interested in having excessive interactions with the world outside.

If you're fine *indoors*, then you're fine *where you are*.

In Rome the tradition of heaviness as a synonym for solidity still survives. Rome is a conservative city, or perhaps it's just a lazy one, a place that is reluctant to give up its customs and its habits, not because it's especially attached to them, but to avoid the psychic cost of change, out of skepticism toward the new. Change is futile or deceptive. It's not that the Romans are afraid of the new, no, rather they deride it, they take it in stride, with a smirk. The law of inertia is respected in Rome when it comes to habits, but certainly not because it's venerated.

In ancient buildings, it was the weight of the cornerstone that conferred solidity.

Here in the QT, on the other hand, the idea of the balcony as a central element of an apartment's quality is widespread. Its decorative motifs are simple and elegant. Prestige, decorum, dignity: but what prevails over all is the theme of the compromise. Yes, compromise is the true key to any understanding of the *train-de-vie*, the lifestyle, the very soul of the QT; it was under the rubric of compromise that this quarter was built, from the first small villa to the last immense apartment house, over the course of eighty years. Very much like its inhabitants, in social terms, the buildings in which those inhabitants live are the product of eclecticism: what with the tireless connecting of different elements, a specific style was created here. Just now, on my way down Via Adige, I walk past a *palazzina* that meets all those criteria, courtly, elegant, urbane, embellished and brightened by every possible figure of the monumental style reduced to a domestic scale: a classical pediment, baroque medallions, just as the motif that highlights the stringcourses of each floor is baroque. Each window has a differently designed cornice and a small balcony, where just one person can look out, maybe two if they squeeze in together.

Other buildings, however, don't even bother to try to lighten any part of themselves, they don't want decoration. They're closed to the world and severe. Travertine on the ground floor, a brick curtain wall on the rest of the façade: signs of the determination to remain firmly planted on the ground (solid, maintaining our position!).

On Via Gradisca, an apartment house has an external staircase that might suggest a turret, but one made of glass: it's not designed to look out from within, rather it seems built to look in from without. At night, I observe it from the windows of my home, it's quite impressive all lit up like that, erect, slender, it looks like a spaceship in an old sci-fi movie. Now I walk past it and I'm struck with admiration.

Via Gradisca, take a left at Via Tolmino, then a right on Via Bolzano . . .

And I finally emerge in front of SLM.

Built like a modern fortress, with walls constructed alternately in cement and brick, dull and neutral colors and a fire-engine-red band that runs under the ribbon windows. Little towers that loom over each building contain the stairwells. And four large internal courtyards, overlooked by the outsized classroom windows: one common courtyard in front of the church, and then one courtyard behind the elementary school, one where the middle school students have their recess, and one for the high school. These courtyards were once connected, even though the student populations were never supposed to mix, at the start of the school day, when they were let out from class, and at recess, never mix—never!—because mixing may be stimulating but it is also very, *very* dangerous. Otherwise the older students might bully the younger ones. Mingling the generations and the sexes, the old and the young, men and women, boys and girls, young men almost fully grown mingling with kids and with children—it's all risky business. Life itself, if you stop to think about it, is terribly risky, made up as it is of contamination and contagion, contact and exchange. The fences are constantly being scaled and the sheep are lost or else clawed, savaged, devoured. If everything would just stay in its proper place, life would be so much quieter, so much more peaceful. But then it happens anyway: the sheep remain shut up in their fold, tame and obedient, but it's the wolf who gets in. And what then? What good are rules then? Just a way of postponing the slaughter? This is what they're good for: so you can say, we did what we could, as if right from the beginning it was just a matter of dotting the i's and crossing the t's, and the prohibitions, the precautions, the sanctions were just there so that, right from the beginning, they could put their mind at rest. We did what we could.

Perhaps this is why the loin-stirring mothers of elementary school children were required to wait outside the gate for them: SLM was a world apart, and inside it, other worlds apart were trying to enter into contact with one another. The courtyard behind the elementary school was the most secret and impenetrable one, small and crowded because back then the classes were all particularly crowded. I spent five years of my life in that courtyard. Then three more in the courtyard of the middle school, and four in the courtyard of the high school.

Yes, a modern fortress, SLM. Its modernity lies in the combination of materials, in the horizontal stringcourses of the ribbon windows, cement and brick, neutral colors and vivid ones, gray, beige, red . . . the relationship between full surfaces and empty spaces, bricks and glass. The emptier, more open walls face the courtyards, while the walls that overlook the street are solid, practically blind. It turns its severity toward the exterior, and that is all. Toward the interior, on the other hand, a reciprocal glance is allowed between those who are in the classrooms and those who run and play in the courtyard . . .

My generation still read the book *Cuore* (*Heart*) at school, as a novel and as a manual of ethics. That was at least eighty years after it was written. Perfect for reading during a school year since it actually takes place over a school year, and is structured more or less like a calendar (brilliant stunt!). Eventually, though, a custom that had endured all those decades died out: I don't think my children even know what the book is about, if we mention Garrone, Franti, Bottini, or de Rossi, or the little Lombard sentry, or the

Florentine scribe. For at least the past thirty years, the book has vanished from circulation. Now I wonder: could it be that my generation was more similar to those youngsters of the late nineteenth century than our children are to us? Because nowadays, a young person reading this book would find it, more than boring or dated, simply incomprehensible.

I've just reread it. Well, it's formidable, with a formidable structure, cunningly devised.

That said, it's the book thickest with misfortune, bad luck, unhappiness, and physical deformities, hunchbacks, rickets sufferers, amputees, deaf-mutes, consumptives, widows, and orphans that I've ever read, and while I have no doubt that this is a faithful or even an optimistic reflection of the society of the time, well, still, all these misfortunes seem to me to have been assembled and distilled in its pages to emphasize more forcefully the ideal of the human ability to withstand adversity. (This, too, is an excellent idea.)

Perhaps its most distinctive feature, now lost, is that it describes a universe in which the most elevated and most intense and most, shall we say, virile sentiment that can be fostered is *esteem*. Yes, that's right, esteem, to esteem someone, feel esteem for them, to be esteemed.

Even back in the day when I was still in school, this somewhat antiquated sentiment still existed, before it was finally drowned in a lake of ridicule.

In any case, it's the only book in Italian literature and perhaps in the literature of all times that, any time you mention it, you must specify that it is a book, to be clear, the book *Cuore*.

At a certain point in this book, a piece of advice is offered that struck me, and that anyone ought to adopt as their own:

AND STUDY CLOSELY YOUR QUARTER; study its streets, its intersections, impress well in your memory that litany of rivers and cities, so that if you were to be hurled far away from it to-morrow, you would be glad to have clearly present in your memory that grid of streets.

2

A MUSEMENTS WERE RARE IN THE QT. They were rare *anywhere*, truth be told.

Breaking down the muffler of a motor scooter, and then reassembling it after emptying it, tensing up your pectoral muscles in front of the mirror, hitting volley after volley against half a Ping-Pong table angled vertically, or else on a full table, four players running around it in what, I can't even remember now, was called (in any case, for no good reason) either "American style" or "German style," a version of Ping-Pong that consisted of hitting the ball when it came your turn, setting the paddle down on the table and rushing around to the opposite side just in time to pick up the paddle left there by your classmate and hit back the ball, which had in the meantime been frantically returned by the three other players, laughing and panting, trying to place the ball where none of the adversaries could possibly reach it in time, with treacherous volleys that would fall short; and then shouting "Whore!" at a nun, collecting trading cards, bottles, flags.

It's not as if there was a lot to do . . . Oh, right, the filthy pulps (the term "porn" would have been too explicit).

These were the chief entertainments of the young boys of the QT, before drugs and political violence became widespread.

OUR EDUCATION was rounded out on trading cards, and not only the cards featuring soccer players, as people seem to think based on the array of superficial accounts that tend to collapse those years solely to images of singers and soccer stars. Instead, the array extended to include what some refer to as general culture, with collections illustrating the nations of the world, the great men of history, from generals to scientists and artists, armies and navies and ships and planes, animals, the continents, outer space, natural phenomena . . .

I remember the trading card of the aurora borealis, the hunt for the extremely rare trading card of the northern lights, with the drapery of its luminous curtains in the Arctic sky, the object of dizzying offers, proposals to trade ten, twenty, or even fifty cards (useless, common doubles, cards that we all had in multiple copies . . .) for an aurora borealis. Then there were the collections of records. Records set for height, speed, weight. We'd write them down and update them, building genuine full-fledged cults around those who had set them. Records themselves became a subject in which records were set, where it was the most fanatical and know-it-all nerd who excelled, memorized the *Guinness Book of World Records*, the shortest midget, the oldest Chinaman, the deepest scuba dive, even if just a month later another scuba diver would come along, beating that record by getting two meters deeper, and then the velocity of supersonic jets expressed in Mach speed, the Olympic gold medals won by Mark Spitz (9) and the number of Motorcycle Grand Prix World Championship titles won by Giacomo Agostini (15) and his number of Gran Prix wins (122) . . . all this was the subject of superficial, meaningless knowledge and aggregations of legend, which when all mixed together created a very particular form of devotion.

Yes, "devotion" is the right word to describe that genre of adolescent fanaticism.

We boys would argue and fantasize endlessly about information concerning the length of sharks and the speed records set on land and water by infernal machines whose pilots often died in spectacular crashes. And off we'd go, reciting the names of the fallen heroes, starting with Formula One racers. I remember that I once had, perhaps as late as middle school, a school planner on the theme of car racing, with all the photos and achievements of the various racers of the time. When I finished high school, I cleared a giant stack of school material from my room, and I found the planner again. We students used to personalize them, pasting in photographs, decorating and illuminating them with markers in various colors, writing random phrases on them, and of course scribbling and scrawling on the planners of our classmates in exactly the same way, until those little volumes would swell until they were three or four fingers thick, an inch or even two. Well, as I leafed through my old "Formula One" planner it dawned on me that the racers depicted in it were *all* dead. When I bought it, they were all daredevils tearing down the track and smiling in photographs; a few racing seasons and a few school years later, and not one of them was left on the face of the earth. The deaths that hit me hardest were those of Jim Clark, Lorenzo Bandini, Jochen Rindt, who posthumously won the world championship with Lotus after dying in a crash at Monza, and the stunningly handsome François Cevert.

I remember that they chose not to come to Lorenzo Bandini's aid while he was being burned alive in his Ferrari, along the waterfront in Monte Carlo—a city that I detest. "Of all the places in the world, the one where the concept of human brotherhood is shared least."

Ah, I want to add a name, Graham Hill, a great racer with a famous mustache, who died not in a car but in an airplane. The Piper he was piloting hit a tree while flying over a golf course, in thick fog.

THE COLLECTIONS OF TRADING CARDS were folk encyclopedias. The cards for soccer players included such statistics as their weight, height, and number of goals achieved or conceded, by such hardworking professional athletes as Cereser, Pizzaballa, or Battisodo. The ejaculatory prayer of the names of the bike racers, on the other hand, was something we learned during the summer, from the half-transparent little plastic balls with their faces sealed inside, balls that we'd launch with a flick of the middle finger along racetracks that we carved out of the wet beach sand by dragging one of our friends along by the heels, if possible a friend with a fat ass so that the track would be nice and wide and the curves parabolic to keep the balls from flying over the sides.

AFTER EXCHANGING TRADING CARDS or winning them in various games and bets, we would argue at length over the accuracy and truthfulness of the captions that accompanied them, whether, that is, the Ganges crocodile *really did* grow to measure twenty-three feet in length, and whether the race driver who drove the Thunderbolt on the Bonneville Salt Flats really did die in the explosion of his wheeled rocket just seconds after smashing the record . . .

A theme that really aroused people's passions at the time: outer space. The conquest of outer space. The most widespread popular epic, which reached its culmination with the moon landing, and its decline precisely in lockstep with the story told in this book. The famous space program, Apollo, carried out eighteen missions in space, and when did it come to an end? In 1975.

AND THEN, as I was saying, there were the pulps, the dirty little magazines, filthy, in full color, with photographs or illustrations or cartoons. The detailed descriptions of sex acts and sexual torture provided the protein necessary for nerds to grow. The pulps! Do they still exist? Or have they been swept away like everything else by the Internet? But maybe it's not all that easy to get online from your cot in the barracks, during your time off from guard duty, and maybe there are still people serving in the military, some horny security guard, some night watchman who has plenty of time to kill—I mean, after all, there are still calendars with naked girls hanging in car repair shops everywhere. Back then, there were pulps of all kinds, war pulps, western pulps, erotic pulps, crime pulps, even political pulps, in short, they covered the entire range of topics that might interest a young boy, from superheroes to cars to the naked breasts of German chambermaids to perverted vampiresses to how to make Molotov cocktails, all the same topics that in other formats would continue to interest (or should I say: obsess) the same boys once they grew up, once they became adults. Yes, I know, I'm talking about males as if they were the only kind of people who existed and females as if they were nothing but pictures printed on extremely low-quality paper, as if they came to life on that porous paper in order to be stripped naked and tortured by monsters, zombies, aliens, gangsters, and masked men, as could be seen on their covers. But, for that matter, the asymmetrical buildings of SLM were populated only by males.

Maybe pulps no longer exist, like so many other things that have lost their functions, like men's hats, jukeboxes, young people's encyclopedias, alarm clocks, ocean liners. All of them objects deserving, if not of regret and lamentations, at least a passing mention, especially ocean liners. Heartbreaking and absurd was the fate of the Italian ocean liners, with their unmistakable silhouettes, the *Michelangelo* and the *Raffaello*, launched when that style of travel was already starting to decline and the sun was setting on passenger liners. I, as a child, had the privilege to board one of the two ships a few days before it was launched, though I don't remember which (they were twin ships, the "twins of the sea" . . .), because an adventuresome uncle of mine who lived in Genoa pretended to be a maritime inspector and managed to smuggle me aboard. No doubt about it, certainly one of the finest experiences of my life. I had never seen anything so magnificent, luxurious, modern, and exciting. There seemed to be no end to it. Until, after touring the ocean liner from beam to beam and from stem to stern up and down its countless decks and right up under the extraordinary funnels (I would urge all those who care to learn more to dig up some vintage photographs . . .), some officer happened to notice us and our inexplicable comings and goings: he stopped us, unmasked my uncle, whereupon the seamen marched us to the gangway and ushered us off the ship.

3

Now, if I write about fascism for the next few pages, it's because several of the protagonists of this book were Fascists, just as the entire quarter was basically Fascist in those years, and also because the Fascists were, in their way—though in the minority, and with highly contradictory attitudes—exemplary specimens of the period I'm writing about, as were for that matter their left-wing adversaries. Actually, though, it is true of the Fascists in an even more distinctive and interesting way, inasmuch as they were deeply anachronistic. That same feverish reaction to the new era that was being ushered in all over the world by left-wing movements became typical of those same years, and in its determination to oppose the advent of the left, practically a constant attribute of the period. By opposing the left, fascism often and eagerly took on its very semblance, though reversing it, distorting it, and deforming it so that it became even more radical than the left at its most radical. This is due to the intrinsically twofold nature of fascism, present from the start: fascism contains within it both repressive institution and impatient uprising, law and transgression, instinct for preservation and childish delight in dilapidating, dispersing, and wrecking the very sandcastles it so lately built . . . the cult of order united with the apex of anarchy. As pure aspiration, fascism is the virtual locus of unlimited enjoyment, absolute, perverse, and therefore impossible, hence maddening, a source of despair, and logically leading to the most rigid repression of that very same enjoyment. Its secret ideal would be the wildest and most uncontrolled promiscuity, whereas its concrete practice took the form of a coercive control over all and any deviancy. Like an image that is distorted in its reflection, thus unexpectedly bringing out its hidden features, invisible to the ordinary line of sight, it is precisely in fascism—obstinate, residual, but constantly seeking rebirth, tirelessly renewed—that we can best perceive the contradictory character of the era in which this story unfolds.

The main problem with fascism is that you can never be Fascist *enough*. You could always be *more* of a Fascist, you could even be more of a Fascist than Mussolini, more of a Nazi than Hitler. There's a sort of frenzy that can never be satisfied, a boundary that is always being pushed forward. Like all mystiques, the Fascist mystique is bottomless. There is always someone who can criticize you for being lukewarm, totalitarian but not wholeheartedly totalitarian, loyal and trusting but not blindly so, fervent and daring but only by half, and if that someone is lacking, then the inner Fascist that can be found in every Fascist will interrogate himself.

ON SOIL ALWAYS READY TO PRODUCE the bitter fruit of derision, fascism did nothing but sharpen the sense of vanity, the sheer vanity of any individual in the face of the potential stature of the hero, and cultivate a contemptuous attitude toward those who did not take part in this faith, those who failed to believe in it or even understand it. Therefore, the die-hard loyalists felt they were condemned from the very outset to a sterile martyrdom, which in the aftermath was bound to go unacknowledged, and in any case, a thousand times degraded with respect to the figures taken as paragons and venerated—ancient Romans, medieval knights, Vikings, patriots . . . while the unfaithful, the infidels, would always be the target of their scorn, because they had been incapable of grasping the depth, the boundless profundity of the Fascist faith, a blind faith, a faith precisely because it was blind, blind inasmuch as it was faith, deep and dark like a bottomless well, into which they let themselves fall, fall, fall.

The constituent unhappiness of fascism, its spleen, its deep-seated bitterness and negritude, all originate in and derive from this long-standing inadequacy in the face of the models, of the hyperbolic watchwords: and who will ever be so evil? so daring? so brainless? so passionate? so ruthless? Who will ever succeed in being sufficiently Nazi, if you stop to consider that the Nazi himself outstrips all conceivable monstrosity? There is no act sufficiently misguided, rash, cruel, obscene, megalomaniacal, arbitrary, or chivalrous to meet that requirement, to fully answer the call. They are all too petty, and they all burn out almost instantly in their accompanying meanness. They become wretched at having failed to achieve wretchedness on a *grandiose scale*. The only haven for this unfulfilled tension is madness. Planting bombs, crashing fatally on a motorcycle, liquidating yourself with heroin, murdering, devastating, shooting yourself in the head. They set out to become knights like Percival, and in short order they became common criminals, and for that matter, grimy two-bit criminals. The stature of the hero remains a mirage, a colossal shadow, not even coming close to heroism, and in the meantime taking on, to a caricatural degree, all the vices, the excesses, the brashness, the nefarious deeds. Like fleas on a dead horse.

✦

THE GRATIFYING CULT OF ANNIHILATION: life gleams at its greatest splendor at the instant in which you suppress another's existence, or when you accept without trembling the suppression of your own. Dying in order to become eternal in the cult of the dead: that is the horizon, the pure Fascist mystique, corroborated by countless historical and literary examples. The sacrifice must be witnessed, illustrated, celebrated with commemorations, to make sure it remains exemplary. In the collective Fascist imagination, the dead heroes are still present, more present than the living. To understand that fact, you need only take a stroll through the QT, still today, and read the graffiti on the walls, read the posters . . .

Legionaries, labarums, anthems, recitations: the QT is a notepad of fallen soldiers.

In those posters, the talk is of wolves and slaves, cowards and loyalty, death and noble blood: the language of ancient Nordic poems is borrowed, from *Beowulf* to the Eddas and the *Nibelungenlied*.

What can we acknowledge as an achievement of that culture? A certain graphic style, its extreme stylization, occasionally the ability to choose striking slogans or titles (like the title of the infamous French magazine *Je suis partout*, "I Am Everywhere," which is certainly on a level with the finest avant-garde art of the twentieth century).

THEIR CREDO COULD BE SUMMARIZED in a single brief phrase: "*Viva la morte!*" Long live death! ¡*Viva la muerte!* For them, killing at random, a hail of killing, killing for none but the most futile of reasons, with no particular criterion but in an unquestionable fashion, was even more inebriating than to strike well-chosen targets with a specific political objective. Indeed, the political objective was, in fact, to have no objective, always to veer toward the gratuitous, because it is in gratuitous sacrifice (whether meted out or suffered, each amounting to practically the same thing) that fascism expressed its energy: the absence of any need to answer for its deeds, sovereign acts, which were in fact not open to discussion, redeemed from and uncontaminated by the leprosy of reason. Their most typical motive, the vendetta, almost never struck those directly responsible for the misdeeds they meant to retaliate against. Every action, every deed was justified by the mere fact of having been committed, and any action performed was in any case preferable to inaction. To succeed or to fail were seen as equivalent. WHAT PURPOSE DOES A SWORD SERVE IF IT REMAINS IN ITS SHEATH? WHAT USE IS IT UNLESS IT IS STAINED WITH BLOOD? If violence and death exist (and there is no doubt that they do), then why not exercise a preliminary right to inflict them, even if that exposes you to the risk of suffering them?

THE SPECIFICITY OF FASCISM is that it is, as we say of certain diseases, aspecific, which means that it does not consist of the content of its ideology, but rather in the way it constructs around that ideology an action and an identity. It is not what you believe in that matters, but the fact itself that you believe it, the absolute conviction, not of something in particular, but of the very fact that you're convinced of it. One is convinced of one's own conviction, one has faith in one's faith. The credo of the Fascist is not a doctrine or a specific political program, because a program is for *tomorrow* while the struggle is for *today*. You can therefore behave and think or speak like a Fascist without really being one. Exactly because that credo is a *forma mentis*, a way of thinking devoid of any specific content, or full of any given content in glaring contradiction with all others, it is therefore exceedingly difficult to refute and to abjure. One can, perhaps, abjure a faith per se, but not because its content has been shown to be false, since there never was any content in the first place, or if there was, it was interchangeable, revolution for reaction, defense of the bourgeoisie for overthrow of the bourgeoisie, cult of the past for impetus into the future, and so on (a fundamental difference between communism—which has a doctrine, and a substantial one, however gross and ham-handed and false one may judge it to be—and fascism).

The fact that fascism stubbornly defies definition can be sensed even in the difficulty any writer encounters in formulating statements about it that are anything other than slogans of exaltation, on the one hand, or insults and vitriol, on the other.

Fascism in fact constitutes the dilemma of unrepresentability: and perhaps for that very reason, incessantly, it loved to depict itself in whole, healthy forms . . .

ALSO INTERESTING IS THE IMPUDENCE, the extraordinary insolence that the Fascists show in proclaiming that they act in the name of *injustice*. It is by no means true that all political regimes claim to act justly, that they strive to reform society in order to obtain better conditions for those who live under them: in any case, here, to the contrary, they are openly fighting to establish a *more unjust* society, as unjust as is humanly possible, and they take this struggle as a point of honor.

The kinds of things Fascists used and did in those years:

They had a passion for snakes: they'd keep a python, or else a caiman, in the bathtub

Sharp-toed boots

Thor's hammer

Rugby, Tolkien (before they made the movies), the Holy Grail (before *The Da Vinci Code*).

(There was a famous incident in which one of them—while the police were arresting him and beating him soundly, so soundly that he died of it— invoked the god Odin.)

THE RIGHT AND THE LEFT AREN'T SYMMETRICAL. In a society like Italy, in spite of appearances, they were almost always in the minority. It was their spectacular presence in the world of youth culture that made them seem stronger, which in politics, only rarely or only for brief intervals, is the same as actually being strong.

The political formula of the extreme right in the seventies: the left (that is, political aggression, revolutionary drive) minus humanism equals pure subversion.

No, there is no symmetry. The extreme right always felt it was superior to the traditional division between right and left (the so-called third position: NEITHER USA NOR USSR was the recurring graffiti on the walls of the QT). Neither right nor left, or else right and left together, as in the very definition of national socialism.

What drove them? Camaraderie, hatred for democracy, the myth of individual courage, scorn for the enemy, the cult of violence and death, pride and despair at being in the minority.

IT IS DIFFICULT to keep from considering the enemy to be a criminal. Reptiles, rats, cockroaches, the demented and the possessed, demons, wild animals, chimps: these are the figures that are often mentioned in the same breath as the enemy. "Fascists are not human. A snake is more human," the Venezuelan president Hugo Chavez rapturously declared, receiving vast approval.

If what reined in the radical thrust of historical fascism was the need for a compromise with the monarchy and the Church in order to govern, neofascism had none of those restraints, allowing its militants to cultivate a purely subversive dream, wild and free. But once again historical reality made sure there was a price to pay. The most extremist political action turned into its exact opposite, in the end. The militants murdered people, convinced that they were medieval knights, whereas at best they were serving as guardians of the established order. A fine paradox!

Terrorists on the left and terrorists on the right. The former were vying for the dictatorship of the proletariat, and they did everything they could think of to make sure the nightmare became reality. They failed in that effort, okay, but what about the latter, the right-wing terrorists? What was it they wanted? It's not clear what project or utopia the terrorists on the right had in mind, if they had anything at all—and I'm limiting myself to the ones who weren't being manipulated like puppets on strings by the intelligence services. Steeped in the myth of the hero, they killed or got themselves killed or wound up serving life sentences without parole in order to defend the future rights of matrons in the exclusive neighborhood of Collina Fleming to double park. They planted bombs in piazzas in order to make sure those bleached blondes could go to water aerobics classes. They spilled their blood to defend the status quo. The Parioli tennis club and the *Maurizio Costanzo Show*, a popular talk show. To make sure the Communists never got their claws on those precious legacies. They blew up trains and banks—for *that*.

HENCE THE RHETORIC of "one day you'll thank us." We did time behind bars to save you from the Reds. More than the democratic state (which we hated), we defended the state of things.

Aside from their own legacy, there's a great deal of the anarchist school (and further back, Christian rigorism) in the scorn for danger and death flaunted by the neo-Fascists. Their typically funereal tone derived from the very nature of their ideology, but to an even greater extent from their awareness of defeat, which therefore demands a sacrifice, unlike Christian ideology, devoid of hope, an end to itself, sterile.

A FEW DAYS AGO, I saw one of these killers on television, for the first time after thirty or so years behind bars. In the interview, concerning his past offenses, he spoke of heroism and the quest for a beautiful death. I have no reason to doubt he meant what he said, that is, that he was genuinely convinced of the things he claimed. The whole truth, though, is that the murders committed by those political groups were ambushes, laid for helpless or unprepared people, who were shot in the face and, even before they could understand by who and why, were dead. They called them by name to make them turn around, thus making certain they were shooting the right person. When you shoot someone in the face, you're killing them, but more important, you're *deleting* them. If an encounter with another person consists of the perception of their face, in the reciprocal acknowledgment of a certain humanity, then to devastate their features with a metal-coated projectile while their eyes meet yours deletes in an instant that option. At first, in front of you, you have an anonymous silhouette, and after you've pulled the trigger, there is *no one*: their face, their life has already been sucked into the void, and you can walk away.

THEIR OBJECTIVE WAS to turn peacetime into a disagreeable misunderstanding, a meaningless intermission. A lukewarm bath in which the hero only grows soft. Against this languid and pacific image—the struggle, the challenge, a stiffening defiance, a venturing beyond, a provocation... There are enemies in every camp and they must be flushed out: in politics, liberalism (even the Communists are more worthy of respect, almost admirable, because they, too, battle against the liberal), laxity in the field of education, Petrarchism in literature, faggotry in terms of customs and lifestyle—these are the enemies. It is necessary to bring war, and its mythical protagonist, the warrior, in peacetime. One must violate peace, useful only to merchants and shopkeepers, fertilize it. Protract a condition of war ad infinitum.

THEY FANATICALLY SUPPORTED any act capable of shattering the individual. They believed that by breaking a person, something new and superior would emerge, something authentic, savage, and pure. It was an idea naïve in its premise, crude in its implementation, nefarious in its consequences. Anything, anything at all, as long as it could be used to crack the shell of normality, conventional identity, in short, the habits that flatten man and render him stupid, when instead he should be reawakened, whatever it takes: you could do it with boxing, drugs, beatings, prayer, gunshots, workouts in the gym, choral singing, hiking, summer camps, anything. But then this same fragmented individual sooner or later would have to be reassembled, strengthened, given discipline: after mystically losing himself in the nothingness, he had to rediscover himself. "For nothing can be sole or whole that has not been rent."

The ideal moment to complete this sort of recruitment-training-indoctrination was between the ages of fourteen and seventeen. I mean, back in those days: nowadays that age would be too late, or maybe the effort would be wholly pointless: adolescents have countless distractions and it's harder to focus their energies, I mean to say, to focus their energies in a single fanatical direction. The blindness of an adolescent of today may be very profound indeed, but it's almost never total: that young person can be seduced and deceived, no doubt about it, but by many things at once, very rarely by just one. In the darkness of their cavern, many flames flicker and gutter, many illusory will-o'-the-wisps may dance, but it is unlikely that all at once the powerful floodlight of a supposed truth will switch on. So much the better, I believe. And here I'm talking once again about the males, that's right, the males, the poor miserable males, miserable about the simple fact that they're male and therefore foolishly proud and fond of their misery. The female readers of this book will, I hope, forgive me for the monotony if at least they're able to recognize in the characters populating these pages some distant reflection of their fathers, brothers, male friends, sons, and those men they may have chanced to fall in love with and who seeded their lives with insecurity. A woman thinks that she's found a bulwark, but instead it was a cabin with walls as thin as rice paper, or perhaps it was a castle, yes, but an illusion of a castle, a trick castle whose walls, as soon you turn your back, vanish in the blink of an eye.

WHILE I TOOK PART in the political meetings on Via Spontini, with a couple of comrades outside on the lookout against possible Fascist incursions, I noticed how every twist of the discussion corresponded to a step in their radicalization. The line of reasoning would snap and then be resumed from a subsequent point that matched a higher level of virulence, exactly like a round of hands in poker, with each player seeing and raising the previous bets, so that with each hand the pot necessarily grows, and grows, the ante continuously piling up, richer and richer. A verbal risk is almost never associated with the actual risk, and that is how certain players tilt into bankruptcy without noticing. Betting a higher sum when you're in the throes of vertigo, in the trance of total detachment from reality. More, more and more and more. Just for the giddy inebriation of that endless tailspin. The thread might have snapped at the sound of a mocking phrase, torn by an insult or a curse, or else by a paradox, which almost inevitably gets the better of all the arguments brought to bear. How so? By its sheer incongruity, which caught your interlocutor off guard, leaving him defenseless, at least temporarily, pawing helplessly at the air. By leaping from one verbal plane to another, you create a void into which your interlocutor—who was following you closely, marking you man-to-man, eager not to let you outdistance him—helplessly tumbles. It's the best way to silence your adversary: leap from one topic to another, attack him on a level or a subject that has nothing to do with the matter at hand, passing from the rational plane to the emotional or the physical, both impossible to refute. Logic crumbles if contaminated by hatred or passion or ridicule, all that remains of its various delicate passages is a grid of threads burned to cinders, like Loki's net. In a dispute, one theory can be opposed by another, one mental broadside can be met with a proportionate response, until someone throws the mechanism out of whack, tosses all the cards into the air. Until someone pulls out a whiff of folly, a handgun, a succession of absurd questions, low blows, flashes of genius, a beating, something unspeakable.

Superior to the philosopher who reasons (Hamlet) is the philosopher who does not reason (Nijinsky).

4

'M LEAFING THROUGH the photocopies of an interview with Cubbone that was published in 1987, while he was a prisoner in France, awaiting extradition to Italy.

The highlight of Cubbone's criminal career—he was so called because of his massive physique—remains his breakout from Rome's Rebibbia Prison on November 23, 1986, an escape that lasted twenty days, until they caught up with him in Paris. A helicopter had landed in the exercise yard, in the criminals' section, on the soccer field during a match, and a French criminal and Cubbone both climbed quickly aboard, while their accomplices aboard the aircraft fired at the guard towers, to prevent the correctional officers from interfering. Both the pilot and the helicopter had been taken at gunpoint from San Camillo Hospital, where they were part of the emergency air ambulance service. Cubbone says that his cellmate tried to join the escape by hanging on to the helicopter, but that Cubbone kicked his hands until the man lost his grip. "If I had let him climb aboard, I wouldn't have been his friend." A couple more years and the man would have served his full sentence, so it struck Cubbone as a bad idea to ruin it all with a prison escape. "He isn't like me and my comrade, wedded to life sentences without parole." Cubbone doesn't know at the time that he won't spend much more time in prison. He would be found dead ten years later, in Florence, apparently of an overdose. He was hiding under the alias of Davide D'Olivia, born in Los Angeles. In reality, Cubbone was the eldest son of a concierge at the Hotel Plaza, as a boy a student at SLM, and with a younger brother also at SLM, a friend of mine. I remember him as likable and nice, and a pretty good Ping-Pong player. We played doubles in the tournament that was held during SLM's ski week, in the Dolomite Mountains, at Lavarone.

THERE ARE STRIKING COINCIDENCES between the spectacular escape of my ex-schoolmate and other events in my own life, less vivid, certainly, but significant of something, something I can't quite pin down, and which the writing of this book intertwines without being able to explain. For example, the fact that I first set foot in a prison (a place where I would go on to spend time for many years and where I still work today) in the criminal section of Rebibbia, in fact, just a few days after the spectacular escape by helicopter, and that my baptism into incarceration was marked by the image of the guard towers with their bulletproof glass, which had withstood those Parabellum bullets, cracking slightly in a sunburst around the points of impact from the bursts of automatic weapon fire.

Even stranger is the fact that, no more than a month ago, I happened to meet an eyewitness to the escape. He's a building surveyor and land officer named Alfredo Rocchi, who, at my behest, is trying to settle a classic cockup at the Rome land office. Issuing from divisions of property dating back to who knows when, there survives a "*relitto cortilizio*" (that's right, a "courtyard relic," that's the legal description) of roughly fifty square feet in the Talenti quarter, of which I am officially co-owner, in equal shares with my cousin, and I can't seem to get rid of it, to resolve it: the issue has been dragging on for what seems like forever, twice yearly I get bills for condominium fees of €7.50, and by now I'm the only real relic, so I'm starting to think that that corner of a courtyard in Talenti is going to be further split up among my heirs, who will receive little more than five square feet apiece, unless Rocchi manages to put an end to this legal farrago, thanks to his contacts at the land office. I don't believe there was any reason aside from telepathy, but the last time that I met with Rocchi, as we were going over the papers and forms, I started talking to him about Cubbone's famous escape. Maybe I'd started with the fact that I work there, at the penitentiary . . . and Rocchi all of a sudden livened up, and in his intelligent light blue eyes, the kind of blue that only certain Roman eyes can possess, a vision glinted into life.

"Ah, but I saw it, that helicopter, did you know that? I was there too, when it landed . . ."

"What do you mean," I asked in amazement, "were you in prison?"

"Prison? Well, no, I was just thirteen."

"Oh, of course, sorry."

"Sorry for what? It was after school, and I was playing at the soccer field in Giardinetti . . ."

"Where, you mean the neighborhood on the Via Casilina? You're from Giardinetti?"

"Yeah, born and raised."

"What was the name of your team?"

"Real Giardinetti."

"Real, like Real Madrid . . ."

"Exactly. And in fact we also had Atlético Giardinetti."

"No kidding. Nice! In Giardinetti, just think."

"In fact, it was the local Giardinetti soccer derby that we were playing . . . when this helicopter flew right overhead. We thought it must be a police helicopter. Someone up in the copter leaned out and displayed a machine gun, waving for us to leave. That was the last thing we kids were going to do! We were scared, sure, but we were fascinated, too . . . until it landed right in the middle of the field, kicking up a cloud of dust, and those guys got out, armed to the teeth . . ."

The old volcanic ash soccer fields on the edge of town.

Cubbone, in fact, remembers that once they took to the skies above the prison, the escapees got lost over Rome. "When you're up in the air, everything looks different, it gets confusing, we couldn't find the place we'd agreed on." Then he saw the only shape that is immediately clear, even from overhead. Rectangular. "There, down there," and he pointed to a soccer field, "put the copter down!" he shouted at the pilot. The kids in shorts and T-shirts scattered in all directions. The helicopter landed. The escapees, guns in hand, flagged down cars, and they were gone.

The interview with Cubbone is bedecked with eloquent headlines and written in such a way that it offers a portrait of a wild-eyed subject, arrogant yet almost likable. A brash yet chivalrous criminal. After the escape, his sense of liberty goes to his head. "I'm too much for the cops, I don't even consider them my adversaries . . . and all those judges who wanted to interrogate me, who wanted to divvy up my remains . . . those armored doors, those gates, those prohibitions, *poof*, all of them, gone."

His brief time on the loose ended with a siege by the French police. His two fellow escapees threw down their guns and put up their hands, whereupon what did he think? "No, fuck, not like this. What should I do? Cock my sidearm and go out in a blaze of glory? But then they'd shoot the other two like sitting ducks . . . so go ahead and kill yourself, you fucking coward. What are you waiting for? I turned my pistol around and aimed it at my chest, a split second, an eternity. I heard them shouting, give up, throw down your guns. More tear gas, they were about to blow the door. What the hell! Better a living dog than a dead lion . . ."

So he put up his hands, too.

I CONTINUE to leaf through "May the Force Be with Me," the interview that my old classmate gave to *Panorama* nearly twenty years ago. I use my highlighter to mark a few paragraphs, where he makes an interesting and self-interested distinction between violence and force. The former is alien to him, it's pointless and gratuitous, while the latter may serve a purpose. What purpose? To defend against the former. And who is it that commits the violence? Institutions. It sounds like an anarchist proclamation. And yet, at the same time, Cubbone is someone who declares that he believes in law and order, in discipline: "God, Fatherland, and Family are three words I capitalized, they weren't antiquated words for me, they were true, they were alive." Europe needed to be united against the red menace. He was a paratrooper in Pisa and he thought all that was great, "the jumps, the patrols, the shooting, the hikes, I liked it all, the smell of the equipment, the rifle on my cot. I didn't give a damn about going back home on leave. That was where I wanted to stay, in the airborne, forever." But then they expelled him from the corps: they'd discovered his criminal record, his involvement in an armed robbery, even if he'd been acquitted in the main trial and the lesser charges had been amnestied. At that point (after an unhappy interval working as a tile and bathroom fixture salesman) he enlisted in the French Foreign Legion, at Fort Saint-Nicolas, Marseille, but there, too, in spite of his revived enthusiasm for "the cots, the uniforms, the smells, the paths of war," they kicked him out after a few months. He just couldn't do it, he couldn't work a job like everyone else, put on a coat and tie and sell bathroom fixtures. He sniffed around, exploring every cause and hot zone where there was an opportunity to wear a uniform: South Africa, Libya . . . Israel or the PLO, it was all the same to him. "That was the life: a good weapon, something hot to eat, a good pair of shoes . . . I'd have been willing to enlist as a private, but they wouldn't take me," and so he built a profile as a sort of soldier of fortune. But soldiers without an army turn into bandits: Cubbone is the first to realize the fact.

So he replaced his dream of fighting a war with fairly standard criminal activity. When he was found dead, he'd been wanted by the law for crimes that had little enough glory to them: kidnapping a child, an armed robbery in a jewelry store, the murder of an officer in the anti-terrorism unit.

I REMEMBER SEEING the newspaper photographs of his first arrest, on the island of Ponza, in a swimsuit . . . I was stunned . . .

LATER YOU WILL HEAR more about a life story that can be compared in many ways with that of Cubbone, with reference to one of the protagonists of the CR/M, whom I have dubbed, in fact, "the Legionnaire": the extreme right, youthful crimes, time on the run, the Foreign Legion, heroin, and finally, a mysterious overdose and death.

"I'M THE SON of an era without medals, without heroes, without causes to believe in and fight for."

5

SOME TIME AGO, a magazine asked me to contribute to a special issue in which each writer was expected to indicate three keywords of their being, or feeling themselves to be, leftists, and to explain the reason for their choice. By inviting me to take part, they took it for granted that I was a leftist; I imagine, in fact, that the request was made to all the intellectuals, writers, directors, etc., with the same implicit assumption: it's obvious that you're a leftist, even if you're disappointed now, skeptical, even if you're not marching anymore, even if . . .

After mulling it over, and not for a very long time, truth be told, I decided to turn down the invitation.

I was at a loss.

All the left-wing words that came to my mind could have been taken for right-wing words.

Let's take, for instance: "liberty" or "courage."

And then, "minority," a word I'm sincerely fond of.

But I'm not at all certain that it's a left-wing word.

What coloration can we give this word?

In the political world I lived in as a young man, and in big cities like the one I grew up in, what was in the minority was unquestionably the right wing. It was in the minority just about everywhere, among students, in the schools, in Italy, even in Rome, which has never been a city with a great Socialist or Communist tradition. Being a right-winger meant you were in the minority everywhere, except for certain quarters, certain schools, among them, SLM.

SLM was necessarily a right-wing school, and therefore being a leftist there meant swimming against the stream, trying to stand out, and yet cultivating your own beliefs in the quasi-secrecy of a clandestine sect, like those worshippers of the goddess Kali, the Thugs.

Yes, we left-wingers at SLM felt we were thugs.

What a delightful paradox: Communists at a school run by priests! In a quarter overrun by Fascists! There was something almost snobbish, ostentatious, about this choice.

And so our way and our reasons for being left-wing were, basically, right-wing in nature, or at least they tracked back to those values and feelings which, what with a long history of being scorned by the left (let one example serve for all the others: courage—for instance, the courage displayed by the mercenary Fabrizio Quattrocchi in Iraq, as he was about to be executed by his captors, in uttering the phrase, now famous in Italy: "Now I'll show you how an Italian dies," which, taken literally, in that murderous context, I consider to be the most enigmatic and interesting statement conceived and uttered by one of my compatriots in the past several years), and after being derided at every level but, above all, in intellectual and journalistic circles, those values were handed over to become the appanage of the right.

Aside from everything else, how *does* an Italian *die*? If he does stand out for the way in which he lives, will he also differentiate himself for the way he dies—his own special way of dying?

WE FEW STUDENTS, who distinguished ourselves at SLM because we were leftists, were proud of our scanty numbers, we made a religion of it, and saw it as yet another reason that our positions were right, few of us but the best, few but outstanding, so few that we could all fit into the living room of my home, where we gathered to discuss the age-old question: what is to be done?

Even more than the question posed by revolutionaries, it is in fact the question asked by any adolescent.

I'D LIKE TO NAME, one by one, these young Communists of SLM, in the early seventies, but I'll limit myself to mentioning just four of them:

Folinea
Falà
Marco Lodoli
Angelo Pettirossi

Folinea and Falà weren't in the same class as me; they were in the scientific high school.

I've forgotten their first names, specifically because we always called them by their last names.

Folinea was skinny but athletic, with broad shoulders and taut, bowed legs, student champion in the specialty event of the 110-meter hurdles, though he'd given that up because "there was too much of a whiff of competitiveness about it," and when he let his beard grow out, to our collective amazement, it was thick and dark veined with red like on an Oregon lumberjack or one of those hippies you can see dancing under the stage at Woodstock. He didn't talk much and he'd nod peaceably at the things other people said, or else he'd shake his head, digging at his chin under the thickets of his beard, and that's the one way we were able to tell what he was thinking.

When he finished school, he wanted to be a truck driver.

I don't know if his family went along with that.

FALÀ WAS MORE OF AN INTELLECTUAL, with round eyeglasses over a pair of chilly light blue eyes in which you could read no other emotions than a certain impatience to see the rapid attainment of his political projects on a grand scale, projects that were bound to revolutionize the structure of society around the world. On narrower, more specific topics he had some difficulty and so he'd put on a resigned, bored demeanor.

While Folinea was likable as a person, Falà was objectively obnoxious, but they were both serious young men. Very serious. One time, when I asked him what his favorite novel was, just to break the ice before wading into our political discussions, Falà replied:

"Novels? Never read one in my life."

"Why not?"

"I don't have time to waste."

"So then what do you read?"

"Nonfiction."

So what nonfiction did Falà read? It's a strange thing that I should remember those titles, have them at my fingertips now, or at least some of them, perhaps because I borrowed them, one after another—and Falà was terribly worried the whole time, inquiring on a daily basis, practically, about when I'd be returning them—and read them myself.

Georgi Plekhanov, *The Materialist Conception of History*
Ludwig Feuerbach, *The Essence of Christianity*
Friedrich Engels, *The Housing Question*
Georges Sorel, *Reflections on Violence*

Louis Antoine de Saint-Just, *Terror and Liberty*
Ivan Pavlov, *Conditioned Reflexes*

(Only after finishing it did I bother to wonder what the last title in the list had to do with the others and whether it had wound up on my friend's bookshelves only because the author was Russian.)

With these topics Falà trained his mind and secured it from the lazy temptations of the novel.

"When all is said and done, though, what do these novels even talk about?" he asked me once. In fact, you can say what a nonfiction book is about, it has a subject, which may or may not interest you, whereas it's hard to say whether a novel is interesting or not, whether it's worth reading, you can add that it's well or poorly written, good or bad, but its story and its plot can never be presented as subjects worthy of being delved into, as such. The social conditions of Sicilian fishermen? The life of the bourgeoisie in Trieste during the first quarter of the twentieth century or the life of the proletariat in Rome in the years after the Second World War? Presented in these terms, there would be nothing particularly attractive about the novels. And in fact, tucked inside Falà's naïve question there was another one, far more profound and even harder to answer, "Why even bother reading a novel in the first place?" a question that glints in the eyes of middle school students when their Italian teacher, male but more often female, unfurls the customary list of titles and characters, Zeno, Mattia Pascal, the Baron in the Trees, perhaps seeded with a few other names rounded up from the current listings of bestsellers or the various other thematic subsectors— novels on temp workers, on the Camorra, on Auschwitz, and so on—in the context of some noble project designed to encourage students to read: but after all, what's the point of reading novels, to learn? for fun? to experience indirectly other people's adventures? or is it actually to gain a better understanding of things that have happened to us? Because we're too shy to tell or confess the same things? In order to be able to spend time alone?

I was unable to give Falà an answer, at least not an answer that rose to the level of objective seriousness with which he had asked me the question in the first place, and today, if I were forced to choose among the canonical replies, perhaps I'd say: "To pass the time of day." Perhaps that's the main reason we read novels, or why I read them, at least. Passing the time of day has always struck me as a difficult undertaking, noble in its way precisely because it's difficult. And God bless those who invented arts and tools to do so, who were capable of devising texts and practices, games and disciplines, calculations and stratagems, deceits and seductions and exercises, meditations and contraptions, spectacles and amusements capable of making the time go by, of using it up. If it hadn't been for their inventions, time would have been stuck in one place, jammed, and it would swell up until it exploded. But my friend Falà wasn't interested in the slightest in "passing the time of day." Letting it flow like the water in a river. Instead he wanted to gaff it on a hook, he wanted to bend time and hammer it until it took on a useful shape, turning time into a weapon, in other words, like a blacksmith tempering a harpoon destined to catch and reel in a whale.

His readings formed part of a five-year plan where there was no room for entertainment. No Sabbath, no Day of the Lord, consciousness raising doesn't go on vacation or take holidays. More than a sin, to Falà's way of thinking, amusement was simply an incomprehensible state of mind, by no means desirable. I mean, really, with all the forms of reality still to be measured and understood, with vast prairies of reality that practically twist before our eyes with the desire to be possessed by our analyses, what need was there to seek escapism with made-up stories like the ones found in novels? Since we knew almost nothing of the real world, why dream already of running away from it? The kind of thing we didn't know about firsthand, such as the condition of factory workers, for example, could be acquired through study, but real study, not the kind you get at school, which was nothing but a waste of time and served only to fog and blur our consciences— which was why Falà didn't love school, and in fact held it in contempt: more than a repressive institution, an astute delaying tactic that served to convey young people, blithely unaware of what was being done, from the moist darkness of family ignorance into the black box of work, into the unfree and unchosen condition of either exploiter or exploited. Free time was the cross of those days. An obsessive topic of reflection that could even condition the choices you made of how to spend your Saturday evenings: go out with your friends or stay at home reading, studying, inquiring? Could you inquire about reality by studiously avoiding it?

An ideological cross. When I took my final exams at Giulio Cesare High School, the first question in the philosophy exam was: "Talk to me about the conception of leisure time in Karl Marx." If asked that question today, I wouldn't know how to answer, but back then I did. Nowadays, we couldn't even conceive of a question like that, but in those days we could. Many of the things I knew or was capable of at age eighteen have been lost. I found an old book of quizzes to help you calculate your IQ. It dated from those years, and on the last page I found notations in pencil of the scores of those who had taken that test, including my father's score—he was a man of great intelligence—and my own. I tried taking the test again. This time my score was twenty points lower than the score I'd achieved back then. At the apex of his mental brilliance, when a young man is about to leave school, he finds himself on the highest point of the curve, and it is from there that he looks out upon the world: perhaps he doesn't understand it, but he sees it, clear-eyed, all the way out to its far-flung borders, and his gaze has a sharpness it will never get back. (NB: among the scores in the booklet, I noticed Arbus's . . .)

In other words, Falà, though he was still only a high school student, and what's more, a student attending a school run by priests, sidestepped the exploitation by reading Plekhanov instead of Hemingway, using his free time to ready the overthrow of the system that allowed him that leisure time strictly to keep him under control, administering carefully controlled doses of soccer matches, Giro d'Italia bike races, discos, and short skirts.

I have always admired, from a distance, those who react to suffering by adding further suffering, rejecting all and any consolation. I admire them, though I fail to understand them. And I admired Folinea and Falà, but I failed to understand them. They struck me as so *serious*. That meant that I, reading my novels, *wasn't* serious. Now I read fewer novels than I did back then, and yet I still haven't been able to be entirely *serious*. Clearly, a lifetime isn't enough. And putting on a gloomy face isn't, either.

We were few but good, we Communists at SLM. Or maybe we were few and not particularly good.

THE CASE OF ANOTHER LEFTY STUDENT FROM SLM, Marco Lodoli, was even more intriguing than those of Folinea and Falà, because his father, Renzo, was a genuine Fascist, and until age fourteen so was his son, under the paternal influence that fed him a romantic veteran's syndrome. As a young man, Lodoli was convinced that his beliefs would lead him sooner or later to a firing squad, back against the wall, eyes blindfolded, and a bullet between the eyes, executed like those collaborationist writers that were being rediscovered and reappraised in those years, in part thanks to Louis Malle's morbid and beautiful film *The Fire Within*. But then this blind innocence came to an end, and political disagreements began to proliferate between the old man and his son, culminating the evening that the elder Lodoli theatrically ripped to pieces and threw into the trash a copy of *The Autobiography of Malcolm X*, which Marco and I had bought (or shoplifted,

I can't be sure) at the Feltrinelli bookshop on Via del Babuino. An unaccustomed thing for the old veteran to do: he was normally a mild-mannered, civil person, but he can't have found it easy to accept the presence of that book in his home, a book that marked the advent of his son's ideological emancipation. The exemplary punishment, however, wasn't very effective: if anything, destroying a book only reinforces the faith of its owner, the conviction that he is in the right, as well as his instinct to resist. The funny thing was that from then on, Lodoli (who was lanky and shambling, wore glasses, and had his kinky hair up in a sort of afro) also physically became the paragon of the nonconformist, leftist student, at SLM, highly noticeable for his ragtag clothing, practically a flashing signpost, a bull's-eye in the crosshairs, in case it occurred to anyone to give him a lesson meant to make it clear that there was no oxygen in the atmosphere for communism at SLM. He became the ideal target.

ANGELO PETTIROSSI was a great drummer and record collector. He introduced me to Soft Machine. Now he's a cardiologist.

THE HAIRSTYLE COUNTED, the clothing was decisive, and how. A pair of pointy-toed shoes or a shoulder-strap bag were part of the destiny of many of the young men in the quarter, in the seventies. Fashion had nothing to do with it, there was no such thing as fashion, those were *uniforms* and that is how and why they were donned. Among the best-loved scenes of the time is the opening sequence of the movie *Electra Glide in Blue*, the motorcyclist's vestition: leather details, chrome-plated buckles that fasten the suit of armor; then *Taxi Driver*, when De Niro sets his shoe polish on fire before applying it to his boots. When you put on a pair of camperos boots, you entered a different world. "Murdered for a pair of boots" sounds like pulp journalism, but it describes a fate that is by no means random. The quarter in which SLM was located was a hinge between opposing worlds, contested ground, an ideal battlefield because the Fascists were a full-fledged presence there, and their shadow loomed over the tree-lined boulevard of Corso Trieste.

ONE EVENING I WENT to Villa Torlonia to see an Alan Stivell concert, and half of the audience was ready to start a brawl with the other half because those Celtic plaints could be claimed by equal rights by both Commies and Fascists.

Back then it was called folk music, today we call it ethnic music, but it amounts to the same thing.

I witnessed a comparable phenomenon during the showing of Lindsay Anderson's film *If*: toward the end, when the students huddled on the boarding school roof are firing down at their headmaster, who is meanwhile inviting them to come down, in the friendliest manner, "Boys! Boys! *I understand you!* Listen to reason and trust me! Trust me!" and he catches a bullet in the forehead, in the film forum the exultation of the Fascists and the comrades, right and left, was the same. We all leapt to our feet.

The willingness to engage in violence was palpable, fluid, violence was the glue that held all ideas together, it was the backdrop against which the figures moved, like the landscape with trees and mountains in paintings from the Renaissance. In a meeting held in a bar, during an afternoon of school-days boredom, you might decide to murder someone, without having to be hardened criminals. And there was no shortage of good motivations, there was always a vendetta that needed carrying out, a lesson to be imparted, a reckoning that had been waiting for years to be settled, a debit sheet of offenses and wrongs that needed to be rectified. There was always justice to be served on an express basis. It's incredible how words are able to support, to give shape to any plan, someone once said that words weigh as much as stones or lead, but that's not true, words are featherlight and elusive, if they had shape and weight they would be unable to treat subjects like life and death with such nonchalance, and instead they flutter and dance and dart around the most extreme subjects. Words are fast, perhaps faster than ideas, and in fact, sooner or later, they leave ideas behind. They're launched into orbit by the flame tongues of reason, but then they're perfectly capable of proceeding all by themselves into the stellar void. From one paradox to the next, you ought to reach a point beyond which you will not venture, it ought to be enough to stop and listen to the words you're saying to be unable to dare to venture any farther, and at that point even the most daring or threatening ideas freeze to a halt . . . but by then the words have built up too much momentum, and they drag the ideas along behind them, crashing through all limitations. They come out of our mouths by themselves and venture where reason is ashamed or afraid to tread. They say the unspeakable. It's an almost poetic internal mechanism, verbal virulence is a particular form of eloquence. Many discourses or articles of political sloganeering are more drunken than the maddest poetry could hope to be, more taboo-shattering than any literary avant garde, more visionary than a mystical trance. If you read them years later, they're quite horrifying, but then and there they simply slip away. Once anointed with the oil of words, they gather headway and there is no act—however barbaric or criminal or bloodthirsty or simply idiotic—that they are incapable of, not merely justifying, but even exalting. The true automatism preached by the Surrealists is there, not in the innocuous poetry of Éluard or Desnos. Murder becomes an elevated act of humanity, extermination a hygienic operation, beatings and clubbings cheerful and good for your health, massacres an instance of perfect geometry, and enemies become rats, insects, worms, and filthy carrion.

I WROTE IT about a hundred pages back: novels live on what no longer exists, has vanished or will soon vanish. Ways of speaking, loving, dressing, and fighting, ways of kissing, buildings, fortunes, witticisms, streets, ribbons and waistcoats, pistols, hairstyles—all sealed in transparent amber to be held up against the light. Even if it unfolds in the contemporary world or the world yet to come, every novel comes into existence already half-buried, the minute it's built it's already a heartbreaking ruin, an enigmatic legacy, a ghost city that will return to life for the brief time—as exclusive as it is illusory—that it takes to read it: everything that appears in it is in any case destined to perish. Everything. Its materials deteriorate rapidly, crumbling like fabrics, unlike the eternal, immortal materials that make up lyric and epic poetry, tragedy and philosophy.

The reader experiences the tragic struggle of an organism as it prepares to enter the domain of nothingness. As its sun sets, as it fades and loses color, after having been alive and pulsating before our very eyes. The wonderful things offered by a novel are therefore always on the verge of cessation.

Whereas there are other artistic forms that treat things that are destined to endure, that which has a future, and which can withstand the onslaught of time.

I HAD NO DIRECT EXPERIENCE with Fascists except for a single case, that of my grandfather, whose tempestuous personality I prefer not to discuss here and now.

Let me just say that for many years my grandfather came by our home every single afternoon.

He and my beloved grandmother would drop by around five, and stay until Papà came home from the office, before dinner.

While my mother and my grandmother would chat or have tea or play cards, my grandfather would get on the phone and begin a series of lengthy, mysterious, and often agitated calls, the angry echoes of which would reach us through the glass door he'd shut behind him.

It was a pointless act of discretion.

As in many bourgeois apartments, and before it became such an important appliance to family life that it began to appear in multiple locations, the single telephone was in a hallway between the bathroom, the kitchen, and the dining room, and it made it necessary to make phone calls standing up, in that pass-through area, which meant you were usually limited to brief, utilitarian conversations—but when it was my grandfather who made the calls, a few minutes after arriving at our home, he would shut himself behind that door, blocking all access to the kitchen, since no one dared disturb him by passing through.

And so we'd loiter in the front hall, waiting for him to finish so we could go into the kitchen and have our snacks, and through the arabesque of the glass door, we'd watch his silhouette as he gesticulated and flailed, dark in the short, brightly lit hallway, waving his free arm, but also the arm that held the receiver, and we could hear his outbursts of wrath, prompted by reasons that remained mysterious to us.

Who was it he called so insistently?

What business matters was he discussing, and why did those calls so frequently end with a receiver slammed down into its cradle?

We encountered numerous instances of his fury but never an explanation, not once.

Of his many frustrated attempts to do business, there remained, tucked away in a nook, a sheet of cellophane that, when applied to the TV screen, was supposed to give the impression of a color TV, back in the day when broadcasting in Italy was done only in black and white.

It worked reasonably well with landscapes, since the upper half was light blue and the bottom half was green.

Much less well with the faces of actors or close-ups of a show's hostess.

Sometimes when he came over, he was accompanied by extremely elderly gentlemen wearing lugubrious black overcoats, and together they'd huddle in the living room behind closed doors, scheming and plotting.

We would sit in the dining room watching TV, in black and white, which at the time hardly struck us as an especially grave handicap, wondering who those guests might be: some of them had a prosthetic hand or an eye patch, just like the old men we'd see stroll around the institute for disabled veterans across the street from our apartment building, until my father would return home from the office, and then his patience and courtesy would be sorely tested because my grandfather, instead of hightailing it out of there, would make a point of introducing his son-in-law to his various companions, one of whom was referred to as "the general."

Despite the fact that he was tired and hungry, my father would join them in the living room, behind closed doors. The conversations could last a few minutes or they could drag out long enough to conflict with dinnertime.

ONE TIME, the general arrived in the company of a young man in a blazer and black turtleneck.

I must have been thirteen, and my brother eleven, so we were still practically little kids, and yet that dark and serious and already mature young man was separated from the old Fascist officer and sent, for generational reasons, to my bedroom, "to spend time with the boys," as my grandfather put it.

Once he entered the bedroom, he looked around with great interest at the furnishings and decoration, the posters on the walls and the books on the shelves, tilting his head to one side to read the titles.

Every now and then, he'd pull one down and leaf through it.

More than looking at the book, he seemed to be looking for something hidden between its pages.

He thoroughly studied the three large bookshelves on the wall, then, after taking off his jacket and carefully folding it over the back of the chair, he sat down on the far corner of my bed, in an extremely uncomfortable position, and started asking us questions.

He had an artificially pitched voice, like someone who has to make a continual effort to control himself, and he spoke in a low, grave tone, with an accent from the north of Italy, clearly enunciating each word without moving a muscle of his face; he stared at us fixedly, first at me and then at my brother, deep into our eyes, as if trying to read our secrets back there and determine whether or not we were telling the truth.

But not the truth that corresponds to the facts, something else.

He was curious to know what school we went to, what we did in our spare time, whether we played any sport, and if so, how many times a week, and why we had chosen those specific sports to play.

THE CATHOLIC SCHOOL 601

And then he asked us if we had made our choice.

What choice? I wondered.

I was surprised and intimidated by that interrogation, just as I had been by the close inspection of my books.

While I was trying to elude the inquisitive gaze of this stranger, letting my younger brother naïvely answer him, my eyes came to rest on his folded jacket, and I noticed a lapel pin, surprised that I hadn't seen it before, so brightly did it glitter.

It was a shield with a cross on it, the ends of which opened out into the shape of arrowheads.

He complimented my brother on his answers about soccer and exercise. "Sports are healthy," he said, clenching a fist, ". . . but they alone aren't enough!" and he opened his hand in a caress with a sort of final pat on the back of my brother's head; he, being less mistrustful than me, smiled.

As he made these gestures, the first ones since he had sat himself down on my bed in that position, he was so rigid that he didn't seem to be sitting but rather hunched on his thighs, his snugly fitting black turtleneck, which till then had made him seem skinny or even frail, puffed up around his chest and arms.

Actually, none of us was especially athletic, but seeing that the stranger cared so very much about staying in physical shape, my brother Riccardo had placated him with a lie.

"What about you, have you made your choice?" asked the young man again, in that gloomy voice of his.

HE SHOWED US HIS HANDS, the knuckles big as walnuts and two or three fingers that wouldn't straighten out.

He told us about his fights, using a cold, dismissive tone that was, at the same time, exalted and detached, as if the scenes of violence were being projected for the umpteenth time on a screen in the back of his mind and he was trying to decide which stills to show, and in what sequence, in his narrative.

He spoke in a laconic manner, so laconic that it was practically incomprehensible, presenting us with only the preliminaries of his stories, or else the conclusion, usually bloody, from which he derived an abstract and indisputable moral.

"But they were forced to repent . . . that's right, bitterly repent . . .

because even if you outnumber the enemy ten to one, it's not necessarily the case that you have victory within your grasp!"

His omissions and ellipses forced us to ask him questions to find out more, and it was at that moment that he, in a calculated manner, would withdraw, as his gaze became even more dark and distant.

"No, you're too young, there are certain things that you shouldn't know about yet . . . but you'll learn, yeah, you'll learn on your own . . . *very soon!*" and he'd shake his head.

The maxims with which he larded his stories were built around such words as "courage," "honor," "loyalty," "battle," and "death," but above all, "honor," which recurred constantly and was coupled with the other words as if it were a sort of invariable part of the discourse: "Honor in battle is what survives of a man." "Those who prefer death to infamy preserve their honor." "Honor does not limit itself to doing only what is allowed." "I choose to be faithful to honor rather than to money." They all tracked back to a dramatic moment in which it had been necessary to choose, to opt among difficult alternatives, choose a side without hesitation. And he had made that choice. For someone like him, a battle began every morning when he woke up. And in order to face up to it, there was no way other than to draw on extreme resources. "Even when I shave in the morning, I wonder whether this might not be the last time." What he wanted us to take away from his stories, the thing that he wanted us to be struck and impressed by, was the sheer *disproportion.* The adversaries to fight against were always twice or three times as many, or else they possessed overwhelming physical bulk, or they made use of superior logistical resources. They had heavier clubs and cudgels, newspapers with greater circulation, political connivance, cash contributions, a more extensive, fine-grained organization. But most important of all, they always outnumbered, there were always more of them, a human tide. This inevitable, chronic disproportion of strength was however offset by the virtues that formed the core of his proverbs, namely, courage, honor, loyalty, defiance in the face of death, all things that were capable of overturning the certain outcome of the clash, in fact, to hear him tell it, you almost felt a twinge of pity for that mass of helpless adversaries who wound up taking a beating in spite of their superiority, at least on paper. And however the battle wound up going, it still ended in glory: if you won, obviously, but even if you lost, because a defeat at the hand of overwhelming and unfair opponents remained in any case a form of moral victory, which cast its glow even brighter and farther, like a bonfire on a mountaintop. There was a special savor in defeat, and in mantling it with nobility through a reconstruction of events that seemed to focus on the moment at which the hero would be betrayed, surrounded, and wounded, but as he fell that hero would drag his adversary down with him, subjugating him morally, triumphing over his vulgarity and mediocrity. I was struck by the resemblance between the stories he told and the singular military history of Italy, which was still taught at school in my day, entirely made up of acts of individual heroism against vast and powerful armies. That history traced back to ancient Rome, or even further back, to Thermopylae, and then given that running start, hurtled all the way up to those young heroes, little more than boys, who threw sticks or crutches or hand grenades at heavily armed soldiers, or scrambled under tanks bare-handed, or rode torpedoes like horses to blow enemy ships sky-high, or let themselves be blown up in order to prevent the invasion of their city, or held off armies ten times their number in the snow. Always fighting against hopeless odds, always martyrs, men lost in the farthest-flung outpost, rebels against destiny. And I, overcome with emotion though I might be, in the end couldn't help but wonder: but we Italians, didn't we ever once manage to win a war just *because our army was more powerful*? Could it be that we always had to rely on a bold exploit that could he handed down to posterity, engraved on a plaque, after the hero had been killed in the process?

And that emotion began to be tinged with suspicion.

ASIDE FROM HIS REASONS for proposing such a bellicose vision of life to us, which were inevitably to remain utterly obscure, there was something about our guest's words, gestures, and glassy gaze that left me baffled. As if his effort, his incessant striving drained any energy he might have to savor the result obtained by that effort. In his carefully calculated, pompous words there never echoed even the slightest smidgen of joy. Everything seemed simply to cost sacrifice, and the sacrifice merely to illuminate in a sinister gleam a charred, incinerated panorama. When all is said and done, if the struggle itself is a value, why shouldn't the opposite also be a value in and of itself? Peace and quiet, abandonment, flight, or tenderness? And if, when the struggle was over, the highest that you can obtain is the preservation of what was there before, the unbreakable position assumed from the very beginning (obsession with loyalty, attachment to values), doesn't the struggle itself become only apparent motion, a deception, or, in the final analysis, nothing more than a way of passing the time of day?

AT THAT AGE, I began to scratch the surface of values with a jackknife. In truth, I had already started to do it as a boy, it was my favorite game. The gilding came off immediately.

ONE TIME, he had been chased and surrounded. They'd started beating him with steel rods. As he hunched down to protect his head, he'd been unable to pull out his pistol, and by the time he got his hand into his pocket to pull it out, his hands were so badly fractured that he couldn't get his finger into the trigger guard. But it was enough to see the weapon appear in his hands for his assailants to desist and take to their heels.

He said that he was sorry he hadn't been able to fire, he would have put down at least one of his assailants.

"After all, maybe it's better this way."

My brother asked him if he had the pistol there with him.

"Would you let me see it?"

He smiled and answered no, he wasn't carrying it today.

"After all, it wouldn't make any difference. If they seriously want to do it, they can kill me before I have time to say amen."

And he gave my brother another sporting pat on the back of his neck.

"And I won't even have time to realize it's happening. In the end, it won't make a bit of difference."

They were all phrases uttered in a hollow, important tone of voice.

He needed to display authority, since authority was his religion.

His black turtleneck made him look like a priest.

He never smiled and his sermon intimidated us without convincing us.

He left, calling us *camerati*—"comrades," but specifically and exclusively *Fascist* comrades.

6

ALL YEARS ARE CONCENTRATED in a single year, the entire twentieth century and a fair chunk of the twenty-first boil down, are foretold, are stowed away, take refuge, are present, and verge on the ridiculous—all in the year 1975. That year makes a succession of other years snap to attention, it makes them scurry along. There's nothing like abuses and excesses to contribute to the advancement of time, and therefore to its fixation. Abuse and abuse alone is memorable. Time stretches out and sways over a point where bands of prerequisites and consequences converge. A dust cloud of events settles over that frozen image, the way the snow settles over the landscape in a snow globe.

I mean to say that, along with what happened from January 1 to December 31 of that year, there also fluttered down on 1975 the events our parents had witnessed when they were children, and others still that had yet to occur and even those that, someday, we may ourselves still be capable of glimpsing with bleary, rheumy eyes, now old men and women with taxidermically stuffed souls and internal organs replaced by spare parts. Every generation ought to have reserved front-row seats to be able to say: "Those times, those times there, those times there were *mine* and mine alone." Hands off. But that's not the way it works. Time belongs to everyone. And in every single instant of it, it manifests itself in its punctuality and its entirety: if only we had been capable of understanding that in a single point of time everything is concentrated and revealed! If we were only capable of it *now*!

Before the seventies, the eighth decade of the twentieth century, there had never been anything interesting in the world. Nothing, ever. No noteworthy event. The Egyptians and the Maya and the countless wars of the Romans and Frederick Barbarossa and Magellan and the bombing of Hiroshima or man on the moon offer little that is comparable to that spectacular decade, that crucial, axial year, around which our little orbits revolve.

I WANT TO OFFER an example that everyone will be free to judge from the angle they prefer; an experiment that aside from me (and my contemporaries) has as its protagonist my son Leone, a smart, curious young man, the way I was at his age, or perhaps even more so. Leone and his contemporaries, in other words. I asked Leo to draw up the most complete and scrupulous list possible of the movies he saw in the past year, 2012. By which I mean first-run films, in movie theaters, with a ticket and not on TV. And I'll put it side by side with the list I reconstructed of the movies I saw when I was the same age he is now, that is, eighteen, in 1975. Maybe I saw others, but the ones listed below I definitely saw. In some cases, I could even list the movie theaters where I saw them.

MOVIES SEEN IN 2012 BY MY SON LEONE, AT AGE EIGHTEEN:
The Avengers (Whedon)
Snow White and the Huntsman (Sanders)
The Hobbit: An Unexpected Journey (Jackson)
Ted (MacFarlane)
Skyfall (Mendes)
The Dark Knight Rises (Nolan)
Moonrise Kingdom (Anderson)
Men in Black 3 (Sonnenfeld)
Seven Psychopaths (McDonagh)
The Raven (McTeigue)
The Dictator (Charles)

MOVIES SEEN BY ME, AGE EIGHTEEN, IN 1975:
Barry Lyndon (Kubrick)
Three Days of the Condor (Pollack)
Picnic at Hanging Rock (Weir)
Amici miei (*My Friends*, Monicelli)
The Passenger (Antonioni)
Dersu Uzala (Kurosawa)
Night Moves (Penn)
Nashville (Altman)
Dog Day Afternoon (Lumet)
We All Loved Each Other So Much (Scola)
The Phantom of the Opera (De Palma)
Chinatown (Polanski)
The Enigma of Kaspar Hauser (Herzog)
The Conversation (Coppola)

Love and Death (Allen)
Lenny (Fosse)
Alice Doesn't Live Here Anymore (Scorsese)
The Man Who Would Be King (Huston)
French Connection II (Frankenheimer)
Kings of the Road (Wenders)
The Sunshine Boys (Ross)
A Slave of Love (Mikhalkov)
The Texas Chain Saw Massacre (Hooper)
Immoral Tales (Borowczyk)
Shampoo (Ashby)
The Suspect (Maselli)
Cría Cuervos (Saura)
One Flew over the Cuckoo's Nest (Forman)
The Lost Honour of Katharina Blum (Schlöndorff and von Trotta)
Adele H (Truffaut)
The Longest Yard (Aldrich)
Scent of a Woman (Risi)
Bring Me the Head of Alfredo Garcia (Peckinpah)
Deep Red (Argento)
The Front Page (Wilder)
Tommy (Russell)
Young Frankenstein (Brooks)
Fantozzi (Salce)
Jaws (Spielberg)

Note: there is no question that we went to the movies a lot, far more often than people do nowadays. Aside from being the most classic form of entertainment (not that there were many others), watching movies, watching *lots* of movies, watching *all* the movies that there were, was considered an integral part of any curious young man's or woman's education, like listening to records and reading magazines and comic books: indeed they were, in those years, the essential component of that education. Film was still the art of the century, it pulled the twentieth century behind it like a mighty titan, his feet braced on the ocean bed, pulling a broken-down ocean liner behind him. How short was its cycle! As brief as the century itself. But what catches the eye in the respective lists isn't so much the demand, as it is the supply: that is, the quantity and the quality of the films that a young man could see back then. And to think that we were already out of the legendary age of the silver screen, in theory, on the downward slope.

Second note: in the list drawn up by my son, there's not a single Italian film.

AN EXPRESSION that was used back then in political argumentation was the "weld point." Perhaps because of its metallic connotation and the sensation that it sprayed sparks. The clanging sound of a metal workshop, but it also had echoes of wartime, of operative language. Tactics and strategy, application and execution of orders. Both Marxism and Fascist rhetoric loved steel.

They imagined, they predicted, they devoutly wished for weld points between material interests, between antagonistic groups, between concepts, between levels of command, between theses about literature and revolution.

For at least a decade, at the dead center of which we can place the culminating events of this episode, Italy was enveloped in the billowing smoke of conspiracies. Secret plots, military coups planned or aborted or reconsidered, mysterious explosions, bloodbaths, murders and reprisals, intelligence services variously sound and hacked, national and foreign, threatening letters killings espionage subversive plots betrayals and ambushes and conspiracies settled soupily over the nation like a dense cloud, no one could see anything, to the point that the best way of moving forward was to just not give a damn, the way we adolescents all did, while the grown-ups obsessed over it, racking their brains about why a certain bomb had been set off and who had planted it and at whose orders. For those who had no blood on their hands, who neither shot anyone nor was shot, who clubbed no one with heavy metal bars nor was clubbed, those were fantastic years. And the smoke-filled air appeared crystalline to them.

AT THE TIME, it was impossible for me to talk about the time. I was in it up to my neck. The losses left me speechless, the conquests filled me with elation: both conditions make any comment superfluous.

The year 1975 was the year of the elections: may I venture to say, the most eagerly awaited, the most grimly feared elections in Italy, since 1948? Of course, I can say so, and even if that weren't true, they'd still be the most important elections in history because they marked the first time that

I was able to vote. The first time that eighteen-year-olds voted, and they were only able to vote by a whisker, because it was only a few weeks before the elections that adulthood was lowered from twenty-one to eighteen, and from one day to the next, to our astonishment, we were no longer minors. At school, the effect of that change made itself felt in the form of a small but significant detail, namely, we could sign our own excuses for being absent, instead of having to get them signed, with a written explanation, by our parents. They ought to have been abolished entirely, for us eighteen-year-olds, what did those old formulations even mean anymore: "for health reasons," "for family obligations"? The members of Collective M of Giulio Cesare High School immediately took advantage of the opportunity to write in the excuse box on the form such provocative and yet realistic phrases as: "She didn't feel much like going, so she stayed in bed," or else: "On account of heavy precipitation," "Because the spring day promised to be beautiful," and underneath that, your very own signature, to be displayed diligently to the first-period teacher, who of course had no desire to engage in discussions of first principles that would only expose them to the ridicule of everyone in the class, unified in their opinion, and of Collective M, which spoke as one, and so the teacher limited himself or herself to accepting that buffoonery and, grumbling under his or her breath, transcribing on the ledger the name of the self-excused student.

The things that our teachers, both priests and non-priests, let us get away with back then! How many times they completely overlooked the most insolent of provocations, because they understood that resistance, fighting the point to a standstill, meant going against the times, making themselves ridiculous, "handing out speeding tickets at the Indy 500" (the famous line from *Apocalypse Now*, which would come out shortly thereafter).

The fact remained that the old formulation "for family obligations" still had its delicious charm, and it was fun to trot it out to justify a day's absence, the kind of absence that has no explanation save for the unwillingness to get out of bed. Mysterious formulation, all-inclusive justification! It would appear that in Italy, adducing the "family" is the one sure way of justifying any behavior or shortcoming, from absenteeism to outright corruption, from tax evasion to bloody vendetta.

BUT TO COME BACK to the elections: that was supposed to be the year of the Communists. The Communist Party was by far the leading party in

Turin, Naples, Venice, in Emilia and in Tuscany. In certain cities, two thirds of the population voted Communist. The Communists even picked up votes in the ranks of the classes that communism had historically declared its determination to abolish, and perhaps those classes voted that way out of a subconscious desire to contribute to their own destruction and finally eliminate the mark of distinction that in other historic phases they had striven ruthlessly to attain. There was a bourgeoisie that defended tooth and nail the prerogatives acquired and a bourgeoisie that fought, at least to hear them tell it, against the regime that had hitherto always protected, coddled, spoiled, and cherished them. These two souls of the bourgeoisie, mirror images of each other, would soon come to a final reckoning. And that final reckoning was expected to come with these elections. When I talked, socialized, argued, made friends, made love, or went to the movies it was almost exclusively with Communists. Of various varieties and degrees, some of them authentic Communists, some less so, and a few who were unquestionable fakes, but all of them *red*, members of the PCI, the FGCI, Lotta Continua, Manifesto, PSIUP, Marxist-Leninists, anarcho-Communists (as we members of Collective M proclaimed ourselves), renegades of the extraparliamentary world, Trotskyites, adherents to the First, the Second, the Third, and the Fourth International, Socialists even farther to the left than the Communists themselves, and a vast number of so-called *gruppettari*, members of grouplets whose political militancy made explicit reference to movements that there is not enough space here to mention, so frequent were their schisms and reconciliations and breakaways and fragmentations, by the end of which there were increasingly extremist and sectarian formations. The only one that I'll cite, if only for its exemplary name, and because the older sister of my first girlfriend was a militant in its ranks, was Serve the People. I, too, was a Communist to all intents and purposes, I was one even if maybe I wasn't one, I hadn't been before and I wouldn't be afterward, I was one even though the ideas of communism failed to persuade me back then any more than they do now, that is to say, almost not at all, and their practical applications actually disgusted me, to the point that I could much more readily say that I'm an anti-Communist than a Communist. So how can an anti-Communist proclaim himself to be a Communist, and act and vote and even wade into brawls, feeling himself wholly to be one, and I mean sincerely, with full conviction—so I ask myself, how can that be? My sole anchor of salvation and my one way of scuttling out from the dilemma of that contradiction was, in any case, to proclaim that I was opposed to Stalin—whom I considered a criminal even then and have ever since, and one of the worst criminals ever to have existed on the face of the earth—and against the Stalinists, and in that way I managed to carve out a virtuous little niche for myself in that ocean of bloodthirsty events and behaviors. All the same, I already know that, no matter how hard I try, no matter how I explain it away, I'll never be able to understand and justify the contradiction that deep down still drives me, even now that I've stopped rooting for one side, now that I've even given up voting, the contradiction that still sometimes drives me to take the positions of a free-market gentleman, and on other occasions unleashes within me the delight of being implacably, coldly Marxist. A disenchanted bard of the status quo ready to turn into an equally disenchanted analyst of man's exploitation of his fellow man. How can that be? And yet it most assuredly is. For that matter, I exist, there's no doubt about it. And I sway, back and forth. I hardly think I'm alone in this.

Perhaps the fact that I sway can be attributed to the profession of writing, which tends to make me adopt different positions from case to case, different ways of looking at things. It's a collateral effect of this calling. Or else, perhaps, I chose this line of work precisely in order to afford myself the luxury of swaying, in order to encourage it, so that I could impersonate first this person, then that one, that idea . . .

> Savor pineapple
> And dine on pheasant
> No future for you, bourgeois,
> So hold on to the present!

WHEN, DURING MY SCHOOL DAYS, and later at the university, I was a militant—albeit one with a great many uncertainties—in what was then described as the "extraparliamentary left," or at least I rooted for them, seeing that as a militant I really didn't do much at all, I was deeply struck by their leaders and deputies and their attitude, copied from the models of historic revolutionaries, although it was shrunk to the appropriate student protest scale, with an added touch that was, shall we say, typical of the period, which couldn't have existed in the time of the Soviet revolution or the time of the Italian partisans. Almost all of them posed as inexorable executors of a political mandate that history had placed in their hands. In a highly affected manner, they were cutting and ruthless, and what's more, ruthless *in words*. I'd like to describe one of them.

TALL, GOOD-LOOKING, with fine hair already starting to thin and a thick blond mustache. Charming, vicious. Swollen with contempt. Peremptory. The peremptory manner is perhaps the principal characteristic of revolutionaries at every level. The last time that I saw him, that I saw him in action, I mean to say, on the street (now he shows up on TV to offer sarcastic comments on current events: he's old and wrinkled and smiles a great deal more than he used to, still full of allure), was during the demonstration in which Giorgiana Masi was killed: May 12, 1977. He was carrying a Beretta MAB rifle under his duster coat. He was running back and forth along the Lungotevere, the Tiber riverfront, and his coat would flutter, eloquently revealing, rather than concealing, that manageable and rather inaccurate submachine gun which was a regulation weapon of the Italian army. A weapon that, a couple of years later, I would handle myself during my military training in Taranto, firing off bursts of gunfire at a floating target fifty yards from the waterline. I couldn't say now whether those who changed their viewpoint are worse or better than those who remain unchanged.

ASIDE FROM A FEW genuine intellectuals who actually verged on erudition, and a substrate of uneducated cannon fodder, the extremist ideologies of the period recruited their militants from a semi-intelligentsia: students and the self-taught, semi-intellectuals, the scholastically cultured of the seventies, people who were ignorant but not entirely, or else cultivated but with enormous gaps, perhaps specialized in a narrow sector, say, "Celtic myths," and ignorant of everything else, possibly the most unstable and dangerous breed, that is, the species of *the ignoramus who has read a few books*, because those books, air-dropped into the void, have landed with a tremendous uproar. Better, far better, far less harmful, in that case, though these days rare and hard to find, would be total ignorance . . . the truth is that certain books land like a massive boulder on weak minds, or anxious minds, starving, thirsting, far too eagerly, for the truth. Thus engendering fanatical infatuations, generating ironclad convictions, as confident as they are unfounded, fomenting murderous certainties. Instead of broadening horizons, they narrow them to a core of miraculous answers . . .

These days it's trendy to ask: What book changed your life? Well, seriously, I'm afraid that those who had their lives really changed by *one* book, by *that* book, it's most likely because they've failed to read many others. And that one book, in all likelihood, would be *Mein Kampf.*

IT WAS A TIME and a way of life that were so chaotic and violent that even in the most trivial and day-to-day matters, even in our amusements, in the passing kerfuffles, in the thoughts and plans of high school students, we constantly and unfailingly veered close to murder. Yeah, that's right, murder—rub out, liquidate, eliminate, or teach a lesson that, given the tools with which that lesson was being taught, might easily turn out to be the last lesson of them all. That eventuality was there, ever present, alongside the chitchat and normal activities, such as playing soccer or doing crossword puzzles. A group of students would meet up at a schoolmate's home to discuss political matters, nothing more or less than the typical afternoon spent working on a paper about the Cuban revolution or Russian futurism, and after a mid-afternoon snack, the talk would turn to plans to shoot a journalist. Instead of eagerly discussing Mayakovsky's broken verse or the price of sugarcane, in a brisk half hour they'd come to terms on a murder. From summary lists jotted down in felt-tip pen, names were drawn, pretty much interchangeable, of the people whose lives it seemed fair and just to take. The motives for doing so seemed obvious, and whatever reasoning might be involved led to them in a few simple moves: any obstacle that loomed up along the way simply had to be moved aside, and if the obstacle was a human being, well, that obstacle had to be removed. That removal would also serve an exemplary purpose, a warning to anyone who might get it into their head to meddle or interfere. It all was supposed to seem like an inexorable political deduction. The less time passed between the handing down of the sentence and the corresponding execution, the greater the exemplary effect, until the impression was that the reprisal simply took place automatically: you publish an article, and the next morning you could already expect to be shot at the bus stop, or the minute you got in your car, even before you turned the key in the ignition.

AT THE TIME, two opposing conceptions were facing off, in every field of human endeavor, but almost no one had the hardheaded stubbornness to align themselves definitively with one side or the other, while practically everyone wound up mingling their views or alternating them, on a case-by-case basis. These two opposing theories could be summarized as follows: "The path to happiness entails returning to a state of nature" and "The path that most limits suffering lies in the ability to transcend the state of nature." The two major philosophers who had theorized these two points of view had lived respectively two and a half and three and a half centuries ago, which meant that their ideas had taken a hell of a long time to come to the final and decisive clash, you might say, perfectly matched, with equal strength. In the meantime, nature herself had already started to go crazy, with forests and waters being poisoned and dying, yet her followers had tried everything imaginable to restore harmony with her, stripping bare naked, living in the woods, fucking like rabbits, developing a new appreciation for ignorance and naïveté and the plow, just as technology was getting ready to integrate our vital functions one organ at a time, and the majority of mankind had already begun to live in a setting where there was not so much as a blade of grass that hadn't been grown artificially, a chicken or a mushroom that hadn't been grown in a battery, surrounded by a high barrier of virtual images.

The two doctrines faced off, in the fullness of their strength and yet, at the same time, at the height of their crisis, feverish, aggressive, spasming convulsively . . .

WHAT WAS ONCE DONE without discussion now has to be thrashed out, negotiated, and revoked if the negotiations fail. The rules change constantly, continually transforming and intersecting, coexisting; take, for example, the laws of love: we tell each other everything, each of us has his or her own life, if you betray me I'll leave you, I'll kill myself, you can fuck anyone you want, as you long as you don't French-kiss them. How was an amorous awareness formed in the first place? Through song lyrics, advertising sketches, psychoanalytical commonplaces, which ended up establishing a pugnacious everyday religion with its commandments and its ethics, that is, its desires, which demanded obedience like the articles of faith of some new fundamentalism. The same thing, more or less, happened with politics and morality. For example, I grew up with a moral sense that was as compelling as it was uncertain, fumbling in the dark, and I always had to wait for the waves of remorse in order to ascertain whether what I had done was wrong. Unfortunately, however, there is no equivalent feeling to confirm that I've done the right thing. And what was the typical venue for this hybridizing? The family. A blend of periods and styles, fragmented and reassembled, the venue for tenderness and anger and indifference, a genuine hotel (and yes, it is, *it is!*) where travelers of all ages stop and stay.

> *Up till then the way things worked had been:*
> *the husband earns the bread*
> *the wife spreads butter on it*
> *the children eat it. The butter*
> *on my bread wasn't spread by my mother*
> *but by young ladies paid to do so, nannies*
> *or housekeepers: and if occasionally it turned out to be*
> *my mother who spread the butter herself*
> *in the first person, this constituted*
> *a special occasion, a great*
> *and unconditional act of love.*

CORPORAL PUNISHMENT was ruled out entirely, while sanctions of an economic nature ("No allowance for a week") were dismissed as vulgar, and prohibitions ("No motor scooter for you, it stays in the garage for a month": sure, but then if your son used it anyway, without telling you, how could you react to that without availing yourself of punishments that had now been abolished? Once overthrown, it's not as if the ancien régime springs back to its feet at a word of command . . . once the institution is liquidated, the servants of the glebe don't just come trooping back, in dribs and drabs, one day on, one day off . . .) were deemed counterproductive or impracticable, so parents were left with minimal room to maneuver in terms of punishing their children—without stopping to delve into the merits of their transgressions or whether the youngsters deserved it, which is a separate chapter. No one knew any longer what was right and what was wrong, or perhaps we should say, what common sense concurred was, in principle, *absolutely* right and *absolutely* wrong. The sacrosanct school of dialogue had taught that every single point of cohabitation and way of life, every so-called value or duty or principle was subject to negotiation; but if, when all these civil discussions drew to a close, you had been able to come to an accord, a compromise that could make the punishment superfluous, then what? What punishment would then be applied, and how—and most important of all, in the name of what, given that the punishment in and of itself contradicted the path followed to reach it? The age-old family art of scolding and punishment would have to be rewritten from scratch but, instead of a new edifice, solid and consistent, what emerged was a tangled mess, an eclectic tangle of different pedagogical styles, old repressive adages mixed with liberal slogans, screaming fights and scenes and scoldings, the occasional face-slap administered for the most part out of exasperation and received as a personal offense devoid of any educational value, sob sessions, not only for the children, but also for the exhausted parents. The cold administration of punishment is replaced by a generalized state of nervous irritation. When we no longer knew what to do and who was supposed to do it, since our fathers by now recoiled from what till then had been considered a privilege but also a duty, the exercise of the punishment power, something they had held on an exclusive basis for millennia, a new attitude surfaced in the history of family relations, namely, indifference, a reluctance to interfere, to judge, and consequently, to impose sanctions on one's children's behavior, indeed, a preference not to know what that behavior even was, to intentionally remain ignorant of it, limiting oneself to a policy of *laissez faire, laissez passer* that, translated into domestic language, was something along the lines of "oh, just do whatever the hell you think best," sometimes pushed out to the edge of "as long as you don't bust my balls," roughly equivalent to the vague precept "for the love of God, just don't get into the kind of trouble that could lead to serious and lasting consequences." Let me say it again, aside from some families that are truly and stubbornly old-school, and some other families that are instead so progressive as to create a sort of latter-day phalanstery, what prevailed in nearly all of them was a hybrid, a sort of patchwork of rules, customs, prohibitions, and obligations of various extraction, veering and fading and in perennial transformation, so that what was forbidden one day might be allowed a week later, and so on for several weeks, only to return to its previous outlawed status, or maybe that was true for a son but not a daughter . . . Some parents were convinced that they'd discovered that putting on an afflicted and discontented attitude with their children, without saying a thing, or almost nothing to explain their attitude, was more effective than the open display of anger . . .

IN THOSE YEARS, the intoxication of defending tradition to the furthest extreme and the opposite thrill of shaking off tradition were mixed: generally we think of only the latter approach as somehow exalting, capable of generating euphoria, an unstoppable wave that rises higher and higher, until it sweeps away the old state of things. But truth be told, reactionaries and religious bigots were starting a riot all their own, a visceral response, a savage sentiment that came from the gut . . . that fed on desire much more than it was fueled by reality. In fact, *nobody* gave a damn about reality. It wasn't a situation with (demented) idealists on one side and (prudent) realists on the other: everyone was equally deranged. And in the demonstrations that filled the streets, where one might expect the community spirit, the collective soul, to prevail, in reality everyone was fighting for themselves alone, shouting and marching for themselves, seized by the thrill of liberty, a delirious fever of the ego that lusted for its independence, its own enjoyment. Even those seized by a nostalgia for order and authority were shaken by the violent fever of individual initiative, the determination to triumph whatever the cost—be it one's own life, or someone else's. Everyone could afford the luxury of desires, but these individual desires were further fueled by shared actions. One mistreated oneself and others with the same indifference. Everyone was alone, facing off with the dizzying risk of "living life."

Alone, and yet together with many others, lifted high on a collective wave.

THE SAME YEAR as the principal event around which this book revolves, the maximum concentration of simultaneity of the nonsimultaneous was attained, to use the brilliant expression coined by the philosopher of history Ernst Bloch, and that is to say, the miraculous coexistence and convergence in the present instant of large slabs of the past, dating back to the postwar years, and an equally substantial chunk of the future, at least extending forward to the turning point of the millennium. Half a century was compressed into a single year, in such a way that an observer could turn his gaze backward or forward, with an incredible depth, experiencing a sense of continuity and one of rupture, neither of them ever previously experienced. Time had extended, covering a very broad span, and then, suddenly, contracted, crushed, the sort of thing you see when those boulders are cut open revealing subsequent layers, forming serpentine curves of different colors.

After the fireworks celebrating the famous New Year's Eve of 2000, time stretched out again and events began to return to a spacing that corresponded to their actual cadence, the events that hadn't crossed that barrier, if even by a short span of time, slid backward down the steep slope of the past millennium, and the future returned to its process of churning up prophecies.

THEY SEEMED LIKE DEMANDS that sprang from difficult living conditions, but in fact they were the product of at least a partial liberation from those conditions. The student protest movement is living proof of the matter. That such a vast social group could dedicate itself to protesting against the established order meant that they, in plain fact, that is to say, in their condition as students, not laborers, had been freed of the basic necessity to provide for their own subsistence, a necessity that had been taken care of by the preceding generation. The established order against which they were rebelling was, in fact, the first in human history to create spaces of freedom, first of all, freedom from need, sufficient to *facilitate* the rebellion instead of *hindering* it. Whereas in the past the rebels, in small clandestine groups, challenged oppressive regimes, and their struggles almost always ended on the gallows or before a firing squad, in the mass student movements of the prosperous nations, they were fighting against a system and an economic model that had allowed those who were protesting against it to find themselves at age sixteen or eighteen or twenty in a school classroom or a university lecture hall, instead of in a manufacturing plant or tilling the fields. (In Italy the successive transition, trying to emerge from this contradiction by resolving it in a radical manner, was to go back in time, in a certain sense, tracking back thirty years or a century or even a century and a half, that is, to the old custom of underground groups, and the armed struggle. The student movement, as such—undermined by its own incongruous social composition, and the fact that it had too long breathed the overrich and inherently unstable mixture of demands for freedom and pleasure, on the one hand, and violent practices and authoritarian aspirations, on the other—dissolved, handing the initiative to paramilitary vanguard groups that fought their battle, taking inspiration from the Carbonari, the nihilists, or the partisan formations. And sure enough, after roughly a decade of relative tolerance, the state police and judiciary unleashed a campaign of repression, and this time it was the real thing, inflexible, nineteenth-century in persuasion and method, uninterested in the fine print, unconcerned about spilling blood, but with one main difference: instead of being sent to the gallows, the rebels who were captured alive were given life sentences. And so, in the course of just a few years, this alleged revolution failed.)

THE PROBLEM AROSE when the things that had been thought or said till then also began to be *done*. The threatening slogans began to be implemented. It marked the end of a hypocrisy and the beginning of a collapse. The structure was unable to withstand the impact of the truths that it had been built to guard against; and so quite soon it was inevitable that people would begin to yearn for the old hieroglyphic world, whose sloppy arcane rules, for better or worse, had held up for multiple generations, specifically because they had rejected any embarrassing truths.

WHAT IS IT that we were searching for? What was everyone looking for back then, what is it they're still looking for, or at least so it seems, searching, still searching for? Aside from justice, an idea so generic that it includes versions of opposite polarities, I believe that what each and every individual was seeking with all his might was Recognition, Acceptance, Indulgence, Approval, Redemption.

AND THE QUESTION "Who am I and what am I doing in this world?" even before it ever expected an answer, was really designed to find someone who might listen, hoped to be taken seriously by someone, a friend, a couple of friends, comrades, classmates, a girlfriend, a priest or a doctor, or anyone who might answer a call dialed at random. People who found not one of these figures, because they were as shy and prickly as a cactus, or more demanding than an English lord, would eventually address that question to a book, or else in the darkness of certain film forums, in the presence of a black-and-white film, like say *L'Atalante* or *Day of Wrath* or *The Killing* or *Destiny* or *Pierrot le Fou* or *Wild Strawberries* or *The Lost Weekend* or *Antonio das Mortes* (which was in color, however) or *Fists in the Pocket* or *The Red and the White* or *The Swindle* or *Gioventù, amore e rabbia* (called that only in Italian, originally known as *The Loneliness of the Long Distance Runner*).

THERE, THAT'S RIGHT. There was an age. That age. The age of the saturnalia. The golden age. There was an age when no prohibitions existed, no punishments existed, no laws, either, and the ones that did exist were confidently ignored or broken. An age when all social differences had been abolished, not in reality, of course, but in words, threats, and dreams. That's already something, in fact, it's a great deal. If something's easy for you to say, then you go ahead and say it. You face up to the intolerable with words, if there's no other way. It was a primordial age in which you could easily lose your life and just as easily take ownership of it, take possession of the life that others told you was already yours, but it wasn't, and the only way to seize it and call it your own was by sheer force. You had to reach out take possession of your life, by force. Force counted for a lot. It's not that punishments no longer existed: but now, instead of suffering them, you were the one who had conquered the right to administer them to those who deserved them. Who made that decision? Who were the guilty parties? And guilty of what? That was up to you, you decided, you and your handful of comrades. From the base. In a meeting. There was a general proliferation of spontaneous tribunals. Tribunals that issued sentences, and then carried them out. Some of those sentences were death sentences. Sometimes, only a few seconds passed between sentence and execution, that is, the person sentenced to death learned of his sentence at the very instant it was carried out. From a blessed absence of law, we therefore slid into an excess of it. Everyone judged everyone else. And sentenced them, too. It was a vast open-air tribunal. The state regained control and judged all those who had set out to judge in its place. There was an exponential proliferation of warrants, arrests, verdicts, sentences, mandatory life sentences, exemplary executions and punishments, and reprisals. "Strike one to educate one hundred."

7

THE PROBLEM WITH CONTEMPORARIES is that they're with you for the rest of your life. It's not like any of them age any faster or slower than you, so that you can somehow break free of them: not a bit of it, if someone is the same age as you when you're fifteen, they still will be at age fifty or sixty. From your desk at school till the day you retire, the distances remain unchanged. And this is ridiculous and tremendous. Whatever you might do to try to differentiate yourself, the chronological alignment persists, the clocks all tick in unison. You can go to the South Seas, become a slave dealer, change your sex, have six wives, or become a priest, but your contemporaries follow you outflank you wait for you around the corner, their faces covered with synchronized wrinkles. The gap in all the various aspects of life can become enormous in the meantime: there are some who are millionaires and others who don't have enough money to buy dinner, this one's on the front pages of the newspapers for murder, for bribes, because he's a cabinet minister or because he won first prize at Cannes: no matter what, next to each of them, invisible, are his classmates, as if for the year-end class picture. Certainly, there are those who might stumble, sprawl by the side of the track, fall sick or even die, but that's simply the exception that confirms the rule that the others continue marching along in line so that, seen in profile, you'd say they were all one single person.

There was a time when this unbreakable generational affiliation was marked by the intervals between wars: the ones you fought together with your contemporaries or narrowly avoided, as well as the wars you witnessed with the clear eye of childhood. Entire draft years recognized themselves and one another in the flickering light of a bombing raid. I think it was Heinrich Böll who commented ironically (in all seriousness) on the fore seeable employment crisis among the makers of gravestones in Germany that would begin in the mid-eighties, when one might have expected a wave of deaths by old age from the generation of Germans that had instead been mown down during the Second World War. A shortfall of millions of graves: a missing link, a glaring gap in the ranks of time. And, in the final analysis, a considerable spike in unemployment among the marble cutters and engravers. The dead walked arm in arm with their dwindling number of living contemporaries. In the last half century we continued, out of inertia and habit, to imagine that the dotted lines of the generations would fall along the fault lines of outbreaks of war. In the absence of wars in the West, a number of evocative surrogates have been identified: the student revolt of 1968, and then in certain countries, the years of terrorism (the "years of lead"), that is, events that resonated powerfully throughout society, even though they directly affected only a minority of the population, giving those who lived through them the sensation of experiencing a time that brought them all together, especially once that time was left behind them and, in spite of it all, missed. Key dates from which you could reckon and recount a "before" and an "after." Hence the typical postwar phenomenon, of *reducismo*, or veteran's syndrome, which marked the so-called *sessantottini*, or sixty-eighters, so indelibly: the line of the awkward slogan, "those years were formidable." Jesus, yes, it must have been hard to shake loose of that band of brothers of their contemporaries! Scratch away the demographic proximity that continued to push them forward, all in a single line, like the croupier's rake pushing the chips along the green felt, even when their fates had diverged to an inconceivable degree: one had become the undersecretary for agricultural policy, another is a television host, a third is in prison, but they're all united by the bags under their eyes and the old gray locks of hair, hallmarks of an era that was thought, rightly or wrongly, to have been heroic.

I'M TEMPTED to wonder what impact we had on the world, or, to take it down a notch, on Italy, on the city, on our quarter, on our workplace, in my circle of friends—there must be some circle, however small, where my presence left a mark, for better or worse, an imprint . . . and, for that matter, the 1970s, a decade I entered at age thirteen and left at age twenty-three, decisive years, what did they produce that was any good? Any good for the collective, I mean to say, and not just for that teenager and that young man?

IT ISN'T TRUE that feelings and dreams are always subjective. There are such things as objective feelings and dreams, especially collective ones. What do we lose by being born in a certain year instead of, say, not even an entirely different generation, but just three or four years before or after the year we actually were born? Or, for that matter, what do we gain? Into what events do we slide unconsciously or happen to lurch into unexpectedly, and what kind of a moment was it: the right one or the wrong one? Does the wave of the new hit us and drown us, or does it lift us upward, into the heights, if we have the right age to ride it, neither too young and naïve but also not too mature and already part of the mechanism, cynical?

My father, born in 1926, was too young to go to war, and then he caught the economic boom times that followed, at the prime of his strength and energy, at its full. I, theoretically, could have done the same thing, in the years when so many of my contemporaries stuffed their pockets (I was born in Rome in 1956), during the new twenty-year era of expansion between 1980 and 2000, since I was the exact same age as my father was when he stuffed his pockets full, but the miracle wasn't repeated. Why not? Perhaps for two essential reasons: the first is that the family pockets were in fact already sufficiently full that I no longer felt such a powerful urge to stuff them any fuller; and yet, for that matter, those family pockets were not stuffed so *extraordinarily full* as the pockets of a genuinely wealthy man, of someone who can live off the interest of their estate, or a captain of industry, that I might feel the obligation to compete in the amassing of wealth, or the need to hand down a mighty financial empire. None of all this. As the scion of the family, in other words, I had no obligation, of the sort one might have felt either toward great poverty or great wealth—to emancipate oneself from the former, or to conserve and grow the latter. Neither a poverty to be stamped out nor a prestige to be expanded could influence my decisions. And so I chose a nonprofession, a noncareer.

AND FROM THE POINT OF VIEW of the literary generation? I think it over . . . and all of a sudden, I have a flash, the doubt occurs to me that practically no great Italian writer has ever been born in the middle of a century, so that they would have been about fifty when their century was coming to an end. Never once, in eight hundred years of Italian literature . . . Could that be?

This brilliant thought occurs while I'm teaching a lesson in prison (in fact), and I'm dying to check it out immediately: and so I set my class of convicts an exercise in analyzing the parts of speech in a sentence, and while they struggle with the task, I sit down and leaf through an old textbook on the history of Italian literature to check out my hypothesis.

Here we are, Manzoni, certainly, 1785 . . . Ludovico Ariosto, 1474 . . . Parini, 1729 . . . Dante, Petrarch, Boccaccio, and Leopardi, it goes without saying . . . and Moravia, Montale . . . Ungaretti, Calvino, Fenoglio, Dino Campana, Foscolo, no need to check . . . Let's take a look at others I'm less sure about. Guinizzelli: between 1230 and 1240. Machiavelli: 1469. Let's try Giovan Battista Marino . . . exactly a century later, 1569. Giambattista Vico: 1668. Pirandello: 1867. They were thirty years old, or younger, when their century turned.

. . . Galilei? 1564. Guicciardini? 1483 . . . Nievo, 1831. Carducci, 1808. Goldoni, 1707 . . .

Hmmm, let's try with the author of *Pinocchio*, Carlo Collodi, I haven't the slightest idea of when he might have been born . . . no good here, either, 1826. I would have thought later.

I leaf furiously through the history of Italian literature, opening here and there at random.

Giovanni Battista Guarini . . . 1538. Jacopone da Todi . . . 1232. Luigi Settembrini, 1813. Ruzante, 1496, with a question mark.

I start looking for specific names.

Metastasio? 1698.

Pico della Mirandola? 1463.

Lapo Gianni . . . no one knows when he was born or when he died.

Pomponazzi? 1462.

Fuck, I can't find a single one born in the fifties of any century!

Rummaging through patriots, prolific authors, sonneteers, novelists, not a single one! There could be Savonarola, but can we really consider him a writer? And the lesser authors, Arrigo Boito (1842), Guido Gozzano (1883), Grazia Deledda (who is hardly a minor figure, she won the Nobel Prize), 1871 . . . Carlo Gozzi (1720) . . . Let's try Aleardo Aleardi . . . he's not in the book (I'll check later, at home, on Google: 1812).

Among the greats, there's only Tasso (born in Sorrento, March 11, 1544) who comes close, and perhaps it's no accident that this teetering between two ages is what drove him mad . . . and then, by a hair, Italo Svevo, 1861, misses belonging to the decade that I'm seeking, but he's a unique, isolated, misunderstood author . . . he had to wait until he was old, a very old man, to . . .

In the end, I find my man: it's Pascoli. Giovanni Pascoli, born in San Mauro di Romagna, on December 31, 1855! A century and a year before me.

(If you like, Marco Polo, too: Venice, September 15, 1254.)

It wasn't easy to predict what could come, whether for better or worse, out of a generation whose ears had been filled with such sounds and lyrics as (untranslatably) *precipitevolissimevolmente, quel motivetto che ti piace tanto, tu sei simpatica, tango delle capinere, tipitipitipso col calipso, violino zigano, ma le gambe, ho un sassolino nella scarpa, ahi!, abat-jour,* and Nicola Arigliano's discouraging *venti chilometri al giorno.*

For that matter, at this point in the new millennium, that generation ought to have shown the best and the worst it had to offer.

HISTORY (whether we spell it with a capital or a lower-case "h") in any case, begins in a school run by priests on Via Nomentana, which at the time was a relatively outlying area considering that, just a few minutes of traffic farther out, once you'd left the populated settlement of Montesacro behind you, you found yourself in the open countryside. Via Nomentana, lined with pine trees and therefore shrouded in perennial shade, wound on through fields inundated with light, climbing and dropping as, every Wednesday afternoon, or else on Mondays, or Tuesdays, or Thursdays, depending on your age and the class section you were in, at 2:30 p.m., aboard a school bus, a certain number of students from the SLM Religious Institute were taken to the playing fields for a couple hours of physical education. What was primarily meant by physical education was chasing one another back and forth across dusty red fields, kicking up clouds of the stuff that, during periods of drought, were thick enough to screen the runners from sight, as they chased after an old leather soccer ball, dry and hard, which almost always seemed to be retrieved only to be sent sailing toward the opposite side of the field. Except for a few skilled soloists, who managed to keep the ball between their feet for a few seconds, the others, including yours truly, immediately rid themselves of the ball with a sharp forward kick, lofting it through the air like in rugby. The game as it is played today, with its spiderweb of passing in all directions, was unknown to us.

WHEN I FOUND my old quiz booklet *Take Your Tests*, with the scores written in pencil on the last page, I was able to gauge the abyss that separated me and Arbus. I had an IQ of 118, while Arbus was 27 points ahead of me, with an intelligence quotient of 145. And what did he do with all those extra points? Nothing, it seems to me. Have you read Arbus's name in any newspapers, in any professional journals? What did he invent, how has he distinguished himself? When you're already very intelligent, maybe there's no point to becoming even smarter. That surplus, it would almost seem, is designed to be frittered away along the way. And come to think of it: what have *I* achieved, with the score I managed to rack up?

Intelligence isn't useful in the slightest. I've come to that conclusion after spending a lifetime hearing people tell me that I'm intelligent. The real meaning behind those declarations, variously charged with affection, admiration, envy, love, pity, scorn, and even hatred, consisted of a "but," and it rested on that adversative conjunction, suspending the phrase and filling it with unknown elements, "You're intelligent, but . . . ," ". . . too bad that . . . ," and anyone could fill those ellipses with a conclusion at will: too bad that you're lazy, you're cold and remote, you're so uneven, arrogant, spoiled, too bad that you lack the balls, that you squander your opportunities, you meander, you don't know what to do with that intelligence, you don't know how to communicate it, to share it, to put it to good use, concentrate it, donate it, that fucking intelligence of yours . . . ! In other words, why don't you take your intelligence and stick it up your ass! Now, if this is what happened, or at least in part what happened to me, only partly a dropout, then we can just imagine how things went for Arbus!

He truly was a wasted genius.

What happened to him was not so much that his intelligence was recognized, as that it was charged as a crime. He was accused from dawn to dusk every day of being intelligent. Whatever his test scores, his teachers never tired of pestering him, insisting that he could do more, even more, much much more. "Someone with a brain like yours, eh . . . !?" His mother seemed to scorn his gift, overabundant but useless, seeing that it wasn't accompanied by such basic virtues as good looks and charm. On the rare occasions that he was willing to speak, after the initial burst of astonishment on all sides, his classmates couldn't wait for him to shut up again, since the things he said immediately demonstrated the paucity and stupidity of all the things they had said and thought: his statements then either provoked surprise or weren't understood in the slightest, making his classmates either fall silent or laugh, which are our instinctive reactions in the face of all forms of greatness. Whether it was brimming over with admiration or contempt, the way that we, his classmates, invariably reacted after Arbus had had his say amounted to this: "The egghead has spoken!"

"WHAT AM I SUPPOSED TO DO, hit myself in the head so the other guys won't feel so stupid?"

SPEAKING OF IQS, by the way: I don't remember whether I've mentioned him in the preceding pages, and if so, probably in passing, but we did have a classmate who was an idiot, a real idiot, Crasta, also known as Kraus, or Three-Toed Sloth, whom I ought to mention. During lessons, he had a habit of cleaning the inside of his ears with the cap of his ballpoint pen. He'd alternate the top of the cap and the sharp edge of the clip that held the pen to the shirt pocket, to clean out the really stubborn chunks of earwax. It was pretty disgusting. Until one fine day, while Kraus was turning and twisting the cap in his ear, we never did figure out just how, the pen got stuck in there, first the whole thing, then just the cap, and it couldn't be extracted, no matter how hard we tried to pull it, till we were afraid we'd hurt him. So he had to be taken off to the emergency room.

NO ONE EVER PAID the slightest attention to Kraus, but it's precisely with this existence devoid of any particular details or interest that God was setting us a problem, placing us all face-to-face with an insoluble enigma. Who was Kraus? Why was he in the world? The enigma of Kraus remained one in part because, in fact, no one had bothered to delve into it, explain it;

its solution attracted no one, and our classmate appeared so nondescript and insignificant, and his personality so weak and superficial, that it would have been a waste of time even to suppose that he concealed anything profound in his depths, anything to look for.

IN OTHER WORDS, his life must have a significance of some kind, but it isn't visible to the untutored eye. It's pretty nondescript, like a worm or a rock along a trail, the kind of thing you're not sure whether to crush underfoot or kick into the woods or just leave there, after all, it makes no difference, it amounts to nothing, there's no point in savaging it or pitying it . . . But if the Creator, who assigns such importance to each component of the universe, even the tiniest and lowliest particle, and who blows His vital spirit every day into the universe to preserve it, surely ought to have tried harder with Kraus, then He ought to have told us loud and clear that this was a boy like any other, and not, say, a stone or an insect or I don't know what else.

8

AT SLM, the Italian teacher, Giovanni Vilfredo Cosmo, constituted a unique case. Tall, gangly, slightly stooped, he frequently wore red pullovers and checked jackets. He had a smile, or rather a grin, stamped permanently on his wrinkled face; it didn't seem to be due to anything in particular, except the protruding and smoke-yellowed set of teeth that his negroid lips struggled to contain, reminiscent of an actor who was popular in those years, the star, after costarring in lots of other movies, of the extremely violent and delirious western *Bring Me the Head of Alfredo Garcia*— Warren Oates. Aside from his sarcastic smirk—which never, however, expressed his true feelings, if anything, it concealed them, tucking them away behind the armor of his encyclopedic culture—Cosmo gave the impression that he was mocking the priests, us students, his lay colleagues and his religious ones, and ultimately himself, as well. He never dropped that cheerfully disenchanted attitude and was the only one who seemed capable of maintaining it even around the headmaster, whose arrival in class for the ritual lectures or the distribution of report cards he was accustomed to hail with bows and hyperbole, like a courtier greeting the passage of the Sun King. "Boys, please welcome in a manner befitting Himself, the incarnation, both in his physical and in his symbolic body, of the power that towers above us all. Up, up, on your feet!" and we would all rise and stand in an equally solemn fashion, though with faint smiles on our lips. "Don't make fun, teacher, please don't mock . . . they won't understand," the headmaster always retorted, flattered but also a little intimidated by and worried about Cosmo. Irony is a double-edged sword, and in his presence the headmaster realized that he lacked any exclusive rights to it. "Good heavens! I'm deadly serious!" our teacher would continue his skirmishing. "We all are here, aren't we, boys?" and meanwhile, with a gesture, like the director of a symphony orchestra, he'd have us sit again. The only thing he actually treated seriously was his profession, that of a high school literature teacher, however much everyone might continue to proclaim their astonishment and puzzle over why such a brilliant man could ever have wound up on the payroll of a private school, instead of occupying an endowed chair at some university, or some other prestigious position. With the mind he possessed, the very idea that he'd spend his days lecturing to a room full of apathetic pampered brats about Arcadia, correcting with strokes of a red ballpoint pen the twisted syntax of essays about a day at the beach or Dante's Count Ugolino. "Pausing in his savage meal, the sinner raised His mouth . . .": for the past thirty years he had done nothing other than to unfurl those immortal lines and comment upon them to audiences that might vary in level, but which were always and inevitably unworthy. He'd never moved on: Why not? What is that had blocked him there, stranded at SLM, like Robinson Crusoe on his desert island? We should point out that he never seemed discontented or frustrated, truth be told. Given his great worth and illustrious reputation, which in turn reflected favorably on the school, there was a persistent rumor that the priests paid him a salary almost twice what any of the other teachers earned. What's more, they allowed him to cluster his classes in the first few days of the week so that he was free to zip around in his Lamborghini, attending jazz concerts; he was in fact a respected and widely recognized expert on jazz. He possessed, actually, one of the most complete and valuable private jazz record collections, and word was that he was a first-class percussionist, an implacable rhythm machine, or had been before arthritis took the drumsticks out of his hands, useful now at the very most for turning the almost impalpable pages of an old edition of the *Divine Comedy*, tattered and dog-eared from years of lessons. Always the same lessons. The golden, featherlight burden of literature. The ritual office of scholastic repetition. There were others who would hint darkly at some very grave incident that had taken place when Cosmo was still young, something that had forced him, so to speak, to withdraw from the world, like a sort of latter-day Fra Cristoforo; but instead of in a monastery, he had locked himself up in the modernist fortress of SLM, mortifying himself in the humiliating role of anonymous high school teacher, safe from the temptation of undertaking a brilliant literary or academic career. Except about jazz, he'd never been willing to write a line of his own, at least that anyone knew of or that had been published; nor had we learned the nature of the terrible sin of Cosmo's youth that he was laboring to expiate.

I owe him a great deal, far too much. If I write books, I owe that to him, and I think the same could be said for the other writer who emerged from that class, Marco Lodoli. Not that we didn't already have a passion deep inside us when we were assigned Cosmo as a teacher our first year of high school: but it was only when we met Cosmo that that passion found the recognition and nourishment that it required. The libraries of books we had at home, bookshelves lining wood-paneled walls, suddenly came to life, and Cosmo made sure to add the pinch of salt of a myriad of titles our parents could never have thought of while they were assembling what they reckoned to be the necessary array of books for the apartment of a family of educated professionals (both our fathers were engineers, Lodoli's and my own), considering the aesthetic effect, the spines bound in morocco leather, the prestigious collections of classics purchased wholesale, and which filled entire shelves in their orderly array. There is nothing that can offer such a restful and powerful visual rhythm as a collection of Loeb classics. Things were slightly different for Arbus. He already had a genius-level academic at home, at least theoretically, since in fact his father was never there. Music, his sister the pianist, etc., completed the intellectual array. And then, as I have explained more than once, it was unlikely to think of Arbus being swayed by anyone's allure. I mean to say, of any flesh-and-blood human being. And there can be no doubt that a teacher exerts his authority in the form of an allure, his fascination as a conductor of impulses: the allure of the things he says, of his eyes as they sweep the classroom in search of other eyes, of the natural gestures that accompany a reading or an explanation, and then there's the timbre of the voice. Cosmo, truth be told, didn't have an especially lovely voice, in fact, quite the contrary: it came from the depths of his throat and sometimes squeaked into a strident, overexcited pitch, like an owl's cry, and then dropped back down to grave and somber tones, which almost made the windowpanes rattle. Perhaps it was precisely this continual and quite theatrical oscillation, and his vivid and vigorous activity, that kept us glued to his lessons, or at least, I should speak for myself, because other classmates, for example Scarnicchi, who by no accident was also known as the Dormouse, would sleep through Cosmo's classes the same way they did with De Laurentiis or Brother Gildo and just as they would have done with Gas&Svampa if the blows from the wooden pointer hadn't kept them awake and alert. Arbus was extremely focused and attentive, he listened to and evaluated the concepts, ignoring everything else, indifferent to the pantomime and the seduction. As if he were able to pass unscathed through the aura of emotions until he reached the core of the formulations. And he recognized that, in effect, many of the concepts expressed by Cosmo were indeed interesting and deserving of examination and in-depth exploration. But he certainly wasn't *captivated* by him. And he immediately dropped everything that would normally be classed under the heading of "personal opinions." Arbus detested "personal opinions" in general, and in particular those purveyed by teachers. He'd confided that fact in me alone. "Do we really have to sit here listening to his likes and dislikes?" he would ask, polishing his glasses with the tail of his shirt, untucked from his trousers. "Plus, also, *exactly* what does beautiful or ugly mean? True or false? Explained like that, or perhaps we should say, *not* explained, it means very little, this is idle chitchat, not teaching, phrases tossed out then and there by an individual who is clearly concealing problems of some kind." He was thinking about the emotional tirades of poor De Laurentiis, the soliloquies of Mr. Golgotha, the irritated and slightly hysterical retorts of Brother Gildo, who whenever one of us, either out of a scrupulous desire to understand or a devious wish to annoy, raised a hand and said they hadn't clearly understood a certain passage, never had anything to say, other than to repeat, enunciating clearly, every single word that he had just uttered, never altering so much as a comma, exactly like a student who has learned a chunk of the book by heart.

But Cosmo understood that what Arbus was talking about wasn't the kind of nitpicking that the smartest kid in class engaged in on a whim, but rather a very specific cognitive system. And he did his best to explain to him that literature couldn't be subjected to that system by its own specific nature. Whoever found themselves talking about it or interpreting it could not hope to avail themselves of clear and certain laws. And so one is forced to remain in the field of detestable "opinions." Something that's changeable, wobbly, not entirely subject to verification.

"And you know something, Arbus? In the final analysis, that a certain poem pleases you or doesn't please you is something that no can determine in advance, just as they can't force you to like it or keep you from liking it. No one can hinder your pleasure or transmute your dislike into anything else but a false consciousness. Do you understand that, Arbus? And the rest of you scamps and scoundrels, do you understand that?"

He often called us that, scamps and scoundrels.

Terminology with a delightful hint of desuetude, nowadays.

I confess, this thing that Cosmo said sometime around 1973, I only finally grasped around 2013, very recently, in the time, that is, since I have lulled myself into thinking that I've not only grasped the true meaning of the term "false consciousness," in general, but also that I've identified what constitutes *my own* false consciousness, where it resides, what it is, in other words, what is so irremediably *false* in me, because it is generated by the anxiety to cover over what can only be covered over, in fact, with a lie. Forget about literature, it is only an exemplum or a field of application of this mode of proceeding: it is the glove that covers the hand, it's not the hand itself, it's a delightful artificial hand, made of hides skillfully tanned and stitched to fit an ideal hand. We're not talking about literature here, but rather any pleasurable or elevating or mortifying or dolorous experience of ours . . .

I don't know whether or not Arbus ever understood it. Perhaps he grasped it instantly, because his prodigious intelligence was capable of accommodating paradoxes, or perhaps he still roams this world (wherever he may be: *O, brother, where art thou?*) devoid of this understanding. A prisoner of his own limitations, boundaries that were erected by a mind too powerful to surrender, to allow itself to be overwhelmed by superfluous elements. Pleasure is invariably superfluous, puerile, and hence unacceptable. Cosmo's wisdom lay not in his erudition, disproportionate for a high school teacher, but rather in the fact that he had chosen to lay down his arms. That he had unbuckled his suit of armor: the armor of his sarcasm, which he exercised so frequently, but not to the point of making him inhuman. In this (but only in this, let me be clear) he resembled somewhat Courbet, the pornographic artist who taught phys ed at Giulio Cesare High School.

I believe that each of us has been given a Cosmo in his life, in the canonical role of teacher, or else athletic coach, uncle, poker player, tramp, manicurist, busker, therapist, big brother, an older brother even if he happens to be younger, and their influence has been decisive, for better or for worse. The Cosmo that you happen to run into is responsible for nothing other than to have made us become what we already were.

9

REALIZED ALL OF THIS much more clearly when I changed schools. They told me that Cosmo made a sarcastic comment about my decision. "Bravo, Albinati! He screwed up *big time*." I couldn't say whether, buried deep in this hasty, acid, and from a certain point of view irrefutable wisecrack there might not have been a hint of regret, seeing that at a single fell swoop, the teacher had lost two of his finest students: a genuine disciple, yours truly, and the multifaceted brilliance of Arbus, whom he couldn't perhaps claim as a follower, but it was certainly better to have him in your class than kids like Three-Toed Sloth or the perverted d'Avenia or rebels without a cause like Chiodi or Jervi. In the case of my super-gifted classmate, Arbus, Cosmo at least could grasp his frenzy to leave the school, to be done once and for all, and in haste, with that cycle that had proved so mortifying for him. My decision was more controversial, and could be viewed as a betrayal, an abjuration. One that had been leveled directly at him. It was, after all, Cosmo I was turning my back on, not the priests and holy mass and the swimming pool, or, say, Gas&Svampa. Cosmo was the teacher I was disavowing. What's more, I had chosen a delicate moment, I was leaving just when things were getting good: Cosmo had been patiently revving his engine for two years of high school, waiting to launch himself on the modern authors, the ones who were closest to us, when the Italian curriculum would turn incandescent for an apprentice man-of-letters like me, from Leopardi to the Romantics and on up to Baudelaire's flowers of evil and the Surrealists . . . and just then, of all times, I was turning to go. But maybe he really didn't care all that much: he'd had bright students before me and he'd have others after me. In the meantime, he still had Lodoli to talk to about poetry, Rummo with his uncrushable seriousness, young believer that he was, the miniaturistic zeal of Zipoli, Modiano's good cheer, Picchiatello's tics to keep under control, and a few others to usher respectably over the finish line. That was the role that Cosmo had chosen for himself: ferryman.

IT'S A SHAME that the notes I took at school have been lost. Especially those stunning summaries and outlines of philosophy and Italian under the protection of whose array, as if beneath the shields of a Roman tortoise formation, we took our final exams, marching forward in serried ranks, grinding through one author after another and leaving the field behind us littered with them: Schleiermacher, Jacobi, Fichte, Schelling, Hegel, Feuerbach . . .

Official sheets of graph paper teeming with concepts and notions, as dense and heavy as honeycombs fresh from the hive. The ramifications of the square brackets that multiplied and proliferated, forming funnel diagrams.

They were handed over to the girls who took their final exams the year after we did at Giulio Cesare. They wound up being sold between the pages, overloaded with underlinings, of textbooks on the used-book stands.

But a few years ago, something popped out of the second volume of Sapegno's *Compendium of the History of Italian Literature*, which had surfaced in a cellar carrel that had to be cleared out in the aftermath of a death in the family, several little pages ripped out of the heart of a notebook and folded in half, with notes that hadn't been jotted down, but rather painstakingly copied, in the handwriting I had as a teenager: slanting to the right, in an effort at regularity and a display of character. Rereading those notes, I realized that they were copied from notes taken by none other than Arbus during Cosmo's lessons on Machiavelli—he had let me borrow them afterward, so that I could copy them for myself.

The block-print heading, likewise leaning at close to a forty-five-degree angle, read: THE PRINCE.

No easy matter, at first glance, and without going back to check, to say which of those concepts, numbered progressively, belonged to the original text, or to what extent they might instead be Cosmo's own thoughts, or even whether Arbus might have added something of his own, in his processing of them. Like a fairy tale when you tell it to a little child, the concepts are formulated in an ever-changing fashion, until they're no longer even the same ideas, and their paternity becomes hopelessly muddled. They become *public domain*. Recopying them below, forty years later, I can hardly withstand the temptation to modify them and add a few things of my own, a dozen or so lines scattered here and there, but for one specific reason: it may be an impression induced by all the time I've been neck-deep in the story, but some of the observations of Machiavelli-Cosmo-Arbus are reminiscent of the murder that this book is based on.

1. If you are going to insult someone, then you might as well do it in a serious fashion; because he will be able to take revenge for minor insults, but grave or mortal ones, he will not. In the CR/M (as in many other crimes and murders, for that matter), it is only by eliminating the victims, only by "snuffing them out" (this is the eloquent verb used by Mac.), that we can avoid being prosecuted for them. Death makes those who have suffered a wrong incapable of paying it back in the same tender. As Stalin liked to say, after issuing orders to liquidate someone: "No man, no problem."

2. It is by no means true that time heals all wounds; quite the contrary, more often than not, time makes things worse.

3a. Every man's natural desire is to acquire, not to lose; to increase, not to diminish; to grow, not to decay. Possession is the unmistakable end that everyone seeks; in various fashions. There are, however, things and even persons whose possession can only be secured (or the illusion of whose possession can only be secured) in one way: by destroying them. Like the spendthrifts in Dante's *Inferno*, who celebrate their patrimony by squandering it, they are owners only when, in fact, they cease to own. For them, destruction becomes a radical form of possession. It is nothing more than an even cruder variant on Oscar Wilde's famous line: Each man kills the thing he loves. Each man possesses that which he annihilates, and so, a man is rich only in that which he squanders and devastates.

3b. You possess only that which you are free, at any time and on the slightest whim, to spend, give away, disown, or destroy. Any limitation on your free will to make those choices or perform those actions is a limitation on your genuine ownership.

4. One's patrimony outlives one's paternity, survives the father. It represents proof of the durability of the legacy of blood. Therefore, men mourn the loss of it far more bitterly than they ever will that of their parent.

5. Love depends upon the one who loves; fear depends upon the one who strikes it into the heart. Love cannot be aroused by us; fear can. We can far more easily arouse fear in someone than we can make them fall in love.

6. Chiron, the preceptor, is half man and half horse. Why that half-beast in the preceptor?

7a. What you truly are deep down, you cannot change; what you merely appear, you can when needed transform, modify, adjust, if the situation so requires.

7b. Truly being what you seem to be may prove risky or even pernicious.

8. There is more life, more hatred, more thirst for vengeance than you'd ever suspect by considering the "tranquil" and "peaceful" existence of humanity: a teeming mass of violent and senseless and filthy desires is concealed beneath that scab.

9. Like archers, you must aim beyond the targets that you mean to hit.

10. It is easy to persuade a people, much harder to keep them firm in that persuasion.

11. Some never stumble along the way only because they fly above the path.

12. Like certain diseases: which would be easy to cure when they're hard to identify, and then become easy to diagnose but, by now, impossible to cure. (The irremediable contradiction beyond knowledge and action.)

13. While philosophers and priests cannot do it, artists will be required to "speak well of evil." (If, that is, "of evil one can rightly speak well.")

14. Acts of violence must all be done at once; kindnesses a few at a time.

15. It's easy to make the people your friend if they wish nothing more than to allow themselves to be oppressed; it is easy to oppress the people by giving them the impression that you are not oppressing them.

16a. There are sins; but they are never the same as the sins you accuse yourself of.

16b. People willingly accuse themselves of any and all sins, except the ones they've actually committed.

17. Slow acquisitions, lightning losses.

18. Referring to invisible entities, and precisely because they are concealed in the depths and rarely verifiable, among all human qualities, the most external and the easiest to simulate is religiosity; that is why it runs the risk of seeming hypocritical even when it is authentic. And so it comes naturally to mistrust priests in general and devout Catholics.

19. To be armed is to be gratified. A weapon expands your consciousness and enhances the physical and mental dimensions of he who holds it in his grip. A weapon multiplies his possibilities. All at once, he can become rich, be revered and feared, rectify that which strikes him as wrong, reach that which is distant, put an end to stories that have been dragging on for too long, and settle accounts once and for all. Those who have ever leveled a firearm have experienced sensations that the unarmed man can't begin to imagine.

20. You engender hatred both with bad deeds, that much is obvious, and with good deeds, Machiavelli opines. At the opposite extreme, I conclude, you can gain gratitude and love both by doing good and by doing evil. That's right, even by doing evil you can win love, perhaps even in a more profound and visceral fashion. We are, in fact, disproportionately grateful to those who do harm to our enemies. And sometimes we're even grateful to those who do harm directly to us. Thank you! Thank you for having mistreated us, humiliated us, kept us in chains, submissive and degraded. If only this weren't considered a pathology, but a common disposition of the human soul, just think how many forms of behavior that are apparently inexplicable would instead become as clear as daylight!

21. What is offensive is not so much the fact of dying but the way in which you die.

22. You invent an enemy to fight him, defeat him, and become great, or at least feel you are great.

23. Arms are sacred only when they become your last hope.

24. If everyone starts telling you the truth to your face, it means you are no longer respected.

25. In Italy there is never any shortage of material to give shape to, in fact, there's an overabundance. It would take centuries to work through it all, taking on its various challenges. The problem is that a great deal of this material already has a shape, and it's a mediocre one at best; and the rest of the material yet to be given a shape is so horrible, in and of itself, that you're afraid of giving it one. That is why writers wind up talking about nothing at all; or if they do talk about anything, they don't rise above the level of idle chitchat. They lack the courage to give shape to what is formless: and what they find already clumsily expressed in clichés and commonplaces, they prefer

to leave as they found it, or at the very most, they simply reinforce it. The only contribution writers bring to bear is a surplus of formal vehemence, which almost never even dreams of delving into the substance of the thing. And in the meantime, the mountain of material continues to grow and grow . . .

10

DO YOU SEE THIS RED?" asked Cosmo, plucking at his usual sweater. "Well, they were convinced that that's the way my sympathies tended. Which is why they feared me and they respected me. They hadn't understood a damned thing. But that misunderstanding happened to come in handy for them and for me. I maintained my Olympian detachment from the rest, and they could show the world how open-minded they were, how liberal they were, to have a Communist teacher in their ranks. A Communist, but a first-class teacher. Without ever openly using the term 'Communist,' at SLM they boasted that they had a left-wing teacher who served as a counterweight to the right-wing teachers. It's the same thing that happened at the major bourgeois newspapers: they'd include articles in their op-ed sections by some writer or other who'd launch a ferocious attack on the bourgeois system. The truth is that in Italy, anticommunism never had an easy go of it because, deep down, more or less everyone admires the Communists, even those who fear them and hate them. And so they made use of my youthful transgressions to invent a character who doesn't exist, Cosmo the Red. Everyday open-mindedness is such a scant commodity that all you need to do is express half an uncommon idea, no, a quarter of an uncommon idea, and you'll promptly be taken for a subversive intellectual. Using this yardstick, Plato, Nietzsche, and Leopardi would be taken for Communists. Intelligence in and of itself is subversive. That's why I don't mind that they continue to think the wrong thing of me. It means that they respect me, they fear me, and they consider me to be precious. A school's teaching faculty is like a soccer team: every position has to be covered. Here at SLM, I'm the left wing, lightning fast, versatile, unpredictable. But it is their preconceptions that demand this of me. Catholicism demands completeness, it feels it must be inclusive, herd opposites together, close the circle. Embrace, always embrace. Its most powerful symbol is the colonnade of St. Peter's Square. And I, in my red sweater, am easy to spot in that enormous square . . . It's him! Yes, that's him, they say, the Communist! And they strike up a hymn of thanks."

He's different, which means he's someone *like* us . . . one *of us* . . .

THIS IS WHAT Cosmo revealed to me in a dream that I had about a month ago. Perhaps it's a reverberation from the work I'm doing on this book and the mnemonic effort that is transmuted into oblique inventions. In actual fact, I don't believe that Cosmo ever said anything nearly so explicit, or if he did, it wasn't to me. Maybe he didn't even think these things. In the dream, we were in a rowboat, just he and I, in the middle of a volcanic lake with steep, wooded sides, it might have been Lake Nemi. I was fore, rowing, and he was aft, reasoning aloud, recounting, with a bemused tone. At a certain point I noticed that there was several inches of water in the bottom of the boat. "Don't worry," he told me, "we can always walk." Walk *where*? I thought to myself, walk on water, like Jesus? And I burst out laughing. As if he'd read my mind, Cosmo nodded, baring his yellow teeth in a broad goofy Warren Oates smirk, which this time wasn't a bit ironic, just sweet, gentle, faintly melancholy. From the lakeshore came the rustling of reeds. A light breeze was blowing. The boat sank lower and lower in the water and by now my elbows were getting wet as I rowed, the oarlocks were underwater, the oars were four-fifths wet. "Jerusalem! Jerusalem!" Cosmo said, pointing toward the shore. "Where? Where?" "Down there." But all I could see was a cabin with fishing nets hanging out in front, tossing in the evening breeze. He took off his sweater, thinking I might be cold, and told me: "You put it on. I'm sure it will fit you perfectly."

"What about you, teacher, what will you do?"

"I'll do what I've always done."

You don't ask anything more of a man than to do his duty. In the snow or the wind or on horseback or a racetrack with fast cars zipping by just inches away. "I'll do what I've always done." Which is what? What is it that you did, Cosmo? Why didn't you ever tell us, loud and clear? Why didn't you at least tell me, in secret, I who was your favorite pupil? He who does good in concealment, without boasting of it, is surely admirable, but in that way he'll never teach anyone a thing. You ought to be able to see him, imitate him, learn from him. Sooner or later, discretion will kill the discreet man. Cosmo's red sweater, as it turned out, fit me perfectly. It kept me warm, in spite of the fact that it was soaking wet. It helped me to stay afloat, even after darkness fell and I could no longer see the shore, or the boat, or my teacher.

II

THERE'S A TYPE OF mental or spiritual Fascist who believes he can forge reality with the strength of his will. With his resolute spirit. Forge, that's right, "forge" is exactly the right verb: it gives the idea of the blisteringly hot temperatures, of the sledgehammer blows, of the showers of sparks with which one bends a recalcitrant material to one's will. The examples are of Roman origin, such as Mucius Scaevola, or else they're Asian—the master of martial arts who smashes stacks of bricks with his forehead or remains solidly planted on both feet while seven others try to shove him aside.

In our class there was one like that, still in the apprenticeship phase.

Ferrazza was a pudgy boy, his nose sprinkled with freckles, who had a fuzzy pronunciation of the letter "r," so that it sounded like a "v," quite effeminate. His fascism consisted in an adoration of the real man, and a real man is what he decided to be, no two ways about it. Decisive and disciplined. There are no limits that can stand in the way of a real man's will if it is driven by an authentic inner strength, calm and unyielding. All sensations can be manipulated: they are under our control and it's entirely up to us whether we enjoy or suffer, dominate or be dominated. Therefore Ferrazza came to school in January in nothing but shirtsleeves. A light shirt made of multicolored silk, always the same. He never wore an overcoat, not even a sweater. In order to ensure that people took note of his imperturbability, his utter indifference to the foolish conventions that lesser souls call "winter" or "spring," he would stand, arms folded across his chest, in shirtsleeves, motionless in the middle of the courtyard during recess, where all the others, however soundly bundled up they might be, kept moving urgently to warm up, slapping their hands against their thighs. Not him, he stood there unruffled, with a faint smile on his face, a smile veined with scorn. If someone asked him, "Hey, Ferrazza, aren't you cold standing there in shirtsleeves?" he'd reply, condescendingly, in that accent of his that put "v" in place of "r": "Cold? Cold, me? Why on eavth should I be?" and then he'd extinguish his laughter, turning serious. "Maybe *you've* cold, but I'm cevtainly not."

"Ferrazza, I'm cold because it *is* cold . . ."

Ferrazza would shake his head.

These stupid materialists, he would think, when will they learn their lesson? When will they take off the blinders that keep them from seeing?

"No, you've cold because . . . because you *believe* that you've cold, because *you want* to be cold," he replied with a patience inspired by his spiritual compassion. "You see all the others weaving an ovehcoat, you know that it's winteh, so you convince youhself that *it's vight* to feel cold . . . not because you veally feel cold. You go along with what the masses believe, ov actually . . . what the masses demand that you think."

"Masses? What masses are you talking about?"

Ferrazza would respond with a shrug.

"Maybe so. You might be right, Ferrazza. Even so, though, today it's *fucking cold out.*"

Arbus and I avoided him because we felt sorry for him. Except for touting his philosophy of imperturbability and spiritual control, he wasn't capable of doing anything at all, he was practically flunking every subject, he was a terrible soccer player and he swam like a marionette, in part because he insisted on attacking every challenge, so different each from the other, with the same identical samurai spirit, the spirit of a rigid and solemn samurai. Whenever he got his hands on the ball, in volleyball, he'd unfailingly send it straight up to hit the gymnasium ceiling.

Almost no one could stand being around him, yet he had convinced himself that it was he, with his magnetism, who rejected all the others and kept them at a safe distance. There was no joking around on this matter. "Pvoximity vendehs evevything so vulgah. Because . . . *only at a distance can you be my stah,*" he loved to state with an air of mystery.

HE STRUCK THE POSES of a shaman or a dictator. He believed he was capable of summoning up whatever he desired with the sheer force of his mind. He declared that he was capable of controlling himself whatever the situation, however critical. And then he extinguished within himself all passion, all emotion, with a simple act of will. This was the Fascist comrade Ferrazza.

FERRAZZA HAD HIS MOMENT when he turned in his essay in Italian class; in it he claimed that the greatest man in history had been ADOLF HITLER. Signor Cosmo read it and threw it in his face.

12

THERE'S NOT REALLY ALL that much to be said about the general outline of the politics of those years. In the administrative elections of 1974 the votes for the Christian Democrats (Democrazia Cristiana, or DC) fell and fell, while the Communists' kept rising . . . until their respective shares were so close as to graze, almost to touch: only a couple of percentage points separated them. The Communists seemed bound to overtake their rivals, the next year there would be a major political election. The DC had governed the country without a break since the end of the Second World War, and now the levers of power were about to be reversed. What would the Communists do once they took power? Pajetta, Longo, Natta, Ingrao, Berlinguer, and Amendola. Perhaps even they had no real, exact idea. They were still old-school Communists who wore the ushanka hat and kissed Romanian and Bulgarian dictators three times on the cheeks, and went on their summer holidays to the Black Sea, but at the same time they were democratic parliamentarians with years of elected service behind them . . . Looming over their shoulders was the specter and the myth of the USSR.

My father sat with the big De Agostini–Novara atlas open wide on the living room table, studying the latitudes and seasonal temperatures of Canada, making plans to move us there before the Communists could seize control. We needed to move quickly, take care of everything in a few months' time. "Anywhere they've taken power, legally or otherwise, they've refused to leave . . . And we know what their methods are like." Canada was immense and virtually uninhabited. The whole family was going to emigrate to Canada, except for me; I could remain in Italy "to enjoy the delights" of the Communist dictatorship. This search for a country to run to lasted for a winter, this attempt to find a city less chilly and hostile. Papà was forty-eight years old: he devised a plan to get out of his business obligations, sell everything even if it meant a loss. Then the project was silently set aside, perhaps he just felt he was too old to start over again, that we were too fond of Rome, or else the red specter turned out not to be so threatening after all, and a strange fatalism won out. At the same time, along with the fear, there spread a realization that the Communists might not outstrip their rivals after all, that the takeover wasn't inevitable: quite the opposite. The well-known and deplorable slogan was coined: "Let's hold our noses and vote Christian Democrat," and my father and mother obeyed that call, they who had always voted for the Liberal Party or the Republican Party, voted for the Christian Democrats to throw up a levee to hold off the Communist threat. Once again the crossed shield had been raised to halt an enemy from the East. In the 1975 elections (when I, too, was able to vote, for the very first time, thanks to the new law: and I voted for Proletarian Democracy) both parties took bigger shares of the electorate, but the Christian Democrats sprinted ahead, reaching close to 40 percent, thanks to the votes designed to throw up a barrier, the votes of people like my parents—and they left the Communists in the dust. Four points behind, a collective sigh of relief. Back then in Italy, practically everyone voted Christian Democrat or Communist, without actually being either Christian Democrats or Communists. Those who wanted to defend their pocketbooks obviously voted *against* the Communists, but even a fair number of people who had money, a little or a lot, voted *for* the Communists, caught up in a sort of intoxication of change, or a spirit of self-punishment, as if they considered their good fortune to be a form of injustice, but they did so seemingly with the hope that in the end, the ones they were voting for wouldn't win; or that if they did win, things might change, yes, but *not too much*. The founder of communism had decreed that the bourgeoisie has no reason to exist unless it subverts the given social relationships, and that view was confirmed once again, with the advent of a Communist bourgeoisie that still exists today, however ragtag and disheartened. The petit and middle and haute bourgeoisie, and the intellectual bourgeoisie, proves to be ubiquitous, capable of fighting both *for* its interests and *against* its interests, with the same impetus.

THIS GOES FOR THE POLITICS OF PARTIES, the parliament, elections, etc. Among us boys it was all far more schematic in nature. You were a right-winger or a left-winger. On the right or on the left, full stop. Impossible to avoid that choice, which was mandatory at every level of life, not merely in terms of political ideas, peremptory and also left frequently shrouded in vagueness after an initial pronunciamento, but even more so when it came to the language we used, the clothing we wore, the shape of our shoes, the way we wore our hair, the kind of school we attended and the model or color of the motor scooter or moped we rode to school and our tastes in music and movies, right or left, right or left, imposing a clear choice of alliance, once and for all, as it were. I know very few people who had the strength to resist the pull of these two poles, or perhaps they were merely driven by misanthropy or maladjustment, I couldn't say, or even a general disinterest in life itself, because in those years, a boy's life revolved around that aspect. I am not one of them. It's not as if I repent or I'm ashamed now that I took a side, quite the contrary, and if I'm not ashamed it's not because I'm convinced that I necessarily was on the right side, since doubts remain open and justifiable (as is the case in any given conflict, for that matter), that both parties to the conflict might well have been at fault, but rather because I have realized, only now, many years later, that the most authentic dilemma of those years wasn't which side to fight for, but whether to fight at all.

Nowadays, rather hypocritically, it is stated that the real problem wasn't even this, but rather a matter of which means ought to be used to fight: for example, whether or not to use violence? If you've used violent means, then the struggle was a mistaken one, whereas if you used peaceful means, then the struggle (the same struggle!) was right. Beats me. As if violence were optional, like having fog lights or a GPS navigator, which you can decide whether or not to turn on, when the time comes, or else leave them off entirely. To consider violence as something purely instrumental, a weapon, which you unearth or, to the contrary, you set aside, never entirely clarifies its meaning, and in truth makes it always possible, constantly imminent, you can always haul it out again, seeing that it has nothing to do with the essence of the ideas at whose service it is placed. According to pacifists, violence taints those ideas, according to others it makes them more tangible, and that is why at the same demonstrations in favor of the same ideas you will see protesters who allow themselves to be clubbed and other protesters who do their own clubbing, one group with cracked heads and the other group destroying everything in sight—perfect mirror images of each other, precisely complementary. Violence unfortunately cannot be added or withheld at will like a spice, violence just *is*, and it ought to be enough to examine ideas a little closer to see clearly that violence is not an element somehow alien to them, but rather a necessary component of them, even though you might disavow it, reject it out of hand. The conviction that violence is somehow only a means, a technical means, is typical of those who dream of how you can technically rid yourself of it entirely, just as we have eliminated progressively over the years so many other barbaric customs, thus displaying their ideals purified and innocent and immune to criticism. Often violence survives in those proponents in the form of an extreme and uncontrollable verbal virulence, a *rabies* that emerges in arguments and debates: eyes rolling, voice strident or choking, lips pulled back to bare the teeth (what is described in physiognomy as "miserable laughter," indicative of outbursts of fear and anger). There are those, on the other hand, who imagine they can make use of it without scruples as long as they consider it appropriate, whereupon they can liquidate it from one day to the next, having attained the goals they had set themselves, and then there are those who enjoy it for what it can offer them at the moment: excitement, intoxication, play.

To make others into tools of your own will—that brings boundless pleasure. To constrain or convince (which are two very different things . . .) others to act as I please, as I choose—and contrary to what they please and choose. To win by all means against their resistance. *By all means.*

In politics, your adversary is whoever you inveigh against, and not the other way around. At the very moment you attack someone, that person automatically becomes your adversary. Adversaries can therefore be created in any and all occasions, and one can easily be replaced by another or several others, alternating them or taking them on all at once.

For that matter, if violence per se is a simple tool, what specific purpose is it being used for? What is it that we wish to attain by using it? Almost no one is capable of offering anything but the vaguest of answers to this question. The objective is almost always unspecified or generic while the concrete violence itself is right here, before us—fists, injuries, death.

(Let me open a parenthesis: in the CR/M, what was the actual purpose toward which the violence was employed? What was there that could not be obtained through other methods?)

If, on the other hand, violence is an end in itself, the only true objective of the action, then to what extent can that end be said to have been attained? At what stage of suffering on the part of the victim, seeing that there could always be a further stage, at least theoretically? With the victim's death? Does death placate the violence, can it be said to have fulfilled its goal? With the victim's death, the violence *ceases*, but it is by no means clear that it has thoroughly spent or vented itself. In a certain sense, then, one might say that death, instead of completion, constitutes an obstacle, a thwarting, the chief antidote *against* violence, its most ruthless and determined adversary—that when death ensues, it kills the violence along with its victim. If the purpose of violence is enjoyment, then death is the most unenjoyable mishap along the way, putting an end to the suffering of the victim, who indeed calls for it as a form of liberation. Perhaps this is what the defense lawyers in the CR/M case meant when they spoke of "accidental death"? Were they trying to say that never on earth would their clients have intentionally put an end to their amusement? Perhaps a murderer wants nothing from his victims.

IN THE MEANTIME, in my family we were always taught to minimize.
Always.
To normalize.
"Nothing's happened."
"No, please, don't go to any trouble."
"It's absolutely not a problem for me."
"Don't think twice."
"Never mind" (*a rather mysterious expression, this "never mind," what does it really mean?*).
"Am I here at an inopportune moment?"
"Please, come right in."
"It's nothing, nothing a glass of water won't take care of" (*even if you've just been hit by a truck*).
"I'll get over it."
"Let's drop it."
"Let's just forget about it."
Drink without choking yourself eat with your mouth closed don't talk so fast don't talk nonsense sit properly facing forward chew your food thoroughly early to bed clean up your toys.

RESPECTABLE ACCEPTABLE SOBER discreet affable patient, in every public act he proceeds with the hand brake judiciously applied. It is solely by means of a thoroughgoing self-control that one can win respect, that same sentiment once in fact obtained by a lack of control, through freewheeling acts of strength or folly. The very same resentment that in a nobleman provokes an instant reaction, in the bourgeois seethes and simmers, lacerating the soul, daring to manifest itself only rarely. Infrequent occasions of venting: suddenly bursting into tears, a father's profanities at the family dinner table, straight-armed slaps, insulting your relatives during holiday get-togethers.

AND SO IT IS: so many and so great are the limitations self-imposed on the freedom of our behavior and our speech, that we are practically only able to express ourselves in angry outbursts, in drunken binges, in nervous breakdowns: that is, by revealing ourselves, once and for all, not the way we really are, but as caricatures of ourselves. And so we weep, we foam at the mouth, we throw punches, we complain bitterly. In some cases, we lash out, we even kill. If we release our grip for even a fleeting instant, which happens only rarely, then we collapse, we plunge straight down in a power dive, losing all the self-restraint so laboriously constructed over time, its profoundly contrived nature revealed all at once. We are thus condemned to appear in one of two extreme figures, the one ordinary and imperturbable, the other exceptional and aggressive. Neither one is authentic, let's be clear about that, not even the image of the troublemaker, a reactive image, likewise created as a sudden crack in the effort at self-control. In other words, forced never to act naturally, never to experience a single instant of truth. He lives immersed in the exterior, extraneous reality like a fragment of shrapnel deep in the flesh. Although he's a champion of introspection, occasionally assisted by expensive sessions of psychoanalysis, he doesn't have the faintest idea of who he really is and, above all, *what he's capable of.* Since it is not really him acting in those fits of rage, even those outbursts tell us nothing significant. If he hasn't committed too much mayhem during this vacation from his own image of respectability, then he can return home on tiptoe, like an adulterous husband sneaking home in the shadows, slipping into his conjugal bed and turning affectionate, caressing his sleeping wife, gazing at her with something approaching tenderness.

INCAPABLE THEN of letting loose entirely in the throes of vendetta, of being evil in a continuous, ongoing manner, we concentrate that evil and choose targets symbolic in their random haphazardness against which to vent, or else we ask for their execution, turning to professionals or idiot brothers.

IN MANY OF THOSE who have practiced violence in a systematic fashion, even after they have renounced it and desisted, or simply ceased practicing it, there survives a sort of hidden pride; sometimes they shake their heads sagely as if they were far too wise by now to delve back into truths long since buried, but which still remain obvious to them; even if they almost always take great care not to do so explicitly, they offer the impression that they are still laying claim to the authenticity of their past actions and choices, their sincerity in the face of a legal world that generally tends either to stigmatize or camouflage violence, even though in point of fact its very foundations rest upon that same violence. Upon domination, bullying, and the abuse of the weak by the powerful. Everyone knows it, right?

With the murderous simplification of their actions (beatings, kidnappings, terror attacks, murders), they would be doing nothing other than to reveal the violent substance of human and social interactions, turning them inside out, revealing their hidden side. Like all prophets, they're guilty of having announced an excessive, embarrassing truth, and were banished for having put it into practice. Instead of the usual hypocritical chitchat, instead of mortifying compromises, they've brusquely put an end to the conversation and let the concrete facts speak for themselves. And there can be nothing more concrete than a Walther sidearm. When you face the barrel of one of those, when it winks at you, chitchat is over. And after all, the pistols they used so ruthlessly are in no way different from the ones that on a daily basis defend the great power structures founded on arrogant abuse. If viewed solely from this point of view, then bandits and security guards are really no different. In short, a paradoxical logical consistency is heralded in those who engage in crime, a more authentic, more intense way of life. Violence is a powerful existential accelerator. And intensity remains the sole antidote to the dull flatness of bourgeois life, intensity is what everyone yearns for, and if evil is the only way to get your hands on it, if evil is the only option to keep you from feeling defeated by and complicit with this machine . . . at the risk of being annihilated, what does it really matter . . . annihilate the scruple, stop lingering over scruples . . .

They would have done anything to roil the placid waters of the pond that was the QT.

Those who practice the clarifying virtue of violence believe that they are breathing a purer air. A blow with a metal bar or a gunshot can put an end to useless chatter, and finally it becomes clear who has a pair of balls and who does not, whose hand is trembling, who is brave only at spouting words. Automatic weapons bring a whole philosophy with them . . .

Only those who have killed understand the meaning of an irrevocable act.

"IT IS AS IF THE VERY LIFE of the species, immortal because nourished by the continuous dying of the individual specimens that make it up, emerged especially powerfully due to the use of violence."

IF, THEN, THE MIDDLE CLASS is by its nature prudent and moderate, silent and reserved, occasionally it explodes. It uses violent methods to gain an audience, to tell the world, "I exist." And it's an announcement seething with rage. It's a mistake to underestimate its ferocity, as the brutal and boastful Cornishmen know all too well after being methodically eliminated one after another by the mild-mannered Dustin Hoffman in *Straw Dogs* (in Italian, *Cane di paglia*, a case in which a misleading translation actually creates an extraordinary title).

This must be the third or fourth time during the writing of this book that I've been reminded of the movies of Sam Peckinpah, and in particular, of *Straw Dogs*, 1971. Like a background buzz, an obsession. Which is due primarily to a notorious and controversial scene: when the Cornishman, who was a youthful lover of the petite blonde, now married to Dustin Hoffman (Susan George, how she lit my fire!), finds her alone in the house, buzzes around her, then tears her clothes off her, literally, dressing gown, T-shirt, torn cotton panties, then gives her a good hard smack because she's objecting, and then fucks her on the sofa, in a way that is undoubtedly brutal, but remains unclear whether it's actually a rape, seeing that after her initial resistance, she seems to enjoy the roughhousing of her intercourse with that hunk of man, in comparison with whom her little American nerd of a husband seems like a complete wimp (or, that is, until the epic finale . . .), and so she gives in, sobbing in pleasure and gratitude, until we wonder whether what we've just witnessed is a rape, or rather a confirmation of the theory that first women kick up a fuss and raise objections, but in the end they like it. Or else, perhaps, the reason is that, after all, that man is her ex-sweetheart, and she is his ex-lover, which means that if you've been with a woman once, you'll always be able to fuck her again, even years later, by a right acquired once and for all, and if she says no, it's only a contrived resistance that can be dissuaded with the back of your hand, and you have every right to beat her because in the end she'll enjoy it even more than you will, or at least, so it would seem in the movie.

Whereas there can be no doubt that what ensues shortly thereafter is a rape, while the mathematician's wife is still lying there, her eyes liquid with pleasure, and the friend of the first rapist comes in carrying a shotgun. This one, aside from being armed, is much cruder and more sinister, as well as armed. Threatening both the ex-boyfriend and the wife, he waves his friend to one side, then turns the young woman onto her belly and, while she screams and the other man does nothing, sodomizes her.

This is what I saw at the movie theater; when the film is shown on TV, the scene is cut because it's too upsetting; there's a break immediately prior to the sodomy scene.

In the meantime, the incompetent mathematician has been left out on the moor, shooting at pheasants, unable to hit even one of them.

SOME OF THE MOST RESPECTED SCHOLARS of violence maintain that there is no violence more bloodthirsty than bourgeois violence. No revolution has ever been as ferocious as the ones led by intellectuals of bourgeois extraction and education (such as Pol Pot). The bourgeois inflicts cruelty. Savagely. He applies his utmost zeal to mete out as much pain and harm as possible. A proponent of boundaries, but look out if he steps across them. A bourgeois with bloodshot, enraged eyes is the most dangerous kind of wild beast, a stuffed dog who suddenly morphs into a Doberman. He suddenly springs to life. And he attacks. Being attacked by a bourgeois is like being ripped limb from limb by a plush dog. I've always tried to imagine the astonishment of the two girls when, all at once, these new friends of theirs, so well spoken and courteous, suddenly changed their tone of voice, the light in their eyes.

TO WHAT (HALLUCINATORY) EXTENT, and in what (symbolic) way did that crime and others committed by the gang display the distinctive traits of a *vendetta*? What were they avenging by kidnapping and torturing? In whose name were they unleashing these reprisals? Had someone hired them, appointed them, legitimized them? Or had they believed that someone was hiring them, so that they felt they were his henchmen, his paladins? Can you hire someone to commit a crime or incite them to commit many crimes without ever showing your hand? Are there orders that never even have to be given and yet are faithfully carried out? And why did they feel such a powerful impulse to demean, to degrade their victims? To profane them, the way men do in ethnic wars, to destroy the enemy's identity? In what sense were those girls "the enemy"?

THEY TOOK THE WOMEN'S VIRGINITY. At the time when these events took place, that was still a priceless possession, although in those years also the subject of fierce debate. With that penetration, a brusque act especially if performed with brutality (more or less like wringing a chicken's neck), a place in the female body considered rightly or wrongly to be sacred is suddenly violated, turning into the filthiest and most contaminated thing. What was intact is now lacerated, what was pure is now heaped with filth.

FOR YEARS THE ITALIAN LEFT WING has done nothing but parody or mock the fear and resentment of a population of helpless citizens who are, literally, at the mercy of their attackers, displaying only contempt for the little old lady who has an armored door installed and hides behind it, closing all three locks and dead bolts, for fear of the Albanian immigrants in the street . . . Assigned to this systematic campaign of denigration are numerous satirical writers and authors of op-eds and think pieces. As if the real social problem, in the final analysis, was the little old lady, to be pilloried and scorned, rather than the Albanians, to be thrown behind bars. Certainly, the first solution is cheaper and easier to implement.

After all, is it so deplorable that what matters most to the members of our bourgeoisie is to live and die in peace? What is so disgusting about this desire, not especially romantic but, in the end, understandable? Why should an honest person not have the right to expect that his legitimate interests have a prior claim over those of a criminal?

To borrow a phrase from the most famous theorist of violence, the honest man has every right to prefer not to let himself be killed just because he is honest . . .

I've said it before: "bourgeois" is a word that nearly all authors, myself included, struggle not to utter or write without a subtle hint of scorn, a faint smirk of contempt.

THE EXTRAORDINARY ABILITY to construct stark and dramatic scenarios in the mind, elaborating on the slimmest evidence of danger, is paid for with a permanent state of anxiety. The laughable aspect of this nightmare is that there is absolutely no need for it to come true in order for it to throw us into a state of panic: the source of terror is the expectation itself. Human beings are probably the most fearful creatures in all Creation, and the bourgeois is the most fearful of all men. Fear keeps him company every minute that marks the passing of both day and night. In the face of a limited prospect of physical suffering, caused by material necessities that are by and large well taken care of, the bourgeois possesses a virtually bottomless capacity for mental suffering. He adds to whatever real threats face him those mass-produced by his tireless intellect, and it is these latter fears that pain him like so many stabbing knives, indeed, even worse, because the hypothetical blade never once stops being brandished over him, brought down to stab, stab, stab, just like in *Psycho*. The incalculable stab wounds of fear, the apprehension of suffering makes us suffer even more than the actual suffering when it arrives. Apprehension, sorrow, distress, alarm, uneasiness, suspicion: the image of the comfortable life of the middle class like some placidly flowing river is the purest myth. The bourgeois is worried about himself, his family, his possessions, and his savings, which he fears are not safely and permanently secure against harm, about the social order and his own moral and psychic equilibrium, that is, the two symmetrical faces of security, which however rests on too many varied factors, none of which can be said to be warranted in perpetuity. He feels threatened from without and within, by those who are worse off than him but also by those who are better off. The powerful and the miserable are using every weapon known, treacherous and outright, to assault the safety, the respectability, the property, and even the life of the helpless specimen of the middle class: the state robs him every bit as effectively as do burglars and thieves and the phone company and insurance companies. High consumer prices and the churnings up and down of the stock market, illegal immigrants and dope peddlers, even the members of his own class conspire against all the other members of the class—and likewise lawyers, doctors, dentists, and notaries do nothing but conspire to embitter the life of the bourgeois man. Court orders and tax bills poison that life, at the hand of the postman. The bourgeois fears solitude every bit as much as overcrowding, he has every bit as much fear of being abandoned as he does of being intruded upon, in his thoughts as well as in his possessions, indeed, perhaps this last-named fear remains the most powerful and the oldest, one is afraid of strangers as one fears the snakes and wild animals that our ancestors fought against, as they defended their caverns. This fear must be exorcized at all costs. Perhaps the most effective option to be wielded against that fear is neither fight nor flight, but rather to play dead. To change into a stone, blend in with the cement, cancel oneself entirely. Suppress all emotional reactions until you have the heart of a fakir. It had always worked. There were people who lived perfectly well as if they were dead, they walked, they signed checks, they watched TV, they drove their Fiat 1100s, they went to the movies or the soccer stadium, and they even died, even though they had already been deceased for some time. Only an early death made a decent life possible. That, after all, is what philosophies and religions tell us.

But after the CR/M, things were suddenly different, a new feeling spread through the QT, a generic anxiety about the meaning of one's presence in the world, the thread of anguish that binds and squeezes the life of the middle class was transformed into terror, an all-consuming sentiment that refuses to be deciphered or neutralized. Previously, death had poked its head up in the quarter in the guise of old age and disease, or else in infrequent car crashes: now it was turning into a widespread possibility, palpable even as it remained abstract, a constant daily topic, something you could never feel didn't concern you because there was never any specific reason either way. A violent fate no longer limited to the narrative of individuals, but rather looming over one and all. Once it had slithered its way into the quarter, that shadow never went away again. In a setting that was by definition "peaceful," it was impossible to calculate the risks. What elements could one use in making such predictions? Which streets were dangerous, which people should we avoid, what behaviors were now inadvisable? Apparently, *none*. *Everything* looked innocuous and deadly at the same time. Everything lent itself to a twofold interpretation. Nerves shot by false alarms. All it required was the creaking of a rusty weather vane, the flat report of a motorcycle starting, a backfiring exhaust pipe, to sow panic. As a result of that unprecedented crime, they had learned that under the outer semblance of a respectable young man, a murderer might be lurking, and there was no way to identify him ahead of time. In other words, they "are among us," they "are just like us." So what do people do, instinctively? They lock themselves up in their homes, turning the lock and the dead bolt, but instead of basking in that safety, they wind up falling prey to the violent propaganda from the TV. Barricading yourself indoors only makes your fear grow exponentially. That's what happened to a great many residents of the QT, especially the ones who were middle aged. Taking a stroll after dinner down little streets like Via Gradisca or Via delle Isole had become more frightening than venturing into a deep dark forest. Heaven forfend you should run into a gang of kids. They might shoot you, or they might just walk past, talking about their Latin test, paying you no mind, because after all, they really were harmless little kids on their way to the pizzeria, not out to commit a crime. Who could know for sure? The most unnerving aspect was the fact that you were always and inevitably at the mercy of what other people chose to do. You were in their power, in thrall to their inclinations and moods. No longer could even the tried-and-tested bourgeois therapy of "doing" be brought to bear: in order to leave less room for anxious thoughts, one overwhelms one's consciousness with practical pursuits, one stuns oneself with hard work. Work has always been the wheel to which the bourgeois nailed himself, in a martyrdom to the eyes of his neighbor, thus earning their respect, while at the same time keeping them safely at bay.

A curfew settled over the QT, that is to say, an extraordinary state in which the simplest and most harmless actions were prohibited while those that were horrible became quite routine. A curfew is first and foremost a state of mind.

THE STUPIDEST THING I did in those years was this: my girlfriend and I would ride around the quarter on a Vespa, her driving and me in back, carrying a water pistol.

The water pistol was shaped like the baby elephant Dumbo and it sprayed the water out of its trunk. We'd zip along the sidewalks at low speeds and if we saw someone walking along with their back to us, we'd slow down even more, come even with them, and fire. I'd aim with my arm held straight and I'd hit them in the face with a jet of water. The trigger would release quite a substantial spray. If the target was too far away to allow for precision fire, then I'd just fire volleys recklessly. There were those who weren't fast enough to notice our incursion and were drenched before they realized it. There were others who instead had a presentiment of the shadow at their back, turned their head, realized they were in the crosshairs, and for the fraction of a second before I pulled the trigger, an expression was painted on their faces that was a blend of astonishment and disbelief, perfectly idiotic, in part because they weren't able to realize immediately that it was only a water pistol. All right, a water pistol with the ears and trunk of Dumbo; but the act was still

the same, straight-armed, aiming a weapon, like the black-and-white pictures everyone had seen, starting with the oldest and most famous photograph of them all, taken in Genoa at the turn of that decade, on March 26,
1971, during an armed robbery carried out by the revolutionary Gruppo
XXII Ottobre, in which you can see two militants aboard a Lambretta, and
the one riding in back shoots a courier (his name was Alessandro Floris) and
kills him for having resisted their attempt to steal his bag full of money.

It had just been the beginning of a long trail of blood that those who are
curious can read about separately.

AT THAT MOMENT their mouths and their staring eyes were just asking
"Why?" Why *me*? Otherwise, their gazes were empty. Then came the spurt
of water into their faces.

We reloaded Dumbo at a drinking fountain and started over. It was odd
that we never encountered people we knew, it seemed as if the QT was populated by cameos and walk-ons who just strolled back and forth on the
sidewalks. Immediately after we fired at them, as soon as they recovered
from their shock and astonishment, they would be seized by outbursts of
rage, they'd shout appalling curse words, two or three even took off running
after us, whereupon we poured on the gas and raced away, laughing and
displaying the toy with which we'd hit them, but the majority of our victims just stood there, amazed and dripping.

Once, on Via Tolmino, instead of taking them from behind, we crossed
paths with a couple out walking arm in arm, enjoying a bracing stroll before retiring for the night, they were well dressed and beaming, an old married couple who realized they were still happy to be together, in spite of
everything, this is the life, enjoying a pleasant walk before dinner, arms
locked with your husband. I had the water pistol, practically empty, when I
spotted those two unhoped-for targets, already close at hand, just a few
yards away, I decided to empty the rest of the water right on them, I leaned
out with my arm held straight and aimed at them, telling my girlfriend,
"Brakes! Put on your brakes!" They spotted us and then a singular thing
happened. The man fell to his knees, dragging his wife with him, because
he still had her tightly in his grip, while she put her hands together in prayer,
begging us: "No, please, don't! We didn't do anything!" The man seemed
resigned or else on the verge of fainting while his wife was screeching with
a voice that stirred pity in us. My girlfriend turned around to look at me
with a grimace beneath the lipstick, though I was hard-pressed to say

whether it was of amusement or horror. My water pistol was already locked and loaded and I was by now inclined to do the job without thinking twice. My finger pulled back on the trigger, repeatedly. I'd only aimed at the man, who was about to pass out, and I brought him to with three squirts of water, on his forehead and his eyeglasses. The woman was spared.

13

THE CR/M, then, might be to the QT what Nazism was to the quiet and artistic Germany, the land of bannered villages and picnics on meadows, the fabled Bremen town musicians and other fairy tales that turned suddenly dark. It might seem like its polar opposite, but in reality it's a precipitate of its essence. The technique involved in cutting a hog's throat can still prove useful even after the animal hanging head-down from a hook has stopped squealing and its blood has all dripped into the bucket; the knife still gleams even after the carcass has been transformed into sausages and slices of cured pork, treats to be enjoyed at Sunday afternoon picnics; there it sits, on the sideboard, glittering, ready, razor sharp, and each time, the scream echoes through the flowering valley. The echo isn't an amusement for hikers and day-trippers, it's the heartbreaking last trace of a disappearance. The QT had been built expressly to evoke, at once, tranquillity, somnolence, and scorn. Everything in it appeared "so small and so hidden," starting with the little villas behind Giulio Cesare High School, dripping with wisteria and geraniums. Little apartment houses, saplings and yearling trees, cunning little gardens, cute balconies, lapdogs and puppies, mopeds, adorable bars, little old pensioners, clerks, handicapped war veterans . . . mini-pizzas, *tramezzini* sandwiches . . . there was more than enough mediocrity to arouse the final wrath and punishment. The being most resentful of all this false peace is, in the final analysis, God Himself. He doesn't need Sodom and Gomorrah to wax indignant. The only peace possible in reality and not in dreams comes at this price. Peace is *always* hypocritical, just like the peace that reigned in the QT. A desirable sham. It is the kind of peace advocated by someone with a boot planted firmly in the face. If they weren't threatened, they wouldn't sign up. Only war is sincere. When you no longer accept unworthy compromises. After what happened

happened, the entire diplomatic corps of the QT activated itself to hinder excessive reactions and level obstacles once again, but by now it was too late, common sense was no longer enough to put to sleep, negate, dilute, avoid, silence, shut one eye or both, evade, smooth over, skim past . . .

What with all the dust that had been swept under it, a mountain had formed beneath the carpet, and atop it, the table started to wobble, the candlesticks overturned, the cabinets tipped over, and the heap of little misdeeds rumbled to the floor.

A MATURE CIVILIZATION is in an ideal condition to break down. As soon as it is complete, it begins to degenerate. The "tranquillity" of the QT concealed or, perhaps we should really say, fomented the development of a growing aggressivity, it nurtured it, like well-seasoned chestnut wood for a fire, which catches easily, with absolute propriety, one might almost say, joyfully. That fire would char acres and acres of the QT in the few hours that followed the rapes and murder.

The priests, for their part, did everything they could think of to limit the damage. They clenched their teeth and bore their cross, while the press hurled headlines at them that were as defamatory as the spit in the face that Our Lord received on His way up to Golgotha. Come, come! Religious educators grooming young rapists, priests rolling in cash ready to shut an indulgent eye on their sadistic young scholars . . .

After a profound reflection that actually lasted no more than a tenth of a second, like a blink of the eye on the only possible truth, among the various metaphors that emerged as a key in which to read an event that was otherwise devoid of any possible explanation, they chose to go with a reference to *bad apples*—but apples that had always been rotten, that were rotten from birth, rotten to the core, there was no possibility that they had grown rotten during their stay in the bushel basket of the school. They had to be, those alumni of SLM, psychopaths at the very least. That was the explanation. Instead of teachers, what they really needed were psychiatrists and guards. And sure enough, they got them. Insanity offers a justification for everything.

THAT CRIME WAS OF A RARE and extraordinary type that seemed to require that those who had committed it were not subjected to the rigors of the individual laws that they had violated, but rather, so to speak, must submit to the law itself, the law in all its terrifying entirety, the Law, in other words. A flaming colossus, which once set in motion no longer bothers to weigh the unmistakable facts or the guilt of individuals, but rears up in all its crushing vastness. The backlash spread well beyond the narrow circle of criminals and victims, and beyond the legal machinery that worked tirelessly to stitch up the enormous vulnus that had been produced. But instead of scarring over, the wound festered. Certainly, the punishment of the guilty parties would not be enough to heal it, not even if they had been burned at the stake. The entire community was shaken by what had happened, the maelstrom dragged it down into its core, reawakening a need, indeed, a lust for sacrifice with respect to which life sentences without parole and the indignant verdicts with which they were handed down seemed like too puny, too scanty a thing. At first, you might think that after a crime so vicious that it ought to have used up the whole stock, savagery would lie low for a while. In sheer statistical terms, there ought to have followed at least twenty years of peace and quiet in the QT. Not another burglary or brawl or breach of the peace, not even a slap should have flown within the bounds of that community, chagrined and contrite. Instead this was only the beginning, the start of a series of plagues that slammed down one after another, as if the vase that had contained them were shattered, and it wasn't clear whether the violence that was unleashed from that moment on in the QT was simply an unprecedented crescendo of delinquency and crime, or on the contrary whether it was part of the punishment for the initial crime, that it was, so to speak, a concurrent penalty. Hard to understand, for those upon whom it is inflicted, whether the suffering is an act of evil or of good. There are in fact moments when the law and the transgression of the law tend to resemble each other with stunning ferocity. The chain of murders could take on some meaning only if placed within a larger, apocalyptic vision, in a collective ceremony of expiation or in a spectacle offered to heaven. Every death meant a sacrifice, and "every evil is justified in the sight of which a god finds edification."

There is a law, and it seems to be applied severely, though no one really knows what it means; not even its own executors seem to know. And in fact, when their turn comes before the judges, after having usurped their role, they stammer out vague and flimsy reasons for their murderous actions; we need only quote a few phrases from their testimony at trial: motivations that wouldn't justify a punch in the face, much less serial murders. More than repentant, they seem astonished at the trivialities that issue from their lips. A little word balloon of nothingness. "Why did you kill him?" "Because . . . the time had come to send a signal." "We had to make it clear that we were still alive." "We couldn't just stand there twiddling our thumbs." And so they kill the first person to happen by. A policeman, a random person from the other side of the political barricades, or even from the same side who might have gotten some strange ideas into his head. All it takes is a shadow of suspicion—and he's a dead man. Thus, its rational content reduced to the zero degree, the sheer power of the law that drove them to kill emerges. These phrases are by no means rare, phrases in which laws apply that no one understands, which must nonetheless be obeyed, in which orders are carried out that no one ever issued, and yet they ring out as peremptory: but these are by no means times of anarchy, you might say that never had so much legislation been produced as during those periods, the citizenry were overwhelmed with measures, prohibitions, restrictions, and injunctions, as numerous as they were reciprocally contradictory, so that inevitably one ran afoul of the law whatever one did or didn't do: the state produced special laws, and in the meantime the murderers administered a power of life and death in their street tribunals, where the trials hadn't even begun before the jury had already issued its verdict and sentence, always the same, "To death with them!," so what was the point of going to the trouble of a trial? The oppression could be felt at every instant of the day, and you could feel the transitions between one jurisdiction and the other: in the office, I obey the bureaucratic law, at home I obey the family law. The social space and the environment of the quarter is governed by yet another law, and I'm wrong if I try to ignore it. If I venture behind Giulio Cesare High School at night, I don't realize that I've broken it, by crossing a border.

POWER ALWAYS ESTABLISHES ITSELF as absolute, and it is only later that it is mitigated, moderated by forces that prevent it from putting people to death on a whim: that is, when it is asked to account for its actions. Asked by someone who, in his or her turn, must necessarily have at least a little power, the power to demand—and it's certainly not enough to just ask a simple question, "Why?" in order to bring reason to bear on power.

The power over a kidnapped girl is exercised even when you're not exercising it. "I *can* kill you" is such an exercise at its highest level. "I can kill you whenever I feel like it." "In a certain sense, I'm killing you now even if I'm not really doing it, because I'm not killing you *yet*." The power to kill, being able to kill are tantamount in every sense to killing. Just as we once considered a bandit "already dead," a corpse waiting to be redeemed, a dead man walking, likewise a kidnap victim is already killed right from the outset. In the cases we're talking about, what's more, the solemn expression "power of life or death" loses its meaning: the only actual power that can be exercised is the power of death, life has already been given and can only be taken, torn away. It lies beyond the faculties of the murderer. The power therefore of anyone who isn't our parent is only that of killing us; and, really, once we're born, the only power even our parents can exercise is a power of death. After bringing us into the world, they can only send us back out of it. In the first years of our lives, they give us thousands of reprieves.

The only power to which we are always subject, then, is that of being put to death; and the only power worth claiming is that of giving death or revoking it. Perhaps for that reason (especially in the phase when they will be unable to do anything more in political terms, as their grip on reality becomes increasingly evanescent), terrorists affirmed their power *by killing*. They had no weapons other than their lethal ones. In the infinite and gradual array of initiatives that could be taken, all that remained to them was the supreme act, the regal essence of power; they were moribund creatures forced to feed on their last fleeting drops of nectar and ambrosia, endowed with a power as funereal as it was residual. In their puny parliaments they scrutinized from on high their future victims, but they could touch the lives of other men in no way other than by killing them. They had sunk to the level of having less influence than a tourism commissioner at a beach resort, or a traffic policeman with his pad of blank tickets, or a fence who receives stolen cars, less charisma than a high school principal or a small-time drug dealer, and in terms of their impact on the real lives of people less than the doorman of a large apartment house—but to make up for that, they could sentence to death whoever they chose. The sheer number and gratuitous nature of their murderous operations grew in inverse proportion to their wait. There were never as many murders as when the armed groups no longer counted for anything. The limitless authorization to kill was given to them precisely by their diminished influence and by the endurance of a myth of violence as a potent accelerator of destiny.

THEN THERE'S THE JOY OF GOING (perhaps only briefly) unpunished. In fugitives from the law, in those who have not yet been caught in spite of the manhunt, alongside the anguish, there is also the frenzy of being out and on the loose—a very paradoxical form of liberty.

In democratic nations, people have very little freedom to act, in fact, they are not free to act at all. The ties of rules and regulations constrain every single action, especially in the city, where the authorities have decided where you can walk, how long you can park, how long you can linger to gaze at a painting and at what distance, whether or not you're allowed to swim in the sea, how much you have to pay to get from one place to another, the number of grams of drugs you can buy, where you can scatter your father's ashes and where your own ashes can be scattered. Every breath of urban life is regulated by figures on a chart, signs announce prohibitions, broken lines separate, and all the while video cameras record it all, in a hail of fines, deadlines, registration fees, alternate days, schedules, and traffic-free zones.

You're not free to do a thing without a special permit, a stamp, a coupon, a card, a password, a ticket, a collar, a receipt, a badge, a magnetic strip; which you constantly have to renew because it expires, it's expiring, there you go, it's already expired, and now you have to start over from scratch. You're always an outlaw even though you chase after the law every blessed day in order to make sure you obey it. The envelopes unopened with notifications of infractions and summons and reminders pile higher on the table by your front door. On odd-numbered days only cars with odd-numbered license plates can be driven, but they can only park on the right side of the street, provided they are equipped with catalytic converters, from 1 to 6 p.m. Someone's keeping an eye on you wherever you turn. Regulations are heaped on other regulations, like posters glued over other posters, and while you sit there doing nothing at all, on a park bench, you're actually complying with at least a dozen codes of the law, each nesting inside the last like so many Chinese boxes.

There's only one exception: bums and criminals. As long as they're not tossed into prison, criminals are the only free men in our society. Or at least they attempt, death-defiantly, frequently getting the worst of it, to impose and exercise their liberty, to the detriment of the freedom of others, as if they were the one law, taken into their own hands, which is never entirely the case, because you cannot call law something that is valid only for a single individual. A law, if it is to be called a law, must oppress lots and lots of people, but in fact it oppresses only those who respect it, who therefore end up being oppressed twice, crushed between two powers: on the one hand the state, whose frequently ill-advised laws they nonetheless obey, and on the other hand, criminals, petty and grand, who impose their own laws upon them. To say nothing of other nonstate organizations that are by now like Spectre: banks, phone systems, and insurance companies, hunkered down in their glass-front bunkers, defended behind telephone numbers where no one ever answers, structured in layers of secrecy impenetrability and impersonal remoteness borrowed and copied from the machinery of state and, also, from the Mafia and organized crime in general.

A citizen always pays his tribute at least twice. It's a fixed double or triple taxation.

(Mmm, let's see in my case . . . apartment burgled and ransacked, car and mopeds stolen or vandalized, an unknown number of digital devices and cell phones stolen from my children and therefore necessarily replaced by me, at my expense, as well as bags "with everything in them," that is, ID, cash, house keys . . . just to cite the most significant items: there, I believe that over the past several years I've turned over to the criminal element at least the same amount as I have paid to the state in the form of taxes and fines. And I've never been reimbursed a cent by either of those two institutions. At least the state, though, however unreliably, does provide me with some minimal services.)

THE GREATEST UNRUFFLED TRANQUILLITY in taking someone else's life can be found in someone who has little interest in safeguarding his own. This attitude is sometimes called courage. In the heart of any hero, a contempt for danger. If there is a desire for suffering and death, it is attained by inflicting suffering and death upon others. A murderer causes death while waiting to experience it in person. Friends of Death, friends in Death. In the letters that Angelo and his accomplice exchanged after the CR/M, we can detect the presence, all-powerful and morbid, of this bond of the Negative.

THE SPECTACLE OF DEATH isn't offered to the one dying, but to the one who survives. In the first place, the murderers, certainly, who enjoy an early screening of it, but also strangers. Before they leave the scene of the crime, it is to strangers that a murderer consigns the bodies of his victims. After which, so to speak, he "has nothing more to do with it," he can move on to other things. The message has been sent, and it may take some time; but as far as being delivered, it will eventually be delivered. The meaning of the death of the two girls (yes, two: the one who was alive was virtually dead) was entrusted to a public decipherment. It constituted the genuine bond, the authentic challenge of the whole story. Murderers vs. society: that turned out to be the interesting axis, the girls, raped and murdered, didn't really count for much in the final analysis; they were the short end of the triangle, and this immediately became clear both to the one who survived, who was never capable as long as she lived of doing anything other than to mumble out her bereft helplessness, and to those who took up her cause—indignant public opinion, feminists, newspaper op-ed writers. A great many hastened to suffer and level accusations on her behalf, in her name, well aware that her personal suffering was unquestionably profound but still, little in comparison with the collective drama orchestrated by that infamous crime. What had the murderers been trying to say? Practically nothing to their victims, but a great deal to everyone else. A great deal of *what*?

The truth is that if the victims have no appeal, no one pays any attention to them. It's sad to say it, but that's the way it is. Youth, working-class origins, homeliness, and naïveté only serve to emphasize how brutal were those who inflicted their savagery on these nondescript facial features, but they constitute nothing interesting in and of themselves. Those are just preliminary facts that tend to refocus the attention on the perpetrators. Out of ten parts of curiosity aroused by the event, nine belong to the murderers.

14

It wasn't hard to kill.
It wasn't hard to find someone to kill.
It wasn't hard to find a good reason to kill someone.
Any reason would do. It wasn't hard at all.

THE DIFFERENCE BETWEEN a little boy and a young man is that while the former may wish to kill someone, the latter *can do it*. An adolescent finds himself suddenly capable of acting out violent fantasies that have hitherto been, necessarily, strictly innocuous. This power, never before experienced, confers a new meaning to the sentiment of hatred. Your impulses have now become potentially murderous. They, too, so to speak, have come of age. The destruction of the other, so longed mulled and longed for, so long that it has turned into a sort of consolatory singsong (*I'm going to kill him . . . I'll kill him . . . I'll kill him*), emerges from the world of fairy tales and becomes a concrete possibility. Childish cruelty is finally given the tools to vent its frustrations.

Violent attitudes may be due to an inability to adapt, to compromise, to bring a little hypocrisy to bear in order to resolve conflicts. Like schizophrenics, adolescents are often unable to accept compromises concerning what's true and what's false, what's right and what's wrong, their morality rejects commonsense solutions, temporary stopgaps. Looking out for one's own best interests, smoothing out problems, avoiding the worst outcomes, not exacerbating contrasts—all these things constitute, to their mind, hypocritical conduct.

(Arbus, for example, was like this. Implacable. His sarcastic laughter submerged any attempt at reconciliation . . .)

But who in all honesty could seriously say what the thoughts of an adolescent are? The personal, profound thoughts? We didn't feel real, but made up of emptiness, air, we had no consistency, we didn't have a home, because the home we lived in was our parents' home, we weren't children but we weren't grown-ups, either, no one liked us, no one wanted us, no one came looking for us. The sensation was that everyone wanted girls, their parents spoiled them, the teachers at school coddled them, we'd never heard of a girl flunking a course, a girl who got three Ds? They'd help her out because "she was just going through a rough spot," a boy with two Cs, well, he would flunk "because he hasn't lifted a finger all year long."

We didn't have the slightest idea of what we would become, and for that matter, we weren't particularly interested, it made no difference to us, after all, we were nobody.

The only thing that seemed real to us were the things we did that were wrong, that were bad. That was what mattered. Suddenly everyone snapped to attention. Then they noticed us. We all at once became important.

Violence gives rise to behavior that seems real because it prompts negative consequences. The positive aspects are more elusive, they're only noticed much later and no one really takes them into account; negativity generates immediate responses, clear-cut reactions. Rage and pain are tangible. If nothing happens after we pass that way, if everything remains the same as before, it means that we count for nothing. To ensure that you notice my absence, I'm willing to pay any price, I don't mind in the slightest the fact that you might consider me a piece of shit. A thousand times better to be a piece of shit than to go unnoticed.

WHEN YOU'RE ALIVE *and there's a dead man next to you, you rejoice. You can still do all the things that he no longer can. A person who's kicked the bucket is no longer a person, he's no longer anything. Things are always better for the living than the dead.*

FROM THE POINT OF VIEW of an individual's self-interest, being very aggressive, ostentatiously aggressive, constitutes a disadvantage. An incessant aggressiveness arouses in one's surroundings reactions of much greater intensity than a single individual is capable of deploying, however bellicose they might be. The life stories of the perpetrators of the CR/M tell us that from their misdeeds, they obtained nothing more than a grim, difficult life, made up of prison time and time on the run. They may not have paid with their lives, but they certainly wasted their lives. In exchange for what?

One of them died of a heroin overdose at age forty after serving in the Foreign Legion; another escaped from prison, was caught, then was released, only to be sent back to prison for good after killing again.

It's clear, in short, that they acted *against* their own self-interest, not only destroying the lives of others, about which they cared little, but also the lives that you might have supposed were dearest to their hearts, their own.

What strange kind of superman complex leads someone to live a subhuman life? Those who do evil do so because they believe they've been victims of that evil in the past, or else they expect that soon they'll be subjected to it. He believes that he's already paid in advance for the crimes he commits. Those who have suffered want to exact vengeance, those who haven't yet suffered want to make sure they shoot first. It's rare to find someone who deep down in his heart is truly convinced that he's going to enjoy impunity. Whereas there are a great many who, albeit indirectly, inflict today what they suffered yesterday. Unfortunately, the vendetta almost never strikes the actual culprits of the harm done, instead, most of the time, it just strikes other innocent peers. A vendetta is always imprecise and transferrable, the wrong suffered is often imaginary.

VIOLENCE CAN BE UNLEASHED for any number of reasons, for a single obscure motive. For the CR/M, we might list a series of factors a page long. Loss of values, herd mentality, superiority complex, fanaticism, widespread atmosphere of violence, ideological scorn, sociopathy, spirit of revenge. In more or less the same conditions as Angelo & Co., at the time, there must have been at least ten thousand other people in Rome, in our school alone, more or less, we all started out from the same basis, so did that mean that we were all destined to become murderers?

HUMAN CRUELTY RARELY BURSTS forth in a rage, in an instant, in an "eruption of uncontrollable passion." On the contrary, it is bound up with planning and cool calculation. The CR/M is a perfect example of this, though, over the long term, the plans devised by the murderers might have been clumsily thrown together, contradictory, ineptly framed, or merely idiotic, but that in no sense takes away from their methodical spirit. There may be madness to your method, but it doesn't mean it's not still a method. If you set aside the brutal aspects of his modus operandi, the torturer still behaves in a scrupulous, Chinese fashion, and it is this coolness, bound up with his so-called beastly acts, that leaves us speechless.

In order to kidnap someone, you have to study their daily routines, their movements, their habits, then you come up with a plan, and you put it into operation. Although the newspapers, in their distinctive moralizing and indignant style, like to say so, very rarely is bestial cruelty actually *blind*. Quite the contrary, it is shrewd, appraising, and farsighted, and what makes it more powerful is the element of calculation, the premeditation, even a certain prudence, all prerogatives not of instinct but of reason. Nothing mindless about it, then. Certain types of torture require dedication and hard work to even imagine them, and cold blood to put them into effect. Nothing blind about it: it takes the meticulous devotion of a surgeon, the patience of a sniper. It requires creativity and commitment to dream up new ways to destroy your fellow human beings. The worst crimes are actually carried out in an almost total lack of emotion, thanks to a dead calm in the heart, in the soundproof room. In a film that came out that very same year, which I can remember frame by frame, Max von Sydow played a contract assassin. He remained perfectly detached as he carried out his assassinations, and that's why they paid him. In his spare time, he painted lead toy soldiers.

BEASTLY CRUELTY: rarely is a term used so inappropriately. What we call beastly in a human being in no way corresponds to any aspect of a wild animal; indeed, it is the opposite, a purely human characteristic, so that, when a man behaves in a way that we are accustomed to calling "beastly," we ought rather to say that he has behaved in a distinctly human fashion.

WHEN I SPEAK ABOUT REASON, I'm talking about the faculty of committing the most clamorous of errors while attributing a motivation to them. Reason has very little to do with intelligence, which can almost entirely be tracked down in the realm of instinct. The plans developed by the reason of murderers are almost inevitably absurd lucubrations: that does not mean they don't apply a certain method to their madness. I have always given this interpretation to Goya's famous etching: it's not the sleep of reason that produces monsters, but rather the *dream* of reason (*sueño* in Spanish can mean either thing). That is to say, its plans, its projects.

IN REALITY, there is no *reason* the CR/M should have been able to happen; neither the actions of the torturers and murderers nor those of the victims help in any way to shed light on the logic of the events as something that came about as a result of causes in view of objectives. Objectives, in fact, are entirely lacking, and from the outset. What did the girls want, *exactly*? Whatever it could have been: friendship, amusement, fun, and perhaps even a boyfriend? But what is even less evident is this: What did Angelo and his accomplices want? Did they want what they finally got? And what on earth was that?

THE THEORY OF INVOLUNTARY EXCESS explains nothing, with its references to an orgy that "ended badly," "got out of hand" (a theory that was recklessly set forth by the counsel for the defense)—the unexpected outcome of a violent game.

That situation was not generated by a specific cause nor by an order of causes; nor do I believe that it was planned out the way it actually played out, so twisted and incongruous is it in the comings and goings of its protagonists, its perpetrators; you might just say that that situation at a certain point came about, that those events occurred, the decision made in that villa by the sea wasn't for those events to occur in this or that manner; rather, the decision was made to go along with them, to let them happen, literally to *execute them*, and once they were inside this internal sequence of causation, in its way unstoppable, to carry them to completion (which, despite the acrobatic argumentations of the counsel for the defense, could have no conceivable outcome but the deaths of the girls). What happened in the villa at Monte Circeo is unmistakable proof that, when everything is possible, everything, inevitably, happens.

(IF YOU CAN DO IT, then you *must* do it, and you *have the right* to do it.)

THAT WAY OF THINKING AND ACTING cannot be reproduced, because it is devoid of logic. More than having a crude syntax, it obeys no syntax whatsoever. Impossible to deduce a plan from the confused tangle of actions that unfolded in that villa and afterward, not even if you change the chronological order, in the hypothesis that the pieces of the story might have been assembled in the wrong order. It's no good, the brainteaser has no solution. Once it makes its debut, violence frees itself of the reasons that brought it there. Like the Red Death in Poe's famous story, once it's inside, it's inside, and it no longer needs a mask.

15

TODAY, SUNDAY, too late for mass at SLM, I brush along the wall on Via Parenzo—the wall my father jumped over to beat it through the fields to escape a Nazi roundup, the very same wall against which our antihero Angelo, I read somewhere, once hurled a Molotov cocktail, in retaliation for a bad grade, even though among the many more-or-less legendary episodes concerning his bad-to-the-bone evil, many of them cultivated by none other than him, this one might be an interpolation, because in point of fact things actually were burned along that wall, and I myself remember taking part in some of those burnings, specifically, the bonfires of assignment books and diaries at the end of the school year. On the last day of school, the minute we walked out the front door, we'd pile up our assignment books at the foot of the enclosure wall, sprinkle them with gasoline, and set fire to them. Then, and only then, could we really say that school was out for good. With that bonfire we'd leave behind us a year of our lives, and we all burned our assignment books (Jacovitti assignment books, Peanuts assignment books, Gran Prix Racing assignment books, B.C. assignment books—and so on), both the ones who were doing well at school, like me, and the donkeys who waited anxiously for test results to be posted so they'd know whether they'd flunked the year entirely, or which and how many subjects they were going to have to brush up on during the summer and retake at the beginning of the next school year, but none of that mattered, there was the same identical flame of joy in us all, and when those real flames began to leap high and a billowing cloud of black smoke and an asphyxiating stench filled the air, we would do a sort of dance, inciting the flames to leap higher, like Jimi Hendrix setting fire to his guitar. I don't know, perhaps this ceremony had a certain violent, Nazi aspect, reminiscent of the notorious bonfires of forbidden books, or else it might have been an Indian or anarchist or hippie catharsis, whatever the case, it was lovely to watch those pages burn, with their essays and lessons assigned for further study, pages and numbers of exercises and examinations and reviews and research topics. Seldom have I ever felt such pure joy.

People say that to keep from suffocating under the burden of the past, a person ought to burn the residue: dry leaves, long-since useless documents, old newspapers, or else they should simply watch a candle burning, calmly observe the wax as it melts.

And breathe.

AN EMPTY SUNDAY. Empty like this quarter, where the first thirty years of my life unfolded.

Everything appears placid, peaceful, even a little too peaceful, fixed in a timeless mediocrity. The perfect theater in which to have nothing happen at all.

And so I ask myself why this thing happened here of all places; why in this quarter of Rome and not somewhere else? Why would so many killings have occurred, so many murders have been committed, and so eagerly, in the streets around Piazza Istria and down the tree-lined boulevard of Corso Trieste? The fact that this was a quarter devoid of any particular identity might perhaps have made it the ideal terrain, a sort of neutral ground upon which to test the highest possible level of political violence that could be attained without necessarily breaking into a full-fledged civil war. Because in Italy, in the seventies, no matter what the veterans of those battles might say in order to justify the crimes they committed, laying the blame on the "climate of the time" or "that epoch," there was no war. There really was no war. It would be interesting to understand why on earth they were so certain that there actually had been: they truly were convinced of it, and they were at no loss for words to construct that illusion. It was all in their head, the war. Can you call something a war if it is recognized as such only by those who fought in it, but not by the rest of the population? Is the person who declares a war also in charge of the meaning, the modalities, and the objectives of that war? All the same, this war invented by its own warriors did leave a considerable number of corpses on the ground, and not all of them had agreed to take part, indeed, some of them didn't even realize that they had anything to defend themselves against, there was no visible trenchworks dug into the middle of Corso Trieste, everyone else was minding their own business, heading home from work, going downstairs to buy the newspaper, like the gentlemen with their impeccably coiffed hair tucked under the checkered flat caps that I saw strolling slowly through the quarter this morning, without the slightest notion that they'd been sentenced to death. Rome wasn't exactly Sarajevo. It's no easy matter to dodge the sniper's bullets when you don't even know you're under siege, when you wind up in the crosshairs of those who are playing at War of the Worlds— if you happen to cross Paul Street in the middle of an armed struggle.

Even though they were dangerous times, even though in terms of physical appearance (hair shoes and bag and girlfriend of a certain type, herself likewise wearing shoes and bag and skirt of a certain type, etc.) I might be a plausible target like so many others for the political violence of the opposite persuasion, I never once was afraid, not even for an instant, in the QT. I never had, over ten years' time, as much fear as I had in Brooklyn at night, in the ten minutes' walk from the subway station to where I lived.

IN ITS MID-TWENTIETH-CENTURY NEUTRALITY, the QT became the ideal territory for murderous rampages. Among its nondescript apartment houses, violence could be unleashed with an untethered crudeness that tended to steer clear of other quarters endowed with a more distinct urban and social personality. Sprawled like a demilitarized zone, a no-man's-land between what back then constituted the outskirts of town (Tufello, Talenti) and the *buen retiro* of the historic Roman bourgeoisie (Pinciano, Parioli), the Quartiere Trieste was used as a buffer zone or a hunting reserve, divvied up every night like a little Poland between its invaders. Still today, when we think of the prototype of the *fascistello*, the petty Fascist, the word we use is "*pariolino*," which back then rang more or less as the Roman equivalent of the Milanese "*sanbabilino*," a term for the denizens of Piazza San Babila. The very perpetrators of the rape/murder this book talks about have always been classified as "*pariolini*," in spite of the fact that none of them actually lived in or came from the Quartiere Parioli; odd, isn't it? because they actually lived in the QT and fit perfectly into the identikit of that quarter. As Giorgio Montefoschi, the historic bard of that quarter, has pointed out, Parioli, well-to-do and therefore by and large conservative by persuasion, was certainly never a particularly Fascist neighborhood, either in its roots or its local customs; in fact, it was precisely its solidly bourgeois characteristics that inoculated it against the nihilism of the watchword *¡viva la muerte!* Proof of the fact is that the Fascist *picchiatori*, or hitters, had given up their effort to garrison the neighborhood's true center, its historic heart, Piazza Ungheria, and instead deployed to the outlying margins of the quarter, far less distinctly branded by the mark of respectability and bourgeois self-control: that is, instead, as is well known, in the very grim and drab Piazza Euclide, an outpost on the edge of nowhere, and in the partial wilderness of Piazza delle Muse, which was a gravel-lined park overlooking the flat expanse of the playing fields, the Campi Sportivi, over near the Acqua Acetosa and the river. And it still stands there, commemorating the outlying position of Parioli, for those who might have got it into their heads that living there might authorize you to think you're the king of Rome. The Fascist hitters happily garrisoned these areas surrounded by or bordering on nothingness, on these platforms without qualities, and launched their attacks from there, whereas they would never have dared to bivouac on the civil Piazza Ungheria. *Far too* civil.

It is an interesting characteristic of the twentieth century, this insistence on places devoid of history, the nondescript, the anonymous, the interchangeable, moral indifference, the grayness of the shaven skull, the void, the mistrust of culture, the aphasia, in short, the century's chilly passion for nothingness. The penitential character of the twentieth century, from the Cubists to Samuel Beckett, by way of the concentration camp, always needs to operate on a tabula rasa. More than the outcome of any process, inhumanity is its point of departure: the stranger, the indifferent one, the man without qualities, the monochrome, the subhuman, the de-evolved, the *arbeiter*, the *muselman*, the man-machine, the cyborg, pieces of body art, the replicant, the corpse, the fossil, the excrement, the cockroach, the murderer without a motive and the rebel without a cause . . . behold the perfect protagonist, the hero forged in the foundry of the last century. Any residue of humanity only hinders the course of the racing mind and slows down all action, to be rid of that human burden only makes us faster, lighter, more automatic. The pressure of a finger on a trigger comes more easily if you avoid getting tangled up in the back roads of feelings and consideration. I was convinced, as was everybody, that it was hatred that dictated these acts, but hatred acts only as an initial driving force, and should never be set aside from reason, which can temper it, bringing together and mingling causes that are frequently theoretical and effects that are concrete. However strong the hatred, it's never enough all by itself to get you all the way there. As long as it's a matter of trading punches, adrenaline helps, but if you're setting out to kill, then indifference, neutrality is much more effective. The impersonal approach that has nothing to do with the inhibitory brakes of character. True professional killers are cold, just as a seducer, a womanizer has to be cold. Hatred would get in the way of the killers, just as love would be an impediment to the lotharios. Perhaps that is why the QT was the favorite gymnasium for political violence, the chosen playground: because, exactly like a gymnasium, it was empty, devoid of memories. It offered no cultural or historical resistance, it possessed no traditions of any kind, nor did it claim any. Discreet, quiet, neither beautiful nor ugly, devoid of the aesthetic enchantment of central Rome, devoid of the incandescent rhetoric of its *borgate*, the outlying working-class suburbs. Nothing but a residential grid of tree-lined, sleepy streets. A square, in other words, a boxing ring, a tatami, a chessboard for chases and ambushes. I would even venture to say that the unfortunate murdered victims of Via del Giuba and Via Montebuono and Piazza Trento and Piazza Dalmazia and Piazza Gondar would never have died, never like that, at the foot of the Colosseum or on Piazza Navona, nor even in the Mandrione or in Torlupara.

> *Behold, the explosive form of life*
> *peaceful, monotonous, the void that draws*
> *and sucks into itself the flame . . .*

GLEAMING IN ITS WHITENESS along Corso Trieste, there stands an immense square building, unmistakably Fascist in style, weighed down by an expansion in the postwar years that sealed off its entry court, adding above the colonnade a new three-story wing: the giveaway is the shift in spacing between the windows on the façade, the clear break where the new wing attaches to the previously existing building. They needed new classrooms, there had been a demographic surge in the student population. This is the Giulio Cesare State High School.

AT GIULIO CESARE HIGH SCHOOL, when I got there, in 1974, the legend of Signor Razzitti was still circulating. He was a much-feared math teacher. To my great misfortune, he was also *my* teacher, and I can safely say that he fully lived up to his reputation. That year he mistreated us in every way imaginable, using his twin subjects, math and physics, which by the way he taught very well indeed, as the tools of a very painful initiation. His students had to suffer through a continuous and gratuitous mortification, and learn to withstand it without surrendering or mutinying, like Richard Harris when he is hung in midair by straps that pierce his shoulders in *A Man Called Horse*, a mediocre film that went down in history on the strength of that sadistic scene alone. A hundred yards of film made up for six reels of boredom.

Just think, Razzitti had assigned each of us students of class 3M a playing card from the Neapolitan deck, and when it was time for a classroom quiz, instead of running his finger down the classroom ledger, he'd shuffle the deck and have one of the girls choose a card, he'd very slowly reveal it, then he'd slap it down on his desk.

I was the Ace of Clubs.

The card that was called upon had to go to the blackboard. His or her surname, their identity, no longer existed. They never really had. Just like in *Alice's Adventures in Wonderland*, we really were playing cards, unfortunate playing cards who were about to have their heads cut off at the first mistake, indeed, there was no need to even make a mistake, since we ourselves were mistakes from the outset. The arbitrary way in which we were questioned was a prerogative of an irresistible power, which answers to no logic or right. It's that way just because it is, period.

Perhaps the mental association of Razzitti with the movie about a white man who becomes an Indian came to mind from the episode that made him a legend forever when, I've been told, in 1968, the students in revolt grabbed him by the ankles and actually hung him out a window. The only thing is, as they were in the midst of playing this game of intimidation, which was supposed to mark the abolition, once and for all, of the odious authority personified by the most desperately feared teacher in the school, the bell had rung, marking the end of that period's class and the start of the next one, which as it happened was one of Razzitti's classes, and that exact class had long since been scheduled for the written physics test, whereupon the students hastened to retrieve their teacher from his uncomfortable position, hanging head down, and set him, safe and sound with his feet on the ground, and he, straightening his tie and adjusting his clothing with a few brisk moves, and pulling out his pack of cigarettes, which luckily hadn't fallen out of his pocket during his defenestration, had immediately set about dictating the text of the classroom physics exercise, from memory, with his raucous voice, in a cutting tone, as if excluding categorically the mere possibility that a single student in that classroom might be capable of getting it right. He had jammed a cigarette in his mouth, state monopoly brand, MS, the cheapest and harshest, and had started his nervous pacing back and forth across the classroom. And in the meantime the very same students who had half-defenestrated him were sitting there, good as gold, once again terrified of him, of his authority, his charisma, bowed over their desks, intently writing away.

Razzitti smoked uninterruptedly, burning his cigarettes all the way down to the filter, sucking on them with an angry, neurotic lust. If you want to get a physical image of him, I can say that when I saw *The Shining*, I was astonished at the amazing resemblance between the bartender at the Overlook Hotel—the one who pours Jack Nicholson a drink in the midst of his hallucinations, and is of course a hallucination himself—and the math teacher at Giulio Cesare. The same smile, the same haggard cheeks beneath the Altaic cheekbones and the slicked-back hair.

The episode of Razzitti's defenestration + physics exercise had been recounted to me on the first day of school by my new classmates to give me an idea of just what kind of teacher I'd lucked into.

THIS, IN OTHER WORDS, was the level of connivance, of coexistence in the QT between conventional decorum, on the one hand, and sheer anarchy on the other. Incredible yet entirely possible. The students ready and willing to throw their teachers out the window are afraid of getting a bad grade. However hard it is to imagine it as a unified movement, the same kids who had gotten their hands dirty beating their political opponents would go home at night and wash those same hands before sitting down to dinner, eating the vegetable puree their mothers had made and quietly paying mind to her scoldings, "Don't make that noise when you eat," "We don't slurp our soup in this house." The general etiquette and routines remained largely unchanged, modest, slightly parochial, prudent, all of them mirroring a style that can be summarized in the single word "dignified." To live, speak, earn, and dress in a "dignified" manner. What does dignified mean? How deep can this concept penetrate and permeate a person's character, whether preserving it or ruining it? When I was boy, and my mother bought herself a pair of nice shoes, too nice, too expensive, and most of all, too *shoey*, in a shop on Via Bellinzona that by no accident was named Follies, I expressed my disapproval of these superfluous outlays and told her, judiciously, that when I got married I'd only let my wife dress in a "dignified" style, nothing more—meaning, no shoes from Follies, or at the very most, a single pair, for important occasions, not the kind of collection my mother had: to my eyes, she was a sort of Imelda Marcos. My father, on the other hand, still madly in love with Mamma, was happy to shower her with gifts.

For that matter, it was always my mother who warned us against squandering money: "It's not as if your father just finds it lying around in the street."

We also made fun of my mother for her preaching:

"Honesty is the first thing."

"Cleanliness is the first thing."

"Courtesy is the first thing."

"Education is the first thing."

O Mamma, just how many of these first things are there?

But maybe that's a story I've told before.

THE QT WAS AN AQUARIUM. The apparent placidity of its little traditions, the muffled resistance to any changes that filtered through the families and the schools, the tendency to reproduce the same ineluctable gestures, such as the Sunday pastries from Marinari or Romoli, and the weekly permanent at the beauty shop. All of a sudden, that smooth surface had been ruffled by a gust of gratuitous violence. Only an instant before, we would all have sworn that such a thing could never have happened, nothing in particular could ever have happened. Among the most mysterious episodes, I remember a proletarian expropriation—as we called what amounted to a loosely organized raid on a shop, a sort of gang shoplifting—that was carried out to the detriment of the casual clothing shop near Piazza Verbano. The owner's last name was Paris and he introduced jeans to Rome and pioneered the jeans store in the process, just like Bartocci on Via Castellini; he had begun in the years after the war with a market stand, and had then opened a shop near Piazza Vescovio, then expanding further with a second shop, called Paris 2, on Via di Villa Ada.

A proletarian expropriation was a form of ideological looting wide spread in the seventies, marking the most spectacular high point of other struggles, more serious and systematic, such as the occupation of public housing, the auto-discounting of rents and utility bills. It consisted of entering en masse into a shop and simply ripping off everything you could get your hands on and fill your arms with, without any particular method, whereupon everyone just ran out of the shop with everything they could carry, usually stuff grabbed at random, occasionally carefully selected on counters and shelves. Only rarely did the militants need to avail themselves of violence, both because of their overwhelming numbers and because of the astonishment of the sales clerks, who weren't fast enough to organize any kind of resistance (and in many cases, they wouldn't have done it anyway because, whether explicitly or implicitly, they generally felt a certain solidarity with the expropriators), and because of how quickly it was all over, usually within one to three minutes, at the very most. I'm not going to belabor the doctrine according to which this did not constitute theft or robbery but was instead *expropriation*, and therefore a legitimate act, albeit brusque. Proletarian legality with a view to the redistribution of wealth. As effective as it was symbolic. Already, by the advent of the following decade, there was no more talk of proletarian expropriations, indeed, the very use of the phrase was lost, save perhaps in an ironic acceptance, thefts had gone back to being the work of thieves, and private property became once again an inviolable concept. So it remained until episodes of proletarian expropriation sporadically began to present themselves again, at the behest of Italian social centers and antiglobalization groups, targeting shopping centers and malls. In those impersonal settings the feeling that there is a legitimate owner of the merchandise, a flesh-and-blood individual, from whom you might be stealing or expropriating, is already null and void, since for the most part the stores are part of anonymous multinational chains. From what I read in the press, the favorite targets of the expropriators have lately been plasma-screen TVs. The bread the poor are stealing for their tables, in other words, was baked by Sony. Back in my day, the owner of the shops existed, and how. His name was Paris, and he had scraped together his little fortune by the sweat of his brow. One day I'd like to meet him, at his shop, and hear his account of the way things went.

AT GIULIO CESARE HIGH SCHOOL, I became a member of the anarchist-Communist Collective M, after my class section, 3M, where I had been sent in durance vile. That section of the class was the last in alphabetical order, and was considered the high school's Devil's Island, a motley crew whose ranks had been decimated by flunkees and failures. That's the main reason I had ended up there myself, as a discard from the school run by priests, and therefore looked down upon as a genuine piece of human garbage. But for us members of the collective, instead, that letter was a badge of honor, or dishonor, reminiscent of M, the monster of Düsseldorf, who was our negative hero, especially because of two scenes in Fritz Lang's masterpiece: the one with the balloon as it flies out of the little girl's hand, only to be tangled in the electric lines, and then the other in which Peter Lorre looks at himself in the mirror, or else in the plate glass window of a shop, I don't remember exactly, and notices that he has the damning letter written on his back. M, for *Mörder*. We felt like monsters ourselves. The unsettling capital letter of "Collective M" was a logo that made us different not only from the Fascists and the tepid young men of the moderate and Catholic center (one in particular, distinguished by an Abraham Lincoln beard, future cabinet minister of the Italian Republic and European commissioner Franco Frattini), who took punches from all sides in their stubborn efforts to intervene and reconcile the warring factions, but in general different from the other classmates who gravitated around the usual political formations: the radical group Lotta Continua, the Italian Communist Youth Federation, FGCI, il manifesto, written in all lowercase letters, and a scattering of Socialists who often found themselves to the left of everyone else—an interesting phenomenon if you stop to think where the Italian Socialists ultimately wound up. We members of Collective M were just a minority sect of pains in the ass. Intransigent and sarcastic. Obtusely faithful to the banner of negativity. Like abstract painters, we sought out the purest forms, untethered to issues of utility. Therefore, ours were genuine provocations. When elections were called for members of the student council, the first in the history of Italian schools, our campaign slogan was "Let's defecate in the ballot boxes" (note the use of the latinate verb, rather than just "Let's shit in the ballot boxes"): unredeemable in our disagreeability, refined in our vulgarity. We were determined that an inexplicably demented spirit must distinguish all our initiatives, leaving those who witnessed or were subjected to them in doubt as to whether they were a prank or something

deadly serious: like when we took the headmaster's office by storm to protest against a custodian.

What had he done that was so terrible?

Nothing, he'd just been *rude*.

"We can't go on like this! Enough is enough! This is too much! Something must be done! Cestra *(that was the custodian's name)*, Cestra . . . is
discourteous!"

"What are you talking about?"

"We're saying that Cestra basically *spits in our faces!!*"

There, the only reason for our occupation of the headmaster's office was
so we could shout, eyes wide open, that senseless phrase: CESTRA . . . SPITS
IN OUR FACES!

The actual Italian phrase, *ci prende a pesci in faccia*, conjured up a surreal image, of someone using a fish to slap someone in the face.

Our obsession with fish, in this particular case, eels, had also led us to
reject the idea of the end-of-year field trip unless we were allowed our preferred destination, the valleys of Comacchio. Why? Why, of all the places
there were to go in Italy, necessarily Comacchio? What was there in Comacchio that appealed to us with such utter exclusivity? Nothing. Except for
the idea that no one ever went there. Florence, Pompeii, of course . . . the
royal palace of Caserta, the Piazza del Palio in Siena . . . but not for us: either
the valleys of Comacchio, or no field trip. And in fact, there was no field
trip. No teacher was willing to accept our diktat, and we stayed home, the
only class in the school that didn't go somewhere. Comacchio was an abstract name, a scholastic notion, like the borax-rich geysers of Larderello,
the steel mills of Cogne, the Liri River, and bauxite mines in general. Every
country on earth has bauxite deposits. In the country files in our geography textbook, under the country's resources, whether it was in Africa or
South America, you could bet your life, there would be bauxite. Or guano.
During quizzes you always knew what to say, and there was no teacher who
would dare to contradict you. Nations such as Suriname, or Rhodesia,
which later changed its name to Zimbabwe, or New Guinea, or the island
of Bali, were primarily rich in bauxite and exported tons of guano. The
world economy rested on these twin pillars, guano and bauxite.

ONE TIME, my father tried to prove to me that communism and anarchy
are irreconcilable. It's one of the few political arguments that I ever had
with him, one of the very few arguments in absolute terms. Communism

and anarchy cannot coexist, in fact, they're historical enemies, and he brought up the example of the Spanish Civil War, during which the Communists liquidated thousands of anarchists. Communism is an iron state, it's the state that controls the lives of the individuals, their ideas, my father said, forget about the libertarian spirit . . .

Not me, though, I refused to listen and I clung to my pride in being a militant in Collective M, in part because, deep down inside me, I maintained, and I maintain still, a certain margin of detachment, a sort of mental and emotional reserve which by no means keeps me from taking part in group initiatives, but nevertheless pushes me out toward the edges, in a marginal role, where instead of being a protagonist, you tend to become an observer. I don't know how to explain it: it's like playing a dual role, at once inside and out, believing and at the same time disbelieving. That is the story of my life. It meant that I could call myself both an anarchist and a Communist but still keep a substantial chunk of myself empty, ready for use. Rather than between two ideologies, the contradiction was inside me but, instead of resolving it, I cherished it. I dwelt in that space, in that hesitation. It's always been that way, even at the times when I was most fully, wholly involved, I always sensed that *something* was carrying me away. My gaze would turn glassy, remote. Total and unconditional adherence sends you straight to heaven, or to hell. I've always been and remain a purgatorial spirit. I can't seem to reason without ifs, ands, or buts—and especially buts, lots and lots of them. Communism and anarchy appealed to me (who has never, at least at one point in their life, been attracted to them? who possesses such clear-eyed, hardheaded realism?) but I was never able to make them wholeheartedly my own, and if I stood up for them, defending them against my father's critique, it was entirely out of a love of argument, not because I was really so sure that he was in the wrong. You wind up taking one side to resist the other, not merely in imitation. And so, if I was contentedly passive as I joined the herd of my classmates and their left-wing ideals, in spite of the doubts I felt, I also gained a fair amount of independence and courage in the act of defending those ideals (taking them entirely as my own at that moment alone) from my father's corrosive criticism. I soon realized that the education the priests had given me served the purpose admirably; and that the very articulation of my thoughts in demolishing or defending a concept is religious in nature. It tends to take the form of a sermon or a confutation. I tried it out at political assemblies, during occupations of high schools and universities, when I held a megaphone up to my mouth: when you speak in public your voice becomes external, as if someone else were modulating it. Before you, you have a community asking to be inspired and, in a certain sense, redeemed. All the same, that community sets up a great number of obstacles, some of which must be ground to dust, others sidestepped, yet others still flatly ignored. You need to bring home a result, whatever the cost, moving among the arguments with your eyes shut. And just what is that result? Persuasion. At that point, the rhetoric works on its own and you must simply let it flow. It really can take you far, so far as to state things you're not entirely convinced of, that would never come to mind if your mouth were shut. I wonder whether extremism feeds more off the maniacal and vindictive thoughts of the solitary man or the speeches prodded by the excitement of the crowd.

THAT WHICH CANNOT arouse faith can arouse curiosity.

AND AFTER ALL, how could we members of Collective M *not* declare ourselves to be Communist and anarchist? Deep down, two things that are equally absurd cannot by their very nature conflict with each other. One set of dreams cannot contradict another set of dreams. In fact, they often encapsulate each other. To dismiss as a dream a political doctrine with hundreds of millions of followers seems reductive or else rings out as a romantic justification of its failure. The crimes committed in its name are passed over in silence or dismissed in a few words, or even avowed openly to celebrate the courage of those who did not hesitate to commit them in order to give shape to their ideals—and in comparison with ideals, facts are always relegated to the level of disagreeable incidents. Idealism certainly isn't going to stop in the face of information and numbers, the accounting of those incarcerated, those deported. But it was a beautiful dream! We believed in it and we believe in it still, in spite of everything! Faith shatters all arguments. Dreams possess a miraculous continuity that bridges all contradictions. And pairs of opposites reveal their intimate bond far more than their difference.

THE FAIRY TALE is defended by treating every objection and critique more or less like a fairy tale. Since the cruelty and violence perpetrated were truly incredible, well, that means in fact that they are not credible, they're clearly an invention. The survivors of the concentration camps were often met with the objection that what happened was too much, an exaggeration, as if the excess of inhumanity was somehow their fault. "If you don't believe it, take it as a fairy tale," runs a wry proverb of Russian criminals, quoted by Varlam Shalamov. While I take your last piece of bread or I strip you naked in the snow, just take it as a bad dream, from which you're sure to awaken sooner or later.

THE YEAR I WAS BORN, 1956, the year of Miguel Bosé's birth and of the uprising in Hungary, those who attended Giulio Cesare were offered few opportunities to express their rebellious spirit. I'll describe here—exactly as it was described to me by an eyewitness, who took his final high school exams that same year—an episode that represents the most daring transgression of school discipline that could be tolerated in the Italy of the 1950s.

While the philosophy teacher was reading aloud from the book resting on his desk, his eyeglasses perched on the tip of his nose and his head bowed, the students lifted their desks and moved them forward, without producing the slightest sound, and then did the same with their chairs, taking care not to drag the legs on the floor, then another half-inch forward, followed by another tiny movement. The entire class thus moved steadily forward toward the desk in practically imperceptible increments, so that when the teacher finally looked up when he was done with his reading, he found himself completely hemmed in by desks, suddenly intimidatingly close, with the students all staring at him. At that point there was a sort of tacit understanding that he would say nothing and that the students would pretend everything was normal, whereby the teacher, after a few brief explanations, resumed his reading of the passage from Hegel or Benedetto Croce, and then, like a wave subsiding, the students would beat their slow retreat, moving backwards with their desks in tiny steps, or hops, if you will, until they had returned to their initial position. The teacher was able to monitor their progress with a rapid glance and then go quickly back to his explanation. The tide of desks rose and fell three or four times during the course of the class. All without the lesson being disturbed even minimally, nor was its efficacy undermined, as the students emerged perfectly well prepared.

The boys were thrilled by their audacity and by the amusement they'd enjoyed in this harmless game. A miserable burst of laughter.

FOR YEARS I'VE HAD the sensation that this was an experiment, or a sort of board game. A number of superpowers, whose catastrophic force could simply never be unleashed in direct, frontal conflict, at the risk of the total destruction of both parties to the conflict and of the whole world (as will happen at the end of times in Ragnarök, the Twilight of the Gods in Nordic mythology), agree to reproduce their clash on a smaller scale, on a neutral field of battle and with simplified rules, manipulating actors who are partly or entirely, blithely unaware, individuals convinced that they are living their own lives, in the first person, making decisions of their own free will, and therefore they struggle, they suffer, they weep real tears, and in the end they go down, they die or they succumb, with no idea that they were ever pawns played, or trading cards swapped, by others. In international politics this conflict is called a "dogfight": instead of you and me fighting, we let our dogs fight in our place. The political battle between the US and the USSR. This kind of an accord between the superpowers has something laughable and yet starkly dramatic, because within the perimeter where the clash actually takes place, the battle is authentic, war is still war: a narrow field, but all-out war. Maybe it's limited to a single quarter of Rome, but it's still "war with no quarter given." Among Ferenc Molnár's *Paul Street Boys*, a rock thrown was tantamount to the launch of a nuclear missile. Frequently, the savagery of the combatants is inversely proportional to the scale of the conflict. People will kill each other, for real, over *nothing*, a line drawn in chalk on the street, to defend a ghost, over a single word. The way it is in certain minor literary prizes: little if any prestige, no cachet to speak of, and yet the nominees strive their hearts out, and they're certainly not fighting for a kingdom. I swear that I have witnessed in those settings some of the most wretched acts of which humankind is capable, precisely because they were absolutely gratuitous, incomprehensible in the light of the ante that was at stake. A real reward somehow blunts the eagerness, domesticates the impulses, while a paltry nothing only whips them up. If there is nothing concrete to be hoped for, then the challenge gets bloody. People who go on TV these days, stubbornly reciting the mantra that "violence has nothing to do with sports," really seem to know nothing about either violence or sports. In a hand of cards played in a tavern, there are those who can pick out the entire spectrum of political acts, the trickery, the ambushes, with a clarity you might not hope to find in a royal court or a parliament, as well as the authentic reasons that men run to oafishness. The whole affair turns even more ridiculous if you imagine that, after all, there's actually no player moving the pawns, in other words, there are no higher powers in the struggle, as if there were an international soccer tournament among teams that belong to no nation. No homeland, no national anthem to fight for. The colors of the jerseys assigned at random. Then there wouldn't even be the excuse of having been manipulated. The marionettes will just go on moving with their wooden gestures not because there's someone up above, invisible, pulling their strings, but because that's their intrinsic nature— they're made of wood. It was an experiment, but one that had become an end in itself, with no scientist monitoring and studying the results. Devoid of real-world applications. There are no masters standing outside the corral where the dogs are battling to the last drop of blood, no one is laying wagers on you or on me, we've been put to the test, in the final analysis, we have won or we have lost, but nothing more than that is going to happen. It seemed like a scale depiction, done in miniature, of a heroic life: the loves and the bouts of madness and hand-to-hand combats and duels and the crossing of rivers in spate on our mighty steeds, which were, in reality, Ciao mopeds and Vespa 50cc scooters, the ruthlessness and the random chance by which the fallen met their fates, and now the survivors are doctors and lawyers, the betrayals and the trickery and the surprises and the excursions seemed like so many defiant challenges of fate, witnessed by the very gods on high, looking down from the clouds, as in ancient times. They amused themselves with our follies, but our follies mirrored theirs, that was the hidden meaning. As if we boys of the QT had been assigned to act out *The Last Days of the History of Mankind*, an accelerated film of a course on ideology, Napoleonic battles to be fought on the pavement between Via Panaro and Via Topino, forced marches and retreats, Doctor Zhivagos on Piazza Istria, a theatrical troupe made up of schoolboys, in other words, who find themselves acting out the Meaning of Life without yet having lived: with vivid enthusiasm and vertical plunges of tone, lavishing on it all the tremendously serious force of immaturity. This is how I've attempted to explain to myself how so much sound and fury could have been unleashed in such a narrow space and time, in the thoroughly nondescript place that is the quarter I grew up in: with the idea, that is, that it was somehow a miniature theater or a laboratory, a workshop.

A guinea pig dies, really and truly dies, even though the disease they injected it with had been administered on a strictly experimental basis.

Instead, it was life, with its pat and meaningless outcomes.

16

THERE IS A PIAZZA IN THE QT, or really, I should say, a traffic circle, which was once overlooked by the Cinema Triomphe, now a McDonald's, and which serves as gateway into the so-called Quartiere Africano. Some consider the Quartiere Africano to be an integral part of the QT, at least from the administrative point of view, seeing that the offices of the II Municipio, where you go to get your ID issued, is right there, on Piazza Gimma, in the midst of the grid of streets with exotic names, Giarabub, Galla e Sidama, Migiurtinia, Amba Alagi, Gadames, all names of places in Italian East Africa, and also because it is a basically commercial section of the quarter, where you can buy a Swatch or a book or a pair of pants; the purists or, if I can use the term, the fundamentalists of the QT reject this latitudinarian territorial interpretation and are convinced that the Quartiere Trieste is one thing and that the Quartiere Africano is quite another. These same fundamentalists, though, ought to consider a further geopolitical paradox that might give them pause. While it is true that the main thoroughfares conveying automobile traffic through the paradoxical Quartiere Africano on their way out to the periphery of the city, thoroughfares along which stand the large intensive apartment blocks which, in fact, have very little to do with villas and *palazzine*, the more genteel apartment houses, have names such as Viale Eritrea, Viale Libia, Via Asmara, and Viale Somalia, that is, the names of colonies to which we bade farewell a long, long time ago, it is also true that the QT itself was once known as the Quartiere Italia (if I'm not misremembering, that's what it's called in the magnificent scene in *La Dolce Vita* in which Marcello's father, passing through Rome, flirts with his son's girlfriend and comes close to having a fling with her, but then falls ill . . . ah, the geniuses! the unequaled geniuses! a genius dreamed that scene up and imagined it from start to finish, a genius wrote it, a genius shot it and edited it, geniuses performed it and dubbed it!), and the history of the twentieth century has seen to it that the names of the streets and the main piazza in this blessed quarter, named Italia and synonymous with Italianness, should refer to places, regions, mountains, and lakes many of which are *no longer* part of Italy or in

Italy, no longer Italian, after being Italian for barely a quarter of a century, just the interval between a world war won and a world war lost.

In any case, whether or not it forms part of it, Piazza Annibaliano is one of the symbolic places in the QT, and it is no accident that it is precisely on that piazza that there now stands the unsightly new metro station that you'll soon run into in the course of this story.

AND IT WAS THERE, on Piazza Annibaliano, on the sixth floor of the apartment house in whose bowels Big Macs and Crispy McBacons are now cooked and devoured all the livelong day, that Maldonado lived, and in the drawing room of his family's apartment an interesting, peculiar cultural project had taken shape. There were those who called it a cult, or a sect.

The leader of the sect was called, in fact, Maldonado, George Ares Maldonado. I couldn't say why he had an English name and a Greek one, followed by a Spanish surname: but they made a perfect series, so perfect that they made you think he might have made up two of them to go with the only one that was authentic. He was a diminutive young man, extremely nervous, with round wire-rim glasses, prominent cheekbones and lips, and a broad forehead already creased with wrinkles. Mongolian eyes, a little like Lenin's, and in any case, typical of the revolutionary. And just like a revolutionary, he spoke in a cutting, peremptory fashion. He'd cut other people off, with a contemptuous chuckle, when they were talking, looking down on them from the heights of a knowledge that he took great care not to expose and which was, as it were, taken for granted, assumed once and for all, at some point in the past as vague as it was concentrated, seeing that he was only twenty years old and, however many of those years he might have spent poring over books, it still seemed impossible that he could have accumulated so much learning in such a brief time, and stored it away behind his pale white forehead, in his bulbous electric eyes that flickered behind the metal-rimmed lenses.

He was in the last year of high school at Giulio Cesare, which he scorned however as an inferior school, when he founded a philosophical-scientific-literary journal that also treated theology and politics, or theological politics (don't ask me exactly what that term is supposed to mean, but Maldonado sometimes claimed that theological politics was the publication's chief point of interest), and which he named *L'Encefalo*. On the cover, under the masthead, ran the mysterious and polemical slogan: "If I smile, it means I'm angry." The cover with title and subtitle was in its turn inscribed within a fine line drawing of a cranium. This approach, so closely bound up with physiology and neurology, was willfully provocative.

For that matter, everything that Maldonado did, said, or wrote was provocative. His artistic proclamations were provocative, his black boots with twelve eyelets for the laces, rising above his ankles, resembling orthopedic footwear and yet, after a fashion, quite elegant, were provocative, and always gleaming, since Maldonado rubbed and buffed them every day with extremely expensive English shoe polishes, and he would brush and shine them for hours at a time. That was one of the few subjects that Maldonado would discuss willingly and explore at length: shoe polish—Meltonian, Kiwi, Lincoln, cream polishes, stains, and leather waxes.

To what sort of provocation did this notion of the high, tightly laced boots buffed to a high sheen belong, who was it aimed at? We didn't know, we didn't understand: but we found it striking. Or at least, I found it striking, I who am unable to venture far on pure imagination alone, who feel as if I've had very little direct experience of things and people, and even now am regularly astonished by a bunch of situations and objects and events that strike others as nothing special and instead seem to be stunning new developments, sensational discoveries, stuff whose existence I never even remotely suspected; that is why, when I was between sixteen and nineteen years old, I was the ideal subject for the influence of someone like Maldonado, perfectly suited to fall under the sway of his charisma and disconcerted by his whims and eccentricities. It was what I didn't understand that fascinated me and won me over, and only now do I realize that anyone who wishes to wield the power of attraction over others must never make himself entirely understandable, never stoop to the level of clarity, never, in short, *reveal himself.* Maldonado relied on this technique, tossing out obscure allusions. In his rare speeches, he would mix banal, everyday considerations with others that, enigmatic and sibylline, lent themselves eminently well to be taken for prophecies. In that which eludes our understanding, we are obliged to seek a secret significance, and the more stubbornly we seek it out, the deeper it hides, the more precious and captivating it becomes.

There, that's more or less the way it worked, *L'Encefalo.* In at least half of the articles, poems, and essays published, Maldonado (who under various pseudonyms was the regular author of all the columns), with diabolical patience, would encode meanings until they had been rendered virtually incomprehensible, and it was readers like me who were then faced with the task of deciphering them. I must say that this school of interpretation and translation proved useful to me, if for no other reason than that it accustomed me to the idea that comprehension entails an almost physical effort, a persistent, repeated effort, to be undertaken especially when the results seem to be lacking: sooner or later the coffer will spring open, the lid will lift, and the hidden meaning will glitter like a treasure trove, or it will produce the delicate music of a carillon. Every single article in *L'Encefalo*, even if it was barely a couple of pages in length, cost an unspeakable effort to read, two or three read-throughs weren't enough to make sense of it. Only those who had willingly run that gauntlet could truly claim to be intelligent.

The first issue, dated January 1975, is right here before me as I write. Sixteen pages obtained by folding and stapling eight normal sheets of copy paper.

The table of contents features:

- an editorial in which Maldonado (that is, assuming it was he who wrote behind the pseudonym of Arimane, but there's no real doubt that it was him) announced an imminent break in time, an epochal turning point of such scope that there is no human language capable of describing it;
- an account in verse of a pilgrimage by six of the magazine's editors to Mount Fumone, where Pope Celestine V had been confined;
- a number of translations of Lucretius and Gottfried Benn;
- a study of Chinese ideograms that have to do with the concepts of exchange, earning, and usury;
- an artistic composition in the form of a collage, with overlapping and intermingling sheets of a score by the musician Buxtehude, images of carafes, anvils, animals bedecked in garlands for a sacrificial ceremony, and a number of words handwritten in a tremulous calligraphy, perhaps the original handwriting of Hölderlin himself, after he lost his mind: *Aus Höhen glänzt der Tag, des Abends Leben / Ist der Betrachtung auch des innern Sinns gegeben*;
- an essay whose main themes were: the battle of the dry against the moist, of fire against water; how fire tends upward; how water rushes downward.

❖

I WASN'T INVITED to the ceremony. But I wasn't forbidden to participate, either. I was an outsider, but not the kind they'd shut out if he tried to enter or who is sent away when they find out he's a nonbeliever, like an infidel ushered out of a mosque. It's the usual story, which I've mentioned before: I hovered between detachment and participation around groups, events, situations, circles, teams, factions, ceremonies, initiatives, and parties, and my role was never at all clear. Member? observer? sympathizer? witness? spy? party crasher? intruder? guest of honor? Never quite close enough to the heart of the matter, and yet not a stranger, or not entirely a stranger, inside but still an outsider, in other words, outside but practically an insider . . .

Politics, work, literary universe, family/families, social settings, vacations: in no place have I ever truly been *at home*—and yet, how many settings I have brushed past, sniffed at, sampled, circumnavigated, how many I have courted, maybe for no more than a day or a month, and by how many I have been courted, in my turn!

Tai chi chuan, vegetarians, the Russian language and Castilian Spanish, humanitarian agencies, monarchic circles, left-wing terrorism, literary salons, kidnappers, yachtsmen, psychiatrists, priests, philosophers, neoclassical poets, refugees, newspaper newsrooms, film sets, recording studios, urbanism, the *borgate*, the ecological brigades, high luxury . . . I skimmed past all these places and categories and activities without ever fully forming part of them, like a guest, with my bags already packed to head out, or rather, never actually unpacked since my arrival. What was to other people a value, a faith, a discipline, a duty, a damnation, a job, a way of getting rich or getting poor, was nothing more to me than a curiosity. I never belonged to an inner circle, no one was ever able to say of me with certainty, "He's one of ours!" and if they did, they were wrong, though possibly that was my fault, because I had given them reason to believe otherwise. In no place, no schoolroom, no hallway of any publishing house, no backdrop on any theater stage, not even at my dining table at home, did I ever venture to say, "This is my home." But at the same time, and without a doubt, I was there, and it was me, not someone else, and I was involved, I had to do with it, I spoke and acted in some cases in an even more intimate and appropriate manner than those who really lived there, and always had, a more intimate and appropriate manner than those who could truly claim to practice those professions, to do those jobs, in fact, those who truly know how to *be there*. I have been *welcomed* far more than I have been *rejected* in my life, but I've always in the end disappointed a little bit those who opened the door to me, hoping for my adherence, my inscription, or my conversion, fooling themselves that I would stay forever. I've never had colleagues, or comrades, or classmates, except for those back at school. And maybe that's why, in the end, school is what I talk about.

AND SO—EVEN THOUGH I was not a member of the editorial staff of *L'Encefalo*, and indeed, truth be told, I deemed many of the ideas propagated by the magazine to be ridiculous, puerile, or just flat-out wrong, and as for the poetry, nearly entirely ugly, some verging on the pathetic, the articles incomprehensible, and the illustrations bizarre, albeit, occasionally, evocative (while verbal incomprehensibility annoys me and nothing more, when it is images that produce incomprehensibility, now *that* at times can be fascinating)—I was still invited in a backhanded fashion to take part in the ceremony. It was Numa Palmieri, also known as Prezzemolo ("Parsley"), a student at Giulio Cesare High School—as was for that matter Maldonado—the youngest and perhaps least intolerant and fanatical of all the editors of *L'Encefalo*, who summoned me with a phone call that was nonetheless brusque and sibylline: "It's going to be tonight, at three a.m., at the Sedia del Diavolo."

THE SEDIA DEL DIAVOLO. Literally, the Devil's Chair. The reader should not be misled by the name of this place, which has nothing satanic about it, or actually, yes, it does, because in bygone times, when it stood, isolated, in the midst of the countryside, the Roman Campagna, and the wayfarer spotted it from a distance as he traveled the Via Nomentana, it really could strike one as sinister. In the dark of night, you could glimpse the flickering light of fires set by those who had taken shelter within; hence the origin of its infernal nickname. Now, though, it is enclosed in a little piazza lined with ugly apartment houses dating from the fifties. It is an ancient Roman ruin, a two-story building, an entire façade of which has collapsed, while all that remains standing on the upper story is a single wall, so that the entire gnawed-away hulking brick structure (rising perhaps twenty-five feet? or even more) has indeed come to resemble a chair, yes, a gigantic chair: fashioned by a titanic carpenter for an enormous creature. It is the most incongruous, dirtiest, and most desolate monument in the QT, a quarter that has grown up around it, practically suffocating it: when you emerge onto the little piazza, your first sensation is one of bafflement as you try to figure out just what that heap of rubble might be, which looks like nothing so much as a house that's been bombarded and burned, with its narrow blackened windows and its missing walls. The Devil's Chair is its apt popular name. I've never known what the structure was originally, nor do I believe that anyone who lives nearby it knows. Back then it wasn't enclosed, but now it has a gated metal fence around it.

I'd set my alarm clock. It's a strange thing, when it goes off in the middle of the night and you've only slept for a couple of hours. I arrived at a quarter to three. It was cold out, there was no one in sight. Not even the officiants. I hunkered down as completely wrapped up as I could in the duffle coat I bought at the Paris jean store the year before. I lifted the hood, and its rough wool tickled my ears. After waiting for a while at the corner of Via Homs, I headed for the Devil's Chair. It was completely dark out . . .

BACK THEN, as I mentioned, it wasn't surrounded by a fence and not just stray cats, but people, too, could enter it freely. The interior was pitch dark. Once, when I was a boy, I had noticed that there spread inside it a dense and damp growth of grass, and something that looked like tropical ferns: but now I noticed, to my astonishment, all the vegetation had been uprooted, and even the crumbly soil that had been formed by the slow rotting of the plants had been swept off the floor, which now appeared clean and dry, by the faint light of the streetlamps outside that poured in through the three high windows. Who had done this? Who had tended to the Devil's Chair? Unlikely that it had been city groundskeepers or attendants assigned to the upkeep of archaeological structures, so numerous and widespread in Rome that, aside from the usual grand tourist attractions—the Colosseum, the Forums, the Pantheon (and not even all of the major ones, suffice it to think of the semi-abandoned Mausoleum of Augustus)—they generally lie in a state of complete desolation, beneath the shelter of the occasional corrugated sheet-metal lean-to, with a flaking informational sign posted out front.

I also ruled out, with equal certainty, the idea of a neighborhood committee or other association of do-gooders. The idea of a community of people acting altruistically for the collective good, even if that good is a small, narrowly circumscribed one, was practically unknown in Rome, and in this the QT, which claims to be a clean and spruced-up district, was no exception. Acting for the common good, the so-called good deed, the associative impulse—these things are virtually unknown in this city. When they do exist, they frequently conceal ulterior motives. Everyone, where they are able, has always taken care to look after their own interests, and so it has been for centuries. The only ones who promoted communitarian initiatives have been the priests. The priests, and maybe a few sports clubs and soccer teams with their entourage of fans, are the chief or sole possessors of any community spirit.

YES, of course, for some time there existed political movements, but their culminating initiatives always tended toward a demonstrative statement of some kind, circuslike, spectacular, and brutal, designed to intimidate or exalt, with the clamorous excitement of the assemblies, the demonstrations, the processions, the mass events; ten thousand or a hundred thousand or a million people, gathered together to protest, mourn, brawl, sing songs and shout slogans—certainly, yes, the "oceanic mobs," those certainly—in the name of grand ideals. Instead, what is rare are groups of a dozen people held together by a limited objective: to clean up a neglected, outlying park or distribute food close to its sell-by date to the hungry. Not that there have never been or are not now Romans who have done so or still do, or are willing to do so (if only someone would ask them), but in that case we are talking about, one might say, an imported, exotic custom that has little to do with the spirit of the city itself, a place where no one does anything for others, but then neither do they expect anyone else to lift a finger on *their* behalf; and actually where people do little even for themselves. The shortcomings of the political powers that be and the public administration are so wide-ranging and deep-rooted that in other cities they would cause a popular uprising, but not so in Rome, because the Romans neither expect nor demand anything much from the administrations that govern them, and they in return expect virtually nothing from the citizenry. To cite one example: when it snows (something that happens every twenty years or so), it is surprising to see how no one lifts a finger, witnessing the white miracle first with astonishment, then with joy, then with boredom, and ultimately with resentment (the entire rainbow of emotions spanning a period of eight to twelve hours, at the very most, a single day), once inconveniences and accidents put the city on its knees. You see no one, literally no one out shoveling snow, at least in front of private residences or to ensure some traffic can circulate on the streets: the citizens passively expect the authorities to take care of it, and the authorities demand, with haughty arrogance, that the citizens see to it themselves. Those few who actually make a stab, after a few desultory shovelfuls, take shelter in the warmth of their home or office. They hunker down, in other words, waiting for the trouble to subside and, sooner or later, for the snow to melt, at the first gust of a southern wind . . .

INSIDE THE DEVIL'S CHAIR I felt comfortably at home. Nothing could feel more right to me than that noble and ramshackle ruin surrounded by drab and dreary apartment houses. There was, in that down-at-the-heels monument, a sense of *coexistence* and *contrast*, a blend of the sublime and the laughable, a dense aura of mystery destined to prove to be, in the final analysis, a total absence of mystery, in short, there were all the things that attracted me back then and that would continue to attract me for the rest of my life, things that still inspire joy, discomfort, and a glittering pinwheel of largely unserviceable meditations in me. The power of that useless and menacing agglomeration of stone set down in the midst of a nondescript open space in the QT put me at my ease. That was my time, yes, and these were my spaces.

But was it the right place for the editors of *L'Encefalo*? You bet it was.

I saw them arrive, right on time, at last, as the clocks struck three in the morning, on the dot. They were walking down Via Scirè, in single file, dark, silent, like the Thugs in Salgari's *I misteri della giungla nera* (*The Mystery of the Black Jungle*), in fact, more than walking down the street, they seemed to *slither* down it. There were ten or so of them, and leading the line I recognized Maldonado, wrapped in a cloak. I identified him by the glitter of his small wire-rim glasses. Each of them had a bag over their shoulder, so they descended Via Scirè bent over with the weight. Bringing up the rear was a slight, slender figure. I felt how out of place I really was when they crept, one after the other, into the Devil's Chair and set down their bags. Except for the minute, warmly bundled figure I had noticed a short while before, in fact, I was the only one who had brought nothing.

And yet it was to me, of all people, me, the outsider, that Maldonado spoke.

"Are you ready?"

I nodded, though I had no idea what I was ready for.

Of the others, there were three I knew: one had been my schoolmate at SLM, though in another class, I'd played soccer with the second one, and in fact it struck me as curious to see him again not in shorts but rather in garb for officiating at the ceremony, and the third was Numa Palmieri, who had published an essay in *L'Encefalo* of which I still remember the opening sentence, lapidary and enigmatic: "The scream disorients the act of listening."

I WAS READY. I was trembling with curiosity, though it was riddled through with veins of skepticism. Deep down, skepticism always aspires to be given the lie by some miracle, and therefore it does nothing to undermine one's expectations, indeed, if anything, it enhances them. It creates fertile terrain for a stunning revelation.

Once my initial bewilderment subsided, I felt like a privileged attendee. The staff of *L'Encefalo* considered me to be a sort of valuable hostage, like the princes raised at the court of an enemy king, so that they might learn and thereafter be well aware of that king's splendor, remaining for the rest of their lives intimidated by his great power. Perhaps that was why Maldonado had summoned me to the ceremony: in order to impress upon me once and for all the depth of the research they had done, their spiritual superiority with respect to the trivial topics we in the QT might be wrapped up in, however relatively cultured we might be: politics, novels, movies, or even perhaps motorcycles or tennis, or even love, and then, inevitably, politics, in other words, a futile clash among ideologized little factions, while they instead devoted themselves to the interpretation of millenarian phenomena, metaphysical currents that bestrode the centuries, persisting like flimsy sheets of onionskin paper: the epochal movements, the great traditions. Yes, I was ready. I always had been. Like a sprinter who lives on the starting block. Maldonado gestured to his companions, and they began to empty their bags. I was careful to refrain from offering to help, well aware I might contaminate the ritual. Indeed, they didn't simply spill the contents wholesale out onto the stone floor of the Devil's Chair, but instead pulled items one at a time out of the mouths of their bags.

They were pieces of wood. They were branches and sticks, about ten or twenty inches in length, and they pulled them out and laid them on a broad cloth that Maldonado had unrolled on the floor. So that was the bulge I had glimpsed under his cloak.

Noticing my curiosity about those sticks, Prezzemolo handed me one: evidently my hands were not so impure that I was forbidden to touch them. So I, too, was ready, yes, I was ready. I grabbed it: it was white and featherlight, and it smelled good. I'm not capable of distinguishing odors, except to classify them as good and bad. But the scent of that wood was sweet and penetrating, and once the officiants had covered the cloth with a pile of light, dry branches that glinted white in the darkness, their perfume spread, really overwhelming and inebriating and exotic. Only many years later did I remember and recognize it for the classic essence of perfumery that it was: sandalwood, where on earth could they have found it? And how could those branches be so dry and light?

After delicately laying out those branches on the red carpet, the others took a step back, leaving Maldonado to sort through the pile. The impression was that they all held their breath while my high school classmate arranged the wood. I have to admit that I, too, instinctively breathed more slowly, as if I were afraid that the chilly, bracing air passing through my nostrils might make noise and disturb the ceremony. Kneeling on the edge of the carpet, Maldonado placed the perfumed wood, one stick at a time, composing a very particular shape on the floor of the Devil's Chair.

On a square base, he erected four walls made of branches, intertwined in such a way that they supported one another, meeting at the corners. On this fairly solid base, which stood about a yard high, he laid a number of longer branches horizontally, as if to close off at the top the cube formed by the floor and the walls of intertwined branches. I could not say how this game of patience—which had required at least half an hour of work, during which no one present spoke a word—managed to stay up without collapsing, but not even a twig of sandalwood tumbled to the ground. Maldonado arranged the wood with a delicacy that I had never detected in his customary acts or speech, which were invariably brusque and arrogant: as he assembled that singular pyre that released a sweet and insistent odor, my classmate was displaying hidden qualities. Watching him, and remembering subsequently what I had learned by watching him, I realized that in each of us there lies, somewhere, the exact opposite of the character that normally guides us and with which others identify us—not wrongly, for that matter, since that personality is what governs 99 percent of our thoughts and actions. I mean to say that we are also what *we are not*, that is, the spiritual whole of which we are composed includes, like a chemical formula, an imperceptible quantity of elements that have the opposite polarity to the dominant components, which means that a lazy person will contain a minimal dose (for the most part unutilized or practically unknown) of boundless activism, in the sensual soul there lies hidden a secret behavior, frosty and chaste, and even the most disinterested and altruistic character maybe suddenly reveal itself to be greedy and grasping, while the coward may behave with courage, perhaps out of a simple reaction . . . but a reaction to what? A reaction to himself, as if to contradict himself, to astonish those who expected the usual behavior from him. Countless resources lie hidden, deep within us, completing our essence as human beings with a touch of the opposite, different from all the other elements with which our essence had been originally painted.

Now Maldonado appeared to me to be very distant from the sarcastic know-it-all I had once frequented. His hands continued to transfer the pale-white branches from the cloth to that curious construction, with an unprecedented grace and skill. Had he done it other times before this? From what experience did that ceremonial precision derive? Actually, I knew very little about the business activity of *L'Encefalo*, except to be quite certain that those twelve or sixteen small-format pages, double-stapled together at the center, were the product of endless discussions, volitions, and evocations. On that cheap, porous paper, the dreams and the frustrations, the intuitions, the hopes, and especially the megalomania of anyone who at age twenty aspired to belong to the realm of literature were deposited in a sediment, as they pursued literature, invading, acting out its rituals, attempting to dominate it. The automatism of conceit generates powerful monsters, and these monsters turn the blades of the sort of gratuitous and arrogant enterprise that founding a literary magazine, and then going on to run it, really is.

A FEW MORE CEREMONIOUS and deft turns of Maldonado's hands and I was capable of glimpsing the shape that the pyre he had assembled now held. It was a chair, a throne. Its outline closely resembled, as a scale model, the very same Devil's Chair that now housed us . . . A high-backed chair almost six feet tall, with long, broad armrests, which gave it a sense of solemnity and solidity. The impression was of a piece of work so well made and stout that you felt the urge to sit on it. Who was the king destined to occupy that throne, constructed with such patience and fanaticism? We'd find out soon.

It took only a single match.

I swear, I saw it with my own eyes, it took only a single match.

Maldonado set fire to one of the branches that formed the base of the throne, and the match hadn't yet burned out between his fingers before the flame had already climbed the side of the throne and extended horizontally to its base.

It was a clear, bright flame, pure, as if it were made of nothing but light, and the sound that accompanied it was not the usual crackling of burning firewood, but rather a hush, a breath of air that added—I wouldn't know any other way of putting it—an impression of coolness to that flaming pyre, to those flames so bright that, if you had only been able to touch them, would have felt cold, freezing.

I had never before seen and never would again see a fire spread with such speed: no more than twenty seconds had passed from when Maldonado had lit his match, and the entire throne was burning. Just then a figure joined the scene, with a rope in hand. The figure tied several knots in it, yanked them tight, then tossed the rope into the fire.

In the hooded figure who had been the last to enter the Devil's Chair, when it was momentarily illuminated by the glare, I recognized the clear and delicate shape of the face of Arbus's sister, Leda.

FROM NUMA PALMIERI I later came to learn that the cloaks worn by the adepts of *L'Encefalo* were made of a single bolt of cloth, cut and knotted in a particular fashion. This was in order to ensure that an ancient ritual condition, a symbol of integrity, should be respected: "That there should be no stitching on their clothing."

> *If words are like fire*
> *Every word uttered is a promise.*

THAT WAS THE ONLY TIME I took part in the initiatives of *L'Encefalo*. The following month four of them set off on foot to visit Ezra Pound's wife, or his daughter, in Venice, or maybe it was actually in a castle in Trentino. I never received the definitive version of this pilgrimage. The director Werner Herzog had done and recounted something of the sort in a memorable book (*Of Walking in Ice*), going on foot from Munich to Paris to save a sick friend. It took Herzog twenty-one days; it took Maldonado and his com-

rades from *L'Encefalo*, I believe, less time. The reports on the matter are
hazy because there are no written accounts of the trek or, if there are, I've
never managed to get my hands on them. *L'Encefalo* ceased publication
after just six issues, which came out at irregular intervals. I owned them
all, but then I lost five of them during a move, and there is no record of
them at the Italian National Library, perhaps because the magazine was
never properly registered as a periodical. All I have left is the first issue. I
met a couple of the old editors by chance on my way through life. I met one
of them while going to pick up my scholarship, which at the time was being
deposited in a bank in Montesacro: he was a consultant for the branch office's after-hours trading desk, he recognized me, he was very polite, he
asked me if I wanted to open an account there, so that my scholarship could
be wired to me without any further inconvenience, and added that he'd be
happy to advise me personally on the purchase of a number of interesting
financial products. Perhaps because he assumed that I was astonished to
find him working in a bank (nothing wrong with that, as far as I was concerned), he told me that he still played the piano, as if music was some sort
of redemption, a kind of absolution.

I met another member of *L'Encefalo*, the same Numa whom everyone
had always called Prezzemolo, at a reception for the teachers at the high
school where my daughter studies. I was the one who recognized him, he
hadn't changed in the slightest in more than thirty years—in fact, by
now, nearly forty years. Skinny, beardless, a captivating smile, a shock of
hair, only slightly gray, hanging down almost over his eyes, a piercing
voice with a Roman accent, which he had under control but was still
unmistakable, the same as plenty of intellectuals, including some very
refined ones.

"Numa . . . ?"

"Yes? Excuse me, sir, do you know me? Your face does strike me as
familiar, but . . ."

"There's been a fair amount of water under the bridge."

I don't know why I used that pat phrase. I was delving into the linguistic resources of embarrassment.

"I'm . . . it's me, Edoardo . . . do you remember?"

Before I could utter my whole last name, Palmieri threw wide his arms
and we clutched each other tight in a hug that was far warmer and more
powerful than had been the ties binding us back in the day. But that's what
the old Prezzemolo from Giulio Cesare High School was like: cordial, caring, sincerely affectionate with one and all, and that explained why the om-

nipresence that had earned him his nickname of Parsley was widely appreciated, instead of being a source of irritation, and he was basically well accepted, even in Maldonado's coterie, the narrow circle of those forever young high schoolers who turned up their noses at the rest of the world. The truth is that Palmieri had read more widely and deeply than all his contemporaries put together, in part because he was easily influenced by one and all and obeyed as wish and command every suggestion to study certain books that were "absolutely fundamental," authors and topics that were "crucial." The day after any informal chat he was already in the bookstore or the library picking up books that had been mentioned causally, in passing, with an offhand reference to the title. As a result, his culture rested, so to speak, on a summation and mean of everyone else's, and what with his tireless climbing of bookshelves, he had formed an enormous mental library. Palmieri therefore was the only one at *L'Encefalo* to remain openminded, full of doubts, willing to question, and in short uncertain about what to think and believe. It was his curiosity and his confusion that made him a friend to one and all.

He congratulated me on the books I had published.

"Ah! I'm glad to hear it. So you read them . . . ?"

Prezzemolo showed no sign of embarrassment or the slightest hint of resentment at my doubt. And he immediately moved to prove his sincerity by bringing up a series of reader's notes that were very accurate, citing passages that he seemed to recall with greater clarity even than the author of those works. "Yeah, really interesting when you write that . . . hold on . . . that 'it's not easy to transform a story that's true into a true story' . . . that really made an impression on me!"

Oh, really? I'm always surprised when my writings are the subject of attention: not because I think they're undeserving of it, but because when I hear others report back the ideas and stories of which I ought to claim paternity, they ring commonplace to my ears, not especially attributable to me, interesting perhaps, but written or spoken by someone else.

"Well, thank you," is the best answer that I could come up with.

"Don't thank me. It was a pleasure . . . and an honor." From the very name he had been given, the name of an ancient king of Rome, Numa could well afford to use such a solemn term. If he deigned to use it with me, then that made this an honor within the honor. "Well, yes: you held our honor high." Our honor, who are *we*? We students who had attended Giulio Cesare High School together for just one year? Of the generation that came into the world in the second half of the 1950s? Or was Palmieri including me, admittedly as one of the more peripheral celestial spheres in the system that revolved around *L'Encefalo*? In that case, let's say a meteor more than any planet with a fixed orbit.

Then, however, once he had run through his compliments, he insisted on emphasizing the age-old difference. The gap that still persisted between the literature that I produced, like so many others, however laudable its quality might be, and the variety set forth by Maldonado and his partners at *L'Encefalo*, which elevated itself "beyond literature," as an "overcoming" of it. But he said all this with an understanding, affectionate smile. "Certainly, it's not the genre I generally read, or that I'd ever write myself, but it's still valid . . . and courageous." I know from experience that when someone tells you that something you've written is "courageous," that "you've been courageous," it usually means you've screwed up royally, you've missed the target completely: courage, in fact, is a euphemism, and it stands for an admirable failure. But I maintained my composure and took the punch, smiling, as yet another compliment.

"What about you, are you still doing it?" I replied. I meant to ask: writing. In terms of his affiliation and erudition, Prezzemolo was well versed in any literary form, ranging from poetry to philosophical essays, from aphorisms to critical prose, but as a young man he had exercised his talents in a middle ground among all these: in a mode that certain sarcastic detractors of *L'Encefalo* liked to describe as "oracular." For instance, "The scream disorients the act of listening."

"Oh no, *of course* not," replied Numa, lowering his voice and smiling mysteriously. He no longer wrote, *of course*. This might mean that the literary experiment had come to an end for him, without regrets, the same way you finish school or university or playing a sport, things that belong to a certain time of your life that you cannot just extend as you please; or else he might be alluding to the "overcoming" of literature itself proclaimed by *L'Encefalo*, the momentous turning point, in the aftermath of which to persist in dictating poetry or dreaming up stories was puerile, arrogant, illusory, as so many thinkers had claimed in the wake of Auschwitz and the atomic bomb. *Of course* Prezzemolo had given up writing. But he still bought other people's books and read them and, from the acuity of the observations that he had made, I'd say that he understood them, as well. His intelligence and his curiosity hadn't waned and twinkled out, *of course*.

"I'm in the field of agriculture and food. I work in seeds. Maybe you don't know or you can't remember, but that's what I studied in university."

"Agricultural studies?"

Prezzemolo nodded, proudly. He traveled frequently in Africa for his job. Well, I said ironically to myself, just like Rimbaud, who gives up his delirious poetry and goes off to traffic in weapons and slaves.

Whereas, just to clear up the reason we had both been summoned there that afternoon, I asked him: "So, you have, here at school . . . ?"

"My daughter. She's sixteen."

"Ah! I have a daughter, too."

"Really? What class is she in?"

"What class is yours in?"

"No, tell me about yours, first."

We exchanged details about family and school. We complained a little, but without too much emphasis, just to follow the thread, about the usual topics: the headmistress, a bit of a church lady, a few of the ditzier teachers, too much homework, too little, and so on. But it was obvious that what Numa cared most about was his favorite topic, so I returned to that.

"So tell me about your daughter, Numa . . . Are you contented with her, tell me?"

Contented? He was a happy man.

"Well, yes, we're very lucky," he replied, his eyes gleaming. If he had managed to get past his time at *L'Encefalo* and his verse, deployed like the folds of an accordion, credit was surely due to his love for that child, which sixteen years after her arrival in this world only seemed to continue to grow. Ah, yes, it's love, that's the turning point, it's love, the path, love is all you need, just like the famous song says. And a father's love for his daughter, all the more so.

"She doesn't give us any problems . . . she's a serious girl . . . and she plays the cello."

"*Stella!*" I exclaimed. Little star, an affectionate expression that my grandmother often used, frequently modified, in the idiom of northern Italy, into "*stellassa.*" I don't know why that word sprung to my lips at that very moment, instead of just saying "Good girl!" or "Congratulations!" but Prezzemolo was struck because as it turned out, that was indeed his much-beloved daughter's name: Stella.

I decided that, more than a traditional family name, it was an homage to the goddess Ishtar. And I also decided that life is full of replays and coincidences.

I STOP TO MEDITATE about the fate of the poets who at a certain point quit writing and publishing: and I review them in my mind . . .

One of them runs an extremely refined Asian restaurant, another has retired to live in his parents' house, which is available because they're now dead, near Tricase, in the Salento, and he makes a living by renting out the top floor of that villa by the sea. Yet another, who was very good and promising as a young poet, I'd go so far as to describe him as brilliant, is said to still be writing, wonderful things, but he won't let anyone read them. He doesn't want to. He's not interested.

I heard that Maldonado died in 2012. He had been ill for some time. The pat phrase people use when they want to say that someone has cancer. This piece of news made me think back to a morning I spent at the municipal office, on Piazza Gimma, which I spoke about at the beginning of this chapter: holding my little number, waiting for my turn at the window to renew my expired identity card. It must have been four or five years ago. Meaning that it was before Maldonado died. Since I expected a long line, I had brought a book to read; I looked up at the luminous display: it informed me that there were nine other citizens ahead of me, and I calculated that I would have to wait about twenty minutes, assuming the line clicked forward at a constant and regular pace—which is, of course, something that never actually happens, because it either takes half an hour to take care of a single, complicated case or else, quite the opposite, the numbers start to sail past with a beep, 122 . . . 123 . . . 124 . . . 125, meaning that someone had kept pressing the button of the machine that issued tickets, and had taken a handful, only to give up and leave. I sat down and in a few seconds I was immersed in my reading, lost in my book.

HOW FREQUENTLY *he grew irritated with his own rigidity, which kept him from extending himself to reach the simplest sentiments that were offered to him in a glance by anyone who didn't yet know him.*

It was impossible for him to free himself from those fixations and those emotions that possessed and occupied him to the point of expelling or replacing all other thoughts, as weak and pointless, to such an extent that there were days at the end of which, finding himself almost mechanically summa-

rizing the events as he prepared to go to bed and then trying, in vain, to get to sleep, it seemed to him that he had lived nothing other than that feverish and monotonous excitement . . .

I HAD BEEN READING for no more than a minute and I was already forced to stop, as if I were stuffed, and I lifted my eyes from the book and rubbed them. I wasn't really sure I had understood what I had read and, as often happens, I confused the thoughts I had found on the page with my own, thoughts that had previously occurred to me or thoughts yet to come.

A "feverish and monotonous excitement" . . . wasn't that after all the same thing that I had been living since time out of mind? And even now, in that waiting room, what else was I feeling if not that? With a neurotic gesture I stuck a hand into my jacket pocket to get the numbered ticket I had put in there just a short moment before. It wasn't there. It wasn't in the other pocket, either. I got to my feet to rummage in my trouser pockets, in the right one my fingers touched something that proved to be the receipt for an espresso, and then finally I found in my left trouser pocket the numbered stub, I checked it again, it was still 129, as if I'd been seized by the doubt that I might have reversed the numbers, maybe it had been 192, what the hell, no, it was really 129, and at that moment the sound of an amplified carillon alerted the room that 121 had just clicked onto the display, I could safely sit back down. But just to make sure, and to avoid having to perform once again that shameful operation of rummaging through all my pockets, I kept the numbered slip in my hand, deciding I'd use it as a bookmark. I went back to my reading, even though a voice behind me, raucous and disagreeable, was annoying. Someone was talking and laughing on a cell phone, without the slightest consideration that they might be bothering other people. I tried to ignore that voice and resumed my reading. I've only managed now, and just barely, and at age fifty, to grasp what my more illustrious colleagues conceived freely and wrote at age twenty-two or twenty-three: dazzling, incandescent concepts, stupendously fluid connections, images that stood out clearly.

I STILL LULL MYSELF *in the childish desire that suddenly it should be possible to reconcile all the incompatibilities; the ones that I feel within me, overwhelming, and between myself and the others, for now, incurable . . . And since this dream, the minute it appears, vanishes again, I feel as if I am the unhappiest person in the world, and naturally I exaggerate in feeling this way and in demonstrating those feelings to those who are close to me, I exaggerate in my affliction, and in this lies my principal vanity: because I know perfectly well that the points of view of human beings are far too disparate for there to be any hope of rebalancing their divergence, and yet I feel these points of view inside me, as vivid and inescapable as thorns . . .*

THE MOST ANNOYING THORN, though, at that moment, was the voice of the individual sitting behind me. He continued talking on the phone, in a raucous, stentorian voice, and it seemed as if he offered his interlocutor no opportunity to reply, save for extremely brief pauses. In other words, a monologue. And a fairly agitated one, seeing that his exclamations and his laughter made all the other people awaiting their turn, including me, lurch and sway. In these waiting rooms, the rows of chairs are arranged backrest-to-backrest, and every burst of laughter from this stranger made me sway back and forth. Irritated now, rather than turn around and start an argument, I stood up to move to another seat, and as I did I felt sure I had recognized the old avant-garde activist from *L'Encefalo* in the shrunken figure of that disturber of the peace, just from a glance at his back. Already his voice and his sarcastic snickering had stirred some memory inside me . . . but the final confirmation that it was really him came as I walked around him. He didn't notice me, caught up as he was in his phone call. His long, stringy hair, his yellow-tinged face, the rotting teeth that he revealed when he laughed before delivering each sarcastic wisecrack.

"Imbeciles! Ha, ha! They're nothing but a bunch of miserable imbeciles! We should feel pity . . . !"

"Ha, ha, but how stupid can a man of some wit turn out to be . . . !!"

"A solution is always within reach, never forget that . . . !"

In spite of the fact that his physical appearance was that of a fossil in comparison with the original animal, yes, I imagine that that was Maldonado, that off-putting client of the municipal office, George Ares Maldonado, one of the most brilliant minds that I encountered in the first part of my life, a star of the first order in the QT. His eyes were more bulging than ever, and the only thing that remained unchanged about him were the orthopedic-style shoes, buffed to a gleam, and his little round eyeglasses.

About Maldonado (may he rest in peace) I want to mention this one last thing: that he sent the contributors to his magazine to the Gallery of Modern Art, with the order to stand and concentrate on a certain painting (*Inner Landscape, 10:30 a.m.* by Julius Evola) and, in that painting, to focus on a specific area, convinced that that form and that color had the power to influence their minds: for example, curing them of individualism. Prezzemolo insists that that system worked on him.

Part VI

The Missing Shoulder

I

'VE HAD ONLY ONE Fascist friend in my life, one I made friends with even though I knew he was a Fascist, and not *in spite of the fact* that he was one, but perhaps precisely *because* he was one. He was a Fascist from head to toe and right out to the ends of his hair, which, by the way, was very lovely: he had long, silky black hair.

He was tall and charismatic, like an actor, the way you imagine an actor ought to be, and yet faintly awkward, or at least so it seemed to me, though this slight embarrassment as he moved his long legs and arms only seemed to make him even more graceful. He was Milanese, and in those years the young Milanese Fascists were quite different from their Roman counterparts, who were generally cruder. His was a fascism that sprang from an aesthetic matrix, and it culminated and took form in the ritualized violence of the martial arts; my friend was quite an ace, at the very highest levels, and in fact he might even have been a national champion in Italy in his category.

My friendship with him was of that very particular type that may not exist anymore, for all I know, in its specific form, and that is, an exclusively, rigorously summer-based relationship. Massimiliano was, in fact, a "beach" friend, as we used to say back then, which explains my connection with someone from Milan, the temporary suspension of the reciprocal prejudices that would surely have prevented the development of a friendship if we had lived in the same city—and what's more, the very special parenthesis that is opened during the holidays, when you experience adventures and emotions that have, so to speak, a predetermined half-life, that are bound to vanish come September, that are submerged, like a beach under a stormy sea, or that go into hibernation only to reawaken the following year, in a seasonal cycle that at least until the age of eighteen constitutes the natural punctuation of one's existence.

It was in fact during this gilded interval, this suspension, bewildered by the whir of locusts and sunlight dazzling on water, that my friendship was born, nay, let me say it, my adoration for this impossibly handsome Milanese karateka with the cutting speech and the perfect teeth. Even though several important parts of me (the Roman part, skeptical, the leftist part, egalitarian, the logical part, intolerant of rhetorical proclamations) remained mistrustful of him and from time to time felt irritated by his theories and the stories he told, which always verged on the absurd, both in terms of their content and the hyperbolic way in which he retailed them, lips clamped in a leering grin, the greater part of me was still bent happily toward him, willing if not actually eager to sit and listen to his bullshit and admire the prohibited blows he would strike, without warning, into the air as he twirled through the garden of his villa at Punta Ala, and literally enchanted when, as if to counterbalance his violent passions and displays of force, he would devote himself to the other discipline in which he was surprisingly skilled, and had a very delicate touch: the art of the classical guitarist.

Massimiliano owned a couple of spectacular instruments, always polished to a high sheen and invariably perfectly tuned, a Ramirez like the one owned by the great Segovia, whom he venerated, and a second guitar built especially for him by a luthier in Cremona, red and shiny with dark striations, made of rosewood: perhaps the entire guitar was made of that wood with its mysterious name—*palissandro* in Italian—or perhaps only the finishing touches were. "You see? It has a missing shoulder," Max would explain, showing me the cutaway in the soundboard that allowed him to reach the frets for the highest notes. "It's my crippled girl . . . my little cripple . . ." he said, caressing the guitar's curves, and then concluding, ". . . by Zeus!" which was his favorite interjection.

"SORRY, but I have to ask this, how can you do karate and also play guitar? Doesn't that ruin your hands?"

Max's knuckles, in fact, were covered with calluses, as if he really did nothing all day but shatter stacks of boards with a ritual cry and a sharp blow, as seen in karate demonstrations on TV, as an object lesson of the lethal mixture of force + technique + concentration, which is, if you will, the quintessence and the supreme objective of the quest of the genuine Fascist, the fighting Fascist, the Fascist warrior, in other words, someone just like what Max was and so strongly yearned to be. He had devoted the same maniacal discipline to his guitar studies, practicing until he became a full maestro. And so, hands capable of devastating everything in sight, like in a Bruce Lee movie, but also of plucking exceedingly delicate sounds from "his little crippled girl," his guitar with its asymmetrical silhouette. On account of the "missing shoulder," the guitar's shape was faintly reminiscent of that of electric guitars. But woe betide anyone who dared to ask him: "Have you ever owned an electric guitar?" the kind of idle curiosity that was as commonplace as it was justifiable among seventeen-year-olds, but which to Max was worse than spitting in his face. Max, however, master of self-control that he was, limited himself to reacting with a faint grimace of disappointment. What he felt was not scorn, but rather astonishment, a sincere astonishment that someone like me, intelligent and sensitive, could ever have stumbled into the traps of the period, the cloaca of ordinary tastes, the great misunderstanding of youth, like any ordinary kid, in other words, listening to pop, and rock 'n' roll . . . and who, in their ignorance, when they hear mention of a guitar, imagine Gibsons or Fender Stratocasters.

Well, he wasn't the first and he wouldn't be the last to think that about me. Over time, I have seen numerous replays of this interest on the part of people who considered me to be a step, just a single step away from enlightenment, from salvation: What? You of all people, so intelligent and curious, *you don't understand*? How could you fail to grasp this? I was always just a single step short of taking that decisive move to sweep away the slag of illusion that still dimmed my eyes.

And who were these individuals, who so devoutly wished me to convert, who had already in their minds enrolled me into the ranks of their little army? Well, first of all, of course, Massimiliano himself, the karateka guitarist, and then an esoteric intellectual (Maldonado), a couple of intransigent philosophers, political militants of differing orientation, and perhaps a priest or two. People who had made a great effort to scratch away the gleaming paint on the uneasy young man: underneath, however, there was nothing, or at least, there wasn't what they'd hoped to find. I disappointed them all, or actually, in order, I led them on, disappointed them, and in the end, eluded them entirely.

Maybe at first Max thought that he'd met in me his twin, a peer, a kindred spirit, a mirror soul, in part because there, at Punta Ala, in any ordinary summer of the seventies, you could find two-bit Fascists and oversized Fascists by the dozens, but they were generally the classic pampered brats with upturned collars on their polo shirts, who did nothing more active than to speak ill of those lazy layabouts in the factories who were always on strike, and then pretty little blondes with fabulous bodies who'd been weaned on arrogance, but there was no one who, like Max, preserved his privilege, convinced that he descended from a superior order, the social equivalent of a cosmic hierarchy. Max was stunned to learn that someone like me, who from the very first meeting had openly declared that he was a "Communist," just to make that point clear, should be so familiar with and even enthusiastic about that dandyistic and aristocratic coterie that was at the time an exclusive appanage of the right wing, for example Drieu la Rochelle, with the array of provocative phrases like the ones Jacques Rigaut so artfully launched ("Every Rolls-Royce that I see prolongs my life by a quarter of an hour"), that fragile and self-destructive fanaticism, the negative consciousness . . . and a few years later he would offer his congratulations at the sight of me perusing the works of Nietzsche and Heidegger . . . How could my friend, a virtuoso at flying kicks and guitar arpeggios, not fool himself into thinking that behind my ideological declaration ("Me? I'm a *Communist*.") there lay concealed a secret faith of opposite polarity, a faith long dissimulated by someone who, without even realizing it, actually nurtured it: that is, by Zeus, by me?

When I asked him if he had ever owned an electric guitar, he said nothing, only hunched over his Ramirez and struck up the most heartbreaking guitar piece I had ever heard.

After a few slow, scattered individual notes, he began an insistent arpeggio. The melody was hard to recognize, so suffocatingly did the tremulous accompaniment envelop it. It had been written specifically to bring a lump to your throat and that was exactly the effect it was having on me. There was something endlessly agonizing about those notes repeated to the verge of the spasmodic, in tight sequence; it moved off, it came back, piercing, increasingly shrill, then wandered away again, but without ever offering the slightest abeyance. I couldn't seem to breathe while Max played that piece: no room had been left for me to breathe in. It struck me as eternal, even if it only lasted for a few minutes. "Una Limosna por el Amor de Dios."

I ALSO KNOW THE EXACT DAY my friendship with Max ended. It wasn't when he tried to cut off the tail of his cat with a swipe of the katana, because he actually didn't succeed, Melville (the name of the cat) was too fast, the long sword sliced through the air without striking its target, or perhaps it was Max who intentionally missed, but he wanted me to believe that he had tried. To make fun of me, to send a shiver of horror through me . . . Poor old Melville! He'd come close, it was matter of millimeters in any case, hundredths of a second.

It wasn't when I saw his mother out walking with a silk scarf wrapped around her head, big dark glasses, a glass of vodka in one hand, white bell-bottom pants, a devastating tan, tottering, a ravaged thirty-five-year-old woman, weeping with large teardrops dripping out from beneath the glasses frames the width of her palm, while Max murmured a single word between lips stretched in an icy smile of indifference, "whore," just that word, "what a complete whore, by Zeus!" transforming the comment into a comparative evaluation of his mother as opposed to all the other women in the world. Could it be that she was any more or less of a whore than any other woman? There were plenty of other women like Max's mother in that vacation spot for the well-to-do, truth be told. Spectacular beauties with their hair pulled back into ponytails, sandals with heels, ranging from the elegant to the vulgar, eyes wide open in a perennial and neurotic search for something, anything, clothing, money, sex, psychopharmaceuticals, cocktails, an oasis of peace and quiet or someone to yank them out of that dependency and set them down elsewhere; but most of all, bronzed, tanned, bronzed atop their flesh but also, so to speak, *under* the skin, down to the bottommost layers, practically to the bone, bronzed with the relentless aid of little folding mirrors to be held patiently under the chin, which women's magazines handed out as marketing gimmicks (or maybe I'm wrong there, the fad of shrink-wrapped premiums and gifts with magazines is something that only started a few years later).

"The glare of the dying sun sweetly embraces / all those lovely little cocksucking faces," I heard a lifeguard-poet of Punta Ala declaim to himself, under his breath, as he walked from beach umbrella to beach umbrella, lowering them for the day, while all before us heaved, oily and blinding, the swells tinged golden by the sunset, and a procession of women waist-deep in the water went past, backlit silhouettes, dutifully walking parallel to the beach to tone up their thighs; and I've held them in my memory, those women and the inspired words of the umbrella attendant and lifeguard, but I'm not a hundred percent certain that right now, in this exact instant, hendecasyllabic verses aren't spontaneously forming in my head . . . "The glare of the dying sun sweetly embraces . . ."

The tears that dripped for no clear reason, incessantly, from Max's mother's emerald eyes and the drops that were pearling the drinking glass clenched tight between enameled fingernails, and the vulgar phrases murmured in her direction by her son as he rattled off arpeggios, playing pieces by Barrios and Llobet, did nothing to push me further away from that family so visibly devastated by the lack of ideals or the overabundance of ideals that were simply too elevated and abstract, and therefore unattainable, and therefore destined inevitably to failure and betrayal, leaving the field wide open for tawdry, demeaning forms of behavior; quite the opposite, I felt even closer to Massimiliano's heart, more of a friend, more closely tied to him: the things that distanced me from him, in fact, only brought me closer to him.

Among other things, knowing as he did my political persuasions, however wanly expressed and defended, he met me halfway (a fairly common attitude among the militants of the far right, who have always suffered a sort of paradoxical envy and admiration for the myths, symbols, rituals, heroes, ways of life, inventions, and to put it in a single word, the *success*, at least among the young, of the left—I remember that a right-wing leader once confessed that the finest political song ever written, and he said it grimly, with death in his heart, he had to admit, was "Bandiera Rossa"—because on the right, in spite of all their efforts, they had never managed to come up with anything of the sort, a song that was anything near as powerful, combative, and popular . . .), Max proved to be benevolent and curious toward the ideas and the novelties that were being introduced by the left-wing movements—and well, no doubt, it was thanks to the left that young women walked around without bras and enjoyed considerable freedom, and it had to be said that if it had been left up to the traditionalists of his political affiliation, they'd still all be wearing starched collars and getting engaged with little glasses of sweet liqueur in the fancy parlor, with the future in-laws.

If, in other words, our generation could have its fun and then suffer the vituperation of Max's comrades, Max himself knew full well that that fun was only thanks to his adversaries.

And that is why he told me about the time he ventured into the opposing camp, like a secret agent on a mission to winkle out the enemy's secrets, like an infiltrator who studies the behaviors and moves of his antagonist, passionately and diligently, until he knows them like the back of his hand, more or less consciously admiring them, and even putting them into practice or, in any case, yearning to do so . . .

Particularly memorable was his account of how he attended the Parco

Lambro Festival, the year before this story unfolded, a so-called youth assembly that had marked an era because it was perhaps the first time that radical political movements, new sexual mores, and drugs had all fused together: the first music festival in Italy where people gathered, did drugs, had sex, listened to music and played it themselves with guitars flutes tambourines and bongo drums, all while protesting against the powers that be, *all at the same time.*

"THERE WERE TENTS . . . tents . . . lots of tents . . . in one tent full of naked people, they were giving massages, in another they were doing yoga, standing on their heads . . . and then there were little groups sitting around bonfires, they were trying to roast something that was dripping grease into the fire, sausages, I think, stuck on spits . . . but they just wouldn't cook, or they'd burn . . . and stands with big bowls full of macrobiotic junk, yes, the whole place was filthy, by Zeus . . . and groups doing improvisational theater, cringe-making, with extremely skinny young men, bare-chested, with bow ties around their necks and their faces painted, and girls, half-naked themselves, their tits bouncing. And then there was the stage with a bunch of long-haired hippies up there who were playing music and flailing around . . . and a constant refrain of political statements through a megaphone, the booths where you could sign petitions against this and against that . . . and political discussions, sausages for sale, people dancing in circles . . . and the girls, yes, the girls.

"Girls dressed in short gauzy tunics cinched at the waist with a belt, who'd look you straight in the eye, their kohl-rimmed eyes steady as they hiked or fluttered the hem of their tunic to show you their pussy, inviting you to fuck them. For real, trust me. As if it weren't explicit enough to expose themselves like that, some of them would crook their finger to invite you closer, 'Come here,' 'Come on over and see me' . . . lots of them homely or just so-so, but some of them pretty and a few truly beautiful . . . who seemed the most relaxed of all, stretched out on mats in the dust, who if you ask me must themselves have fucked, in the three days of the festival, at least a dozen young men each, or more, twenty? thirty? Some of them retiring to the privacy of a pup tent, others letting themselves be mounted right there, in the open, from in front and from the rear, where everyone could watch, though everyone was half asleep or high on drugs, and there in the darkness . . . but I swear to you I saw them, by Zeus, yes, and I didn't just see them! In the dark, their white thighs . . ."

Max claimed he had fucked three girls that night he went to the Parco Lambro, that every time he had come *inside* them, that they had told him, "Come inside me," and that they liked doing it, or rather, they liked the fact that they were being fucked, though it wasn't as if they liked it all that much *while* they were doing it, in other words, they didn't have orgasms, they never had orgasms, and in fact that wasn't the reason they were letting themselves be fucked in the first place. "So then why?" I asked, simultaneously excited and curious, and also envious, because Max had been where I would have preferred to be myself; he, the Knight Templar, the crusader, filled with scorn and superiority, had ventured into enemy territory to fuck the infidel wenches.

"How am I supposed to know? To feel they were free, I guess. Shouldn't you be the one to explain it to me?"

"Search me . . . maybe it's because you're so handsome, Max."

He opened his eyes wide.

"Me, handsome . . . what the fuck are you talking about?"

Max reacted by blushing because, deep down, even though he was as handsome as the noonday sun, with the physique of an athlete and the myth of the superman, he was still a shy young man, and he was embarrassed to have anyone pay him a compliment. What's more, a man who pays another man a physical compliment . . . is always somewhat suspect. Max pretended to lash out with a swivel kick, but stopped his foot just a few inches short of my throat.

"Those girls, my friend, were letting anyone fuck them at all. By Zeus!"

Then he went inside to get his sword. It's as if he wanted to show off the beauty that he denied existed, at least in words. He whipped off his T-shirt and in the middle of his backyard he started doing his routines. In fact, he possessed a perfect physique, and I was captivated by the sight. And as he went through his maneuvers and routines, chopping the air with horizontal and vertical swoops of the sword, which he brought up short after having lopped off imaginary hands and arms, Max's long smooth hair danced whipping around his head.

IN THE END, the idea of Max that remains strongest for me is that of the teacher, the maestro. Of the teachers that he had had, and to whom he was devoted, and of the teacher that he would have already liked to be, at not even eighteen years of age, because the thing that mattered most to him was that, the transmission of a specific body of knowledge, but only to those who deserved it, only to those who showed themselves to be worthy of receiving it. By Zeus. For that reason, our friendship was doomed to end: I was squandering his gifts with my distraction. I remember him with the guitar in his arms, in that position, so harmonious, because it gives the impression that the player and his instrument are somehow all one, something I always envied: to handle an artificial extension of the body that at once completes and identifies you for what you're *truly* capable of, like in old portraits—a lance, a paintbrush, a sheet of parchment, a spyglass, even a miserable plow, as long as it renders the act significant and worthwhile. How many lessons he gave me, in just a few summer months, my friend the Fascist guitarist!

"Do you know, Edoardo, what a *rasgueado* is?"

"No . . . but please . . . let me hear it."

And he released his right hand in a progressive movement, faster and faster, fanning his fingers over the strings in a burst, one at a time, each fingernail striking the strings separately, five sharp blows just like an opening fan.

TO CHECK OUT what Max told me forty years ago, I went and watched some film clips about the Parco Lambro Festival. Well, no doubt about it, it was nuts. From the descriptions Max gave me, one detail is faithful, just how skinny many of the participants were: the young men with their emaciated physiques, shirtless, wearing hip-hugging, high-waisted jeans, their hair concentrated on head and face, and only at the center, like a bush, of their underdeveloped chests; the girls, on the other hand, with their jeans slicing into their hips, and also super-skimpy bikinis, just tiny triangles of fabric. They all look like they're hungry, like the main problem at that gathering was food. And in fact, there's a scene where some members of the organization were going around armed with crowbars, in order to go and retrieve a number of frozen chickens that someone had stolen (pardon me: *expropriated*) to then sell at the food stands.

It was practically only the men who danced naked: then there's a redhead, with extremely long hair, a very particular type, completely fried, and more than dancing, she's swaying, wobbling, barely making her small pointy breasts bounce. In the collective nude scenes, it's remarkable that the ones who take their clothes off are almost exclusively extremely pale young women, while the males are dark, with a dark forest of pubic hair from which emerges, shriveled, a wan, pale penis . . .

And then there is a yellowish dog walking around and among the people lying on the ground or squatting in the dirt.

Lots and lots of overalls, frequently worn with nothing underneath—overalls, perhaps the only item of apparel that, with the possible exception of car mechanics and gas station attendants and one famous TV chef, have once and for all been set aside, never again to come back into fashion, thank heavens.

Concerning women's bodies and how they appear to have changed over the course of the years, seeing the documentary about the Parco Lambro Festival reminded me of an instructive exchange I overheard on Via di Santa Costanza, a couple of weeks ago, between two office clerks who were eating a panino on their lunch break.

FIRST OFFICE CLERK: Have you noticed? In the old days, pussies were hairy, tits were smaller and saggy, but with bigger nipples.
SECOND OFFICE CLERK: What is that supposed to mean? . . . That's just what they show you on those porn websites. Women are no different than they were thirty years ago, it's their image that's different. They shave their pussies, otherwise they would be hairy. And they work on their nipples with Photoshop, while their tits are just surgically enlarged.
FIRST OFFICE CLERK: I'd heard that it was a matter of nutrition.
SECOND OFFICE CLERK: What about nutrition? So what?
FIRST OFFICE CLERK: The fact that girls have bigger tits these days. A couple of inches bigger, they say.

As I listened to them, I too wondered the same thing: yeah, I guess, maybe the second, wise office clerk has a point when he says that these are cosmetic and technological effects, but still, as the first clerk pointed out, you really do get the impression, as you look at those images from the seventies, that that race of men and women, boys and girls, with all their specific qualities, is now extinct. That it's vanished, no longer exists. Aside from the details or styles dictated by fashion, it's their bodies, their faces, their hair, their colors that no longer exist, even their tans or their pallors are no longer the same, and those images, dating back after all just a few decades, are farther from us today than the daguerreotypes of the 1800s.

In any case, I saw no signs in the vintage footage of the Parco Lambro Festival of the alluring sirens that Max claimed he had fucked.

HOW IS IT that our friendship ended, then? I'll tell you soon. But first, a brief intermission.

I **WAS HOLDING TWO FINGERS** deep inside her pussy, until my fingertips were shriveled and wrinkly, the way they are if you spend too much time in a hot bath.

I spent a whole month of August with one or two fingers permanently inserted in my girlfriend's pussy, my first girlfriend, that is, the girl I'd asked to be my girlfriend, and who had accepted.

The Olympics were on, and we'd watch TV in the afternoons, spread out on sofas, with other kids, our age and younger, and even little children, and while we watched I'd keep my forefinger and middle finger in her pussy until the skin on my fingertips wrinkled up.

What was I trying to find inside her?

What did she expect from that penetration, which the first time, perhaps, had been exciting or interesting, for its novelty, if nothing else?

Every so often, I'd move my fingers a little.

As if checking to see if anything had changed.

In and out, all the way.

Or else I'd widen my fingers, like a pair of scissors, feeling that the wet walls, when strained, would widen in turn, but only slightly, and I encountered resistance.

I'm not at all sure that she liked this, and if I turned to look at her, shifting my eyes away from the screen, I'd notice that her large dark eyes fixed on the TV were glistening, the mouth hanging half-open, lips swollen, her slightly buck teeth, like those of a bunny rabbit, glistening as well, but then that was my girlfriend's customary expression, slightly vague, vaguely stunned, hard to say, it might have been something entirely independent of the fingers that at that moment I held deep inside her.

It was an exploration, and I had no idea where it might take me.

In order to prevent the other little kids sitting around us from noticing what we were doing (now that I think back, I'm sure that they knew exactly what we were doing, considering how long we did it, they had to have realized and might even have seen), she held a T-shirt or a beach towel in her lap, and underneath my hand worked away, undisturbed, between her skinny bronzed fifteen-year-old thighs. Of course, that length of fabric was there for one reason alone, to conceal my maneuvers, otherwise why else would it be there?

Another expedient was to keep her thighs closed, her knees pressed together, which ought in theory to have blocked all access, while ensuring that everyone else assumed there was no way I was trying any such thing, while in fact I was able to do it all the same, with an unnatural twisting of my arm and my wrist.

And so I tried to pry apart, at least a little bit, her slender bowed thighs, because my wrist started to hurt a little after a while, what with being twisted back, but she wouldn't budge an inch: fingers inside, all right, but only with the thighs clamped tight.

She was embarrassed to spread them wide, all I had to do was glance over at her profile, falsely attentive to the Olympic endeavors, the blush that colored the only cheek I could see. I can say that I spent an entire summer looking only at her profile, as if she were an ancient Egyptian, which by the way is more or less what she looked like, her eyes elongated, rimmed in black, her sharp straight nose, her pouty red lips, or perhaps a Babylonian, the Semiramis of the Monti Parioli district.

Was she ashamed of me? For me? Was she afraid of the other kids?

But the others paid us no mind and kept their eyes focused undistractedly on the pole jump competitions, where for the first time we could see the competitors, or perhaps just one of them, the pioneer of the new technique, trying to ride the pole backwards, racing down the path and taking the last few steps before twisting around and launching into the decisive last backward leap.

It was a somehow unnatural act, as was ours.

What was the reward for that effort, what medal could we hope to receive?

This was research, these were blind attempts.

Neither she nor I really knew what we were trying to achieve, but we darkly understood that there were, there must be, passages, progressive steps forward, we certainly couldn't just stand pat on the level of kissing, and even the kisses themselves could be graded on a scale, depending on how deep one of us slid their tongue into the other one's mouth, but since there is a physiological boundary past which a tongue cannot reach, both because the tongue has its limitation in length, and because whoever is taking in the other's tongue runs the risk of suffocating at a certain point, after the oral exploration, one sets off to discover new parts of the body.

For males, the hierarchy and the resulting series of quests is relatively simple, after a girl's lips there's her breasts, her breasts to be touched, squeezed, hefted, from outside a blouse or a sweater and then (one step up) with your hands tucked under them, then (next step up) the final barrier, the bra, as you shove the cups upward, letting them ride over their contents, or else blindly unhooking them in back (an operation that, as we all know, can be complicated, and which is therefore accompanied by awkward embarrassment or hysterical giggling from both parties, or else snorts of impatience, "Here, let me do it"), or simply slipping a hand between fabric and flesh.

There cannot be, perhaps, a newer and yet more familiar sensation, at once remote, ancestral, that a boy can experience in his explorations than to stumble across the shape of the female breast; and I have always wondered, and more than once I have asked, filled with curiosity, those directly involved, many years after the first time they had them touched, exactly what their symmetrical sensation was in feeling hands make their way toward their breasts and, finally, palpate them. The word "palpate" is midway between the neutrality of a medical examination and a blandly lubricious use, instead, straight out of dirty joke, a piece of high school gossip, which reduces the act to a crude groping, as many women have confirmed they underwent in the years when they were young or extremely young, when their inexperienced lovers think they need to get busy on their counterpart's body in order to manifest excitement, interest, appreciation, and to prove to themselves that they know what they're doing, that it's worth doing, that the time has finally come to do it, and so they do it. Which means that those breasts need to be crushed, twisted, yanked up or out, massaged and manipulated more or less like a material you're trying to give a shape, as if it didn't already have one.

Awkwardness mixed with presumptuousness!

For that matter, if everyone knew everything from the very beginning, we'd avoid a lot of misunderstandings, no doubt, but at the same time, we'd never experience what has to be the only, true, sublime pleasure in life: namely, learning, the transition from the beatific state of ignorance to the impure state of consciousness.

It seems like a step down, a demotion, and in effect, it is, but in the very instant that it takes place, it releases an incomparable pleasure, even if a second later you might plunge into the depths of disappointment and dismay.

To touch a breast or feel your own breast being touched, not just the first time, but the second, and the third, and the hundredth, and even the thousandth time that you touch a breast or feel a breast being touched that has never been touched for the first time, or the same breast but being touched by different hands, or by the same hands and still the same breast but which over the years has changed shape, well, it's always a unique, unrepeatable experience.

When they confided in me, the women never told me about anything other than a sensation that could be broken down into terms of pleasure or annoyance.

"I've always liked having my tits fondled." "He didn't know what he was doing, he kept squeezing them, and it hurt." "It's nice to feel a pair of hands there, lifting them, holding them . . ."

Or else women gave me instructions, made specific requests.

"Tug on my nipples. Hard. Harder!"

"Please, no, not the nipples." "Why not?" "They're so sensitive."

"There, not like *that*, like *this*."

Often, contrasting instructions came from the same person, at different times.

As far as I was concerned, pleasure consisted of doing it, simply doing it, simply being able to do it, in realizing that you were doing it, that a path was open, a ceremony had begun and I was part of it, *I was initiated into it*, I could tell myself, "You see? you're touching a girl's tits. It happens," or even better, "A girl is letting you touch her tits, you, not someone else, those are *your* hands."

That's right, because, according to the mentality of the time, girls never *did* anything, but only *let* it be done *to* them.

The good girls, at least, the so-called good girls, and it is my impression that they constituted the vast majority of Italian girls, of all walks of life, classes, and levels of education (including, for example, the two victims of the CR/M, my classmates at Giulio Cesare High School, the daughters of my parents' friends, my female cousins . . . and so on). There was talk, but in fact, these were mythical exceptions, of incredibly uninhibited and enterprising girls who "did it all on their own," girls who took the initiative, who touched, manipulated, licked, and sucked.

> . . . *back in those days, there were still girls*
> *who wouldn't let you go any further than the thighs*
> *and the tips of their nipples . . .*

✦

(AFTER MANY YEARS, I saw this girl again, at a wedding, a grown woman now. There is an age at which your contemporaries all start to get married. In the meantime, I had had my experiences and she, I imagine, her own. Maybe she had even gotten married, and was there with her husband, I don't remember clearly. At wedding parties, toward the end of the dinner, people start getting up and switching places, sitting down here or there to chat with different people, and she and I wound up next to each other for ten minutes or so. Our legs chanced to brush against each other. Maybe because I was already pretty drunk, I couldn't help but reach a hand out under the table and slip it between her thighs, lifting her skirt, pushing her panties aside, and sliding a pair of fingers into her pussy, which was, just like ten years earlier, the last time I had touched it, very wet. Her eyes opened wide, then she turned her head and started talking to the person sitting on the other side of her; meanwhile, under the table, she spread her legs, rotated her pelvis forward, sitting in a way that allowed me to slide my fingers in deeper, then she grabbed my hand, making sure I couldn't pull away. She must have had at least as much to drink as I had.)

3

THE FOLLOWING SUMMER, there was a monthlong trip to Greece. Upon my return, exhausted, sun-charred, out of cash, in a city oppressed by beastly heat, which back then was an empty ghost town in mid-August, like any spoiled young man I went to the beach to stay with my parents. For several days, I did nothing but eat and sleep, with the occasional plunge into the waves. I slept twelve hours a day. It was the second half of August by now, the period when the summer turns and begins, all of a sudden, to wane, not because the heat subsides, but because a certain vibration in the light and in people's eyes, especially people younger than twenty, tells you that things, everything is accelerating toward a conclusion, and that was when I remembered Max. Of course, Max. The Milanese Fascist. The dark and smoldering Max. The classical guitarist. The champion practitioner of martial arts. Strange that I hadn't yet thought of my gorgeous friend, with whom the previous summer I had spent moments of closeness and intimacy sufficiently intense to convince me, to borrow the jargon of scandal sheets, that there might be "something more than just friendship" between us. I tried to describe some of those moments in the preceding chapter, and I hope that I was successful in conveying the idea that, at least for my part, we were close to an infatuation. During the winter, however, each in his city, it was as if we lived in two different nations, we hadn't spoken, we hadn't written to each other: I had almost immediately lost the scrap of paper with his address and phone numbers, both in Punta Ala and in Milan, and he had never reached out to me either, which I had never expected him to do, for that matter.

The summer back then was a free zone, an open domain that it seemed impossible or imprudent to reproduce at different times of the year, like a rite that must be restricted to its own specific time and place, otherwise it would be blasphemous. The distance wasn't then, as it is today, crowded, pullulating with contacts, contacts that no one felt the need for: we accepted distance as necessary, unbridgeable, and there, in its fashion, a beautiful thing.

And for that matter, even if I hadn't lost his phone number and address, what could I have told him by phone or by letter? What could I have told him about myself and asked about him? "Is the karate going well?" (Or was it tae kwon do?) "Have you been training properly?" "Are you still convinced that fascism is your singular destiny rather than our common past?" Or else: "Have you had any fistfights with anyone? Did you send them to the hospital?" I'd never have had the nerve to ask questions of the sort, or I wouldn't have been interested to read the responses. Not as written by Max, anyway. I have no evidence for what I'm saying, but still I'm convinced that he had no gift as a writer, or that he considered it to be a despicable activity, something for layabouts or little girls: by which I mean the correspondence, the "Hi, how are you?" the petty chitchat. And perhaps writing taken as a whole, the accumulation of words, compared with action, of course, with music—blessed music, superior to all else. In the packet of letters from the years that range from my teenagehood to my young adulthood, I find sentimental messages and confessions, or else discourses on topics such as literature, ideations, and polemics. Aside from a couple of letters from my mother, asking me how I was doing during my military service, the rest of them are about love or books, after all, those were the things I cared about . . . and how could I have shared such things with Max? That pure and contemptuous concentrate of physical acts, noble in his fashion, because utterly useless when it came to communication?

And so I decided to go to Punta Ala and try to find him.

I ALWAYS RODE my moped down the long, almost straight road that runs from the state highway to Follonica and cuts through the pine forest to Punta Ala, singing as I went. In my head, that is, with my mouth closed, to keep from getting a mouthful of mosquitoes.

AT FIRST, I got the wrong house. Villas surrounded by trees all look the same to me. The fact that I could not recognize, just a year later, the place where I had spent so many afternoons and evenings sent a chill down my back. It seemed to be telling me that stories and memories have no foundation: if even a house lacks a foundation, and appears and disappears at different spots in the pine grove, then what are feelings—such as friendship, for instance—even based on? And the pleasure that comes of them? Confused, I went up and down the road I thought Max's villa overlooked a number of times. The road was deserted, and so were the houses, in part because at that time of day, six in the evening, everyone must have headed back down to the beach. I decided to go there myself to look for Max, guessing that he and his mother still went to the same beach club, and even that they were renting the same slot and the same beach umbrella. I had to believe, I had to have faith that things continued to repeat themselves, unvarying.

I WALKED ON THE BEACH, filling my shoes with sand. I made my way down to the water's edge and walked it in one direction and then the other. The impression I mentioned above, that the summer was over, gone now, even though it was still a fair number of days till the end of August, struck me, as it were, right in the face. Perhaps it was because of the sun, low in the sky, enormous, red, warm, and yet melancholy and vulnerable, as if it were about to vanish, leaving no guarantee it would ever rise again: but as it left, it wished to delete the beach with a wave of light. Like the bathers crowding it, and those lounging in the water as slick as oil, remarkably still, motionless, no one swimming, no one diving, I was blinded by the glare. There wasn't a breath of wind and everything appeared definitive and yet precarious in its surreal fixity. Already over. It's strange that that image, overexposed and devoid of a soundtrack, is far and away the most vivid recollection I still have of that summer: the entire, wonderful trip with my girlfriend to Greece, all those columns, the oracles, the ruins, the sea a thousand times more unforgettable, left nothing like the same enduring mark on me. That moment lasted far too long. I can't say why, but it seemed unbearable; so much so that I was forced to stop, panting and out of breath for no reason, my arms hanging at my sides, unable to go on hunting for the beach umbrella beneath which I thought I'd find Massimiliano and his mother. Things were never going to be the same again, I was certain of it in a pungent manner, and I was filled with a pain that would have made me bend over, folding in half, if I had understood more clearly where it was coming from.

Now I understand, I understand all too clearly, and in fact, I'm bent over in the middle.

I WENT BACK TO THE PINE GROVE AND, at an intersection, I realized that I had taken a wrong turn earlier. Max's villa was on the inner road, parallel to the frontage road, and almost identical. Imagination was not the strong suit of whoever built that renowned vacation spot, just as a sense of direction isn't mine. And in fact, there it was, my friend's house, right where it always had been. A long, low building, enlivened by barely perceptible angulations on the façade, with large sliding glass windows, a retractable awning, wooden chairs lacquered white on the lawn where I had listened to Max play his guitar or tell me stories of his fights, with a few surviving pine trees standing there in commemoration of the fact that, until just a few years earlier, there had been nothing but trees. The idea had been to merge with nature, to hide in it: and yet never had an effort at camouflage succeeded so well by making use of elements so diametrically opposed to those it meant to imitate.

It was not uncommon to find holes in the garden that a wild boar had dug with its tusks.

MELVILLE, the gray cat whose tail Max had pretended to cut off one day, comes prancing across the grass toward me. He looks fatter than he did last year, and somehow slightly desperate. He rubs against and between my legs, but the minute I lean down to pet him, he takes off for the woods. Instead of cheering me up, the sight of the cat fills me with anxiety. Nothing is the way it used to be, I tell myself again. The green trees and the sky are mirrored in the plate glass windows, but one sliding window is open, you can see the interior of the house, I want to go find Max, give him a hug. "Is anyone home?" I call. "Can I come in?" It would be disagreeable to enter the house and find Max's mother in her bikini, with the usual wide-eyed stare. But then I notice that a different car from theirs is parked on the driveway, with a Florence license plate. "Max, are you here?" I call out again. I hear music coming from inside. Not the usual classical guitar compositions, but a whining voice from the radio.

> *Sylvia's mother says . . . Sylvia's happy . . .*
> *So why don't you leave her alone?*

A song that I know, though I've never known who sings it. Instead of my friend's mother, the person who comes to the door is a skinny, composed matron, with an inquisitive smile on her face. She's drying her hands on an apron that she immediately unties from her waist, as if excusing herself for having been caught in the middle of household chores, and she slides it over her neck. "I was in the kitchen, I didn't hear you . . ."

"I was looking for Massimiliano . . . Massimiliano, uh, yeah . . ." and it dawns on me that I can't remember my friend's last name. No, that can't be. I've forgotten it. Nothing is the way it used to be. "I'm a friend of his . . ." And it's only been a year. "A friend from Rome," as if specifying the city I come from would assure me the reception people reserve for a wayfarer, a pilgrim tried by the hardships of the road after making a very long trek to reach this place. "Oh, listen, I'm sorry to tell you, but they left at the beginning of the month," the woman tells me in a kind tone of voice, "anyway, you're welcome to sit down for a moment, if you'd like . . ." and she points me to the folding chairs on the lawn. Someone must have repainted them recently, because the white enamel paint gleams against the bright green of the grass. Seeing how stunned I am, the woman is increasingly hospitable and, as if we were in an American made-for-TV movie, she asks me whether I'd like a glass of lemonade. In the meantime, the voice in the song becomes increasingly despairing, almost breaking into sobs.

> *And the operator says, "Forty cents more . . . for the next three*
> *minutes . . ."*

The woman goes in and turns off the radio.

✢

"THEY HAD TO LEAVE IN A HURRY. They didn't say why, or at least, if they did, I don't know myself. Maybe my husband does, when he comes back . . . They'd rented for July and August, like they do every year, and they'd even paid in advance! But we'll certainly find a way to give them back the rent for August, at least, which they had no chance to enjoy . . ."

So they never owned the house, after all, I thought, stunned. And yet Max had shown me around, pointing to each object in the villa and telling me the story behind it: the story of the old rifles hanging on the wall above the fireplace, collected by his father during his trips overseas, and then the rocking chair, the original Royal Navy hammock, the knife that was chipped by a baboon's teeth, the canvases painted by his mother before alcohol had pickled her brain . . . still lifes, I have to admit, rather lovely, with pebbles, candles, necklaces, and bottles. I glanced at the walls to look for them, but they were no longer there.

"We really weren't thinking of coming, but anyway, the house was empty . . ."

The woman handed me a glass and filled it from a pitcher in which the ice cubes, newly plunged into the lemonade, were still crackling and splitting.

"I never go to the beach. I hate lying in the sun. It's bad for my skin. My husband, on the other hand, goes fishing. Maybe next week our daughter will join us. She's married and she lives in France."

The lemonade was unsugared. I took a couple of sips, thinking I'd leave now. "It's a pity, because they had been coming five or six years in a row now . . . they seemed to like the place. We only came in the winter. It's nice here in the winter, you know . . . there's no one around. Some people don't like the solitude . . ."

"Excuse me, though, what about the cat?"

"Oh, Lord . . . Certainly, the cat."

"Melville."

"Melville, right, poor thing . . . what a name, though, how on earth did they come up with it? With all the names to choose from. I say poor thing, but it's not as if he's particularly sociable, at least not with us. But what are we supposed to do, let him starve to death?"

Max and his mamma had been obliged to leave in a hurry, and they'd been unable to find the cat. He'd gone to ground in the pine forest.

They'd been forced to abandon him there. When the owners of the house had come to take possession of the now empty house, they'd seen him wandering around in the vicinity, and as soon as they'd opened the door, the cat had darted inside. And since then, he'd refused to budge from the place.

AH, THAT UNSUGARED LEMONADE! I drank three glasses of it. The lady of the house was in the mood for a little conversation. From the pleasure she showed in entertaining me, I guessed she had no children, then I remembered the one who was about to arrive from France. The married daughter. In that case, what she missed was a son, or just anyone to make it worth the trouble to squeeze all those lemons. A son whose thirst she could quench, a son to watch as he put on a clean T-shirt, a son to scold for some trivial thing, a son to give chores to do, such as "We're out of cat food, could you go and buy some for me? I'm so tired today . . ." knowing that he'll complain about it, but in the end, he'll do it. I've always gone along willingly with these sort of impromptu adoptions. Actually, I was waiting for her husband to arrive so I could talk to him. I would gladly have gone to buy several cans of cat food for Melville, in the meantime. But the fishing must have ended early, because the master of the house came home. My thoughts, which had wandered away from Max, turned back to him and remained there.

HE INTRODUCED HIMSELF with an edge of formality, as if I were an adult. "Marinucci," he said, then he extended his free hand to shake. In his other hand he was carrying a plastic bucket.

Marinucci was a big man, with swollen gut and legs. He wore a faded canvas cap, a checkered shirt open on his chest, and eyeglasses with a pair of dark lenses clipped to the frame, the kind that you can flip up or down; they were pretty common in the seventies but you hardly ever see them anymore.

"How old are you?" he asked me, brusquely. I told him. He evidently decided that I was the right age for a man-to-man talk. He took my arm. "Ada, why don't you go put these in the fridge?" and he handed her the bucket. Only then did I look inside: the bucket contained three fish. I don't know why I remember it so clearly, and yet I'm certain of what I say now, forty years later: there were three fish in the bucket, one of which was still flailing. The clearest images are often these side views.

"Are you listening to me?"

"Yes."

"If you're a friend of the boy, I think it's only right for you to know. I chose to keep my wife out of it. She's easily upset. If she hears of such a thing, and what's more, learns that it happened in our house, it will ruin her vacation. Which would consequently ruin mine."

He had a strong Tuscan accent, which to my ears has always sounded brutal.

Yes, brutal, in spite of all the literature and all the water that has flowed under the old bridges: or maybe it's exactly that original brutality, of ways and concepts, that made the literature that derived from it so powerful, who can say.

"The son phoned me, and told me that they were leaving. I believe they left late at night. They'd received bad news about the father. He was in Switzerland, very sick. Yeah, really sick. He'd checked into a hospital without telling them about it, neither his wife nor his son, but his condition had suddenly worsened. As soon as she received this news, Signora Vera tried to commit suicide."

"What, she tried to kill herself? And how do you know that?"

"Max told me. That is, he didn't actually tell me, but I could tell, all the same."

And he gazed at me, with an eloquent glance.

"*Un so' miha stupido, eh!*" His Tuscan accent thickened, as he snorted that he was no fool.

I shook my head to indicate that I hadn't thought anything of the sort about him.

"But the boy handled it well! Your friend. Who knows what *someone else* might have done instead . . ."

I thought that by talking about that hypothetical other person, Marinucci was referring to me. Well, I certainly would have gone into a state of panic: with my father on his deathbed on the one hand and my mother trying to kill herself. I asked him how she'd tried to do it. He glanced at me with a smirk of arrogance and practically burst out laughing.

"How do you think she attempted it? With a handful of pills, of course!"

I THOUGHT BACK TO VERA, Max's mother. I couldn't manage to separate her from the summer dresses she wore in a spectacular manner, naïve and brazen, as if at a fashion runway presentation or, rather, in the glossy photos in magazines, which depict in unreal poses the gestures and movements that are supposed to appear spontaneous, a greeting, a farewell, a leap for joy, the hand shading the eyes, hugging knees to chest, sweeping back hair, a pensive moment; nor could I remember her gaze hidden behind the big sunglasses with red or white frames, overwhelming her lovely triangular face, shrinking it to the size of a little girl's face, playing in front of the bathroom mirror, dressing up with her mother's accessories. She wore them indoors, too, those sunglasses, so similar to the multifaceted compound eyes of a fly viewed through a microscope, she even wore them to cook or leaf through magazines while sprawled out on the sofa, dangling her wooden clog with the progressive flexing of her enameled toes, from pinky to big toe. I managed to see them only once or twice, her eyes: and they were immense, vain and filled with anxiety, emerald green, but the iris ringed in black, like the eyes of a big cat in the adventure books that I had devoured until just a few years earlier, reading them in close succession, books that in fact told of enormous panthers, fabulous emeralds and rubies, guarded by sects of assassins in their subterranean temples. But at that instant I couldn't see them in my mind's eye, couldn't remember them, struck as I was by an anxiety similar to hers. The news had upset me. What came to mind instead were her dresses, her clothing. Her rumpled gauzy blouses. Her shorts. And then the scarf wrapped tight over her forehead, her heavy necklaces, the spaghetti shoulder straps of skimpy summer dresses, dotted with garish flowers, over her bronzed shoulders, her bronzed back, the neckline that revealed freckled flesh, because Max's mother was fair, with light-colored hair, light complected, but with that special blond complexion that darkens in the sun until it turns into a sort of golden leather, oily. Described in these words, it might seem that she was trying to be seductive and alluring, beautiful as she was and virtually nude, aside from the few square inches of almost impalpable fabric, the hooks, the interwoven knit rings of the bodice, the oversized belts that girded her waist: but instead that exhibition was put on, so to speak, in a void, for no one's benefit. Max had another opinion and was certain that his mother had a lover, or several lovers, there at the sea, and back in Milan. He had told me so more than once and he confirmed it with the insults that he spewed at her through clenched teeth. I personally recoiled from that thought in utter horror, indeed, to tell the truth, I couldn't even bring myself to contemplate it. It was my mind that rejected the thought, a priori, as if it were being asked to make a superhuman effort, or to contradict basic logic, the kind that told you that two plus two makes four, and there are no alternatives to that fact.

Max's mother couldn't possibly betray her husband, whom I had never met, for that matter—she just couldn't, period. Adultery was a thought beyond my intellectual scope. On account of that, the first time I read *Anna Karenina*, during my time as a draftee, I didn't understand, that is, I simply didn't grasp what the novel was about: I literally didn't understand *where the problem was.*

And in any case, the idea that it was all true seemed to worry and scandalize me far more than her son.

If you ask me, Max was a Fascist in part because of it. Hold on a second, I'm not trying to say that he was a Fascist because his mother had broken the marriage bond, but rather because confidently, bitterly, Max could think and accept as established fact that she had, be more than certain of it, that is, that she was cheating on her husband, his father, for the simple reason that he couldn't conceive of the slightest possibility that his mother *wasn't* cheating on his father. That his mother was a slut was something that Max simply took for granted. In that sort of ribald generalization which takes the form of what we call witticisms, it is customary to say that Italian males are convinced that all women are sluts, except for their own mother. They assume that she alone is a saint. Well, that's not true: that is, it isn't true that they believe it. Maybe they pay lip service to the notion, maybe they even tell themselves that it's true, but deep down they don't believe it in the slightest. Quite the contrary—the poor opinion that Italian males have (or had) about the respectability of women is something they originally formed with respect to their own mother. That opinion concerns *her.* Out of jealousy or resentment. When it all comes down to it, your mamma is that slut who denied you her breast. Not always, but at some point, and in a capricious manner, which is even worse, it only sharpens the sting. Dear reader, if there's a woman on earth whose faithfulness you should have doubts about, that's your mother . . .

Max despised his mother, despised her unsettling beauty, her weakness, her madness. The way she dressed ("like a slut"), the cocktails she drank, the puddles of tears she wept. If she had been less wealthy, or if she had been homely, her son might have felt some understanding toward her; but as the poet puts it, it's hard to feel pity for beautiful women, you have to be particularly intelligent and sensitive to do it, while Max had first crushed his sensitivity with his karate chops, and then conveyed it all into the fingertips with which he strummed his shoulderless Cremona guitar. This was just one more reason he was a Fascist. To lose all illusions about life, about the world, a place populated only by wolves and swine, to cultivate like a hothouse flower his fanatical faith in something capable of leading him out of that world, canceling it, draining his swamp. His mother *was* that swamp. I imagined her vomiting up those pills with the same vehemence with which she'd gulped them down . . . and while her son upbraided her, insulting her before trundling her into the car, along with the modicum of luggage he'd managed to assemble. That was certainly no time to be thinking about Melville. And then the drive, through the night, to Milan, and on to Switzerland . . .

THINGS WERE NEVER GOING to be the same as before. Of course not. It's a deeply moving thing to say and, at the same time, a stupid platitude that you could apply to any given point in life.

But here the doubt is even more powerful, and it shakes me from head to foot.

Things were never going to be the same as before.

But here's the thing, and the suspicion that goes with it, maybe things weren't the same *before*, either; they hadn't been the way we thought before, and they wouldn't be afterward: quite simply, that is, those things *never had been.*

MARINUCCI INSISTED ON SHOWING ME how to load the rifles that were hanging over the fireplace. An ingenious system for the times in which they had been manufactured. There was everything you could care to name in those rifles: chemistry, physics, goldsmithery, art, industry, courage, expertise, precision, and the instinct to kill. He took them down off the wall hooks, let me feel their weight, then he loaded them, aimed into the air, fired them, and hung them back up on the wall. Perhaps he, too, missed a son to whom he could impart some technical or moral notions concerning the world. It was no accident that the daughter had married a Frenchman, placing at least five or six *départements*, and a number of mountain ranges, between her new nuclear family and her original one. In vain Signora Marinucci tried to create a preprandial simulacrum with the invitation to stay for dinner. It wouldn't be long, already you could catch a whiff of oil and rosemary from the kitchen. But when I was a boy, I didn't like fish.

4

BACK THEN, time had been greatly foreshortened. Nowadays things last longer, life lasts longer, youth lasts longer, we have children later, at age fifty, women show off their breasts and they're still fabulous. Things don't end, even wars go on endlessly, smoldering, like in the Middle Ages. There's space and time between one event and another.

I think of the music of that period, and I list some examples here.

EXAMPLE A

1969, *In the Court of the Crimson King*
1970, *In the Wake of Poseidon*
1970, *Lizard*
1971, *Islands*
1973, *Larks' Tongues in Aspic*

EXAMPLE B

1970, *Trespass*
1971, *Nursery Cryme*
1972, *Foxtrot*
1973, *Selling England by the Pound*
1974, *The Lamb Lies Down on Broadway*

EXAMPLE C

1970, *Atom Heart Mother*
1971, *Meddle*
1972, *Obscured by Clouds*
1973, *The Dark Side of the Moon*
1975, *Wish You Were Here*

There, in the course of four or five years, it all began and ended, from discovery to abandonment, at a feverish, red-hot pace, you counted the months, the weeks until a new record came out.

☩

I GOT THERE LATE, out of breath and panicky at the front door of the Piper Club, there had been something . . . there had been something at home . . . I can't remember what it was, something must have happened at home, something in my family, which is why I got there late . . . Probably some stupid minor thing, some trivial detail, but families attribute the greatest importance to minor things and trivial details, they turn into matters of life or death. Like when they warn you: "This is the last time I'm going to warn you." Clean up your room, get your helmet out of the front hall, take the pliers (the drill, the wrench, the stepladder) back to the doorman, it's almost always things that have been in the wrong place for months now, and that need to be straightened up, put back, returned, after countless requests, it's the straw that breaks the camel's back, that suddenly makes their patience snap . . . and this unfailingly happens when you're heading out the door, when you're already on the landing but they call you back.

Which is why I crept out stealthily, without a word to anyone, to avoid being summoned back and given warnings, repeated "for the very last time."

Before becoming world-famous, Genesis was popular in Italy. For some reason, they were largely overlooked back in England, but in Italy they already had hordes of passionate fans, after just their first two records, or make that three, although the first album is largely skipped entirely in most discographies, no one includes it, even the band members have forgotten it or disavowed it. I myself start their history with *Trespass*, which is actually their second album, and in those days *Nursery Cryme* had just come out, an absolute masterpiece that I must have listened to, and I'm not kidding about this, at least a hundred times, and the single track "The Musical Box" twice as many.

THE SONG TELLS A STORY that I never fully grasped, but I don't want to go looking for the lyrics now and study them, I'm happy to settle for the residue that remains in my memory, to conclude what I had understood from the very first listen, and that is, that the song is about a rape. Rape, that's right, it seems that that's what it's about . . . In the song by Genesis, a fairy tale (a dark fairy tale, but after all, aren't they all?), it's a little girl who is raped by a jack-in-the-box, or by someone who, like the spring-loaded

puppet, pops unexpectedly out of the box, slips out unexpectedly—Old
King Cole. And after a great many arpeggios and flute solos . . .

> *Brush back your hair . . .*
> *And let me get to know your flesh*

Your flesh, your body, that is.

> *Why don't you touch me,*
> *touch me, touch me*

In a spectacular crescendo.

> *Now, now, now, now!*

I MISSED ALL THIS by arriving late at Piper, the famous club on Via Tagliamento, made famous, in fact, by countless miles of footage and thousands
of photographs, but which in that period had become the venue for performances by cult groups (I saw Soft Machine play there, for example, and
Amazing Blondel). Arbus was there, with a look on his face you'd see at a
funeral, which was actually his usual face: the curtain of long greasy hair
as always framing his expressionless face.

Too late, sold out.

"I've been here for an hour," he said, with his usual approach, the flat
statement of fact that contained no reproof. Having already apologized pro-
fusely for getting there so late, I asked him why, in that case, seeing that
he'd been there when there were still tickets, he hadn't just bought one for
me, as well.

"I didn't have enough money."

Again, an unassailable argument.

"Well, then, you could have just bought the ticket for yourself alone, and
gone in."

He shook his head as if that idea went against the basic principles
whereby the earth orbits the sun. Arbus was too literal-minded, too rigid
to enter the first, fabulous, historical Genesis concert in Rome without his
friend at his side. There was no need for him to put it into words, I understood from the faint shake of his pale, ashen face. This, which had been

THE CATHOLIC SCHOOL   735

meant as a demonstration of loyalty, proof of how indestructible Arbus's friendship for me really was, was something I didn't like one bit. It meant that not only had I missed the chance to see Peter Gabriel, Mike Rutherford, Tony Banks, Steve Hackett, and Phil Collins, and that it had been my fault, it had also been my fault that Arbus had missed it. I was sorry, disappointed, incredulous, a sheet of ice had descended over my heart, and without another word, I stared at the little front door of the Piper Club, which was locked shut, in the idiotic delusion (which was matched by the round and solid certainty that nothing of the sort would ever happen, not in ten minutes, not in half an hour, not tomorrow, in short, never . . .) that suddenly a bouncer would throw it open and announce, "We can take ten more," or five, or just two, and that those lucky two would be Arbus and me.

It didn't happen. In all likelihood, Genesis started playing shortly thereafter, or maybe they were already playing. I thought I felt the vibrations. Perhaps it was the opening bars of "The Knife," or the prelude to the not-yet-released "Watcher of the Skies," which just a few months later would become an unforgettable standard. While I was suffering unspeakable pangs and at least seven different feelings—rage, envy, shame, suicidal impulses, despair, fatalism, and remorse—were swirling inside me, Arbus said, "It doesn't matter," and, sticking his hands into his jacket pockets, he added only, "I'm going home."

IN AN ERA without cell phones and prepaid phone cards, decisions were clear-cut, errors irreversible.

IT WAS ARBUS who had discovered Genesis in the first place, and then introduced me to them. He had bought the records (*Trespass*, faux-medieval, starting with the album cover, with a dagger stabbing and slicing it), he'd recorded the tapes, and he'd given them to me so I could listen to Genesis myself without having to spend the money. He, too, with such a maniacally painstaking attention to detail that it couldn't have been the result of mere affection toward me, but must rather have derived from an abstract love of order and perfection, had recopied on the folded cardboard lining of the transparent cassette case the song titles and the band members' names, and next to each the instruments played, imitating the typefaces used on the album covers, which looked as if they had been typewritten. I don't know whether Arbus regretted missing that concert the way I did, if he still thinks about it. I know that in the course of a few years he lost interest in pop music and went back to his exclusive devotion to classical music—playing it, listening to it, analyzing it, understanding it, in a way I've never been able to do: too complex for my mind, too profound for my soul.

If you ask me, he didn't really give a damn. In no time at all, his head was already grinding through something else, and he never thought back to the Piper Club, the hour he spent for me, on the sidewalk on Via Tagliamento.

IF YOU WANT TO GET AN IDEA of the linguistic swamp we were struggling with all our might to escape from, suffice it to consider that the prose of those writing about it, the words we devoured from dawn to dusk in the pages of *Ciao 2001* (it makes you laugh, nowadays, doesn't it? that futuristic date) or else that we absorbed like sponges from radio shows were of this variety: "Robert Fripp is a fucking guitar surgeon," or "Once again, as if by magic, Rick Wakeman unrolls his sumptuous sonic carpets," or even "I'm an atheist, but Billy Cobham is God."

> *Everything in the universe suddenly turns crystalline . . .*
> *It was . . . it was so beautiful.*
> *I want to hear it over and over again, for years.*
>
> *My eyes turn into water . . .*

. . . That enigmatic record by King Crimson, the cover illuminated with brightly colored allegories, remains stamped on my retina, forever.

WHEN I WAS SIXTEEN YEARS OLD we'd sit and listen to this. We'd set the needle down on the first track of the album and listen to it, *all*. No distractions, no cell phones to check constantly. LPs were the only technology for listening to music, it was a pain to skip a track, you ran the risk of scratching the vinyl. So we listened to albums, forty minutes of music, from start to finish, the A side and then the B side, with the ambient segments, the endless solos . . . And then, frequently, we'd listen to it all over again.

MY CONTEMPORARIES FROM all over the world now write as follows:

> *Recuerdo que salía del colegio e iba a casa corriendo a escucharlo a todo volumen.*

> *Io lo ascoltavo facendo i compiti mentre ero al liceo e, incredibile! mi aiutava a concentrarmi.*

> *I remember when i was 17 or 18 years and i was smoked and i put music something like this, Tarkus! It was real estyle of the life!*

FREE HAND, by Gentle Giant; *Close to the Edge*, by Yes; Jethro Tull's wonderful ballad "Look into the Sun"; the despairing "Nobody needs to discover me!" in "Looking for Someone"; "Book of Saturday," which still raises goose bumps on my flesh; "Manticore," by Emerson, Lake and Palmer; Caravan's "Hello Hello"; Mahavishnu Orchestra's "Celestial Terrestrial Commuters," where in fact the drummer is God; Van der Graaf Generator's "Killer" (from *H to He*) and *The Least We Can Do Is Wave to Each Other*; Mahavishnu Orchestra again, *The Inner Mounting Flame*; the mellotron . . .

"LOOKING FOR SOMEONE" is better to whistle or sing under your breath, its mournful melody, its breaks—better even than listening to the record . . .

EVERY ENHANCEMENT OF PLEASURE is analytical in nature. The culmination of the curve, and it's no accident, is attained by obsessives: by those who fixate on the object of their obsession to squeeze out every last quirk, savoring, thrilling precisely to that endless analysis. A wine connoisseur, an opera lover, a soccer commentator—they all break down the topic of their interest into individual film stills, phonemes, snapshots, scents, impressions, and then they relive them, they review them on a moviola, scrolling back and forth endlessly, tasting and savoring and spitting out. Madness is just a step away, but there is no pleasure unless you venture at least somewhat close to madness, running the risk of falling in. Those who wisely stay away from the brink miss the pleasure. All wisdom is founded on the renunciation of joy.

(And in fact, that was how Arbus and I listened to records. I would say, rather than acolytes or priests, like scientists in a laboratory. And if the method that makes an experiment significant is to repeat it, many times, until validation is attained, we did the same thing with records, listening and relistening to the same record for a whole afternoon, and it was stunning the way that with each new listen we would discover something surprising. By that point, I knew those melodies and arrangements by heart, and yet every time I listened to them again, I would always take another step forward. A step forward into what? Into knowledge, into understanding.)

IT'S POINTLESS TO SAY that pleasure is natural, instinctive, naïve, spontaneous . . . quite to the contrary, there can be nothing more artificial, that is to say, nothing more constructed, artificially shaped. Pleasure is cumulative and comparative, and it is intensified, in fact, by accumulating, comparing, and grading. Anyone who says that knowledge and understanding blunts the shock of discovery, habituates, fosters indifference, is talking nonsense; who knows, perhaps when we're old (though in my case the passage of time has actually sharpened my sensitivity, pushing it to the verge of the feverish, life experiences rendering it morbid and profound . . .), but when you are kids, this is certainly not a danger, in fact, when you're kids what you feel are the pangs of a genuine hunger for knowledge, enrichment, because without knowledge, without repetition, without attention, without dedication, there is nothing. Nothing. No pleasure, no sweetness, no conquest, no heroism.

WE WERE TWO SPONGES SUCKING the liquid out of the music, the lyrics, and the images, swelling up and squeezing out, only to swell up again as we were dipped into the ocean of the new and the unknown.

5

HOW I MISS ARBUS! Once he left school, the fact that I might now be the smartest student wasn't a source of any particular satisfaction. And then, I wasn't the smartest student, people *said* I was, and sometimes I even *thought* I was, but always in terms of *potential* rather than in terms of any actual achievement. I'm condemned and will be for the rest of my life to hear people sing the praises not of the things I've done, but of the things *I could do*. The book that I could write, not the one I've written. People refer to my supposed intelligence as if it were a patrimony that hasn't been properly invested. And which in the meantime is being squandered, devalued . . . Which means that these compliments ring at the same time like criticisms.

With that head of yours, you know the things you could have achieved? And what did you do, after all? Fucking nothing.

Then I, too, left SLM.

NO DIFFERENT from my dear classmate Arbus, I had the clear sensation I was learning nothing. At least, in that case, as the headmaster had advised, I could have learned something by getting to know those around me, my teachers and my classmates, yes, I could have learned something from them, understood their lives . . . their thoughts and their needs . . .

THE REAL PROBLEM is that I lacked a personality. I still didn't know what a personality was. When I found out, I tried to construct one for myself, using segments of movies I'd seen and books I'd read, and striking phrases uttered by the few people I had around me: people a few years older than me, my cous-s-sin, unattainable heroes or secondhand idols. Everything that back then struck me as ridiculous and idiotic, nowadays seems lovely and decorous to me. And the other way around.

THE PARADOX OF SCHOOL is that things are taught too early that are too complicated, things that have nothing to do with the actual lives of those who are learning them at the moment that they learn them. And yet, that moment, and that moment only, is the time to learn them, when you still can't even begin to understand them. At age fifteen you find yourself studying the metaphysics of love, woman made angel, *la donna angelicata*, the *cor gentile al quale rempaira sempre amore*, the noble heart to which love always returns, when you don't have the foggiest idea of what these things are, what love is, much less its subtlest and most extreme declensions, distilled by medieval poets teetering on the brink of lunacy, in the wake of exceedingly complex abstractions that cost them centuries of thought and thousands of miles of burned-out nervous systems. And then there's the difference that runs between substance and accident: the substance, about which nothing can be said, nothing known, that you cannot define in any way, otherwise it would already no longer be substantial . . .

On the one hand, there are these unattainable concepts, which the brightest teacher on earth could never bring within your grasp, because they lie outside his as well, and he, too, struggles with them—and on the other hand is you.

THE FORMULA THAT DROVE us crazy back then was this: "What is, is, and what isn't, isn't." Signed: Parmenides. Sure, let's say it over again: "What is, is . . . and what isn't, isn't" . . . Oh, really?! What a thought. And this is supposed to be philosophy? That which exists, exists, that which doesn't exist, doesn't. "What is, is, and what isn't, isn't." In that case, if my grandfather had had five balls, then he'd have been a pinball machine: why don't you put that in the textbook, too? What is, is . . . and what isn't, isn't: to come up with this platitude, we had to turn to a great thinker? In that case, the subject we call philosophy is nothing more than a scramble of incomprehensible concepts and disconcerting banalities, and the idea that someone should go down in history and that we should still be here, twenty-five hundred years later, mulling over a phrase that really didn't ring all that different from "that dog is not a cat," and especially to exclaim over this scrap of foolishness as if it were the quintessence of the wisdom of the ancient world, necessarily led us to think of philosophy as a fraud; and the much acclaimed Greek Man we'd heard so much about as a poor sap. The problem was that, in fact, we started with things like this, these were the topics of the very first lessons of a brand-new subject that was being presented to us as the art of reasoning, the treasure chest of human wisdom, in short, intelligence in its purest state: and right from the very first pages we stumbled across mysterious personages, of whom all that survives are a few phrases, lopped off in the middle, stating that all is fire, no, wait, all is water, all is numbers, that arrows float motionless in the sky and that atoms fall straight down but then, at a certain point, they change direction, and who knows why. The *clinamen*: what could be more alien, more genuinely distant from the experience and the common sense of a fifteen-year-old boy? What can the *apeiron* be to him, and he to the *apeiron*? Pointless to put the blame on the usual teachers, there is no teacher good enough to popularize something that by its very nature defies reduction. Oracles aren't designed to be explained, otherwise what kind of oracles would they be? The most daunting concepts remain daunting, otherwise they degenerate into tomfoolery. In fact, in fact . . . an honest teacher ought to admit to his students his helplessness in the face of the steepest concepts and emphasize, instead of concealing or minimizing, their difficulty, how hard the knot is, don't think you can untie it with some trick . . . The more you explain and delve into the depths of these concepts, the more you realize that they elude your grasp. To say nothing of Italian literature, which begins from the end, is born already adult, a newborn with a monstrously developed head, with degrees of difficulty inversely proportional to the age of those who study it. So that throughout your entire time in school, the literature almost never intersects with its reader at the same intellectual level. The reader grows, the literature declines. At a certain point the two lines intersect and the student may even become too mature for the material he's studying, such as the various gloomy youngsters who complain about everything, or those renegade Futurists with their sound effects, all *tratatrak, tri tri tri, fru fru fru, ciaciaciaciaciaak.* Whereas at the very beginning it's truly tough. It's as if, in the very first lesson, the diving instructor pushed you onto the board, expecting you to perform a full-twist double pike. It's not the instructor's fault, it's not that he's too demanding. I am still left breathless when I read certain of Dante's cantos, and I try to imagine what it must have been like to confront them as a boy . . . but I no longer remember what that was like.

LEARNING AND UNDERSTANDING don't go together, or hardly ever: for a long time, you learn without understanding and then you understand when it's already too late to learn anything more. This is just one more reason why studying necessarily must be sheathed in a certain dose of coercion.

The same applies to prayers: first you have to learn them, and repeat them over and over, recite them from memory, many many times, as if they were a piece of music and the words didn't count; then, perhaps, years later, you'll understand what they meant in the first place and realize that what you were murmuring actually had significance. Or didn't. Or else you just drop them, stop saying them, period. Religion was founded on traditional practices performed from childhood without any discussion of their meaning, without a meaning ever being grasped: there was no need for that. The meaning would only have constituted a stumbling block. Nowadays, on the other hand, people expect someone to believe in God and explain God and *only then* can they enter a church, otherwise the act would be illogical, but in the old days people used to go to church out of habit until, one day, perchance, they actually ended up believing in it. Once we drop the custom and routine that is a precondition to the experience, then the experience itself dwindles and fails. Only those who gradually become familiar with something are able, in the end, to recognize it. First you pray, then you'll meet God, first you march and you chant and sing, then you'll wind up loving the fatherland, this is the foundation of religious and civil rituals. Nowadays we expect everything to justify itself immediately, giving good reasons. We no longer concede a lapse of time, a decent interval between learning and understanding: the two things must be simultaneous, everything must be clear from the very start, there is no room for boredom or for mystery.

EVEN NOW THAT I am an adult and I have, sadly, stopped learning about any new topic—with the occasional sensation that I am starting to understand something I actually already knew all about, but I hadn't ever really understood—many concepts and a great many issues remain beyond my grasp. I know about those ideas, but I don't understand them. I could even teach them to others without having grasped them in the slightest. Perhaps I have to become old in order to penetrate them, to be penetrated by them, as if by a ray that slices through a material turned featherlight and transparent. I imagine the mind of an old man as something lean, diaphanous, spare, scabrous, fragile, similar to his skin, stretched thin by age. A fabric tattered by too many washings. In the end, thoughts, crossing through this arid room without encountering any further obstacles, will dematerialize it once and for all, with a whoosh and a puff of ashes. This will be *death*. But until that day I'll continue to react with an astonishment mixed with a sense of the ridiculous in the face of many notions learned as a child (only to set them aside in haste), when I was both docile and skeptical, more likely to obey than to be seriously convinced of anything. I can guess at their hidden grandeur, but for now all I grasp is their peculiar aspect. Let's take for example the Myth of the Cave. Is it truly imaginable that men would walk around with statues on their heads, back and forth like the silhouettes of bears in a shooting gallery, and this for no reason other than to deceive other men who lie, trussed up like turkeys in a cave, staring at a rock wall? And that those men deep inside the cave are actually *us*?

THE TRUE AND PERFECT RELIGIOUS SCHOOL could not be anything other than a boarding school. A total institution, which covers every aspect of one's biological and mental existence. The fact that students are returned to their families and the outside world, as is the case in a normal school, only hours after entering the institution, interrupts the work of education, which is far more complex and delicate than a mere cycle of lessons from eight in the morning until one in the afternoon. Every evening, the web is unwoven, rendering pointless everything that was created in the morning. I'm not referring to the topics studied in class—no, those would be forgotten in any case, and they only count at the moment in which the child's intellect sniffs at them, seizes them or rejects them; in the final analysis one is as good as another and mathematics carries the same weight as chemistry or drawing, in other words, these are pretexts, stimuli, prods, there's no point in trying to make sure that a thorn remains buried in the flesh if its only purpose was to awaken you from the coma of indifference. Puncture the skin and you're done, all finished, run along home now. Instead I'm talking about that process of slow persuasion, that imperceptible metamorphosis which only lengthy, empty stretches of time can encourage, actual imprisonment, a lack of practicable or dreamed-of alternatives, the abolition of the very concept of expectation, and therefore of hope, that is to say, in the end, pure despair.

The expression "brainwashing" doesn't mean that the brain is dunked in water for a quick rinse and then taken out and drained. The mind, the human mind must be ground down, marinated at length in the brine of religious education, left there and forgotten, day and night, many many nights and just as many days, until it is thoroughly steeped, after which it will never again lose that distinctive odor, medicinal, astringent, a mixture of sweat, wet wool, aftershave, and at the same time passionately infantile, which emanates from priests of all ages, and from popes, from Paul VI to Ratzinger, including the archbishop of Kraków, I feel certain—though, even after getting in line at four in the morning, I was unable to reach his corpse to find out. Perhaps. Perhaps. Perhaps, repeated twelve hundred times. Perhaps the essence of the religious man lies in the stark wait and expectation, in the empty lulls, perhaps it happens while nothing happens, and it's there that you learn something, in the interval, perhaps you learn or perhaps you forget, the perhaps is mandatory, nothing that exists could be more dubious and uncertain than one's approach to God, Who might in fact manifest Himself in the form of a distancing, and trick you one more time.

The novelties that come out of bewilderment, finding something by chance, which is always a rediscovery, a recognition, a retracing of one's footsteps, a contradiction, turning one's head around, first 180 degrees and then 360 degrees, waiting to see if anything emerges from these blind stabs in the dark.

If someone is making even the slightest effort, then he is immediately released, refreshed, given shelter, if someone is free, the minute the bell rings, to spit out the holy water that had filled his mouth, then what is the point of even giving it to him? If you interrupt a ritual, then you remain only half immortal, and it is the fear of eternity that makes us say, "Let's stop here for today." School, in fact, consists of "that will do," "let's go home now." Let's go home, let's go home. Which is the reason for boarding school.

WHEN THERE ARE TWO OF YOU, *who decides which is to be Batman and which is to be Robin?*

THE FOLLOWING ARE STATEMENTS by my old classmate. The first time I heard them I didn't understand what they meant. They've stuck in memory, word for word.

"Everyone has some wit, some spirit. I have none. To make up for it, I can tell the truth, I can do, that is, what no one else does."

"It's pointless for me to reveal to my classmates what I think, since they are accustomed to laughing at everything."

Often, instead of responding to the witticisms of his classmates, Arbus would grind his teeth, his lips clamped shut, like the dwarf Hop-Frog in one of Poe's most terrifying short stories; you'd have said that he was sharpening them in preparation for sinking them into the throats of those mocking him, but at the same time his eyes, behind his perennially smudged lenses, were gleaming, because he was anything but angry, instead, as was his wont, he was thinking quickly and had already imagined, using what is called in chess "depth of play," the next five or six wisecracks that might well follow the first if he were to choose not to keep his mouth shut and, in fact, grind his teeth.

It should be said that Arbus, actually, wasn't a very likable young man, at least in the usual understanding of the word. Whenever he veered close to being likable in word or deed, you could be sure that he'd add an unpleasant or awkward touch, with the effect of shattering that positive impression.

With his behavior, wholly free of affectation, Arbus never made the burden of his superior intellectual gifts felt by others; but if it happened anyway, since there was no need to point out his disproportionate mental prowess, Arbus would simply cease setting forth his ideas and would just alternate them with a wisecrack or two, adhering to the general line of jokes young men his age tended to favor: about his teachers, soccer, the boredom of school . . .

Hello, is this the Beethoven residence?
No-no-no-nooo! *(to the opening notes of the Fifth Symphony)*

Hello, is this the Mozart residence?
Do me a favor and don't bust my balls / you might find the number on the bathroom walls . . . *(to the tune of the first movement of the Fortieth Symphony)*

Ergazomai ton filon dendron! (in ancient Greek, I care for the friendly tree, but in Italian, sounding very much like: I stick it up your ass)

WHAT DOMINATED in his face was uncertainty. He was inscrutable, either because he himself lacked a sense of certainty about the things he felt, whether he was in a good mood or a bad one, or else because other people didn't understand him. Something ineffable hovered around his face, a face that I cannot say I ever saw genuinely angry, or contented, or frightened. The only overbearing manifestation of himself was his laugh. Arbus's laugh was resounding and chilling, an explosion, and when he laughed (often for a reason that eluded others), my friend would open his mouth as wide as it would go, tossing his head back to display the upper arch of his teeth, white and strong, which he normally limited himself to grinding; when he laughed like that, instead of seeming like the fragile four-eyed nerd that he actually was, he made me think of a Cossack, a savage horseman from the Asian steppes.

CONVERSATION, between Arbus and me, was a more tangible way of thinking. He would express himself with a few laconic phrases, often impossible to share precisely because they were so terse, while I needed a great flow of words to get close to a concept, even the most elementary sort, as if useless words helped me to walk in a certain direction without even knowing whether it was the right way, but just to get out of my stalled paralysis. And so it remains, for me. I confess that I have never known what I think unless I could write it or say it first, and even afterward I still have the impression that my true thought must have been another one, all right, but which? Or that it needed clarification, development, or that I was making that statement only because I had read it in a book or heard someone say it, and all I was doing was repeating it, the way you might do when you're being tested in class, relying exclusively, out of all your mental faculties, on memory.

That dissatisfaction drove me to pursue a line of thought, after remaining silent, trying inwardly to determine what I actually believed, in other words, what I could *swear to*. Concerning life, school, my classmates, politics, music, soccer, in fact, even on topics like soccer, I never sensed that the things I said matched up with what, theoretically, I thought. Because an unexpressed thought too closely resembles a mere sentiment, a desire. What sort of an idea would it be to state that I *hate* this thing and I *admire* that thing, while this third thing just *bores me*? And so, when it comes to priests, capitalism, literature, the law, education, or the right soccer formation to field against Juventus in order to keep from getting pounded, I've never had any clear ideas, just a wavering between roughly held positions, which I buttressed with any number of arguments, none of which were decisive. Arbus, in contrast, gave the impression that he had already formed his ideas clearly in his mind before expressing them, and that he would change them not on a whim or an uncertainty or in the vain pursuit of something personal, the way I often did, but only when confronted with worthier arguments. Ideas didn't remain glued to his person, quite the opposite, they broke off effortlessly.

IN THE ARBUS FAMILY, strange things would happen. When we first became classmates, in fifth grade, those things were still invisible. It was a period of truce that lasted a few years, when children are still too young to either imitate or judge their fathers.

On certain gloomy afternoons, when the rain came down steady and cold, as if to give the lie to those who say that in Rome, whatever the season, "*fa bello*"—the weather is fine—it seemed impossible to start work on anything serious, positive, or even slightly amusing, so our sole ambition was to get through the afternoon, get it out of the way as painlessly as possible and make it to dinnertime. The truth is that it gets cold in Rome and the heating plant in apartments is underpowered, just a few old radiators with elements that provide half the warmth required. Winter Saturdays that ended at five with a curtain of dark and icy rain. It was during one of those afternoons that Arbus told me about his father.

WHAT DID PROFESSOR LODOVICO ARBUS, my classmate's father, study, what did he teach? A subject that stood midway among grammar, logic, mathematics, and philosophy. It seems that he was admired and respected at the university, and that his students venerated him. But often the professions of the fathers remained hovering, hidden behind a veil of indeterminacy, tucked away behind a term of professional respect such as professor or counselor or engineer, which told you little enough about what they really did all day, far away from home . . .

With our fathers, nearly all of us had a remote, detached relationship, or one fed by nervous excitement, fed by fear and admiration, since a father was someone who brought home a salary, inquired about your future, gave you affection provided you showed you deserved it by doing something meritorious—whereas our mothers gave us that affection always, no matter what. But in that phase of life, having passed through a more-or-less-golden childhood, it was obvious that we now had more interactions with them, the great males, our fathers. The period of unconditional affection, of cuddling and snacks (Eleonora Rummo would feed us fresh *rosetta* rolls filled with butter just taken cold from the fridge, not spread, because it would soften as we warmed the roll in our hands), that time dominated by benevolent feminine figures was coming to an end and on the horizon there loomed an imposing silhouette that was, at the same time, disagreeably exemplary, that was going to force us to reason, to strive, to achieve, to size one another up and challenge one another—and no longer merely in play. Almost none of us had ever seen our father at work. We knew that he worked hard and was strong, the best in his field, without a doubt, and yet practically none of us had ever seen him work with our own eyes, if anything we might have witnessed him leaving home in the morning to go to an office, a study, a construction site, a clinic, and again upon his return home in the evening. Never to have had a direct eyewitness experience of their father at work led some (me, for example) to fantasize about the things he did there, others to take no interest in him, others still to hate him for his remoteness or to idolize him for his success, of which we perceive only a shimmering gleam of flattering words and money. My father might have spoken to me five minutes a day, give or take, and, unless he was really very angry (about something at work) or very cheerful (for what reason I couldn't guess), in those five minutes he never expressed any particular emotion. But that was fine by me.

(IT IS SAID THAT EVERY EXPERIENCE left uncompleted leaves a hole, and that this hole then fills up with demons.)

ASIDE FROM THE OCCASIONAL CASE of a mythical or mythologized father, or a particularly strict and stern one, the source of incurable conflicts, I'm afraid that those of my generation have relatively little to say about their sire. We have understood very little about him, and we know just as little. Even the ones who mythologized him know very little, even if what little they know is good. Many of us seem to have had the same father; a standard-format father, an interchangeable father, a fusion of all the fathers available, but one that still remained a shadow, a stranger. In part, still a tyrant, and therefore greatly feared, but by and large a failed tyrant, and therefore at once the object of resentment and commiseration; viewed by us as already old, at age forty; a man ill at ease or out of place in his own home, dominated by his wife without concessions, and required to stay as far as possible from that home for his duties at work, at the office; a man perennially tense and incapable of managing his emotions, though he must have tried, but only to repress them; remembered for certain outbursts of blind rage, infrequent, and for the resentful tenderness of which he occasionally, in an entirely unexpected manner, proved himself capable.

Later on, the men would split up into three categories: the ones who hurt women; the second kind, who console women for the pain caused by the first kind; and last of all, the ones women do their best to have as little to do with as possible.

Lodovico Arbus belonged simultaneously to the first and the third category.

While looking for paste, or a pair of scissors, Arbus had found in his father's bottom desk drawer a collection of pornographic photos. These, however, weren't the usual naked women; these were boys.

And so he went hunting for more, and he found them in his father's books.

6

ID I READ? *Did I read?* I didn't *read* books, I devoured them, I sliced diced and chopped them. I gobbled them all down without leaving so much as a crumb on the table, a line of text that hadn't had all the juice squeezed out of it. Often I didn't understand much, or I didn't understand a thing at all, but only churned through the incomprehensible, done, finished, on to the next book. Only Arbus was as fanatical as I, but, in this like all else, more methodical. We spent one weekend (it might have been the tail end of the Easter vacation, or the long weekend of the Day of the Dead: if you just lock yourself indoors, the seasons start to become the same) in his father's country cottage. Calling it a cottage may be overstating the matter. It reared up in the middle of a completely sere patch of flat dirt broken only by a fruit tree here and there. You couldn't even stroll around the place if you wanted to, the grass was covered with excrement, variously dry and fresh, the sheep devoured and befouled everything, they grazed and defecated endlessly. But in the cabin where Arbus's father had written his fundamental works on linguistic recursivity (and, as we'd only learn later, where he used to bring his occasional male lovers), without TV, without heating, if you wanted water to wash you had to draw it from the well—but we liked it fine, because we'd brought a dozen books and in less than seventy-two hours we'd read them all. All of them. In fact, we read so quickly that on the last day we had nothing left to read, and so we left. I would finish one and put it on top of the stack, and there Arbus would grab it, after doing the same with the book he'd just finished reading. No commentary, we'd just read and nothing more. I think a faint buzzing could be detected, like the sound an electric transformer emits. Two young men stretched out on cots, in sleeping bags, demolishing one book after another. The sole diversion from this marathon reading session was to go outside for half an hour and take turns fielding penalty kicks, treading sheep shit underfoot, one of us kicking, the other one keeping goal, or rather, failing almost uniformly to keep goal, and Arbus practically never, between the goalposts formed by two saplings loaded down with still unripe persimmons, and either because the kick went wide of the goalposts or else because it sailed through the goalkeeper's hands, so the goalie would have to go and retrieve the ball, hopping to and fro amid the manure. We finished reading an hour before the bus left for Rome. The last two books were slender volumes, from the Einaudi Theater collection: Ionesco's *Rhinoceros* and Osborne's *Look Back in Anger*, and they each took us half an hour to read through, tops, forty-five minutes. Cosmo, our teacher Cosmo, had given them to us to read. It was like drinking fresh-squeezed orange juice without sugar.

I REMEMBER ONCE, perhaps in seventh grade, when Arbus sprained his right wrist. The only time I heard him complain and, if I'm not mistaken, I even saw him cry, holding his wrist as if it were broken. His mother massaged it with an ointment that released heat, bandaged it carefully, and hung his arm from his neck in a sling. For two weeks, my classmate was treated with every consideration, at home and at school. "Does it still hurt?" "Do you want me to cut your steak for you?" "Here, give me those books, I'll carry them for you." Actually, Arbus hadn't hurt himself at all, he just wanted to bask in his mother's attention and tender care. He confessed as much to me a year later; and it was one of the few times that he confided to me when we were still kids. Another time was his detailed account of a dream. That happened during the period when it was discovered that dreams have hidden meanings, and he searched for those meanings himself, stubbornly, or else asked me what they could be.

✠

"I DREAMED THAT I was leaving home. My mother was standing in the doorway, wearing an apron. Actually, she hasn't worn an apron once in her life. Twisting and rumpling the apron in her hands, she was begging me not to leave. I didn't answer her, and I just turned my back, in fact, *I turned on my heels*, and I headed off down a long hill, paying no mind to her pleas. I could hear her as she kept calling my name, her voice broken with sobs. Then, when I reached the bottom of the hill, I heard her voice, murmuring in irritation: "Fine, then, go to hell!" and I just couldn't understand how I could still hear her at such a great distance. By now I had left, I was starting a new life, but I couldn't say whether I was happy or sad. The first fact of this new life was a tryst with a woman. She was much older than me. She let me get in her car so she could take me home with her. I accepted willingly. But she seemed confused, she couldn't remember where she was, she'd take wrong turns and I was starting to get annoyed, "Can it be, does she really not know where she lives?" I thought to myself, and I asked her to let me out of the car. Turning suddenly stern, almost vicious, she told me no. "No, I won't let you out of the car," and yet she pulled over and braked to a halt, as if inviting me to try, in other words, just daring me to get out. I tried to pull the door handle, but it was frozen in place. "And now kiss me," the woman said. I gave her a good hard look for the first time: she was pretty, heavily made up, about thirty years old, but she had a deranged look in her eyes. Without any further discussion, I kissed her, and I had the sensation that she was dissolving in my arms, softening all over, turning almost liquid, and it was a very unpleasant sensation, her mouth was hot and gooey . . . and her face, her whole body was gooey and shapeless. I reached out to touch her breast, to find out if it was gooey too . . .

"After that, I don't remember what happens in the dream, but I do find myself making love with her. I have no idea how we got to this point and how it could have happened. All I know is that she doesn't want to, she starts screaming that she doesn't want to. 'Stop it, stop it! I'm still a virgin!' she shouts, in desperation, and at that point I want to tell her that I'm a virgin too, but instead I say to her, in a menacing voice: 'I don't care! I'll show you! I'm the one who decides!' She struggles loose, but I still have a grip on her. The strange thing is that, even though I force her, I don't actually have to make any effort, I don't have to tie her up or beat her, and the thing that's stranger still is that while I'm making love with her, I turn my back on her, as if I didn't want to see her. I don't know how, but I raped her with my back to her . . . and I could hear her whimper. I didn't get a glimpse of my genitalia or hers, I didn't even know where they were. It was a horrible thing."

IN CONCLUSION, I would say that there never was a person as thrifty as Arbus. Not even Zipoli, our classmate who used a single notebook for all his subjects, was quite such a penny-pincher. He had never asked the world for anything for himself but enough food to keep him on his feet, a pair of trousers and a T-shirt to wear, books to read, and a pair of eyeglasses. No joy, no tramping and hoboing on the far side of the stream, never a glorious drunken spree. At least, that's what we thought.

7

ARBUS HAD ALREADY DISCOVERED the fact for himself, but his father, with an act that was rare for the time and exemplary, made his homosexuality known with a public announcement. Without prompting from anyone, he wrote an open letter to the most widely read evening newspaper in Rome. It was read with astonishment by one and all, it was carried by other newspapers, and it began a "debate," as the phrase went at the time, on the subject. Which wasn't exactly homosexuality: there had always been lesbians and queers, and as such they had always been singled out, parodied, ghettoized, coddled, beaten bloody or else considered "very amusing" or "very sensitive," depending on the situation. But also left alone, inasmuch as they were distinctly different. In my own, private opinion, they were far freer then than they are now, but perhaps that's true for all of us. Such a curious phenomenon, liberty: on paper, it has increased, but in concrete, everyday terms, it's only shrunk. Lots of homosexuals occupied prominent posts in the world of culture, as writers, directors, art critics, and so on. One line of the transmission of knowledge and creativity had always worked in this way, and it had worked very well. But the case of Lodovico Arbus, who belonged to that world, albeit as an academic and not as an artist, was more controversial: that is, the case of a married man with children who, having already lived half of his life, now chose to reveal that he was and, deep down in the core of his existence, always had been a homosexual; and he now resolved from that day forth to behave in accordance with his true nature, without forcing it or concealing it anymore. His wife, his children, these were the product of a sacrifice or sheer confusion. Professor Arbus's manifesto shook public opinion, pushing it toward an array of reactions, which we can easily imagine without having to list them here. Those who lived through those times can picture them to themselves; those who didn't live through them because they were too young or not yet born would just be wasting their time studying ways and customs that vanished so suddenly you'd think they really had been just so many castles in thin air. We should in any case mention two opposing attitudes that transcended the merely sexual aspect: either to consider Lodovico Arbus an honest and courageous man, or to consider him a cowardly egotist. He was either recognized for his sincerity in his self-revelation or deplored as a hypocrite for having been willing to conceal his true nature till then. The problem with a double life begins, in fact, when you stop living it. And each of the two parts of that life demand to be acknowledged, at the expense of the other.

LODOVICO ARBUS LEFT the apartment in Montesacro, taking with him only a few suits, some documents, and his personal effects. A short while later, a fire broke out in the apartment that half-destroyed it, including the professor's library, and the bedrooms of my classmate and his sister, Leda, who luckily both survived the blaze: she was sleeping over at a girlfriend's house that night, the smoke woke Arbus up, and he saved himself and his mother, Ilaria. The cause of the fire was never determined. Normally if you're asleep, you die of asphyxiation. Perhaps Arbus was just never a very deep sleeper. His brain never shut off, not even when he was sleeping. Ilaria Arbus struggled to recover from those misadventures. Everyone took it for granted that she had always known her husband's authentic proclivities. She, too, was therefore showered with accusations of hypocrisy and silent rhetorical questions of this sort: "How could she tolerate . . . ?" ". . . right under her nose . . . ?"

I SAID THAT ARBUS was already aware of the professor's true nature. I don't think he cared very much about the fact that he had been sired by a man who, even as he possessed Arbus's mother, was dreaming of wrapping his arms around a muscular young man, instead. The resulting spurt of semen had brought him into the world all the same, and the same could be said for his pretty sister. Two irrevocable episodes concerning which any judgments or comments remained purely scholastic. Once I had heard him set forth a theory, dating back to antiquity, that paternity was a wind that scatters spores where they chance to fall. He had delivered this little speech in class, during the hour of religion, sowing concern and dismay, along with the morbid interest of Mr. Golgotha, who had immediately taken the opportunity to offer a Christian version of that parable: the wind in question was, in fact, God. A sacred wind. The Holy Spirit.

Nor had the duplicity of his father's life apparently scandalized him to any degree, independently of whether Lodovico's lovers were male or female, a secondary issue in light of the oath of faithfulness that both spouses had sworn. My friend had never displayed amorous propensities in any direction, and he remained quite neutral when it came to those of other people. The only aspects that I believe wounded him were the physical abandonment of the family residence on the part of the professor, the absence of his hat, no longer hanging in the front hall, and of his leather satchel from the swaybacked armchair next to his desk, the fact that he no longer heard, through the wall, the voice of his father, who would talk on the telephone, in the evenings, to his assistants, instructing them, in an unruffled monotonous drone: those phrases broken by silences during which the professor listened to his interlocutors, limiting himself to the occasional murmur of assent, perhaps my friend regretted the loss of those things. They proved that his father was capable of some attention.

Some of Lodovico Arbus's possessions, however, remained in the apartment, either because of the haste with which he left or else because they were of no interest to the professor or else because, quite to the contrary, it was his precise intention that they remain where he left them, as if they were testamentary bequests to the family life that he was bidding farewell for good. Among these, there was one strange object to which he had previously seemed quite attached, something he had been given, at least according to him, at the end of a series of lectures that he had delivered in Oslo. It was a sort of imaginary animal carved out of light wood, midway between a bear and a walrus, about sixteen inches tall, smooth, practically without limbs. Beginning from its vast set of teeth, it was impossible to say if it was funny or menacing, like a demon ready to come to life the minute an ancient spell was uttered. While the professor talked on the phone, he would rest a hand on the animal's head. And he'd caress it, he'd give it little taps, tenderly.

Now it enjoyed pride of place in the empty office as if it were its new and exclusive inhabitant. One of the few times that I went to Arbus's house after his father had packed his bags and cleared out, I had the impression that Arbus glared at that odd knickknack with a look of pure hatred.

Then, however, all these things and all these fantasies burned in the fire.

8

DID IT EVER HAPPEN TO ME?

Yes.

Yes and no.

It happened in a hotel in Barcelona, many years ago.

The man was kindly, gentle, and bald.

I was young and handsome.

We had struck up a spontaneous friendship.

It happened at one of these seminars for writers brought together for a few days from different countries.

Together we laughed and joked about our colleagues and many other things.

English sped up the pace of conversation.

Late at night, after the usual excessive drinking, he asked me to come up with him to his room.

We went up the stairs.

The wall-to-wall carpeting, muffled, slightly wobbly footsteps, the procession of doors, each like all the others . . .

For a few more minutes of conversation.

We sit down on the sofa and we drink three or four little bottles from the minibar.

We go on laughing about . . . and about . . . and about . . .

We're astonished at what good friends we've already become.

We agree on everything.

Then he turns serious, he leans toward me, and he kisses me, and I accept his kiss.

I don't know *why* I accept it.

Can I say that I was expecting it?

Yes, I was expecting it.

Not that I was expecting *exactly* that, but I was expecting something, a lunge.

He had a raspy tongue.

He holds his hand against my neck and I hold my hand against his neck too, where he still has some hair, sparse and thinning.

I told him that I'd expected we'd end up kissing, but only at that point did it dawn on me that I was kissing a man.

Not a woman but a man.

Exactly, a man and not a woman.

A man I wasn't even attracted to.

So why was I kissing him?

(I'd later ask myself that question many times.)

I recoiled from the kiss.

He tried to lean close again and press his lips against mine, and I did something that a girl had once done to me, to block my kisses: without turning my head, I slipped my right hand with the palm turned outward between his mouth and mine.

If you wish, it might be an easy barrier to overcome, but at the same time, discouraging and exciting.

He couldn't figure out whether I was rejecting him because I didn't like him, or anyway not well enough to continue with the kissing and go beyond that.

So, if the writer I met in Barcelona had been handsome and if I'd liked him, would I have continued?

Would I have continued? Deep inside, I thought that it wasn't that I didn't like him, it was that I didn't like men.

There, I had gotten confused.

I was getting this all wrong.

It's men, handsome and homely, that I'm not attracted to.

I reiterated the concept to myself.

But I didn't tell him.

Maybe it would have been better for him to know it, that I wasn't rejecting him personally, but I still didn't say it to him.

He was saddened, but that didn't stop him from being polite.

He ceased his advances almost immediately and replaced them with an invitation, which sounded almost like a plea, indeed, a lament: stay and sleep here anyway, with me.

Where would I sleep?

Here, in the bed with me, I won't try to touch you.

I swear . . .

His imploring voice trembled with desire and I finally saw him for what he really was.

A typical middle-aged English queer.

Honestly queer and understandably aroused.

That was the situation, and I had allowed it to come to this.

I could have stopped things sooner.

So what was I, then?

What did I want?

If I wasn't queer, then what?

I told him no.

You don't want to?

I can't.

No way on earth, I thought to myself.

Fifteen minutes later, I was leaving his room.

With an idiotic giggle on my lips.

In reality, this had already happened once before, a long time ago.

When I was very young, when I was very young and reckless.

9

W*HAT WAS IT THAT DROVE THEM? Was it libido? It was the libido that in the city spreads and dusts all things, that you can't tell from friendship, business, jealousy, murder, fast cars—oh, but it wasn't even libido anymore, it was just a frenzied desire for fun, for adventure—but not even that, it wasn't a thirst for affairs and adventures—it was the collapse of the castle of clouds, too heavy to hang in the sky any longer, it was the exterminating angel sent by God to punish us, it was the folly of the angels, the destruction that cannot find so much as a moment of respite, can't stop, must keep punishing and punishing, it must punish sins where it finds them, or transform innocence into guilt so that it can punish it. There, that was the libido.*

ANGELO: never was there a more suitable name. Angel: you might think that an angel is good, you have a guardian angel, to whom you turn your prayers before you lay you down; by a perverse misunderstanding, possibly deriving from the popular image of the little creatures that flutter overhead in devotional paintings, unaware that these are a Christianized version of pagan cupids, namely those adorable curly-haired putti, which are actually sexual symbols, when a child—deplorably—dies, or when many die all at once (a few years ago, for example, in the collapse of a nursery school), we console ourselves by saying that they've become angels and now they're looking down on us from heaven; people even make commemorative streamers that they display at soccer stadiums; forgetting the punitive aspect of that winged demon, the descent to earth of the exterminating angel, and Michael with his flaming sword expelling our progenitors from Eden, and all the other times that an angel has brought us desolation and death, rather than consoling us over desolation and death. In reality, the angel is an executioner, a mere extension of the divine will, a reflection of its light, and often terrifying. And so, in the case at hand, Angelo could not be a more appropriate name.

The protagonists of the CR/M fostered a strong sense of friendship, brotherhood, and camaraderie. They were ready to stand up to the siege, together, shoulder to shoulder. What siege, from whom? The siege of the Communists. They saw Communists everywhere; even their parents, devout Catholics, were taken for Communists in spite of themselves. It's quite something to see a family raise a child to respect certain values without dreaming he might someday use them as a cork dartboard.

In declaring the principle of brotherhood, however, they forgot to point out its origin as a defensive and offensive alliance, which is to say, fundamentally, a careful distinction between an "us" and a "them." Universal brotherhood is an oxymoron or an abstraction whose meaning contradicts how human groups are actually structured; in the real world, there are a great many brotherhoods, and they are, by and large, permanently at odds with one another, not surprising since this is what they were founded for in the first place: to defend one's brothers. It is no accident that the sentiment of fraternity, or brotherhood, originates in particular during wartime, at the front, in the trenches, as poets and writers have taught us: that's right, our brothers are our fellow fighters, the ones we're willing to shed our blood for . . .

Therefore, you might think that the highest level of enmity is to be found among groups of males battling one another. And yet that's not the case at all: among male factions fighting one another to the first blood, if not the last (for example, the hooligans that root for certain soccer teams), there are a hundred times greater levels of similarity than difference. In fact, they often acknowledge one another reciprocally in a sort of brawling symmetry— when a soccer ultra dies, the ultras of the other teams pay him honor. The real gulf is between a band of men and a group of women; even more sharply accentuated, the distance between a band of men and *one* woman. Disparities of gender and number. Maximum asymmetry. The most widely separated points possible, the opposite colors on the spectrum.

Let's add to that differences of class.

A GROUP OF MEN and one woman alone, or perhaps we might put it better: isolated. That's the same technique, elementary and effective, as a pack hunting a flock of sheep: the prey is targeted among the many potential individual prey and then stalked and scattered with a series of tactical moves, at the culmination of which the target stands alone. Or else it's enough to just watch and wait until she, of her own initiative, leaves the more populous and closely monitored locations: at that fatal time of the day, at that crucial moment that marks the end of work or the end of amusements, which for an unaccompanied woman marks the peak of apprehension in urban life: night, darkness, leaving a club, a gym, walking home, a narrow, empty street, a bus stop, a poorly lit lobby . . . All of these are dangers and threats compared with which the offer of a convenient ride from smiling people seems like a good solution.

The fact that in the case of the CR/M the prey was two women instead of one is due to the fact that one woman alone was less likely to have trustingly accepted the young men's invitation. It was therefore a shrewd move on their part, and it resulted in a double scoop.

IF YOU PLAN TO ROAM the city looking to pick up girls in order to rape them, you need to have time on your hands, and that is why gang rapists tend for the most part to be young, unemployed layabouts, petty and mid-range criminals, soldiers stationed in foreign countries, illegal immigrants, misfits and renegades of various sorts, in other words, people who don't know what to do with their days. All right, let's throw in students, too, university students, the children of that singular method we have of running our universities in Italy which consists, or at least consisted in the days when this story unfolds (and I was a perfect specimen of the genre), in attending lessons more or less infrequently and then, back at home, grinding out long and grueling sessions of study to prepare for some major hurdle of an exam, say pathological anatomy or business law. Free time is the curse of the man without purpose, or the man whose purpose lies too far afield and who is looking to find a few other objectives in the meantime.

All right, then. What do these layabouts talk about all day long with their friends? Women and sex. What do they think about? About how to get even for all their time spent dangling aimlessly in that void. Put a knife in their hands and point out to them that 99 percent of the population around them is defenseless, and that half of that 99 percent is made up of women. What do you think will occur to them to do, now? Where are they going to get started?

THE CR/M CAN BE LISTED as a "recreational murder," that is, the kind of murder that allows you to spend a Saturday with your friends, or even an entire weekend. In some parts of the world, it would appear to be a typical pastime of men's days off: build up an ample stock of liquor and drugs, kidnap a young woman, have your kicks with her until you've had enough, and then she dies.

DURING THESE SESSIONS a ceremony of homosexual initiation takes place, consisting of extracting one's member and displaying it to the other men before inserting it into the same woman in whom they have inserted their own.

"Sharing a girl among friends." A homosexual erotic contact attained through a third body.

As is stated in no uncertain terms in "La Marseillaise"—in fact, sung at the top of one's lungs—the value of brotherhood is expressed at its maximum intensity when the time comes to kill someone, when you are *united* in spilling that person's blood: it is the impure blood of the enemy that cements the pact of brotherhood. It is the blood of the adultress that bonds together all those who, as one, as a mob, stoned her to death.

You are blood brothers if you were brought into the world by the same woman, or when, together, you kill the same woman.

By attacking a woman together, males subtract themselves, at least temporarily, from reciprocal violence. The woman cushions and absorbs the aggressivity that the men would no doubt otherwise unleash against one another, and so they turn that violence into a form of complicity. A male's blade loses its edge: by brutalizing women, he forgets how badly he is brutalized and subjugated by other men.

The erotic bond that joins together the men who commit a rape is far stronger than the one that links them with their victim, in fact, we might say that a gang rape is perpetrated with a view to affirming that former type of bond and entirely deleting the latter. There are also nonviolent versions of that same brotherhood, where the male libido focuses for a fleeting instant on a female figure, and then is refracted back at those who first projected it: in a striptease show, the male spectators are much more in contact with one another than they are with the girls who are taking off their clothes. Aside from the exchanges mimed with various obscene gestures, each sex remains segregated, in perfect solitude, to share their excitement.

Raping the same woman is a way of getting closer to the sex, the genitalia, of your buddies, of seeing it and touching it indirectly, wallowing in the semen of your friends, inside a woman.

IT'S A FELLOWSHIP CREATED by mysterious forces, "to which it is pleasurable to give in, in part while experiencing or causing pain." Hence the myth, indeed the enchantment, of friendship, its sacred mystery set against the banality of other relationships, beginning with family ties. Usually, in a family, emotional excesses are unwelcome when they upset the ties of kinship, which have been established once and for all, without any possibility of choice in the matter. You can never desire, nor revoke or reject, the fact that your mother is your mother. The only family tie that can be revoked is the one with your spouse: you cannot cease being a son or daughter or brother or sister or mother. These are ties that prevent all enthusiasm: not just Lenin or Goebbels, but even Jesus encourages the cutting of those ties.

The new bond, instead, is struck by something that lies outside of that bond entirely, the communion of spirits and bodies is aimed at a distant object, to be venerated, a god, a leader, an ideal, a master; or else, every bit as forcefully, as something to be hated, an enemy to be fought. In this virile union there is no personal privacy, no counterpart to one's own initiatives; there is only sharing. In that bond, all the cases are extreme, and if they aren't, they are taken to extremes. Loyalty, the chief surrogate of love.

The more compact and cemented together the group, the more its members will be willing to direct their bellicosity toward those who are not members of that group.

If a male's yearning to copulate with a woman is a sexual desire, no less sexual and no less powerful is his desire to aggregate with other males. Sometimes the two desires can be confused or can even merge. The feminine element consequently becomes totally extraneous, the object of desire and hostility, each more scathing than the other.

LET US IMAGINE a virile universe that feels it has been encircled by enemy forces: indeed, that these forces are already in our midst, that they have infiltrated us. The enemy is a spreading stain, it filters into our social fabric like a liquid. Its infection is spreading, by means of women, foreigners, Jews, and pederasts. What is so dangerous about these categories? What does their threat consist of? Fundamentally, in their lasciviousness. In their potential erotic disorder. And yet it is fascism's erotic impulse that unites it as a body, a corps, a sect.

Just yesterday, while taking a stroll around the Stadio dei Marmi, at the Foro Italico, I realized it as I took in, at a single glance, those sixty nude athletes.

Taken individually, perhaps there would be nothing homosexual about those statues: but it is the way they parade, the circuit of giants that creates a sort of virile enchantment. You are subjugated by that procession of muscle-bound males. Desire is always misguided, both heterosexual and homosexual desire: the latter is only more evident, more spectacular, as is the male nude with respect to the female nude. Once that becomes clear, it's a matter of directing it instead of dispersing it. Dispersion is dangerous.

In the period I'm writing about, young right-wing men brought together a nebulous array of uncertain desires and angers and fears and enthusiasms, forcing them all to converge toward a single monolithic ideal, fascism, which however was composed by those very same pieces, compressed and fused together in the crucible of action; for young left-wing men, on the other hand, who did not for the most part seriously expect the advent of the dictatorship of the proletariat in the near future in the West, communism was a preliminary and generic ideal of justice, against the background of which they could attain far more immediate dreams, to name a few, independence from their families, music, fucking, giving free rein to their instincts, one and all, whether joyous or beneficent or murderous.

A liberatory ideal, while the right-wing counterpart was an effort of concentration. To scatter energy madly or collect and accumulate it madly: that was what lay behind the terminology that once pointed either to the left or the right.

It is not so much the homosexual content of fascism that strikes the observer, as much as the virulence with which that content is denied and repressed. The exasperated cult of virility and the resulting scorn toward everything that is feminine tend to create an entirely male universe: even Goebbels noticed it, and expressed his concern about it!

A masculine, mannish society, formed of equals as only males aspire to be, where all individualistic or familistic impulses, dictated by female demands in the name of a collective that transcends the male-female relationship, are eliminated: the state is ideal, masculine, spiritual; the family is biological, feminine, material. And that is exactly how the good Greek soldier of antiquity rolled: hetero for the family and homo for the fatherland. Intercourse not as a way of dedicating oneself to one's fellow man, but rather as a way of setting him aside: a chore to be gotten out of the way before going back to the one and only virile pursuit, that of the quest for glory.

In the very idea of heroism there lies an implicitly homosexual model, though explicitly disavowed and, indeed, rejected in disgust.

The unmistakable but unusable proof lies precisely in the fact that so many great men were homosexuals, proof that only greatness of soul is able to overcome prohibitions; these men, therefore, were great not because they sublimated their sexual energy thanks to the prohibition, but rather because they overcame the prohibition by means of that energy. Only genuine heroes of thought and art or action are successful in this. Therefore, the hero, too, is fundamentally homosexual: a glorious queer who triumphs over mediocrity and conventions, over the claustrophobic prohibitions of a society of half-men and half-women.

SOME BIOLOGISTS HAVE EXPLAINED rape as the last-ditch strategy of losers who, unless they resorted to violence, would be cut out of the race to hand down their genetic inheritance.

Other scholars have viewed it as a peculiar way that males have of communicating with one another: to establish a friendship or sanction a competition or, as we have said, camouflage a homosexual contact experienced through a proxy, or else, as in the case of wartime rape, to make it unmistakably clear who has won, appropriating for oneself the bodies of the women of the losing side. It is to the latter party, the defeated men, that the message contained in the rape is directed, a message for which the female body is merely a context or a medium.

IT IS RARELY UNDERSTOOD how authentically and powerfully men need to obtain tenderness and love from other men, and how often this unsatisfied need is then brutally turned to women; and likewise how brutal the exhibition of virility can be, when it is directed against women, and perpetrated with the sole objective of winning the respect and admiration of other men, once it becomes clear they will never be able to obtain their love.

Males bond in one of two ways: either by affinity and unresolved love, or else after an initial rivalry, in which case the bond of friendship serves to limit the degree of aggression by turning it toward the exterior. If you don't hurt me, I won't hurt you; if anything, by joining together, we can hurt others—that is the implicit rule in every gang. What we call brotherhood results from the fusion of these two elements, love and aggression, detoured from their actual objects and redirected into political action, war, positive or negative ideals of every kind, or criminality. This is how men court other men. Even when they're flirting with a woman, they're considering the effect it will have on other men whether their seduction proves successful or fails.

IN COMPARISON WITH the madness of women, the male universe appears simpler and more predictable. For that reason, there is a temptation to abandon the skirmishes with the opposite sex and take refuge in the reassuring community of one's peers: at least with them, everyone understands one another, everyone supports one another, and they all feel the same things. They create fewer illusions, fewer deceptions.

The homosexual truce, the nonaggression pact in an all-male club, calls for all hostility to be rerouted outward, toward specific groups of men and all women, without distinction. This pact can also be described as friendship, and it lies at the foundation of many male communities, including the literary community: just think of the Italian writers of the twentieth century and their almost exclusively homosocial environment, with an almost religious cult of "amici"—male friends—and their scorn for women, or vice versa, their formalized cult of women, and their aggression toward all rival groups. In their epistolary exchanges, they employ a hyperbolic phraseology of admiration and devotion far more emphatic than was used toward the idealized ladies of courtly love.

We have the impression, then, that the generous cult of the *amici* and the myth of friendship so celebrated in Italian literature (with a continuous appeal, nostalgic or vibrant or resentful, to comradeship, spiritual brothers, brothers in arms on both the left and the right, with whom were founded movements and groups and artistic schools), as well as the relationship never fully or adequately investigated between so-called masters and pupils, might really have been a form, not even all that well disguised, of erotic relationship, sublimated and translated into less reprehensible behaviors.

THE RITE OF MALE INITIATION entails pain and loneliness: in order to be admitted to the gang, a young man or boy has to show not only that he is capable of putting up with discomfort and suffering, but also ready and willing to inflict them. Upon whom? Upon the enemy. And who can be the enemy of a male group, if not other male groups, which are also competing for a specific territory, or else, in far more general terms, for women? All women? The other males are concrete adversaries, the females are symbolic ones. Women, with their provocative presence, obstruct both the real lives of male groups, on the street, in the schools, in dance halls, and their oneiric and imaginative lives: because there is no place on earth more overrun and infested with women than the brain of someone who is a member of a youth gang. And it is a symptom of very serious insecurity that a young man should be willing to subject himself to painful and exhausting ordeals, or else show himself willing to commit cruel acts in order to gain recognition of his own masculinity, and be officially proclaimed "a man."

When men associate, aggression is released in more substantial doses. It is in fact a rare thing for violence to be an exclusively individual factor. The reasons for committing a crime, or a murder, are almost always directed toward the exterior of the persona. People want to take revenge on others, or attract their attention, or win their approval. Or else they frequently feel obliged to imitate them. It is right that the individual should be the unit of measurement upon which to reckon and attribute guilt and punishment, but in reality, nearly all murders, nearly all crimes have a collective foundation: they originate with a group and their objective lies in a group. This is especially true for the CR/M.

✤

PROTECT EACH OTHER, and strike out. There is no need to swear oaths, because everyone knows deep down that this is the foundation of a friendship. Outside of friendship you live in cold and in danger. Having friends means having a shield. Sometimes a sword as well. If you have no friends, you are naked to the world. If, instead, by friendship you mean knowing people you can chat with at a cocktail party, sure, that's human interaction, too, but it offers damned little protection, and when the time comes to act, you'll find yourself operating solo.

Just as some theorize that the biological reason men make war has to do with the instinct to protect everything they hold dearest, "women and children, land and ideals," likewise you could maintain that they make war in order to take possession of or to destroy their adversaries' women, children, land, and ideals. They never fight for themselves, for themselves alone, but in order to protect what they consider to be their own possessions, and to acquire or destroy the possessions of others. Rather than merely trying to kill your adversary, you must take his wife, burn his cabin, poach his flock, and finally, force him to disavow his dearly held principles. Then he will truly be defeated.

If he was forbidden to rip off his armor and steal his concubines, the Greek would have no incentive to challenge the Trojan . . .

The event can be said to be consummated when it gives rise to a victory or a defeat: the aggressive lunge subsides when the prey has either been killed or has managed to escape. The unconcern with which the young men of the CR/M parked downstairs from their home and went off to get themselves a gelato leaves no doubt about the fact that they were certain they'd killed both girls. That they had two corpses in the trunk of the car.

I've wondered what would have happened if that had actually been the case, if *both* girls really had been dead. How would the rest of the story have played out? Probably the defendants answered questions of this sort in court. But the defense, at least in the early phases of the trail, was based on their conviction that the girls were still alive. So what would they have done afterward, that same night or the following morning? Would they have freed them?

CAMARADERIE AND CLASS COMPANIONSHIP. I think of Giampiero Parboni Arquati, the notorious "Carlo," who pulled out at the last minute, so that his life miraculously avoided being incinerated over the course of a few seconds, in the space of a phone call and by virtue of a decision made while rocking back and forth on his heels, in the narrow hallway where, in bourgeois apartments, the telephone was located. To veer away by a couple of degrees from the route that Angelo and Subdued had charted meant winding up a great distance from those two men alongside whom he had originally set out. Just as in a math problem, you need only get a single figure wrong to wind up with an answer that is wrong by fabulous quantities, likewise even the smallest shift can contribute to great changes in the fates of many people, including the victims, who might not have met the same fate if the makeup of the team of kidnappers had been different. Perhaps they would both have survived, or they might just as easily have both died. It often happens that someone's life is saved by a mere mistake.

I want to examine another of Angelo's buddies, Damiano Sovena. Damiano was a fair-haired young man with freckles. Back then he seemed big and strapping and strong, though not as big as the famous Cubbone, and he would later play American football, in Italy, of course. How tall and strong men are, and how old they look, is something that even those who know them well often have a hard time gauging, those who see them every day: in fact, their wives buy them shirts two sizes too big, their children describe them as old when they're only forty. And it must, in fact, be forty years since I last saw Damiano. It was strange that a guy like him should have been able to stir in others, simultaneously or in extremely rapid succession, both fondness and fear. He was always cheerful, extroverted, and jovial, but later this cheerfulness of his would swell into something so expansive that it became brutal. His friendliness would overflow into violent forms of behavior, it was impossible to wriggle free of one of his hugs, and he would squeeze you harder and harder, as if he wanted to strangle you. His infectious laughter would suddenly veer into something much more menacing. Like the character played by Joe Pesci in *Goodfellas*, it was never clear whether his way of kidding around was benevolent or was instead the prelude to an explosion.

One time we were in a bus on our way to the playing fields and he was standing in the aisle laughing and joking with some younger students, junior high school age, already dressed in soccer uniforms. Back then it was fashionable to wear as part of the uniform the jerseys of the Serie A clubs, but not the Championship jersey, instead the more unusual jersey that the team wore during the European Cup games, and among those teams the Inter jersey was especially popular, white with black-and-blue cuffs and collar, and a diagonal stripe across the chest—the stripe, too, of course, black and blue, running from left shoulder to right hip. These soccer outfits were so cool-looking and sought after that it didn't matter at all whether they corresponded to the team you rooted for (for that matter, it would have been impossible to find eleven kids who all rooted for the same team), and there was none of the fierce sense of soccer identity you have nowadays: whoever wore one of those jerseys was very proud of it anyway.

Damiano, sinking down on his knees to brace as the bus took a curve, was in fact surrounded by kids dressed in that precious jersey, all of them brand new, and with his usual playful, exaggerated tone of voice, he was complimenting them—really nice this new Inter Coppa jersey. Then he wanted to feel the fabric, so he asked one of the kids to stand up, but the kid wasn't fast enough getting to his feet so, still chuckling, Damiano grabbed him by the shirt and yanked him up so brusquely that he tore the kid's collar. "Oh, I'm so sorry!" he exclaimed, but then, instead of letting go of the terrified little player, continuing to hold him up by the lapels, he calmly, almost methodically, began unstitching the diagonal black-and-blue stripe running across the boy's chest, except this painstaking work was starting to draw out because the stitching was really strong, so at a certain point Damiano, fed up, just yanked on it with all his might, which wound up tearing the whole front of the jersey.

The little boy burst into tears. And Damiano, taking him by the chin and delicately lifting the boy's face toward his own, said: "Hey, hey . . . don't worry. I'll buy you a brand-new one."

I NEVER HEARD ANYTHING more about him; only that a few years later he was wounded, shot with a handgun, in Piazza Euclide.

Of the three men guilty of the CR/M, this book talks a little bit about Angelo. The second was a psychopath without any moral brakes or inhibitions. The third was a *natural born killer*.

LET'S FOLLOW THEM from their bad behavior in school to the kidnapping and then the murder: a progressive graduation from level to level and an extension into the domain of serious crime of their "roughhousing and troublemaking." These are selfish, impulsive, dishonest boys, they tend to grab what they want, indifferent as to whether or not they have any right to do so. They can turn violent if hindered, or even if they aren't. By no means worried about the consequences of their actions. Disapproval or the prospect of punishment don't frighten them beforehand from committing their misdeeds, nor do they chasten them in the aftermath. Instead of acting as a deterrent, punishment if anything seems to encourage them, or to leave them cold, indifferent, at the very outside to exacerbate their resentment. More than hostile out of any principle, they seem to be utterly insensible to their fellow humans, they seem to struggle to acknowledge any specific identity, likewise with ideas, feelings, or rights, while others' suffering, even when it was they who caused it, simply doesn't concern them. In contrast with genuine sadists, they don't seem to take pleasure in the pain of others in any direct manner, but instead observe it as a "distance effect," a secondary phenomenon. They tend to act impersonally, and they consider the harm they do on the order of an inevitable natural occurrence that requires no explanation. If other people mean so little to them, why should they feel any remorse for the damage inflicted? If anything, a little astonishment and a hint of annoyance, at the way others exaggerate their objections, their protests, their chagrin, their demands for reparations. The suffering always appears to them as something disorderly, grating, and excessive. Concern and remorse can only spring from an ability to empathize, to identify with others, a faculty for imagination, for projecting oneself into the world, something that they do not possess. We may suppose that when they go to the movies they have a hard time understanding why the audience is so afraid, or weeps, or takes passionate interest in the stories they see projected on the screen, and so they are bored to death or, perhaps, they just snicker into their sleeves at the sight of all that mawkish sentimentalism. They have eliminated from their way of thought any cause-and-effect relationship. They live with only one objective: self-affirmation. They have this impression of the world: a place that is fully available to them, nothing is out of the question, nothing is forbidden. If you want to do something, only the will to do it is required. Because they don't feel loved, they do not fear that anyone might withdraw or refuse their love as a consequence of their bad behavior. Behind them and before them is a void. The truth leaves them cold, it bores them. They have little interest in being honest, and they have a hard time recognizing the actual difference that exists between honesty and dishonesty. And it is rare, exceedingly rare for them to feel even a twinge of guilt.

IF AT FIRST, the CR/M seemed incomprehensible, so vast was its scale and so indecipherable its root cause, little by little people began to understand it, to sense it as something familiar, and most important of all, in line with the times. The odious crime was metabolized and canonized in its form of unrivaled horror, and as a result it came to be considered an event that was by no means extraordinary, but rather, within the ordinary course of things: people might express astonishment both that it hadn't happened before and that this kind of thing didn't happen more often. Like every ritual, that schema, in its way, so classical (privileged young men who torture and abuse young working-class women, rich males against poor females), demanded to be re-experienced, reinterpreted, emulated. Once a case is closed and the culprit incarcerated, there will always be someone else out on the street ready to strike, if the reasons the crime was committed in the first place still apply. That means that in a certain sense the case is still open, it can recur, there can always be another such case, identical or merely similar, and after that another and yet another . . . Which is even more so if the crime was gratuitous, as the CR/M was, in fact. Indeed, how can you eradicate the root causes of an event, to prevent it from happening again, if there really were no root causes, properly speaking? How can you take steps, what antidote can be readied? The more gratuitous the evil, the more likely it is to persist. You can never be certain it won't repeat itself. In fact, repetition seems to belong to its nature: that which has no foundation cannot in any way be revoked or given the lie.

THE CR/M IS NOT ONLY A PRODUCT of its time, but a producer—of times, of course, of history, of concepts, of ways of life. Nothing after it remained the same as before. To some degree, it was an event that had been expected: people knew that it could happen, in spite of the fact that no one expected it, and despite what that sounds like, it's not a logical fumble. In those days, people knew perfectly well that unthinkable things would happen: they knew it, but they didn't know exactly *what*. Of course, the worst things imaginable, the most absurd, the most unheard of: and therefore, to the letter, people expect that something will happen that they don't expect. Reality, the future, these things are unpredictable. Perhaps they always have been and always will be, but I have the impression that in 1975 *they were more so.*

(THE ETYMOLOGY OF THE ITALIAN WORD for rape, "*stupro,*" indicates something that causes stupor, astonishment, something that one wasn't expecting . . .)

10

THE CR/M IS STRUCTURED *like a fable, and it possesses a fable's deceptive simplicity. Two young women are lured into a house in the forest . . .*

A chain of happenstance guides the transition from one stage to the next, almost a slippage, a slow drift.

The sessions of sexual abuse and torture are based on the principle, typically, of intensified repetition, like that seen in Hans Christian Andersen's The Tinderbox, *where the nightmarish dogs that guard the treasure have progressively larger eyes, bigger and bigger—first as big as saucers, then as big as mill wheels, and finally as big as the Round Tower of Copenhagen; the violence is graduated in a progressive crescendo, to put the victim's endurance to the test, her body put through its paces like an engine on a test bench, jolted and beaten, crushed, dislocated. The abstract impulse of the torturer who wishes to penetrate through his victim to the point where that body will stop resisting: the body bruised, wounded, ripped open as if trying to find something inside it.*

The recourse to violence and the rite of submission, however ferocious, may appear as a game that will sooner or later come to an end, whereupon they can take off the uniforms of brute and slave girl and everyone can return home—but no, let's get serious. Only death can free the act of its foolish sexual patina, from the idea that it was all just dumb show, playacting, a distasteful back-and-forth. In gang rapes, at a certain point, there comes a pause in which the actors no longer know what to do: they can't go back, but they can't continue along in the same direction, either. Sexual gratification, if that was really what they were going in search of, can be obtained in just a few minutes—but then what?

During the CR/M, there were these long intervals in which the situation was stalled. As if it had been enchanted. Just as in a fable.

A PROTRACTED DYING, infinitely repeatable. The tortures inflicted serially upon the victims of the CR/M induce the illusion that the afflicted body is able to resuscitate each time, after every blow.

And then a sort of pseudodeath ... there ... maybe it's done ... for long moments it seems that the body has stopped breathing ... but then, instead, it breathes. The chest resumes rising and falling, bubbles of air and blood ooze out of the nostrils. It's supernatural. The clubbings, the injection of disgusting liquids, the head knocked against sharp corners, none of it has had the desired effect. Death won't come, and so they continue to inflict punishment. Death arrives, finally, almost unlooked for, so that the murderers' grotesque claim becomes a hair more plausible, the claim that they repeated over and over during the trial hearings and the appeals, that they believed that the girls, there, in the car trunk, *were alive*. In a certain sense, it might even be true that they believed it, in the light of their overall delirium: if they weren't dead after the treatment they'd been given, then they never would die. Let's be clear, however: not because they ever intended to kill them. Far from it! They did their best to kill them, but then, when they were finally, really dead (or, rather, when one of them was dead and the other pretended to be), it had long since become unthinkable either that they could die or that they could remain alive. In that repetitive game, no one really dies, no one can die. The coyote is bound to emerge for the hundredth time from the canyon into which he has fallen.

Bruised and battered, but *alive*.

Between the real corpse and the fake one who starts shouting from inside the car trunk, there really isn't all that much difference. You might say, as in Schrödinger's well-known paradox, that they are *simultaneously alive and dead*.

The difference lies in an index of probability. The murderous acts are somehow candid, as if they entailed no consequences. For that matter, what could be more childish than to park a car with the victims in the trunk and go to get a gelato? A *gelato*? With two dead bodies in the trunk? The only thing that could be less believable than that would be if they thought they were still *alive*—as in fact the defendants maintained—but even then, even if you have two bloodied girls on the brink of death in the trunk of your car—what the hell, a nice gelato is just what you need. A snack. Among the many expressions coined and publicized by the press, which became grimly proverbial, none seems to fit the protagonists of these merry excursions better than "*compagni di merende*," literally, snackmates. A term that blends a slightly vulgar playfulness, friendship, immaturity—and ferocity. And then there's the prod of hunger, the need for "something sweet," the same urge that overheated, sweaty children felt after a soccer match with their friends, as they ran to Mamma to beg for the snacks advertised on TV. Years later, when he killed again, Angelo would devote just as much care to the making of sandwiches to slake his hunger as he would to the murder of a mother and her daughter. It's true, there is an art of making panini. A pity to waste them after making them. It was said of another famous murderer that, after killing two kids, "he ate their hamburgers." Actually, it turns out, he ate their apple pie. Just one more reason to sentence him to death.

I HAVE BEFORE my eyes a famous image, in which a name is carved into a girl's chest with the point of a knife. Blood sprays from every letter. It's from *The Last House on the Left*, a film I will never tire of coming back to.

Locking two girls in a car trunk is something that the maniacs in the film *The Last House on the Left* did three years before the CR/M: that's how they transported the girls they raped from the city to the countryside, from New York to Connecticut—whereas Angelo and his accomplice were taking them back to the city, from Monte Circeo to Rome. That film has pursued me, obsessed me for years, just as it has obsessed the people who shot it and acted in it. It was originally supposed to be called *Sex Crime of the Century*, or else *Night of Vengeance*. At first it had been conceived and written as a porn film, then someone noticed that the sex scenes were superfluous, and that observation proved to be starkly accurate, because when you mix together eros and violence, to create an exciting blend, the eros acts as a fuse but then it becomes unnecessary, while the violence turns out to be more than sufficient. Violence is more logical, it has more narrative consistency. A succession of sex acts just gets boring.

AS IN THE CR/M, all that was needed to eroticize a scenario destined to accommodate torture and death was the simple premise: two attractive young women, alone (one of them is turning seventeen that very day, and Dad and Mom are baking a birthday cake for her, with her name, Mary, written on it in icing, with lots of little hearts), two attractive young women, alone, at the mercy of a gang of perverts. What could the gang do with them? Rape them, the mind runs straight to that predictable consequence. Sexual abuse hovers over any girl who ventures to become independent, autonomous. The same punishment will be visited on both the naïve girl and the seductive one. Therefore, when the girls fall into the trap, the spectator ritualistically finds himself saying: "Well, you asked for it." But then the story moves on from that point: rape is merely a passage, and not even an especially obligatory one; in this story, the rapists almost seem to be engaging in it against their will . . .

I saw it with my father at the Empire cinema, one August afternoon, and the place was air-conditioned. There were three of us in the theater, my father, me, and a third spectator, and when the movie was over and the lights came up, the other man walked past us on his way to the exit. As he went by, he raised his eyebrows and assured us that "all's well that ends well." Just a few moments earlier, the father of the girl who had been tortured and murdered had cut the rapist's torso in half with a chain saw, spattering blood all over the sheriff, who had finally burst into the house in the very last scene, shouting: "John! For God's sake, *don't!*"

WHEN HE WAS A BOY, the director of the film had been forbidden to watch movies and shows, listen to music, or even play. And this is the result of that puritan upbringing.

IT WAS IN THOSE YEARS that the love generation made way for the hate generation.

First there is the myth of sexual liberation: a party where everybody makes love with everybody else. It's a ballet danced in the nude, all the bodies twisting in slow motion, as if they were underwater. The libido oozes and seeps into the most rigid postures, the severe hairdos or tightly wound buns relax into gentle ringlets bouncing on shoulders and backs. Like the smears of color in psychedelic film clips, everything oozes, pulsates, flows, and spreads. Then the image of sexuality curdles, darkens, with the pretext of taking it back to some savage and predatory origin, unmasking the most unconfessable desires of both male and female. Violence comes into play, but at this point the roles are found to be inverted: it's not sex that has become more vicious, it's the violence that has come to take on a sexual coloration. The criminal enterprises of the young men of the CR/M couldn't have as their sole objective personal enrichment or political reprisal, no, they had to express themselves in a more gratuitous, capricious fashion, which paid profit no mind, and was therefore all the more exciting. In rape, truth be told, there are no profits to be earned, or hardly any. It's an easy crime that yields almost no benefits: you obtain in a frantic, largely unsatisfying manner—at least, speaking in erotic terms—the same thing that for ten thousand lire you could obtain from a professional, with no fuss no muss and no bother, in, say, Tor di Quinto. So *that's* not the thing they're looking for. The *thing* isn't pleasure. The *thing* is death.

The pornographic vision accepts the new stimulus. And it, too, is invaded by death. Instead of the classic Rubenesque sluts, who enjoyed their husky lovers on spring mattresses, there are petite young women who are tortured next to rural irrigation ditches. Not only raped, but penetrated with blades and rifle barrels, burned, their throats cut. Rape itself is a secondary consideration by now, it has become clear that the sexual aspect is entirely subordinated to the venting of ferocity. It is the ferocity that attracts, that excites. The submission of the weak, the punishment of the weak. The punishment that awaits any woman, for whatever reason, be she beautiful or homely, young or old. When you have full and total disposal of someone else's body, then you can't limit yourself to exploiting it with petty erotic byplay. You can't just trifle with the genitalia, like mere adolescent beginners. The sexual impulse has a limited range and duration, and that is why it must be supplemented by further proof of domination. To lose your drive can take seconds, after which the seriousness of the situation emerges, and if you want to give it meaning, you have to take it to its logical conclusion. The only frenzy at this point becomes the frenzy to be done with it. During a rape, if it hadn't been planned from the outset, there always and inevitably emerges the hypothesis that it may become necessary to eliminate the victim.

IT WASN'T AT ALL uncommon for an eighteen-year-old youth in those days to have witnessed many scenes in which women were kidnapped and raped, tortured, and then killed. Where? At the movies.

II

IN THOSE YEARS, there was a steadily growing demand for death. Actually carried out, or as entertainment. At the movies, audiences sat as hypnotized by the spectacle of death. We watched women being killed in all imaginable ways: with an oxyacetylene torch, red-hot metal, meat hammers, electric drills, dildos, boiling water, lobster claws, poisoned sperm, and naturally with razors, the good old-fashioned barber's straight razor, ironically referred to as a "safety razor"—that is, because the straight razor's blade folds away into the handle—broken bottles, falling plate glass windows, telephone cords and violin strings, shovels, pickaxes, hammers, chisels, saws, meat hooks, spits, shears, scissors, spears . . .

Girls' throats are cut, they are drowned in an aquarium, devoured by cannibals or sharks or piranhas, hacked apart with an ax, impaled, throttled, eviscerated, decapitated . . . bitten, chopped up and put into a refrigerator . . . a scalpel slices their faces open or dissects them, reduced to human guinea pigs, laboratory specimens . . .

They are always before the eyes of their murderer.

And the contagion spared no corner of society, it touched the exposed tips of Italy: in one movie, an actress's arm is hacked off with hatchet blows—and then that actress went on to marry our prime minister; in another (actually, in a long and bestial series of films), the wife of the most affable anchor on the TV news broadcast most closely allied with the leading Catholic political party in Italy actually has intercourse with a horse. Practically no one is spared the contamination.

The sweet German girl who brings you a stein of beer offers herself to the murderer in an erotic thriller, her legs spread wide on a sofa: sure enough, she, the pastoral nymph, turns out to be a seething naked body.

It is this ambiguity, this lack of clarity of roles that insinuates the doubt that there may be no safe zones, no people with their integrity intact, no individuals immune to perversion, no events that can be ruled out in advance, no one concerning whom "you can put your hand into the flames," swear to their character with utter confidence. "He would never have done such a thing." "He's always only thought about his family and his work." "He's an outstanding person, a first-rate intellectual, he could never have been the mastermind behind a murder . . ." Every young girl, even the most shy and modest, conceals a dark and infamous dream. The innocuous, the innocent, the mild mannered, the reserved, the decorous, or quite simply the nondescript, can turn out to be, in the blink of an eye, the obscene, the criminal, the abominable. There is no need for any reversal, indeed, you might even say that it is the blushing candor itself that is perverse. Potentially, all children are demonically possessed, all virgins are rutting wild animals in heat, all coeds are nymphomaniacs, all young men in V-neck sweaters are murderers on the prowl, to say nothing of well-to-do matrons, whose lascivious cruelty is simply unimaginable, or their salt-and-pepper-haired husbands, who are corrupt and impotent satyrs.

Precisely because at first glance beyond reproach, the bourgeois, more than anyone else, hypocritically cultivates his own bottomless unworthiness, which almost invariably springs from a sexual neurosis. He controls it and he indulges it, he diverts it or keeps it at bay as long as he is able. Inside every untroubled individual, an out-of-control, obsessive identity may lie concealed. We never know ahead of time. We can't rule it out in advance. No one is safe. All it takes is a slightly stronger stimulus, and the social mask drops. The fever can infect anyone, in fact, the fever is already deep inside, incubating. Ordinary people have no idea of what their genuine desires are: they want to loot and burn, they lust for violent pleasure and their enemy's head on a pike. "A man's greatest pleasure is to defeat his enemies, and to hold their wives and daughters in his arms, as the flames rise high from what was once his home . . ." Every young man from the industrial outskirts is ready to hunt down defenseless teenage girls in filthy, garbage-ridden fields, and those girls will secretly thrill to their rapes. By the light of this revelatory principle, there's not an individual or a social role that saves itself. Every high school teacher might be a Peeping Tom who gets aroused by spying on the derrieres of his female students, or the male ones, as they return to their desks after being quizzed in front of the class. The more their role in society is respectable—teachers, prelates, doctors, senators—the greater the likelihood that behind that façade there lurks and acts, undisturbed, a maniac of some kind.

Or else, no, heavens no, none of all this! It can't be true, and it never happens. Or *almost* never. God forfend that the distinction between good and evil should ever vanish. But by now the seeds of doubt have been planted and the boundaries are hopelessly scrambled.

The decade is marked by contamination. Insecurity penetrates under everyone's front door, impregnating the fibers, like some indelible stain. Sexual and political and gangster violence, kidnappings, torture, cold-blooded elimination of witnesses.

And yet statistics tell us that, aside from peaks for certain specific crimes, the crime rate was high but not all that different from other periods. The unsettling aspect is that the ones committing these crimes weren't Lombrosian criminals. They were unsuspectables.

After the CR/M, every apprehensive mother would scrutinize her son to try to understand whether there was a "monster" deep inside him, too. How can you tell if your son will rape and murder? When he comes back home at night, how does he say hello to his parents, does he display a good appetite, does he eat his bowl of soup, does he stink of tobacco smoke, are there circles under his eyes, are his pupils dilated, are his hands shaking? Does he laugh for no good reason, is he intractable? Mothers spent lots of time deciphering tiny clues. It's easy to get it wrong, to exaggerate or underestimate the importance of clues. Only a glimmer of adolescents' real lives filters through their gestures and their words. Direct questions, if you are angry or desperate enough to ask them, are almost never met with a response, the young people simply close up like hedgehogs. The level of dishonesty rises. Are you taking drugs, are you having sexual relations, if so, who with, what are you hiding from me, what's on your mind, what sort of people are you seeing, how are you spending your evenings, why are you coming home so late?

I recently read a slender volume about the erotic lives of Italian adolescents nowadays, based on "real" interviews, though the names of the interviewees were invented: I doubt that the parents could glimpse their loving daughters and sons in those pornographic thumbnail portraits.

Mass, low-intensity pornography, pictures and videos on their cell phones, the collective imagination on the Internet, it seems today that a general sexual clog has stopped up all the pores of everyone everywhere. And yet it was precisely in the time of the CR/M that we attained, according to some observers, "peak eroticization of the system." No longer the single individual, but society as a whole was "seeing nude."

VIOLENCE OF THE WELL-TO-DO CLASSES and plebeian violence: who likes to rape more, the rich or the poor? The question hovers over the surreal debates that followed the CR/M. In reality, everyone, let me say it again, *everyone* is potentially an audience for and protagonist of violence, both as victim and agent of it. And everyone in any case pursues and claims for themselves broader margins of liberty, sovereign power over their own lives and, frequently, those of others, either because they're accustomed to exercising that power, or else because they've always been excluded from it. In the well-to-do classes, familiarity with power pushes people to appropriate what they desire with a spontaneous arrogance; in the poor classes, brutality is viewed as the only way to obtain the sources of satisfaction: a risky but effective shortcut. Money and sex must be taken at gunpoint, otherwise they would remain out of reach. The power that you don't possess or inherit from your class must be constructed with fists and handguns.

All this sex, all this violence could always be legitimized as a reaction against bourgeois hypocrisy, conformism, the stupidity of the world of television and consumerism. The directors of hard-core and horror films unmask this respectability, forcing the audience to look into their own abyss, where what teems and pullulates is the same filth and violence, barely repressed, as is shown on the screen. Priggish moralism was met with an even more rigid countermoralism. It all formed part of the syndrome of the "exposé." You can't hide from the spotlight of the exposé. If you refuse to see the atrocities or the array of filth, then it just means that you're a hypocrite, or that in turn you have a little something to hide that's every bit as dirty or atrocious. I think I read somewhere that the hooks inserted in a woman's breasts in a cannibalism movie were meant as a form of intellectual resistance against Mike Bongiorno (for those of my readers who may not know the name, a popular television game show host). Okay, maybe so. Certainly, we're all wedged between monsters, monsters over here and monsters over there, and not only do all these monsters frighten us, they also want to give us a lesson in how to live. Any act of gratuitous violence, even the most revolting one, can be rebaptized as a courageous act of rebellion against conformism, every shocking act of cruelty can become a shout of protest, a *j'accuse* against that same act of cruelty and yet others, even greater, that society struggles to conceal, but which the intrepid cineaste instead has the courage to unearth. If logic is the tool of the polemicist by definition, then paradoxical logic works even better, because it has a sharper edge: whereby the profane swearer is actually the man with the most unshakable faith, the adulterous fornicator the purest woman, the coward courageous, since he at least has the guts to confess that he's afraid. A film full of Nazi orgies is actually an anti-Nazi exposé. That way you catch two birds with one stone: that way you stimulate inconfessable appetites by showing a naked blonde being raped, and at the same time you condemn the wickedness of the rapists, etc., etc. Educational intent can be claimed to frame any disgusting image. After all, any depraved act is an open confession that the man is depraved and must beat his chest in repentance every time that he takes a breath. Therefore, the man who admits his dishonesty is an honest man. I've been hearing people turn common sense inside out like a glove ever since I was a boy, and I myself have learned the technique, and how it can always come in useful; and where did I learn it? At the school run by priests.

SURE, I GET IT, I'm as aware as anybody that "evil lives in each of us." And for all the time I've worked in a prison (for the past twenty years, that is), I've had a chance to understand just how slippery the distinction between good and evil can be, or perhaps I should say, not the distinction per se, which to my mind remains bright-line clear, but the definitive and irrevocable assignment of a given individual to one of the two camps that that boundary divides and, at the same time, unites. How easy, that is, to step across that border. By chance, weakness, impulse, curiosity, ignorance, fear, or brashness, imitation, defiance, and for a thousand other reasons that, in their turn, might just as easily be judged good or bad. Since, according to our legal codes, there is provision for the possibility that in certain cases a bad deed might be committed for perfectly just reasons. And that, just as you can cross the border in one direction, so can you cross it going the opposite way. From good to evil, from evil to good. Back and forth. But I find cloying the mind-set, of Catholic derivation, according to which in the face of wicked deeds, committed by others, the observer is obliged to pound his chest and accuse himself. "Yes! Yes! I would be just as capable . . . I'm every bit as guilty!" It's a sterile self-indulgent admission, really. We're all guilty, my rosy ass! I hate to contradict the Master, but it is by no means true that he who sees a mote in his brother's eye necessarily has a beam in his own. Let us further consider that we are in Italy, and just how well has the morality of "we're all guilty" worked out, with its corollary, "and therefore we are all innocent"? In this country, the splendid slogan "Let he who is without sin, etc., etc.," allows the guilty to feel perfectly entitled to preach sermons. Among the hundreds of criminals that I have known in prison, nearly all of them admitted that they were guilty, if not of the exact crime for which they were convicted, of something else, and yet they were all convinced that "those who are out on the street are worse than us." As if to say that the whole world is criminal, and we're the only ones paying for it. That punishment is meted out at random, dealt to anyone who draws the short straw, and that chance falls on one head rather than another. Only rarely does it befall a truly innocent person since, according to this way of seeing things, there is no such thing as an innocent person.

BUT LET'S GET BACK to the sadistic images. In a treacherous, subtle manner, they condemn what, in the meantime, they show. They hypnotize an audience wavering between fear and desire, fascism, religion, lust for vendetta and orgy and contrition. Those things go arm-in-arm. Inextricably.

I remember an old gentleman who took me by the hand in church, and he kneeled, taking his face in his hands and pressing his fingers against his eyes as if he could only pray by hiding himself, and blinding himself, in the throes of a sort of horror, and he remained there, motionless like that, for an hour, waiting to be incinerated or saved. From the pocket of his jacket protruded a roll of pornographic magazines. I must have been ten years old. My cold, gleaming child's eye was scandalized and fascinated by that gentleman who was asking for forgiveness while wearing a jacket stuffed with nude women. It's a lifetime that nude women have been chasing me. Just as they chased my grandfather.

I AM CURIOUS, a Swedish film from 1967. The author of this book was ten years old in that year . . . and he never recovered from the sight of the poster for the film, his imagination is stuck, rooted there, like an arrow quivering in the trunk of a tree, arrested at that point, never to develop past it—or perhaps the poster was for the film *Il primo premio si chiama Ulla*?

It's interesting to scroll through the titles of movies that came out the same year as the CR/M.

Let's take *Fango bollente* (*The Savage Three*), for example. Plot: "Three apparently well-behaved young men, oppressed by their alienating jobs and their disappointing personal lives, are transformed into sadistic criminals."

Or else Mario Mercier's *I riti erotici della papessa Jesial* (original French title, *La papesse*, English title, *A Woman Possessed*), which also came out in the red-letter year 1975. The following misadventures befall the unfortunate female protagonist: during the course of a black Sabbath, she is raped by a man dressed as a gladiator, she is locked up in a stable, she is seared with a red-hot cattle brand, sprinkled with the blood of a rooster, raped again by another adept of the cult, whose sperm, collected in a goblet, is later drunk by the priestess, and then "walled up alive in a cave [from which she will emerge raving mad, after having dreamed she was being raped by a repugnant vulture-man], and in the end, ripped limb from limb by a dog." In comparison, not a hair on the heads of the CR/M's girl victims was harmed. The following year, a film came out in which "first a guy extracts all of a poor girl's teeth so she can perform fellatio upon him, then he shaves her bald, drills a hole in her cranium with a Black & Decker drill, and samples her brain through a straw" (I'm quoting from the thoroughly documented volume *Sex and Violence* by Roberto Curti and Tommaso La Selva). The seventies would go on to build a filmography whose most reassuring title was *Violenza a una vergine nella terra dei morti viventi* (literally, *Rape of a Virgin in the Land of the Living Dead*, original French title, *Le Frisson des vampires*, English title, *The Shiver of the Vampires*, Jean Rollin, 1971).

Rancid, abrasive, unbearable, revolting, and also ramshackle, tarantula-bit and overexcited, slipshod, putrid, and enough to drive you off the rails—all of these are to be taken of course as positive judgments of this kind of cinema. It's the perfect blend, designed to stimulate and scandalize: sex is fine, violence is okay, too, but sex and violence together are as excessive as they are exciting—sex as interchangeable with death.

But why talk about the movies here? Not because they offer bad examples and pernicious encouragements, no: but rather because that is the way the ideational machinery of cinema functions. If cinema is the art that reveals the most massive disproportion between the possibilities it offers and its actual achievements, as Buñuel claimed, the same grievous and grotesque disproportion can be found in sex, where there is a yawning gulf between our fantasies and the reality we experience, and in some cases perhaps it's better that way, since the unbridled nature of those fantasies might do serious harm to those who embody them. It might be a very bad thing, in other words, for the two planes to meet in reality. If fantasies became reality, they would unleash the monsters of *Forbidden Planet*. Foolish, trivial, and violent as is the erotic imagination, sex is a coagulant within which lie curdled the most frantic and bizarre impulses. While at first glance it might seem that everything comes down to the rutting frenzy to fuck, or to be fucked, *inside* that frenzy there is rarely hidden an exclusively sexual desire—something that can be placated in the elementary gymnastics of coitus. Most of the time, sex instead acts as a language, used to express other desires and fears. To simplify them and render them easier to communicate, even if they thus become even more mysterious. Every language at once renders manifest its object and masks it, veils it.

AT AGE SIXTEEN OR SEVENTEEN, Lodoli, Arbus, and I went to the independent movie house to see *Viva la Muerte*, *El Topo*, and Borowczyk's *Immoral Tales*. *Night Train Murders* had just come out, which the *Corriere della Sera* panned as a film of "low slaughterhouse cinema," though it's now considered a classic of the Rape and Revenge genre: addled druggies on a train who rape and murder, only to encounter their nemesis.

In those same years, the most prolific director of sexploitation cinema, revered by connoisseurs as a maestro, Jesús Franco, was producing such films as:

Intimate Diary of a Nymphomaniac
The Erotic Exploits of Maciste in Atlantis
Pleasure for Three (very loosely based on the Marquis de Sade's
   Philosophy in the Bedroom)
Who Raped Linda?
The Devil's Possessed, or, variant title, *Sexy Diabolic Story*
The Girl with the Shining Sex
Barbed Wire Dolls, or, variant titles, *Women's Prison* and *Caged
   Women*

No fewer than three films are based to some extent on the CR/M: *Roma, l'altra faccia della violenza* (*Rome: The Other Side of Violence*) by Marino Gerolami, *I violenti di Roma bene* (*Violence for Kicks*) by Sergio Grieco and Massimo Felisatti, and *I ragazzi della Roma violenta* (no English title) by Renato Savino. I was able to see only one of them.

   In the end, everything crumbles and swirls back into pornography. Sex is the door through which we enter, it is also the door we leave by: between those doors is the world. Nothing matters except as a mode of transit. The frenzy is to cross through, penetrate, contaminate, and then dissolve. No one is interested in sex per se, it's used as a bypass, a transcendence, some use it to get as close as possible to the truth, others to death, if death is the only truth, the only throughline of life, and therefore, in the most exacting terms, it's not even death, it can't be, since death doesn't exist, it can't be experienced in the first person, and in fact all these serial killers are seeking in vain to feel it, they make a great effort by killing other people, an effort to sample a little piece of death—that magic mushroom, that magical potion—only it turns out that killing isn't the same as dying, no, it's far simpler than dying, far more illusory, repetitive, it immediately becomes addictive. Killing teaches you nothing, after the first murder, all the others will be a steady diminuendo. They quickly plunge into the prose of the everyday. Sex is a shortcut that sooner or later is abandoned because it's monotonous, not very exciting. Even rape, which represents a distillation of pure violence, in its perfect blend of brutal appropriation, humiliation, and pleasure, even rape is soon downgraded to the rank of a pastime, a half-solved crossword puzzle, a leisure-time activity for those with nothing better to do, for doormen sitting in their lobby booths. Far more erotic is, to put it bluntly, death. The paroxysmal violence of the erotic act ends up eradicating any further desire, if not the desire for death: but, however crude, eroticism succumbs in the presence of the corpse and, like alcohol, cruelty is transformed from exciting to depressive. Eros is a coward, it cuts and runs when it catches a whiff of the stench of death.

IN THE FINAL ANALYSIS, rape is an act of extreme realism. Exactly like murder, which can be vindicated as a demonstration of an individual's mortality, carried out for the benefit of the naïve and the incredulous who refuse to take it into consideration. The victims learn their lesson at the exact instant it becomes of no use to them, as they're dying, much like what happens to Martin Eden in the novel by Jack London, with its spectacular finale. Open your eyes, poor fool, and then shut them for all time. That is why you will find a philosophical vein in certain murderers; in their delirium, wisdom; an aura glows all around their dirty work; they're convinced that they possess a certain depth of knowledge due to their familiarity with death, and that they are, as it were, more honest than many others, the only truly honest ones, since they are willing to reveal the negative roots of life by brusquely accelerating the natural end of its process. What are you complaining about? After all, you have to die, sooner or later, don't you? So *die*! Die now! Without all this blathering about it. *Go ahead . . . make my day!* (Eastwood). Such hypocrisy or naïveté, to hear murderers tell it, in those who cling at all costs to life. Those who refuse to accept dying. As R.L. must have done, shortsighted young woman that she was. A famous and aristocratic murderer of the Renaissance, as he was butchering his adversary with the help of a paid assassin, complained that this man simply wouldn't let himself be killed. He urged his victim, for the love of courtesy, to cease his foolish resistance. Often a murderer works meticulously, with great diligence, like a pupil completing an assignment. He is the head of the class, when it comes to death. And if death is the only indisputable truth . . . the only irrefutable fact . . . then clearly the murderer has secured a solid A in philosophy. Ah, the fatal sheen that certain interviews with murderers take on, the aura that surrounds them . . .

In rape, a very simple message is being transmitted. It's directed at women. It asks them to have nothing more than a crumb of common sense, and honesty about themselves. Women, be sincere. Recognize once and for all that you are all so many stupid whores, admit it's true. You know it perfectly well, no one has to tell you. And you know that the fate written for you from time out of mind is to be subjugated and mistreated. A rapist just demands that the filthy phrases a lover whispers to his woman to excite her as he penetrates her should be respected as absolute dictates of the law, and he loses patience if his victim persists in denying that unmistakable fact. He beats her and he tortures her if she resists, but not because she's resisting him, because she's resisting a general principle, a fact of nature that is taken for granted; in fact, if you follow this point of view, then you might say that the woman isn't resisting her rapist, she's resisting herself.

Rapists and serial killers consider themselves, after a fashion, educators, extreme pedagogues, who are imparting lessons to recalcitrant young coeds. To emancipate them from their ignorance or rather from their coquettish naïveté, that is their mission with respect to these women. "You'll see, you'll like it," while the victim is pinned down by both arms, legs spread, the same kind of promise or encouragement that sports instructors or teachers of musical instruments give their beginning students: dismay and mortification or even suffering are obligatory steps along the way in any apprenticeship. The lesson must be reiterated very firmly. Women *necessarily* have to like it. There are no two ways about it. The subordination of a woman lies is this sort of obligation to enjoyment. If she seems to be refusing in her words and her gestures, then you must appeal to her unconfessable desire. She wants it, she's always wanted it. In English: *She's gotta have it.* And if she doesn't, that hardly matters.

The rape is to a certain extent demanded by the woman herself, the brutality accepted as part of a role-playing game, feminine sexuality viewed as insatiable, hence guilty by definition.

The second most common phrase in a rape is: "You asked for it."

THE EDUCATIONAL ASPECT OUGHT to be confirmed by the enjoyment that the victim displays after the initial constraint. In the schema of certain medieval ballads, a knight errant sees a farm girl in a field, takes advantage of her, first with words and then by force, possesses her, in spite of her cries and objections, then trots off on his horse as the farm girl showers him with thanks. The ingratitude of the victim who instead, afterward, continues to complain and sob must be further punished.

Western culture has been constructed on the foundation of these songs and poems.

Pleasure in submission. Sex is the context in which disproportion is most appreciated. Equal treatment gives no one any excitement. In bed, what dominates is the perverse pleasure of asymmetry. In rape, that becomes total. Thus reduced and simplified, the sex act reveals its intrusive roots, its effect of subjugation. As is so often the case with exceptions that prove the rule, the extreme case of rape casts light on relations between the sexes. It is from exceptional edge cases that we can best obtain a rule, best identify a tendency.

And so, in every relationship between male and female, between any male and any female, rape is present. Even where there has been no coercion; even where there is love and tenderness, there is rape. Rape is the simplified paradigm of relations between the sexes, its energy-saving mode, its substantial diagram, and it lies at the foundation of every relationship, of every act of intercourse, not necessarily brutal ones. The violation of the innermost, hidden essence of an individual nevertheless takes place during the sex act, and if it doesn't, the act is in vain, if a fissure isn't opened, if there isn't an existential leak, a calling into question of the very life of those involved, then nothing has actually happened.

RAPE THUS BECOMES THE RECEPTACLE for all kinds of violence; the funnel down which abuses of various kinds flow, conveyed and transformed into sex. For that matter, already at the time, and even more nowadays, sex is the most widespread currency, legal tender, the planetary language, the golden equivalent used to measure all communications and every human interaction. Sex for Money, Money for Sex, Sex for Food, etc. It is becoming the substitute for money, which in its turn was the substitute for everything else. Consider the sexualization of society, work, images, food, clothing, free time, religion, and all our nonsexual desires.

In rape, pleasure is nothing but power, but power at this point has no way to manifest itself, except through pleasure. It is forced to communicate this way. If it is unable to express itself by cutting someone's head off, then power will give itself sheen and luster by eroticizing itself.

And so we live in a society of rape. Hostility, rapacity, and power find a sexual manifestation. Sex is a language, not a thing. It's a way of wanting, not the object of that desire. Any drive can be interpreted through sex: whether it's a drive for revenge, a claim of ownership, an exhibitionistic impulse, a yearning for identity. Boys rape their female classmates and film it on their cell phones. Freedom understood as the faculty to do harm. Liberty = crime. A full realization of ourselves can take place only if we are willing to abuse others, bend them to our will, and are capable of *doing so*. The self fully coincides with power. (Only a prig like Nietzsche could manage *never once* to mention sex, that is to say, one of its most obvious manifestations, in the six hundred incandescent pages of *Wille zur Macht*, or *Will to Power*.)

SOMEONE HAS GONE to the trouble of listing the array of situations in which a woman's violent sexual subordination is depicted or propagandized. When a woman is viewed as an object or as merchandise; when she is depicted as a slave, forced to satisfy all requests; when she takes pleasure in her own humiliation; when she is tied up, wounded, or mutilated in order to give her pleasure or to give pleasure to others; when parts or sections of her body are isolated and displayed as if they were independent of her as a person; when she is penetrated by objects and animals; or placed in a degrading setting and insulted, tortured, dirtied, cut and made to bleed, in order to arouse excitement.

IN A CERTAIN SENSE, in the QT it was as if we were in the Middle Ages. A battlemented, turreted citadel, protected behind its walls, an elite of professionals, merchants, and functionaries with a narrow mind-set, who fear above all other things disorder and any intemperance that might come to disturb the smooth functioning of their businesses. Well-concealed secrets, quiet living. And young people without many distractions. Once school is over or after the hours of study preparing for the ponderous exams for medical school or the department of engineering or law school, with snacks and glasses of milk laid out by the housekeeper, there's almost nothing to do in the quarter, "no form of organization capable of martialing the energy of the strutting young studs, therefore condemned to find their amusements with vulgar pranks, narcotics, and girl chasing." Then there was political militancy, which back then took the form of ideological sessions or paramilitary activities such as patrolling, standing sentinel, security forces, demonstrations, boxing. More than a release of energy, it's useful for winding up the spring. Sports and physical activity are concentrated in the confines of small cellar gymnasiums, where you build up your muscles just to feel them pulsate with the effort.

If morality is severe, then you violate it in order to let off your repressed energy; if it is permissive, then everything seems to be permitted. It is therefore "peaceful living" itself that generates its opposite, it's the river flowing quietly that produces whirlpools in which you can drown. Boredom. There is nothing more fertile than boredom. Brilliant discoveries, masterpieces, demented undertakings, and crimes all spring from boredom. Self-harm and waste.

In one of those films based on the CR/M, the protagonists, who are described as "pampered brats with a Jaguar in search of prey," are chatting in boredom at Bar Tortuga, across from Giulio Cesare High School. The café of the Fascists.

"We need to do something . . ."

". . . always the same faces . . ."

". . . always the same things . . . !"

I watched it on DVD on Christmas Day. The next day, St. Stephen's Day, I watched *Non violentate Jennifer* (literally, *Don't Rape Jennifer*), whose original English title was *I Spit on Your Grave*. The titles of many seventies films are negative imperatives: *Non aprite quella porta* (*Don't Open That Door*, the Italian title of *The Texas Chain Saw Massacre*), *Non si deve profanare il sonno dei morti* (*You Mustn't Defile the Sleep of the Dead*, English title, *Let Sleeping Corpses Lie*), and *Non si sevizia un paperino* (*Don't Torture a Duckling*) . . . which is the most enigmatic title of them all, especially because, where's the duckling, in the movie? Who's the duckling?

I Spit on Your Grave is one noteworthy and very crude movie. Jennifer is raped repeatedly by a gang of four lowlifes, one of whom is actually retarded, but she survives the rapes and torture and takes her revenge by seducing them and then murdering them one by one, first of all the village idiot, perhaps the least guilty, who is hanged by the young woman as he is in the throes of making love with her and just as he is having an orgasm, for what may be the first time in his life. His moans of pleasure are transformed into a death rattle when the rope lifts him up and leaves him hanging from a tree.

During one showing of the movie in America, someone in the audience called out: "That was a good one!" after the girl's first rape. Upon the second rape, "That'll show her!" and, after the third: "I've seen some good ones, but this is the best." When the other three men try to make the retarded man rape Jennifer, too, there were shouts of encouragement from the audience.

"There is no reason to see this movie except to be entertained by the sight of sadism and suffering," wrote a reviewer.

The viewing public (male, but not only) has a dormant criminal mind. Depictions of abuse reawaken it.

UNDER THE STRICTURES of a repressive morality, a man lives in a state of permanent sexual misery. This much is clear. But actually, things go even worse with a liberated man. He winds up becoming indentured to his own freedoms, the inclinations that were once censored, the proliferating attractions, the law of desire that demands satisfaction; slave to the countless possibilities that his liberated life now offers him, and which in the absence of inhibitions he is in some sense *obliged* to take advantage of, otherwise he's just a miserable loser. He must necessarily *find fulfillment*, and that means taking advantage of every opportunity, offered or imagined, making the most, exploiting—that's the imperative of the free world. Perennially stunned by the variety of erotic supply, if he suffered when his instincts were repressed, now that they no longer are, he howls in pain, caught in a vise grip of unbridled yet unsatiated desires. Individualism and consumer ideology mean just one thing for him: the whole world is his to fuck. So it's up to him to fuck it.

Unfortunately, no one seems to be up to this grandiose task.

A FAMOUS GYM of the period was right across from my home. I've already talked about it, in the chapter devoted to my gym teachers. I went to it regularly for a few months, together with Arbus, in hopes that we'd toughen up—abs, arms, our intentions in life. The idea was wrong but the place was right. Its cold lighting and the creaking of the plastic-coated floor eliminated any illusion that you might be there to enjoy yourself. This wasn't a way of letting off steam: gymnasiums concentrate, they compress, they're buzzing accumulators like the fluorescent ceiling lights. Instead of being released, the energy builds up, and the serial enjoyment remains within the body, the rush of blood that pumps into the muscles makes your head spin. Mechanical gestures repeated twenty or thirty times, rapidly.

The gym was famous for its proprietor and instructor, whose hoarse shouted slogans accompanied us as we did our exercises, almost all of them based on painful, exhausting series of push-ups. But you had to keep going, you couldn't give up. The slogans were like the ones the Marines used in boot camp: hyperbolic, shouted until there was no voice left.

The one that echoed through the gyms most often was "Man is a beast!!!" Do you remember it? And the instructor, the legendary, hirsute Gabriele Ontani? According to Ontani man was a beast, so it was only right that he should suffer. To gain what? A perfect physique?

NO, suffering was an end in itself.

"Go . . . go . . . go . . . go . . . come on . . . come on . . . come on . . . come on . . . come on, again, go, go! again! go! go! go!" Ontani would shout in a hoarse voice, stepping up the pace of the push-ups still to be done, and culminating with: "Man . . . is . . . A BEAST!!!"

That maxim was the signal that we could stop now, to our relief, massaging our muscles, which had crossed the threshold of pain. Also, remember the clause that supplemented the concept, buffering it and rendering it enigmatic, less preemptory: "Man is a beast . . . and woman . . . is *a work of art!*"

That rounds out the meaning. This was the secret and our condemnation: we were beasts destined to meet works of art. Outside the gym (where the schedules were rigorously divided up between men and women, back then there was no sexy promiscuity, no intermingling, then the proprietors wised up and the exercise outfits grew skimpier), beyond the confines of the tatami and exercise mats, works of art teemed, just waiting to meet us, to let us admire them. But, I wondered, how are so many beasts going to copulate with so many works of art?

I was seized by a lurking doubt: could it be that . . .

Ontani's slogan revealed an unbridgeable difference between men and women.

12

NUDITY HAS SOMETHING *to do with death. It's always bound up with death. Not a point of departure, your start as a newborn, Adamitic, but rather a point of arrival. Final destination. Denuding is never a spontaneous act, but rather the consequence of a brusque, convulsive, revelatory movement; even when you take your clothes off to go to sleep, you relive the stark aspect of every discovery, therein included the one that takes place every night, in a bathroom or a bedroom.*

WHAT DID THE MURDERERS of the CR/M see, what were they seeing when they looked at the young women they had denuded? What was there *underneath*, what lay before their eyes, what lay deeper beneath that nudity which by rights ought not to have had anything more to conceal? Two attractive bodies? Two victims of mistreatment and abuse whose nudity was just the most explicit way of saying that they were defenseless? The first thing you do to someone you capture to make it clear to them that they are at their captors' mercy: you strip them bare. So were those young women now prisoners in a concentration camp as in the imaginary world most beloved of those who had kidnapped them? (The school of Nazi-sadist pornography.) A girl's naked body throws open a question that has nothing to do with her and everything to do with whoever is looking at her. With how and why they are looking at her. If there is no erotic purpose, then the sight becomes unbearable. If that objective was lacking, therefore, then it was necessary to create it, somehow. After which, hands had to reach out, onto the girl's body or onto one's own, one had to take control of a hunk of flesh so that the otherwise unbearable sight of nudity might be transformed into a concrete act, so much the better if that act was brusque, violent, unpleasant, like the act of someone pinching themselves or pricking themselves with a pin to make sure they are truly awake. Looking at a nude girl is like looking at her dead, it's like looking at her *already* dead, it's like looking at her *murdered*. Suffocated, unbreathing, white, abandoned, inert, that is how a nude girl always looks in any image, be it pornographic, artistic, or domestic, it's always Ophelia drifting in the current of the river in which she drowned herself: perhaps that is why those who take those pictures sometimes try to obviate the funereal aspect of their nudity by artificially warming it up with vulgar poses, forced smiles accompanying obscene acts with the naïve intent of infusing a little liveliness into those bodies that might as well be laid out in a morgue, into their buttocks, into their breasts, into their belly smeared with semen, it, too, quickly cool. Despite all the efforts of erotic prose and erotic photography, a naked body will never be *throbbing* . . .

Being a man, what does one do with a woman's nude body, if it is not the object of love, or fond attention, protection, attraction, or even of perdition?

A MAN MAY MAKE USE of a female body in one of four ways: by paying the woman for her services; by viewing an image of her body, nude or clothed, in still photo or film; by seducing her; or by kidnapping her. Among these four possible modes, which seem to be alternatives to one another, there are actually subtle strands of connection (far more than common sense might be willing to acknowledge) and intermediate conjugations; in some cases, they even coincide, overlapping, especially the last two, seduction and abduction, based on a differing use of force, or rather, a use of differing forces—in the first case psychological, considered to all intents and purposes legitimate (even when it is preponderant over the target of its intent), in the second case physical in nature, which is deemed illegitimate in all cases, and therefore forbidden and sanctioned. The first two modes, in contrast, call for an investment that is purely economic in kind. A man must therefore spend money and energy to obtain his pleasures, to an extent and according to protocols that range from a prudent investment to gallantry to rape, in some cases by way of love, which can however also be adapted to the purpose like any crowbar or burglar's jimmy.

There was once a fifth possibility, namely matrimony. By marrying a woman and bringing her to your home, you were once able to assure full availability and access to the asset constituted by her body, as if it were an exclusive piece of property. Nowadays, however, this is no longer the case, and a husband is required to start over from scratch every time in order to obtain the consent that was once deeded to him on a permanent basis, intrinsically and in perpetuity, on his wedding day, much like an unlimited usufruct, to be enjoyed at any time, without condition. In traditional matrimony, there coexisted without any evident contradiction aspects of purchase and sale, abuse and exploitation, and simple abduction, in terms of both the facts on the ground and the symbolism in the air. A sixth possibility, facilitated these days by the customs attendant upon youthful amusements, and which might be defined as not merely seductive or abductive but rather inductive, involves battering down any and all inhibitions against sexual consent, by the use of a variously dosed blend of instant courtship, psychophysical constraint, and the use of such substances as alcohol and narcotics. This contemporary mode of courtship is supported by massive social conditioning, as powerful as any ideology and widespread as an advertising campaign, which deems that the sexual offering and performance of a young woman's body is an obligation and a duty. Which makes our so-called sexual freedom something very similar to sexual oppression, reformulated to new standards that are perhaps even more binding and restrictive. What was once forbidden is now not only licit but obligatory. Even the pornographic enjoyment and exploitation of the female body, which until a few years ago was the subject of a commercial transaction, is nowadays given out free of charge, also in obedience to the same diktat, in the form of amateur videos and compromising photos. The diffusion of images of women of all ages taking off their clothes and coupling is now part of an amorous ritual that it is practically impossible for them to refuse, because it forms part of the dowry, the endowment, of that body, whose conveyance, free of charge, to anyone who asks must be total and irrevocable.

In practice, that's the way it works, even though the laws try frantically to restrict the possession of women's virtual bodies, no less precious than their physical body, and every bit as eagerly exploited. Overvalued, targeted as the object of morbid curiosity, obsessive attention, drawn and quartered in its anatomical details by the dissecting gaze, stripped of clothing and garbed in desire—and, at the same time, devalued, reduced to an interchangeable zero, a pallid ghost, an off-white blur on the screen with pinkish buttons and a dark triangle and red lips. Money, charm, physical force, emotional extortion, pornography that generates excitement far more than it placates it, obligation to submit always and in any case to desire, captivity, gossip, bullying, and abuse: who can be such a hypocrite that they fail to recognize that the methods men have for obtaining women's bodies always wind up being the same, conjugated in variants of greater or lesser chivalry or brutality, variously romantic formalized or no-nonsense—as the phrase goes, "wham, bam, thank you, ma'am"? If this is at least somewhat true (just as the claim that it is entirely true is clearly false), then how can you blame those who rush to conclusions, who employ, that is, bruising, overbearing manners? And who take what they want? The whole world, after all, is encouraging them to do so.

THE NUDE BODY VIES for primacy with the face, and deletes it. A nude body, in point of fact, is headless; a body that strips naked or is stripped naked instantly becomes headless; and then if you use force to strip it naked, the face disappears even before the body is completely unclothed. That is why, in pornographic poses, the women being photographed or filmed as they allow themselves to be sodomized or grip various numbers of cocks in their hands have some difficulty in getting their faces to take on the appropriate expression. Because, in point of fact, there is no expression, it doesn't exist, the face itself ceases to exist, and it would make more sense just to blur it or cut it out entirely with some digital graphics effect, or else put a mask on it, or a hood; which explains why the girls either put on idiot smiles or lick their fingers, feigning arousal, appearing either frightened or pained at the hugeness of the members that loom over or are inside them, or else even remain expressionless: in reality, they have no idea what to do with their faces, because their faces, at that moment—even as all the rest of their body is visible, open, spread-eagled, thrown wide, unhinged—their faces simply *don't exist*.

WHEN A MAN'S DEAD BODY is found, it's almost always fully dressed, when a woman's dead body is found, it's most often naked. And if by chance the woman is wearing clothing, then the first thing that is assumed is that she was stripped and then, once murdered, reclothed. A woman's body must be nude by definition, and a murdered woman's body all the more so; that reveals how she died and why. Denuded and murdered, murdered and denuded. The two actions are thought to be inseparable, indeed, they practically coincide, to such an extent that it makes one think that anytime a woman's clothes are taken off, the possibility that she is about to be killed draws closer, either by allusion or in far more concrete terms. It's a sort of introduction to the topic. Only in death camps were both men and women naked in heaps. In much the same way, in advertising, or movies, in fashion, and now even in operas, it is a female body that is denuded—driving home the point that at the beginning and end of all stories, topping the scale of desires, in the stimulus to and the purpose of every purchase, at the foundation of any exercise of seduction or practice of sexual violence, one will find a nude woman, or parts of her body, her nipples, hips, eyes, buttocks.

WE ENCOUNTER NUDITY at three decisive moments: at birth, in the sex act, and at death. The dead body is naked even when it's wrapped in a shroud or under the suit in which it's being buried. Death itself is nothing other than a final form of nudity, replicating in a chilling fashion the nudity of birth. Once expelled from Eden and thrust out willy-nilly into the world, nudity will have lost its splendor and its innocence, it will walk in the shadow of an element of tragedy, so to speak, it will be hemmed in by death. For this reason, and perhaps for this reason alone, nudity is obscene, and hence forbidden. Naturism and nudism are naïve or hypocritical attempts to go back to an origin no longer attainable by canceling that shadow, pretending that there is no secret and no shame, that this custom of wearing clothes is nothing but a foolish convention . . .

ASIDE FROM THE MORGUE, there's another place where women are unclothed, and that is museums. Hanging on walls or standing in the middle of hallways or sprawled in languid poses, there are countless unclothed young women. Some are beautiful and attractive, there are others who move you to pity in their skinniness, others still buxom and corpulent, painted to take up a great deal of room with their pink flesh.

AND IT ISN'T TRUE that we're used to it. It isn't true that the visual and verbal tempest that has been gusting without a moment's pause for at least forty years has swept away all sensitivity to the subject. There is still a certain shock effect (on me at least), not only at the sight, but even the mere sonic contact with phrases that contain "a *nude* girl" or "the man was *naked*," "she was left *naked*," "the bodies lay *nude . . .*" or "they lay *naked* on the sand."

And even the innocent nudity of children strikes the eye and captivates the imagination, and feelings of admiration, excitement, disgust, uproar, and astonishment are all churned together in a single rush of blood to the face when we are faced, unexpectedly or after long yearning, with the nudity of a body, whatever the sex or age.

Nude: in the two vowels of that little word, "my useless head gets lost."

13

THE ANGUISHED REACTIONS *of respectable families when they receive notice of new crimes committed by their children: "Oh no, he's done it again, the same thing all over again!" And then they latch on to an ancient conviction: "Money can make all problems go away . . ."*

THE MONEY IN QUESTION is necessary to hire good lawyers, to offer reparations to the victims, to stave off criminal charges: as long as they have existed, well-to-do brutes have been the beneficiaries of the indulgence or even the complicity of their judges. This age-old pattern suddenly changes in the years during which this story unfolds, and to a considerable degree because of *this* story. The leading role was played by the press, which still largely called the shots and controlled the weather when it came to public figures and whether they would be praised to the high heavens or nailed to a cross; the newspapers knew how to turn a crime story into a sensational saga, exploiting its violent and morbid content while simultaneously feigning indignation in their denunciations, attracting men and women, who read those broadsheets like flies drawn to honey, the men magnetized, the women scandalized. The CR/M brought together reactionaries and progressives at a single blow. Until this point, rape had been punished within a system that oscillated between harshness and almost wholesale tolerance. Judges seemed uncertain. Then, all at once, privilege was turned upside down, suddenly becoming a disadvantage.

In the campaign that followed the crime and accompanied the trial, what counted was not so much the weight of the sexual conflict (men against women) as that of the class conflict (rich against poor). What really stirred public opinion was the murderers' social affiliation. A petit bourgeois jacquerie revolted against the supposedly privileged young men and their supporters, while in reality they were revolting against themselves. And it was the death of one of the two victims that magnified the impact of the case. *That* death, in particular: the isolated villa on the beach, the car trunk. In truth, this had always been the case in traditional judicial practice and conscience: rarely was a rape punished unless the victim was seriously wounded or killed. Only the raped woman's grave injury or death seemed capable of suddenly awakening consciences, stimulating the courts to issue stern verdicts against the crime committed, punishments that could range up to the death penalty. That meant a case, however, where the more serious offense, murder, ended up absorbing and camouflaging the rape. In the face of the macabre evidence of the corpse, people tended to forget that, before being killed, that body had also been raped. Rape became a moot point. But in this case, the sexual violence and its degeneration into violence, plain and simple, into torture and finally murder, were all considered as a whole, as a horribly coherent and unified process, with preliminary acts that worked their way right through to the final outcome, powering it along, making the whole thing truly unbearable to the consciences of one and all—investigators, relatives, judges, jurors, and public opinion.

For centuries rape had been considered in accordance with a scale of gravity proportional to rank, the social classes to which the rapist and the rape victim belonged. The rape of a servant girl by her master was likely to draw nothing more than a fine; while a tramp who raped the daughter of a prominent family might find himself walking the steps to the scaffold: as if the crime to be punished was first and foremost an assault on the existing social hierarchy. That paradigm was suddenly overturned, in the wake of the calls for political change in those years, and in a sort of Dantean *contrappasso*, what we might call tit-for-tat, or eye-for-an-eye, it was transformed into its exact opposite, formulated as follows: rape is all the more grievous and abominable when it is inflicted by the "well-to-do" upon "working-class girls." The bourgeois extraction of the culprits—which had so far protected them from the gravest consequences for their actions, and might yet spare them again (good lawyers, plea bargains, substantial reparations paid to the victims and their families, in other words, the old-school approach mentioned above, "money can take care of everything")—was now overturned into an aggravating factor. These were no longer just wild young men sowing their oats, they were now ferocious murderers. In the language of organized crime, *ci era scappato il morto*—there'd been a collateral victim. Specifically, a dead woman. A poor young woman, dead. A young woman, from a poor family, dead. And that upends the old pact, according to which what counts is the social standing of the culprit and that of the victim. It upended it with overpowering thoroughness. The social affiliation of the rapists now made them all the more odious, monstrous, and guilty, since they couldn't even attempt to invoke the mitigating factors of ignorance or having grown up in a depraved environment: nothing, they had no excuses to cling to. And so, before you knew it, the articles in the crime sections of the popular press had been transformed into declarations of social conscience: and when you give the press an opportunity to whip up a blend of such succulent ingredients . . .

THIS WAS BOUND TO HAPPEN. Social inferiority has always been one of the ideal conditions attendant on domination, and the young men accused of the CR/M did nothing but perpetuate an age-old scorn for the weak. They considered themselves to be untouchables, above the law. And they considered young women to be property with which they could do as they pleased. Only they'd picked the wrong historical era, by a couple of centuries at least. Whatever else you might say about it, our era does provide tools to the weak with which to demand justice. Power does encounter an objective limit in the law. Only the law, and only a posteriori, can provide a counterweight to the inequality that made the rape possible in the first place: inequality of age, experience, social standing, role, number, and physical strength. There can be no doubt that the victims were abused not because they were particularly attractive but because they were defenseless. Proof that rape has nothing to do with any excess of sex drive on the part of those who commit it and those who suffer it can be found in the fact that many rapists are impotent and that their victims are devoid of any physical attraction, homely, nondescript young women, women in their later years, or with unremarkable sexual features, and who do nothing to dress provocatively. A rapist's penis is often tiny. That is not the basis of his power, and in any case, it can be substituted by surrogates of all kinds, clubs and various other implements, used both as physical objects and as symbols of domination.

The motif of rape is predictable—indeed a venerable old tradition even considers it to be inevitable—in which an isolated, defenseless young woman is left at the mercy of a man or a number of men. Young shepherdesses with their flocks, goose herders, little washerwomen, barely older than children, who go from one village to another carrying food or linen, serving girls and handmaidens are the historical target of these abusers. In the old French ballads to which I referred previously, the story is told in a lighthearted fashion. Things that are inevitable often ring as casual, disillusioned. A knight spots a young shepherdess, approaches her, lays her down on the meadow, lifts her blouse, finding her flesh is white and her breasts are firm, and, in spite of her protests and her pleas, he takes not only his own pleasure, but also the virginity of the sheepherding girl. Then he rides off on his steed, in no hurry, perhaps after giving her a gift of a silk sash or some other trifle. In the bourgeois setting, the characters of the story change, instead of peasant girls we have college coeds, shopgirls, office clerks, telephone switchboard operators; and the landscape becomes urban or suburban instead of pastoral.

THE TRUE MYSTERY of the CR/M is not the identity of the murderers, about which writers have outdone themselves: the black hole of that crime is the identity of the victims. The fact that they were "ordinary girls" is the most mysterious, enigmatic definition imaginable: what does it mean to be ordinary? Reading the morning papers, in the days that followed the CR/M, threw most Italian families into a state of consternation, as they discovered from one day to the next that their beloved sons might actually turn out to be rapists, and that their daughters were wide open to the tender mercies of sex maniacs every time they went out in the afternoon "with friends." Which friends? Going *where*? To do *what*? The questions were relentless and went unanswered. Danger was everywhere, on every side. Just outside the front door, there lay a vast, unknown territory. Till then, we were certain that we knew it, but now streets and piazzas were no-man's-land.

The account of the murderers' exploits, spiced up every day with new details, as casual as they were bloodcurdling, suddenly undermined all moral defenses, to utter collapse. The press exploited the morbid aspects of the story (innocence violated, sex, blood, wealth) to draw in readers and then to chastise them with moralistic tirades that, in their turn, did nothing but kindle new life into the reader's morbid fascination. When you bring out the rot—even with the noblest of purposes, that is, to cleanse and purify ourselves of it—it's almost impossible not to be infected by it. As you denounce it and shine a bright light on it, to some extent you are forced to acknowledge its inevitability. The carrion has been unearthed, and its guts befoul the air. An authentic love of truth cannot be separated from an unholy passion toward truth's discoveries, however obscene they may prove to be. And so, if you want to learn more, you must be willing to overlook the very same moral laws in the name of which you have prepared yourself to investigate.

From this point of view, the CR/M was a scandal, a genuine scandal. The kind of scandal that disfigures in an indelible fashion the space that it lays open to the glare of daylight. That which was revealed gave others the opportunity to fall into the same errors. Instead of protecting *from*, they encouraged *to*. The scandal served at the same time as a warning against the evil detected, but it also implicitly instigated others to commit the same crime by the force of a negative example, suggesting that by now the world was contaminated and there could be no respite from corruption and violence. Either you were victims or you were perpetrators (the slogan "We are all responsible," which dates back to distant Catholic roots, has had an incredible popularity in our country, and caused the damages I've already discussed: by summoning us all to accept glaring or hidden guilt, at the same time it dilutes that guilt in a sort of generic collective sin, which can be condoned equally collectively), or else both things together, perpetrators and victims, which leads to a sort of general amnesty. Stigmatized in words, the horror became accessible, within reach of one and all. A scandal is never beneficial, it can never restore the thing that has been lost, though it has proven illusory, seeing that the sickness had already spread before the fever spiked.

It is right not to conceal the truth, but if the truth is rotten, it will infect anyone who comes to know it.

Innocence was ruined for good. If innocence had ever existed.

No one could be further from death
than two ordinary eighteen-year-old girls
but at the same time no one could be closer
and better suited for the role of victim: that's
right, suited to dying, fittest for death.
Their immaturity makes them a tastier fruit
unripe and yet ready to break off the branch.
Their fall will cause a thud
that can be heard echoing in the distance
fatal and dramatic in a way that it wouldn't be
if the fall were due to natural ripening.

They weren't ready for death. This wasn't their season.
Their souls unconfessed, unshriven, great or small
though the sins committed in a short lifetime might have been.
It's not part of the plan for an afternoon outing
to end your life drowned in a bathtub
after long hours of abuse and torture. Untimely death.
The one comforting thought is that an individual
can only suffer pain and misfortune within certain limits
beyond which they will either be annihilated or fall senseless.
This is the ironic observation that Dante makes concerning
the centaur Cacus, killed by Hercules with a hundred
blows of a club, of which he may have felt the first ten, certainly
     no more.

LIKE ABEL IN GENESIS, who is there practically only so he can be slain by Cain, a similar role is played in the CR/M by the two girls. The attention is wholly directed upon the guilty party, rather than the victim. What interests Holy Scripture is the drama of the malefactor, his torment, his headlong flight, the way he will be punished and, at the same time, preserved from punishment. Once he has been killed, the mild-mannered Abel shuffles off the stage. That in general is the victim's problem: no self-respecting actor would be willing to play a character who disappears fifteen minutes into the movie. It seems that the very name Abel means, in Hebrew, "nothingness." Were the two girls in the CR/M nothingness? If I say little or nothing about them in this book, am I every bit as unjust as the anonymous author that Bible scholars have identified with the letter "J"?

SEX CRIMES CREATE A MORBID COMPLICITY that bleeds its color onto anyone who has anything to do with it. The first to be contaminated is the victim, involved in the indignity of it, which often leads her to keep the rape,
or the violence suffered, a secret in order to avoid suffering its shame. This
extends to the families of the perpetrators and of the victims, who were unable to educate, inhibit, or protect, and to its witnesses, direct or indirect,
each of whom carries within them a fragment of responsibility: and if we
extend the concept of witness to include anyone who has learned about
what happened, by reading the newspapers or watching TV, or those hybrid forms that are books but especially movies (by its very nature, rape
lends itself more to a visual reconstruction than a verbal description), then
you can see that the degree of moral involvement in a rape can stretch out
to touch the whole of society. You need only open a newspaper to become
part of this corrupt community.

AS LONG AS RAPE was considered a crime against morality and not against
a person, it was inevitable that the victim should be bound up with the rapist in the same aura of shame. You become impure not only for acts committed but also for acts suffered, like a plague victim who has contracted
the disease against his will; he may just be an innocent victim, but he
arouses the same disgust nonetheless.

THE MINDS AND PRIVATE LIVES of sons and daughters become an impenetrable jungle. That's what it always has been, true enough, but, with the
exception of a few special cases, the parents never thought they had anything particular to worry about. As long as the kids didn't flunk school
or say too many dirty words, the rest was routine business. But now,
behind the routine, anything could be lurking. Indeed, routine normality had become frightening, peace and quiet an unsettling sign. There, in
their rooms, the kids might be scheming, coming up with something
horrible: rapes, ambushes. Or maybe they were just working on a translation out of Latin. Some of the victims of political terrorism were singled out and then murdered as a result of afternoon meetings not much
more focused and thought through than ordinary discussions of what
movie to go see. The decision was made of who needed to be taught a les-

son, by breaking their legs, who to rub out, who to shoot. And if you weren't one of the murderers, you could always be one of the victims. All girls had turned into potential prey, now that you could no longer trust "polite young men." Some said that an anthropological mutation was under way, others claimed that the bourgeois class's frenzy for domination was no longer reined in by the hypocritical counterweights of restraint and one's good name.

And then there's the crisis of the family. Ah! Perhaps no notion has been called upon so frequently to explain such a wide varieties of phenomena as the "crisis of the family" . . .

THIS SENSATION WOULD SWELL until it became paranoid in the years that followed, with political violence striking right to the threshold of the home and often even inside. Flaming gasoline leaking in under the front door. Apartment house atriums where adversaries were hunted down and finished off. Dead bodies sprawled on the stairs, splatters of brain matter on the plaster. The visual documentation never takes in open fields of view or long perspectives, they're always apartment house gates, parking lots lined with mopeds, low walls, rest areas, bus stops, front doors of large apartment buildings, narrow sidewalks, manholes, car doors, shattered driver's side windows through which you can see, half tangled in the steering wheel, the murdered victims. The leatherette front seat of a Fiat 750 is no longer a comfortable, familiar setting.

While kidnappings for ransom frightened only a minority of the wealthy, and Mafia and Camorra murders back then were restricted to the south, political violence could strike anywhere and anyone: you could be blown sky high in a train, in the branch office of a bank, at the station, someone might crack your skull open because of the length of the hair covering that skull, or the style of your shoulder bag, and if at home one of your children was interested in politics—and in that period, more or less everyone was interested in it, impossible to remain neutral—the evenings when that child was still out were chilling, the possibility remained wide open he might have been stabbed, knocked off his motor scooter, kicked repeatedly in the head.

IT PROBABLY WASN'T actually the cause of it, but the decline of the traditional family did allow the violent manifestation of problems that had previously remained within its confines, imploding there in silence, causing less alarm or remaining entirely invisible. In the past, many prosperous males had experienced their sexual initiation and had maintained the possibility of letting off their sexual steam within the perimeter of the domestic setting. These were the "ancillary love affairs," a singular blend in household customs of sex abuse, the duties of the household help toward their employers and masters, hierarchic relations, and prostitution diluted and masquerading as workplace interactions, all of them practices that would send you straight to prison nowadays. These were long considered an acceptable solution or even a source of domestic stability, since they warded off far riskier and more uncontrolled sexual adventures. With the drastic reduction in size of housing and household staff, and the consolidation of the civil rights of even young women of working-class extraction, if a male now wishes to vent his libido between the walls of home, he has no option but to turn to his wife, provided she is still attractive to him; and, unfortunately for him, his wife nowadays can meet his advances with an unchallengeable rejection. Another door is now barred shut. Previously, one could comfortably indulge in various forms of sexual abuse, but now you have to go out onto the street. The first-mentioned phenomenon was less clamorous and glaring than the latter. The latter proves more violent than the former.

14

A JOURNALIST WHO WAS WILLING *to help me, Carmela G***, had the opportunity to read some transcripts from the questioning of Angelo, dating back to late 1993 and early 1994. She was not allowed to make copies of them, only to read them and make recordings on her cell phone of what she thought might be interesting to me. The alarmed tone of her voice cannot be reproduced here. Listening to the recordings, it is clear that these are in many cases first-person statements that Angelo himself made; at other times the transcripts speak about him and his accomplices in the third person; in yet other cases, it is Carmela herself who reports on and summarizes what she is reading, or else makes her own comments (which I have marked here in italics). I couldn't say which of Angelo's statements are true, or which* *of them was taken by the investigators to be true. By and large, I'd have to guess, very few of them. I have transformed many of the names mentioned in the interview sessions of questioning, or else I camouflage them, omit them, or abbreviate them with asterisks to avoid legal problems. Aside from the person being questioned, there are numerous mentions of his accomplices in the CR/M, whom I have previously referred to as the Legionnaire and Subdued: the full reason for the first nickname will be illustrated below, I adopted the second nickname in reference to the defense strategy employed in the CR/M trial. That strategy was to pass off their client as a young man whom his companions instigated, subjugated, and practically forced to join them, a classic figure in rape cases, so much so that we find it punctually recurring in every filmed depiction: the weak, reluctant one. Personally, I doubt that the real person was like that at all. But in a book, the nickname worked nicely. Some may point out the unsettling correspondence with a well-known brand of girl's clothing: adorable little dresses and rompers, shorts, tops, and tees. And then there's Cubbone.*

... **AFTER JOINING** Avanguardia Nazionale [National Vanguard], at the start of 1971 I was recruited into the Fronte Nazionale [National Front] by Dalmazio Rosa, who had been my teacher at SLM and was the son of Major Rosa, *repubblichino*, an adherent of the Fascist Social Republic of Salò, and one of the those investigated in the Golpe Borghese coup attempt.

... I was treated like a child prodigy (I was just sixteen years old) and that climate of conspiracy excited me.

The National Front meetings were held on both Via Angela Merici and Via Tolmino, though not at MSI headquarters, but in a secret office that was located in the same building as the embassy of Nationalist China.

... contacts with Nuova Europa, Fronte Studentesco, Lotta di Popolo ...

... the distribution of counterfeit dollars and cocaine ... and then arms trafficking with the Legionnaire in Bordighera. The weapons were concealed in trunks in the cellar of a villa (later identified as Villa Donegali) that had once belonged to an SS officer.

... **MEMBERS** of the National Front had been responsible for the murder of ***, a treasurer for the National Front, drowned and thrown down a well with his dog in December 1969 in the neighborhood of Ammazzalasino (*Affogalasino??*) probably because he was on the verge of revealing details about the bombings of December 12 (Piazza Fontana), with which he was said to be quite disgusted.

WHAT IS STRIKING is this willingness of theirs, the fact that they were ready for anything, capable of anything . . .

THE DRUGS WERE STORED on the farm of *** in Colonna where I would processs it and cut it. Also involved in this traffic was another classmate of mine, Scataglini, who was at the time in class 5B at the scientific high school (the same class as Cassio Majuri), and whose father owned a pharmacy on Via Rovereto. Scataglini supplied me with milk sugar to cut the heroin. He had an apartment in Casal Palocco that we used as a place to store the already refined heroin.

ALONG WITH SUBDUED, the Legionnaire, and Cubbone, they constitute a cell of the Dragon's Eggs, an organization founded on the ashes of the Second World War and which linked together militant groups ready to spring into action, bent on antidemocratic and anti-Communist struggle. The Dragon's Eggs, as an organization, was responsible for four other murders, described vaguely and incoherently by Angelo, three of them at the hand of Subdued, and to be specific, the murders of an ex-convict named Carletto ***, a Roman hotelier, and then one other person, who knows what their name was or when they were killed, in the course of a robbery, while Angelo was behind bars (*but if he was behind bars for the Circeo crimes, then how could Subdued have taken part? Ah, right, it's the time he spent behind bars prior to the CR/M . . .*), and then one last murder that took place in Mantua in the summer of 1975, committed, according to Angelo's testimony, by the Legionnaire, together with certain others, and the victim was said to be another ex-convict who had been bothering a Fascist matron with attempts at extortion, a woman who had ties to the National Front, and who owned a factory that produced the well-known game of pick-up sticks called Shangai.

. . . THEY RENT AN APARTMENT near Piazzale delle Province, and there a class is taught on the use of explosives, run by an ex-officer of the OAS [Organisation armée secrète] and by a very serious Tuscan who would show up with his briefcase, deliver his lecture, and then leave; this man was later identified as Mario Tuti, after his photo was published in the newspapers for the Empoli double murder. One lesson in particular had to do with how to activate an explosive device through the use of an ordinary garage door remote control.

INTERROGATION SESSION OF DECEMBER 16, 1993. Angelo talks about his time on the run, from his escape from Alessandria Prison on August 26, 1993, until his arrest in Paris twenty days later. It was an escape strictly from a legal point of view, not in the traditional sense of the term: in fact, Angelo simply failed to return to Alessandria Prison at the end of his furlough.

He claims that he was in Paris, Brussels, Antwerp, London, and Barcelona . . . and to have been in touch with Armenian bankers and Middle Eastern criminals. He spends time in offtrack betting parlors, spends time with narcotics dealers, the Magliana Gang (*inevitable!!*). At the residential hotel in London, he registers with the name of a friend.

THEN, *let's see what else he says . . . ah, here we go:*

. . . I WANTED TO HELP some people in Sarajevo, I gave three thousand marks to some smugglers so they could get a young woman out of the country; she had written to me asking if I could save her . . .
    . . . I had planned two major armed robberies, one in London and one in Biella, though I never carried them out . . .

WHEN I CHOSE not to return to prison, I only had a couple of million lire [a couple of thousand dollars] that my parents had given me, plus a sum in foreign currency that was worth roughly 100 million lire [roughly a hundred thousand dollars], from two secret bank accounts, one in Switzerland and one in Austria.

ON AUGUST 30, 1993, Angelo phones Subdued from London, or rather he has Subdued call him at a phone booth near the Ferrari dealership in Kensington. "What have you done? Did you betray me?"
    There were moments of coldness . . .

THEN SUB INVITED ME to join him in South America, promising that he'd give me half of his cash, so I could get plastic surgery done on my face in Brazil and then go live in Argentina. I was a wreck. I needed money weapons and identity papers. Subdued told me that he was in Goa, India, on a spiritual retreat. As to where he was actually calling from, I couldn't say . . . *(to offer a more complete array of information: Subdued had escaped from San Gimignano Prison after serving five or six years behind bars for the CR/M. Two years on the run and he had been arrested again in Buenos Aires. While awaiting extradition, he had once again managed to escape, from the prison hospital where he had been admitted for hepatitis, in 1985. In 1994 he would be caught by Interpol in Panama, and extradited to Italy. He's been a free man since 2009).*

OR ELSE I COULD HAVE GONE to Hong Kong under the protection of a very powerful manager of casinos and gambling dens . . .

Or another possibility was Tijuana, in Mexico . . .

But were these real, solid possibilities? I couldn't tell.

I INTEND TO OFFER the greatest possible collaboration in order to bear out my absolute credibility . . . I will therefore abandon all my reserve on the subject and tell the full story, down to the smallest details . . . I have decided to shine a spotlight on my misdeeds.

I WAS A SCHOOLMATE of Cubbone's for thirteen years, and with him I carried out two armed robberies and a murder.

. . . ROBBERY OF A GUN collector on Via Panama in Rome, October 30, 1973. Angelo, the Legionnaire, and Cubbone use as their inside man a friend of the gun collector's son. At trial, Angelo was acquitted because the Legionnaire assumed all responsibility and was sentenced to five years. The three of them entered the apartment, armed, with the excuse of returning a book to the gun collector's son. The wife was at home, with two housekeepers, one of whom was a Filipina. We were armed, with our faces uncovered, when we knocked at the door, but before anyone answered we slipped hoods over our heads. We stole weapons and jewelry, including a .22-caliber long rifle that was found years later (in 1977) in a duffel bag on Piazza Augusto Imperatore immediately after the murder of Giorgiana Masi. (??) and an MP 40 submachine gun . . . I recognized it as my own.

. . . ROBBERY ON VIA NOMENTANA in 1974 with wounding of the jeweler ***.

. . . BANK ROBBERY on Via Nomentana/Via XXI Aprile: aside from the usual Angelo and Cubbone, there was also Renatino de Pedis (. . . *Banda della Magliana, the transcript annotates: now deceased*) and Spezzaferro (from Tufello). Angelo armed with an Uzi. Twenty million lire was the take.

Fall 1974, robbery in Avezzano (jewelry store) carried out by Subdued and an ex-convict named "Capone."

IN OCTOBER OR NOVEMBER 1974, Cubbone and Subdued, together with a couple of guys from Cinecittà, organize but fail to successfully pull off the kidnapping of A*** A***, from in front of a boarding school run by nuns. They have a station wagon with a hidden cargo compartment in which to hide the hostage. But the girl manages to break free while they are trying to capture her, and she manages to mingle among the female students of the boarding school.

. . . (IT'S A *MONOTONOUS LIST* . . .) umpteenth armed robbery at the Tiburtino post office, June-July '75, the usual crew plus two others. Angelo does not take part but they give him a share of the loot (30–40 million lire) because he provided the weapons: two .357 Magnums, an MP 40 submachine gun, two RCSM35 hand grenades.

. . . RAPE OF A.B. AND L.C.: Angelo is arrested. While he is in prison, in the winter of '75, armed robbery of a shylock.

... **ARMED ROBBERY OF A BANK** at the Bologna wholesale markets between January and June '75 ... Subdued and Cubbone pulled it off while Angelo was in prison, and when he gets out they give him 4 or 5 million lire.

IN THE SUMMER OF '75, armed robbery of the Marina di San Nicola post office: the usual four-man formation. After the robbery, they take refuge in the villa of a classmate from SLM where Ezio Matacchioni would later be kidnapped and then released.

... **ARMED ROBBERY OF A BANK** in Lacona (Monte Circeo) at the end of August '75 ... I planned this robbery personally ... I was the lookout and I was armed with an Israeli Galil rifle and a Colt .38. The take: 50 million lire.

CUBBONE, the Legionnaire, and Subdued, in September '75, kidnap the son of the builder Francisci. The hostage was held for five days in the villa at Monte Circeo and the ransom paid was 300 million. They gave me 20 million even though I hadn't taken part.

LIQUIDATION OF THE FUGITIVE Amilcare Di Benedetto for having broken a rule. I killed him myself in a farmhouse near Riccione, with two shots from a .38-caliber handgun, and the corpse was wrapped in oilcloth and transported to the garage of the villa of *** (*another SLM classmate, as found in the class ledgers . . .*), and then taken out in a pilot boat, also belonging to ***, and presumably dumped in the open sea.

THE MONEY PILED UP BEFORE we were sent to prison for rape went into the hands of three "clean friends," one of whom was ***, mentioned above, who invested the money profitably in mutual funds. (At the time he lived in Locarno with Swiss citizenship.)

AFTER THE CR/M, the Legionnaire relied on Cubbone's logistical support to remain on the run. With Cubbone, he attempted an armed robbery at the Italgas office near Piazza Barberini; it was unsuccessful, though, because after tying up the guards and setting to work to cut a hole in the safe—which was thought to contain 600 million lire—with a thermal lance, the billowing smoke forced them to stop. We were told about this episode by Cubbone himself, the day that he was captured on Ponza and found himself transiting through Latina Prison, where we were incarcerated. Cubbone had been arrested for the Matacchioni kidnapping.

THE FANTASTIC FOUR in the summer of '75 prepared the kidnapping of F*** S***, daughter of the owner of a company traded on the stock market (*namely?!*) and who lived on Via della Carminuccia (*would that be Via della Camilluccia . . . ?*).

WHILE WE WERE PREPARING FOR THIS "JOB," at Circeo we met Ezio Matacchioni, who suggested that we kidnap him and demand a ransom of a billion lire [roughly a million dollars], money that his uncle had managed to smuggle to Switzerland in the course of bankruptcy proceedings. We ignored the suggestion since we were preparing the kidnapping of F*** S***; but then when I read that Matacchioni actually had been kidnapped, I thought that it was as a result of that plan, even though Cubbone, again during his short stay in Latina Prison, told me that the kidnapping had been carried out against Matacchioni's will, and that he had been treated in a fairly brutal manner. Subsequently, Cubbone went on the run from the law and the Legionnaire went to Sweden and then to Argentina.

WHEN THE LEGIONNAIRE WAS ARRESTED for the armed robbery on Via Panama, I was promised that I would be introduced to a highly placed official in the intelligence services. I wanted to help the Legionnaire, but it struck me as dangerous for me to meet an officer in the services, since I had actually committed the robbery in question, so in my place I sent my trusted friend *** (*one of the names mentioned most frequently by Angelo, who brushed close to the CR/M, which, by pure chance, he had not participated* *in because "he had some studying to do"*) to the meeting, and he was taken to the villa of Frank Coppola in Ardea . . . the individual identified himself as an officer in the intelligence services and a Fascist comrade, *** was convinced that he had met him before at the home of the cabinet minister ***, who was a family friend, but once he learned the names of the judges who were conducting the pretrial investigation of the Legionnaire, the secret agent said they couldn't be approached because of their honesty and because their political ideas were diametrically opposed to the right wing.

. . . DURING HIS TIME ON THE RUN, the Legionnaire was certainly in Italy in 1977, where he had taken part in the kidnapping of Stefano Scarozza, a Roman.

. . . THE LAWYER WHO WAS DEFENDING ME and Subdued during the time of the appeals trial for the CR/M (1980) brought us reports about the Legionnaire, with whom he was in contact. For instance, he met him on Viale Libia in the company of two Fascists. Sub and I, who were a couple of reckless fools, had it in for the Legionnaire, in prison we felt he had abandoned us, he'd allowed us to be lynched by the Communists and the feminists at various demonstrations without carrying out any reprisal. The lawyer told us that that wasn't true, that the Legionnaire had taken action, and he made some reference to the killing of Giorgiana Masi. When Subdued, too, escaped from San Gimignano Prison, he got word to me about how tough life was as a fugitive from the law, and that really, all things considered, the Legionnaire hadn't treated us that badly after all . . .

HERE IS A STORY *that sounds interesting* . . .

CASSIO MAJURI ATTENDED SLM, he was a few years older than us, from a very rich family, and he, too, was a Fascist comrade. He vacationed on the Côte d'Azur and in Versilia and during these trips he was in contact with the Marseille organized crime families and with groups of Fascist comrades. He was delivering large shipments of heroin and was involved in the actions carried out by the extremist group known as La Châine, made up of former militants in the OAS. Majuri fell into disgrace: he behaved like a bully, he skimmed off the top of the heroin imported from France, during one delivery I noticed that a certain amount was missing from each bag. Politically speaking, he didn't act like a good Fascist comrade anymore, he was even friends with some Communist comrades, and word was that he had failed to deliver some letters sent from France, containing lists of activists, and that he had set them aside, in hiding, as an insurance policy in case of trouble. One evening at Bar Tortuga a number of leaders took me and Sub aside and informed us that at this point Majuri had become untrustworthy, that it was necessary at all costs to recover the material now in his possession, and then implement a definitive solution. They ended their summation against Majuri with this statement: we need to shoot this guy in the mouth. The straw that broke the camel's back was when Majuri pulled up in front of the Fronte Studentesco [Student Front, a Fascist youth organization] on Via Tagliamento in his Mini Minor, and without a word to anyone, and with a defiant, mocking attitude, laid down rubber and took off, tires screeching. That same evening, the leaders, among them D***, asked us to arrange to recover the letters that Majuri had hidden and to find a definitive solution to the problem, which was actually not an explicit request to kill him, though we took it that way. Sub took it upon himself to reestablish friendlier relations with Majuri, so as to win his trust, but in the meantime, the three of us, with Cubbone, had already decided to take the matter to the bitter end. We were just seventeen, but we were very determined. One time, when I went to Cassio's place, I noticed that he had very thick walls and that sounds couldn't be heard outside. Subdued and Cubbone managed to steal a bunch of keys from him, and while he was away, searched his house for the letters, but the only interesting thing they found was a Bob Dylan record with a note written by Majuri inside it. The note said something along the lines of: "You all shouldn't have left me alone," and maybe it was nothing but the translation of a line from a song, but it could come in handy as a fake suicide note. On Sunday, we SLM students usually met in front of the school where the "beatnik mass" was celebrated. On one of those occasions, we overheard Majuri making admiring comments about the sister of another SLM student (*the girl's name is redacted in the transcript, perhaps because at the time she was a minor, but from here on we'll refer to her conventionally as Perdìta, with the accent on the "i," like the Shakespeare character . . .*). Angelo thought we could use that girl to lure Majuri into a trap. Sub and Cubbone went and suggested a gang rape, to be done at his house, and Majuri was pleased at the idea, and added that there was no need to bring weapons to hold on the girl, because he already

THE CATHOLIC SCHOOL   813

had a double-barreled shotgun. The evening agreed upon, Angelo went to get Perdita, who had told her parents that she was sleeping over at the home of a female cousin on Via Fogliano, and the two of them went to the appointment on Piazza Verbano with the others . . .

Subdued and Cubbone were armed with handguns with silencers and they had given Perdita a Colt .38, for the most part to make sure she was involved in the caper, so she'd feel like one of them. Then they went to Majuri's house . . .

Majuri was already in bed, naked, ready for the rape, his friends had acted out what was supposed to happen when the girl came upstairs, but then Sub leveled Majuri's own shotgun, aimed it at his chest, and pulled the trigger. No one heard the shot or noticed them when they left. At the time his death was filed away as a suicide and the family did its best to cover up the scandal, hushing up any other theories, but in the milieu of Fascist comrades, it was a well-known fact that Majuri had been murdered, and even D*** himself once asked Angelo, "What on earth did you do, did you kill him? . . ."

. . . AND I ANSWERED that we had just done what had to be done, and he replied that it wasn't something that could be resolved in such a hasty manner, and that it should have been thought out more carefully. A few months later we were in the headquarters of Lotta di Popolo [a left-wing extremist group] and we were planning a reprisal against the Communists in the Department of Architecture. I commented on the conversation I'd had with D***, "That guy is really an idiot," I said, and my friends added that if anything came out that suggested the Majuri death had been a case of murder, not suicide, then we ought to rub out D***, as well. Perdita was very upset after Majuri's death, and when, a few months later, I, ***, and Subdued raped a girlfriend of hers, G*** P***, who lived on Via Cortina d'Ampezzo, no. 3***, who chose not to go to the police to file a criminal complaint, Perdita had a nervous breakdown and started running her mouth off to anyone who would listen, all things that I did my best to minimize with my friends because I was afraid they'd make up their minds to get rid of her, too.

ANGELO ALSO CLAIMS to have had interactions with Giusva Fioravanti, Facchinetti, the CIA, Gelli, the Lebanese, the Syrians, Turkish and Armenian terrorists . . .

He claims to have been in contact with Roberto Calvi (*banker found hanged under Blackfriars Bridge in London, June 1982*), works as a debt collector for the Mafia . . .

IN CONCLUSION: Angelo's accusations and self-accusations are not very credible because his references to events and people are "in appearance rich in detail which, however, no one has verified or which cannot be verified" and lack any indication that makes it seem certain, or at least probable, that the information comes from someone who actually took part in the criminal acts in question, about which Angelo might have learned "through a thousand other channels."

FOR ANYONE WHO HAS BEEN PATIENT enough to read this far through this tangled and astonishing account, I'm going to paste in excerpts from an interview that Angelo gave in 2001, and a few other curious and significant documents.

ACCORDING TO THE JOURNALIST who did the interview, Angelo "has lost the gaze of a chilly robot" that he had at the time of the CR/M.

AND HERE IS WHAT HE REVEALS about himself: "I've stopped loving violence, only thanks to my love for my fellow humans, only once I understood the beauty of being a man among men." As a boy, with his gang of classmates, he pulled armed robberies, "as many as four a week." And this is how he explained those youthful intemperances: "We felt we were knights at war with the world, invulnerable and unbeatable . . . life is a charge, a furious, desperate careering charge in which you push your horses to the utmost of their strength, to sweep aside enemies and obstacles." And then the usual (all too familiar to me) nursery rhyme about rehabilitation: "In prison I have had time to read, study, and think . . ."

THE EDUCATORS AT CAMPOBASSO PRISON understood it:
    "Angelo has worked with profit as a scribe. He took part with interest in the course of English language and literature, was part of three theater proj-

ects, two computer courses . . ." What's more, "he possesses a natural instinct for poetry."

Angelo has faced the challenges of the last several years of his confinement "with a sort of positive, problem-solving approach, directed toward an exploration of the aftermath of his wrongdoing. He took advantage of the privilege of his considerable intellectual gifts to focus on changing and renewing himself . . ."

As a result, "we recommend adopting more expansive measures of freedom, in order to allow him to strengthen his relationship with Città Futura, which has been positive and fruitful."

(CITTÀ FUTURA, literally Future City, is the association in Campobasso where Angelo was working as a psychological consultant for troubled young people when he strangled two women, a mother and daughter; those murders took place in April 2005.)

IN THE REPORT FROM PALERMO PRISON in July 2004, which helped to win him a regime of partial freedom, you can read, among other things:

"ANGELO IS A SOCIALLY USEFUL individual . . . a specialist in the treatment of alcoholics and in the integration of Roma into society, with particular focus on the scholastic reintegration of children . . . he shows willingness and openness to dialogue, exhaustive and eloquent . . . he has sincerely repented . . . in fact, he appears to be undertaking a psychological journey of expiation and reparation for the harm and offenses done to others . . ."

FROM A HANDWRITING ANALYSIS, the following observations emerged, in sharp contrast with the views expressed above:

- a tendency to present himself endlessly in the same manner, with stereotypical behavior;
- an inability to express openly his own state of mind, which leads the subject to repress his aggressive impulses to a pathological degree, with a corresponding risk of an explosion of violence;
- little if any emotional and relational involvement;

- in order to feel he is alive, the subject needs to experience strong feelings and excitement, including perverted ones;
- stubborn determination in constantly adopting the same attitude, typical of those who "will stop at nothing."

15

ONTE CIRCEO, like so many other places in Italy, for that matter, became a vacation spot by mistake. Almost without realizing its menacing nature. In reality, it's a frightening, mythological, doleful place. An immense magnetic rock. An Indian burial ground that someone built their house atop. Strolling along the beach at Sabaudia and approaching the mountain's black bulk, down there, in the distance, where the beach ends in a gorge, you walk and walk for miles, and everything looks the same, until all of a sudden there it is, looming right above you, sheer, a vertical massif, shrouded in darkness and greenery, but that greenery is a green blacker than ink. Only here is it clear that a crime of this kind could never have been committed in Rome, too shallow, too lazy, and instead it took place at the Circeo, a place of the horrid and the supernatural.

I have been telling myself for years that I should take a tour of the house where the CR/M unfolded. I hesitate, I keep putting it off. I doubt that it would be useful, dotting that particular "i," crossing that particular "t," in other words, would be very useful, to be able to say, "I was there," "I saw it." Direct experience is more useful when it's involuntary, the product of random chance . . . and my eyes see better when I'm not obliged to observe. And so, today, I made up my mind once and for all: I'm not going. I'm not going to go. I asked Tano, F.'s son, who's been going to the beach there since he was a child, to tour the house in my place and to give me a report. Here are his notes.

THURSDAY

It was six in the evening.

At that time of night in Circeo we can say that we've done almost everything there is to do here. In the morning we wake up, have breakfast, then hang out on the rocks by the water until two in the afternoon, then we eat, we go down to the water again, then when you're tired it's back up to the house, shower, chess, dinner, and bed. At the very most, you might go dive off the Gabbianella or the Batterie, but by the twentieth dive you've run out of the adrenaline from the first dive, and you keep diving just because you have nothing better to do.

But yesterday was different. In fact, at six o'clock we decided to change our daily routine.

Carlo, Bernardo, Lavinia, and I decided to go see *the house*. That's right, the Circeo house.

We'd heard about the story of Circeo since we were kids, the *Monsters of Monte Circeo*, about all the terrible things that happened in that house, but we were always afraid to go see it.

Certainly, there was nothing particular about its appearance: it's just a waterfront villa like any other. It's a few minutes away from the house where I've spent my vacations since I was a child, and it was exactly this proximity that has always made me steer clear of it . . .

We started off, following the signs. They are strange signs, red letters "I" in circles. Ten minutes on foot and we were there: two large red I's told us we were in the right place. After hesitating briefly, we climb the dirt road that leads to the gate, and suddenly we see it.

The black gate, shaped like the tentacles of a giant squid, makes your legs shake. But there is nothing frightening about the house itself, it isn't abandoned, indeed, if anything it's in pretty good shape. The shutters are closed but the lights burning in the garden are meant to convey the idea that someone was there until recently and will return anytime now. I don't think twice, I just climb over it, and the others follow me. Carlo cuts his hand on the rusty gate.

Once we got in we took a stroll around the garden: it felt as if we were in that movie, *The Goonies*, four friends entering a house where a murder took place thirty-five years ago . . .

The house isn't pretty, a small two-story villa with a view of the water, nothing extraordinary. Children's toys scattered in the courtyard. After walking around it, we stopped on the terrace to admire the breathtaking view of the Pontine Islands, but we soon realized that the owners might be back at any moment and that we really shouldn't linger. What sounded the alarm was a pack of cigarettes on the table in the living room, which we saw through the window: they must have just gone out for a few minutes to buy some food, we said to one another, we'd better get out of here!

On our way back, we wondered about who the new owners might be.

There was talk of a couple of Germans. Who wants to live in a house where those things happened?

It wasn't frightening the way I expected. When I was a kid I had nightmares just at the thought of going by there, the *Casa del Circeo*, and I imagined it as monstrous, like in a horror movie, but now I understand that when you hear people talk about something terrible without ever having seen it yourself, there's a good chance you'll be even more afraid of it because your imagination pushes you a lot farther out there.

The house at Monte Circeo isn't scary, but I only just realized that.

FRIDAY THE 13TH

The road there is deserted. It always is. The curves full of potholes, skirting the sheer drop to the sea. The aqua-green gate, with the guard who happens to be on duty standing watch, not particularly authoritarian, and clearly with no desire to work. The asphalt turns into gravel and the vegetation grows thicker. On the left side, there are no houses, just wild trails that run down to the Batterie: natural rock stacks at different heights, perfect for diving off. The man-made berms are speed bumps, to slow down cars though there are none in sight, and even when they pass, they're gone immediately in a cloud of dust.

SUNDAY

I remember the exact point. From there on, the mountain became the protagonist, you could start to feel its weight . . . The sea was out of sight . . . The road ran uphill in blind hairpin curves. The House was there. At the foot of the mountain. It stood there, suspended in a limbo between rock and sea, two forces of nature that may meet but that can never synchronize. You could perceive a powerful energy in that place, and it was both frightening and pleasurable at the same time . . .

MONDAY (BACK IN ROME)

Monte Circeo is, for me, an oasis of peace, though I come out here only in the summer, usually toward the end, so that I can enjoy the last few days of bright sunshine. I eat, I drink, and I sleep well. Nothing more than that. I feel isolated, I see no one, I'm a young hermit in search of peace after my summer adventures out and about in the great big world. I read books, I watch movies, I play chess, I do puzzles . . . I distract myself and perhaps I bore myself. The biggest charge of adrenaline comes when I dive off the Gabbianella cliffs or I play Pictionary.

The tragedy that occurred just a short distance from here still hovers in the air. The people who come here to visit like to ask which is the famous villa so they can go and take a look at it and wet their pants a little, maybe to stave off the boredom of playing cards, but I'd rather avoid it. I'm afraid of that house. When I was little, my older female cousins would go there at night and they'd tell me about seeing strange shadows and otherworldly sounds from the beyond. It was a sort of baptism of fire, out at Monte Circeo, to sneak into that house at night, but I never did it. I just limited myself to going to see it in broad daylight, kept at bay by my fear of the unknown and the darkness of the moonless nights.

I play cards and I listen to music on the rocks, then I take a swim and do some push-ups, I climb back up to the house, hiking up the ninety-one endless steps, I eat some stuffed pizza with fresh mozzarella and cherry tomatoes, a nice gelato, and a nap in front of the TV. If friends come by, then we can go have a drink together on the roof, we chat about things, we feel good, carefree. But if we shift our gaze just a little farther up, the sinister shape of that house, now the property of Germans too cold-blooded to be afraid of it, a chill runs down our backs. Horrifying thoughts get the upper hand, you try to find a distraction but it's hard, you read a few pages without understanding, your mind is otherwise occupied. Another nightmare tonight? I hope not. And so, before falling asleep, I try to focus on the filled doughnuts from Casa del Dolce that await me in the kitchen tomorrow morning.

Part VII

Vergeltungswaffe

I

SOMEONE WAS RINGING the doorbell.
Someone was ringing.
The doorbell was ringing . . .
I woke up, I got up from my desk, and I went to answer.

It was a diminutive priest with an open, honest face, neatly brushed red hair, a clear gaze, and a northern Italian accent, who had come to give my home an Easter blessing.

This ceremony always embarrasses me and if possible I avoid it, making sure not to be home during the times listed on the announcement posted in the window of the doorman's booth roughly a week in advance. This time I'd overlooked it.

The priest asked in a low voice, "May I come in?" and I couldn't think of any reason to say no. But we remained standing in the front hall. "I'm Father Edoardo. A pleasure to meet you." Astonishment: Father Edoardo. I'd never heard of a priest with my name, it sounds . . . it rings strange to my ear . . . stranger than Jeremiah or Rehoboam.

He asked me who else lived there, and whether those other tenants were at home.

"No. I live alone."

Unfortunately.

"I understand. But even living alone there can be happiness, contentment. And therefore, let us pray together, the two of us, intoning the Our Father," and he opened his arms wide, holding the palms of his hands turned upward, while I joined my hands together, interlacing my fingers, even though I'm afraid that's not done anymore. Perhaps no one but a few little old ladies prays that way anymore. I felt I was suddenly a child again, and I bowed my head, fearful I might not remember the prayer, but then I limited myself to mumbling along, while Father Edoardo clearly and audibly enunciated the words and phrases.

Having finished the Our Father, the priest blessed the apartment, sprinkling holy water left and right, that is, toward the bookshelf that held the *Enciclopedia Treccani* volumes that had belonged to my grandfather, then to my father, and now to me, and then toward several cases of wine, stacked there, ready to be consumed.

I was confused and, at the same time, contented that this holy water should have come into my home, at just the right time. Maybe it's always the right time, there's really never a wrong time.

Father Edoardo rummaged in his black leather satchel. He handed me a flyer with the program of Easter services at the parish church. Since he'd never seen me there, maybe he imagined that I was a nonpracticing believer, or a lazy Catholic, or a little lost sheep, or maybe even someone who had recently moved to the quarter, or else an atheist: and I was none of these things and yet I was all of these things together, at the same time. I expected that at that point he would ask me for an offering in exchange for the benediction, but he didn't. I was surprised and I appreciated that, since I thought it was up to me in any case to decide whether to make the gesture. I reached back to the rear pocket of my trousers, where I keep my cash, bills folded, since I've never owned a wallet. I don't know if the priest had noticed my act and meant to stop me, or whether he actually was in a hurry, but he grabbed my other hand and said: "I'm terribly late, I really have to run," and added an apology for the unusual time of the evening in which he'd knocked on my door.

Right he was, it was 8:20, time for dinner.

He snapped the buckle on his bag and said goodbye the way any scrupulous professional would have done, a physician, for example, after a house call.

As soon as he left, I went back to my computer and closed the various pages, stacked one atop the other, of the porn sites I'd been surfing when the doorbell rang. Then I turned off my computer.

I SPENT GOOD FRIDAY working on a screenplay. The story we were developing was about a king whose wife has died young, whereupon he gets the misguided and corrupt idea into his royal head of marrying his own sister: "flesh of his flesh, breath of his breath." The young woman, whose name is

Penta, refuses, disgusted by that incestuous proposal. But the king won't give up. He absolutely must make her his . . .

"If your sense of honor as a man doesn't stop you, at least restrain yourself in the name of the love that has bound us since we were children."

"Penta, it is precisely this that I dream of, every night. And that is why I desire you. After all, it's just a matter of being together again, the way we were when we were little . . . playing together, amusing ourselves in the same bed . . . Only, now we'd be closer . . . a little closer . . . one inside the other, that's the only difference."

Having been rejected for the umpteenth time, the king has Penta locked up in prison, in one of those underground cells called "oubliettes" (a frightening name, a "forgetting hole") with just a single opening in the ceiling, letting in a shaft of light, and through which food is lowered to the prisoner. The part of Penta's body to which her brother is most attracted, in a morbid fashion, are her hands: and so the girl, in order to put an end to his desire, has a servant cut off her hands . . .

THAT NIGHT ON TV I watched the finale of the third season of a series set in Atlantic City, during Prohibition, featuring corrupt politicians and a gangster on the rise. Even though the series abounded in frontal nudity and explicit violence, it was very well written and directed, with a well-constructed story, fantastic actors and dialogue, in short, that kind of enviable commercial product, brilliantly produced and well acted. But the final episode is a bloodbath. They try to kill the main character, played by Steve Buscemi, but are unsuccessful, and so other gangsters gallop to his rescue, and it's a massacre. Tommy guns spit flames in the dark of night. People are disemboweled, there are shotgun blasts to the face. One veteran of the Great War, whose face is half-masked to conceal the horrible disfiguring wound he suffered, manages to get into a brothel where he murders seven people in order to rescue a little boy being held captive there by the boy's grandmother, a heroin addict, who a few episodes earlier had killer her lover, who she'd chosen specifically because he resembled her dead son, drowning him in the bathtub after fucking him and then giving him a fatal overdose of heroin. The true bad guy in this third season, whom we had seen in previous episodes engaged in every imaginable sort of brutal violence (including decapitating with a spade a man buried up to his neck in the sand, because he was guilty of having lost a shipment of whiskey at sea), dies stabbed in the back while he's pissing on the beach.

That is how I celebrated my Good Friday. With lots of blood. Fake blood. On the third day, Easter Sunday, I wanted to go and attend Father Edoardo's mass, but because of some confusion over the timing (daylight savings time had just gone into effect), I missed it.

ANOTHER YEAR WENT BY as I wrote this book, and Easter rolled around again, a late Easter, almost at the end of April. No one understands why it is that Easter wanders like that through the springtime.

And roughly a week before Easter, Father Edoardo appeared once again at my door, about seven thirty in the evening, when the street door downstairs is closed, so that if someone rings my doorbell they're already in the building, someone else has let them in, the way it happens with salespeople from the phone company, Jehovah's Witnesses, and volunteers for UNICEF. Seeing Father Edoardo's fine honest face I suddenly realized that a year had passed, *a year* had passed (good God, what have I done in the past year?).

"Good evening, my dear sir, I'm here for the Easter benediction. Do you mind if I come in?"

"Certainly, come on in," I said to him, stepping aside, and I felt a surge of happiness at his arrival. We lingered in the front hall, just like the last time. For someone who's carrying out a pastoral mission, Father Edoardo still appeared rather embarrassed about what he was doing. More embarrassed than me, even though I was the target of it. I got the sensation that he didn't remember me, while I vividly remembered our meeting of a year ago: for that matter, you really can't say that his visit, as much as it struck me at the time, had pushed me to be much more involved with his parish: in truth, I had gone to Sant'Agnese—the church of Sant'Agnese—many times, but always to the little café inside that wonderful complex, adjoining the catacombs, the boccie and basketball courts, beneath the trees, surrounded by retired men talking about politics in the accents of their home town or playing cards, and where the manager is an exceedingly civil old man with blue eyes.

I had only been once to mass at Sant'Agnese, for my father's funeral, many years ago . . .

(Those fragments of liturgy don't count, the ones you witness when, meaning to tour a church, you discover that a service is under way when you go in, so you sit down in one of the pews all the way in the back . . .)

At any rate, never once to mass with Father Edoardo.

How old could he be? I wondered, thirty-five? He looks like a student, even if his hair is gray . . . or that kind of ash blond that's so delicate and faded that it seems gray.

Ash, a dead, pale, chilly thing, and yet the sign that here, once, a fire blazed.

Wait though, wasn't his hair red a year ago? Could I be getting mixed up? Or had he suddenly aged? "If you like, I'd be glad to say a benediction."

"I . . ."

"Only if you'd like . . . you tell me . . ."

"I . . . Father, I'm not a believer. But maybe . . ."

It wasn't clear even to me whether that "maybe" applied to my claim not to believe in God, which is something of which I'm by no means certain. So I wonder whether it is possible to maintain at the same time that you don't believe, but also that you don't believe you don't believe, in other words, that you are by means convinced that God exists, but neither are you convinced that He does not exist: I'm not talking about the thing itself, whether or not He exists, but only whether I believe or disbelieve.

And so? Do I or don't I believe?

Father Edoardo smiled, his pity aroused by the lack of brashness with which I'd proclaimed my atheism.

"Listen, if you don't care to do it, there's no need," said the priest, "we're here strictly out of friendship . . ."

"You tell me, Father . . ."

"Tell you what?"

I wanted him to . . . I wanted him to tell me . . . I wanted him to be the one to decide whether or not he should bless the apartment. After all, isn't it enough—for a thing to be done—that the person doing it believe in it deeply?

"I mean to say . . . whether you think it makes sense . . . that is, to bless the home of a nonbeliever . . . let's just go ahead. But you ought to tell me if it's right . . . maybe it's absurd."

"Absurd?"

As he asked me this question, Father Edoardo's gaze was *angelic*, and I feel no shame in saying so. Seriously, he seemed to me to be the first good, serious, honest, simple, and straightforward person I had met in years, unshadowed, without ulterior motives, devoid even of that slight hypocrisy that emanates, like a pungent and slightly sickening perfume, from those who devote themselves *exclusively* to the good. To the good of others.

"Does anyone live here besides you?"

I shook my head. He'd asked me the same question the year before. Maybe the priest imagined that I wanted to be consoled in this loneliness of mine, and it might well be that the meaning I wanted to convey by shaking my head was in fact this. I was confused and subjugated by that angelic presence. I almost couldn't stand finding myself standing next to a virtuous person, I was hypnotized by him.

"My children come here, but not even all that often . . ." I added, to make it clear that I didn't live like a hermit, "a few friends . . . my girlfriend . . ."

I thought that with these last few bits of information my portrait as a bad Christian was now complete. But I know perfectly well that it is precisely this figure that good priests, good shepherds, go in search of—find, so to speak, especially delectable. Could Father Edoardo make an exception? Yes, he made it. In fact, he said nothing, neither to bring me over to the right side nor to leave me where I was.

He smiled sweetly.

"Well, in any case, a home has a personality . . . and it mirrors the person who lives in it. It has the same spirit . . ."

"Listen, whether I'm here or somewhere else, it's all pretty much the same to me."

"What do you mean by that?"

"I feel like a guest."

The diminutive priest gazed at me in astonishment.

Perhaps he thought that I was in such bad shape that I had taken advantage of that unannounced visit to appeal to him, to issue a cry for help. Perhaps he thought it was normal for someone like him to live in the solitude of his religious vocation, but not for someone like me, who had no calling, no vocation. Why didn't these children, why didn't this woman live with me? Come to think of it, why didn't they? I wondered the same thing. What could the reason be?

And why is he telling me this?—this priest who shared my first name might perhaps have been wondering—why is he telling me that he feels like a guest in his own home, that he has felt like a guest in every home he has ever lived in?

"It's strange," he said, "you'd think that you have no attachments to anything . . . that's so strange . . . and if you ask me, it isn't true, either."

"No, in fact, it isn't true," I replied, shaking my head again. He smiled faintly.

"And in any case, this apartment, as you told me, does have some passing occupants, from time to time . . ."

"Yes, certainly . . . passing occupants." A perfect description.

That's when I exclaimed, with a sort of sudden cheerfulness, that it made perfect sense to bless my apartment, after all, if it wasn't me in person, still someone could receive that benediction, even if they spent just a few hours there, where I lived like a Fascist official in retirement, or a professor too taken up with his abstract studies for other human beings to have any desire to cohabit with him.

"Well then, let's bless this home, shall we?" asked Father Edoardo, with that ritual question that had already been answered before he posed it, the way it is when you get married, and still it's necessary to answer it, the affirmative reply has to leave your lips as a clear and specific sound . . .

"Yes, I'd like that," I said, and I was truly happy that he was doing it, that he was going to bless me. A benediction, that's what the place needed, yes, a *benediction*.

Father Edoardo reached into his slender bag, which until then he had carried under his arm like an office clerk carrying his documents with him from one office to another, and pulled out what he needed: a sheet of paper with an ancient image printed on one side, which he handed to me, and the aspergillum. Then, staring at a certain corner of the front hall in my apartment, between a small red velvet armchair and the massive cabinet with the Treccani encyclopedia, he made the sign of the cross, reciting, "In the name of the Father, the Son . . . and the Holy Spirit," with that brief pause before naming the third, ineffable mystical personage. I couldn't say whether it was because he was so close to me, side by side, or else because I would have just felt like a worm if I'd let him recite the formula all by himself, or else it was the gesture itself, which these days almost no one employs except soccer players running onto the field to substitute an exhausted or injured teammate, but I crossed myself too, with broad gestures, murmuring, "In the name of the Father, the Son . . . and the Holy Spirit," with just a half-second delay behind the other Edoardo.

"YOU KNOW, my name is Edoardo, too . . ." I said, once the priest was done.

"Ah! Really . . . !" Perhaps he'd remembered me, from his visit the year before. He pointed to the little sheet of paper that I'd transferred from my right hand to my left when I'd crossed myself, and which I was still clutching in a childish manner, as if awaiting further instructions. "There you have the schedule for the preparatory get-togethers for Easter . . . and, of course, for the Easter services."

"Why, certainly . . . thank you . . ." and I looked at the sheet of paper, turned it over: on the back was stamped an Easter oration, and all the rest.

"Well, maybe I could come . . . that is, we'll see you . . . at one of these . . ." I replied, eager to participate, to really go, but at the same time careful not to overdo it, like when they invite me to a cultural event of some kind, a book reading, an exhibition. "If I can, if I'm not out of town . . . I'll certainly make sure to come."

"I'll try to swing by . . ."

With the charming diligence of a seminarian, an annotation that melted my heart a little, he pointed to the bottom of the sheet, where there was a line of print, ". . . And in any case, just in case there are any changes in scheduling, or to make sure," Father Edoardo suggested conscientiously, "you can always go to the parish church's website."

Of course, the website . . .

"I think I really will."

Something told me I wouldn't go.

AND IN FACT I REMAIN virtually paralyzed through all the days leading up to Easter, I don't even notice that it's Good Friday and that the day is going by, in spite of the countless movies about Jesus on television, and when Sunday finally comes and it stops raining, instead of going to one of the services listed on the printout, I get in my car and I head out of the city, I get onto the highway for L'Aquila, I take the Lunghezza exit, I turn onto the Via Polense at Corcolle, I continue along the magnificent road that runs toward Poli across a ridge flanked by brilliant green ravines.

Somewhere along the road, roughly between kilometer markers 26 and 28, the African prostitutes are staked out, as always, in their skintight brightly colored dresses, even today, Easter Sunday. Usually, they extend their rounded asses toward the road and those who are driving along it, and every time that a car goes by, and especially when a car passes slowly enough that it might be reasonable to believe that a potential customer is aboard, they hoist their scanty skirts (in the winter, instead, they lower their pantyhose), bend over, and shake their bare asses in the direction of the motorists. Some of them do it to the rhythm of a dance that they were already subtly hinting at, gyrating to, even before the car came even with them, and which they continue evoking after it drives on, other prostitutes in contrast stand motionless, backs to the road, busy talking on their phones, and these bend over and put their enormous black buttocks in motion only when they reckon that the motorist has a real chance to appreciate the sight, let's say, fifty or so yards before the car rolls past and then, as you can see by glancing in your rearview mirror once you've passed them, they stop all at once, though their asses still wobble up and down with the momentum. I only recently learned that this movement is known as twerking, and it's an invitation to penetration from the rear. Aside from the specific position, I assumed that the African prostitutes were offering themselves to their potential customers for two reasons, one positive and the other negative, that is, to display what is objectively the best portion of their physiques, in fact, I'll go so far as to call it seriously surprising, almost surreal in shape, volume, and elasticity, while simultaneously concealing the least attractive aspect, because their faces are ugly, extremely ugly, bad enough to drive away anybody. So I'm accustomed to driving this road, which is enchanting and deserted, punctuated every hundred or two hundred yards by the stunning naked buttocks of African women, nearly all of them diminutive in stature, in their skimpy red or purple dresses, and with their leggings down around their ankles.

But today, Easter Sunday 2012, I notice a difference.

SOMETHING HAS CHANGED, whether permanently or perhaps just for this holiday, for this special day, I couldn't say. The prostitutes who are lining the Via Polense in great numbers, as if around here we had this custom of sanctifying the holy feast (before heading home for the family supper and sharing a banquet of lamb with relatives, children, or friends, first a quick fuck along the way), this time don't have their backs turned to the road, no, now they're turned toward the traffic, and every one of them in their skimpy dresses made of stretchy fabric scrutinize the motorists, few and far between it must be admitted, as they drive past, but then they make a new gesture, a different one, which I notice only after passing two or three of them: they hike up the hem of their skirt nine or ten inches, and then they swivel their hips no longer back and forth, as if in a sex act, but side to side, sashaying. As usual, they're wearing no panties, and what they're showing off this time is the pussy, but driving along lost in thought as I was, I have a hard time making it out, it's only after a little while that I really notice: black pubic hair against dark black skin. I slow down and now I look at them more closely, and as I do, they assume that I'm interested and am considering whether or not to stop for some sex. The former is in fact the case, while the latter is not. Now I'm rolling along at about 20 m.p.h., instead of 45 m.p.h., and the young women have time to notice my relaxed rate of speed, as well as the fact that there is just a lone man at the wheel of the car, so now they strike up their obscene dance with true conviction, displaying their pussies and swiveling their hips. A couple of them even point to their pussies with an extended finger, as if the message weren't already sufficiently clear. After passing a dozen or so of these girls, I notice another new twist: there must have been an influx of new blood sometime recently, because these girls, and I'm talking about the ones I've had a chance to observe not just between the thighs, are less ugly, in fact a few even have pretty faces, though the obscene gesture tends to push that into the background.

WHILE I WAS DRIVING TOWARD POLI, a big box was clanking in the trunk; it contained a number of oversized combination wrenches. I had bought them online at a discount price when a famous brand of tools was having a sale, but I must have got the order wrong, or they'd made a mistake filling it, and instead of a normal set of combination wrenches for household use, that is, in sizes ranging from an 8 to a 16, I had received four long and heavy chromium-vanadium steel wrenches, in four sizes: a 24, a 26, a 28, and a 30, which is practically a foot and a half in length, making it useful for only one thing, as a weapon, and in fact I thought I would take it with me to the countryside to leave it under the bed in case some ill-intentioned person happened to break into the house, and I had thought of what the effect of something like that would be on the skulls of my political adversaries.

This stuff dates back forty years, but it's familiar to me, proof that I'm an old man now, but also that those street demonstrations really were something terrible and portentous.

When I was twenty-two years old, I had a short—too short, as far as I was concerned—relationship with a young woman, an adorable blonde, who called herself Lou, like Lou Salomé, or perhaps it was me who imagined this learned reference and that was just her nickname; mere suppositions given that I never knew her full name, and this Lou, who took me to bed roughly three hours after we met, in one of the few breaks during the night we spent together making love, when I ran the tip of my finger over her exquisitely pert little nose, which was, however, marked by a blemish about halfway down, a tiny bump that didn't look natural, before I could even ask a question about it she replied, somewhat shamelessly (I was to discover in the days that followed just how shameless she really was, which is fine for a single night, except that our time in bed together was seasoned by her succession of absolutely gratuitous "I love you, I love you," while we were fucking, which had deceived me, leading me to believe that who knows what might blossom between us, while instead it ought to have been obvious from the very start that to her this was a hookup like any other, a one-night stand like any other, seeing that one time I'd overheard her talking on the phone and she was talking about a girlfriend of hers who had gone on a hitch-hiking trip and had fucked seven men, seven different men, in seven days, one a day, or maybe more than one if on other days of the week she had rested), and so, as I was running the tip of my finger over her pert little nose, she smiled in a wry, mocking fashion and said, "So you noticed it, eh? They did a bad job with the stitches, there, at Niguarda Hospital," she said, "and I was so stupid . . ." I was ready to hasten to say that she was by no means a stupid young woman, I find you to be not only pretty but intelligent, and so on, but she me beat me to the punch with a cynical smirk meant to show that she was much older than her eighteen years, "Eh, I wanted to show him, that asshole, that I knew what I was doing with a fixed-head wrench . . ." and she acted out the mechanics of whipping a Hazet 38 wrench over her head. Right then and there, I decided that with her short blond hair she really did look like a medieval knight, a woman-warrior like in the old poems, Joan of Arc leading a charge as she whirled a sword, on the saint's face the same fanatical, defiant smile that Lou was wearing at that moment, petite and audacious, and I wondered who the asshole could have been, the asshole who had had the temerity to doubt her courage.

AFTER THAT NIGHT, I pursued Lou, in vain, with phone calls and stopping by her home unannounced. One time I even went upstairs, but her parents were there and it was dinnertime, and I was invited to stay and eat, and I saw a domestic version of the shameless young woman I liked so much that I had compared her to Joan of Arc, as she helped her mother to make mozzarella and prosciutto bruschetta for dinner, whereupon I very politely declined the invitation. Another time I rang their doorbell and they buzzed me up over the intercom. Lou wasn't there, I found a girlfriend of hers who was lying on the floor and drawing, and this girl's face was puffy because the night before she had slept on Feniglia Beach, with the hood of her K-Way windbreaker tied down as tight as possible, but not tight enough to keep the mosquitoes from savaging the part of her face that had been left exposed, from her eyebrows to her lips. She was scrawling and doodling on large pressboard sheets, erotic drawings that struck me as awkward and unattractive, even though I confess I couldn't devote overmuch attention to them, distracted as I was by her face covered with bug bites, and by her breasts, which I could see in their entirety through the loose neckline of her tank top: a pair of pallid cones with pink tips. "Will Lou be back?" I asked her. "Maybe," she replied, and went on drawing messy but oversized cocks all over the cardboard. No other relatives of Lou were at home. From those fleeting impressions I felt certain that she was the girl who had fucked seven men in seven days, but actually, it could easily have been someone else: that type of girl was pretty much interchangeable in those days. The asshole from Milan, on the other hand, was one of Lou's ex-boyfriends, as I later learned, the head of the enforcement wing of a political group. He'd smashed in plenty of heads in his time, swinging a Hazet 38 wrench.

I never saw Lou again. Wait, that's not quite right. Once I saw her zipping past Piazza Istria on a large motorcycle. She was wearing an extremely short, gauzy white dress. Her legs were bronzed and she was wearing sandals.

ALL THESE THINGS I saw or thought or remembered as I drove down the road toward Poli, on Easter Sunday, the clanking of the oversized wrenches, the gray brain matter spilling out of a split skull, Lou's tiny blond pudendum and the blacker-than-black pudenda that the African women continued flashing with the fluttering hems of their short skirts, doing what a poet of that period (years of the avant-garde, years of extremism and of stories variously tragic and amusing) referred to as "taking the beast out for a breath of fresh air" (Victor Cavallo, R.I.P.).

2

IF YOU BELIEVE THAT VIOLENCE is a strictly male prerogative, then it is also the most significant indicator of virility. It was used very widely among youth groups, especially if they were politicized: both on the right and the left, those who were willing to use their fists were admired by men, desired by girls and women. Violence was a means of simplification, an interpretive key to reality that, while it might be crude was nonetheless eloquent, as one might well say of the notorious Hazet wrenches . . .

VARIOUS PROBLEMS derive from this cult of virility. The leading one is this: by hypermasculinizing the models emulated and taking one's heroes to a practically parodistic level of aggression, we end up in a situation where nearly all real men fall short of the ideal. Real men, in this case, remain a scant minority.

A second problem of these so-called virile qualities is that, even if it were Hercules who made use of them, they are bound to slip sooner or later into the realm of abuse and excess. Rationality becomes cold indifference, calm becomes an inability to communicate, concision becomes aphasia, strength becomes a destructive frenzy, and independence becomes isolation. To have backbone in this case means becoming incapable of adapting. Virility taken as a whole proves to be a form of obtuseness. By using the same faculties that allow him heroically to vanquish monsters and free men from many plagues and blights, Hercules also slaughters his wife and children. Why? It is as if strength, once unleashed, becomes incapable of making distinctions.

FOR THAT MATTER, it would appear that men manage to feel truly close to other men only when they are fighting. In the shared heat of combat. What is it about peace that doesn't work? Are we certain that sports, that is, the most widespread surrogate for outright combat, is sufficient to create a spirit of camaraderie, or does it not rather run the risk of exhausting that spirit in the attainment of mediocre objectives—a trophy on the shelf in the bar, next to the liqueurs and the digestifs?

Are there equivalents to war? Political militancy? The scouts? Serving some cause? Boxing? Criminal delinquency?

Violence is by no means synonymous with force or strength. It may be an aspect of it, or a projection. Violent people are often weak, deep down, and the violence that they field is a disproportionate reaction and a sort of compensation for their own weakness. As if they were afraid—once they abandoned their bellicose posture—that they might cease to exist. A man who runs the risk of vanishing once his rage attenuates, loses its punch . . . I can state that I've seen the same thing in prison: men forced to maintain their pose as a tough guy because, if that aggressive image were to waver for even the briefest of intervals, then all at once the effort that had gone into creating it and making it credible in the eyes of the other men would instantly be undermined and rendered pointless.

VIOLENCE HAS BEEN FOR A LONG TIME the best and fastest-acting technique for making the world acknowledge the masculinity of those who wield it. Using your fists, fighting a duel, etc. There is, however, a decisive difference and a sharp shift between the old days and the present day: male aggressiveness ritually unleashed men against each other, in an attempt to reinforce a hierarchy that had been called into question; what remained indisputable was their supremacy over women. When that, too, began to be called into question, then violence was deflected from rivals and turned almost entirely against this new source of disorder.

CERTAIN MEN DEMAND OBEDIENCE from women by subjugating them; other men may try to do so and fail, while still others allow themselves to be dominated, unable to prevent it, or even because they enjoy it. Men who kill women belong to all these categories of man: they kill them because they dominate them or they kill them because they are unable to dominate them or they kill them because they can no longer stand to feel that they have been dominated.

It's one of the most cutting paradoxes of the CR/M: the only way of getting the better of two harmless girls is to kill them.

If there are few men truly capable of subjugating and manipulating as they please, there are, however, a great many others who cherish that aspiration, or who indirectly take various advantages from the brutal dominion exercised by those former few. This is what sociologists call the "patriarchal dividend," whereby, even without bullying women in the first person, I can still cash in the small share of power that every man enjoys, thanks to the subjugation of women implemented by others; the subordination that was created by other men. To put it in the simplest of terms, I have no need to use violence against any individual woman because there's already someone willing to do it for all men, that is, who arranges to establish an oppressive regime that the individual man can blame while simultaneously, in point of fact, benefitting from it.

A very few of them act like "real men," that is, by treating women roughly, forcing them back into line, showing them who's in charge, but all the other men, saying nothing about it, or even hypocritically criticizing the brutality of those few "real men," enjoy the benefits of this positional dividend ensured by the initiative of those few. Something similar exists in the relationship between pacifistic Western societies and the armed minorities who defend their privileges on the boundaries of the world, often camouflaged as peace missions: the pacifists are often indignant about the warlike approaches taken by the armed minorities, unwilling to recognize, out of either candor or bad conscience, that the latter are quite often protecting the interests of the former.

For that matter, it is difficult to imagine that as massive and pervasive a state of inequality as exists between the sexes could be perpetuated without the use of violence. Not an official, institutional violence, but rather a lurking, petty, potential violence, low intensity yet systematic, a sort of guerrilla warfare, a death by ten thousand cuts ... Its capacity for oppression may even be greater than that of the explicit domination exercised by men in traditional societies. This is a regime perennially being placed at risk: a stable hierarchy between the sexes would have no need to avail itself of a continual campaign of intimidation. Which only goes to show just how far it is from being a "natural" state of affairs ...

(Acknowledged and respected hierarchies do not exacerbate conflicts between individuals; quite to the contrary, they reduce them to a minimum.)

In the period when this story unfolds, women's demands for independence were understood as an undermining of the social foundations, against which immediate steps had to be taken, without delay.

There were those who had the impression that men were surrendering. Not all of them, but a fair number, perhaps even the majority. Tired, weary, on the defensive. They were simply making too many concessions to women's demands. They were softening, beating a hasty retreat without daring to object. What was needed was someone to stand up, hold their head high, and put the female rebels and organizers on behalf of women's rights back in their places. By so doing, they would be riding to the rescue of the entire male gender, now forced into a state of crisis, which meant they would also be benefitting those males who lacked the courage to lift a finger against the rising tide of women's demands, those unmanned men who were going to allow all women to crush them underfoot, to a greater and greater extent every day, starting with their own. In short, what was needed was someone willing to take responsibility for doing the "dirty work" in the name of all those men who rejected the idea or chose not to know about it. This meant wildcat corps of fighters, irregular troops, ready to use guerrilla techniques and brutal demonstrative acts of violence and terror, acts which those who weren't directly involved could conveniently disavow, at least in words; like the sort of thing that happens in those political movements where a party that acts strictly within legal guidelines and recognizes the seated government is, de facto, flanked by a clandestine structure that carries out and targets violent initiatives in such a way that the official party can distance itself, paying lip service to an indignant condemnation, while in point of fact the two distinct versions of the same political movement, one parliamentary version, another terrorist version, march side by side. One of the two parts negotiates, while the other carries out terror attacks and acts of sabotage. One part undertakes in a clandestine fashion what the other part will publicly stigmatize.

The demonstrative act by very definition is the reprisal.

This counteroffensive against women's liberation needed to get under way before matters could move too far forward, get too far out of hand. Before it was too late. The problem is that *it was already* too late. And the two dynamics continued to develop, each on its own: women continued to emancipate themselves, and certain men continued to come up with violent ways of preventing that, symbolically punishing certain women according to the strategy employed by the terrorist groups of those years: Strike one of them to educate a hundred. Strike *one of these women* to educate a hundred.

BY A CAPRICIOUS LAW OF HISTORY, the most revolutionary experiments, the radical shifts, the pivots, the turning points, the exemplary new developments almost never take place in the most advanced and civilized countries, where progress has taken place in a gradual and constant manner, but instead in those countries where archaic structures and customs persist. When these structures and customs sense the pressure of innovative demands or suddenly come into contact with them, like the lava from a volcano suddenly plunging into ice-cold water, they form an extremely volatile and dangerous cocktail that can lead to spectacular reactions, explosions, sprays, uprisings, and the creation of never-before-seen forms that solidify instantly. In less advanced countries, the new and the old face off with a radicalism and a ferocity unknown elsewhere, because they are both "too much": the old is *too* old, the new is *too* new, and neither the one nor the other would actually be suited to the times we live in *now*, while the insecurity of each one's position induces them to turn to the cruelest and most ruthless means to defend and implement them. In the end, what may happen is that the new is drowned in blood, or that tradition is uprooted as if it had never existed at all, but before we reach either of these potential solutions, we will see many hybrid, monstrous crystallizations, where these various aspects coexist, intertwined and compressed, as if in volcanic rock. Against the background of epochal tumult, uprisings that can last as long as the human equivalent of a geological era, and which mark the submerging of entire societies accompanied by the rise of new ones, what remains are individual cases, representing this clash among the seismic faults of the time, while the personal stories are the gems set in the sedimentary layers. That is how an entire historical epoch can be compressed into a single day.

IF WE WISH TO CONSIDER the CR/M from this point of view, it is in fact nothing more than a marginal episode of reprisal in the larger context of a global war, unfolding on a front of lesser importance, in a nation and in a society whose customs and ways of life are backward with respect to other nations in the Western bloc, but where, for that very reason, radical experiments are being carried out on the planes of politics, morality, religion, relations between the sexes—experiments out of which the country would eventually emerge, changed from top to bottom. The one thing, then, that was to remain virtually unaltered for forty years, i.e., until the present-day crisis, would be its economic structure; this tells us a great deal about the political wing that, at least on paper, viewed change in the nation's economic structure as crucial to a reformation of the rest of society: we are, of course, talking about the left. This political formation would experience the paradoxical fate of exercising an extremely powerful influence upon nearly all aspects of Italian society, helping to transform them, indeed, to overturn them entirely: lifestyle, language, music, clothing, religious faith, eros, film-making, while at the same time leaving intact the only aspect that it had set out determined to overthrow.

The duopoly was organized as follows: the Christian Democrats were awarded political and economic power, while the left got everything else, that is, the movies, the books, the professors, the painters, the humorists, the cultural programming on TV—what the very founder of communism himself would have dismissed scornfully as "superstructure."

IN THE COURSE of the hostilities unleashed by the emancipation of women, diplomacy had failed in every effort at reconciliation, and for those who bemoaned the sunset of the old order, no option remained other than total, open warfare between the sexes, with the traditional entourage of retalia-tions and exemplary intimidations. Roughly a quarter of a century from the end of the second millennium, someone made a drastic decision: take no prisoners. The same thing was happening in the realm of politics: the radicalization of the clash. In Italy at the time, there existed practically no conflicts on the basis of nationality or race or religion: the struggle was narrow, and therefore all the more ferocious, restricted as it was to the twin fronts of class and the sexes. The CR/M took place almost simultane-ously with the first proposals for the abolition of the legal acceptance of honor killings (the *delitto d'onore* would not be deleted from Italy's juris-prudence until 1981!), in the year following the national referendum to al-low the introduction of divorce, and the same year in which Italy reformed its family law—the equivalent in terms of lifestyle of the abolition of servi-tude of the glebe.

Those were years in which the importance of sex (talking about it, claim-ing the right to it, doing it or not doing it, rebelling against the laws that had governed it for centuries or else defending those laws strenuously, trans-forming it into a symbol of liberation or oppression) ballooned drastically. In a country like Italy, the impact arrived all at once, while in other Western countries the changes had been gradual, there had been a progressive ac-commodation of this new obsession.

Only in Italy could a film have been conceived and made, and been con-sidered to be credible and specific, under the frivolous form of comedy, as was *Vedo nudo* (*I See Naked*, with Nino Manfredi and Sylva Koscina).

❖

SOME SOCIAL POSITIONS, as soon as they're endangered even slightly, at the slightest pressure or criticism, are overwhelmed with fear of a vertical collapse, fear that they might cease to exist, since they rule out in advance any possibility of transformation. And so, once women's emancipation began, not a few men decided that the only possibility left to males in their dealings with women was to continue to oppress them, but in an even more severe fashion. If the domination of women is an essential attribute of masculinity, it is vital to its essence not to moderate that domination, every bit as much as to refuse to give it up entirely: to do so would be more than an abdication; it would be authentic gender suicide. By renouncing his claim to conduct such domination, a male becomes useless, peripheral, devoid of purpose, a sort of drone; the minute he stops controlling and oppressing women, the male plunges into a ravine of insecurity and solitude, where he realizes that he is redundant, marginal with respect to the continuity of life personified by woman: a biological episode, a bizarre hiccup, whose function is rapidly forgotten. An instant after releasing his grip, he begins his slow drift toward the end, the way a large predator that has lost its claws and becomes tame is immediately overwhelmed by the animals he used to hunt. A law of statistics tells us that a weakened male is more vulnerable than the average female. A sick man, unemployed, impotent, separated, and without a chance of seeing his children, or who has to leap through hoops to do so, with monthly alimony payments that are pushing him to the edge of bankruptcy, depressed, confused, mobbed, is more fragile than any woman. Once they've started down this slippery slope, men have no more hope, since they are less well equipped than women to face up to difficulties: accustomed as they are to delegating their own material survival, incapable of caring not only for others, but first and foremost for themselves.

When you lose your job, you stop producing testosterone.

With their minds infested by the nightmare of that outlook, some have decided that it was necessary to hang tough when it comes to women, resist uncompromisingly. Resistance. That's right, die-hard, relentless resistance: to those who are mythically anchored to that term, considering it a synonym for progress when, by the same token, it can be a synonym for conservatism, if not even for reactionary impulses, we should point out that "resistance" can also be the refusal to give up a privilege.

The end of segregation always creates paradoxical effects. Having long excluded them, kept them in separate classes, watched over their personal movements, to a certain extent men had been protecting women from other men; by including them now, there was an increase of the risk they would be mistreated or abused. With sexual liberation, which was supposed to work in their favor, women had actually been handed over to the spirit of male domination. In a freer society with looser restrictions, threats and dangers actually increased.

AS LONG AS PHYSICAL STRENGTH was crucial to survival, man subjugated woman. When it no longer was, women began to emancipate themselves, but physical supremacy continued to be used by males to keep them from doing so: both as a general theory and as a rough brute practice. It is a vain effort, but it continues to be attempted: physical strength remains menacing even after it is outlawed. Society does all it can to stigmatize it, but cannot eliminate it entirely. Strength has no option, then, but to specialize in minor bullying and mistreatments: otherwise it would have nothing left to it but the occasional opportunity for manual labor and the hamster wheel of gymnasiums. Strength is useless, outmoded, and even a little ridiculous in its claim to matter nowadays, to constitute a boast or an achievement worthy of note. It manifests itself in the form of a caricature, in the muscular figures of bodybuilders, whose physiques are a sort of archaeological museum of strength, the exhibition of its embalmed image, designed only to prompt astonishment. It's one thing to have to go out and hunt a wild boar or a lion, it's quite another to host a television show or to teach at a university. In the first case, the shortcomings of being a woman are considerable, in the second they are nonexistent.

3

FOR THAT MATTER, what should the "respectable" young men of the CR/M have done with a couple of young working-class women who were not, however, prostitutes, but themselves perfectly "respectable"? They couldn't reach for their wallets, and neither could they invite them to dinner to meet their parents. There was room neither for a money-based

THE CATHOLIC SCHOOL   843

interaction nor for a traditional courtship. They feigned the latter strictly as a tactic, overlooking the class differences, instead taking advantage of them to lure the young women into the trap. When the means of the profit motive and the call of disinterested love are excluded from interactions between men and women, the temptation, nonetheless, arises to enliven them with violence. Violence provides meaning to a relationship that is otherwise devoid of it. It represents a way out of sterility. Gratuitous violence awakens one from the torpor of empty, sleepless nights. After the idle chitchat that served only to reel them in, what else were the young men and the young women of the CR/M going to have to say to each other?

IT WORKS LIKE IN A SORT of ongoing military service: you are terrorized and brutally hazed by the "old-timers," to the point that you find yourself hoping and wishing with all your heart for the time to come when you too will become an "old-timer," and you can start terrorizing and brutally hazing other newcomers. The best-oiled mechanism of transmission is that of abuse and mistreatment: in order to make it bearable, I identify with whoever is inflicting it on me, preparing myself in the meantime to take their place. In the old days, the role of father, the virile role, the role of authority in general was handed down according to this tried-and-true script. At the time our story unfolds, this schema had entered into a full-blown crisis; it was caught in a quagmire but it had by no means faded out of existence; it is a well-known fact that when it senses a threat or even realizes that it is on the verge of waning out of existence, a social law grows rigid, and it is applied in an even more inflexible fashion, laboring under the illusion that by so doing it can arrest its decline and reverse the course of time. It is when white supremacy is called into question that the Ku Klux Klan does its worst. The protagonists of the CR/M can be called Italian members of a KKK that was targeting not blacks (in Italy at the time there were still very few blacks) but women, half of the population. *Woman is the nigger of the world.*

BRUSQUE MANNERS AS A WAY of creating a hierarchy among males—acts of bravado, bullying, drag racing and motorcycle duels, beer-drinking contests, escalating rounds of drug-taking, diving off cliffs, rocks tossed off overpasses, massed charges against the police outside the soccer stadium. Skill, but especially readiness in the use of violence have always been valid indicators in the selection of chiefs, from the Stone Age at least up until Achilles, but afterward as well. What now brings only chaos to society once contributed to holding it together, in the days when its survival was guaranteed by such violent activities as hunting and war. Back then being aggressive was more or less a social service.

The primitive hunter that lurks in the depths of every male, then, is unhappy and underemployed. Consigned to the want ads since time out of mind. He sits there twiddling his thumbs, with no idea of what use to make of his natural backlog of aggressiveness, instinct, physical strength and prowess. And he doesn't know what to do with his cruelty and his ferocity, for that matter, which still lie there, available even if unutilized: at the very most, he can hope to play with them in his spare time. He whiles away his time with the violence that once served to ensure his survival and that of his community. He wastes that precious resource on pastimes, and if he wants to make it pay off in any fashion, he has no alternative but to turn to criminal activities. When a war finally breaks out, offering an opportunity to make use of violence without facing legal sanctions—in fact, receiving encouragement and gratitude from those in whose name he fights—who do we find on the front lines but common criminals and soccer hooligans, that is, the ones who kept themselves in training during peacetime. In the former Yugoslavia, for example, they lined up to enlist. A way of transforming reprobation into honor.

If he wishes to survive in a world that has become hostile to the displays of ferocity it once admired, that archetypal hunter must transform his violent exuberance into cunning, his physical cruelty into its mental counterpart, and he must turn his zeal and fury for the hunt against his fellow man in such a way that it becomes profitable, no longer for the entire community, but solely for himself. Instead of the wild stag, he must now hunt women or pharmacists or armored car guards. Or immigrants. He must unleash his killer instinct in squash courts and television political debates. He must tear his adversaries to pieces with legal briefs instead of clubbing them over the head. His war is almost always individual now.

WHAT EXPERIENCE NOWADAYS can take the place of the spectacular deeds of shattering your enemy's skull and raping his wife and daughters? Can we simply delete such an act from our atavistic memory, or does it still have to be substituted, sublimated, surrogated by something else? In what direction must the forces and the strength that once served for hunting large prey or other human beings now be channeled?

IN NATURE, males are predisposed to make use of violence in order to be able to mate, or at least to prove themselves ritually capable of doing so. A biological legacy ensures that they are ready to fall back on it if necessary. Violence remains as an implicit content of coitus, just as the compulsion toward death is intertwined with the vital impulse toward life. The siren song of sex arouses aggressiveness toward those rivals who stand in the way of mating, and in some cases toward the object of competition herself. Since there are no rivals in rape, however, or if there ever were, they have since been vanquished, or else instead of competing they have chosen to form an alliance, creating a gang that operates on consensus, in which case all the aggression is turned against the victim. She is overwhelmed with violence, at least some of which had originally been meant not for her, but for other males. Most of the time, rape is a hunting party that comes to an end all too soon, with the almost immediate capture of the prey, leaving the hunter frustrated, still in need of a way to vent all the energy built up for the chase and with a view to dodging attendant dangers. Rape is a ridiculously simple crime to commit, and the criminal is able to commit it while still in full possession of his physical resources, his strength and all his savagery. The risks to his own safety are almost negligible, the struggle with the adversary is brief. The ratio of strength is unequal. So much adrenaline has been pumped into his blood that he has to find a use for it. To calm down, there is nothing left, nothing remains for him to do but lash out.

I'VE SAID IT BEFORE, but I'll say it again. The objective of sexual violence would be to obtain by force what one is unable or unwilling to work to obtain through courtesy charm or sentiment, or else with a cash payment. The gratification is obtained by other means, with the display of power, the humiliation of the victim, brutality as an end in itself, the application of what is considered a righteous punishment of a woman, of *this* woman and, at the same time, of *all* women: coitus is incidental, secondary, when not actually impracticable, because the rapist is in point of fact impotent, in which case the intercourse itself is surrogated with all manner of torture and abuse. The woman in that case will be penetrated with various facsimiles of the malfunctioning male member.

✦

TO SOME, rape is not simply one of the possible forms of interaction between male and female, but rather its basic substance, its essence, rooted in
history, in myth, in the metaphysical configuration of relations between the
sexes. The men who view it like that, who think about it that way, more or
less lucidly, are at the antipodes of society: either learned scholars or hulking brutes. The former think about it endlessly, the latter not even an instant. This short circuit between those who theorize violence and those who
practice it is a recurring phenomenon in twentieth-century culture. Anyone who says that culture has no influence or is separate and detached from
what ordinary people think and do, especially in the lower sectors of the
population, fails to consider just how hard the learned and the expert have
devoted themselves to corroborating, with an extensive deployment of
reasoning and studies and sources and evidence, the most brutal ways
of operating and the crudest and most simpleminded belief sets. Paradoxically, this doctrine of rape as foundational to relations between man
and woman is also at the center of a number of the more intransigent
theories of feminism.

Certain radical declarations manage to be at once a revelation, an obvious banality, and a falsification. Feminist thinkers have set records for appearing equally brilliant and deranged. Nothing could be less an act of love
and more an act of violent appropriation than a man fucking a woman.
Nothing could be less an instrument of pleasure and more a symbol of oppression than the penis. Nothing could be less an expression of affection
and more a manifestation of dominion than traditional man-woman intercourse. And so on. The reliance on paradoxes is an integral part of all radical language, simplifications as brutal as they are suggestive, which at first
offend, then seduce, subsequently appear true and just, and in the end, dis-
appoint. The hidden truth that is revealed after the unmasking turns out to
be nothing but yet another mask.

The shared trait lies in the perception of an absolute, unyielding female
difference, as if women belonged to another species (this is the so-called
pseudospeciation).

THE THRILL OF POWER IS UNEQUALED. Sexual domination is a primary or
secondary aspect of it, a symbol, the most classic example of it, or else a
caricature. Sex then is merely the ambit or the language through which the

domination is illustrated. The contrary evidence is that what gives enjoyment to the masochist is not so much the suffering itself as it is the submission. To have a master is a delicious, almost poetic sensation . . .

MULTIPLE MURDERERS OF WOMEN are interested in sex only to a relative extent. Since it usually represents an intermediate station on the victim's journey toward death, sex might be rocketed through without even stopping. Like a stop on a tourist itinerary, you may just decide to put that attraction off till the next time you return. Having a woman at your mercy, let's say, during an armed robbery, always includes the option of raping her: even when there is another objective, say jewelry and cash, it is the sheer availability of another person's body obtained with the threat of weapons that leads one to take their pleasure with it, ravaging and raping. If you limit yourself to beating the master of the house, say in a home invasion, then both treatments might very well be meted out to his women. It's as if when the criminals are asked about torture and mistreatments, they were to say, Fill 'er up! or I'll take it all: the economic objectives of their enterprise are momentarily set aside to scoop up some lesser prizes. There must be a paralogism that makes it hard not to take it out on the defenseless. Since it happens regularly and it has been confirmed by a myriad of studies, then it must be taken as a certainty that when a person has a chance to do harm, he will do so (see the story of the Ring of Gyges). Not always, but most of the time; not everyone, but certainly a majority. So it is not so much the *will* to do evil, as the mere *opportunity* that unleashes it. And then, of course, the habit.

For some people, it becomes a habit to use violence as a tool to obtain the things they want, whether those things are property or power or sexual satisfaction. Once you've contracted this habit, it becomes very difficult to break the nexus of I want/I take.

IN THE CR/M, the rape in the narrow sense of the term, the sexual violence itself, had a very limited duration; all the rest of it was torture that had to do with the kidnapping, and served to amplify to the greatest extent possible the sensation of domination that the kidnappers exercised over their victims.

GIRLS WHO ACCEPT INVITATIONS from boys don't realize that they're taking part in a game. The rules of this game aren't clear, but the sanctions against those who fail to respect them are very harsh. It's like looking for a fifth corner in a room: the room is square, there is no such thing as a fifth corner, but if you fail to find it the guards will beat you brutally. Where's the fifth corner? You don't see one? Very bad. And the beatings begin. This is a story told by survivors of the Soviet prison system. The same thing happens to girls: by now they're in the game, they're inside it, and from inside, nothing is ever clear. Things happen, but you can't understand them. A moment after they get into the car, here we go, the game has begun. In the end, they pay with their lives. But what could have allowed them to be spared? No one knows that. Not even their kidnappers. Refuse from the very beginning? Play dead? Resist in some way? Beg and plead? What is the right move, if there even could be one that is better than another? This is certainly not a classic boy-girl courtship, they must have understood that from the very outset, nor is it a reckless adventure, much less a typical kidnapping of the kind that were common in that period, strictly for ransom. They don't have any money. So what *do* they have, what *can* they bet, what *can* they lose? Their virginity, sure, but once that's been taken away, all they have is their lives. They don't have anything else to ante up, they've sat down at the table and now they can't get up and leave. There is nothing preestablished about the game these girls are now taking part in, neither the objectives nor the rules, nor the pleasure of playing it, nothing but what's at stake: their lives. (It later became clear that also at stake in this game were the lives of their kidnappers, at least a good long stretch of those lives: for that matter, the kidnappers hadn't figured it out either, perhaps they thought that they were the referees, rather than the players . . .)

BUT THAT'S HOW SOCIOPATHS ARE, indifferent to pain: they tolerate it, they suffer it, and they inflict it, all while maintaining an attitude of ostentatious nonchalance: "Is this all there is?" they seem to say. They may take pleasure in it, or pretend to, out of a pure spirit of defiance, of contrariness. They want to feel free of the conventional constraints (good, evil, right, and wrong) that are binding upon others.

Included in the concept of punishment as it is commonly understood, is the fault or transgression of which the punishment is supposed to be the juridical consequence. The very fact of a punishment implies a fault: retroactively, the punishment creates the crime itself, it implies it. It therefore follows that every time one is taught a lesson, there must have been a reason for imparting that lesson. Otherwise none of this would make any sense, and the human intellect vacillates in the absence of meaning, of sense. If you don't find a meaning in events, then you conjure it up out of nothing. Often, then, it is the punishment that fabricates the fault from which it is supposed to descend. The positive fact—positive, that is, in the sense of effective, documented—that women suffer violence becomes the very reason they suffer it. The reason for the punishment consists of the punishment itself: it's the greatest possible realism. Feminine weakness serves both as the fault and as the condition of the punishment: it is at once the *why* and the *how*.

The punishment of a woman turns into the reward of a man. If he isn't impotent, the man is rewarded. If instead he is impotent, the woman is punished. She is punished for her own impotence, her helplessness to resist the punishment. Anyone who isn't strong enough to resist a punishment deserves it for that very reason. Therefore, since the woman is physically weaker than the man, she'll be punished precisely for being weaker, and that is a fault in and of itself, a sin to be expiated; in the second place because, weak as she is, she won't be able to defend herself from the punishment. The punishment is a mechanism that self-activates and then goes in search of a fault to punish, and you can rest assured that it will find one, no doubt it will find one, no one but Jesus and the Virgin Mary can consider themselves safe. It's never happened that the weak one punishes the strong one, it's always the other way around, unless in her or his turn the weak one is protected by a strong one (model: *The Seven Samurai*). The reward given to the strong one is to be able to punish the weak one at his pleasure. From this point of view, Jesus's much touted "Turn the other cheek" might prove to be a much less paradoxical and revolutionary precept than it appears at first glance, indeed, nothing more than a realistic adaptation to the world as it is, almost Confucian in approach: tolerate the violence that is done to you without dreaming to returning it, because you would only pay the price in any case. If you have taken a slap, prepare yourself to receive another one, and another after that: then someone far more powerful than you will see to a final reckoning in the afterlife. And it is no accident that for many centuries that is exactly how it was interpreted.

When violence is pure, and it uses sex as the medium through which it expresses itself, women become its targets for a banal reason, even drearier, if possible, than the reason provided by libido, and that is, that their attacker isn't strong enough to be able to face up to a physical struggle with more powerful victims. Women are chosen only because they offer less physical resistance. You might say of certain rapists or serial killers that they raped and murdered women solely because with nine men out of ten they would have gotten the worst of it. In Angelo's case, this is unmistakable. A considerable part of the hatred that he nurtured toward the female sex sprang from his scorn for their physical inferiority, for the ease with which they could be overpowered.

Out of cowardice or guile (which often trace their roots back to the same source) one chooses to direct violence against those least capable of defending themselves. This inability to defend themselves, in turn, often exacerbates the violence being inflicted. Nothing stirs to violence quite as much as the weakness of those suffering it.

And if there is any uncertainty or competition between impulses, the one that prevails is likely to be the impulse that leads one to do harm, to wound, to kill. Rather than raping a woman, the assailant might choose to stab her. Even if she has put up no resistance. In fact, resistance is almost never the reason that violence is unleashed. To the contrary, there is a tendency to inflict greater cruelty on cooperative victims. Giving in offers no assurances that no harm will be done, contrary to what a widespread legend maintains; indeed, it may only trigger further cruelty. A supine person only reinforces the impulse to brutalize, and in a certain sense, justifies that impulse, offering proof that the punishment inflicted wasn't entirely undeserved after all. The dehumanization of the victims allows you to have reasons afterward to denigrate them.

THERE IS NO GAME, for that matter, that doesn't call for a punishment: a sexual game necessarily includes sexual punishments. That is why erotic fantasies so often consist of a punishment. The first form of abduction is oneiric in nature. We dream of kidnapping someone or of being kidnapped. In effect, we sense that there is something wrong about rape, an error, which lies however with the victim. Those who submit, who succumb, are at fault for submitting, for succumbing. The wrong that the victim suffers becomes one with her, it is classified with her, it's even imputed to her. There are countless nuances of the punishment inflicted according to whether the women dream of it, desire it, deserve it, provoke it, need it, suffer it, or delight in it. One theory holds that women aren't moral because they have no fear of castration. In order to punish them, then, it will be necessary to dream up sterner or more painful chastisements, seeing that women seem incapable of recognizing the law, and by breaking that law they have deserved their punishment. Perhaps the sentence itself should be etched in the flesh of the condemned woman, as in Kafka's famous short story.

IT WORKS LIKE THE LAW of the *contrappasso* in Dante's *Inferno*. If she is unwilling, and insists on being unwilling, then sex serves to punish her; if instead she wants to, and then wants more, and can't be satisfied ("she just can't get enough"), then she'll be punished by satiating her with a deadly dose of exactly what she asked for. The typical threat "I'm going to bust your ass!" makes it clear how the first thing that comes to mind to punish someone is sex. And then if the person to be punished is a woman, the idea becomes clearer and more precise, the punishment more appropriate. The reasons may vary, but the method is standardized.

If a girl puts on airs, rape will unmask her.

If a woman gets uppity, if she denies or concedes herself to too many men, then rape will put her back in line. If she likes solitude, or fun, or books and concerts, or if she goes around without an escort in the illusion that she is independent, autonomous, or if she is too demanding because she wants to be loved and understood, then rape will make it clear to her just where she was wrong. When it's time to give her a lesson, rape is always handy, within reach.

WITH THE ADVENT of so-called sexual liberation, it was discovered that the poets had lied. For centuries. All of them, or nearly all of them. Women want sentiment? They want love, pure, eternal love? No, women want pleasure. They want to fuck their brains out. They clamor for cock the way males clamor for pussy. No more and no less. The sexual emancipation of women and the claim of their right to pleasure led to the same conclusions that misogynists of all time had already come to: that they are by no means fainting lilies, but instead they are tremendous sluts, exactly the same way that males are tremendous swine. Many misogynists believed that they had just been offered clamorous vindication by none other than their very adversaries.

And after all, even homely women want cocks. It may sound brutal, but after all, every discovery is brutal to some extent. And the more brutal it is, the more fundamental. The hypothetical link between a woman's beauty and her sexual availability or ability exists strictly in the heads of certain men of whom we can only say that they're either naïve, or aesthetes, or incurable romantics, or else that they're just too ambitious—and maybe I was all those things at once. Committing a logical error, I assumed that those girls were most lascivious who aroused the most lasciviousness in me, confusing object and subject. It was a mistake, but I was warned against it with sage brutality by a friend of mine, a painter, Rodolfo Cecafumo, when he scolded me for snubbing a homely young woman who had expressed an unmistakable interest in me, stubbornly preferring to lavish my attentions on her pretty girlfriend who clearly didn't like me one bit. The homely girl, Maria Elisa, was drooling after me, while the pretty girl, Cristina, couldn't have been any more indifferent. How to emerge from this impasse? Cecafumo fell back on an outside argument, the way philosophers do in their disputations. "Don't start thinking about how homely Maria Elisa is. Instead, think about what fantastic blow jobs she would give you. Often that's the way real dogs are: they know they aren't pretty, so they make an effort to bridge the gap by becoming first-class cocksuckers." I wouldn't know whether this theory is true, I have gathered far too little evidence to be able to build a statistical model. But it was in any case impossible for me to separate Maria Elisa's physical appearance from her claimed skills, at least to a sufficient extent to take instrumental advantage of those skills, and instead I preferred to go on being ignored by Cristina, sighing after her, dreaming of her at night, following in vain the clues that she scattered around the city.

IT SHOULD MOREOVER BE POINTED OUT that penis envy, so central to the theories of psychoanalysis, is something that men experience, not women. Even though they have a penis, they envy another, an imaginary penis, bigger, more powerful, the insatiable cock of the well-known joke, a magic wand that will open all doors, and not only the one between women's legs . . . which solves your problems, procures money, chases away thieves and enemies, and guarantees success. Every man dreams of being endowed with this fantastic organ. The procession of worshippers of this phallus winds around the block and out of sight. In pornographic mythology, the male sex drive seems unstanchable: a brute force that nothing and no one can stem, which sweeps away every obstacle that it finds in its path, morality, decency, feminine modesty, the penal code, even the credibility of its own exploits, until it has vented its load, which by the way, it never seems able to fully and thoroughly vent . . .

And yet, in point of fact, there is nothing that needs encouragement as much as this formidable desire for fornication—it needs encouragement, instigation, support, aid, cuddling, lulling with an endless stream of words, pictures, chemical substances, and complicated ceremonies, because otherwise it will deflate. The slightest trifle is enough to halt this ferocious war chariot in its tracks, to make the uncontrollable urgency that had set it in motion just vanish like the morning dew.

Whittled down to bare essentials, pornography stages the two ways in which men interact with women, namely desire and conflict. The bodies act out attraction and violence, sometimes separately, often together. When only violence is exercised, the sexual context is clearly shown to be a trivial pretext, it is reduced to a stage setting appropriate to the dramatization and, however crude, the story line spools out, with women for victims and a generally male audience. The throughline is a commonly accepted one, given that its only purpose is aphrodisiacal in nature. Once sexualized, the violence becomes attractive. You stop questioning the sense of any of it and you limit yourself to letting the excitement sweep over you. The relationship between sex and pornography is suddenly overturned: you don't excite yourself with the latter in order to complete the former; you practice the former in order to imitate the latter.

4

IT'S TIME TO SAY IT, or say it again. When a dilemma is debated for too long, maybe that means it's false, and that the real problem and its potential solution lie elsewhere. Far more than the generic opposition between the right and the left so often trotted out in order to provide an insignia to power groups battling to attain hegemony, the most original and enduring political discourse of the twentieth century is feminism. It has changed the lives of those who believed in it and followed it, those who didn't follow it, but to an even greater degree, those who are opposed to it: just as the whirlpools produced by a river that flows around the piers of a bridge spin, not in the direction of the current, but in the opposite direction, and instead of dragging objects that they seize downstream, they tend to suck them under. Among the most interesting phenomena of any era are in fact those that oppose resistance, the backlashes, the recoils, the ricochets, the counterthrusts, the anachronisms, the blowbacks, which can attain greater power than the change that generated them. At the point where time warps bump and rub against one another, pushing up ridges and plunging deep into abysses, an incredible state of uncertainty is created, where meanings change places, and the glow of sunset can be confused with the glimmer of dawn. The chief political issue of the twentieth century, then, isn't communism, which originated in the heart of the nineteenth century, nor is it the reactionary alchemies that fought against communism, more or less mingling with it. Much less is it capitalism, which has far more distant origins.

The most innovative political movement of the last hundred years or so, as well as the one that is most starkly relevant, is the women's liberation movement.

As soon as we look more closely, we realize that the societies in which there are strong calls for equality of the sexes and effective improvements in the status of women are the same ones in which the exhibition of masculinity, however rare it may become, is exasperated to an extreme of violence in order to highlight the residual difference, so as to prevent it from shrinking any further. When hierarchies begin to be shaken from below, their reaction is to become even more rigid, and the moderation that they showed when their dominance was unquestioned gives way to the ruthless and even terroristic use of any means necessary. The same thing happened a century and a half ago with the workers' movement. As long as they behaved themselves, there had been no need to mow them down with rifle fire. The difference lies in the fact that the reprisals against the women's liberation movement strike at single individuals, and they can do so at any time and place. At home, on the street, by day, at night, in the workplace or in places of amusement and entertainment. There is no occupied factory to be cleared, no public square to be swept with a cavalry charge. The target of the reprisal, that is, a defenseless individual woman, can be found anywhere. In any house, or out in the world.

MORE THAN AN EVENT out of the ordinary, something exceptional or pathological, rape can be viewed as one of the not particularly numerous modes of interaction between men and women: a "canonical" relationship. In contrast with the theory of the raptus, the fact remains that at least three quarters of all rapists plan out the violence that they then proceed to commit. And the fact that violence is inherently at the heart of relations between men and women can be demonstrated by another statistic, namely that almost half of all women murdered were killed by their husband or their boyfriend, or by someone who was one or the other at some time in the past and could not accept the fact that they no longer were.

ASIDE FROM THE EXAMPLES TREATED at length in this book, let me offer as a further and unique case the killing of a fourteen-year-old girl by a group of boys led by an adult (a certain Erra, someone whose destiny was written in his name: "*erra*" means "goes astray, does wrong") in Leno, in the province of Brescia, in 2002. They wanted to rape her to punish her for having rejected their propositions, they'd targeted her, peppering her with a hail of texts, and in the end they had lured her to an isolated farmhouse, with the excuse of wanting to show her a litter of newborn kittens.

THE BOOK THAT YOU ARE READING, then, treats an episode on the outskirts of this conflict, this long war of liberation that is far from being concluded, with the victory of one side in the struggle: an episode of *reprisal*. In German, of *Vergeltung*. I know that as I talk about it, I will be repetitive, obsessive, but I can imagine that the same obsession, the same morbid curiosity may pulsate in the head of whoever is reading these pages. To write them, I consume shelves full of books and a plethora of cases that actually happened: nearly every paragraph from here to the end of Part VII of this book will be a condensed version. But anyone who has had enough, and is impatient to return to the adventures of Arbus and company (I'd understand it, I'd like to do the same myself . . .), can take a look at chapters 8 to 12 (maybe chapter 24, too, about Angelo, which is very brief, and chapter 18, with the story of a German girl named Bettina, and the battle that we fought together against her virginity) and then hurry on to Part VIII of the book, *The Confessions*, where many of the characters we've met previously return, Jervi, my teacher Cosmo, Leda Arbus, and, obviously, her ineffable brother.

WHEN YOU TRIGGER A CRISIS in a social order based on a low-intensity but diffuse violence, generalized, and by and large accepted by common opinion, like that of the domination of man over woman, then as a reaction there may be episodic bursts of extreme violence that have the value of full-blown retaliations. The latent violence condenses and is channeled toward individuals with an exemplary character of some kind, based on a pretext or a fiction, perhaps, but perceived as such. These interventions are attempts to patch the leaks that have sprung in the system. By attempting to conceal the crisis with spectacular and exemplary acts, they wind up emphasizing it. The violence that was supposed to hold the system together, preventing it from crumbling, instead contributes to its liquidation. The reprisal almost never obtains the effect of restoring things to the way they were, resurrecting the order that existed prior to the crisis, and in fact it only accelerates its dissolution.

THE SIMPLEST METHOD, primal and direct and at the same time symbolic, available to a man to disarm a woman is to subjugate her sexually. Once he has performed this inaugural act, and thereby founded and secured the relationship of domination, he will be able to proceed to extend it onto the social and economic plane, in the form of exploitation, discrimination, and segregation. In those years, the most militant feminists were assembling a theory that was interesting precisely because of its radicalism, which is that the sexual oppression of women was oppression by definition, the original form of violence, the model of exploitation that begat all others: war, class oppression, authoritarianism, racism. Sexuality is the sphere in which the dynamics of power are developed and calibrated, ready to be used elsewhere; it's not erotic language that is borrowed from the language of warfare, but the other way around.

THE WARS FOUGHT BETWEEN CITIES, nations, social classes, guilds, and economic competitors may experience, if not actually periods of peace, at least truces or phases of dormancy; the war, on the other hand, that has never known a single moment of quiet is the war between the sexes. It has been fought on a daily basis at every level for hundreds of thousands of years, from the cave to the tent to the palaces of the royal courts, on almost every occasion in life: when you're born, when you eat, when you get married, whether you're on your feet or flat on your back, at the market, at school, in bed, in the kitchen, when you're writing and painting but also when you're praying and sacrificing. And then in the courtrooms and the army ranks, and when those armies break and run through the streets of a village being sacked and plundered. That war never stops to take a breath. It often, however, goes unnoticed, passing unobserved, unrecorded because it's reduced to a particular aspect, a secondary effect of the wars that will, instead, be mentioned in history books, with dates and everything else. Within the context of any armed conflict, there will always be a subchapter dedicated to the war against women, the specific treatment reserved for them, a sort of war within the war, that sees the men on both sides allied against them, or at least in agreement on one point: whoever wins gets to rape the women of whoever loses, and if the fortunes of war seem to ebb and flow, then they'll just take turns. In the Bible and in the brothels of Bangkok, on TV and in the churches and mosques and synagogues, at the family dining table or in the assault of spermatozoa dancing in a uterus, a permanent and unstoppable conflict is under way, in spite of all the treaties and armistices that seem to establish fixed points, conquests acknowledged and tacitly accepted, new limitations placed upon the sheer power of one sex over the other, or of certain individuals over other individuals, including those of the same sex, seeing that the outcomes of the war between the sexes are reflected in the hierarchies internal to each: depending on his ability to subjugate females, a male will also subjugate other males. While the woman who, in her turn, captures males instead of allowing herself to be captured will earn a status of excellence and become the object of a singular form of respect mingled with desire. It is curious, in fact, to note how a woman's respectability, based on her capacity for seduction (this is true, for example, of actresses, of great beauties, of femme fatales, the most successful women of the twentieth century), is subject to a sort of double standard: she is all the more admired the more she is morally questionable.

WE CAN'T SAY WHETHER this is a hot war or a cold war, consisting as it does of a myriad of episodes, some of them nearly harmless skirmishes, others extremely grave crimes.

A war with plenty of blood spilled in circumscribed episodes which are, however, for that very reason, exemplary. And the blood always belongs to women. While many women may make men spit blood, metaphorically speaking, some men make women spit blood, but in actual terms, and those women are the wives and girlfriends who are sick and tired of them, the ex-wives, the adulterous wives, or even just women they've lusted after but who have turned them down, or women who said okay, unaware that they were saying it to a sadist, or else women abducted and murdered at the height of a bout of sexual violence; that's just limiting the blood to the murders, even if the greatest volume of it consists, drop by drop, of the blood that oozes from the faces of women beaten by family members and spouses, within their homes. Their blood spurts out, staining in a continuous flow the statistics of this low-intensity world war. Or perhaps it's a planetary outbreak of guerrilla warfare, whose singular feature is that the guerrillas are the ones who hold power, not the ones who are fighting that power. They represent a sort of armed vanguard of that power. The bloodshed is too widely scattered across the landscape for a line of combat to be identified, in fact, the problem is that the contenders are almost never separated by a border, a trenchworks, a wall, or a barbed-wire fence. And so, a decisive battle will never take place.

WOMEN, *after all, they're used to bleeding . . .*

THE FIRST CULTURAL INITIATIVE I took part in was the foundation of an art gallery in Rome. It must have been 1978 or thereabouts. The founders were painters, the ones with the strongest interest in establishing a gallery where they could exhibit, and with them poets and writers, plus a few other characters of the sort that orbit around artistic groups, the kind of people that, even after you've known them for years, you keep wondering *exactly* what it is they do with their lives: but they're even more distinctive elements of the milieu than the writers or the painters. Among the artists there were several who will make other appearances later in this story: Giuseppe Salvatori, Felice Levini, Santo Spatola, Antonio Capaccio, Rodolfo Cecafumo, Piero Pizzi Cannella . . . The gallery took its name from Via Sant'Agata dei Goti, in the Monti district. Sant'Agata—St. Agatha—became our heroine and our patron saint, as well as the patron saint of bell-founders: that's because her breasts, when they were sliced off during her martyrdom and set upon a tray, were in fact reminiscent of two bells, two small flesh bells, because of their youthful, unripe, perfect shape.

Perhaps the most perfect prototype of torture inflicted on the female body.

IT IS RISKY TO DO WITHOUT WOMEN, very risky. Only small sectarian communities are able to do it. It is hard for men to give them up, and not only for sexual reasons, but for the fundamental role that they play as conflict mediators; and for the precious fact that they represent, in any case, the lowermost layer of society. Women are in fact the most exploited of the exploited. Poor men are willing to put up with counting for nothing as long as there is someone who counts for less than them, that is, their women. That is why the ones who most greatly fear women's emancipation are poor men: if they were to be bypassed by their women, then they truly would find themselves on the lowest rung of the social ladder. This is the sole point at which the males of different classes can find a paradoxical convergence of interests: any social order is acceptable, as long as there is someone in the end to place underfoot. Traditionalist societies, where women have no rights at all, are based on this principle. That is what women are good for, to make the lowest of men feel like they're the masters of something or someone. Rich men sometimes manage to oppress rich women, since they have no difficulty oppressing poor men and poor women. These two latter categories are likewise oppressed by the rich women. So the poor men have no option but to oppress poor women, while the poor women have no one left to oppress (perhaps their children, but that doesn't last long, and nowadays they can't even do that anymore). From time to time, poor men can mistreat rich women, using violence against them, robbing them and raping them. Poor men, for that matter, do the same with poor women, with the sole difference that the take is more meager. Rich men and rich women can oppress each other reciprocally, for example, making their spouse miserable with their toxic lives together or by taking them to the cleaners in their divorce settlements. For a rich man to rape a poor woman is in the nature of the social order, as is the rape of the rich woman by the poor man; rapes within the same class form part of power dynamics between the sexes, not between the classes.

RAPE AS APPROPRIATION (when I rape a woman I make her mine) or as vandalism (I rape a woman who belongs to another man): in either case, it is a conflict over the possession of something, either in order to obtain her for oneself or else to deprive someone else of her. The satisfaction of the second of the two instincts provokes even greater pleasure: more than obtaining the thing, one rejoices in making it impossible for others to enjoy it from now on. In many places around the world, a raped woman is destined to be cast out, marginalized: expropriated of her own identity, she can no longer give it to others.

RAPE IS A STAPLE PRODUCT like flour, salt, glue, or muriatic acid. Men who feel frustrated and impotent use violent sex to reclaim their masculinity, while men who hold power use it for yet another confirmation of the fact. The ones who have been given little and who have been overlooked develop a need for self-affirmation that they are ready to satisfy by making use of violence if need be; the ones who have been given a great deal and who have been spoiled by abundance expect to perpetuate their privilege at any and all costs, and they are willing to use violence to confirm the fact. The former are vindictive over what they don't possess, the second are eager to show off what they have. People who have been humiliated and overlooked are no more and no less dangerous than those who have been treated to every comfort and attention. The murderers of the CR/M had very few reasons to rape and kill the two young women. The psychology of the murderer is the psychology of *anyone*, of the everyman.

A personality that is by no means special, indeed, rather common, if we consider common—and they are—such characteristics as being cynical, manipulative, egocentric, not to experience feelings of guilt, to think only of the present, which corresponds to a human type that is by no means extraordinary, indeed, quite the contrary, an *everyman*, an authentic pillar of contemporary society. He really can be *anyone*, a colleague at your office, a clerk at the bank, a student of law or engineering, the guy sitting at the next table over in a restaurant or in the row behind you at the movie theater. Not a monster you can recognize from a distance, like an ogre or a werewolf, but an absolutely ordinary individual, nondescript, anonymous. So insignificant that he could pass entirely unnoticed. Maybe a neighbor who even seemed courteous, or at the least harmless, or who never attracted any attention. If that's the way things are, there is no way to protect yourself, and that is what's scariest . . . and it's not just the women who are afraid, but also the men, because if the monster really is such an ordinary type, they are forced to look at themselves in the mirror and worry.

Corresponding to the few actual murderers, there is a corresponding multitude of armchair criminals who mentally rape and strangle their victims. Often wholly unconscious that they're even entertaining these fantasies.

MANY HAVE A HARD TIME RECOGNIZING that they possess something only because that same thing is denied others: that they can feel pleasure only at the cost of someone else suffering. It's mathematical: if there is abundance here, it means that there is scarcity there. Everything that we have we took, and at this very moment we are taking it from someone else. To a substantial extent, the amusements of a part of mankind are made possible by the suffering and misery of the rest. For the most part, this misery is concealed from the view of those who enjoy the better lives: privilege in fact consists of the possibility of pushing away those whose suffering permits their enjoyment: exclusive mansions and country clubs are built expressly to separate the two human categories, leaving outside the most numerous and enclosing behind impenetrable barriers the fortunate few. Sexual abuse, in contrast, brutally puts the person who's enjoying the privilege in direct contact with the one suffering to provide him with enjoyment. In a forced embrace, the one who is enhanced by the privilege is locked together with the one who is diminished by it. In contrast with the case of the children who make soccer balls, who are on the far side of the globe stitching leather while we dribble the finished soccer balls at our country club on the banks of the Tiber, in rape there is no shield or distance. Of all the many ways of exercising power, it is the most direct.

5

So LET'S GRANT that they thought the girls were dead. If one of them hadn't turned out to be alive, by mistake, and hadn't knocked on the car trunk, what would they have done with the bodies, how would they have gotten rid of them? It's not all that easy to get rid of two corpses. Even the Mafiosi have their problems with it, and they have to make use of procedures straight out of horror films. But even if they had succeeded, and had gotten off scot-free, and there had been no report of the CR/M, if there simply had been no CR/M, with the villa at the beach cleaned up and the two girls vanished like so many others (in that same year, twenty-five other young woman disappeared, and nothing more was ever heard of them), the matter would have ended there, or else the young men would have tried it again, sooner or later, they would have continued to abduct and rape and eventually murder young women (having already murdered two, from that point on they might as well murder them all, each time, it's hard to turn back once you've started down that path), and the police would have caught them the next time, or else the time after that. After how many different cases would they have caught them? Especially considering that they were so reckless and bold, in scattering their path with clues and displaying utter indifference, as if they felt certain they would get away with it; or, quite the contrary, actually hoped that they'd be caught. I could—and perhaps I should—work on this hypothesis of impunity. Move the dates later. Imagine a longer career as sexual delinquents and homicidal maniacs. But what actually happened is more than enough.

IF AT THE CULMINATION of a Greek drama or a biblical tragedy, someone doesn't kill their brother or father or mother, they'll go out and kill someone else's brother or father or mother. Once you've averted domestic violence, the impulse to kill spills out into the outside world, toward your *enemies*. If we don't have a woman of our own to kill, or if by this point we're so indifferent to her that we no longer even feel the desire to kill her, to possess her and kill her, to kill her in order no longer to feel obliged to possess her, well, then, there are countless women out there to take it out on. It wouldn't be strange in the slightest if one of the protagonists of the CR/M, instead of killing the girls they took out to Monte Circeo, had instead decided to murder his mother. I ought to check out whether they had sisters at home.

EVEN WHEN IT TAKES PLACE in a secluded location, and there's no one other than the perpetrator or perpetrators and the victim of the rape, a rape always has a demonstrative aspect, the quality of a lesson being taught. It is laid out as a theorem, indeed, it is self-explanatory, it explains itself in its execution. Its paradoxical pedagogy is aimed at the victim then and there and at all those others who will learn of it in the aftermath: the woman, it's unnecessary to explain just why, but with an accent of contempt aimed at her male relatives, fathers, brothers, husbands, who have failed at their responsibility for protection and custodianship, and therefore to other men, to ensure that they learn that there's a brusque and disrespectful way of treating women. There is nothing quite like violence to set forth a thesis, to illustrate a theory, to lay claim to a right. By *ravaging* someone (the Italian word is "*scempio*"), you set an *example* (and in fact, *scempio* is derived from *exemplum*, the Latin root of *example, exemplary*).

I COPY DOWN HERE a few notes jotted on the title page of the philosophy textbook that had belonged to Arbus, inherited by me, seeing that he was skipping the rest of the year. I still own it, torn and falling apart though it is, and I occasionally leaf through it, studying the works of some author or other: the juicy old textbook by Eustachio Paolo Lamanna, *Manuale di storia della filosofia ad uso delle scuole*. Arbus's handwriting is minute and precise. I couldn't say whether these ideas are original with him or borrowed from some philosopher; or whether that even makes any difference, after all.

> *Everything that causes change is violent.*
> *Nothing that is violent is lasting.*
> *Violent change destroys, on the one hand, and on the other, it creates.*
> *Violent change never knows in advance what it's going to create.*
> *That which is frightening and repugnant isn't necessarily false.*
> *The truth often is.*

Rereading these apodictic declarations, written by a seventeen-year-old forty years ago, I am tempted to say that, crude and categorical though they may be, they're nonetheless more interesting than all the chatter you hear grown men spouting these days, every night, on TV. I am beginning to think that the so-called *buonismo*, a sort of Pollyanna-ish bleeding-heart optimism, is this: to refuse on principle that the truth can ever be unpleasant or painful, and in order to avoid that risk, take refuge in the shade of a comforting lie. The ways in which reality can be adjusted, bringing it into touch with a vision in which conflicts either don't exist or can in any case be reconciled, are essentially rhetorical in nature, it's a question of language and careful selection and recomposition of the data to be strung together in the way you talk about it, so that every time you run the risk of finding yourself face-to-face with an inconvenient or unpopular truth, you can always detour in some other direction . . . When this zigzagging progress becomes truly unbearable and the contradictions or the persiflage reveals itself for what it is, nude and crude, then one invokes the inalienable right to produce them. Once unmasked, lies can always be recycled as utopias or noble ideals. The protest against those who insist on demanding the truth and not a fairy tale then becomes: "But you can't try to keep us from dreaming . . . !" "It's your fault that things always remain the same!" When faced with this ultimate argument, any possibility of critical reasoning vanishes, it becomes pointless to specify, "No, that's not how it is," since they know perfectly well that that's not how it is. That's not how it is, *embè*? So what? We can hope that someday it will be!

(*Embè?* The term is a formulation that defies any reply. If the sages of the Middle Ages had ever come face-to-face with it, it would have offered them a perfect opportunity for a theological disputation. Although carrying much of the same baggage, it isn't as grim and aggressive as the American equivalent, "So what?" Instead it's disarming, surrounded by its philosophical aura. *Embè?* clearly states, in just two syllables, that all distinctions are vain. All criticisms and objections are childish. F.V. described having been forced to install a gate at the far end of her yard in Trevignano, which led to a small pier on the lake, because, every single day, people would tie up to her pier and disembark, and with baskets, tablecloths, and bottles, they'd sit down unhurriedly for a meal in her garden. She's old, she lives alone, but the hundredth time that it happened, she finally mustered the nerve to walk the length of the garden and go to tell the intruders, in her unmistakable gravelly voice: "Ex-cuse me, but you're on my pro-per-ty . . ."

The day trippers, with their napkins already tied around their necks, looked up at her in astonishment: "*Embè?*")

REPRISALS AGAINST DEFENSELESS WOMEN, whose fault is precisely that, being soft, whiny, whimpering, disgustingly fragile women, deserving of subjugation precisely because they already *are* subjugated (oppression is always a confirmation of oppression), also constitute a reactive movement and a violent protest against the maternal monopoly during childhood. When, that is, the female figure who now appears so weak was actually extremely powerful. A true goddess. To think about it carefully, that monopoly of care was sweet, tender, a labor of love, the object of infinite yearning . . . but there is an impulse to make a sharp break from it. It is love as such that is targeted as an object of scorn. Some need a brutal act to successfully break away from it; they fear otherwise that they will remain entangled forever in that saccharine universe, stuck in that gooey oatmeal that smells of mother's milk. It is an angry bite to the mother's breast. By brutalizing that breast, we escape from the figure that dominated the most important years of our lives. We take vengeance on our mother by devastating the wombs of women, sparing only the one from which we emerged, and perhaps not even that one. It belonged, after all, to a whore.

When you reach the point of calling your mother a whore, then you can say that your upbringing is complete. The circle is unbroken.

AT FIRST THERE ARE ONLY WOMEN, or a single woman. Then out of this woman another woman is born, or else a man is born, but he, in order to come into the world as a man, must make himself different from his mother, twist and turn, make a special effort, exert an act of will, otherwise from women only women would continue to be born, as one might logically expect. In order to become a man, then, it's not enough to emerge from your mother's belly. You must also disavow that belly, ensure that this origin is erased, as if you had been born out of nothingness.

It's not enough to flee the womb, you must also punish it. The incredible resentment that is fostered toward the feminine sex . . .

A MOTHER HAS TWO BREASTS, one good, one bad. One gives you milk, the other denies you milk. One is gratifying and the other is frustrating. At a certain point, though, you realize that it is the same breast, a single breast that one time satiates your hunger, the next time leaves you wanting more. Your frustration derives in fact from the pleasure that you have experienced, and that you are confident you will experience again, but instead, you are denied. It is the mother herself who behaves like this, not just her breast. Therefore the same person may be just as much the object of love and gratitude as of resentment and rage: in each of the two states, the other is implicit. Satisfaction underpins frustration, frustration is what it is only because it has experienced satisfaction.

We are accustomed to expressing love, need, and anger as an inextricable whole, and have done so since we first began sucking milk from the maternal breast. Love is barely distinguishable from other stirrings of the soul, it really doesn't exist in a pure, unalloyed state, it is manifested through feelings considered to be its opposite, such as hatred and aggression, sorrow, guilt, and scorn.

TAKING VENGEANCE on the false promises of the female body. Yes, taking vengeance is the right terminology. Of all the women who go by on the street, it seems that their bodies are speaking to you, inviting you to take them, it's the individual parts of that body, the breasts, the buttocks, the legs, the lips, that promise great pleasures, a festive, unbridled welcome . . .

Sure, but then? What happens then? *Nothing* happens. Those women and girls, brimming over with all sorts of attractions, whom it would cost nothing to offer you a small portion of their body, a few square inches all considered, for ten minutes, but even five minutes would do, what do they do? Nothing, they do nothing, they just keep walking . . . they shrink into the distance, they vanish for all time, minding their own business. They pay no mind, perhaps they never even notice the trail of promises they've scattered behind them. And the same is true of the high school girls, the shopgirls, the young women on motorbikes and scooters, the girls at the beach, the schoolteachers, the female lawyers in their snug-fitting skirt-suits . . .

(NOW, while all the rest of the things inside me almost always stir only in-difference and apathy, the same cannot be said of a woman's presence. An awakening occurs, an awakening of something, not necessarily something agreeable, in fact, quite the contrary . . .

To stiffen in the presence of a woman, as an uncomfortable reaction to the woman's physical proximity, or even just to her mental presence. The former might be possible to avoid with some basic precautions, the latter, unfortunately, less so.

It wasn't only fear and it wasn't only arousal, and yet the effect was the same, that is, to feel that I was growing petrified, that my respiration was slowing down and even stopping, that my voice was freezing in my throat, my member was stiffening, I was turning to ice . . .)

FOR SOME MEN, the idea that women might avoid their fate, the fate, that is, of being possessed, is intolerable. If they do escape, then they must be killed. First raped, then killed. Raping them, in a certain sense, turns them back into women, gives them back their feminine prerogative. In their turn, they become capable of recognizing a woman's attractions only after killing her: like Achilles with Penthesilea. The death of a reluctant woman restores her to the femininity she was trying to get out of.

To kill is an extreme way of making someone yours. It is in principle a form of acquisition. If I desire someone, I can make them wholly mine by taking their life. I'm the last one to have had them, and in this radical form, the only one. Of the right that only I can exercise I deprive all others forever, which is the requisite of any full ownership. To rape a woman is not enough to take ownership of her: only with her death is the mere usufruct rejoined with the naked ownership. You enter into possession of the entire person only when it ceases to exist. In the corpse.

This explains why so many ex-husbands or ex-boyfriends murder their women. When the women refuse to get back together with them or even just to make love with them, they have no other way of possessing them than to kill them.

THE RAPIST-MURDERER DESTROYS what he meant to take possession of. His crime lies midway between simple violence and robbery, mixing hostility toward its object and desire for the same object. You might think that he wants to take possession of a woman in order to destroy her. But it's more likely that he destroys her because only by doing so can he boast that he possesses her.

And so, to kill a woman to get rid of her, or to get her back.

6

ASYMMETRY I
In the CR/M, we came to know everything about the murderers, even the brand of their tennis shoes; about the victims, aside from the generic and oft-repeated emphasis on their modest social extraction, nothing.

ASYMMETRY II
General law: we often think that others feel for us what actually *we* feel for *them*. We muddle and confuse grammatical persons: the one who is the object of desire is mistaken for its subject. In this way, we can fool ourselves into thinking that just because we desire a woman, she in turn feels desire, that the desire to be possessed actually begins with her. Take me! you seem to think the woman says, whom you're staring at in a frenzy to take her. That is why we tend to attribute sexual availability to a pretty woman: because she is *attractive*, we imagine that she is *attracted*.

ASYMMETRY III

If what you seek is equality and the parity of rights and duties, forget about
sex. It's not what you want to look at. A very honorable principle, equality—
but utter nonsense when it comes to sex. Everything in sex is asymmetrical. Excessive, unbalanced. And everything is a losing bet, an exuberant
fiasco. In erotic relations, the thing that dominates gleefully is injustice—
at least until you run headlong into the penal code.

It's a question of being either a slave to another's body, or else its
master.

The sexual shiver of injustice derives, by a reversal of terms, from the
unjust shiver of sexuality.

Only a few elect spirits in this world are capable of drawing pleasure
from egalitarianism. An absolute leveling of conditions instantly lowers all
desire. Yes, perhaps the occasional saint, some deep thinker in love with
pure abstraction . . . Everyone else, however, takes at least as much joy from
disparity as they do misery: they hate being in disparity, and yet they yearn
for it, to abide in disparity, at least temporarily slaves or masters of something or someone, and they experience delight not only when they get to
be on top. Even the one being dominated may take pleasure in the disproportionate upper hand held by the other, indeed, perhaps, the image of
someone being subjugated is the better depiction of the state of bliss: a
work of portrayal verging on the impossible even for the greatest of artists,
who in fact are obliged to avail themselves of metaphors. This position is
best and most fittingly exemplified by the inamorato, the swooning lover,
as well as the acolyte, the true believer, the die-hard fan, the son with his
mother, the adept with his teacher: all these figures are grateful to those
who loom over them, showering them with their strength, and so abandon themselves trustingly to the pleasure that they draw from that relationship, without reservations, without complaint. As if standing in a warm
August rain . . .

One is unlikely to attain equality and equilibrium by going to bed with
someone. I wonder what someone really desires when they desire such a
thing. If what they're looking for is 50 percent control of all shares, if they're
interested in getting 50 percent of the profits, then let them start a company.
But the most beady-eyed accountant with a green eyeshade and bifocals
riding low on the nose would be hard put to balance profits and losses, *who*
profits and *what* they gain, and to draw up a final balance sheet for an act
of intercourse: those reckonings would always and inevitably be found to
add up to zero. In sex, no one in the final analysis gets *anything*, except

perhaps for a taste of their own annihilation. Splashes, flashes of annihilation. The only moments that are truly worth living are moments of abandonment, of loss, of boundless possession, and of the utterly gratuitous, of being useful and idiotic slaves to another's body, even if you receive a big fat nothing in exchange.

ASYMMETRY IV

The only way that any equilibrium could be restored is if women gave birth to girls and men gave birth to boys. Instead, they're all born to a woman. It is hard to imagine two peoples in incessant and permanent conflict when one of those peoples was—and always will be—given birth by the other, and therefore will depend on them for their own very existence.

7

A COCK IS A TOOL with all the sensitivity of a hammer. And in fact during a rape it can be substituted by other objects that serve the same purpose: to humiliate and cause suffering. Just as in consensual sex, various stand-ins or proxies or prosthetics can be used to give and receive pleasure, similarly in a rape, bottles or clubs or broom handles (from some wartime accounts: grenades, mortar shells, and, where there was a hint of blasphemous excess, crucifixes) can be used to inflict suffering. In such cases, the only reasons that these are considered acts of sexual violence is because they concern certain areas of the body. In the CR/M, the objects used were an ashtray and a car jack.

(IN CERTAIN POLICE DEPARTMENTS the preprinted form to be filled out in case of a criminal complaint of rape includes a box to be checked off next to the phrases "insertion of objects into the vagina" and "insertion of objects into the rectum").

THE ONLY PERSON who can claim to be the master, the owner of something is he who is free to destroy it. As in the legendary contests of profligacy and squandering recorded by anthropologists, where tribal chiefs face off, ready to smash to pieces everything in their possession, the supremacy of wealth is acknowledged only at the moment in which you destroy it. An owner answers to nobody where his property is concerned, and proof of that fact can be seen in his willingness to do without it.

He squanders, dissipates, wastes, and purchases, only to destroy immediately that which he has purchased, and that is the true luxury of possession: to discard what you have just made your own. Both moments are pleasurable and brutal: through robbery you accumulate, rapaciously you squander the booty, the plunder, the swag, you devour your prey, you devastate your assets, disposing of jewelry, slave girls, horses, foodstuffs, groaning banqueting tables, Indian brides, kidnapped girls, executed prisoners, dynamited bridges, the jigsaw puzzle you just finished which is voluptuously thrown in the air and returned to the state of chaos whence it came, the cash from the cracked safe pissed away on narcotics and whores. Two moments in the metabolism of power, to acquire and discard, to steal just to burn and leave charred . . . It's a sort of party, a feast, a meal, a pigout, a house set on fire just to enjoy the show. *Tout doit disparaître!* announce the nihilistic signs advertising sales in Paris shops: Everything Must Go! These signs aren't so much urging you to buy as to sweep away, liquidate, eliminate . . . After all, what else does the verb "consume" mean, if not that? Away, away, away with everything. Even what you love; above all else, what you love.

Pathology is the correct lens through which to view and understand physiology. You can best understand how an organism functions when it stops functioning. And the same is true of the mind: when it breaks down, falls apart, or spins out of control, racing into the void, that's when you can see how it's built. The exceptional state is the only one that tells us something interesting. But there is no need to cross over into the territory of pathology to perceive the nexus between sexuality and destruction, separated by the thinnest of veils, if by anything at all. Suffering, desire, hatred, attraction, and pleasure rarely appear to be distinctly separate, least of all in the context of intercourse, indeed, it is only through an intertwining of them all that an event takes place which would otherwise be inexplicable or grotesque. People subject themselves to practices that, if considered outside the context of that specific ceremony, and viewed with even a smidgen of detachment, would be ridiculous or disgusting; assuming postures that are incredibly aggressive, the poses of two wild animals fighting to the death. Lucretius's phenomenology still scandalizes because it shows in a crude manner, devoid of flattery or niceties, the rabid frenzy of lovers: but no one can seriously cast doubt on the accuracy of this description.

> *Quod petiere, premunt arte faciuntque dolorem*
> *corporis et dentes inlidunt saepe labellis*
> *osculaque adfigunt, quia non est pura voluptas*
> *et stimuli subsunt, qui instigant laedere id ipsum,*
> *quod cumque est, rabies unde illaec germina surgunt.*

> *The parts they sought, those they squeeze so tight,*
> *And pain the creature's body, close their teeth*
> *Often against her lips, and smite with kiss*
> *Mouth into mouth, because this same delight*
> *Is not unmixed; and underneath are stings*
> *Which goad a man to hurt the very thing,*
> *Whate'er it be, from whence arise for him*
> *Those germs of madness.*

IN MUCH THE SAME WAY that you can leap directly over love in the sex act, you can also skip the act entirely and move directly to the cruelty, to the destructive frenzy implicit in the act, which only needed to be extracted and purified and made manifest, without wasting any more time on those genital manipulations, those sideshows typical of oversexed kids. After all, sex is just a drooling digression, a futile pastime, perhaps really an excuse to distract us from the real task at hand. An idle amusement, in other words. But if the objective is to penetrate a body, wouldn't it be easier to just go ahead and use a knife? Cut open that body at any point you choose? Sadism wouldn't be very interesting at all if it didn't help bring to light that buried element. To break the sensual hesitations and sweep away all that emotional equivocation. After all, what you're looking to do is hurt someone, period. Let's be done with all the hemming and hawing. Once you've unearthed all the violent implications of sex and cleansed them of their sentimental implications, they appear as so many steel objects, gleaming, simple, chilly, and sharp-edged; and it's not as if the sadist brought them along in a special satchel: they'd always been there. Right there, next to the bed. The toolbox of suffering is within reach of one and all. A bed is ideally suited for resting, reading, making love, dreaming, fighting, and torture. Another person's pain arouses a sadist not only because he is, in fact, sadistic, but because he is also, at the same time, a masochist, he identifies with his victims and thrills to their pain. He takes twice the pleasure: in the pain that he inflicts and the pain that, through a third party, a proxy, he inflicts upon himself.

I HAVE READ OVER and over again Tolstoy's *Kreutzer Sonata* and I still haven't understood it, or perhaps I should say, I don't understand if I've understood it. And if I have, then I'm not sure to what extent I agree with the author, and whether I've ever experienced in my life what the author describes in such painstaking detail: that revulsion toward the sex act, the disgust prompted by the sex act, that is, the very same act that we all desire more than any other and which, nonetheless, Tolstoy tells us, is the cause of the deepest revulsion.

If there is a form of sex act in which this repugnance manifests itself in full, that would be rape. Careful though, the disgust is not just for the victim, but also and especially the rapist. His sexual violence does not express attraction for the body he is appropriating by force, but rather a paradoxical repulsion. Desire thus reveals its distinctively destructive bow wave: while experiencing attraction to something and, at the same time, finding it disgusting, it angrily demands that that thing be wiped off the face of the earth. In order to react to the humiliation of feeling fascinated and therefore in a certain sense bound and dominated by something repugnant, one mistreats it and destroys it. To a rapist, there is nothing wonderful about a woman's body; quite the opposite, it's a filthy sewer, and he can feel himself sinking into it. Her genitals are repugnant, her moaning mouth is repugnant, her lips, above and below, are repugnant, her breasts are disgustingly soft, her tears are contaminants . . .

This explains the gratuitous brutality that often accompanies and completes sexual violence, once it has guaranteed the rapist the attainment of his minimal or apparent objective, that is, to force the victim into coitus: if that was the true purpose of rape, then why the fists, the blows, the cigarettes crushed out on the flesh, the objects jammed into the vagina and anus, and the torture and abuse that can lead to death?

Hating the frenzied need to do it, hating doing it, hating the woman you do it with, the woman who is forced to do it, while you do it and after you're done, hating the body that is the cause and at the same time the target of the depravity, hating yourself: the sum of all this hatred is crushing.

Perhaps that is how I manage to grasp one of the paradoxical points of the *Sonata*, namely that the only way to *keep* from killing women is to stop going to bed with them: abolishing the occasion for contact and therefore the friction between the sexes, the root of the reciprocal disgust and the engine driving a violence that is otherwise unstoppable. The chastity preached by the now elderly Tolstoy, a chastity that he never actually put into practice. I'm not actually sure that the prescription works in the real world, as opposed to on paper or in vows or in prayers (". . . lead us not into temptation . . ."), not only because even its proponent lacked the strength of will to apply it, limiting himself to a description of the deplorable effects caused by a failure to observe that chastity. Husbands who sexually oppress their wives, or who cultivate their most depraved tendencies in order to squeeze a few drops of pleasure out of them, men who pervert their women and themselves in order to gratify a frenzy that lasts only a few instants but then, shortly thereafter, rears its ugly head again, only intensified. There can never be liberty and equality between man and woman as long as sex is involved . . . Maybe the old Russian writer had a point . . .

A DESIRE WITHOUT A SPECIFIC OBJECT, blind, furious, the desire for a woman, but not a woman in particular, just any woman, the body of any woman, the nude body of a woman, a nude portion of the body of any woman at all . . . a detail, hypnotic and mysterious the way that only details can be, enlargements under a magnifying glass, the close-up, grainy image of a piece of anatomy concealed between the thighs, under the armpits, in the recesses where the limbs are attached and where they form folds, mucous layers, membranes, something that glistens, moistly . . . that protrudes, extends from the body . . . or that burrows into it in depth, like a sinkhole.

Even in the most episodic encounter, an intense experience, unconsciously desperate, like a battle between beasts in the depths of a forest. A violent surge, a tense frenzy, the chilliest indifference to the personality the rights the faculties of the individual, no respect for limits, a vindictive bitterness the minute one has satiated one's lusts, often followed by disgust and then by a renewed frenzy, the frenzy to be elsewhere, a dulling, a sense of solitude, or the melancholy desire for solitude.

As soon as the excitement subsides, animosity hostility and coldness take its place.

In its very pantomime, in its outward appearance, the sex act possesses a dangerous affinity with the act of murder: a man penetrating a woman seems to be establishing a relationship no different than that between a murderer and his victim. This similarity of posture makes it easy to confuse or substitute the one thing with the other. This mimicry may act power-fully upon a weak or troubled intellect. And especially on someone who is untouched by such feelings as tenderness or love. Those are emotions that cause a person to recoil, after once experiencing it, from the diabolical re-semblance. If, however, you are immune to them, coitus is restored to its deathly surgical blatancy, as if it were taking place under the glare of the lights in an operating room or a morgue.

. . . AND COPULATION WAS ORIGINALLY not the happy and willing joining of the two sexes, but instead a violent act to which the woman submitted because she was weaker than the male. Only with the passage of time, a great deal of time, centuries or millennia, did that brutal embrace start to lose its mark-edly offensive character and begin to be enjoyed by the female, as the male's blind and exclusive drive toward the woman's sex organs began to spread over the entire surface of her body, the painful blows became tender caresses, the penetration lost its aggressive intent. And yet, like a subconscious memory, a trace remains of the primitive assault and the struggle and the abuse, indel-ible, it cannot be eliminated from the encounter between a man and a woman, even in those suffused in the gentlest sweetness.

IN THE ELIMINATION OF WOMEN, impure by nature or by garb, there is an overwhelming obsession with purity. It starts with prostitutes, habitual and, in a certain sense, designated victims for those who nurture this sort of frenzy, but then it continues, extending a moralizing edict to all women, in whatever walk of life or class, who can in any case be tagged as prosti-tutes, de facto or potential, or even unconscious prostitutes, that is, unaware that they are prostitutes by the simple fact of belonging to the female sex.

A cynical proverb says that a woman's best way of avoiding rape is to submit to it. From a logical and descriptive point of view, in fact, consent would have the power of eliminating violence on the spot: without coer-cion, how can you talk about rape? Whether this witticism hits its target or is merely awful and inappropriate, it is unquestionably false. If we took the absurd argument to its logical conclusion and assumed that a woman agreed to consent in accordance with a calculation of this kind, the rapist would instantly cease to go along. What he is looking for in that coitus, in fact, is nothing other than domination, which is not a means to an end but the end itself. Depriving him of that domination with a stratagem would serve no purpose whatsoever, and indeed it often only stokes to new heights the rage that impels the rapist. These are people who pay little attention to paradoxes and who have never read Oscar Wilde. The logic by which in order to reduce thefts we need only hand over our possessions to the thief can only be said to work in a philosophy class, the same kind of class where they teach that arrows stand still in midair, that a respectable man must not lie, even if that means telling a murderer where his intended victim is hiding, that being dead is preferable to being alive, or else that it's the same thing, that a barber cannot shave himself, that I cannot state that I am lying, that not all things that are not black are not crows, or all nonblack objects are not-crows, that if I replace all the parts in my car I have to wonder if that is still my car, that a donkey will starve to death rather than choosing between two equal stacks of hay, and so on. How much does a brick weigh if it weighs three pounds plus half a brick? Well, only Polyphemus was stupid enough to believe that his enemy was Nobody. These reasonings, at once logical and absurd, warm my heart because they take me straight back to our high school desks. We were tireless, ferocious hunters of contradictions . . . and of mysterious meanings concealed beneath the most ordinary objects. I remember the immense pleasure it gave me to get to know Freud. Suddenly the world proliferated, beneath every single thing there was another, and beneath that, yet another . . .

I hardly need tell you that it was Arbus who introduced me.

THIS PROLIFERATION OF PARALOGISMS is due to the singular status of sexual violence as a crime. Rape, in fact, is the only crime that in order to be considered as such requires its victim to resist. If the victim doesn't resist, then all of a sudden it ceases to be a crime. No one would call into question an attempted murder just because the intended victim had failed to put up a fight.

REJECTING THE SENTIMENTAL AND SICKLY sweet versions of the encounter between man and woman, the various saccharine endearments, either corrupted by the search for reciprocal pleasure or else stale and stagnant in the convention of endless engagements and pseudoconjugal cohabitations and compromises in exchange for a few crumbs. Instead of all this inconclusive buffoonery—rape. The perpetrators of the CR/M had done nothing other than go straight to the heart of the matter. Everyone else was beating around the bush, they had plunged in the knife. The blade had sliced through the soft butter of rules, family ceremonies, and scholastic hypocrisies based on study intelligence good behavior cooperation personal maturity God the Madonna etc., all fine things laid out in order to conceal a very simple truth, that if you want something you only need to go and take it—provided you're strong enough to do it. All the chitchat was there strictly to discourage the cowards, to muddle people's ideas about ends and means, minimizing the former and selecting among the latter only the licit ones, which are notoriously far less efficacious. Violence, either a little violence or a huge amount of violence all at once, could make things clear, put them back in order. Violence is immediate, concrete power, all the rest is just the gossip and chitchat of priests . . .

> *Every woman is a stranger, a deep*
> *and narrow well. She is put into the world*
> *to increase the number of men and the amount of their treachery.*

8

THERE ARE TWO MUTUALLY EXCLUSIVE WAYS *of rejecting the female body: keep it far from oneself by means of chastity, or else seize it by force. In both cases, what is preferred to any real intimacy with the woman is a safer, deep down more masculine, interaction with one's own gender. You cannot lower yourself to interact with women on the path chosen by them. To accept the rules of courtship, seduction, the frivolous game of love, makes a man effeminate: the brusque manners of either chastity or rape keep him intact.*

A REAL MAN ought to be insensible or indifferent to pleasure. Pleasure is something strictly for debauchees, or simpering little girls, just like sentiments. The most famous playboys of the world said that love is for housekeepers. If the essence of the female organism lies in its pathicity, in its extraordinary readiness to experience pleasure and pain, an openminded man can set out to explore this abyss of extreme sensations, using a woman's body as a laboratory: if he cannot or will not provoke the former, he can always provoke the latter. If a woman is insatiable for pleasure, she certainly will likewise be insatiable for pain. It is her receptive nature that disposes her to this.

Virgins tortured and murdered are subjected to a kind of pain that in the natural order of things they ought to experience only in childbirth: and that pain is replaced with a sterile and derisive suffering.

CHASTITY—SEXUAL PROMISCUITY DEVOID of emotional involvement—rape: there's a fine thread that connects these three very different attitudes toward women: at the very least, the fact that all three resolve the problem of intimacy with a woman. How? By deleting it. Intimacy is liquidated, negated from the very outset, either within the practice of sex or by keeping oneself at arm's length from it. In their interactions with the feminine, there are a far greater number of points of contact than there are differences among a chaste man, a womanizer, and a rapist. It is the one who lives in a middle ground who finds himself in trouble: for example, the married man. He is expected to establish and maintain a relationship, otherwise what did he get married for? If even he can't attain it with his spouse, then it means that this question of intimacy is a pure myth, yet another invention of Romanticism and its fanatical poets. Those who steer clear of it (priests, homosexuals, Casanovas, whoremongers, rapists) are doing nothing more than to acknowledge this impossibility and ready countermeasures. (The female body negated by those who desire it, those who mistreat it, those who reject it.) Chastity is a very particular variation on sexual brutality. Perhaps the most refined form of physical violence. Refined because bloodless and because an individual inflicts it upon himself, freely, which by our moral standards has something heroic about it, and deserves the respect we attribute to those who sacrifice themselves. The appreciation of what is difficult rather than what is easy. Discipline.

A FEW DAYS AGO, I visited Fossanova Abbey with my daughter, who was suffering the pangs of unhappy love. On a late August afternoon, at three o'clock, there was no one but us, and on the front door of the church hung a sign that said OPEN, but the door was still locked. We walked around the abbey. My daughter was sad, tormented. I tried to lift her spirits but I didn't say much, I didn't have much to say, since there is nothing more inexplicable than the feelings she was experiencing and that I too, reflexively, was feeling, and there's practically nothing that can alleviate them. So-called sensible remarks are even less useful. We were told that the abbey would open at four o'clock and, since we hadn't eaten lunch, we ordered something to eat at a refreshment stand that, in perfect counterpoint to the abbey, looked closed but was actually open. It wasn't hot out, clouds were sailing past overhead, borne across the sky by a brisk wind, and the tall trees were tossing their leaves: these delightful sights and sounds might allay her pain at least a little. But my daughter's pretty face remained sullen and her mind full of dark thoughts.

Around three thirty, the place started to liven up. Two couples of tourists arrived, waiting like us for the abbey to reopen and then, a few at a time, appearing from around a corner of the collection of houses surrounding the abbey, came a line of young priests, many of them with cameras on shoulder straps. In the end, we counted a dozen or so, in little clusters of two or three at a time: they'd collect and then scatter, wandering around the massive block of the abbey, snapping photos, chatting in low voices. From their appearance and from the occasional phrase picked up here and there, I understood that they were Americans: ranging in age from eighteen to twenty-five, aside from a couple of older ones and the dean of the group, probably in his early fifties. They were all slender in their black tunics and with ash-blond or reddish or chestnut hair, worn short but not too short, I'd have to guess cut by a skilled barber, a careful job. One of them, extremely young and not very different in his facial features and physique from a girl, was already thinning around the temples, his fine angelic hair destined to fall, his enormous clear eyes set far apart like in Orthodox icons. A young St. Paul, I thought, or else an Alexei Karamazov, Alyosha, perhaps very weak, or maybe very strong, who could say. Only time would tell.

"YOU SEE, Margherita, what their life is like? How different from ours? You can imagine a few centuries ago, when everyone's destiny was different, each from the other. A vocation or a trade or the simple fact that you carried a certain name would point you down a path marked in advance. Lives were all different. There were a thousand uniforms that whoever wore them never took off. A sailor, a money changer, a soldier, a prince, a priest—they all led lives that had practically nothing in common. Someone might spend twenty years away from home, and there was nothing surprising or strange about it. Nowadays they're the only ones left who are different, who wear a uniform. And they chose it themselves, all on their own. The single life, no family, and yet by no means free. And if by chance it starts to resemble the lives of others, then it's all over.

"If they keep faith with their pledge, they'll never have a wife, they'll never have children. They'll never be able to find themselves in a situation like this one, you and me, right here, a father and a daughter out on a day trip. They'll always be with one another, and soon they'll no longer be young, and the people they'll be in touch with will be the people who come to tell them their woes, to confess their sins, to pray, to have their newborn children baptized. They'll be able to help them and give them advice, and they can even love them, but they'll never be able to kiss them and touch them, and if they do, then they're filthy pigs. They'll sleep their whole lives in a single bed. Just think! Their whole lives!"

I sensed that as I spoke I was growing emotional. And I was full of admiration and compassion for those young priests, whom I also found beautiful, pleasing to look at. My daughter turned to look at me, trying to understand why on earth, after so much silence, or only brief consolatory or exhortatory phrases addressed to her, I had suddenly become so eloquent, inspired by the chastity of young American priests. Her eyes studied me, slightly astonished but also, for the first time since I had swung by to pick her up in my car and take her away from the site of her emotional affliction, for the first time she had been distracted from the center of gravity of her sorrows. It was as if I were telling her that, deep down, those sorrows were a privilege, when compared with the emotional sterility induced in those young men in black tunics, one of whom might perfectly well have become my daughter's boyfriend, an ideal boyfriend . . . indeed, I thought, if only one of these reliable and serious young Americans would take her, if only she were free to fall in love with one of these boys before us who, I went on to imagine, would certainly be intelligent and kind and probably very affectionate . . .

I'd be delighted to invite a young man like that to come have lunch with me and her and speak to him and listen to him speak. But he would have to be just like them, so different from their contemporaries, but at once the same as all the free, unmarried young men of the world. Which is impossible.

I fantasized for about a minute, rapt, about the idea of a couple formed by my daughter and one of those young men in tunics.

But she wasn't free, and neither were they.

I MUST HAVE WRITTEN this five hundred pages ago, but I'll write it again right here: in the protagonists of the CR/M, there is a projection in paroxysmal terms of the problem of the entirely male identity of SLM, of its teachers, religious or not, and its students. During classtime, that place truly became Mount Athos.

The only woman who wasn't an intruder at SLM was the Virgin Mary.

THE FACT THAT WOMEN, at the trial and afterward, hated them, seems clear and unmistakable to me. But the hatred and scorn that ordinary men declared toward those perverts, I don't know, there was something about it that doesn't quite ring true, as if it were a sort of exorcism, an expedient that allowed them to call themselves *out* of an event *into* which, without quite realizing how or why, they had found themselves dragged, involved, almost interrogated, by the presence of an unsettling sexual undertone or innuendo, stigmatized with words of fire lest it come to the fore to unmask identities and complicity, even with those who were nattering on about exemplary punishments, death sentences (the refrain of calls for castration had not yet taken center stage). The only thing you're in a hurry to put at arm's length is something that is close, uncomfortably close. Certainly, one might reasonably suppose that many of the fieriest speakers feared that the same fate that had befallen the two young women at Monte Circeo might be visited upon their sisters or daughters, but theirs did not seem like a preemptive rage or the furor of an empathetic identification with the suffering of the victims . . . rather, it seemed like a very different and quite dangerous kind of identification, to be discarded with disgust should it ever surface, and namely with the murderers. To be lumped in with them, to share even a single cell of the same tumor . . . as if, among men, the CR/M had a singular power of contamination . . . as if it somehow transmitted from the barbarity of the crime to that of the punishment invoked, preserving, in fact, an identically morbid erotic twist. The venting of instincts is not much more vicious than their repression, especially if that repression is howled for by the mob. The public scourge yawping for the punishment of the sadist may turn out to be a sadist himself, except that the whip his hand is raising high in the air bears the brand of probity and rectitude. Therefore, the hatred served to conceal a substantial complicity, albeit sublimated or experienced backwards, as repugnance. Rape fantasies echoed in the outraged prose of the press: the more they deplored what had happened, the more they celebrated it. The culprits of the CR/M were lifted on high by the choruses of "Down with them!" The sexual murder feeds these paradoxical circuits where, through a twist not unlike that of the Möbius strip, there is no break between the two opposite faces. Along with the universal condemnation, it pumps up a maniacal attention to the details that loom and flash in the journalistic accounts, indignant and aroused to the same degree: "two days of uninterrupted rape and violence on the poor thing . . ." and so on.

Sex maniacs constitute a risk for women and children, but also, indirectly, for respectable men: the risk of revealing their unexpected proclivities. That is why they are obliged to thunder even louder and with greater indignation against deviants: to prove they haven't been infected by them.

INDIGNATION IS A SENTIMENT that conceals things rather than reveal them. A veil descends over the indignant person's face, preventing him from seeing clearly and preventing others from seeing clearly into him. He is inclined to consider aberrant things that as often as not are ordinary, and therefore much to be feared. In a heartfelt tone, he hastens to declare alien the sort of things that are often dangerously familiar, and the passion that he puts into decrying scandals reveals his fear that anyone might suspect he's involved. Instead of venturing closer to the source of the scandal, in order to comprehend it as clearly as possible, he recoils from it, striking a horrified pose. But in fact, what he fears above all else is comprehension, because comprehension entails involvement. His exorcisms are almost never successful in expelling the devil, because they consider him an intruder, rather than an age-old inhabitant of our minds and our homes. Very little can be achieved with indignation, and it does very little good, except to assuage us with the temporary relief, the fleeting complacency of feeling that we are in the right, that is to say, one of the most deceptive and childish satisfactions that can be enjoyed.

THE SAME VIOLENT INSTINCT, then, can be present in attacking women as in protecting them from the violence of others: women find themselves caught in the middle, suffering the abuse of both their assailants and their protectors, in fact, it often happens that the latter are actually the most obstinate ones. Their oppressive guardianship is continuous and real, while the danger that comes from the former is often intermittent at best and hypothetical in any case. It may be that in the end (Machiavellian lesson to be learned) it is the protector who turns into the aggressor.

SOME MEN THINK THAT THEY'RE GODS, with a right to take the women of the earth, leaning down and snatching them up, the way Zeus and his brother Hades did, and as Apollo tried to do, more than once, in vain (the only god I know of who failed to complete a rape: a would-be rapist who may have devoted himself to the arts for this reason, after all—that is, a pursuit in which one learns to make profitable use of one's frustration); other men instead place themselves on a plane so low that they judge it impossible to imagine that a woman would yield to their courtship voluntarily. Fearing that their sexual advances might be destined to failure no matter what they do, they feel justified in proving them right. In other words, force is used by those men who feel that they are too high above or too far below all women; but in fact, it is the entire history of our culture that places a woman either high above (in some cases) or far below (more frequently) a man, but never on the same plane. A sublime variant of misogyny is, in fact, chivalrous love, which transposes the woman onto a mystical, transcendental plane, rendering her almost as odious as she is in her degraded version of sinner and diabolical temptress, or witch, or object to be possessed. In the courtly literature of the troubadour, in fact, knights would put themselves at the service of ineffable *dames san merci* with angelical demeanors, who like authentic dominatrixes would force their humble vassal to submit to mortifications of all kinds; but in the meantime, the very same knights in thrall to love would forcibly have their way with young shepherdesses, gooseherders, wayfarers—all of them girls, with an average age of twelve. Chivalry is in fact the presentable face of brutality; it represents an exterior form of reparation for injustices as well as the most elegant way of concealing them. A rich rhetorical indemnity, in other words. It is quite likely that the courtly poets simply invented it all out of whole cloth, and that the much-declaimed enslavement of the knight to the lady of his heart never actually existed. The knight, on the other hand, went his merry way along country paths deflowering peasant girls alone and unaccompanied: a pursuit celebrated by troubadours and court poets in their ballads, in a dreamy, playful tone. Music forgives, it forgives *everything*, it forgives *always*. The swollen river of amorous poetry rolled on, flowing free of any relation to reality, and in that freedom resided its loveliness and the lie at its heart.

LET ME SAY IT AGAIN: unlike other crimes, rape isn't an expression of dissidence, revolt against norms and tradition. If anything, it represents a confirmation of it. A blind, absolute confirmation. In case anyone had forgotten, a norm is illustrated from time to time in the act of imposing it by force. Every time that a rape is committed, a principle is reiterated. Rape, in fact, serves to defend an order, that of the dominion of man over woman, or to reestablish it if woman were ever so ill-advised as to call it into question. By tradition, women are accustomed to being bent to man's will by an instrumental force: either paid, or violated, or seduced, or wedded against their will, or else they fall in love (that is, vanquished by love). Money, fists, family authority, charm, and last of all passion—these were the forces arrayed in the field to deprive a woman of control over her own body. Even romantic love was invented by a group of writers feverishly trying to justify—by bringing to bear an element that was at least in appearance nobler and irresistible—the idea of a woman setting aside her principles and giving in to a man's sexual advances. It is no accident that the second part of Romanticism was devoted to a painful and dolorous unmasking of this deception created by the first.

9

A VIOLENT DEATH can be the product of the brutal nature of things and people, or else of the application of a law of mankind; in either case, the person dies as the victim of a greater force, but it's one thing to be murdered, it's quite another *to be executed*. In the first case, *you die* and that's that; in the second *there is an expiation*. This means that someone has exercised something resembling a right. To be the victim of a crime like the CR/M may entail both aspects, however paradoxical that may sound: the victims suffer the most infamous abuse which, however, to some extent also claims to present itself as an act of justice, that is, as the implementation of a sentence meant to restore a state of equilibrium: and that, without a doubt, is the objective of the law. Certainly, it's a perverse justice, one that is administered by criminals, but that doesn't mean they can't act as if they were actually carrying out the sentence of a court. I've previously said this elsewhere: it may be an internal spring driving it, or an unacceptable justification, or a ghost haunting someone, or a demented delirium, but in any case the guiding idea is that someone is doing something that is, in the final analysis, *just*. And for that matter, it rarely happens that even the most horrible misdeed fails to conceal, deep inside, at least a speck of justice, actual or imagined. Any one of us, with the exception of Jesus, at least deserves a little bit to die for the crime of having come into the world in the first place, an act whose inevitable consequence is death, and we thereby pay the price for sins committed by other men and other women, sins that will fall on our heads for the rest of eternity. After all, we're still working off the penalty for that business with the apple . . . But in truth, as Plato saw it, we are all brothers and therefore, like it or not, we are all accomplices. Sin contaminates the guilty every bit as much as the innocent.

What were the girls of the CR/M expiating? Whose crimes, aside from the obvious ones of the actual culprits? It seems unbelievable that the victims should be paying the price of a crime committed not *by them*, but *against them*: and yet this, too, is a paradoxical form of guilt. Aside from some venial sin they might have been guilty of, the girls were charged with the supposed crime that can be imputed to all women, plus the actual crime perpetrated by their murderers. It would be much more difficult to do evil if you weren't convinced, as you commit that evil, that you're applying at least a crumb, yes, at least a speck of justice . . . Many of those responsible for very serious crimes like to present themselves as victims, as someone "more sinned against than sinning," who has in other words suffered more wrongdoing than they have committed. Sometimes it's true, or it is only if you take into account the suffering perceived rather than any real harm suffered. A series of small but continuous humiliations to which one might have been exposed, for example, can be experienced as if it were an interminable process of torture; and one might react to it disproportionately, even by committing murder, which appears as an appropriate measure, a crime that is not all that serious after all, or not even a crime but rather an act of justice, putting an end with a simple pistol shot and a fleeting instant of pain, on the one hand, to an endless calvary of torment, on the other. Some of the wrongs to which these criminals have reacted are real, many are created out of the whole cloth of paranoia. Certain vexations or violent acts that they claim to have suffered, as a justification for their acts, exist only in their heads . . .

This sort of upside-down juridical reasoning covers all kinds of crimes, from theft to kidnapping to swindling to murder; in a rape it often lurks implicitly, and just because it's tacit doesn't mean that it's not present. The idea then that the act of kidnapping, raping, and even murdering somehow serves to right a wrong and restore justice; that these brutal acts are appropriate sanctions, that the guilty parties are judges and the victims defendants, found guilty and sentenced, that the entire process of the trial took place in the blink of an eye, without hearing or summation or lawful appeal, in the very instant the trigger was squeezed or the hands pressed around the throat, throttling out the life. No one in the world can deprive certain criminals of the intuitive conviction that their victims, in no uncertain terms, "deserved it." Ah, if it were only common criminals who thought like this! The bloodier the crime, the more this twisted logic tends to surface in even the most placid minds ("they deserved it"), as we saw on a vast scale after 9/11 and on a staggeringly vast scale after the Holocaust ("well, if that's the way it went, they must have deserved it"), perhaps because people refuse to believe that so much blood could be shed and so much suffering unleashed without a good reason of some kind. If it happens, that must mean there was a reason. "They must have been asking for it." In the case of rape, this logic is even more relentless. The girls and the women had been asking for it, and that is why they were (justly, or at least somewhat justly) punished. "She really was asking for it . . ." It's important to note that it's not only rapists who think this way: it's a common opinion, perhaps expressed under their breath, of a great many observers, and not all of them men. So, what was it that the young women, D.C. and R.L., were expiating, what crimes, and committed by whom? Because this is far less clear, and yet every bit as glaring, as the guilt of those who raped them.

In the approach that newspapers took to sex crimes, it was always implicit that the victims were, to some greater or lesser extent, responsible for what happened, whether that was the rape and violence they had suffered or even their death. Either because they had provoked it, or else because they had failed to take sufficient precautions to prevent it happening, taking excessive risks, failing to take into account that . . . fooling themselves into thinking that . . . Even where the writer hasn't openly taken a stance against the women, the guilt imperceptibly creeps over and washes down upon them, sliding from the figure of the assailant onto that of the victim. What is taken under close examination and probed and plumbed is the victim's behavior. How was she dressed? What was she doing there? Why did she listen to them, why did she accept their invitation/ride/offer? Why on earth didn't she defend herself with greater determination, etc. These arguments—once upon a time adduced explicitly; nowadays, in an era of pseudocorrectness, still filtering through the wrinkles of language like a subtle murmuring instead of an open statement—are the cells of thought that proliferate around the core of rape, connecting all the protagonists, the perpetrators as much as the victims, and if the former are not a matter of chance, then neither can the latter be. The victims, too, are subject to the principle of responsibility: if it hadn't been for the victims and their behavior, either brash or provocative or naïve or stupid, then the crime wouldn't have happened, or it would have happened to someone else. Among the array of crimes, rape is the one that seems least willing to remain inexplicable, the one whose causes people are most vociferous about emphasizing and underscoring, in part because they are reasons that appear obvious, the relationship between cause and effect leaps immediately to the eye, and if the effect is the targeted violence perpetrated by the rapist, the cause can't be anything other than the woman. The reasoning is this: if you leave a steak out unguarded, you can hardly complain when the dog wolfs it down.

A great many women, by education, temperament, intelligence, and experience, outstrip most males: and they're capable of holding them at bay by virtue of these qualities. But the victims of the CR/M were doubly or triply disadvantaged in comparison with their kidnappers, in terms of physical strength, age, social standing, education, and simply being outnumbered. And let's throw in malicious innuendo. In veiled terms, as almost always seems to happen, the young women were accused of having delivered themselves into their captors' and torturers' hands, having sinned by naïveté, to put it mildly. It's a textbook objection, and leveled at young women who at first had displayed a friendly willing and compliant attitude toward the rapists, accepting a date with them, taking rides in their cars. It is remarkable how in common opinion the victims are always blamed in hindsight, and with a hint of complacency, for a lack of caution that winds up making them in some sense accomplices in the trouble they got themselves into. People hasten to rummage through the accounts of their behavior to find faults or shortcomings sufficient to allow an attribution of at least some share of the guilt to the victims. That is because it would be intolerable to accept the idea of their utter innocence. Everyone would find that unbearable. The guilty are always more acceptable than the innocent.

But if you consider carefully, all of the protagonists of the CR/M, culprits and victims, display an extraordinary recklessness. Farsightedness really wasn't one of their gifts. And then, if we consider the behavior of the murderers, once they had committed their misdeeds and were back in the city, then you really have to conclude that they were by no means evil masterminds, but just a trio of pathetic idiots.

THEY THINK THEY'RE SO CLEVER that they'll never stumble into the hands of the police. Or else they know they will, but they're not afraid of winding up like that, they just don't care, who gives a damn, that's all she wrote.

IF ONLY THEY'D BEEN NOTHING but idiots! Idiots lack sufficient imagination and initiative to conceive what they actually carried out. Instead, they were that exact blend of wickedness and imbecility that makes people truly dangerous. They were stupid enough not to feel fear and repugnance for what they were preparing to do, but clever enough to concoct a plan, however half-baked. They brashly assumed they would never, ever be caught. Their idiocy rendered them unfeeling, their wickedness made them arrogant and cruel. It's the same blend that we find, on a sublime level, in Satan. The light of the spirit allows itself to be made an instrument of blindness, its gaze twists and then turns sullen. The satanic modus operandi calls for agility of means and weightiness of ends. For that matter, these were decent students, in high school and later at university, with passable grades. They studied for their exams. There were even those who claimed that Angelo had a superior mind, that he was a genius, though an evil one, mistaking the insane gleam in his eye for the light of true intelligence. The obstinate error of those who, observing the enormous bulbous blue eyes of the no-longer-young criminal—not unlike a cartoon character who has seen a ghost or a monster and whose eyes pop out in surprise—mistake that wide-eyed stare for a sign of presence of spirit, while instead it points to a lack of it, because those eyes see nothing in particular, nothing hidden, nothing ulterior, and above all, there is nothing to see *inside them*, beyond them: as enormous as they are, they have no depth, they have never known second thoughts, which constitute the very essence of thought in the first place. They seem to be nervously wide open, focused on the present, like the eyes an uneasy bird rotates incessantly in search of prey, or intent on not becoming prey itself. A perpetual watchfulness that adds nothing to one's consciousness, if anything thinning it out, rendering it a pure nervous vibration. Melancholy, sadness, hope, disappointment, happiness—all of which, in order to develop and be expressed, require an emotional space sufficiently broad and deep to allow past and future to coexist—are unknown to this gaze.

ANOTHER DOCTRINE PROPOSED is that of the sowers of chaos. Accelerate evil, unveiling it, bringing to light the dark side of everything: that is the task to be accomplished, as far as these missionaries are concerned. It is with prophetic punctiliousness that they rape and strangle, to ensure that the violent nature they harbor in their hearts is not hidden from the eyes of men or inadvertently forgotten. Murderers, then, are the midwives of evil; their task is to bring to the surface nightmares that lie on the seabed of consciousness.

Buried in the heart of the universe, almost forgotten, is its underlying principle, namely chaos. At least as a faint trace or glimmer, it still persists in every living thing, diluted in each individual particle, to such a degree that it remains unrecognizable, invisible. And yet it's there. Its being and its nonbeing amount to the same thing. The nonbeing of chaos is always present, lurking in ambush, in that which exists. All order hangs together practically by a miracle, teetering on the brink of an abyss of disorder, on the verge of collapse. The body of each individual, each destiny, whether a personal destiny or the destiny of an entire society, is a grandiose and precarious construction in which chaos lies dormant, a cold cell. But once it reawakens, the entire organism is infected in short order and begins to crumble. Whether or not they realize it, the agents of chaos are those individuals who, through their crimes, put the process in motion, they bring it to light, they restore chaos to its sovereign role. Following their passage, the lines have been twisted, the design has vanished, the house has collapsed, the wells are dry. "Chaos reigns." By killing a child or a defenseless young woman, they are tapping on the vein to make it swell and come to the surface. That vein is chaos.

> . . . the summer will be full of fury
> men with two faces will come
> the plowed fields will not be mown
> the women will have horns . . .

FOR THAT MATTER, if destruction is the first and most obvious law of nature, murder isn't a crime, but rather an article of that law.

10

IN *THE ROAD TO OXIANA*, Robert Byron writes, concerning several immense monuments: "But while the mountains last, the rock-maniacs who commanded these things must be remembered—and they knew it. They were indifferent to the gratitude of posterity. No perishable aestheticism or legal benevolence for them! All they ask is attention, and they get it, like a child or Hitler, by *brute insistence*."

That's right, attention. To get attention. Not to chase after psychologisms (even if that were the right approach, it would already be a well-trodden one . . .), but unless you grip in your fist both the murderers' ferocity and their recklessness, you'll never be able to understand the disjointed sequence of their actions, which led them to be caught immediately, while the body was still warm, the blood still fresh. Brashness? Imbecility? Indifference to the consequences of their actions? Such a misbegotten murder cannot have a motive that entirely excludes the secret desire on the part of those who committed it to be found out. Otherwise there's no explaining it. No one is stupid enough to behave like that. So stupidity isn't the explanation, or at least not the only one, it's not enough, it's necessary but not sufficient. You need to hypothesize that anyone who undertakes such a senseless enterprise (let's leave aside the morality and the feelings, let's just talk about logistics) is doing it with the objective of attracting the attention of the police, their families, the press, the world. Instead of concealing the evidence, they scatter it and exhibit it, or perhaps we should say, they put it where anyone can see it. Attention: perhaps this is the keyword. The young men of the CR/M, when they were boys back at school, were already trying to get attention, with their continual provocations—provocations the priests had decided not to react to, taking no disciplinary measures against them, practically pretending to ignore them, convinced that if they took them seriously, they'd just be playing along with the provocateurs. The priests believed that by acting in this manner, they'd let them fall flat, they'd take the wind out of their sails, little by little, depriving them, in fact, of the oxygen of attention. It's the school of thought behind mitigation, the approach of farsighted passivity, according to which the best way of getting someone who's acting like a lunatic or stirring up trouble to stop is to pay them no mind, ignore them, turn your back or shrug your shoulders, making it clear that you are by no means impressed: that is to say, no reaction. Wisdom of this kind, widespread in the Catholic world but elsewhere as well, may perhaps allow you to win a "war of position" as defined by Gramsci, but rarely does it work if the attackers are launching their assaults in sudden episodic bursts. I don't believe people when they say that if you're swimming and you encounter a shark, all you need to do is remain motionless and you'll be perfectly safe. (Though I, too, far too many times, have chosen not to react, in order to avoid giving satisfaction to whoever had provoked or insulted me . . .)

The method didn't prove to be particularly effective. If given little or no consideration, when considered unworthy even of punishment, those people simply resumed their demand for attention, aiming higher this time. Those who aren't met with firm opposition take it personally, as an offense. Hey, you, I'm not a ghost, you know, I'm not a scarecrow, take me seriously, or I'll show you what I'm capable of, and I'm not talking about schoolboy pranks! You'll see. They used what a hardened traveler and explorer like Robert Byron attributes to the Achaemenid emperors, that is, insistence, brute insistence. They demand attention and they obtain it, "like a child or Hitler," that is, by sheer bullying. Brutality becomes noteworthy and memorable: you can't just take it in stride. Nothing makes a stronger impression than sheer savagery. It is true, however, that when an impression is made in the soft wax of public opinion, it tends to melt and turn indistinct as soon as it is heated and reshaped by some new excitement, by subsequent scandals or horrors or vile deeds, things that are described as inconceivable but, it soon becomes clear, are anything *but*, given that they continue to happen, day after day, year after year they recur, they replicate, they present themselves over and over, and behold, the inconceivable is something we ought to conceive once and for all, instead of remaining astonished and scandalized each time, and then again, and then yet again, starting over from scratch each blessed time. Exceptions, when multiplied by a thousand, cease to constitute exceptions: they form a substantial chunk of reality. The state of exception presents itself, in effect, in every single instant and in every convergence of events, it constitutes the ordinary, the everyday, you might even say the familiar, the domestic. If horror exists, it is routine, everyday. Madness is the order of the day in the life of any individual. Madness lies within us, in our brothers and sisters, in our parents and our children and our acquaintances, in even clearer form in our spouses, to say nothing of that gang of misfits we call friends, it's just that it manifests itself variously, in a more or less ostentatious manner, sometimes it lurks, nesting, other times it explodes into view, it can be paralyzing or violent, and in its turn the violence may be directed toward others or it might ricochet, like a curved arrow, back on whoever first released it. Are those who cruelly ravage themselves any less deplorable than those who do it to others?

Just yesterday I learned that a fellow who was to all appearances entirely ordinary, a jovial and nondescript person, succeeded in obtaining the management of his wife's money, and then ran through the entire fortune before she was able to notice a thing, and just as he was on the verge of being found out, on the eve of a cruise with his wife, who was convinced that he had actually reserved and paid for the tickets, well, rather than confessing to his own lies, admitting that there were no tickets for the cruise in question, and that he had in fact promised another woman that the two of them, also the following day, would set sail aboard a two-masted sailboat on a different cruise, a vessel he had hired with his wife's last remaining money, the boat and crew and enough provisions for fifteen days and iced champagne, all ready to depart, instead what he did is he locked himself in the bathroom while his wife was in the next room packing their bags, and he cut his throat. That's right, he *cut his throat.* Just writing this phrase, between "cut" and "throat," I can't help but take my fingers off the keyboard and lift them to my own throat. And gulp.

The unpredictable, therefore, is eminently predictable: we don't know to whom it will happen, but it will surely happen. It is impossible to rule out any outcome. Nothing can ever be taken for granted. The future might be written in *n* different ways. Three young men born to good families (or else four or six, it makes no difference, if their friends didn't get dragged into this mess, it was by sheer happenstance) proceed to kidnap and torture to death two young women, and two others might just as easily have been in their place.

AND YET IN THE END, Xerxes or Genghis Khan or Hitler will be remembered down through the centuries—while the perpetrators of the CR/M will not. This book of mine, unfortunately, is no equivalent for the monumental tombs that maniacal emperors built for themselves, carving them into living rock to ensure they would be remembered. But I'll do my best. In order to be listened to, I too will have to employ some of that all-too-deplorable "brute insistence."

YOU GET CAUGHT, often, due to a mistake made upstream of or in the aftermath of the crime.

One day, many years ago, in the cell in Rebibbia Prison where I teach school, during a cigarette break (the prison equivalent of recess), two or three students are leaning against the bars, looking outside, toward the internal courtyard where prison visits take place; then they turn around and gesture to me, they want to point someone out to me. I walk over to the window.

"You see that guy?"

Yes, I see him.

"He's the worst," and they smirk.

Since I'm at the beginning of my career as a prison teacher (if we can call it a career, since twenty years later I'm at the exact same point I started from), I imagine that the guy the inmates are talking about must have stained his reputation with some infamous crime, and in fact, as it happens, that is exactly what he did, since, in spite of his inoffensive appearance, he is a kidnapper. Among all the crimes that can be committed, this strikes me as one of the most revolting. Especially vile when people try to doll it up with a veil of social conscience (it's a way of striking the rich, etc.). Even before taking on connotations of rape and murder, wasn't the CR/M first and foremost a kidnapping?

In any case, it wasn't for moral or juridical reasons that my students were stigmatizing that prisoner. I was still too naïve to appreciate that their negative judgment ("He's the worst") was exquisitely technical in character. In discussions of crimes and the meaning of punishment, people often misuse the term "error" to describe the crime they committed, as if it were exclusively moral in nature, a slip, a wandering from the straight and narrow: however faded it might be, our Catholic education tends to fudge, loading that word with a meaning very similar to the traditional significance of sin. People forget that the reason most criminals wind up in prison is an error of a practical, logistical nature, technical—in fact, in other words, because they left evidence behind them, didn't notice that they were being followed, because they forgot to keep their mouths shut, because during their getaway they took one street instead of another, as that spirit says so sadly in Dante's *Purgatorio*: Ah, if I had gone that way, I'd still be among the living! So the error is something many criminals intend first and foremost in a concrete sense: that phone call, the reasonable precautions overlooked, strutting around with the money from the caper, going to see a woman afterward, misjudging the situation, scattering clues and evidence, choosing the wrong place or time for a meet, or letting it slip out . . . so that in the end, when you get there, the Carabinieri are waiting for you, submachine guns leveled.

That was the case with the convict my students were discussing. They told me the story, or really, the decisive anecdote, at once repugnant and ridiculous.

HE'D KIDNAPPED a businessman and held him prisoner in the countryside, handcuffed to a tree. I don't remember the reason, whether it was out of necessity, because he was forced to leave him untended frequently, or out of inhumane cruelty, but the kidnapper gave his prisoner very little to eat. And so the man began wasting away, so rapidly that it was visible to the naked eye.

"So guess what happened, why don't you?" I shake my head. The fate of the starving hostage fills me with anxiety.

"Well, after all that time he decided not to give him anything to eat . . . the guy gets skinnier . . . losing weight, wasting away . . ." and all of a sudden the narrator snickers, shaking his head, disappointed at the foolish, reckless management of this kidnapping, while the other prisoner does nothing more than to gesticulate: he curls two fingers around his wrist and then slides his hand out from between them . . .

"In the end, he got so skinny that he slipped out of his handcuffs, and just like that, he got away!"

At that point, even I couldn't help but laugh at the misfortune of the hapless kidnapper. Foolish or inhumane, or both?

The moral of the story is that you have to feed your hostages, if for no reason other than to keep them from starving to skeletal skinniness and escaping when you least expect it.

ASIDE FROM BEING the struggle of males eager to camouflage their uncertain identity by inflicting brutal acts on defenseless women; aside from being the venting of frustrated wealthy young men upon poor people, forced to pay for the sin of their social inferiority, the CR/M is a punishment of weakness, both physical and psychic. Even before being poor and female, the young women caught up in the CR/M are weak, weak of course inasmuch as they are women and of working-class extraction. Torturing them means concealing the torturers' own weakness, nailing it to a cross that you relegate to others to carry. The impotent man is the greatest bully of them all, when he finds himself face-to-face with people even weaker than him, whom he selects, in fact, identifying them from the outset as disadvantaged categories: naïve virgins, of modest economic conditions, perhaps the only creatures even weaker than the murderers—murderers whom the press never seemed to tire of presenting from the beginning as so many powerful Bluebeards, almost invincible personalities, diabolically brilliant, whereas in reality these were just neurotic defectives, who in a school any different from SLM would never have had a chance.

Ah, yes, what did the priests of SLM think of these singular individuals? What did our modern and liberal priests think of their openly displayed fascism, and what did the young Fascists think of the priests? Forget about it. A priest, to a Fascist, is the ideal man to scorn and mistreat, he's not even a man, he's less than a man, an *untermensch*, a faggot in a tunic, a skirt-wearing lunatic who wears pinned to his chest the image of the famous crucified acrobat, that ragtag preacher in the desert, hypocritically good or, even worse, really and truly good.

(In order to construct that last sentence, I made use of expressions that I heard out of the mouths of the young men of the CR/M, their classmates, and used, with intentions more playful than blasphemous, by other students at SLM. I myself thought and used similar statements. Even though I could never really laugh at the men in skirts, and in fact, a little bit, they always fascinated me, they aroused my curiosity; and not just once, more than once—especially in elementary school, while the young teachers would play with us in the courtyard, kicking up those skirts and hiding the soccer ball beneath them, so that we crowded around their legs, kicking like lunatics to make the ball come back out—I found myself imagining that one day I, too, would wear it, that tunic. And that thought filled me with a warm wave of pleasure.)

IN DEFIANCE OF IDLE CHATTER and the time-wasting—murders are an exceedingly effective argument. They brusquely cut off all the chitchat. They are often a form of ultracompliance. Those who kill, as I've already pointed out, are convinced that they're carrying out an order, which might have been framed generically or was simply a verbal conjecture, a resolution: "That guy is giving us a real pain in the neck," the boss happens to say—and off they go to kill him. Thus they are demonstrating their zeal, showing they won't shrink in the face of extreme solutions. Once you've pulled the trigger, there's no going back. That's the only time you can really talk about a fait accompli, a truly "done deal," an accomplished fact: the others are never entirely complete, but death is.

THE MYTH OF ACTION as an end in itself, devoid of any purpose other than the individual's pure affirmation of self, culminates in the moment when he accepts his cessation as an individual: the supreme and perhaps only value of life coincides with death. Not only in accepting the risk of it, but in actually going out in search of it, in consciously procuring it, that risk. In admitting the eventuality, the probability, or even the certainty of it. Hence the aura that surrounds mountain climbers, bullfighters, acrobats, Formula One racers, and anyone else who puts themselves at risk for a reason that cannot be aligned with common sense, that has more to do with will and emotion than with necessity and thought. The death of others at this point becomes a secondary fact along the path of a quest for one's own death. Once one sets out to achieve one's own annihilation, the annihilation of others becomes a secondary contingency.

What prevailed in the CR/M was this secondary aspect: the impulse toward death took it out on other bodies. Once the heroic path was blocked off to them (and like all the fanatics of the extreme right of the time, the perpetrators of that bloody crime fantasized about that path in degraded ideological terms), all that remained to them were the unseemly extensions of that path, the appendices, the paraphernalia, namely cruelty, sheer arbitrary actions, indifference toward the deaths of others: instead of suffering themselves, they inflicted suffering on others, instead of dying, they killed. It's by no means the same thing, but the sensations one draws from it are at least related.

Like little children who experience death by killing small animals: when they see them in their death agonies, they get a taste of their own.

THE REPERTORY ABOUNDED with expressions of this kind: "annihilate oneself to the last spark," "hurtle toward death," "training to die."

A hero is someone who has the courage and the folly necessary to really do what others limit themselves to imagining, using it to fuel their secret fantasies, or which they achieve only in a small part or on a diminished scale. Which of course includes the great exploits, the dangerous escapades that redound to the benefit of all, glory, triumph, the noblest sacrifice of all, but also the most frightful crimes that the human conscience is capable of conceiving, and which, in fact, the hero takes it upon himself to carry out, making them emerge from the dark side where a reasonable worldview had relegated them and cowardice kept anyone from putting them into action. It is the same force the hero makes use of for his more elevated purposes that awakens demoniacal instincts and dreams. For that matter he could hardly avoid them, since this is the very task he has assigned himself: the gigantic Unspoken and Undone of mankind—that instead is exactly what the hero declares and performs, making those things frighteningly real, and he never does them on a personal basis but always in the name of those who had limited themselves to merely suggesting, or wishing, or fearing them. He truly is the personification of a collective nightmare, he is the perfect machine of *Forbidden Planet*. A human heart, amplified, turbocharged. Far from representing a capricious individual will, his deeds are always the expression of a shared state of mind that has finally found its champion. Its formula.

THEY WERE THE EXACT OPPOSITE OF HEROES, but they worshipped them. Just like the Christians who venerate Jesus but do the exact opposite of everything that He did. Over time, I've grown gradually more certain that this is exactly what veneration really consists of: dedicating your entire soul, putting it in an ideal place, up high, very very high, and so getting rid of it in such a way as to set your hands free. The bicameral mind houses, on the one hand, theory and, on the other, practice. They're not so much at odds with each other as they are allies, in the sense that each tends to its own affairs, without interfering in what the other one gets up to. Similarly, honor and infamy can go together, faithfulness and betrayal. The hero is satisfied by death alone: at the peak of gratification there ought to be his own death—magnificent, glorious—but in the meantime he rejoices in that of his enemies, he savors in their dying agonies a prefiguring of the death that awaits him. Humanism and utilitarianism consider this to be a crime, or, even worse, sheer nonsense. But if it's nonsense that we are looking for, the behavior of the young men of the CR/M will suddenly appear perfectly sensible. If it is senseless actions, deeds that outstrip or annul entirely the calculation of self-interest, that make those who commit those actions exceptional, then the CR/M reveals its objective, even if it fails to attain it, and shows a logic all its own by sweeping away all logic.

Violence is an unpredictable god, blinding and blinded. True, pure bellicosity lays waste to friends and enemies alike. It doesn't distinguish among its adversaries, it simply destroys them; and only in the act of destroying them does it dub them adversaries. It unhinges all order, including the order of battle, it recognizes no tactics, at the very outside, it doesn't know how to wage war precisely because of an excess of death-dealing force. Fundamental, wholesale bellicosity has no objective, no homeland, no rules, and no purpose. Like certain warriors from archaic times described in mythology, who fought and killed with such indiscriminate fury that it was no longer possible to say which side they were on. They were on the side of death, of destruction in and of itself. Their heroic individualism ruled out any communitarian spirit, which would have meant being and feeling themselves to be members of one army rather than another. The desire to be first, to stand out, leads people to dominate their friends as well as their enemies, and defies any and all logic, except perhaps for the inverted logic of disproportion and waste.

As a long-ago French knight puts it, neither meat nor drink satisfies me, I am not placated unless I hear the sniveling of a girl taken prisoner, unless I see the blood spraying from her white flesh, and my own semen dripping down her thighs mixed with that of my fellow warriors, and I finally see her lying dead with a wooden stake driven through her temples. There is no greater delight than the sight of a virgin body tortured and ravaged in a holy scene, as when I contemplate paintings in church, with dying female saints torn limb from limb, bloodbaths, the gratuitous offering of suffering. In this insane and visionary world, the greatest pleasure a man can take is to have his way freely with a naked woman hanging on a rope from the ceiling.

THAT WAS WHY THEY "wanted to be found out" . . .

Bellicosity in its purest state does not actually pursue any objective, save for that of revealing in full those who act it out; it produces neither pleasure, nor profit, nor utility; it leaves no creation behind, for the most part it undoes existing creations. It is therefore gratuitous, which makes it by and large inexplicable. For that matter, from the point of view of this mind-set, *anything that can be explained is worthless.*

THE TARGET REMAINS the utilitarian spirit. If you place importance only on actions for their own sake, which have no practical objective, that produce nothing outside of the fame or the infamy of whoever commits them, if you imagine that nothing is noble but that which serves no purpose, the following step in your reasoning will be that what is noble is not merely that which is useless, but even that which is harmful. The supremely free act, and therefore the beautiful act, the act that is truly superior because free of any obligations to obtain a positive outcome, then, will become the negative act: the acts of those who commit gratuitously evil deeds. For no reason, with no objective.

II

THE STORY OF THE LEGIONNAIRE is not a topic for this book. He comes on stage with the CR/M and immediately exits in the opposite direction, like a viper crawling through a wall. Anyone interested in pursuing further reading into this character, at least as fascinating as Angelo, but far more mysterious and, so to speak, hypothetical, starting with his appearance, of whom we have photos taken when he was eighteen years old, and then various identikit sketches layered on them, depicting him as older, with mustaches, eyeglasses, and beards.

The obsessive loquaciousness, the verbal and subsequently criminal activism of the accomplice finds its extreme opposite in the mute and oblique shadow of the fugitive, Signor Jacques, the man about whom nothing is certain except for his sheer evil. Overlooking his criminal record, the only trace of his presence here on earth that I'd like to adduce in this context is that of his death (real or alleged, which is still the topic of debate, the kind of debate that inflames the airwaves on television shows), and of his burial.

ON THE SHORES OF THE MEDITERRANEAN, in the Kingdom of Morocco, directly facing the Kingdom of Spain, there are two fortified strongholds under Spanish sovereignty. One is Ceuta, directly across from Gibraltar, the other is Melilla, almost two hundred fifty miles to the east. It is here, in the cemetery of Melilla, that a veteran of the ranks of the Tercio de Armada, the Spanish Foreign Legion, named Massimo Testa de Andrés, lies buried. From the photograph taken upon his enlistment, he has been identified as the one perpetrator of the CR/M who was never captured. In spite of the fact that the cross adorned with symbols of the Spanish legion bears the date of April 11, 1994, the corpse of Massimo Testa was actually found by the Spanish police on September 9, 1994, in a drab one-room apartment, and his death, from a heroin overdose, was dated to roughly a week previous. The body, in an advanced state of decomposition, was lying facedown, balanced over a stool, with one arm dangling and the chin jammed into the drawer of the nightstand. He was in his underwear. On his right arm were three tattoos: an arrow piercing two hearts, a scorpion, and the words "Amor Madre." Under one knee was the syringe assumed to have injected the lethal dose.

The mini-apartment where Testa lived is cheap and bare. Over the bed hangs a banner with a portrait of Bob Marley framed in the outline of Africa, and at the lower corners are a marijuana leaf and a lion run through by a sword. On the armchair is a kaffiyeh.

There are more syringes still sealed in their packaging on the edge of the bed.

According to records, Massimo Testa de Andrés had been released from the legion in 1993. At the military hospital, where he was taken after a collapse, he had confessed to the doctors that he was addicted to heroin.

ELEVEN YEARS LATER, November 2005, the grave in Melilla was dug up to exhume a femur and a fibula so that genetic testing could be done on them, in order to establish whether Massimo Testa was in fact simply an alias of Angelo's accomplice, who fled in the aftermath of the CR/M and was never arrested. The femur was sent back to Italy in the custody of the medical examiner and assistant district attorney who had come to witness the exhumation. The fingerprints taken by the Spanish police when the dead body was found did in fact match those on file at police headquarters in Rome in the aftermath of the CR/M; and the DNA result was positive. One singular detail is that the skeleton emerged from the coffin wrapped in a blanket, the same one that had been found in Testa's apartment, and in the folds of that blanket was found the syringe used to shoot up for the last time, as if corpse, blanket, and syringe had been hurriedly or perhaps, quite to the contrary, religiously assembled prior to burial, like old-fashioned grave goods.

AS I'VE SAID, the Legionnaire is not the subject of this book, perhaps because his story is excessively overflowing and teeming with conjectures, rumors, contradictions, investigations and counterinvestigations, and borderline hypotheses.

Let me try to recount a glimmer of his enigma by transcribing a number of wiretaps recorded by the investigators, where the voices recorded were not those of the protagonists themselves, but rather two supporting actors, who were however very close to the heart of the Legionnaire's family, so close that it would not be wrong to say they had every right to claim membership in that family, out of long habit if not of actual blood: namely two elderly housekeepers, one still working for the Legionnaire's mother, the other now retired after many years working in the house of his aunt. They are respectively Severa Acutillo, sixty-five, and Adelina Porru, eighty. All of the landline phones and the cell phones of relatives and connections, thirty years after the CR/M, were placed under surveillance in order to gather information that might lead to the capture of the fugitive, or else establish once and for all whether he had actually died and been buried there, in Melilla, under the name of Massimo Testa de Andrés. These transcripts are the result of months of listening and patient decipherment. By sheer chance, so incredible as to seem like something more, the two phone conversations recorded through these wiretaps took place just a few days before and roughly a month after the double murder committed by Angelo in Campobasso, in April 2005.

Thirty years later, the network of the CR/M reemerges, bringing to the surface both corpses and facts that ought not to have anything to do with each other: but which that network takes in and exposes to the light.

FIRST PHONE CALL, from the wiretap on the home phone of the Legionnaire's mother.
Hello? Adelina?
Yes.
I'm calling before I go out because I don't know how late I'll get back . . . yesterday, did you see . . . I mean, did you see the program . . . ?

Which program?

The program on TV.

No. Or actually, yes, I was watching it, but then . . .

They revealed the whole story about the young man . . . the signora's son.

Who do you mean, Leo?

What Leo are you talking about, Adeli' . . . the son of my signora, not the son of your signora . . . the one who had . . . come on, Adeli' . . . he was there from start to finish . . . how they did, what they did . . .

Are you serious?

Yes, I sure am!

Okay, but that guy didn't do a single day behind bars . . .

Exactly . . . that's why they've been looking for him high and low and they have their doubts . . . but anyway, they'll talk about that next week.

What are they going to say?

Eh no, they still can't say.

But why, can't they find him?

Eh?

Severa, I'm asking you, can't they find him?

No, they're not going to find him. They can look . . . they can look all they want! He's dead!

Dead . . . ?

Dead.

What do you mean, dead? Who? Him? Do you really mean it?

Yes, I really mean it. But the family didn't want that to get around.

Are you sure he's dead?

How am I supposed to be sure? They never told me so to my face. But I heard them talking to each other: he's dead now, isn't he?

Then that must mean he's dead.

His mother is having a mass said for him. In his memory.

That's certainly news to me.

I've known about it for a couple of years now.

So he's been dead for a while?

A few years, yes, it must have been.

And where was he? Where is he buried now?

I don't know. He was in Spain . . . maybe there.

But then why are they still looking for him . . . ?

They're looking for him, but they can't find him. Next Monday there's another episode. Maybe they'll explain it.

Let's hope so.

Did you see the finale of the broadcast?

I . . . no, I didn't, I got tired after a while, it was past ten, by the end I'd already fallen asleep, sorry . . .

Well, that's a pity. They told the story, from start to finish. And they showed his picture, too.

Oh, they did? That boy was really a young criminal.

Yes, yes, he was, a criminal.

But handsome.

Handsome, you say? Yes, a good-looking young man. No question about that.

SECOND PHONE CALL, same phone line. (Between the first call and the second, Angelo committed his new murders and was arrested: the newspapers are full of articles about this new crime, and of course the story of the CR/M is dragged back out, and with it the Legionnaire and his run from the law, which has been going on now for thirty years. A TV program that specializes in the pursuit of missing persons is featuring him.)

Last night, you watched it, I hope!

Yes, from start to finish, this time. We all watched it.

And thanks be to God . . . have mercy on his soul . . . I saw the whole thing, too.

And they put it in the paper.

And on the TV news, on the TV news . . . they were talking about him . . . but I changed channels . . . they were talking about what he'd done.

Yes, they mentioned him and the other guy they put back behind bars.

But this is already two episodes they've featured him.

More than two! Three!

But I only saw two.

Three, I tell you. From start to finish they were talking about him.

Just think how the signora must have felt when she saw it!

Eh, yes, Madonna . . .

Seeing him . . .

And the photographs, too . . .

Yes, but Severa . . . it isn't true at all that he's dead. That's a big fat lie.

But who told you that?

That he isn't dead?

Who told you that he isn't dead?

I heard someone say that he was dead . . .

Of course, you heard someone say it, Ade', you heard it from me! Don't you remember? I told you myself, for Pete's sake!

Sure, sure . . . whatever you say . . . but the thing is he's definitely not dead. He's been seen . . . he's been seen around . . . in December when he was walking, in that place, there . . . on the program!

But it could have just been someone who looks like him!

No, no . . . this woman they talked to was certain it was him . . . that guy's no deader than I am, he's actually in Rome . . .

Well, I don't know about that, the one who says he's in Rome is that girl who . . .

No, they said for sure that now . . . and everyone knows it, that he's in Rome . . . and at the beach, near Anzio, I think. Anzio.

That's a lie.

Why do you say it's a lie, come on, Adeli'!

Oh, Severa!

Adelina!

Oh!

Listen to me, I'm telling you! I'm telling you, and I know. His cousin even went to see him! She went all the way to Spain!

Where did she go?

To Spain!

But who went to Spain?

Oh, you know: a cousin of his.

Not his mother?

No, not his mother. They sent his cousin.

To see him.

To see his grave.

And was he really in Spain?

Yes, in Spain, but it wasn't his name on the headstone.

Well, of course, he certainly couldn't have kept his real name.

Obviously not.

But in that case, why don't they say so?

As long as the mother is alive, they aren't going to say it.

As long as she's alive?

That's right. As long as she's alive.

But why?

You got me. That's what they decided.

But it would be better if they said something about it. They've been suffering from this thing all their lives.

All their lives, that's true. What are you going to do about it?

And it would be better for the government, since they're still looking for him.

The government, look. They should just put their minds at rest.

What are they still looking for?

Don't ask me, it must be the law.

And now her, poor thing . . .

They're all crowding around, outside the house, have you seen? With TV cameras, too . . . but she won't open the door.

I can imagine that.

And she won't even answer the phone . . .

Of course not.

In other words, a grim time.

Certainly, poor thing. She ought to move away.

Ever since that criminal's out and about, they've started searching for him again.

But isn't he behind bars?

Sure, but they dragged out the whole case again.

Well, of course they did . . . every time they bring up one of them . . . they're going to bring up the other.

And out comes the whole sad story.

Maybe so, but as far as I'm concerned, this idea that he's dead . . . I don't know . . . anyway, if you tell me that the cousin saw him . . .

Whether or not she saw him, I couldn't say, he was already buried, but . . . it's not like I can swear an oath.

Huh . . . it must be like you said, Severi' . . . I can't really question it . . . if you heard it . . . right?

I told you: his mother has a mass said for him. The mass for the dead.

That doesn't prove anything . . .

Then what does it prove, in that case?

No, no, I'm not questioning . . .

First she was having it said here so that the nuns wouldn't find out about it . . . then she went to see the nuns, "That way I can have them say mass for him, too." What do you think that means?

Adelina, I'm not questioning your word, it's just that . . .

My word is no better than your word. And anyway, it's a secret. They didn't want anyone to know.

Eh, eh . . . but it would have been better if they had spoken up, with all the problems they have now!

In fact, even the cousin says: Let's just tell them, that way it's taken care of. Let's hope so. But we have to wait. We have to wait for her to die.

If that's the problem . . .

When the mother dies, maybe they'll talk.

To stop them from looking for him anymore.

Let them go on all they like . . . they won't find him.

In fact, why do they care if they're looking for him?

Well, what I want to know is, are they really looking for him? Really really looking for him? Because if they were really looking for him, they would have found him.

Are you sure of that, Seve'?

If they never found him, it's because they weren't looking for him.

But he moved around so much . . .

Eh, he was spotted here and there . . . they saw him in Rome, they saw him in Venezuela . . .

At first he was in Rome, right?

Then they saw him in Africa, in a hundred other places . . . it must mean he didn't feel safe staying in one place for very long.

But who was giving this boy the money?

No doubt, his mother was sending it to him.

So she knew where her son was staying?

Exactly. But if all this boy did all his life was dress up and preen, then who was sending him the money?

She was.

So she had to know where he was staying.

Certainly. But we didn't. No one ever knew. Even though, maybe . . .

Maybe what . . . ?

Nothing, Ade', I was just saying.

All right, we've talked till it's late.

All right.

Time to get some sleep, Severi'.

Mamma mia! You're right, it's time. Give my regards.

You, too, ciao.

Ciao, eh.

12

LISTEN. *Are you listening to me? Maybe it's pointless to go in search of psychological explanations: it's pointless to try to narrow down and connect the nonhuman to the pathologies of the human, to its farthest fringes. Here we're in the presence of behaviors that can't be explained by childhood, education, or brain damage . . . It's almost offensive to rummage around in those dresser drawers, offensive. The word "monster" should be taken seriously, and not as a metaphor.*

THE ADVANTAGE IN TALKING about someone like Angelo ought to be not having to waste a lot of time explaining who he is and what he did. Certainly, forty years ago there would have been no need, when his name was stamped in letters of fire in the Italian consciousness, and the sword of the archangel who had expelled him from the ranks of humanity still blazed, and even ten years ago, when he returned to occupy the front pages of the press with his wrecked, debauched face, for a crime perhaps even more frightful than the one before it, and yet he already seemed faded, blurred, like an absurd rerun (absurd the context, absurd the return to circulation of Angelo, that was what struck the mind most powerfully), like a ghost coming back to haunt a house whose occupants thought they were rid of it for good; like an old actor treading the boards again with his old routine that's been seen a thousand times. "Oh, no! Not him again!" So that now I'm not so sure I don't have to explain it all from scratch, once again. But I'm not going to do it in excruciating detail.

BETWEEN THE CR/M and the 2005 murders, there's a certain redundancy.

After the first one, everyone was talking about him, his name was everywhere, his name became synonymous with evil, he was famous, on the lips of the people. After the second crime, as the hubbub over his reappearance in the summary at the beginning of the TV news began to subside, among the five lead stories of the night, and in second place among the crime news, by the time of his new conviction, no one came to cover him, there were no more mentions of his name, it fell out of the ready conversational vocabulary that people had (the lexicon that in those years saw expressions such as "*tracimare*," "*tsunami*," "*tesoretto*," "*bipartisan*," "*quant'altro*," and "*rottamare*," rise and fall, etc.), perhaps now people would have a hard time summoning that connection when they heard or read his name in passing, only to add, "Ah, yes, of course . . . that guy . . . the one from *Monte Circeo*," but only making reference to his first rape and murder, the one that made him famous, while the second crime instead condemned him to lie buried in the file of forgetfulness—and I, too, in the final analysis, am writing with the same objective, not to make that name live on, but to bury it. Which would be the purpose of all writing: to delete, burn, leave behind, whereas nowadays everyone says the opposite, and namely that we write to preserve, keep, remember . . .

Our capacity for scandal is limited, it cannot replicate itself on the same topic, the first time it's morbidly attracted, the second time it records it and files it away, to move on to something else. When faced with the repetition of a monstrosity, a peculiar indifference surfaces in the observer . . .

Which is why no one paid him any more attention, with the exception of a crazy woman who actually wanted to marry him.

*. . . of shame or remorse for what he had done
not a trace was ever found . . .*

AND THEN THERE WAS Angelo's act of mockery, when he became a "psychological counselor" (by the way, the famous serial killer Ted Bundy was one also).

This means that there's a willful delight in putting victims into the hands of the perverted—minors, weak people, people in need of assistance. It's enough for a person to become an even slightly charismatic figure and others begin to believe that he might be the ideal choice to help others. Let's consider the case of that guru in Prato, known as the Prophet, who for twenty years was financed by the regional government of Tuscany to house minors in a community where, right from the very outset, it had been determined that they were being abused, and in fact the Prophet was convicted of various criminal violations, and yet the family court continued to assign minors to his community. Where he could abuse them.

I think back to that very strange Christmas, which I spent watching a DVD of the movie *I ragazzi della Roma violenta* (1976), based on the CR/M.

The film begins with a series of man-in-the-street interviews, with pass-ersby calling for the death penalty. That's pretty plausible, since if you take the sampling of man-in-the-street interviews as representative, 90 percent of Italians are in favor of the death penalty, execution by firing squad, or hanging.

Then the respectable young men are agonizing in the boredom of the bar.

This, too, is realistic, the idea that one progresses from boredom to murder.

Afflicted by *tedium vitae*, they'll warm up their lives with brutal acts.

Anyone who has never experienced anything other than safety, peace, and personal comfort will thirst for danger, challenges, and violence.

13

CRIMES SERVE AS A COUNTERBALANCE *to the intolerable burden of virtue; the graver the crime, the greater its exemplary usefulness, to keep the world in a state of equilibrium, lest it slip into the abyss of goodness. According to this piece of economics, a misdemeanor, a minor crime, which is therefore not all that different from a virtue, serves no purpose. Pointless to sing its praises, pointless even to bother committing it.*

TO WHOM SHOULD we attribute the thought that I have paraphrased here?

Would you like a single episode, just like that, picking at random, let-ting one of his novels fall open to a given page?

Here you are. They apply a holy wafer to the asshole of the unfortunate protagonist, a monk sticks it in and then sodomizes her, after which, among the numerous profanities, he takes pleasure "upon our Saviour's very Body," spurting upon it "the impure floods of his lubricity's torrents."

Who invented and wrote this sacrilegious episode? And who, in the opinion of many, actually carried it out? Do you really need to ask?

I READ THE MARQUIS DE SADE for the first time at the military hospital in Taranto, where I was waiting in vain to be declared unfit for service. The mornings and afternoons slipped past, empty and hot.

I knew that the Marquis had been described as "divine" and that the Surrealists adored him, but the books that the student from the DAMS Institute who occupied the bunk next to mine let me read consisted of nothing but exceedingly long and monotonous tirades on natural philosophy, interspersed with journeys through France, and sexual abuses whose mechanics I was honestly unable to fully understand, so minute and acrobatic were they, with straddlings and kneelings, pilings up of bodies in postures that were difficult to picture, like in descriptions from yoga manuals, such as, "He straddles me on all fours, on top of me with his head turned toward my back, and he forces me to spread . . ." etc. Between one abused and another, the learned torturers engaged in disquisitions on Nature, there was a great deal of talk about Nature, natural instincts, natural laws, they spoke of nature and organs, using rigorously rational argumentations, which were therefore completely mad, as reason always is when it is purified and set free of all emotions. Moreover, on every page they glorified the order of things, inscribed, carved, and crystallized, according to which it is written that the weak must give in to the wishes and desires of the strong, as it always has been and always will. So it may be, but if it's such an obvious statement of fact, why flog it to death, repeating it a thousand times?

IN THE MIDST OF ALL THOSE PAGES of virtuosic perversion, necessarily dull, what struck me was a more subtle and enduring truth. Namely, that pain is sincere, authentic, as impossible to avoid as it is useless to simulate or feign. Acute pain is a powerful and specific sensation. The sensation of pleasure on the other hand is dubious and in any case limited over time: you cannot take more than a certain amount of pleasure, nor can you effectively pretend to do so. Whereas if a person is being subjected to torture, there can be no doubt about them suffering: and there are no limits to their pain, in either intensity or duration, except in the obstinacy of the person inflicting it.

And I understood another thing at that point, which cast a retrospective light on the CR/M: what arouses a pervert is not a woman's beauty but the crimes that can be committed against her body. As a result, something that no longer has anything to do with sex but rather with domination as such, in every field, at every level: and that is, that the more criminal a power, the more it excites whoever exercises it and takes pleasure from it.

Hence the following Sadean principles:

Cruelty is nothing other than uncontaminated energy.

The man who takes pleasure from a woman kidnapped by force from her husband or her family experiences far greater pleasure than the man who legitimately takes pleasure from his wife.

From an incentive to sexual pleasure, crime little by little reveals itself to be a pleasure in and of itself, even greater than sexual pleasure, from which it breaks away, becoming autonomous.

Kidnapping a young woman, therefore, is a pleasure in and of itself, and not merely in terms of the pleasure that one can expect to enjoy while abusing her.

(I believe that this was the most intense shiver that ran down the backs of the young men of the CR/M: when the two girls accepted their offer and got in the car with them.)

The more respectable the ties, the greater the delight one takes in breaking them.

(Indeed, they believed that they were free men, authorized to break all laws, all conventions, all shame, all pity, all fear of punishment; which are nothing other than the "knots that fools use to bind themselves." Those who feel themselves constrained by these rules are simply weak and cowardly. Selfishness is the only nonhypocritical form of action. On the planes of both individual pleasure and the general economy that governs the world, the suffering of a single creature is irrelevant. Anyone unwilling to do whatever is required to obtain that which is useful to him or gives him pleasure is fainthearted.)

REMORSE? Nothing more than the murmuring of a soul too weak and sluggish to shut it up.

You can only repent of something that you do exceptionally or rarely: in order to quench your remorse, then, it will be enough to repeat over and over whatever it is that prompts it, as often as possible, until it is transformed into a habit, until one becomes completely habituated to crime and murder. By the third or fourth crime in a row that you commit, the sense of guilt begins to wane, by the fifth or sixth, it will vanish completely.

NOT ONLY IN PRACTICING, but especially in preaching violence, terror, and mistreatment as the highest objectives of man, there is always a powerful pedagogical ambition, which aims to clear the field of the misunderstandings and clichés that hold in their thrall the naïve, the respectable, hypocrites, and those laboring under illusions—all of them deserving of an exemplary lesson. The reader—who if he is of the male gender might or ought to identify with the various monsignors and gentlemen, and take pleasure alongside them in their erotic misdeeds—instead finds himself in a position similar to that of the young girls who have been abused: he undergoes unbroken violence and so he learns. He learns that the pursuit of an individual's liberty entails the fact of enslaving a second individual: the radical liberty of one takes concrete form only in the radical enslavement of the other, as two complementary facts, two mosaic tiles whose shapes fit together.

It is rare that a rape fails to offer this aspect, a mix of the philosophical and the pedagogic. Edifying, illustrative, in its manner, like a crash course in degradation and corruption. In order to teach you quickly to accept that, in fact, degradation and corruption, and not order and peace, are the rules that govern the world.

ONCE I ASKED MY TEACHER Cosmo what he thought of the Marquis de Sade.

"Sade the apostle of liberty? Only a gang of wankers like the Surrealists could have thought such a thing."

ONE ASPECT, not new, that struck me for its virulence was the polemic against Christianity. I'd already read such things in the thinkers of the Enlightenment, among whose number Sade, when all is said and done, could be counted, as well as in Nietzsche, who wrote with far greater profundity but also with his typical German heaviness. Sade, on the other hand, moves briskly, with a dismissive, Voltairean flair. Jesus: an impostor. The apostles: frauds and corpse thieves. Their prophet writes nothing, because he is profoundly ignorant; he speaks little, given his stupidity; he does even less, given his sluggishness. When scoundrels of his sort find an audience, however, their success is guaranteed; a lie spreads faster and farther than the truth: that's the story of errors throughout history.

Last of all, the mediocre and inane story of his life as an impostor, also known as the Gospel.

FROM THE SO-CALLED LUST MURDER, lust disappears, leaving only murder in its place. Homicide no longer becomes the tragic outcome, but rather the substitute for coitus. The sexual phase is skipped entirely because it was a pretext in the first place (unquestionable proof of this are the murders committed by Angelo in 2005). If the purpose isn't sexual, if the desire is not for physical pleasure, the excitement in violently possessing a woman does not change whether she is young or old, ugly or pretty, seductive or recalcitrant, it's all the same thing, just as there is no difference between possessing her and murdering her. You can experience greater erotic satisfaction in strangling a woman than in masturbating, or else in masturbating after strangling her than in penetrating her when she is still alive. The sexual enjoyment is situated at unthinkable points along the way and in the body.

People imagine that a rapist pines after sexual intercourse, finds it so desirable that he's willing to break every rule in order to obtain it; in reality, though, that act disgusts him, he perceives it as something filthy and abject, so why shouldn't he replace it with an equally deplorable act? Torture instead of fornication. Or else merge them into a single act. Coitus is a peculiar act that is at once replicable and *substitutable*. We are perennially engaged in a search for its equivalents. There are those who find them in the amassing and display of money and clothing, or automobiles; others, in power, some in art or violence, which can all be a surrogate or a support: we gain access to sex through its substitutes, you take someone to bed after impressing them with a display of the collateral attributes of sex, first and foremost, power. There are others who find substitutes for sex in self-sacrifice and altruism, or else in perversion, that is, by doctoring coitus until it can only be practiced in the form of submission, outrage, punishment, affirmation of one's power, or erasure of the world. From the fairly simple and basically repetitive act that it is, no different from eating and sleeping, coitus lends itself to any transmutation, and it is not uncommon to find it camouflaged or transferred into other ordinary acts and situations. Except for playboys (forgive me the anachronism, I know that there is no longer any such thing as a playboy, or that if there is, that's certainly not the term we use, but I don't know the present-day term for it) and for prostitutes and gigolos and porn stars, coitus occupies a very limited portion of the time available in a person's life, almost laughably small, a few minutes a day, or a month, or even less . . . and is consequently far more present in substitute acts than in real ones.

Its specter haunts our everyday lives, but it is rarely embodied. Preparatory acts, substitute acts: ninety-nine times out of a hundred, we limit ourselves to those.

IN IMAGINARY SHAPES, it was present in our minds when we were boys.

SEXUAL THINGS ARE PANTOMIME. Comedies, farces, melodramas, mystery plays, interludes, blackout gags, grim dark tragedies, the *Oresteia, Romeo and Juliet, A Streetcar Named Desire, No Sex Please, We're British, Il magnifico cornuto, Senso, On ne badine pas avec l'amour, The War of the Roses, La mandragola, Othello* . . . Pure theater. Disguises. Betrayals. Women dressed as men. Men transformed into beasts. *The Dresser. The Servant. Les bonnes. Macbeth.* Desire and impotence and vengeance. Murderous fantasies, suicidal, delirious, romantic. The Queen of Sheba and Vlad the Impaler. The death of Procris. The man who didn't know how to love, the man who knew too much, the man who loved women, the French lieutenant's woman, the woman who lived twice, the sign of Venus, the gentlemen who prefer blondes. *Last Tango in Paris* and elsewhere. It is only in these forms codified by theater and film and novels that we can begin to express a certain number of narrative lines in that extremely tangled thicket. Who can claim to have revealed their own sex life in its entirety? What they have done, and what they have yearned to do, dreamed of doing, attempted, feared? In the spectrum of an ordinary life, and even of a chaste life, there's more passion and obscenity than in any *Emmanuelle + Werther + Portnoy + Wuthering Heights +* the complete works of Henry Miller Bukowski Erica Jong and Tinto Brass. It's a vast, endless field, and not even the individual who lives there knows it thoroughly. The most ardent confession, the most out-of-control novelistic invention will not be up to the task of revealing it in its entirety. Artists, therefore (so many blind Tiresiases with withered dugs), devote themselves to one of these lines and reconstruct it, extracting it from the welter. They know everything, and they have either a presentiment of it or have actually seen it, but they tell only a tiny sliver of it.

THE SIMPLEST of these lines is rape.

WHATEVER EFFORT IS MADE, you always fall short of the mark, or else you push past it in a programmatic, hyperbolic, exponential manner, that is, in the mode typical of pornography. In order to cover a boundless field, you must divide it up into quadrants like a land office, composing a textbook of perversion that is to the reality of an individual's sex life as a book of grammar is to the language that person speaks.

COERCION CANNOT BE ELIMINATED from the concept of intercourse and in the very hypothesis of pleasure: even where there is no violence to be detected, if there has been pleasure, that is because a temporary domination has been established, an illegality has been committed, a forcing open has been perpetrated, one will has surrendered to another. Or even surrendered to itself. The loss of dignity is a crucial condition of any sexual enjoyment.

14

RAPE STANDS ROOTED IN SEX *like the Tree of the Knowledge of Good and Evil at the center of the Garden of Eden. We are not allowed to lift our eyes and gaze upon it; to taste of its fruit would reveal all at once the true nature of all that surrounds it. Of sex, rape constitutes the unspeakable secret that, if it were once made public, would degrade the world, blighting for all time relations between men and women, between humankind and Nature.*

OBJECTS AND HUMAN BEINGS have for us the value that our imagination attributes to them: this is true of love, friendship, fidelity, and of the vilest ideas and fantasies, so that a person, the dignity of their life and the integrity of their body, lose all importance in comparison with the pleasure that we can experience as we caress the notion of torturing them. From a fantasy to the actual attainment of that fantasy, the path is usually long, so long that almost no one ever really travels it even once in the course of a lifetime, even though when you stop to consider it more carefully you discover that it's a relatively easy tight spot to get through, as is shown by the CR/M;

in truth, nothing could be simpler to undertake and complete than the kidnapping and rape of a girl or young woman on the part of a group of men; it's a crime that demands only a minimal effort and entails at most a trifling risk to one's personal safety, if you compare it with the risk entailed, say, in robbing an armored car.

However you calculate the take from a rape—far more difficult to establish than the plunder, say, from an armed robbery, where the loot is tangible—the cost of committing it is practically zero. It is precisely that minimal outlay of effort required that gives some the impression that, deep down, it's not really a crime at all: Why should there be any punishment at all for an act that can be committed with such nonchalance? Against which there are no safeguards of any particular nature? It's practically like finding a wallet lying in the street: can it seriously be considered theft to pick it up and pocket it? The same thing as taking a woman against her will. Once you've established that her wishes are secondary or exist specifically to be overruled, what else is stopping you? And an act that won't run into any obstacles, isn't it therefore basically legitimate? Where are the steel bars, the armored doors, the alarm systems, the guard dogs, and the firearms that are usually set to guard whatever it is that criminals generally venture to steal?

Just about anybody could attack an unaccompanied woman. One paradoxical consequence of women's emancipation is that, taking as a given women's right to freedom of behavior, and understanding that they have won the full and peaceful possibility of exercising that right, the defenses provided by a more traditional social conception have been reduced or eliminated entirely: a repressive system of precautions and controls over women which, though by and large ineffective, nonetheless, by limiting their freedom of movement, also limited the occasions in which they were in danger. Women, then, are now more exposed than they used to be; and so they remain, in spite of the growing awareness that they're on their own now.

That period was, in short, a dangerous limbo in which the old social protections had been dismantled and swept away, the age-old precautions now considered so much garbage, and the culture of self-defense had not yet become widespread.

Twenty years earlier the young men of the CR/M would never have dreamed they could invite a couple of young women out without first being put through a meticulous family screening process. Twenty years later many doubts would have stood in the way of the fatal outing, and the technological means necessary to report the dangerous sideshow would have been available. The rape and murder could certainly still have transpired, of course, but not with the same modality. I therefore have the sensation that I'm telling an age-old story that happens over and over again, but which that one particular time happened the only way it could, the way that the times dictated it had to.

Anyone is capable of attacking an isolated woman. And erotic ideation often circles around that very image, the rape sequence, it embroiders countless active or passive fantasies on the theme: it is a theme with a limitless array of variations, perhaps there is not a single person in the world who hasn't imagined being a protagonist, either as rapist or rapee, there is no body of erotic literature that doesn't feature rape, as a fantasy, dream, nightmare, terror, or unconfessable desire.

In particular, a woman's pubic area can be viewed as provocative—not of erotic impulses but rather of irritated and violent reactions. It is its incongruity, its shapeless appearance, undefined, that prompts what is often a sort of angry curiosity, an astonishment that is transformed into rejection (and it is no accident that the term used in vulgar Italian to describe the female sex organ is the image of an animal that arouses the same type of reaction: the mouse. Some say that the fear triggered by such a small animal is due to the unpredictability of its appearance, its dark color, the odd way it has of moving around . . .).

The feminine sex organ sits there, anonymous, dark, concealed beneath layers of fabric but, so to speak, always present, always perceptible in its hiding place between the thighs, another hole just an inch or so from the hole that everyone has, even men. There are those who go crazy at the thought of that hole, but then there are others who go crazy at the sheer thought that that jagged hole must be honored, revered, that we must lavish attention on anyone who possesses one, that it is necessary to ask permission to enter it, that a particular woman so arrogantly acts as a guard and custodian of that piece of nothing as if it were something that only she has, when in fact all women have one, and they're all identical, and in this detail, all women are the same, and they're all proud as punch to have that piece of nothing and show it off or hide it, promise it or deny it to men who lose their heads over it, willingly subjecting themselves to a series of stupid rules and conditions, when all it would really take is a couple of good hard slaps to . . .

That is why it seems necessary to punish that sex, for its obscene reluctance and shyness and its even more shameless exhibition, when it opens up, displaying the forbidden interior of the body, its slimy channels: it must be forced, pounded, stabbed, surgically removed. Considering that it already looks like a wound, let it become one for real. Those who violate it seem to be trying to find something in it that's not there, like certain burglars who rampage through houses, wrecking the place only to find that there was never any loot in the first place; the angered astonishment in the presence of a woman's genitalia is perhaps similar to that which Emperor Titus must have felt when he penetrated into the Sancta Sanctorum of the temple of Jerusalem: and found it empty. There was *nothing* inside, neither a god nor a spirit, nor gold or precious stones, not a statue—nothing. Nothing to worship, nothing to plunder. In that case, in the name of *what* had he even fought? When the rapist discovers this, he really can lose his mind, if what had guided him up to that point was a sort of practical reason bent wholly on obtaining that which he desired; at the moment in which he discovers that a woman's sex is not the garden of delights he'd dreamed of, a place it was worth committing a crime just to enter, his rage is vented upon that which *is there*, whatever projects and can be seized and yanked and crushed and upon which he can take out his fury, which is to say the face, the hair, the breasts, the buttocks, the delicate or fleshy and in any case defenseless, and therefore provocative, feminine forms. The same anatomical part that for a lover is the source of excitement is the same for a sadist, except that in his case it is an angry, resentful excitement: instead of admiring that part, he detests it, instead of celebrating it and blandishing it, he considers it to be his enemy. There is no difference, in terms of the nervous system, in the buildup to excitement, while there is a great deal of difference in its many possible outcomes, in its consequences and conclusions. Nerves stretched to the breaking point give rise to comparable gestures and deeds but of inverse polarity. Instead of caressing a pair of breasts, one crushes or punches them, instead of lightly slapping the buttocks one claws them or cuts them. The hands reaching out toward a woman's body are always filled with either tenderness or violence. In an unstable equilibrium. An underlying misunderstanding persists. Even the lover most wholeheartedly devoted to his sweetheart's pleasure might imagine heightening it by having recourse to brutality. Even the woman who has most confidently abandoned her body to the attentions of her lover may be swept by the lingering suspicion that, at the high point of these pleasurably solicitous efforts, he might just go a step further, transforming himself into another man, forcing her into positions or coercing her into acts that might prove disagreeable or painful, going so far as to hit her or wrap his hands around her throat . . . or even headlocking her into a position from which she can free herself only by satisfying his frenzy. And sometimes even that's not enough, and it doesn't do a lot of good to protest or beg. Domination always lies latent in a sexual relationship, it's there even when it's not, all you need to do is shift the weight of a gesture by a gram in either direction and redirect by a degree or two their intention, and before you know it a caress has been transformed into a brutal blow. Lucky are they, men and women, who have never experienced that equivocal moment of finding themselves teetering between one and the other: even though in all their good fortune, they may still lack the fundamental experience of amorous ambiguity, knowledge of the dark side, the implicit battle that unfolds in the shelter of love, when the bodies are joined and they compenetrate, and yet still, deep down, they are battling. And you can just imagine when there is no love! When what is running the games from the very outset is deception and hatred. Rape is merely a dogmatic, unilateral, *literal* interpretation of one of the possible meanings, a way of destroying any ambiguity by consigning coitus to a clear and simple significance. Old-school feminists and rapists of all ages come together on the idea that penetration is a violent act in and of itself. You have to *do* something to that body, you can't just leave it the way you found it and took it, it must necessarily emerge transformed, transfigured by pleasure or, otherwise, disfigured. How many options, how many modalities of interaction present themselves, once you get your hands on a feminine body! Strip it naked, explore it, cover it with kisses and saliva, cuddle it, experiment with different instruments to determine how it experiences pleasure, reacts to stimuli, writhes in agony, trembles in fear at the sound of threatening words, and allows itself to be deceived by reassuring ones: in other words, *anything* to keep it from lying there inert, indifferent, *anything* to make it correspond to your own excitement. Sometimes, however, the rapist is not even slightly excited or paroxysmal, instead he is calm, icy: in this case it will be his victim's nervous excitement that will fill the emotional void. If the victim suffers, then her tormentor gets proof of his own existence, even if he is incapable of feeling and thought: it will be the victim who feels them and thinks them for him, in his place. To behave in an inhumane manner in order to feel that you are alive, to prove that you exist, is a contrivance as old as the world, and it can be found in countless situations, it is the underlying foundation of a great many experiences, war, criminality, authority, education, even respect itself, even honor itself, even so, the so-called inviolable rights of the individual emerge out of that individual's potential to turn violent. A helpless creature has no rights, or else yes, it does, but only on paper, so really, it has none. It begins to have them only in the course of a struggle, when in fact it proves that it exists, perhaps associated with other creatures like it, capable of reacting to brutality with equal brutality, proving itself at the very least able to return the blows. What we nowadays pompously refer to as rights, as if they'd always existed, there at our disposal from the very outset, nicely assorted, a nuptial dowry laid away in a drawer where you go to get clean linen, but instead they are the result of battles, tests of strength, rebellions, bloodshed. I exist because I, too, can hit, overwhelm, demand retaliation. Therefore, nothing could be less surprising than the use of violence as an affirmation of self: to offend, to defend yourself. Let me say it again: the very inviolability of the domicile originally means that on the threshold of his home stands a man armed with an axe, and with his children backing him up. The specific element of the story that I'm telling is, nonetheless, the private use of brutality: the story of single individuals who bring out a latent tendency and train its fire in exemplary acts. The conflictual character circulating in relations between the sexes bobs to the surface in its entirety in a few clamorous episodes that cast light on countless other insignificant episodes of that same conflict.

If all men hate women, well, there are certain men who hate them more, much more than those who hate them a little or perhaps a fair amount can even distantly begin to imagine.

NO FORCE IS SPARED, no money, no mental effort, no imaginative resources, nothing is spared, indeed, one willingly squanders it all, ruining oneself just to satisfy that frenzy. Lives are ruined, one's own and other people's, patrimonies and matrimonies, professions, families, all of society is devastated as prisons are filled and pages of infamy and ridicule are scrawled in order to quench that frenzy. "All that mud for three minutes of letting off steam!"

How our sex lives influence all the rest of our lives—how they influence life itself! Either because they absorb it or because they are ejected from it;

and even when they unfold in a balanced manner, because in fact equilibrium is a signal of the greatest imaginable lack of equilibrium: in short, it is a signal of danger.

Shy, modest, apprehensive individuals can be driven to knock down all manner of obstacles, starting with their own conscience and dignity. Laws, bonds, affections, piety, decency, human bodies: it's all swept away, all sacrificed. There is nothing left except a frenzy, and indeed in the end not even that exists any longer. Once the ceremony gets under way, in fact, there emerges a certain mechanical coldness: the kind that drove Angelo to perform the act of suffocating his last two victims, mother and daughter.

THOUGHTS, *words, deeds, and omissions: the catechism that we were taught at SLM put these things on the same plane, and it was possible to commit a grave sin in each of these categories, assuming any of these attitudes whatsoever, that is, by doing something or not doing it, or just saying it or thinking it. Now, in our sadistic fantasies what is most frequently lacking is the opportunity or the courage or the effective will to put them into practice: they remain on the level of words, thoughts, and images. If sadistic fantasies suddenly became real the world would become a bloodbath, a paroxysmal torture chamber. Leaving aside the catechism, which was rightly concerned with covering all aspects and all human activities, both physical and mental, in an effort to identify the possibility of sin even just in the form of intention, it remains clear what distinguishes a fantasy from an act: How many degrees of separation, however, are there between the two things? What equation links them, transforming one into the other? Can you perform a brutal deed without having premeditated it in the slightest? And above all, when you become accustomed to indulging in violent images and taking pleasure in them, are you really sure that there is no risk of their ever taking shape in real life, no danger in other words that you might just do those things, instead of dreaming them and nothing more?*

15

I READ SOMEWHERE that a young man aged twenty-two tried to rape a woman aged fifty-three. Because she put up fierce resistance, he killed her, raped her corpse, and tossed it in a lake. Then he fished her back out and raped her again.

Ah, how many stories I've stumbled across in the course of this research project of mine! For instance, the story of a man who violated the cadaver of his beloved sister, laid out in her casket for the viewing and wake; he had come in her mouth and his relatives found him that way, with his trousers unbuttoned right next to the loved one's smeared face, in the throes of a pleasure so intense that he hadn't even noticed their arrival in the chapel of rest.

These things would be incomprehensible and yet I try to understand them all the same, and I almost succeeded, if not in actually understanding, that is, making entirely my own, an act of the sort, well, at least I manage, so to speak, to *conceive of it*, it forms in my eyes while still remaining mute and awaiting meaning. The preference accorded a dead body rather than a living woman has its point, as fine and subtle as a human hair, but hair can grow thick and strong, never break, still resist years after you're dead, attached to something that is no longer a head but basically a cranium . . . the lack of any heartbeat or scintilla of energy, the immobility, the passivity of the dead body, these are all elements of stimulus toward an act that is thought to be irresistible, that cannot be halted or mitigated, and is therefore a perfect instance for a depiction of fatality. The corpse is the only human figure completely deprived of any will of its own. Not even the most docile and thoroughly subjugated masochist can match a corpse in terms of availability. The caresses of a living body are always restrained or guided by that body's reactions and can't bring you the unrestrained pleasure that you feel as you clutch a corpse to your chest and shower it with amorous effusions. Once you have committed the supreme violence of murder, a world of delicacy may open up, there is no longer any place for brutality: when the body of the obstreperous baby doll finally settles into peace, then you can lavish a thousand caring attentions upon it. There is a story of a man who had taken home a woman's decapitated head, and covered it with kisses, sweetly calling it "my wife."

The pungent desire to see, in contrast with the immobility, a liquid organic spurting on the inanimate body . . .

Like those Japanese perverts who would rape a goose and, just as they were on the verge of coming, cut its head off with a kitchen knife: a perfect synchronicity of pleasure and death.

BACK IN THAT PERIOD, at beach resorts, topless bathing was becoming more common and so, to a lesser extent, even though it had always existed, was nudism. Nudism, however, has the peculiar wrinkle of demanding an adherence that is ideological in nature, while no proclamation needs to be made in order to take off your bikini top, nor do you have to wave any flag other than your own two mammaries, and in fact this way of exposing oneself on the beach has become one of the common habits of the population even in Italy, until it has become so insignificant that it is starting to become almost rare again, I would say, with a tendency specific to generational categories, so that nowadays it is less common to have twenty-year-olds sunbathing with their breasts bared than fifty-year-olds and up, that is, the twenty-year-olds of back then, who were accustomed to doing it in their youth. Far more than nudism, in any case, it was topless sunbathing that shifted the traditional boundaries of feminine shame. Some theorists had hypothesized that the reticence derived from the fact that a woman's genitalia are hidden, practically invisible. Hence the male frenzy to explore them, to violate their secrecy. Let's leave them secret, protected in the darkness between the legs. But the breasts? The pussy may very well be invisible, while the tits can be seen clearly, and when naked, big tits, but also small tits and soft tits and sagging tits, can be spotted from a distance. In spite of efforts at deliberate disattention, it is impossible for a male not to notice them, not to take notice, and even a detached observer like Italo Calvino's Mr. Palomar strolled up and down the beach to peer at them. What was true for a man born in 1923 was also true and remains true now for a man born in 1956. I don't know how things work for the succeeding generations . . .

We get it, you might be saying, we understand. If women must be treated like sexual objects to use and discard, it may be difficult to get aroused unless you render them, in fact, just like objects. Therefore, a woman who speaks, who thinks, who reacts, protests, or weeps can become unbearable, to the point that a rapist has no alternative but to eliminate her.

That said, there can be no doubt that a considerable portion of the pleasure that derives from the sex act consists of the universally, and wrongly, vilified *reification* of your lover's body, as well as your own body, bodies that are broken down in the sex act, fragmented, made wonderfully independent of the whole, restored to the pure material of which they're made and the pure form in which they're shaped, with the individual anatomical details that become autonomous of the general meaning claimed in order to hold together the individual, free even of the identities of those who are participating in the amorous disporting in question. Thanks to this process, the woman lying nude next to you, the curve of her hips, may look like a mountain range, and her breasts may resemble pomegranates, and all the hyperbole of the Canticle of Canticles will fade in comparison, and the metaphors of the Baroque poets and those uttered by Ariel in *The Tempest* will no longer be stupendous rhetorical figures, but objects, real objects, real as only objects can be—things, simple things, matter, pure physical expanse, because that naked body is finally and blessedly an object, which certainly doesn't push us to hold it in disdain, but rather to admire it, cherish it, venerate it. And play with it. Objects weren't made to be destroyed, you know! Unless they fall into the hands of a demented child. More was done during wartime to save objects than human lives! Porcelains and paintings were sealed in lead crates while thousands of children were burned alive with white phosphorus bombs. Are we sure, after all, that it's always and in any case a good thing to be treated like *people* rather than *objects*? It is rare that anyone intentionally destroys a Meissen soup tureen—but how many women have been murdered with malice aforethought? Hatred seems to have an easier time of targeting people.

That is why I jotted down a few lines of a "Hymn to Sexual Reification."

> *Oh, the splendid autonomy of the anatomical parts*
> *of which the body is composed!*
> *To lay one's gaze lightly*
> *for just an instant on his or her neck:*
> *what on earth could this be? We can ask for no greater delight*
> *and in it we swim as if in a boundless sea.*
> *Oh, the wonder of headless torsos in museums!*
> *All the chatter about personality, the integrity*

and inviolability of the individual (but which individual? where?
who??) when quite to the contrary a religious sense
capable of respect toward the human creature
emerges far more powerfully from the anonymous
splendor of a corporeal detail, the hair, a breast
toes and fingers to be gazed upon and kissed, the fissure
between the buttocks and the fold beneath them, fine as a thread . . .
Oh, the dorsal muscles of a man lying facedown!

it is true that a body reduced to a thing is the image that comes closest
to that of a lifeless body . . . for that matter, the sex act has *this* in its destination, desire burns in view of *this*, in *this* it finds its achievement, that is,
in finally feeling itself to be lifeless, exhausted, stripped of all meaning and
higher sentiment to lie as an object among objects, a thing among things,
matter no longer in search of redemption. "Perhaps you and I are no longer
people, but things . . ." says a love poem that compares the beloved's body
to a landscape, to a still life. Otherwise intercourse would be an activity like
any other, useful or fun, productive, while it is the exact opposite of any
productivity and utility. In the case of an actual outcome, a consequence of
the coitus, its productivity is in fact paradoxical, almost a mockery of the
original premise, with a long-term effect that is as spectacular as it is disconcerting: I make love to annihilate myself, and instead I reproduce myself.
I'd like to delete myself and instead I multiply and proliferate. Having joined
together into the same act two such opposing tensions has been considered
by a great many thinkers as a wise deception of nature, the seductive trap
of reproduction. The Romantic pairing of love and death has its polarity
inverted into love and life. Well, okay, I'm not going to argue with that.

THE IRREPLACEABLE FUNCTION of intercourse is to liquidate (at least temporarily) the obsession, at once most catholic and most rational, with the
individual, with the accompanying retinue of qualities, uniqueness, dignity, rights, etc., all those things that are useful to the municipal registry or
in court or at work but which, in bed, are nothing but a deception and a
hindrance. No blessed abandonment is conceded to those who stand watch
on the ramparts of their own personality. Whoever takes that psychological or juridical burden with him under the covers will always sleep alone.
Luckily every so often sex passes by and clears the field, resets the results to
zero, like the great blade of a snowplow. In sex, you start from scratch every

time, that is to say, from your body, this soft machine. Yes, I'm talking about the miracle of people changed into things. If it's not to exploit them, to sell them, or to make them suffer, the fact that people are transformed into things, then where would be the harm in it? Why consider a nightmare something that to me, for instance, is a daily aspiration, perhaps the only truly religious aspiration of my life, that is, to escape from my person? Can it be that anyone should mistake this sacred need for anything abject? To happily become objects: if only! It would take years of practice, not even a Brahmin or a hesychast can do it . . . To become nothing more than a plant, a rock, a desert flower, or rather an apple, no, better yet, that apple's shadow on a windowsill . . .

IT IS INEVITABLE THAT THIS PROCESS entails a risk. These are experiments done on the crater's rim. It may be that you never wake up at all, that a wish is granted whose scope you hadn't really entirely understood in the first place. The suspended animation stretches out until it becomes permanent. That's the risk. The story is told of a personage in antiquity named Hermogenes, who was able to leave his body: his soul wandered through the world as it pleased and only when it was satisfied with all the things it had seen would it return to its home, in his body. What happened, though, was that some bad people noticed this magical ability of Hermogenes, and were jealous of him. So while his soul was out wandering the world, they burned his body. When the soul returned, it found its residence was gone . . . and it fell into despair . . . .

EVERY KEY POSSESSES a combination of cuts that makes it suited to one and only one lock. In the same way, every individual pursues a distinctive form of gratification. As a result, it's almost always impossible to obtain that gratification in perfect accord with someone else, rarely does the required profile match up exactly. Sexual encounters are therefore often frustrating or forced, for at least one of the two lovers, if not for both: you're always a little too high or too low, you make compromises or sacrifices, willingly or unwillingly, you renounce a great deal from the very outset, and other things necessarily along the way. You'd like more or less, faster or maybe slower . . . What with all the compromise, you end up meeting on a sort of no-man's-land, unfamiliar and alien to both of you; if concessions aren't made, then one becomes the mere instrument of the other's pleasure, but when someone is reduced to that state, soon she or he will be destroyed and replaced, worn out and replaced, compared and replaced. Once a human being has sunk to the role of a tool, however sophisticated and functional a tool, they will soon become sheer wreckage.

IMPLICIT IN THE SEX ACT, in any sex act, even the most joyous, is the possibility that it will end with a lifeless body: it's a symbolic possibility, which one can access through the image of the "little death" of the orgasm, and whose catastrophic outcome is continuously grazed, acted out, and at once indicated and concealed in its corporeal nature; you approach it with audacity and recklessness or as a game, and you disengage from it with a shiver; in any case, it's present and up close, as a sort of radiant center to the act itself. However remote or dreamlike it may appear, this possibility of death exists every bit as much as the chance of starting a new life, it hovers on the horizon of possibility, constituting one of the indispensable elements of pleasure: uncertainty. An indicator of precariousness that for this exact reason drives lovers to seize as much, each of the other, as they can. The force of gravity of the sex act attracts opposites, it's the eye of the storm, the center into which all energy is sucked and swallowed: it is there that the squandering of energies is conveyed. That is what the coupling of individuals consists of, this is what their annihilation constitutes: in that bonfire the identities are dissolved and a new one may begin to take shape, only to see the light many months later. Among the countless declensions and gradations of this theme, there are murderous ones, where the possibility of death elsewhere staged as a game suddenly looms as an unexpected outcome, or at an ever purer and more extreme level, when the intention is to kill, and sex serves only as a protocol of execution. Just as the government might use the guillotine or the noose, likewise the single maniac uses the sex act, which alone, it's true, is not sufficient to cause death, but might, so to speak, inaugurate it, it is a preliminary phase just as fasting and ablutions are in certain religious ceremonies that lead to the decisive vision through stations of approach; instead of placating the aggressor, sex only pushes him toward a higher level, the next step, which is murder: it is there that he wanted to arrive right from the beginning. And so, that which lies deep in the sex impulse as an obscure implication, in a form that could barely be distinguished from the other motives, is brought out into the light, purified and powered up, until in the end it's so strong that it can stand out against the background where it was resting, it becomes entirely autonomous, in fact, it becomes its exact opposite, its negative stand-in, its own double. This is how inside the erotic universe (and not outside it, as people tend to think) a zone is created where, in place of reciprocal joy and pleasure, what triumphs is death. Death, which is nothing other than the hidden fold, the minor key of the act of love, which turns into a dominant chord.

IN ANY CASE, it's still a dismemberment. The dissection of the female body undertaken by the photographic gaze, in pornography every bit as much as in artistic photography. Pieces of woman, obscene and slobbery and painted red or else icy like marble in the stupendously grainy imagery of the masters of the black-and-white print: the objective is different, but the process of decomposition is quite similar.

THAT ANATOMICAL DETAIL you see so close up, during the sex act, isn't a thing, nor is it a person. It's something alive that however possesses no individuality. Although it is shaped in a particular form, a breast, an ear, a nipple, the veins that pulse in an arm or in the erect male member or that can be glimpsed beneath the translucent fair white flesh, the peach fuzz, the pubic hair, the belly button, an ass cheek, an asshole spasmodically contracting or gaping open, the eye beneath its eyebrow, aren't really all that different from every other eye, buttock, wrist, asshole. Really, they could belong to anyone, and this is the source of their infinite wonder: in the fact that they're impersonal. I'm not saying they're *all the same*, but rather that they *belong to no one*. Sex renders those who practice it beatifically anonymous, as they writhe intertwined and the horizon of their vision is wide open; or in the blank relaxation that ensues after their spasms. When you exhibit, when you expose or hand over your nude body, the person disappears, swallowed up by their own physicality. They are ready to be taken by another, by their gaze or their hands, seized, possessed, rejected, used, or abandoned. In an advanced civilization, where slavery does not exist and minors are supposed to be protected from the abuses of adults, this is the only occasion in which you can take possession of an individual. *Make it mine*, as you might say of an inanimate object. Because you cannot possess people, only things, there would be no reciprocal possession if lovers didn't deliver themselves into each other's hands. It's by becoming a thing in another person's hands that you allow him or her to fully become a person, that is, a subject capable of exercising possession. By being possessed you allow the elevation of rank of the person possessing you: by losing your individuality, your own name, you allow the other to acquire it, as if by some miracle. Whether this exchange (person for thing, thing for person: I became a thing in order to make you a person) is the result of violence and abuse or is done as an act of free will, a loving exchange, or else as a pure exercise of perversion, none of that changes its substance, only its modality: being treated as an object, then, can be a wonderful experience or a risky form of fun or a human being's worst nightmare.

> Anyone who has never seen you nude cannot understand
> what a landscape really is, what the profile
> of mountains and rivers, and canyons, the immense plain
> of flesh stretched between the iliac crests
> now brown now white or speckled with snow
> depending on which season is passing overhead.
> Pure phenomenon, pure material, laid out, stripped bare
> by years of eroticism of every sense:
> and yet, yes, that famous poem about the giantess
> ("To wander over her huge forms . . .
> To sleep nonchalantly in the shadow of her superb breasts . . ." etc.)
> now indeed I remember it and even, a little, understand it.

> Perhaps you and I are no longer people, but things.

THE CONSEQUENCES OF THIS PROCESS of reification can lead so far that you can never retrace your steps. Since people can always be reduced to things, while things can never become people (at least not until we have thinking robots, but I mean genuinely thinking ones), the number of things in the world is constantly increasing. To keep this number from becoming overwhelming, many things are *eliminated*. Like junked cars, tossed into dumps. The same thing happens with people: first we arrange to reduce them to objects, then we eliminate them on account of their status as things, that is, discrediting them as no longer having anything human about them. This is the circuit of degradation that mortifies beings so that we can then hold them in contempt for having been reduced to this state. If a body is available as a thing, then that means it is interchangeable, whereupon we can confidently dispose of it. If we can do what we like with something, then it no longer has any intrinsic worth.

THERE, that anatomical detail becomes a portentous battery in which it is possible to store up endless amounts of pleasure or pain, real or imaginary. What renders sacred any given portion of a man's or a woman's anatomy is precisely its impersonality, its anonymity, like that of the marble torsos you see in museums, often far more admirable than the entire bodies. What do we care if it's a Hercules, rather than any other god or hero? The intertwining of the muscles, the density of the flesh, the hemisphere of the buttock of a Callipygian Venus—all these things have lost contact with the original name, history, and meaning.

IN THE SAME WAY that in medieval statuary the hands and the eyes and the face were out of proportion with the rest of the body because through them the sculptor depicted the spirituality of the man, and artists back then cared more about meaning than optical appearances, likewise pornography is very attentive to meanings, it takes little interest in the realism of the entire human figure, and instead deforms the anatomy, with the selection of a certain lens or a startling close-up, emphasizing the parts and the moments in the purest, most stylized state: the cock, female orifices, a mouth gaping open, the spurting semen.

MOTIVES FOR AN ERECTION can be found by the dozens. Every young male builds up over time—more or less entrusting himself to random chance, or else through a pedantic quest—an iconography made up of bodies and details of bodies, especially the exclusively feminine parts, that is, the breasts. The tits. The big tits. The great big boobs. And he learns to direct his excitement, his arousal, to that anatomical gallery, to devote to it his erections, which at first occurred in a chaotic, disorganized fashion: by so doing, little by little, he acquires the certainty of his actual sexual tastes. The same thing happens with prayer and sacrifice, which are primordial impulses but, at first, aren't well directed. You feel the need to pray but you don't know to whom, especially because frequently the gods are the recipients of an offering that exists prior to them: first comes the offering and then you decide who to dedicate it to, just as first comes the erection and then you create a gallery of bodies to which that erection will be devoted. Those bodies aren't the cause, they are just the destination. You can have a stiff dick out of anger or fear, while riding a sled, drawing a tree, hearing a report of gunfire, being called to the blackboard, while reading Mickey Mouse or Roy Rogers, running after the family cat to stomp on its tail, when the news vendor gives you the wrong change, or while a skin forms on your milk at breakfast when it gets too hot. Fear and desire mingle, and they always will.

If you choose the tits, it's because they are the obvious emblems of femininity, and they are assumed to qualify as a male, beyond the shadow of a doubt, anyone who is attracted to them.

... *THE NUDES OF THOSE YEARS are hardly ever fully nude, stark naked, in the sense that you never see the body stripped bare from head to foot: instead it is garbed in articles considered seductive, nylon stockings, fishnet stockings, baseball socks and tennis ankle socklets, white socks and leg warmers rolled down on the calves, yes, lots and lots of leg warmers indicating the hard work done in the gym to get a body like that, and work on the bar to make it this firm yet graceful ... dance slippers or gym shoes ... or else corsets, bustiers, garter belts, lace ... lace and embroidery, everywhere ... thick, dark furs used as a bedcover upon which the candy-pink or snowy-white body stands out, lazily nude ... and, around the neck, scarves, shawls, bandanas, chokers, necklets, tight collars or pearl necklaces, or heavy collars strung with large stones, or geometric objects dangling between the breasts, practically down to the navel, and even farther down, all the way to the luxuriant pubic area, lots and lots of necklaces in every size and shape ... and the abdomen gleefully crisscrossed with objects designed to break its continuity, like leather belts, bathrobe sashes and nightgown ties, ribbons, suspenders, men's neckties, towels and sheets draped over the body as if in some mischievous coquettish burst of modesty ... the shoulders almost never uncovered, but instead half dressed by skimpy blouses or translucent camisoles, and ballet wraps and boleros thrown open to show off the overexuberant breasts ... checkered cowgirl blouses fetchingly knotted at the waist, even though right above that knot the tits made the buttons pop open ... over which in some cases tumble the adorable blond braids of a country girl, the residue of innocence lost or never even known ... fringed capelets and Indian buckskin bikini tops and hippie halters, always shoved aside by those insolent perky breasts ... and on their heads were those big floppy-brimmed hats, canvas sun visors or transparent plastic shades, terry-cloth sun hats, ushankas, woolen ski caps ...*

16

T HE MONSTER BY OMISSION remains indifferent to everything but a
single detail, a portion of the anatomy. Female virginity intimidates
him, challenges him, and only encourages him to use violence in order to get out of the impasse which that virginity itself represents for him.
To rape a virgin demands a determination that you can't have unless you
have the ferocity to go with it. In the face of virginity, a perverted man gets
excited, gets vexed, and runs the risk of impotence. At that point he will make
use of any means or instrument if it allows him to act upon that body, which
he can't leave as it is. What may well be the most chilling circumstance of
the reports and the transcripts: when you run into phrases in quotation
marks such as "ravaged with a broom handle" or "the insertion of a beer
bottle," as if using objects instead of the sex organ to penetrate the victim
were an indication of a particular savagery and determination, which is
probably true, but it also constitutes a facilitation of the act, and not just an
amplification of the cruelty. You might say that taking someone's virginity
with a tool or an object denatures and more clearly reveals the nonerotic
nature of the deflowering: the intention becomes more unmistakable, the
fact that it has very little to do with the gratification of an instinct but instead resembles nothing so much as a ceremony, sadistic and necessary.
Just as in certain primitive communities a special tool was used, a horn or
a bone, to ensure that the initiation of femininity was performed by no
single person but in a certain sense by the community as a whole, likewise
the impotent rapist girds himself to the task of deflowering as it were a
mission that exceeded his physical strength, and uses other means to break
the seal, to render profane, that is, to give back to the world, from which it
had heretofore been withheld, that portion of the feminine anatomy that
stood for innocence, symbolizing it and with it the fact that the whole person was unsuited to society. Something powerfully anonymous is at work
in the rapist's act, a force that goes well beyond his desires, certainly awakened by his arousal and his own personal lack of scruples, but not explica-
ble solely by those factors. It's a sort of fatalism, as if deep down he thought
of himself as an executor, someone who implements a mandate. Through

him cruel and ineluctable laws find their implementation. This has nothing to do with the "quest for pleasure." Indeed, rapists almost view it as a job. A job that has to be done. In other words, someone's going to have to do it, and so they roll up their sleeves and get it done. Putting on the leather apron worn by serial murderers, made famous by the movies. In the letter in which he first signed himself "Jack the Ripper," dated September 28, 1888, the unknown killer, who before then had been dubbed by the popular press Leather Apron, insists on using work-related formulations: the last job, do a bit more work, I love my work . . . job and work, these are the recurring words, work and job, that is, a task he performs scrupulously, out of a sense of duty. Since his identity never has been uncovered, the Ripper remains, so to speak, a collective figure, anyone can don his mask and apron, remaining anonymous while still impersonating his salient features, the ferocity and the gratuitousness of his acts and, at the same time, the inscrutable necessity of his work, his contempt for the law, in other words, all the traits that made him a popular character. Exactly, *popular*, a popular murderer, popular precisely because he was despicable. Despicability is a garnish to fame, not its antidote. For those reasons, the character of Jack the Ripper will never die. He lurks in the heart of everyday life.

17

TO DIE IMMEDIATELY after losing your virginity. To die as you're losing it. The site of fecundity associated with the time of the funeral rite. A grape crushed and pressed can represent a life being born and a life coming to an end. Nuptials are blood nuptials, nuptials with death, like the nuptials of Persephone, sucked back down into the underworld with Hades, the god who welcomes many souls. The girl passes from one dominion to the other without intermediate phases. Hades rends asunder the earth in order to offer Persephone a kingdom bursting with wealth, and with fear: the offering is so rich and dangerous that it sweeps away the woman for whom it was meant. We are aghast, overwhelmed. All understanding is steeped in panic. If this transition to awareness is inevitable, then it may seem legitimate or even necessary to shorten the timeline, with a burst of violence. A brutal act may even seem more honest than indulging a stream of saccharine endearments, waltzes and daisy chains of deceptive words . . . to wean the girl, kicking her out of the nest, cutting short her fantasies in no uncertain terms, her naïve hopes and dreams.

"NOW YOU'RE A WOMAN." "When you lay down on the meadow you were a little girl / but when you got up you were a woman." That's what people said of a girl after she had her virginity taken. Or else she said it of herself, "I am a woman now," in songs. That was the exact expression in Italy back then: to take someone's virginity, or have it taken, almost like having a wisdom tooth removed to keep it from crowding the rest of your teeth.

There is a special ferocity taken out on a virgin girl, as if they wished to punish her for her pride or for her naïveté in choosing to remain one, for having cultivated her virtue. Virtue is seriously a reason for misfortune, when it encounters its enemies, who are bound and determined to make it pay dearly, as we have said, with a paradoxical pedagogical intent. Virtue shown off ends up becoming a "splendid sin." For that matter, there seems to be no way out for women: they are raped either because they tempt men or because they reject men. Both attitudes are considered provocative. Except, in the first case, they are punished by going along with what seemed to be their wish, only taking it beyond all reason; in the second case, they are punished by having taken from them what they had so strenuously defended. The goal is the same, whether it is shamelessly offered or jealously denied: to a man eager to punish a woman, the objective actually doesn't interest him all that much, only as a pretext for inflicting a punishment.

18

A FUNDAMENTAL PSYCHIC RUPTURE COMING on the heels of a negligible physical laceration. This happened to me once, with a German girl, experiencing both phases of this passage, but over a considerable span of time. The interval between made the experience extraordinary. Usually, you meet a virgin girl and then you either leave her as she is or else you make love with her and together with her you experience the passage from the life that precedes to the life that follows. The girl will get up no longer a virgin (that is, deprived of something, and yet completed by that privation).

But I experienced the following, rather improbable adventure. I beg you to believe me when I swear that it really happened to me, exactly as I am going to tell you. And the reason I'm telling it is that I believe it has something to do with the other stories gathered in this book, which all have to do with the spilling of blood, like Freud's famous anecdote from his study on the lapsus, what came to be known as the Freudian slip.

. . . EXORIARE ALIQUIS NOSTRIS EX OSSIBUS ULTOR . . . (Let an avenger arise from my bones . . .)

HER NAME WAS BETTINA. I've had four German girlfriends in my life and three of them were called Bettina. She was eighteen when I met her, I might have been twenty-three. We were in Salamanca, Spain, where I had won a scholarship for summer studies, and she had come to study Spanish. She was very pretty, her hair blond and silky, and there was a small space between her two upper front teeth, which gave her a sweet and slightly childish smile, as if her family had decided not to get them straightened with orthodontics, intentionally leaving her with that mouth of a child. In her case, the family mattered, it mattered a great deal. Bettina in fact was the youngest daughter of a hero of the Second World War. A fighter pilot who had been awarded the Iron Cross at the age of twenty-two for his extraordinary courage. Bettina would tell me about him as she lay stretched out naked in the bed of my dorm room, arms wrapped around me, after I had tried in vain to take her virginity, I had tried, I had given it my utmost determination. I really liked Bettina a lot, and she aroused me, I had tried gently but decisively, but as I began to penetrate her, she would moan with the pain. "It hurts! It hurts so much!" she would moan, because even though she was there to improve her Spanish, which for that matter she already spoke fluently, with that enchanting German accent which was not the least of the reasons—along with her beautiful eyes, her breasts firm and erect, and the impalpable blond peach fuzz that covered her all over like a pelt and in the hollow of her sex only grew a shade denser—that I liked Bettina so very much, whenever we were with other people we spoke Spanish, but between us, in English. It was easier, more direct. "It hurts!!" she would complain, as soon as I so much as began to push into her. And this happened once, twice, three times, ten times, sobbing and wriggling out of my arms, until I had even thought of trying to hold her still by the arms, pinning her down with all my weight and thrusting it in by force, but then I hadn't had the nerve. And so after a week of doughty attempts we'd given up: we'd lock ourselves in the bedroom, we'd take off our clothes, we'd embrace and kiss, but went no further than that. I remember my sex organ, swollen to immense size with my arousal, after an hour of these hugs and kisses. To have a beautiful caring young woman in your arms, naked, but not make love with her (it seems to me we didn't have recourse to any other solution as an alternative to penetration, I don't remember ever coming on her or in her hands, and I'd fleetingly kissed her between the legs just to try to soften the obstacle that barred the way to that dingus of ordinary size but which, in effect, did appear outsized with respect to the minuscule fissure just lightly dusted with blond peach fuzz, indeed, perhaps that was the only real reason, to feel the tickle of that fuzz on my lips, that I had knelt over her, and never for more than a few seconds at a time), to hold that German delight in my arms without making love with her remains one of the most heartbreaking sensations that I've ever experienced in my life, and in fact it created an indelible memory in me, a memory that resurfaces every time that chance establishes a random connection between words and images such as girl—Germany—blondness—pain.

I REMEMBER THAT AMONG THE GODDESSES of antiquity there are some who will forever remain virgins, such as Athena or Artemis. They are unwilling to come into contact with males, and we ought to spend a moment considering the reason, certainly no accident, that the first goddess to abhor all sexual contact should be the daughter of Intelligence and the second should reign over the boundary between the civilized world and the world of savagery. Then there are goddesses that, in contrast, seem to know and belong to their spouse, whether that is spouse singular (Hera with Zeus) or spouses plural (Aphrodite), as if they had always been possessed by them. They know what sex is, what a male is, and they seek him out incessantly, either to mate with him or to prevent him from mating with other females. Only one deity, Persephone, changes her condition, from virgin to bride, she alone passes through and personifies the phases of female life, which in the other female deities are alternative, either/or. (How could there be a goddess of love who remains chaste? Or a huntress with offspring?)

And now we come to the second phase of Bettina's sex life. As much of it as I know about, of course. I beg you to believe me when I tell you that the further portion of the story I'm about to tell you, like the part I've told you thus far, and in general all the stories, with the exception of a few minor details, collected in this book, is true, it really happened, it actually took place . . . somewhere, at some moment in time and someplace on earth, if not to me, to someone, which makes the task of telling it so easy and agreeable to me. This book is so quick to write that not even a god could keep up with the dictation. Am I exaggerating? Perhaps a little, but it's much easier to write when what you're writing is the truth. And nothing is invented except for a few passages here and there, transitions that memory has deleted or ignorance has left obscure, or imagination has now taken upon itself the pleasant task of developing as it pleases: not lying, not twisting the tale, but rather magnifying: a detail, a face, a series of exchanges, the place where certain characters met, which might be lifted up and flown from one location to another, just like the house of the Virgin Mary, which from Nazareth was transported by angels to Loreto.

I ran into Bettina again, by pure chance, in Rome, a year and a half after my futile attempts to work my way into her womb in Salamanca. Her crotch remains one of the most enchanting things I've ever seen in my life: and a woman's pudendum isn't always so charming. Most of the time, it's a rather anodyne thing. Those who claim that women are inferior to men always bring up, as a visual example, the insignificance of their sex organ, its virtual invisibility, in other words, the fact that it *doesn't seem to be there*. It's an old argument, so I'm bringing it up again. But Bettina's was simply wonderful, although also impenetrable. And the opportunity I was afforded to try to enter it again was an extraordinary one.

I happened to be at Piazza del Popolo—yes, I know, what could be more obvious, a clichéd tourist stop, but that's exactly where I happened to be, on that large and beautiful piazza, sitting on the steps of the church that's on your right as you look down Via del Corso, right at the corner of Via di Ripetta, and I was talking to a friend of mine who was a painter, about some artistic topic, focusing on the words being spoken while at the same time distracted by the usual spectacle of the piazza, which is a common characteristic of many intellectual conversations that take place in a setting already fully charged with beauty; you talk, you listen, you try to follow the thread of the reasoning, but in the meantime your eyes are captivated by something that contradicts, cancels, or outdoes what you're saying. This happens all the time in Rome, it's part of the constant dialectic between the unparalleled results achieved in the past and the muddled apprenticeship of those who stroll through an artistic creation, knowing that they've already lost before they start fighting. Beaten, yes, but not humiliated, indeed, almost consoled, as if the young artist could feel at least a little bit of the force that crushes him, vibrating inside him as he's borne down to the ground and swept away.

I was sitting on the steps with a painter friend of mine, talking, I believe, about conceptual art, when I felt someone embrace me from behind, or perhaps merely touch me on the shoulder but in a way that struck me as an embrace, as warm and unsettling as an embrace. And it was Bettina, whose face appeared from above and whose blond hair spilled over my own. She told me that she had stopped to talk with us only to ask a question, to get directions, and not because she had recognized me. In fact, she had a tourist map in her hand and a girlfriend at her side, the classic girlfriend you travel with, the kind you go around visiting monuments with and letting local boys try to pick you up, and they were a pair, as were, in fact, the painter and I. But I didn't need to try to pick up Bettina, I'd already taken care of that, two summers ago, in Salamanca, I'd already chatted her up, foolishly and seductively, I'd already kissed and undressed her. And we had rolled and tumbled for hours on a single bed. From the moment I saw her she seemed different to me. I don't know if she was prettier or less pretty, but certainly far from the ethereal maiden I had repeatedly attempted to deflower in the Castilian dorm room, before giving up that quest as too challenging, because in order to achieve it would have demanded either an extra dollop of patience, a specific skill, or perhaps a brutality that I did not appear to possess. Perhaps I only needed to ignore her pleas to desist ("Please, stop . . . It hurts so much!"). Anyway, Bettina was thrilled and excited about our chance meeting. And so was I. But perhaps I can analyze my own excitement better than I can hers. She seemed to be brimming over with joy and astonishment. I felt oddly at fault, as if I owed her an apology of some kind, and also a little worried, worried, I mean to say, about what to do next; unsettled by that beautiful young woman whom fate had brought back in touch with my life for the second time now, at a distant point in Europe. And on that exact spot in Rome. In those days it was common practice to meet with friends to discuss topics you cared about, topics that we seriously thrashed out, studying them, weighing them, delving deep, and in the absence of any real masters, we wound up teaching one another. Those who knew a little more about something would deliver improvised lectures, quite frequently holding forth on a set of steps, seated in the sunshine that in Rome allows these open-air lessons as early as March and as late as the end of November. Our favorite steps were the immense ones, vast and deserted, seemingly built expressly to stimulate discussions on topics of an aesthetic nature, in front of the Gallery of Modern Art, in Valle Giulia, or else the steps in front of some of the less popular churches, such as Santi Pietro e Paolo al Celio, San Gregorio, likewise on the Caelian Hill, or the one on the slopes of Monte Caprino, I don't remember what it's called. Out-of-the-way places in the city, in certain cases practically abandoned (the plaza in front of San Gregorio scattered with condoms dumped there by those who come to fuck in their cars after sunset), well, if that day I were to have decided to arrange to meet in one of the usual places with my painter friend, I'd never have seen Bettina again, and the last image I would have cherished of her, enchanting even if it was the fruit of a failure, is that of her naked on the narrow bed of my dorm room in Salamanca, as she lay with one arm flung crosswise over her eyes, a melancholy pose that how-ever perfectly highlighted the silhouette of her proud breasts, spilling to-gether, almost jostling each other, as she wept silently in mourning for having failed to make love with me, because I hadn't been able to make love with her: a young Italian, healthy, dark-haired, virile, and a mag-nificent young German woman, blond, lithe, passionate, the two of us to-gether had been incapable of doing something that was, after all, so simple, so ordinary, managing to insert one of us into the other, fitting together two parts of our bodies, complementary in size and shape, one into the other, however willing and even frantic to do so we might have been; and the tears dripped from beneath her arm onto her chin and neck. She was ashamed, and I was ashamed too, my virile obstinacy evidently much weaker than her own desire to put her condition as an as-yet-untouched maiden behind her. My determination only went so far, I was happy enough with Bettina the way she was, a virgin in spite of herself, sad and weeping and beautiful, and I'd be able to handle the fact that I hadn't fucked her, that we hadn't fucked, that our fucking hadn't happened (three ways of teasing out the exact same verb, indicating three actions, each dif-ferent from the others—and which in any case had *not* been accomplished), I was still happy with the way things had gone, because of her beauty, which made up for everything. Yes, it may ring contrary to all logic, but I might be happy to give a very beautiful woman a kiss or just touch her breast, or to see her naked, naked just for me, even without being able to have sex with her, maybe because I'm a fucking aesthete, some might say a half–ass wanker, or half-a-queer; while a less beautiful woman, or a woman who is not beautiful at all, not even pretty, or even ugly, well, with that woman it's practically a duty to fuck her, I mean, you are duty-bound to fuck her once you've started the procedure involved in doing so, it's not acceptable, there is no way you can settle for failing to achieve that result, once you've put it on your agenda, however incautiously you may have done so. The luminous beauty of Bettina's naked body was, on the one hand, an abundantly rich reward for my eyes, almost too lavish in a sense; and on the other hand, it induced a state of serenity in me, a delicacy, something verging on a melancholy languor, in other words, an array of sensations by no means ideal for someone running up against challenges in the quest to deflower a young woman.

BUT THERE, on Piazza del Popolo, we couldn't immediately state in explicit terms the most obvious thing. And what would that be? That we were going to give it another try. That we *had* to try again. There was no other way to interpret that extraordinary coincidence than as an obligation, a clear and precise commandment to go to bed together once again, and this time to enter one into the other. It is upon this idea, and upon this physical, me- chanical detail, upon penetration, that the very concept of sexual inter- course is based, from a point of view that may be, varying from one case to another, symbolic, juridical, emotional, as is shown by dozens of illustri- ous instances; I don't know why but I know that's the way it is, that's the way it works, that's how we talk about it, and until we had completed the story with the penetration of my sex into hers (oops! by mistake I just wrote: of *her* sex into *mine*), it was as if none of this had ever happened, that it had merely been a dream or a trumped-up claim. Anyway, we immediately made a date to meet that evening, but since we had to conceal the real rea- son for our meeting, and since she couldn't ignore the duties of friendship, the date was with her and her friend, whom Bettina could hardly leave all alone on that first evening, which, as far as I was able to determine, was also the only night they'd be spending in Rome, since the very next day they were planning to leave the city. To depart. Heading for some other fucking city brimming over with art. Which meant I was going to have to procure a partner, a date for her girlfriend. That was demanded by the protocols of the time: libertine our customs may have been, but not excessively so, lib- ertine but still drawn on the foundations of the old and well-established schema of a mirror image: a couple of girls + a couple of boys. So I invited the painter to join us, though at first he was reluctant to come . . .

In a flash, as I was saying goodbye to her, a number of images from our incomplete sexual relations flashed through my mind. I'll spare the reader, given their sheer awkwardness, the efforts I made with my fingers to open a passage into Bettina.

THE EVENING WAS PRACTICALLY A DISASTER. The dinner, with me as the half-hearted chef: pasta, salami, and salad. The painter was nervous and spoke in a ridiculous manner the various languages in which the conversation unfolded, in dribs and drabs, whereas I could think of nothing but the moment when the others would finally leave and only Bettina would remain, and all the while she smiled at me shyly, and yet, I could have sworn, with a hint of mischief, looking at me in a way that was utterly different from her gaze of two summers earlier. The change that had come over her was as subtle as it was spectacular. In Salamanca she spoke very little, her voice slow and raucous, with that faint accent that made every sentence she uttered sound pure and naïve, at least to my ears, steeped as they were in lessons on German Romanticism, but at the time that had seemed like a sign of shyness if not actually candor. Her lovely appearance was matched by an extreme simplicity of thought and manner, and it was with that simplicity that she spoke to me as, for a while, we abandoned our less and less determined and increasingly sporadic efforts to fuck, instead just lying there, intertwined, kissing and caressing, in spite of the intrusive and persistently bulky presence of my member, which simply would not deflate, prompting a series of "Oh, pardon me," "No, please pardon *me*," and her blushes whenever it slapped against her or was bumped by accident or popped between us like the third that interrupts company and makes a crowd, determined at all costs to get attention, and at that point we tried, as the expression goes, to "get to know each other a little better," and since we had proved to be unable to do so carnally, at least we could do so in words, and what she did in particular was to ask me a series of very basic questions full of genuine curiosity, about myself, my family, my brother, and my sister, what their names were, the color of their hair, the hue of their complexions, astonished to learn that they were fair-skinned, and about Italy, and Rome, and why I had chosen to study languages other than German, while I, to tell the truth, aside from the story of the twenty-two-year-old fighter pilot enthusiastically tilting his Messerschmitt into a power dive against the British bombers (I can just picture him, his hair buzz-cut high on the nape of his neck, icy-cold eyes, absolute contempt for danger, atavistic, inborn familiarity with death), could sincerely not care less about everything concerning Bettina's place of origin and the schools she attended or the plans she was nurturing for her future, about all *that* I cared nothing, or really, less than nothing: I was interested in *her*, that's right, her and her alone, at that moment, in my bed, and if anything I thrilled to the extravagant idea that I was holding in my arms the last-born daughter, brought into the world by mistake, sired by a weary, fanatical hero, old and defeated but covered from head to toe with medals, while she lay there, defenseless and white as snow in my arms, eager to allow herself to be run through by a strapping young southerner who seemed not to be up to the task: how stupid I was, how I liked this contrast, I even luxuriated in the objectively frustrating fact that I had been unable to complete my task, so that I richly deserved a bit of scorn, like a knight unhorsed, his lance shattered along with his pride. This impotence, in fact, struck me as romantic, the absolute obstacle laid between our union, as if a razor-sharp sword had been placed between us to halt our lust, a fact that had united us more than any mere act of intercourse could have. Her adamantine sex had emerged intact from the ordeal of reciprocal desire. The maiden's frenzy added to the youth's lust had produced a neoclassical statue in the mold of Cupid and Psyche.

At age twenty-three, your every thought gallops recklessly off in all directions, toward the horizon and beyond, all manner of senseless pursuits offer a fascinating, adventurous side, which only later will appear for what it truly is, complete crap, by the cruel light of adulthood.

BUT NOW BETTINA WAS CALMER, more direct and, at the same time, more complicated, grown up in a sort of awareness that even made her look physically bigger, taller, perhaps even prettier. The delicacy that I had come to know and touch in Spain had evaporated from her, and what had been then a vague albeit intense desire had been transformed into a very precise will. We glanced at and watched each other frequently, in silence, our smiles abounding in tacit messages, while the two other guests labored to carry on the evening's socializing, in bits and pieces, a get-together that need never have taken place, a pointless picture frame that we had insisted on placing for the sake of convention around an image that could so easily have done without it, radiant and promising as it was, a picture of our miraculous new Roman encounter; and especially her friend, Heidi, who on any other occasion I would have considered really likable, and in her way, attractive, though she was very skinny and ridiculously tall and freckly and a little bit mannish, the redheaded Heidi talked and told stories, waving her arms and laughing, a vast array of amusing anecdotes and adventures she'd had as she traveled the world, and she made it clear that she knew lots of things, had traveled to various countries, had tried nearly all the drugs there were and dabbled in a wide variety of sexual experiences, or perhaps I should say, experiments, to which she unfailingly referred in an ironic tone, as so many minor accidents or mishaps along the way that still had been worth living (this more or less summed up the dominant philosophy of the time: anything I might do or get up to, I will own up to it later, I won't deny it: whether good or bad, it was in any case *an experience*. Recklessness, therefore, elevated to a cognitive method. Those who survived all that can, in fact, boast precisely of the fact that they survived it and can recount the stories in a memorable manner: that time they injected who knows what shit into their veins, that other time they fucked eight people in a single night, or how they tailed a stranger to give a report on their habits to whoever would later shoot them. All of them liminal adventures, the kind of thing that leaves a mark on whoever experiences them, that become human and inhuman personal baggage, so that if someone manages to surface, of course, not to drown in it, be overwhelmed by it, if they don't lose their mind or get sick or die or end their days in prison, and even if they do, then one day I'll tell the story . . .), and from the anecdotes that she told, in just twenty-one years of life Heidi really must have gotten up to just about everything imaginable, and all the while my friend the painter tried to keep up with her, to come up with retorts that showed how incredulous and ironic he was in response, though he was hindered in that attempt by his school-taught English and his jury-rigged French, both languages that Heidi spoke fluently and comfortably. Up to a certain point, the painter kept pace with the young German woman, trying in fact to come off as even more extremist, more nihilistic, and more world-weary than she was, jamming his foot down on the accelerator, answering everything she said with expressions that were even more virulent and radical, or more comical, and overlaying the laughter she produced as accompaniment to her stories with loud sarcastic bursts of hilarity, then all at once there seemed to be a shift in his mood, or rather, in his direction, as if he'd suddenly veered around and headed the opposite way, as if, having failed to outdo her in the field of her choice, he had decided to veer around on the opposite bearing.

Heidi had spoken of her father, in a grotesque manner, as a megalomaniac Sixty-Eighter, a child of the revolutionary year of 1968, a stunningly handsome man but an utter failure.

"Hey, listen, 1968 wasn't such a failure," my friend retorted.

"Oh, it wasn't? You ought to take a look at my father. That would change your mind. Or maybe not, seeing that you kind of resemble each other."

Bettina nodded with a grin, and the painter clearly didn't care for the comparison.

"That's who you reminded me of, now that I stop to think . . ." Heidi went on, "*mein Papa* . . . and you're pretty easy on the eyes yourself, as men go, and you will be for another four or five years, but after that . . ."

"Why, how old is he now?"

"Thirty-nine."

"So he was just a kid when he . . ."

"When he had the misbegotten idea of bringing me into this world, with that misbegotten wretch of a mother of mine!"

"Listen, if he hadn't believed in certain ideas, you wouldn't have been able to lead the life you have," said the painter, suddenly serious, in an almost grave tone.

"Why, what kind of life have I lived?" Heidi asked, and then laughed.

Bettina laughed, too, and looked over at me.

"Well, a pretty nice life . . ."

"Are you saying I'm unprincipled?"

Heidi had used the English word, "unprincipled." I had to explain it to my friend.

"The life I lead is a free one," said Heidi.

"Sure. Maybe it's too free. Certain people can't handle too much freedom."

"That's a nice reactionary thought."

"Well, who knows, maybe I've become a reactionary . . . but it's not as if I'm ashamed of it."

"Don't you like freedom anymore?" Bettina asked him.

"I like the kind of freedom you conquer for yourself."

"And you did a lot of fighting, didn't you?" Heidi prodded him, having the time of her life mocking him. "And now you're tired."

"I'm not tired in the least . . . it's just that . . ."

"Isn't this, after all, the best of all possible worlds?" Heidi asked, clapping her hands.

"Maybe so . . . well, yes, the least worst, anyway," the painter said, hesitantly, using an old piece of Italian slang, unexpectedly compliant, in part because he couldn't be certain what Heidi was driving at with her logical leaps. Bettina looked at me and shook her head. Her glistening eyes told

me that she had other things in mind, but that matters would have to follow their course. I, too, thought that it was right, all things considered, to
waffle.

"What I mean to say is, there are certain attitudes that just annoy me,
there, I said it. *Stop.*" The painter ended his sentence in English with the
word "stop," which in the context made little sense. It's time that I say his
name. It was Santo Spatola.

The two German girls exchanged a glance and put their hands over their
mouths. When Heidi took her hand away, she was no longer smiling, her
lips were compressed, a stern look on her face.

"But in that case, excuse me, if you ultimately just think I'm a whore,
then why do you defend the morality of those who taught me to be one, that
is, my father and mother?"

"I don't understand," he said, confused, and he really hadn't understood
a thing.

AROUND TWO IN THE MORNING, they left. But Bettina went with them, and
I was shocked. I neither made a gesture nor uttered a word to keep her from
going, as I accompanied them all to the front door and said good night,
that's how stunned I was. It meant that up till then I really hadn't understood a single thing: What she wanted that night wasn't to be with me, so
what *did* she want? What had been the meaning of the looks we had given
each other at the dinner table? As soon as they left, it started raining. The
windows rattled with thunderclaps. Perplexed, tired, and half drunk, determined not to wallow in doubts and self-interrogations, which I preferred
to put off till the following day, I undressed and, after wandering around
the apartment in a state of stunned confusion, I got into bed.

That's the way it had gone, it was pointless to rack my brains over it,
though my overexcited mind refused to obey and, as I lay there in my bed,
it continued to spew out hypotheses, images, memories, and fantasies about
the German girl. In particular, I would say figures, figures of her, of her
hair, her lips, the impalpable golden fuzz that covered her body . . .

I HAD BEEN ASLEEP for half an hour when I heard someone knocking on
the door, and I woke up. Those were definitely knocks on the door, not bolts
of thunder, because the thunderstorm had ended and by this point all it was
doing was raining, with a light dense buzzing of drops, in that uniform

manner that can go on for hours. I got up and went to answer the door. It was Bettina, drenched from head to foot. I let her in, took her to my bedroom, took off her dripping clothing, ushered her into my bed, and then lay down on top of her to warm her up, since she was cold as ice; the minute she opened her legs, I slid right into her. My member had already been hard even before she got there, while I was sleeping. After a while, her body had warmed up and softened. Bettina still had a tight, narrow opening, as she had in Salamanca, but now I could fit inside her completely: still, I felt the need to check and see that this wasn't just a mistaken sensation on my part, so I reared up, straightening my back until I rose almost vertically above her and looked down at where our two sexes were joined, lifting her thighs and then crushing them down atop her, but not to penetrate her more deeply, which is the usual objective of assuming that position, but only to see whether it was really happening, that I really was all the way inside her.

"I'VE HAD A BOYFRIEND for the past year, in Bochum, and he is dear to my heart. He's handsome, too. He's my same age. I never had any difficulties with him, I mean to say, no difficulties in making love. The first time, it happened immediately, and it didn't hurt me. Since then I've been in love with him, and he loves me. Whereas I had no special connection with you. I liked you, but that was all. I liked you a lot. Maybe that's why we weren't able to do it. I'd like to go on loving him in the same way, if I'm able. Now I really care about him, and I'm sorry to betray him. That's why I left your place, earlier. Heidi was glaring at me and she told me, 'You're crazy, completely crazy!' and I felt like crying. I no longer knew what I wanted, whether to leave or go back . . . We walked toward the bus stop while Heidi went on scolding me, as if I'd committed some terrible mistake, 'No, but really, I already have a boyfriend!' I objected, but she didn't care, she kept scolding me as if I were an idiot, then it started raining, coming down harder and harder. We took shelter in a doorway, right in front of the bus stop. The thunder was terribly loud. It seemed like the bus would never come. I hugged Heidi and she stopped berating me. I don't know how long we were there before the bus finally came."

"And did you board the bus?"

"Heidi wouldn't let me. She pushed me away and jumped aboard."

"Couldn't you have boarded too?"

"Sure I could have . . . I could have done it. But I hesitated. While the door was closing, Heidi shouted, 'Go to him! Right away! What are you waiting for?' and even before the bus pulled out I had turned around and was running in the opposite direction, running back to you. Only it was pouring rain and I got lost. I wandered for a long time before finding the apartment building. And when I found it, I didn't know what buzzer to ring."

AT THIS POINT SHE TEARED UP and began to cry, and her lovely eyes welled over with salty tears, and in order to stop I pulled her on top of me, hugged her tight, and kissed her on the neck and ears and, while I was doing it, I slid my erect member inside, my cock which wouldn't hear of turning flaccid. Then I lay there, motionless, holding her there like that. She began to moan and as she did, she continued to cry, but she wriggled loose of my embrace and sat bolt upright on top of me, spreading her thighs, knees bent, with my sex straight up inside her, and as if she didn't want to let me see her tears, she bowed her head forward so that her hair covered her face, and I saw only that blond curtain waving back and forth.

Then she started moving, not up and down but rather back and forth, keeping her pelvis pressed tight against me and dragging it so that my sex changed angle inside hers. I could feel the difference when she pulled back and my cock, bent downward, rubbed against her clitoris, and when she came back forward I could feel with the tip of my penis the depth of her tight aperture and with the base the proximity of the other orifice, which must have given her pleasure, seeing that it was precisely in the wake of that movement that she issued a loader moan. I pondered how Bettina had changed in that year. And how I had changed, too. And so, after she had come like that, straddling me, I turned her over on one side, still moaning, and laid her flat on her belly, with me on top, pressing down on her with all my weight, and I fucked her in the ass. A dozen or so deep thrusts, and after I had spurted the final strand of come into her ass, I felt that at last my sex was starting to unstiffen, as if it were liquefying, and without even having to slide it out, I found myself outside of Bettina.

Her buttocks gleamed white in the darkness, and she seemed dead, she wasn't moving, she no longer seemed to be breathing.

if you want to turn this page
first you have to have read it

19

I HAD PLENTY OF FRIENDS who were painters, some of them quite good. More friends who were painters than in any other single category. They were nearly all of them interesting young men. The sculptor Nunzio had a thicket of hair and deep-set fiery eyes. Mariano Rossano was the classic young Neapolitan with fine, melancholy features, measured gestures, doubts, and a hint of laziness. Giuseppe Salvatori's blue eyes and close-trimmed blond beard made him a late-nineteenth-century Frenchman, like those wearing Zouave knickerbockers and carrying everything they needed to paint in a leather rucksack tied to their back. What caught your attention in all of them were their eyes: the mocking, wide-eyed stare of the very skinny Felice Levini, Spatola's inquisitorial look, Pizzi Cannella's light eyes, the eyes of a praetorian guard, and Cecafumo's eyes, full of terror and tremor, peering into the darkness, scanning an imaginary score, in pursuit of the notes of Charlie Parker's solos. "I need to detach them," he'd say, obsessively, "separate them one from the other," and it was impossible, like trying to separate drops of water in a mountain stream rushing down into the valley. It finally drove Cecafumo mad.

And then there were Giancarlo Limoni, Marco Tirelli, Beppe Gallo, Gianfranco Notargiacomo, Bianchi, Gianni Dessì, and Mimmo Grillo, Gianni Asdrubali, Vittorio Messina, and others still. It was fun for an outsider as ignorant and curious as I was to go and mingle with this school of painters. They led a life that was similar to and yet, at the same time, completely different from mine: no university, a far less vague, much more concentrated apprenticeship than any writers ever served, and immediately, or almost immediately, they plunged their hands deep into their work, as in fact it ought to be for everyone, into real work: painting, canvases, studies, installations, or performances, videos, shows. The ones I call painters, using an old-fashioned term, knew from their school days on that they wanted to be artists, that they wanted to spend their lives making art: and outside of that material vocation there were the trattorias, the poolrooms, pussy, interminable discussions of art, for some of them, drugs, and nothing else. It was a more severe, practical education, more "focused," as we might say today, than what we writers did, wasting endless amounts of time chasing after words, immaterial elements. Break down, reassemble, break down, reassemble . . .

They had to produce objects, figures, corporeal masses, surfaces, applying all their ingenuity and industriousness like so many blacksmiths and carpenters, sawing, nailing, painting, getting smeared with pigments, dust, wood shavings, and varnish. Their work filled them with hunger and thirst, and a lust for distraction, once they'd shut the door of their studio behind them, while the ascetic nourishment of the word has always just confused me, pumped me up with air while at the same time thinning me out. Working with words is never really working, it's an endless dripping, closer to prayer or a soliloquy than to genuine work, instead of working you think, you fantasize, you form clouds of vapor steaming from the readings you've done, you pile up and discard vague ideas. In the end, these vague ideas, thanks to a monotonous, never-changing gesture that you repeat endlessly using just a few fingers and allowing the unutilized rest of your body to grow stiff and waste away, these intuitions, if God is willing, will find a form, which however, even if it comes to life, will never be embodied, and will always, in the end, remain virtual, dormant, locked between pages. A breath dried on paper. For that reason, too, you never get a break from this nonwork, not even when you're tired, and you can't take it anymore, when, as Flannery O'Connor writes with great precision, after a few hours spent striking typewriter keys, "I'm sick of talking about people who don't exist with people who don't exist."

PAINTERS, on the other hand, as in the famous and chilling diary of their illustrious colleague Pontormo, have to have produced *that* at the end of the day, or to be more precise, have to have fabricated it: *that specific thing*, an arm, a head, a forearm, a little clay man, a revolving mass of things, a first layer of collage, the repainting or soldering of specific useful objects, or even maybe the canvas of a future canvas, still to be painted.

AMONG THE PAINTERS THERE WAS A TALL, fair-haired young man, born in Lichtenstein, very wealthy, who had come to Rome especially to be an artist. He looked like Helmut Berger, Luchino Visconti's actor. Leda Arbus, my old schoolmate's sister, who also frequented painters as I will recount later on, was quite taken with him, I think. For that matter, so were we all, more or less: with his beauty and with his holy naïveté. His name was Leopoldo van Sigmaryngen, which he had abbreviated in his career as an artist to Sygma, though the rest of us, more familiarly (and with that hint of cutting sarcasm that is inevitable in Rome), only ever called him Poldo, the Italian rendering of Wimpy, the endlessly ravenous, hamburger-crazed office clerk from the Popeye comic strips and cartoons. The crushingly handsome and aristocratic artist smoked a brand of cigarettes that was impossible to find, De Bruine, which came in a red-and-blue pack, holding them poised at the tips of his long fingers, drinking and offering shots of a specially aged twelve-year-old malt whisky, instead of the usual Johnnie Walker, and he schemed to mount luminous signs high atop the city's pitted monuments, with phrases in English along the lines of: THIS IS FILTHY, ISN'T IT? or else NOT IN SPACE, NOT IN TIME: OPPORTUNITY, though God only knows what they were supposed to mean, what they alluded to, but in the meantime he was just building castles in the sky, no one would ever have let him actually do it, and it was precisely that impossibility that stimulated him. No practical considerations can act to brake ideas that are out of this world. Only once, as far as I can remember, did he even come close to achieving these magniloquent plans of his, or perhaps I should say, he didn't even come close but at least he made an effort, submitting an application to a competition for an artwork intended to embellish a public swimming pool in Vaduz. He didn't win. Nor was his project even given an honorable mention or called out as a noteworthy candidate. Once again, his proposal was a phrase spelled out in neon letters, roughly sixty feet long, which said:

WEH DEM DER AUCH NUR EINEN EINZIGEN TROPFEN ZUM ÜBER-LAUFEN BRINGT!

which means:

WOE BETIDE ANYONE WHO MAKES SO MUCH AS A DROP OVERFLOW!

WHILE OLD AND NEW LITERATURE still interests me as much as ever, nowadays visual arts interest me less, every day a little less, absorbed as it is in the language of communications and advertising campaigns and practically indistinguishable from them, all the way down to the very nature of the conception. When I see an exhibition of works by the best-known and most brilliant Italian artists working today, I have a hard time seeing what about them is fundamentally different from the gags in a joke magazine.

SANTO SPATOLA WAS ONE OF THE FINEST of those painters, but when it came right down to it, one of the unluckier ones. The time, at least, was a propitious one: he launched himself while the wave of the so-called return to painting was still building, but he was soon swamped by others who were cleverer and more inventive, though less gifted than him, and who were catching the very crest of that wave. He reacted to what he perceived as an injustice, but which was actually a matter of pure chance, making sure his shows were less and less frequent, hoping to make them rare and eagerly awaited events, but the only result was that he slowly drifted out of view of the gallery owners, art collectors, and critics—he fell, as the saying goes in Italian, "out of their hearts," where for that matter he had never really found a secure place. The art world reached the conclusion that it could easily do without Santo Spatola, but not the other way around, as he had fooled himself into believing in the course of his—truth be told, ever less confident—roller-coaster rides of megalomaniacal hope. In art, in the movies, in the world of books and journalism, there are inexplicable phases in which one person is mentioned continuously, cited, invited to speak here and there, nothing can be done without them, they are sought after until it's considered a miracle just to be able to speak with them, they become indispensable, unquestionable, selected without a doubt as the first— or if not the first, at least *one* of the top three or five names to come to mind the minute anyone starts putting together an initiative of any kind, be it an exhibition, a survey, a festival, an anthology, a roundtable; and then before you know it, their name starts plummeting in the rankings until it's dropped out of the bottom; it's no longer on anyone's lips; and even if it came to mind, no one would dare to bring it up, because at the mention of that name the others at the table, or in the room, would react with a grimace, an unconvinced "Huh . . . ," accompanied by the hand-and-wrist gesture of someone discarding a crumpled piece of paper, "Oh, Lord, no, no, for the love of God!"

That's what happens, and that's what happened for no specific, exact reason to my friend Santo Spatola.

✤

AMONG THOSE YOUNG MEN, there were a great number of remarkably creative minds, forced to bang their heads against the wall to come up with
something new to say, a new way of painting, or of stopping painting, or of
starting to paint all over again. They considered everything that had been
done right before them to be tremendously important, and they felt a responsibility to renew it. They had to burn their bridges with the recent past
or else, contrariwise, pay homage to it, in all seriousness or in jest. In effect, when you visit any collection of twentieth-century artwork, with its
halls organized thematically, it is shocking to see the implacable histori-
cizing tendency of the works of nine artists out of ten, year after year, decade after decade, the shifting succession of styles, of periods, of the
movements they joined or turned away from—without being an expert or
a specialist, any museumgoer ought to be able to assign a certain canvas
to the year it was painted, or come within a good approximate range, so
"dated" is it, for the most part. All of a sudden, one fine day, everyone or
nearly everyone starts painting a certain way, and then just as suddenly
they stop. Just as is the case with fashion, they can tell that behind the
scenes there pulses a fickle marketplace that demands the new, the updated. Now, there is far less of a compact front in literature, there are fewer
movements and wholesale shifts every decade or five years, a writer can
perhaps go on writing the same way for forty years, or else change with
every book: they'll find followers or be ignored individually, on a case by
case basis. At least that's the sensation I have about it.

Whatever the case, it was perhaps precisely in the period I'm telling you
about that, in the visual arts too, the scholastic compactness of the various
movements cracked and then shattered, and the artists began advancing in
scattered order, each following her or his individual path, paths that inter-
sected and often became tangled, forming switchbacks and knots, but certainly didn't march along in parallel. It was a lucky thing and to the same
extent, a catastrophe. Artworks ceased to come to each other's rescue, the
way they do in museum halls dedicated, say, to Cubism or Informalism,
where you find paintings side by side that justify each other, the good ones
save the ugly and insignificant ones, the insignificant ones form the backdrop, the horizon of the understanding against which the good and beautiful ones stand out. Outside of the surrounding context of mediocre
artworks and ham handed attempts, even certain masterpieces would remain,
so to speak, mute, uncommunicative, while all the rest would be swept

away. I wouldn't know, honestly, whether among the works of the painters I spent time with there are any that deserve the description of masterpiece. Perhaps that designation at this point can be used only in a relative or specialized acceptance (for example "a masterpiece of the horror genre," "a masterpiece match-winning goal"), thereby distorting the original meaning of an *absolute* value.

Santo Spatola never painted a masterpiece, but on more than one occasion he expressed a quality that was decidedly out of the ordinary. He liked to dream up titles for his canvases, or else his friends would find them for him. I coined a few myself, for example, *L'arto fantasma* (*The Phantom Limb*, my favorite), and then *Troppo umano* (*Too Human*), *Cul-de-sac*, *Il sogno rosso del coraggio* (*The Red Dream of Courage*, a punning title, where in Italian *segno* and *sogno*, badge and dream, are close cousins), *Lutto incompleto* (*Incomplete Mourning*).

It was easy and it was fun. The title was conceived separately, and if it sounded good, it could be paired with a canvas in an enigmatic manner, leaving those who viewed it the job of establishing a relationship, or really, the absence of any relationship.

But his finest painting is still *Domenica è sempre domenica*.

20

I T WAS A DARK PAINTING, even though it was done with bright and vivid colors. It depicted a battle, being waged in uncertain fashion: first of all, it wasn't clear who was fighting whom and why. Rushing in from the left, men in colorful uniforms were bursting into the middle of a wood, whirling swords and daggers, but they were blindfolded, so they were having a hard time regaining their orientation. Also on the left, in the extreme foreground, were two of those men, richly arrayed, perhaps the generals of the army launching the charge in the background, or else a couple of deserters, with very tall plumed hats. As if utterly indifferent to what was occurring behind them, they were killing time by showing each other two small round hand mirrors like those that women carry in their purses to check their makeup, but any attempt to see their reflections in these mirrors was foiled by the fact that these two men, like all the others, were in fact blindfolded.

Seen from up close, the blindfolds covering their eyes were actually made of flesh, or skin, a skin speckled with scales, and yet almost transparent, like the skin a snake sheds. On the right, perched high in the trees, or bound with ropes to the trunks of those same trees, or else clinging to lianas that dangled from above the treetops and even beyond the rosy clouds that quilted the sky (these dark lines cut the scene at angles, giving it a visual rhythm), were a number of adolescents, boys and girls, smiling as they watched the soldiers attack, resisting their onslaught by pelting them with such household objects as chairs, cushions, flowerpots, shoes, watering cans, transistor radios, kitchen utensils, and bathroom accessories, depicted down to the smallest detail. Also in the foreground, almost obstructing the center of the painting with their masses, a number of slaughtered horses, belly up, and numerous victims of the clash, both young people and soldiers, some of them seated or lying face downward, with their hands tied behind their back.

The whole thing might have been taken for a game, like hide-and-seek or blind man's bluff, in a particularly sadistic version, given that the soldiers, the boys, and the girls all seemed blissfully contented, and smiles also flickered on the faces of those who had been taken prisoner, tied to the tree trunks, or who lay bleeding and dismembered on the ground, so that you wondered if their wounds were only feigned or else if they might be healed at the end of the battle.

Because of its surreal grandiosity and the movements of mass and the details, as well as the hovering brutality, *Domenica è sempre domenica* reminded me, adjusting for the necessary differences, of the cover of a well-known Frank Zappa album, *The Grand Wazoo*. But when I told Spatola that, he wasn't best pleased. Perhaps he would rather have heard his painting compared with a battle scene by Paolo Uccello, which is certainly where he had taken the terrified horses from, or else to the mosaic depicting Alexander the Great victorious at the Battle of Issus, his eyes elongated all the way to the temples.

"But how did you come up with it?"

"I just did."

"You don't even know yourself."

"Sure I know. From my fears. You see them?"

I thought he was referring to the prisoners and all the blood spilled. Or the blindfolds over their eyes.

"They're right here," and he pointed to two men in the foreground.

"Look closer."

I leaned in toward the painting and those two enigmatic figures. I saw nothing.

"It's the plumes."

"Those are your fears?"

"Yes. The colorful plumes on the hats."

Shivers ran down my back. In effect, it was a very childish work of art, almost naïve, though still technically impeccable. As I admired it, I felt the certainty, as in fact I was saying above, that it would not establish the career of its creator. It was out of step with its times, painted in a classical style, with the chilly composure of, say, Poussin, without, sadly, possessing his splendor, with the animated vigor of murals from the twenties or thirties, and it was totally devoid of that pop detachment, it didn't relish the facile advantage of citation or reference that would have made it possible to treat that material like any other, that is, with a fatalistic, ironic shrug.

Precisely because it was candid and explicit, its playful violence was unbearable. It left viewers horrified and discontented. And then there was the title. This time, it had been coined by Spatola himself, and it was in effect very distinctive, very representative of his way. *Domenica è sempre domenica.* Upon a second reading, and even more so, upon a third or a fourth, it didn't sound at all ironic, as you might well have guessed upon a hasty viewing: that painting by Santo Spatola really was any ordinary, tragic Sunday in life.

THAT WAS THE DEADLOCK in which Santo Spatola found himself, only a little older than me, once he passed the age of thirty.

I continued to see him until about fifteen years ago, then we fell out of touch.

Of the painters mentioned and their entourage, many are in the vanguard, some are barely eking out a living, or they're doing something else, I couldn't say whether some of them have given up art entirely.

I've had limited success with my books, but among writers I can hold my head up high, figuratively speaking, because I'm not among my colleagues very often, nor am I able to display any particular pride; still, when I'm among them, I don't feel that I'm a pariah.

It's different for painters: a painter who doesn't sell his canvases, who has shows in second-ranked galleries, by the time he reaches fifty or sixty, it's as if he no longer existed, and he runs the risk of dropping, or being downgraded, almost to the level of those who paint as a pastime and keep their easels in their broom closets at home. Since it is permeated, impregnated with money in every single pore, the world of the visual arts is the most violently hierarchical of them all: yes, certainly, in literature there are awards or the number of copies in print to serve as gauges, but it's still theoretically possible that you could be a fine writer, or at least a decent one, or even an illustrious writer, and recognized as such, even without winning prizes or while selling only small numbers of books . . . since it is difficult to measure literary worth, and there exist no pitiless market quotations to certify it.

21

ACCORDING TO CERTAIN PHYSIOLOGISTS, cruelty and aggression are nothing more than the degeneration and intensification of the survival instinct: seeing another person's blood flow guarantees that I'm not seeing my own. The pleasure of witnessing harm done to others, with the assorted accompanying Latin proverbs, nowadays considered to be so many disgusting relics of the past, derives from the comforting sensation of not being the victim of that same harm. Certainly, from this sort of relief it's only a short step to actual enjoyment, for its own sake, caused by the suffering of others, also known as sadism, or one's own suffering, also known as masochism. The delicate nexus of pleasure and pain is thus established and perverted for all time.

One proceeds by way of intensification. Intensification causes a continual series of shifts between levels until the senses are overthrown. You start with tickling and you wind up being burned alive. Intensification can lead from the noblest sentiment to the most benighted frenzy. Loving with all your heart, you take one thing for another. A kiss turns into a bite. Did I kiss her? Did I kill her with a kiss? Did I kiss her or did I tear her limb from limb? If it was a mistake, which of the two things was mistaken?

Her breasts arouse me
only if I can ravage them.

NOW, THERE IS A HYPOTHESIS that explains sexual cruelty as a form of atavistic throwback. According to this theory, the stimulus of hunger would be analogous or even identical to the sex drive, evidence for which can be found in those lower orders of animal species where individuals devour their sex partner during copulation or immediately afterward. It is no accident that we talk about a sexual appetite: the functions of copulating, killing, and feeding have only divided in later stages of development, in which animals learn to keep them separated. Only in nature it is the females that kill the males: it wouldn't make any biological sense for the male to kill the female after inseminating her. So that's a theory we can dispense with.

ACCORDING TO OTHER SCHOLARS, what sex and violence have in common is the state of exaltation, excitement; they seek their object with lust, they want to take possession of it at all costs, they manifest themselves in physical action generated by psychomotor agitation. A sex act, if the witness were to be imagined as having no idea of its purpose, if this witness were completely and entirely clueless and naïve, say, a Martian, might easily be taken for an act of violence. Exactly as it is described by Gioacchino Belli, for example, in a famous sonnet: as a physical clash between glassy-eyed beasts, who puff and clash, beak to beak, "*e ddajje, e spiggne, e incarca, e strigni e sbatti*" ... ("It's knock, push, poke n' squeeze, a thrashen a twat n' tool") the gestures, the sounds and noises, the mechanics of the thing might seriously make up the picture of an assault, offer proof of some great suffering. One of a pair of lovers might sometimes be unsure whether the moans of the other are caused by pleasure or pain. And a child who may have chanced to see his parents having sex, through a crack in the door carelessly left ajar, will interpret this scene of love as this: "Daddy is hurting Mommy." What arguments could we bring to bear to persuade him otherwise? Sex chooses the same forms in which to express itself as do hostility and suffering: the body is riven by the same convulsions, the nerves at play are the same, and so are the muscles, whether we're embracing someone or strangling them, and in the final analysis they are gradations of the same force. Pleasure quickly veers off into annoyance or pain, in the taut strings of the nerves, capable when plucked of producing an angelically sweet sound or an anguished scraping drone, with the slightest shift in pressure. The tendency is accentuated in psychopathic subjects, who are frequently incapable of distinguishing between their own actions in terms of meaning, or gauging them in intensity, frequently devoid of moral or rational inhibitions. Brutal acts therefore become indispensable to their sense of pleasure, they integrate with it or replace it entirely. It may well be true that, as a philosopher once stated, sexual desire is brother to murder: but only a psychopath can revive that family kinship.

A couple of months ago, the streets were full of posters advertising what we might call an art house porno, based on the confessions of a nymphomaniac, featuring photographs of naked actors as they were having, or perhaps we should say, *acting out* orgasms: they all seemed to be experiencing, in the midst of their pleasure, something painful, a stab of pain, a spasm of anguish and disgust. As if a misfortune had befallen them. Which is, actually, pretty realistic.

WE STRUGGLE AGAINST INHUMAN TEMPTATIONS with the assistance of two different forces: one supplied by reason, capable of overcoming negative impulses by means of a process of reflection, while the other rests on our sentiments, which are instinctively repelled by certain malicious or obscene acts. Heart and brain, rational and moral ethics summon up more or less the same precepts, and they are almost always obeyed, otherwise any given individual's life would be nothing but a succession of criminal acts. And so giving in to evil and brutality is by no means a simple matter: it requires battering down a double barrier of inhibitions. You would have to be at least one of the following things: a) incapable of reason, an idiot; b) devoid of feelings and emotion, that is to say, an affectless sociopath; c) both things.

The emotionless imbecile will therefore be the ideal subject, the perfect actor of any and all cruelty.

UNLIKE THOSE WHO MURDER their wives out of jealousy, or their fathers out of hatred or some vested interest, or their business partners, or their personal enemies, or whoever it is they feel betrayed them, or those who get in the way of their objectives—the emotionless imbecile is not *interested* in the slightest who he kills: his brutal intentions aren't directed *at anyone in particular*; if they were, he'd be less pure somehow, he'd be entangled in resentments and calculations and it would become a personal matter. Within given categories (for example: women) his victims are interchangeable. Just as anonymous as the force that drives him to kill are the individuals that he targets. He wants to act, act, and only act, and murder is, without a doubt, the most effective action available, in the sense that its effects are indelible, unlike what happens as a result of any other action. The prerogative that constitutes the primacy of murder is the fact that it is *irreparable*: there are no replacements, there can be no reparations, it isn't possible to carry out some sort of exchange, and what is contrived by the institution of the vendetta and the reprisal, or their stylized version, what we refer to as justice, does nothing at all to erase what has happened—if anything it reprises it, it causes it to proliferate. It is a fire that refuses to be extinguished. A mark. The murderer is at the same time the one who wears the mark and the one who inflicts it. He may have the sensation, therefore, that his is a specific task, which he does nothing more than to carry out, like those who transmit a message without being expected to know or understand it, exactly as a courier ought in fact to do: do nothing more than to deliver it, taking to the recipient what has been entrusted into his hands. Choosing that recipient is above his job description. But who is the sender, what name goes on the return address?

The sadistic act, then, is imperative and iterative.

By tormenting her, he wants to induce three sensations in his victim: terror, dependency, degradation. And it is fundamental that there never, and I mean never, be *any* element of reciprocity. Reciprocity would be an indicator of something normal, something healthy in the relationship, which is a notion he abhors to the greatest degree.

As much as he delights in the sufferings of his victim while she suffers from his torture, that is exactly how indifferent he is to her death. The suffering gives him shivers of pleasure, the death merely bores him. (That is what happened in the CR/M, dictating its hasty conclusion.)

If he is impotent, he will still take pleasure from whipping or stabbing his victim, or subjecting her, often in an incredibly stupid and ridiculous way, to all sorts of abuse and torture, degrading and humiliating her. His scanty erotic prowess is made up for by an even greater savagery. The more he seems to be out of gas sexually, the more brutal he becomes. Instead of thrusting with his pelvis, he batters with his fists or sticks: surrogates for the physiological act he is incapable of performing.

The victim interests him solely as a temporary extension of himself. The girls of the CR/M could have been replaced by any other girl. The future victim is almost always deceived by nonsensical or paradoxical lines of patter, with fanciful promises, where the words—affectionate, enthusiastic, jovial, alluring—make a strong impression with their sparkling brilliance, but what matters is what's left unsaid, held back (which, for that matter, is true of any discourse).

("They seemed like such nice guys . . . unpretentious.")

There is nothing different from any other process of seduction about it, only that it's more concentrated, so to speak, tightened up: in order to approach people, you don't need to overwhelm them with attention, but you don't need to starve them of it, either: the ideal is to offer intermittent com-

pliments, which get the hook into the recipient while at the same time inducing a continuous and anxious expectation of receiving more. Another
technique is that of self-pity, a confession with an implicit request for help.
The victims, in that case, fly to the rescue of someone who is going to be
their executioner, they console him, they cuddle him. Any potential latent
aggressivity on the murderer's part may be viewed naïvely by his victims as
something they'll be able to cure him of . . .

A VIOLENT IMAGE and sensation hover over the sex act from the very outset, due to the spilling of blood in the first act of coitus, and throughout the
whole arc of time that leads a woman through the entire span of sexual
initiation, from deflowering to childbearing, marked therefore by suffering
at the beginning of the process every bit as much as at the end. All of these
pains are unknown to the male. Men are tempted to experience through
the female body the suffering they know nothing about, and thus feel it by
proxy. They never forget the inaugural mark of their virile activity: the
spilling of blood. In tradition, that fact safeguarded the honor of the male,
a worthy man, and confirmed the honor of his bride, unviolated. It is unlikely that the traces of spilled blood ever disappear entirely.

INTERCOURSE LEAVES A MAN UNCHANGED. Which makes him either envious or concerned about the spectacular changes that the same act can instead produce in a woman. If he wishes to gain any understanding of those
phenomena, those emotions, those feelings, including hope sorrow and terror, he necessarily has to pass by way of a woman's body. Full enjoyment is
the woman's prerogative, if we are to rely on the famous declaration of Tiresias. The sadist acts on a woman, therefore, because a woman is reality, and
only by so doing can he feel every bit as real, alive, and active as she is. If a
man were capable of remaining chaste, women would cease to exist, they'd
vanish on the spot. In order to make a woman alive and concrete, and deserving of existence, she must be brutalized; in order to make her alive, then,
it is necessary to kill her; and in that fashion, by killing her, feel alive oneself.

THERE IS ANOTHER KIND OF BLOOD that no one seems to have any hesitations about shedding. Not in rivulets, but in gushing gobbets, in waterfalls.
A torrent of blood. In the archaic world, it happened a few times a month,

when the hunters caught some large animal that was destined to feed an entire village. In the present-day world, every five seconds, in automated slaughterhouses. From the moment that man becomes a carnivore and starts systematically slaughtering animals for food, the pleasure bound up with the slaking of our hunger is indissolubly tied to the pain caused in the killing, or to be more precise, the pain experienced while being killed, a pain that contaminates both parties, killer and killed. That infernal passageway of pain and suffering becomes incorporated into the person who caused it, until it is part of his or her way of being. Which forms the conviction, eventually by subtle degrees transformed into an uncontestable law, that the only way you can assure your own survival, gain your own living, is to take the lives of others. *Mors tua, vita mea*: Your death is my life. That same point of view creeps obliquely into the sexual realm: you can take pleasure only by inflicting pain upon those giving you pleasure. For that matter, as with food, the union can take place by incorporating, ingesting the body with which that union takes place. Let's turn once again to mythology: it's what Zeus does with Metis. In order to mate with her, he eats her.

FAMILIARITY WITH THE SPILLING OF BLOOD undermines the sense of a relationship with the divine, it overturns it. You are no longer giving up a precious good in order to sacrifice it as an offering to a cruel and demanding god, thus winning his favor; on the contrary, the sacrifices constitute an attempt to make the gods complicit in killing and devouring animals, by offering them a part of the plunder. The gods would soften their wrath if they were invited to the banquet that is supposedly the reason for their fury in the first place. If that were the case, the gods' resentment at the slaughtering of beasts would only be caused by the eventuality of being excluded from the feast.

IN ITALY, roughly three thousand people are murdered every year, which means fewer than ten a day. And in spite of the sensation of spreading violence, the number is actually in continuous decline. On that same given day, along with the human beings—and without there being any corresponding police investigations or newspaper headlines—it is estimated that a million other living beings are killed, an assortment of cattle lambs calves horses pigs birds and fish: killed chopped up and quickly devoured. There are so many killings that they cannot be counted with any precision: they take place by suffocation, throat-cutting, boiling, freezing, electric shocks, decapitation, or with a bolt fired into the brain. How can we think that a society will abstain from spilling human blood and be able to keep from being contaminated by it, when it wallows in animal blood like this? The slaughter is so pervasive and uninterrupted that we don't even notice it, in part because it is kept carefully concealed from our eyes, which wouldn't be able to withstand so much as a minute of the mayhem. Far from our eyes, but not from our mouths! This is the true assembly line, forget about Ford, forget about Fiat . . . The assembly line of killing and disassembly of animals to be eaten. And then a person is supposed to be shocked and aghast if for every hundred thousand animals murdered, one man dies at the hand of another man? How is that an exception to the rule?

LOVE AND VIOLENCE ARE INSTINCTS quite similar in terms of intensity, they both set out in pursuit of the object of their desire, of the prey, seeking, whatever the cost, to take mastery of it, to possess it, and they culminate in the feverish physical action turned against that object. Their specific form is excitement, which can attain peaks of frenzy. An unrestrainable impulse to react against the object that causes the stimulus, in the most astonishing manners and with the greatest intensity. By virtue of this hybrid, lust can drive us to acts that are usually an expression of hatred, anger, and brutality. In our handling of the bodies of others, if it isn't love that guides our actions, it's possible that what will be manifested is ferocity. Unless affection, attraction, and desire are awakened toward that body, it is quite likely that the impulse will arise to *destroy it*, as if to punish it for failing to arouse positive feelings. Just for the sake of feeling something, out of the yearning emotional desire for warmth at whatever cost, there springs a bestial instinct, hatred gushes—it's still an emotion, a sentiment, after all. Hatred is a perfect antidote to nothingness. It is capable of establishing an alternative relationship to love, and an even more effective one. A person can reject love, but can't reject hatred, it always hits its mark, it invariably strikes the target. There are men who, if they do not love a woman, have no alternative but to murder her. In any case, they feel obligated to make a strong statement to her. Otherwise her body becomes intolerable, her breasts and her thighs a derisive provocation, her very existence an insult.

IT'S NOT JUST A CURSED, Romantic cliché: there is a bond, as powerful as it is mysterious, between lust and death, between sex and murder, but also between sex and suicide, especially during adolescence, when it's by no means an easy matter to tell one impulse from another and every emotion sweeps over us like a crashing wave.

The desire to make others suffer often springs from the desire to suffer, projected outward. By exchanging our own sensations with those of others, and taking those of others for our own, we live and experience in the first person what they live and experience, and we attribute to them what are in fact our own thoughts and sensations.

TO PRODUCE IN ORDER TO DESTROY: an incessant activity to which we tend laboriously, like a spider spinning its web, that tiny scale model, that miracle of engineering suspended in midair, to capture and cocoon and kill. The act of self-affirmation is a violent one. The desire to live, to reproduce, to acquire space and time and strength, is steeped in violence. Mating is not something of which all are assured: it's something you must win for yourself. In nature, most males never copulate even once in their lives. The degree of aggressiveness necessary to win a female isn't directed against her alone, but first and foremost against the other males competing for the chance. In any case, the spectacle of violence is for the benefit of one and all: if it is directed against the woman, it sends a clear message to all the other women, to make sure they understand who's in charge; if it is directed against the men, it serves to ensure that the woman realizes she's dealing with a dominant male, and will give in. (Instead of physical violence, we can just substitute power or money, that is, more sophisticated and complex forms, sublimated through many successive stages, which give the impression of shifting away from their predatory origins until they are forgotten.)

A MALE MIGHT HAVE IMAGINED that his sex organ was the most natural thing in the world, that animals spent their days copulating with whoever happened along; while it's only men and women who make things difficult, invent rules and obstacles and interdictions, from courtship to marriage to the prohibition of obscene acts in public places, from "Not tonight, dear, I have a headache" to the taboo against incest, and to religious, moral, and legal prohibitions. Nothing could be further from the truth. The sex life of the poor beasts varies from the grim to the nonexistent.

NOTA BENE: it is not only the female who is subjugated to the cult of the phallus. In fact, the first who must bow down to the phallus are the very ones who wear a phallus themselves: the small phalluses must submit to the Great Phallus. Does the Great Phallus exist?

Yes. I've seen it. I've seen the object of this cult materialize when, squatting in a latrine, I was abruptly called upon to bow my head at the passage of a wooden pole, like the ones that surveyors hold up for their measurements, known as the "pool cue," carried in procession by senior soldiers (that is, soldiers who had been in the service longer than me, even if they were a few years younger than me), and then to kiss it.

"Kiss the pool cue, insect!"

And I kissed it. I kissed the Great Phallus, during my *naja*, or mandatory military service, in a gesture of submission.

Who can say if this ritual still exists in the barracks of Italy. One thing is certain: the term "*naja*" no longer does.

THE MEMBER OF A MALE COMMUNITY, who lives in it for a long time or even for his entire life, is generally sadistic, narcissistic, obsessed with the power that he exercises and submits to on a daily basis, and homosexual, either practicing or latent. Otherwise, he won't be able to hold out. Even those who spend only limited periods in these communities (for example, obligatory military service) are subjected to the ethos in question: hierarchical and homosexual in tendency. They adjust to it, they submit to it, passively or with great discomfort, they incorporate it with enthusiasm or genuine wickedness, they rebel against it: these are all possible attitudes that, however, do not so much as scratch the structure of an exclusively male society, where the addition of the countless differences among individuals only tends to add up to a sum that never varies. Indeed, all the contrasts that may crisscross it only end up strengthening the structure, since it inevitably wins over the singularities, transforming the exceptions into exemplary cases. Whether you accept it or reject it, the dominant morality remains the same. The eccentrics exist precisely to confirm the law of virility.

IN ORDER TO ENJOY THE RIGHT TO MATE, you have to *get the better* of someone, in a competition that can unfold at levels of extreme violence or else where the violence is reduced to a minimum, left masked, stylized, silenced, transformed into a skirmish, both verbal and ritual, until it is transformed into its opposite, that is, courtesy. What we call chivalry encompasses and fuses together the entire range of possible attitudes, from the most sadistic to the most delicate. Your adversary, in this duel, as imaginary as it is real, is not only the object of your desire, to be won both in the sense of defeat and of gain, that is, the woman; but you also have other adversaries, namely all the men near that woman, close either in terms of kinship or social group, or else because they enlisted in the competition that features her as first prize. To rape a woman not only means bringing aggression to bear against her, violating both her and her body, but also breaking the general rules governing the competition among males for the possession of females. This competition is already tilted unfairly in favor of the handsome and the rich, and it allows for the use of forms of psychological domination that go by the generic name of seduction: but it rules out the use of full-fledged coercion. Anyone who takes a woman by force must therefore be met with sanctions, not only in the name of that woman and all women, inasmuch as they are potential victims of the same crime, but also on behalf of the men whose right to attempt to possess that woman by legitimate means has thus been violated. And that's not to mention the men from whom that woman has been, so to speak, or in some cases literally, stolen, abducted, because she formed part of a nuclear family or relationship: that is to say, the fathers, husbands, brothers, and sons. In the exemplary instances of rape that occur especially in wartime, or in those scale models of wars that are gang wars, rape is perpetrated intentionally before their eyes, and the men look on, helpless, bound, and beaten, to make it obvious just how incapable they had been of protecting their women. The schema unfolds, never changing. Armed men burst into a home, they separate the woman from her family members, who are then chained or clubbed senseless or held prisoner at gunpoint, they tie her to a radiator so that she is forced to bend over or kneel or else they lay her down, holding her by the arms and ankles, legs spread-eagled, and they rape her in front of her people, taking turns. She will suffer, her mother will suffer, her small children will never be able to forget this scene; but for the adult males present, who can glimpse it through the red of the blood oozing down from their forehead, from the blows they received, the grief and pain will be slightly different, no greater certainly, but more significant, more eloquent, because the real message of that violence is directed first and foremost at them. They are, to some extent, at least symbolically, jointly responsible, accomplices. They must come to an understanding that what is happening to their wife, or daughter, or mother, or sister is really their fault.

Feminine society reacts by identification with the victims. Masculine society, on the other hand, reacts as if it had been challenged, menaced at the very core of its existence, the heart of its authority. Rape affirms the criminal authority of some males, thus defiling and disenfranchising the authority, considered legitimate, of all the others. One day a prostitute managed to escape from Sade, who was whipping her bloody, by lowering herself out a window, stark naked. The Marquis pursued her across the fields, but soon his pursuit was transformed into headlong flight, because a howling mob of furious peasants was hot on his heels, determined to avenge the mistreated whore, who was a member in good standing of their community.

THE MAN WHOSE WOMEN (wives, mothers, daughters, sisters) are raped is forced to confess his helplessness. Instead, a man is worthy of being considered a real man if he proves capable, at the same time, of protecting his own women and ravishing with impunity the women of other men. The body of raped women is nothing more than the physical medium used to send a message to their men: clear, brutal, and mocking. That is the reason it's often the husband or father or boyfriend, bound and gagged, who's forced to witness the rape to which she's subjected: it's not just an excess of sadism, it's the genuine meaning of the act. A quintessential affirmation of supremacy.

> . . . in the profound experience that belongs
> to the collective memory, every penetration
> reproduces the rapes that women suffered
> when enemies invaded the village,
> consummated in the midst of the bloody bodies
> of their brothers and father, murdered,
> in a final attempt to defend them.

THIS WAS THE SOURCE (and still is in traditionalist communities) of the oppression of women within the nuclear family, on the part of father or husband or brothers. "If you want me to protect you, you must obey me. If you don't obey me, I'll leave you to the tender mercies of other men."

ONCE, when I was studying with his brother, Angelo came in and asked me, in fact, ordered me:

"Hey, you!"

"Yes?"

"What do you like about girls, hmmm?"

Right then and there, I didn't know what to answer. What a ridiculous question.

"All right then, if this is easier for you: what is it about guys that you don't like?"

I turned to look at my classmate, hoping that he might help me out in that strange interrogation.

Angelo went on without waiting for me to answer.

"Is what you don't like the body hair? The whiskers?"

"Well, no . . . that's true . . . the body hair . . ."

"Now, tell me loud and clear: what you don't like is *the cock*. Say it. Say it! Say: I don't like cocks. Because if you do, you're a queer."

I hastened to say I didn't.

23

FEAR AND PAIN, in deeds and words.

Violence is always accompanied by words. Yes, words again, still more words . . . There's a very close link between words and violence. Mocking the enemy or a prisoner, insulting him, deriding him, threatening him, terrorizing him—all these things give meaning to brutality: you might say that the entire spectrum of truculence is experienced only to create the occasion suitable for the occasional derisory or cruel word, even crueler than the accompanying actions. Violence and eloquence are made for one another. Publicly insulting the enemy, from "*Vae victis!*" to "Drink, Rosamund!" and "Let us allow the young prince to go first..." which echoes in the *Nibelungenlied*, before the son of Attila is seized and has his throat cut by Hagen, the mockery that echoes in the ears of the tortured man ... all these things are integral parts of torture. Did you know that Italy, the birthplace of rhetoric, is the only country in Europe to insist on refusing to acknowledge the fact in legislative terms? Fear and suffering can be experienced as well from words alone, that is, the words that threaten to inflict fear and suffering. You suffer just from hearing them. A prisoner can go mad before his captors touch so much as a hair on his head. With macabre comic humor, the torture chamber was called the "Fun House."

SUFFERING IS MANIFESTED *FOR* SOMEONE, before the eyes of someone, either on their behalf or to bring them relief.

It has been said that the suffering of the torture victim undoes the reality around him. I read those words somewhere, that pain "unmakes the real."

In the case of the CR/M, the reverse happened: for the two young women, something unreal took shape, became tangible ("It made real the unreal"): their suffering constructed around them a world that would once have been unthinkable. The nightmare materialized. Perhaps in order to be able to understand what it means to be tortured, you need to try imagining undergoing an operation without anesthesia.

The victims, then, reduced to being their miserable bodies and nothing more, just tortured bodies, a mass of pain-racked limbs.

And the pain propagates in various ways: through violent physical acts and in words, in the circuit of the mind. Imagining the suffering and expecting the worst aren't just anticipations or prefigurings, but rather direct experiences of suffering. You suffer while waiting for suffering just as much as you do while experiencing it, and then while reliving it in your memory. The punches you receive hurt in the same way as those threatened or recollected.

Rapists use doubled fists and flat-hand slaps or wrap their hands around the necks of their victims both to overcome their resistance and because it's part of the pleasure of tormenting them. The best way to put an end to a struggle is by strangulation. The lack of ability to breathe induces an indescribable panic in the victim and paralyzes her.

The screams of one girl terrorized the other
making her feel the same physical pain
inflicting upon both of them the same wounds
even when it was just one of them being tortured.
The terror of waiting to be hit can hurt
more than the blows themselves when they come.
The fear of being killed was enough to kill them.
In your imagination is already contained every torture
and it is there, and it is then, that we become inhuman, we descend
below the threshold of humiliation and dishonor:
suffering in advance the terror of suffering . . .

PEOPLE WHO ARE SUFFERING get on other people's nerves. The ones who were bothered most of all by the screams and begging of the young women were their kidnappers: the girls were crying and shrieking, and that just made them even more unbearable. It has been shown that many killings take place when the murderer simply can't take the sound of the whining anymore, as if he himself wasn't the cause of those cries of pain, and was just bored or disgusted at the victim's lack of self-control.

NOW, TO GET BACK TO SEX: in the sixties, it was liberatory, in the seventies, punitive. You can detect this in the pornography of the respective decades. This is not a contradiction, it's a natural development, or rather an evolutionary leap. The step from liberation to punishment is far more logical than you might imagine: you punish those who have liberated themselves, doing it with the same weapon they used to attain that liberation, sex, and you chastise those who were emancipated—namely, women—by showing them the dark side of that very same emancipation. Each and every conquest of territory by freedom is paid for with exposure to a recoil, a backlash, that is usually inflicted with the same tool that had been used to advance, to progress. Liberty, technology, money, prosperity, oil, airplanes, plastic, TV, computers—they all turn against their discoverers and inventors, like HAL 9000 in Kubrick's film *2001: A Space Odyssey*. The cock, celebrated as a fungible pleasure-giving device for young women, finally liberated, in the course of just a few years was transformed into an instrument of anger and punishment.

I REMEMBER how some of my female classmates at Giulio Cesare High School imagined, speaking aloud, the sexual dimensions and performance of a classmate of ours (now a television journalist): "He must have a cock like a Stalin."

A typical piece of demonstration equipment, the Stalin was a pick handle around which a banner was wrapped: of the two components that made up the object, the banner served a symbolic purpose, to be waved and displayed, and the pick handle was to be used in case of a street fight. One thing was light and impalpable, the other was stiff and good and solid and heavy.

It wasn't just in their left-wing bird brains that a cock was associated with a blunt, heavy object. Oh, yes, hardness, the quintessence of masculinity. Books have been written on the subject. The stiff as opposed to the soft, etc.

WHO CAN IDENTIFY the source of the feeling that intercourse conceals something dangerous, at the very instant it is undertaken, or later, in a disastrous consequence? Every seduction is fatal: just as the eventuality of pregnancy is implicit in the act, and therefore of a new life, likewise you can sense the danger of death. In mythology, we find countless cases that make the point: a woman avoids her wedding, or refuses to consummate it, or else consummates it with the knowledge that she will thus be killing the man with whom she lies down; the man on his part hesitates, perplexed, afraid that in the depths of that trivial act there may be lurking something murderous, fatal. A trap. Every time a knight strips off his armor to lie with a maiden, he is putting his life in danger. The funny thing is that they're both in danger, whether it's the knight who accepts the maiden, or if it's the maiden who agrees to lie with him, or even if either he or she refuses to lie with the other, thus arousing the fury of their wounded pride! In any case, it opens a wound that cannot be healed, either the wound of the virgin who is one no longer, or else by tarnishing the knight's honor, damage is done in his breast or her womb. Every time that Sir Gawain reaches his hands out to touch the maiden who has ordered him to spend the night with him, swords stab out from the bed to run him through; for having done the same thing, Holofernes loses his head, Samson loses his hair, and so on. A flicker of suspicion had put them on their guard, and yet they went ahead . . . blinded by their libido. If they don't kill each other, lovers still choose a victim to sacrifice on the altar of their intercourse: my dear man, if you want to go on fucking me, then cut the head off that crazy preacher, Yohanan. Directly or obliquely, sex leads to a beheading. Men fall asleep, never to reawaken, or to find themselves prisoners, helpless, contaminated, sent straight to hell. Sex is the most powerful weapon of all magic and artifice: by threatening her with his sword and taking her by force in her bed, Ulysses strips Circe instantly of all her powers. By entering her, he enters another world. Penetration is the riskiest act you can commit: things will never be the same as before. You might be imprisoned like that necrophile gravedigger of Moscow, trapped in the vagina of a dead woman, or else be greeted the morning after with a message on the bathroom mirror in lipstick, WELCOME TO THE WORLD OF AIDS; but even when husband and wife go to bed together, they're running the risk of contamination, endometriosis, fibroids . . . the penis given a chemically induced erection at the cost of a heart attack . . .

SEX IS A SINGULAR SORT of prison whose bars keep you from getting in, rather than getting out: what you want, what you desire is *inside*, it's a secret, hidden the way that genitalia normally are. I know few people who haven't been obsessed with this for most of their lives and, without fear of contradiction, I think that I can state that intelligent people, and especially the most intelligent ones, the most curious and creative ones, either were or still are.

24

I REMEMBER LISTENING to Angelo's confessions on TV. Face-to-face with a woman whose brow was furrowed but who was willing to take note of his delirious statements. And then there was the myriad array of spontaneous statements in which he declared that he had been guilty or else a witness to a great number of crimes, a latter-day confirmation of what I had once read in Dostoyevsky's *The Idiot*, and namely that "it is indeed possible to feel an intoxicating pleasure in recounting one's foul deeds, though one has not even been asked about them," to which I would add, without even having necessarily committed them. The pleasure of self-accusation.

✣

"ANGELO, yes, an angel, the angel of evil . . . but still, a well brought-up angel." He kisses the hands of the ladies who come to confer with him in prison . . . women interested in his crime.

He has always cultivated the sentiment of friendship, of brotherhood.

And the family, deeply Catholic, brings up their son in accordance with their values, certainly never dreaming that . . .

His friends, his peers, his accomplices: the first is a psychopath (*editor's note: the only one currently out on the street, a free man*); the other was brought up in the heart of his family in such a stern and strict manner that he went out and started committing armed robberies to be able to put in his wallet the money that his parents, though rich, stingily refused to give him.

Angelo speaks with a drawling Roman accent.

He claims credit for himself as a "well-known hitter."

In his youth he was avowedly in favor of the Nazi concentration camps.

The first passion of his adolescence wasn't love for a specific woman, but hatred for all women.

And then the idea of dragging someone else into the crime, to make them vulnerable to extortion, get them involved in something grave, serious . . . which means the murder was planned upon, premeditated . . .

Now he admits it, while back then, at the trial, of course, he didn't: "Things went the way they went, the way these sort of things go . . . we threatened them . . . we scared them . . . we had sex with them . . ."

One girl dies, the other one survives by a fluke of pure chance . . . "Good luck from her point of view . . . bad luck from ours . . . certainly not because we took pity!"

"But now I've changed . . . I've *changed* . . ."

Thirty-five hours of torture . . . the sense of domination . . . "Who knows what was going through their heads? We were prisoners of a role, no one wanted to look weak, we had a pact of blood . . . and it pushed us to become increasingly ferocious . . ."

And then there's the lie, which makes such a good impression on delicate souls: "Prison did me a *lot of good* . . . in prison I was brought into contact with reality . . . I've finally become *human*!"

At the trial he could sense the hatred that was building up against him.

"As long as I've been behind bars, I've been living in a state of complete indifference about my own fate."

The girl who survived speaks with a lisp, maybe she always had it, or maybe it's because of the teeth that she had broken . . . "You hit me in the teess, 'at'th what you did!" "It's obvious that she's acting . . . and she's doing a bad job of it, too!"

Once in prison, Angelo took part in roughly a hundred trials as a witness (always found to be unreliable, even though some prosecuting magistrates with a thirst for revelations at first believed him).

After the CR/M, 1975, and before murdering again, and for certain two women this time, in 2005, he'd confessed to seven murders.

"Yes, I'm ashamed to be the way I am."

"To the lawyers, I want to tell you that I never deceived you. I was seriously convinced that I'd brought under control all the negativity that I had inside me . . . I was certain that I would be able to live a happy life close to those I hold dear (*editor's note: what on earth is he talking about?*) without causing any more pain to anyone . . . Perhaps I was fooling myself first of all."

Why did he do this? What are the real reasons? Well, it's not easy to say. "Things happened *that made these two women drop out of my heart.*"

"At the mere sight of them, *my heart and guts froze solid.*"

Once again, he insists on involving someone else in his crime, he wants accomplices, he wants to commit a grave crime together, "something that will bind them to me forever."

The accomplices have to be weak, easily influenced; and that is why he loves them and has no bad thoughts about them: because they're weak and foolish.

"When I was alone with A***, I fantasized about *walling her in, alive, in a corner of the office.*"

"I'd made sandwiches so we could all eat lunch together, the four of us," but then he ate them alone, while drinking a Coca-Cola.

BUT THEY COULDN'T TURN *their backs on nature, on life itself; after the pain and the weeping, they ate a meal, like men always do.*

"TOO BAD. Before too much longer, we would have been happy. We would have been one big happy family."

The TV journalist becomes self-critical and admits it: "Yes, I had believed him."

25

THERE ARE THOSE WHO SAY that the murder in *Psycho* is the first eroti-cized one in the history of film (the young woman naked in the shower), or perhaps, that that scene depicts a murder "too erotic not to give the viewer pleasure." Voyeurism in fact consists of placing in the service of the audience's pleasure images that they declare, in words, to be horrible and deplorable.

It is no accident that Alfred Hitchcock thought that an actress's most important quality was her *vulnerability*, the sensation that they inspired of being in danger. At any moment, someone might hurt them. The spectator was supposed to fear for them. Looming over their glamour was destruction, their desirability increased the more their beauty was threatened, indeed, you might say that it was precisely that desire that represented the threat: it meant that they would end up becoming the victims of impulses comparable to the ones that the spectators felt toward them. It was desire that menaced them, and that menace constituted their desirability.

What we discovered with the CR/M was that the victim of a rape need not be even somewhat attractive. The press, accustomed to spicing the daily bowl of soup (suffice it to scan the right-hand column of the online editions of Italy's most respected newspapers, nowadays consisting almost entirely of women half-naked, with the excuse that, variously, they are in Miami, they're presenting a new collection of lingerie, a wardrobe malfunction allowed a nipple to escape from their T-shirt while out shopping—or else, if we return to the period in which this story unfolds, the pretty naked girls on the covers of the two biggest-selling political newsweeklies, girls who were slapped on the covers to illustrate an endless array of in-depth articles, from birth control pills to political corruption, from terrorism to the drain of capital to foreign countries), found itself at a loss for titillating topics and was forced to hit the accelerator of political and moral resentment. Unlike in other news stories where sex served as a magnet (the most notorious of which, when I was a boy, was the Casati murder, in which perverted games were interrupted by shotgun blasts, with a great deal of brain matter spattered on the walls: but then I could also reference the famous Amati kidnapping, in which the kidnapped girl was seduced by her kidnapper and photographs circulated of the two of them having intercourse), the CR/M was less titillating because of the victims' total lack of sex appeal and the instinctive repulsion inspired by the rapists. The only way to stitch together an appealing story is if there's at least one attractive character involved, or at least, if not attractive, of some interest, whether the victim or the torturer, even better if they both are: a handsome bandit (cf. either the Marseillais kidnapper of Giovanna Amati, or Renato Vallanzasca, a.k.a. *Il bel René*), or a fashion model dragged down into perdition (Terry Broome), a female student of great beauty and a teacher who was a bit of a Casanova (Popi Saracino and his pupil), a wealthy and powerful man (here the line stretches out the door and, as we approach the present day, the list of names is endless, knights of industry, political leaders, champion boxers, soccer champions, basketball champions, high prelates, TV hosts . . .), stewardesses, hostesses, and so on. There, the ideal would be a beautiful airline stewardess, non-Italian, found dead, naked, etc.

It was not pity that drew a veil over the ravaged bodies of the girls, but rather the unmistakable fact that those bodies could in no way be garbed in glamour and then sold with morbid objectives, not even to a necrophiliac public.

In the tempest of interpretation of the CR/M, there raged in particular the theory that the rapists had chosen those working-class young women in order to inflict upon them a full-fledged class vendetta, in the tradition of the Roman senator who has his runaway slave crucified. In the binomial "poor girl," it was rather the adjective that unleashed the punitive violence on the part of the wealthy kidnappers. The punishment they administered, then, was political even more than sexual. There is no doubt an element of truth in this interpretation, as long as you keep track of the fact that it wasn't a choice, and that there is very rarely a choice in the target of a rape, because the rapist only rarely finds victims that perfectly match his preferences. Except for the ones who murder their wife, or the neighbor whom they hate or the business partner who defrauded them, or else the ones who shoot an armored car guard or rub out an informant, for the most part, criminals take what comes along. They almost always fall back from one target to another or another still . . .

In rape, the targets are interchangeable: it depends on opportunities.

Proof of this is the fact that when it was a matter of abusing well-to-do young women, before the CR/M, the boys certainly hadn't been shy about it. You can find just as many reasons to rape a rich little bitch as you can to rape a working-class slut. In different but every bit as intense ways, you can feel provoked and challenged by both categories of girls, you can get the same itch on the palms of your hands, the same yearning to crush them underfoot, humiliate them, punish them.

THE LEGENDARY SCENE OF *The Shining* in room 237. Inexplicable. Two minutes and fifty seconds that are *inexplicable*. People say that Kubrick edited it in various ways to give it a certain logic, but it has no logic. It does, however, have a meaning. By embracing a nude woman, a man embraces death. The spectacular young woman who emerges from the bathtub, pale, long-legged, high-breasted, is actually a rotting corpse. A living cadaver . . . There are some men who say that when they're with a woman they feel as if they're suffocating. They feel as if they're in a trap, either when they enter a woman or else are simply in her arms or even when it is they who are wrapping her in their arms, when they are hugging *her* . . . they feel besieged even when it is they who are laying siege. There must be a reason for such a paradoxical feeling. Perhaps they're just afraid of getting her pregnant and thereby being caught in a trap. Even certain men who forced a woman to have intercourse later accused her of being the one to entrap them. What they said might be a lie or a deplorable self-deception, but it still tells us something deep and strange.

MOREOVER, men fear or are actually terrorized by the expression of feminine feelings because they can sense that, in the dark depths concealed behind layers of tenderness or more-or-less affected fragility, a tremendous rage lies hidden. If rage is the root of all emotions, in the sense that all emotions contain within them at least a certain proportion of anger, and even in joyous exultation you can sense a hint of ill-concealed rage trembling, it's likewise true that any emotion is ready to be transformed back into rage, that it can conceal or unleash rage, prove to be rage: first and foremost, this is true of love. In feminine love, some men see a temporarily benevolent Erinys, a Fury. They see, in other words, Medea.

Some feel that women's original sexual task would be that of channeling the disorderly and promiscuous sexuality of males toward the purpose of reproduction and establishing a family order. This aspect, whose significance cannot be denied, is however in direct contradiction with a feminine faculty pointing in the opposite direction: there is in fact nothing that has fewer limitations (which means that it's potentially unlimited) than a woman's sexual availability, that is, the potential to copulate with countless males, or, in theory, countless times with the same male, something that is impossible—and therefore deeply upsetting—for him.

AT FIRST MEN complained of women's lack of willingness to engage in sex; then the fear spread that they might be *too* willing, and that their drive for pleasure was limitless. At the time when this story unfolds, men could complain of both things. Whatever the case, women are the cause of anxiety and upset for any neurotic man, and if he wasn't already neurotic, then sooner or later this is bound to turn him neurotic: either because he is convinced that they are threatening him with their now manifest sexual independence and superiority, or else because they might contaminate him with their intellectual inferiority, or because they loudly proclaim their total lack of dependence on him, or else, the other way around, because they trap him, they suck him in, they weaken him, they immobilize him in a spider-web of seduction. Against such a tricky and treacherous enemy, you have no alternative but to declare a preemptive war, before they succeed in over-turning their social inferiority into a state of biological supremacy, by virtue of their inexhaustible erotic potential. And that is when they must be struck, that is the vulnerable target, that threatening arsenal must be destroyed. In that light, the exploit of the CR/M has, as we have previously seen, all the earmarks of a counteroffensive. But if only it was really a war, just a war and nothing more, the classic war of the sexes! Open war, no quarter given, with an official declaration and perhaps at some point a cessation of hostilities, a clear, well-defined front, unequivocal acts, a clearly articulated strategy. Instead the flags are tangled and confused. This conflict manages to intertwine atrocities worse than any civil war, piling up mistreatments and torture with the most delicate tender mercies, the pleasure of spending an hour together with flaming love, reciprocal admiration with the gift of one's defenseless nudity, continually mingling and blending, so that even the bitterest of enemies won't stop seeking each other out in search of a hug, since they seem to have a desperate need of each other, the one for the other, and yet, once they have found each other, they can't seem to do anything but hurt each other. Never has there been such a tangled, confusing war in which the members of the opposing armies continue to couple and mate, producing the children of war, the orphans of war.

✦

WHEN A REPRESSED IMPULSE FINDS AN OUTLET, obtaining a substitute source of satisfaction, it provides not pleasure, but anger or disgust. Vendettas, for example, dictated by resentment, poison those who carry them out, no less than those who are their victims. Vengeance ruins your life. The pleasure that we are convinced we will obtain through a violent and liberatory act instead collapses in on itself, exactly like what becomes of the walls of a volcano during an eruption, with disastrous results, because the materials that plunge down into the raging furnace below only trigger new and violent reactions. What they call a venting or a letting off of steam never really is. Nothing is vented at all, all that happens is more steam gets built up; and then that steam gets amplified, condensed, refined, until it becomes self-aware and theatrical. Once unleashed, a violent impulse can easily be re-created, and then it is again released and again re-created, and once it has been constituted in serial fashion, it demands immediate and continuous satisfaction, in rapid-fire manner. If you abuse a girl and get away with it, the temporary disgust and sense of guilt will quickly be transferred to the victim of the abuse, and as if through some kind of miraculous multiplication, you look around and realize that all women are abusable, the entire female gender is at your mercy, you can stalk any woman at all, kidnap her, torture her, taking advantage of certain times of the day or certain solitary locations with lower risk, and the anger that has by no means been abated or vented, but actually exacerbated by the first abuse, will drive you to replicate it again, time after time. The world has suddenly been populated by potential victims, and what you must do is take a deep breath and hold down in your lungs your enthusiasm for this discovery, your hands start to tingle, your blood pumps quickly through your veins, a foxy cunning suddenly seems to be produced in your imagination, ordinarily so lazy . . .

And so the impulses and drives that had previously been so incompatible with the rest of an individual's personality because of the high-handed arrogance with which they pursued violent and obscene objectives, and which had therefore been only at the cost of great effort restrained to lower levels of development and deprived of satisfaction and attainment, band together into a sort of independent republic, autonomous from the rest of your personality but still capable of attracting certain components of it, breaking away a section at a time, with the revolutionary promise of ever greater satisfactions, exactly like what actually happens during a state of civil war, until they are able to become even stronger than the original personality and triumph over it. By now, this is the dominant personality, victorious over vain scruples, animated by a growing column of anger, striving spasmodically toward its new objectives, while all that remains of the prior persona has been funneled almost entirely into drives that were previously thought unspeakable. And thus a serial rapist is born.

The confirmation of one's own identity through repetition (in this case, of repugnant acts, but it would be no different if we were talking about pious good deeds) is a source of pleasure, it instills a sense of security. One's own suffering and that of others procure the same sense of enjoyment.

AH, ANY KIND OF EXPERIENCE that takes you out of the humdrum banality of ordinary life, and lets you float in another dimension, producing a special feeling of giddy intoxication and triumph in defiance of the aridity of the life you've broken away from, a crushing victory over the part of you that had flattened against the walls of that life, lurking in concealment, and over those who never escape from it, don't dare to leave its confines, wouldn't even begin to know how, can't even attain a conception of the idea of liberation, prisoners of the humdrum rat race that they believe to be life, without alternatives: for example, in bourgeois families but also in those of many honest blue-collar workers, people who work like slaves for years without ever once lifting their heads, their own parents. This sensation of liberty is so exhilarating that it immediately becomes irreplaceable, and therefore a monkey on your back, an obligation, it demands to be sought out at every moment of the day and at all costs, and it produces a parallel feeling, a sort of vicarious impulse that can accompany that triumphant intoxication or replace it when you aren't able to achieve it, namely scorn, but a scorn ribbed internally and structurally with reasonings, motivated, ferocious, against the poor and the hypocrites who haven't the faintest idea of the way you feel when you're "*de fori*"—on the outside, to use the Roman slang—and yet recriminate ceaselessly against the dangers and the harm of that condition, who are frightened or scandalized by it. Your parents, of course, are in the front row, followed by all the other representatives and guardians of ordinary existence. If fostered and nourished in a continuous manner, scorn soon consolidates into hatred, while the people it is directed against are soon reduced to a subhuman level.

Once you've gone into that corkscrew spiral, it will take a dose of some controlled substance or the exercise of a given activity to allow the excitement to be vented, to release the unbearable tension.

Drugs and sex are the obvious answers to this requirement, and they are given, like medical pharmaceuticals, in doses calibrated to attain the desired effect, which is the achievement of a temporary narcosis: a shot, a shot, a third shot, or else a series of lines to snort, or else a fuck, a second fuck with the same subject or else with another, depending on the variable needs of those who are already high and want to stay high or else come down but, if possible, not in a nose dive.

Then there's a third activity capable of releasing powerful doses, and in unlimited numbers, because the body suffering its consequences isn't the body of the person practicing it, who runs no risks, who suffers no damage, who doesn't plunge into the abyss, neither consumes nor exhausts their own strength, but rather that of other bodies. Here is an activity that will never lead to an overdose: gratuitous violence. In other words, the kind that is unleashed on helpless bodies. The circuit of this addiction involves a frantic stimulation of one's sensibilities in such a way as to procure at least a brief interval of utter insensibility.

OUR ALWAYS ALERT, unflagging sexual attention by no means derives from a hammering, abnormal physical need, but rather from the fixation on noting everywhere we turn our eyes, encountering, like so many personal provocations, the unmistakable signs of feminine difference, the breasts peeping out of the ice cream vendor's neckline as she hands you your cone, the slender swiveling hips atop a pair of lanky legs of the young girl in a sweatshirt sent by her mother to take the dog out for a walk before leaving for school, the red lipstick worn by the woman in her fifties to whom you've offered the last shopping cart available, and you do it in order to see those shiny red lips turn up in a smirk of gratitude, and her pretty eyes glitter with a wateriness that might be due to an erotic desire repressed too long, just as it might be a result of the irritating fluorescent lights in the supermarket, so that she hastens to put on a pair of dark glasses. Each of these details, which can be found in half the population, is stored away in a mental silo, each one striking the man in question right in the face like a glove announcing a duel, an intolerable transgression, or as confirmation that all the women who emit these signals—signals they cannot help but emit the instant they show themselves in the public street, in school, at home, everywhere and anywhere, creating a massive, frightful interference, a buzzing network of stimuli and provocations—all these women, in short, are nothing but *sluts*, goddammned *sluts*, who march down the thoroughfares of the city rubbing their thighs together, the thighs where their perennially damp sex is lurking, and bouncing their breasts, even if they are small, even if they don't bounce in the slightest, compressed and immobilized by their brassiere as they are, well, that makes no difference, it's as if they were, it's as if those breasts were bouncing, up and down, up and down, *nodding and winking.* The messages that they launch into the air are even more subtle and duplicitous when they deny what they state, when the sources of those messages are chastely dressed women, nondescript, showing off none of their sexual differences, well, sure enough, they're even bigger sluts than the rest of them, since underneath their modest flower-print dresses and in the filthy swamp of their desires they know that they're concealing a perverse frenzy, insatiable sex organs, it's all so clear! The more they act like nuns, deep down the more depraved they are. As for the ones that dress like sluts, with their thighs bared for all to see, well, they're obviously sluts. Eleven-year-old girls are just future sluts, women in their sixties used to be sluts, and they're suffering and seething because they just can't act that way anymore, they can't show it off ("Well, so, when are the rapes going to begin?" the old women of Cyprus wonder, impatiently, as the siege progresses and it looks like the city is about to be stormed by the Turks . . . Lord Byron, *Don Juan*).

AT THE TIME, there was a constant pressure on women to say yes, to be "accommodating"; these days that pressure extends down to thirteen-year-old girls, for them to be suggestive and available, if they don't want to risk becoming outsiders. Young girls whose mothers wear such low-waisted pants that the elastic strap of their thong is visible, T-shirts with slogans like TOMORROW I'LL BE A GOOD GIRL (today, clearly not), or else SAVE A VIRGIN, DO ME INSTEAD, or GAME ROOM with a large arrow pointing below the belt, or else LIMITED TIME OFFER wobbling on the surgically rebuilt tits.

26

GOOD LUCK EXPLAINING a murder with the criterion of utility or rational motivation! Let's take Hagen, who, in the *Nibelungenlied,* when confronted with reactions of horror at his deed, argues rationally the reasons he betrayed and murdered Siegfried, in political, coldly realistic terms: the elimination of an ally who was too powerful, the cause of continual unrest, the source of endless envy. It was necessary to put an end to Siegfried's tyrannical sway; and Hagen did it without scruples. "I care very little for the weeping." His speech is crude but concrete, and yet no one listens to him, or gives a sign of believing in what he says. When you kill someone (especially a hero, or a virgin), whatever valid reasons you might have will fade into the background, your motives will pale or appear trivial in context; issues of appropriateness or convenience no longer count; when you kill a symbol there are other motivations, more powerful, profound, tragic, or demented. There is no rational consideration that can hold up. Realism is actually banished from every murder, and not only those committed during a contest for political power. Only Machiavelli, with a special effort at abstraction, was able to reduce murder to the outcome of a rational calculation.

THE PROBLEM WITH PEOPLE like that is that they don't perceive the limitations of their own person and their own actions. Their fear must be truly great if they are to renounce doing what is prohibited: well, sometimes the frenzy of doing it is even stronger than fear.

WHILE WE MAY HAVE LEARNED how to defend ourselves from others, rarely are we capable of withstanding the sudden shock wave that is generated within ourselves. When we are standing watch, we look forward, away from our encampment, peering into the darkness, not behind our backs. And yet the deadliest sirens are singing into our defenseless inner ears, to which we cannot apply any wax plugs; and when all is said and done, the effort at self-control will prove even more costly and demanding than that involved in defending ourselves from external threats. And that is precisely why it is the first mechanism to break down when overloaded. What's more, the threatening impulses that rise from within provide tangible proof that we are alive, that in any case a force of some kind inhabits us, if not a good one, an evil one: instead of putting up resistance to these temptations, feeling shame at them, there are some who are happy to feel them awakening, to hear their summons, as if it were the clarion note of a horn blown by an angel, and little does it matter that the angel in question is the angel of death. There are many ways to feel you are a man: one is to spare yourself the neurosis of self-control, allowing those forces to overflow without worrying whether the consequences will be noxious or harmful. To go on a bender, to take drugs, to take random potshots, to steal other people's property and women, to risk your life for no good reason, idiotically, to rape and ravage, this transgression of the limits allowed to an individual, accompanied by a terrible sense of remorse, or else in perfect indifference, as if you didn't even notice that you had broken those limits—all this can undeniably unleash moments of the purest joy. I don't give a flying fuck about the price I pay. First I'll make others pay, then I'll pay, sure, I'll get sick, I'll wind up in prison, my veins and my brain will both burst, I'll turn into a walking corpse, everyone will turn their backs on me, and it may even be that some demon will return to flutter through the halls of that dreary ruined castle that was once my conscience, tormenting me. But you know what I say? I still don't give a fuck. I've been to the top of Mount Everest with the devil himself, and from all the way up there, to fall and smash against the rocks after a long drop pumps so much adrenaline into your veins that I wouldn't trade my inglorious death for any other destiny.

Nothing is more powerful than the longing to embrace a negative destiny, I mean to say, *totally* negative.

HOW IS IT THAT THIS WORKS? The way it works is that we seek out experience even though we know it's unpleasant because, if it is we who are seeking it and provoking it, the pain it causes will be far less than if that experience were to catch us off guard, or because it might even be able to be turned into a pleasure, or even better, into the sovereign conceit of being masters of the event, having produced it intentionally, instead of depending upon it as slaves. Pointless to await tremulously for violence to be unleashed when it can be we ourselves who activate it. Pointless to wait for the courtship of a girl to give its results when it can simply be decided in advance with the use of force. You will feel like masters of your own life, masters of your own destiny, while you plunge into the evil that the others all hasten to avoid when it originates with their peers, or to repress within themselves. If there is pain in the world, and it seems that there is and there must be, then anyone who can afford to decide how much pain, and when, and how, and who will suffer it, will feel themselves to be divinely gratified, in contrast with those who find themselves unexpectedly experiencing it, with no way of exercising any choice in the matter.

Along with goodness, but perhaps even more exemplary than it, there exists nothing more sovereign and gratuitous than evil savagery, which one exercises even against one's own best interests or even one's personal well-being and safety, even when you're certain that it will provoke retaliation; when you're sure that you will be punished for what you have done. If that evil savagery often appears stupid or mad, that's because it has no good reasons outside itself. Let's say that it depends on nothing other than a mood . . . a propensity, an inclination . . . just as there are people who love cats, who can't do without a cat, stroking a cat, talking sweetly to a cat . . .

THEY KNEW NO GREATER SOURCE of amusement than to relish the favors they'd extorted, savoring the reluctance with which they were yielded up. What does it take to receive a pleasure or a kindness from someone who loves you? Far more satisfying if the person who is forced to offer it actually hates you, or fears you, and is disgusted by their own cowardice. Forcing people to act contrary to their own nature is the utmost proof of power.

SINCE THEY WERE BASICALLY mediocre individuals, the dream of the young men of the CR/M was to strike fear into others. Since they were incapable of being truly powerful or noble or authoritative, nothing remained to them but to become pitiless. Sowing terror not in whole populaces, as in the old days of Sargon of Akkad or Genghis Khan or the times of more recent dictators, whom they venerated, but instead among a few underage dirty-blond women, girls to whom they show their implacable cruelty. Their eyes grew bloodshot at the sight of the weak. It is a singular thing that almost invariably those who have adhered to the doctrine of the superman have been unremarkable individuals, among the least gifted from every point of view, people of mediocre intellect, not particularly manly and even less courageous or, practically—you might say, to use their own categories—Übermenschen. It is a characteristic of the last century that it produced in so many petty, grimy men such a frenzy to make themselves at least somewhat noteworthy through their evil. Before then, evil might boast a certain magnificence, incarnating itself in monumental figures, but then it crumbled into a porridge of widespread white-collar sadism, the work of routine torturers, petit bourgeois monsters or serial killers who exercise their capacity for oppression upon increasingly defenseless targets, within reach, whom they could terrorize and murder with the least outlay of effort. The desire and then the pleasure of feeling themselves to be the cause of terror must have seriously obsessed the young men of the CR/M, and others like them, who failed to carry through only because the jaws of their inhibitory brakes had caught them just in time.

> *... What I can't obtain from them with love and in friendship*
> *I can always take from them by force.*

TO HUMILIATE AND CRUSH the two young women served this exact purpose. As confirmation of a belief that can be fully grasped only by spilling blood, otherwise it remains vague, abstract, namely that the life of any single individual is worthless, has no value, serves no purpose, can be eliminated without upsetting the equilibrium of the world, without causing even the slightest shift of the needle, and all the more so if the existence of the individuals in question seems, so to speak, a matter of random chance: beings devoid of any notable personality, special qualities, as are in fact most individuals, and as were those two young women. An abundance of blood. Blood is the one element that is excessive by its very nature. A single drop is always too much, much too much. The fact that under normal conditions its circulation takes place in a closed circuit, inside invisible vessels, ensures that when it suddenly does emerge and spray in all directions, or drip, or ooze, it seems like an unstanchable flood, a river in spate.

> *I wanted there to be someone who needed me.*
> *I wanted there to be someone who was afraid of me.*
> *I wanted there to be someone who remembered me*
> *for the good things they had seen me do*
> *or for the bad things I had done to them.*
> *I wanted to live more but I didn't know how.*
> *I wanted to leave an indelible mark on someone.*
> *I wanted them to talk about me for a long time.*
> *I wanted someone to cry on account of me.*

Part VIII

The Confessions

I

I's **LIKE IN PLATO'S DIALOGUES.** *Socrates speaks and all the others do is confirm what he said: "By Zeus, that's certainly correct!"*

TO EVERY QUESTION ASKED, sooner or later an answer is given. Months or years may pass and the person who answers may not be the same one of whom the question was asked. Or else the reply may even self-generate, as in Asimov's blasphemous short story about universal entropy, "Nightfall," which made such a big impression on me when I was a boy, and which, as some of you may recall, ends with "Fiat lux"—"Let there be light"—uttered into nothingness.

Words serve no purpose other than to restart the world.

There was a period of time when my surname was well known in the QT, or at least to its mailman, when my father's company was still up and running and a considerable volume of mail was delivered there daily. That must be the reason, around the middle of the nineties, when the Albinati & Bro. construction company had been sold off for years and the ashes of its last managing director were resting in Flaminio Cemetery, an envelope with my name on it and the simple address "Quartiere Trieste, Rome" was able to be delivered to the doorman in the apartment building where the company had once had its offices. The doorman held on to it for me.

It was from Massimiliano, my friend from Punta Ala. That's right, *him*, Max, the Fascist guitarist. The only young man I could have given myself to, the way a woman gives herself to a man, and I use this antiquated verb because it exactly matches my state of mind at the time. I believe, in fact, that Max was the only man I was ever attracted to, first and foremost for his stunning beauty. I had thought of him, I confess, in those terms as well, though without nurturing any specific desires, just remembering his lithe, perfect body, mourning his unexpected disappearance, and then, finally, forgetting him entirely, with the whole baggage of things that went with him, his sword, his guitar, the long enchanted afternoons spent admiring his displays and listening to the vast loads of bullshit he spewed. A phenomenon that never happened a second time.

I read his letter in astonishment, due both to the span of time that had elapsed since the last time we'd seen each other, more than twenty years earlier, and to the discovery that Max knew how to write, and wrote well. From certain clues, such as his use of tenses, I had the impression that a first draft had been tossed off just after the events in question, but then left there, unmailed, and then finally taken back up and revised or else rewritten from scratch. And also, moreover, that this new version was due, I might say, to a certain literary ambition, that is to say, Max's story hoped to go beyond the objective of communicating something to me, his old friend from the summer. Or maybe I'm wrong about that, maybe he really had only meant to reach out to me, but to show me something that transcended the mere exposition of the facts, of events; something more important still about himself and about his inclinations: to prove to me, that is, that he was capable of captivating with words, by ordering them in a row; capable of captivating me. That is primarily what knowing how to write consists of: and it has an allure completely different from knowing how to talk or dance or sing or play an instrument, that is to say, it's an indirect, discrete attraction, one that is released slowly, as if it's a colorless mortar that you need to leave in place for several days so that it can set.

MY FRIEND, *I heard from the Marinuccis that you came looking for me in Punta Ala. Yes, I know, you shouldn't be astonished or angry, it was many years ago, it's true, it took me all this time before I reached out to you again. I needed to wait until both of my parents died before I could do it. They died not yet old, my father at age fifty-nine, of a heart attack, my mother not long after, she didn't cross the finish line of sixty either: it took less than two months from the diagnosis of a very widespread tumor to the day she passed away. They were divorced and I don't think they saw each other again even once after they signed the papers: my father in Switzerland, she in our big house in Milan, all alone. Maybe it will strike you as absurd that I should get back in touch after all this time to tell you about them, seeing that I don't believe you ever met "il papi" in person, and you may remember what I thought of my "mamma," Vera. Did you ever once hear her open her mouth and speak? Say something, I mean a logical discourse, string together a sentence with any meaning to it, I mean to say? When you came to visit me, did she ever address you with anything more than those desperate smiles of hers, with that mouth, those perfect, white teeth . . . why, of course, certainly . . . "with a mouth like that, you can say whatever you want."*

The two of them are the two missing pieces of the story, and I'll start from there because now I really have been left all alone. I have no one above me, at my side, or beneath me, and I say that the last item is a good thing because I doubt that I would have been capable of raising children, considering the haphazard job that they did raising me. I never married, then, nor will I ever in the future. I'm a lawyer by profession and I work mainly for a large religious organization that reaches out to laymen. Its objective is the construction of a truly Christian society in which every community, small or large, and at whatever level, is bound by the same ties of faith; and this starts with the family, as is right and self-evident, rising up through the workplace, the office, the various professions, leisure time, the arts, various sports: in order to make it clear that laymen, and not just priests, can contribute to a wide-spread and fine-grained evangelization, exactly like the circulation and diffusion of blood in our bodies. In my law office, I work on the legal aspects of this undertaking, but I can say that I subscribe in whole to the overall plan. Perhaps the only way to keep the whole world from collapsing under the weight of the lack of faith.

I can imagine the first question you would ask me if we were to meet. No, I no longer practice martial arts (even though I might still be able to surprise you with some of my moves, because physically I haven't changed a bit, the same as I was, could it be a miracle . . . ?) and I gave up the guitar, and I no longer listen to records either, because they just distracted me. They would instill agitation and vague, elusive feelings: an inexplicable sadness. Do you remember my favorite guitar, my little crippled girl? Well, I gave it to a music school for children. Blind children. In exchange for the promise that they would treat it with consideration. No doubt, with all the hands it's passed through, it must be a wreck by now . . . But oh, don't think for a second that I've become a pious soul! A latter-day St. Francis or, even worse, a Communist! In fact, in that donation there was actually a hint of the sadistic and the sublime: that is, the idea that from that moment on, whoever laid their hands on the crippled girl would themselves also be missing something, could hear her but never see her. Construct an image of her by touching her, taking her in their arms, caressing her . . . feel her vibrate in their hands and ears, with-out ever tarnishing her with their eyes.

A kind of suffering, in other words, or else an even purer sensation, I couldn't say.

It was easy to get rid of that guitar, love ends the way it begins, and little does it matter that in the meantime there were (I did the numbers) ten thou-sand hours of practice, more or less. Every day, at least three hours, for ten years . . . and then from one day to the next I stopped. No more music. All these changes started in Punta Ala, on the last day of vacation that summer, but I might as well say the last day of my life. It took some time before I could figure out what had happened and what was still happening, but then it dawned on me, and that's what I want to explain to you, in part because I can imagine the bullshit that Signor Marinucci might have told you, or any-one else. Poor man: when I came back to get Melville, I saw his eyes glittering with a ferocious curiosity, typical of those who feed their curiosity with the misadventures of others. The last thing I ever would have done was to satisfy that curiosity. And his wife, who made the gallant gesture of trying to give me back the money from the August rent, or maybe she actually wanted to pay it back. That certainly wasn't why I came back, I just wanted to pick up the cat. I know that when you went there you discovered that that wasn't my house. We rented it, like so many others do. I couldn't say why I lied to you and told you that it was ours: it corresponded better to the image that I wanted you to have of me, of us, and my ideals of that time, really, every-thing. You see, Edoardo, I loved you and I respected you more than perhaps you could ever have imagined. And I wanted to make an impression on you: a powerful, indelible impression. You seemed like a young man made of wax upon whom I needed to impress my form; and therefore I had to have a clear, sharply defined one, at the cost of constructing it with a lie or two. But it's time I started picking up the pieces and putting them back in place.

The things you already know or that someone might have told you about this story, sweep them all aside.

My father was almost always in Switzerland for problems with his work. By now, even at home, we referred to him as "the Swiss." He had dealings with banks, and I never knew if it was strictly on the up and up. Most likely, there was no need to actually break the law. The borderline with the laws is a mov-able one, undulating, which entails curves in its outline to leave room for business deals and the men who know how to get around things. The laws step aside as they go by. And if, as I'm guessing, the Marinuccis told you that he was sick, and that his condition had suddenly worsened, the reason we had

had to leave without warning that summer (it was 1973, right? I'm not sure, even now), well, I just want you to know that it wasn't true. Until the day that, many years later, he was cut down by that heart attack while he was leaning on the railing of his chalet, smoking a cigarillo and enjoying the view of the enfilade of lakes in the Engadine valley, half-covered with iridescent ice, "il papi" was as healthy as a horse. Clear-minded, energetic, full of life, brutal, never a wasted shot. Keep moving, keep moving, keep moving, moving his mind, that is. That was exactly why he wanted nothing more to do with my mother. And it was for that very same reason that you never saw and never would have seen him there at Punta Ala, with us: he stayed up there in the mountains, where the air was cool, moving his funds around with a phone call, to avoid the boredom of his needlessly gorgeous wife and his fanatical son, and having to take them out in a boat to get away from the summer heat, the island of Elba on the horizon, unattainable. There's nothing like a woman's beauty that can wear out a man who married her for that and that alone.

So, that night, the call that came in from Switzerland conveyed no news about a sick man on his deathbed; there was no clinic, no doctor with a voice taut with concern; it was a husband standing solidly on his own two feet, informing his wife of his irrevocable decision to divorce her, a classic and well-codified boilerplate format for that sort of message, I believe. Which could also have been done in Italy, there was the new law, in fact, the boundary had been shifted just that margin to leave individuals free to do as they pleased. Another margin of space for their own fine thoughts, their personal wishes. My mother's reaction was every bit as classic. Do you remember her—Vera? I'm sure you do. Now that she is dead, and she's no longer my mother, just as I am no longer her son, our ties of flesh have dissolved and I feel I have the right to talk about her as I would of any ordinary woman—well, can I tell you that she was pretty impressive? All you need to do is take a look at an old picture, in case your memory is faulty. Dazzling. Something midway between Jacqueline Bisset (everyone told her the same thing, back then, the minute she took off her sunglasses, "what a stunning resemblance!") and anyone you might choose among the statuesque beauties that when we were boys always seemed to marry a succession of famous men, oh, I don't know, Barbara Bach, Britt Ekland, Elke Sommer, I just remember all those k's and those heavily made-up eyes in the photos in the fan magazines: light blue, violet, or green, like my mamma's eyes. Not just open: wide open, agape. Enormous bright eyes. Now that she's gone, I'm fond of her memory, I think of her, I miss her, I even come close to tears: back then I hated her, nothing more. I scorned her, just as I believe my father did. It was a duty to scorn her. While Vera listened to the verdict being issued over the phone by the Swiss, no differently than he might have dictated any ordinary banking operation, from time to time she would pull the receiver away from her ear and press it against her forehead, as if she were trying to make my father's words go straight into her brain, and I understood what was happening without having to listen to a single phrase: it was obvious, it was natural that the moment of truth had finally come. I'd been waiting for it since I was a boy, that is, since the day I had realized I'd never have any siblings, and the reason . . .

I STOPPED READING for a moment and went to drink a glass of water. There was something that didn't add up, but I couldn't put my finger on it. I picked the pages of Max's letter back up and examined them closely. There was nothing odd about them.

CAN I JUST GO ON CALLING HER VERA, *rather than my mother? A woman like her, nowadays, isn't on the market. She's priceless, out of print. You can't reproduce her with the name of "Mamma," or at least I don't seem able to do it. I know that you've written and published books, Edoardo, over the years, and I confess without shame that I haven't read even one of them, but maybe you'd be capable, I mean to say, you'd be sufficiently skillful and detached to bring to life a beautiful woman like her, as if she were a character invented for a movie or a novel, with the trifling detail that you yourself had come out of her, out of her outspread thighs. A writer brought into the world by his own character . . . It's thoughts like these that turn my stomach: where I emerged from, other men entered. Many others, before and after the Swiss: her screaming in pain, her moaning in pleasure. Vera's shrieks and moans, her tears real and false, have always thrown me into a rage. They wore on my nerves. If I say that I wanted to kill her when she threw her tantrums, made her scenes, it's no vulgar exaggeration. I really did feel that desire, deep down, a clear, simple wish, and entirely within my reach, eminently attainable.*

When she hung up the phone, she seemed calm, almost indifferent. She wandered around the house, moving objects from here to there, tidying up. As if she were seriously considering whether that giant seashell looked better here or there, the lantern for when we ate outdoors in the garden after dark. She unfolded and hung out to dry the wet beach towels and blankets. She filled the ice trays with water and put them back in the freezer, as if by routine. I fol-

lowed her from room to room. She was wearing a purple band that held her hair back from her forehead and behind her ears, and the blond wave bobbed on a line with her shoulders. Her movements were slightly rigid, and that was the only piece of evidence that she was sunk in other thoughts. In a provocative manner, I asked who that had been, just now, on the phone. With a contrived voice, she replied: "Oh, just a wrong number." So, now she was trying to get my goat! It made a surge of rage rise up in me, different from usual. I was shaking. "Don't spout bullshit!" As if she hadn't even heard, she traipsed back to the kitchen in a series of small leaps and went to see if the ice was ready, which was impossible, of course, since she'd only just put the water in the freezer a minute before. "It doesn't matter," she said to herself, and went back into the living room and poured herself a glass of whiskey. One of those glasses that's so wide and heavy that you practically can't hold it in your hand. She did it constantly, several times a day, a glass at least two-thirds full. She threw back a gulp and immediately afterward smiled. "It's delicious warm, too . . ."

"You disgust me," I told her. She raised the glass as if to drink to my health. "I couldn't agree with you more," and down went another long swallow, "in full agreement. There are at least three of us who think so." I walked over to her to take the glass out of her hand, but she started back to the kitchen with that same little series of leaps. I managed to grab hold of the strap of her dress, but she twisted out of my grasp, and as she did so, she tore it, and the dress opened up both in front and behind. Taking advantage of my disorientation, she got into the little utility room behind the kitchen and locked herself in. "What are you doing . . . what are you doing . . ." Then she started sobbing and shrieking.

To have to listen to her making all that ruckus from behind that door, and not be able to see her, was driving me crazy. "Get out of there," I snarled, "open up. Open this fucking door, open up immediately!!"

It was no good, she just stayed holed up in there, shrieking through the door. "Stop it!"

Once she'd drained the glass, what could she do? Her shrieks grew ever stronger, ever more resonant, deeper and deeper, like a wild animal. "Open this door, I swear I'll knock it down!" But she wouldn't listen to me. After a few minutes went by, the shrieks turned into a moaning, a sort of singsong. It was like listening to a little girl, sick and tired of sobbing, trying to console herself.

"Come on, Mamma, enough's enough, please," and I changed register, because I was scared at this point, that scene really terrified me, and maybe for the first time, it dawned on me that I was alone with her in that house, with no idea of what to do and no one I could turn to for help. "Open up, I'm begging you," I implored. I heard my own voice saying things that I never *would have dreamed of saying. It was really another person, another son speaking in my place.*

"Come on, we'll work this out."

"We can do it, Mamma, you and me."

I even went so far as to whisper words to her that, I swear, horrify me just to write them down: "Come on, Mamma, let's talk."

Let's talk, sure . . . of course . . . Vera and me, me and Vera, me talking, her listening, me listening, listening to her anguish, her sorrow, me consoling her, and then maybe me confessing my own anguish to her . . . such a thing never happened once in our lives together!

I pounded my fists against the door, loudly, to frighten her and make her desist from whatever it was she was getting up to in there. After that series of blows to the door, Vera really did stop her wailing. She was still crying, but almost soundlessly, I could just hear her sobbing. I continued talking to her through the door. And at last, the door swung open.

Vera was sitting on the cot in the utility room, as if she were the maid, exhausted at the end of a hard day's work, so tired she didn't even have the strength to get undressed. The torn strap was hanging down in front, leaving one of her breasts uncovered, white and separate from the tanned flesh above and below it. I felt aroused and ashamed of that arousal. Her face, twisted into a grimace and yet still very pretty, was a mess of tears, kohl, lipstick, and freckles. I had never seen her eyes glittering like that. She looked at me as if I were a perfect stranger. I got her to stand up and I reknotted her strap, covering up her nudity, then I led her into the living room. She didn't say a word but just started sobbing again, as if a crashing wave of emotions had knocked her down where the last one had subsided. Sitting on the sofa, with her head thrown back and the thin clear stripes of her bronzed throat as it jerked up and down.

"No, nooo . . ." I murmured, and I seized her by the shoulders and shook her. "Let's not start again."

But she continued, louder and louder.

I shouted at her and threatened her, but her only reaction to my threats was to pump up the volume. Now her sobbing was a savage noise, full of gurgling and racking moans, with nothing human about it at all, sounding almost like a donkey's braying. I swear, I couldn't take it anymore. No one could have. Just when she seemed to be on the verge of quieting down, she'd start all over, and it seemed as if it was going to go on forever, exactly like the waves that never stop rolling up onto a beach, one after another. The devastated beauty of her grimaces rendered that woman utterly repugnant. I tried to out-bellow her roars, and I insulted her in the worst ways I could think of, but Vera, staring at me wide-eyed, while I called her nothing better than a stove-in whore, just responded by howling louder. I went into my bedroom and got my sword. I wanted to scare her, and I was more scared than anyone else by what I was doing. I doubted, once I was armed, whether I'd be able to control myself. I went back to where she was, raised the sword, still in its sheath, above her, as if it were a club, and shouted with all the breath I had in my body: "That's enough!!!"

At that point, she let herself slide off the sofa, with her knees on the floor now. And finally slowing the pace of her gasping sobs, she looked me in the eyes, spoke, and, in the midst of her weeping, uttered an absurd statement.

"I never once cheated on him . . ."

I've already told you that I was beside myself with rage, despair, and a bloodcurdling sense of helplessness that was unlike anything I'd ever experienced before, I, who considered myself the strongest young man in the world. I was experiencing a misfortune that had no remedy and, rightly or wrongly, I felt that I was responsible for it. That was what was driving me crazy. But when Vera made that reference to her supposed faithfulness to my father, it was the last straw that made my fury break its bounds, the weightless snowflake that settles on a branch and finally breaks it off the tree. Faithful? You were faithful to him?! I thought, and that unassuming phrase sounded to my ears both ridiculous and offensive, whether it was false or it was true. Because if it was a lie it was deserving of punishment, and if it was the truth, I was even more profoundly disgusted by the idea that this unbelievable woman could have treasured and guarded for twenty long years this petty morality of hers, leaving exclusive rights to it to the Swiss, and it turned my stomach that she should drag it out now, in front of me, as she kneeled there, the last good reason he never should have left her . . .

I screamed and unsheathed my katana, assuming the stance, gripping the hilt with both hands.

Vera looked up at me towering over her and, through the layer of tears and saliva covering them, her gleaming lips took the shape of an ecstatic, demented smile.

"Yes," she said.

Maybe that smile was ironic.

"Kill me."

I STOPPED READING. I stuffed Max's letter in my pocket and left my apartment. I tried to think of something else, but I couldn't. At the bus stop I touched the folded sheets of paper in my jacket pocket. I started reading again, standing in the crowded bus. I wasn't breathing, as if I'd been intubated.

WHEN YOU ARE ABOUT TO DELIVER *a sword stroke, the muscles of your shoulders and arms relax, otherwise the blow will arrive, hindered by its own force, while instead it should sail whistling like a slashing razor that cuts through the air without any weight. Even though I couldn't have any real intention of killing my mother, I could sense that my shoulders—entirely involuntarily— were releasing the energy that my rage had built up in them, my muscles were losing their stiffness, growing elastic, as if I actually were getting ready to release the blow. That's how my masters had taught me, and this is what I had learned in thousands of hours of training. "Kill me," she had just told me. I knew exactly how to do it, my well-trained body was preparing to do it. The nicely balanced katana, my fingers open wide and then clenched tight with the greatest possible adhesion to the hilt, the twisting of my torso against my legs, which were slightly spread and bent: I shut my eyes and let the sword fly.*

The weapon hurtled down at an oblique angle. It wasn't me who was controlling it. It fell of its own volition, free to execute the stroke. When I felt the blow come to a halt, I opened my eyes, and I saw that the blade had stopped right between my mother's jaw and neck, and that it was glittering just beneath the earring that dangled from her left lobe, but not in time to keep the flesh from opening with a scratch the length of a finger: tiny though it was, blood began to flow from it immediately. I couldn't say what force had opposed its counterthrust to make the sword stop right there, a few fractions of an inch from the choke point where blood, breath, and thought all crowd together. The sword had halted at the very edge of Vera's own life. She who was still my mother.

THE THING THAT MOST ANGERED ME was the doubt that Max might have kept me breathless even though it was all invented. Why would he have done that? I had a knot in my throat as I went on reading.

2

WHY ARE YOU ANSWERING THE PHONE? Where's your mother?"

"In the bathroom."

"Doing what?"

"Putting on her makeup."

"Oh . . . that's right. She's putting on her makeup. Is she planning to go out later on?"

"I don't think so. Her mascara ran down her cheeks. You know, from the tears."

"Oh, no, please, not the waterworks. What a prima donna."

"Not a chance. I hate music when there are all those singers standing around."

"What singers? What are you talking about?"

"All those fat prima donnas. I hate them."

"Does this strike you as the time to start rambling on about musical genres?"

"No. Not now."

"Then tell me if she's calmed down."

"Do you really want to know? Are you *seriously* interested in knowing?"

"Well, at least if she has calmed down a little."

"Maybe so. Frozen solid. All credit goes to me, Papi."

"She needs to accept it. Unfortunately, that's just the way things go."

"It's the honest truth, by Zeus."

"Are you trying to make fun of me, Max? Trust me, it's not a good idea."

"Actually, if you ask me, it's an ideal situation for it."

"What's the matter with you? It sounds like you're having trouble breathing."

"It must be the heat."

"Is it very hot there?"

"Hot enough. Listen, so are you planning to come back?"

"Come back where?"

"I don't know. Back home. To Milan."

"Not anytime soon."

"Got it."

"Now put her on."

"No."

"I said, put your mother on."

"That's not a good idea, by Zeus."

"Cut it out, Max. I want to talk to her."

"You already talked to her once. Wasn't that enough for you?"

"I need to clarify a couple of points."

"It seems to me that you're no longer in any position to express your own wishes."

"What is all this? Have you suddenly gone over to her side?"

"Just one second after picking up the receiver and hearing your voice. 'Who is it?' 'The Swiss . . .'"

"Ha! Very funny. None of this concerns you, it's between your mother and me. You're a big boy, you ought to understand."

"I understand, Papi, I understand, believe me, I understand."

"It seems to me that you don't understand a fucking thing."

"And yet you ask me to understand."

"It's not that hard to grasp."

"Speak for yourself. I'm hanging up now."

"Hold on a minute: Is it about the money, is that what you're worried about? Is it for the money?"

"For the money?"

"You're not going to have any problems with money."

"What money?"

"My money."

"You can keep it."

"Massimiliano . . ."

"How strange. You never call me by my full name."

MAX'S LETTER, which had previously been so detailed in its account of that "last day of vacation," resurfaced toward the end, becoming almost hasty, strictly informative, as if it were a normal thing for him to get back into touch after all those years. He returned to his initial theme, which was clearly dear to his heart, his devotion to the cause that was supposed to bring laymen to live once again in accordance with religious precepts.

But I didn't care much about that stuff.

3

AND JUST AS HE'D VANISHED, he returned.

You don't stay offstage for long, as long as you don't die. And Arbus was still alive, somewhere out there. He found my number and called me. "I'd like to resume relations with you," he said, making me think how little he had changed, at least in the way he spoke.

"Wait, are you in Rome?"

"No. I come every so often to see my mother. I'll be there next week."

"How is your mother?"

"Depends on the day."

"Well, then, come by and pay a call, one afternoon, if you like."

"Just any old afternoon?"

"Give me a day's notice."

AND HE SHOWED UP. We shook hands. I led him into the living room and offered him a seat. He was still skinny, slightly bowed, his hair long, a pair of eyeglasses. Jacket, tie, and black trousers. Shapeless shoes with thick rubber soles. I asked if he wanted something to drink but he said no. If it weren't for the myth that trailed behind Arbus, the beginning of our first meeting in all these years wouldn't have been all that different from when a door-to-door salesman comes in with an attractive offer for a new contract for electricity or natural gas or the Internet. Or maybe there was something different, because I never feel so awkward with a Folletto vacuum cleaner salesman. My heart doesn't race like this. I don't expect my life to rewind.

Arbus noticed my discomfort and with a smile decided to accept my offer of a drink.

"No, wait, I changed my mind, yes . . . I'd gladly drink a chinotto, if you have one."

A *chinotto*?

He bared teeth and gums in a broader smile, narrowing his eyes, and there I recognized my old classmate more clearly, oh yes, Arbus, skinny old fishbone, Arbus the disbeliever, despair and pride of our baffled priests, disposable genius, sinister and useless relic of those effervescent years, the least sentimental young man who ever knelt down before a religious relic.

"You don't have chinotto, do you?" He added, in English, *"Never mind."*

The marks of his long-ago acne had remained, but I can say that they almost looked good on him, like on certain actors who play the tough guy. His haggard pockmarked face peeked out through his long hair, almost entirely white, and it had taken on a strong, decisive character. And his gaze had, so to speak, hardened with a hint of viciousness; the peculiar and lively intelligence that emanated from it no longer seemed to wander through abstract spaces, but instead seemed finally to have landed in this world, where it had encountered obstacles, frustrations, defeats; and it gave the sensation that it had managed to survive, thanks to the resources of stark wickedness each of us possesses, even without imagining it. A naïve intelligence that offers itself naked to the aims of others is quickly devoured. Already, at school, Arbus's intelligence had clashed with petty cruelty. The cruelty of us, his classmates, not up to his level, the typical cruelty of the priests, small-minded, lurking, slithering, conciliatory—the master of ceremonies of it all was the headmaster, and then there was the petty cruelty of the school in and of itself, Catholic or non-Catholic, a place of watered-down knowledge and intermittent discipline and boredom that remained instead in the purest state: you might say that only the woman who sold pizzas at recess, on some occasions Cosmo and just possibly Brother Curzio himself, who in the gym treated him without any false pity for the graceless awkward being that he was—only these few individuals had confronted Arbus in a direct, frank manner, had either appreciated him or else had clashed openly with him. I myself, on some occasions, had concealed our friendship from the others, in order to avoid being associated in the mockery and criticism that they reserved for him. I was glad to see him so manly and calm, now that he was well along in years. I was only partly aware of the bulldozing that life had lavished on him, running over him again and again, crushing him under red-hot weights. Certainly, the burning of the apartment, the painful story of his father . . .

"I READ SOMEWHERE THAT YOU WORK in prison . . . that you teach writing classes."

"No, I don't teach writing classes . . . nothing creative, believe me. I'm just a standard Italian teacher. Grammar, object complements, subject complements, *The Canticle of the Creatures* . . . the Hundred Years' War . . . the same things people study out in the civilian world."

"It must be interesting, though."

"Reasonably. But why do you ask about prison?"

"Because I was in prison myself."

PRISON. *An unexpectedly commonplace topic. It ought to be unusual, in this social class. All right, let's see: I've been working in a prison for twenty years, fine, Arbus tells me that he served time, even if not a very long sentence, fine, Stefano Jervi would have ended up behind bars sooner or later, if he hadn't blown himself or been blown up, and Subdued and Cubbone spent long periods in prison, other classmates of ours and theirs, shorter periods. Fine, fine. And Angelo will be in prison till the day he dies. What an absurd connection between prison and the school we attended.*

4

ALL DAY AND EVERY DAY *we are in intimate contact with air and water; a little less so with earth, unless we live in the countryside; practically not at all with fire, if we leave aside lighters and gas burners. Have you ever turned up the gas on your stove and observed the flame, without a pan or a pot on the burner?*

The ardent crown of tiny light-blue flames, alive . . .

Fire is the great absent presence in our lives and it causes agitation when it appears—the way it darts, dances, caresses things . . . destroys them . . .

From an ordinary fireplace, blazing like a devastating house fire, the sensation that you obtain is of an extraordinary event. A portent.

"THE FIRST TIME, I burned Leda's dollhouse. Do you want me to tell you about it? It was a little house built by our father, when he had an obsession with the coping saw and balsa wood, for a couple of years, an obsession that of course he got over. Considering the developments that ensued, you might insinuate that he had built it for himself to play with. It is said that fathers, in general, buy electric train sets for their children for utterly self-ish reasons.

"I recently had a revelation, when I read somewhere that, when we were boys, we all loved building model kits for a reason that never would have occurred to me: namely that we got high off the airplane glue. The glue we'd brush onto the wings of a Spitfire or a Stuka, before attaching them to the fuselage. We were junkies, in other words.

"So that's the explanation for the feelings of euphoria we got from that hobby.

"Dad had made the little house for Leda with almost no glue, and using interlocking slots and tabs, on a modern model. It looked like the apart-ment building where we lived in Montesacro, you remember? Four stories tall with little terraces on the front. The wire railings gave it a touch of sin-ister realism. In order to help Leda put in and take out her dolls, the entire façade with windows and terraces swung open and lifted up like a lid, but once it was put back into place, the dolls really did seem to live in there, in the various furnished rooms, kitchen, living room, bedroom, so that in order to see what they were doing, you had to get close and peer in the windows like a nosy neighbor. And just who was that nosy neighbor? It was me. When Leda wasn't there, I'd go into her room and, throwing open the shutters that Papà had carefully attached to each window, with tiny hinges, as if to protect the dolls' privacy, I would witness the little scenes of domestic tranquillity that unfolded inside that apartment house.

"Leda had not only put all her dolls in there, but she had also let all her plush toys and puppets and marionettes live there too, of different sizes and materials, as were the dolls for that matter, and the fairies, and the result-ing mishmash was unsettling. In one dining room, for instance, sitting around the table was a little family consisting of a Barbie dressed lavishly, and then a nondescript little baby doll whose hair, however, had been chopped off with a pair of scissors while on her face a beard and mustache had been drawn with a ballpoint pen. What's more, this shaven-headed, bearded doll had no clothes on, and her rosy nudity contrasted with the re-gal attire of the Barbie next to her. I felt a strange heat on my face at the sight of that nude baby doll. Completing that family meal was a man in a suit of medieval armor and a squirrel with an acorn in its paws. In the kitchen of the same apartment a small teddy bear was cooking a meal. The rest of the house was inhabited by dolls dressed to the nines and other dolls that were naked. Also, there was Baby Jesus and Little Red Riding Hood having tea from a tiny set of cups, saucers, and spoons, and in front of them, in the living room where real paintings hung on the walls (my father had constructed them, using matchboxes with Italian landscapes on them), in a rocking chair, sat resting what was perhaps Leda's favorite plush toy, a porcupine dressed in Tyrolean attire.

"On the third floor, on the king-size bed in the master bedroom, lying next to each other and staring at the ceiling with their little painted eyes, were a wooden Pinocchio with movable limbs and a naked baby doll, her round mouth open wide. I knew that doll: more than a baby girl, she looked like a Neanderthal, her hair hanging messily over her apelike shoulders, her legs short and bowed, her feet oversized. Like Polyphemus in the cavern, when he tries to seize Ulysses's comrades, I reached a hand through the window in the plywood wall and pressed on her belly, and out of the obscene orifice in the middle of her face there extended a long red tongue, more obscene still, only to retract, vanishing, the minute I released my thumb from her belly. Pinocchio, motionless, showed no signs of caring that I was groping his wife.

"Well, in spite of all the inappropriate canoodling, it was clean and tidy. Leda liked things to be tidy.

"I liked that tidiness and cleanliness myself, I was almost jealous of it. Just for fun, I moved a few dolls around.

"Since there was no one in the bathroom, I put Little Red Riding Hood in there and, hiking up her cape, I sat her down on the toilet.

"I felt like laughing at the thought that Leda would find her like that, with her underpants pulled down. Once again I felt a burning heat rising from my neck to my cheeks. Then I felt ashamed at this thought of mine, and I felt a burst of rage. At age fifteen, the idea of wasting time fooling around with my little sister's plush toys! I was seized with a terrible fury and I put the blame, deep inside me, on that stupid dollhouse with all its various idiotic characters inside, it was their stupidity that had passed into me. They were so . . . so immobilized, lying there abandoned in their little rooms, living their dreary lives (by now Leda had stopped playing with them, and limited herself to tidying up the dollhouse and keeping it clean . . .) and then my own life was pretty dreary, seeing that I was spending it studying and rummaging around in my sister's dolls and teddy bears. I got the idea in my head of grabbing Leda's dollhouse and shattering it to bits. Until a short while before, everything about that dollhouse had expressed love and satisfaction: everyone in there *loved one another*. But now, instead . . . so I went into the kitchen and got the butane stove lighter."

Arbus's face had contracted into a grimace as he told his story. He continued more or less mechanically to sweep his hair behind his ears as he described in minute detail how he had set fire to his sister's dollhouse, with such intense concentration that he gave the impression that he still had that scene before his eyes, the flickering flames reflected in the lenses of his eyeglasses. His account went on, lurching, fragmented and intense, and he focused on certain details that were apparently secondary: to name just one, the way that the hands and feet of the dolls melted in the heat. While those tiny fingers and toes melted, drip-drip-dripping, until their gauzy little outfits caught fire, I could have sworn that I'd seen a sparkling tear emerge from under the heavy oversized glasses frames and run down my friend's cheek, but maybe it was nothing but a drop of sweat.

"I burned my eyebrows and the tips of my hair. I got too close to the fire. But I wanted to see, see it all . . . and warm up, by that merry, crackling little fire."

"And then?"

"And then . . . I tried to study, to understand what was happening to me. It was incredible and hard to explain the tension that I felt. Every nerve in my body was quivering. My senses became extremely acute, as I imagine an animal's senses must be, until they hurt, until I was being tortured by the sensations: my eyes were burning, and so were my ears, hands, nostrils, and tongue; I could hear a hiss, a buzz on the surface of my organs as if my body were electric . . . and some interference were passing through it. Then suddenly the tension slackened all at once . . . transforming itself into intense pleasure, as soon as the flames began to burn brightly."

"Arbus, do you know that poem by Walt Whitman?"

(*There, another cultural reference . . . could it be that I have anything— that I think nothing—of my own . . . ?*)

"Which poem?"

"'I Sing the Body Electric.'"

"No, I don't know it. Is it nice?"

"Yes, but that doesn't really . . . never mind. Go on."

"An electric body . . . interesting, though, and you ought to . . ."

"Go on, don't stop."

"If you like. Yes. The flames . . . When the flames leaped up I felt happy and strong. I was big . . . I was whole. But while I was watching things being destroyed in the fire, I felt the sensation of dissolving myself, and in that way, of being able to rejoin that from which I've always been separated. I couldn't say what that was, but I knew that I was returning to the forgotten, hidden source, from which I originally come. From which, perhaps, we all come. At least, all those who have my same blood. No, it's not my mother, but something or someone who was there even before . . ."

"Before *what*?"

"I don't know, before her, *behind* her, even deeper . . ."

"Maybe I understand you," I said, and I meant it.

"Let's say this: that, illuminated by the fire, I finally felt that I understood everything. That was . . . it was the light of truth. Excuse me, it may seem obvious, but to me that light is irreplaceable. It purified everything that it made glow."

"And in the meantime it went on burning . . ."

"Yes, but that wasn't why, that's not why I was doing it. That was a secondary effect. Fire, instead of destroying, helps me to penetrate, to insinuate myself into that reality of life from which I've always been excluded. It sounds bizarre, but I never thought I was destroying anything by burning, but rather that *I was making it live*. Or bringing it back to life. And feeling alive while I was doing it, while I was in the process, and that I was performing an act of great joy. After they arrested me, I had to submit to a series of sessions with psychologists: there was no other way to regain my freedom. Interesting people, these psychologists . . . and like many well-meaning people, rather stupid. They were convinced, and consequently, they wanted to convince me, that I had set the fire out of frustration, as revenge, because I'm a misfit . . . in order to compensate for who knows what sexual privation, which might be true, I don't deny it, sure, I'm a miserable wretch, even if I'm certainly not the only one: but the point that these people missed completely, that they couldn't even begin to imagine, was the joy, the light . . . the purity, the intelligence, the truth . . . the simplicity. All things that in fact I succeeded in touching in the presence of a fire. Started by me."

"Did they believe you?"

"Believe . . ." Arbus shook his head and sighed. "'Believe' is a burdensome word, don't you think? They believed me the same way I believed them, not a jot more, not an iota less. It's a preliminary pact. After all, the things you think don't change a bit from what you believed before. No one really listens to anyone: maybe you're not even listening to me right now. Forgive me . . . I know that's not true. They were convinced that I was using fire as a weapon, while for me it was just a show. That's all. I didn't want to prove anything or obtain anything, by setting fire to things, except that there are various different ways of taking care of things, and that was how

I did it: and it was magnificent. I've never done anything spectacular in my life, except for that. From my background, from what little I had told them about myself and my family, the psychologists deduced that I was a solitary individual, easily offended, with resentments against the world and against everybody . . . True, all quite true . . . but also false. A person could size up my criminal profile just from the fact that I wet the bed at night."

"What do you mean? You were peeing your pants . . . ? That's normal, in boys . . . until how old?"

"Oh, I don't know, fourteen, fifteen. Sometimes even *later*."

Arbus burst into a loud laugh. I can't remember the last time I saw and heard him laugh, and I had forgotten what his laugh was like.

It was bloodcurdling. But contagious. And in fact, I too started chuckling along.

"They assured me that wetting my pants was my way of manifesting my repressed emotions . . . of giving voice to my *malaise* . . ."

As he laughed, he revealed his long teeth, which had grown blackened and jumbled, tossing his head back, until his noisy prolonged neighing was suffocated by a series of almost mute hiccups, his throat spasming.

"So anyway, I did eight months behind bars for arson."

RIGHT AFTER ARBUS LEFT MY APARTMENT, I went online to find the psychological profile of the pyromaniac: and I found a number of clear-cut definitions, some of which corresponded with great precision to my friend. The extreme isolation, the immaturity, the search for a clamorous affirmation of an identity they had always sought to keep hidden, misunderstood, suffering but perhaps to some extent delighting in the lack of understanding from others . . . Yes, I recognized my old schoolmate in these traits. I remembered the profanities with which he had covered his desk the day before leaving the school for good: Hadn't that been the act of an incendiary, albeit in figurative terms? Weren't those eight banner-headline letters, after all, the opposite of what the divine flame had carved into the stone tablets, in the movie that the priests had projected for us roughly half a million times, *The Ten Commandments*? (And then there was *Miracle of Marcelino, King of Kings, Ben-Hur* and *Quo Vadis?* and even Pasolini's *The Gospel According to St. Matthew*.) Our Christian education, in other words. The redemption from our own personal misery, in those demented images . . .

Yes. That's the way Arbus was, it was him, that's our man. In the flesh.

I thought I could see him now, sculpted, ragged and tattered, his long hair plastered to his cheeks, as he dragged the cross in one of the stations of the Via Dolorosa.

(A Via Dolorosa that many years later I would walk in the middle of the night, in Jerusalem, my eyes full of tears . . . for the cold, for the stirring emotions. That long, sweet, painful, and unforgettable steep flight of stairs.)

I focused, reading more carefully the information available on this singular pathology: case studies, statistics, timing. Among the motivations that can drive a pyromaniac to set a fire, which are usual either/or and rarely coincide, I found some that might have acted on Arbus simultaneously: having ruled out the entries "vandalism," "personal profit," and "concealment of a corpse" (at least I hope . . .), the others rang familiar to my old classmate's character: " excitement" . . . "mental disturbance" . . . "extremism" . . . "discouragement" (whatever that term is supposed to mean . . .), and then perhaps "vendetta," yes, vendetta . . . but a vendetta against whom, exactly? Against what?

Discouragement . . . But had Arbus ever once been discouraged in his life, or perhaps I should put it, had anyone or anything ever once actually managed to discourage him? Perhaps this was the chief detail of the whole story: from age thirteen on, from as much as I had been able to see of him and understand, nothing could intimidate Arbus, nothing and no one was sufficiently powerful or threatening or seductive to sway him from his intentions. In a certain sense, not even he could meddle with whatever direction he had set off in . . . For this reason as well, at school we considered him not to be entirely human, and it was also for this virtue or character flaw of his that I had made friends with him, and that I admired him and, to some extent, feared him. This world did not contain a valid deterrent, a threat, or a penalty of sufficient gravity to inhibit him. He was proof against pleas, promises, rewards, warnings, and intimidations. Deep down, I thought, with a shiver of appalled realization, he wasn't all that different from another protagonist of this book . . .

On one thing, I am in agreement with the psychologists who had been keeping him under observation: his almost total inability to express his emotions. And the shame that he felt, by proxy, when it was someone else who did it for him: first of all, his mother.

"LIKE NERO . . . ?!"

"Yes, Nero. Lucius Domitius Ahenobarbus, who went by Nero, an underestimated emperor . . . slandered by history. I know that this will make you laugh, but it was him I was thinking about . . . that textbook figure, the madman from the movies, who plucks at his lyre, rapt with inspiration, while Rome is in flames. I was every bit as inspired, and in fact there was a music playing inside and outside me, I could distinctly hear the melody above the crackling of the flames, or perhaps it was as if that sound of cracks and pops were following the rhythm of a dance, a village dance, first slow, then faster and faster, its pace picking up . . . as if possessed by the devil. I was incapable of resisting the impulse: in fact, it seemed to me that it was neither useful nor even reasonable to try. And once the fire was raging, I was proud that it had been my hand that had caused it all, and I rejoiced as I gazed at the consequences . . . in observing that if I set out to do a certain thing, well, then, that thing happened . . . it was *real*, and I was real, too, seeing that it was only thanks to me that it had happened. Everything was burning, burning . . ."

THE CONNECTIONS IN THE NETWORK of my mind can be extremely fast or quite slow, depending on whether the elements to be connected are or are not dear to my heart. When the material it's working on has no immediate importance for me, my brain zips along at stunning speed, a matter of nanoseconds and the most unthinkable relations are established, the farthest-flung notions come barreling in on me en masse; but just let the matter at hand have something to do with me, and my mind seizes up, gets distracted . . . when I have the person I would have liked to tell X and Y in front of me, just like that, X and Y vanish into thin air, and my mind turns blank, empty. I can say nothing.

Without the idea of asking him while he was here, visiting me, even grazing my mind, and getting a confirmation of the fact from him directly, two or three days after his confession, I had a sudden and unsettling flash in my head, accompanied by an unusual cold tremor in my hands, and the instantaneous certainty that the fire that broke out in the Arbus home, when he was still just a boy, and which had destroyed half the apartment, all his mother, Ilaria's clothing and her possessions and her memorabilia, as well as all that remained of his father's library, after the professor had abandoned his family in order to pursue his (ridiculous) dream of sexual happiness, was due not to a short circuit in the electrical wiring as had always been claimed, but had been intentionally set by my classmate. Why, of course, of course . . . *of course*! I said to myself, while my hands, rubbed vigorously back and forth on my thighs, regained their warmth and finally stopped trembling. Why are the simplest things always explained in incongruous and mysterious ways, when all you'd really need to do is keep your eyes open and apply basic logic to work your way back to the true causes? Knowing my classmate as I did, and his many eccentricities, why had it never occurred to me that he was guilty of that arson? The spotlight on what had happened that day should have flicked on instantly, when he had told me about the blaze he had set, when he pitilessly burned all his sister Leda's dolls: all that had changed was the order of magnitude of the fire, from the balsa-wood dollhouse to the apartment inhabited by flesh-and-blood human beings. The members of his family. But if that episode from his adolescence hadn't been enough, still, how had I failed to see when he told me about how he had set fire to the woods?

"SUNDAYS ARE TERRIBLE. I didn't know what to do. For that matter, up there in the mountains a Sunday is a day that's no different from all the other days of the week, and yet I felt the crushing boredom as if I were in the city, in August. And at the same time, I felt a strange excitement. If it weren't for the fact that the language those damned priests taught us simply turns my stomach, I'd say that I had fallen into a mystical state of mind, that's right, mystical, or else prehensile, on the alert. The woods were silent: just a faint breeze passing through the beech branches, a creaking sound here and there, the rustling of those wonderful places. And that murmuring tore at my heart and I pricked up my ears, trying to hear something inaudible . . . a hiss, a hidden lament . . . the presence of something alive that wasn't just the sound of the trees and of the animals hidden in their trunks or high in their branches. It almost annoyed me to see the incredible towering height of those trees, my head spun when I looked up at the light piercing the lofty foliage of those beeches. Seventy-five feet . . . a hundred . . . massive trunks rocketing upward, like so many accusations leveled against the sky, pointing heavenward. Hundreds of beeches all around me, nothing but beeches, such incredible monotony. Why all this squandered space, why this repetition?

"I was on duty all alone, that day, since in fact it was a holiday, and I was driving aimlessly around in my jeep, like a layabout with no idea of where to go. Driving at random I found myself emerging, in defiance of probability, in the same clearing, as if I'd been driving around in circles. I was supposed to monitor an area so vast that the very word 'monitor' loses its meaning. And monitor what, after all? Make sure that the ants were doing their jobs? Or that some wing nut wasn't lurking behind a boulder, wearing a checkered hat with earflaps, ready to gun down some unsuspecting bear? I hadn't seen a single bear or wolf in months. They must have moved to higher altitudes to escape the heat. I like the wilderness and the solitude, but that day I perceived it like a fault, some burden of guilt. Guilt for what? Of the many greater-or-lesser possibilities, perhaps the sin of not loving. Failing to love myself, first and foremost, and also failing to love other people. And if I'm going to be truthful, failing to love even the places into which I had withdrawn, fooling myself into the scornful belief that woods and animals were less hostile and unpleasant to me than human company. I had thought they were ideal subjects for my study and devotion. But who was I to take upon myself the duty to protect them? Wasn't I, rather, the creature who needed protecting, who needed care? And yet the very idea made me laugh. Yes, certainly, me, me, me . . . what's the sense of saying it, thinking it? Me, me, me . . . what does this obsessive first person singular even mean?

"The stillness of the summer day was reaching an unbearable point. A breaking point. I stopped the jeep and got out. The dense layer of dried twigs, leaves, and ferns crunched under my boots. Then I sat down on a rock, my head bowed. I tried to remember, with fury, with care and precision, undertaking an immense effort of the will. And, I don't know how, I remembered *everything*, all of it, from the first minute of my conscious life until the very instant I had stepped out of that jeep. It was the only time that I managed to see and grasp all at once my entire existence. A portentous thing, it all appeared to me, laid out in the correct order. Things had gone exactly as they were meant to go, up till then.

"As I raised my eyes, I noticed one tree that stood out from all the others, a particular beech, ancient, stout, with massive limbs, concealed beneath sparse foliage. As it had grown, it had managed to keep the other trees at a distance, creating beneath it a circular clearing at least fifty paces deep.

"I've never smoked a cigarette in my life, neither before that day nor since. But I suddenly had an urge for a cigarette and so I went back to the jeep to see if my work colleague had by any chance left a pack in the door pocket. He had. I pulled out the pack and opened it: it contained four national-brand cigarettes and a lighter. It was against the rules to smoke, of course, since that was one of the main reasons for forest fires, but my co-worker smoked anyway, taking all conceivable precautions. I would do the same thing. As I leaned forward to shut the door of the jeep, my gaze darted behind the passenger seat, where there was a two-and-a-half-gallon gas can. Practically full. My coworker had filled it up down in the valley, seeing that there would be two holidays in a row, the Saturday and the Feast of the Assumption, and there was a chance we'd have to use the chain saw. I put the pack of cigarettes back, after extracting the lighter, and, gas can in hand, I went back to the rock where I'd been sitting before.

"I looked around again: the woods were stupendous but inanimate, it looked like a charming photograph, odiously beautiful, artistic, in short. And I, as you know, *hate* poetry. I hate it. I wish I could put it to death. We'd be so much better off if beauty just vanished, replaced by something simpler. Right there, before me, reared up that beech tree unlike all the others, with a monstrous array of branches beginning just ten feet off the ground, while all its neighbors simply rose smoothly into the air. It had to be at least two hundred years old. Arrogant, vain. For centuries it had been standing there, pushing upward, elongating its increasingly massive and heavy scaffolding of branches. Muscular branches. I went over to the base and poured at least a quarter of the fuel can onto the dry kindling that surrounded it. The foliage and litter, dry as paper, drank up the gas, the wet stain vanished in an instant. Then I moved two hundred paces farther on and did the same thing, pouring another quarter can at the foot of a second beech, and a hundred paces off to the right, the rest of the can at the base of the only fir that had grown in that stand of trees: that's why it had caught my eye, bright and smooth among the darker, gnarly trunks.

"I gave the fir tree the honor of going first. Like any conscientious forest ranger, I carried in the breast pocket of my shirt the booklet with the park regulations: I tore out a couple of pages and crumpled them up, then I patted the trunk of the fir and lit the ball of paper.

"The fir tree burst into flame in an instant. The fire enveloped it and started creeping around the trunk. It seemed to lick the bark without touching it, as if it were running upward like a liquid, with some misguided understanding of gravity . . .

"I followed the same procedure with the second beech, which struggled to catch fire, perhaps because I had only sprinkled it with a little gasoline, half a gallon at most. As a gesture of encouragement, I tossed the manual of park regulations into its flames: it fanned out, spreading the remaining pages, and then lifted into the air, charred in an instant. At that point, I turned to go back, climbing up toward the huge beech with the frightening branches. Behind me I began to hear the unmistakable crackling of the dry twigs and leaves scattered across the ground and a truly wonderful, harsh scent began to fill my nostrils, nothing like the stench of plastic from that time I had burned Leda's dolls: a living, animate perfume, an essence so inebriating that I felt stunned at the thought I'd been able to even call the time I'd existed until then, before filling my lungs with that aroma, 'life' . . . you're welcome not to believe me, but I swear to you that there's no experience on earth so delicate and intense.

"Having done what I'd set out to do, I sit back down on the rock and look up at the old coppery tree. At its base, the flames leap high . . . twisting . . . the red . . . the red . . ."

IT MUST HAVE just been an effect of the light pouring in through the window, but once again I had the sensation that the gleam on the smudged lenses of Arbus's eyeglasses was a reflection of flames. His voice quavered.

". . . THE BRIGHT COLOR OF BLOOD . . . but it's *my* blood being spilled . . . and this hemorrhage is perhaps the happiest event of my life."

"WHEN THE BLAST OF HEAT became unbearable, and the flames on the ground began to draw closer with furtive, serpentine movements, I grabbed the empty fuel can and ran toward the jeep. I drove uphill, as far as possible from the fire, and then abandoned the jeep and continued on foot, clambering up a rock ridge. Having reached the summit, on a barren outcropping, I turned back to observe the panorama.

"My deed had begun to transform it.

"At least a dozen big trees were burning right out to the tips of the highest branches swaying in the air . . . the incredibly long arms seemed to be trying to hail some rescuer, but instead they managed only to transmit the fire to the neighboring trees. Where the trees were close enough that they almost touched, the flames leaped from one to another, and on the tree that had just been set aflame it blazed with an impetuous vigor. Crushed and suffocated under the scaffolding of branches, the plumes of dark smoke from the burning underbrush suddenly burst forth in fearsome pillars, spinning around their center . . . animated internally by reddish glows, struggling to make their way through the foliage, shoving it aside in their furious ascent, as if yearning to breathe . . . and as I watched them rise toward the sky, scattering sparks in all directions, I thought to myself that

that was just the beginning. The beginning. I uttered those words over and over again, through compressed lips. Then I sat down on the fuel can to enjoy the show."

"AFTER A FEW HOURS, the fire had spread in all directions. It was methodical. Toward evening, the wind began to blow, produced by the immense heat. It was blowing toward where I sat, from on high I could see the front of the fire marching along, with the flames leaning forward and suddenly shaking with fury, like waves in an ocean storm, heading straight for me. As they gradually drew nearer, I could make out the windmilling flames that burst out of the gray cloud, whirling around on themselves before vanishing, swallowed up by the smoke, like flashes in a summer tempest. Even though I was high above, I felt a scalding blast dry the evening's humidity, and it warmed me up. I also noticed, to my amazement, that a number of large long-plumed birds, instead of fleeing the flames, seemed to be attracted by them . . . they floated above the fire like garishly colored kites, and then fluttering in an irregular and awkward manner, they dropped lower still, perhaps lured in by those sudden bursts of light, and at a certain altitude, stunned by the smoke and hit by a blast of unbearable heat, they were instantly burned alive, mummified, and, still beating their charred wings, they plunged headfirst into the fire. One after another. Playfully, I pretended that I was shooting them with a rifle and bringing them down. I'd take aim at one, line it up in my crosshairs, following the zigzag pattern of its suicidal flight, wait for the right moment, when the feathers of the incautious bird were just about to be incinerated by the blazing gust of the flames, and then I'd pull the imaginary trigger, making a noise with my mouth, ptew-ssh! and the bird, hit dead center, would stiffen, and then drop in a nosedive into the fire.

"I killed dozens of them like that.

"The night was every bit as surprising: a charade of fire accompanied by a sound I'd never heard before. It was a dull roar formed of tiny sputters, pops, hisses, lacerations, that wound up turning into a wind. I felt no fear, not even when a sharp explosion roughly two hundred yards from where I was sitting signaled that the flames had reached the jeep and taken possession of it. In my soul, the euphoria had been replaced by an absolute sense of serenity, which allowed me to stay up all night without feeling any emotion whatsoever, placid, self-contained, focused.

"The next morning there were no longer pheasants flying over the blaze, but instead helicopters and—with a deplorable delay in their arrival, for which I at the time was grateful, because it allowed me to enjoy the show much longer than I already had—a couple of large firefighting aircraft. They came roaring out from behind the mountain and for the rest of the morning, slow and noisy, they kept passing overhead, roughly once every half hour, dropping boxcar loads of liquid onto the fire, but the minute they dropped it that liquid seemed to vaporize into the air, and to hit only such a small and imprecise part of the blaze that not even a hundred of those airplanes opening their bellies all at the same time would have been capable of dousing it. No, my fire would never be extinguished. My battle was just beginning, I decided . . . it was just beginning. But suddenly I felt tired. Terribly tired. Hollowed out. Something wasn't adding up anymore. What was that? What battle had I been talking about? Was there a war raging or had I just dreamed it? There's no such thing as a fire that burns forever: either someone puts it out, or it will burn out on its own. Thinking back on what I had done, from the moment in which I had first laid eyes on the gas can, I didn't think of it as a mistake, on my part, or a crime, but something worse, far worse: an act of idiocy. I was nothing but a pathetic loon, that's what I was. My exhaustion and emptiness were transformed into dismay. The chain of events was made up of a series of weak and deformed links. A stupid little maniac . . . a cowardly, solitary cretin . . .

"My strength failed me, I could feel my shoulders bowing. They were already slumped, but now they slumped even further, as if my arms were literally about to fall off. The lenses of my eyeglasses were so dirty and smeared with smoke that I couldn't see a thing. I took off my glasses and burst into tears. As I was wiping off my face, using my own tears, hot and sooty, I heard someone call my name, and I turned around. Not far away stood three out-of-focus figures. The words they said to me were out of focus as well. I recognized one of them by his voice. It was my coworker. He came toward me. Yes, that was him. He put a hand on my shoulder, and as he did, he was talking, he was talking to me, but I couldn't understand what he was saying. The roar of the flames had burrowed into my head, it was inside my head now, its crackling covered up every thought, and a damp and dirty smoke enveloped it. He bent over to pick up the empty gas can, unscrewed the cap, sniffed at the mouth, and then dropped it, disconsolately, and kicked it across the ground.

"'What on earth have you done?' was the only phrase I managed to discern amid the chaos that was crackling in my mind. I put my glasses back on. My coworker's face, so close to my own and suddenly crystal clear, was cut clear across by a grimace of incredulity or disgust, and suddenly he looked to me far older, almost decrepit, as if he were my grandfather and I were an incorrigible child. A few yards farther on stood another forest ranger and a firefighter in full gear and regalia. The forest ranger had snapped open the flap of his holster and his hand was resting on his pistol.

"AND SO, in that very same magic instant when I was supposed to become uncatchable, I was caught. I put up no resistance. At my trial, they gave me a light sentence because I had no prior criminal record but, since there was no mistaking how dangerous I was, they kept me behind bars. I believe that was the only way they had of continuing to keep me under observation. The aggravating factors were the sheer vast expanse of the fire that I had set and the danger to human life and limb: in the four days it took to get the flames under control, they'd had to evacuate a campsite to eliminate all risk, and some of the campers had suffered psychological damage on account of the emergency. The prosecution went so far as to maintain I had willfully intended to cause a grave disaster with ensuing loss of human life. That affirmation was rejected by the court but it cast a shadow over the trial. My lawyers pointed out, in vain, that the campsite was four miles from the most extensive front of the raging fire."

STRANGE THAT IN that one SLM high school class there should have been not one but two students who later became writers: me and Marco Lodoli, who was an earlier beginner and more of a regular producer, and who published a lot of books, building himself a recognizable career, a profession, in a way I was never able to do. Still, the real writer was neither me nor Marco Lodoli, the real writer was Arbus, or at least he could have been. But I have the impression that he considered writing—unless it was strictly necessary, something that happens only rarely—a leisure activity, a waste of time.

When Maldonado was publishing L'Encefalo, that magazine was the only thing to come out of the QT that was anything more than the usual political disquisitions . . . and Arbus would easily have been able to master those topics, the only one among us, perhaps, capable of understanding them and calling them into question. But he wanted nothing to do with literature.

AND THEN I ALSO REMEMBER, during the ceremony at the Devil's Chair, a young woman wearing a cowl making knots in a rope, and then tossing it in the fire. That was Leda Arbus. In the instant she drew near the flames and her face was illuminated by the glow, if ever so briefly, I thought I recognized that limpid gaze.

5

THE SECOND TIME he came to see me, in my home, he told me without shame and in brief summary what his life had been like from age twenty to age forty. He took a degree in engineering with the highest possible grades. He very quickly abandoned the Nazi-Maoist groups, which by that point in any case were already crumbling under the blows of enmity from without and within. He got married to an anarchist shopgirl, who worked at a store that sold mountain equipment, where he had gone to purchase some hiking boots. The marriage lasted little more than a year. In that period his love of solitary, inaccessible places began to grow. After her initial enthusiasm, his wife refused to go up to the mountains with him anymore, which spelled the end of their marriage. He spent eighteen months in a cabin in the Apennines observing the lives of wolves: he followed them in their travels, he photographed them. In particular, he studied one specimen, a female, who was, however, killed by poachers. During this period of isolation, strange to say, he met another woman, who also had a passionate interest in wolves. The only other human being in the mountains besides him. He came to her rescue at one point, when she was freezing to death. He married her, his second marriage, and this time the marriage lasted five years, even though it was practically never consummated. He became a teaching assistant in the Department of Robotics, and then an associate professor, at the University of Bari, but then he was suspended from his teaching duties after a suspicious episode. At that point he took the civil service exam for a position as a forest ranger and got the job, perhaps the oldest and most highly qualified forest ranger ever hired. After that, the forest fire he set, and then prison. After serving his sentence, he was forbidden from going back to work in the woods, but he did resume teaching in the field of robotics. His second wife left him and a tendency that had previously only been hinted at began to rear its head and become predominant, in time absorbing nearly all his attention and energy.

HE BEGAN REPLYING, by mail, to classified ads that read: "*Dame sévère demande élève*" ("Stern lady seeks student"), and realized that he tremendously enjoyed the demented correspondence that ensued.

He wasn't really interested in meeting a woman, he wasn't looking for a relationship, he only wanted to picture parts of her in his mind, work with his imagination. He dreamed intensely of female buttocks of every size and shape, and how he could spank them.

"With respect to reality, the good thing about fantasies is that you have no need to actually put them into effect . . . worst case, even the most violent and perverse ones, you just jack off to them and be done with it."

I listened to him raptly.

Then he told me that one day he had groped a woman on the street, in the midst of a knot of pedestrians waiting to cross at a traffic light. She didn't even notice. And from that day forward, he was unable to stop.

"Grabbing women's asses in the crowd, you have no idea how many men do it. Discreet men, above suspicion, well-mannered and properly brought up, just like me. Certain women know it, what with having been groped for years, groped the minute a big enough crowd gathers to make it possible for them to do it without being identified. The yearning to touch wins out over any prohibition. I've given it a lot of thought, and I've tried to figure out why. Deep down, it's basically something so stupid, but it's as if the stupidity of that act were in fact the reason to do it, the exciting aspect, doing something as stupid as putting your hand on a woman's ass, just brush it with your fingers and while you're doing it, think, 'I'm touching it, yes, I'm touching it, I'm touching her ass, let's see whether she even notices,' which she almost instantly does. See if she starts, if she turns around, if she darts away . . . suddenly lifts her head, swivels her head suddenly . . .

"Then the high point of stupidity and excitement is to touch four or five in a row, passing through a crowd of people with their backs to you, whispering, 'Excuse me, excuse me,' and pretending to be in a hurry, so that the contact seems unintentional, or can at least be claimed as such in case an argument breaks out. There are jutting, hard asses, wrapped in tight jeans, or else the skirt of a skinny woman with practically nothing but bones underneath, and that's exciting too, and it doesn't really matter if it's a young girl or an old woman, like I said, it's such a stupid thing, and there's a special satisfaction in doing something senseless, a thrill in being attracted to something that isn't attractive, or that's attractive only because it's forbidden or because of its name, 'ass,' yes, an 'ass,' the satisfaction of grabbing and squeezing the ass of a woman who's a perfect stranger is the same as the thrill when we were kids of repeating the word 'ass,' even though your mother had forbidden you to say it, because it was rude. I remember hearing grown-ups use the expression 'dead hand,' for someone touching on the sly, 'dragging the dead hand,' I understand what it means, of course, but I doubt there could be a less apt and suitable expression: that hand is actually all too alive, it's like a lopped-off lizard tail moving on its own, though it's severed from the body . . . if anything it's the rest of the body that's dead, but the hand, the hand that's touching, that's quite alive, indeed, my whole life, all my heart, my sex organ, my brain are in that hand. I've never felt as much life as what pulsated in my hand while it was fondling the ass of a female university student or sliding edgewise into the long, deep cleft between the buttocks of a Cape Verdean cleaning woman . . .

"Pointless to go out looking for the prettiest girl. What a foolish idea! That was the mirage that adolescents chased after: not me. I read about a guy in a brothel who would always choose the prettiest girls and found that he couldn't really get aroused with them; so he changed strategy; he'd pick a perfectly ordinary whore, neither pretty nor ugly, in fact, preferably ugly, and he'd have her whip him: and then he would get aroused, excited to the moon and stars! I've learned that beauty, true beauty, serves as an anesthetic. Beauty is the road to chastity. I could never have anything to do with very beautiful women, and luckily I've encountered very few, which isn't something I regret, in fact, I'm very glad about it. Beauty, in fact, embarrasses, dumbs you down, paralyzes, enchants, and most important of all, there are very few who understand it and appreciate it for what it is, and nothing more. I'm not one of these. But I do understand that beauty is untouchable and the best thing you can do is leave it where you found it. The man rapt in admiration won't move a finger, he almost can't breathe. I understood that, not with women, which aren't really my field of expertise, but with the mountains."

"I'VE OFTEN FOUND MYSELF incapable of doing my work, carrying out my everyday tasks, enjoying the simplest and most normal interactions with others on account of the obsessions that filled my mind. They'd saturate my mind, holding it hostage, leaving me free only for brief intervals, a few minutes at a time, during which I didn't even have a chance to start on any real projects because I knew that before long I'd once again be overwhelmed by obscene imagery and desires as foul and filthy as they were puerile and ridiculous, the sort of thing that would only cause me affliction and shame. I felt comfortable only when I sank to the lowest levels. Once I became a miserable wretch and I behaved like a miserable wretch, I realized that I was finally myself, and this gave me a tremendous sense of relief and, at the same time, it tormented me . . ."

THE INCIDENT, then, that put an end to his university career partook of that nature. An insistent, prolonged caress of the ass of a young female student bent over peering into a microscope. Impossible to claim that physical contact was involuntary or accidental. Moreover, there were witnesses.

I was very surprised by Arbus's confession. When we were classmates back at school he had never, not even once, expressed sexual desires or yearnings. Now this interest, which had turned into a frenzy, was manifesting itself in an intense, spasmodic fashion.

"And I'm chiefly attracted to ugly women," he reiterated. Maybe that was his real perversion.

WHILE HE WAS TELLING ME about his exploits—which I was unable to entirely dismiss as sad and tawdry, though they undoubtedly were that and more—Arbus kept grinning. Yes, grinning and grinding his teeth. The pockmarks dotting the skin on his face flushed red. He seemed at once giddy and mortified. Probably deep down he was taking pleasure in the degradation of revealing his inner nature to me. It's an innate mechanism of confession, without which it would never happen at all. I wonder to what extent he was conscious of the fact that those revelations were music to my ears, certainly not celestial harmony, but still, perfectly in tune. With what? With whom? Well, with him, with me, with our whole friendship in which all was crooked, nothing had been straight and smooth, with all the things we had witnessed and taken part in, with our deeply twisted natures, with the relationships everyone at once seeks out and avoids, the ones that they all fear and yet to which they are morbidly attracted. While my friend told me all about the time in his life during which he'd regularly board a city bus, just any old bus, in order to be able to press up against the specific warmth of a pair of flesh-toned pantyhose, I suddenly saw the entire Arbus family before my eyes, starting with Ilaria and running all the way down to the languid Leda, by way of that odd fellow, the father, Lodovico Arbus, professor of mathematical logic, with his wooden walrus, the souvenir of a night spent in a sauna with several pale and bearded giants, and a final roll in the snow, and I couldn't say where the follies of one ended and the peculiarities of the other began. All of them special, all maniacal. A long, sweet slide into pathology. I remember a screwball movie from the seventies, *Fire Sale*, directed by and starring Alan Arkin. Arbus's erotic fixations, my own fixations on the attractive women of his family, his father's fixations with young philosophers of language with tweed jackets and tousled hair, Ilaria's aphrodisiacal uneasiness, which also came straight out of a film from the seventies . . . all formed a circle in which everyone desired the wrong thing or the wrong person, or a part of that wrong person, the hair, the buttocks . . . the voice . . . the wooden walrus . . . the fingers performing an arpeggio on a piano keyboard . . . fair flesh spattered with semen . . .

Maybe only a milkman dies with a healthy mind, and maybe not even he.

I UNDERSTOOD THAT ARBUS, as long as he was a kid, had managed to rein in the erratic impulses that surged inside him. His fresh, still intact adolescent energies were even stronger than those impulses, if allied to a sense of duty and his inborn shyness. Once he became a man, however, paradoxically more mature and freer of restraints, and therefore weaker, those impulses had gained the upper hand. In the name of what was he supposed to go on sacrificing them?

The path of liberation, and of his new enslavement to his impulses, might well have begun the day of that profanity written on the desk, his last day of school, the last day he spent with us.

I saw before my eyes, once again, that tall, skinny young man, at once glacial and on edge, who wore the mask of awkwardness and intellectual superiority, and I understood the protracted effort that he had made to control himself. Lust. The demon that I naïvely thought had never yet tested his defenses. Because back then I hadn't understood that that demon can attack in many ways, above and beyond the pure and innocent imagination that can't conceive of anything more complicated than sexual intercourse.

Even in that unexpected confession of his, a serpent's tail still whipped, vibrating menacingly. For what reason had Arbus sought me out and come
to see me? Was it to tell me those stories, if not to prolong that humiliating
pleasure? Nothing could be as morbid as the retailing of a bad habit abandoned: it's the best way to relive its excitement, blamelessly, a thrill you
claim you no longer wish to experience.

"SO IS THERE ANYTHING ELSE?" I asked ironically.
    "Well, yes, there is . . ."
    "So, tell me the truth," I asked when Arbus was done with his confes-
sions, "were you the one who set fire to your apartment?"
    "No."
    "Then who did?"
    "Leda."

LEDA!
    Oh, Leda, Leda, St. Anthony's fire of my youth. My flesh still burns,
there where you *never* touched me. I never imagined that I would have occasion to think of you again. And revisit my early twenties.

6

THERE WERE TIMES *when Leda stared at me, for long minutes on end,
but there was something singular about her gaze, she seemed to be
looking not at me, but at some object that was miles away, or else a portrait of me that had been hung there on my shoulders for her to contemplate
in place of my own real face. Those eyes of hers, so lovely, seemed to have
been given to her not to look through but rather to astonish anyone who
looked at her.*
    *(I was scared at the thought of what must have happened to her to give
her those eyes.)*

✦

BUT WHAT WAS IT I had had with Leda Arbus? A friendship? A friendship with kisses? An emotional relationship without love, a sexual relationship without sex? Can a boy and a girl be friends? If they can, can they be lovers? If they become lovers, can they remain friends? If they don't, is it because one of the two decided not to?

WHAT HAPPENED between me and Arbus's sister can't really be called a love story or even a friendship—a friendship, for that matter, still being an unusual thing between a young man and a young woman in those days, when there was practically only room for such binding and aggressive feelings as love, desire, devotion, and scorn.

Maybe it wasn't even a *story*, but a *situation*, with two characters between whom certain things could happen. Whether or not they actually did is a matter of chance.

So what happened between me and that girl? From the very first time I went to Arbus's house, it was clear that there was a bond between me and his sister, that is to say, a bond that already existed, that had been there even before we met. I believe that you would call the thread that appeared between our two persons Destiny, when I saw her seated at the piano, with her back so straight that it actually appeared curved to me, concave, the line of her shoulders thrown back compared with her pelvis, and she turned, and the thread twanged, vibrating between our eyes. Equally marked by destiny was her position with respect to me, which can be summarized in the somewhat lurid definition "my best friend's sister."

She was playing Debussy's *Children's Corner*. I remember it quite exactly because when her brother informed me, the following day, of the name of the piece, I ran, and that's not a figure of speech, I literally slingshotted myself to the *ricordi* store on Piazza Indipendenza to buy the record. Performed by Arturo Benedetti Michelangeli. And that was the first record of classical music that I bought with my own money.

AT FIRST GLANCE, there could be no doubts whatever about Leda's family ties. But all the facial features that were excessive in Arbus, and therefore unpleasant, as if they'd been composed on his face without taking into account the proportions and distances between one feature and another, were in perfect harmony in his sister, Leda, to such a degree that perhaps the sole defect of that assemblage of eyes, lips, nose, and hair was precisely its per-fection, making Leda look like a doll, a painting, a drawing traced with a pencil rather than a flesh-and-blood girl.

When I first met her she was fourteen; two years later you'd expect me to write that she had changed . . . but no, she hadn't, she looked exactly the same, just a little taller, a little bigger, and she played the piano better. The scene was the same: she, facing the piano, with her back, erect, to me, and her shoulders loose, playing Schumann this time, the suite *Papillons* (it was she who told me so, after she finished playing the piece), while I listened to her from the door of the living room, leaning against the jamb. The suite is played continuously, without hesitation, and as far as I could tell, without the slightest mistake; but when Leda turns around, surprised by my ap-plause, which comes of my sincere enthusiasm, and yet, perhaps, out of an incurable male shyness mixed with a certain aggressiveness, is also meant to ring faintly ironic, I realize that everything has changed in her, while still remaining the same. Her gaze is calm, pellucid, apparently devoid of any emotion, and in this, only in this one aspect, she reminds me of her brother as he removes his eyeglasses to rub his eyes after solving—in just thirty sec-onds, practically without removing the chalk from the blackboard—the physics problem that three other classmates labored over in vain, until the teacher, out of patience, summoned him to put the matter out of its misery: clearly, in the Arbus household, emotions were banished entirely, or it was forbidden to display them, or perhaps they simply didn't exist, and Leda had played that deeply moving piece by a half-mad composer without a twinge of real feeling, nothing more than the satisfaction of having played it well, and possibly not even that.

But the absence of feelings or any manifestation of them in Leda, I don't know why, was something I liked, it attracted me very much, just as it had magnetized me in her brother. I felt as if I were falling into a deep and won-derful void; and what's more, the calmness and lack of reaction in Leda's eyes allowed me to gaze into them without inhibition, admiring their beauty in perfect tranquillity.

Later, at the university, I would study hundreds of pages of art history, aesthetics, and philosophy that attempted to express in concepts an ideal of uncontaminated, pure, placid beauty, undisturbed, in other words, clas-sical: but never in any statue, painting, or poem have I ever found the calm—so close, truth be told, to chilliness and yet by no means cold—that I saw in Leda's eyes when she turned to look at me after playing the last notes of Schumann's suite. Even the word that she said to me, the most ordinary word in the world, seemed to come from a distant universe and sounded singularly precise to my ears.

"Hi," she said to me.

"Hi, Leda."

What's so memorable about this very brief dialogue?

The fact that it contained everything that we had to say to each other, she and I. In fact, I'm convinced that Leda was aware of our bond, even though in the unmistakable light of the facts there was no bond between us at all: I was just another of her brother's classmates who occasionally came to their house to study, in the afternoon, to get that class genius to explain what I hadn't understood that morning. The smile that she gave me was pure, too, so pure that it seemed false, considering that it didn't go with any particular feeling. In fact, I don't think she was happy to see me, but rather that she assumed it was something inevitable: that I was there was fate, and therefore a normal thing. Therefore, why be astonished or get worked up?

I understood as I watched her get up from the piano bench, amazing me with how tall and skinny she was, close her sheet music, lower the lid over the keyboard, and then walk past me with a handful of musical scores on her way to her room, I understood at that moment that one day we would kiss, she and I, that it was entirely inevitable, the two of us were destined to kiss, even though I had no idea of when it would happen and what path would lead us there, indeed, I was so certain of it that to me, it was as if it had already happened, which is why I felt free of the anxiety of having to imagine the steps necessary to reach that point. That point had already been reached and bypassed. As she brushed my shoulder with hers and walked past, and I watched her go, following her with my gaze down the dim light of the hallway, I was in fact convinced that it was every bit as clear to her what I had seen and understood, as if it were there before her large dark eyes.

It would be reasonable to doubt that Arbus and Leda were brother and sister. As I think I have said before, my friend had raven-black hair and small blue eyes, while Leda instead was blond and her eyes were dark, such a deep clear brown that you'd say they were practically black. The contrasting colors seemed to have drawn at random from a contradictory genetic patrimony, as is the case, for example, with my family, where there's a bit of everything—tall and short, blond and brunette, slender and muscle-bound.

And yet there was something unmistakable in the Arbus family that made it clear that they were brother and sister, specifically the way they had of tilting the head, leaning slightly forward, so as to toss the hair hanging on either side of the face, Arbus's hair long dark and dirty, Leda's blond, fine, and gleaming. In both cases, locks of hair escaped from behind the ears where they'd been tucked, and wound up dangling over the face, concealing the eyes, grazing and covering the corners of the mouth . . .

"WHAT ABOUT ARBUS?" I asked her. "Isn't he home?"
    "No."
    "Do you know when he'll get home?"
    She shook her head.
    She pointed me to my classmate's bedroom.
    After fifteen minutes he finally arrived.
    "Sorry," he muttered. His hands were black and he seemed upset.
    The door to Leda's bedroom was shut.

THE TIME CAME when what had been clearly prefigured from the very beginning finally happened, but not the way I'd imagined. In a certain sense, it was better the way it turned out: more interesting and unique, and nonetheless quite absurd. I've often wondered if certain deeply unsuccessful or aborted experiences are at least as significant as those that are fully consummated, whether it was worthwhile to live through them as they were, rather than in a more fully achieved and yet unremarkable realization. Most of my amorous experiences bear the seal of incompleteness, of absurdity, but maybe that's why I remember them in particular, because they spoke to me or taught me something, because they pushed me to shed tears, but far more frequently, perhaps many years later, they have made me laugh out loud because of how ramshackle and misbegotten they were, off-track, partial, funny, exhausting, either because of the way they played out or failed to, in whole or in part. Even though sex is something fundamental to me, something I've thought about perhaps every day and every hour or fraction of an hour in my life, including times when other important and dramatic things were happening, in fact, especially during those times, as if sex was the perennial distraction, there to help me face up to and overcome every challenge, a sort of promise on the other side of the obstacle, an indirect and hallucinatory compensation for the all-too-real annoyances we are forced to put up with, if I think back on how my interactions with nine out ten women in my past have actually gone, if I remember the times I've developed a crush, or just a fondness for, or even fallen seriously in love with a woman, or even just been aroused, well, I can only conclude that what prevails in the entire affair is the demented, mad, lunatic aspect, and it often takes the form of a prank, a mockery. And yet, as far as these pranks and mockeries are concerned, in some cases pranks played by the women, more frequently suffered by them (and not just women . . .) but more often experienced jointly with them, as if we were reciprocally playing pranks, taking turns mocking each other, each with the same impression, I believe that what we're doing is something eccentric, odd, in defiance of all logic, and about which, if it weren't for the arousal that clouds the mind, or a speck of self-respect, or a sort of tacit understanding that instead of recognizing the ridiculousness of the situation we should just go ahead and kiss and take off our clothes, as per the standard script— if, as I was saying, it weren't for that, it would be more appropriate to just burst out laughing together.

What the fuck are we doing, you and me?

The list of surreal situations would be too long and might be mistaken for a confession or a parody.

. . . WHAT ABOUT the one who started doing a belly dance to get me excited, and came close to making me burst out laughing right in her face? (Shamelessly erotic undertakings have only one outcome, they depress me, and let me inform you, brash and enterprising ladies everywhere, I am not alone in this, many males share this view with me, men who are reasonably capable, they are left appalled, or choking back a snicker, so look out for those lacy outfits, those hyperbolic offers, those feline moves, because they can achieve the desired effect, but if they fall so much as a millimeter short, they will plunge the situation deep into its implicitly farcical aspects . . .)

. . . and the young Rhenish woman who had to go pee every five minutes? Maybe because of the excitement, or perhaps it was a case of cystitis, even in the flower beds in front of the church of San Giovanni a Porta Latina at three in the morning . . .

. . . and the one who was decidedly too beautiful, too beautiful for me . . . who had loaded her armpits down with heavy applications of stick deodorant and when I had the unfortunate and misguided idea of licking her there, to seem like quite the fiery lover, my tongue dried out till I couldn't even speak . . .

. . . or the one who was playing hard to get, indeed, didn't even notice the invisible bonds that I was launching and drawing close around her, until one day, to strike a blow to her heart, I decided to leave a note for her, tucked into the seat of her Piaggio Ciao moped, a scrap of paper with a poem by a Surrealist poet, ". . . *et je neigerai sur ta bouche*," realizing only too late that this was no brilliant poetic image, but rather a filthy metaphor, which, seeing that I had never yet succeeded in placing a kiss on those lips, that mouth into which I was now suggesting I might go so far as to "snow," disgusted and offended her, driving a wedge between us once and for all?

. . . and the one who threw the dice to decide whether or not I was going to sleep with her . . .

. . . and the one who kneeled down at my feet, sucking me off as she stared up at me, her mascaraed eyes wide open, imitating something she must have seen in some porn film, in the mistaken belief that it was every man's fondest dream to be gazed at like that . . .

. . . and the one who lured me into her room, after I chanced to walk past it, by leaving the door ajar, so that I was able to see her as she stood at the window, her back to me, scantily dressed, looking up at the full moon . . .

. . . and the one who told me, the first night, "Sodomize me, I'm having trouble getting to sleep . . ."

. . . and the one who exclaimed, ardently, "Take me!!" thus demolishing once and for all my already wavering erection . . .

. . . and the one I pursued with a full heart, and whose little toe was the only part of her that I ever managed to touch, just the little toe, not even the foot, and none of the rest of her lovely honey-colored body . . .

. . . and the one I still love insanely, because unfortunately there is no other way to love?

> Her image appeared to me in the night
> and I was so frightened that I experienced at once
> desire and the fear of dying. I don't know
> which feeling was stronger (perhaps
> the first). I've always experienced greater attraction
> than repulsion: if there was something that
> I would have been better advised to avoid and ward off,

it was exactly what I liked best. With her, too,
that's how it was and continues to be: even
at night, even beside her or embracing her,
even when I'm inside her, I can't
free myself from this infernal attraction:
and I continue to plunge toward her.
But, I ask you, how can you get any closer than that?
Once you have reached the center of the earth
what could be deeper than that?
Shouldn't the force of gravity suddenly cease?

HOWEVER YOU WANT TO PUT IT, my encounter with Leda, Arbus's younger sister, was memorable.

I still remember with great precision every instant we spent together, first in an apartment where she lived with her mother, Ilaria, after Arbus had left and their father had left, too, in the wake of his notorious declaration that he was homosexual, and always had been, and then, some time later, when she had gone to live on her own in a garret that she called "the studio." We saw each other for six months, practically on a weekly basis, once or twice a week, but toward the end, less and less, and in the last month we might have seen each other only a couple of times, and yet I have the impression of remembering every single instant of our times together: but not because anything extraordinary happened, who knows what wonderful things, in fact, little or nothing happened, six months that converted my curiosity into, first, affection, then passion, and at last, a sweet sickness.

I'll try to recount that little or nothing.

I'VE SAID THAT I REMEMBER EVERYTHING, with the exception of the first time that we met again, after I fell out of touch with Arbus, their little house in Montesacro, the four-handed piano recitals. From the account that I have laboriously reconstructed, extracting segments of memory and pasting them together, it would seem that I ran into her again at the Gallery of Modern Art in Rome, but not inside the museum, instead on the monumental staircase leading up to the front entrance, and specifically on the steps where everyone camps out, smoking, sunning themselves, talking about the art that already exists and the art that hasn't yet been made, the privileged domain of those who are lazing about on those steps. That apparent leisure, those idle yet impassioned conversations, constitute the incubation of artistic careers. I believe I've already mentioned Giuseppe Salvatori, Felice Levini, Marco Tirelli, Ceccobelli, Santo Spatola, Cecafumo, Pizzi Cannella, Mariano Rossano, Biuzzi, but they are only a few of the artists I spent time with on those steps. And then there was the art dealer Giovanni Crisostomo, also known as Boccadoro, which is the translation of his name from the Greek.

Back then, the books of Hermann Hesse were very popular, as they are now, especially *Siddhartha* and *Narcissus and Goldmund*, and I believe that Crisostomo's name came from there, rather than from the etymology of his surname. I wonder why I never read Hesse, everyone read him back then, I mean everyone read at least *Siddhartha*, that is.

Maybe to stand out.

Boccadoro in any case claims that it was he who had come accompanied by Leda. That she was twenty years old. And I didn't recognize her. Spatola and Pizzi Cannella immediately tried striking up a conversation with the young female painter. Back then, Pizzi Cannella had the chiseled profile of a Roman centurion, Tirelli and Biuzzi were both charming fellows. Boccadoro claims that I didn't exchange so much as a word with Leda that day. And that was exactly the clue that I had made an impression on her, and that in turn I had been deeply struck by her. And he was right.

IT WAS STRANGE to lie next to her.

On the bed, fully dressed, a man and a woman, in a deeply intimate position that was therefore in need of further developments, because there's only so long that a person can lie there without doing something, changing state, trying something . . .

The horizontal position is for sleep, otherwise you necessarily have to start talking, or caressing, or undressing.

We invariably ended up stretched out on the hard, thin mattress on the floor of her studio; she would lie down first, then I'd join her, easing myself down next to her supine body, perhaps a foot apart, her shoulder next to my shoulder, her hip by mine, her gaze focused on the ceiling. At that point, it wasn't all that different from being alone, alone but with a woman next to me, whose scent I could smell, whose quiet breathing I could hear, a woman who was beautiful, among other things, a woman with her body and thoughts and feelings. Just what Leda's thoughts and feelings might have been I never found out, she never expressed them in any shape or form, or at least, not one I was able to decipher. The fact that we were lying together on that mattress meant there must be some reason, on her part, I have to guess, maybe she liked me, or she didn't dislike me, or else (I'm going by trial and error here) that position and that nonaction already meant something to her, perhaps it meant everything, or perhaps she didn't think there could be anything else.

I'm torn between two hypotheses: the first is that she expected me, out of the clear blue sky, to turn and kiss her on the lips, climb on top of her, start fondling her breast, in other words, that I would do what other boys and girls normally do, the things that I, too, when I find myself in a similar situation, had always done: kiss, or try to kiss, fondle, or try to fondle, unbutton, unzip . . . and so on, ordinary, obvious things, things you take for granted, but things that were anything but obvious when it came to Leda, in part because it's unusual to start from such a well-defined, static situation, lying in bed without looking at each other . . . with any other girl you arrive at that position only after already kissing and fondling, and as a transition to something else . . . whereas the two of us already seemed like husband and wife lying on the carved stone lid of an ancient tomb, sculpted in that position for all eternity.

After opening the door of her home to me, and then the door to her bedroom, while she still lived in the little villa with her mother, and before stretching out on the mattress on the studio floor, Leda would always do just one thing, a single action: she'd put on a record. Invariably, a piece for piano solo. Which meant we were assured of twenty or so minutes of unbroken piano music ahead of us, the duration of one side of the record, before having to get up and turn it over or put on a different disk.

DURING THE FEW MONTHS OF MY . . . how shall I put this . . . of my time frequenting Leda, no longer as Arbus's sister, but as a young woman and nothing less or more, I didn't have any other girlfriends, nor did I make the slightest effort to get any, because I felt, though without any basis for that feeling, that I had a commitment with her. Time and again I found myself wishing that she would reject me, break up with me, so that I might feel free to look for another girlfriend, or else other girls I could just have some *fun* with (I use this expression without ever having actually put it into practice—certainly not as *fun*, but as a sort of predation, a venting, an obsession or a form of deceit, anything you can think of, in other words, but *fun*). For that matter, in order to be able to reject me, Leda would have needed me to put myself forward in some explicit manner, something that actually never happened, and so the equivocal situation stretched out. And yet I continued to secretly wish that she would put an end to it by rejecting me, which would have brought me every bit as much relief as a positive outcome.

In that case, why go on seeing her?

Inertia is a disease: witnessing from outside, from above, what the body does or doesn't do, without intervening, without *wanting* to intervene, waiting for things to happen on their own, because in the meantime (this would be the underlying idea), if something's going to happen, it will happen in any case, and if not, oh well, it wasn't meant to be.

Cursed fatalism! Sometimes you've made my life easier, but far more often you've ruined it! How I have been stupidly indolent and perhaps even cowardly, letting things and people flow over and past me instead of seizing them or decisively rejecting them! Because of the sweetness, the gentleness, which was in fact unequaled, of a handful of occasions in which everything occurred *naturally*, without any effort, in how many other situations have I failed because of my inertia, my inaction, expecting the river to reverse course and start flowing toward me, to bathe me with its waters?

(And then, of course, my doubts, which aren't really all so much a matter of: Will I be capable? as, rather: Will I be able to get to the point where I'll be able to prove that I'm capable? At the appropriate instant? If it's not the instinctive reflexes of the world's Don Giovannis, what is it that actually drives a *man* to try to hook up with a *woman*, with a *certain* woman, with a certain woman at a *given* moment, in *that one* specific situation? Is it really nothing more than a question of putting your hands on them or pursing your lips until they meet and lock with other lips? Isn't it this and nothing more?)

AFTER A WHILE, I kissed Leda, but this didn't inaugurate any change, if anything, it was a new stretch of stasis.

Between Leda and me, the kisses were so long and drawn out, you couldn't really call them kisses anymore. Anything, any event, in order to be given a name, must have a beginning and an end, a shape or a duration: if the lips never break apart, then how can that be a kiss, and if one never ends, you can never give another, and another, and yet another, to paraphrase Catullus's well-known wording, and his equally well-known phrase about "thousands of kisses" doesn't mean the lips remain locked for hours, without ever parting, because in fact that would no longer be a kiss, just as the ones we exchanged weren't really kisses, with our eyes closed, wrapped in a moth-eaten blanket, Leda and I, that was by no means a kiss at all, but rather a morbid or childish or animalistic contact, the likes of which you might see in documentaries, on the verge of insensibility, of catatonia, like the incubation of an insect's eggs in another insect's body or the exhausting intercourse between shellfish that lie there, glued together, sucking on each other's membranes for days at a time. More than once, Leda, with her lips attached to mine, dropped off to sleep, in a state of peaceful abandonment, and I realized it from the fact that her breathing slowed and grew regular, and she was breathing into my mouth, the only significant signal, seeing that as she kissed me she already had her eyes closed and her arms lay slack at her sides.

ON OCCASION I WOULD TAKE ADVANTAGE, in an extremely limited fashion, truth be told, of these little catnaps of hers. We were under cover of the usual tartan blanket because it was cold in her studio. I placed a hand on Leda's belly and I pulled her shirt from her trousers. Leda always and only wore pants. I never saw her in a skirt or a dress. I lifted the shirt and touched the flesh of her belly. It was soft and cold. Skinny though she was, if I pressed down, I could feel my fingers sinking into her skin. Since I couldn't descend beneath the belt of her trousers, which were very snug and high-waisted, as was the style in those years, I raised my hand ever so slightly to where Leda was skinnier and the flesh was more taut. In the meantime, she went on breathing into my mouth, caressing my face with the breath that issued from her nostrils. I hesitated to raise the blanket so I could see what my hand was getting up to down there, I might easily have awakened her, and the mystery of that flesh, so chilly and insensitive, pumped so much blood into my face and my abdomen that I had the impression, in contrast with her, of burning, of being scalding hot; and so I overcame my hesitation and uncovered her, first lifting the blanket and then sliding it down over her legs. And I saw that her belly was snow-white and smooth, like a little girl's. But when I tried to lower those skintight corduroy trousers, as soon as I unbuttoned them at her waist, I realized that from that point down, a scar began, running vertically, slightly raised, and I immediately abandoned the idea of finding out how far it went.

THIS DETAIL STIRS IN MY MEMORY, obscenely open to allowing itself to be corrupted by trivial juxtapositions, the umpteenth ribald joke that circulated back in school days.

"Do you know what Princess Anne has six inches below her belly button?"

"No."

"The socket for her Philips."

(A pun on the surname of Mark Phillips, the queen of Britain's son-in-law, and the well-known brand of electric appliances.)

ONE TIME I CAME ON HER. Breaking the state of paralysis, I climbed on top of her. Leda neither rejected me nor welcomed me, making such a show of her passivity that it made me think it might have been a tactic. She can't have been utterly indifferent to that act of mine. As was her custom, she shut her eyes and let out a sigh. The fact that she didn't look at me, wasn't encouraging me, stopped me again; it killed my initiative aborning. Leda turned her head to one side, still with her eyes shut, but not as if she were displeased or disgusted. And then she smiled in a fleeting fashion and said in a whisper: "Do as you please." As I please *what*? I thought to myself. She hadn't told me, "Do *what* you please," but rather "*as* you please," and what difference is there, what does it mean? At that point I stopped bracing myself and let my whole weight sink down on top of her, forcing her to spread her legs just enough so that I could lay my member atop her sex and rub mine against hers. And as I continued rubbing the crotch of my pants against the crotch of hers, I could feel that I was about to have an orgasm, in spite of the fact that my member had barely started to swell, but the idea of coming in my pants seemed ridiculous to me, so I unbuttoned them just in time for my member to spray a spurt of semen onto Leda's white pullover, right between breast and neck. Feeling me crush her, Leda had just opened her eyes again, and she witnessed this development as if it were a natural phenomenon, limiting herself to lifting her pullover between thumb and index finger, to keep my semen from soaking through to her blouse. Then she got up and went into the bathroom without a word. When she came back, she had changed out of the white pullover and into a red V-neck sweater. She smiled and lay down next to me again; I was properly dressed again, and she took my hand, not the one that had held my member during the orgasm, but the other one.

Then she asked me:

"Have you ever been to Switzerland?"

"Switzerland? Yes, a couple of times."

"What do you think, is it nice there?"

"Yes, very nice."

"Are there mountains?"

"Yes. Lots of them."

Those are the exact words we exchanged.

I couldn't explain why, after that one time, I was stuck with the obsessive thought that I might have gotten her pregnant. And that thought never abandoned me until after we stopped seeing each other.

7

ABOUT LEDA AND ARTISTS. From what I know about her, and that's very little, she had been in love only once before our relationship. With a very strange young man, tall and gawky, taciturn, conceited, who tormented her not so much because he mistreated her but because he was too caught up in allowing his soul to be tortured by problems of all sorts, foremost among them his almost total ineptitude at interacting with the world, understanding others, and making himself understood. Gustavo Herz was his name. From this inability of his, along with an intelligence that was acknowledged by and large as a virtual reparation, perhaps, for his odious and all-too-concrete shortcomings (in fact, those who maintained that this was the case tended always to place the adverb "still" before the compliment: he may be an ugly lunk, he may be a solitary and maniacal egotist, he may be a blight on humanity . . . "Still, how intelligent he is . . . ! You have to admit"), Herz had deduced that his was an artistic personality, distinctly artistic, and therefore, necessarily, misunderstood. An artist cannot help but have all of society arrayed against him: therefore, if society is against you, you're an artist. Even though he had never once actually heard its siren call, he never ceased telling Leda all about his "artistic vocation," the need to follow it at all costs, sacrificing to its requirements any and all things or persons (by which he meant, first and foremost, her), and he laid upon that vocation blame for all his difficulties, with his family, with his fellow man, with the system, with his depressing classmates (he was in fact attending, intermittently, either the first or second year of university), with the people in power, the bourgeoisie, the ignorant and the learned, motorists and pedestrians, and with anyone who tried to give him a hand, invariably rejected, with those who ignored him, dismissed as shallow, and finally with all those, and they were a great many, who couldn't stand him, and to them Herz, as if repaying in the same coin, tit for tat, and with a certain smug complacency, never tired of providing them with fresh and excellent reasons to detest him. And thus the cycle came back around, since he could sense the dislike and even hostility growing around, he had persuaded himself that he was simply sharing the fate common to every radical artist, surrounded by Philistines, and hindered by a wall of general misunderstanding.

(People who are unilaterally convinced they are on a mission tend to make those who are close to them pay the highest cost, even more than their adversaries: in Gustavo's case, those were the members of his family and Leda.)

He had enrolled at the university, majoring in chemistry, a department he'd chosen on the basis of a whim, really, rather than any true interest or predilection, but he soon abandoned the idea of taking the exams ("Those are tests for stupid people, they're worthless and meaningless, the worst students always pass, I don't have time for that"), and therefore also the fantasy of even studying for them, by going to class or just reading the textbooks. He delighted in the consternation of his parents when he announced his intent, their opposition offering proof that he was doing the right thing. Like a patch of mold on food gone bad, Gustavo thrived on disapproval: letting human relations rot was, for him, the best way of putting them to the test, and that is what he did with Leda. And yet she remained attached to him. Perhaps she thought she'd found in Gustavo certain traits of her brother or of her eccentric, wretched father, except that those two members of her family were truly geniuses—while Gustavo Herz was anything but.

WAS GUSTAVO AN ARTIST? As he weighed what medium he might choose to express his talent, he decided that literature was a domain that demanded too much time to gain the confirmation of one's gifts. As for classical music, the apprenticeship was even longer, and he by this point was too old to undertake it, while the field of the visual arts seemed to have been homesteaded by a band of wily foxes, and it was inadvisable to try to compete with them, either because they were better prepared than him in technical terms, even if that was in the execution of the crap they came up with, canvases ambitious and frivolous and that sort of thing, or else because they were capable of justifying their work with a pile of nonsense, in oral or written form, which served as a side dish to their performance art, installations, piles of dirt, or rusty heaps of iron.

That's when Herz figured out that the shortest path involved songs.

Songs, yes, songs, the fantastic twentieth-century shortcut in which various geniuses expressed themselves who might have lost their way or been lost to posterity if they had been forced to negotiate more complex and articulated forms. A popular genre, and therefore attractive, which in the course of three minutes manages to condense centuries of theater, thousands of pages of literature, symphonies, and concerts, plus the peculiar sense of the present day, which has a special beat all its own, a pulse in which you can sense the quiver of youth, fashion, adventure, dance, seduction, all those things, in other words, whose heartbreaking beauty consists of an absolute state of ephemerality, from which a superconcentrated emotional juice is squeezed, and if and when it works, it casts a spell on the listener, churning and troubling in a way that the more complex arts can only dream of. And all this, thanks to a short and simple melody, played by a few basic instruments and accompanied by a few rhyming verses.

WITH HIS GUITAR, which he could strum and pluck like anyone else, and on the piano, where he could spread his fingers mechanically to form the chords Leda had taught him (at least the dozen basic ones), Gustavo composed three or four songs, then, as he became increasingly fond of humming and singing them all the livelong day, he came up with as many more, which brought him up to the canonical number of songs to make up a record, at least the way LPs were produced at the time, and therefore to be able to claim, and not only to the mirror on his armoire, that he was now "a composer." A composer of songs. The first two songs he wrote were called "Dieci lire" (Ten Lire) and "Ballata per una Hoover" (Ballad for a Vacuum Cleaner) and I listened to them in a bar during an open-mic night. Herz sang those two songs so quickly that in five minutes he was done and had already hurried offstage, without even saying good night. Well, I have to admit that it wasn't bad. Verging on the annoying, on the whiny . . . but there was no question that Gustavo had managed to capture the audience's attention, especially with his "Hoover" song, during the performance of which he imitated the sound of a vacuum cleaner. He was right, after all: that combative nature of his had a certain magnetic je ne sais quoi.

WOOO-WOOO-WOOO . . .

FIRST HE CALLED HIMSELF GUS. Then Gus-To. Then he changed his surname to Herzmutter, which I believe means nothing in German, but it
sounded good. When he was tired of coming up with stage names by deforming his real name, he founded a group that he dubbed Weed, composed of just one musician, him, who did everything: he wrote words and
music, he played all the instruments, he sang or, really, he whispered,
because the songs were spoken more than anything else. With that handful
of tracks, eight in number, and working on the opening and closing arrangements so that the overall running time didn't seem too scant, he put
out his first album, *Hoover*.

IT'S ONLY NOW THAT I've reached this point that I feel I can talk about
Leda. The story of Gustavo Herz's career could continue to be told separately, with no need to intertwine it with any other character, since that's
exactly how Gustavo wanted to run it: alone, imagining this solitude as a
gift and, at the same time, as a cross to bear, typical of the true explorer,
the pioneer, the innovator. That aside, I confess that I have some serious
problems with talking about Leda, in general, and with having her talk to
others, with imagining her wrapping her arms around Herz, talking to
him or smiling at him, or having her clothes taken off by him, or else showing him, as she spreads her slender fingers, how to finger an A minor chord.
I'm jealous, I'll confess it, even if I have no right to be, and I'm terrified at
the idea of contaminating her with the secretions of other creatures, with
the glistening slime trail left by their passage through her life. They might
be words or deeds, conversations, scoldings, embraces, mistreatments:
everything that has to do with Leda troubles me deeply as if she weren't
Arbus's sister but my own and I were touched in my own body by everything that happened to her. In fact, I never find myself thinking about what
she did, but only about what *other people* did *to her* . . . The verbs that have
Leda as their subject in my mind are all conjugated in the passive form.
Does that mean she had a place in my heart? Does that mean I loved her,
that I'd fallen in love with her—all of this? Maybe so. We give the provisional
name of love to far too many contradictory sensations all jumbled together,
while waiting for further developments to clarify what we're dealing with.
The developments that emerged between the two of us ought to force anyone

to withdraw that conjecture. And so why do I bring it up myself now, after all these years?

Maybe I just wanted to protect her, and I haven't been able to. And now I feel remorse for not having persisted with my efforts, for example, my quest to steer her clear of the malevolent influence of Gus, which continued even after they broke up.

He used her the way a knife-thrower or a magician uses the girl he saws in half, but demanding that everyone's attention converge upon him, upon his hand ready to let fly, on the immense responsibility resting on his shoulders lest something go wrong. None of the things that the two of them did together could be normal, routine: and in his opinion Leda should only be grateful for the fact. Grateful, that is, if during the week of Ferragosto, for example, in the middle of August, when instead of going to the beach like everyone else, they spent those days in the attic organizing the stamp collection that his grandfather left him when he died. "They're incredibly valuable," Gustavo would assure her, with a gleam in his eye, "and someday I'll sell them. That day, I'll give you a nice gift, since you've helped me. Or maybe I won't, maybe I'll just keep them here with me . . ." and he patted the side of the dusty stamp albums. "Yes, and I'll leave them intact, an inheritance for my own son," he added with a hint of bitter pride, without bothering to wonder or ask her whether she was interested in being the mother of that fortunate heir. Leda in her turn was so alienated that she was incapable of realizing what Herz was offering her as a life, as a tattered rag of a life, as a cerebral surrogate for what two young people can do when they are together. If he called her before dinner, announcing that they wouldn't see each other that night, in contradiction of what they had planned, he wasn't honest enough to tell her, "Listen, I just don't feel like it now, I'm tired," far from it, he'd tell her that he was very busy, that's right, he had important things to do, even if in reality those commitments consisted of lying on his bed with his guitar on his belly, staring at the ceiling.

"So, what did you do last night?" Leda would ask him the next day.

"I thought," Herz would have the nerve to reply. And he was utterly serious. He actually believed it. He was seriously convinced that he had *done* something while lying there sprawled on the bed, wallowing in his frustrations . . .

Only once did the two of them do anything together, but it was such a singular undertaking, so senseless and dreary, that instead of breaking the siege to the citadel behind the walls of which Gustavo had shut himself up, it confirmed once and for all just how impregnable it had become; and, an even more singular fact, that Leda, too, was now outside its walls.

A trip. Yes, it's from the trips taken together that we can better understand the two individuals who make up a couple, and what the sum of the two produces, provided that it's a sum and not a subtraction. Leda and Gus took a trip to Brazil, but (and here I imagine that it was for a specific request on Herzmutter's part, I can glimpse in this decision his distinctly self-destructive trait, as well as the way that it was punitive toward the person traveling with him) they chose to go to the unhealthiest and most squalid spot in that whole magnificent nation. Namely, to an immense swamp, extending over thousands of square miles, where people live on stilt houses, doing their best to avoid snakes and diseases, where any living creature that could make it interesting to visit the place lurks unseen beneath the surface of the muddy water, invisible. Leda and Gus spent two weeks there. As was predictable, within three days they had already fallen sick and they spent the rest of their time throwing up and experiencing fulminating diarrhea, emptying their bowels down a hole in the floor of the stilt hut where they were staying. Gus was unwilling to cut short their stay in the villages of that disgusting backwater, in spite of the fact that however badly the fever and the diarrhea might have hit Leda, in him they took a far more worrisome form, often pushing him into bouts of full-blown delirium. Every time he regained lucidity, however, when Leda implored him to leave that place and go to a halfway civilized city, where they could get proper medical care, he replied that "that would ruin everything," that "you don't abandon a project just when the challenges are bringing it close to what you were looking for in the first place," that Leda's attitude was just "her typical way of setting false stumbling blocks in her own way."

"But *what* are we looking for, here?" she asked, "what is it you're trying to find?" still laboring under the illusion that there was some logic behind his obstinate childish insistence on staying, and that there really ever could be—in that corner of nature, that patch of Creation shaped especially by the Lord to resemble an urban cloaca, only a thousand times more vast—anything worth discovering, something only Gus knew about, as if he had stored up a surprise finale when he had brought her all the way down there. In fact, there are those who like to conceal the true objective of a journey from their partner, so that the discovery, when it comes, is so much more amazing and delightful. Herz refused to answer that question, simply shaking his head and breaking off all interaction, instead getting up and going over to vomit down the hole.

There can be no doubt that the couple were risking their lives in that place, or at least were in danger of returning with indelible repercussions from that misadventure. Permanent damage to their health, both physical and mental. Something about Leda never fully recovered, some part of her was never healed. Certainly, her love emerged shaken, though reinforced more than undermined. She could boast that she had saved Gustavo, that she had guided him out of that hellhole when, during the last few days, he was frequently unconscious or delirious from the fever, and if he'd been alone, he never would have made it: she had managed to get him onto one of those unsteady native pirogues, she had nourished him, getting into him what little Gus was able to keep down without spewing it out again immediately, and she had dragged him practically senseless though the obstacle course of the airports and, finally, having arrived by God's will back in Rome, safe and sound, she had cared for him for a couple of months in a ward of the mysterious tropical diseases wing of the Polyclinic Hospital, and there Gus had gradually regained his health. Even a hasty reader of the works of Ariosto will recall that Angelica falls in love with Medoro, who lies wounded, and will surely remember how in the princess's heart there opened up a depiction of the wound while, day after day, the wound in the body of the young Saracen warrior healed and scarred over. Let's just say that something of the sort happened to Leda, or rather: the love that in the heart of anyone else would have been utterly crushed by that misadventure, only to be replaced by resentment and scorn, in her heart instead was revived and warmed, by the daily task of caring for the man who was chiefly responsible for those very same mishaps. In caring for Gus, Leda forgot to care for herself, and this makes me think back on so many qualities of hers that I would learn to know in later years. Was this not, however, exactly what she had been looking for? The perverse and powerful mechanism of love invariably pushes those who love closer to the source of their discomfort, their problems, investing them with the mission of saving the person who will ruin them. I don't believe for a second that Leda was blind, I think she knew perfectly well what kind of a person Gustavo was, though she did not possess a plumb line long enough (there couldn't be a sufficiently long one on this earth!) to measure the abyss of his selfishness and egotism. So powerful was her desire to get away from herself that, in the end, Gustavo actually turned out to be her ideal man . . .

From the fog of a long and serious illness, Herz emerged with a single idea in his mind: the title of his next album. The one that would introduce him to a much broader public: *Pantano*. Morass.

✦

THE ALBUM'S SUCCESS, though it was more a matter of critical acclaim than of impressive sales, was a blessing for Leda: as soon as he became even slightly famous, in fact, Herz entirely gave up the already minimal attention he had been paying his girlfriend, concentrating his renewed energy on coordinating radio interviews and concerts, at first in tiny clubs but soon in larger theaters, where Leda almost immediately gave up going to see him, because in public he ignored her as if he didn't even know her. This attitude, rather than offending or wounding her, only reassured her that Gustavo no longer required her devotion: and together with that new confidence, the love that had been rekindled, in the tropical disease wing, for that gravely dehydrated young man, began to dwindle; meanwhile his innate rudeness was regularly repaid in kind by the nurses, who made a moral point of it. Still, their affair wasn't quick to die. Herz and Leda, in fact, continued getting back together and breaking up, breaking up and reuniting for close to a year, with a week-on, week-off cadence, month-on, month-off: a seesawing relationship that was so inexplicable and confused, there were times that one of them was convinced they were still dating while the other was certain they weren't. And the truth is that there wasn't such a sharp difference between the two states of affairs.

When I started seeing her in the assiduous and singular manner that I described in the previous chapter, I was by no means certain that she had broken up once and for all with Herz. The two of them went on with their game of Fort-Da, the way Freud describes it: toss it, pick it up, toss it, pick it up, toss it even farther and then wait to see if the object will be picked back up . . . From listening to just a couple of tracks from the album *Pantano*, on the radio, I should have understood in advance that a girl who had placed her heart and (a chill runs up my spine at the thought) her delicate body in the hands of the composer and lyricist of those songs must certainly have some serious problems: whether they were cause or consequence of the fact that she was in a relationship with a guy like him, I could not say at the time. The most widely listened-to hit of the second album, "Hole in the Sand" (I admit that I liked it, actually, when it first came out, and I found myself humming it under my breath, what could I do about it, it had wormed its way into my head . . .), ran as follows:

> *Not a word you say—that I don't know*
> *For its basic grimness—slimy and low . . .*

And down on the beach
Don't you dare steal my pail!
Or I'll bury you under a ton of sand
There's really no need—of red fury's hand
To lay you out dead with a hammer blow
That'll stay in your head
When the guests—when the guests—when the guests—
Have all gone to bed . . .

"To lay you out dead with a hammer blow," da, da, da . . . had really dug its way into my mind.

A hole in the sand
To hide all the problems
Your old plans, all that boredom
The emotion, so canned . . .

IN POP MUSIC, the rule is to put out record after record after record. Produce songs, one after the other, collect tour dates, fill each season with hits before the competition can do it, saturate the airwaves, crowd the playlists. The profession of pop singer, which looks like an endless vacation from outside, actually demands that you work very hard and behave like a solid professional. They're serious people, the ones who work in pop music, and they can't miss a trick, or else they're right out of the business, cast into the outer darkness, dead without having to overdose, after the first burst of flame and shower of sparks, they burn out like a roman candle at a village festival. At least, that was the case in the time when our story unfolds. Now the very word "record" has no meaning and no one is in any danger of being forgotten: there's no such thing anymore as being forgotten. When the widespread but fleeting popularity of *Pantano*, like a thin layer of fresh snow, vanished, and Gus had nothing to follow up with because he was struggling to find inspiration for a new raft of songs, and the few lame chords he could paste together understandably disgusted him, his inability to relate with himself, let alone with his fellow human beings, gained once again the upper hand. He immediately put the blame for his crisis on the recording industry, capable only of squeezing the talent of its artists until they gasped out garbage, and even his audience, in spite of the fact that they had shown that they liked his music, indeed, the positive response that *Pantano* had enjoyed (a record that Gustavo now, a year after its release, considered crude and infantile) became, to his eyes, something like proof that the newly acquired fans of Weed actually couldn't tell good music from a hole in the ground, and that they were fickle and disloyal seeing that they hadn't hesitated to abandon his band the minute it hit a dry spell. Actually, no one had abandoned Gustavo Herz at all, and if he'd been capable of writing even a minimally decent song in the first place, they would have sought him out, and listened to him, and applauded, and whistled enthusiastically: but you could hardly expect them to buy the same record twice (especially if it was, according to its own creator, "half baked and poorly performed"). That meant it was the right time for Herz to get back together with Leda, in accordance with the classic pattern. In other words, time for more nausea and hypercritical rants. But this time, she put her foot down. She rejected him. Herz was stunned, breathless. He could not understand how such a thing was possible. Leda was my girlfriend now. Herz's bitterness and laziness and vacuity pushed him out of circulation. He disappeared, from the city, from the world, from the picturesque and highly remunerative field of pop music. Could it be that a new life was beginning for Leda?

> *I dig a hole in the sand*
> *To hide all the problems*
> *The old plans, all your boredom . . .*
> *Da, da, da . . .*

I'LL MAKE USE OF A NOTE found in certain notebooks I'll talk more about later. The author: Giovanni Vilfredo Cosmo, G. V. Cosmo, that's right, my old literature teacher from SLM.

> To those who cause us pain, we are immensely grateful if they cease to do so. Our gratitude, then, winds up being turned toward those who have hurt us. That explains why some women remain bound to husbands or lovers who mistreat them: it is the moment of truce that binds them to their men with an even tighter knot, to make them love those men more than ever because they have been so generous as to temporarily stop mistreating them. The alternation of brutality and consolation creates a driving emotional rhythm that's like a

dance, in which one of the two dancers is first clutched by the other in a suffocating embrace, and then thrust away with something approaching brutality, expelled, thrust aside, only to be gathered back up and wrapped once again in his arms.

8

THE INCORRIGIBLE NEGLECT by the author of the book you're reading has deprived it of a chapter that might have been interesting, and instead adds a different one that's brief and melancholy.

The neglect consists of having put off and postponed (thinking: "There will always be time, later . . .") the opportunity to interview Signor Paris, the owner of the clothing shop just above Piazza Verbano, a historic establishment of the QT, even though it actually was a replica of the older, original shop, which was close to Piazza Vescovio, and that was why it was called Paris 2, like a sequel to a movie. I go by the place frequently, Piazza Verbano is an obligatory transit point in any travel around the QT, and each and every time I told myself I ought to go in, but then I never did, until one fine day I made up my mind, I stopped, and I entered the shop.

The last time I'd set foot in there might have been twenty-five years ago.

Signor Paris was there, old but in fine fettle, surrounded by display cases of the articles that had been his specialty: the casual apparel that, still, when I was a kid, at least in Rome, was rare, and that few shops carried. The famous brands, Levi's, Lee, Wrangler, etc., jackets boots leather belts and so on, which, with the passing years—like everything else for that matter—became more refined and costly.

I introduced myself and asked whether, one day, he might be willing to let me interview him, concerning an episode that had transpired many years before . . . and specifically in 1975, the year of the CR/M. A proletarian expropriation that had been carried out against his store, and which I knew a number of my classmates from Giulio Cesare High School had taken part in. I'd always heard people talking about it, and I asked Signor Paris if he would be willing to tell me about it. He burst out laughing. "My wife was running the store that day . . . you ought to get her to tell you what happened." "But is it true that they mostly took boots?" I asked: boots were very fashionable at the time. Camperos. "Ah, the stuff they took . . . the miserable wretches!" And he laughed with a bitter grimace.

I promised him that I'd soon come back by to make an appointment.

Then months went by, perhaps as long as a year.

In the meantime, I wrote other things and I wrote nothing. The proletarian expropriation could wait. I'll do it next week, I'll start working on it on Monday, I told myself. After all, it's a separate chapter. When I finally go back to the store, a very courteous woman greets me, the proprietor's daughter. "I'm sorry, Papà isn't here, he's at the hospital for some exams, but you'll find him back here starting next week." I expressed my best wishes to the woman. "Please give your father my regards and tell him that I came by to see him, if he remembers me."

Again an interval of neglect ensued.

Neglect, neglect . . .

A couple of months, more or less, had gone by when a young woman who works at the De Paolis Film Studios, on the Via Tiburtina, to whom I had chanced to mention the shop near Piazza Verbano, the story of the proletarian expropriation, and the fact that I was planning to interview the elderly shopkeeper, since she was a close friend of Signor Paris's family, told me, deeply moved, that he had recently passed away.

9

*T*HIS STORY INCLUDES OTHER STORIES. *It's inevitable. It branches out or is already full of branches at the moment it begins. It overlaps the way people's lives do. You can't say where they begin and where they end, these lives and these people, since it is all, naturally, relationships, triangles, knots, transmissions, intersections, and the beginning is never the beginning because there was always something else before that beginning, just as there will always be something else after it ends. And so in this book you almost can't glimpse the main story: a forest has grown up around it, a forest of wheres, whens, as ifs, and meanwhiles, and the protagonists have become no longer the young men at the center of the grim events, but many other young men who are every bit as much the protagonists, and their mothers, their* *sisters, their high school teachers, the guitarists and drummers they used to listen to and the manufacturers of the motorcycles they rode and the architects who designed the buildings these young men lived in and the authors of the books that pushed them to become allies, to become couples, to kill each other, or to break away in search of truth, or isolation to escape it.*

THE AMUSEMENT IN THIS STORY LIES *in its random nature, but its tragic aspect also lies in its random nature. What is tragedy, after all? That which can't be put back together, fixed in any way. That which can never find a state of equilibrium, ever, not even after the end has come, with its naïve claim to even up the reckoning: there's always something left over in tragedy, an unpaid debt, an excess of right and wrong, as there is in amusement, for that matter, which is always based on an unbalancing of oneself toward others, or of others inside oneself. You intrude and you are intruded upon, like in demented laughter, which once it gets started no one can restrain. There's not much to be done about it: where harmony reigns, no one can get a laugh. That's why practically no one goes in search of it, harmony, except on drawing paper. This story amuses me and makes me suffer, both, as I tell it. I'd like to get it to attain a state of equilibrium so that I could feel nothing, and let the reader feel only the sensation of it unfolding, like a fabric tumbling to the floor, rustling through the hands of someone in pitch darkness, who tries to grab it: but I know I won't be able to. The way it goes corresponds to an underlying truth of the facts that I can't change, no matter how absurd it may be. Even less can I modify the parts that I made up myself. Which parts are those? you might ask me: the ones that don't sound quite as absurd as the others.*

10

AND IT'S CHRISTMAS AGAIN. Like every year, I thought about going to the midnight mass at SLM but then I didn't. Instead of going to church, I sat up in bed reading a novel by Sven Hassel. Up wide awake until three in the morning reading a paperback. I bought copies of the Hassel books I read at fourteen, back then I stole them from my father: I wanted to see if I still liked them. Today no different than forty years ago. This one I'm reading in the middle of the night is nothing special, *Wheels of Terror*, but the two I read hungrily on Christmas Eve were fantastic. *The Legion of the Damned* explains how the main characters, who will reappear in all the other books, wound up in the punishment battalions in the first place: some of them common criminals, expiating their death sentences by fighting desperate battles where the likelihood of getting out alive isn't all that much better than the narrowly averted gallows, others are opponents of Nazism, others still, like Hassel himself, deserters, while there are some, like the notorious Julius Heide, the Jew-hater (that name has always been for me, since I first read it, the prototype of a Nazi), pro-Hitler fanatics who have somehow managed to fall into disgrace, and are therefore all the more ferocious... in other words, a perfect handful of lost men, an outpost of gallows birds and psychopaths and the dregs of society hurtling against the enemy but, at the same time, well aware that they are the worst enemy of all, that evil is on their side, that there could be no more ill-omened ideal than that homeland whose surrender they all devoutly wish for on every page of the book. Fighting literally tooth and nail, they defend their own skin and that of their fellow soldiers, let us say, the less infamous and the more generous ones. Read him, Sven Hassel, read him at age eighteen or at fifty, read his crude masterpiece *March Battalion*: I realized that I remembered whole passages practically by heart, words that had been impressed in my memory for decades, a sign that the things you read at that age are truly unforgettable.

ALL HELL WAS PROMPTLY *let loose about our ears, but in that instant Porta fired and a long flame snaked out toward the nearest T-34. The tank seemed to rear up in an effort to avoid it. It moved forward a short way, then stopped. An answering flame shot skywards from the turret. A man appeared in the opening. He pulled himself half out into the open air and then fell back again, with blue flames licking greedily at his body.*

THE RUSSIAN TANKER ENGULFED by the blue flames. The men sentenced to death, detained in Torgau. "I think by now the bedbug must be crushed." The canister of *mastica* (aquavit) engraved with the red star. "Then we saw the green cross, the death's head of the NKVD." If I compare these clear and lucid memories with the swelling tide of books consumed over recent years, many of them much more interesting and far better written than Hassel's, I find that, nevertheless, I can't remember so much as the shadow of a phrase, not even the title of the book . . . in spite of all the dog-ears and underlinings I left in them . . .

Especially formidable are the scenes in which our antiheroes, aboard a tank tearing along in full flight, rumble at top speed through Russian villages, crushing or sweeping aside any obstacle that rears up before them, trampling under the treads Soviet soldiers but also German ones who try in vain to halt their onslaught, waving their arms and asking for help. I remembered them for forty years, and then found them and re-read them exactly as I remembered them, the instantaneous vision of the little Russian girl, terrorized, in pajamas and braids, who appears in the tank's periscope as it's breaking open her poor house like a walnut shell, because a second later the Tiger that had crushed her with the rest of her family had already driven on, in the roar of the diesel engine and the smoke, punching through a circle of flames, and on into the stained snow.

The scenes of combat between the German Tiger tanks and the terrifying Soviet T-34 counterparts (with the numbers of the aiming mechanism for the turret cannon that dance until they line up . . .) are thrilling. It would be pointless to ask me why I'm so fond, excited, and engaged in these scenes of battle.

Around three thirty in the morning I stopped reading and turned out the light, incendiary bombs and Nazi salutes whirling in my head, and fell asleep, all alone, in the last few hours of the night of Christmas 2012, like the Baby Jesus freshly placed in his manger, he in the hay, me under the quilt I'd bought from Chinese street vendors.

WHEN I WOKE UP, I wondered why I still needed war now, and why I had needed it at age fourteen, why I'd needed its sarcastic inhumanity, which Sven Hassel so loved and portrayed, and to which his readers have thrilled for various generations. Morbidly attracted to the reiterated scenes of violence and dishonor.

Let one scene stand in for them all: when the soldiers of the punishment battalion, at the peak of an orgiastic stay at a brothel on the Black Sea, hang the madame by the neck until dead, having discovered her misdeeds: a fat slut who dangles, lifeless, completely naked, from a flagstaff, until her neck stretches and stretches . . .

(This capo had arranged to deport her girls, and she'd had some of them executed by firing squad . . .)

PORTA TORE DOWN SOME VELVET CURTAINS and ripped off the heavy cord which operated them. Little John snatched up a discarded pair of stockings and tied a gag round the victim's mouth. One of the Rumanians bound her hands together with a red silk brassière. [. . .] One end of the curtain cord was attached high up on the flagstaff. The other was formed into a loop with a slip knot. [. . .] The loop was placed round Mme. Olga's neck.

"JUMP," ordered Little John. Mme. Olga balanced precariously on the edge of the windowsill, all her fat white flesh quivering and threatening to unbalance her. "Jump!" roared Little John, for the second time. She jumped at last; or fell; or was pushed. Her body wrapped itself round the flagpole, hanging at the end of the cord. Her double chins seemed to swell up like so many balloons, and then her neck stretched out very long and thin. A silence fell in the upstairs room. Some of us turned away. Some of us leaned out the window and stared with globulous eyes, hypnotized by the horror of that fat white body swaying to and fro at the end of the cord . . .

AND THERE YOU GO, before you even know it, another year has gone by. It's Christmas, a new Christmas, the Christmas of 2013. Who knows why I spend the holidays immersed in sadistic themes, whether it's pure chance or a choice. Today is Christmas and, yesterday afternoon, after wrapping the presents and cooking something for the family dinner, I sat down to read an article titled "On Cruelty" by Judith Butler, in the *London Review of Books*. It's a review of a book by Jacques Derrida on the death penalty. Without entering into the merits of the points argued by the various authors reviewed in the article, from Nietzsche to Freud and Lacan in his paradoxical essay "Kant avec Sade" (where Lacan claims that Sade is the closest follower of the Kantian categorical imperative, by filling the empty commandment with concrete acts), and then, naturally, Derrida, I gain a powerful impression of the diffuse violence in all aspects and at all levels of crime—obviously—but also of punishment. In short, that a "festive cruelty" can be found in the violation of the law but also in the application of it. Morality can be every bit as violent as those who break its laws: indeed, in order to ensure that the Ten Commandments are respected, almost as much cruelty is deployed as is lavished in the infraction of them in the first place, and at the same time as much suffering as enjoyment is generated. If the suffering of others causes exultation, as is the case when a malefactor is punished, then even the just punishment of the culprit is clearly sexualized. If that culprit is also guilty of a sex crime, as in the case we're examining, the CR/M, then we have a twofold sexualization of the violence: that committed by the rapists, and that implicit in their incarceration and sentence, which cause widespread enjoyment among the respectable citizens, the hotheads, the feminists, the fathers and heads of household, the newspaper readers, in other words, among everyone, or almost. The pleasure of seeing another person punished, another person suffer (prison is an only slightly more civilized and diffuse way of inflicting suffering, when compared with whippings or mutilations or killings), is not in and of itself different, by the sole fact of its being legitimate. In short, sadism occupies the whole of the stage, in both the first and second acts of crime, from prologue to epilogue, and it warms the hearts of each of the characters in the drama, the guilty parties, the survivors, the judges, the public, the chorus of commentators. Crime, vengeance, and justice are all merged into an indistinct enjoyment, which might culminate and then subside only at the instant when those responsible for the murder cease to live: by means of the death penalty, the implementation of which, in fact, in certain of those countries where it is imposed, can be attended by the relatives of the victims, in a sort of psychic reparation intended at least to compensate for the grief and pain suffered with a form of enjoyment, intense but definitive, experienced in witnessing the death agonies of the culprit; whereas extended incarceration would be a far more diluted delight, though also a longer-lasting one. Cruelty can be exhibited, so to speak, naked, or else behind the mask of justice, that is, rationalized and transformed into a moral duty; and hostility against life appears inherent to life itself, entailed in life's own formation, only presenting itself in different forms, some of which are so pure and abstract that they start to resemble, in fact, laws of necessity. The pleasure principle and the death impulse basically are striving for the same thing. This, then, would be the paradoxical Kantian legacy in Sade and, more in general, in the Sadists, who operate on the basis of a principle that establishes itself well beyond that of pleasure, or the satisfaction of a need: because if the violent sexual impulse goes above and beyond the interests of those who feel it, if it no longer aims to achieve any recognizable gratification but instead acts in an impersonal fashion, if, in other words, it truly is *disinterested*, then it can be considered an absolute, moral act and can be seconded and implemented almost as if it were a duty or a mission, that is to say, in fact, a categorical imperative. It is therefore not moral behavior that is secretly based on selfish and pathological impulses (an unsurprising unmasking that anyone, after Freud, is capable of carrying out), but rather its ostensible opposite, that is, desire, which acts impersonally, dispassionately, in a *disinterested* and supraindividual manner, in short, the way one would expect of a pure moral action, whose criteria it matches perfectly and whose profile it ends up fitting. Desire acts *against* the most elementary interests of both those who experience it and those who are its object. Who is the beneficiary of it, who has a vested interest in it, come to think of it? No one. That is why the sadistic fantasy develops gratuitously, beyond all realism and any calculation of interest, outside the logic of cost and benefit that one ought to consider when committing evil instead of good, and imagines itself being applied to a virtual body that can be tortured and killed ad infinitum, a body capable of withstanding a cascading chain of suffering and humiliation, and which is reborn each time intact, to be tortured and abused, on and on, as in *Justine*, as in the CR/M: an *immortal* body.

(In that case, if that's the way things stand, the thuggish guards in the famous song by Fabrizio De André weren't seeking "the soul with a thorough beating" in the atheist's body, but they were seeking his body, the immortal depths of his body, a body capable of allowing unlimited violence to be inflicted upon it . . .)

I WAS SHAKEN FOR A LONG TIME by the reading of that article. The fact that sadistic topics, that my morbid interest in the scandal of violence should reemerge with the approach of religious holidays is, I believe, pure random chance but, perhaps, not entirely without its root causes: the man-God whose birthday we commemorate today will die on the cross just a few months later, his legs shattered and his shoulders racked and his arms yanked out of their sockets. And so it goes, starting over again from scratch every year.

On Christmas Eve, in the midst of the ceremony of gift-giving (usually, I give a *great many* gifts and receive *very few*: it's a law I can never quite resign myself to), I consider abandoning relatives and children to hurry over to the midnight mass at SLM: it's probably the last chance I'll have to witness it and describe it, since I'm hoping to finish this book sometime during the new year, but in the end, I don't go. Nor will I finish the book, come to that. I think and think about it, but I don't go.

I TRY TO MAKE UP for that on the morning of the twenty-fifth by going to Sant'Agnese. Maybe I'll find Father Edoardo there, the priest who blessed my apartment not once but twice. Before leaving, I checked the timing of the services on the parish's online website, and I chose the last mass of the morning, at eleven o'clock. I search for a parking spot around Piazza Annibaliano, taking care not to let my gaze stray to the metro station, a blight and an eyesore that might give the last and decisive blow to my mood, already teetering precariously, and then I drive up Via Bressanone with my eyes turned obstinately to my left, toward the gently sloping hill with the basilica and the baptistery, restful sight, balm for my soul. After a fruitless search, I end up parking my car with all four wheels perched on the median dividing the service lane running along Via Nomentana from the central flow of traffic. It's a rude and uncivil act of parking, I know that inwardly. I sidestep the main entrance to the basilica from Via Nomentana, where two beggars have taken up position, and I turn down the little side street alongside Sant'Agnese, crowded with people who like me are hurrying to get to the service in time and others who are walking the other way after attending the previous mass.

And in front of Sant'Agnese, in fact, there is a considerable throng of the faithful entering and exiting the church. Bells are ringing, variously deep and piercing notes, everyone is exchanging hugs. Well, I certainly never expected such throngs and such fervor, such a pitch of festivity. Inside the church, full as I've never seen it before, there is a general clamor, voices and the cries of children, exchanges of greetings, the wailing of more than one newborn. Those who attended the mass that had just ended showed no intention of leaving. Can I say that I, too, was happy in this situation? But "happiness" isn't the right word: from the depths of my grim darkness I feel a weight lift. Maybe I can lay the boulder I'm hauling down for a moment and rest before lifting it back onto my shoulder and setting off again, to carry it aimlessly to and fro. That might be why I'm happy to sit down in an empty chair, next to a family that has occupied an entire pew: the parents on either side, young, serious, but cheerful, and three children between them, who don't seem at all bored or unhappy at having been brought to church instead of to the park. Looking around, I'm positively struck by the assortment of humanity that is preparing to attend mass. There are also many non-Italian women, with scarves over their heads, nearly all of them in their early forties, but worn and tired, eyes red as if they'd just stood up from a floor after scrubbing it with lye. They clasp their hands in their laps. As the mass begins, people are still exchanging greetings and farewells and hugs and grandparents are steering their little ones to the front row to gaze at the manger scene, where last night, at midnight, I imagine, the Christ Child was given pride of place. The priest officiating, however, is not Father Edoardo, but a powerfully built man of the cloth who reveals, the instant he opens his mouth, the usual accent, with no attempt to conceal the cadence, if anything, in fact, seemingly accentuated as if to proclaim a working-class extraction, unpretentious, as for that matter, are the things he says. The service begins with "Adeste Fideles" (Oh Come, All Ye Faithful), the lyrics to which appear at number eleven in the program, and it is an excellent idea to start with a song, as if a theatrical trick, allowing the audience time to get settled, covering up the noise of those leaving the church and those who ("Excuse me, excuse me . . .") are still finding a place to sit. If they are unable to find a seat, they remain standing in the side aisles. Before the first two verses of this Christmas carol with the lilt of an Irish ballad have been sung, I find myself joining the chorus, at the top of my lungs.

"Natum videte—regem angelorum" . . . Come and behold him, Born the King of Angels . . .

Even if I haven't crossed myself, even if I don't pray and I don't take communion, can I still sing, or not? It's so simple, anyone ought to be able to do it. (I'm reminded of the words of the oblate at the church of Santa Francesca Romana: "In order to participate you need only believe in God . . . *or maybe you don't even need that."*)

The mass unfolds with its singsong rhythm, which corresponds to the way the faithful rise to their feet and sit down again, like a wave in a stadium. A number of elderly readers follow one another up to the microphone to enunciate select passages on the topic of the Annunciation, I struggle a little to keep up and I make use of the sheet of paper to find my way. Words like a buzzing, a murmuring, beneficent no doubt, but practically incomprehensible, where there is talk of angels, a great deal of talk of angels . . . of the holy arm of the Lord bared before the nations . . . they say how beautiful on the mountains are the feet of the Messenger of Peace, but what a daring image, practically surreal . . . the image of the lovely feet of He who announces salvation. Isaiah, St. Paul, Epistle to the Hebrews . . . until we reach the Gospel according to John, and there, not even if I follow along line by line on the paper (1:1–18) am I able to penetrate beyond the sound of those words, heard and repeated so many times before: the Word, the shadows . . . the Word made flesh, the glory, the fullness. That is the stunning manner in which John begins his Gospel.

The priest's homily does its best to meet the faithful halfway, reassuring them, confirming the difficulty of those words. His own words have the rough effect of a bucketful of water tossed onto glowing embers.

"After a reading like this, you might as well just phone home and let them know: listen, I'm not going to be there for lunch . . ." Then he smiles to let us know that he's exaggerating, ". . . because here we'd have things to talk about until dinner . . . in fact, till long after dinner, before we'd even come up with a single clear idea!"

All I seem able to retain from that Gospel is a phrase that occurs close to the end of the passage: "No man hath seen God at any time."

The homily continues without any particular interest. The priest skates along through a succession of commonplaces, every once in a while warming up with a patch of dialect ("*Dovremmo sta' contenti, no? che Iddio ce vole tanto bbene*"; We should be happy, shouldn't we? that God loves us so well) the thin ice of those topics. But the atmosphere in the church, all the same, is so full of light and harmony that no word could either perfect it or ruin it. I glance over at the children in the next pew, sitting between their parents, their silhouettes so attentive, their noses straight and their eyes glistening, as they listen, as they nod: Can it be that I am the only one subject to distraction? The only one who *really doesn't understand*?

When I emerge from this strange and in any case pleasant state of torpor, the moment for the Credo has suddenly arrived, and everyone in the church takes up the words at the top of their lungs. A chorus of rhythmic affirmations. I'm seized by a profound sense of uneasiness: I know it by heart, from my childhood, but I don't want to recite it with others, that would be a deception, this isn't a damned song, it's a declaration, and in any case I'd be committing perjury by saying "*credo*"—I believe; but I don't feel like remaining silent, either, while all around me proclaim their faith, article by article: so I slip between the chairs, behind the columns, and make my way to the exit.

> . . . *begotten, not made,*
> *being of one substance with the Father* . . .

I wait for the pledge of faith to be completed, and then I leave.

OUTSIDE THERE IS ONLY ONE PRIEST, dressed in white. He has his back to me. I walk by him and he turns his head ever so slightly and he acknowledges me, lifting his eyes from the smartphone on which he'd been busily tapping out a text.

"Good morning," we say to each other, almost in unison, after which he adds, with a smile, ". . . and Merry Christmas to you!"

"Certainly, thank you, and Merry Christmas to you, too . . ."

He's lost weight, his hair is whiter, his eyes are bright: yes, it's Father Edoardo. It was he I had so hoped would be saying mass, but instead he was out here, perhaps catching his breath after the ten o'clock service. Officiating is tiring. I immediately move a few steps away, as if I'd been burned by that brief interaction. Before heading off to the café near the basketball courts to get an espresso, I look at my watch: I held out in Sant'Agnese for twenty-five minutes. Technically my presence at the Christmas mass wasn't valid, that's the way we used to say it when I was a kid, because if you didn't stay to hear the Our Father at mass it was as if you hadn't gone. Father Edoardo is just finishing his text, using a single finger, then he sends it with a final touch: as he does it, closing the case of his phone, he smiles faintly to himself.

LAST NIGHT I RECEIVED AS GIFTS a shirt and a pair of socks bought at Paris, the shop just above Piazza Verbano. Then I received on my smartphone a photograph that provides a thorough illustration of the spirit of the city where I live and of its inhabitants. The photo frames a balcony on an apartment house on the outskirts of town. For the holidays, someone has installed a message, hanging off the railing, in large luminous letters:

MERRY CHRISTMAS MY ROSY ASS

The most concise possible response to season's greetings in this time of economic crisis.

When I got home from Sant'Agnese—which is, as you'll remember, the church of St. Agnes—I transcribed the hymn that you will read in the next chapter.

II

THE LEGEND OF ST. AGNES

They say it all happened when she was a girl,
in fact, a young girl, in the earliest years of her adolescence,
still too much of a child to be engaged or married but already
     ardently
filled with the love of Christ, wherefore at the request to prostrate
     herself
in adoration of idols, disavowing the true faith, the young Agnes
replied with a terse refusal. And even though she was drawn out
and tempted with great cunning by a judge, who variously
     blandished her with
honeyed words, or threatened her, warning of atrocious torment,
she remained firm in her choice and went so far as to offer up
her body to be tortured, with absolutely no fear.
At that point the pitiless prosecutor said to himself:
"If it strikes her as easy to tolerate the pain
because she holds her own life in no high esteem,
perhaps she'll be sorry to lose something even more precious
     to her:
her virginity. So I'll have her tossed into a brothel
until, eventually, she'll repent and implore Minerva's forgiveness,
the virgin whom she, in spite of the fact that she herself is a virgin,
     she nonetheless
stubbornly continues to scorn. The men will flock from all
     directions
to see the brothel's newest acquisition, they'll come to blows
to get first shot at this new toy . . ."
"Christ won't allow it," Agnes thought, "Christ
won't forget us, Christ won't abandon us. He defends
those who keep themselves chaste and won't allow the sacred body,
kept intact, to be violated. Bathe your sword in my blood

but you won't sully my body with lust!"
And she announced her proud intention. The magistrate had her
    placed
on the Via Nomentana, at the crossroads
with a dusty country track
where the passersby could see her, nude, as if she were there
to sell herself: but the crowd avoided looking at her, they all
cast their eyes down or turned their backs
as if repelled by her innocence. Only one wretched oaf
failed to respect the sacred aura she emanated
and dared to turn his insolent gaze on the young woman,
he let a lascivious gaze linger upon her
and immediately a bolt fell from heaven that blinded him.
He rolled in the dust, both eyes gone.
His friends hurried in vain to his aid: he was dead.
In the meantime, the virgin triumphed, still chaste
after her first day as a harlot. Not even the street,
not even the brothel had contaminated her. Her virginity
had won the duel. For this she thanked her Lord.
Asked by the friends of the thunderstruck oaf, she began
to pray to God that He might restore the young man's sight and
    life,
until the young man's soul returned to his body
and his lifeless eyes glowed once again with light.

But this was only the first step on the path to heaven.
Soon Agnes was given an opportunity to climb the second step,
so great was the bloodthirsty frenzy exciting her adversary.

"I'm losing the battle," he mused. "All my efforts
against this virgin are proving vain . . . And so, hurry,
soldier, unsheathe your sword and carry out the orders
of our emperor!" the magistrate commanded.

When Agnes saw the grim figure
looming above her, his sword unsheathed, her happiness
suddenly swelled. "I rejoice to see this man
armed, barbaric, ferocious, ready to take my life, rather

than some sweet-scented young man come to destroy my honor.
This murderous lover is certainly the one I like best! So I confess.
I'll meet him halfway, welcoming his desires, and I'll extinguish
his hot lust for death by giving him my own.
I'll welcome the full length of his sword
into my breast, I'll lure it in. I, bride of no man but Christ,
will leap the width of the gulf of shadows and find myself right in
    heaven.
Open to me the doors once locked against the children of the earth!"

With these words, she prepared her neck, bowing her head, to
    receive
the impending wound. The executioner's hand granted her wish,
lopping off her head at a single blow, so that death
came instantly, forestalling pain.
Her soul, disincarnate, now floats surrounded by angels
along a glittering path . . . she is amazed to see
the world beneath her feet and, as she continues to climb, distant
    now,
all those shadows . . . and she laughs at the sight of the
solar orbit, and the countless universes spinning intertwined . . .
the life of all things, the welter of circumstances, all the vanities
that the world chases after, kings, tyrants, empires, high offices and
    honors
puffed up with stupid pride, gold and silver piled up
in fury, by every means, and the splendor of the palaces, the richly
embroidered garments, the rage, the fear, the oaths, the risks,
the long-drawn-out sorrows and the all-too-brief joys, the smoky
    ember
of rancor that dirties all hope, all human decorum . . .
and finally, far worse than any other ills on earth,
the dirty clouds of disbelief. All this Agnes
trod underfoot as with her heel she crushed the head of the serpent
that poisons everything, who now no longer dares to rear his head,
now that the virgin has cast him down to hell.

And God encircles your head with two glorious crowns
in place of the nuptial crown you never wore . . .

Oh, blessed virgin, oh, new glory added to the heaven
you now inhabit, you whom the Father allowed
to render chaste a den of iniquity, turn your glowing
gaze upon us, fill our hearts,
make us pure with the ray that emanates from your face
or with the touch of your immaculate foot!

12

THE STORY I'M ABOUT TO TELL NOW will clarify (or perhaps further confuse) the dynamic of an episode described many pages back in this story.

Until some time ago, I was a teacher, working in the maximum-security wing (MS) of Rebibbia Prison in Rome, where Mafiosi and Camorristi are among the inmates. That wing is isolated from the rest of the penitentiary. As a number of my colleagues maintain—and in fact they work year after year to keep their assignments to that wing—those are great classes to teach, in fact, they're better than the others, it's an objective fact, the students are, on average, better disciplined and more eager than in the wing where common criminals are locked up, full of out-of-control young men and demented mad dogs of every ethnic persuasion: of course they are, the people in the MS wing are solid, straight-ahead folks, who respect hierarchies, and in their midst the simple fact of having a college degree assures you a certain traditional type of respect, that has evaporated everywhere else in Italian society. A teacher, of whatever gender, is still "someone": maybe deep down, that's not really true, and their modest salaries tend to lower their standing down to the threshold of the ridiculous, but at least in their explicit demeanor, the students of the MS, with their legacy of ceremonious manners, still give every sign of holding old-fashioned views, and they comport themselves with a courtesy that may well be contrived, but what courtesy isn't, after all?

What with the tireless demeaning of external niceties, in Italy, we've all been plunged into the inferno of authentic feelings. Which, most of the time, are as authentic as a hock of spit or a fart.

❖

NOW, IN THE MS, among the many unusual students, there was one who was more unusual than the rest, even though in many ways he was perhaps typical, categorical. Diminutive in stature, elderly, though probably not as old as his appearance might have suggested, bespectacled, with an almost incomprehensible way of speaking, both because of the thick dialect and because of his raucous voice, he kept insisting that we had to write a book together, he and I. He asked me about it at the end of practically every class I taught: "*Allora, prufesso', quann'è c"o scrivimm' chist' libro? Ch'agg'a fa', tutt' i' solo?*" (All right then, Professor, when are we going to write this book? What, do I have to do it all alone?) "Excuse me, what did you say?" And he'd say it all over again, with his singsong drawl.

This man was known as Prince, or the Prince, sometimes with, sometimes without the definite article. His plan, inspired by the crackpot idea of righting the wrongs that he felt had been done to him, and with the mirage of earning a mountain of cash, was to write a sort of response to Roberto Saviano's formidable bestseller *Gomorrah*, which, to hear my student tell it (and he was named in the pages of that book, by given name and surname, as the perpetrator of odious murders, that is, the very reason for his being incarcerated, and therefore, my student), was riddled with falsehoods, and so it was imperative that the truth be established at the earliest possible opportunity. My student, then, hoped to undertake what was once known as a counterinvestigation, by the light of his own firsthand experiences, and publish an *Anti-Gomorrah*, a *Counter-Gomorrah*, a *Gomorrah à rebours*, turned inside out like a glove, narrated from the point of view of the Camorristi. And he wanted me to be his mentor, his editor or ghostwriter. "*Che ne dice, prufesso'? Ce finimmo anch' nuie, primm'n classifica?*" (What do you think about it, Professor? Do you think we'll wind up at the top of the bestseller list, too?)

A subtler motivation that I later gave some thought (and about which I'm still thinking as I write this book of mine, all mine, *nearly* all mine) was that the student in MS claimed to hold a sort of copyright on the crimes he was involved in and guilty of. An author's copyright in the narrow, legal sense of the term.

"*Inzomma, chill' i mmuorti l'agge fatt'io . . . iooo, colle mani mie . . . e li quattrini se l'ha dda fa' qualcun altro?*" After all, I killed those men myself, with my own hands . . . and now someone else is going to make money off it?

"Well, I guess that . . ."

"*Ma pecché?*" But why?

Among my Camorristi students, this expression was widely used, at once disconsolate and mocking, when confronted with the absurdity of life: "*Ma pecché?*" A question destined inevitably to fall into the void, to be greeted with silence, the great universal vacuum devoid of explanations, and yet it had to be asked, both hands pressed together almost as if praying, then rocked up and down, all the while turning the corners of the mouth down in a grimace of almost amused disgust. "No, I ask you: *ma pecché . . . ?*"

ANTI-GOMORRAH, or *Gomorrah Unchained*, in the end, was never written by the odd couple formed by the vindictive student and his all-too-clever Italian teacher, so it never skyrocketed to the top of the bestseller lists, either. I'd dismiss the thought that he might have gone ahead and written the book alone, or with the contribution of some other man of letters, though you never know, and it might be on the verge of being published . . .

I'm not going to bother to explain here, with what patience and evasive maneuvers, dully, I managed to let the matter drop, each time the book we were supposed to write together came up, changing the topic relentlessly. Since he is an intelligent person, he understood and in his turn, slowly, stopped asking. But every now and then, as if he were still trying to tempt me toward his project, showing me all the wonderful material I'd be missing out on by not giving him a hand with his book, he would relish telling me some never-before-heard criminal episode that could have made the book succulent and even edifying.

For instance, the time that he had shot his eldest son, then seventeen, in the legs because he was hanging out with disreputable individuals, tangled up with drug dealing: an exemplary act, from his point of view, which had been meant to show that, of the many crimes he might have committed, trafficking in narcotics was not and could not be one of them, by his very ideology. Or the miraculous episode of a five-story building thrown up in complete violation of code overnight. Or else the stakeout mounted by a gang of paid assassins, come all the way from Smyrna, on the Anatolian coast, to surveil a modest villa near Bacoli, actually inhabited by two old women, the owners of a dry cleaner and now retired, the Montesano sisters, upright citizens, well known in the quarter, and not at all the debt-riddled drug dealer that the Turks had come to kill.

And then there was a varied body of anecdotes involving former soccer players from SSC Napoli, open-sea speedboats, five sisters, all of them sluts, shipping containers full of immigrants, perfectly counterfeited Rolex watches, street sweepers paid faithfully by the city government for thirty years without ever having held a broom in their hands, and then little by little he'd work his way up to episodes of violent crime: woundings and murders planned, committed, misfired, called off, or carried out by mistake or in too much of a hurry. *La prescia, ah, la prescia*, haste ruins everything, my student would sigh, with no idea that Franz Kafka was convinced of the same thing.

(But the deadly sin Kafka speaks of isn't haste, it's *impatience*.)

UNTIL ONE FINE DAY, during the cigarette break between lessons, Prince made a fleeting reference to a side business in fireworks. The Camorra was even interested in such leisure-time pursuits as fireworks: making them, warehousing them, peddling them, and setting them off at parties and festivals. For that matter, these were objects that belonged to the same family as guns and bombs. My student, however, had exited the business after a certain point in time.

"For me, they're practically bullshit" (*author's note: from here on in, for the reader's convenience, I'll just report the Prince's statements in proper Italian, instead of dialect*). "That is, I mean, fireworks themselves, per se: really, just complete bullshit."

"Why? I like them!"

"Oh, you do? Well, good for you, good for you. *I* don't. Those blasts, those explosions . . ."

"You ought to be used to them . . ."

"You never get used to them. They get on my nerves. They make my eyelids quiver, and then they just won't stop. I've got delicate nerves, actually. And I don't like chaos."

"You'd never think you come from where you come from . . ."

"I think you might be misunderstanding. I'm not talking about the *schiamazzo*, the ruckus and voices. The confusion is something else, and it's much more serious: you hear from a distance those shots and those blasts, and who can say whether it's someone involved in serious business, or if it's just for fun?"

"Ah . . . now I get it."

"I don't have anything against having fun. But in that case, go fishing, if you're looking for enjoyment, or get a dog. Take a woman to bed, I don't know. Don't go around blowing up *everything in sight*. That's stuff that's made to kill people. And sometimes it does."

"By accident . . ."

"What accidents are you talking about! By stupidity. You know how much gunpowder there is in a Bomba Maradona? Enough to knock down an apartment building. Ten kilos!"

"Boom!"

"You sure are being funny today, Professor."

"Oh, come on, I just felt like kidding around . . ."

"But people get hurt. And they get hurt for no good reason . . . no benefit to anyone. That's what I can't stand."

I understood his line of reasoning because I had heard it many times before, in prison, in particular in the maximum-security wing. It was an argument that was Machiavellian in its purity, one that you find distilled to a similar degree of purity only in certain implacable pages of the great Florentine political analyst or distilled into the famous saying that's variously attributed to Talleyrand or Fouché, concerning the deplorable execution of the Duke of Enghien with Napoleon's approval: "It was worse than a crime, it was *a mistake*." That which legitimizes an act, or makes it deplorable, is strictly its efficacy with respect to the chosen objectives, whatever they may be. If it is successful, it is good. If it fails, it is bad. If it serves a purpose, it's beneficial. Otherwise, it's harmful. It's a flat, simple morality, which instead of corresponding to a complex table of values, obeys one and one alone: self-interest, results. Blowing up ten kilos of plastic explosive, unless it's under the car of a business rival—can anyone tell me what the hell good that does? To celebrate *what*? Blasting powder is supposed to destroy something, otherwise it's just plain buffoonery. Once an operation has been completed the way it's supposed to, in and of itself, it becomes a positive thing. In other words, shooting guns, blowing up explosives, these are serious matters and need to be done with care and judgment, with the objective of wounding and killing.

I was following his line of reasoning but I took care not to give him the impression that I agreed with it.

"Then I gave up the whole thing after an accident. That's right, it was thirty years ago. I never wanted to hear a thing about fireworks, rockets, and roman candles after that. I lost so damned much money . . ." And he made a gesture, imitating a bonfire that burns a pile of cash to a crisp. "It ain't as if I lost an eye or a finger . . . a hell of a lot of money is what I lost!"

Once again, we were talking about matters economic . . . transparent and hard as fine crystal. You can lose a hand if you're involved in a business deal, but you can't lose money, otherwise what kind of a deal are we talking about here? So, not Machiavelli, then, but maybe Bentham, or Adam Smith . . . ?

"A whole warehouse blew sky high . . . and the explosions lasted for the rest of the night. We could see it from a distance, flaming, screeching . . . not even the fire department could get close to it, with all those rockets sailing through the air!"

In spite of the scorn he'd originally manifested toward firework displays, he couldn't keep from smiling.

"But where was this warehouse, in the countryside?"

He gave me a wink. "Well, you'll never guess . . ." he said, waving his hands in the air and winking first one eye, then the other.

And then a curious thing happened, odd but not all that uncommon, and typical of inmates, even the shrewdest and wisest ones: the perverse love of storytelling got the better of discretion and caution. What the Camorrista revealed to me quavered with a tone of pride and defiance: all the supposed rationality of criminal activity gave way with a thump to the pleasure of having put together a scheme so astounding that it almost seemed like a practical joke, and to the delight of explaining it to an outsider, running the risks that went with that.

"Ah, you won't believe it . . . forget about the countryside! We'd put the warehouse on top of the loony bin! Now, that's some crazy shit, am I right or am I right?" And he started laughing in a guttural fashion. "Ka, ka, ka . . ."

A series of hacking coughs is what his laughter sounded like, or the noise you make when, deep in your throat, you collect a gob of phlegm in preparation to spit it out. Two or three inmates stepped closer to us, clinging to the thin plumes of smoke rising from their cigarettes. Unlike his Neapolitan compatriots, and their famed cheery character, it was fairly rare for the Prince to show any sign of hilarity.

"The crazy house, the loony bin, ka, ka! That one was *truly* crazy!" he went on, beating the pun to death.

"You mean that the fireworks . . ."

"Yes, yes, the fireworks . . . and what fireworks! Real bombs, rocket ships, space missiles . . . Katyushas . . . ka, ka, ka!"

". . . were *where*, again?" I asked, determined to get a clearer explanation. "What do you mean . . . by the crazy house?"

"What do I mean? What do I mean . . ." and the others around us started laughing too. It must have been a well-known story, this one with the loony bin and the fireworks. One of the new arrivals slapped me on the shoulder.

"The insane asylum!"

In collusion with a number of corrupt male nurses and correctional guards, my student and his gang had used as a factory and warehouse for illegal fireworks the structures on the roof of an old criminal insane asylum. As absurd as that choice might sound at first, it was perfect in its way: no one ever went up on the roof of the insane asylum, the washhouses had been abandoned for years, and you could work there in blessed peace, and what's more, undisturbed, carrying material in and out: a building contractor based in the area, and also under the Prince's control, had obtained a regular permit and contract to clear the roof of asbestos: water tanks, plumbing, roofing, corrugated panels, and so on.

"It was all legal! It was all legitimate! Ka, ka, ka . . ."

And the amazing thing is that all this madness had taken place, as the Prince had said, in the "loony bin," with the real loonies and the alleged loonies and the serial stranglers and the paranoids and the ones who believed they were Satan, the illegal structures and the Bin Laden bombs and Maradona bombs all together in the insane asylum, one floor above another, like in some satirical short story.

Maybe that's why the Prince had thought of it in the first place, this ramshackle piece of madness, the idea of setting up the fireworks factory there.

In spite of the fact that the story was amusing, the umpteenth episode of a paradoxical reversal of the proper order of things (just like the time that the Carabinieri discovered, by their surveillance films, that certain Mafiosi were regularly meeting in the offices of the Giovanni Falcone and Paolo Borsellino Commemorative Association . . .), I still felt a sense of discomfort, a powerful, creeping, growing sense of uneasiness, which was not however due to the usual twisted use of a government institution, it was not due to any misgivings of that sort, I haven't had any such worries for a long time now, or else I sift through them very painstakingly before letting them prey on me, before I start expressing vacuous and hypocritical pangs of indignation, and after all, there in prison, you have a genuine professional obligation to set them aside, between parentheses . . . what the hell, even as I chuckled along while listening to the story of the Prince's fireworks factory ("ka, ka . . . ka!"), deep in my heart, in fact, even farther down, in my stomach, I felt a twinge of cold and fear for something slithering out of the past straight toward me, slyly, treacherously, like a bleeding creature whose limbs have been lopped off. It continued inching along, yes, right toward me . . .

"Then I went out of business, and that was that . . . all because of that asshole."

The shiver traveled out to my hands. I could feel them tingle. My voice spoke of its own will.

"Whose fault . . . who . . . all because of *which* asshole?"

The answer to that question was already present, just lurking behind the scenes of my consciousness, which was refusing to allow it in, to let that name make its appearance onstage, even though it was pressing, pushing, to be uttered. The name was there, and it was pressing dolorously on the membrane of my awareness. That name, forgotten for years, and yet familiar, surprising how well known, the way an old pencil case from school days discovered in the cellar might have been: you remember that, don't you? you used it every blessed day for years, you opened it a million times and dropped it on the floor and picked it back up . . . before retiring it. And yet it remained yours, and yours alone. Forever. I stammered, in a faint voice: "Who . . . who was this asshole, excu-scuse me? And why was he an *asshole*?"

The Prince was no longer snickering and he had resumed his usual ferocious expression. Grim, disgusted.

"Because he managed to blow himself up with the whole warehouse!"

His lips curled into a grimace of contempt for such boundless idiocy.

I asked for no clarifications about how the accident had unfolded. From that instant on, I had no doubt that he was talking about Stefano Maria Jervi, my old classmate from my days at SLM, the precocious youngster, the adolescent sultan with the flaming eyes. Jervi, the brother of the stunningly beautiful Romina, identified, once he was nothing more than a corpse, as a militant of the UGC, the Unità di Guerriglia Comunista—the Communist Guerrilla Unit.

"The criminal insane asylum of Aversa . . ." I murmured, pensively, while I was reminded of an episode that might have dated back to the last year of middle school, or even my sophomore year of high school, when all of us, I, Jervi, Arbus, Pik, Rummo, Regazzoni, and everyone else, would have been sixteen.

AT ONE O'CLOCK IN THE AFTERNOON, when we got out of school, on Via Nomentana, there was a young blonde astride a motorcycle. I remember that pressed between her legs was a Ducati Scrambler with a yellow gas tank and a tall spreading set of handlebars, really an oafish motorcycle for a girl, and such a pretty girl. I was standing next to Stefano when she spotted him and waved at him, I couldn't say exactly why but it was immediately clear that she was waving specifically at Jervi out of the dozens of youngsters who were shoving and bumping against one another in their haste to leave school: rather than simply leaving at the end of the day's lessons, we seemed to be trying to stage a mass prison escape. Stefano recognized her and went straight over to her, striding briskly, and then when he reached her he hauled back and gave her a smack on the face, hard and sharp, the kind you see in the movies and the commercials of the time, the ones shot in unnatural, pumped-up colors, he knocked the motorcyclist's long blond hair to one side, and I had the impression that her locks floated in the air in slow motion. Again, as if in a movie, like, say, *Carnal Knowledge*, I, playing the role of the friend (Art Garfunkel), clapped my hand over my mouth, paralyzed by my astonishment. Without saying a word, he, Jervi (Jack Nicholson), turned and stalked off down Via Nomentana, while the girl bowed her head and covered her face with both hands, out of pain or shame, and presumably burst into tears, because I could see her petite shoulders covered with her long blond hair shaking and lurching.

"STEFANO . . . THIRTY YEARS AGO . . ." I murmured, forgetting entirely where I was at that instant and in the company of whom: in a cell in the maximum-security wing of Rebibbia Prison, surrounded by foot soldiers of dangerous Mafia-type organized crime families, that is, my fond students. I was too caught up in the memory of the students that we had been back then. The young woman that Jervi had slapped had attracted me for countless reasons: because she was beautiful, because she owned and drove a motorcycle, in those days an almost exclusively male appanage, because she was in tears, because she wore purple pants, snug at the top and wide at the bottom, because Jervi had hurt her, and because Jervi had certainly kissed her and fondled her.

"How do you know it was at Aversa?"

The Prince's tone of voice as he spoke to me now had changed. It was inquisitive now, I would say.

THE BLOND GIRL HAD TO BE AIDED, comforted, and I was the one to do it, inasmuch as I was a reader of hundreds of novels and *fotonovelas*, devouring

Grand Hotel and TV movies, one of the clearest and most agile minds of SLM, a classmate of Jervi, the guy who had hit her, and I therefore had every right to weigh in, this was obvious to me, and I acted almost without thinking: I had to make up for the harm done by my classmate, so I moved toward her.

"I just made a wild guess," I replied to the Prince. "Is it or isn't it the most famous criminal insane asylum in Italy?"

The other convicts nodded.

"Certainly . . . of course it is. Aversa. A nasty place."

"A nasty, nasty place . . ."

"You can go in . . . but you won't necessarily come back out."

"ARE YOU OKAY? What happened?" I had asked the girl on the motorcycle, who didn't answer. "Can I do anything for you?"

It goes without saying that a girl who lets herself be slapped around like that just loves rough guys and tends to feel little regard for those who instead go out of their way to be caring and kind, if she doesn't actually feel utter contempt for them: that's one of the many unjust laws that govern relations between the sexes. Hence my eagerness to help her hadn't been the right move: for that matter, there wouldn't have been any right move for me to make. And yet I persisted.

"Did he hurt you?"

She took her hands off her face and I was able to get a better look at her. The smack had reddened one of her cheeks and swollen her upper lip, which already must have been naturally turgid and arched. Her light blue eyes had deep dark circles around them, and were full of tears. She had freckles. The way the old songs say, something worth giving up living for, right then and there.

"Don't interfere," she replied, brusquely.

By the transitive property typical of morbid passivity, just as she delighted in letting herself suffer Jervi's abuse, likewise I delighted in letting myself be treated the same by her. Which stoked my thirst for further humiliations.

"No, that's exactly what I intend to do," I told her, with a frivolous spitefulness on the verge of homosexual hysteria.

It's strange how the instantaneous attraction that I felt toward that very beautiful girl, an unmistakable sign of my heterosexuality, led me to behave like an impudent little faggot, instead of revealing me in all my virility. I have noticed that feminine seduction has this effect on me.

"Get out of my hair, you have nothing to do with this." Then she looked at me a little more closely and from her scowling face there emerged a cruel half smile. "Get out of here, kid . . ."

I took a step backwards as if I was the one who had taken the slap.

Still half-smiling and half-crying as well, she stood up over the seat and gave a powerful kick to the starter, then another, and then yet another, even sharper, until finally the Ducati responded.

"Little kid!"

IN THE PRESENCE OF MY STUDENTS IN PRISON, I also frequently feel like a well-intentioned kid, or maybe just a kid, period, who has gone and gotten mixed up with much bigger and more experienced people. Bigger not so much in terms of age (now I'm older than nearly all of them, after all), but in terms of overall human stature. And why on earth did I do it? Out of a punctilious point of honor, out of a sense of playfulness, out of sheer boredom—in fact, all of them kid reasons to do something. The aspiration to experience something constantly new is driven from the very outset by an illicit principle, it leads you to the borders of the illegal, and often beyond. Maybe that's what happened to Jervi. How did he ever end up on that roof-top? And how could I ask the Prince and get more information from him without letting him figure out that I already know about that story and that it already concerned me personally? The guy that he referred to as "that asshole" was an ex-classmate of mine, no less. But with people like him, it's very difficult to bluff, in fact, practically impossible.

I TRIED TO CIRCLE BACK to the topic in the days that followed, but my student, from the moment he realized that I was interested, and for real, not like with his goofball publishing projects, withdrew. Curiosity had aroused his suspicion of my partial familiarity with what had happened and alarmed him. Or maybe he was just doing it out of spite.

As for how Stefano Maria Jervi really died, I was left with the doubts I had had initially, still intact, and a series of theories arranged one atop the other, and hidden each from the rest, like the layers of a cake: composing an unknowable truth.

Perhaps something that had been nothing more than criminal activity had been mistaken for the maneuverings of a terrorist cell: the illegal fabrication of fireworks for New Year's Eve, which Jervi was taking part in.

Or else maybe Jervi really was a terrorist, because back then, in that convulsive phase that was to accentuate the movement's decline, the various revolutionary groups had chosen to form alliances with common criminals and with the Camorra, to commit kidnappings and murders: and the supposed fireworks business was nothing other than a cover for the management of a genuine, full-fledged arsenal.

Maybe Jervi really had made some blunder that blew him sky high or maybe someone had lured him onto the insane asylum roof by some deception. In those days, there were countless scores being settled with spies, real or presumed: anyone might wake up one fine day and just decide to turn informant. Had Jervi simply not had a chance to squeal yet? Had he planned to? Or had his confederates simply made a mistake? Back then, everyone was suspicious of everyone else.

Or maybe the Prince had just told me a lie, and that was that.

He'd done it for the fun of it . . . just to watch me fall for it . . .

Ma pecché? But why?

Perhaps, as is so often the case, he was telling half a lie. Maybe both things were being warehoused in those abandoned washhouses, bombs and New Year's Eve fireworks, Tokarevs, Sig Sauers, Glocks, Škorpions, along with ordinary firecrackers.

Maybe Jervi had been killed elsewhere and then transported up there and blown up with all the rest, to mislead the investigators.

It isn't easy to distinguish in Italy between the two phases that, according to Marx, succeed each other when the same event occurs in history: first as tragedy, then as farce. Rather, these two phases overlap, merging into a single event, at once dramatic and grotesque. He had jotted this down in his papers, my old and beloved teacher, the only person I've ever had and acknowledged as a master in my life, Signor Cosmo: Tragedy and farce are, in our country, tragically, comically simultaneous.

Maybe Jervi had committed suicide.

But deep down, what does it matter?

EPILOGUE. It's been a number of years now since I stopped teaching at the MS. If you're interested in life behind bars, I invite you to read the article below that I had the unfortunate idea of publishing in the weekly magazine of a prominent daily paper. It is the story, saccharine sweet and picturesque (soap and water, in the modest opinion of its author), of a typical morning of a teacher in prison. The names are all fictional, except for one. This is a detour from the main body of this book, so anyone who does not wish to read it is welcome to skip the chapter, they won't have missed a thing. It is in any case on account of this semi-innocent article that I no longer teach at the MS, and once you've either read it or left it unread, I'll tell you the reason.

13

To GET TO THE CELL in the maximum-security wing where school is taught, you have to go through eleven checkpoints, a combination of iron gates and armored doors. The first six open automatically: a guard gives you the once-over, either in person or by a video camera, and pushes the button. The next three gates have to be operated by hand, by an officer in the roundhouse: with a large yellow key he opens the gate for you and, as soon as you've passed through, slams it shut behind you, with the usual distinctive bang. (In fact, the roundhouse, from which all the wings extend, with their cells, and that unmistakable metallic crash are the most garish signals of prison, the icons acquired by the habitual visitor—but they hit you like a punch in the nose if you're going in for the first time.) The last two gates are left ajar, and I slide through, squeezing myself thin and dangling in one hand the transparent plastic book bag containing the roll book, the ruler, the official notarized pages, the tiny Hoepli edition of the *Divine Comedy*, the pencils—in other words, the accoutrements of a normal teacher in a normal school.

Practically all of my students are standing near the whiteboard where they're commenting, ironically or pityingly, on their classmate's efforts; he stands there, marker in hand, swollen with doubts, trying to solve a math problem. A couple of them are over by the open window, smoking. The teacher, a woman, is trying to steer the student toward the correct answer with a few comments: she can't just abandon him to the anguish of those numbers, but she can't spoon-feed him either, otherwise what good would the exercise do him, what's more, the others would make fun of him—

pitiless mockery. Actually, though, the ones cracking funny, if they had been at the whiteboard, would be just as helpless. It's incredible to watch a hardened bandit turn helpless in front of a piece of homework or a math problem. Accustomed to acting tough when being grilled by the cops, they turn into marshmallows when given an exam. Even certain Roman hard-asses, accustomed to pulling off armed robberies . . . One time I had a student who was taking his final exam in literature, and he came close to tears in shame, tangled up halfway through a poem by Pascoli.

If everyone stands up in this cell-classroom, it's in part because there is no heat, the heating doesn't work, it never once worked this winter—and so they mill around, stamp their feet, rub their hands. The mathematics teacher wears an overcoat, as well as a woolen skullcap, fingerless gloves, and un-failingly yellow-and-red oversized scarves, the colors of the AS Roma soccer club; there's a tall, neurotic Sicilian who seems ready to go skiing with a Jean-Claude Killy style of cap, dating more or less back to that pe-riod, the late sixties, faded from repeated washings. It is brutally cold in there, even though the February weather is mild. It's damp—I can't figure out why, but it's always damp in prison, even in the dog-day summer heat.

Since the bell doesn't ring in here to mark the end of the hour and I came in stealthily, it is several seconds before I am noticed, whereupon the ironic, festive ceremony of greetings begins, along with the ritual of offer-ing coffee.

"*Aho!* Americano! The professor's here, aren't you going to make some coffee for the professor?!" someone calls toward the cell across the corridor from our classroom.

Until just a few weeks ago, the Americano's voice would ring out in re-sponse, in a heavy Roman accent: "*Nooo! Nun je lo preparo er caffè ar vostro professore . . .*" No! I'm not making coffee for your professor . . .

"And why not?"

"*Perché è daa Lazzio!*" Because he roots for Lazio, instead of Roma.

But then, within minutes the steaming pitcher of coffee would arrive, along with the little plastic cups so we all could have some. A thin line of coffee at the bottom of each little cup.

"Fine," after we've had our coffee, "let's get down to business," and I start the lesson by handing out photocopies with the epigrams of the Palatine Anthology, in Milo De Angelis's lovely Italian translation. You need only read the first three or four poems and the atmosphere starts to warm up, a strange languid feeling starts to spread as everyone's attention grows intense.

Ieri, con la testa appoggiata alla mia spalla
piangeva, in silenzio. La baciai. Le lacrime scendevano
come da una fonte misteriosa sulle nostre labbra unite . . .

One day, she leaned on me—I knew not why—
And, resting on my neck, she gave a sigh.
She wept; I kissed her, and our lips grew wet
As streams of dew flowed on them as they met.

We speak of pagan Eros and Christian Amor, of the lyrical tradition that begins with Sappho and ends up at Sanremo Song Festival, of the demon that possesses men and leads them to escape from the self that imprisons them. The inmates fight among themselves for the chance to read poems aloud, putting theatrical emphasis into their reading. Where regret or sensuality are strongest, their voices reach the appropriate pitch and vibration, and I decide that literature actually has meaning.

"Now, I want to read this one, though," with an arch expression, and I start in:

Doride, culo di rosa, l'ho distesa sopra il letto . . .

Having stretched out Doris the rose-bottomed on top of a bed.

After an hour spent like that, as the temperature in class rises steadily, I decide the time has come for a bucket of ice water.

"Now we've had enough of those faggots the ancient Greeks, let's move on to some grammatical analysis of simple sentences . . ."

"Nooo!!"

The classes in Rebibbia are widely variegated. Nigerians, Romanians, Slavs, and a fruit cocktail of Italians. Here in the maximum-security wing, I have, among others, two Romans, an elegant Colombian, a Sardinian, and then various subjects of the Kingdom of the Two Sicilies. Faces, voices, personalities, physiognomies. I want the lingua franca to be Italian but frequently Sicilian and Spanish gain the upper hand—nearly all of them, in the course of their illegal trafficking, have had to learn some amount of Spanish.

And then, of course, there's Wilmo.

Every year, inevitably, in every class, there's a young man like Wilmo.

Wilmo is truly unrestrainable. In his small, light blue eyes, the thousand ideas that pass through his head burn like electric discharges, the observations, the answers to questions never asked, the objections, the wordplay, the anecdotes—and it is all transformed into an explosive burst of laughter. Despite the fact that he has been in prison for years, he has not yet assumed the hieratical calm typical of the older prisoners, the ones who have learned to control their movements, to slow their respiration in order to avoid being touched by what happens around them in prison. Wilmo does not want to slow things down, in fact, he constantly accelerates. The words pour out of him, he wants to answer all the questions, solve all the problems at the whiteboard, read aloud, correct mistakes . . .

A few years ago, the members of a rival gang tried to stop him, with fifteen bullets. "Fifteen?!" I exclaimed. "And they all hit the target, Professor!" Wilmo laughs, as if proud or just amused at the astonishment he's caused.

"Excuse me, though, they must have been small-caliber bullets . . ."

Not at all—9 mm! When the surgeons got to work on him, they couldn't believe that that colander lying there on the operating table, that fountain of blood could still be among the living. So what does Wilmo do? Are words enough to tell the story? No. He pulls up his T-shirt to show me the scars of his entry and exit wounds. Then he comes closer to me and points out a couple of pale marks on his face, a streak that runs along his jaw, and, at the right corner of his mouth, a crease that I just thought was a wrinkle of expression: instead it's the point where the bullet entered his mouth.

"I just swallowed it!" He laughs.

The lesson, which up to that point had sailed along as taut and direct as a violin string, bends, collapses, plunges into the void: but I know what to do about it, I let the fishing line hang slack, I let the lure bob easily, and in just a few minutes' time I'll hook all my little fishies again with a good hard yank. Another go at the parts of speech will bring them back to the fold of reason.

To keep the prisoners in line, others use billy clubs, I use syntax: subordinate, relative, and concessive clauses.

What good does it do to study, here, in prison? Does it do any good, help anyone? I couldn't say. I have no assurances to offer in that connection. I've wondered for years, and with some personal torment, and then I've stopped asking myself, the hell with it, I just settle for life as it is, and I enjoy those glints of intelligence and pleasure that I can see passing over my students' faces as we read, as we argue, the sizzle of a concept that is transmitted like an electric bolt, from one head to another. The buzz of minds at work. I can't be certain that I'm really taking them anywhere with Petrarch and modal adverbs, and most of all, that I'm steering them away from the reason they ended up in here in the first place.

Reintegrate, reeducate, resocialize . . . all these "re-somethings" guarantee nothing, I'd have sufficient evidence to say that this method works and enough to say that it's a failure. There's a high rate of recidivism in crime. Among my former students there are those who now have gainful employment, who, in short, "rebuilt their lives"—and others who went merrily off into a hail of bullets just ten days after being released from incarceration. And the strange thing is that often the ones who fell right back into it, into the mayhem of drugs or armed robberies, were the first in the class . . . you would have "bet your life" on them . . .

Before I leave, and before they go back to their cells, to make their lunches, as they stream out of the classroom they insist on shaking hands with me, and I shake hands with them even though it seems a little absurd, given that we've been seeing one another regularly since September, and tomorrow I'll be back here, so why this theatrical farewell, this ceremonial salutation? Perhaps it's because, in prison, you never know, maybe they'll transfer you tomorrow, or they'll send you to trial, they'll release you, or maybe . . . A certain caution suggests never taking any future event for granted. Perhaps that comradely salutation is because we've just spent a few hours together that were less inhuman than usual.

Wilmo thinks he needs to give back the photocopies of the poems. "No, keep them, just remember to bring them tomorrow." Without textbooks, the school in here relies on the wheezing, limping photocopying machine downstairs: if it breaks or runs out of supplies, forget about classes. Two years ago, in September, before school began, I had made up my mind to buy a couple of reams of paper with an accompanying supply of toner, beating my colleagues to the draw: and I had selected, cut out, assembled into a collage, and photocopied a hundred or so poems and other famous pieces, such as Hamlet's monologues or the face-off with Polyphemus, or Palazzeschi's nursery rhymes, in short, a little anthology, created with one student in mind in particular who passionately loved reading: Scarano.

Last year, every time I entered the classroom, this elderly Neapolitan, Scarano, with his long white locks, nicknamed "Archilochus" since the day we read the famous poem by that Greek poet describing how he abandoned his shield and took to his heels during the battle, would ask me, in a faint, ironic, and slightly wheedling voice: "Can we read some really nice poem today, what do you say, eh?" Scarano never wanted to study history, or grammar, or do abstruse and tiresome exercises, all he ever wanted was to enjoy "some really nice poem," the way you might listen to a serenade or a canzone. He'd enjoyed Ariosto's knights, and the death of Clorinda . . .

On the first day of school I show up with my stacks of photocopies to hand out, and then I call roll, so, let's see who's still here from last year and what new students we have . . . I run down the list, Scarano is on it but I don't see him in class, so I ask: "What about Scarano?" How can it be that the poetry connoisseur isn't here today?

"Where's Scarano?"

I suppose to myself he must be talking to his lawyer or in the visitor's room, seeing family.

"Mmm . . . *professo'* . . . didn't you hear about Scarano?"

"Hear what?"

"He *died* a week ago."

For months he had been hearing a whistling in his ears, and had had pains in his chest, he kept asking to be seen by a specialist, but they wouldn't arrange for it. They weren't taking him seriously. I remember, in fact, that in class he'd hold his hand to his temple, trying to stifle that incessant shrill noise. He was pale, tired. And then, one night, he up and died. His heart gave out. In the outside world, it's called "medical error" or "malpractice," while in prison it's part of the punitive routine, which in spite of all the fine words about the objectives of reeducation still remains the deep-seated underlying reason for the very existence of prison: a punishment that is first and foremost corporeal in nature. Prison, and everything that's in it—in terms of health, work, food, human interactions—must necessarily be much worse than can be found in the outside world, where people live in freedom: otherwise what deterrent effect would it have against crime? And there's no need to go all the way to the verge of tragedy: the most unremarkable toothache can turn into a nightmare if they won't give you the pill you need. Will they give it to you? Won't they? Well, it all depends, if you're in luck or you're clever or you count for something. The only therapy they'd never dream of skimping on involves psychopharmaceuticals. The plastic *bicchierini*, or cups, the "*goccine*," or drops (who knows why in the brutal world of Italian prisons there is such rampant overuse of these coy little diminutives: the "*spesino*" or gofer, the "*domandina*" or application form . . . as if the convicts were being infantilized into some sort of oversized nursery school). And so the prisoners, sedated with horse-pill doses of sedatives, lie helpless on their cots, bothering no one, mumbling, furry-tongued, especially the junkies who would otherwise spend their night howling at invisible moons . . .

You try teaching a class to a guy like that, stuffed to the gills with Lexotan.

But today, I don't want to think about Scarano, no.

If you want to work here in prison, you have to let everything flow over and past you, let it flare and burn the instant after it happens. Shake off mistreatments and pain. The convicts learn it right away, and I've learned it from them. From Alfredo Muntula, for example, who just a few days ago kept his cool while the police inspector who had come to serve him with a judicial injunction, which Muntula refused to accept, shouted into his face that he could take that document and "stick it up his a—" "I'll write to my lawyer," Muntula had replied, remaining calm, whereupon the inspector blurted: "Well, then, write to your lawyer and tell him that he can take the penal code and stick it up his . . ." etc.

If you react to these provocations, they'll file a report on you, and then you can say farewell to various benefits automatically assigned by law: your sentence, virtually shortened for good behavior, suddenly stretches out again as if viewed through the wrong end of a spyglass. Your release recedes into the future. Is it worth it? Nooo. That's why you learn to put up with things.

I've gone back down to the ground-floor roundhouse, and I stand, swaying, waiting in front of the locked gate. I'm waiting for an officer to come and open it for me. You can wait a long time, there, in front of the bars lined with a sheet of plexiglass. Theoretically, if no one shows up, or if the officer is on the phone, or maybe even has his back turned, pretending he hasn't seen you, you could use an iron ring hanging from the bars and bang against it, once, twice, three times, until someone comes to open the gate for you, but I personally hate that sound. I *hate* it. It always depends on who happens to be in the roundhouse, the likable officer or the jerk, the one who will never go out of his way to notice you're there. My teacher's badge only partly protects me from their rudeness. The main thing is to remain calm, take deep breaths. I usually hum to myself to take my mind off it, and to ready myself for the fresh air of the outdoors.

Today, luckily, there's a kind, solicitous officer, the nicest one, short, quick, smiling, and he has the key in his hand immediately.

After this, just five more gates, and then I'll be a free man.

14

T**HAT'S ALL, FOLKS.**

The effect of the publication of this article, a mix of the sentimental and the giddily foolish, with a dollop of candor of which I'm now rather ashamed (if you really wanted to lay it on, with the hyperrealism of the grimmest events of life behind bars . . .), was the beginning of my troubles. I managed to turn everyone against me. The day after its publication, I walked through a black cloud of hostility. I received a threatening letter from the warden. Too bad I didn't keep it, it might have come in handy, who knows . . . but instead I decided, after reading Marcus Aurelius's *Meditations* and being swayed by its point of view, to discard unpleasant things. Immediately.

Are there thorns on the path home? Then step around them! A bitter cucumber? Spit it out immediately.

That's what the wise emperor suggests.

But that wasn't enough: at the MS they'd started to make my life bitter (and I couldn't just spit it out . . .) in the daily routine, which isn't that hard to navigate, all you need to do is comply with the regulations, which slows down all procedures: painstaking searches on my way in and out, locked gates with guards who pretended not to see me or who would tell me, "Just wait there," for no good reason, for a good fifteen minutes. Endless rigmarole before I could bring an ordinary rubber eraser to class so I could correct papers, turned over and over in querulous hands as if trying to theorize some potential criminal use. Certainly, a boycott is the greatest pressure that can be brought to bear on someone like me who, when all is said and done, is a free man and will be going home in just a few hours. But the saddest thing is that the very same officer I've described as solicitous had suddenly turned hostile: he was probably embarrassed to have been cast in a positive light in my article, his coworkers must have thrown it in his face: "Nice job! So you treated that piece of shit with kid gloves?" I had written that he was nice to me, and he'd taken it the wrong way. *Me*, nice?! Forcing himself, he'd transformed his innate personality and done what he could to come off as a tough guy.

The splash of cold water of my piece of journalism had little if any effects on the students, except for the comic effect caused by the name I'd used to rebaptize the young Sicilian, here referred to as Wilmo: I'd come up with it when I remembered Fred Flintstone's wife and the phrase he shouted so loudly that it echoed through the cave: "Wilma! Get my club!!"

In other words, with my edifying little account, I didn't even win for myself among the inmates the title of their paladin and defender, a title that I don't even aspire to, nor did I gain the stripes of avenger of the rights trampled underfoot: from that article I gained nothing but headaches, which reinforced my belief in the old adage that it's better not to write about such things. But we did at least have some laughs about Wilmo, and from then on that became his nickname.

In the end, I received the message: "Get out." Got you, loud and clear. I applied the sage precepts of the philosopher-emperor. So I bided my time and bit my tongue and then, in September, I applied to go back to teaching the rank-and-file prisoners, transferring out of maximum security.

TO CONCLUDE THE EPISODE: I later met the blond girl Jervi slapped around outside the school, first and last name and proper introductions, a dozen years ago, more or less, around 2001. Rosetta Mauri, known to her friends as Rosi. She was no longer pretty, almost all her good looks wasted away, terribly skinny, wrinkles around her mouth, etc., but her eyes were bright and lively and she still wore her hair long, blond, too light colored to be natural, as it once had been. How did I manage to recognize her? Well, you might not believe it, but she was dressed *exactly* the same way she had been that day, when she had sat sobbing astride her Ducati, and then had roared off down Via Nomentana, leaving the kid who had tried to comfort her in her dust: she wore a stiff white Scottish cable-knit sweater, flared purple pants, and ankle boots. Thirty years in which everything had changed, and yet nothing had changed: it might still be the same sweater, I thought to myself . . . it had withstood all the laundry cycles, which was more than could be said of her complexion, sadly. As ill-tempered as she had been that day in the distant past, that's how welcoming and compliant Rosi was when I met her again. I knew her by reputation, in the meantime she had become a talented television producer, working in a team with her second husband, and she knew me by name as well, but neither of us had ever put face to name, never shaken hands, never exchanged phone numbers, much less had we ever (I immediately formulated the thought in my mind, accustomed to leaping to conclusions, recklessly, as if the words and corresponding images were hurtling out of a slingshot, in the presence of an attractive woman) brushed lips, sad to say, nor had our bodies ever been joined. I refrained from saying that I had recognized in her the girl on the motorcycle who had had her face slapped by Jervi (R.I.P.), something I was only certain of, one hundred percent, when she burst out laughing at some stupid joke I had made—thus proving, since Rosi was by no means a stupid woman, that she was doing it to butter me up—and she *hid her face in her hands.* That's right, just before she started laughing she put her hands up to hide her face. As if it were instinctive to conceal it when she laughed or while she cried or when she was faking it: feelings, ideas, cheerfulness or sadness, unconfessable thoughts, to be revealed only behind a scrim of fingers. Her fingers were skinny and long and she plunged their tips into her bleached hair. I very much liked this gesture of what might be either shyness or cunning, but in any case it was seductive. At that point I could no longer resist and I asked her: "So, do you still have the Ducati?"

I TOOK ROSI MAURI TO BED THREE TIMES. The first time, a month after we'd met, was in Milan, where I happened to be for meetings with my publisher, while she was working on a television show. It was no particular challenge to arrange to meet, and clear to both of us what the purpose of that meeting was to be. I was a guest in the studio of an artist I knew indirectly, a messy place crisscrossed with cables, multiple electric outlets, clamp lights, paintings turned around to face the wall, metal shelves, stacks of CDs and DVDs, and a powerful-looking double-screen video-editing device; and in the middle of the big room, a bed with a very hard mattress and a double headboard, which I had covered with clean but unironed linen sheets. Fifteen minutes before she arrived, having finished all her meetings, around six in the evening, it started to snow, at first lightly and intermittently and then in increasing gusts, so hard and violent that you could hear the loud thumps of the flakes hitting the panes of the old, ramshackle windows, slapping resoundingly. Luckily, the heaters in the studio were purring along famously, so that the minute Rosi entered the studio, bundled up and covered with a dusting of fresh snow, on her scarf, her chest, her woolen cap, she felt the immediate, stunning blast of heat, and her face went from dull, leaden, chilled, bewildered, all at once to tomato red, bright as a rose burning in the winter fire. One yard into the studio, that is, just far enough to be able to shut the door behind her, and I had wrapped my arms around her, freeing her at least of the cap and scarf, letting her hair, blonder than the last time, fall around her shoulders and onto my chest, tips drenched with snow, and then indifferent to the fact that frozen crusts of snow were raining onto me, I undid the bottom two buttons of her long woolen overcoat, spread open the two sides and thrust in a hand, lifted her skirt and discovered that, underneath, she was wearing those stockings we call Parisians, or over-the-knee socks, with elastic at mid-thigh, which have the effect of keeping deliciously cool the flesh that is left uncovered, the way a bottle of champagne might be if left in an ice bucket. Instinctively, Rosi bent and lifted one leg and laid it against me, with her knee above my hip, baring the stocking and the portion of thigh, nude to the crotch, which was white, no, really, colorless, as if there could be something in nature that was paler than snow or ice, and then she hopped along backward toward the wall in the front entrance, and leaned back against it, clutching me even tighter and searching confusedly for my mouth with hers.

THE NEXT DAY, in a chilly-looking Japanese restaurant, where I ate little or nothing, or at least nothing that I considered edible, paying no serious attention to those little rounds of cold, raw fish, I met with my publisher, jollier and more cynical than ever, who made use of the expression "*Non c'è trippa per gatti,*" literally, "there's no tripe even for cats," reasonably appropriate to the type of restaurant, to make it clear to me in no uncertain terms that he wasn't dreaming even for a second that he'd be able to sell a single copy above initial sales projections of my wonderful new book, no more than the tiny print run, in other words, nor did he intend to lift a finger to push it, to bring up sales, because in the meantime ("You hadn't heard? That's on you. You live out of touch with the real world, *caro* . . .") another book had come out, with almost the same plotline, far worse written but with much greater commercial potential than mine, a book that—the week after its author appeared on TV—had sold no fewer than ten thousand copies a day and promised to go on selling at that clip, actually, even better than that, much better, better and better. But I was still half dazed from my encounter with Rosi, steeped in a blurred sensuality, my mind too dulled to cultivate any specific wishes or claim my rights, and I couldn't bring myself to take it personally, or at least if I did I didn't show it—though deep down inside I was truly miffed, because of my dulled senses mixed with my usual foolish pride, I didn't let so much as a hint of dissatisfaction seep through, indeed, I acted superior and detached—and that was wrong, terribly wrong, because the minute the publisher realized that I was will-ing to stop short when presented with a fait accompli, when he saw that I wasn't protesting, wasn't demanding, that I didn't seem determined to fight for something, something more, something better, he seized the op-portunity and changed the subject, and *arrivederci Roma*, it was straight to anecdotes, which took up the rest of the forty-five minutes allotted to my audience with him.

The "sporting" attitude that I've always adopted in these situations, playing the gentleman *"qui se pique de rien,"* is unsuccessful. All things (in-cluding money, success, and love) come to those who really want them and fight to get them, with all means necessary, get it?

THE ELECTRIC HEATERS had raised the temperature in the studio to the threshold of the intolerable, while outside, in the darkness, a blizzard was battening down all of Milan under a blanket of snow. I've never gotten used to it, nor will I. In Rome, the apartments are always left on the verge of be-ing chilly, and that's how I prefer it: in the tropically heated apartments of Milan, I'd prefer to throw open the windows and let the snow come in, but with that snow, at least, a breath of cool air . . .

Thanks to the overheating, though, Rosi was lying naked on top of the sheets, on her tummy, dangling one leg bent in the air, and her face buried in the pillow, swamped by the highlights of her hair. Which I liked. Then she rolled onto her back, displaying her front to me, her breasts and her belly relaxed by her pregnancies. I could now look at her as I pleased and finally get to know her. I thirstily admired at some length the devastation that time had worked on her body and face, in spite of which she remained an attractive woman, actually, a very attractive woman, as if that lost beauty were especially alluring precisely because it was no longer there, and was present only as a preliminary sketch or a ruin in the aftermath, forcing the observer to make an intense, inspired, melancholy effort of the imagina-tion that was also exciting, sharpening one's sensual faculties in the recon-struction of what must once have existed: the magnificent beauty that Rosi must have been as a girl. Think of her breasts, at age twenty . . . wonderful, superb . . . think of those long legs, now broken down at the knees, and what they must have looked like at twenty . . . think of her beautiful mouth, whose upper lip, thinned out now and riven with tiny vertical clefts, think of what that mouth must have been like when those lips were full and prominent, in fact, don't think of it, remember, O mind of mine, remember clearly, O eyes, because you've seen those lips yourself, swollen and puffy after Jervi's fist had smashed into them.

"IT WASN'T MY MOTORCYCLE, it belonged to my brother . . . I'd taken it without asking . . . I wanted to impress that asshole . . . (curious, isn't it? that Rosi, too, just like the Prince, should have used that word to describe Jervi, my former classmate, subsequently disgraced) . . . and I didn't have the registration, much less a driver's license, I've never gotten one . . . I still don't have one now . . . later on the police stopped me while I was racing around Rome like a lunatic, I wanted to go jump off the bridge over Corso Francia . . . can you imagine a Roman policeman saying anything to a sixteen-year-old girl, blond, and in hysteria . . . ? Before you knew it, he might just as well have gotten down on his knees and proposed to me. When you're pretty and you're in love, you can make everyone fall in love with you, with just a snap of the fingers, everyone . . . except for the guy you really love. And I was head over heels in love with that friend of yours . . . No, there's no need to tell me that he wasn't your friend, I already know that, Stefano didn't have friends, male, much less female . . . he had women, women who were older than him. He had gone to bed with the mother of one of your classmates, he told me so to get me jealous, as if there was any need for that . . . what an asshole . . . and I was so in love with that asshole, you wouldn't believe how much . . . ! Two or three years must have gone by and I still loved him, I was out my mind with love for him, but he didn't even have my phone number anymore, it was as if I was dead to him . . . and I would wait for him outside his building, I'd look up to see if the light was on in his bedroom, and if it was on but turned down low, I'd imagine that there was a girl up there with him, that he'd put her colorful bra over the lamp on the night table, just think what an idiot . . . I felt sick at the thought . . . and then if there was no light on at all, I'd wring my hands in anguish, trying to imagine where he could be . . .

". . . so one time I followed him, on the Ducati bike, which had a broken headlight at that point, in order to see who he was going to visit, and I staked out the building where he had parked, and waited for him . . . and then I got the idea of wrecking his car, and taking my revenge in that way, even though the car didn't belong to him, it was his father's, an armor-plated Mercedes-Benz, but what difference does that make, I told myself, now I'll go and break all the side mirrors, I'll key the hood . . . my signature, R-O-S-I . . . and just for a change, I was crying.

"Time passed, and I still hadn't made up my mind to take my revenge, when I saw a car pull up, and a young woman got out, tall, made up, and dressed as if she was going to a party. She had a bucket in one hand, and she strode briskly toward that asshole's Mercedes . . . I couldn't believe my own eyes . . . it was a can of paint that she was carrying, and she started pouring it over the roof of the car, over the windshield and windows, onto the hood, but not angrily, just methodically, taking care not to get any on her dress and shoes, until she had covered almost the whole car. The cream-colored Mercedes was now black. I sat there open-mouthed watching that woman take her vengeance, a vengeance that she had planned much better and more dispassionately than I had—what's more, she had implemented her plan against Stefano before I had a chance to lift a finger. She threw away the empty paint can, giving it a kick so that it rolled all the way to the sidewalk, and that was her last angry gesture. Then she climbed back into her compact car, started it up, and tore out of there.

"So that meant he didn't have just one woman, aside from me, he had at least two or three, or who knows how many more. But I was incapable of doing anything about it, I just went on loving him and suffering over him. I was seized with a wave of panic, instead of snickering at his misfortune behind his back, when I thought about what would happen with his father, on account of the car. I was so worried that I was tempted to call his parents' house and ask for his father and say that none of it was Stefano's fault, just take the blame for the car myself, tell him that it was me who had ruined it with the black paint . . . and I did, I called Stefano's parents that very same night, but there was no one home. They were all out on the street looking at the charred car, with the fire department and the police. In fact, Stefano had somehow managed to drive the paint-covered car all the way to his home, and then he had set it on fire with a tank of gasoline he'd found in the garage. The police theorized that it was a threat or a warning or an act of retaliation against his father, who for a while went everywhere with a police escort.

"I've never been in love with any other man. Not even with my first husband, or with the second, that's for sure. And not even with my children, though I do love them deeply . . . The feelings I had for Stefano outweigh any thing and any person, I mean to say, the feelings I might have for any person. Because they include the wicked things, the crazy ones. The things you dream when you have a fever. With him, I could easily have committed a murder, if he'd asked me to, if I'd had even the vaguest notion that it might please him, and bring him back to me . . .

"I don't think I've ever been quite so stupid as I was when I loved him. For a certain period, I even stopped washing. I lost twenty pounds. I cut my hair almost down to the scalp, thinking that I'd appeal to him again, like that, again, again . . .

"I didn't give a damn about how he had left me all alone to face the most difficult moment, how cold and arrogant he had been. He was just so beautiful, so beautiful and wicked . . . Stefano Jervi, your classmate.

"My husband, on the other hand, is a good man . . . he is close to me, he understands me. I don't need to think about him. I can go days on end without thinking about him, because in any case he's *there*. You, too, were kind and thoughtful that time he hit me in front of your school—at least, from what you tell me, because I don't remember a thing about you, that day. Were you really there? But that smack he gave me, that stayed with me.

"I couldn't see anyone but him, I didn't understand . . .

"Then when I found out that he was dead, I had already been married and divorced, and I had a young daughter . . . I can't say that I was still obsessed with him, that wouldn't be true, I hadn't thought about him for a while, it had been ten years, I'd started another life, and after that, yet another life, my little girl, my job . . . but when I heard about it, I was seized with a violent pang of pain, as if someone had driven a sword through my body . . ."

IT WAS ONLY AT THAT MOMENT that I realized Rosi was crying, but not from the raucous sound of her voice, as she went on telling her story at the same monotonous pace, in the same remote tone of voice, but rather from the fact that the hair behind which she was hiding her face was wet again, like when she first came in out of the snowstorm. I didn't interrupt her, nor did I try to dry her tears, I just started stroking her, from her shoulders down to the small of her back, dotted with stretch marks above and below her skinny butt cheeks. I noticed two small dark bruises right above her jutting sharp pelvic bones, which practically broke the surface, and there I concentrated my caresses for the longest time.

". . . IT WAS AN INTOLERABLE, senseless grief. Stefano had vanished from my life, ten years it had been by that point, what did it matter to me that he was dead, and that he had died in that way, after all? What better occasion could there be to think that it served him right, it really served him right, such an absurd death! And just think: He was someone who had never given a damn about politics anyway . . . The most selfish egotist of all time . . . dying as a revolutionary combatant—come on, now! I couldn't accept that, it was unthinkable, it made me want to laugh. All the same, that sword twisted ever deeper into me, into the pit of my stomach, taking my breath away, I was breathing as if my ribs had been bent inward . . . and all of a sudden I decided, with great clarity of mind, that I, too, wanted to die, like him, in just as senseless a manner, by blowing myself sky high . . . the apartment . . . my little girl, the high chair, the juice boxes, the sofas, the clothing and the shoes in the clothes closets . . . just blow it all up.

"I fastened all the windows, I went into the kitchen to turn on the gas on the stove, I took my daughter in my arms and, with a lighter in reach, I sat down at the kitchen table, waiting for the right moment . . . the point of saturation. But the pain wasn't diminishing, in fact, it became intolerable, piercing, I thought I'd die of it, not from the gas. In the meantime, my little girl started yawning and rolling her eyes. I don't know what was wrong with me, why I was doing it. I'm a calm woman, I'm self-reliant, I know how to make decisions. I know how to say yes and no. I told you yes, I told some other guy no, and I know the reason. At work they actually consider me a snake, a cold-blooded reptile, heartless, maybe you've heard people say it around town, and all just because I'm a *thinker*, because I know how to *think*. You don't know me, and I don't know you, all things considered. But if we're here, it means that we know each other and we know what we're doing, we know that it's wrong, but we're doing it anyway. That day, though, I was beside myself, something else was making decisions for me . . .

"When I looked at my little girl again, she had shut her eyes. She was asleep. Maybe because of the gas, which I could barely smell. It looked to me as if she was luminous . . . her flesh looked phosphorescent. I got out the lighter, ready to flick it. Outside the window, the stars were shining in the clear night sky. Steady, motionless. I looked down at my daughter once more, and she had changed again: a little corpse, motionless, swaddled in winding cloths, a statuette, you know, like those Madonnas, those tiny little Madonnas that glow in the dark . . . and suddenly everything was clear to me again, simple, the way it was supposed to be, I set the lighter down on the table, I stood up, I threw the window open, I twisted the knobs on the stove to 'off,' and with my daughter in my arms I went to throw open all the windows in my apartment, and five minutes later the gas had all flown out into the night sky, and my daughter was breathing normally. I went to lay her down in her little bed, it was all over now, the piercing pain in my belly had vanished, replaced by a bubble of nothingness, and the thought of Stefano as someone with whom love had been made, long long ago, sure, a good-looking young man, a special boy, my first sweetheart . . . but nothing more . . .

"I got off easy, and since then I've lived my own life.

"So that now, I laugh at certain memories with him. I laugh, and that's all.

"I remember when he'd talk about your school and about the priests. He hated them. He hated all of you, his classmates, truth be told, or at least that's what he told me. He wanted to run away from your school and from the priests. And from his family. But from the school, most of all. I don't remember him ever saying anything about you, but in general he considered you all a herd of idiots. Except for one, a genius, he said that there was a genius in your class, an absolute genius . . . Do you know who he was talking about? Was that you? No? But there's nothing you can do about it, Stefano was a wicked guy. Evil. One time he told me about how he injected poison into a plant . . . that you had a queer teacher who was in love with that plant, and he killed it, as a joke, by injecting it with poison . . . Was that true?"

"Yes. It really happened. But it wasn't him who did it . . ." I said, to defend his memory. I don't know why I said it. I had been reminded somehow of his large, dark-rimmed eyes . . . his gleaming white teeth. I stopped caressing Rosetta's back and she whipped around to look at me.

"Ah, then . . . the usual liar!" and she laughed. "Let me tell you about something, which was just my last piece of lunacy. But a simple one, risk-free. So risk-free that it wasn't even worth the trouble of trying it. Did you know Stefano's sister, Romina? Do you remember her? If you met her, you surely liked her. She was the prettiest girl in Rome, in my opinion, or at least, the prettiest in her quadrant . . ."

"Her quadrant?"

At this point, in much the same way certain guidebooks do, splitting cities up into zones to make it easier to find monuments or restaurants, Rosetta Mauri ventured into a rather curious theory she had about Rome and the young women who were beautiful and famous, famous for being beautiful, the beautiful young Roman women of thirty years ago, the beauties of the schools, that is, of the high schools, the dance clubs, of the families of good-looking people, the most sought-after and desirable young women, about whom Rosetta knew everything, unlike me. According to her, there were actually different physical types, almost as if they were distinct species or breeds, depending on the quadrant they belonged to. The hair, the eyes, the mouth, etc. A persuasive theory, corroborated by numerous examples, which I'm not going to list here at any length because it would involve mentioning too many people, by their first and last names. I saw something of the sort on TV once, on a program (cruel, intelligent, and in fact, that program was taken off the air almost immediately) in which they went back, many years later, to dig up various beauty queens from school years, or a certain vacation spot, or a volleyball team.

In my city, in any case, and for fifteen years or so starting from the period when this story unfolds, Romina Jervi had illuminated with her beauty the entire northern quadrant, with a light so dazzling that, according to Rosi, she had dimmed the glow of all the others, "and I was among the girls that she made disappear, and I wasn't exactly chopped liver, now, was I?"

I shook my head. Rosi was a perfect personification of the type of off-hand appreciation that I must have read about in a book translated from the English: "I wouldn't kick her out of bed," a sentiment I was confirming to the letter at that very moment.

"Maybe it was to take revenge on Stefano, or else because I still loved him and I wanted something of his, something that belonged to him or resembled him. That resembled him *closely*. I'd had a lot to drink . . ."

You lovely thing, what are you talking about? I wondered to myself. Rosetta was one of those people who enjoy telling stories by tossing out broken, mysterious phrases to arouse their listener's curiosity, so that the listener in question is therefore obliged to ask questions and act eager to know more, so that he practically has to beg the person who started the story in the first place to go on. It's an old trick, I knew how it worked, so I didn't ask a thing. After a lengthy silence, as if astonished that I wasn't demanding further clarifications, she continued: "Well, there she was, in the same club . . ." In the meantime, she'd cupped her breasts in both hands, as if she no longer wanted me to see them. It was hellishly hot in that studio.

"You understand who I'm talking about, right? Romina Jervi, Stefano's sister . . ."

Instead of nodding, I shut my eyes. That's the best way to listen.

"I'd always wondered if she liked men. If she really liked them, I mean. Appearances or habits aside, it's hard to tell, and even harder with Romina. What does it really tell you that someone has a boyfriend or a husband? So I decided to put her to the test. And then I thought to myself that kissing her would be like kissing her brother. She had the same mouth, in fact, her mouth really was Stefano's mouth. As if they switched: one day he had it, the next day she did. After all, what's the difference? A pretty mouth is a pretty mouth. Can two people have a single mouth? Yes: if they're brother and sister. For that matter, your classmate's mouth was the part I liked best about him. Okay, go ahead and think that I'm crazy . . . that's what you think, isn't it? And you also think that I'm not a very good girl, that I basically threw myself at you . . . I know that, but I don't care . . ."

I took her hands off her breasts, and each one fell to the side. With one finger, I traced the stretch lines that radiated toward the armpit.

"You like them anyway?"

I nodded.

"Well, anyway, Romina, yes, Romina, the beautiful Romina . . . was rather stupid. For that matter, so was Stefano. Courageous, impetuous, and dazzlingly handsome . . . but stupid. Back then, Romina was dating a guy who was filthy rich and had taken her to a deserted little island, between Corsica and Sardinia, for two months, with nothing and no one, except for his jeep and his villa, and he'd leave her there, he'd fly away in his helicopter . . . maybe for a week, for business, and then he'd come back . . . he'd leave and come back, you get it? Even though she was already pretty dark, she'd lie out in the sun all day until she turned practically as dark as an African; for that matter, what else was she supposed to do on that fucking deserted island? Swim naked and lie in the sun. When I saw her in the club, she had just finished spending the summer like that. The asshole was drinking champagne with some noisy friends of his, and Romina was all decked out in jewelry, glowing in the shadows, and she was drinking too, but just taking small sips, as if she didn't like it. Without even bothering to say hello, I just sank into the tiny space between her and the arm of the sofa she was sitting on. I took her glass out of her hand and drained it to the last drop. "That's the way you do it," I told her, and she was so surprised that she gave me a beautiful smile, filled with astonishment. Ah, that mouth, those teeth . . . I just had to kiss her, and right away. I pulled her head close to mine and I kissed her. Romina opened her eyes wide, dark-rimmed like Stefano's, but she didn't take her lips off mine. I don't know what got into me, or really, I know exactly what it was. The interesting thing is the way that Romina responded to my kiss. Totally. With passion. As if she were kissing her man, who was sitting on the sofa next to ours, and as if I were kissing the man who had once been mine, namely Stefano. Then the asshole noticed what we were doing. "Hey, hey! What's going on here?" he cried, and abandoning his noisy friends, he came over and squatted down in front of us, with the glass of champagne still in his hand, and the same grin on his face he had had before. He didn't seem scandalized or jealous, quite the contrary. "Did I miss something?" he asked, looking at me in a provocative fashion. Romina gave him a slap in the face, which he pretended to take as a joke, even if it made him lose his balance from that filthy squatting position he had assumed and his champagne glass spilled onto the floor. In the meantime, Romina turned back to start kissing me again . . .

"What are you doing? Aren't you interested in what I'm telling you?"

"Certainly I'm interested, you can't imagine how much," I told her, "but right now, if you don't mind, I'd like to fuck you again."

"No . . . no, I don't mind."

I slid into her. She gasped. She held her breath. And with her voice in a falsetto she asked if it had excited me to hear about Romina, about the two of them together. Had she done it intentionally?

"Do you . . . do you want me to tell you more . . . ?"

"No. Shut up now." That wasn't why.

But she went on talking. And I went on fucking her.

AND IN THE MEANTIME, the snow kept coming down heavier and thicker, exactly as the TV weather reports and the daily newspapers had said it would, there was a blizzard over Milan, all of Lombardy, the railroad tracks were freezing over, the trolley cars came screeching to a halt, their regular runs at an end. When day dawned, the city was a crystal forest. I went to the appointment with my publisher on foot, sliding along the sidewalks, the only means of conveyance, all vehicles and buses were out of service.

I FUCKED ROSI FOR VARIOUS REASONS. The first and the most important one remains the absence of reasons: those are things that you just do, for the sake of it, and that's that. Then there's the fact that she was even more beautiful, even if 90 percent of her beauty had to be backdated to an age that had to be imagined, dreamed of, like when you're masturbating: it's a morbid aspect whose importance I couldn't measure, a strange blend of excitement and contempt, perversion and heartbreak. Then there was her prompt willingness, reciprocal to my own. And then there was the fact that something which, whatever way you choose to look at it, would still have only made sense to have happened ten or twenty, or even thirty years earlier, but which instead didn't happen, if fate decides that the possibility of it happening finally does present itself thirty years later, well then, this time it absolutely *has* to happen, you have to make it happen: in such a way that the loop of time closes in on itself, leaving no doors wide open or even cracked just slightly ajar. That door needs to be *sealed shut*, in other words. Rosetta Mauri and I had gone to bed together the number of times strictly necessary to open, consummate, and close the case. Last of all, there was perhaps a lesser, but still decisive, motive clamped in my twisted mind, namely, that she had been my classmate's woman, that's right, Stefano Jervi's girlfriend, and *he* had taken her virginity. I entered Rosi thirty years after my screen-idol-handsome classmate did: in the same pussy where he had first come, getting her pregnant, I too had come, even though there was no longer any danger of my doing the same. She had made that clear to me an instant before my orgasm, when I had asked her in a choked voice if I needed to pull out: she was lying on one side with a twist of her torso that, if she hadn't been so bony, I would have described as Michelangelesque, so that she could look me in the eyes while I loomed above her, penetrating her from behind, perhaps the finest position in which to make love with a woman because you have a view of both her face and her breasts and you're in contact with her ass, and you can touch and kiss *everything* because her body, so to speak, turns into a single unbroken surface, and in response to my frantic query, she, who had already come violently and was quite tired, matted with sweat, indifferent, had replied merely with an ironic, complicit smile, baring her teeth, as if to say, "Go ahead and come inside me, kid, don't worry . . ." whereupon, understanding that contemptuous smile as the signal of an experienced, knowledgeable woman, perhaps even happy to be out of the perverse circuit of childbearing, I thrust my sex deep into hers until I had filled her sex with semen. Just like a kid.

I LATER WONDERED just which classmate's mother Jervi claimed to have taken to bed. I gave no consideration to the idea that he might just have been boasting: it had happened as he said, perhaps just once, or else it had gone on for who knows how long. I modestly ruled out my own mother and, gradually, all the other mothers, except for two. Actually, though, I didn't really have to do all that much work to exclude the candidates, because it was clear to me from the start that it could only be either Ilaria Arbus or else Pik's mother, Coralla Martirolo.

THE GIRLS OF MY GENERATION and Rosi's who had abortions at age sixteen, right after their first experiences of intercourse, or in some cases right after the first and only one, are numerous. Abortion was illegal in Italy, but you could always find a way. Well-to-do families, simultaneously disapproving what was being done but every bit as much considering it necessary, would either convey their daughters out of the country or turn to doctors who were as costly as they were discreet. Poorer families just made do, one way or another.

(THE MONEYBAGS WHO USED to squire Romina Jervi around every summer, taking her to his island by helicopter, and whom Rosetta never called. anything other than "the asshole" in her account, well, I'm afraid I know who he is. Once again, blood ties, family ties, and school ties. He is, in fact, the big brother of another classmate of mine, the umpteenth SLM alum, the perfect prototype of the rich young idler upon whom the Catholic school conferred a gilded patina that, with the passing years, flaked off, what with all the incessant rubbing . . .

I've talked before about this thing with brothers at SLM.

Romina and Denis Barnetta, Gedeone's brother, were together for four long years; she was sixteen when they met, twenty when they broke up once and for all, just before their relationship could culminate with a trip to the altar, then children, then divorce. One of those classic cases of the alternative: "Either we get married or we break up." So they broke up.

Further consequences of that senseless kiss between Rosi and Romina at the discotheque, a precursor of the lesbian vogue of these past few years: Denis Barnetta reacted to Romina Jervi's slap with a hail of punches that made her cry and left their marks, then her brother Stefano found out about it and, like James Caan in *The Godfather* with his brother-in-law, tracked Barnetta down and, once he had found him, managed to drag him out of the car where he had locked himself in, in a frenzy of terror, and beat him silly, shouting threats, after which he threw a terrifyingly jealous scene with Romina, over both the asshole she was dating and the kiss with Rosi, a single occurrence but passionate and deep, a full French kiss, and with his own old girlfriend, for that matter; last of all, he pestered Rosi with a succession of phone calls asking to see her, with the obsessive idea of fucking her one last time, years after he had dumped her, but Rosi turned him down, told him to get that thought out of his head once and for all. And that is the last event in the life of Stefano Maria Jervi that I know anything about, until the night he lost that life in the explosion on the roof of the insane asylum.)

ONLY NOW, as I reread what I have written in the preceding pages and at the end of the previous chapter, do I realize that, for the lovely Rosetta as well, it must have been Jervi, young Jervi, Stefano Maria Jervi the way he was back in his golden years at SLM, the true point of contact with me, the phantom that led her to seek me out, that made her call me in a playful but explicit tone of voice, convinced her to come visit me, let herself be fucked, standing up, in the front hall of that chaotic studio of a Milanese artist. There was the stunningly handsome olive-skinned prince, seventeen years old, between us, while we rolled and tumbled on that uncomfortable bed, a bed that would leave our backs broken and aching the following day, and she must have thought intensely about his hands, his eyes, his always-erect sex, his arms, while we were making love and my arms were wrapped around her, embracing her in the same way that so many years before on a dusty soccer field those same arms of mine had embraced Stefano after he had scored a goal, with the exact same thrilled jubilation, a sort of enthusiasm mixed with joy of which I am capable nowadays only because in that enthusiasm youth is eternally revived, not *my* youth, but youth itself, the youth of the world, of the whole world when it is still young, like water gushing up out of the earth in the dark depths of a cavern, in powerful spurts.

Upon that bed, as hard as rock, lay the naked bodies of three attractive adolescents, strong, dazzling, unconscious, with three wonderful gradations of skin tone and hair color, from honey blond, mixed with ash blond, to corvine hair with bluish highlights, fixed in the light of a perfect age, sealed in upon itself like a translucent shell, vanished now, dead, dead, dead even to those of us who were, thank heaven, still alive—and not a graying man and a no-longer beautiful woman, both accustomed to adultery.

15

YOU MIGHT JUST AS EASILY SAY *that this story is of no interest to any-body as that this story is of crucial interest to all of us: both things are true. Take me, for instance: I don't give a damn about it anymore, and I never really did give a damn about it, not even at the time when it first un-folded. So why am I writing about it? one of you might justifiably object. Maybe because I know a fair bit about it, that's an answer that could be permitted me as sufficient, does it satisfy you? Because I know a fair bit about it and I think that I know even the things that I don't (and that's what writing is good for, after all . . .). Or else, perhaps, contrariwise, because I don't know about it, or else because I don't yet know enough? Or else because the time has come to write about it—now or never? If not now, when? Come on, forty years is long enough to tie it up in a bundle and forget about it. I write about it, in fact, not to commemorate it, but in order to ensure that it's sealed and forgotten once and for all. By me, at least. I'm enclosing it in this book as if I were burying it. Amen.*

16

I'M SORRY, Edoardo, am I bothering you?"

"No, I . . . wait, who is this?"

"Were you asleep?"

"Well, actually . . . what time is it?"

"A quarter to seven."

"A quarter to seven . . . !"

"Too early?"

"No, the alarm clock was just about to go off . . . but you, excuse me . . ."

"It's me, Rummo. Gioacchino Rummo."

"Oh, Rummo! Ciao . . . what . . . did something happen?"

"I thought you ought to know. At least you. About Cosmo."

"Cosmo . . ."

"Our Italian teacher at SLM."

"Right, of course, I understand, Cosmo."

"Because, you know, Cosmo . . ."

"He's dead. Is he *dead*?"

"I wanted to tell you that Cosmo . . ."

"No, please, don't tell me that he's dead. Rummo, please, don't start my day like that. Not like that. Otherwise, I'll hang up, I'm telling you, I'll just hang up immediately."

"No, he's not dead. But he's sick, he's very sick."

ONE THING ABOUT PSYCHOPHARMACEUTICALS is that they take the sting out of waking up. Reality struggles to break through. And I say that's a good thing. Especially the one I'm taking now, which has a long half-life, too long to work merely as a nighttime sleeping pill, which is why the doctor wanted to prescribe me another one, and also why I said, no, thanks, I'll just keep taking this one and processing it in my own sweet time. The fact that it overlapped, also covering a piece of the following day under the cloak of indifference, was something I didn't mind one bit.

But as soon as I was sufficiently lucid to understand what Rummo had told me and why, I was glad he had called me. Glad that he had chosen to call me, even if it wasn't to deliver a particularly good piece of news.

Rummo told me he had encountered our old teacher again, this time as a patient, because he was treating him for a serious case of depression. Reduced to a state of something approaching poverty, Cosmo had withdrawn into isolation from everyone. When Rummo had gone to pay a house call on him, he had been stunned at the wreckage, the desuetude.

"He sold off his legendary record collection . . ."

Rummo assured me that he had seen plenty of similar cases. A couple of times a week he volunteers, providing medical and psychological care to the poor, the forgotten and abandoned elderly, the homeless. Ah, good old Rummo! A stout, unadorned pillar of our Catholic school. Tirelessly faithful to his calling. Admirable. But Cosmo's case was different, and it had struck him, not merely because this was our beloved teacher.

"Do you remember? He seemed old to us already!"

"Wrinkly as an elephant!"

"With that cough!"

"Always scratching his neck . . ."

Cosmo had fallen so far that he was living in a miserable little hovel on the Roman beachfront. Two rooms, with books stacked high along the walls, floor to ceiling, a sofa with the springs sticking out, a single mattress on a swaybacked iron bedstead, no TV, no radio. A velvet armchair of some indescribable, nondescript color. Empty wine bottles lined up under a low coffee table heaped with newspapers, in a space that could be described as a kitchen only because of the presence of food-based grime: rice stuck to the bottoms of pans, eggshells, that sort of thing. But aside from the filth surrounding him, and his black mood, according to Rummo our old teacher was still the same man we'd known at SLM. Devastated but lucid, the last man on earth, a figure straight out of Giacometti, his eyes gleaming in his haggard face. He had recognized his old student almost immediately. Not from the name, Dr. Rummo, mmm, Rummo, Rummo, yes, that rings a bell . . . but rather from Rummo's face, the face of a boy who'd grown old.

"But had he been treated?"

"Yes. With electroshock."

"I can't believe it."

"No, really."

"Who told you this?"

"My colleague, who saw him before me and then referred him to me."

"I didn't think they used electroshock anymore."

"No, believe me, there are still people who administer electroshock therapy. And those who are subjected to it."

"I know my grandfather got electroshock treatment lots of times. But that was many years ago, and I was just a kid."

"And did it work on your grandfather?"

"I don't think so. He just kept going, up and down, up and down. And one time, when he was pretty down, he threw himself over the railing and down the stairwell."

"Good God. I'm sorry to hear that."

"Pretty horrifying, yeah. I only learned about it years later, when they gave me his watch."

"Wait, what happened?"

"Well, it's a story that . . . I wrote a poem about it once."

"Would you let me read it?"

"You really want to read it?"

"Certainly. I'd really like that."

"I'll send it to you by e-mail . . ."

"Please do. Don't forget."

RUMMO HADN'T MANAGED to pull Cosmo out of his state of depression, only to keep him suspended in that dark state of lucidity, like the bubble of mercury in a thermometer, preventing him from dropping any lower, from plunging into the depths. Sometimes when he made his calls, our old teacher would receive him with a grimace of disinterest and refuse to say a word to him. Other times he'd flash a grin, thanking him for his devotion. "I don't deserve it," he'd say, then add: "Though no one deserves it, probably, so I don't think I'm depriving anyone with a greater right." In effect, my old SLM classmate had started visiting him more often than was strictly necessary, and someone at the charitable association who had sent him to see Cosmo pointed out to him that he couldn't devote his few, precious hours of volunteering to a single patient who, all things considered, wasn't even in such critical shape.

"So I took a few days off, to go see him."

"That was nice of you."

"I just wanted to spend time with him, be near him. I had the impression that, in spite of his brusque manners, his indifferent act, deep down he was glad that someone might look after him. Me in particular."

I didn't remember Rummo being especially fond of Cosmo, back in our school days. I was, though: all the same, once I left SLM, I forgot all about him. He exited my life, no different than Gas&Svampa and Brother Gildo and the disgraced Mr. Golgotha, or the ancient literature teacher, the ineffable De Laurentiis, with his little concerts of ancient Greek music played with a single finger. And what should I say about Impero Baj, the custodian, dubbed Ottetti after the quantity of pasta, roughly a pound, that he ate every day? Ottetti, whom we loved so well, whatever became of him?

A door that opens in one direction only.

And the same goes for many of my classmates from school. Vanished into the breeze. Incinerated. And yet I can safely say that those were my friends and that Cosmo was my first and most important teacher. What does this mean?

"He said that he didn't want any treatment, that it was a waste of time."

It's as if life had reduced the past to ruins, pushing them up and forward only to ride roughshod over them, crushing them beneath the pressure of the moving present, continuing forward. Onward, straight ahead.

I've always gone blindly *forward*.

"He had a perfectly respectable attitude, even if stubborn and wrongheaded: but then he proved, in the end, willing to yield, to let me do what I thought best, because obstinate attachment to a negative conviction would have been every bit as foolish as optimism. And believe me, Cosmo is still an intelligent man . . ."

"Wait, Rummo, are you telling me that you persuaded him to accept treatment?"

"To do the minimum indispensable to suffer less."

There, I recognize my old teacher in this attitude. And—in the way he respected it—my old classmate.

"After all, his intelligence will never be snuffed out. Even when all the rest will have rotted away."

Even if I abandoned Cosmo unceremoniously, even if I betrayed him by leaving for another school and then forgetting him, till today I've never done anything other than respect his intentions. For himself and for us, we who were his favorite students. I'm talking about Marco Lodoli and Arbus, of course, and the others he'd encountered during his years at SLM, all of them pierced by his method of teaching: a continual spray of stimuli, an incessant poking in the ribs. It was he who had set us off down the road that way: lunging, lurching forward, as if we were young calves being buffaloed out of a corral, and who need to be sent on their way speedily, and if they feel a little pain in their hindquarters, they're unlikely to turn around toward the source of that prodding jolt. I believe, in other words, that Cosmo meant to be abandoned, that he preferred it, in fact, that he had planned it. He was putting a great deal of distance between himself and us, in effect, already during our time at school, he was never agreeable or cordial or indulgent with us students the way teachers are who love only because they want to be loved in return. There was no special warmth in his lessons. He was the exact opposite of Golgotha, in other words, and of poor De Laurentiis, both of whom attempted desperately to "involve us." Abandonment was his objective as a teacher.

Perhaps that was why Rummo's assiduous but neutral presence didn't really bother him. With Rummo there was never a narrowing of the margin of safety that someone like, let's say, Marco Lodoli, or me—one of the disciples, in other words, that he, too, had done everything in his power to avoid assembling around him, one of the illegitimate children that he had in any case brought into the world—would have done their best to cross. Especially now that the maestro might be about to impart his last lessons.

"But a month ago we got a nasty surprise from the routine tests we ran on him. Cosmo isn't just depressed: he has a tumor."

"Oh, fuck, no."

"I'm almost tempted to say that the depression concealed the more critical illness. Or even that it staved it off, reined it in . . . slowing its development."

"What are you saying? Could that really be?"

"I'm just speculating, it's nothing but a hypothesis. Or maybe it's just a wisecrack. We have no idea how long he's had it. It's at an advanced stage, but it might progress slowly, given his age . . ."

17

LISTEN . . . would you come see him, with me?"

"I'm . . . oh, sorry, Rummo . . . I'd rather not. This isn't a good time."

"*Pas de problème*. If you like, though, I'll keep you posted on his progress . . ."

"Of course, no doubt about it, in fact, call me whenever you like. Let me know how he's doing. Or else I'll call you. It's just that . . ."

"There's no need, you don't need to say a thing."

ACTUALLY, it's never a good time when someone is sick. When someone is *so terribly* sick. It's not a good time to die and it's never a good time to spend time caring for someone who's dying. The good time may perhaps come when all is said and done, once the enormous, vain agitation comes to an end, and "the book full of anxieties, sorrow, and pain" will be shut in the darkness. Which means it will no longer be a good time.

In the last few years, I had witnessed the rapid decline and death of people very dear to me. And my act of coming too close to that inglorious mystery—out of an excess of boldness and false confidence, almost as if I wished to prove that I was courageous enough to look *someone* who was on their way out right in the face, and to see just *what* would take their place, on that face forever deprived of expression—instead of making me stronger, as I had naïvely fooled myself into believing, naïvely and at the same time arrogantly, like someone who might turn to his audience with a shrug and brazenly declare, "Pshaw! He won't even tickle me!" before taking on a giant in single combat, it had drained me completely. Proximity to the dying had taken a great deal of life out of me. The nerve had grown thin and now it twanged at the slightest excuse.

Better to leave my old teacher to the more appropriate care of his willing ex-student, I thought. Though, from what he told me, Rummo wasn't giving him any actual treatment. And it hadn't been Cosmo who had refused treatment, this time, but Rummo who'd understood how pointless it would have been. No shock therapy, then, much less mild or palliative therapy: only the application of a medical protocol to limit the most painful effects of the condition. A minimal, simple, humane attitude. Sage, just as Gioacchino Rummo had always seemed sage to me, in his unshakable faith. Caught in the maelstrom of the controversy, one might imagine that Catholics erect their bulwark in the die-hard, extreme defense of life as such, at all costs, always and inevitably. An ideological bulwark, more than a religious one. And it is certainly true that there are some vociferous paladins defending this position. But it would be every bit as Christian, indeed, even more so, I believe that it would be a hundred times more so, to accept without too much chatter the will of God. Let blessed death come, in other words, when it must come: seeing that sooner or later it's bound to come in any case. There probably isn't a religion on earth that places such faith and hope in dying; and that makes it impossible to understand the position of those who demand that we struggle to forestall death's arrival, as if allowing a Christian to die Christianly were an outrage. Equally impossible to understand that death (which in the sermons of condolence will be described by those same Christians as a simple transition toward the true life, and something approaching a cause for jubilation) should be pointed to as a shameful defeat and the triumph of malevolent forces. Truly, I cannot understand it, I can't bring myself to understand this. Luckily, though, Rummo belonged to the empirical school of those who know how far to venture and where to stop. Where to stop to catch your breath.

"We see each other every week," he had told me about those assistance protocols. "And I get the impression that our teacher smiles, almost without moving his lips, every time I let slip a verb conjugated in the future tense."

"So, anyway, how long does he still have to live?" I asked him.

Rummo lowered his voice on the phone.

"Well, to hear him talk about it, still too long."

WHEN COSMO TOOK A TURN FOR THE WORSE, I made up my mind to go see him. I turned onto Via Aurelia, my head stuffed with thoughts I wanted to avoid at any and all costs. The dismay I expected to experience at the sight of him, after forty years, and my likely repugnance at his current state, was something that I acrobatically replaced with a bucolic fantasy in which he, younger though still wrinkled and bowed, and I, a long-haired, overgrown boy, as if we were Socrates and Alcibiades at a symposium, discussed and debated in a leisurely fashion, while he stroked my hair and there issued from my mouth, in response to his comments, simple and truthful statements that, sadly, I immediately forgot. Nothing could be further from the reality that had held sway back during my school days and from the present-day situation. According to what Rummo had told me over the phone, I already knew we wouldn't exchange any more than a word or two, that by now he no longer spoke, not because of any physical impediment, but because anything that could be said would be superfluous. Any urgent need to communicate that he might once have had ceased within him some weeks ago: he would placidly gaze at the doctor or the nurse, he'd let them do what they would, he'd let them wash him, he listened to the few ritual phrases of encouragement to turn over or lie down: but he said nothing, if not the occasional interjection, "yeah," "okay," "yes-yes," "oh, yes," "no-no-no." Sometimes he seemed to sort of sing to himself. Whatever he might have to say, he had already said. And apparently he had also written.

Rummo had confessed to me that his first phone call, early one morning a month earlier, had been on account of that. As he was sorting through the little apartment and doing his best to tidy up a bit, under the gaze, now impassive, now mocking, of its tenant, Rummo had noticed a pile of notebooks with black covers, extremely ordinary, cheap pocket notebooks, extracted from the general chaos and held together by an appearance of order, as if whoever had crumpled their covers through much handling cared very much about them. When he opened the one on the top of the pile, he saw that it was filled to the middle pages with a regular but practically illegible handwriting, spangled with crossing out and overwriting.

Every page contained short blocks of writing separated by blank spaces.

Some jottings and parenthetical notes filled the margins above and below and sometimes along the side of the page, continuing vertically only to resume at a point in the block of text already written with a shaky but precise line. With the notebook in hand, Rummo had turned toward its author, who at that point was sitting in the faded velvet armchair, clutching at the armrests that must have been used in the past by some cat to sharpen its claws, and had displayed it to him, with a questioning look.

"Is this your writing," that gaze had asked, "did you do this?"

"Sure, yeah . . ." Cosmo had murmured, and on his face there appeared a smile, at once chagrined and sly, impudent, as he lifted one hand from the armrest and waved it in the air as if to say, "Leave it there, forget about it . . ." as if, instead of notes, Rummo had just stumbled upon a collection of lewd photos. A minor secret vice that he might have been ashamed of, in other words, if there had still existed even so much as a glimmer of decorum in his surroundings, and inside him: something that Cosmo clearly was ruling out, with that smile and that gesture. Rummo had counted twenty or so notebooks. And other times, never formulating an explicit question, and not daring to peruse them or even peek inside them, he had questioned Cosmo in a silent dialogue as to exactly what those notebooks were, and whether they contained anything significant or precious, receiving in reply evasive glances or else an X traced in midair that meant, without a shadow of doubt, "oh, nothing, just junk," and "throw it all away." If Rummo continued in his display of curiosity, the old man reacted by huffing in annoyance and growing agitated. All the same, even in those same glances and gestures of annoyance, Rummo felt sure he had glimpsed an implicit denial of that disinterest and scorn toward those notes on the part of their author.

It had seemed to him, in other words, that Cosmo wanted to put his instincts to the test by simulating a total apparent detachment from something that, in fact, deep down, he considered very important.

"I DON'T WANT TO KNOW ANYTHING more about it. I'd be ashamed to poke my nose into it. But if Cosmo dies without having left any specific instructions to destroy those writings, it's going to be your responsibility to take those notebooks. Then you can decide what to do with them, even if that means throwing them away without reading them."

As usual, I hesitated, and Rummo summed up brusquely.

"I believe that you, you in particular, *owe him that.*"

SO I FOUND MYSELF DRIVING along a coast road from which I could glimpse the sea only in snippets here and here, a good hundred yards away, between one apartment building erected in defiance of the zoning code and the next, diseased palm trees, auto mechanic shops, parking garages. I thought about what old Cosmo might still have to say to me, and whether I had ever really loved him, aside from admiring him and swallowing his indications. Yes, that's what I'd call them, the things he conveyed to us at school, not lessons, or instructions, or information: but *indications*, gestures that pointed out far into the distance and revealed the existence of entire continents, invisible beyond the horizon, jagged-edged archipelagoes of names and ideas, characters, stories, disputes, struggles, battles between angels and demons, armies and philosophers, caravans of merchants in the midst of their journeys, adventures and precious substances and knots of stars and schools of deep thinkers and forests and diseases that raged and prisoners dragged into the snow and the lust for supremacy that had dragged them there, until you had worked your way back to an ampule of some sort filled with a pulsating liquid from which that phantasmagoria had originated in the first place, the wisdom that had spilled out of the heads of men, the rite of passage, the nectar that makes you sage and immortal or the poison that kills in a few seconds.

My hope was accentuated by an illusion as banal as it was sincere, almost invariably destined to prove vain: namely that sick men, men whose end is approaching, either rapidly or almost imperceptibly, are ready to dispense a deeper and more sincere truth, that they have, in other words, a final, extreme message to give us before saying farewell forever: a message that, while it might not illuminate the secret of life in general, still ought to give some meaning to the life they have lived. Well, that is in fact an illusion. And it shows just how appropriate the well-known negative argument really is, according to which either this ulterior truth does not exist at all, or even if it does exist, we never come into contact with it, even in the proximity of death, or else, even if that truth were shown in its entirety to the eyes of the dying man, as one final grace bestowed, he still wouldn't know how to communicate it to others: he wouldn't know how or he wouldn't want to, he'd lack the strength, and his words would dry up in his mouth.

Even so, I couldn't extinguish that illusion.

Surely Cosmo had something in store for me, and for me alone. Let it be his mocking grin resting on some rare word. Not even for a moment did it occur to me that it might be me who was supposed to tell him something. It certainly wouldn't be me who sat there telling him "what I'd been doing with myself," "all the news" (of the past forty years?).

But had I really loved him or not? And had he loved me? And if so, how much?

UNFORTUNATELY, I got there too late for confidences and revelations. There was only one revelation, the same one you have in the presence of certain paintings, where the figures become independent of the characters they are portraying, and are nothing more than a head, a torso, some limbs: a *thing*, that is, that you can see, that you can see *clearly*, but that is not uttered in words. Corporeal evidence.

I ENTERED THE SHACK. Rummo was there, with a woman. Cosmo had lost consciousness.

"He's been like this since yesterday."

"He never comes to?"

The woman shook her head.

I still hadn't looked at him. The room was cramped, a few square yards, and yet my gaze wandered above and around the corner where I knew he lay sunken in his mattress, somehow managing to avoid seeing him, or seeing him only as an empty space. I could list the details that my eyes perceived in that circumnavigation, but they were insignificant. I have no idea how to describe poverty without a hint of complacency, as if in a genre painting, a special effect. I noticed the notebooks, stacked on the sill of the casement window, only one sash of which could therefore be opened. Had they always been there, or had Rummo put them there? When he saw how hesitant I was, Rummo threw his arms around me. He hugged me and I hugged him back, hard. "Too bad," he said, "it's a pity," and that made it clear to me that, in all likelihood, Cosmo was never going to emerge from that sleep again. But there wasn't a hint of reproof in the voice of my old SLM classmate, if anything, perhaps, regret, regret for me and for the aged teacher, for the boundless array of confidences and reflections that he and I might still have been able to exchange. The last words, famous, fatal, that hadn't been uttered, and in fact, never are, save in the imagination of posterity— those last words ought to have been spoken to *me*, or so thought Rummo. Only then did I think back to the precocious grief of the man who was hugging me with such transport; I thought, that is, of just how old Giaele would have been now, if her family had returned from the outing to Angel Lake tired but happy with their rucksacks full of twigs and branches for Eleonora Rummo's collage, and one more berry than the ones that actually wound up in the trash can, once they did get home. She would have been forty-five years old, or so, Giaele. She'd have children of her own, blond perhaps, however recessive that characteristic might be in theory. Or perhaps she would have died before her time anyway, falling off her boyfriend's motor scooter back before helmets became mandatory, from an aneurism or a routine operation on the wrong ear, perhaps it was her fate to remain forever *small*. Not to grow up. With my chin resting on Rummo's shoulder, opening my eyes again after that tight hug had made me close them, to hide the tears, which instead now sprayed forth, I finally glimpsed through a damp veil the bed that Cosmo lay in.

LET ME WRITE SOMETHING AWFUL: he was exactly the same as I remembered him from school, even if he was twice that age and was dying.

18

FOUR DAYS LATER, Rummo called me back. Cosmo was dead. He had died without any particular suffering. Rummo had cared for him right up to the end, with the nurse whose presence Cosmo had become accustomed to, and a third person whose identity he was unwilling to disclose.

IT WAS RUMMO WHO HANDED me the keys to the little house. With the unorthodox assignment of removing the notebooks and the rest of whatever original handwritten material I might find. But I would need to move fast: at the end of the month, the hovel where our teacher had lived and then died would return to the jurisdiction of the Cerveteri city office for affordable housing. Rummo had managed to persuade the local functionary to wait two more weeks in exchange for the promise that the place would be left clean and emptied out. He would send two Romanians around with a pickup truck: except for a few suits and a couple of pairs of shoes that needed to be resoled but which were very well made, everything else was to be taken straight to the dump.

"I WANTED YOU TO KNOW SOMETHING about our teacher . . . the last thing."

"Okay, tell me."

"It's something you might not imagine."

Nothing could be more likely, I thought. I have a harder and harder time imagining what the people I know really do, that is, the people I *think* I know . . . who they *truly* are.

"Okay, Rummo, I just hope it's not yet another terrible thing . . . I've had my fill."

All I want now is joy and happy, lovely things around me. Is it a naïve desire, worthy of a spoiled child? Yes, yes it is.

"Oh, no, it's not terrible at all . . ." Rummo smiled. "On the contrary, on the contrary . . . but it's a singular thing for someone like him."

"Well, what is it?"

"Before losing consciousness, he asked for the comfort of religion."

"Cosmo?!"

Rummo nodded.

I can't believe it. I can't bring myself to believe it. Cosmo, the teacher . . . the most unreligious man. In the History of Mankind. There was a priest at his side, watching over him as he passed away.

DURING THE SAME STRETCH OF DAYS during which Cosmo was dying, a great technological innovator also died, perhaps the greatest and most famous in the field of computers. He, too, had fallen sick with cancer, though he was much younger than my teacher, and even younger than I am now, as I write this, and as I periodically gently touch my balls to ward off bad luck. His name is easy to guess and his slogans too popular for me to think of repeating them here. I read about him that, after "battling with courage," he had been "defeated" by his cancer. People had spoken on TV and in the newspapers about his "lengthy defiant struggle." Athletic and military metaphors were lavished. The account of any disease is nowadays translated into terms out of soccer or tennis, taking it for granted that the sick think like athletes, so that in the end, those who died did so only because they gave up. But that's not how it is. There really is no struggle, except for the struggle that well-meaning people stuff into the heads of the sick, trying to convince them to fight with all the strength they no longer have.

I LACKED THE NERVE, because it would have been insulting, to ask Rummo whether the priest really had been the dying man's request or if Rummo hadn't brought him there of his own initiative. Even though I think only the best of my classmate, the doubt was still rattling around.

19

IT IS POINTLESS AND STUPID to deplore and mock fear, because it is always linked, a mirror image, to hope, which means that to laugh at the fears of given individuals means denying them all hope.

FEAR DOESN'T ALLOW ITSELF to be defeated once and for all. A man seeking advice within himself will find his privileged interlocutor in fear. In order to conquer it, it is necessary to approach very close to death, even, one might say, cross through it. He who triumphs over fear gains access to the kingdom of the dead, just like Christ. In a variant of the wonderful poem "The Green Knight," Sir Gawain, one of the knights of the Round Table, who has faced death and has escaped with a scratch on the neck instead of being beheaded entirely by the mysterious knight of the title (who reveals himself to be none other than Death, in the green attire of a chatelain), finds himself wandering, befuddled, in a world he cannot recognize, estranged, where things are no longer what they used to be, where voices ring differently, and likewise colors and sounds.

It is the world of the dead.

Because you, my dear Gawain, that threshold you were so sure you'd managed to avoid, you actually crossed it . . . without noticing.

And there is no apparent exit to make your way back. Until he meets Merlin, that is, likewise the prisoner of an enchantment that has chained him forever here in the world of the dead. Merlin's voice hovers in the air like the rustling of branches . . .

MERLIN: *Gawain, neither will you ever return among other human beings.*
GAWAIN: *What are you saying? I'm already among other human beings, I'm free, the Green Knight spared me!*
MERLIN: *You don't have to lose your head in order to be lost forever.*
GAWAIN: *What else am I supposed to have lost? Are you referring to my honor?*
MERLIN: *Oh, no, you have more than enough honor left over, good knight, but where you are now, honor counts for nothing. This isn't the world of the living, Gawain. Are you still struggling to grasp what's happened to you?*
GAWAIN: *Then . . . I'm . . .*
MERLIN: *You've been ferried over, Gawain! You're on the other side.*
GAWAIN: *My brothers, the knights, will come to get me. I'm sure of it!*
MERLIN: *To them, you're a ghost, they can see you only when they're asleep, at night, as you brandish your sword in vain, and in the morning they rub their eyes to erase you from their sight.*

Now that I, too, have passed through the straits, through the grindstones of doubt and sorrow and fear, and I've emerged from them, far weaker and much reduced, what is left of me? What are the forces upon which I can rely? By now it's obvious I cannot place my reliance on anyone other than myself, and this causes me a tremendous sense of anguish because I feel that I have been reduced to the minimum viable state of existence by the ordeals I have been put through, alive, certainly, alive but weakened far more than rendered wise and astute. My bewilderment is clear evidence of how little the school of life has taught me. It is true, I have withstood the test in the presence of nothingness, I withstood its impact, and yet I have the sensation that nevertheless, nothingness has taken possession of me. While I was defeating it, it was penetrating me, that's right, I managed to defeat it only by virtue of its forces, forces that I had taken as my own, forces that had become *me*. The nothingness that I had—now in front of me, now beside me, like an adversary attempting to catch me off guard—is now inside me.

A PART OF THE EDUCATION RECEIVED was focused on death. Or really, on a life that wasn't, however, this one. The priests' continuous referral to the extrasensory world, in class, during mass, in prayers, in the explanations of the catechism, did nothing but emphasize the void that we felt around and inside us. It wasn't clear what good it did to live or not live, what difference there was, seeing that, after all, eternity was somewhere else entirely, afterward, at the end, and the life we were living now was just a hasty parenthesis. And if the material world was devoid of meaning, well, the promise of heaven struck us as equally empty (and we wouldn't have known how to populate it with sighing words or vague and glittering images like that of the angels, feathered, golden-haired youngsters), the World Supernal, which awaited us at the end of the exercise, that sort of training ground to which the priests, in their discussions, always overbrimming with promises, reduced life. Theology could teach us to become aware, become conscious of our condition: but not how to get out of it.

(Someone must once have said of the angels that they were actually dead children who had flown up into heaven.)

WHY AM I WRITING ABOUT THIS NOW? About fear and death? Because the news that Cosmo is no longer among the living shakes me down to the roots of my being.

In every modern story, a mythical element is always present, implicit, as if lying in ambush, ready to step forward and take over the story itself.

THE POEM ABOUT MY GRANDFATHER that I never send to Rummo is titled "Steel and Gold" and it focuses on the wristwatch that he was wearing when he threw himself down the stairwell, just like Primo Levi did. It was a Rolex dating back to the thirties or forties: not even the specialized watch repairmen I talked to could tell me the exact name of the model. The model that most closely resembles it is familiarly called the "Ovetto."

> As I tap at the keyboard, glittering on my wrist
> is the steel-and-gold Rolex that belonged to my grandfather, the
>   Fascist
> who killed himself. The hours are practically illegible on it.
> It was fastened to his wrist when he jumped
> down the stairwell with its handrail, black
> and mournful as his political convictions:
> whose values, in the final analysis, he didn't so much believe in

with any rational conviction as much as he incarnated
them due to a matter of nerves, a mood swing
at the bottom of his dark and tortured heart.

Six floors straight down. No one saw it, but the thud
was heard in every apartment.
Upon impact in the darkness at the foot of the stairs
the fragile gearings of the watch shattered
as did the organs of the man wearing it.
Today a highly paid craftsman, drawing on a supply
of spare parts and cogs now out of production,
managed to get the Ovetto going again, he gave it back to me
insisting on fastening it to my wrist in person
as if it were the shackle on a convict's wrist:
and as I write its widowed hands
spin around the dial, seeking in vain
traces of the lost hours.

20

AH, MY GOOD SIR, we don't sleep like we used to, in the old days ... When
we slept *like dormice* ...

WAKING AT FOUR *to soundless dark, I stare* ...

NO MATTER WHAT TIME I've gone to bed the night before, I wake up too
early, when it's still night out and daybreak is far away, at say four, or four
thirty, I open my eyes in the darkness and I'm pervaded by anxiety; I
take half a tablet of a well-known psychopharmaceutical and wait for it to
take effect.

The first times that I took it, within fifteen minutes it made me so indifferent to whatever problems I had, that out of gratitude I wanted to dedicate a poem to it ...

Now because of overuse, it takes much more, no matter how much I toss and turn in the sheets.

For many years now I have been afflicted with the habit of waking up early. What afflicts me most of all is its uselessness. Since I am neither a baker nor a farmer, much less a poetic soul, I don't know what to do with the dawn. The bards of early-morning hard work ought to explain to me what they get done in the afternoon, when, that is, they've already been at it for eight or ten hours, how they spend their time until dinner, are they still able to work then, do they trot along, spraying energy in all directions? If so, where do they find it? Aren't they already dead to the world by the middle of the day? And in that case, what benefit have they gained?

Waking up when it's still dark out scares you.

Now that it takes so much longer, I've transformed the time I spend waiting for the benzodiazepine to lay me out into an opportunity for some reading: a rather hallucinatory reading session, gluttonous, unfocused, which gradually relaxes—the body chemistry starts to function, the effect of the pill that I've dissolved in my mouth, under my tongue, begins to arrive in short waves, one upon the heels of the other, subsiding each into the next, as I absorb it as if I were sand—there, the waves stop interfering, entangling, it becomes linear, and the relaxation of my nerves starts to correspond with the relaxation of the sentences that line up in orderly fashion without any particular effort or snags, one follows another, while their content becomes less pressing, less important, or maybe it just appears to be what it is, neither more nor less, but just what it *actually* means, without my having to overload that sentence with meanings, without my having to comment upon it or reject it or be struck by it as a revelation: it passes through me and goes out the other way. Page 123 of the book has leafed past to become page 148 without my being fully aware of just how I got there, who pushed me there, and finally the sublime detachment that I've been waiting for starts to set in, detachment from the individual sentences, from the book that I hold in my hand, from the story told in the book, from the story of my life, which I no longer need to reconstruct, and from the lives of all those around me, and from the toil and tribulations that will begin again when the cell phone alarm goes off, well, I no longer feel any of that, dawn has come and it filters in through the windows but it doesn't cause any particular fear, it's just a source of light, it doesn't give any hope or illusions that might later be painfully given the lie, I no longer expect or fear anything from the new day that's dawning and I feel no other desire than to go back to sleep for another delicious hour or so, until the alarm goes off again, my head heavy on the cool pillow, the reality around me clearly defined in what is its authentic dimension: meaninglessness, insignificance.

>   . . . and all the uncaring
>   Intricate rented world begins to rouse . . .

THE XANAX + NOVEL METHOD (better if it's a long one, many hundreds of pages . . .) has been working for a long time now, I can safely say that I have not yet been strangled by my dependency. The fact remains, though, that for the past several months, since I bought a digital tablet, and I stopped being able to find large and engrossing novels, or else I began to be frightened by their sheer mass, instead of reading literature I've started to peruse online newspapers. Not the news, which at that hour I wouldn't even understand, but rather the reader comments. I've discovered that they are a genuine genre all their own, perhaps not exactly literary, but pretty close. If I've developed a dependency, it's not so much a dependency on the pharmaceutical that tranquilizes me, as much as a dependency on the comments that alarms me. They inform me about the state of things, about the way the world works, about what people think, much more than do the articles they're only there to gloss and rebut. I have the impression that that's really the point: not so much the things that happen but what people think about them, how they react, what words they use. And how pissed off they seem to get. Because the commenters are almost always pissed off. Their comments are 90 percent overflowing with rancor and resentment. You would say that rancor is the feeling that these days inspires nine out of ten Italians, nine out of ten human beings, it gets them out of the house in the morning and brings them back home in the evening, makes them breathe and think, and then sit down at the keyboard to twist names and invent nicknames, threaten retaliation, mock, promise the other commenters that they will all soon be "swept away." Still half asleep, but already sufficiently lucid to be amused and at the same time, horrified, I run my finger down the tablet's screen, skimming through dozens and dozens of bitter wisecracks, accusations, remonstrances, and retorts along the lines of: you're all just abject slaves, thieves, miserable lackeys, sellouts, brain-dead, sodden drunks, spies, jack offs. The term "troll" is widely used, a piece of pejorative online jargon that means "an individual who interacts by means of messages that are variously provocative, annoying, off topic, or meaning-less, with a view to disrupting communication and sow discord."

"TROLL": a word I was fond of and that has always stirred a subtle thrill within me, ever since the days when I first read *Peer Gynt* in an illustrated children's edition, which I found at my family's beach house, a book that I am looking at even as I write, published by Aristea Editrice, translated by Rossana Bagaloni, and I leaf through it now, my emotions at a high pitch . . .

But now I hear that trolls have appeared online? Who are they talking about? Who is it that's talking? The comments would seem to refer to the original article, which gave rise to the dispute, but by now that's a hundred or two hundred comments away, the spool of thread has become hopelessly tangled, falling very far from the beginning of it all, and who can even remember what that was about in the first place? By now people only address those who commented right before them, commentaries pile up atop commentaries, in a spiral where you can get the upper hand only by being more aggressive or more sarcastic or funnier . . .

ONE OF THE THINGS that's been keeping me from sleeping lately is the fact that I'm writing this book. Its subject. Its phantoms. The crime that triggered it in the first place. I hadn't thought about the CR/M in years and years . . . then someone got back in touch. Came knocking at the door.

When I was a boy, my insomnia was much different, pure, uncontaminated. Preliminary. It was impossible to fall asleep.

At age twelve, thirteen . . . at age fifteen . . . sleepless nights with my heart churning and my mind noisy with clashing thoughts, an enormous, inconclusive, uninterrupted hive of thinking.

In the darkness, continents of thoughts smashed into each other, with a crunching sound, enormous slabs of ice drifting freely. Vain, incessant thought . . . The body calling out for rest . . . the mind hungering. What was I thinking? Actually, *nothing*. It wasn't me thinking, it was the thoughts themselves that arrived en masse, swirling like flocks of birds in the winter sky, every so often forming a figure that gave the impression of having meaning, only to dissolve almost instantly.

21

WELL, FINE, the time came. The necessity for this book was born, or perhaps came back to life, ten years ago. It was reawakened like a mummy in a budget horror movie.

ON APRIL 29, 2005, near Campobasso, two dead women are found buried in the garden of a small villa.

AMONG THE PROTAGONISTS OF THIS STORY is Dario Saccomani (the inmates called him "*il truffaldino*"—the con artist: his projects with the prison had only one objective, to secure public financing).

SACCOMANI: "I am a person who acknowledges in his existence the hand of God." He founded in Campobasso the association Città Futura, which works in four different fields of social importance: alcoholism, prison inmates, at-risk youth, and sexual problems.

IN THE MEANTIME, in the Palermo prison, the theater and writing workshops were being run by Giuseppe Pittà, a cultural activist who, according to the prisoner Giovanni Maiorano, whenever he heard Angelo tell about his criminal exploits, would simply laugh.

Angelo is the author of a novel, one of whose chapters is entitled "*Uccidiamo le pischelle*," "Let's Kill the Young Girls." Pittà helped him write it. According to Pittà, most of the things described in Angelo's book are "products of the imagination."

❖

LUCA PALAIA, a pimply young man. The son of a Calabrian lifer serving his time in prison with Angelo.

Palaia and Angelo meeting in August 2002 while out on furlough.

ANGELO: "I was captivated by Palaia. Despite the fact that he'd had an unhappy, troubled life, the evil he'd faced seemed to have slipped right off him, he was always cheery, always smiling. Other people in his place would have become embittered, but not him. I developed a crush on him, even though I want it to be clear that there was nothing homosexual about this attachment of mine to Luca. He was like a son to me."

DURING FURLOUGHS, in Campobasso, after eight in the evening, Angelo lived at the Roxy, a four-star hotel, where he held dinners for his guests, as many as ten people at a time, including (he claims) members of the parliament of the Italian Republic.

PALAIA WAS PREPARING to spend the night with Angelo at the Roxy when the police came calling, for a routine check. A report was filed on that "unclear, turbid situation." The officers found Palaia's pajamas in Angelo's hotel room.

ACCORDING TO THE CHIEF of the Mobile Squad of Campobasso, Angelo, while being interviewed, had no hesitation admitting his homosexual tendencies. Saccomani says that he was bisexual. Guido Palladino (the other accomplice) said that he liked little boys. "Palaia was his type." It was in any case a morbid relationship, even if Angelo Izzo denies having had any physical relations with him.

AS A RESULT OF THIS INCIDENT, Izzo loses his work-release status and is sent from Campobasso back to prison in Palermo, in the Pagliarelli maximum security prison.

THERE HE ESTABLISHES TIES with Giovanni Maiorano, whom he had previously met in various prisons. Maiorano, from Puglia, had murdered a drug dealer and, it is said, had played ball with his head.

MAIORANO WASN'T THE FIRST to be ensnared by Angelo's intellectual profile. What profile? one is tempted to enquire. The one established by the fact that he comes from a good family, that he attended university (just one year, actually, then prison). The crème de la crème of magistrates and journalists, both male and female, fell for it, so why not a few hoods and criminals possessing little or no schooling?

"He gave me advice, he'd give me books, and I'd cook for him, I'd give him lunch." Maiorano becomes convinced that Angelo is a gifted entrepreneur and expert in finance, well connected, and he decides to entrust him with his savings, he's confident that Angelo will help his wife, Antonella Linciano, and his daughter, Valentina, who happen to live in Campobasso, once Angelo is able to go out on work furloughs again, leaving the prison for his job at the association run by Pastor Saccomani. And in fact, it is none other than Maiorano who urges the two women, mother and daughter, to entrust themselves to "Uncle Angelo," which is what the young girl will soon call him. He states that he is not jealous, in this case, because it is a well-known fact that Angelo likes young men, not women.

ANGELO MINIMIZES HIS RELATIONS WITH MAIORANO: "We talked and walked together . . . we ate a bowl of pasta together . . . that sort of thing."

"He wanted to commit crimes with me . . . but I have much more impressive criminal connections, there's no reason for someone like Maiorano to think he can go into business with me."

GRADUALLY, as Angelo moves closer and closer to obtaining work-release status again, Maiorano becomes more insistent. According to Angelo, it is Maiorano who tells him to "make use" of his wife—who is a clever sort— however he sees fit, and in exchange to lend a hand. Lend a hand to her and to his daughter outside prison, and lend a hand to him, behind bars.

AT THE TRIAL, Saccomani talks about himself as a cultural organizer, an "*operatrice*," in the feminine gender. His path to becoming a woman in full has reached an acceptable point. The evangelical pastor Saccomani, founder of Città Futura, is in fact on the verge of a complete sex change when the murders take place. Yes, I know, that's incredible. If a screenwriter wanted to add this touch to the plot of a film, the other writers would mutiny. "Oh, come on! The last thing we need now is for a priest to become a woman. We already have a murdering rapist who works as a psychological counselor . . . Let's not go overboard!"

"I HAD A CHOICE, whether to take on the challenge or turn away from it . . ." (the challenge, that is, of helping Angelo Izzo to get out of prison, that interwoven web of self-interested and slightly oily friendship that, under current operating guidelines, allows one inmate to leave prison and another, less facile and practiced, to rot in his cell) "and I chose to take it on because I start from a very specific presupposition . . . a presupposition of faith . . . some might mistake that for sheer folly, for a state of religious and mystical exaltation . . . but it isn't."

"I am an extremely rational person . . . *but* I'm a believer," says the pastor. He has signed a (fake) employment contract with Angelo for the "development and production of a newspaper," at a monthly salary of 500 euros.

JUDGE: *How much did Angelo earn a month?*
  Saccomani: *Five hundred euros.*
  So he was an employee of yours?
  Yes.
  And how could the association afford to pay Izzo a regular salary?
  Well, I was able to bring in the sum necessary to pay him thanks to donations, including one from his family . . .
  Was that a regular donation?
  Yes.
  Monthly?
  Yes.
  And how much did the monthly donation from Angelo's family amount to?
  Five hundred euros.

But that's the exact same amount as the salary you paid him!
Yes.

WHO WAS IT THAT TURNED to Città Futura in search of aid and support? "Gypsies, the jobless, lots of women who'd been dumped by their husbands for younger women, and who therefore found themselves in difficult straits," Angelo replies. The psychological support he supplied proved effective. "I can brag a little bit that I resolved sixty, seventy percent of my cases . . ." Angelo finds work for many of those seeking help and he encourages abandoned women. He plans to defraud Maiorano and his wife by inventing a story involving a restaurant that needs to be renovated, to con him out of money; but at the same time he actually dreams of opening a real restaurant "to create jobs to give to the needy," saying that he's "grown sincerely fond" of his beneficiaries.

IN NOVEMBER 2004 he's once again awarded partial release by the Palermo parole board. Oh, it was about time. (You can find the parole board's reasoning laid out in chapter 14 in Part VI of this book.) At the end of December, Angelo is released. He gets Città Futura to hire Palaia, paying his salary of 300 or 400 euros a month out of his own funds.

ANGELO BOUGHT HIM CLOTHING, gave him a car, then he meets Maiorano's wife, whom the convict in Palermo had so highly recommended to him, and Angelo convinces her of his intention to open an imaginary restaurant in Frasso Telesino, in a family home ("a castle"). Maiorano's wife, Carmela Linciano, known to her friends as Antonella, lives with her daughter, Valentina, in a nearby town that has the absurd name of Gambatesa, literally, "Stretched Leg"; Valentina, not yet fourteen, was in middle school. Everyone in town shunned the woman, except for Angelo, though he has an ulterior motive; he plans to con her out of the money to renovate the restaurant ("The restaurant project was a con job, I had no intention whatsoever of opening a restaurant, it was just a way of getting her to give me ten or fifteen thousand euros and pocketing the cash"); in the end, Antonella Linciano gives him 5,500 euros, unwillingly, at the insistence of her husband, who's behind bars.

Maiorano wrote to her that Angelo is "a person deserving of absolute trust." There's no need for a receipt.

"What do you want, it's a miserable sum," Angelo declares.

THE RELATIONSHIP BETWEEN Angelo and Maiorano's wife is a short, perverse novel, of which only the murderer's version survives. And that
murderer stacks up a vast quantity of statements, insinuations, allusions,
embellishments (Angelo himself uses the term to describe them), as he
had previously done in his account of the CR/M and many other episodes.
By his account, Antonella Linciano pursues him tirelessly. She phones
him constantly. She often goes to see him at the offices of Città Futura. She
always brings that blessed daughter of hers along with her. "She wanted
to do everything you can think of." It was only when the topic turned to
her producing money that she turned mistrustful and uncooperative. Angelo takes over the role of husband with her, handling family matters: dealing with the lawyer for her nephew, Daniele, who is under house arrest, an
eviction, her unemployment check. And even though he claims he detests
her, he starts to enjoy "being the man of the house for the two women."

The relationships that Angelo gets tangled up in always have something hallucinatory about them. They consist of brief fanciful impulses
of transport or disgust. According to him, the relationship with Antonella Linciano deteriorates because she soon shows herself to have "a
greedy and extortionate nature." She was "a witch without a drop of
sensitivity."

And always with that girl tagging along after her . . .

"EVERY TIME I LAID EYES ON THEM, a chill ran through my heart and
my guts."

"I began to hate them. God, I prayed, take these two out of my life."

ONE DETAIL, on the other hand, of the relationship between Angelo and
the utopian pastor who's about to undergo a sex change: the photographs
of Vietnamese children charred by napalm that Angelo would show Saccomani, asking him: "Can it be that God allows such a thing?" (the same
question that Ivan Karamazov asked his brother Alyosha, if I may venture
to note) and the evangelical pastor replied, in religious inspiration: "It's not
true that God does nothing . . . God created you precisely to put an end to
these injustices."

(**GOD CREATED ANGELO** to prevent *this . . .* !)

WHILE THE STORM RAGES IN HIS IMAGINATION, buffeting his soul, Angelo realizes that his friends Palaia and Palladino are entirely consumed by their own problems, not his. Angelo's inner torments go unnoticed. And he finds himself alone again. He thirsts for love, to be really and truly loved, in fact, he demands it. He's shut up in a corner, and he wants to get out of it. That's when the idea penetrates his "damaged mind" of dragging the two wing nuts into something that will bind them to him irreversibly. "I was so terrified of being abandoned!" In a confused, blurred way, though, he begins to glimpse a possibility . . .

"**THE IDEA OF A BLOOD PACT** that would force them to love me forever."

A QUARTET IS THUS CREATED which Angelo wants to direct after his own fashion. And he will succeed. Two females and two males. Antonella Linciano and Valentina, on the one hand, Luca Palaia and Guido Palladino on the other. By murdering the two females, starting with the elder ("When we were together, in a state of intimacy, I dreamed of walling her up alive in the office"), and then, if it seemed appropriate, her clingy adolescent appendage, and by so doing, tying the two men to himself, with the bonds of complicity. Just as he had thirty years earlier.

"**ENOUGH IS ENOUGH.** Now I'll pretend to give in, I'll pretend to go away with those two females and then I'll get rid of them."

THERE ARE SOME WIRETAPS.
    It's well known that wiretaps are like a trawl net: you toss the net into the water thinking you'll catch certain fish but something else, something unexpected, always winds up getting tangled in its meshes. The Mobile Squad was investigating a drug smuggling ring. The wiretaps on

THE CATHOLIC SCHOOL   1121

Paladino and Palaia instead talk about a pistol that was used in an armed robbery . . .

GUIDO PALADINO IS DETAINED BY THE POLICE. They convince him that they know everything. He speaks of two corpses in his grandmother's little villa. The policemen are astonished, at which point he changes his version of the facts and tells them that there are two pistols in the villa. The next day, the investigators find the pistols and then discover a well-trodden path in the backyard that leads to some recently excavated soil. They start to dig and they find some quicklime. "At this point Palladino realizes that we wouldn't be leaving the place until we'd found out everything, and he confesses: underneath, mother and daughter are buried" (a phrase that Angelo considers a "cute invention" dreamed up by the Mobile Squad).

DIGGING DEEPER, they find Linciano's corpse, fully dressed, her hands fastened behind her back with a pair of handcuffs.

The duct tape on the mouth and over her nose (though her nostrils weren't completely covered over) and the handcuffs were all put on when the victim was alive and conscious. Wrapped around her head was a black nylon bag fastened around her neck with more duct tape: that's what suffocated her, causing her death after roughly five minutes of agony.

VALENTINA WAS NUDE, her arms handcuffed behind her back and a pink-and-white sweater wrapped around her arms, a black nylon bag over her head, fastened with packing tape and sealed around her neck with surgical tubing. The body was wrapped in two green nylon bags.

"BIG WHORE AND LITTLE WHORE," Angelo used to call them, because "all they cared about was money."

AT THE OFFICES OF CITTÀ FUTURA, he says, "I had a customer window and I'd talk to them there. If I needed to talk about private matters, I'd go take them to the office nearby. If we were going to have sex, I'd go down to the office at the far end, which was enclosed and which we called, in jest, the room of gallantry."

Here Angelo claims he had three-ways with the victims.

THE FIRST TIME that Angelo met Maiorano's wife, he had kissed her hand. He employed the same gallant gesture with the female journalist who went to interview him, several years earlier, and on whom he had made such a favorable impression.

ANGELO ON THE PHONE WITH VALENTINA (a few days before killing her): "You sound a little sad . . . what's the matter, a sad love affair? Heh, heh, heh . . ."

"**HEY**, you really are a wonderful daughter."

HE SAYS THAT HE HANDED over some emeralds to Linciano. "By now she was my accomplice . . . a bad, greedy woman. She had started blackmailing me."

ACCORDING TO THE MEDICAL EXAMINER, Valentina's hymen was intact, fibrous in nature, such as to rule out any penetration, even a partial one.

Angelo's DNA was found in the girl's mouth (maybe he kissed her, or something else, before strangling her).

THE HANDCUFFS FOR EROTIC BYPLAY: who bought them? They were found to have been purchased at a shop called Cose belle, "Nice Things," in Campobasso; Palaia had bought the surgical tubing for Saccomani, who used it for a tourniquet for the injections he was giving himself, to become a woman.

SURGICAL TUBING . . . again . . . (go back to page 468).

"I'M A PERSON WITH GENDER-IDENTITY ISSUES," says Saccomani, as he prepares to have a sex-change operation and change his name accordingly. "My journey to this transition has been going on for ten years now." On his PC the police found hundreds of photographs of child pornography.

ANGELO ALLUDES TO INCESTUOUS and pedophilic relations between Maiorano and Valentina. "The plaintiff has a raw nerve when it comes to this topic . . ." he says at the trial, with a brilliant flash of malevolent cunning.

SACCOMANI: "I did what I ought to have done. Those who serve God are already satisfied with their service, they have no need of any further gratification . . ." (*What the fuck are you talking about, dude??*).

ANGELO CLAIMS: "In 2002 I'd already had Palaia buy some quicklime to bury a pistol that had been used in a murder, so it was dirty. I didn't give Palaia any explanations, he just did what he was told, without asking."

According to the defense, that monster had Palaia under his thumb. Maybe he is the real Subdued. For that matter, it was Angelo who told Palaia that he reminded him a lot of his old friend from the CR/M, in fact, he's his spitting image.

By the way, that's not Luca Palaia's real name: he changed his identity as a child, because his father was sentenced to life without parole and began cooperating with the prosecution. In twenty-three years, he might have seen his father once. As a boy he had served six months in the reform school of Latina for a "two-bit armed robbery" (description offered by Angelo), with a sawed-off shotgun in a pharmacy, for which he was later acquitted.

At the trial, when Luca Palaia's father was asked, "On what terms are you with Palaia, Luca?" he chose to avail himself of his right not to reply.

MAIORANO STATES that Angelo told him he had been to Rome with Palaia and a girl: Palaia had sex with her and Angelo watched.

ANGELO IS TALKATIVE AT THE TRIAL, he enjoys telling stories, he laughs, he's boisterous.

"I wanted to buy him a Porsche, because I loved him, I wanted to put a McDonald's in his name."

"Actually, it was Angelo himself who had fallen under the spell of this loveboy!" (blurts out the plaintiff's lawyer).

"Palaia was weak, by his age, out of insecurity . . . because of his IQ . . ." (here Palaia's lawyer calls his client an idiot to save him). "Palaia's criminal depth? *What criminal depth are we talking about?!* Palaia has no depth, and I'm not just talking about criminal depth, he has no depth of any kind!"

"ANYONE WHO'S EVER HAD ANYTHING to do with Angelo has ended up trapped in his web . . ." (again, it's Palaia's lawyer who's speaking).

THE PROSECUTING MAGISTRATE: "The murderer killed to teach Palaia how to kill. To train his godson."

"ANGELO LIVES ON HIS CRIMINAL ANNIVERSARIES, Angelo battens off the evil he does!!"

OUT OF THE MISTS OF THE PAST, ghost ships reemerge . . . drifting hulks of memory . . . pieces that resemble other pieces . . . they can be disassembled and reassembled in different forms . . . the constellation of crimes can be varied ad infinitum.

". . . WHEN WE KILLED Piero Castellani, a.k.a. the Slobberer, we went there to kill him and his wife was there, too, so we had to kill her, too . . . so now I say, gosh darn it, there are times when you're forced to kill people who have nothing to do with it, like the girl, because it's not like I'm a lunatic, or a serial killer, for that matter, I know she was innocent, I had to kill her *because there was nothing I could do about it . . .*"

22

THAT MORNING *I'd made some sandwiches. I'm reminded of a rape in which I'd made sandwiches. Maybe the first rape I'd committed in my life. And I remember that that time, too, I'd made some sandwiches. We'd gone to a villa over near the Castelli Romani, taking a director's daughter with us, and I remember this detail of the sandwiches. But this time, no one was eating. It was awkward. So I went into the kitchen, I opened my bag, and I pulled out the duct tape and the surgical tubing. Then the handcuffs. I called Antonella, "Could you come in here for a minute? I have something I want to tell you." Then I told her to lie down, I had to search her, and not to make a lot of noise or she'd scare Valentina. I had the gun in my hand. I got her to lie down on the ground and then I told Palaia to handcuff her. He put them on. "Now gag her." That is, duct tape over her mouth. She seemed dead already. In the meantime, the girl was in the other room. With duct tape over her mouth, Antonella was helpless. Luca was pale and shaking. I shove him aside and put a bag over the woman's head and strangle her. How did I do it? I sit on top of her. She starts struggling. Just as I start to feel better, she starts struggling. I don't know how long it took her to die. At first I wasn't planning to kill her, I just wanted to knock her out. But with the bag over head, she was definitely going to die. All I wanted was to make sure that she didn't struggle too much, because it had become clear that I couldn't count on Luca, he was a wreck. I tell him to calm down, I help him to sit down. The girl in the other room was relaxed. We hadn't made any noise, and it only took a few minutes. What did I feel after strangling the woman? I felt joy. I had rid myself of a burden. In life, you have problems sometimes, even major ones, that get taken care of all at once. It was as if I'd cleaned off the filth and grime of thirty years in prison. Then I thought: I need to take care of the girl, and I went to where she was. But first I needed to calm down Luca. If he sees the girl being killed, he might raise objections. I guarantee him that I won't do anything to her. "Stay calm and don't move." I tell her that there's been a change in plans and that I'm going to have to wrap her up. I have to take her away without anyone seeing. I don't know if she fell for it, but she had a gun trained on her, what was she supposed to do? So I put the handcuffs on her.*

You found her nude because at first my plan had been to strip them both na-
ked and stick them nude in the plastic bags, get them to the grave, and then
bury them after taking off the bags, so that the bodies would decompose
quickly. With clothes on, it takes longer, and they can always be identified.
But I'd already messed up the plan with her mother. I had Valentina sit on
the sofa, I put handcuffs on her wrists and then duct tape to keep her from
screaming. I put on plenty, maybe three or four pieces, I put tape over her
eyes, too. Then I stripped her, but since she was already wearing handcuffs,
I couldn't get the sweater off her entirely. I took off all the rest of her clothes,
I bound her legs, I put the bag over her head, and I sealed it around her neck
with the surgical tubing. Then I turned away. And she suffocated to death. I
had wrapped duct tape around the bag, too. How much air can there be in a
bag? The girl didn't struggle, tied up as she was, hands and feet and gagged,
with a bag over her head. She didn't struggle like her mother. I turned away
because it bothered me. And I drank a Coca-Cola.

Part IX

✥

Cosmo

I

GLANCING OVER THE NOTEBOOKS taken from Cosmo's house, I almost immediately identified the last one compiled, in which he must have written until the disease silenced him, until, in other words, a few days before he died, or at least so I believe. Rummo told me that he had never seen him handle the notebooks. If Cosmo still did it, then he must have waited until he was alone or else he did it in the presence of the nurse, Jelena, with whom he must have been on more confidential terms.

The notebooks bear no dates or any chronological indication. I figured out which was last from the handwriting. It was very dense, with infrequent erasures and very few corrections. It contained more than four hundred annotations, each separated from the next with a dotted line. I copied them into my computer and numbered them in the order in which they had been written. In the following chapter, I cannot publish them all, for considerations of space, but I have included a fair number of the ones that struck me most forcefully or which might mean something in connection with these stories: even if he never speaks about them, Cosmo gives the impression that he might be referring to them, here and there.

In a more opportune context I will make public the entirety of this notebook, and if there is time and a chance to do so, and people interested in reading, I'll try to do the same with the others.

In a few cases, I've added notes of my own.

2

1. The readers of daily newspapers in Italy are not interested in learning what they don't already know or don't expect; they have no interest in being informed or kept abreast of events; they prefer, if anything, to have someone confirm the convictions they already hold. If a person hates someone, then they want the brilliant op-ed writer for the newspaper they buy every morning to prove to them how right they are to hate that person, want them to bring them fresh arguments daily in favor of hating them.

5. A practical man is driven either by self-interest or vanity, which in any case comes under the heading of self-interest, since it has to do with an ambition to increase one's personal prestige and therefore, by reflection, that of one's commercial or professional activity. While it may seem like a squandering of money, vanity is actually a sound investment.

6. It often happens at a dinner or a party where things are rather dull that there is someone who tries to liven things up with a bit of indignation in a conversation that is otherwise flat. At least by so doing, you can always be sure of standing out at a meal, and the situation in Italy, whatever the historical period (though now more than ever), offers opportunities for invective. People try to ward off boredom or things that have already been heard and already been said with virulent tirades or sacrosanct outbursts, ranging from A to Z. Often those who light into these rampages aren't doing so for the first time, they've already tried them out, these same monologues, in the presence of different audiences, these are reruns, items from the repertoire, greatest hits and golden oldies that are trotted out when interest is waning and people are glancing at their watches. All that's needed is a hook and a line, a fuse you can light and set off. You can improvise on the topic of the day. Intellectuals more than anyone else indulge in this sort of exercise, and the sheer love of words, enthusiasm for the squandering of words and rhetorical aggression outstrips the love of truth, it matters not at all whether what triumphs in the end is wrong or right. In fact, if what tri-

umphs in the end is the most spectacularly mistaken point of view, in defiance of logic and common sense, then that just means that the speaker's sheer prowess overpowered them. For that reason, great orators, truly great and magnificent orators generally uphold misguided arguments, which they are able to justify only with their sheer mastery. They pursue the wrong, they adore the wrong, they attain the wrong, the wrong is their point of pride, their permanent existential position, and if a concept is by any chance right, they manage to twist it so massively that it is useless for anyone who thinks straight, they give it a hunchback, they make sure it's wrong. By making sure the wrong side of the argument triumphs, it is the speaker who triumphs, not his argument.

Transferred onto the verbal plane, it is the same exercise as that practiced by those who wish to break up the monotony of their evenings and therefore go out and set fire to Dumpsters or throw rocks off the overpass, the thrill is very similar and they're convinced they're actually not hurting anyone.

The defining characteristic of this kind of verbal extremism is in fact its total harmlessness.

7. Can there be a regeneration that has nothing to do with violence? How can anything be reborn if it hasn't first been destroyed? Can you pass from one order to another without there being an interval of chaos? Those who point the way to salvation glimpse it through a wall of flames. The higher those flames leap, the sooner we will burn, and the sooner we will be restored. The field must burn so that it can be fertilized. The sole salvation from disaster is a still greater disaster.

8. Since only destruction allows transcendence, since only by passing through some catastrophe can one perceive the existence of more advanced stages of consciousness and sensitivity, and attain them, it is possible to persuade some that every destructive act facilitates an elevation. It is the mysticism of annihilation: of the raging bonfire, the cleansing massacre, the violence that transports man beyond himself, transfiguring him. It is a mistaken syllogism. Transcendence originates in a violent break, which alone however is not sufficient, it is a necessary condition but not sufficient alone to allow transcendence of the ordinary state of consciousness, indeed, most of the time it only dulls, it doesn't elevate. Those who practice violence and those who suffer it are both dulled by it.

9. Where there is justice there is a struggle, where there is a struggle there is at least a hope of justice. But this hope is based on the possibility of destroying that which is unjust, he who is unjust. Justice, therefore, is nothing but conflict and struggle.

10. In the present-day triumph of the materialist culture of the body, the body is actually debased, maltreated, shaped to comply with the whims of fourth-class aesthetes as if it were an inert material, mere clay devoid of any original quality and form. Capriciously, its sex is changed, along with its features, size, even the color of its skin, blacks lighten theirs while whites tan theirs, in other words, it's just a backdrop, a landscape to be carved and sculpted, where you can hang hooks or upon which you can scrawl any garbage, the way graffiti writers do on subway cars, in other words, an Italian garden to be clipped and sheared, forcing its plants to take on the desired shape, however artificial and absurd it may be. After all, what is to stop us? How can the body rebel against the dictatorship of the mind that demands it be remade in its image and semblance? The body cannot. It's mute. A prisoner. A slave to manias. An unfortunate machine. It will patiently go on submitting to the whims of that idiot woman who's decided to have her tits enlarged, that moron who guzzles steroids and then builds up his arms while he destroys his joints. His joints, the articulations of his body, which sits silent and suffers and is deformed. To say nothing of professional athletes: the true, authentic enemies of the body, which they massacre for money, until they're finally stuck in a wheelchair. What exaltation of the body are they talking about! It's not the triumph of the flesh, it's the triumph *over* the flesh. Employed as a parade ground for symbolic maneuvers, military processions. Never so much in human history as today, *crushed underfoot. Our* flesh.

11. Systems of power can be understood best not at their high points, but rather in the phase of their deterioration, at their sunset. Morality, ideas, fashions, political regimes, religious principles, all reveal their true nature when they are on the verge of succumbing to the thrust of new things. Just before they are replaced, they unleash their essence into the twilight in the purest and most dramatic fashion, becoming wholly understandable, under the galloping onslaught of events that they could never have foreseen, and therefore all the more instructive. Since there is no real stimulus to understand that which is imagined to be immutable, our understanding always

sniffs around the proximity of destruction. A man's character, a family's actual economic resources, an army's strength, the depth of a love can all be manifested in their entirety only in a state of crisis. When that crisis becomes irreversible, however, there is a further revelation: namely, that it is abuses and excesses which contribute more than anything else to the advancement, the evolution of the times. Only if extreme deterioration takes place, touching low points never before seen, only *then* can anything different and new come about. The excesses play an important role in evolution, they shatter the barriers between the sexes, between the classes, between individuals, making energy circulate. It is the excesses that cause the decline of an era, and it is the decline of an era that explains its excesses.

12. An indirect way of delighting in evil and harm, of enjoying harm by proxy, in a fantastic, and yet functional key, immersed in a sort of waking dream crowded with bloody images, witnessing the catastrophe of skyscrapers in flames or airplanes crashing or the devastation of entire cities, ravaged by enormous apes or implacable aliens or the living dead or freak waves or asteroids or nuclear contaminations, sucking greedily every day on the press and the TV, gobbling down an immense quantity of news having to do, for the most part, with murders, massacres, terror attacks, floods, hurricanes, epidemics, all of them typical of a society not only ready but in fact eager to savor its own annihilation; perhaps willing to forgive or even to assist those who are carrying out that destruction, and grateful to those who depict it in a spectacular manner, allowing them to enjoy it in advance, on a virtual field. Contemplating destruction while undergoing it provides an unexampled aesthetic pleasure.

13. In those bottlenecks where the recourse to violence is decisive in changing the direction of history, a certain kind of criminal henchman comes in handy. It's not even necessary to recruit them: without any explicit request being made, those who have direct experience in subjugating and killing, and no inhibitions about doing so, spontaneously offer their willingness to enter into action. That explains why, alongside the noblest idealists or simple fanatics, you will almost always find a certain number of enterprising gallows birds.

14. It is never the situation in and of itself that *creates* ferocity, what it does is *allow* that ferocity to be unleashed.

17. Any state, once created, tends to place its men face-to-face with the choice between concealing, with some embarrassment, the episodes of violation of the law and sheer violence that attended its foundation (the collapse of the preceding regime, a revolution, a military campaign) or else vindicating those acts as heroic. In either case, whether hiding them or embellishing them with high-flown rhetoric, one mystifies them. The bloody side is praised and exalted, because it is too disgusting if described in a frank manner for what it actually is, and it is thus ill-suited to encourage the coherence of the new social structure. Volleys of rifle fire and executions by firing squad must vanish without an echo into silence or else be echoed in salvos of blanks at special ceremonies evocative of the past. Many years later, historic revisionism finds its place, often with a fairly ham-handed spirit of polemic, rectifying the picture of the past with stunning revelations that are touted as objective, but thus creating not a salutary effect of truth but rather an indiscriminate revulsion toward one's own history, which suddenly reemerges, spangled with murders and infamy. But now it's too late, the truth ought to have been told sooner.

19. While only elected politicians can enter the Palace, the halls of power, *anyone* can venture out into the street. It is foolish therefore to ask oneself with irony as abundant as it is futile why major protest rallies and demonstrations continue to be held, with marches and processions. Those who do so clearly fail to understand or at least underestimate their aspect, at once festive and menacing. In order to understand certain community rituals, it is necessary to recognize the way that they blend till there is no distinguishing between enthusiasm and furor, obligation and hypocrisy, the spirit of adherence and the spirit of sharing, nonconformism but also conformism, excitement hope and fear. It is every bit as much a mistake to take them for innocuous and salutary exercises of democracy, healthful processions with copies of the Constitution in hand, an error due perhaps to mere naïveté. The individual vanishes if he seriously believes that "he has a say in the matter," by his rights as an individual. What most fascinates about street demonstrations is the grandiose and quivering spectacle of anonymity, laid out in the nude viscerality of its components, as pure life without specifications, and therefore fearsome, too. Those enormous glistening clouds of fish that spin wheeling away from the hand of the scuba diver, only to become compact again, are certainly not what I think of when I utter the adjective "democratic."

20. Techniques of insurrection have been theorized, preached, and war-gamed by the left; and then almost invariably put into action by the right. The left readies the subversive laboratory with all its tools and instruments, but the Fascists are the ones who actually use it. They quickly and eagerly learned the lesson about how to mobilize crowds, how to overwhelm strongpoints of control, prefectures, police stations, barracks, tossing in their own extra pinch of military training and the mental habitus of war.

21. The Fascists perform experiments on life and in history with the same spirit of curiosity and cruelty that can be found in children vivisecting a lizard with a pocket knife. They want to know what it looks like "inside," whether it can walk with its little paws cut off, how long it will go on living with its guts spewed on the ground. It's not even wickedness in the strict sense of the term, but rather a brutal and crude experimental method, like in the times of Sir Francis Bacon, who throttled chickens and then froze them (and thus caught the pneumonia that killed him).

24. The ideal narrative figure to intertwine the threads of different and contradictory stories, so as to unify them, is the *renegade*.

25. Two canonical approaches of Italian intellectuals to the relationship with power: homage or outrage, sometimes both things together, since any outrage against a political faction serves as an homage to another one.

26. However blind or ridiculous or unpleasant they may seem, those who cultivate a boundless dedication to an idea always inspire a certain respect, I repeat, even in cases where their idea may seem absurd or even repugnant, the fact that they pursue it with all their might, willingly taking on any and all sacrifice, still stirs admiration. Martyrdom loses none of its splendor and transcends the ideals in the name of which one immolates oneself. Let us say, then, that it has a dark splendor.

28. It is pointless to invoke common sense, the spirit of justice, or sentiments of equity when what is acting on men are forces that appeal to the unfathomable depths of the soul, sidestepping entirely the virtuous and tortuous circuit of reason in favor of an emotional shortcut. The first victim of these forces is, in fact, logic, consequentiality, the link between

cause and effect, the deductive capacity and, most particularly, the inductive capacity: it all collapses. That which *is*, that which *could* or *should be*, and that which is *not* all become the same thing. Error rises to the rank of supreme proof of what is just, if you are convinced in advance that what is just is superior to any error, in fact, feeds on errors in order to grow. Mistakes, lies, misdeeds, and patent injustices all serve to confirm the goodness of an idea if it is able to outlive the negative consequences that that idea itself has unleashed. It is the paradoxical truth of Boccaccio's novella where the Jew converts to Catholicism after seeing with his own eyes that the Vatican is an open cellar and all priests misbegotten scoundrels—because if a religion can tolerate such a miscarriage of morality and still endure through the millennia, then surely it must be true! That is the same faith that invites Abraham to commit the most odious crime there is: it doesn't matter whether or not he commits it, only that he be *willing*. A man of true faith "must always be ready to sacrifice himself or to kill," or at the very least to allow himself to be killed, if that is what his faith tells him. Between killing (sacrifice) and allowing himself to be killed (martyrdom) there isn't really all that much of a difference, there is always someone who is brutally deprived of life in obedience to a supreme will, more or less the same thing that is demanded of a soldier in wartime. Faith cannot be anything other than obedience to a diktat: the minute you begin to examine the reasonable basis of that order, whether or not it corresponds to exterior criteria of justice or logic, well, by that point faith has already fled.

30. Ideological oversimplification is used by the learned specifically to feed to the ignorant.

31. The profane is the setting in which our lives unfold, the sacred is the very source of life. If life aspired to remain in the sacred where it originates, it would perish; if life depended exclusively upon the profane, it would never be born at all.

32. Goodness is concentrated, evil is diffuse.

33. If you take a given point or moment at random, on average you will find more bad than good; but if you choose certain areas, or individuals, or eras, or instants of life, or customs, or actions, or places, you will find there boundless deposits of goodness.

34. Some textbooks about war and books of history tell us that, in battle, the first ones to turn and run from the enemy are almost always the soldiers in the rear ranks, not the men in the front lines, who, for that matter, would be killed on the spot by the enemy if they did turn to run. The paradoxical corollaries of this observation, applicable to many fields and situations, are that the first to flee are the ones in the least immediate danger; and that the courage that circulates in the front lines is the fruit of the same spirit of self-preservation that guides the footsteps of the cowards in the rear lines.

35. I count religion but a childish toy, And hold there is no sin but ignorance (*it is a Machiavelli in the shape of a devil who expresses this maxim in the prologue to Marlowe's* The Jew of Malta).

36. The sacred is in fact the place or experience or activity in which there have been unreserved compromises, without any possible reconsideration. Now there is nothing more compromising than to give origin to a life or to put an end to one. To conceive or to kill.

37. The italian state: a monstrous and vulnerable system, an arbitrary and vindictive machine on the verge of openly avowed illegitimacy, but at that same time recklessly lax, a veritable administrative colander. Its laws often have the look and feel of offhanded reprisals. Since the state assumes that you want to defraud it, it goes ahead and defrauds you, even beating you to the draw, so now you have no option but to be even faster, and extract your handgun to defraud the state first, necessarily becoming, this time for real, the con man that the state first took you for. In other words, nobody cares whether the citizen is honest or dishonest: he is given the shakedown on the assumption that he's out to shake down others, so that in the end, what with the succession of reciprocal extortions (this must be the underlying reasoning) between state and individual, you wind up breaking even in the end.

39. Cursed be this entirely literary obsession with "the best of youth," that nucleus of untainted hopes and innocence: everyone convinced of course that it was theirs, the best of youth, the most luminous and courageous— the winged ideals, the "stupendous passion" . . .

40. Two quotes from saints about Italy's two capitals: "Milan fears gods but little, men not at all" (St. Ambrose) and "the Romans devour one another" (St. Jerome).

41. What a pain in the neck is the constant daily journalism exercise of anti-Italian rhetoric! As old as Noah's ark, embellished with a variety of contemptuous rhetorical flourishes. What a relentless annoyance, the refrain that we, poor we, "never had the Protestant Reformation"! Well, Germany had it, in fact, a German invented it, that Protestant Reformation, and the starry sky overhead and the moral law below—and yet how the Germans waved their arms, tossing flowers at the SS troops marching past! Whereas we . . . ancient, dating back to time out of mind, but still too recent; decadent for centuries now but still spoiled rotten by the economic boom and terrorized by the recession; overloaded with culture, every sort of culture, especially the kind that can be transformed in a single night from "ruin" into "rubble"—and yet deeply ignorant, the true donkeys of Europe, the last in the class, with a university system worse than anything you can find in the Third World, overtaken even by countries with mass starvation, where the women go around with their heads covered; illiterates poisoned by a steady overdose of TV; eloquent and aphasic; with the complex of the dominators and the vices of the dominated; cheerful and "*simpatici*" but at the same time afflicted by a continual regret, moaning in a lament that never seems to come to an end . . .

42. The chief characteristic of the hero is certainly not purity, if anything *im*purity, bound up with the violence that he exercises and by which he is contaminated. There may be knights, free of fear, but there are none, absolutely none, free of sin.

43. There are demented stories that, as you tell them, the more you exaggerate, the closer you come to the truth. Normally it is best to beware of overemphasis. Anyone who has a great deal to say tells a great number of lies. But only with demented stories can you begin to understand demented situations, embrace them, even if only to get them as far from you as possible.

44. Heroic characters who draw their bow to the quavering utmost, horses racing at a full gallop, towers set atop the highest walls, clashes between armies with glittering suits of armor—sabotage, reprisals, ambushes, looting and plunder, summary executions. You can fool yourself into thinking that war is the former—but it almost always winds up turning out more like the latter.

47. The hero is a dead man walking, who has taken a vow to death, wedded to it, without death a widower, a blind man. He is a prince straddling two realms, alive among the dead who march in their serried ranks, already deceased and yet present, like El Cid, riding at the head of his armies. Temporal continuity and spatial contiguity between the dead and the living. But the confusion engendered by the indiscriminate cult of death at a time when no one knows any longer what death even is ensures that nowadays we call a "hero" and celebrate as such any person who has fallen, even if he performed no memorable deeds of any kind. The title then is awarded to those who ought more properly to be described as victims.

48. To write books about the faults of the Italians, against the Italians, to show just what fools the Italians are, how corrupt, what scoundrels, how cowardly and shameless they really are, has always been and becomes constantly more fashionable, to the point that it has given rise to a full-fledged literary genre or tradition, with shelves dedicated to the category in every bookstore. Those who specialize in this category are sharp-eyed, disenchanted journalists, reasonably good stylists, tireless collectors of stories of turpitude from judicial sources, as well as historical and literary authorities, great writers of the past and politicians embittered by the realization that every effort to redeem the Italians seems to have been in vain. Using doses of indignation alternating with or blended with humor and satire, they plunge their hands into the abundance of materials within reach of anyone who wishes to demonstrate that this people cannot, will never be able to succeed, will never change, never discount its atrocious, sad, or ridiculous sins.

49. Whatever behavior the Italians might engage in, they target it for sarcasm or scorn: some particular custom meets with their disapproval, but then so does its diametric opposite: if the Italians save, it's because they are afraid of the future, they're mistrustful, they hide their money under their mattress; if the Italians squander their money and run up debts it's because they're slaves of the false myths of consumerism, corrupt and facile. They can be accused at the same time of cowardice and recklessness, of being terrified of the slightest risk and of living on the razor's edge. They scold them for having short memories and being flighty and superficial and, at the same time, of being chained to the past.

51. There is only one common enemy: weakness. And immediately following, two lukewarm virtues: prudence and patience. The seventies tried to be everything except for these three much hated things. No doubt, there was very little prudence or patience in circulation in those years, and very few practicing either quality. Weakness, since it cannot be uprooted from the souls of individuals, was more generally concealed, disguised, camouflaged, like a voice trying to avoid being recognized on the phone. Many of those who acted like tough guys in those years were trying to conceal something squeaky or neurotic in their character, overcome their weakness with swagger, blow themselves up, brace themselves . . . When they tried to raise their voices, what came out was a *falsetto*.

52. In Italy, apparently, it is only with violence and threats that the status quo can be defended and only with violence and threats that the status quo can be modified.

53. Not just demonstrations in the street, but also religious processions have, when you look carefully, a menacing tacit undertone. The faithful address their patron saint with an extortionate and impudent devotion: either you answer our prayers (send us the rain, erase our sins, free us from the cholera outbreak, etc.) or else you can forget about this nice festival, the votive candles, the chants, the flowers . . .

55. A country where every social issue becomes a criminal matter; and where every criminal act can be given a social explanation. An army that has more often been given the order to open fire on its own people, during demonstrations and strikes.

58. There are moments, historical phases, winters, springs, when *everyone* engages in political violence: demonstrators, reactionaries, revolutionaries, terrorists, the police, the Carabinieri, security forces, intelligence services, ordinary citizens, criminals, vigilantes by day and night.

59. A revolutionary blend: professionals of violence + dilettantes of violence + young men driven by fanaticism/idealism/romanticism/athletic spirit + poor intellectuals driven by resentment + rich intellectuals driven by esthetic scorn + the alienated, driven by alienation.

61. The quality of divinity, if exiled and repudiated, returns in the form of the demoniacal.

64. Certainly there is something stupid, but there might also be something profoundly noble, in stubbornly ignoring reality and holding it in contempt. Don't pay too much attention to reality, flying *over it* or running headlong *against it* are both attitudes worthy of a noble spirit.

65. The time that we ought to use for action, we waste on preparation.

70. If you want men to be eager to rush into war against each other, to spill rivers of blood, all you need to do is "capitalize words that mean nothing."

71. Enthusiasm and fanaticism go hand in hand. Only those who lack all enthusiasm are in no danger of becoming fanatics. It is said that the only ones who have a reasonably realistic view of life are the depressed, that is, those who have pathologically ceased to harbor any illusions about their state. When they wake up every morning, they see the world *the way it really is*, an unbearable vision, and that is why they're tempted to dive back under the covers and just never get out of bed, and so how are they supposed to believe, what are they supposed to hope for?

72. It is not possible that everyone forms all their own opinions, beliefs, and certainties, or even just the indispensable rules of behavior to live by; therefore, even the freest, most independent spirit ends up adopting, unevaluated, a vast number of precooked, received notions. While that is true, it is especially true in politics: the domain in which the greatest number of dogmas prosper and thrive. Even more so than in religions, which, by comparison with many political convictions, appear far more open, changeable, flexible, and infinitely less based upon precepts. There the truth is slippery and elusive.

73. In reality there is no contradiction between an authentic need of faith and its instrumentalization, in fact, these two things almost always go *together*.

74. Faith is real even when its object is false.

75. In religions, the instrumental aspect and authentic faith, the anxiety for salvation and the lack of scruples, holiness and the abominable, miracles and cheap tricks, fanatics and illumined visionaries and charlatans and real prophets and false prophets all get mixed up together, sometimes overlapping, that is, they are sometimes the same thing, and equally circumfused. The halo glows around the blessed head that emits a wafting aroma of holiness with the same light that exists only in the eyes of those who look at it as a splendid cult effect. The object of devotion and at the same time, an effect of *that same* devotion.

76. Of both politics and religion, only one thing is asked: redemption.

79. Purity cannot exist as innocence. If it did, then only the innocent would be pure. And the innocent don't exist. Not even the innocents in the "Massacre of the Innocents" were innocents, since they had borne the burden of sin from birth, or really we should say, it was birth itself that constituted their sin. It is coming into the world, per se, that is sin, and at the same time, sin's expiation. Instead of "In sorrow thou shalt bring forth children!" an angry God might just as well have shouted at Eve, "Thou shalt bring forth children!" and nothing more, since that was the punishment, to give birth and be born, to enter the world only to end up sliding down into the maw of death, Holy Scripture is quite clear on the point! The penalty to be served for the sin committed is, quite simply, life. But life the way it *really* is, once the veil of the Earthly Paradise has been rent asunder. That is, with pregnancies, diseases, old age . . . And so if that innocence is denied us from the very outset, it can only be obtained with forgetfulness and the various means available to attain that oblivion. By forgetting who you are, where you come from, in short, by forgetting your chains: denying that you were ever born.

80. When a childhood has been too happy and carefree, you drag it through your adolescence as a burden. One's past happiness is an intolerable weight to carry: what you've left behind your back becomes a monkey *on* your back. And a considerable portion of my current unhappiness as an adult and, I can imagine, soon enough, that even greater, if residual, unhappiness as an old man is due to the excessively great and powerful joy I once experienced, only to see it vanish.

81. During my adolescence I felt that nothing could protect me from my anguish. When it came, the black phantom wholly possessed me. A knot

blocked my throat, my heart rose until it kept me from breathing, I couldn't stop sighing incessantly, there were no more sounds around me, except for the dull roar of my blood, a muffled, fearsome silence descended over the room, I felt alternately hot and cold, my eyes filled with tears for no good reason, tears that couldn't seem to tumble out. I felt like crying and vomiting. I was clogged, saturated with grief. I went into the bathroom, but I couldn't do it. I knelt there, with my face hovering over the pot. Then I hugged myself in a disconsolate embrace. Everything appeared unfriendly, hostile. That's not right: everything appeared distant and pointless. Even that's not right: everything seemed ridiculous and nothing more. Finally, a few tears rolled down my cheeks, scalding them, burning them, my tears were boiling hot. The most terrible thing for me was that even amid the immense sorrow I remained aware that there was no reason in the world for me to feel like that. This endless sorrow had no cause. Nothing terrible had happened, at the very most some minor displeasure and sometimes not even that, and a black curtain descended over the day, time stopped, all my strength vanished at once, there was no longer enough energy to string one minute together with the minute that followed.

82. The principal element, the true protagonist and, at the same time, the internal enemy of Italian society and culture: rhetoric. It is on rhetoric and by rhetoric, making use of well-established, well-tested rhetoric or else inventing new variants, that politicians, journalists, and writers, make their living, in a so-to-speak professional manner, but so do industrialists and magistrates and factory workers and mothers and students and all the corporations and guilds that, like so many colorful swatches of cloth, make up the clothing of the nation. Politicians cannot dream of doing without rhetoric, and that is obvious, but neither can the journalists who criticize what those politicians do. The so-called man in the street, moreover, is usually a champion at rhetoric, especially if he is interviewed on television, a medium that either intimidates or amplifies the emphasis of those who express themselves on it. The Italian rhetorical tradition is unbeatable and pervasive: during the first half of the twentieth century it was by and large an appanage of the right wing (thunderous, pompous, turgid, hyperbolic to the verge of the purest surrealism), in the second half, on the other hand, it belonged to the left wing (menacing or whiny, depending on the topics discussed), and on a continuous basis, dusting everything with its fine haze, odorous of grief and goodness, we can turn to the rhetoric of Catholic origin. Thanks to the power of rhetoric, it becomes possible to say

everything: rhetoric does not hesitate in the face of falsehood, much less in the face of the truth, which it overwhelms and chops fine and blends and utilizes freely. You can be every bit as rhetorical when telling lies as speaking the truth: even when telling the truth, you can't always tell it stark and naked, the way it is, you can't help but garnish it with rhetoric, which means that you wind up being false even while you tell the truth: you falsify the truth to make sure that it's having the proper effect, perhaps because you don't have too much confidence in it, you believe that it's a petty, tawdry thing, that it's not enough, unless it is pumped up, reinforced, hammered, fired skyward, made to resonate like a clashing gong and flutter in the breeze like a flag. It's an instinct that's too strong: the writer and the journalist and the orator and the preacher, in Italy, even when they're right, when they're absolutely right, when they're right in a sacrosanct way, and their rightness would be more than sufficient to uphold their point of view, they can't help but bedeck it, armor it, impregnate it, and saturate it with rhetoric. The words of our language, so rich and so spectacular, are an irresistible temptation; and their prehensile syntax seems designed expressly to hook together and pile up as many as possible, as if trying to build a barricade around their own truth, to protect it, only ultimately concealing it, instead.

83. There are two rhetorics that are mirror images of each other and equivalent: the rhetoric of consensus and the rhetoric of dissent, since in a universe consisting of two opposing poles those who dissent from something automatically find themselves consenting to the opposite thing, so that it's immediately clear in which direction the contentious spirit is veering. For that matter, the various contenders know that it's a skirmish, a verbal entertainment at the end of which the victor will be determined only by measuring his skill at presenting his own arguments and attacking the arguments of others: in fields as complex as, for instance, the economy, economic meltdown, economic recovery, recipes for economic recovery, which are debated and discussed relentlessly on TV shows, who among the spectators and home audience is going to be capable of evaluating the arguments on their own merits, independently, that is, of the persuasiveness of their patter, their confidence, the impression they give off of being perfectly at their ease? *Almost* no one, I'm afraid, or perhaps no one *at all*. I certainly wouldn't be able to. I'm the classic case of someone who understands *nothing* and makes up his mind strictly based on likability, obnoxiousness, or partisan affiliation—the true pillars of my ethical convictions.

84. Usually, people speak of Italy as the land of illegality. A place where laws are constantly being broken. Probably that's true, I can't deny it. And yet I can't help but be astonished at how seldom it actually happens. How rarely, that is, anyone actually violates a rule, even in a country as disrespectful and inclined toward the illicit shortcut as is ours. Perhaps because it happens in an automatic and almost unconscious manner, we have a hard time realizing the enormous number of rules and regulations that we do observe, I'm not even saying every day, but every hour, perhaps every minute of our passing lives. For one single rule that we might be breaking, in fact, there are ten others that we have obeyed, or even a hundred, without even noticing it. I'm talking about every sort of law: from traffic regulations to conventional greetings, standards of hygiene, the most unremarkable prescriptions about how we walk, look, eat, breathe, speak, add and subtract, and even the rules of any sport or profession. In fact, when we make love, we're respecting certain procedures. This virtually constant obedience is much, much less visible than the episodic infraction: we have incorporated the routine in our lives to such an extent that we forget how extraordinary and unnatural it is. Our default setting, it turns out, is actually to walk the straight and narrow, and in comparison the transgression stands out as an event. That is why I'm astonished that every time I'm stopped at a red light and there is no one coming from either direction, all the cars and motorcycles don't simply take off at top speed, given that the red light at that point is superfluous; I'm amazed that every evening ninety-nine convicts out of a hundred on a day pass return tamely to prison after spending the day out, whether it's on a furlough or because they're on partial liberty; I'm amazed that adultery isn't a frantic, everyday practice; I am stunned that the blond lady I see crossing the street, there, isn't immediately robbed of her purse and jewelry. Could it be that out of the hundred people she crosses paths with, there isn't one, I say, not *one*, who thinks of doing it, and then does it? How many blond women with purses and fine embellishments *weren't* robbed today? Shouldn't that statistic be much more surprising than the ultimately trifling number of successful purse snatchings? And this, in fact, even in Italy, where it seems as if everyone does exactly as they please and obeys nobody and nothing. Anarchists and individualists and heretics that we think we *are* but actually *aren't*. Even in Italy, autopilot for the most part steers individuals away from transgression; not out of goodness, or because anyone is convinced of the justice of the laws that they are respecting; just out of sheer self-preservation. Transgressing, over the long run or even the short run, always causes much more trouble than does obedience. Crimes subversion and madness are, in other words, relatively rare things: most of the time we conform, we adapt, we

submit to laws written and unwritten, we comply with codes that tell us, Do this! Don't do that! at furious pace, even if we hardly notice it.

87. We should investigate precisely what strikes us as already familiar and well known—known to the many, and even to those who gird themselves to investigate. Instead, it isn't even slightly well known. We know much less than we think we do. In that which we consider super familiar, and even obvious, discounted, the most interesting mysteries lie concealed. Deceived by its smirking familiarity, it is in ordinary life that we can handle the unknown.

88. If we suppose that man is reasonable, that is, endowed by nature with reason, then by becoming reasonable and behaving reasonably, he achieves no progress, accomplishes nothing noteworthy.

90. What holds a community together is what is taken for granted in it. What there is no need to argue about, what was discussed and agreed upon once and for all in the very act of founding the community, and which it is assumed will last long enough before having to go back over it and reexamine it. But when *nothing* is taken for granted, then nothing holds that community together anymore. The parliament, understood as a debate over ideas, is not allowed to call *everything* into discussion. Free opinions can be exercised from time to time on a given topic, but not on all topics simultaneously: that would be the equivalent of having the ground give way beneath your feet during an earthquake. The very field upon which the social structure was founded would no longer exist: its surface ravaged, its perimeter shaken, rendered indistinct. For that reason, a community cannot rise, prosper, and preserve itself on the basis of critical thought, which, by definition, takes *nothing* for granted. And that is why in any human community, those who exercise critical thought without setting aside some topics are viewed askance or considered a certain concern, if not with outright hostility. A human society is not based on doubt. It can be enlivened by doubts, provided they do not undermine it as a whole.

92. People say that social relations are underpinned by a supposed contract, but who's ever seen it, who's signed this contract? Of all the social pacts and contracts hypothesized by political philosophers, who are the actual parties to the agreement? Where is the populace, where does it live,

what is it called? Where are their signatures, the dates, the embossed validation stamps?

93. Modernity is the era in which prophets are false prophets. All equally false. Typical of the modern era are both those who believe blindly in false prophets and those who unceremoniously unmask them.

95. Why is it, I ask myself, dispassionately, when analyzed closely and rationally, that fascism always appears so ridiculous? Grandiose, perhaps, or terrible or sometimes tragic, even admirable, but always and inevitably ridiculous. Every time you are left agog, stunned, as you read through accounts, watch footage, listen to speeches. You are inevitably driven to parody what you see, as if it were, however, the conscious and mocking basis of that parody. It hardly seems possible that what stirred so many illusions and such vast tragedies, what drove hearts and clubs and daggers and hand grenades and, finally, tanks, could have been such a piece of *buffoonery*. No, that can't be. And yet, yes, it *can* be, it *is* possible, it was possible, and perhaps it always will be. Which means that it is the emergence of fascism into the light of reason, its discovery or revelation or extraction from the concrete material of historical action, to be scrutinized by measured reflection and critical analysis, it is precisely this cognitive process that alters its essence, that transfigures it, reducing it to that sideshow skeleton, good only for eliciting shrieks of fright and bawdy laughter. Like a fish of the abyss that loses its mysterious luminosity if brought to the surface, where it resembles nothing so much as a pathetic little monster. Was that miserable object really what aroused such fear, what triggered such delirious excitement? All that remains of the tragedy and the epic are little heaps of cinders, and what little survives has the general tenor of a stage set after the show is over: painted trees, cardboard swords, plaster chickens. After a thousand books on the topic, fascism remains mysterious. Mysterious in what is most evident, in its essence, which so stunningly coincides with its ostentatious appearance. Exactly the opposite of communism (which is always as duplicitous and Machiavellian in its practices as it is crude and monolithic in its principles), fascism is exactly what it seems: explicit, manifest, proclaimed, and yet incomprehensible. Perhaps certain aspects of our lives are destined to remain unknown, or else known but not understood, since knowledge, in fact, with its ascensional and reductive movement, can only transform its discoveries into the objects of mockery.

Knowledge, in other words, does nothing to the subconscious by dint of knowing it, neither alters it nor unlocks it, at the very most, it destroys it, rationalizes it to the point of making it a skeleton of its former self. The most extraordinary characteristic of fascism remains the fact that it is a subconscious that has been everted and exhibited, transformed into a thunderous voice, into an enameled surface . . . *Knowing* doesn't matter, *modifying* matters: and the modifications take place in a mysterious fashion.

96. In vain the attempt was made to combat it. I mean to say, with means other than weapons, which, when the time came, proved effective. But it was hopeless to try to fight it with ideas or words! That would amount to so much wasted time. Fascism is what by its very nature cannot be subjected to criticism. Its shadow cannot be illuminated, and in fact, if it ever is, it simply vanishes. Since a place of such a nature that it remains wholly impermeable to knowledge or the calling into question or discussion does not exist (just think, not even God could make such a claim!), it is invented instead out of whole cloth, and this is, no doubt, a brilliant move, and only intellectuals could ever have thought of such a thing, only people capable of formidable abstractions but also endowed with the common touch, a little like Giotto's frescoes and the invention of Pinocchio. The whole history of Italian intellectuals can be summarized in the perverse pleasure taken by such a subtle and skeptical mind as Leo Longanesi's in inventing the slogan "Mussolini is always right." Not since the time of Zeno and his unbeatable tortoises had such a self-sufficient, well-rounded, one-dimensional paradox been created! Like the logical brainteaser of the phrase "I am lying." When reason has a hard time keeping up with rapid change and the world around you begins to waver and shimmer, then what's needed is an act, an invention. A brilliant intuition. While all of European science oscillated in the cloud of probability, and even the pope could feel the fullness of the divine mandate trembling in his hands, and the pillars upon which the weight of the world rested were starting to crumble, in that chaos of incredulity and skepticism, certain Italian literati were able to restore a modicum of certainty! Even Luigi Pirandello with his sophisms, his "maybe like this, maybe like that," and the various contortions about identity and doubts about who is who and who did what, even Pirandello, more skeptical than Gorgias and more of a Taoist than Zhuangzi, who dreams of being a butterfly who dreams of being Zhuangzi . . . even for Pirandello, one certainty existed: MUSSOLINI IS ALWAYS RIGHT!

97. Pointless to scold fascism because it refused to submit to analysis, because it refused to behave in accordance with the categories so dear to its critics, who therefore denounced it as guilty of irrationalism. Irrationalism is no vice, it is something of which fascism boasts. And fascism is not even guilty of irrationalism, when you stop to think, but rather a singular form of mystical materialism, a roughhousing spiritualism, a proteiform entity that can get the better of its adversary because it's capable of commandeering its appearance and stealing its strength, adding it to its own, and turning it in a different direction. If what is normally emphasized in fascism is its sectarian spirit, its rigidity, the extremist purity that demands the elimination of all impurity, the cult of the healthy body that shakes off of itself all contaminating elements (foreigns, blacks, Jews, Communists, renegades, draft dodgers, etc.), what I instead see from the very outset is an extraordinary and eclectic collection of contradictory attitudes and fragments of disparate doctrines, a mimetic fury that is by no means exclusive, quite the contrary, in fact, a reckless and paradoxical attempt to be at once reactionary and revolutionary, men of order and of disorder, of the right and of the left, defenders of the bourgeois and the antibourgeois, traditionalists and extremely modern, profoundly Catholic and ferociously, Nietzscheanly anti-Christian, ascetics and yet men of action, proponents of vitality above all other values and at the same time prophets of death, fans of death, wooers and courters of death, in other words, everything that it is possible to think and do as long as it is all fused together into a single lunge of vitality. The subconscious is a machine that cannot help but produce. Consider Pierre Drieu La Rochelle's diary, in which he says a thousand times that he is a Fascist but that he wants to become a Communist, to be bourgeois, or perhaps the only aristocrat still in circulation, and at the same time an aesthete, a shut-in, and an implacable man of action and a mystic and ascetic, but also as simple and pure as was the French peasant of bygone days, an impotent seducer, a refined barbarian, a hard-living saint, in other words everything, but absolutely *everything*, in a savage all-inclusive ambition, provided that this frenzy finds an adequately aggressive, insolent expression, capable of astounding, seducing, frightening . . . Fascism doesn't explain itself but it functions, it functions as long as it functions, like an animal before it falls ill or is killed. It's not only praise of the body, it is a body itself, whose life cycle almost always coincides with the life cycle of its Duce's body.

98. More than on the purely political plane, where it hybridizes watchwords of disparate origin, Fascist ideology, or perhaps we should say the

distinctive and unmistakable flavor of fascism, can be found in its purest state in the writings of a philosophical or mystical nature, when they explore such archetypical or abyssal subjects as sex, destiny, honor, courage, the rise and decline of civilizations, the metaphysical tradition, the Oblivion of Being, race, and death. More than dealing with the forms of state or government, issues that he willingly leaves in the hands of jurists, on these fatal themes, the Fascist truly has something to say and, above all, a distinctive way of saying it, suddenly soaring high above the political arena, where he is always forced to take borrowings from and crossbreed in hasty fashion with the languages of the other traditions, socialist, nationalist, anarchist, grassroots activist, accentuating now one now the other aspect in accordance with contingencies and needs, as did the Fascist movement's original opportunistic founder. As it swerves and fishtails from right to left, a celebration of absolute modernity and a religious cult of the past, revolution and reaction, so that it's never clear what its activism aims at (whether, for example, to overthrow the bourgeoisie or stand as a mighty bulwark in its defense), Fascist thought moves at greater ease in the spiritual dominion of metaphysics, erudition, the philosophical polemic, and therefore in the field of the symbolic. And in fact, the Fascist doctrine isn't—or it isn't *only*—a political doctrine, but rather a declension of symbolic thought. It interprets the world in accordance with a specific reading and it tends to express itself through symbols, or rather, it wouldn't be capable of expressing itself in any manner other than through symbols. Hence the cause of its attraction to more erudite repertories, the inexhaustible mines of the history of religions, the mysteries of esotericism.

99. And since everything that you desire is real, real even if it doesn't exist outside of your desires, so fascism can be real even when it lies, in fact, especially when it lies, because its falsehood is a real desire. The same can be said of the hatred that engenders it, that engenders fascism and that, in its turn, is engendered by fascism. Desire doesn't spring from the absence of something but, quite to the contrary, from its presence, even if that is in the form of an image, a phantom, which is as real as all the rest. The production of phantoms and specters by the Fascist machine is stunning . . . a love of truth obliges us to say that no one could ever have complained about being deprived of phantoms during the two decades of Italian fascism, the *Ventennio*, and even more so in the aftermath of the war, right up to the present day, and today more so than ever. The masses that it stirred by exalting them were by no means deceived, what they desired they obtained,

exactly what they desired, and in great abundance. Did they want excitement and death? They got them. Like those who dabble in S&M games, it would just be childish to get scandalized afterward if every so often someone wound up choking themselves to death while hog-tied. You can only smile pityingly at those, some of them respected intellectuals, others ordinary citizens, who declare that they were "disappointed" by fascism, that is, that they would have liked it to be more leftist, or even more ferociously rightist, Hitlerian, Stalinian, less plebeian and vulgar or less bourgeois and sanctimonious, more anticlerical or Mussolinian or grassroots-driven or social or mystical or aristocratic or racist, or maybe they wanted it to be nonracist ("Yeah, after all, that's the one mistake that M. really made . . ."), in other words, that they would have preferred it to be like this or like that . . . Since it's a recipe with many ingredients, some of which can be alternated with each other, or used in variable quantities, the result is that everyone can cook their own fascism for themselves in their own mind, removing or adding at their pleasure anarchism or eugenics, charisma or the Middle Ages, to taste.

102. When it comes to concrete matters, political and religious movements veer so sharply away from the ideas of their founders that they can be fought by making use of quotes from those same founders. And so people are able to denounce Christianity and the Church in the name of Jesus, and His "authentic message"; ditto for historical communism, with verbatim quotations from Marx; while select passages from Nietzsche are used against the philosopher's most fanatical followers. It is natural that this should take place within the context of ideologies sufficiently vast or contradictory to give rise, within their own confines or in the course of their larger spread and diffusion, varying practices and even ones that are entirely at odds with each other; just as there can be no doubt that the fringe groups that have moved farthest away from initial principles, almost to the point where you'd say they'd turned them on their heads, would simply never have existed without those principles, from which they undoubtedly first took their inspiration. That the inspiration might have been perverted is something intrinsic to the very nature of all inspiration: it is, in fact, the way that all theories have of modifying and updating themselves, thus giving rise to entirely new ideas, over time and space, that is, throughout the course of history and in the specific locations around the world where they have been accepted and applied; as well as, to use the words of the philosopher in question, the apparent decay that takes place in the passage from

ideal purity to concrete implementation which responds to no other necessity than that of "no longer [burying] your head in the sand of heavenly things, but [carrying] it freely, an earthly head which gives meaning to the earth!" The meaning of the earth will be very different then from that imagined with eyes closed, head buried in heavenly sand . . . and no farther from the truth than its ideal formulation would have been.

103. The most current and clamorous example of this multiplicity is to be found in Islam, when, that is, verses of the Qur'an are cited to condemn acts committed in the name of the Qur'an.

104. The generic idea of brotherhood or fraternity (Enlightenment), but also the more concrete idea of neighbor (Jesus), seems to ignore or put little stock in the fact that it is in fact proximity that most engenders hatred, and that discord and rivalry among equals can push humans to persecution and to murder. It is not the Other, the one who is different, but rather the one who is most similar who unleashes conflict. So it always has been from the most remote and mythical origins, and it still functions in that exact way. It is your next-door neighbor who drives you crazy with his dog that barks the whole night through, not an Aboriginal in far-off Australia. As always, Jesus with His precepts seems to announce the obvious, what's taken for granted, while His teachings remain that much more daring and provocative, wrapped as they are in that quasi-childishness: He knows perfectly well that you hate your next-door neighbor and that you'd gladly hang him from the highest tree, and so He orders you to love him. He never talks about the grand clashes between nations, but rather of the small and incessant conflict that is unleashed on a daily basis in a few dozen square feet: the room where brothers sleep, the boundary of a field of alfalfa. To say "Love thy neighbor" actually means "Love who you detest."

105. Being-close, that is, being-neighbors is the foundation upon which hatred is built and where it flourishes.

106. Hatred is by no means turned against those who are different, but rather against the dangerously similar: the anti-Semitism of Drieu la Rochelle is never turned against the bearded man with long curls and a fur hat, but rather against men of letters and journalists like him, whom he encounters in restaurants . . .

107. Hatred isn't a reaction to something, it's a basic need.

108. The nightmare of acquaintances: exactly who are my acquaintances, *really*? And if I've known them for a long time but in reality I frequent them only sporadically, running into them by chance or obligation, is that because, deep down, they get on my nerves? Otherwise, why haven't they become my friends, genuine friends? And why, instead of "acquaintances," aren't they called, as would be more logical, "acquainteds"?

111. The doctrine of "But we didn't know" ought to be replaced with the admission "We knew everything, but we just didn't want to acknowledge what was obvious."

114. Political ideologies are not perfect doctrines rationally conceived for the good of humanity, even if they more often than not choose to present themselves as such. They are, instead, formations of struggle that have emerged from hostility and resentment, in periods of crisis, where what counts most are enthusiasm and anger.

115. Contradiction in the morality of strength, in the figure of the warrior. He is invoked as the defender of society and tradition, whereas he is actually their disintegrator. There is nothing more savage and ungovernable than a warrior, caught in the purity of his one exclusive deed, namely, killing. His essence is found in devastation, certainly not in preservation. *Marte* (Italian for the god Mars) means nothing other than *Morte* (Italian for "death"). The same thing happens in Latin, *Mars* and *Mors*. Similarly in English, "martial" and "mortal." And in all herculean figures, that is, those figures characterized by the use of force, force itself knows no limits, nor any preset use that can be called in advance either good or bad; it is nameless and directionless; it can be used to alleviate the destiny of humans, in beneficial undertakings, as well as to commit horrible and senseless massacres. The warrior is always impure, always bloodstained, and often the blood in question is the blood of innocents. The hero kills not only dangerous monsters who threaten the helpless, but also the helpless themselves, defenseless women and children and men, or even his own family, in the throes of the same blindness that allows him to hurl himself against his enemies and destroy them. It would just be too easy if you could put force on a leash! Like any other superhuman energy, just like birth, death, and

love, the warrior fury defies regulation, and when it submits to it, that means that in its turn it has taken on the character of a brutal vendetta. The guilty are slaughtered by others every bit as guilty. The warrior is a crazy horse who yearns to die; his chivalrous morality inclines him to gratuitous violence: how could he be the defender of a moderate and stable society? He is one only to the extent that he is *instrumentalized*.

116. Heroic initiatory separation from the family, from one's home: it was necessary to leave and stay away for years in order to become men. Today the hero can do nothing other than return home, otherwise, where would he go?

118. Aside from a few old-school gentlemen's clubs, deep down the Catholic priesthood is nothing more than the last of those strictly male clubs which, until not all that many decades ago, loomed like fortresses, like control towers on the horizon of our society. Male separation formed not one but many untouchable Mount Athoses, in the army, in academia, in finance, in government. They've all been dissolved except for the priesthood. Who knows how much longer this communitarian model based on exclusion can hope to endure.

119. To me, the subjugated should not be exempted from criticism for the simple fact that they have been subjugated, indeed, this is the first criticism that ought to be directed toward them. And the last, it's high time they stopped lazing around comfortably in the evangelical promise that they are going to be the first.

120. As boys, forging our identity in the fire of the cruelty of others or, even worse, of false friendship, or the false willingness of some adult or other, right there and willing to help you, to reach out a hand, but only in order to lead you where *he* wants you to go. Therefore, either you succumb to wickedness or you resist it by finding every bit as much grit and wickedness inside you, or else you let yourself by seduced by advisers with ulterior motives, until you start thinking things that you believe are your own, your own convictions, your own hopes, your own plans but which aren't in fact yours at all, but most of all you start to hate someone whom or something which your adviser had been trying to turn you against from the very outset. The chief characteristic of the bad adviser is his sweetness, his kindness.

THE CATHOLIC SCHOOL 1155

In the midst of so many wild beasts it starts to become natural to listen to him, entrust yourself to him.

121. The private school where I taught for so many years housed a male contingent who combined the privilege of their birth into well-to-do families with a solid education capable of preparing them for a position of prominence in the adult world. All of that tempered by a catechism that, on paper, preached almost the exact opposite. It is a singular characteristic of Italian Catholicism that it carries forward an age-old tradition of defending the last and the least while, at the same time, allying itself with the worldly interests of the first and the highest. Perhaps this contradiction lies at the basis of its grandeur and its solidity. But it can't really escape anyone's notice, and the first ones whose notice it didn't escape were in fact the lucky enrollees: my students.

122. If you stop to think about it, the fact that someone might harbor a baseless fear, however ridiculous it might seem, is always better than being frightened for good and solid reasons. Even if they wear at our nerves, false alarms should be preferred to the ones that precede a genuine bombing raid. This is from the point of view of cold hard reality. From the point of view of our feelings, well, it's very different, given that we can even feel a certain sense of relief when the worst does happen, when after so many groundless worries, an authentic disaster looms on the horizon, when we stop by to pick up the medical exams we undergo periodically for routine prevention, and the values that for years had come back normal are suddenly all over the place. Damn it, but also, hooray! At last! These tragic reports are a form of reparation, at least making us appear less ridiculous to the eyes of those who have always considered our worries to be overblown— worries that we, first and foremost, had always been a little ashamed of— finally making our fear respectable, as it should be, always and in any case.

123. If you want to obtain recognition, you have to give something in exchange: even your life, in exchange for a word, a medal, a caress . . .

124. Some feelings are original, others are derived, but they are not for that reason any less powerful or lasting, if anything, more so. Italians are accustomed to taking their courage from anger, which can also rapidly vanish, but only after bringing to light a formidable audacity. The sentimental

and personal side is so sharply accentuated that for many, in the final analysis, it becomes more important to take revenge than to win. Private passions get the better of public ones, or else they are converted into them, triumphing in the form of civic attitudes. Internal revolts do not cease to be what they are merely because they march behind a flag, and the same is true of resentment and ambition. Scratch the surface of any public statement you care to choose, and scant fractions of an inch beneath the scab of logical reasoning and a general motivation, you will find the maggot that was burrowing into the speaker. Often, there's really no need to even scratch!

127. There's a proverb that says: a holy place never remains empty. Perhaps it's even more credible that an empty place sooner or later becomes holy. If material appetites overlook it for a long time, it's destined to be occupied by holiness. Holiness and emptiness and silence and absence (of humanity, words, and signs) are by now synonymous. Thus, for example, by now the few square miles of the Italian landscape that haven't been thoroughly ransacked are holy: they weren't at first, often they were just barren and inhospitable places with no real significance (that's why they were spared: they offered nothing to exploit), but now they are. Paradox would have it that the most beautiful places, overrun and captured on account of their beauty, are now the most frightening, the most horrible.

132. Homosexuality (whether latent, open, or repressed) is at the basis of immense cultural and political groundswells, from Neoclassicism to Nazism, from the Renaissance to Fashion, from the myth of the uncorrupted child to Catholic schools to the Spartan army, from attending gyms to civil rights.

133. There was a sect whose leader had announced that the world was about to be destroyed by flying saucers. The date announced for the end of the world came and went. Nothing happened. After the leader's prophecy was shown to be wrong, the number of proselytes joining the sect, instead of declining, increased.

134. Many people who have been deceived continue to believe in the deception they fell for. Not even the most massive batch of evidence can undercut your faith in a lie, if it's a true faith. Let's take religious relics: even if they weren't authentic, the fact that they have been venerated for so long and with such faith is enough to make them sacred.

137. They say that misfortune is a good school: perhaps. But happiness is the best university (*quote from a letter from Pushkin to his wife, Natalia, March 1834*).

138. Instinctive annoyance toward what is "too close," fascination with what is "moderately distant," fear toward the "absolutely remote."

139. I realize, now that I am about to die, that I can no longer stand it when people come talk to me or argue with me about anything serious or grave. Nor can I stand to listen to them on television or read them. I prefer the sound of words to have little meaning or none at all, and do nothing more than remind me what the human voice is like, and not the concepts that it utters. In certain cases, perhaps in nearly all, it is pious and just to speak without saying anything.

142. However far back you may be able to venture with your memory and forward with your hopes, and however much you may be able thus to move along the axis of time, the present is not easily stripped of its immense power of attraction.

143. Ideas should always be developed to the full extent of their range, out of a curiosity to see where they lead us, and to discover that the most interesting ones lead to a dead point, while those which at first seem less brilliant have greater possibilities of leading to a genuine revelation. You can only run into a genuine revelation along the way, or near the end point, while many naïvely believe that that's the starting point.

145. The more dismal the life we actually lead, the greater the alluring distinction between ours and the life we're convinced we have every right to live. The dreary realism of everyday existence serves as a propellant for our fantasy lives, the products of which are entered into the ledger of not only possible things, but things that are due us, things that sooner or later we will attain, once we have removed the temporary stumbling blocks.

146. First they fired their guns and then, depending on what they had hit, they would say that that was the target.

147. Prisoners of heuristics: which presupposes that there is a meaning to every individual thing just as to the whole, and that you can, indeed that

you *must* find it. And what if there is no meaning? What if no meaning ever existed? If we no longer had any obligation to seek it out, then what would become our duty?

149. Ability, confidence, brilliance—all deployed for the creation and diffusion of garbage. That is the way the lion's share of talent is invested. Since technical skills are in and of themselves praiseworthy, independent of the field in which they're applied and the ends to which they're put, you will often hear people say that this or that person is "outstanding," "truly at the top of their game," or "a serious professional," that they're "freaks of nature," because in point of fact they show great ability at their trades, they tend to complete their projects successfully—something that, all things considered, could also be said of Jack the Ripper and Adolf Eichmann. Dominated as we are, even in the domain of our imagination, by the considerations of success, efficiency, and productivity as applied to every walk of life, we wind up admiring anything that has been "well done," "accomplished." But if at a certain point you grow impatient and blurt out that a certain person is a "genuine piece of shit," both because of who and what they are and because of the things they produce—be they TV programs or buildings or clothing or songs or newspaper articles or TV commercials— all too often the response is the disarming argument, "Hey now, the one thing you can't say is that they're stupid!"

151. Adolescence is the period during which we are most acutely incapable of recognizing an all-too-simple principle, namely that our actions and our thoughts aren't actually tremendously and wonderfully *unique*, but instead ordinary, all too common. But then, perhaps, we might say the same thing of adults and even old people, as well as every other intermediate phase that goes to make up existence. After all, life is made up of passages, intervals, crossings, so that we never occupy a sufficiently solid position to be able to judge all the rest objectively: they strike us as obstacles and battles, but if that's what they seem, then that's what they really are.

153. What an enormous waste of intelligence there is, both in understanding and in refusing to understand.

154. Those who love humanity with an abstract love almost always love only themselves.

155. Like in the first century in ancient Rome, likewise in the years I've been assigned to live in, so many illogical faiths teem throughout society, populating the world with demons, deceiving enormous masses of people about the imminent advent of portentous new developments, promising this and threatening that and brandishing evocative enchantments, so that many naïve people were defrauded by the false prophets and charismatic leaders who were propagandizing these ideas. Unlike in ancient times, when cultivated souls were able to withstand the spread of these lies, really suitable only for fools and the illiterate, in the contemporary era many intelligent and learned people, variously intellectuals, philosophers, writers, artists, and scientists, instead of taking care not to be deceived by these fairy tales, quite to the contrary, chose to pay them heed, embracing them as if blinded and preaching them with an even greater enthusiasm than that manifested by the ignorant, thus contributing to the credibility of the most deluded illusory ideas with the force of their intellect and the arguments of their culture. Culture served in any case not to give these lies a proper critical examination but only to reinforce them with lines of reasoning as defective as they were convincing: intelligence used its resources to elevate nonsensical persiflage to the status of theories, and its arrogance to defend them against any objections.

156. I've come to the conclusion that the Trojan War was really fought to take back Helen. It wasn't about commercial hegemony! She was the reason, just as the myth tells us, and in fact mythology always tells the truth, and may occasionally be even more realistic than history.

157. Even many years later, after reading many books and doing much hard thinking, I'm still stuck with the impression I had as a boy, perhaps unfounded but very powerful, namely that the Greeks produced far greater depth and meaning in their mythology than with all their renowned philosophy. I'm not talking about mere beauty of language. I'm referring to an intellectual contribution, an effort at the interpretation of the meaning of life, the depth and originality of a view of the world. The fact that the stories in question are fairy tales does nothing to undercut their meaning; if anything it enhances it. Further evidence supporting this view is the fact that the most relentless detractor of the ancient myths and their bard, Homer, should never have done anything other to illustrate his theories than to come up with new myths, and that is how he is remembered, starting

in classrooms: the Myth of the Cave, the Myth of the Androgyne, the Myth of the Horses That Pull in Irreconcilable Directions: which frankly strikes me as fairly improbable . . . drab . . . their images, peregrine . . . when compared with ancient myths. Unless, that is, we are to consider philosophy itself as something not so much as a break with the mythical vision, but rather its mere continuation, sparer, more faded, bureaucratic, specialized, sterilized with respect to the carefree overabundance of the origins.

158. For some individuals, only violent action can wholly restore the sentiment of freedom: it is at that point that the sexual impulse and the political frenzy converge (*here it seems unmistakable that he is referring to the perpetrators of the CR/M*).

159. Nowadays, in our horror to see either of the contenders annihilated, we intervene to counterbalance the outcome of any battle. Thus, wars without victors go on endlessly.

160a. The law, reduced to a scarecrow, instead of sowing terror, becomes something familiar and habitual, so that the crows use it as a perch.

160b. The law, reduced to a scarecrow, upon which, through habit, by no means frightened, the crows use it to perch upon (*this thought is formulated twice in a row in the notebook and I have decided to transcribe both versions, imagining that my teacher couldn't make up his mind, and seeing in his indecision a great deal of his personality, perfectionist and, at the same time, open to possibility*).

161. Power engenders pleasure, limits it, represses it, negates it, exalts it, and sometimes is instead exalted or erased entirely by pleasure. Both those who exercise power and those who are overwhelmed by it can experience one of these positions in the relationship of pleasure. There was a time when these warps and wefts had a place in which they could be woven into a story, in fact, to be exact, two places: one private, the confession booth, the other public, the novel. The novel is nothing more or less than the commercialized transcription of the confession, and for that reason, it so often preserves the same formal aspect as the original: which is to say, in its continued use of the first person singular.

162. The experience of grief and pain and the indelible memory that accompanies that experience constitute the principal barrier thrown up to hinder the flow of life: only a truly rampaging narrative, only a genuinely impetuous flow of words can sweep away such a stubborn obstacle and reopen the path that leads to a happy state of forgetfulness. It is in this that the essence and the function of the confession and of the novel coincide.

164. Unlike stories, ideas have no end. In reality, even stories should never come to an end, except that at a certain point in the course of them, the storyteller simply stops telling them. But where, exactly? And why? Because the storyteller decides that she has said all that she had to say. But that's really not true. Every drama could easily be followed by another, further drama, and each generation could be followed by the one that replaces it. You can always write a sequel. Conventionally, the end of the adventures are made to coincide with the end of their protagonist. When Hercules dies, his skin flayed by the famous shirt, that death puts an end to the Labors of Hercules. And the movie ends with Carlito Brigante in his death throes on the train platform, putting a final end to his flight, which is the same thing that happened to Accattone and Macbeth, the Consul Firmin and Martin Eden, Michel Poiccard in *Breathless*, Bluebeard, and Anna Karenina. Or else it might be a wedding that spells the end of the story, that is, a good point to draw the moral of the story, or the number of pages that can easily be printed without crushing the reader under their weight. Ideas come to an end only when the thinker is worn out.

165. What renders adolescence unique and inimitable, giving it its original and vital spirit, is by no means the thing about it that is strongest and best able to withstand the passage of time, but rather that which is destroyed by that passage of time. The most precious qualities are bound up with fragility, its precarious nature: the recondite meaning of things is concealed in their transitory nature. You'll never understand a thing if you stubbornly insist on seeking out *that which lasts*, that which endures and does not wither away; if you're at all capable, watch and seek, rather, that which sooner or later *vanishes*. Adolescence is no exception to this rule, if anything its first and more precocious application: in fact, adolescence is exactly *that which is eventually dissipated*. Its principle resides not in that which continues to live, but rather in that which is destined irremediably,

naturally to perish. (I once thought this, while observing my students, and now I think it while remembering them.)

167. For a sociologist, mediocre literature is always more interesting than fine literature, which is less representative of the times, of society, of common thought.

168. I've long observed my best students, which is to say, those with the greatest natural gifts and those who show the greatest application and determination, two heterogeneous categories that, in fact, are almost the opposites of each other, but which often produce similar academic results and therefore might as well be considered as a single whole.

Well, I have noticed that in excessively reasonable behaviors the embers of rebellion are always there, ready to leap into flame *(I can't get it out of my head that here Cosmo was referring to Arbus).*

169. As is demonstrated by memoirs—such as, for instance, the impeccable memoirs of Marshal de Grouchy, who was one of the officers responsible for the French defeat at Waterloo by stubbornly insisting on attacking the Prussian rearguard far from the main battlefield—the quality of the prose rises when the person writing feels called upon to justify their mistakes. In the act of excusing themselves (just as, sometimes, in the opposite exercise of self-denigration) many writers attain their highest levels.

170. Liberty is an exciting game and an anguishing burden: in cases where you have the option of choosing, you will be tormented by the nightmare of having chosen poorly, the doubt that you may have made a mistake and that you will live to regret it. That which is imposed upon you, you will be able to tolerate to the limit of your resources, and you won't feel any responsibility for it, while that which you have chosen to suit yourself, or out of a whim, can soon become intolerable, and the fault is entirely yours. It's a law of statistics: coercion starts from the lowest point and it is perceived as intrinsically negative, so that under its yoke there may sometimes be improvements; free choice, in contrast, must necessarily be positive, and therefore has a high probability of deteriorating.

172. Often, what is stated is obscure, but what it means is clear.

174. It is a problem to be slow on the uptake, but not as much of a problem as it is to grasp things too quickly, because it is this excess capacity that generates boredom in those who possess it and exercise it. If you can understand everything in the blink of an eye, all the rest of the time your resources lie idle: dead time. I had a student who was like that. His name was Arbus. I don't know what ever became of him, and I therefore deduce that he never wound up achieving anything significant. Probably he was killed by all that dead time.

175. From my past as a teacher, one thing I remember is how uncomfortable it made my students when they were being examined to be asked the one question that ought in theory to have been the most benevolent, the most encouraging: the easy question by definition, since it's not really a question but an invitation to a party: "Talk to me about any subject you like." I would ask it when I was tired and I just couldn't think of yet another quiz. Well, when I asked it some of them panicked: that was because, if they get the answer wrong to a question that they had actually chosen themselves, that they'd asked themselves, their failure would have just been that much more spectacular. Who is such a donkey that they don't even know what they know? Not even one thing out of a thousand, one page out of an entire textbook? And after all, it wasn't even true, because this singular syndrome struck those in particular who had studied, at least a little; in other words, the ones who I thought were actually reasonably well prepared, but who were caught off guard, wrong-footed if I let them talk about whatever they liked. The freedom to choose unraveled all their plans. The first few times I was taken by surprise. Then I started to understand, and I stopped asking that vague and embarrassing question. Rather: "What is the ideal of solidarity that Leopardi suggests in his short poem 'La ginestra' (Wild Broom)?" "Who killed Julius Caesar and why?" "Speak to me about the Counter-Reformation . . ." "What do the three wild beasts represent that Dante encounters while climbing the 'mountain of delight' in the first canto of the *Inferno*?"

Why, of course, it's better like that, much better that way.

176. In his effort to understand the world, man runs into an excess of signification. He collects too many signs and he has too many at his disposal. There are countless hints and nudges, indications that the world offers, hinting that it's trying to tell us something, compared with how much of it we're actually capable of understanding. Everything seems to mean

something, but maybe it's only an appearance, it might be a misunderstanding caused by the frenzy to understand, and many of those coded signals don't mean anything at all.

179. Perhaps, when we're depressed, as I am now, we have a far more realistic vision of what surrounds us; or perhaps we should say, we're less inclined to be blinded by illusions devoid of any basis. Or perhaps even this attempt to find melancholy to be advantageous is an illusion, a meager consolation.

182. I have performed my duty only because I was ill-suited to do otherwise, and therefore because of a limitation and not a choice.

183. The light of a person you're in love with passes through a prism.

184. The value of an action is independent of the fact that one might have been driven to perform it by sheer will, ambition, whim, or desire.

185. Time renders legitimate what was originally criminal.

186. The only truly new thing in life is birth.

189. *E il povero insetto che sbadatamente schiacciamo*
     Nella sua sofferenza corporale prova una fitta forte
     Come quella di un gigante che muore . . .
     (*I've managed to track down the source of this, which in fact struck me as a quotation: these are several lines translated into Italian from Shakespeare's* Measure for Measure, *act 3, scene 1, 82–84:* And the poor beetle that we tread upon / In corporal sufferance finds a pang as great / As when a giant dies . . .)

190. For a teacher, it's a matter of changing the people that you observe, or of seeing the people that you observe changing. For the most part, what's happened to me has been the second thing.

191. It's unbearable, the struggle that we have to carry on every day with people who ought to be coming to our aid: our lawyer, our plumber, the insurance agent, the tile layer, the surgeon, the mechanic who fixes our car, and, albeit indirectly, the politician for whom we voted. All people we have

to pester to get them to do the work we consulted and compensated them to do, to get them to finish it, or to do it over from scratch, because they did it badly the first time, or sloppily, or less than painstakingly, or else to get them to return their fee. Most of the disciplines and trades and professions that they exercise remain unknown to us in their fundamentals and their details: therefore we'd like to be able to have boundless faith in those who are experts, we'd like to be able to say to them: "Do as you think best to solve the problem." Instead, unfailingly, we are forced to choose, by the so-called experts, among various options, basically blindly, given our ignorance, obliged to make a decision, while pretending we know what we're doing: in such a way that we will not only bear the consequences of the errors committed by others, which are bound to redound to our harm, but we will also bear the responsibility. We must constantly find remedies for our remedies: every dentist who peers into our wide-open mouths unfailingly asks how it can be that his predecessor did such disastrous work. Every notary laments the sheer quantity of oversights or foolish mistakes contained in the document compiled sometime earlier by some colleague of his. And so we are surrounded by support figures whom we know in advance we won't be able count on, who seem to grope their way blindly, jury-rigging provisional solutions, overrunning their budgets, delivering a day late, a month late, a year late, or never, who wouldn't dream of replying to voicemail messages, and often just vanish entirely. Into thin air. Concerning the plumber who had installed the faucets backwards and so close to the wall that they scrape against it whenever I turn them, and whose cell phone number seemed to be out of service, I was actually told that he had left the country. For where? For *Australia.*

192. My job as a teacher: like a farmer who labors to prepare a field, weeding and clearing it, breaking the soil, planting seeds, watering . . . then, when after months of hard work, wearing his fingers to the bone and breaking his back, the green shoots spring from the soil and from those stalks the flowers, and the flowers in the end are transformed into fruit, wonderful, swollen, juicy, ripe, and lovely to behold . . . he doesn't harvest them, seized by a sudden weariness that might just as well be lack of interest . . . and he lets them rot in the field, on the branches, he watches day by day as they rot away, without ever lifting a finger . . .

194. The stupidity of certain ideas is by no means redeemed by the stubbornness with which people remain faithful to them.

195. Money is always an excellent reason. But it's almost never the real reason.

196. The enemy is so powerful that even the dead will have reason to fear if the enemy wins.

197. The instructions of the mystics—that in order to attain a purer and more intense and perfect second life you must snap the thread of the first one, that is, the ordinary life—can be extended in many ways also to those who stain themselves with the crime of murder, so that, aside from their own lives in a figurative sense, they literally snap the thread of the lives of others, and the sense of the terrible and the powerful, the clear and the definitive, the cruel and the wonderful, the fatal and the limitless, which appeared to be veiled in ordinary life, are now suddenly revealed to them in all their sharpened clarity, in their untranslatable lucidity. The perverted life and the perfect life resemble each other in this way: that they have broken their bridges with the ordinary life.

200. Certain things become mysterious only once you begin to feel the desire to understand them. Until then, they seemed obvious. They were just there, and that was that. Their very appearance was reassuring. It gave the impression that there was nothing about them to be discovered, no enigma. In much the same way, the people who seem to have the fewest secrets have the most. And the attempt to cast a beam of light upon them makes them withdraw into the depths, just as the shaft of light from a flashlight when shone into the mouth of an underwater den makes the fish hiding in there pull back into the shadows.

201. As long as you hurl your accusation against the world, instead of submitting to it yourself, you are in line with the world.

202. I know that truth and justice are quite invaluable things, certainly, I know that: but when I hear other people complaining, each from her or his own legitimate point of view, about personal matters or the larger, general situation, focusing on nitpicking accounts of misdeeds, wrongs done . . . I start to think that I have too little time on my hands to worry about who is right and who is wrong. The catalogue of misdeeds that nowadays makes up the content of discussions, conversations, television broadcasts: what

can I do about it? It all just bores me. Let me make it quite clear, I too do nothing but complain all the time.

203. In order to be conceived in the first place, even the crudest and falsest of doctrines must contain in principle a tiny dose of truth. It is out of that grain of truth that the most dangerous and misguided ideas develop. Error grows thickest around a slender but truthful green shoot.

204. Among some primitive peoples, the name of the chief deity means "He Whose Existence Is in Doubt." That same name evolves in religions, taking on the meaning of "He Whose Existence Is Unquestionable." Right up to the present day, when it means "Great Big Lie."

205. In certain books, in certain writers, including some I dearly love, I end up detecting the automatism of style and qualities allowed free play: in other words, bravura, or shall we say, skill. From skill, which by no accident is often described as "consummate," the authentic dramatic content is often removed, while in the same process being countless times reoffered and repeated, only in forms such that, instead of bringing that content to light, they conceal it, burying it ever deeper, where it can never again be attained. What with the constant insistence on grazing the thing that needs to be said, what with the constant saying of the thing without saying it, hinting at it, alluding to it, the heart of the thing is pounded away to a pulp. The real problem with repetition is that it distances and uses up the object meant to be grasped, making it with every attempt a little slipperier, until it backs away to the far end of its lair, its hole, just like what happened years ago to that little boy who fell to the bottom of a well, when too many people frantically tried to save him, and when the right person finally arrived, it was too late, it was as if the poor boy had shrunk, squirreled away in the mud . . . In writing, every time you repeat something (a turn of phrase that was felicitous the first time, a well-tested invention), another shovelful of dirt is tossed onto the intimacy of the possible discovery: and the authentic thing will no longer be said, buried instead beneath a dense layer of words.

207. The world should be taken in small doses. An intuitive person ought to need no more than a small sampling.

212. My ideas and my convictions never aspired to possess the one quality that would make them worthy of widespread circulation, namely, certainty. As

it was, they stayed here with me, in my vicinity, never venturing too far away, like pet cats, who simultaneously belong to the household and to no one, and often run away from their owner, but not because they're looking for another one.

216. If the object of desire is one, then there isn't much difference between being gratified by obtaining it and being punished by having it denied you, since that gratification produces a sense of guilt and therefore a frenzy for punishment, which can in its turn be rewarding. This ensures that punishment and satisfaction are frequently intertwined, mistaken one for the other, put one in place of the other, so that one winds up taking pleasure in suffering and pain, and sorrow in gratification. This happened to some of my students.

217. There was a time when men could live their whole lives continuing to do what they'd always done until then, that which it had been their duty to do without any other option or choice, without wasting time questioning themselves about the meaning of what they were doing, since before them countless generations had done the same, no more and no less. Only in recent years have we incurred the need to discover and understand ourselves, who we are, what we really want. Into our inner selves, the realm of controversy, only the occasional hero would venture, and not even all of them, far from it, the majority of great men steered well clear of that area, considering ridiculous or superfluous, and perhaps even offensive, the question "Who am I, really?" just a way of dirtying oneself with the mud of doubt, of uncertainty, the way a foundling might do, a nobody, the son of nobody. Today, on the other hand, the condition of nameless orphan is the starting point for each and every individual, and we are all expected to set out on a lengthy quest to find our own personality and destiny, and before each of us there is no beaten path, no road to give us direction. Of every young person, nowadays, we say, benevolently, with a nod to the pleasure of the liberty that is thought to come with and facilitate the young person's choice, that "they just need to find their way," yes, *his* or *her* way, as if we all had different ways, different roads, and only one of those paths, a single route, was destined to each individual—had been laid out and paved exclusively for him or her, like the Door of the Law in Kafka's famous parable, so that he and no one else might travel it. But if there are millions of virtual roads, of which one and only one was intended for each of us, what vanishingly improb-

ably stroke of luck is supposed to allow us to choose, unerringly, the right one?

219. The epic is for the rich, the fable is for the poor.

220. You feel disgust for that which you need, then for that which you desire too ardently, then for that which you love, then for yourself.

221. I have been reduced to a state of human existence so dismaying and demoralizing that what now dominates my life is disorder, which I once struggled to combat, and which instead I now allow to weigh down heavier day after day, seeking in it a sort of bitter and almost grimly vindictive satisfaction. I plunge greedily into the chaos of my home. My books, which to tell the truth have never been especially dear to me, instead make me snicker with glee when I see them stacked high, from floor to ceiling, swaying and collapsing and tumbling down . . .

(I was able to identify, by a lucky chance, the source of the following thoughts, numbered here from 222 to 238, nearly all of them brief; they come from Tolstoy's novel War and Peace, *which I happened to start reading again, after many years, at night, while during the day I was perusing the thoughts of my old teacher. I believe that the Italian edition he had before his eyes, when he jotted down these notes, was the same one that in the meantime I happened to be reading, that is, the 1942 Einaudi, republished in 1990 as a two-volume paperback, considering that some of the words and expressions found in the translation by Enrichetta Carafa, which actually dates back to 1928, correspond to the wording used by Cosmo. I realized that the source must have been* War and Peace *from fragment 229, where it is clear that the subject is unmistakably Nikolai Rostov, brother of the famous Natasha, on the eve of the Battle of Austerlitz: from that moment I went back and forth in the book in search of tidbits that had caught Cosmo's fancy, and the task was fairly easy, even though in a few cases my links are just guesses, when my teacher's reflections wander very far from what might have been their origin, which might just as easily have come from somewhere else. The spark could have been struck anywhere. It's singular, in any case, the way that he collected and appropriated, from the colossal novel, fragments, a few individual phrases or observations made by this character or that, often expressing them in the first person, while completely forgetting to comment on the magnificent scale of the work with all its historical and metaphysical implications,*

which seem to be of no interest to him. Or else he just thought there wasn't much more to add.)

222. In drawing rooms, the few times I have had occasion to set foot there, I felt like "either a housekeeper or an idiot" *(this, reformulated by Cosmo in personal terms, is the recommendation that Prince Andrei offers Pierre Bezukhov against marrying, because he would wind up right in the midst of the social whirl of dances and gossip).*

223. On the faces of unctuous people you can see that, depending on what you say to them, they're equally ready to burst into laughter or tears, and sometimes they can be so quick to change expression that they can anticipate what they think they've understood, but have instead misunderstood. At that point, their face will remain uncertain, their eyes speculating about the best next move while their mouth tightens into a seesawing succession of smiling or sorrowful grimaces *(Mademoiselle Bourienne, p. 109).*

224. "What I need, I won't ask for; I'll just take it for myself" *(a phrase uttered in a contemptuous tone by Dolokhov—while we're on the subject, one of my favorite characters in* War and Peace, *along with Nikolai Bolkonsky and the beautiful Hélène Kuragina—on p. 137. This pride very much matched Cosmo's character. He was convinced that everyone had to make their way under their own power, that they should not complain, that you should just take the things you desire and be done with it, if you have the strength to do so, that all art was like that, and so was life: there was no point in waiting for kind concessions, if anything, a stroke of luck, for example, to have a little talent, or beauty, or intelligence. One time, commenting on an essay I'd written in class, Cosmo said: "Never offer explanations. Don't try to justify yourself. The things that you do must be self-evident as you do them, adding them later is a form of deceit. One sentence can't be helped out by other sentences. You should take your essay and* throw it in the rubbish and write it over again from scratch. *You should throw it away precisely because it isn't bad. I know that you write well, but I also know that that's your main shortcoming. It's as if your writing is justifying what you wrote, as if it's absolving it of all sins. Often the ones who write about something are the very people who know and understand least about it, while the people who know remain silent. A superficial experience is easier to report than a profound one, and*

you are driven to communicate by a force that is inversely proportional to the force of the thing that you are communicating. Those who communicate a great deal, communicate very little.").

225. I'm not interested in the whys, but the hows *(p. 175).*

226. The closer we get, the less we see *(in this, which could be a general rule of sight, perhaps we can see an implicit reference to the episode of the Battle of Schöngrabern, to whose chaotic unfolding the Russian commander, Prince Bagration, accompanied by Bolkonsky as aide-de-camp, attempts in vain to give a certain meaning with his orders: in the slaughter and smoke and roar of the artillery, no one is any longer capable of understanding what is taking place: "The colonel . . . couldn't have said with any certainty whether the attack had been repulsed by his regiment or his regiment had been destroyed by the attack." Uncertainty, random chance, mass scenes that are actually the unpredictable aggregation of individual acts).*

227. The things I say seem intelligent while I am preparing them in my mind, and suddenly stupid when they come out of my mouth *(Pierre, p. 235).*

228. Strange, but I think that perhaps I could have been a good parent. Me? Yes, me. And how? By imitating other parents. Not naturally gifted that way, and possessing no personal inclination, I might easily have chosen the best examples and shamelessly copied them, the way my most ignorant students used to do. The ones who run the greatest risks of failure are, in fact, those who think they know something about it, who think they're up to the task *(if this is a consideration based on* War and Peace, *I haven't been able to track down the source in the book with any confidence. Cosmo's thoughts, like for that matter anyone else's, hurry quickly away from the source from which they were drawn. Unless the source lies in a note about Prince Vasili Kuragin, accustomed to addressing his daughter Hélène with a tenderness that, Tolstoy writes, did not come spontaneously, but that "in his case had been worked out by imitating other parents," p. 245).*

229. Before the Battle of Austerlitz, Rostov half asleep on horseback, his drowsy head irresistibly sinking down against the animal's mane: here we have, a good fifty years ahead of its time, and condensed into twenty lines, the famous internal monologue of Molly Bloom in *Ulysses (p. 307).*

230. Other people's cheerfulness can be very tiresome and, in the end, induce melancholy *(p. 542)*.

231. At peace, at home, warm and dirty *(Pierre in Moscow, p. 627)*.

232. There are men who purposely put themselves into the most dismal conditions of life in order to have a right to be dismal *(about Marshal Davoust, p. 723)*.

233. When you are asked to forgive something, it means that there was something deserving punishment *(p. 739)*.

234. Take no prisoners: this alone would make war less cruel *(paraphrase of thought of Prince Andrei, p. 911, who puts the blame on our hypocritical magnanimity and sensitivity: "Take no prisoners, but kill and be killed!" War should be this and nothing more, without rules and without rights)*.

235. Every great war aspires to be a war of peacemakers, endowing those who fight with a definitive security and harmony. Every great war is inspired by sound common sense *(see the page in which Tolstoy transcribes from Napoleon's memoirs from St. Helena certain considerations about the Russian campaign, ". . . la plus populaire des temps modernes . . . celle du repos et de la securité de tous," p. 959 of the Einaudi edition)*.

236. I believe I know how to die no worse than anyone else *(p. 1168)*.

237. When a child falls and hurts himself, to console him and to bring a smile promptly back to his face, his mother will scold and smack the floor where he landed *(p. 1176. Ah, smacking the floor: how long since I last thought of this delightful practice . . .)*.

238. Very often in history great armies have ceased to exist without losing any battle *(p. 1206. In this last notation taken from* War and Peace, *perhaps Cosmo wasn't thinking of military history alone, but rather of single individuals, of their inclination toward self-destruction, each in his fashion. Perhaps he was thinking of himself)*.

239. The self-suspension of justice has a name, and it is called a pardon. A pardon is always profoundly unjust, arbitrary, capricious: those who re-

ceive it have no reason for it to have been given, those who administer it place themselves above all laws.

240. Comforts, luxuries, lavish wastefulness, exclusive rights, and privileges are things you can enjoy only if you're already filled with joy, only if you are already disposed by your nature to a limitless increase of joy, wealth is a gift that you deserve only if it goes onto a pile of countless other gifts, if in other words the good fortune that has come to you is shameless, boundless, capricious, sublime. Only in that case do riches manage to vanish into an estate, into a vaster, more boundless fortune, until they almost seem part and parcel with the essence of those who enjoy them. In the case, however—and it is a far more common state of affairs—where privilege falls upon someone incapable of accepting it and absorbing it, of letting it vanish into himself because he is made of the exact same material, much as light disappears into a greater light, merging with it, then it remains an excrescence, an outgrowth, an ornament, the display of which has something painful about it. One ought to *be* that splendor, not just own it. What we often call well-being is a state that is really only well-*having*. There are some who wear richness like a hunchback, like an artificial limb.

247. As in the story of the merchant who flees to Samarra to escape Death, the original course of one's life takes detours, twisting, turning roads and random side roads, before reaching its destination, its point of arrival, which, in contrast, has always remained and still remains the same. The effort to stand out against nothingness, which lasted the whole first phase of your existence, is followed by the effort to return to it, disguised as a flight, while it is actually a return.

248. Obstinacy and pride ensure that each of us demands the right to find his own way to death.

249. A part of us pursues the natural route that leads to the terminus of our development, which is to say, extinction, and in the meantime another part tracks back toward the origin, toward the mysterious beginning of that development. A single individual is dragged downstream by the current of the river, like a log, while also wriggling and leaping upstream, trying to climb that same river, like a salmon. These equal and contrary movements are present with equivalent force in sexual desire, which is a lust at the same time for annihilation and for reproduction: it traces its path back to the

source of life and rushes headlong toward the earliest possible encounter with the boundaries of death.

251. I have crossed the sea of awareness. How was I able to do it? It was easy: the sea had dried up. Many decades since, perhaps even centuries. The human mind had drunk it dry.

252. When you are immersed in total darkness, the way I am now, it wouldn't be the wisest thing to reject any offer, albeit of minimal light. But this offer leaves me indifferent. Not, let's say, skeptical, but cold. Even wisdom strikes me as a pose, or an excuse. Like a mouse caught by surprise, and which looks around wildly for even the tiniest hole in which to take shelter, the excuse in its turn seeks a reason for the fact that it's failed to gain any hold on me, and ends up finding it precisely in the darkness it was supposed to brighten, and blames it for everything, for my confused mental state, for my reluctance to indulge in revelations. All right, then, in that case, it's become clear to me that in the darkness I move along at an even greater clip.

253. I hope that nothing of me survives. And yet there is no one so ephemeral, so fleeting, no one of whom not even the slightest trace remains.

254. That which I am not allowed, I desire ten times more ardently. The unattainable glows, full of life: and so that which is dead, that which has vanished forever, is animated with the most intense life.

255. "I love you." Having said it in my life always meant I was in a state of turmoil, agitated, excited . . . very excited . . . and ready to die.

256. The bourgeois spirit is an ascetic spirit that can never seem to rid itself of the world, in fact, its purpose is to remain there, only at a slightly higher level each time.

257. The people we most detest are those we have done wrong. We no longer want to have anything to do with those to whom we have done some harm.

258. The thing that most often spoils literature is sentimentalism. The second most often, ingenuity.

259. I danced around the Golden Calf as long as there were other people dancing with me, joyously and enthusiastically, intertwining legs and arms, then once I was released from those embraces, I continued to spin and whirl for a while on my own, in the darkness that the torches, now close to flickering out, were no longer bright enough to illuminate, and then I raised my eyes, glazed with the wine whose effects were starting to wear off, gradually, against the glow of dawn that was rising in the wrong part of the sky, and then I realized that the Golden Calf, too, was now gone.

260. You cannot linger at length on the heights of heroism. The excess of virtue that allows a hero to win his magnificent victories, the excess that makes up the splendor in which his figure is shrouded, leads him outside and beyond justice and reason, hurls him into the depths of abuse, perdition, and infamy. And in the end, into death, always a horrendous death. If it were any other way, a cruelly statistical law would intervene in any case, the law of reversion to the mean, according to which once you've attained the loftiest summits, you can only go downhill. Glory does not proliferate ad infinitum, otherwise what would be miraculous about it? Little by little, a hero loses his extraordinary qualities, he shrinks, his powers fade, until he has returned to normality. And for a hero, normality is damnation.

261. If they asked you to choose, you'd want to be the man hanging up there from the cross. The hero, that is, alone before his fate. But it's far more likely that you'd be one of the many mingling in the crowd at the foot of the cross.

264. The exclusive sentiment of love, from Romanticism onward, has replaced and surrogated religion, has substituted the religion of love, which is to say, Christianity, leaving space on earth for only one religion that can be practiced collectively, the religion of hatred. The religion of love, therefore, survives as a personal cult, which links single individuals together, in couples or in restricted numbers, while hatred is capable of binding together much vaster groups and entire communities.

265. The very least that you can expect of someone like me who is about to die, who can see the end coming over the edge of the horizon, is that he stop, once and for all, being Manichean.

266. A more boring conversation than the one you might have with a person who does nothing but list the things they like might perhaps be a conversation with someone who instead denounces all the things he detests. The enthusiastic tone of the former is in any case less annoying than the contemptuous smirk of the latter. If we really have to distinguish ourselves according to our tastes, I'd much rather talk to someone who does it with a series of "I just love it!" than someone who unfurls his "I just hate it!"

267. When nostalgia disappears, it doesn't give way to serenity, it yields to the void. Having forgotten many things from my past doesn't bring me any particular relief, in part because nothing can justify the bizarre selection according to which I continue to remember some all too vividly, those and those alone, and why? The willful ways of memory are an ironic and disconcerting phenomenon. No one will ever be able to bring order to that archive where the important things have vanished, so that trifles and trinkets become important, indeed, precious, priceless, and only because they are still there.

269. If I have ever met a person I'd never known before and I have found them to be special, I have always had the sensation of "seeing them again." The encounter has taken place now, but that person had always been in my life, at a point not yet explored.

270. Every single conversation we have or story we tell always runs the risk of being incomplete but at the same time excessive. We spend half our lives examining the other half.

271. If God is distracted, if He isn't listening, then we turn to His adversary. There is no invocation of the devil that fails to receive an attentive and interested hearing.

272. I'm afraid that it is the devil who imparts many of the lessons that lead us to know ourselves better.

273. Instead of trying to achieve fantasies and dreams, nowadays it would be advisable to take real facts and convert them into fantasies.

276. Living one's life to satisfy the needs of another, to absorb their bad

moods and malaises, to carry the train of their sickness, to earn a martyr's crown in assisting them, while never making a point of it, never complaining, never demanding a thing in exchange for one's mute sacrifice: well, deep down, I'm happy not to have a person like that at my side, so wonderful, so devoted, and instead to be allowed to kick the bucket in blessed peace.

279. That which is visible is also vulnerable.

280. Everything that is indispensable, from a certain point on, seems to have been lost forever: motherly love, for example, precious motherly love. We'll spend the rest of our lives surrogating with other emotions the one emotion that can never be replaced, and the problem is that we do a passable job of it, going so far as to forget that indispensable sentiment entirely and thus, at the very instant we do so, sadly, becoming people who are no longer indispensable. The indispensable is what we regularly dispense with and then replace, substitute, surrogate, until what with all those replacements, there's not so much as a gram of gold left in the statue, even if its divine and regal appearance remains unchanged, at least from a distance.

282. What makes the world turn is a gigantic compensation machine that works tirelessly.

283. Disaster is the consequence not of some wrong done, but of some joy experienced.

288. On special occasions, like those that I have been experiencing for the past couple of months, apparently the last or the penultimate moments of my life, reason becomes entirely independent of those who exercise it. And it begins to strike hard against its adversary, hard against even its allies, and last of all, even against itself. Delicacy by this point is a stranger to it.

290. I'm too busy regretting certain individual events from life to have time to regret life as a whole.

291. I was calm. But if someone comes along and tells me to calm down, then all of a sudden, I get worked up.

293. The crater on the edge of which the saints sit waiting is extinct now.

295. In the phases of a man's life, there are migrations from one point of sexuality to another. Schopenhauer states that after age fifty, males generally turn homosexual, because the wisdom of Mother Nature wishes to prevent old men from getting women with child.

298. The Muses were savage at first. Then Apollo taught them everything. All education, even as it seems to eliminate it, only refines and empowers barbarity.

299. Some appreciate silence as the highest spiritual manifestation, placing it in opposition with the word understood as chatter. But there is nothing more menacing than silence. Garrulousness offends, but silence kills.

303. For an Italian, it was so natural to be a Catholic that, if an Italian wasn't one, he was thereby rebelling against the very spirit of his blood. That is why atheists in this country are so angry and punctilious. Far easier to try to destroy the Catholic faith than to replace it. The problem with the project of overthrowing it is that, along with the Catholic faith, you have to sweep away all the rest; soon nothing is left standing of Italian culture, not even its most pugnacious opponents.

305. They explained to us how the world for quite some time now has been disenchanted and governed by reason. That wasn't true. It isn't true. The twentieth century was surely the least rational century in history, even less rational than the year 1000. Its movements were spasmodic. Its faiths, absurd. Its crimes: monstrous, unequaled. The only rational thing it had was the organization needed to commit them. Forget about *Beowulf*! Forget about *Das Rheingold*! Forget about flagellants and stylites and pillar saints! A society that wanted to present itself as rationally optimized on a scientific and economic basis was actually functioning like a crystal ball, a magic sphere of pure enchantment, and everyone was inside it, even the atheists, even the philosophers and the scientists, who had been turned back into sorcerers, all of them delighted at the chance. The twentieth century was a century of hypnosis and trance. How else can you explain the marches, the oceanic assemblies, the respectful silence of visitors when confronted by any old piece of crap in a museum, the rapture and tears with which great criminals were heard and venerated, the worship-

ful reception accorded megalomaniacal impostors, the idiotic smile of ambitious exterminators and the murderous smile of film divas . . . A century of sleepwalkers, of nightmares and evil spells and magicians.

306. Hatred in belief, and then resentment in the cessation of belief.

307. Effort always produces rancor: that is why some of the works of literature longest labored over and polished (e.g., those of Flaubert) seem to address the reader with a certain degree of spitefulness, as if scolding her or him for not sufficiently appreciating the sacrifices made to please her or him.

311. At times I have thought that I have attained, with respect to other people, say, my students, for example, a true and perfect goodness, and, in listening to them and advising them, an absolute objectivity. The fact that they have almost never paid any real attention to me in no way undermines this sensation, indeed, implicitly, it confirms it.

312. Lies are of no importance when both those who tell them and those who hear them know the truth.

314. We are convinced we love certain people and hate others: instead, most of the time we love and hate the same people.

317. Politics in and of itself is leftist, culture and religion in and of themselves are right-wing.

318. Since Mazzini's time, every new political development in Italy originates outside the bounds of legality, so it makes perfect sense that subversive politics (first to establish fascism, then to overthrow it) would in time struggle to produce a leadership class.

319. Riches without men, and men without riches.

320. In the world of today, the possibility, nay the likelihood, practically the certainty of any given individual being at odds, in disagreement: so countless are the subjects, so infinite the number of variables in which that disagreement can surface. Even just the brand of cell phone you should buy, the best type of plan to choose. As choices increase, affinities diminish.

324. Life is a tortuous labyrinth, like the viscera concealed within the body.

325. Before dying, I'd like an explanation of just one thing. Anything at all.

326. I've noticed that at the recurrence of anniversaries of deaths, you no longer see headlines in the newspapers like, say, this one: "Ten Years Ago Lucio Battisti Died," and instead we have "Ten Years Without Lucio." As if to say: How have we managed without him, what sense have the past ten years even made, so empty now? After my own death, which will come soon enough, the small space that I have occupied will be filled immediately, just like a seat in a crowded streetcar (I'm reminded of those old trolleys, with shiny wooden interiors, that still circulate in Milan, slow, elegant . . .), where as soon as someone shows even the slightest intent of getting up to leave the trolley at the next stop, the passengers packed around them take advantage of the opportunity to spread out a little, relaxing with their elbows and bags and legs.

327. Knowing how to wait, accepting deferral, ought to be the adult way of facing up to things; demanding immediate gratification, instead, the childish way. The fury of the suckling infant who's had the breast taken from him . . . Now I find myself in an utterly new condition in which I can't tolerate deferral, and yet at the same time I demand it: I'd like anything, whether good or bad, to be pushed farther away, postponed ad infinitum.

328. Death comes no differently for those who whine and whimper and those who wait impassively (*this is a paraphrase of a line from Philip Larkin's cynical poem "Aubade," difficult to render in Italian because of the participial construction, so typical of the English language: "Death is no different whined at than withstood." While it's reasonably clear why Cosmo might have chosen to translate an excerpt from the poem, having read it recently, or else because it had suddenly come to mind, resurfacing in view of his own impending death, what still remains to be understood, in the final indifference between those two attitudes, is which of them he'd actually adopted, in which of them he recognized himself; or whether he simply alternated them, sometimes "whining," at other times firmly withstanding the ordeal; or whether there might exist yet another possibility, a different approach that*

entails neither complaint nor virile acceptance; something I can't quite pic-
ture to myself, but which perhaps Cosmo had discovered and adopted).

329. I don't know how to conceive of the future. I don't have the faintest idea of the afterlife. I could have founded the Church of What's Happening Now.

331. Having to tend every day, in fact, every hour and every minute, to the needs of the body is already in and of itself the greatest and the most terrible of diseases: in this sense, the body is sick even when it's healthy, given its incessant need to drink, eat, rest, defecate, breathe, spit, wash itself; it is no less sick in its desires and its lusts than in its requirements. Therefore the true diseases, the one that doctors diagnose with a particular name, are by no means exceptional states, but rather moments when the body, so to speak, finally stops deceiving us, abandons the fiction of health, and reveals clearly its true condition, pathological from the outset. Whatever the disease, therefore, it's incurable, given that so was the health.

332. Everything can be seen as a progressive mechanism of expulsion. In order not to have to admit the existence of evil, which nonetheless existed in Him, God expelled it, creating Satan. In order to eliminate it from his heart, sin was extracted from man's rib, and from that rib woman was made: so she will be the cause of the Fall. Out of fear or disgust at having to interact with our fellow man, we Italians invented the formal pronoun "*lei*," whereby we speak to an imaginary third person in which we house the personality that has been expelled from the flesh-and-blood interlocutor before us, reduced to a servile spokesman for that respectable virtual master. We have subcontracted many of our duties, thoughts, decisions, and desires to the exterior, to collective institutions: let them take care of them. The impurity of feces is evacuated. Even psychic suffering can be expelled with a pill: but once expelled, where will it wind up, will it dissolve into thin air or will it go to live in some other being, like the legion of demons in the Gospel of Matthew that inhabited a herd of pigs? To save the rest of the body's life, a gangrenous leg is amputated. We lose the integrity of the whole in order to safeguard it. Now, will that leg be buried in a grave? Does it still belong to someone? Is it *someone?*

333. All studies are preliminary studies.

334. The two best-known italian novels of the early twentieth century have two assholes for their main characters.

335. Zeno Cosini/Mattia Pascal 6–1, 6–0.

336. She was cross-eyed right down to her thighs (*I found the source of this image, too, while leafing through* Zeno's Conscience, *where the character of Augusta is described*).

339. Asking for protection, demanding protection, everyone understandably wants to be protected. Children first and foremost should be protected, and likewise the weak and the infirm, women demand that they be protected by and from men, meaning that they want a man at their side to protect them, and that they need protection against men, who are often violent and oppressive. But men, too, ask to be protected, from being fired, from disease and death, and they feel frustrated when the state does nothing to help them, when their friends abandon them, when their leader instead of guiding them betrays them. The police, the law, ought to protect us: and instead we become their target. If you fall into the crosshairs of the law, you won't get back out until you've gone through a long nightmare. That is why, in Italy, we always need protectors, mediators, intercessors, beseechers, godfathers, saints to call on in heaven. No one has even the faintest hope of getting by on their own. The only thing you can do alone is kick the bucket, in fact, not even that. And when neither your family nor associations or guilds will protect you, and not even your friendships or the state will protect you, then who do you turn to, if not heaven?

340. I don't think there's anything wrong with asking for a little help. It is from heaven that light pours down, from on high, and it's only from on high that light can descend. Don't tell me that I talk like a priest. I haven't talked to anyone for a long time, it was useless, all that came out of my mouth was heresies. The tongue is a vehicle of iniquity, a world of errors, as long as you use it to communicate. When you stop expecting to communicate, on the other hand . . . I'm sorry to say it but, perhaps, whether I were to speak or remain silent, I might deceive all the same.

341. If you're looking for miracles, here they are: errors prove fertile, disease becomes a way of stalling for time. The waves of the stormy sea have driven the boat into port, chains stretch like rubber bands, an urgent need

becomes a hopeful expectation. The true miracle, in other words, isn't that all this evil and pain should be erased; the true miracle is that all this evil and pain becomes acceptable.

342. A miracle is a perfect story, because it brings together a terrible misfortune with a wonderful salvation.

343. The ignorant and the learned. The ignorant are never *entirely* ignorant, while the learned are never learned *enough*.

345. The true miracle takes place continuously, in such a way that it produces the sensation that no miracle is taking place.

348. Doctrines that offer man guarantees against loneliness can be very successful.

350. I'm the least free man in the world. Believing I would enhance my life, I've given myself death: privation, indigence, desire, dependency—that is the perennial condition of my spirit. Admiring beauty, I generated new aspirations and therefore new sources of pain.

351. It would be appropriate for thinkers, scientists, and philosophers all to die at age sixty, because past that age they start to oppose new ideas. Perhaps only artists might be allowed a few extra years, as long as they are devoid of prejudices, or sufficiently flexible and lively to come up with new ones: it is, in fact, quite amusing to watch political infatuations among the elderly, for example. Ordinary people like me can live as long as they want, it makes no difference. In fact, I've grown old without causing any harm to the progress of knowledge (*no one has ever understood why such an intelligent and gifted man should have withdrawn to that private school, to become a teacher . . . that is the great question that hovers around Cosmo . . . the great rationalist who ended up teaching in a school run by priests!*).

352. I've tried not to get too fond of my ideas, so that I can rid myself of them relatively painlessly as soon as someone comes along who can prove to me that they were false.

353. Why should creatures that do nothing but suffer, desire, with such great frenzy, to reproduce? No one should feel any desire to perpetuate an

unbroken state of suffering. There therefore exist, and cannot help but exist, certain pleasures, and even those who have never experienced them intuitively know what these pleasures are, they know, in other words, that however few and far between, they are still possible, and that they might alleviate their inferno from one moment to the next. Ironically, the most intense of these pleasures is the one that is experienced in the act involved in reproduction: thus the circle is closed and the initial question receives a mocking response.

357. The malleable parts of my spirit have grown stiff or dissolved entirely, just like the malleable parts of my body.

358. The things I've seen, the things I remember and believe that I've seen, the things I've imagined seeing are all one with the things I dream.

359. I experience moments of great objectivity. They last for half an hour, at the very most an hour or so. In them, things appear for what they are and oddly enough they turn out to be identical to the way they ought to be, there is no gap between images and definitions, nor is there any regret or hope. In those moments, the only activity I'm aware of carrying out is breathing. Breathing. I'm still capable of doing that with no particular effort, and I do. I breathe, I fill up my lungs, I empty them out, the breath enters and exits regularly, and the castle built on clouds that is reality doesn't collapse, it doesn't dissolve all at once, nor does it glitter in the distance like a fabulous miracle, but just hangs there, dangling in midair, and I, too, like anyone, inhabit it, at least for a brief interval I have the right to inhabit it. And how did I gain that right? By choosing to stop asking any more questions. This, in fact, was the last question I asked myself, before objectivity, instead of answering questions, extinguished this, too.

360. I don't believe that God has forgotten me; rather, He would have every reason to suppose that I have forgotten Him. And so, for Him to receive a prayer from me now will arouse His astonishment. Perhaps He will think that I want to ask Him, decidedly far too late, for a favor. From the position of someone on death row, any appeal has a tang of desperation and a whiff of hypocrisy. So you, too, now? Why are you wasting the scant time still remaining to you? When you had vast and limitless amounts of time at your disposal, you didn't seem so interested in heaven, or frightened of hell . . . But that is not why I am turning to Him: it's just to reestablish a

connection. When was this line last hung up? Many years ago. I couldn't have been more than fourteen or fifteen . . .

361. In any case, I have the feeling that it will be God who will make the first move. Whatever attitude I might have and whatever state of mind I am able to induce in myself, whether of disbelief or skepticism, it won't be me who asks but, if anything, He who offers. He is the doctor who goes to pay a call on the sick man, unasked. If not in his room and at his bedside, let's just say that He is waiting outside the sick man's house, where the snow is starting to stick on the sidewalks and the breath turns to vapor in front of the faces of the passing pedestrians.

362. At the cost of ruining the fable, I can't help but imagine a version where, after the little match girl strikes the last match, a benefactor comes along.

363. The axe at the base of the tree will be withdrawn, and the trees will be allowed to go on growing for some time at least, because even the apocalypse needs to be heralded and then allowed to slip away, so that there is time to meditate on its deception and become thoroughly disabused of the illusion. The first time we were caught unawares, the second time we'll already be tired of waiting.

364. You can come to know God without recognizing your own misery. Many, contrariwise, know their own misery in great detail but do not therefore come to know God, indeed, it is precisely the fact that they're miserable that precludes them from finding the path to know God, who, if He existed, would be nothing more to them than the target of their rancor, because He would be thought to be responsible for their misery. If it were ever to happen, the meeting might last no longer than the arc of a profanity. The misfortunes that befall us can bring us closer to God or distance us light-years from Him, as if what had already happened weren't bad enough, as if celestial clouds and clusters and nebulae formed of millions of stars weren't enough to separate us from His being, but He still had to precipitate even farther from us, even deeper into the remote abysses, withdrawing from the disaster that He has caused us. Practically speaking, on the lam, taking it on the run. For that matter, if the world is so cruel and absurd, why would anyone be interested in getting closer to its Creator? Much less worship Him? And therefore, between God and human misery there is an abyss that cannot be bridged, or else it is obvious to suppose that it might

be bridged only by hatred: hatred of the Almighty who crushes His unsuccessful creations; the hatred of creatures who cannot stop cursing Whoever brought them into the world. The curser is a singular figure of connection. By filling the void with contumely, he makes it practicable, like someone who throws rocks and junk into a stream. He isn't all that different from someone who prays: he seeks, in other words, to establish a relationship, however brutally. But we seriously do need a high-level mediator between God and human misery, and that would be Jesus Christ, Who is at the same time God and human misery, the problem, the cause of the problem, and its remedy. Therefore it is completely useless to seek God without following the path of Christ. The God that you might encounter by following a different route all alone would be incomprehensible or frightening because devoid of any humanity: a God for theologians or philosophers or mathematicians, a God for kings and high priests who need to subjugate the masses by terrorizing them. Those who set off on this solitary path can only end up crushed or hurled into the depths. Your own personal suffering, sealed into your individual dimension, would just be useless ballast weighing you down on this steep climb, while the suffering of Christ, once His cross has been acknowledged, would help you to lift that burden, or rather, it would invert the polarity of that weight. Instead of hindering you, the pain would serve to provide signposts. Let us allow Him to carry at least a little of our pain. Let Him blaze the path for us. Let us mirror ourselves in His pain, let us learn to recognize in it the entire spectrum of our pain and sorrow: when we suffer, we are insulted, mortified, betrayed, when our friends abandon us and our home is destroyed and our bed is invaded and our body tortured. These are all things that happened to Him, and He experienced them one by one. He who doesn't know and acknowledge Christ, then, knows nothing. He knows nothing of God, he knows nothing of the world, but he also knows nothing of himself. Or perhaps we should say that he can only know his own senseless misery and his own equally senseless pride, as if they were incommunicable elements. In fact, only that which establishes communication can be understood: between one thing and another, between oneself and oneself, between oneself and things, between one person and another, between oneself and people and things. Only affliction, without consolation, only tenacity without honest recognition of one's own weakness: if you leave these elements disjointed, the world remains incomprehensible. Jesus is the only connecting figure. Of ourselves to ourselves, first and foremost. And then to others.

P.S. If I were a pastor, what I have just written might provide good material for a sermon. Since I'm not one, however, who am I preaching to? My pulpit is the kitchen, my congregation, a line of tuna cans.

365. However much it may annoy me how Christian rhetoric gives inspired definitions of disasters and human suffering as "gifts of God," precious opportunities supposedly offered us expressly to understand, grow, mature, open up to others, etc., etc., things that appear to me at once fanatical and consolatory, if not actually hypocritical seeing that they are trying to palm off an objective misfortune as an advantage, there is no doubt that the most solid communities are formed in resistance to sorrow and grief, by passing through them. Those who pass through them alone, then, what benefit can they gain therefrom? And what benefit will they transmit to others? I'd like to say none, but it's of this "none" that I'm afraid, I'm afraid even just to say so.

368. Like a shooting star, hope passed over their heads.

369. To love those who hate you, as Christ preaches, is a very difficult thing, but maybe you can give it a try, you can make an effort, it's an experiment that is still conceivable; but to love those *you* hate, no, that's just not possible, unless you choose to camouflage and twist an emotion, palming it off as its own diametric opposite, thereby becoming a whited sepulcher. At the very outside you might try to hate them a little less, or forget about them, dislodging them from your mind and your life.

370. Let's put it this way: the only visible and indisputable law that has been imposed upon us is injustice. And who are we to dare to strip ourselves of the only law we possess? *(from the turn of phrase and the subject, I presume that this thought was inspired by Franz Kafka).*

372. Who am I? Tell me. And if I like being the person you tell me I am, I'll come. Otherwise I'll stay here.

373. Feelings become stronger when they contain something horrible.

374. Telling a story of which you're the main character is a sign of either great confusion or arrogance.

377. Even happiness leaves its trail of victims behind it, because the happy individual is often happy at the expense of some other individual: the rich man, the beloved man, the chosen one, the winner, the pregnant woman— they're all happier than the poor man, the unloved man, the discarded one, the loser, the sterile woman. Therefore happiness produces unhappiness, and unhappiness reproduces itself.

378. There are very few occasions in which we are conscious of the real reason for our joy; it is even harder to understand how often it is caused by someone else's pain, and how often we enjoy something only because we took it away from someone else; there are practically no pleasures that don't make someone else suffer: the animal that has been slaughtered, the peasant who gathered the bunch of grapes, the bunch of grapes that was squeezed, the woman we cheated on, the woman we cheated on her with, and even the one we remain faithful to: to say nothing of ourselves, the very first ones to be devastated by our wishes, by those ungranted as well as those attained. More tears are shed over answered prayers than unanswered ones *(that last phrase is a quotation from St. Teresa of Ávila, used by Truman Capote in the opening of his unfinished novel* Answered Prayers*).*

379. We are not only capable of concealing a part of ourselves from others, but also of housing it inside us as if it were a stranger. That concealment, then, is above all a concealment of ourselves from ourselves: seeing that the boundaries of our own selves laid out by our brains can easily include objects that are not part of them at all (see, for example, the experiment known as "the rubber hand illusion"), likewise the brain can be persuaded that some parts of one's own identity are actually extraneous, alien, intrusive elements.

380. An American writer once tried to tease out the suffering due to illness in all its possible meanings, as various metaphors: as a contract, an inheritance, a promise, a task, a gift, a mistake, an ornament, or a dream (I imagine, a nightmare, in that case). Depending on how we interpret it, we can respond by: fighting, reacting angrily, resigning ourselves, surrendering nicely, expressing our thanks, trying to come to terms with it through any of various moral, religious, or intellectual instruments, that is, through deception, forgetfulness, illusion, disillusionment, narrative, sublimation. I believe that I have assumed at least once and for various amounts of time each of these attitudes, rotating them. Lately, I tend to see it rather as an

ornament, or maybe I should say a garment, which means: something that doesn't belong in the narrowest sense to my physical person and which I wear, because I am required to, but appropriately, in other words, like a uniform. It distinguishes me from others while at the same time establishing a bond with everyone else who wears it. And like a genuine uniform, suffering can't simply be taken off from one day to the next: it would be as if you'd been stripped of rank, your decorations ripped from your chest. It would be a dishonorable discharge.

381. My last words, I'm almost certain, will be negligent and negligible. Perhaps that is what scares us: not silence, or a scream, or a nice weighty phrase, but rather, "Oh, good morning to you, Doctor," and that those might be our last words.

382. If I no longer experience genuine proper emotions, that may be because they have been transmuted into physical sensations, which the body may interpret as cold, heat, annoyance, the need to urinate or vomit, relaxation of the muscles, air in the belly, falling asleep, sugar on the tongue. All things that I might once have called by such names as hope, or anger, or sweetness, or fear. I wonder what physical shiver friendship is equivalent to: a sentiment or rather an attitude truncated forever but which might perhaps resurface in some specific point in me as a perception of which I'm barely aware: maybe as the breeze that comes in suddenly through the window on a stifling hot day.

383. I don't have too much of a reason to complain about physical pain. In that sense, I can consider myself lucky. If this illness hits one in a hundred, that is, me (bad luck), then I'm the further one in a hundred of that 1 percent, who, once sick, suffers little or almost not at all (good luck within the bad luck). Moreover, I wouldn't know what to say about the pain I do suffer, I wouldn't venture to describe it, it would be pointless, in fact, the few times that I seriously do suffer, before squeezing the dose into my body, the last thing that would occur to me is to force myself to find the words to explain what it's like, in order to tell someone about it or write it down here. With the shift nurse who comes to give me my treatment, we have an understanding by now on a mute signal that I give her to let her know how things are going and how much pain I'm feeling: I raise an arm to a certain height and she understands. When I am no longer capable of administering the necessary doses myself, she'll take over, and in the meantime my

growing extraneousness will, I trust, make it an automatic, almost bureaucratic process, which I'm happy about—or, to avoid using a word as out of
place as "happiness"—which I'm satisfied with. Even now. Even now, in any
case, the whole thing is rather impersonal. The random nature and the patent injustice of this disease, of any disease that strikes anyone at any age,
with or without good cause, whether you went looking for it or else it came
looking for you, out of the blue, instead of getting me worked up, reassures
me, lightens me, and if it weren't for the fact that I'd feel a certain shyness
at being mistaken for a courageous or defiant person, it almost makes me
laugh. The many many senseless things that punctuate our lives and even,
as in my case, bring those lives to an end, free us of the obligation to find
an overarching meaning for this exhaustion, this agitation that we call life.
It seems sufficiently faithful to follow its wave as it rises and then crashes,
letting myself be taken and then overwhelmed. Does it make me seem too
wise to think this? Do I seem like a wise old Chinese man? Screwing just
like a Chinaman, as the man says in that movie?

385. This is how it is: I don't want to add any pain to the pain of being
unable to express the pain. Not a drop more than what I deserve. Reflecting on his impotence does nothing to redeem the impotent man, if anything, it expands the range of his impotence from the corporeal to the
intellectual.

386. In order to obviate the poverty of our way of expressing feelings like
love and suffering, literature was invented. But it, too, makes an effort with
great ingenuity and much effort to obviate that poverty. The bodies tormented by pain or in the throes of ecstatic pleasure plunge into silence or
cliché.

387. The more civilization perfects itself, the higher the number of madmen
and suicides, which some blame on the spread of narcotics use, but which
might actually simply be the plague against which those substances were
simply an attempted and temporary remedy.

392. (Machiavelli, Leopardi.) The obstinate and haughty realism that was
the pride of all the greatest Italians, at an even higher level opens up to the
realm of possibility in those same spirits. The determined insistence spent
on proving that there are no alternatives to the acceptance of the harsh-

ness of reality, except in a lie, gives way to a more flexible, fluctuating vision, open to the "maybe," the "you can't rule out the fact that," the hypotheses even just barely hinted at, when the various theses have grown arid with the fury devoted to sustaining and defending them, and they have therefore suddenly become as fragile as dry leaves.

393. Though it's not a sure thing, we should certainly hope there is a God who sees and remembers everything, taking note of every tiny overlooked act of goodness, and threatening punishment for the crimes that men never even noticed or whose culprits couldn't be tracked down. The community would feel more protected, and bad men would feel pursued everywhere and always: in such a system they could no longer get away with things, scrutinized by God's all-seeing eye and eventually punished, perhaps not in this world but certainly in the next one. Whether or not such a thing actually happens is of no real concern, if what we were looking to obtain was a deterrence effect in the here and now, a way of discouraging evildoers. So God really ought to cut it out, once and for all, with all this hiding of Himself: all He'd need to do is show Himself, threateningly, maybe once every thousand years. Then, in the end, He could even forgive everything, it hardly matters.

394. Four different eventualities of repentance. Repent while resolving never to repeat those mistakes. Repent specifically to be able to repeat them again, then repent of them, and then fall back into them, and so on. Not to repent at all, and just to go on as before. Not to repent, and yet stop making those mistakes, because sin has become dull and boring or else it has used up all your energies, it has even worn out its own name, and even if it were to be repeated, it would no longer really even be a sin.

399. Why does pleasure always have to be followed by its opposite? Why is it discarded and abandoned almost immediately? Perhaps it is its unexpected nature that is so upsetting. Most people don't know what to do with the unexpected. It's simpler for them to just adapt to its absence. As quickly as they can. Happiness makes people uncomfortable. Do you want to compare it with the tranquillity of being frustrated? Its linear nature, its complete consistency? The way most people have of dealing with a pleasure that has taken them by surprise is to hide. One's own vitality and that of others are impending threats.

400. If they are observed from close up, if one attentively turns them over in one's hands, all the imperatives of philosophy, religion, and morality are utterly empty: inside the translucent coffer of their propositions, which claim to be necessary and universal, there is everything but also, at the same time, nothing, nothing specific at all: anything specific and concrete would undercut their totality. Whatever the case, as soon as they receive those commandments, people immediately fill them with contingencies, provide their abstractness with practical contents, succeeding sometimes in achieving the exact opposite of what the commandment prescribed.

401. The cadaverous obedience of the Jesuits. The mechanical obedience of all bodies to the laws of physics, and of the elements to the laws of chemistry. Dispassionate and impersonal obedience to moral law. Obedience to the perverse law of pure desire. Obedience to the party and its leader. Obedience to the principles of liberty, which also demands obedience, and might indeed be the most tyrannical mistress.

403. The centuries are too short.

404. If Oedipus actually murdered his father in order to have sex with his mother, and nothing more, it would mean that the homicidal impulse moves economically, rationally, to attain some specific satisfaction: however, there must be subtler, more hidden reasons than this banal objective with a sexual undertone, more unpredictable motives that may, who can say, also be sexual in nature, but which have to do with destructiveness in a less mechanical fashion than this rustic idea of simply eliminating a rival. The idea of gratuitously destroying an individual (much like the idea of *not* destroying him even when to do so would serve one's self-interest or the more general collective interest) transcends all logic and any economic principle. To kill someone or spare them might mean to follow a rule or break one. An example? The one provided by people of goodwill who stand ready, rock in raised hand, to stone the adulteress, that is, to implement a measure of justice prescribed by law, or else to gratify a homicidal impulse conveniently transformed into a moral instrument, all the more implacable precisely because it is legitimate. By putting down that stone instead of throwing it, they will give rise to the controversial relationship between Christianity and justice, as if to say, between disproportion and proportion.

405. It is pointless for the saints to kiss the pustulent sores of the filthy: not only us, but even God himself is disgusted to see them seeking paradise through such repugnant proofs of faith.

406. In the state I'm in now, I'd feel only pity and scorn for someone who, even if it were with the noble intent of communicating a sense of brotherhood to me in my pain, displayed any particular sense of transport toward my rotting body. I would much rather stir an appropriate repulsion or, at the very most, that this objective disgust might be held at bay, professionally, by the nurses who treat it with the necessary technical detachment, cleaning it, disinfecting it, emptying it with businesslike, uncharitable gestures, the way you would with a trash can, suppressing your natural disgust behind a routine smile. True compassion lies in doing your duty and in the meantime thinking about other things, say, a tropical beach. I'm the first to turn away and let myself be lulled by the escapist, childish fantasies in the minds of those who take care of me, whereas I would only be depressed by a fanatical devotion, completely focused on my aching guts or my Christian soul, about to flit away.

407. The body is treated by the person who inhabits it like a house, that he or she can freely renovate, altering the original floor plan or even leveling it, to rebuild. There isn't all that much difference between people killing themselves and people deforming themselves with plastic surgery or a sex change: in all those cases, a living human being is liquidated, the body as it once was, the difference lies only in whether they decide to replace it with another body, or not to replace it at all.

408. What need is there for death to take possession of my life in such a treacherous and complicated fashion? I'd have preferred to hand it over willingly, rather than have it snatched away from me.

409. I'd gladly settle for a cheap amnesty, obtained through institutional laxity, or by some subterfuge or error. A solution straight out of a comedy of errors. It would bring bottomless joy to be left alive in the place of some other random individual, undeserving of death.

410. Does a gaze capable of going beyond things see things never seen before, or does it see the same things but in a different way? Or does it fall upon itself because there is nothing more to know? I'd like to know so I can

understand whether or not it was right to stop my investigations—but I want to know soon, in fact, right away. Okay, yes, I admit it, I'm insatiable. That's because in the final analysis I was interested in this good old world. I was even amused by its cynical spectacle, precisely because it was reprised, with some considerable technique, on different stages, and every time the audience willingly allowed itself to be taken in, aghast at its own docility. To object is a more childish attitude than to allow yourself to be persuaded. I admit that I fell for it myself, to have done nothing more than to protest, even though I knew it was sterile, as are nearly all ways of getting noticed. Every word added at the bottom of these lines is nothing but a protest, however weak, that risks being mistaken for praise, is likewise too timid and faint to be accepted by the One it was meant for.

411. Among the wreckage, my mind has remained intact like certain dainty little drawing rooms that you can just glimpse after an earthquake on the fourth floor of an apartment building that has had its façade torn off. But you can't get in there, if you do, the whole place will collapse.

414. Depending on the voice in which it is delivered, the same announcement can sound like a threat or a promise.

413. My mind shakes the ocean (as far as I can tell, this is the last sentence Cosmo wrote before dying).

3

IN A SEPARATE SMALL NOTEBOOK, a more diminutive format, pocket-size, with handwriting grown uncertain and irregular, Cosmo tells how he grew attached, in the last month of his life, to a nurse, Jelena: he asks the association that is seeing to his care to send her, and only her, to tend to him, none of the other nurses; he hires her, paying her under the table, to spend nights at his home, in a jury-rigged bed; for a brief moment he even considers marrying her, so that once he's dead his teacher's pension can be transferred to her. I seem to understand that she, Jelena, was there, with Rummo and the *priest, when Cosmo died. I'm only going to feature one passage from this small notebook: I'd be uncomfortable transcribing the whole thing. The thoughts by Cosmo that I've offered above have a value that I consider anything but private in nature. His notes about Jelena, on the other hand, the shy trepidation of his novella, which is perhaps a love novella (I wouldn't know what else to call it), will remain unpublished. For how much longer, I couldn't say.*

JELENA IS THE ONLY EUROPEAN NURSE caring for me. The others are all Latin American or from North Africa. Very good at their jobs and kind, certainly, and brisk, almost cheerful, I'd say, in the performance of their duties, twice a day. For that matter, since I've renounced any therapy worthy of the name, it's only a matter of administering the palliatives and supplements prescribed for me and performing the few hygienic operations that help to keep me from falling apart or, at least, not falling apart immediately: half an hour, what with the IV and all the rest, then they leave. I'm the one who encouraged them to speed up the IV infusion by squeezing the bag. "We're really nodda sposeto, eh, Prof!" but they went ahead and did it. Everything becomes much more elastic when in the final analysis you're just talking about letting someone die the way they please and choose, I mean to say, the protocols, the restrictions on schedules and doses with the accompanying scoldings if you go astray . . . what's the point of insisting? They know it better than I do. We understand each other clearly on this point. As I said, it's all very, very relative.

They alternate in shifts that do not seem at all regular: the Peruvian caregiver, for instance, came three days in a row, while I was waiting for it to be Jelena's shift at least once between morning and evening. She is the least prone to smiling, perhaps because she has a reserved character.

With her, I feel like joking around. Smiling. I'm sure that she would smile, too. I'd certainly understand it. Who knows why the sweetness in me is buried so deep. And why the same thing must have happened in her. But she doesn't have the excuses of old age and disease, which I hide behind. I wouldn't want to reveal to anyone else the anxiety that seizes me when another caregiver comes in her place, such as the Peruvian, for example, who is good at her job and very polite, the poor thing, but she isn't Jelena, she doesn't have that same light in her eyes. By now it's become a hard task to wait for her, and it's exactly the kind of thing I do not want anymore:

any feeling of yearning toward life, anything that summons me back. By now I've gone too far to turn around. Just now, when everything's about to end, I wind up getting a crush on a nurse just because she comes to take care of me a few hours a week, because she's silent, because if I look at her in profile she reminds me of nice things, from behind, of desirable things, and if she stands facing me, I see a melancholy human being who works to make a living. What does Jelena think about while she wipes me down, while she washes me?

Why don't I care about learning the same thing of the Peruvian? Is it because she flashes me the occasional quick smile, while Jelena doesn't?

Well, that is the last thing I need: this turmoil. Prompted by a woman who could be, not even my daughter, but my granddaughter. The blood that surges in my veins for a change, instead of stopping once and for all, that is what hurts me. And it fills me with shame and anger. Without wishing to, under the mechanical pressure of the years, I had been forced into wisdom, imperturbability, the virtuous contemplation of people and things, as if what had bent me were sermons in preparation for death. The presence of Jelena beside me acts like a powerful poison. But it doesn't kill me. Jelena isn't beautiful, she isn't fetching, she's just simple, and alive. She won't manage in the end to make me yearn for my life back, will she?

THE OLD MAN WEARS *his new love on his shoulders like a harp: he's strong enough to drag its weight along, but the effort keeps him from playing it.*

Part X

Like Trees Planted Along the River

I

Y<small>OU TURN AROUND</small> *and your brother's hair has grown suddenly long*
You turn around and your sister has become suddenly beautiful
You turn around and your brother's hair is brushing his shoulders
You turn around and your father is dead and your mother stops smiling and you have your first car crash luckily not a serious one and you get your girlfriend pregnant and she has an abortion and you feel as if you're about to kill yourself because you're a useless and unhappy creature and you even try but you're unsuccessful and the world hasn't stopped spinning while you were in the hospital, it went on spinning neither slower nor faster

You turn around and with the next woman you meet at a party you'll have children and then you'll leave her and your children will curse you for the rest of your life even if they hug you affectionately when you go to pick them up at school one week on and one week off

Then the doctor says that he's diagnosed an infection and you're given an emergency operation and they just manage to save your life, another twelve hours and you would have been dead, and though you were ready to kill yourself before now you're pretty contented that you made it out with your skin on even though you're tired, very tired, and you don't make enough money, and you're in the hands of lawyers who continue to file appeals on your behalf without achieving anything clear and the roof of the country house inherited from your father collapses because of the heavy rains and the limited maintenance done on it or, to tell the truth, none at all

You never even went there

You turn around and your sister isn't beautiful anymore, she teaches French in a middle school, she never married, she's an old maid before her time, she has recurring panic attacks

Your brother went to live in Panama. Actually, he fled the country. He left behind a wife and a son who has serious vision problems. You avoid getting too attached to that little boy because you're afraid that you'll have to take care of him even though, in the meantime, no one is taking care of you

Whereupon you turn around and you see a woman, free and unattached and not bad-looking either and after spending two or three nights together you decide that things could develop into something with her, she's a serious person, she's serious about it, she seriously wants to do this, she's already planning a vacation together for next summer and the summer after that, on account of which you start to withdraw, you gradually withdraw, you stop answering her calls, and before the month is out you've definitively broken up with her

2

MY ALL-CONSUMING ANXIETY has led me to scrawl out "Human Life in the Last Quarter of the Twentieth Century," which you read in the preceding, exceedingly brief chapter. Does it have anything to do with the events described in this book? Yes and no, it could run on a parallel track, as an alternate plot. It expresses the fantastic desire to tell of an ordinary life in just a few words instead of a great many.

I promise: the chapters that follow will be just as short or extremely short.

So let's start over again from the very beginning, from the QT.

3

QUARTIERE TRIESTE, tomb of courage, prison with transparent walls, cradle and decline of civilization!

Seized by a loneliness and an unhappiness brimming over with unspecified desires, which pricked me to get up and move, no matter what the movement in question, on this brilliant and icy winter Sunday I left home early to penetrate once again, in search of who can say what novelties, given that your essence as a quarter of the city is that you never offer anything new, and even though I knew that so sharp and clear a light could hardly help but blind me and thrust me back into the mental enclosure inhabited by the usual thoughts, the usual memories, the same novel that I read and write, that I write and imagine, that I imagine and erase.

Instead, my outing was interesting because there was a new development, a novelty after all, finally something new to see, even though it would have been far better never to have seen it, so graceless absurd incomprehensible and a blight on the landscape. On the slopes of the hillside that runs up from Piazza Annibaliano to the high point on Via Nomentana, where the basilica of Santa Costanza and its wonderful baptistery lie concealed among the trees, behold the brand-new station of the Rome metro: after years, it is done and it has come to light, since they took down the barriers that sheltered the secret project that had been toiling onward.

It's a sinkhole, a chasm, a sort of quarry of unfinished cement from the depths of which looms upward the tower of a gratework elevator that, once it reaches ground level, towers upward another dozen or so yards into the air, sticking right into the space that was once destined for a view of Santa Costanza by anyone covering the last stretch of Corso Trieste. Before they barricaded the entire area for the construction work (with a view, one might suspect, of concealing the horrible surprise still to come) between the looming apartment buildings of that last stretch of road and the dull brown housing projects, ten stories tall, on Viale Eritrea, which begin right at the edge of the piazza, the sudden opening of light and space almost obliged the passerby to turn his gaze to the right, toward Via Nomentana, and the promontory where, for time out of mind, both Sant'Agnese and Santa Costanza stood sheltered, a verdant nursery deep in the shadow of the tall holm oaks, a preschool, and a happy tennis club with terraced courts punctuating the slope of Via Bressanone.

Now, right in the center of this lovely archaeological oasis in the QT, at the exact center of the painting that one might paint in commemoration of the martyrdom of the young female saint, willing to suffer her beheading, garbed only in her hair, on Via Nomentana where they had set her out as a prostitute, stands the gray thorn of the elevator tower of the Annibaliano metro station, topped by a red M so large that it could be seen from an airplane and could serve as the target of a bombardment which, for that matter, it would so richly deserve. From this piece of signage, a passerby might reasonably feel almost threatened, as if by any other outsized totalitarian emblem, so out of scale is it, and it seems to allude to the existence, down below, of the largest metro station on earth, where countless lines intersect and overlap, and you can easily get lost on your way from one to another: I don't know, the way you might at Châtelet, Charing Cross, Grand Central . . .

And instead it's just an ordinary metro stop on the B1 line, though it's been given this monumental appearance, as if it were an entrance to the underworld. Perhaps they were worried about solving the problem of what would be seen of the sad old Piazza Annibaliano once the excavations were covered back over, they had the brilliant idea of not covering it up at all, but instead exalting it, hailing it, that abyss, rendering it as grandiose as a monument to the Holocaust or to the War Dead.

(Aren't the stations on the metro line supposed to be *underground*, though? Isn't that where they belong? Like in London, *Underground*, isn't that what the English word means?)

And the real kicker is that, when they decided to name the new station, which could certainly have just been called Annibaliano, since it stands, or really, sinks down into a corner of the old piazza, they insisted on adding the name of the monument the sight of which the station itself, with its tower looming up out of the crater, roundly defaces and obstructs. Which is why the metro stop is called Santa Costanza–Annibaliano . . .

BUT ONCE I'D LEFT that monstrosity behind me, just a few steps farther along, the rage had already vanished, the indignation, deep inside me, had already dwindled: after all, what can I do about it now? And I realized that I'd immediately transformed that collective insult into a private sentiment. I'd immediately focused down into myself, into my own problems, my desires, and I couldn't say whether this selfishness consoled me or made me even more intolerant. From the narcissistic point of view, that unsightly mess of a metro station seemed to have been built specifically for me, for me and me alone, as the sole future user of the system, either as a personal slight or else to take me away to the far side of the city, as quickly as possible, that's right, they had spent billions just so that I could take that trip underground in just ten minutes . . . and then and there I swore to myself that I'd never take the metro, not from that station, I wouldn't descend into that grotto as garish and ostentatious as an amusement park.

Then that fantasy vanished entirely and I went back to thinking . . . brooding . . . yearning.

And as I was walking along, narrowly skirting the massive walls, drunk with the winter daylight, I thought that when all was said and done, there was only one thing missing from my life, missing even when I had it, in fact, missing *especially* when I had it, because the fact of having it only sharpened the pain of each successive instant in which I'd no longer have it, making it all intolerable, making me suffer for the fine-honed awareness of the difference that runs between having it, this thing, and no longer having it, having let it slip through my fingers. And this thing is woman, *a* woman, that *special* woman.

I never yearned for anything else in all my life but to have a woman. No sooner had I emerged from the affectionate arms of my mother than I began dreaming of nothing other than a new embrace. But this time I wanted to be the one who embraced, who surrounded, who pulled a body close. I never cared about anything else and I don't now. I don't give a dried fig (as the delightful saying once ran) about literature, money, personal satisfactions and dissatisfactions, the past, the future, friends and enemies, justice, the fate of the world at large. I don't care about God or the nothingness that stands in His place. Without the love, without the body, the attention, or the mere sight of a woman, my life has never meant a thing, that is to say, had any significance, or for that matter a minimal direction. And in fact, that is what I thought as I strolled all alone through the QT: that the woman I love was far away, and this was intolerable, it strangled me, it took my breath away. That women stir my blood and fog a mind already far too confused, too prehensile and distracted, at age twelve I couldn't concentrate, speak, understand, or think if there was a young woman or a girl in the vicinity, in close proximity to me, or even if I saw her in the distance, passing by. Which meant that I really could never think at all, I never understood a thing, I was perennially upset and confused and the only instants of lucidity I could have hoped to attain would have been at SLM, where there were no girls or women. But even there, sure enough, if not in flesh and blood, in the image, in my imagination, all the space around me was populated with female figures, girls who weren't there but might as well have been; it made no difference whether that figure did or didn't exist, whether it was pretty or homely, whether I liked her or not: it was enough just to have a person of the opposite sex next to me or in my eyes or in my mind's eye, to disturb me to an indescribable degree. I could feel the surge of blood in the veins of my arms, my legs, drenching my abdomen, and a flush at once icy and hot would stun me, rushing into my head, which was suddenly full, as if stuffed, padded, so that I was all at once both blind and deaf, my tongue lying dead in my mouth, paralyzed, precisely as in that famous poem. The senses, no longer coordinated, exclude one another, so that if I can see, I can't hear, if I listen I can't see, or my visual field shrinks to the few square inches of a detail, and if the girl that has so captivated my mind is close to me, I can give the impression that I'm enchanted by her mouth, or the wave of hair that having escaped from behind an ear now floods around it, and in fact, I see nothing but that, and in the meantime I sense nothing else, I hear nothing else, I don't think, I don't speak . . . my words are disconnected from my thoughts, my feelings, peeled away one from another . . .

SINCE I WAS A BOY, I always felt this way. And since I still do, and I feel it deeply, I believe it's true. Look, it's simple. The presence of a woman next to a man is an event. Something happens between them, whether it happens or it doesn't. Even if there is no contact, it's as if there *had* been contact and, in point of fact, as if *there were*, even if it was an invisible contact, even if not on the physical plane. I've always felt this thing in the strongest imaginable way.

4

IN THE FOLLOWING DREAM *("The Vigilante of the QT") there is a blend of an unrequited lust, the piercing yen to go into action after so many ritualistic complaints, a parodistic myth of chivalry, the need to administer exemplary punishments in a way that will ensure that the populace understands and rises up in rebellion, but rebellion against whom? Against itself, that's obvious, because it is the populace that without noticing it has been oppressing the populace, in this intolerable battle we wage of each against all, all against all . . .*

I IMAGINE AND PLAN with maniacal care, snickering as I conceive the scene in my mind, donning a mask and mounting my scooter, and then zooming up and down, back and forth through the QT with the mission of punishing the motorists who have double-parked their cars: the ones who, wanting to go grab a before-dinner drink in one of the bars along Corso Trieste and do some shopping, taking their own sweet time, just leave their car there and off they go, for example, abandoning it at the intersection with Viale Gorizia, heading down toward Piazza Istria, and with Via Topino, on the way back up. The inanity or the sadism of the joker who chose to redesign the traffic flow of the QT, alongside the rude indifference of the owners of double-parked Smart cars, ensures that every hour of the day small but decisive traffic jams form, through which the city buses are unable to pass: now, listen carefully, this isn't a traffic jam created by hundreds of vehicles, not a bit of it, all it takes is a couple of cars trying to turn off Viale Gorizia and onto Corso Trieste, another couple that need to turn left onto Via Topino (and that is the only point, incredibly! the one and only point where the extremely long central median, useful only as a place to let your dog take a piss, offers a gap so you can change direction), there, all it takes is four cars plus the usual Smart car double-parked and any of the countless city buses, route 80 or 88, stuck behind the Smart car, and traffic is paralyzed.

And so I, possibly with an accomplice behind me on my scooter, though I might be able to do it on my own, if I were fast enough and careful not to tip over or let myself be caught by the enraged motorists and pounded to a pulp, once I'd carefully obscured the license plate of my scooter and my identity with a full-face helmet or a ski mask (certainly, it would be better and more appropriate to wear a suitable uniform, with a flowing cape, the mask of the Avenger of the QT), armed with a can of indelible spray paint (at first I'd thought of using a screwdriver, but I thought it over and the risk of hitting the pavement if the screwdriver happened to catch on a door handle or a side mirror is really too great), so, tricked out like that, I'd patrol up and down along Corso Trieste, using my can of spray paint to mark the cars parked incompetently. *All of them.* Without once releasing my finger from the spray-paint button, in five seconds I'd paint five or six cars, one after the other. I'd do it once, twice, for a week, for a month in a row, reckoning an average of twenty motorists punished every day, always miraculously avoiding capture. I'd be pursued in all likelihood by hulking irate citizens, by screaming matrons, who would show up at that exact moment, ready to retrieve their vehicles after taking their own sweet time about it, only to see their cars given a flying paint job by this masked guy on a scooter, maybe, at first, in the first few days of my vendetta, without a clue as to why I'd ruined their paint job, assuming that it was a random act of hooliganism, carried out by a young criminal, while instead it was in fact a just and exemplary punishment behind which lurks a middle-aged man, so that in the course of a week it would become clear, to the entire QT and to the city, just what those defacements meant, regular and systematic, it would become clear, that is, that these are targeted punishments, by no means arbitrary, which isn't hooliganism but the exact opposite, it's *justice*, it's an archaic yet elevated form of justice that, since none of the authorities delegated to deal with it (traffic cops, municipal police, normally otherwise occupied in ticketing scooters that cause no hindrance to traffic whatsoever) seem willing to mete it out, it's up to me to take it into my own reluctant, but in the end decisive, hands of a private citizen sick of suffering abuse and mistreatment. I know perfectly well that it's only a short step from there to Charles Bronson or else *Falling Down*, and in fact I can't rule out a further escalation. The next target would be Rome's dog owners, the ones who refuse to clean up after their pets—*smerdatori*. I still don't know how I would punish them. But these are people who take their dog out and bring it home after smearing the sidewalks with its excrement. I've never stepped in so many different dog shits of every shape and color as since I've come back to live in the QT. Next would be graffiti taggers, even if they're hard to catch, those miserable jerk-offs, while they trace out their monotonous logos: SFAZ and SMUARK.

5

THE DECISION TO COME BACK to live in this quarter provoked a landslide in time, a seismic shift. As I walk along, the same wind pushes me that blew back then. If I look down now, to sidestep the plentiful dog turds, I have a pair of stained and shapeless Clarks desert boots on my feet, which lightly leap over the puddles. My step has become lithe and carefree. That's how I walk, good-looking, twenty-two years old.

THE TERRITORY OF THE QT was marked by a series of challenges.

This piazza belongs to me, that street is one that we conquered, there you'd be advised not to set foot. Mark the boundaries of your own living space and expand it through an array of provocations. Spitting, threatening, graffiti, posters, swinging chains.

In ethology, it's called "spacing," in bullfighting, "querencia."

Knuckleheads
make no noise
if you use a club

IN PARTICULAR the graffiti on the walls indicated that the space had been violated by interlopers at the same time courageous and cowardly: there can be nothing more futile, and therefore heroic, than going in the night to scrawl a few insults that your enemies will find under their noses at breakfast.

Every day, it was necessary to update the map of territorial control with new data. Woe betide those who wander into the wrong zone, thinking it's still safe! Like in any war, the greatest number of casualties was caused by disinformation.

What remained above and beyond any dispute was the domain of the Fascists, their stronghold and outpost, Piazza Trasimeno, that is, the little opening in the thoroughfare created by the left-leaning curve that Corso Trieste hints at as it passes in front of Giulio Cesare High School, only to continue to climb toward Via Nomentana. That piece of territory (nothing more than a little tree-lined excuse for a piazza) seemed to have been assigned from time out of mind to the Fascists and it served as their base or presidio, on the opposite side from the high school, where Bar Tortuga still stands. There the sidewalk is broad and deep, and perfectly suited to the tables out in front of the bar and the scooters parked in their rows, and there's also a photo booth. The little strip of photographic paper, with four pictures one atop the other . . . which, a couple of minutes after the glare of the flash, drips into the exterior slot . . . and then just sits there drying, if you're not too curious to be willing to wait. The result: eyes invariably wide open, dazzled by the flash of light. Inevitably, the face of a terrorist, with or without a mustache. For at least twenty years, on all of my IDs I always had the photo of a terrorist. And like me, thousands of other young men and women.

I find nothing quite so amusing as the idea that entire generations that set out from the QT have been recognized at the borders of half the world, from Checkpoint Charlie to the Khyber Pass, by displaying a passport photo taken at the little photo booth in front of Bar Tortuga. The flashes of their wide-eyed faces have left the customs officers of every nation scratching their heads. They've always pulled me aside for further examination, even at border crossings where others were simply waved through without a second glance.

I emanate pulsations that engender suspicions.

In the QT, the boundary lines were modified in accordance with a shifting field of forces. The expansions took place promptly the minute the adversary loosened his control over the territory, scattering the garrison that he exerted, the patrolling on scooters, the activity of putting up posters. In terms of political clashes, playing with home team advantage meant you could make up for the possible disparity in strength and numbers. As was once the case with soccer teams, which were mainly unbeatable in their own stadiums, the ones who were fighting on their own territory, even if they were outnumbered, almost always won. But at this point, the singular characteristic of the QT emerged: it didn't belong in any stable fashion *to anyone*. It was to all intents and purposes a no-man's-land, a neutral field. Day after day, anyone could seize a slice of it and declare it their own; but that declaration and the possession that went with it never managed to take on a definitive character.

The war being waged in the QT was a war of position. A single night, and the enemy lines had shifted without you knowing it. When you woke up, just like Vittorio Gassman and Alberto Sordi in the film *La grande Guerra (The Great War)*, you found yourself surrounded by the enemy.

6

The yearning is great
there is no pussy
I grab my dick
feeling tired and wussy

Aside from dirty poems, what still remains in my head after years of school, years of Catholic school, after a lifetime spent in a Catholic country, listening to radio stations with the rosary recited in a singsong by nuns and TV news shows where the pope appears punctually every evening, greeting, saying benedictions, smiling, admonishing, expressing regret or rejoicing, hoping that the war will end soon and that all violence will soon cease (over the course of my own lifespan I have had six popes who spoke to me, looking out from a TV screen, they were speaking to everyone, and I was there too, among all of them: John XXIII, about whom all I can remember was the collective sadness when he died, Paul VI with his quavering voice and the appeals he launched that went unnoticed, the falling star of Pope Luciani, Wojtyla in his various phases, the magnificent and much vituperated German pastor Ratzinger, and now Pope Francis . . .), landing in a distant airport, pushing his way through the crowd in his armor-plated automobile, washing the feet of young black children . . .

And in fact, what I am left with are those iterative clauses, the Christ Who wins, the Christ Who forgives, the Christ Who saves, the Christ Who restores to life, the Christ Who accompanies and consoles us . . . the sermon that I feel like I've been listening to since before I was born, unchanging, a sort of whisper diffusing from the grate of a confessional or the grillwork of a loudspeaker, always raucous, hoarse, perhaps as a result of a tireless preaching and preaching . . . patiently, almost dully, in the presence of an audience formed of one or two or two hundred or two hundred thousand faithful, it makes no difference, and even now that it's Sunday morning and I'm driving with the radio on there are, in fact, on the Third Network, those extremely learned biblical exegetes who, with the psalmodizing voice mentioned above, interpret passages of Holy Scripture. More than explaining them, they seal them into hermetic formulas overbrimming with tremor and enthusiasm, humble enthusiasm swollen with faith and doubts, enthusiasm for a mystery that refuses to yield to any attempt to unveil it, not even the most intelligent and dashing and impassioned . . . "It is the enigma of the love of God," they say, or else, "It is the love for the enigma of God" or "It is the enigma of the God of love . . ."

For the umpteenth time today, they announce that they are ready to listen, and they suggest that we follow suit, we, the radio audience, we too should stand ready to listen. Ready to listen is the key phrase. It is necessary to know how to listen to the word, listen to your neighbor, to others, listen to God, listen to Him especially when He does not speak, listen to silence, listen to the silence inside of us . . . Listening to those plummy voices, often colored by a foreign accent or intonation that falters on such Italian words of Greek origin as "*pneuma*" or "*càrisma*" (with the accent on the first *a*), "*paracleto*," "*parusia*," I am lulled, enchanted, and in the meantime the panorama flows away on either side of the car.

MY SKEPTICISM TOWARD PREACHERS of any kind comes from a film I saw, in fact, at SLM, at the legendary film forum organized by Brother Barnaba, namely *The Ballad of Cable Hogue* by Sam Peckinpah, him again, the director of *Straw Dogs*: and it's a humorous and blasphemous scene, in which the Rev. Joshua Duncan Sloane, played by David Warner, a filthy and deranged preacher, invites a young woman to pray with him, lifting both arms to the sky, and she, her eyes filled with tears for the death of her beloved, lifts her arms to the sky, and as she does, the pastor, from behind, slips his hands into her dress and squeezes her breasts.

ONCE, the oblate of a church in the center of Rome (Santa Francesca Romana) asked me and F. if we were interested in taking part in a session of reading and interpretation of passages from Holy Scripture. The monks who were running the session were learned and levelheaded, and by intercession of the oblate we could get permission to observe. The idea interested me but I doubted I possessed the prerequisites, first and foremost, genuine faith. The readings would take place within a monastic community. And I, who haven't taken communion since I was fourteen . . .

"But what's necessary to take part? I don't know if I . . . if we . . . are up to it," I objected, dubiously.

"Well, it doesn't take much . . . you only have to believe in God."

In fact, I thought, maybe that's the problem.

The oblate looked me in the eyes. His were light blue and bloodshot.

"Actually," he added with a smile, which you could see more in those bloodshot eyes than in his mouth, twisted in an ironic smirk, "you don't even have to believe in God." Then he gave us a wink. "Who knows, maybe that comes later."

WE'VE COME BACK TO THAT CHURCH because today is the feast day of the saint in question and tomorrow F. is going to be admitted to the hospital. We went there to pray. Just what good that praying will do isn't clear to me, but as in many similar cases, it's the sort of thing that it is better to do than to waste time wondering about why one might do it. At the end of the service, after going to see the imprints left by St. Peter's kneecaps on the basalt paving stones of the Via Sacra when he knelt down to pray as Simon

Magus was levitating in midair, a hundred feet off the ground (F. insisted on placing her hands in the hollows of those two dark imprints), through a providential intervention of the oblate, we were allowed to slip into the sacristy, where the prelates were doffing their vestments after officiating the mass for St. Frances of Rome, and we were able to find a moment of time to address a hasty prayer to the Virgin Mary that is housed in there, the oldest Virgin Mary in the world, to her sweet broad face made of wax, with asymmetrical eyes. It's one of the few images before which I've ever felt the presence or at least a spark of the sacred, which is something quite distinct from aesthetic appreciation, indeed, it is in direct opposition to it. The others are: the Madonna dell'Orto in Venice, the niches of the Buddhas destroyed in Bamiyan, Gethsemani, Dante's grave in Ravenna, the Alyscamps in Arles, the Mithraeum beneath Santo Stefano Rotondo, places where I think I've done something like praying, spontaneously, without having a clear idea of to whom and why, and asking or promising what.

In the meantime, while we were looking at the Virgin and She was looking at us, with her sweet, almost cross-eyed gaze, Simon Magus, the braggart, was released by the devils who had lifted him high into the air, and he plunged downward, smashing onto the pavement.

1

LET'S ALSO SAY THAT THE STORY of the CR/M tucked away in this book wasn't the only story. Alongside a given account and intertwined with it there are others, which branch out in every direction, like in a family tree, you can never say where one ends and the next one begins, so closely connected are they, origins and filiations. All around the CR/M there grows a dense forest of perverse and criminal ramifications. Not all of them bloody, none of them venial. Some of these appendices are invented, others are legendary, others still so obscure that there's not a person now alive who knows what really happened, or else they do know but they can't prove it, or they could prove it but are afraid to. Forty years later, there are very few around who saw with their own eyes and heard with their own ears.

So many different things have been heard . . . in dishonest confessions, deliriums of criminal megalomania, exhibitionism, boasting . . . People say, word has it.

Crimes have a tendency to feed off each other, they strive to outstrip each other, creating a certain continuity, replicating a character or else the backdrop against which he moves, in such a way as to highlight him; in other words, a single crime is not enough, it isn't sufficient to create a worthy and complete figure, and that is why criminals commit more crimes, or if they don't commit them, they dream them up, which amounts to the same thing with respect to the personality that they intend to construct for themselves: and so they multiply their stories, they vary them, they amplify and add on . . . They *always* throw more meat onto the fire, when it's not the judges tossing that meat on for them. At Rebibbia Prison, in the wing where common criminals are confined, where the crimes are burglary, armed robbery, peddling narcotics, and similar offenses against property and person, when you talk with an inmate willing to open up to you a little bit, well, there's practically not a crime out there he doesn't know about in considerable detail, either because he's heard about it, or else because in one way or another he actually took part in it, or else because he was excluded from it or else he ruled himself out of it at the very last minute. The network of criminal accounts is fine-grained, extremely dense, and it's practically impossible to distinguish between the threads of the truth and the legends that form around each case. Certainly, there exists a written tradition, in the form of the verdicts issued by the various courts, but it's very fragmentary: the restricted nature of investigations tends to shoehorn the story into a specific lapse of time, or a circumscribed physical space, framing it and detaching it from the network of events that represented its initial premise, or its natural aftermath, as well as the contiguous, parallel events. Those links have been severed and, after bleeding for a while, they have been cauterized, they've scarred over. At least in appearance. Because in the oral tradition resected stories have gone on living, sprouting new branches, like a tree after it's pruned, and gradually, as the text of verdicts dried up and mummified, dwindling practically away to dust, dust that no one paid any attention to, until one fine day the decision is made to sweep it away, but in the meantime the oral versions thrived and blossomed, becoming increasingly vital and, so to speak, fresh, dewy with credibility, because of the fact that they are heard from the living voices of men, rather than having to track them down in the archival files where any statement sounds falsified, forced into the schematic structure of bureaucratic language so as to comply with the investigative hypothesis.

If I think about the effort involved along the way when you write a novel or a treatment for a film, striving to eliminate to the best of your ability the numerous inconsistencies that tend to pop up, I can imagine the extent to which conjecturing the perpetrators of a serious crime will require you, in your efforts to solve the case, to take shortcuts, skip over unclear transitions, construct daring bridges from one point to another in the tangle of events. In order to get things to add up, I'm pretty sure that investigating magistrates, in perfect good faith, find themselves twisting the facts, starting with the way they are laid out: they emphasize certain sources and overlook others that would conflict with the first, picking and choosing among the available evidence to favor those that support a plausible theory, a reconstruction of events that holds together, and backgrounding all the rest. Only through a violent effort, similar in certain ways to the aesthetic striving involved in writing a short story or shaping a statue, can a verdict attain a minimum of internal consistency: even though I personally have read my share of verdicts that truly didn't make a lick of sense.

It's no accident that Kafka saw the trial as the greatest possible concentration of logic and, at the same time, of absurdity: the sheer consistency with which you can develop a nonsensical premise. It's a matter of lining up a series of difficult-to-understand events, among which the ones that actually happened may very well prove to be even more mysterious than the ones concocted out of thin air, indeed, I'm convinced that the chief use of invention is to fill in for the shortage of logic in factual reality; not so much therefore to escape the strictures of a fixed and rigid world, but rather to give some meaning to a world that fluctuates to a fault. Inventions and lies serve to inject a smidgen of logic into a world that appears devoid of it; they serve in other words to create, through sheer artifice, the passages between different zones of reality, because reality as it stands is too riddled with holes, too earthquake-battered, too riven with crevices of the nonsensical, which means that imagination is required to step in to build bridges that might allow the human mind to span the dizzying abysses of the absurd, the abysses into which that mind, if it lacked the imaginative faculty entirely, would surely plunge. We don't use imagination to flee this world, but rather to inhabit it without going mad, and in order to attempt to live in it by giving it the meaning that it lacks.

And so it is that in the oral tradition, made up as it is of muttered stories and discarded conjectures or legends pure and simple, something *close to the truth* can circulate.

❖

THE STORY I AM ABOUT to tell is an appendix to the CR/M, even if it takes place *before* it. The chronology of understanding and fame arranges events as it pleases along the axis of time: a clamorous event, as the CR/M was, brings all the others from the past bobbing to the surface, illuminating them with its meaning, or even *creates* them, so that, while these events took place *before*, in reality they only began to exist *subsequently*. The principal event catapults them into the future. Which is typical of scandals, which only begin to arouse outrage at the moment that they cease. As Karl Kraus put it: "The scandal begins when the police put a stop to it." Many things have their beginning in their end, and take to their wings at sundown, like the owl of Minerva. Things that happen before but only acquire significance afterward. The sorrowful revelations and the discoveries about the past sow the future with shocking or consolatory images.

I might say, for example, that my friendship with Arbus became authentic and powerful only when we parted ways, when our lives separated. At first it was a scholastic friendship, perhaps an alliance or a refuge, especially for me, someone who was all too easy to influence.

8

THE INFORMANT'S FRENZY is that of *explaining, connecting,* establishing connections between events and people. A selfish and narcissistic disposition, placed however at the service of others, who must be enlightened; the point is to reveal to them what is concealed under the official version of things, invariably false. Precisely because the Italian mysteries are so numerous and obscure, there is a widespread syndrome among those who avow they possess the formula that can explain them. Usually these individuals describe themselves as being in a perennial struggle against the version of events supplied by the authorities or against common sense, which holds tight to its misguided convictions. They set themselves up as apostles of the truth: a truth that has managed to slip under the noses of investigators, or which has shown itself off almost provocatively, practically waving and gyrating to obtain notice, under the eyes of public opinion and yet unable to win full consideration, remaining ignored, overlooked if not actually mocked and derided. The individuals in question, instead of taking umbrage at the fact, actually boast of it, because the greater the resistance to the truth of which they are proponents, the more fundamental the revelations they herald.

What can rival the pleasure of knowing something that the others, clueless simpletons, don't? The behind-the-scenes stories, the secret reasons why things went the way they did, the names of those behind it.

In Italy there is a teeming mass of these super-well-informed and contemptuous souls, who have been able to turn the ridiculous inside out, into the stigmata of those who continue down their path, the path of truth, and claim to know who really kidnapped Aldo Moro, where Emanuela Orlandi is hidden, who planted the bombs and why, blew up churches, banks, trains, railroad stations, the cars of police escorts . . .

People who know, in other words, what went on *behind the scenes*. Italy is the country where what happens in the light of day necessarily sinks its roots into the obscure, the occult; where nine out of ten criminal cases, among the most spectacular ones, those discussed on TV and in the newspapers, remain unsolved, unpunished, or else involve convictions of people whom many consider innocent, as if the verdicts had no value as anything other than suggestions, hypotheses, and in that case, one hypothesis against another, each might as well hold on to their own; where instead of one version of events there are at least two, or three, or ten, all of them valid, arguable and defendable, it hardly matters how improbable and ludicrous. Pirandellism, relativism, the "right you are (if you think so)," the infinite interpretation and hermeneutics, the intelligence services, the dossiers, the gossip, the Machiavellianism, the idea that behind and beneath everything, even the fact that a team wearing solid-colored jerseys instead of striped ones might have won the championship, there is a plot, a conspiracy, a Masonic lodge, the CIA, the mysterious and powerful Elder, the Vatican, the Soviets (when they still existed), the Israelis, or the omnipresent Banda della Magliana. Alternative and unofficial truths, the countertruths, are so diffuse and widespread that they themselves have become official.

THE AUTHOR OF THE GREATEST NUMBER of stories running parallel to the CR/M is one of its protagonists, Angelo, brother of my classmate Salvatore. The investigators have spent years thumbing through the thousands of pages produced by his statements, where he revealed crimes committed on his own or with accomplices or else put the blame for them on other criminals, more or less well known, intertwining pending cases and providing them with a solution obtained thanks to prison confessions or confidences shared in a cell, and to a baggage of direct experience that Angelo, even though he had spent almost the totality of his adult life behind bars, wanted others to think was as boundless as that of public enemy number one. The investigating magistrates found themselves face-to-face with a strategic mind that had collected and collated the entire criminal activity of the seventies and eighties into a single shifting and delirious reconstruction, they listened to it, tried to follow the leads that that fertile mind, mixing together things that were well known, unprecedented details, and sheer inventions, produced incessantly, with the aim of earning for himself the status, then widely sought after, of cooperating witness; or perhaps those accounts issued in a continuous stream on account of a personality disturbance; or perhaps we were in the presence of an artist, a creative spirit, who shapes alternate structures to reality. A predisposal or a frenzy to confer meaning, to restore order, to make known and, therefore, to attribute to himself the truth of "the way things actually went," in a way that no one had ever previously guessed, or confessed. It is the syndrome of revelation.

In parallel with this, there is instead the optical illusion of proliferation, the house of mirrors in which you can vanish without a trace, the labyrinth.

And yet there are judges who have taken Angelo seriously, deeming him to be a "gold mine of information."

(Often the inmates I work with, out of discretion, out of prudence, or else by falling silent, allow those who are curiously listening to them a much broader field of possible revelations, horrifying or paradoxical, and they stop just as they get to the good part of their stories, with a sibylline *"Nun me fa' parla' . . ."*—Don't get me started.)

❖

WHERE ARE THE EGGS the dragon laid? How many of them hatched?

How many pages would it require to draw up a complete list of the people that Angelo claims to have killed or to know who actually killed them? It is remorse that has driven him to confess: "I have personal reasons for speaking, my decision is due to the convictions developed in prison, the need to make reparations for a repugnant murder" (namely, the CR/M).

Among the stories that I haven't yet mentioned, there are these:

The military training on how to build timers for bombs by using plastic alarm clocks; instructions received from a French military officer, "standing six foot seven, powerfully built, olive complexion, mustache, sunglasses," that is, a pure comic-book cliché of a retired soldier. Which means it might very well be true.

The truth about nearly all the great massacres that took place in Italy between 1969 and 1980, from Piazza Fontana to Piazza della Loggia, to the Italicus train bombing, to the bombing of the main train station in Bologna.

In 1986 he declared that the murder of Piersanti Mattarclla, the late brother of Italy's current president, was committed by the NAR so that the Mafia in exchange might free neo-Fascist Pierluigi Concutelli.

That same year, he claimed he was guilty of the attempted murder of a jewelry salesman, committed twelve years earlier. The victim was only wounded, and Angelo said that he had threatened to murder his six-year-old son, because he wouldn't stop crying.

He claimed that he had witnessed the killing of a typesetter at *Il Messaggero*.

He provided details on the attempted murder of Bernardo Leighton of the Chilean Christian Democratic Party; and the rape of Franca Rame, wife of the late Nobel laureate Dario Fo (carried out by the Fascists at the behest of the Italian Carabinieri).

A criminal complaint for defamation was filed against him by Judge Giovanni Falcone: according to Falcone his confessions were inspired by "ambitions of notoriety."

He accuses Massimo Carminati of killing Mino Pecorelli.

He says that he knows who killed Peppino Impastato: a guy whose last name is Miranda, a.k.a. "Il Nano"—The Dwarf.

He claims that the person who shot Giorgiana Masi (by the way, that day, May 12, 1977, among the demonstrators on the Ponte Garibaldi, Marco Lodoli and I were there, too) was the Legionnaire, his accomplice in the CR/M.

Fausto and Iaio, left-wing militants: they were murdered by Massimo Carminati, a.k.a. "Er Cecato," the One-Eyed Man (that's right, him again).

And again in 2005 he claims responsibility for the killing of a Turin prostitute, Franca Croccolino: a murder he supposedly committed thirty-five years earlier.

Et cetera.

10

AMONG ALL THESE STORIES there's another one that concerns me in particular (having come this far together, I'm tempted to say, that concerns *us*) because it contains a couple of unsettling elements that are exemplary of the period in which they took place. When: two years, perhaps twenty months prior to the CR/M. Where: on the outskirts of the QT, which is to say in that quarter that can rightly be called its twin, in both a spatial and an anthropological sense, because it extends, a mirror image of the QT, along the eastern edge of Via Nomentana, and revolves around Piazza Bologna, the way the QT does around Piazza Istria, the two piazzas reasonably similar except for Piazza Bologna's monumental post office, designed by the architect Mario Ridolfi, a building that characterizes the otherwise insignificant roundabout from which five or six streets run away in a spoked radius, streets with an inexplicable assortment of names.

What, in fact, does Via Lorenzo il Magnifico, named after Lorenzo the Magnificent, have to do with the home provinces of Via Livorno and Via Ravenna? Or for that matter with Viale XXI Aprile (namely, April 21, a date that marks Rome's Christmas, the anniversary of its ancient foundation)?

And who on earth were Michele di Lando and Sambucuccio d'Alando?

Behind the barracks of the financial police, known as the Fiamme Gialle, or Yellow Flames, for their distinctive logo, on Viale XXI Aprile, there lived an eighteen-year-old youth who will be known in this book as Cassio. Cassio Majuri. Like many other young men of the Nomentano quarter, a district that is in fact so similar to the QT that it is often mentioned in the same breath or even considered to be a part of it, Cassio was a right-winger. He'd been born into the right wing, he thought of himself and proclaimed himself to be a right-winger. His family belonged to the right wing, the school that he attended, the SLM Institute, was a majority right-wing establishment, and so for Cassio it was neither easy nor difficult to think and believe the things he thought and believed.

He played rugby. He studied very little. He frequented in a sporadic manner the local office of the neo-Fascist Movimento Sociale Italiano. He was theoretically shy around girls, but as he built up his physique by playing sports and by treating them rudely and crudely, in his imagination he believed that he could have not just one girl, but many. He met Angelo during a political assembly at which a mid-level official had been provided with a detail of bodyguards, given that at the time it was common for right-wing headquarters or offices to be targeted by sudden and violent attacks. There was no need for any particular organization or degree of planning on the part of the groups behind those attacks: even I—always quite skeptical about this sort of symbolic operation, designed specifically to do physical harm to some adversary or other, chosen at random—found myself taking part in similar actions a couple of times, with no planning aforethought: all it took was for there to be, during any ordinary political assembly, which might have been called to discuss the exploitation of miners in South America, say, or some other such subject, a sudden piece of exciting news, for instance, a badly beaten comrade who claimed to have been attacked by a group of Fascists, or a girl who claimed to have seen a certain right-wing enforcer enjoying an espresso at the café on Piazza Istria, all alone and apparently not looking for trouble . . . and there you had it, a perfect opportunity for a retaliation or an emblematic operation, and off went a commando mission, ready for action. Usually, without advance planning, which meant lacking any of the necessary equipment, such as clubs or helmets, except for the very few helmets that might have been worn by those who had come on a motor scooter, but back then helmets weren't required, so they were few indeed . . . and within ten minutes or so you found yourself on a war footing outside one of those places known at the time as *covi*, or Fascist lairs. You could count on sheer force of numbers, rather than armaments and the fighting quality of your combatants.

BUT NOW LET'S GO BACK to the office on Piazza Bologna where Cassio has been assigned to protect the personal safety of one of those old walking fossils, and I'm using the term in a technical sense, without a hint of malice, who formed the backbone of the neo-Fascist movement and its leadership, backing up the affable mustached mask of their national leader, Giorgio

Almirante. When they heard him make his calm and unruffled arguments on television, on political talk shows in the lead-up to elections, even the viewers who were opposed to his party had to admit: "Still, you have to say, he's a good speaker." In reality he was by no means either calm or reasonable, and even less so were the other officials of the Italian Social Movement, the Movimento Sociale Italiano, or MSI, which was often pronounced like the English word "miss": men with an unmistakable appearance, who were determined to emphasize their difference from the run of the mill by, so to speak, wearing that difference, the way you might pin a badge or a button to your lapel. They were often fat and powerfully built or else, to the contrary, skinny and ascetic, like sad knights, always rather funereal, as was, for example, my grandfather. The man who got out of the party-issue car, and whom Cassio escorted into the chapter office, was bald and wore a slightly shiny black turtleneck, with a pinstriped double-breasted jacket over it, and he concealed his eyes behind a pair of dark glasses—dark but not impenetrably so, very much like the headmaster at SLM. To Cassio and the other young men, among whom it appears that Angelo, too, was present, he limited himself to offering a ritual encouragement, out of context to the setting in which it was delivered: a semideserted street, a quarter that was minding its own business, no attack, no ambush, no enemy on the horizon . . .

"Bravo, comrades, bravo! Hearts striving upward!" Whereupon the young men snapped into a straight-armed salute, and so did Cassio, a little late.

Sensing the agitation swirling around him, Cassio was astonished to find he was inwardly so cold and detached.

"Weird: I should be having goose bumps. I can see that the others are excited, on edge, ready for anything. And I love them, my fellow Fascist comrades. And I can feel that I, too, am ready to do something. But is this *it*?"

What good is a single act if there is no physical result?

"To be afraid but manage to control that fear without effort makes me feel grown up, a little more of a man . . . but I don't know what to do with these few extra inches, if they don't take me any closer to what I truly desire."

It's reasonably easy to understand when you're playing rugby: you have twenty yards to the goalpost, or ten, or just a few short steps, before you're knocked backward by a long kick into touch. There, at least, the object is clear, you know where the line runs.

"But what is it I want, what is the goal I'm seeking? What am I looking for? Fascism? My father is a Fascist, my grandfather is a Fascist, sure, both of them . . . they know what they believe in, but I . . . I'm just a guy looking for an opportunity."

II

So CASSIO DECIDED TO DEDICATE himself to criminal pursuits, under the guise of his political faith. It was a faith that allowed a criminal sideline, indeed, that identified illegal activity as an appropriate and necessary means of carrying on the struggle, if not its actual objective. And then there was the thrill of taking up arms, the courage necessary to do so: those things could perfectly well be pursued for their own sake, divorced from any specific objectives. The Majuri family, well-to-do, vacationed at Cap d'Antibes, and there, through certain right-wing extremists, Cassio was introduced to members of the Marseille underworld. After a few test runs, in the course of which he proved himself to be reliable and punctual, he became a regular narcotics courier: he transported heroin and made plenty of money. Theoretically he ought to have put that money at the disposal of his political activity; the earnings from the drug trafficking were supposed to be plowed back into the purchase of weapons, to finance training camps, for travel abroad, to pay the utility bills of the lairs used for meetings or to store guns and bombs, as well as the fees of the lawyers to represent Fascist comrades whose families couldn't pay for them. They weren't all rich, in fact, there were quite a few comrades who came from the working class. Guys like Angelo and Majuri and the Legionnaire and the so-called *pariolini* were well known, but they didn't make up the mass of the movement: many militants came from the poorer outskirts of town. But Majuri started to develop a taste for that money; he soon discovered that he preferred pocketing it instead of devoting it to the cause; even worse, he started to believe he could get away with pilfering small quantities of heroin from the shipments he was delivering; he kept that surplus for himself and resold it. Seeing that the shipments were huge, he fooled himself into believing that the amounts he was stealing hadn't been noticed. But they were. His employers, though, said nothing, waiting to see what else he might get up to. Still, sensing that his bosses were keeping an eye on him, and noticing that along with the narcotics shipments, there were also reports being sent concerning certain Italian, French, and Spanish militants, Cassio thought it would be a smart move to make copies of them and conceal them, so that he could use them in case matters came to a head. Little did he suspect that, instead of protecting him, these sneaky moves were only accelerating the decision to eliminate him.

All the while, he went on with his life as a young Roman, in accordance with the standards of the time in the milieu of the right wing. He played rugby, he made sure he was seen in the right places in his gleaming new automobile, he did his best to appear self-confident, to put on the appropriate tone. The money from trafficking and peddling heroin and cocaine came in handy in this. His behavior became increasingly arrogant. He paid prostitutes to avoid going through the effort of courtship and the risk of rejection from girls his age. So they decided they could strike at him from that angle. They realized that they'd need to find a girl to bait the trap to catch Cassio. By now, the decision had been made: he had to die. In those circles, no one even dreams of trying to reform a guy like that. You get rid of him and be done with it. But first they needed to find out where he had hidden his copies of the compromising documents. Angelo and his men got ready to lay a trap. Since Majuri had expressed interest in the sister of a student at SLM, whom he had spotted one day outside school, they convinced the girl to take part in the deception. The girl was named, it seems, Perdìta, which is a strange name but seemed perfect for her, that is, for a lost girl, a girl on the road to perdition. She was fifteen years old. They had persuaded Cassio Majuri that they would bring the girl to his apartment, for a gang rape. He suggested a day when his family was traveling and the apartment would be empty. For certain gang rapes, Angelo and some of his friends would later be tried and convicted: but we'll never know how many they had carried out before the one at Monte Circeo, much less who was involved. In any case they were nearly all SLM students or alumni.

Dealing and consuming narcotics, marching in the honor guard at the funerals of dead comrades, violent retaliatory missions, kidnappings, variously real or with the complicity of the victim, handling weapons, breaking his relatives' hearts, living a double life, black flags, rugby, rape, and the occasional euphoric reading of this or that manifesto: that is the circuit Cassio Majuri plunged into, and it was there, in the end, that he met his death.

Perdìta was taken by car to Cassio's apartment building. Probably under the effect of illegal substances. It wasn't clear whether she was supposed to act as if she were a willing participant or pretend to have been forced unwillingly into the group sex. Cassio had told the others not to bother bringing weapons because he already had his father's hunting shotgun in the house, and armed with that, they'd easily be able to force the girl to comply with their wishes. He greeted them, already naked, in his parents' bed, the shotgun within reach. This was the first time he'd taken part in this kind of orgy. He'd been told the way these things worked: the girls were forced to undress at gunpoint or else by starting to strangle them to overcome their resistance, forced to drink alcohol, to take the members of the various males in their mouths, in turn, and then they were raped and sodomized. Last of all, threatened at gunpoint to make sure they told no one. The thought of what was about to happen filled Majuri's mind to the point that there was no room for doubt or suspicion. Nor did it occur to him that, if a girl like Perdìta had caught his eye, he might consider approaching her by more conventional means. Even though there was something at the bottom of Cassio's heart that didn't entirely rule out the idea that he might even be able to fall in love with a girl like Perdìta, he was willing to rape her just to avoid the humiliation of a potential rejection. He was getting ready to rape a girl he might have been able to love, under normal conditions. But there are no normal conditions, they don't exist. Everything is always an exceptional case. Cassio suspected nothing when they rang his doorbell. He stripped naked and ran to his parents' bed, where he'd already laid out the shotgun, loaded. He wanted to make sure that the muscles he'd developed playing rugby were on full display.

PERDÌTA DIDN'T UNDERSTAND what was about to happen. They had shown her some pistols and that aroused her curiosity rather than frightening her. Some of the gang remained in the car downstairs to wait. A couple of others went upstairs with her in the elevator. The door to the Majuri apartment was left ajar. Three of them went in, Perdìta and two young men. As soon as they were inside, one of them grabbed her and twisted her arm behind her back, clapping a hand over her mouth. She laughed as she felt that hand almost suffocate her, because she assumed this was just make-believe. "Stop laughing, you idiot!" said the one who was holding on to her. "Come on ahead!" they could hear Cassio's voice from a room at the end of the hallway. And they did. They opened the door and saw Cassio in the bed, naked, with his legs under the sheets. He pulled the sheets aside to make it clear just how aroused he already was. "What's her name?" he asked the one who was holding the girl. "Let her talk, I want to hear it from her." The guy took his hand off her mouth. "Go on, tell him." "Why do you want to know? What's it matter to you?" Perdìta retorted. Cassio was struck by the girl's brashness and his visible arousal immediately began to subside. He wanted to say a tough guy's phrase of some sort, but his voice came out quavering: "Oh, no reason . . . just that, before getting started, it might be better to know it." "Getting started with *what*?" asked the girl, but the guy holding her put his hand over her mouth and gave her a shove, and she whined in response, because this time the guy had hurt her for real. She tried to wriggle free. Cassio Majuri wasn't sure about what to do next. He felt like fucking that girl, and right away, but he didn't want her to be hurt, or at least not too badly. "Hey," he called to his friend, "take it easy . . ." and then, "come here, we're not going to hurt you," to the girl. All of a sudden, he felt awkward about being naked while the other three were fully dressed. He felt a little ridiculous. And defenseless. His arousal had vanished completely by now. In the meantime, his other friend had walked over to the bed and had taken the shotgun. "There's no need for that," said Cassio, but the look in the eyes of the one who had taken the shotgun told him otherwise, and namely, that that shotgun did need to be used. Majuri's brain had never been lightning fast, and even in that situation it took him a while to put together that look, his own weakness at having let himself be caught naked as a worm while the others were fully dressed, wearing shoes and hats and leather gloves, the odd reason why his old friends, with whom he'd interacted so infrequently in recent months, should have decided to involve him in this kind of orgy, entirely new to him, and the fact that the girl he wanted to fuck and his other friend who was holding her tight, with his hand over her mouth, had in the meantime retreated to the door and had now backed away through it, vanishing into the hallway. At this point he felt as if he could see before him, as if they were the answer to all those peculiarities, the two bundles wrapped up with packing tape, that is, the portion of the last shipment of heroin that he'd scraped off before delivering it, and the hole in the wall behind the metal cabinet down in the garage where he had hidden them, and the stacks of cash that the sale of that shit would bring in, and the foul mood that would come over the person who learned about all this through the lateral channels that twist and wind like capillaries through the criminal underworld, perfusing it with information, and that's when a flash of awareness opened up a path inside him. Another fraction of a second of painful concentration ensured that Majuri's mind, a weak mind perched inside a powerful, healthy body—two entities that were both destined before long to be dissolved one from the other—was able to stitch together all the singular aspects of that story, but as he glimpsed all these various connections, his father's double-barreled shotgun had already completed a 180-degree rotation and was now pointed against his hairless, muscular chest, in fact, was almost grazing it, and had burst into flame with a roar, punching a gaping hole through it. And so it happened that Cassio was able to put together in a single point, microscopic but extremely dense and heavy as lead, all the salient elements of the last dangerous year of his life, at the exact instant that that life ceased to exist. He had just enough time to regret that laziness and to make a resolution to be smarter and more careful in the future—only he'd never have a future in which to keep that resolution, because he was already dying. He also had enough time to ponder the fact that the girl had never told him her name, and that he was therefore dying without knowing it, and without having fucked her, in fact, without even having a chance to run his fingers over her flesh, and during the rapid expansion of the globe of flame that charred the edges of the gash that had just frighteningly torn open in his chest, that is to say, the chief piece of evidence that would later lead his death to be filed away as a classic case of suicide, he even managed to formulate a doubt as to whether or not she was in cahoots with his murderers.

That point was to remain an unanswered question mark.

HEY, DO YOU REMEMBER *those rugby jerseys made of rough fabric with horizontal green and white stripes, purple and white, yellow and violet . . . ? In London, Lillywhites was a legendary address for well-to-do young Italians, they lusted after those jerseys, both as an emblem of strength and because of the way they always looked rumpled, down-at-the-heels. They lent themselves to both interpretations and these two aspects, from being opposites at first, soon merged into a single entity, which was after all the perfect figure of corresponding quality, at once full of energy and precarious, bullying and vacillating, feminine and virile, powerful but very fragile: youth.*

The torsos of the adolescents that those jerseys would wind up adorning with horizontal stripes, were, in fact, eminently vital and yet transitory, placed in great danger—so easy to wound, riddle with holes, crush . . .

Young Fascists wore them with the collar pulled up, while the lefty com-rades wore them unironed, and probably unwashed, never washed or almost never, using them as pajamas or letting their girlfriends wear them after sex or under a jacket purchased at the flea market.

12

I KNOW WHO'S CONCEALED under the name of Perdita. Now I know. I first learned it several months ago. That is, since Arbus has come back to inhabit my life. All those that I had kicked out or who had packed their bags on their own account have come back. A few years ago, historians coined the expression "the past that doesn't pass" to describe those stalled situations where a people or a nation (in particular, Germany) are incapable of processing great catastrophes, war, guilt, war crimes either committed by or against those unable to get beyond them. Meanwhile, in psychotherapy a technique has become common, the subject of endless dispute and controversy, namely the use of "recovered memories," because in fact it aims explicitly at bringing to surface memories buried in the subconscious, especially concerning sex abuse suffered in childhood. Authentic abuse, or the product of outside suggestion? That is, created by the very same therapy that should do nothing more than recover them?

I don't know to what I owe this backwash of so much material, such a wealth of lived experience. It was Arbus who first triggered the process, no doubt about that. But who, in turn, triggered Arbus?

He told me the last time we saw each other. There was no need of it. Maybe he thought that he needed to complete a picture. Out of the blue, he just started telling me the story of Cassio Majuri, a story I did not know: Cassio was too much older for me to remember him at SLM. And the only way you might find out the story of his tragic death would be by reading Angelo's unabridged confessions, something I never fully did, they're as long as the *Mahabharata*. But the story of Cassio was interesting in any case, and it caught me up. I found it deeply disturbing. The fake rape and suicide . . . I listened without understanding why Arbus was telling me about it, and this was just the source of further uneasiness. The corpse of a young man lying in a bloodstained bed, with a shotgun lying next to it.

I couldn't imagine that Arbus would finish his account by revealing Perdì-ta's identity.

"I know who the girl is," and he fell silent.

It struck me as strange, and frivolous, that he should want to create suspense.

"And how do you happen to know that?"

"She told me."

I felt a singular wave of awkwardness. As if I were ashamed. It often happens to me that I cringe with embarrassment over things regarding others, not me. For instance, when I'm watching a bad movie, it occurs to me that the actors uttered those lines and I'm ashamed for them, telling myself deep inside: "No, please, no . . . don't say that . . . don't do it." Or else when I hear a writer on TV commenting on current events and using the same emphatic style as politicians and journalists, or even worse. The same thing happened to me in the run-up to the revelation that Arbus was about to make.

"WOULD YOU LIKE AN ESPRESSO?" I asked, suddenly leaping to my feet. We had already had one when he arrived. "Gladly," he replied, and gave me an up-from-under look. I had just made an excuse to get away for a moment. In the kitchen, I caught my breath. I focused on the espresso pot, I carefully filled the little basket with coffee grounds, slowly, taking care not to spill any, though in spite of my painstaking attention I put a couple of spoonfuls more outside than inside the basket, spreading a light carpet of finely ground coffee onto the counter. My hand was shaking a little. My gestures were imprecise. Let me assure you, dear reader, that I'm not dragging this out intentionally to create suspense: but I would like to bring you as close as I can to the way I arrived at it. I twisted together the top and bottom of the espresso pot and set it on the burner. In reality, I'd already come to it for some time, but I couldn't formulate the exact phrasing, the complete sentence, as if I wanted to let Arbus have the right to say it to me, a perverse pleasure that he was clearly experiencing in hesitating, prolonging the pangs of that pleasure to the point of spasm. I was staring at the flame under the pot when I heard him behind me. He had joined me in the kitchen.

"I'll keep you company while you wait."

No, my friend, you're not keeping me company. It's that you don't want to let go. I know what you want to tell me: that the young girl they used to lure Cassio Majuri into a trap and kill him was your sister, Leda. I know it: Perdìta is Leda Arbus. Leda, pale fire of my youth, moonbeam that imparts no warmth! An abused young girl pretending to want to abuse in her turn, that is, a form of abuse so refined that not even a Chinese or an Ottoman expert on torture or a Jesuit in a libertine novel could hope to come up with it. Abused in the mind, the place where the most unspeakable misdeeds are perpetrated. In a part of me, I had understood it from the very outset: hence my profound shame now, hence the long, silent afternoons I spent as a boy next to her rigid body, admiring her chest as it rose and fell with her respiration. Leda was the only point that could stitch together all the others in the constellation of her brother's account. I imagined grabbing the espresso pot, which was by now half filled with coffee, and hurling it into my old classmate's face. I imagined the boiling spray of liquid scarring the few places left free of acne, his screams of pain and astonishment. Maybe he expected to get some reaction out of me, because he knew that Leda and I had been an item, in other words, that there had been something between the two of us.

Your friend's sister is an important chapter in your life, possibly more than the friendship itself.

"How much sugar do you want?" I asked him, turning around with the handle of the espresso pot pinched between two fingers, taking care not to burn my hand, and filling his demitasse.

"I take it bitter, thanks."

WHEN WE RETURNED TO THE LIVING ROOM, and he had explained it all to me, I looked at him in relief and gratitude. The same colorful fragments of the kaleidoscope changed position, giving life to new figures. It was hard to believe that the shy pianist had passed through those ordeals. But the lives of girls are full of blank spaces, suspended moments during which, unbeknown to their parents, but also to their friends and classmates, they frequent "a rough crowd," they get stoned out of their skulls, they bury in silence risky or demented behavior. Then, from one day to the next, if they're lucky, that phase comes to an end and they go back to being who they were before. At least in appearance. Leda had been initiated in that way. I don't know whether Angelo and his friends had raped her, and I didn't ask her brother whether they had. The masquerade that ended Majuri's life might just have been an isolated episode. It scared her enough to steer her away from them.

"I think my father must have found out about it," said Arbus.

"And what did he do?"

"Nothing."

Arbus was shaken by a wave of sarcastic laughter. His elderly father is still alive, spry, perfectly lucid, coldly realistic. One night, on one of those educational channels, while I was waiting for the half tablet of anxiety medication to do its dirty work on my consciousness, I watched one of his lectures on generative grammar. Not the whole thing, but at least half. As I progressively understood, I just as quickly forgot what I had learned. Well, no two ways about it, Professor Arbus really was a good teacher, I thought to myself, before the pill altered my perception of reality and my imagining of unreality, shoving them both away to a safe distance. A good professor, why not, a dedicated educator . . .

Too bad that he'd retired years ago.

"How about your mother?"

"My mother was kept in the dark. Understanding other people has never been her strong suit. When my folks broke up, she went back to school and got a degree in psychology on account of it." Say what? She was working as psychologist because she was incapable of understanding other people? Or because she wanted to finally be able to understand them? Arbus hadn't changed since we'd been students together: his statements could always be understood in at least two different ways, often two opposite ways, and he never retraced his steps.

"Where is Leda now? What is she doing?"

"She died three months ago."

The grim matter-of-factness of that answer drained me of all energy. I told him how sorry I was.

"So am I. She had a tumor."

"Where?"

"In the pancreas."

I curse the very existence of this organ with its absurd name.

13

A COUPLE OF YEARS AGO I received an e-mail, in fact, a series of e-mails in which an old classmate from SLM wanted to have a reunion of class 3A, and the invitation was kindly extended to me as well even though I had changed schools, not finishing my education there.

March 13, 2012
Ciao Edoardo
    happy to hear from you (or at least to hear what you're up to) . . . I'm "scraping together" all the old classmates . . .
    I'm attaching the information I've managed to pull together so far, if you have any other contacts not mentioned in the e-mail . . . reach out to them and see if you can get their e-mail address and cell phone number . . .
    when we've found them all . . . let's see what we can do!!
    Gigi Regazzoni

I never answered Regazzoni, except for his first e-mail. Why not? I couldn't say. Aside from whatever desire I might have for an old home week, which in fact might be limited at best, I was writing this book, so it might have been useful to see all the old classmates I hadn't encountered since then, find out what had become of them, ask a few quick questions about SLM, maybe, little by little, work around to also asking a little something about the CR/M, about what it had been like for them, how they remembered it, the relations they had had with the murderers, if indeed they had had any at all. Instead I just didn't respond to the new e-mails. I avoided that which I ought to have been most curious about. Maybe it was precisely the fiction of this book that made me steer clear. So that I could feel I had a free hand.

New appeals poured in from Regazzoni, rather astonished that his idea had gathered so few adherents, a fairly lukewarm enthusiasm.

June 1, 2012

Ciao, I'm still having trouble tracking down a few people. I've been working on it since December 2011 . . . and I have no intention of giving up.

Exert some pressure on the people who have yet to give me their contact information, maybe we can put something together . . .

It would be good if you could also contact the classmates whose e-mail address or cell phone number I have but who haven't replied . . .

All those with whom I've had personal contact have said that they're happy to see each other, with just one doubtful and another pessimistic about the atmosphere of the get-together . . . I can't wait . . . but we are going to need a little bit of cooperation.

Let me know, talk soon, Gigi

6/24/2012

Ciao alumni!

Nuntio vobis gaudium magnum . . . mission (almost) accomplished . . .

Between Monday and today, I caught up with Barnetta, the most impossible to track down, I talked to him on the phone (and "shot the shit" just like in the old days).

Now I just need to lay my hands on the e-mail addresses of Giuramento, Sanson, and Zipoli (and I wonder if I could ask those who talk to them most often to do it), and the cell numbers of Busoni, Crasta, Izzo, Sdobba, and also Scarnicchi (does anyone know what became of Dormouse?)

My intention is to organize something for September!

For those who live outside Italy, for those who live outside Rome . . . and for those who are "out of their minds": I'd really appreciate it if you'd start thinking about passing through Rome and, if you are thinking of it, informing yours truly (self-appointed organizer) as soon as you possibly can

To the people who live in Rome: can you put anybody up in your home?

I have an extra bed . . .

I can't wait to hear the echoing war cry of the old class . . . and to shoot the shit again over a nice steaming bowl of carbonara . . .

Talk soon, Gigi

Battle cry? Reading this euphoric message, I was tempted to think: What are you talking about, Regazzoni, when have we ever shot the shit, you and I, in front of or not in front of a bowl of carbonara? I started to wonder whether this idea of his was going to go anywhere.

September 7, 2012
Ciao guys,
   I'd like to try to set a date for the "pizza party"; I'd start by suggesting two days, pick one: Friday, September 25, or Saturday the 26th, so that those who don't live in Rome can let me know what their chances (or interest) might be in getting together on one of those dates . . . or else they can suggest some other date . . . thanks, till next time, Gigi

September 19
Ciao everyone, not having yet received answers from:
   (there followed a list of nineteen names in alphabetical order, starting inevitably with my own name, immediately after which came Arbus's)
   I'm going to cancel the effort to organize a get-together for September 25 or 26 . . .
   let's try again with a date in late October, and we can see if everyone is reading their e-mail
   I'd suggest October 31, a Saturday
   I'd appreciate replies, even if they are negative, and may God smile down on our venture . . .
   (To those who have already replied, I'd recommend waiting for the others to reply . . . after all, I already know their position . . .)
   See you soon (I hope) Gigi

But even these subsequent reminders did little to stir my ex-classmates: it was still just the same names, there were no new ones added to the list, in spite of the organizer's best efforts. Regazzoni had split up the old class roll into four columns: Those Who Are Coming to the Dinner, Those Who Can't Come, Those Who Haven't Even Answered, Those We Can't Track Down. The provisional roster said that eight were coming, seven couldn't come, twelve hadn't answered, and the rest couldn't be found. I, in fact, belonged to the third category, a little contemptuous, a little depressed and concerned, a little supercilious, and a little bit ashamed at what an asshole

I was being *not* to want to see my old classmates. All of them together, no! Two or three at a time, maybe, but all at once . . . ! I thought of those whose last name was all I could remember, not even their first name, because it was strictly the surname that was used by the teachers, but also by the rest of us. That was how we were known. It was by the surname, and therefore in the class ledger, in the roll call, in the oral exams, and on the outside, in the number that we wore on our back while playing soccer, that a boy became recognizable. Well, sure, that's the way school was: a destiny, a vocation, a list, a string of surnames, all different, while there were countless repetitions of the given names, the first names: so many Marcos, so many Fabios, so many Francescos . . . but just one Gedeone.

Regazzoni gave up any dreams of unanimity and decided to settle for a gathering of the most enthusiastic alumni. To build up numbers, he even tried to recruit old classmates from elementary school or middle school, with whom we'd studied even if only for a year. I followed his convivial efforts via e-mail, like the coward that I was, leaving the messages I continued to receive unanswered, like someone coldly observing the attempts of a cockroach lying overturned on its back to get back upright onto its legs: ready to weigh in but never doing so, waiting to see if it could do it on its own . . . a slightly disgraceful entomologist, in other words.

IN THE E-MAIL DATED OCTOBER 15, Gigi informed us that he had received twelve positive RSVPs (including his own), plus five "almost certain" and two "probably," and then there were three who had yet to answer (including my name), and five certain no-shows. Among them there was one who worked in Zurich, Galeno De Matteis, and then there was the one who had fled to Costa Rica. I don't think that Regazzoni had spoken to him in person, but maybe he had realized the unlikelihood of a fugitive from the law returning home for a class reunion dinner. The message ended with these words:

> I wonder if anyone who lives near SLM could try to find a place for dinner, anyplace will do, someplace we can reach on foot, if possible, and where we could make reservations for twenty or so people . . . I'll wait to hear from you . . .

The e-mail that came on October 19 contained a stunning new development.

Ciao everyone, I've managed to track down Arbus, who's even reserved a flight to join us that day . . .

A dinner actually did take place, in a trattoria on Corso Trieste. Very few people took part. Arbus didn't show up. He didn't take any plane. And from where, after all? Here was Gigi's commentary after the meal.

November 2
Ciao, everyone, I join in the preceding thank-yous for the lovely evening . . . I'm just a little disappointed because I was hoping to see more of you . . .

As for the rust and ruin . . . it seems to me we have nothing to complain about, I found everyone to be in excellent shape (and what the f***, we're in our fifties, not in our damned eighties!)

I uploaded here: http://www.amilcarecenterforsafety.com/ (don't pay any attention to the name, it's a free site I happen to own, Amilcare was my grandfather) the photos I took and I'm waiting to receive the ones taken by Modiano and Kraus (send me 10 MB or so a day, zipped into a single file!!!)

I went to take a look at the photos on the site. Probably they had been taken by a waiter with Regazzoni's cell phone. I counted six men around a table, in a restaurant that must have been dimly lit because the flash had gone off automatically, turning the diners into so many hallucinatory specters. If there hadn't been a list of participants in Regazzoni's e-mail, I would have had a hard time recognizing anyone. In the days that followed I continued to check the site, but apparently no one had added any other photos. Regazzoni's e-mail went on:

As for my minor "disappointment," I've decided that we can try again next year, on the second Sunday in April, during the day, at my house or Gedeone Barnetta's place; he generously offered to have us over . . .

For all the assholes who didn't bother to show up . . . you have another five months to make your plans, do your best to clear your calendars for that date . . . Pilu said he'll come with his 26-year-old "caregiver" . . .

Matteoli, if you're reading this . . . let us know you're still alive!!

(editor's note: Matteoli, on the run from the law in Central America)

*If, in the meantime, we manage to track down anyone else who
graduated in 1975 . . . the more the merrier . . .*

A hug to you all, Gigi

*P.S. I was forgetting: for those of you who live in Rome and still do
some sports . . . I have a little amateur volleyball team that plays on
Mondays and Thursdays at 8 p.m. at Sant'Agnese and we're looking for
players . . . it isn't obligatory to come twice a week . . . and anyway
anyone who wanted to come try it out could make their minds up
afterward.*

On November 26 we got what even in Italian the insider jargon terms a
"reminder."

Hey, none of you sent me even one photo!

Crasta sent in two, but they were out of focus . . .

*Let me remind you that the pictures I took can be seen at: http://
www.amilcarecenterforsafety.com/*

see you next time! G.

March 2, 2013

*Ciao guys, I'd like to remind you all that during the dinner we had a
few months ago now, we agreed that we would all get together again on
the second Sunday in April, that is, 4/11/2013, at the home (presumably)
of Barnetta in Casal Palocco. This time with our respective families, for
those who wish to or can . . . so that those who have little kids have no
more excuses not to come, because the wives will be there to take care of
the young ones . . .*

*This time, again, I'm letting you know in plenty of time, hoping
attendance will improve . . . get organized, I don't want to hear any
excuses!! If there's anyone who just doesn't want to see any old
classmates, they can tell me to go fuck myself, but loud and clear!!!*

*For the photos I took, I transferred them to http://gigiregazzoni
.xoom.it/ because the other site just vanished from one day to the
next . . .*

*anyway those two assholes Pilu and Crasta couldn't even see their
way to downloading theirs onto a CD and mailing them to me . . .
because the idea of sending them over the web . . . well, that's completely
out of the question . . .*

a big hello to everyone, G.

P.S. Has anyone else been contacted? I'd also like to know if—once we've established the day—I can also invite the headmaster, I have his e-mail address . . . I don't think his presence would bother anyone, would it?

March 11, 2013
Ciao everyone,
following on what I wrote before, I suggest a change of date to May 16 . . . (among other things, d'Avenia wasn't available for the date we had chosen previously).
Now there's more time available . . . Let me sincerely ask those I didn't get a chance to see on October 30 to make sure they take part in this second get-together (with or without family accompanying)

April 13, 2013
Ciao everyone, I'd like to get some confirmations of who will be there at Barnetta's house on Sunday, May 16, I assume after 10 in the morning . . . (and the exact address, too, Gedeone), and especially from:
Albinati, Edoardo
Casorati, Francesco
Giuramento, Alessio
Iannello, Riccardo
Lodoli, Marco
Rummo, Gioacchino
Sdobba, Enrico
And all the others who weren't able to attend last time . . . Seeing that we'll have to put in an order with a cathering [sic] service. Unless everyone decides to just each bring a sandwich for themselves :-)
We'd need to know the total number of people who will be attending, seeing that this time it's open to the families, as well . . . After all, there's no point in just wasting money and food for no good reason . . .
And also whether you've managed to get in touch with anyone else . . . I may be able to get in touch with Pierfrancesco Blasi and D'Aquino, but I couldn't track down Marco Morricone . . .
A hug to you all

Regazzoni's e-mail dated April 20 has a faint whiff of desperation about it.

I thought I had already agreed to the change in dates from Saturday the 15th instead of Sunday the 16th . . . in the name of one and all . . . but as it turns out, there weren't many replies and most of them were to say they wouldn't be able to make it . . . anyone who hasn't written in yet, could you let me hear from you?

I also wanted to know if anyone had managed to track down any other alumni, maybe even not just from the last year??? talk soon, Gigi

At this point in the long-drawn-out negotiation Sandro Eleuteri pipes up.

Dear friends,
  a couple of details:
  1) ORGANIZATION: I have an idea that's a little more demanding but also a little more personal. I'd like to suggest a "porta-party"; that means everyone would bring a hot dish or something ready to eat, breaking the attendees down into four groups:
  —PRIMI PIATTI (baked pasta, insalata di riso, chicken salad, etc., etc.)
  —MAIN COURSES/SIDE DISHES (big salads, vegetable casseroles, frittata, etc., etc.)
  —DESSERT/ICE CREAM
  —WINE
  All of these are things you'd bring cooked or ready to eat. The master of the house won't cook a thing; he'll just make his home available, along with paper plates/napkins/disposable cups.
  From my own experience . . . porta-parties are a lot of fun, you laugh, you eat, and you drink.
  2) DATE: I don't know if anyone noticed, but Sunday the 16th at 3 p.m. is the last day of the championship. I don't know how many of you are interested but it really would be a crime to miss out on it, seeing how things are turning out. Couldn't we do Saturday the 15th??? And anyway, who's even coming?? I haven't seen this groundswell of enthusiasm . . .
  Ciao, ciao, Sandro

At this point Gedeone Barnetta weighs in.

Dear friends,

I have a slightly different suggestion, one that I think is more in line with the needs and abilities of all of us, for this coming May 15.

Not far from my house there's a good restaurant, it's called Il Gnocco Traditore, and they do some delicious dishes (meat—it's famous for its steaks, which it serves on a soapstone grill—and fish) and it's reasonably priced (30–35 euros, max).

Here's what we could do: meet at one o'clock at the restaurant, then we can go to my place, where, for anyone who wants to hang out into the evening, we can whip up a big bowl of spaghetti (with a side dish!).

That way we can avoid the pitfalls of catering (Gigi, what were you thinking . . . sandwiches!!!) and the traffic on Via Cristoforo Colombo. What's more, we can accommodate people who want to sleep in a little (not me, I sleep 4–5 hours a night, tops).

What do you say? If you're all good with it, all I need is to know about a week in advance the approximate number of people attending so I can make a reservation for a private room at the restaurant. If you want, we can arrange for a prix fixe meal, but I don't see the need. The one sure thing is that you eat well at Il Gnocco Traditore.

Last of all, an important notice for the gentlemen who took and then published a photo in which one of you is making the sign of the horns behind my head: as promised, I printed mug shots of both of you and put them in the doghouse of my dog Frisk, so that, come May, he'll be able to identify you both and take appropriate action.

Let me know, and a big hug to everyone,

Gedeone

The next e-mail from Regazzoni has a worried, disappointed tone.

May 9, 2013
Ciao guys, let's summarize and flesh out all the various points:

we moved the date to this coming Saturday (May 15) at Gedeone Barnetta's house, and we're waiting for him to let us know the address and time to show up there . . .

Here's who's coming . . . (followed by a list of names, which has now shrunk to nine, including Regazzoni)

Sanson and Dormouse were on for the 16th, I hope they still are for the 15th d'Avenia couldn't come on the 16th but I hope he does come, now that we moved it to the 15th . . .

Ferrazza, Zipoli, and Rummo haven't responded but I hope they can make it . . .

We haven't heard a word from Albinati, Arbus, Lodoli, Sdobba, and Zarattini . . . but I hope we see at least a couple of them . . .

Let me remind everyone that the family members are invited, too (wives and children; but leave your other relatives at home :-))

The Headmaster sends his regards and thanks one and all but he won't be able to make it; too many aches and pains!!

For the menu, it's a mess, so let me try and organize things a little myself:

Barnetta: beverages

Crasta, Busoni, Regazzoni: primi piatti

Scarnicchi, d'Avenia, Zarattini, Zipoli: main courses

Lorco, Modiano, De Matteis: side dishes

Ferrazza, Puca, Iannello: desserts

if anyone wants to switch up, do as you please . . .

others I haven't mentioned here because I'm not really expecting to see them, I'd be only too happy if they proved me wrong, bringing whatever food is easiest for them to procure . . .

as for the quantities, I wouldn't bring any more than four reasonable portions, otherwise we'll have tons of food . . . anyway, anyone who has any better ideas, just pipe up . . . see you Saturday!!!

May 11

Dear friends, I'm canceling the get-together on Saturday the 15th on account of a greater number of absences than presences. The following, with a 100% or 99% likelihood, won't be coming: Busoni, Crasta, d'Avenia, Izzo, Lodoli, Scarnicchi.

No replies from: Albinati, Arbus, Ferrazza (after we moved the date from the 16th to the 15th) and Rummo . . .

. . . in any case I'm going to Casal Palocco to have lunch with Barnetta, at the trattoria Il Gnocco Traditore, and anyone else who wants to come along would be mighty welcome.

Later on, I'll send you the exact address for Il Gnocco (or else you can find it yourselves online) and the time I'm meeting Gedeone, unless his Internet connection starts working again and he can do it himself . . .

*in future, considering the objective challenges and, in some cases,
the general unwillingness to use e-mail . . . I suggest we establish a date
to observe on an annual basis so as to make it possible for those who are
willing and able to spare the time to plan for it*

*I would suggest the first Saturday in October, when the weather and
daylight savings time ought to make it easy to get together in the
afternoon . . . we'll work things out better in future . . . in particular
from those who missed both the last get-together and the one we just
canceled, I'd welcome any suggestions you might have—if, that is,
you're interested in taking part!*

For now, all of you take care, Gigi

It was easy to guess what happened next: the insistence of Ragazzoni's
messages did nothing to achieve the desired effect, in fact, the defections
followed thick and fast. His e-mail dated September 14, 2013, under the
jesting manner concealed a truly pained note. Reading it, I thought of Chiodi and Jervi, who were no longer among the living.

*Ciao guys, this is to remind you that we had agreed to meet up on the
first Saturday in October . . . I'd say at 9 p.m. out front of SLM!!!*

(Again Regazzoni writes the name of our school as an acronym, the way
I have throughout this book . . .)

*Those who failed to make the last get-together can jot it down in their
datebooks, or put a reminder in their cell phones . . . or tie their dicks in
a knot . . .*

*Find a way to get free of your obligations for 3 hours . . . On that
Saturday . . . And then if you really don't want to . . . just tell me to go
fuck myself!*

A big hug, Gigi Regazzoni

Here Regazzoni signed the e-mail with his first and last names. A significant slip. With the infelicitous wisecrack "tie their dicks in a knot," he
has also, without even noticing it, signed his letter of surrender. He never
was a funny guy, my classmate. To watch him try to be funny, now, at age
fifty-seven, online, only makes it clear how heartbroken he really is. Just
three days later, on September 17, he finds himself forced to write to us all
again.

SO TO SUMMARIZE
Second consecutive get-together canceled
I'm stepping aside as organizer
Anyone who feels like it can get busy and come up with some new
dates
A hug to you all
Regazzoni

That was the last time we heard from him.

AN UNSETTLING DETAIL: in importing this paperless, one-sided correspondence, I've been forced to reduce it all to the same color, point size, and font; but Regazzoni's original e-mails were written in various colors, and with an alternation of different fonts. I wouldn't know how to explain this eccentric whim. In fact, he used:

Arial Narrow green italics and blue roman
Times New Roman bold and dark blue, green, light blue italics
Consolas 10.5 point
Verdana 13.5 lime green and dark blue

The e-mail dated March 2, 2013, is in a muted green Arial 12 bold italic; on March 11 (perhaps because of his discouragement) he goes back to a black Consolas, all lowercase; from April 13 on, he uses a black Consolas, with the exception of May 9 (Arial 12 dark blue) and May 11 (dark blue and red lowercase, green uppercase).

14

TO THINK BACK TO MY OLD CLASSMATES. *To think back to that time. I'm sorry I had to do it. Why did Regazzoni get so stubborn about it? The words bob back to the surface . . . the phrases, the manners of speech, the expressions, which we still remember even if we use them little if at all. They were the legacy of our parents.*

IF SOMEONE WAS GOOD at some particular subject, we'd say he had a *bernoccolo*, the bump on the head used by phrenologists. For instance, "*il bernoccolo della matematica*," literally, "a bump on the head for math"; if they had a passion, or a predilection, practically a fixation, with a certain thing, especially something trivial or futile, we would say "*ne aveva il pallino*" (they had a "little ball," which might describe a polka dot or a cue ball or a Ping-Pong ball or even a BB). *Il pallino dei go-kart* or *delle piste per i modellini*. A fixation with go-karts or, say, slot-car tracks.

A WORD THAT WAS USED a great deal back then and almost never nowadays: "*fesso*," meaning, literally, cracked, to call someone a "fool."

IF SOMEONE WAS A BIG COMPLAINER, people would say, "*non fare il pianto greco*," something approximating "don't be a Greek mourner."

A VAST NUMBER OF NEGATIVE EPITHETS: *screanzato, villanzone, buzzurro, filibustiere, lestofante, manigoldo, lazzarone, mascalzone*, roughly equivalent to scoundrel, oaf, highwayman, or churl.

. . . WHEN PEOPLE SAID of a homosexual that he was "*un invertito*," a cross between "perverted" and "twisted," or else that he was "*dell'altra sponda*," literally, "on the far side."

. . . WHEN YOU WANTED to describe someone who was in trouble or in bad shape, who might, say, have been in a crash or beaten black-and-blue, we'd use the mysterious expression "*È proprio combinato per le feste*" or "*conciato per le feste*" (in shape for the holidays, or tanned for the holidays, or perhaps parties—but what parties or holidays could the phrase have been referring to?)
. . . Back then words that are nowadays lighthearted and meaningless— words like, say, "*lavativo*" (lazybones) or "*spendaccione*" (spendthrift)—were enough to brand an individual negatively, the equivalent of a scarlet letter. Moral transvaluation, after almost entirely accomplishing its circuit,

makes those words practically incomprehensible today, and would keep us from picking up on the quavering note of contempt in the voice of those who uttered them (normally, the head of the family).

. . . words like "*fandonie*," or "*frottole*," or "*frescacce*," all of them meaning, roughly, balderdash, and now swept aside by the more vulgar and generic "*cazzate*," or "bullshit."

It's been a long time since I've heard anyone use a word that was uttered quite frequently by my parents: "*mentecatto*," or mental defective, as in someone is nothing more than an unfortunate mental defective: "*è un povero mentecatto*."

> DITTIES AND NONSENSE RHYMES
> (to the tune of "Kozachok")
> *Oh, Natasha*
> *How did you like the kasha?*
> *I loved it, Pavel, I pooped it on the gravel!*
> *You've really made a mess of the steppe, etc.*

> (to the tune of "Bibbidi-Bobbidi-Boo," also known as "The Magic
>   Song," from the film *Cinderella*)
> *Bibbidi-Bobbidi-Boo*
> *What the fuck is the matter with you, etc.*

(or else, to the same tune, the blasphemous ditty on the Crucifixion, which I previously included in the chapter on our religion teacher, do you all remember him, Mr. Golgotha?)

> *Take a little nail . . .*
> *And a little hammer . . .*
> *Come and join us, drive a nail or two . . .*
> *Come nail up Baby Jesus*
> *Make sure he never comes down again!*

> (to the tune of *Leichte Kavallerie*, in pidgin Spanish)
> *Le currieron detras*
> *Le currieron detras*
> *Le pusieron un palo en el culo . . .*
> *Ai que dolor! Pobre senor!*
> *No se lo pudiera sacar!*

These were mixed up with the nursery rhymes useful for learning, for example, the names of the Alps from Tuscany to Friuli: *Ma Con Gran Pena Le Reti Cala Giù*, etc. A mnemonic that incorporated the names of the various Alps, from Maritime to Julian: Maritime, Cottian, Graian, Pennine, Lepontine, Rhaetian Noric, Carnic, and Julian Alps.

CARDUCCI: "Sei *nella terra fredda* . . . Sei *nella terra negra* . . ." The riposte, playing on the fact that "you are" (*sei*) and the number six (*sei*) are the same word, was: Hey, what, did this guy have *twelve* children die on him?!

LAST OF ALL, the learned quotation (from the *Aeneid*, which we read in late middle school), previously referenced:

> *This is Lavinia*
> *your future bride*
> *feel her down under,*
> *slip your finger inside!*

THE MOST FAMOUS and inappropriate contrary-to-fact sentence was this: "If my grandfather had had five balls, he'd have been a pinball machine." This is to say that there's no point in formulating hypotheses other than the actual state of affairs, you can't build history with ifs and buts.

> *Hasta la vista!*
> *I pissed on the pasta!*

AND THEN there was an endless supply of silly and obscene ditties and rhymes, nonsense, and schoolboy puns. Arbus was greatly amused by them. I would never have believed that he enjoyed this foolishness, in fact, I thought he held them in contempt (but how wrong we are in our judgments and, to an even greater extent, how wrong we are in our beliefs about how others judge *us*! It's an incredible chain of misunderstanding: the mistakes we make in our beliefs about ourselves, the mistakes others make in their beliefs about us, the mistakes we make in our beliefs about others, the mistakes we make in our beliefs about what others believe about us, the mistakes others make in their beliefs about what we think of them.)

> *Cos'è una banana?*
> *Una ba-donna ba-piccola ba-piccola.*
> *E una tartaruga?*
> *Una tarta-piega della tarta-pelle.*
> *Un cavillo?*
> *Un animile che galippa galippa.*

> *+ me lo –, + vengo –: x non venir + –, non me lo – +*

This array of miniaturistic gems of absurdity, by definition untranslatable, as they're based entirely on word structures in Italian, partake of the protocols of ciphers. "*Nana*" means female dwarf, a *banana* then is a ba-very ba-small ba-woman. And so forth, from the punning use of "cavil" (*cavillo*) and "horse" (*cavallo*) in the same way, and finally the obscene references to masturbation using plus and minus signs.

By the way, zippers were called *chiusura-lampo*, or "lightning fasteners."

NEVRASTENICO: this term, "neurasthenic," straight out of nineteenth-century psychiatry, was still used as a pejorative to describe an intolerable individual; and the equivalent of antianxiety medicines were "tranquilizers."

FARE UN REPULISTI (carry out a thorough cleansing, that's what my mother would say when in the throes of the cyclical, maniacal urge to do a deep clean and straighten up, for example, in the cellar or the garage: "*È ora di fare un bel repulisti*"—but you'd also hear political extremists use it when the time had come for radical solutions against their political adversaries: "*Assaltiamo la loro sezione e facciamo un bel repulisti*" ("Let's attack their offices and clean them out") or else "*Il QT ha bisogno di un bel repulisti*" (literally, "The QT needs a thorough cleansing").

IN ROME, something of little worth or a small object whose name you don't know is offhandedly dubbed a "*cazzabubbolo*" (a mix of the obscene "cock" and the old-fashioned "sleigh bell"), and a small person or child, a "*soldo di cacio*," literally "a pennyworth of cheese."

Traffic police were called "*pizzardoni*," a term that may have referred to their caps or to their resemblance to certain aquatic birds.

Roman dialect expressions I haven't heard since:

"*Ha fatto un grifo!*" ("He pulled a griffin," meaning he fell off his bicycle or motorcycle), "*è annato a scroscia' contro un palo!*" (and hit a lamppost!)

La pula (the police).

Andare a fette, to go on foot, where "*fette*" (slices, as of bread or pizza) means feet.

Mannaggia alli pescetti, a minced oath, like darn and heck, involving a comical imprecation against little fishies.

In Rome, at least, if something was useless or broken, one would ask, rhetorically: "*E con questo, che ci faccio? La birra?*" ("What am I supposed to do with this? Make beer?)

"*Fate voi*," literally, "you do it," for "be my guest," would be latinized into: "*Fate vobis.*"

IN ROMAN DIALECT: "*gajardo!*" to mean nice, impressive, noteworthy, impressive. I haven't heard it in years. It was once very common. Everyone said it.

A sly and undisciplined young man would be compared to a fishing line: "*È proprio una lenza!*"

The classic Roman curse, involving contemptible dead ancestors, or *mortacci*, would be tuned up with the Italian name for Disney's Goofy, Pippo: *Mortacci de Pippo.*

And then there's the surprising etymology of "*mortanguerieri . . .*" a variant on "*mortacci*" with the added suffix of "warriors."

MOREOVER:

Porca l'oca (a comically minced oath mixing a swine and a goose)

Vattelappesca (beats me, literally, "go fish for it")

Mi ha buggerato (he screwed me, interestingly from the same root as the English "bugger")

Che sagoma! (what a character! from "*sagoma*," meaning silhouette or cardboard cutout)

Roba da chiodi (a comical variant on *Roba da pazzi*, already an exasperated equivalent of, say, the English usage of looney tunes!)

Le zinne (breasts), *una zinnona* (a shapely woman)

È uno scorfano (the word for scorpion fish, to indicate a homely young woman, a pejorative term, more extreme than the companion insults, "*cozza*" or "*racchia*")

Stai fresco (you're out of luck, possibly a learned reference to Dante, see *Inferno*, canto 32, line 117).

Sei una schiappa (for someone who's bad at a game or sport, especially tennis: *una vera schiappa*)

Papale papale (verbatim, literally, from the emphatic use of "papal")

Costa uno sproposito (something expensive is "disproportionate")

Un bel gruzzolo, un gruzzoletto (from the Lombardic, a funny-sounding term for a pile of cash)

Marcantonio (from the name Mark Antony, a big strong man)

Faccia da impunito, race d'impunito: a broad use of the adjective derived from "impunity," tantamount to "shameless."

Vai a farti friggere! (Go fry your head in it!)

Vai a farti un bagno! (Go take a bath!)

Va' a fa' l'ovo! (Go lay an egg!)

Non mi dare il cordoglio! (Spare me the grief!)

Mannaggia a Nerone (Darn that Nero!)

Che c'hai le paturnie? (A phrase roughly equivalent in sound and meaning to the "screaming meemies": "What's up with you? You got the screaming meemies or something?")

Guarda quanto ben di dio! (Look at this cornucopia of delight!)

Se non le è d'incomodo . . . (If it's not too much of a bother, an inconvenience, in a piece of quaint phrasing)

A EUPHEMISM FOR PREGNANCY, to say a woman is "*in stato interessante*," in "an interesting condition."

To say someone was a prostitute, the phrase was "*fa la vita*," or "leading the life."

If a girl wouldn't "play ball," then you'd say, "*Manco fosse Maria Goretti!*" ("She thinks she's St. Maria Goretti!" The saint in question is an Italian virgin-martyr, and one of the youngest canonized saints, murdered by her would-be rapist.)

A restless person was "a breakneck," as in "*scavezzacollo*" or "*rompicollo*."

Going to sleep or just lying down for a quick catnap took the verb "*coricarsi*," for example: "*Sei stanca? Perché non vai a coricarti un po'?*"

Mopping the floor was termed "*dare lo straccio*," or "passing a rag."

To laze about was to "*stare in panciolle*," literally, to lie "belly-up."

Whenever anyone was interviewed about young people, on TV or in the press, who knows why, they always felt called upon to specify, "the young people today."

Denatured alcohol was called "*spirit*," as in English "spirits."

UN TIPO DA SPIAGGIA (a peculiar character, literally, "a guy off the beach")

· *Stagnino* (old-fashioned term for plumber, from tin, in Latin: *stannum*, symbol Sn).

Rivoltella and *rivoltellata* for, respectively, revolver and revolver shot.

Tonto, tontolone, and *tontolomeo* (terms for a simpleton; my mother and my grandmother would use the latter variant with a certain fondness: "*Sei davvero un tontolomeo!*")

Ellalléro! (a word trotted out when someone was exaggerating, saying things that stretch credulity).

Metti giudizio, porta pazienza (be judicious, exercise patience: here, it is the underlying concepts that have vanished).

Squattrinato, mattacchione, pelandrone, scorbutico, pruriginoso (five colorfully quaint terms for being, respectively: penniless; cheerfully eccentric; lazy and slow; grouchy; and itchy or prurient)

IN ROME, at least, without thinking twice about it, we would use the gravest diseases, sicknesses, and handicaps as insults. "What are you, a spaz?" we'd upbraid someone incapable of performing an elementary task; we'd say that a skinny boy had a case of rickets; from the bleachers at the soccer stadium you'd hear voices shouting out, "Hey, Encephalitis!" when the referee missed a call.

AND THEN THERE WERE A FEW FRENCH WORDS whose disappearance marked the international decline of that language, but which were still widely used in our parents' day: *vedette, entraîneuse, gigolo, chaperon, exploit, mannequin,* to say nothing of the dusty lampshades, or *abat-jours,* the *paletots* (overcoats), *secretaire, negligée, refrain, consolle,* and *frigidaire.* Advertisements were called *réclames*: "Have you seen the *réclame* for Ovaltine?" And an advertising campaign was called a *battage.*

"*MI PUÒ FARE LA PREMURA*" (or else: "*Mi può usare la premura*"), polite-ness entailing the use of a word roughly equivalent to "solicitude" (to, say, put aside a small loaf of bread for me . . .)

"*UN BEL GIORNO* . . ." (literally, one fine day, to indicate one particular day, any ordinary day, but which had proved decisive): ". . . *e un bel giorno dico basta coi capelli lunghi, decido di farmi la frangetta*" (". . . and one fine day I say to myself, I'm done with long hair, I'm going to get a page-boy"), etc.

That was an era when adjectives were applied to things that were usu-ally used for people, which meant our mothers might call a dress "amus-ing" and the fabric used to upholster a sofa "likable." A slender young woman had "*un bel personale.*"

"HOW DO YOU KNOW?"

"*L'ha detto il giornale radio.*" (I heard it on the radio newscast.)

15

IT'S THE END OF THE YEAR 2015. Thousands have drowned trying to cross the Aegean Sea. Now that it's winter, the seas are high and the crossings are even more dangerous. The refugees are trekking across Europe en masse. One day they're turned back, the next they're welcomed. An elderly archaeologist had his head cut off, and his decapitated body was strung up from an ancient column. Lazio, the soccer team, was unable to make it into the Champions League, instead being eliminated in the preliminary games by a German team named after the company that makes aspirin. With all his vast experience and his precious contacts at the land registry office, the surveyor Rocchi has yet to come up with a system to free me of the twenty square feet I own, unwillingly, in the middle of a courtyard. These are all pieces of purely bad news, but there has been good news as well. There must have been, no doubt about it. Only I can't think of any right now. It's Christmas. I'm at the midnight mass at SLM. I did it, in the end; and Don Salari is there, celebrating mass.

He's older and more twisted than ever, but he is a stout and durable man. He has quite a way about him. Maybe he's sick, maybe he's old: but he bears his cross magnificently, the way all the recent pontiffs, old and in pain, have done—and as the current pontiff is already doing, because he's in much worse shape than he appears—limiting to a barely perceptible grimace on his already haggard face the discomfort that he feels as he turns to face the altar, handling the accessories for the mass and turning the pages of the book on the lectern, just gesturing in the direction of kneeling, that tiny bow. He is so weary and rigid, Don Salari, that you'd think he's at risk of breaking in two from one moment to the next. Even his phrases have become rigid, the syntax that strings them together is always on the verge of crumbling, produced as it is by a mind that has long since dried up, and a pair of desiccated lips.

"Not only would we never know God if it hadn't been for Jesus Christ, we wouldn't even know ourselves. It's only since the advent of Jesus that man has existed, that man, indeed, that men taken one by one, have had any importance and become worthy of attention. All of them. Before Jesus no one cared about his fellow men, much less about themselves, or their own inner life, which was nothing but a filthy and repugnant pit. That is where the heroic inhumanity of the past lay. Show no care for other men. I tell you that without Jesus the world would be a living hell. Someone might retort: But it still is! I would reply to them: Friend, don't curse! Hell truly is another matter entirely: here we have only pale and provisional examples . . . imitations . . . miniatures . . ."

I STARTED LISTENING, for once, seriously and intensely. That evening, Don Salari was truly inspired.

"AS A RESULT, everything in a man is open to question, every single claim to be worth something is open to suspicion. And so, in order to prove himself better than others, he must fall back on hairstyles, clothing, buildings, ancestors . . . If I walk down the street and a man looks out a window, should I think he is looking out the window so he can see *me*?"

❖

WE COULD NEVER UNDERSTAND ANYTHING if it weren't first, as a necessary condition, incomprehensible to us. Understanding is a process, a change of state. It is therefore necessary that a truth be well hidden before it can reveal itself. You must first be unaware, only then can you comprehend. In fact, you might say that only that which is mysterious can to some extent be rendered intelligible.

At the time, back then, I understood and I didn't. I saw and I didn't. That night at SLM the faithful who were attending mass weren't strangers to me, I didn't feel they were different. And yet I didn't know any of them. Certainly, in among them there must have been some old classmate of mine or other.

I started looking around at everyone present in search of some familiar facial features. I wouldn't have been capable of connecting them to a specific name. Children from forty years ago who grew up and became men and are now almost old. There was one, however, who really stood out. He responded, in a voice that was both loud and clear, to the formulations launched into the congregation by Don Salari at the microphone. He didn't mutter under his breath, but replied to the ritual appeal of the old priest in a direct and, how shall I put this, *confident, trusting* manner. Those words had a real meaning for him, they weren't just a formula to be mechanically repeated. He would have uttered those words, even if they hadn't been written in the booklet or the prayer book. Those words were destined to produce a concrete effect. This, after all, is what prayer is supposed to be good for.

I observed him more closely. He was a big tall man with white hair and a translucent complexion, he looked like an old Swede, well seasoned, decorous, like those in the audience in the overture to *The Magic Flute* as filmed by Ingmar Bergman. I thought I recognized him: this was Ezechiele Rummo, the older brother of my classmate Gioacchino. I hadn't seen him in years and years. I know that his little publishing house had folded a few years earlier, it could no longer stand up to the costs of production. The Sardinian author, Rummo Books' biggest seller, had suddenly become a pill in the marketplace, from one title to the next; and so she had decided to change publishers, moving on to a much more commercial house which was capable of paying her large advances and undertaking a major marketing push, but the popularity of her early novellas had never returned. Sitting next to Ezechiele, who already looked elderly to me, there was a genuinely elderly man, skinny and dried out, but with a beautiful head of silvery hair and round tortoiseshell eyeglasses. Only Le Corbusier himself could have carried off those glasses, I thought to myself, without making them seem like an architect's cliché. I almost immediately repented of this sarcastic notation. Sitting next to him in the pew were two extremely good-looking young people, who both resembled their grandfather to a stunning extent, a man in his early thirties and a younger woman, who held a little child in her arms, a little boy with a perfect, marvelous head of hair, so blond it looked white. They really could have been brother and sister or husband and wife, those two, with their young child; or else a little brother born from a late second marriage of Ezechiele's, I speculated. The Rummo mold was so strong and distinctive that it was even able to influence the spouses; or perhaps they were chosen precisely because they had such a strong resemblance to start with, they had chosen as their wife or husband someone who already belonged to their same race: that is to say, blond, tall, Catholic, altruistic. And so the blond woman at the end of the row of Rummos at midnight mass might perfectly well have been Ezechiele's wife, or perhaps one of the sisters, Elisabetta or Rachele, or maybe even a grown daughter of Ezechiele's, but it was impossible to say, because, while the others were sitting, she remained kneeling and praying, holding her face buried in her hands. She had a short red coat from the sleeves of which extended her long pale fingers, and behind those fingers she was hiding her face. I thought a stupid thought. Yes, very stupid. Perhaps this, simply this, was the reason I'd stopped going to mass as a young man; because during the course of the service I could never seem to stop a flow, stunning in its sheer volume, of thoughts that had nothing at all do with the mass, alien, a great many of them stupid, others that would make you blush, sinful, others still just funny and nothing more.

I thought, then, that I would have been tremendously lucky and undeservedly pleased, when entering the SLM church, to have gone and sat, by purest chance, next to that woman in the red coat, simply because when the time came to exchange the sign of peace, at the end of the recital of the Our Father, I'd have been able to shake hands with her. I would have held her hand, warming it for an instant, because it was surely cold. I'd have made peace with her. And, since I would have been the last one sitting in the pew, the end of the row, I wouldn't have had to make peace with anyone else. Just with her. I felt a pang of sorrow because it hadn't happened. And I certainly couldn't move now, putting myself at the end of the row of Rummo's, forcing them to scoot in tighter in their pew to make room for me, while Ezechiele responded to Don Salari, who had just exhorted his parishioners, "Let your hearts be raised":

THEY ARE TURNED TO THE LORD.

"Let us give thanks to the Lord Our God."

IT IS A GOOD AND JUST THING.

"It is truly a good and just thing to give thanks always and everywhere to You . . ."

AND IT WAS TRUE, in Ezechiele's case: his heart was turned to the Lord, as was the stolid yet sincere heart of his father, the architect Davide Rummo, now well into his eighties. At last the woman in the red coat took her hands away from her face and I realized that she, too, was old, like the architect, and that in fact she was the other architect, his wife, Eleonora, mother of Ezechiele and Gioacchino and that vast litter of children who were all now at least fifty years old. All but one. I guessed that she had just finished praying for the distant memory of Giaele. Her bloodless hands, which I'd so regretted not being able to grasp, were the hands of a little old lady, and her face was haggard. Her eyes were red and distracted. It broke my heart to see her.

Well, yes, I wish I had the strength, I alone, for that entire family, the strength to shape the divine will with my invocations. Restore the lost happiness. Renew the oath. And obtain an easy forgiveness for having coveted my neighbor's wife, even though all I wanted to do was touch her hand during a religious ceremony. It had happened to me at certain funerals, where I had decided to try to judge which woman was the most desirable among all those present, which one looked best in tears. Instead of thinking about the dead man, and mourning for him, I was totting up rapid rankings as if I were at a beauty pageant. Beauty + grief, an irresistible formula. Someone like Don Salari was certainly well briefed on the distractions that are generated in your mind. Did he condemn them? Did he lump them together with the other sins? Did he teach how to master them or was he all right with them as they were, because he, too, had understood that from brute death we all recoil in search of softer, gentler thoughts, more pleasurable, sensual, vital ones—like touching, kissing . . . ? Spying on the neighbors?

There was a time when you were supposed to repress these things, repress them—period. But nowadays?

I REMEMBER THAT, before I simply stopped attending, the phrase I liked best in the holy mass was "Kyrie eleison."

> *Kyrie eleison . . .*
> *Christe eleison . . .*
> *Kyrie eleison . . .*

It was the sound that appealed to me.

When it began to say "Lord, have mercy" and "Christ, have mercy," it was then that the litany lost its allure for me. It became whiny, when we understood what it meant. Then I got lost. And no formulation in Greek was ever capable of taking me back there.

"I CONFESS TO ALMIGHTY GOD and to you, my brothers and sisters, that I have greatly sinned, in my thoughts and in my words, in what I have done and in what I have failed to do, through *my fault*, through *my fault*, through my *most grievous* fault."

Even after the Confiteor was translated into and recited in Italian, when I was a boy I loved to pound my chest three times repeating the word: *colpa, colpa, colpa.* Fault, fault, fault. It was such a theatrical gesture. I didn't feel guilty of a thing, but I still pounded hard, fist clenched, *colpa, colpa, colpa . . .* until I felt genuine pain, for a genuine fault. There was no need to know which fault. The authentic confession goes well beyond the specific sins: one time it will be one sin, the next time it will be another, what difference does it make?

I TRULY DON'T KNOW what is worse: whether it's worse to believe and later discover that you have believed in vain (but that's impossible, since after life there is nothing, our consciousness will be null and void, whether you were wrong or you were right), or rather not to have believed, and in the end discover, too late, that He exists.

16

I T WAS ONE OF THOSE WEEKS in the mountains, those ski holidays known as *settimane bianche*, "white weeks," that SLM organized in the Dolomites, at Lavarone. I remember a massive, unlovely hotel outside the town, on the side of the mountain, about which I must have previously written elsewhere. Aside from skiing—a sport that I've never loved, and at which I've never been very good, since I could successfully take curves only in one direction—I do remember with pleasure or heartache the ferocious tournaments of Ping-Pong, the soccer goals kicked in fresh snow, the evening projections of edifying films (that's right, that's exactly what I wrote about, how *The Miracle of Marcelino* led me and the other overexcited children to the verge of a nervous breakdown, like a horror flick, which is after all what it was: a Catholic horror flick), and I remember the teeming and festive refectory and the ruddy cheeks and the sealskin ski boots and the coughing. The evening before the races, the older kids and the talented skiers (therefore, not me, though I looked on in fascination, as if I were in the cabinet of Doctor Faustus) were applying and reapplying wax to the bottoms of their skis, tips pointing at the floor, in the large gloomy storage area under the hotel. The faces brightened by the cold and by the flames over which they were heating the blocks of ski wax. I remember the loving care lavished on the Kneissls, the Rossignols, the Atomics, the Völkls, and the Heads. I have specific memories of the tiniest details, and approximate overall memories of the rest.

Toward the end of the winter vacation, just a couple of days short of my return home, I got sick, with a fever. It's a classic for little kids to get sick while away from home on trips. "Let's hope he doesn't get sick," people say about a little kid before he heads off to camp, a week on horseback, the WWF center, the educational field trip, the tennis camp in the Apennines. I've never understood whether this facility for getting sick is caused by excitement, fear of new things, disruptions to routine, changes in climate, or changes in what they eat and where they sleep . . . by the effervescence of a different lifestyle than the usual. Children are creatures of habit, much more than old people. The classic outcome of disruption: the flu or bronchitis. Maybe I'd just been wet after countless tumbles in the snow and, when I went back to the hotel run by priests, I'd climbed into bed without changing into something dry, and had dropped straight off to sleep. When I woke up for dinner, my back hurt, and so did my legs and every bone in my body, and I was trembling. At dinner I didn't feel like eating anything, not even the soup. "Your eyes are glistening," a priest told me. "Come over here," and he put his hand on my forehead.

He had a big hand.

"Jesus, you're burning up!"

This priest wasn't from SLM, but a different religious school in Italy, so he wasn't a teacher or professor of ours, but by now we knew him well, seeing as how he'd been with us since the beginning of our holidays at Lavarone. We'd found him already there when we got off the long-distance bus from Rome. He was friendly, kind, quick to laugh, and joked with everyone, but it was clear that he was also greatly respected. He had freckles and fine, thinning fair hair, and a pair of frameless glasses, the kind where you can't quite figure out how the lenses manage to stay on. He was called Father Marenzio. I couldn't say whether he was a supervisor or exactly what his position might have been. For sure, he counted for something in the organization of that week in the mountains: he was the one who had decided many specific details, from the calendar of the Ping-Pong tournament to the operation of the medicine and liquor cabinet, and it was he who called the start in the timed downhill races, which we had done in the few preceding days to work up to the race finals. I had fallen midway down, because of my usual problem with handling right-hand curves, which meant my race time hadn't been taken into account. After all, I never would have taken part in the downhill race in any case.

"You'd better get to sleep right away, otherwise you'll just wear yourself out," said Father Marenzio, and at a gesture from him I got up from the long refectory table. A number of my friends said good night. Arbus wasn't there, they never sent him up for the week in the mountains. "Come," said the priest, and he extended his big hand, I put my hand in his, and it vanished in his outsized grasp, then we headed off down the long hallway that ran the length of the hotel like a subterranean tunnel. We fetched up in the end at the small office with the first-aid cabinet. Made of wood and glass, it was fastened with a padlock that had a long, tall, narrow shackle (in fact, these are the details that I remember as if they were utterly indelible: the glass panes of the cabinet, and behind them the little curtains concealing the vials containing the medicines, that extremely long padlock whose shackle extended upward through four hasps). He found a thermometer and gave it a few vigorous shakes. In the meantime, he'd sat me down on a bench.

"Let's take your temperature."

I took the thermometer and, after pulling aside the neck of the sweater and the collar of my shirt, I was about to lower it down into the hollow of my armpit, when Marenzio shook his head.

"No, not there."

I immediately pulled the thin glass tube back out and sat there, baffled. A feverish shiver ran through me and I was afraid I'd drop the thermometer. My mouth was dry.

Marenzio pointed to my crotch.

"Down there is better," he said, "you'll get a more reliable reading."

I don't know what kind of a face I made, but the priest just broke into laughter and plucked the thermometer out of my fingers. "You don't have to be ashamed. You're a sick boy. We just need to take your temperature, see how high the fever is. Shall I turn around and look the other way?" And he turned to look at a depiction of the blessed founder that hung over his desk, with a little dry sprig from an olive tree tucked into the frame. He kept his big freckly hands clasped behind his back, under the sash that held his tunic at the waist, tapping his fingers against his palms.

"Ready?" and he handed me the thermometer with the tips of his fingers. "But don't take an hour now, eh!" and he laughed again.

I unbuttoned my pants hastily and stuck the thermometer right into the fold between my underwear and one of my thighs. It was piping hot and sweaty in there.

I buttoned up my trousers again, and he turned around to look at me.

"Oh, good. In five minutes, we'll know everything."

He held out his hand to caress my face. His hand seemed cold to me, and big. His caress ended when he had tucked my long locks of hair behind my ears. "Eh, you know, it's about time . . ."

And with two fingers, he imitated a pair of scissors.

"Snip!"

I HAD A FEVER OF 103. When I opened my eyes again, they were puffy. I was in pajamas, lying on my back, in our six-bed bunk room, and at the foot of my bed sat Father Marenzio. He looked at me, with a smile on his face, an arm resting on the side of the bed. He said: "Well, what are we going to do?" I tried to put a half smile on my face, in a vague apology. A child who gets sick in the mountains is just trouble. It doesn't seem to me that he had given me any medicine. I had no cough now, no stomachache, just a fever. But he had made me herbal tea. I remember that I was forced to drink it, with the priest lifting the rim of the mug and me gulping it down to keep from suffocating. It was scalding hot and it reeked of rotten grass. The other five beds around me were empty. My classmates were downstairs playing or watching the usual black-and-white film, about some heroic feat of mountaineering, or else *The Ten Commandments*. In the big bunk room, Father Marenzio had switched on only the little light above the sink. His face was backlit, therefore, dark, but I could see that he was smiling, and every now and then, the gleam of his eyeglasses. I could hear his voice speaking to me, but from a distance, muffled.

"Keep your hands on top of the blankets . . ."

I pulled them out. They were damp, because I'd been holding them wedged into my steaming hot crotch, inside by pajama bottoms, to protect me.

"There, good boy . . . *good boy* . . ."

Maybe there were other "good boys" uttered by Father Marenzio, but they reached my ears fainter and fainter. He had taken one of my hands.

I don't know why I thought that in the meantime Moses's beard and hair must have turned white and grown disproportionately, and that he will never reach the Promised Land: he'll glimpse it from afar, and then he'll die. "You're very hot," said Father Marenzio, holding my wrist, "but you needn't worry." I told him, "Thank you," the way my mother had taught me: always say thank you. "Tomorrow you'll be all better, wait and see."

He looked at the watch on his wrist, and his eyeglasses gleamed, and also his fine blond hair, pushed back on his rosy cranium. "But now your classmates are about to come upstairs, and they'll have to turn on the light, they'll make a noise and they'll wake you up, they'll bother you." To tell the truth, at that point the pain had almost subsided and the blazing fever was putting me into a passive but not disagreeable state of mind. The bed had turned soft again. Soon, Barnetta, Zarattini, and the others would come back upstairs into the bunk room. Especially Stefano Jervi, who slept in the bed next to mine—I'd be happy to see him, before falling asleep, and to hear him tell with his usual arrogance about his plans to win the slalom race. He was a young champion. He had a brand-new pair of skis, yellow with a purple lightning bolt running the length of them, and magnificent ski boots, with hooks that snapped shut, unlike mine, which had extremely long laces that were a lot of work to tie. "I want to say hello to them," I murmured to Father Marenzio, running my tongue over my dry lips. He went over to the sink, rinsed the glass that stood under the mirror, filled it with water from the tap, and brought it to me. "Drink." I needed to drink a great deal, he said. "That's not a very good idea, for you to see them, you know that? You could infect them all." He laughed silently. "And then to-morrow we'd have six boys in bed with the flu, instead of just one!"

FATHER MARENZIO WAS BIG AND STRONG and he carried me easily in his arms. I had my arms around his neck and my head rested on his shoulder. My slippers were dangling from the tips of my feet. I've always found shameful an object like slippers: their shape, their function, those tawdry colors. The priest's shoulder was cool and my eyes began to droop and shut. Once again, I was dreaming of Moses with whirlwinds of fire carving the Ten Commandments, one after the other, etching the letters into stone, and Moses angrily shattering the tablets, hurling them at the idolaters. The blast of heat I felt was that of a sandy desert being beaten by the wind, and once again my mouth was dry. I don't know if I would have had the courage to continue forward, or whether I, too, would have mutinied to return to the land of Egypt. "Let's turn back, let's go home . . ." We climbed a flight of stairs. Moses's staff was coming alive, transforming into a serpent. The serpent was slithering, and it curled up in the water under the stilt house. There was water under the desert, so much concealed water; once upon a time, the desert had bloomed with all that water, there had been huge buildings with stairs and terraces and gardens and fountains. The water pitchers were overbrimming and cool. The serpent spat out a spray of water from its mouth. We rested in the shade of a room with the shutters pulled to, the sun had bronzed us and wearied us, and our games had exhausted us, the sheets were white and cool . . . the sweat on my forehead dried off on the fabric of Father Marenzio's tunic. He alone insisted on wearing his tunic even up there in the mountains. The other religious were all wearing check-ered shirts and heavy sweaters. The serpent breathed in the shadows and a naked woman listened to him, then followed him. "Eat this apple. There's nothing wrong with doing it." There's nothing wrong . . . there's nothing wrong . . . and she obeyed him. I felt every bit as obedient. It took no effort to obtain my obedience. My right slipper fell off my foot and Father Maren-zio bent over patiently to pick it up, while I clung to his neck, then he stood up, and we looked into each other's eyes. He smiled at me. He was strong and calm, and determined. His eyes were full of love. "You know that you're as light as a feather?" he asked. He didn't slide the slipper back onto my foot, but held it tight in his fist. He was crushing it. "An angel's feather, maybe," and he laughed merrily.

If there was an angel between us, that was him, actually. Father Marenzio. The guardian angel who watches over each of us. Who guides you in the darkness, who teaches you who you are, and in the end who flies down and saves you. Your luminous shadow against the wall, even your name, finally clarified. Edoardo . . . guardian of all that is good. That goodness, always threatened. Some want to steal it, others intend to destroy it. "Edoardo, come on, wake up . . ." but I kept my eyes half shut. The light in the attic hallway was turned off, and the floorboards beneath Father Marenzio's feet were creaking with every step. "Here we are," he said.

HE HAD PUT ME IN HIS BED. On the little side table, there were books and a water pitcher. A faint light came in through the curtains on the window, perhaps moonlight glinting off the snow. He wanted to check my temperature again, to see if the fever had gotten any worse, and this time he did it himself. He lifted the rough brown blanket and pulled down my pajama bottoms. I cooperated, lifting my back so that the elastic band could slide under my bottom, and I spread one leg, my right leg. I thought he wanted to slide the thermometer in there. Father Marenzio did slide it in, and narrowed my leg. The thermometer stood up straight. Not even my mother had ever done that, I don't think. I had always done it on my own, ever since I was a little boy. Then he covered me back up, with just the sheet, and together we waited five minutes, then ten.

"**WHAT A HANDSOME BOY YOU ARE . . .**" said Father Marenzio, caressing me. "You really are beautiful . . ." and I could see his face close to mine. He'd moved the chair over next to the bed. He was smiling at me. "You're so handsome . . . so kind . . ." His freckles had lit up on his face, and behind the lenses his large light-colored eyes glistened with emotion. After pulling the thermometer out of my crotch, he hadn't told me whether my temperature had risen any higher, to me it seemed as if it had, but that wasn't important right now. I imagined Jervi at that moment, snoring with all the others, in our big bunk room. He was dreaming about tomorrow's downhill race. And, of course, he was dreaming about winning. I fell asleep for a while and then woke back up. The great big angel standing at heaven's gate held a flaming sword, but instead of turning people away, he was waving them in with his sword. I drew close, full of curiosity, even if the light that poured out of the gate, and from the sword, and from the angel, was blinding me. But I still wanted to enter. "Wait, wait." Padre Marenzio rubbed his face and his eyes behind the lenses, "Wait," he said, panting, "wait!" and when he started caressing my face and neck again, I felt his large hand was wet. And this contact gave me pleasure. I told him I liked it. And then he wetted his handkerchief under the faucet of the sink in the room, wrung it out, and applied it, folded and refolded, to my forehead. "God bless you," he was saying, "God works miracles . . . on this earth."

I believe that at this point it was the middle of the night. And that it went on like that until daybreak.

17

ARBUS HAS GONE MISSING AGAIN. Maybe he sensed that he was done with me. The following week I made an appointment with Paris's elderly widow to get her to tell me the details of the proletarian expropriation at the shop on Piazza Verbano. She'd been there that day.

But I mustn't let myself be distracted from the mass, this time, I want to stay until the end of the service. I want to listen and participate. This Christmas mass has to work, it has to be valid, this time, at least this one. The clock strikes midnight.

Behold, the clock strikes midnight, He is born. He is born. I lack faith. I've never found it. To be honest, I've never made any great effort to search for it. I certainly haven't wrung my soul to save it. I assumed it would come on its own, faith, strike me without warning, like an illness or a lottery winning, but clearly that's not the case. It takes preparation, you have to lure it in, like some unwary prey, the way you'd seduce a girl, or make a show of being willing to be seduced by it, preyed upon by it. Am I ready now? Is this the moment? Is *this*? How many moments present themselves in life? Or is there just one, to be seized, now or never? Does it bloom only once, like the plant murdered by my classmate Jervi? And when it dies, do the tears shed by whoever loved that wonderful unique flower serve to water something, help it grow?

How Svampa sobbed over that withered stalk!

You damned faggot of a priest, are you finally going to succeed in stirring my emotions?

Even walls built to protect can collapse and kill us, even the steps built for our comfort and ease can be lethal. That's what I had read among the thousands of thoughts that Cosmo had stored up in his notebooks. What good had they done? And good to whom? Perhaps to him? Why had he died without being willing to communicate them to anyone? What did you die for, my old literature teacher? Your resurrection is a distant mirage. Your body will be stolen away. I knew very well what no one asked me. If they had asked me, I would no longer have known it. My thoughts wandered among the images of bygone times and the times still to come, while awaiting the reawakening.

THE CONGREGATION LINED UP to take communion. Not all the Rummos went up. The elderly Eleonora remained kneeling in her pew. She watched the others. The young woman with her son in her arms, when her time came to stand in front of Don Salari, opened her mouth and let him place the wafer on her tongue. The little boy tried to do as his mother had done, but it faded into a long yawn, whereupon he shut his eyes and fell asleep. The elderly priest seemed to smile at the youngster, abandoning his customary severity. The grimace engraved in his furrowed brow could, in fact, take on various meanings. I'd have liked to join the line. That night seemed inexhaustible: as soon as the line started to shorten and seemed to be on the verge of dissolving, someone always joined it, someone who had waited till the last minute to leave their pew and join the line, the way experienced travelers do at an airport departure gate, to avoid needlessly spending time standing. Perhaps everyone in the SLM church took communion, except for Eleonora Rummo and me. Don Salari gave himself communion last of all. He popped the wafer into his mouth as if it were a treat, and his mouth vanished with the whole wafer.

IT WAS LATE BY NOW, the middle of the night. In the black sky, thunderclouds followed one after the other. The sky loured dark and heavy over the church's modern, copper-sheathed roof. The rain poured down. The cross flamed.

In each of us, reason acts slowly, while sentiment can be triggered in the blink of an eye: fear, love, resentment, cheerfulness all spray upward and then evaporate. Desires burn up in moments. Whereas in my friend Arbus, as a boy, the exact opposite happened: his intellect was lightning-quick, his heart was slow. But once it was set in motion . . .

The memory of Arbus and his sister, Leda, suddenly stopped obsessing me and became clear and simple. Perdìta was me, I was Perdìta, the small pale flame that glows on the night table, the sky-blue cloak, the downcast eyes full of sadness, the bare feet.

We don't understand other people. We may not have the patience necessary to do so. We judge them overhastily, awkwardly, there is so much left that we do not know, so much left to suffer and enjoy, while we're stranded here, in number, in time, in dimensions, in the confinement of a single mind.

We ought to work more on uncertainty, turn it to our favor, that's right, work for uncertain results. If what we are looking for should never make itself known, that would mean that it doesn't exist or that we're unworthy of finding it. But instead, it does sometimes appear, and its very rarity cancels all equivocation.

ONE SONG AFTER THE OTHER, the Christmas mass at SLM was drawing to its close. And my heart finally overflowed with joy.

September 29, 1975–September 29, 2015

Author's Note

The Catholic School is based on events that actually happened, events to which, in part, I was a direct eyewitness. Working from those actual events, I've intertwined episodes and characters with varying percentages of fiction: some are concocted out of whole cloth, others owe a considerable debt to things that actually took place, to people who exist or once did. I had no hesitation in mixing the true, the allegedly true, the fictional but plausible, and the true but implausible; I freely interbred memory and imagination. The same character who narrates the story in the first person singular may well differ to some extent from the author cited on the cover.

Just to be clear, in my reporting on the crimes in question, I made use of police reports, deposition transcripts, wiretaps, interviews, and legal verdicts concerning the protagonists of those crimes, cutting and stitching where I thought necessary and omitting or replacing certain names, for the most part because they would have sown confusion or stirred up pointless and tiresome controversy. This book makes no claim to any accurate historical reconstruction or to propose an alternative version of events: if anything, it hopes to restore an atmosphere free of rhetorical contamination. The only episode in which I've wandered freely away from the official version of the events I took as my model—developing in my own fashion several confessions that at the time were deemed unreliable by the investigators—is the death of Cassio Majuri, behind which name lies concealed a controversial case of murder: and I did so strictly for reasons of narrative expediency, for which I take full responsibility. The contents of human life and human lives is what literature shapes for its own specific purposes, and it tends not to be overtender in its treatment.

If, in my handling of personal truths, I have caused any shame and suffering, I neither suffer nor feel shame at the thought, unless the result is judged to be mediocre, in which case I feel I owe an apology to those who have fallen victim to my reckless inadequacy. To my readers first and foremost.

The list of texts and people who can claim credit, small or large, for this book would be endless. Nine out of every ten lines in *The Catholic School* owe a debt to some outside contribution—whether conceded, gifted outright, or pilfered. To paraphrase the lines of a poet friend, if I were to return that which is not mine, I'd have nothing left.

Among the many debts I owe to those who helped me to revise such a long text, I will limit myself here to mentioning the generous advice of Margherita Loy and the punctual severity of my daughter Adelaide, who also helped me to transcribe the parts of the book that I wrote by hand. To them, and to all those who worked professionally on this volume, my gratitude.

The Catholic School would never have been conceived, written, rewritten, and—most important of all—finished, if I hadn't had Francesca d'Aloja at my side.

Translator's Note

To a translator, the well-known line "The past is a foreign country; they do things differently there" rings with a special resonance. Translation is a quasi-industrial process, taking semifinished "foreign" products and buffing and polishing them into a new and "legible" form. The choke points in this manufacturing process are the stubbornly foreign concepts, the ones without a web of known cultural references. Just as we have a hard time extracting ancient humor, with its sly winks and puns, from, say, Greek Old Comedy, likewise does a translator struggle not to overexplain a text's nostalgic references to an earlier period of a foreign culture: a popular singer who committed suicide backstage at the Sanremo Song Festival, or a national craze for a racing game played on beach sand with oversized marbles. No "untranslatable words," perhaps, but many "untranslatable *worlds*."

The word "foreign" is itself a translator's conundrum: How would you translate it? If an Italian in an Italian book uses the word, how would that translate in English? "Non-Italian?" Or do we use "foreign"? Alfonso Cuarón, in his Oscar acceptance speech for the Best Foreign Language Film Award for *Roma*, slyly pointed to this paradox when he said, "I grew up watching foreign-language films and learning so much from them and being inspired, films like *Citizen Kane, Jaws, Rashomon, The Godfather,* and *Breathless.*"

When Don DeLillo wrote *Libra*, he wasn't writing about an "American" political murder, with its ensuing conspiracy theories and fever dreams. He was writing about a global story, the most powerful man on earth brought down by the nephew-in-law of a Soviet colonel. Not so for this story set in the Italian 1970s.

The case at the heart of *The Catholic School* is one that still resonates in the minds of Italians. The kidnapping-rape-murder at Monte Circeo was as much as or more than the sum of its parts. What we Americans mostly know about Italy in the 1970s is the Red Brigades, a terrifying, shadowy left-wing terror cell that kidnapped and murdered Aldo Moro, former prime minister and party chief. What we know less about is the neo-Fascist nemesis to the Italian revolutionary left, committing murders and bombings in what amounted to a barely controlled civil war, with the tacit approval of the Catholic

Church, the "renegade" Italian intelligence services, and their CIA big brothers. Literally, the Red and the Black: Marxist-Leninist Red and neo-Fascist Black.

All this in the midst of the eruption of a "nostalgic" wave of toxic violence and masculinity, on both sides of the political spectrum. As Albinati himself puts it, groups of men rape women to keep from killing *each other*. In the past, in a foreign country, they may do things differently, but there are enough universal similarities to make this complex and breathtakingly savage exploration of male dysfunction an absorbing read.

About the Translator

Antony Shugaar is a writer and translator. He is the author of *Coast to Coast* and *I Lie for a Living*, and the coauthor, with the late Gianni Guadalupi, of *Discovering America* and *Latitude Zero*.